Lives and Moments

AN INTRODUCTION TO SHORT FICTION

Hans Ostrom
University of Puget Sound

Holt, Rinehart and Winston, Inc.

Fort Worth   Chicago   San Francisco   Philadelphia
Montreal   Toronto   London   Sydney   Tokyo

Publisher: Ted Buchholz
Acquisitions Editor: Michael Rosenberg
Developmental Editor: Martin Lewis
Senior Project Editor: Dawn Youngblood
Production Manager: Annette Dudley Wiggins
Art & Design Supervisor: Vicki McAlindon Horton
Text Designer: Tom Dawson/Duo Design Group
Cover Designer: Michael Niblett
Illustrations by: Chris Hoover

Library of Congress Cataloging-in-Publication Data

Lives and moments : an anthology of short fiction / [compiled by] Hans Ostrom. — 1st
ed.
    p.   cm.
  ISBN 0-03-030374-5
  1. Short stories.   I. Ostrom, Hans A.
PN6120.L59 1990   90-31237
808.83′1—dc20   CIP

Printed in the United States of America

1 2 3 4   0 1 6   9 8 7 6 5 4 3 2

Copyright acknowledgments can be found on page 941

Holt, Rinehart and Winston, Inc.
The Dryden Press
Saunders College Publishing

# Preface

THE PURPOSE OF THE BOOK

Lives and Moments is aimed at a college-level audience that is writing fiction, embarking on the study of literature, or familiarizing itself with the short story as a distinct genre. The anthology is also appropriate for introductory and intermediate courses in composition that include the study of short stories.

In editing this anthology, I sought to provide a context for the selections. Many anthologies I have encountered as both student and teacher have presented stories in something of a vacuum. They have provided little historical or cultural information, and they have said little about the development of the short story. Some anthologies merely arrange stories alphabetically, according to the last name of the author. It seemed to me that this approach reinforces the sense some students may have that literature comes out of nowhere to appear on the shelves of college bookstores.

ERAS OF SHORT FICTION

To provide a context for the stories in this collection, therefore, I have divided the anthology into four "eras" of the short story: early, modern, contemporary, and emerging. "Early Voices" contains stories from 1835 to 1910. The dividing lines between "early" and "modern" are fairly clear, not just because of the Great War and the Bolshevik Revolution, but also because writers like Joyce, Kafka, and Hemingway deliberately set out to write a new kind of story, however much they still owed to early masters like Chekhov and Poe, and however "modern" a writer like Conrad seems.

The last two sections, "Contemporary Voices" and "Emerging Voices," contain stories from the early 1950s to the present. These two sections overlap more than the other two, partly because the historical and literary lines of demarcation simply are not as bold. However, "Contemporary Voices" tends to include writers whose reputations are well defined—writers like Updike, Cheever, O'Connor, and Fuentes. It also includes stories that have become enduring expressions of contemporary life, such as Updike's "A & P" and

O'Connor's "Everything That Rises Must Converge." Such stories seem as representative of their era as Joyce's *Dubliners* stories are of theirs.

As one might imagine, "Emerging Voices" includes many stories from the 1970s and 1980s. However, "newness" was not the only criterion of selection here. The section also includes writers who may be well-established poets but whose "voices" in short fiction are still emerging. And it includes writers who are redefining an established area of literature—in the way Louise Erdrich is redefining Native American literature with a story like "Snares," for instance. Finally, the section also contains work by accomplished but undervalued writers from parts of the world that have only recently gained a higher profile in the world's "literary scene." The South African writers Elsa Joubert and Njabulo Ndebele are but two examples.

THE DETECTIVE STORY AND THE HORROR STORY

The anthology includes one "detective story" in each section because I thought that some students might be interested in "tracking" one subgrenre of short fiction through several periods. Also, the development of the detective story runs roughly parallel to that of the short story because Poe and Conan Doyle are often credited with creating this type of story. The stories by Conan Doyle, Chandler, and Grafton are more or less traditional detective stories, though each one adds distinctive elements to the form. The story by Joyce Carol Oates is on the far boundaries of the form and does not include a detective in the usual sense.

For several reasons, I have included a story by the popular writer of horror fiction, Stephen King. Because many college-age students read his work, I thought it might be useful for them to see one of his stories in a different context. It also seemed important to include one example of a subgenre that is extraordinarily popular in America, that is controversial because of its subject matter, and that has ties to an early master, Poe. The stories in these two subgenres will also raise issues concerning "popular" versus "literary" fiction.

DIVERSITY

An awareness of diversity has guided the selection process. *Lives and Moments* represents a spectrum of ethnic backgrounds, cultures, nations, and social classes, and it features diverse voices from both genders. My view is that the short story belongs to the world and that translated fiction is a great gift to American students.

THE SHORT STORY EVOLVES

The anthology includes an introductory essay about the evolution of the short story from the nineteenth century forward. The essay mentions several precursors to the short story as we know it, but the focus is mainly on the "reinvention" of the genre by Poe, de Maupassant, Hawthorne, Turgenev, and others. Following this section is a brief discussion of how the form changed as subsequent writers took it up.

My goal, however, was *not* to provide an indisputable version of this genre's evolution. Instead, the main purpose was to convey the idea that the connections between history, culture, and art are important, and that the notion of a literary history can enrich our interpretation of a single story. The essay is only a point of departure, from which students can begin to shape their own views about the remarkable history of "the short story." If students and their instructors take issue with my particular sense of how short fiction has evolved, so much the better, for my aim was to start a dialogue of sorts.

Additionally, the anthology includes an alternate table of contents that lists stories according to their date of publication. This chronology will further help place stories in history and connect them with events and eras that students encounter in other classes.

Each of the four sections also has its own introduction, which contains background information about a particular era, defines terms like *Modern* and *post-Modern,* and draws connections between certain stories.

Believe me, as an editor I know very well that few will read or refer to every story here. This knowledge gave me second thoughts about writing comprehensive introductions. Nevertheless, it seemed important to discuss stories in relation to one another, to provide background and context.

The headings in all the introductory material will allow students and teachers to locate a brief discussion of a certain story, author, or topic quickly—without having to read a whole introduction if they do not wish to do so. This arrangement should be useful both to those who find background and context helpful and to those who want to get to the stories with minimal delay.

WRITING ABOUT STORIES AND WRITING STORIES

This anthology is intended to be useful to students of literature and students of creative writing alike. Therefore, I have included one essay on how to write critically about short fiction and one essay on how to start writing fiction. These essays discuss both the purpose and process of writing essays and stories. The practical advice in these pieces springs from my own experience writing criticism, poetry, stories, and novels. More importantly, though, it springs from my experience teaching writing and literature to a wide variety of college students. Many of the ideas about writing also reflect my experience with writing centers at a large state university and at a small private college.

In addition, I believe writing stories to be not just a form in which students may write imaginatively about the world but also a way for them to study literature through "imitation." What better way to understand plot and character than to have to invent a plot or develop a character?

As with the other introductory material, however, I do not offer this advice as commandments, only as places to start the difficult processes of writing critically and writing imaginatively.

ADDITIONAL "APPARATUS"

After each story appear questions for discussion and suggestions for writing. Some of the questions are "formalist" in nature. They help students examine the conflicts, points of view, narrative structures, symbols, images, scenes, resolutions, and so forth, of stories. Others have a psychological or social focus. They will help illuminate relationships between characters, conflicts between social groups, motives, obsessions, reactions, and personalities that are evoked on the page. Other questions involve basic issues of "reader response" and rhetoric. Still others are "practical" in nature. They ask about the originality, the significance, and the ambitiousness of certain stories.

My essential approach in these questions is to avoid second-guessing the author's intentions and instead to help students articulate and refine their interpretations. These questions also encourage students to be aware of the way different critical approaches generate different interpretations.

The suggestions for writing include possible essay topics, ideas for informal pieces in a notebook or journal, and ideas for stories. As with the discussion questions, the goal was variety and flexibility. (Many of the topics for informal writing can be adapted easily to collaborative activities in the classroom—in pairs or in groups. The instructor's manual accompanying this anthology also contains a list of possible collaborative activities.)

Up front in the anthology are alternative tables of contents that arrange stories chronologically and thematically. There is also a checklist of stories that exemplify certain techniques (dialogue, closure, flashback, for example) or points of view (first, second, third, limited omniscient, and so forth.) The latter is not a comprehensive alternative table of contents but a checklist for quick reference.

BIOGRAPHICAL NOTES, GLOSSARY, CHECKLIST OF BOOKS

In the back are biographical notes on each author arranged alphabetically by last name, a glossary of literary and critical terms, and a checklist. The checklist includes anthologies of short fiction, books on writing and the art of short fiction, as well as collections of short fiction by North American, Latin American, European, Asian, African, Australian, and New Zealander writers.

SUMMARY

I hope the structure of the anthology, the introductory essays, the questions and suggestions for writing, the biographical notes, the glossary, and the reading list will help students and teachers when help is sought. Nonetheless, the strength of *Lives and Moments* lies in the great originality and diversity of its stories and of the writers who produced them. The short story is a remarkable genre with a rich history that is tied to England, Ireland, America, and the Continent and that has been enriched further by writers from Latin America, Asia, Africa, the Middle East, Canada, Australia, and New Zealand.

ACKNOWLEDGMENTS

First I want to thank the students in my many literature and writing classes who have studied the short story with me and who have enriched my knowledge of this genre and its development.

The following manuscript reviewers provided timely, generous, and perceptive comments: Patricia Belanoff, SUNY at Stony Brook; Tom Collins, University of Arizona; Nelliemay Hellenberg, Spokane Falls Community College; James Helvey, Davidson County Community College; Betty Hughes, Beaufort Community College; Angela Ingram, Southwest Texas State University; John Iorio, University of South Florida; Helen Marlborough, Depaul University; Mildred Miya, Weber State College; and Betty Towsend, University of Maryland.

I also want to thank my colleagues in English at the University of Puget Sound, with a special word of gratitude to Beth Kalikoff, Bev Conner, Laura Laffrado, Barry Bauska, Peter Greenfield, Tim Hansen, Florence Sandler, and Frank Cousens. Shelley Bott's advice and assistance throughout the project have been indispensable. The late Esther Wagner enriched my knowledge of short fiction immeasurably.

A residency at the Ragdale artists' colony in Lake Forest, Illinois, let me get a lot of work done on this book, and I am grateful to the staff there and to the writers and painters from whom I gained insight and energy. At least two selections in this anthology sprang from discussions with fellow writers there.

The advice and support I have received from the people at Holt, Rinehart, and Winston have been superb, and I am deeply grateful to Charlyce Jones Owen, Michael Rosenberg, Steve Delancey, Tod Gross, Dawn Youngblood, Timothy Westmoreland, Robert Griffin, Mary Pat Donlon, Martin Lewis, and Cassandra Coats.

My greatest good fortune is to have the support and encouragement of Jacquelyn Bacon Ostrom and her associate, Spencer.

Hans Ostrom
Tacoma, Washington

Contents

Preface . . . .   *iii*
Alternate Table of Contents (Chronological) . . . .   *xiii*
Alternate Table of Contents (Subject Matter/Theme) . . . .   *xxvii*
Technique: A Checklist of Stories . . . .   *xxiii*
The Evolution of the Short Story: An Introduction.   1
Writing About Stories: An Introduction.   9
Sample Student Essays.   19
Writing Stories: An Introduction   25

PART ONE: EARLY VOICES

Introduction to Early Voices.   37
Edgar Allan Poe, "The Tell-Tale Heart".   45
Nathaniel Hawthorne, "Young Goodman Brown"   50
Herman Melville, "Bartleby the Scrivener: A Story of Wall Street"   60
Guy de Maupassant, "The Necklace".   86
Ivan Turgenev, "Bezhin Meadow"   93
Leo Tolstoy, "The Death of Ivan Ilych"   110
Anton Chekhov, "Gooseberries"   150
Henry James, "The Pupil".   159
Kate Chopin, "The Story of an Hour"   190
Charlotte Perkins Gilman, "The Yellow Wallpaper"   193
Arthur Conan Doyle, "A Scandal in Bohemia"   206
O. Henry, "The Gift of the Magi"   224
Sholem Aleichem, "On Account of a Hat".   229
Stephen Crane, "The Blue Hotel"   236
Joseph Conrad, "The Secret Sharer"   257

Overview: Additional Questions for Discussion
     and Suggestions for Writing.   286

PART II: MODERN VOICES

Introduction to Modern Voices   291
James Joyce, "Araby".   300
D. H. Lawrence, "The Horse Dealer's Daughter"   305

Ernest Hemingway, "A Clean, Well-Lighted Place"   318
Franz Kafka, "A Hunger Artist"   323
William Faulkner, "A Rose for Emily"   331
Frank O'Connor, "Guests of the Nation"   339
Luigi Pirandello, "War".   349
Tadeusz Borowski, "The Supper"   353
Aya Koda, "The Black Kimono"   357
Sherwood Anderson, "The Egg"   371
Katherine Anne Porter, "The Jilting of Granny Weatherall".   379
John Steinbeck, "Chrysanthemums".   387
Eudora Welty, "Petrified Man"   396
Willa Cather, "Paul's Case: A Study in Temperament".   407
Ralph Ellison, "King of the Bingo Game"   422
Langston Hughes, "On the Road"   430
Zora Neale Hurston, "Sweat"   435
Raymond Chandler, "The Wrong Pigeon".   445
Katherine Mansfield, "The Fly".   469
Yasunari Kawabata, "The Mole"   474

Overview: Additional Questions for Discussion
   and Suggestions for Writing.   481

PART III: CONTEMPORARY VOICES

Introduction to Contemporary Voices   486
John Updike, "A & P"   494
John Cheever, "Goodbye, My Brother"   500
Janet Frame, "Insulation"   516
Alice Munro, "Miles City, Montana"   521
Ann Beattie, "In the White Night".   536
Hisaye Yamamoto, "Yoneko's Earthquake"   541
Richard Yates, "Doctor Jack-o'-lantern"   551
Cynthia Ozick, "The Butterfly and the Traffic Light"   563
Flannery O'Connor, "Everything That Rises Must Converge".   571
Tim O'Brien, "The Things They Carried".   583
Margaret Atwood, "Rape Fantasies"   597
Ray Bradbury, "2002: Night Meeting"   605
Carlos Fuentes, "Aura"   612
Lars Gustafsson, "Uncle Sven and the Cultural Revolution"   634

Bernard Malamud, "The Jewbird" 643
Heinrich Böll, "My Melancholy Face"...................... 651
Donald Barthelme, "The Author"......................... 657
Joyce Carol Oates, "The Murder" 660
Luisa Valenzuela, "The Censors"........................ 668
Richard Brautigan, "The Ghost Children of Tacoma" 671
Shirley Jackson, "The Lottery" 674
Amos Oz, "If There Is Justice"......................... 682
Alice Walker, "Everyday Use" 692
Raymond Carver, "Errand"............................. 700

Overview: Additional Questions for Discussion
      and Suggestions for Writing.......................... 709

PART IV: EMERGING VOICES

Introduction to Emerging Voices........................... 714
Louise Erdrich, "Snares" 717
Keri Hulme, "One Whale, Singing" 726
Sue Grafton, "She Didn't Come Home" 735
Susan Engberg, "A Daughter's Heart"..................... 748
Jayne Anne Phillips, "Bess"........................... 758
Matt Ellison, "Civil Engineer" 767
Elsa Joubert, "Back Yard"............................ 778
Liliana Heker, "The Stolen Party"....................... 787
Richard Cortez Day, "A Chagall Story" 792
Shawn Hsu Wong, "Each Year Grain" 800
Rick Demarinis, "Under the Wheat"...................... 805
Stephen King, "Graveyard Shift"........................ 814
Tess Gallagher, "A Pair of Glasses"...................... 828
Alberto Alvaro Rios, "The Iguana Killer" 836
Njabulo Ndebele, "Death of a Son" 846
Fiona Barr, "The Wall-Reader"......................... 854
Sesshu Foster, "The Street of the Fathers" 860
James Welch, "Fools Crow" 866
Gyanranjan, "Our Side of the Fence and Theirs"............... 875
Madeline DeFrees, "The Ventriloquist's Dummy" 881
Martin Amis, "Bujak and the Strong Force" 888

Overview: Additional Questions for Discussion
and Suggestions for Writing. 903

BIOGRAPHICAL NOTES. 907
GLOSSARY OF LITERARY AND CRITICAL TERMS 919
SELECTED CHECKLIST OF ANTHOLOGIES, BOOKS ON
WRITING, COLLECTIONS OF SHORT FICTION,
MAGAZINES 928
INDEX OF AUTHORS. 947
INDEX OF TITLES. 949

Alternate Table of Contents

(Chronological)

Note: One way to understand the history of short fiction is just to get a sense of the chronological relationship between certain stories. However, please remember that this chronological table of contents is based on *date of publication,* not on *date written.* In some cases, a story was published much later than when it was written, so one needs to be careful about making generalizations based solely on the date of publication.

1835	"Young Goodman Brown," Nathaniel Hawthorne
1843	"The Tell-Tale Heart," Edgar Allan Poe
1852	"Bezhin Meadow," Ivan Turgenev
1853	"Bartleby the Scrivener: A Story of Wall Street," Herman Melville
1884	"The Necklace," Guy de Maupassant
1886	"The Death of Ivan Ilych," Leo Tolstoy
1891	"The Pupil," Henry James
1892	"The Yellow Wallpaper," Charlotte Perkins Gilman
	"Gooseberries," Anton Chekhov
1893	"A Scandal in Bohemia," Arthur Conan Doyle
1894	"The Story of an Hour," Kate Chopin
1896	"On Account of a Hat," Sholem Aleichem
1900	"The Blue Hotel," Stephen Crane
1905	"The Gift of the Magi," O. Henry
1910	"The Secret Sharer," Joseph Conrad
1914	"Araby," James Joyce
1921	"The Egg," Sherwood Anderson
1922	"The Fly," Katherine Mansfield
	"The Horse Dealer's Daughter," D. H. Lawrence
1924	"A Hunger Artist," Franz Kafka
1926	"Sweat," Zorah Neale Hurston

1930   "A Rose for Emily," William Faulkner
           "The Jilting of Granny Weatherall," Katherine Anne Porter
1932   "Paul's Case," Willa Cather
1933   "A Clean, Well-Lighted Place," Ernest Hemingway
1937   "Chrysanthemums," John Steinbeck
           "Guests of the Nation," Frank O'Connor
1939   "War," Luigi Pirandello
1941   "Petrified Man," Eudora Welty
1944   "King of the Bingo Game," Ralph Ellison
1946   "Goodbye, My Brother," John Cheever
1948   "The Lottery," Shirley Jackson
1950   "2002: Night Meeting," Ray Bradbury
1952   "On the Road," Langston Hughes
           "The Wrong Pigeon," Raymond Chandler
1954   "Doctor Jack-o'-lantern," Richard Yates
1959   "The Supper," Tadeusz Borowski
1960   "The Mole," Yasunari Kawabata
           "The Black Kimono," Aya Koda
           "The Censors," Luisa Valenzuela
1961   "Everything That Rises Must Converge," Flannery O'Connor
           "The Butterfly and the Traffic Light," Cynthia Ozick
           "A & P," John Updike
           "Yoneko's Earthquake," Hisaye Yamamoto
1962   "Aura," Carlos Fuentes
1963   "The Jewbird," Bernard Malamud
1964   "The Ghost Children of Tacoma," Richard Brautigan
1967   "My Melancholy Face," Heinrich Böll
           "If There Is Justice," Amos Oz
1968   "The Author," Donald Barthelme
           "Our Side of the Fence and Theirs," Gyanranjan
1973   "The Murder," Joyce Carol Oates
           "Everyday Use," Alice Walker
1974   "Each Year Grain," Shawn Hsu Wong
           "Graveyard Shift," Stephen King
1977   "Insulation," Janet Frame
1980   "Uncle Sven and the Cultural Revolution," Lars Gustafsson
1981   "Back Yard," Elsa Joubert
           "A Daughter's Heart," Susan Engberg
           "One Whale, Singing," Keri Hulme
1982   "The Stolen Party," Liliana Heker
           "Under the Wheat," Rick Demarinis

1983   "Rape Fantasies," Margaret Atwood
        "Death of a Son," Njabulo Ndebele
        "A Pair of Glasses," Tess Gallagher
1984   "Bess," Jayne Anne Phillips
        "In the White Night," Ann Beattie
        "The Iguana Killer," Alberto Alvaro Rios
1985   "Miles City, Montana," Alice Munro
1986   "A Chagall Story," Richard Cortez Day
        "The Things They Carried," Tim O'Brien
        "She Didn't Come Home," Sue Grafton
        "The Wall-Reader," Fiona Barr
        "Fools Crow," James Welch
1987   "Bujak and the Strong Force," Martin Amis
        "The Ventriloquist's Dummy," Madeline DeFrees
1988   "Errand," Raymond Carver
        "Snares," Louise Erdrich
1989   "The Street of the Fathers," Sesshu Foster
        "Civil Engineer," Matt Ellison

Alternate Table of Contents

(Subject Matter)

CONFLICT BETWEEN SOCIAL CLASSES

Guy de Maupassant, "The Necklace"
Anton Chekhov, "Gooseberries"
Herman Melville, "Bartleby the Scrivener"
Henry James, "The Pupil"
Ivan Turgenev, "Bezhin Meadow"
Ralph Ellison, "King of the Bingo Game"
Sherwood Anderson, "The Egg"
William Faulkner, "A Rose for Emily"
Richard Yates, "Doctor Jack-o'-lantern"
Alice Walker, "Everyday Use"
Gyanranyan, "Our Side of the Fence and Theirs"
Liliana Heker, "The Stolen Party"

RELIGION/SPIRITUALITY

Nathaniel Hawthorne, "Young Goodman Brown"
Leo Tolstoy, "The Death of Ivan Ilych"
Frank O'Connor, "Guests of the Nation"
Ernest Hemingway, "A Clean, Well-Lighted Place"
Franz Kafka, "A Hunger Artist"
Louise Erdrich, "Snares"
Martin Amis, "Bujak and the Strong Force"
Ray Bradbury, "2002: Night Meeting"
Carlos Fuentes, "Aura"
James Welch, "Fools Crow"
Richard Cortez Day, "A Chagall Story"

DEATH AND DYING

Leo Tolstoy, "The Death of Ivan Ilych"
Henry James, "The Pupil"

Kate Chopin, "The Story of an Hour"
Ivan Turgenev, "Bezhin Meadow"
Aya Koda, "The Black Kimono"
Frank O'Connor, "Guests of the Nation"
Ernest Hemingway, "A Clean, Well-Lighted Place"
Franz Kafka, "A Hunger Artist"
William Faulkner, "A Rose for Emily"
Luigi Pirandello, "War"
Njabulo Ndebele, "Death of a Son"
Ann Beattie, "In the White Night"
Hisaye Yamamoto, "Yoneko's Earthquake"
Katherine Mansfield, "The Fly"
Raymond Carver, "Errand"
Richard Cortez Day, "A Chagall Story"

THE INDIVIDUAL AND SOCIETY

Herman Melville, "Bartleby the Scrivener"
Franz Kafka, "A Hunger Artist"
Joseph Conrad, "The Secret Sharer"
Heinrich Böll, "My Melancholy Face"
Luisa Valenzuela, "The Censors"
Shirley Jackson, "The Lottery"
Martin Amis, "Bujak and the Strong Force"
Joyce Carol Oates, "The Murder"
Ralph Ellison, "King of the Bingo Game"
Fiona Barr, "The Wall-Reader"
Njabulo Ndebele, "Death of a Son"
Elsa Joubert, "Back Yard"
Stephen Crane, "The Blue Hotel"
Louise Erdrich, "Snares"

INSANITY

Charlotte Perkins Gilman, "The Yellow Wallpaper"
Edgar Allen Poe, "The Tell-Tale Heart"
Joseph Conrad, "The Secret Sharer"
Ralph Ellison, "King of the Bingo Game"
William Faulkner, "A Rose for Emily"
Madeline DeFrees, "The Ventriloquist's Dummy"
Joyce Carol Oates, "The Murder"
Willa Cather, "Paul's Case"

COMING OF AGE

John Updike, "A & P"
Jayne Anne Phillips, "Bess"
Liliana Heker, "The Stolen Party"
Tess Gallagher, "A Pair of Glasses"
Matt Ellison, "Civil Engineer"
Alberto Alvaro Rios, "The Iguana Killer"
Susan Engberg, "A Daughter's Heart"
James Welch, "Fools Crow"
Hisaye Yamamoto, "Yoneko's Earthquake"

CONFLICT BETWEEN WOMEN AND MEN

Charlotte Perkins Gilman, "The Yellow Wallpaper"
Arthur Conan Doyle, "A Scandal in Bohemia"
Kate Chopin, "The Story of an Hour"
Yasunari Kawabata, "The Mole"
Eudora Welty, "Petrified Man"
John Steinbeck, "Chrysanthemums"
Zorah Neale Hurston, "Sweat"
D. H. Lawrence, "The Horse Dealer's Daughter"
Katherine Anne Porter, "The Jilting of Granny Weatherall"
Keri Hulme, "One Whale, Singing"
Sue Grafton, "She Didn't Come Home"
Sesshu Foster, "The Street of the Fathers"
Carlos Fuentes, "Aura"
Hisaye Yamamoto, "Yoneko's Earthquake"
John Updike, "A & P"

CONFLICT IN FAMILIES

Anton Chekhov, "Gooseberries"
Bernard Malamud, "The Jewbird"
Susan Engberg, "A Daughter's Heart"
Jayne Anne Phillips, "Bess"
Tess Gallagher, "A Pair of Glasses"
Alice Munro, "Miles City, Montana"
John Cheever, "Goodbye, My Brother"
Hisaye Yamamoto, "Yoneko's Earthquake"
Sesshu Foster, "The Street of the Fathers"
Alice Walker, "Everyday Use"
Donald Barthelme, "The Author"

MATERIALISM

Guy de Maupassant, "The Necklace"
O. Henry, "The Gift of the Magi"
Herman Melville, "Bartleby the Scrivener"
Henry James, "The Pupil"
Sholem Aleichem, "On Account of a Hat"
Eudora Welty, "Petrified Man"
Sherwood Anderson, "The Egg"
Franz Kafka, "A Hunger Artist"
Janet Frame, "Insulation"
Amos Oz, "If There Is Justice"
Cynthia Ozick, "The Butterfly and the Traffic Light"
Alice Walker, "Everyday Use"

CONFLICT BETWEEN HUMANS AND NATURE

Keri Hulme, "One Whale, Singing"
Rick Demarinis, "Under the Wheat"
Lars Gustafsson, "Uncle Sven and the Cultural Revolution"
Ivan Turgenev, "Bezhin Meadow"
Shawn Hsu Wong, "Each Year Grain"
Stephen King, "Graveyard Shift"

CRIME

Arthur Conan Doyle, "A Scandal in Bohemia"
Edgar Allan Poe, "The Tell-Tale Heart"
Joseph Conrad, "The Secret Sharer"
Tadeusz Borowski, "The Supper"
Frank O'Connor, "Guests of the Nation"
Martin Amis, "Bujak and the Strong Force"
Margaret Atwood, "Rape Fantasies"
Raymond Chandler, "The Wrong Pigeon"
Joyce Carol Oates, "The Murder"
Sue Grafton, "She Didn't Come Home"

THE HOLOCAUST

Tadeusz Borowski, "The Supper"

VANITY

Sholem Aleichem, "On Account of a Hat"
O. Henry, "The Gift of the Magi"
Eudora Welty, "Petrified Man"
James Joyce, "Araby"
Liliana Heker, "The Stolen Party"
Tess Gallagher, "A Pair of Glasses"

CONFLICT BETWEEN RACES OR ETHNIC GROUPS OR NATIONS

Tadeusz Borowski, "The Supper"
Ralph Ellison, "King of the Bingo Game"
Frank O'Connor, "Guests of the Nation"
Langston Hughes, "On the Road"
Shawn Hsu Wong, "Each Year Grain"
Hisaye Yamamoto, "Yoneko's Earthquake"
Elsa Joubert, "Back Yard"
Njabulo Ndebele, "Death of a Son"
Fiona Barr, "The Wall-Reader"
Bernard Malamud, "The Jewbird"
Lars Gustafsson, "Uncle Sven and the Cultural Revolution"
Cynthia Ozick, "The Butterfly and the Traffic Light"
Sesshu Foster, "The Street of the Fathers"
Gyanranyan, "Our Side of the Fence and Theirs"

LOVE AND SEXUALITY

O. Henry, "The Gift of the Magi"
D. H. Lawrence, "The Horse Dealer's Daughter"
Yasunari Kawabata, "The Mole"
James Joyce, "Araby"
John Steinbeck, "Chrysanthemums"
Rick Demarinis, "Under the Wheat"
Hisaye Yamamoto, "Yoneko's Earthquake"
John Updike, "A & P"
Jayne Anne Phillips, "Bess"
Carlos Fuentes, "Aura"
Sesshu Foster, "The Street of the Fathers"

WAR

Tadeusz Borowski, "The Supper"
Luigi Pirandello, "War"
Aya Koda, "The Black Kimono"
Martin Amis, "Bujak and the Strong Force"
Fiona Barr, "The Wall-Reader"
Frank O'Connor, "Guests of the Nation"
Tim O'Brien, "The Things They Carried"
Richard Brautigan, "The Ghost Children of Tacoma"
Rick Demarinis, "Under the Wheat"
Amos Oz, "If There Is Justice"

CHILDHOOD AND ADOLESCENCE

Jayne Anne Phillips, "Bess"
James Welch, "Fools Crow"
Richard Brautigan, "The Ghost Children of Tacoma"
Liliana Heker,"The Stolen Party"
Hisaye Yamamoto, "Yoneko's Earthquake"
James Joyce, "Araby"
Sherwood Anderson, "The Egg"
Richard Yates, "Doctor Jack-o'-lantern"
Alberto Alvaro Rios, "The Iguana Killer"

Technique:

A Checklist of Stories

Please note that the following is not a complete alternate table of contents but only a checklist for quick reference.

FIRST-PERSON NARRATION

Edgar Allan Poe, "The Tell-Tale Heart"
Herman Melville, "Bartleby the Scrivener"
Arthur Conan Doyle, "A Scandal in Bohemia"
Joseph Conrad, "The Secret Sharer"
William Faulkner, "A Rose for Emily"
Sherwood Anderson, "The Egg"
Alice Munro, "Miles City, Montana"
Jayne Anne Phillips, "Bess"
Gyanranjan, "Our Side of the Fence and Theirs"
John Updike, "A & P"

SECOND-PERSON NARRATION

Carlos Fuentes, "Aura"

THIRD-PERSON NARRATION

Nathaniel Hawthorne, "Young Goodman Brown"
Leo Tolstoy, "The Death of Ivan Ilych"
D. H. Lawrence, "The Horse Dealer's Daughter"
Zora Neale Hurston, "Sweat"
Anne Beattie, "In the White Night"
Shirley Jackson, "The Lottery"

Hisaye Yamamoto, "Yoneko's Earthquake"
Richard Cortez Day, "A Chagall Story"

PERIPHERAL NARRATION

Arthur Conan Doyle, "A Scandal in Bohemia"

UNRELIABLE NARRATION

Edgar Allan Poe, "The Tell-Tale Heart"
Joseph Conrad, "The Secret Sharer"
Joyce Carol Oates, "The Murder"

NAIVE POINT OF VIEW

James Joyce, "Araby"
Hisaye Yamamoto, "Yoneko's Earthquake"
Liliana Heker, "The Stolen Party"
Matt Ellison, "Civil Engineer"

SETTING

Ivan Turgenev, "Bezhin Meadow"
Stephen Crane, "The Blue Hotel"
William Faulkner, "A Rose for Emily"
John Steinbeck, "Chrysanthemums"
Ray Bradbury, "2002: Night Meeting"
Carlos Fuentes, "Aura"
Hisaye Yamamoto, "Yoneko's Earthquake"
Shawn Hsu Wong, "Each Year Grain"
Sesshu Foster, "The Street of the Fathers"
James Welch, "Fools Crow"

IRONY

Guy de Maupassant, "The Necklace"
Henry James, "The Pupil"
Sholem Aleichem, "On Account of a Hat"
Franz Kafka, "A Hunger Artist"
Sherwood Anderson, "The Egg"

Langston Hughes, "On the Road"
Alice Walker, "Everyday Use"
Lars Gustafsson, "Uncle Sven and the Cultural Revolution"
Luisa Valenzuela, "The Censors"
Matt Ellison, "Civil Engineer"
Martin Amis, "Bujak and the Strong Force"
Fiona Barr, "The Wall-Reader"

SYMBOL

Nathaniel Hawthorne, "Young Goodman Brown"
Anton Chekhov, "Gooseberries"
Charlotte Perkins Gilman, "The Yellow Wallpaper"
Stephen Crane, "The Blue Hotel"
Aya Koda, "The Black Kimono"
Yasunari Kawabata, "The Mole"
Ralph Ellison, "King of the Bingo Game"
Katherine Mansfield, "The Fly"
Ann Beattie, "In the White Night"
Heinrich Böll, "My Melancholy Face"
Alberto Alvaro Rios, "The Iguana Killer"
Fiona Barr, "The Wall-Reader"

PLOT

Joseph Conrad, "The Secret Sharer"
Leo Tolstoy, "The Death of Ivan Ilych"
Arthur Conan Doyle, "A Scandal in Bohemia"
John Steinbeck, "Chrysanthemums"
Raymond Chandler, "The Wrong Pigeon"
Flannery O'Connor, "Everything That Rises Must Converge"
Raymond Carver, "Errand"
Njabulo Ndebele, "Death of a Son"
Madeline DeFrees, "The Ventriloquist's Dummy"
Sue Grafton, "She Didn't Come Home"

PROSE STYLE

Henry James, "The Pupil"
Joseph Conrad, "The Secret Sharer"

James Joyce, "Araby"
William Faulkner, "A Rose for Emily"
Ernest Hemingway, "A Clean, Well-Lighted Place"
Willa Cather, "Paul's Case"
Raymond Chandler, "The Wrong Pigeon"
John Cheever, "Goodbye, My Brother"
Ann Beattie, "In the White Night"
Cynthia Ozick, "The Butterfly and the Traffic Light"
Donald Barthelme, "The Author"
Sharon Hsu Wong, "Each Year Grain"
Richard Brautigan, "The Ghost Children of Tacoma"
Raymond Carver, "Errand"
Tess Gallagher, "A Pair of Glasses"

CLOSURE

Anton Chekhov, "Gooseberries"
Kate Chopin, "Story of an Hour"
James Joyce, "Araby"
Ernest Hemingway, "A Clean, Well-Lighted Place"
Tadeusz Borowski, "The Supper"
Tim O'Brien, "The Things They Carried"
Flannery O'Connor, "Everything That Rises Must Converge"
Shirley Jackson, "The Lottery"
Susan Engberg, "A Daughter's Heart"
Madeline DeFrees, "The Ventriloquist's Dummy"

The Evolution of the Short Story:

AN INTRODUCTION

EACH STORY IS CONNECTED TO OTHER STORIES

As you read and interpret individual stories, you will begin to develop your own definition of *the short story,* you will begin to establish your own criteria for a successful story, and you will begin to get a sense of this literary form's history and development.

This essay is designed to begin the process. However, it is intended only to sketch the development of short fiction—to give you an outline that you will fill in and extend according to your own reading. This or any other particular version of short fiction's development is less important than the *notion* of that development. It is vital to remember that this form of art, like any other, has a complicated past, and that any story written today—by you or someone else—is attached to a vast web of fiction in our own culture and in others.

A WORKING DEFINITION

What is a short story? One working definition is "a short prose narrative in which 'fact' has been transformed by the imagination." This working definition only gets us started in the process of exploring this form of art, however. The more we think about and read stories, the more refined our sense of "narrative form," differences and similarities between prose and poetry, and the workings of imagination will become.

THE ANCIENT ART OF STORYTELLING

In one sense the short story is an ancient art that is rooted in human beings' propensity to recount, embellish, and purely invent "what happened." Every time you share your experience of a national disaster, report gossip, tell a joke, or explain to someone how your day has gone, you act out a storytelling impulse that is much older than recorded history. Virtually every culture on the planet is based in part on a tradition of transmitting stories orally, and when these stories were written down in some form, literatures flourished.

Babylonian creation myths; Norse, Greek, and Roman myths; Chinese and Egyptian tales; narratives and parables from the Bible; Buddhist parables; fairy tales, fables and folk tales—these are but a few examples of narratives from early societies. Closer to our own time, Boccaccio's *Decameron* and Chaucer's *Canterbury Tales* (both written about six hundred years ago) are essentially collections of short stories. These and other narratives form the rich, distant ancestry of the short story as we know it. Many of them, especially the myths, are stories that attempt to explain how civilizations came to be, and they often deal with superhuman figures.

Therefore, we can detect in such precursors of the short story the desire to shape experience—to explain human behavior, to represent patterns of behavior, to order chaos, and to address universal issues such as death, love, war, power, and evil. Short stories written today may not be as comprehensive or grandiose in what they attempt to achieve, but with myths, fairy tales, fables, and folk tales they share the impulse to shape experience with the tools of imagination and language.

THE REINVENTION OF THE SHORT STORY

In another sense, however, the short story was "reinvented" about a hundred and sixty years ago, meaning that many writers began to see the short story as a unique narrative form and to experiment with that form. Many definitions of the genre spring from this rebirth of the form. Russian writers such as Leo Tolstoy and Anton Chekhov, French writers such as Honoré de Balzac and Guy de Maupassant, and American writers such as Nathaniel Hawthorne, Henry James, and Edgar Allan Poe were among those that deliberately redefined this kind of imaginative writing. Writers from the British Isles had comparatively less influence on the short story form at this time, although a few decades later the influence of British and Irish writers would be enormous. The British contribution to the novel at this time, however, can hardly be overestimated. To see how the short story changed in the nineteenth century, let's briefly consider the contribution of two American writers.

Edgar Allan Poe and Henry James

Poe's essay "The Philosophy of Composition" (1846) had such an enormous impact on writers and critics that it is still considered a key document of literary theory. It deals specifically with how a narrative poem ("The Raven"), not a short story, was written; nonetheless, it shows how deliberate Poe was about achieving certain effects and about creating a powerful, compressed narrative. The essay is one significant example of how self-conscious nineteenth-century writers were about how and why they wrote what they wrote.

Henry James's essay "The Art of Fiction" (1884) has endured for much the same reason. It remains the source for many of our current ideas about point of view, "showing versus telling," and other narrative strategies. It also articulates James's view of fiction as a complex, multilayered replication of life itself, and so the essay tells us much about how ambitiously James approached short fiction.

The Short Story as a Distinct Form of Literature

Two of the ways nineteenth-century writers redefined the form may seem contradictory. First, they sharply distinguished the short story from other kinds of literature—novels, plays, poems. In theory (when "writing about" the art) and practice, they treated the short story as a unique form of literature that enabled writers to achieve effects and interpret life in new ways. But these writers also placed the short story in the company of novels, plays, and poems by suggesting—in theory and practice—that this genre was in no way more slight or less powerful than these other kinds of writing. In other words, a short story could achieve as much as a novel, play, or long poem. It could do justice to significant experiences and big ideas. It could have the same impact as a novel or a play.

The common effect of these two seemingly different phenomena was to elevate the short story. It became important, even indispensable, to writers. It became a form on which writers could depend, a form with its own distinct identity and power. Even writers like Poe (who wrote poems, a novel, and essays) and Tolstoy (who wrote novels and essays) saw stories as essential, not secondary, to their careers.

Literacy and Publishing

The birth of the short story as we know it occurred not just because powerful voices like those of Poe and Tolstoy used the form, however. Like the rise of the novel and journalism in the 1700s, the rise of the short story in the 1800s resulted partly from events in society—specifically, increased literacy and improved printing technology. Many more people were reading, and societies had found ways to deliver "reading matter" to the public in greater quantities, at cheaper prices, and at a faster pace.

This situation was particularly true in Europe and America. Between 1780 and 1840, the publishing "industry" was transformed; in fact, it *became* a genuine industry during those years. Machine-made paper, power presses, faster methods of binding, and faster distribution all emerged in these six decades. At the same time, the population of cities was virtually exploding, creating a massive market for newspapers, periodicals, and inexpensive books.

It is worth remembering that writers write to audiences via publishers; the expanded audience and the spread of publishing broadened the readership of the short-story writer and made the career of writing fiction more possible if no less precarious. It is no coincidence that the short story began to flourish at the same time as the number and quality of literary and popular magazines began to rise.

The "reinvention" of the short story in the 1800s happened, then, because of individuals we can name, but also because of social, historical, and technological changes we can trace.

SUBJECT MATTER: PSYCHOLOGY AND "ORDINARY LIFE"

As the short story was reinvented, so was its subject matter. Suddenly two subject areas seemed particularly suited to treatment in short stories: psychology and "ordinary life."

Inasmuch as the late nineteenth and early twentieth centuries saw the emergence of Freud and other modern psychologists, it should not surprise us that psychology—the study of the mind—influenced literature. However, no one probably could have predicted how extensively Poe, Hawthorne, Tolstoy, Turgenev, Chekhov, James, Gilman, and others would explore the mind. To be sure, these writers were not the first who were interested in the subject; Chaucer, Shakespeare, and Austen are but three examples from British literature of earlier authors who were astonishingly perceptive observers of the human mind and emotions, the "interior life." But psychology as a social science came into its own in the 1800s. Partly as a result of this development and partly as a coincidence of it, short-story writers addressed the subject more fervently than ever.

As you will see, in many of the stories from this period the significant action is not physical or even external but instead is emotional, mental, internal. The short story proved to have a unique power to suggest an interior voice and to magnify crucial psychological moments; consequently, it helped these writers explore self-doubt, faith, desire, guilt, madness, and alienation in ways that literature had not tried before.

Indeed, even the modern detective and horror stories, for which Poe and Arthur Conan Doyle refined prototypes, can be seen as products of this interest in psychology. For Poe and Doyle are fascinated not so much by violence, heroism, and spectacular pursuit, but by the criminal mind, the processes of detection, and a dark psychological atmosphere. Later writers of detective and horror fiction, such as Raymond Chandler and Stephen King, have made the forms more violent and extreme, but they have also preserved this interest in psychology and atmosphere.

As Conan Doyle was creating the world's most famous and possibly most eccentric detective, Sherlock Holmes, and Poe was exploring extreme states of being, other writers were depicting characters that were neither famous, nor extreme, nor even exceptional. Hawthorne, James, Chekhov, Melville, de Maupassant, Tolstoy, and others plucked characters from everyday life and placed them under the microscope of the short story. Because of this, many of these writers are associated with the broad literary movement of *realism.*

Here is where the modern short story differs most severely from its ancient precursors; instead of writing about gods or heroes or legendary figures, these writers implied that the real stuff of literature was the common person—clerks, wives, husbands, students, teenagers, prostitutes, ministers, and so on. Indirectly, the authors were saying that a character's being larger than life was not a key to the appeal of the short story. They were saying that the story drew its strength from the ways it could see into ordinary lives with extraordinary force and perceptive power. These writers began a tradition that has persisted to this moment: They used the short story to illuminate our lives for us.

As with psychology, "ordinary life" as a subject for literature was not a new invention by the realistic writers of the 1800s. For example, folk tales—tales of "the people"—are by definition about ordinary life, though they may have fantastical elements. The Romantic movement in literature, which began about the time of the French Revolution (1789), also expressed a renewed interest in common people. One aspect of British Romanticism, 1789–1830, was its interest in democratic ideals. In fact, the British poet William Wordsworth at this time deliberately set out to prove that great poetry could be written about rural life and that rural life was just as interesting and important as royal life. Consequently, to some extent his brand of Romanticism contributed to the development of gritty realism. Nonetheless, in terms of sheer emphasis, the short-fiction writers of the 1800s were unsurpassed in their desire to transform everyday life into literature.

THE MODERN PERIOD AND AFTER

As writers in the late 1800s and early 1900s confronted alienation, meaninglessness, world war, and the numerous problems of industrial society, the short story inevitably changed, but psychology and everyday, unspectacular life remained crucial to the art and are still important to writers of the late 1900s.

From the late 1800s through the 1930s, the short story underwent its "modern" phase—"modern" both because society was changing more quickly than ever before and because writers stretched the form for a range of purposes, including the purpose of making the form responsive to changes in society.

James Joyce and Ernest Hemingway

The Irish writer James Joyce published a collection of short stories *(Dubliners)* in 1914 that still ranks as one of the most widely read and widely influential books in the genre. His concept of *epiphany*—a moment of overwhelming but not necessarily beneficent insight on the part of a character—transformed the theory and practice of short fiction. Further, his unsentimental look at the city of Dublin articulated many of the changes all cities had undergone; in this sense his fiction was modern because it looked at life in industrial society and explored the several ways in which people were alienated—cut off from their own families, cities, religions, and cultures.

For his part, the American Ernest Hemingway developed what may still be the most recognizable style in short fiction. The spare style evoked a terse, unsentimental, and sometimes brutal point of view that has been widely imitated, sometimes scorned, and often parodied. Like Joyce and other *modernist* writers, he also grappled in his fiction with problems of alienation, of living in a world that some claimed was "godless," and of feeling dissociated from one's nation and culture.

Although it is important to recognize what Joyce, Hemingway, and others did for the modern short story, it is equally important to note what it did for them. Although the reputations of Joyce and Hemingway rest in part on important novels like *Ulysses* and *The Sun Also Rises,* their careers owe a huge debt to the short story. Such is the case with D. H. Lawrence, Eudora Welty, Katherine Anne Porter, Katherine Mansfield, Franz Kafka, and dozens of other writers whose work has lasted. The case of Kafka, whose stories go well beyond the world of Poe to depict a world of futility and absurdity, is particularly instructive, for his remarkable reputation as a writer is founded almost exclusively on his short fiction. In a sense, the respect accorded the short story in the 1800s paid enormous dividends to later generations because many writers of remarkable vision and talent felt free to depend on the short story as a mainstay of their artistic expression.

Women's Experience

The short story proved to be extremely valuable to women writers. Kate Chopin and Charlotte Perkins Gilman are but two examples of nineteenth-century writers who illuminated women's experience in new ways by means of the short story. As with these writers' male counterparts, psychology—particularly the psychology of "domestic" life—proved extremely attractive as a subject of fiction. Since then the genre has remained essential not just to writers who happen to be women, but also to women who are deliberately attempting to establish feminist perspectives in literature—perspectives that push us to reevaluate relationships between genders, the influence of gender on art, and the meaning of gender itself.

The use of fiction to reevaluate definitions of gender anticipated how important fiction would become to all groups of people who at some point find themselves defined as "secondary" or as "outsider," either because of ethnic origin, economic status, or color. The voice of fiction is often one of protest, identity, and redefinition. One might argue that during the modern period, the political edge of the short story grew sharper.

THE CONTEMPORARY SHORT STORY AND "EMERGING VOICES"

Perhaps the most important observation to make about the short story since the 1940s is also the most obvious one: As much as if not more than any other literary form, the short story has continued to flourish. It has remained useful to the nations that helped reinvent it in the 1800s: Russia, France, England, and America. But it has also proved essential to writers in Africa and Scandinavia, Australia and New Zealand, Canada, Central and South America, Eastern Europe, the Middle East, and Asia. Voices from virtually every economic, social, ethnic, and national background have used the form to assert views of the world. Subgenres such as science fiction, horror fiction, and detective fiction have appropriated the short story. Short fiction seems to be the most inexhaustible and resilient form of literature. Indeed, whereas critics and writers alike have periodically decried the "death" of the novel or the poem, the short story has generally escaped such doom-saying. If anything, short fiction in America has been revitalized by the vast increase of women, black, Hispanic, Asian, and Native American writers. The genre has also flourished because of the greater impact that writers from outside Western Europe and North America now have on the global literary scene.

Some issues that affected the short story in the 1800s still affect it. For example, its vitality still depends on the marketplace—on magazines and the reading public. The influence of mass-market (large-circulation) magazines has decreased, either because magazines have dropped their fiction departments entirely or because they print stories aimed at an extremely narrow segment of a middle-class audience. No doubt television has played a part in such changes, as it has in so many other areas of life. Small literary magazines have taken up the slack somewhat, however; the twentieth century is *the* century of the "little" magazine. This phenomenon has no doubt allowed for more experimentation in narrative form, point of view, and subject matter.

Also, the growth of creative writing programs, chiefly in America but also in many other nations, has produced not just more writers but also a continuing audience for short fiction. From the 1940s forward, writers have been supported and developed by the literary magazine, colleges, or some combination of both. Some literary critics have claimed that this support has stunted the growth of the art, yet others have observed that the support is but a different version of the social and economic realities that helped the short story to flourish in the 1800s.

New collections of short fiction from virtually every corner of the globe appear almost daily. This abundance can cause momentary confusion, but in the long run it is a tribute to the art form and a comment on how interconnected the world's literary communities have become. The "emerging voices" represented in the last section of this anthology only hint at how varied and rich the world of the short story is late in this century and how the genre is being redefined all the time.

The division of the anthology into four eras of the short story—Early, Modern, Contemporary, and Emerging—is intended to reinforce the sense that short fiction is an art with a history and many traditions. Any such division is bound to be arbitrary to a degree, and it is bound to become even more arbitrary as one assesses stories written closer to this very moment. However, the purpose of defining four eras is to make the history of short fiction easier for you to define on your own, not to force that history into four "boxes." Indeed, one of your pleasures in exploring the anthology and the art of short fiction in general will be to identify continuities and patterns that run throughout the eras and across boundaries of culture, nation, race, belief, and gender.

Two other introductory essays follow. They address the topics of analyzing and writing about stories and writing stories yourself. Additionally they define the short story in more detail, building on the working definition with which we have started.

Each section also begins with a brief essay that will elaborate on many of the ideas hinted at in this discussion of short fiction's evolution. However, no amount of introductory commentary can replace the knowledge of short fiction you will cultivate merely by reading as many short stories as you can.

Writing about Stories:
AN INTRODUCTION

In 1798 the British poet William Wordsworth published a poem in which a speaker expresses an attitude toward analyzing "beauteous forms" in nature and art; the attitude is one that most of us have shared at some point:

Sweet is the lore which nature brings;
Our meddling intellect
Mis-shapes the beauteous forms of things;
—We murder to dissect.

from The Tables Turned

Often it does seem as if we "murder" a piece of art when we "dissect" it, and at other times it seems doubtful whether any amount of analytical "meddling" will alter our first impression of a story, poem, painting, concert, or play.

However, we should remember that the view expressed in Wordsworth's poems is only one side of a playful, speculative dialogue about "books and learning" versus "nature and art." We should also remember that analysis need not be "murder," and that it can have the opposite effect of enriching—breathing life into—our understanding of the thing analyzed.

Before we analyze and write about stories, therefore, we should ensure that the process is more than cold dissection, and that it never be merely a fulfillment of an assignment or a repetition of a formula. Analysis should serve the author of the story, the story itself, you the writer of the analytical essay, and your reader. It should do justice to all four.

WRITING BEGINS WITH READING

In a sense, then, writing about stories begins before you ever put pen to paper or push a cursor across a screen. It begins with your attitude toward analysis, with what *you* want out of interpreting a story.

It also begins with your attitude toward reading. To write well about a story, one has to read a story well, meaning that one has to read *actively*. One has to be alert to the effects, large and small, that the story produces. Reading a story is a transaction between the printed words and the reader. This kind of reading may be more difficult for those of us conditioned by television, radio, film, and other electronic media that seem to surround us and to depend sometimes on our passivity. Reading a story requires more than sitting back and absorbing words; it asks us to take part in "the continuous dream" (as the writer John Gardner called it) of a story.

Once you have finished reading a story, you may want to read it once or twice more because rereading itself is a kind of analysis, particularly if you have a strategy for rereading. "Strategy for rereading" may sound abstract and complicated, particularly if you are used to reading a story only once. Basically, though, the term merely implies that you should look for something different in a story the second time around. For instance, you might focus on characters instead of plot; you might concentrate on one scene that seems important; you might examine dialogue, or images that might be interpreted as symbols; or you might go back to a place in the story that confused you and try to clear up the confusion.

PREWRITING

After these readings, you may want to write a spontaneous response to the story. It is a good idea to keep a notebook of such responses. You may wish to begin with the most basic question: Did you like the story or not? Remember that the answer to this question is the beginning, not the end, of your analysis, however. Disliking a story or claiming to be bored by it may spring from a misunderstanding or a misconception on your part. Further reading and analysis—or discussing the story with others—may very well allow you to break through your dislike and boredom to an appreciation of the story. In any case, this spontaneous response may contain virtually any remark you think is worth making about the story.

After writing such a response, you may want to keep generating ideas by doing more brainstorming. In this process you may be guided by a paper topic that an instructor has provided. Make lists of ideas, issues, questions that the story has made you consider; list problems you had with the story, pinpointing things that confused you; list elements of the story that struck you as important or memorable; identify qualities of the characters, the conflict, the crisis, the resolution, or the theme. Definitions of these terms appear in the Glossary. Talk about your impressions of the story with a classmate or a friend. Jot down crucial words or phrases from the story.

But remember: The idea here is not to formulate a thesis or a point of view but to generate as much material as you can. Therefore, it is best not to prejudge what you write down. Keep the pen, pencil, or cursor moving. You will have plenty of opportunity to toss out unwanted material later. Remember, too, that brainstorming can be useful at any stage of the writing process. For example, after you have written a draft, you may find that a paragraph or a section of it needs further development. At that point you may find that some additional brainstorming will help you.

Topic and Thesis

How long should the prewriting stage last? The glib answer is "as long as it takes." In the ideal world, all of us would have as long as we need to come up with satisfactory ideas for an essay. Unfortunately, in the world of college—and elsewhere—deadlines loom and force us to shift our emphasis from the "process" of discovering what we think to the "product"—the essay the instructor wants by a certain day. No matter how near the deadline is, however, allow yourself at least a few hours to brainstorm, make lists, doodle, and take other steps to get ideas and clarify them before you start thinking about "product."

One way to bridge the gap between "process" and "product" is to focus on a topic for your paper as well as a thesis. A topic is "the subject matter," an area you want to emphasize in your analysis of the story. A thesis is your point of view or opinion about this topic. A thesis is the viewpoint that your paper will try to convince a reader to accept. For example, a topic might be "Symbolism in James Joyce's 'Araby,' " and the thesis might be "The symbolism in Joyce's 'Araby' mainly involves images of light and dark." The chief purpose of your essay, then, would be to demonstrate the thesis, to convince your reader that *your* interpretation of the topic is useful, and that *your* view of symbolism in the story is worth considering.

Sometimes you will be given a list of topics, and at other times you will discover a topic while you're reading a story or writing an informal response. Your instructor may also suggest specific ways of finding a topic and developing a point of view, either on your own or with other students in class.

Questions to Help Generate Topics and Theses

In any event, there are some categories of questions that will help you to define the kind of analysis you want to pursue and to focus a topic more precisely. Two words of caution: These categories are not meant to be exhaustive; they are only some of many kinds of analysis. Also, the categories are not mutually exclusive. You may wish to use questions from two or three categories to help focus a topic. You may also want to use these questions as springboards to other questions you invent on your own. The main thing is to be aware of the critical approach you use; to remember that the questions you ask about a story will "frame" your reading of it.

Technique/Form

1. What is the point of view? Is it third person or first person? Through what character's or characters' "eyes" do we perceive the action? Are you sympathetic to this point of view? Is it a "reliable" one?

2. How well does the story capture and hold our interest? How does it attempt to capture and hold our interest?

3. What images and details seem particularly memorable or striking or shocking or grotesque? Why? Begin by listing several details—without actually looking at the story again.

4. What individual scenes seem important? Are some confusing? Why? Choose a scene that seems important and list the reasons for its significance.

5. How well do you feel you know the main characters? Are you sympathetic to them? Why or why not? To what extent are characters stereotyped in the story?

6. How effective was the end of the story? The resolution of the conflict?

7. What is the plot of the story?

8. How effective was the author's use of dialogue? How is the author's use

of dialogue different from that of other authors'? What did you learn about the characters from what they said and how they said it?

9. Are there clearly identifiable symbols? What do they signify? How successfully are they used? Choose one image, object, or place in the story that you think may be a symbol and explain its symbolic quality.

10. How much does the setting affect the story and in what ways? What is unusual or especially vivid about this "place"? You may want to begin by describing the place.

Subgenre/Mode/Type

1. Is the story science fiction? Fantasy? Horror? Detective? Is it a mixture of subgenres?

2. Is it realistic? Surrealistic? (These and other terms are defined in the Glossary at the back of the book.)

3. Does the story deliberately violate conventions or readers' expectations?

4. Is it satire? Comedy?

5. Is the story easily placed in a category (love story, coming-of-age story, story of family conflict, story about confronting death, and so forth)? Is it too easily placed in a category? That is, is the story predictable? What other works of literature does it remind you of?

6. If this story is about "the future," what will the future look like? Do you agree with this vision/version of the future? Why or why not?

Ideas/Issues/Themes

1. Directly or indirectly, does the story make a political statement? What is it? You may want to begin by determining whether the story addresses a particular political or social issue or problem.

2. Does the story address a social problem that is still relevant today? In what way?

3. Does the story criticize or celebrate certain kinds of behavior? Explain.

4. Does the story express or attack certain religious or philosophical ideas?

5. Does the conflict in the story seem old-fashioned or dated to you? Why or why not?

6. Is the story concerned with a certain phase of life? Adolescence? Leaving home? Marrying? Growing old?

7. To what extent does the story concern good and evil, right and wrong?

Gender/Class/Nation/Race/Religion/Ethnicity

1. Can you identify stereotypes of women, races, classes of people, religious backgrounds, or nationalities in this story?

2. To what extent is the story concerned mainly with women's experience or men's experience?

3. To what extent is the story linked with a specific culture? To what extent is this link an obstacle in your reading of the story?

4. To what extent is the story tied to working-class or middle-class experiences?

5. To what extent does the story deal with conflicts between genders, generations, beliefs, nations, races, classes, or ethnic backgrounds?

History/Literary History

1. How clearly is the story connected to a specific period in history? What are the clues?

2. Is the story about a certain war or a certain period of political or social

upheaval? What more do you need to know about the historical background to make your reading of the story clearer?

3.   Compare and contrast this story with another one written at about the same time.

4.   Compare and contrast this story with another one that is about a similar issue/conflict/theme but that was written much earlier or much later.

5.   Have other critics placed this author or this story in a particular "school" or "period" or "movement" of writing? What were the reasons for this placement?

6.   If the story is considered a "classic," what do you think *makes* it a classic? Would you call it a "classic"? Why or why not? If you were editing an anthology, would you include this story? Why or why not?

PURPOSE

Once you have gone through the reading and prewriting processes and settled on a topic, it is advisable to ask yourself whether your topic can be covered adequately in the number of pages for which your instructor has asked. It is also a good idea to ask yourself what the purpose of your paper will be. By "purpose" I mean not "to get a good grade" or "to fulfill an assignment for English 258," although these are undeniably worthwhile purposes. By "purpose" I mean *what will your paper attempt to demonstrate, and how will it demonstrate this?* If your paper is about "Desperation in Ralph Ellison's 'King of the Bingo Game,' " for example, the purpose will be to show your reader the ways in which desperation figures significantly in the story, the ways in which it reflects oppression and racism, and so on. Without a focused purpose, papers become nothing more than a mechanical fulfillment of an assignment, and ironically they then fail to fulfill the assignment.

A FIRST DRAFT

The way to go about producing a first draft of the essay should be entirely up to you because writing is an idiosyncratic enterprise. If you have a favorite time to write or a lucky pen, so be it. If you need to have absolute quiet or music blaring, follow your instincts. However, make sure you think of the first draft *as a first draft*—as a draft that might be heavily revised later. Also, remember that writing is a process not just of putting words on paper but of discovering what you think. In other words, the very act of writing down your ideas may force you to change your ideas, think of new ones, or alter the topic and thesis of your paper. Such discovery and change is natural and will probably result in a richer analysis of the story or stories.

Should you outline the paper before you begin to write? If outlines have helped you write successful papers before, then continue to use them. But do not force yourself to write an outline if you know that it will have no bearing on the actual writing of the essay. And do not imagine that you need to follow rigid rules of outlining that include lots of Roman numerals. The purpose of an outline is to give you a map of your essay, and if a quickly scribbled list of subtopics achieves this purpose, then that is all the outlining you need to do.

One other way to outline is to wait until you have written a draft. Then underline each of your topic sentences and produce an outline based on these sentences. This outline will be a map of what you have already written, and it will tell you where you need to rearrange the order of topics or to introduce new ones. This kind of outline can be a useful bridge between a first and second draft.

If you are writing a paper on an assigned topic, check your rough draft against this assignment. Force yourself to answer the following questions honestly: Does my draft fulfill the assignment? Does it answer the questions my instructor has asked on the assignment sheet? Sometimes we produce well-written, insightful essays that are nonetheless off the topic. The time to bring the essay back on target is during the first-draft stage.

EVIDENCE

Because an analytical essay tries to convince a reader of a thesis, you will need to gather evidence to support the thesis. In a sense, you may need to repeat part of the prewriting process by returning to the story after you have developed a thesis, looking for parts of the story that will be most useful to you, marking the margin or making lists of potential "evidence." Returning to the story in this way may also lead you to revise your thesis slightly. Writing is a recursive or cyclical process, meaning that we often return to so-called "prewriting" techniques when we are in the middle of a draft.

Essentially, there are two kinds of evidence that will be useful to you. One is "internal." Internal evidence comes from the short story itself. As you read and reread the story, and as you begin making notes and doing other kinds of prewriting, you will need to identify scenes, passages, lines of dialogue, and segments of the plot that will help you demonstrate your opinion of the story. Later you will quote from these parts of the story. A word of caution: *Quotation is not analysis.* Reprinting whole chunks from a story does not take the place of analyzing the story. The usefulness of a quotation depends on what you have to say about it, so you will need to tell your reader how to connect the quotation with a view you have expressed. You will also need to select quotations carefully, for too much quotation may give your reader the idea that you are getting close to reprinting the story in full.

Another kind of evidence is "external." External evidence consists mainly of what other readers of the short story (often called "critics") have already said about it. This kind of evidence will be less useful than internal evidence when you are writing a fairly brief analysis of a story, but it will become increasingly useful as you write longer, research-oriented papers. The checklist of books at the back of this anthology is one starting place for discovering external evidence.

External evidence also includes the connections you will make between the story and your own experience. For example, if the story involves "loss," you may want to explain how the story relates to a particular experience you have had with "loss." External evidence includes cultural and historical information as well.

Using either kind of evidence brings conventions ("rules") with it. You will need to know when and how to use quotation marks, how to set off quoted material in the text of your essay, how to acknowledge the work of other critics, how to avoid various kinds of plagiarism, and so on. One place to start finding out about these conventions is in a handbook of college English; another source is the *Modern Language Association Style Sheet,* which should be available in your library, bookstore, or writing center/writing lab. (Many college handbooks on writing contain this style sheet in some form.) Conventions vary, however, so be sure to follow the ones your instructor prefers.

REVISING

One important thing to remember about revising is that it is different from editing or proofreading. Literally, *revising* means "seeing again"; practically, it means that you will probably have to change your first draft more significantly than by only rewriting sentences or checking for typographical errors. You may have to move, delete, or change whole sections of the essay. You may also have to change your original thesis significantly.

To "see" a first draft again is no easy matter, however, because all of us tend to like what we write, at least when we first write it. Therefore, you need to develop strategies of revision. One effective strategy is to have someone else read the draft and comment on it—not someone who loves everything you write, but someone who can be critical and fair, and someone who is somewhat familiar with analytical essays. This person will likely see elements of the essay that need changing or developing. If you ask a friend or a classmate to read your first draft, however, make sure that this person is not proofreading; you may need to ask the person to look at specific elements, such as how convincing your evidence is, or how clear your thesis is stated. Otherwise, the person may only check your spelling, which is an important consideration later but an unimportant one early in the writing process. Also, make sure that the person does not rewrite the paper *for* you; what you want is a response to your writing, not a replacement of other writing for yours.

One other way to get the distance you need from your first draft is just to set it aside for awhile. This technique is not so easy when the due date for the essay is near. Even if you can fit in several hours or a day into your writing schedule when you will not look at the essay, however, you will be able to look at the draft with more critical eyes.

Whatever method of revision you use, be sure to concentrate on such crucial elements as the topic, thesis, purpose, and evidence of the essay.

Most important, remember that analysis need not mean the destruction of the story you are analyzing. Analysis should repay you for the hours and energy you put in. It should make you a better reader, and it should make a story come alive for you. On the midnight before a paper is due, these principles may not be uppermost in your mind, but they should always be nearby, because, above all, they are practical; they will result in good papers.

Sample Student Essays

Here are two essays by college undergraduates about Charlotte Perkins Gilman's story "The Yellow Wallpaper" and Ann Beattie's story "In the White Night." (Both stories are included in this anthology.) These sample essays are presented not as "perfect" examples but as ones that provide coherent, interesting analyses supported by evidence.

The first student, Katie Jenkins, has chosen to address the issue and meaning of suicide in "The Yellow Wallpaper," and one of the rhetorical strategies she has chosen is to compare and contrast the story with a novel that addresses similar issues. Through these choices, this student has focused her analysis and has provided additional literary context. Her thesis is forceful, even controversial, but it is also reasonably stated and anchored to specific passages in the works discussed.

The second student, Shelley Bott, provides a close reading of Beattie's "In the White Night." She focuses on the connection between imagery and setting, on the one hand, and the nature of loss and grief, on the other. Obviously, there are innumerable ways in which one might write about such a story, but Bott's clear focus provides one intelligent and useful way to approach the story and, indirectly, to approach Beattie's writing in general.

Awakening to Wallpaper

M. KATHERINE JENKINS

Most people consider madness and suicide to be horrible endings to lives that held promise. Nowadays madness is treatable and, in many cases, curable, but during the nineteenth century it was in many instances as final as death. Suicide, then and now, holds frightening connotations: the fear of going to Hell for taking one's own life, permanent separation from loved ones, and the transition from the known of life to the unknown of death. In two nineteenth-century works by women, however, the perception of madness and suicide is unusual and unconventional.

Curiously, in Charlotte Perkins Gilman's story "The Yellow Wallpaper," madness is Jane's escape from the desolation of everyday life. Similarly, in "The Awakening" by Kate Chopin, suicide is Edna's "logical" alternative to the life she has discovered holds nothing for her. Jane and Edna decide on a course of action that ends their former existence. In each case the decision is an attempt to gain a separate existence, apart from the pressures on their former selves. The extremity and irrationality of their actions is a measure of how difficult and exacting some women's lives were during the 1800's.

Both Jane and Edna are trying to produce from the turmoil of their daily lives their essential selves—the entity that is free and independent from all other persons and ideas, strong and self-sustaining, not needy of the succor of others to become complete.

Strikingly, Jane and Edna attempt similar means to gain this elusive self, most obviously through men. Jane seeks her self through her husband and his understanding of what her role should be. John is a doctor, and so Jane's nervous condition is seen by him as a common "female ailment" that his wife should easily conquer. He treats her like a child, calling her "little girl (449)" and commands her to stay in bed for her own good, having Jane "lie down for an hour after each meal (450)." She accepts his treatment, but continues to write a journal without his knowledge. However, in this journal she expresses herself using John's language. It is startling how often Jane uses the phrase "John says."

On the other hand, in "The Awakening," Edna fails to find expression through her husband, partly because he is unsure himself what her role should be: It would have been a difficult matter for Mr. Pontellier to define to his own satisfaction or any one else's wherein his wife failed in her duty toward their children. It was something which he felt rather than perceived, and he never voiced the feeling without subsequent regret and ample atonement (181). Because Mr. Pontellier is unable to define his wife's role, she cannot perform it. Edna begins to have a love affair in his absence, yet even then she is no closer to her self than she was with her husband. When Edna finally confronts her passion for Robert (not the subject of her affair), whom she believes understands her struggle, she realizes "that the day would come when he, too, and the thought of him would melt out of her existence, leaving her alone (350)."

Keeping all this in mind, we might consider suicide and madness from a different perspective, not as endings but as beginnings. Jane's madness is seen as an end to her previous life. Yet it should be viewed as the start of self. Jane, John, and their baby go to the country for the summer because of Jane's recent nervous condition. They stay in a rented summer home in hopes of improving her health, and Jane is often left alone in a large room of the house decorated with a fading yellow wall-paper. During their stay, Jane becomes certain that her husband doesn't understand how serious her mental unbalance is: "John does not know how much I really suffer (445)." As her fascination with the wall-paper grows, Jane feels better about herself because she has "something more to expect, to look forward to, to watch (451)." As the story progresses, she becomes certain that the wall-paper contains a special secret for her. Jane hides her obsession from John and their housekeeper so they will not discover the secret before she does. She has achieved an interest outside of John and the baby, a natural and healthy interest in herself. But in order to maintain this interest, Jane must sever herself permanently from the trappings of "wife and nurturer." Her obsession ends with Jane's release of the woman she sees trapped in the wall-paper—the woman trapped within herself—and the madness that belongs to them both. However, this madness is not an end insofar as it has released Jane irrevocably from John and from the submissive being she was before. Now she is free to pursue her self without the constraints of John and the discarded Jane.

Similarly, Edna is initially unable to swim and cannot "get the hang of it." She suddenly gains her balance in the water after an emotional experience that awakens her to music. When she returns home she makes an even greater discovery about herself. She realizes that she will not be able to complete herself as long as she must deal with the responsibilities of husband and children. Edna's return to the water, her walk into the sea, is an awakening similar to her response to the music. "The voice of the sea is seductive; never ceasing, whispering, clamoring, murmuring, inviting the soul to wander for a spell in the abysses of solitude; to lose itself in mazes of inward contemplation (190)." Edna finally gives herself to an entity that will allow her to become her self, without the fragments and opinions of others. It is a tragic ending, but it is also a wonderful beginning, full of promise.

While it is natural to see madness and suicide as condemnation to a kind of Hell, we must nonetheless take into account the point of view of both Edna and Jane. For Edna and Jane life is a form of imprisonment by a school of thought that forced women into a role of subservience and surrendered their identities to their husbands and children. Edna's decision is the only one left to her and should be thought of as the natural progression from awakening to individuality. Thus, suicide can be viewed not as a loss of salvation but as an escape from the hell of a dominating society. Similarly, Jane's "loss of sanity" is actually a gain of self. She has forever left the caged character of "wife and mother" to become an individual on her own terms. Hence, madness can be thought of, not as a state of mental chaos, but as a cunning release from a life of subservience.

Without a doubt, both Jane and Edna have ended their previous existences to attain the self. Jane cannot find it through her husband nor through deceit, only through madness. Edna cannot discover it through her husband or through affairs with other men. Only through suicide, through the sea, can Edna find her self. Both women continue on in an isolated state to pursue peace and individuality in another realm.

The appalling paradox of their predicaments, of course, is that both women are driven to destroy themselves in order to obtain the freedom they so desperately want. Their decisions are at once "logical" and "unacceptable"—unacceptable in the sense that no one should be driven to such "logic." Therefore, we must view "The Awakening" and "The Yellow Wallpaper" not merely as tales of self-destruction, but as tales of extreme reaction to psychological and social oppression.

All references from: Chopin, Kate, "The Awakening," Random House, 1981; Gilman, Charlotte Perkins, "The Yellow Wallpaper," Trimmer, Joseph F., and Jennings, C. Wade, *Fictions,* 2d ed. Harcourt Brace Jovanovich, 1989.

Setting: Seeing In The Dark

SHELLEY S. BOTT

Setting in short fiction often plays a major role in establishing the tone and even the theme of a story. In Ann Beattie's story, "In The White Night," setting suggests the ways in which loss and grief are at once inevitable and unpredictable. Curiously, it is a white night, not a dark night in which Beattie places grief and loss and thereby mirrors human experience. The unique light that snow creates enables us to see in the dark, and we can sometimes emotionally "see" things differently in the quietness of night, too.

Beattie's title and imagery lead us into a night full of brightness and silence when "Time might even be frozen." Snow fall often evokes a response of awe for the natural forces of the world we live in. We cannot stop the snow; we cannot hear it fall. It just happens. And Beattie's character, Carol, recognizes that in real life certain things just happen no matter what she does. "What happened happened at random. . . ." Being human simply encompasses not only joys but sorrows. Just as the snow falls without warning and slows the travel of Carol and Vernon, the death of their child altered the movement of their lives, and the memory of her often intrudes to "stop" their lives.

Beattie's fictional setting also helps to capture the idiosyncratic way Carol and Vernon cope with change and loss. Divided between the frozen outdoors at the beginning and the cold living room of their home at the conclusion, the story involves scenes of stillness and sadness, and Beattie reinforces the sense of loss when she moves us from the outdoors to the indoors. Withdrawing physically from the cold seems natural, and withdrawing mentally into grief seems natural too as we watch Carol and Vernon. Further, Beattie uses the "largest, coldest room in the house" to reveal two people struggling with their emotions. Vernon falls asleep on the sofa and drapes Carol's coat over his head and shoulders to keep warm, or perhaps to somehow "touch" his wife and understand what she is feeling and why she is crying. Carol responds by stretching on the floor next to him and covering herself with his coat.

As she drifts off to sleep, Carol imagines her daughter as an angel passing by in the snow-filled night, and her vision leaves us feeling not cold, but warm, because we recognize the need, as Beattie writes, for "necessary small adjustments" in sleeping arrangements, in memories, and in visions. There, in the cold, silent, snowy night in a cold, large room of a big house, together two people form a small focus of warmth. Two humans cope with their common grief.

Ann Beattie obviously knows human nature and plays on our emotions by using a "cold" setting and title to great advantage. Like the characters in the story, we like to huddle inside something comforting and familiar too, a protection against the reality of life. Beattie uses the setting as a stage for recalling the painful loss of a child and for exploring how the parents deal with that experience. It also allows Beattie to conclude the story with an especially poignant image. The night begins "white" because of snow, but it ends "white" because of the imagined angelic light only a daughter's spirit brings "for the second that she [the daughter] hovered." And somehow as we visualize the closeness of Carol and Vernon's forms in their living room combined with this momentary visit, we can almost sense that although they've coped this night, tomorrow and the next day will bring with it fresh memories and new, unexpected ways to cope.

Writing Stories:
AN INTRODUCTION

WHY WRITE STORIES?

There are at least two basic impulses that lead us to want to write stories. One is the belief that we have a story to tell. The other is a need to try to do what someone else has done—the need to imitate.

Both impulses are certainly healthy and worth paying attention to. Wanting to tell a story means wanting to share a view of the world, or at least a view of a piece of it. It means wanting to record and shape experience. Wanting to imitate a story means wanting to take part in a tradition—to try your hand at an art form that others have established.

Whether one of these impulses, or both of them, or another impulse has led you to write a story, you probably have questions about how to start writing. Or, if you have written some stories, you may have encountered problems about which you would like some advice.

DEFINITIONS

You probably know what a "short story" is, and the previous essays have introduced definitions with which to work. But just so we can begin a discussion on common ground, we ought to define what it is you want to write.

What does "short" mean? "Short enough to read in one sitting" is one definition, but it is not all that helpful, because the length of a "sitting" may vary considerably, and some people might not sit through even one page of a boring story. Five, ten, fifteen, thirty pages? Yes—though many successful stories are shorter than five and longer than thirty. Nonetheless, five to thirty pages is the range in which many writers of "short" fiction work.

However, "short" applies not just to length but also to scale. Consequently, we can usefully contrast a short story with a novel. Whereas novels typically have numerous characters and several episodes, short stories usually focus on one or two main characters and on one key episode. And a novel may present hundreds of scenes, but a short story may present as few as one or two. In general, then, "short" describes the scale of a story as well as its length.

And now for "story," which may be the more difficult term to define. "The Evolution of the Short Story," another brief essay in this anthology, defines it from the perspective of the reader. From a writer's point of view, however, we may want to emphasize different characteristics, and the most important of these is probably *conflict*.

A short story presents characters—people—in conflict: people at odds; people who want something from one another; people who want to control others; people who do not know how to or do not want to get along; people unsure of who they are. In other words, short stories are about people who are in trouble of one kind or another, and the trouble can range from "problems at work" to living through a time of war.

Are there stories that don't involve conflict or trouble? Undoubtedly, but they aren't memorable, because fiction, unlike advertising, seeks to expose problems, not to gloss over them. In a sense writing fiction is a problem-solving art, or at least a problem-presenting one. Apparently, readers (and listeners) have always wanted it that way. Consider the romance novels that are sold by the millions in supermarkets chiefly because of their perfumed depiction of life. Even this kind of warm-and-fuzzy "escape" fiction puts its characters in trouble first before it lets them live happily ever after.

For you, the writer of a "story," the idea of conflict means that your stories will have to be more than portraits or sketches of interesting people or of interesting places, although your ideas for stories may very well *begin* with a place or a character you have imagined. You need not have a conflict in mind immediately to start writing. However, not until conflict occurs between the people or in the place will you have a story. Not until your interesting person runs into trouble will you be writing a story. In fact, when you engage in the process of "getting ideas" for a story, you are engaged in the process of defining a conflict out of which a story will spring. Think of John Updike's "A & P," included in this anthology. Its first line, spoken by Sammy the supermarket cashier, is "In walks these three girls." The girls walking in mean trouble; the story—and the conflict—begin. A few pages further in the story—a few moments later in Sammy's life—he has quit his job for reasons even he doesn't entirely understand, and his life will never be the same again.

LYING

In addition to remembering that a story ultimately involves conflict, writers need to remember something that is painfully obvious but also easy to forget: A short story is *fiction*. To put the matter more crudely, the short story is a lie. It is made up, invented. The difficulties you may have with this notion are considerable.

For example, you may want to write a story that recounts something that really happened to a member of your family—your grandmother, let's say. After you complete the story, you may have someone read it, and this person may say, "This part of the story doesn't seem quite right. I think you should change it." And your response will likely be, "But that's the way it happened." Such a response is entirely natural because you will want to be loyal to the original facts of the story and loyal to your grandmother. Unfortunately, the response has little to do with writing fiction. The lore from our families and other kinds of "true stories" are different from fictional stories, and when you say, "But that's the way it happened," you're talking not about the story you wrote but about conversations and "facts" that you remember being told. When your reader says that "This part of the story doesn't seem quite right," he or she means that the *fiction* you created is flawed, not that your family or your grandmother is flawed.

Even if you begin with an idea that seems nearly complete, then, you will have to lie—to make things up. Moreover, until you can comfortably break from "the facts" and from "what really happened," you will not have control over your story. You may need to change grandmother into a grandfather, for example. You may have to place the story in a city and not in a town. You may have to change the way it all turned out. Most importantly, you have to intensify the conflict; that is, you may have to be more cruel to your grandmother than you imagined you could be. To write a successful story, you may have to put your grandmother in very serious trouble. But remember: Once you begin to write *fiction,* your grandmother is no longer your grandmother. She is a character created entirely of words. As a writer of fiction, you must mold this character the way a sculptor molds clay. You must manipulate and change the original material of the story. Keep some of "the facts" if you think they are useful. Throw others out. Invent others. Fiction concerns itself with essential truths, not with replications of actual events.

Much of the other writing you do—in college or elsewhere—involves reporting and analyzing facts. Consequently, this writing of fiction will seem very different at first. However, the main thing to remember is to make the fictional break from "what really happened." You're *making up* a story by creating characters and placing them in conflict, even if the story springs originally from something that "really" happened. In the writer's mind there is always a healthy tension between perception and invention, between what a writer sees and makes up.

CRISIS AND RESOLUTION

Once you start making up a story and putting your characters in conflict, you will want to keep at least two other basic ideas in mind. One is *crisis,* and the other is *resolution.*

Essentially, the crisis of a story (sometimes called the climax) occurs when the conflict is at its most intense. Put more colloquially, the crisis is when "the stuff hits the fan." Let's go back to Updike's "A & P." The conflict develops when the young women walk into the supermarket scantily clad. They disrupt the routine; Sammy and his boss must react to this trouble. Most readers would probably say that the crisis occurs when Sammy's boss, Sammy, and the young women all collide (figuratively) at the check-out stand. At that point, Sammy is forced to make a choice between loyalty to his boss and loyalty to the young women. This is the point in the story when Sammy is under the most pressure and when we the readers wonder how it all will turn out.

The conflict and the crisis are resolved when Sammy says, "I quit." When we say that a story has reached a resolution, however, we do not mean that everything has turned out all right. Everything could turn out all wrong, and still the conflict could have been resolved. In fact, in Sammy's case everything has, to some extent, turned out all wrong. He has lost his job, the girls have ignored his gesture of chivalry, and he doesn't feel particularly good for having stood up to his boss. Nonetheless, he has made a choice and taken an action, thereby resolving the immediate conflict of the story. Has he resolved his attitude toward young women and bosses and himself? Probably not. Resolution in fiction does not mean a resolution of all problems; it means that events in the story have played themselves out, one way or another.

One more word about crisis and resolution: The "opposing forces" need not be extreme, all good or all bad. What makes Sammy's choice difficult and believable is that his boss is not entirely bad and the girls are not entirely good. Sammy's choice is difficult and confused, and in a way he can't win. Ironically, if his boss had been an evil tyrant and one of the girls had been Sammy's true love, the conflict, crisis, and resolution would all be less complicated, probably less interesting, certainly more like a cartoon than a story.

GETTING STARTED

So far, we've talked about what "short" and "story" and "fiction" mean. We have talked about such basic elements as conflict, crisis, and resolution. In essence we've begun to sketch out what it means to write a "short story." But there are even more basic questions that you may want answered: How do I get ideas for stories? How do I get started?

If you have already written a story, and it turned out all right, then you know at least one way to get started. If it worked, try it again. Here are two more ways of getting started, opposite ends of a spectrum, and only two of many ways to start.

Choose a friend or an acquaintance. Write a factual sketch of the person: physical description, details of personality, background, occupation, and so on. Then start to "fictionalize," to invent and imagine. Keep at least one essential characteristic—shyness, for example—but change other things. Move the person to another state. Change the person's age, background, occupation, gender. Keep making these changes until you have created a specific character different from your friend or acquaintance. You may even want to write a monologue for the character—a page or so of the character speaking in first person ("I") to no one in particular.

Then start brainstorming a list of possible conflicts that somehow seem appropriate for the character. When you find a conflict that seems significant and that "feels right," start writing a story or sketching out scenes. You're on your way.

Another way to begin is to start with someone, something, or some place that you do *not* know. Look at a picture of someone in a magazine and make up a character. Describe an object and then make it figure in a story, not as an overt symbol, but maybe as something two characters argue about. Go to a place in your town or city that you have never visited before. Watch people. Describe the place. Invent some possible conflicts that might happen there.

Whether you use either of these two ways to begin, variations thereof, or other ways, remember that you're in charge. You're the inventor, the maker of the story. Remember, too, that one useful way to think of a story is to think of *characters in conflict.*

Ten Ideas

Here are ten other ideas to consider as you begin and continue to write stories.

1. In a book about Zen Buddhism, Shunryu Suzuki wrote, "In the expert's mind there are few possibilities, but in the beginner's mind there are many." Don't bemoan the fact that you're a beginner; celebrate it; use it. Try to write many different kinds of stories. Experiment with many different kinds of characters and conflicts. A writer of fiction is one who invents, and beginners are no less likely to be inventive than experts. Keep a notebook and jot down ideas, images, conversations overheard, people observed, and so forth. Inevitably, a story will emerge from such notes.

2. Conventions (or "rules") in fiction are meant to be bent, if not broken. In this discussion we have identified such conventions as conflict, crisis, and resolution. As you write stories, however, don't turn these conventions into formulas. In fact, as you'll see from reading some stories in this anthology, many writers deliberately ignore, undermine, or redefine these conventions and their readers' expectations. You may or may not want to go that far at first, but remember to make conventions work for you; don't become a slave to them. For example, if you have an interesting character but no conflict yet, don't force yourself to invent a conflict. Just keep working with the character until the right conflict emerges.

3. Writers read. Read everything you can get your hands on: fairy tales, myths, folk tales, translated stories, stories in languages you know, stories in magazines you pick up, poetry, novels, plays, science, history, journalism, graffiti.

Some young writers claim they don't like to read when they're writing because they don't want to be influenced by someone else's style. There is a minute grain of sense to this: The last thing some science fiction writers need to read is more science fiction. But this does not mean that they should stop reading fiction altogether. Reading other writers is absolutely essential. It helps you place your own work in a context. It lets you see how others manipulate conventions. It makes your sense of language more powerful. It gets the rhythm of sentences in your head. Most important, reading good fiction—and defining for yourself what "good fiction" is—are inherently worthwhile.

4. Books on writing are often helpful, if not now then later. I'll mention a few: Janet Burroway's *Writing Fiction* (second edition, 1987); John Gardner's *The Art of Fiction: Notes on Craft for Young Writers* (1982); Rust Hills's *Writing In General And The Short Story In Particular* (1979); and Natalie Goldberg's *Writing Down the Bones* (1986). There are many other books on writing listed in the bibliography at the back of this anthology. One quality these books share is that they are not just "how to" books but instead are books that will enlarge your ideas of fiction and help you place your own work in a richer context. They will help you generate ideas and refine the ones you have.

5. Writing is mysterious. Advice on getting started, books on writing, and writing classes are all helpful. They save steps, they help you solve problems, they begin the long journey. Nevertheless, the process of writing is endlessly mysterious, and all writers learn by writing. You set out to write a story about justice, but your character may change on you and turn it into a story about going home. You may get stuck on a story, give up, and go do some laundry—only to have the idea that gets you started again pop into your mind. You will be unable to make writing *not* be mysterious, but you can find a productive way to work within the mysterious process, and you can avoid the trap of using the mysterious nature of the work to avoid the work.

6. Writing is hard work. It doesn't look like hard work, but then neither does the smooth stride of a champion marathon runner. Writing involves spending hours alone pushing a pen across paper or a cursor across a screen. It means "showing"—creating images in your readers' minds—only by means of arranging ink on paper. Most of all, like much of the other writing you do, it means revision: finishing a draft, putting it away or showing it to someone, getting a response,

writing it again, and so on. But please know that for all
writers writing is hard work.

7. Because writing is mysterious and hard, and because we are
    inevitably blind to parts of our own work, it is important to
    find a "live audience" for your work. Taking a workshop is
    one way but not the only way. Merely showing your work to
    a reader you trust (not to a reader who always loves every
    word you write) is another way. However you choose to
    present your work-in-progress to a live audience, try not to
    accept or reject everything the audience says. If you find
    yourself defending every word of your story, then you are
    probably too close to the story or you have convinced yourself
    that you are a genius. In either case, try to open your mind
    and let the response in. Mull it over. It could be that your
    audience is telling you something valuable about your writing.
    On the other hand, if you accept all criticism and automatically
    make all of the suggested changes, you aren't trusting your
    own judgment enough. An audience is a sounding board, a
    place to "try" your story. Be able to distinguish between
    your*self* and your story.

8. You do not have to have a license to write. Some people may
    say that one should, but let's face it: they're snobs. You do
    not have to dress or act or talk or look "like a writer." All you
    have to do is write. Pen to paper, fingers on keys, cursor on
    screen. Few people publish stories regularly. Fewer still are
    genuinely professional writers. The census tells us this. Even
    if you write only a few stories, you have done something
    worthwhile. You have found out what it's like to write a story,
    and this knowledge will likely make you a better reader.
    (Imitation has long been a valuable way to study literature.)
    Also, you have written more, and the very act of writing
    more will strengthen other writing you do. And finally, you
    may have written a story you needed to write, for numerous
    reasons. In any event, you don't need anyone's permission to
    sit down and try your hand at writing.

9. A story doesn't really exist until it's on the page. When ideas
    come to you, jot them down. During the prewriting process,
    it may be fruitful for you not to write but to let your mind
    turn ideas and images over. However, at some point, you will
    have to write if you want the story to be written! It is part of
    the hard work. Try not to fall into the habit of "talking stories
    out" and never writing them. A beret or a cigarette or
    keeping odd hours does not make a writer. Writing does. The
    more regularly you write, the better; as with other arts or
    sports, practice is essential.

10.   "Real life" versus "school." Some people may tell you that if you want to be a writer, you should forget about books and writing classes and go out and "live." By "live" they may mean fighting bulls or going out to sea or doing something else that's supposedly rugged. If you are headed for the bullfighting arena or out to sea anyway, go ahead. But if you're not, don't imagine that you'll be a better writer by going out to "live." These rugged activities are no more real than your life as it is right now. The material for fiction is, literally, everywhere. Right beside you now there is a story. All you have to do is find it.

Of course, you do not have to take a writing class to become a writer. Writing classes aren't for everyone. Mainly they're there to get you started, to put you in touch with other "workers" (hence the term "workshop"), and to save steps and time.

If—for whatever reasons—you feel that you would rather write in a less formal or less "social" situation, do so. You may still want to find a "live audience" of some kind, but it need not be a writing class.

Most of all, do not believe that there is a barrier between "school" and "real life." School is real life, and real life is school. What you'll find in a writing class is other people interested in writing, plain and simple. For a more extensive and highly sensible discussion of this subject, read "In Defense of Creative Writing Classes" in Richard Hugo's *Triggering Town,* which is listed in the bibliography at the back of this anthology.

After you have written for a while, you may want to try to publish something. If so, send a story to a school magazine, a local publication, or a regional journal. For more information about how to submit stories and about publishing in general, see the section on "Publications on Publishing" in the Checklist of Books at the back of this anthology.

Part One

Early Voices

Introduction to Early Voices

Most of the fifteen stories in this section have been anthologized hundreds, maybe even thousands, of times, and all of their authors are—to put it simply—famous.

Frequent reprinting of stories and established reputations of authors can create problems for students, however, for often the stories and the authors' names simply appear in anthologies, with no accompanying mention of why the names are well known or why the stories are oft reprinted. One implied message this situation sends to students—to anyone—is that Hawthorne (for example) is famous because, well, just because he's famous, that's all. This implied message goes on to tell us that one should read a Hawthorne story simply because Hawthorne wrote it.

To be sure, many of these stories are as self-evidently excellent and memorable as any literature is. Nonetheless, it is essential to consider precisely what these stories add to the history of short fiction, and precisely why so many people have considered them crucial to that history.

It is also worth considering how these stories helped reinvent the genre of short fiction in the nineteenth century and how they interpret that century for us. It is important to think about why certain stories almost insist on being reprinted, why others have appeared less frequently, why still others may have fallen out of favor with readers.

Above all, it is worth your time to cast a critical glance at the term *classic story,* which has at one time or another been applied to each of these stories. As you read them, you will begin to define more clearly for yourself what a short story is, and you will begin to formulate your own history of the genre. You should also decide for yourself which stories deserve to be called classics, which ones do not, and what that term means.

Edgar Allan Poe

Of all the authors in this section, Edgar Allan Poe is the one we can be sure that everyone knows. He is widely considered to be an original master of a subgenre of short fiction—the tale of horror. With "Murders of the Rue Morgue," he also helped invent another subgenre—the detective story. And of course, he is famous as a poet, too, "The Raven" being one of the most widely read poems in the world. To some extent, then, Poe is famous for being famous, and—like Arthur Conan Doyle—he is an author that appeals to adolescents and scholars alike. His tales are morbid and sensational, complicated but also accessible and entertaining. As much as any other writer of short fiction, Poe used the genre to explore extreme states of consciousness.

Like many of his contemporaries, he is also important to the theory of imaginative writing, chiefly because of essays and reviews such as "The Philosophy of Composition." Poe went about his art in a calculating way, fiercely concerned about the effects his poems and stories would have on his audience. Other writers in this section wrote more complicated and socially pertinent stories, but no other writer defined his or her niche in literary history as boldly as Poe. His fiction remains startling, psychologically acute, and entertaining, as "The Tell-Tale Heart" demonstrates.

Nathaniel Hawthorne

Purely as a writer of short fiction, Nathaniel Hawthorne has a reputation that is less sharply defined than Poe's, though his general importance to American literature is indisputable and secured mainly by the novel *The Scarlet Letter*. Huge differences exist between Poe and Hawthorne, but one subject they have in common is evil. As "Young Goodman Brown" shows, Hawthorne preferred to address the subject in the context of Puritanism, the religious movement greatly responsible for creating the America we know. Hawthorne combines Poe's interest in psychology with an interest in religion, particularly religious fanaticism and how communities based on religion operate. As this story also shows, Hawthorne's fiction involves itself with symbol and allegory, and there is often a deliberately fantastical element in his stories. In any event, "Young Goodman Brown" shows that Hawthorne relied on the short story and not just the novel to explore significant issues of evil and morality.

Herman Melville

Moby Dick, the famous white whale, may be slightly better known than the captain (Ahab) who stalked him, and Ahab may be better known than another sailor created by Herman Melville, Billy Budd. Bartleby the scrivener (or "clerk") is less famous than these seagoing counterparts, but in many ways his tale is as powerful as *Moby Dick* and as morally significant as *Billy Budd*.

Were it not for this single story, Melville would not rank highly as a writer of *short* fiction, nor would any of his short fiction be reprinted nearly as frequently. Because of "Bartleby the Scrivener"—and a single line of dialogue in it—Melville's reputation as a short-story writer is secure.

"I prefer not to," the meek, hermetic Bartleby repeats; the simple utterance—and the iron will and complicated motives behind it—make Bartleby a haunting fictional character like no other. Just when America was becoming an economic and political giant, Melville gave us "a story of Wall Street" that concerns an invisible clerk who "prefers not to" participate. In so doing, Melville crafts a myth of nonconformity and passive resistance that reminds us of his own century's *Walden,* by Henry David Thoreau, but also reaches forward to the century of Mahatma Ghandi and Martin Luther King, Jr., and Nelson Mandela in South Africa and Rosa Parks in Mississippi. Certainly, Bartleby is antisocial and apolitical; he is the furthest thing from a *leader* of a passive-resistance movement. But paradoxically, his story has astounding social and political implications.

The Americans Poe, Hawthorne, and Melville have left indelible marks on the history of the short story, then. The nations of France and Russia shaped that history just as powerfully, however.

Guy de Maupassant

The French writer Guy de Maupassant masterfully captured the lives of working-class and lower-middle-class people. Perhaps more than any writer, he made short fiction *the* art of the lower middle class. "The Necklace" is a superb example of how astutely de Maupassant observed the frustrations and motivations of "ordinary people." It is also an excellent example of how he could forge real tragedy, which was once reserved for kings, from the circumstances of a young married woman who yearns to have just a bit more money. Ironically, the very element of the story that seems at first to resist tragedy—pettiness—is the one out of which de Maupassant spins genuine pathos. De Maupassant is not one to flinch; in a different way, he can be as morbid and cruel as Poe, as the fate of Mathilde Loisel makes clear.

Ivan Turgenev

From France we travel to Russia to visit that country's counterparts to Poe, Hawthorne, and Melville: Turgenev, Tolstoy, and Chekhov.

Ivan Turgenev's "Bezhin Meadow" is part of his *Hunting Sketches,* a book of interrelated stories that writers learning the craft of fiction often consider a "must read." If one hallmark of the nineteenth-century story is its preoccupation with "ordinary" life, then the contribution of Turgenev to this trend is as crucial as de Maupassant's. In "Bezhin Meadow," Turgenev depicts peasants vividly, honestly, and generously. He treats "folk wisdom" sometimes with irony, sometimes with simple acceptance. He shows not only how important oral traditions are to the nineteenth-century story but also how powerfully the nineteenth century transformed such traditions.

Most of all, Turgenev immerses us in the language and earthiness of Russian peasants. Of all the writers in this section, he seems most comfortable writing about nature—the woods and fields and their inhabitants. (It is especially revealing to contrast Hawthorne's use of "the woods" in "Young Goodman Brown" with Turgenev's use of them in "Bezhin Meadow.")

One might think that a hunting sketch would involve action and danger worthy of Daniel Boone, but "Bezhin Meadow" is surprisingly cerebral. Although it is lush with nature imagery, its "plot" consists chiefly of a man listening to boys tell campfire stories. Many critics have pointed to a "revolt against plot" in nineteenth-century short fiction. The term is probably too melodramatic, but writers like Turgenev did experiment with plots that had not the "rousing action" of some popular tales but the subtler "action" that can occur, for example, simply between a speaker and a listener.

Leo Tolstoy

If de Maupassant and Turgenev give us illuminating glimpses of ordinary lives, Leo Tolstoy gives us a painstaking, exhaustive study of an ordinary death in his most famous short story, "The Death of Iván Ilych." With a cold, unsentimental eye, Tolstoy shows how the friends, relatives, and coworkers of an obscure lawyer respond to his death and dying—and how the lawyer himself responds. He shows us how self-centered, distracted, and calculating humans can be, and, like de Maupassant, he examines with clinical clarity the motivations of a middle-class person.

Tolstoy is less subtle and experimental than his Russian compatriates, and even in this masterful short story, it is easy to see that his predilection was for longer prose forms, such as the epic novel *War and Peace*. Like Melville, Tolstoy is a powerful novelist whose reputation as a short-fiction writer rests primarily on this one story, which may still offer the most unwavering look at the appearances and reality of one person's death.

Anton Chekhov

It would be difficult to overestimate the importance of Anton Chekhov to the development of the short story, for many of his innovations seem as fresh today as they were in his era. And it is no coincidence that a recent master of the short story—America's Raymond Carver—chose to pay homage to Chekhov by writing a short story concerning Chekhov's death. More than any other writer in this section, Chekhov masterfully combined complicated subject matter with a deceptively simple surface.

His story "Gooseberries" is representative of his work in many ways. The idea of plot it exhibits is, like Turgenev's, nontraditional. Two friends visit a third friend and take a swim, and most of the story is taken up with one friend (Iván) telling the other two men about his brother. In one sense, "nothing happens" in the story, but in another sense, everything does, for in the compressed form of a short story, Chekhov manages to address issues of epic proportions: human contentment, inhumanity, and class conflict, among others.

As with many of his stories and plays, the characters of "Gooseberries" are from the middle class—dissatisfied professionals, small landowners who pretend to be great land barons. In "Gooseberries" Chekhov weaves a subtle "story within a story"; he uses dialogue and imagery deftly; he explores psychological and social issues that remain pertinent; and most of all, he continues to show us just how much can be achieved with the form of the short story.

Henry James

Henry James may be the preeminent theorist of short fiction among this group. His essay "The Art of Fiction" was widely influential and still constitutes the foundation of much literary criticism; it also helped create much of the terminology that springs from "the rhetoric of fiction," including the notion of "showing versus telling," "limited omniscience," a narrative "voice" distinct from the author's, and so forth.

Like Tolstoy, James sometimes strained against the limitations of short fiction, and he almost always pushes the form toward novella length. Part of this impulse seems to spring from his desire to give us a fictional world that is as rich and layered and detailed as life itself. He is a master of subtlety and nuance; he never rushes through a scene or takes shortcuts. The very first paragraph of "The Pupil" demonstrates this quality.

In both his novels and his short fiction, James extensively explored the predicament of Americans abroad—abroad in Europe. His fiction—"The Pupil" included—is anchored to a specific moment in American history, when friction between America and Europe was increasing. James usually explores the social and psychological manifestations of this friction, not the political. He is the most important recorder of that segment of nineteenth-century American society whose wealth was substantial but precarious and whose identity and sense of social custom were often pretentious and confused.

Kate Chopin

Kate Chopin's "Story of an Hour" offers a striking contrast to the fiction of Henry James. Instead of an overwrought, dense presentation, we get a story that is like a single brutal thrust of a sword. In sheer length it is slighter than many of the stories included here, but it is no less substantial. In some ways it is a feminist parable, a glimpse into the life of a woman who has been smothered by her husband's will. It also anticipates the wealth of experience women were to bring to the genre and the way women were to address psychological and social issues through short fiction. "The Story of an Hour" is a landmark feminist short story, but it is also a landmark short story in general.

Charlotte Perkins Gilman

Charlotte Perkins Gilman's "Yellow Wallpaper" is also something of a key feminist story, and like "The Story of an Hour," it examines the domestic imprisonment of women. It also shows that Poe was not the only writer among this group to probe extreme states of consciousness. Both the social causes and the private effects of the woman's madness in this story are memorably rendered, and the wallpaper becomes an extraordinary symbol of desperation.

Arthur Conan Doyle

A. Conan Doyle is one author we may thank for developing a subgenre of short fiction, the mystery (or detective) story. And he is the author we must thank for giving us the detective's detective, Sherlock Holmes, whose pipe, violin, cocaine habit, address, sidekick, carriage rides in the fog, and obsession with solving puzzling crimes have gone beyond fame to worldwide familiarity.

"A Scandal in Bohemia" is in many ways a classic Holmes tale: Because it involves royal secrets, it has the air of the exotic and—more practically—it gets the police out of the way. Further, it shows us Holmes's predilection for disguises and sting operations and for keeping Dr. John Watson mostly in the dark.

In other ways the story is uncharacteristic, and refreshing: Holmes (surprise!) is outwitted for once—and by a woman, a fact he can hardly bear. Also, the crime (blackmail) is "softer" than the murders and robberies he often investigates.

In any event, the story gives us a remarkable sense of Watson's voice, Holmes's personality, and the other ingredients that have made Doyle's stories the most widely read in the subgenre. It also presents us with the essential paradox of most detective fiction: Although the plots of such stories are intricate and action-packed, most readers fall in love with the subgenre not because of plot or action but because of the detective's personality.

O. Henry

O. Henry (William Sydney Porter) is more infamous than famous for some readers because his stories are such a contrast to the others in this section, with the possible exception of Doyle's. Whereas these other writers deemphasized the single, obvious trajectory of a plot and emphasized character, psychology, and the complexity of social forces, O. Henry wrote "old-fashioned" tales with plots (and plot twists) so clear that they are predictable, with characters who are types, and with bald "morals" at the conclusion.

Essentially, O. Henry created a formula story that was enormously popular and that represents a nonexperimental strain in American fiction. In a sense, O. Henry's fiction still represents "what sells" in mass-market periodicals and on television. "The Gift of the Magi" exemplifies the O. Henry style and world view, and it helps us define the contribution of these other writers by contrast.

Sholem Aleichem

More than any other story in this section, Sholem Aleichem's "On Account of a Hat" shows the extent to which an oral tradition informs the genre of short fiction. In many ways the story reads as a transcript of a storyteller's performance in a village or small town. In addition, the story exemplifies the wit and sense of irony that characterize much of Yiddish fiction, and it reveals an exuberant comic voice that is characteristic of Aleichem's fiction. The story may be the earthiest and most unassuming of the group, and it speaks for a European ethnic culture different from the ones for which Turgenev, Tolstoy, Chekhov, Conrad, Doyle, and de Maupassant speak.

Stephen Crane

In Stephen Crane we encounter an American writer much different from his predecessors Melville, Poe, and Hawthorne—and from his contemporary Henry James. As in his famous novel *The Red Badge of Courage* and his story "The Open Boat," Crane in "The Blue Hotel" casts a cynical eye toward the behavior of human beings and the purpose or design of their fate. For Crane, "fate" is often a matter of accident, a product of blind forces and unpredictable violence. "The Blue Hotel" allows him to link this notion to a setting that is perfectly suited to a writer preoccupied with cynicism and violence: a small town in the American frontier.

Crane is by no means a pure stylist in the way Chekhov and James are. He often intrudes on his own narratives, and his sense of structure is not as elegant. In place of elegance, however, we get writing that is focused on large questions of fate, morality, and heroism, and we get writing that is vivid, earthy, and raw. We also get a world view that prefigures the perspectives of Ernest Hemingway.

Joseph Conrad

Joseph Conrad was a professional sailor before he was a writer, and a speaker of Polish before he was a speaker of English. These circumstances make his renown as a writer unlikely, they add authenticity to his sea stories, and they add originality and surprise to his prose.

"The Secret Sharer" is as unorthodox but undeniably original as its author. Like "Bartleby the Scrivener," "The Secret Sharer" presents us with a simple situation—a new captain hides a stowaway on his ship—that becomes inexhaustibly rich in its implications. It is a serious tale of life and death, but it is also a comic story of awkward physical situations. It is a tale of the sea and a story of the mind. It is realistic and fantastic. It is rooted in a nineteenth-century fictional world of masculine adventure, and it anticipates a twentieth-century world of alienation, fragmented personality, and disorientation. Like his novella *Heart of Darkness* (on which the film *Apocalypse Now* drew heavily), "The Secret Sharer" confronts basic questions of good and evil, real and unreal, truth and falsehood—as well as the maddening question, "What really happens in this story?"

SUMMARY

Each of these stories makes a particular contribution to the history and development of short fiction, and each speaks for a different experience. Collectively, they give us an extraordinary view of the nineteenth century: its social conflicts, its emerging struggles of power, its preoccupation with identity and psychology. Most of all, like explorers in uncharted regions, these stories revealed to later writers not just what it was possible to do with the short story, but *how much* was possible. Although this section presents only fifteen stories from a century that produced thousands of stories in many languages, the range of topics, techniques, and points of view is astonishing, and it suggests how much the nineteenth century expanded the potential of the short story.

The Tell-Tale Heart

EDGAR ALLAN POE

T rue!—nervous—very, very dreadfully nervous I had been and am; but why *will* you say that I am mad? The disease had sharpened my senses—not destroyed—not dulled them. Above all was the sense of hearing acute. I heard all things in the heaven and in the earth. I heard many things in hell. How, then, am I mad? Hearken! and observe how healthily—how calmly I can tell you the whole story.

It is impossible to say how first the idea entered my brain; but once conceived, it haunted me day and night. Object there was none. Passion there was none. I loved the old man. He had never wronged me. He had never given me insult. For his gold I had no desire. I think it was his eye! yes, it was this! One of his eyes resembled that of a vulture—a pale blue eye, with a film over it. Whenever it fell upon me, my blood ran cold; and so by degrees—very gradually—I made up my mind to take the life of the old man, and thus rid myself of the eye for ever.

Now this is the point. You fancy me mad. Madmen know nothing. But you should have seen *me*. You should have seen how wisely I proceeded—with what caution—with what foresight—with what dissimulation I went to work! I was never kinder to the old man than during the whole week before I killed him. And every night, about midnight, I turned the latch of his door and opened it—oh, so gently! And then, when I had made an opening sufficient for my head, I put in a dark lantern, all closed, closed, so that no light shone out, and then I thrust in my head. Oh, you would have laughed to see how cunningly I thrust it in! I moved it slowly—very, very slowly, so that I might not disturb the old man's sleep. It took me an hour to place my whole head within the opening so far that I could see him as he lay upon his bed. Ha!—would a madman have been so wise as this? And then, when my head was well in the room, I undid the lantern cautiously—oh, so cautiously—cautiously (for the hinges creaked)—I undid it just so much that a single thin ray fell upon the vulture eye. And this I did for seven long nights—every night just after midnight—but I found the eye always closed; and so it was impossible to do the work; for it was not the old man who vexed me, but his Evil Eye. And every morning, when the day broke, I went boldly into the chamber, and spoke courageously to him, calling him by name in a hearty tone, and inquiring how he had passed the night. So you see he would have been a very profound old man, indeed, to suspect that every night, just at twelve, I looked in upon him while he slept.

Upon the eighth night I was more than usually cautious in opening the door. A watch's minute hand moves more quickly than did mine. Never before that night had I *felt* the extent of my own powers—of my sagacity. I could scarcely contain my feelings of triumph. To think that there I was, opening the door, little by little, and he not even to dream of my secret deeds or thoughts. I fairly chuckled at the idea; and perhaps he heard me; for he moved on the bed suddenly, as if startled. Now you may think that I drew back—but no. His room was as black as pitch with the thick darkness (for the shutters were close fastened, through fear of robbers), and so I knew that he could not see the opening of the door, and I kept pushing it on steadily, steadily.

I had my head in, and was about to open the lantern, when my thumb slipped upon the tin fastening, and the old man sprang up in the bed, crying out—"Who's there?"

I kept quite still and said nothing. For a whole hour I did not move a muscle, and in the meantime I did not hear him lie down. He was still sitting up in the bed listening;—just as I have done, night after night, hearkening to the death watches in the wall.

Presently I heard a slight groan, and I knew it was the groan of mortal terror. It was not a groan of pain or of grief—oh, no!—it was the low stifled sound that arises from the bottom of the soul when overcharged with awe. I knew the sound well. Many a night, just at midnight, when all the world slept, it has welled up from my own bosom, deepening, with its dreadful echo, the terrors that distracted me. I say I knew it well. I knew what the old man felt, and pitied him, although I chuckled at heart. I knew that he had been lying awake ever since the first slight noise, when he had turned in the bed. His fears had been ever since growing upon him. He had been trying to fancy them causeless, but could not. He had been saying to himself—"It is nothing but the wind in the chimney—it is only a mouse crossing the floor," or "it is merely a cricket which has made a single chirp." Yes, he has been trying to comfort himself with these suppositions; but he had found all in vain. *All in vain;* because Death, in approaching him, had stalked with his black shadow before him, and enveloped the victim. And it was the mournful influence of the unperceived shadow that caused him to feel—although he neither saw nor heard—to *feel* the presence of my head within the room.

When I had waited a long time, very patiently, without hearing him lie down, I resolved to open a little—a very, very little crevice in the lantern. So I opened it—you cannot imagine how stealthily, stealthily—until, at length, a single dim ray, like the thread of the spider, shot from out the crevice and full upon the vulture eye.

It was open—wide, wide open—and I grew furious as I gazed upon it. I saw it with perfect distinctness—all a dull blue, with a hideous veil over it that chilled the very marrow in my bones; but I could see nothing else of the old man's face or person: for I had directed the ray as if by instinct, precisely upon the damned spot.

And now have I not told you that what you mistake for madness is but over-acuteness of the senses?—now, I say, there came to my ears a low, dull, quick sound, such as a watch makes when enveloped in cotton. I knew *that* sound well too. It was the beating of the old man's heart. It increased my fury, as the beating of a drum stimulates the soldier into courage.

But even yet I refrained and kept still. I scarcely breathed. I held the lantern motionless. I tried how steadily I could maintain the ray upon the eye. Meantime the hellish tattoo of the heart increased. It grew quicker and quicker, and louder and louder every instant. The old man's terror *must* have been extreme! It grew louder, I say, louder every moment!—do you mark me well? I have told you that I am nervous: so I am. And now at the dead hour of the night, amid the dreadful silence of that old house, so strange a noise as this excited me to uncontrollable terror. Yet, for some minutes longer I refrained and stood still. But the beating grew louder, louder! I thought the heart must burst. And now a new anxiety seized me—the sound would be heard by a neighbor! The old man's hour had come! With a loud yell, I threw open the lantern and leaped into the room. He shrieked once—once only. In an instant I dragged him to the floor, and pulled the heavy bed over him. I then smiled gaily, to find the deed so far done. But, for many minutes, the heart beat on with a muffled sound. This, however, did not vex me; it would not be heard through the wall. At length it ceased. The old man was dead. I removed the bed and examined the corpse. Yes, he was stone, stone dead. I placed my hand upon the heart and held it there many minutes. There was no pulsation. He was stone dead. His eye would trouble me no more.

If still you think me mad, you will think so no longer when I describe the wise precautions I took for the concealment of the body. The night waned, and I worked hastily, but in silence. First of all I dismembered the corpse. I cut off the head and the arms and the legs.

I then took up three planks from the flooring of the chamber, and deposited all between the scantlings. I then replaced the boards so cleverly, so cunningly, that no human eye—not even *his*—could have detected anything wrong. There was nothing to wash out—no stain of any kind—no blood-spot whatever. I had been too wary for that. A tub had caught all—ha! ha!

When I had made an end of these labors, it was four o'clock—still dark as midnight. As the bell sounded the hour, there came a knocking at the street door. I went down to open it with a light heart—for what had I *now* to fear? There entered three men, who introduced themselves, with perfect suavity, as officers of the police. A shriek had been heard by a neighbor during the night; suspicion of foul play had been aroused; information had been lodged at the police office, and they (the officers) had been deputed to search the premises.

I smiled,—for *what* had I to fear? I bade the gentlemen welcome. The shriek, I said, was my own in a dream. The old man, I mentioned, was absent in the country. I took my visitors all over the house. I bade them search—search *well.* I led them, at length, to *his* chamber. I showed them his treasures, secure, undisturbed. In the enthusiasm of my confidence, I brought chairs into the room, and desired them *here* to rest from their fatigues, while I myself, in the wild audacity of my perfect triumph, placed my own seat upon the very spot beneath which reposed the corpse of the victim.

The officers were satisfied. My *manner* had convinced them. I was singularly at ease. They sat, and while I answered cheerily, they chatted familiar things. But, ere long, I felt myself getting pale and wished them gone. My head ached, and I fancied a ringing in my ears: but still they sat and still chatted. The ringing became more distinct:—it continued and became more distinct: I talked more freely to get rid of the feeling: but it continued and gained definitiveness— until, at length, I found that the noise was *not* within my ears.

No doubt I now grew *very* pale;—but I talked more fluently, and with a heightened voice. Yet the sound increased—and what could I do? It was *a low, dull, quick sound—much such a sound as a watch makes when enveloped in cotton.* I gasped for breath—and yet the officers heard it not. I talked more quickly—more vehemently; but the noise steadily increased. I arose and argued about trifles, in a high key and with violent gesticulations, but the noise steadily increased. Why *would* they not be gone? I paced the floor to and fro with heavy strides, as if excited to fury by the observation of the men—but the noise steadily increased. Oh God! what *could* I do? I foamed—I raved—I swore! I swung the chair upon which I had been sitting, and grated it upon the boards, but the noise arose over all and continually increased. It grew louder—louder—*louder!* And still the men chatted pleasantly, and smiled. Was it possible they heard not? Almighty God!—no, no! They heard!—they suspected!—they *knew!*—they were making a mockery of my horror!—this I thought, and this I think. But any thing was better than this agony! Any thing was more tolerable than this derision! I could bear those hypocritical smiles no longer! I felt that I must scream or die!—and now—again!—hark! louder! louder! louder! *louder!*—

"Villains!" I shrieked, "dissemble no more! I admit the deed!—tear up the planks!—here, here!—it is the beating of his hideous heart!"

Questions for Discussion

1. What motivates the narrator to commit murder?

2. What part of the narration is reliable? What part is not?

3. " 'The Tell-Tale Heart' is just a frightening story; there's nothing more to it than that." Explain why the story is more than just a "scary story."

4. What makes the narrator confess?

Suggestions for Writing

1. Write an essay in which you compare and contrast Poe's "I" narrator with other "I" narrators in this section.

2. Write an essay that explores how much contemporary horror fiction (such as Stephen King's) owes to Poe's example. Start by contrasting two specific works.

3. What is the attraction of horror fiction? Write a journal entry that examines this question.

4. Write a monologue from the point of view of someone who is in an extreme state of consciousness, as Poe's narrator is.

Young Goodman Brown

NATHANIEL HAWTHORNE

Young Goodman Brown came forth at sunset into the street of Salem village; but put his head back, after crossing the threshold, to exchange a parting kiss with his young wife. And Faith, as the wife was aptly named, thrust her own pretty head into the street, letting the wind play with the pink ribbons of her cap while she called to Goodman Brown.

"Dearest heart," whispered she, softly and rather sadly, when her lips were close to his ear, "prithee put off your journey until sunrise and sleep in your own bed to-night. A lone woman is troubled with dreams and such thoughts that she's afeared of herself sometimes. Pray tarry with me this night, dear husband, of all nights in the year."

"My love and my Faith," replied young Goodman Brown, "of all nights in the year, this one night must I tarry away from thee. My journey, as thou callest it, forth and back again, must needs be done 'twixt now and sunrise. What, my sweet, pretty wife, dost thou doubt me already, and we but three months married?"

"Then God bless you!" said Faith, with the pink ribbons; "and may you find all well when you come back."

"Amen!" cried Goodman Brown. "Say thy prayers, dear Faith, and go to bed at dusk, and no harm will come to thee."

So they parted; and the young man pursued his way until, being about to turn the corner by the meeting-house, he looked back and saw the head of Faith still peeping after him with a melancholy air, in spite of her pink ribbons.

"Poor little Faith!" thought he, for his heart smote him. "What a wretch am I to leave her on such an errand! She talks of dreams, too. Methought as she spoke there was trouble in her face, as if a dream had warned her what work is to be done tonight. But no, no; 't would kill her to think it. Well, she's a blessed angel on earth; and after this one night I'll cling to her skirts and follow her to heaven."

With this excellent resolve for the future, Goodman Brown felt himself justified in making more haste on his present evil purpose. He had taken a dreary road, darkened by all the gloomiest trees of the forest, which barely stood aside to let the narrow path creep through, and closed immediately behind. It was all as lonely as could be; and there is this peculiarity in such a solitude, that the traveller knows not who may be concealed by the innumerable trunks and the thick boughs overhead; so that with lonely footsteps he may yet be passing through an unseen multitude.

"There may be a devilish Indian behind every tree," said Goodman Brown to himself; and he glanced fearfully behind him as he added, "What if the devil himself should be at my very elbow!"

His head turned back, he passed a crook of the road, and, looking forward again, beheld the figure of a man, in grave and decent attire, seated at the foot of an old tree. He arose at Goodman Brown's approach and walked onward side by side with him.

"You are late, Goodman Brown," said he. "The clock of the Old South was striking as I came through Boston, and that is full fifteen minutes agone."

"Faith kept me back a while," replied the young man, with a tremor in his voice, caused by the sudden appearance of his companion, though not wholly unexpected.

It was now deep dusk in the forest, and deepest in that part of it where these two were journeying. As nearly as could be discerned, the second traveller was about fifty years old, apparently in the same rank of life as Goodman Brown, and bearing a considerable resemblance to him, though perhaps more in expression than features. Still they might have been taken for father and son. And yet, though the elder person was as simply clad as the younger, and as simple in manner too, he had an indescribable air of one who knew the world, and who would not have felt abashed at the governor's dinner table or in King William's court, were it possible that his affairs should call him thither. But the only thing about him that could be fixed upon as remarkable was his staff, which bore the likeness of a great black snake, so curiously wrought that it might almost be seen to twist and wriggle itself like a living serpent. This, of course, must have been an ocular deception, assisted by the uncertain light.

"Come, Goodman Brown," cried his fellow-traveller, "this is a dull pace for the beginning of a journey. Take my staff, if you are so soon weary."

"Friend," said the other, exchanging his slow pace for a full stop, "having kept covenant by meeting thee here, it is my purpose now to return whence I came. I have scruples touching the matter thou wot'st of."

"Sayest thou so?" replied he of the serpent, smiling apart. "Let us walk on, nevertheless, reasoning as we go; and if I convince thee not thou shalt turn back. We are but a little way in the forest yet."

"Too far! too far!" exclaimed the goodman, unconsciously resuming his walk. "My father never went into the woods on such an errand, nor his father before him. We have been a race of honest men and good Christians since the days of the martyrs; and shall I be the first of the name of Brown that ever took this path and kept—"

"Such company, thou wouldst say," observed the elder person, interpreting his pause. "Well said, Goodman Brown! I have been as well acquainted with your family as with ever a one among the Puritans; and that's no trifle to say. I helped your grandfather, the constable, when he lashed the Quaker woman so smartly through the streets of Salem; and it was I that brought your father a pitch-pine knot, kindled at my own hearth, to set fire to an Indian village, in King Philip's war. They were my good friends, both; and many a pleasant walk have we had along this path, returned merrily after midnight. I would fain be friends with you for their sake."

"If it be as thou sayest," replied Goodman Brown, "I marvel they never spoke of these matters; or, verily, I marvel not, seeing that the least rumor of the sort would have driven them from New England. We are a people of prayer, and good works to boot, and abide no such wickedness."

"Wickedness or not," said the traveller with the twisted staff, "I have a very general acquaintance here in New England. The deacons of many a church have drunk the communion wine with me; the selectmen of divers towns make me their chairman; and a majority of the Great and General Court are firm supporters of my interest. The governor and I, too—But these are state secrets."

"Can this be so?" cried Goodman Brown, with a stare of amazement at his undisturbed companion. "Howbeit, I have nothing to do with the governor and council; they have their own ways, and are no rule for a simple husbandman like me. But, were I to go on with thee, how should I meet the eye of that good old man, our minister, at Salem village? Oh, his voice would make me tremble both Sabbath day and lecture day."

Thus far the elder traveller had listened with due gravity; but now burst into a fit of irrepressible mirth, shaking himself so violently that his snakelike staff actually seemed to wriggle in sympathy.

"Ha! ha! ha!" shouted he again and again; then composing himself, "Well, go on, Goodman Brown, go on; but, prithee, don't kill me with laughing."

"Well, then, to end the matter at once," said Goodman Brown, considerably nettled, "there is my wife, Faith. It would break her dear little heart; and I'd rather break my own."

"Nay, if that be the case," answered the other, "e'en go thy ways, Goodman Brown. I would not for twenty old women like the one hobbling before us that Faith should come to any harm."

As he spoke he pointed his staff at a female figure on the path, in whom Goodman Brown recognized a very pious and exemplary dame, who had taught him his catechism in youth, and was still his moral and spiritual adviser, jointly with the minister and Deacon Gookin.

"A marvel, truly, that Goody Cloyse should be so far in the wilderness at nightfall," said he. "But with your leave, friend, I shall take a cut through the woods until we have left this Christian woman behind. Being a stranger to you, she might ask whom I was consorting with and whither I was going."

"Be it so," said his fellow-traveller. "Betake you to the woods, and let me keep the path."

Accordingly the young man turned aside, but took care to watch his companion, who advanced softly along the road until he had come within a staff's length of the old dame. She, meanwhile, was making the best of her way, with singular speed for so aged a woman, and mumbling some indistinct words—a prayer, doubtless—as she went. The traveller put forth his staff and touched her withered neck with what seemed the serpent's tail.

"The devil!" screamed the pious old lady.

"Then Goody Cloyse knows her old friend?" observed the traveller, confronting her and leaning on his writhing stick.

"Ah, forsooth, and is it your worship indeed?" cried the good dame. "Yea, truly is it, and in the very image of my old gossip, Goodman Brown, the grandfather of the silly fellow that now is. But—would your worship believe it?— my broomstick hath strangely disappeared, stolen, as I suspect, by that unhanged witch, Goody Cory, and that, too, when I was all anointed with the juice of smallage, and cinquefoil, and wolf's bane—"

"Mingled with fine wheat and the fat of a new-born babe," said the shape of old Goodman Brown.

"Ah, your worship knows the recipe," cried the old lady, cackling aloud. "So, as I was saying, being all ready for the meeting, and no horse to ride on, I made up my mind to foot it; for they tell me there is a nice young man to be taken into communion to-night. But now your good worship will lend me your arm, and we shall be there in a twinkling."

"That can hardly be," answered her friend. "I may not spare you my arm, Goody Cloyse; but here is my staff, if you will."

So saying, he threw it down at her feet, where, perhaps, it assumed life, being one of the rods which its owner had formerly lent to the Egyptian magi. Of this fact, however, Goodman Brown could not take cognizance. He had cast up his eyes in astonishment, and, looking down again, beheld neither Goody Cloyse nor the serpentine staff, but his fellow-traveller alone, who waited for him as calmly as if nothing had happened.

"That old woman taught me my catechism," said the young man; and there was a world of meaning in this simple comment.

They continued to walk onward, while the elder traveller exhorted his companion to make good speed and persevere in the path, discoursing so aptly that his arguments seemed rather to spring up in the bosom of his auditor than to be suggested by himself. As they went, he plucked a branch of maple to serve for a walking stick, and began to strip it of the twigs and little boughs, which were wet with evening dew. The moment his fingers touched them they became strangely withered and dried up as with a week's sunshine. Thus the pair proceeded, at a good free pace, until suddenly, in a gloomy hollow of the road, Goodman Brown sat himself down on the stump of a tree and refused to go any farther.

"Friend," said he, stubbornly, "my mind is made up. Not another step will I budge on this errand. What if a wretched old woman does choose to go to the devil when I thought she was going to heaven: is that any reason why I should quit my dear Faith and go after her?"

"You will think better of this by and by," said his acquaintance, composedly. "Sit here and rest yourself a while; and when you feel like moving again, there is my staff to help you along."

Without more words, he threw his companion the maple stick, and was as speedily out of sight as if he had vanished into the deepening gloom. The young man sat a few moments by the roadside, applauding himself greatly, and thinking with how clear a conscience he should meet the minister in his morning walk, nor shrink from the eye of good old Deacon Gookin. And what calm sleep would be his that very night, which was to have been spent so wickedly, but so purely and sweetly now, in the arms of Faith! Amidst these pleasant and praiseworthy meditations, Goodman Brown heard the tramp of horses along the road, and deemed it advisable to conceal himself within the verge of the forest, conscious of the guilty purpose that had brought him thither, though now so happily turned from it.

On came the hoof tramps and the voices of the riders, two grave old voices, conversing soberly as they drew near. These mingled sounds appeared to pass along the road, within a few yards of the young man's hiding-place; but, owing doubtless to the depth of the gloom at that particular spot, neither the travellers nor their steeds were visible. Though their figures brushed the small boughs by the wayside, it could not be seen that they intercepted, even for a moment, the faint gleam from the strip of bright sky athwart which they must have passed. Goodman Brown alternately crouched and stood on tiptoe, pulling aside the branches and thrusting forth his head as far as he durst without discerning so much as a shadow. It vexed him the more, because he could have sworn, were such a thing possible, that he recognized the voices of the minister and Deacon Gookin, jogging along quietly, as they were wont to do, when bound to some ordination or ecclesiastical council. While yet within hearing, one of the riders stopped to pluck a switch.

"Of the two, reverend sir," said the voice like the deacon's, "I had rather miss an ordination dinner than to-night's meeting. They tell me that some of our community are to be here from Falmouth and beyond, and others from Connecticut and Rhode Island, besides several of the Indian powwows, who, after their fashion, know almost as much deviltry as the best of us. Moreover, there is a goodly young woman to be taken into communion."

"Mighty well, Deacon Gookin!" replied the solemn old tones of the minister. "Spur up, or we shall be late. Nothing can be done, you know, until I get on the ground."

The hoofs clattered again; and the voices, talking so strangely in the empty air, passed on through the forest, where no church had ever been gathered or solitary Christian prayed. Whither, then, could these holy men be journeying so deep into the heathen wilderness? Young Goodman Brown caught hold of a tree for support, being ready to sink down on the ground, faint and overburdened with the heavy sickness of his heart. He looked up to the sky, doubting whether there really was a heaven above him. Yet there was the blue arch, and the stars brightening in it.

"With heaven above and Faith below, I will yet stand firm against the devil!" cried Goodman Brown.

While he still gazed upward into the deep arch of the firmament and had lifted his hands to pray, a cloud, though no wind was stirring, hurried across the zenith and hid the brightening stars. The blue sky was still visible, except directly overhead, where this black mass of cloud was sweeping swiftly northward. Aloft in the air, as if from the depths of the cloud, came a confused and doubtful sound of voices. Once the listener fancied that he could distinguish the accents of towns-people of his own, men and women, both pious and ungodly, many of whom he had met at the communion table, and had seen others rioting at the tavern. The next moment, so indistinct were the sounds, he doubted whether he had heard aught but the murmur of the old forest, whispering without a wind. Then came a stronger swell of those familiar tones, heard daily in the sunshine at Salem village, but never until now from a cloud of night. There was one voice of a young woman, uttering lamentations, yet with an uncertain sorrow, and entreating for some favor, which, perhaps, it would grieve her to obtain; and all the unseen multitude, both saints and sinners, seemed to encourage her onward.

"Faith!" shouted Goodman Brown, in a voice of agony and desperation; and the echoes of the forest mocked him, crying, "Faith! Faith!" as if bewildered wretches were seeking her all through the wilderness.

The cry of grief, rage, and terror was yet piercing the night, when the unhappy husband held his breath for a response. There was a scream, drowned immediately in a louder murmur of voices, fading into far-off laughter, as the dark cloud swept away, leaving the clear and silent sky above Goodman Brown. But something fluttered lightly down through the air and caught on the branch of a tree. The young man seized it, and beheld a pink ribbon.

"My Faith is gone!" cried he, after one stupefied moment. "There is no good on earth; and sin is but a name. Come, devil; for to thee is this world given."

And, maddened with despair, so that he laughed loud and long, did Goodman Brown grasp his staff and set forth again, at such a rate that he seemed to fly along the forest path rather than to walk or run. The road grew wilder and drearier and more faintly traced, and vanished at length, leaving him in the heart of the dark wilderness, still rushing onward with the instinct that guides mortal men to evil. The whole forest was peopled with frightful sounds—the creaking of the trees, the howling of wild beasts, and the yell of Indians; while sometimes the wind tolled like a distant church bell, and sometimes gave a broad roar around the traveller, as if all Nature were laughing him to scorn. But he was himself the chief horror of the scene, and shrank not from its other horrors.

"Ha! ha! ha!" roared Goodman Brown when the wind laughed at him. "Let us hear which will laugh loudest. Think not to frighten me with your deviltry. Come witch, come wizard, come Indian powwow, come devil himself, and here comes Goodman Brown. You may as well fear him as he fears you."

In truth, all through the haunted forest there could be nothing more frightful than the figure of Goodman Brown. On he flew among the black pines, brandishing his staff with frenzied gestures, now giving vent to an inspiration of horrid blasphemy, and now shouting forth such laughter as set all the echoes of the forest laughing like demons around him. The fiend in his own shape is less hideous than when he rages in the breast of man. Thus sped the demoniac on his course, until, quivering among the trees, he saw a red light before him, as when the felled trunks and branches of a clearing have been set on fire, and throw up their lurid blaze against the sky, at the hour of midnight. He paused, in a lull of the tempest that had driven him onward, and heard the swell of what seemed a hymn, rolling solemnly from a distance with the weight of many voices. He knew the tune; it was a familiar one in the choir of the village meeting-house. The verse died heavily away, and was lengthened by a chorus, not of human voices, but of all the sounds of the benighted wilderness pealing in awful harmony together. Goodman Brown cried out, and his cry was lost to his own ear by its unison with the cry of the desert.

In the interval of silence he stole forward until the light glared full upon his eyes. At one extremity of an open space, hemmed in by the dark wall of the forest, arose a rock, bearing some rude, natural resemblance either to an altar or a pulpit, and surrounded by four blazing pines, their tops aflame, their stems untouched, like candles at an evening meeting. The mass of foliage that had overgrown the summit of the rock was all on fire, blazing high into the night and fitfully illuminating the whole field. Each pendent twig and leafy festoon was in a blaze. As the red light arose and fell, a numerous congregation alternately shone forth, then disappeared in shadow, and again grew, as it were, out of the darkness, peopling the heart of the solitary woods at once.

"A grave and dark-clad company," quoth Goodman Brown.

In truth they were such. Among them, quivering to and fro between gloom and splendor, appeared faces that would be seen next day at the council board of the province, and others which, Sabbath after Sabbath, looked devoutly heavenward, and benignantly over the crowded pews, from the holiest pulpits in the land. Some affirm that the lady of the governor was there. At least there were high dames well known to her, and wives of honored husbands, and widows, a great multitude, and ancient maidens, all of excellent repute, and fair young girls, who trembled lest their mothers should espy them. Either the sudden gleams of light flashing over the obscure field bedazzled Goodman Brown, or he recognized a score of the church members of Salem village famous for their especial sanctity. Good old Deacon Gookin had arrived, and waited at the skirts of that venerable saint, his revered pastor. But, irreverently consorting with these grave, reputable, and pious people, these elders of the church, these chaste dames and dewy virgins, there were men of dissolute lives and women of spotted fame, wretches given over to all mean and filthy vice, and suspected even of horrid crimes. It was strange to see that the good shrank not from the wicked, nor were the sinners abashed by the saints. Scattered also among their pale-faced enemies were the Indian priests, or powwows, who had often scared their native forest with more hideous incantations than any known to English witchcraft.

"But where is Faith?" thought Goodman Brown; and, as hope came into his heart, he trembled.

Another verse of the hymn arose, a slow and mournful strain, such as the pious love, but joined to words which expressed all that our nature can conceive of sin, and darkly hinted at far more. Unfathomable to mere mortals is the lore of fiends. Verse after verse was sung; and still the chorus of the desert swelled between like the deepest tone of a mighty organ; and with the final peal of that dreadful anthem there came a sound, as if the roaring wind, the rushing streams, the howling beasts, and every other voice of the unconcerted wilderness were mingling and according with the voice of guilty man in homage to the prince of all. The four blazing pines threw up a loftier flame, and obscurely discovered shapes and visages of horror on the smoke wreaths above the impious assembly. At the same moment the fire on the rock shot redly forth and formed a glowing arch above its base, where now appeared a figure. With reverence be it spoken, the figure bore no slight similitude, both in garb and manner, to some grave divine of the New England churches.

"Bring forth the converts!" cried a voice that echoed through the field and rolled into the forest.

At the word, Goodman Brown stepped forth from the shadow of the trees and approached the congregation, with whom he felt a loathful brotherhood by the sympathy of all that was wicked in his heart. He could have well-nigh sworn that the shape of his own dead father beckoned him to advance, looking downward from a smoke wreath, while a woman, with dim features of despair, threw out her hand to warn him back. Was it his mother? But he had no power to retreat one step, nor to resist, even in thought, when the minister and good old Deacon Gookin seized his arms and led him to the blazing rock. Thither came also the slender form of a veiled female, led between Goody Cloyse, that pious teacher of the catechism, and Martha Carrier, who had received the devil's promise to be queen of hell. A rampant hag was she. And there stood the proselytes beneath the canopy of fire.

"Welcome, my children," said the dark figure, "to the communion of your race. Ye have found thus young your nature and your destiny. My children, look behind you!"

They turned; and flashing forth, as it were, in a sheet of flame, the fiend worshippers were seen; the smile of welcome gleamed darkly on every visage.

"There," resumed the sable form, "are all whom ye have reverenced from youth. Ye deemed them holier than yourselves, and shrank from your own sin, contrasting it with their lives of righteousness and prayerful aspirations heavenward. Yet here are they all in my worshipping assembly. This night it shall be granted you to know their secret deeds; how hoary-bearded elders of the church have whispered wanton words to the young maids of their households; how many a woman, eager for widows' weeds, has given her husband a drink at bedtime and let him sleep his last sleep in her bosom; how beardless youths have made haste to inherit their fathers' wealth; and how fair damsels—blush not, sweet ones—have dug little graves in the garden, and bidden me, the sole guest, to an infant's funeral. By the sympathy of your human hearts for sin ye shall scent out all the places—whether in church, bedchamber, street, field, or forest—where crime has been committed, and shall exult to behold the whole earth one stain of guilt, one mighty blood spot. Far more than this. It shall be yours to penetrate, in every bosom, the deep mystery of sin, the fountain of all wicked arts, and which inexhaustibly supplies more evil impulses than human power—than my power at its utmost—can make manifest in deeds. And now, my children, look upon each other."

They did so; and, by the blaze of the hell-kindled torches, the wretched man beheld his Faith, and the wife her husband, trembling before that unhallowed altar.

"Lo, there ye stand, my children," said the figure, in a deep and solemn tone, almost sad with its despairing awfulness, as if his once angelic nature could yet mourn for our miserable race. "Depending upon one another's hearts, ye had still hoped that virtue were not all a dream. Now are ye undeceived. Evil is the nature of mankind. Evil must be your only happiness. Welcome again, my children, to the communion of your race."

"Welcome," repeated the fiend worshippers, in one cry of despair and triumph.

And there they stood, the only pair, as it seemed, who were yet hesitating on the verge of wickedness in this dark world. A basin was hollowed, naturally, in the rock. Did it contain water, reddened by the lurid light? or was it blood? or, perchance, a liquid flame? Herein did the shape of evil dip his hand and prepare to lay the mark of baptism upon their foreheads, that they might be partakers of the mystery of sin, more conscious of the secret guilt of others, both in deed and thought, than they could now be of their own. The husband cast one look at his pale wife, and Faith at him. What polluted wretches would the next glance show them to each other, shuddering alike at what they disclosed and what they saw!

"Faith! Faith!" cried the husband, "look up to heaven, and resist the wicked one."

Whether Faith obeyed he knew not. Hardly had he spoken when he found himself amid calm night and solitude, listening to a roar of the wind which died heavily away through the forest. He staggered against the rock, and felt it chill and damp; while a hanging twig, that had been all on fire, besprinkled his cheek with the coldest dew.

The next morning young Goodman Brown came slowly into the street of Salem village, staring around him like a bewildered man. The good old minister was taking a walk along the graveyard to get an appetite for breakfast and meditate his sermon, and bestowed a blessing, as he passed, on Goodman Brown. He shrank from the venerable saint as if to avoid an anathema. Old Deacon Gookin was at domestic worship, and the holy words of his prayer were heard through the open window. "What God doth the wizard pray to?" quoth Goodman Brown. Goody Cloyse, that excellent old Christian, stood in the early sunshine at her own lattice, catechizing a little girl who had brought her a pint of morning's milk. Goodman Brown snatched away the child as from the grasp of the fiend himself. Turning the corner by the meeting-house, he spied the head of Faith, with the pink ribbons, gazing anxiously forth, and bursting into such joy at sight of him that she skipped along the street and almost kissed her husband before the whole village. But Goodman Brown looked sternly and sadly into her face, and passed on without a greeting.

Had Goodman Brown fallen asleep in the forest and only dreamed a wild dream of a witch-meeting?

Be it so if you will; but, alas! it was a dream of evil omen for young Goodman Brown. A stern, a sad, a darkly meditative, a distrustful, if not a desperate man did he become from the night of that fearful dream. On the Sabbath day, when the congregation were singing a holy psalm, he could not listen because an anthem of sin rushed loudly upon his ear and drowned all the blessed strain. When the minister spoke from the pulpit with power and fervid eloquence, and, with his hand on the open Bible, of the sacred truths of our religion, and of saint-like lives and triumphant deaths, and of future bliss or misery unutterable, then did Goodman Brown turn pale, dreading lest the roof should thunder down upon the gray blasphemer and his hearers. Often, waking suddenly at midnight, he shrank from the bosom of Faith; and at morning or eventide, when the family knelt down at prayer, he scowled and muttered to himself, and gazed sternly at his wife, and turned away. And when he had lived long, and was borne to his grave a hoary corpse, followed by Faith, an aged woman, and children and grandchildren, a goodly procession, besides neighbors not a few, they carved no hopeful verse upon his tombstone, for his dying hour was gloom.

Questions for Discussion

1. "Had Goodman Brown fallen asleep in the forest and only dreamed a wild dream of a witch-meeting?" In your view, what does the narrator of the story want us to believe in response to this question?

2. Assuming that the events of the story occur only in Goodman Brown's mind, what kind of person is Hawthorne depicting? Are there twentieth-century examples of such a person, or is this story strictly confined to Puritanism?

3. Assuming that the events all really happen, what kind of community is Hawthorne depicting?

4. Summarize Goodman Brown's attitude toward "the Indians" and "the wilderness." To what extent do they represent more than just "different people" and "the forest and rivers"?

5. Look up the word *allegory* in a glossary of literary terms and then explain in what ways "Young Goodman Brown" fits the definition. (The glossary in this anthology includes a brief definition).

Suggestions for Writing

1. " 'Young Goodman Brown' is about Puritans; it has no relevance today." Write a journal entry in reaction to this statement, explaining ways the story relates to current discussions of religion, faith, and good and evil.

2. (a) "Goodman Brown didn't meet the Devil in the woods; he met his own suspicion and paranoia." (b) "Goodman Brown did meet the Devil in the woods, and what Goodman Brown believes about his community is correct." Write an essay that develops a thesis similar to one of these.

3. Invent a retelling—orally or in writing, on your own or in a group—of "Young Goodman Brown," choosing an alternate point of view, such as that of an Indian, Deacon Gookin, Goody Cloyse, or Faith.

Bartleby the Scrivener: A Story of Wall Street

HERMAN MELVILLE

I am a rather elderly man. The nature of my avocations, for the last thirty years, has brought me into more than ordinary contact with what would seem an interesting and somewhat singular set of men, of whom, as yet, nothing, that I know of, has ever been written—I mean, the law-copyists, or scriveners. I have known very many of them, professionally and privately, and, if I pleased, could relate divers histories, at which good-natured gentlemen might smile, and sentimental souls might weep. But I waive the biographies of all other scriveners, for a few passages in the life of Bartleby, who was a scrivener, the strangest I ever saw, or heard of. While, of other law-copyists, I might write the complete life, of Bartleby nothing of that sort can be done. I believe that no materials exist for a full and satisfactory biography of this man. It is an irreparable loss to literature. Bartleby was one of those beings of whom nothing is ascertainable, except from the original sources, and, in his case, those are very small. What my own astonished eyes saw of Bartleby, *that* is all I know of him, except, indeed, one vague report, which will appear in the sequel.

Ere introducing the scrivener, as he first appeared to me, it is fit I make some mention of myself, my employees, my business, my chambers, and general surroundings; because some such description is indispensable to an adequate understanding of the chief character about to be presented. Imprimis: I am a man who, from his youth upwards, has been filled with a profound conviction that the easiest way of life is the best. Hence, though I belong to a profession proverbially energetic and nervous, even to turbulence, at times, yet nothing of that sort have I ever suffered to invade my peace. I am one of those unambitious lawyers who never addresses a jury, or in any way draws down public applause; but, in the cool tranquillity of a snug retreat, do a snug business among rich men's bonds, and mortgages, and title-deeds. All who know me, consider me an eminently *safe* man. The late John Jacob Astor, a personage little given to poetic enthusiasm, had no hesitation in pronouncing my first grand point to be prudence; my next, method. I do not speak it in vanity, but simply record the fact, that I was not unemployed in my profession by the late John Jacob Astor; a name which, I admit, I love to repeat; for it hath a rounded and orbicular sound to it, and rings like unto bullion. I will freely add, that I was not insensible to the late John Jacob Astor's good opinion.

Some time prior to the period at which this little history begins, my avocations had been largely increased. The good old office, now extinct in the State of New York, of a Master in Chancery, had been conferred upon me. It was not a very arduous office, but very pleasantly remunerative. I seldom lose my temper; much more seldom indulge in dangerous indignation at wrongs and outrages; but, I must be permitted to be rash here, and declare that I consider the sudden and violent abrogation of the office of Master in Chancery, by the new Constitution, as a—premature act; inasmuch as I had counted upon a life-lease of the profits, whereas I only received those of a few short years. But this is by the way.

My chambers were up stairs, at No. ____ Wall Street. At one end, they looked upon the white wall of the interior of a spacious skylight shaft, penetrating the building from top to bottom.

This view might have been considered rather tame than otherwise, deficient in what landscape painters call "life." But, if so, the view from the other end of my chambers offered, at least, a contrast, if nothing more. In that direction, my windows commanded an unobstructed view of a lofty brick wall, black by age and everlasting shade; which wall required no spyglass to bring out its lurking beauties, but, for the benefit of all near-sighted spectators, was pushed up to within ten feet of my window panes. Owing to the great height of the surrounding buildings, and my chambers being on the second floor, the interval between this wall and mine not a little resembled a huge square cistern.

At the period just preceding the advent of Bartleby, I had two persons as copyists in my employment, and a promising lad as an office-boy. First, Turkey; second, Nippers; third, Ginger Nut. These may seem names, the like of which are not usually found in the Directory. In truth, they were nicknames, mutually conferred upon each other by my three clerks, and were deemed expressive of their respective persons or characters. Turkey was a short, pursy Englishman, of about my own age—that is, somewhere not far from sixty. In the morning, one might say, his face was of a fine florid hue, but after twelve o'clock, meridian—his dinner hour—it blazed like a grate full of Christmas coals; and continued blazing—but, as it were, with a gradual wane—till six o'clock P.M., or thereabouts; after which, I saw no more of the proprietor of the face, which, gaining its meridian with the sun, seemed to set with it, to rise, culminate, and decline the following day, with the like regularity and undiminished glory. There are many singular coincidences I have known in the course of my life, not the least among which was the fact, that, exactly when Turkey displayed his fullest beams from his red and radiant countenance, just then, too, at that critical moment, began the daily period when I considered his business capacities as seriously disturbed for the remainder of the twenty-four hours. Not that he was absolutely idle, or averse to business, then; far from it. The difficulty was, he was apt to be altogether too energetic. There was a strange, inflamed, flurried, flighty recklessness of activity about him. He would be incautious in dipping his pen into his inkstand. All his blots upon my documents were dropped there after twelve o'clock meridian. Indeed, not only would he be reckless, and sadly given to making blots in the afternoon, but, some days, he went further, and was rather noisy. At such times, too, his face flamed with augmented blazonry, as if cannel coal had been heaped on anthracite. He made an unpleasant racket with his chair; spilled his sand-box; in mending his pens, impatiently split them all to pieces, and threw them on the floor in a sudden passion; stood up, and leaned over his table, boxing his papers about in a most indecorous manner, very sad to behold in an elderly man like him. Nevertheless, as he was in many ways a most valuable person to me, and all the time before twelve o'clock meridian, was the quickest, steadiest creature, too, accomplishing a great deal of work in a style not easily to be matched—for these reasons, I was willing to overlook his eccentricities, though, indeed, occasionally, I remonstrated with him. I did this very gently, however, because, though the civilest, nay, the blandest and most reverential of men in the morning, yet, in the afternoon, he was disposed, upon provocation, to be slightly rash with his tongue—in fact, insolent. Now, valuing his morning services as I did, and resolved not to lose them—yet, at the same time, made uncomfortable by his inflamed ways after twelve o'clock—and being a man of peace, unwilling by my admonitions to call forth unseemly retorts from him, I took upon me, one Saturday noon (he was always worse on Saturdays) to hint to him, very kindly, that, perhaps, now that he was growing old, it might be well to abridge his labors; in short, he need not come to my chambers after twelve o'clock, but, dinner over, had best go home to his lodgings, and rest himself till tea-time. But no; he insisted upon his afternoon devotions. His countenance became intolerably fervid, as he oratorically assured me—gesticulating with a long ruler at the other end of the room—that if his services in the morning were useful, how indispensable, then, in the afternoon?

"With submission, sir," said Turkey, on this occasion, "I consider myself your right-hand man. In the morning I but marshal and deploy my columns; but in the afternoon I put myself at their head, and gallantly charge the foe, thus"—and he made a violent thrust with the ruler.

"But the blots, Turkey," intimated I.

"True; but, with submission, sir, behold these hairs! I am getting old. Surely, sir, a blot or two of a warm afternoon is not to be severely urged against gray hairs. Old age—even if it blot the page—is honorable. With submission, sir, we *both* are getting old."

This appeal to my fellow-feeling was hardly to be resisted. At all events, I saw that go he would not. So, I made up my mind to let him stay, resolving, nevertheless, to see to it that, during the afternoon, he had to do with my less important papers.

Nippers, the second on my list, was a whiskered, sallow, and, upon the whole, rather piratical-looking young man, of about five and twenty. I always deemed him the victim of two evil powers—ambition and indigestion. The ambition was evinced by a certain impatience of the duties of a mere copyist, an unwarrantable usurpation of strictly professional affairs, such as the original drawing up of legal documents. The indigestion seemed betokened in an occasional nervous testiness and grinning irritability, causing the teeth to audibly grind together over mistakes committed in copying; unnecessary maledictions, hissed, rather than spoken, in the heat of business; and especially by a continual discontent with the height of the table where he worked. Though of a very ingenious, mechanical turn, Nippers could never get this table to suit him. He put chips under it, blocks of various sorts, bits of pasteboard, and at last went so far as to attempt an exquisite adjustment, by final pieces of folded blotting-paper. But no invention would answer. If, for the sake of easing his back, he brought the table lid at a sharp angle well up towards his chin, and wrote there like a man using the steep roof of a Dutch house for his desk, then he declared that it stopped the circulation in his arms. If now he lowered the table to his waistbands, and stooped over it in writing, then there was a sore aching in his back. In short, the truth of the matter was, Nippers knew not what he wanted. Or, if he wanted anything, it was to be rid of a scrivener's table altogether. Among the manifestations of his diseased ambition was a fondness he had for receiving visits from certain ambiguous-looking fellows in seedy coats, whom he called his clients. Indeed, I was aware that not only was he, at times, considerable of a ward-politician, but he occasionally did a little business at the Justices' courts, and was not unknown on the steps of the Tombs. I have good reason to believe, however, that one individual who called upon him at my chambers, and who, with a grand air, he insisted was his client, was no other than a dun, and the alleged title-deed, a bill. But, with all his failings, and the annoyances he caused me, Nippers, like his compatriot Turkey, was a very useful man to me; wrote a neat, swift hand; and, when he chose, was not deficient in a gentlemanly sort of deportment. Added to this, he always dressed in a gentlemanly sort of way; and so, incidentally, reflected credit upon my chambers. Whereas, with respect to Turkey, I had much ado to keep him from being a reproach to me. His clothes were apt to look oily, and smell of eating-houses. He wore his pantaloons very loose and baggy in summer. His coats were execrable; his hat not to be handled. But while the hat was a thing of indifference to me, inasmuch as his natural civility and deference, as a dependent Englishman, always led him to doff it the moment he entered the room, yet his coat was another matter. Concerning his coats, I reasoned with him; but with no effect. The truth was, I suppose, that a man with so small an income could not afford to sport such a lustrous face and a lustrous coat at one and the same time. As Nippers once observed, Turkey's money went chiefly for red ink. One winter day, I presented Turkey with a highly respectable-looking coat of my own—a padded gray coat, of a most comfortable warmth, and which buttoned straight up from the knee to the neck. I thought Turkey would appreciate the favor, and abate his rashness and obstreperousness of afternoons. But no; I verily believe that buttoning himself up in so downy and blanket-like a coat had a pernicious effect upon him—upon the same principle that too much oats are bad for horses. In fact, precisely as a rash, restive horse is said to feel his oats, so Turkey felt his coat. It made him insolent. He was a man whom prosperity harmed.

Though, concerning the self-indulgent habits of Turkey, I had my own private surmises, yet, touching Nippers, I was well persuaded that, whatever might be his faults in other respects, he was, at least, a temperate young man. But, indeed, nature herself seemed to have been his vintner, and, at his birth, charged him so thoroughly with an irritable, brandy-like disposition, that all subsequent potations were needless. When I consider how, amid the stillness of my chambers, Nippers would sometimes impatiently rise from his seat, and stooping over his table, spread his arms wide apart, seize the whole desk, and move it, and jerk it, with a grim, grinding motion on the floor, as if the table were a perverse voluntary agent and vexing him, I plainly perceive that, for Nippers, brandy-and-water were altogether superfluous.

It was fortunate for me that, owing to its peculiar cause—indigestion—the irritability and consequent nervousness of Nippers were mainly observable in the morning, while in the afternoon he was comparatively mild. So that, Turkey's paroxysms only coming on about twelve o'clock, I never had to do with their eccentricities at one time. Their fits relieved each other, like guards. When Nipper's was on, Turkey's was off; and *vice versa*. This was a good natural arrangement, under the circumstances.

Ginger Nut, the third on my list, was a lad, some twelve years old. His father was a car-man, ambitious of seeing his son on the bench instead of a cart, before he died. So he sent him to my office, as student at law, errand-boy, cleaner and sweeper, at the rate of one dollar a week. He had a little desk to himself; but he did not use it much. Upon inspection, the drawer exhibited a great array of the shells of various sorts of nuts. Indeed, to this quick-witted youth, the whole noble science of the law was contained in a nutshell. Not the least among the employments of Ginger Nut, as well as one which he discharged with the most alacrity, was his duty as cake and apple purveyor for Turkey and Nippers. Copying law-papers being proverbially a dry, husky sort of business, my two scriveners were fain to moisten their mouths very often with Spitzenbergs, to be had at the numerous stalls nigh the Custom House and Post Office. Also, they sent Ginger Nut very frequently for that peculiar cake—small, flat, round, and very spicy—after which he had been named by them. Of a cold morning, when business was but dull, Turkey would gobble up scores of these cakes, as if they were mere wafers—indeed, they sell them at the rate of six or eight for a penny—the scrape of his pen blending with the crunching of the crisp particles in his mouth. Rashest of all the fiery afternoon blunders and flurried rashnesses of Turkey, was his once moistening a ginger-cake between his lips, and clapping it on to a mortgage, for a seal. I came within an ace of dismissing him then. But he mollified me by making an oriental bow, and saying—

"With submission, sir, it was generous of me to find you in stationery on my own account."

Now my original business—that of a conveyancer and title hunter, and drawer-up of recondite documents of all sorts—was considerably increased by receiving the master's office. There was now great work for scriveners. Not only must I push the clerks already with me, but I must have additional help.

In answer to my advertisement, a motionless young man one morning stood upon my office threshold, the door being open, for it was summer. I can see that figure now—pallidly neat, pitiably respectable, incurably forlorn! It was Bartleby.

After a few words touching his qualifications, I engaged him, glad to have among my corps of copyists a man of so singularly sedate an aspect, which I thought might operate beneficially upon the flighty temper of Turkey, and the fiery one of Nippers.

I should have stated before that ground glass folding-doors divided my premises into two parts, one of which was occupied by my scriveners, the other by myself. According to my humor, I threw open these doors, or closed them. I resolved to assign Bartleby a corner by the folding-doors, but on my side of them, so as to have this quiet man within easy call, in case any trifling thing was to be done. I placed his desk close up to a small side-window in that part of the room, a window which originally had afforded a lateral view of certain grimy backyards and bricks, but which, owing to subsequent erections, commanded at present no view at all, though it gave some light. Within three feet of the panes was a wall, and the light came down from far above, between two lofty buildings, as from a very small opening in a dome. Still further to a satisfactory arrangement, I procured a high green folding screen, which might entirely isolate Bartleby from my sight, though not remove him from my voice. And thus, in a manner, privacy and society were conjoined.

At first, Bartleby did an extraordinary quantity of writing. As if long famishing for something to copy, he seemed to gorge himself on my documents. There was no pause for digestion. He ran a day and night line, copying by sun-light and by candle-light. I should have been quite delighted with his application, had he been cheerfully industrious. But he wrote on silently, palely, mechanically.

It is, of course, an indispensable part of a scrivener's business to verify the accuracy of his copy, word by word. Where there are two or more scriveners in an office, they assist each other in this examination, one reading from the copy, the other holding the original. It is a very dull, wearisome, and lethargic affair. I can readily imagine that, to some sanguine temperaments, it would be altogether intolerable. For example, I cannot credit that the mettlesome poet, Byron, would have contentedly sat down with Bartleby to examine a law document of, say five hundred pages, closely written in a crimpy hand.

Now and then, in the haste of business, it had been my habit to assist in comparing some brief document myself, calling Turkey or Nippers for this purpose. One object I had, in placing Bartleby so handy to me behind the screen, was to avail myself of his services on such trivial occasions. It was on the third day, I think, of his being with me, and before any necessity had arisen for having his own writing examined, that, being much hurried to complete a small affair I had in hand, I abruptly called to Bartleby. In my haste and natural expectancy of instant compliance, I sat with my head bent over the original on my desk, and my right hand sideways, and somewhat nervously extended with the copy, so that, immediately upon emerging from his retreat, Bartleby might snatch it and proceed to business without the least delay.

In this very attitude did I sit when I called to him, rapidly stating what it was I wanted him to do—namely, to examine a small paper with me. Imagine my surprise, nay, my consternation, when, without moving from his privacy, Bartleby, in a singularly mild, firm voice, replied, "I would prefer not to."

I sat awhile in perfect silence, rallying my stunned faculties. Immediately it occurred to me that my ears had deceived me, or Bartleby had entirely misunderstood my meaning. I repeated my request in the clearest tone I could assume; but in quite as clear a one came the previous reply, "I would prefer not to."

"Prefer not to," echoed I, rising in high excitement, and crossing the room with a stride. "What do you mean? Are you moon-struck? I want you to help me compare this sheet here—take it," and I thrust it towards him.

"I would prefer not to," said he.

I looked at him steadfastly. His face was leanly composed; his gray eye dimly calm. Not a wrinkle of agitation rippled him. Had there been the least uneasiness, anger, impatience, or impertinence in his manner; in other words, had there been any thing ordinarily human about him, doubtless I should have violently dismissed him from the premises. But as it was, I should have as soon thought of turning my pale plaster-of-paris bust of Cicero out of doors. I stood gazing at him awhile, as he went on with his own writing, and then reseated myself at my desk. This is very strange, thought I. What had one best do? But my business hurried me. I concluded to forget the matter for the present, reserving it for my future leisure. So calling Nippers from the other room, the paper was speedily examined.

A few days after this, Bartleby concluded four lengthy documents, being quadruplicates of a week's testimony taken before me in my High Court of Chancery. It became necessary to examine them. It was an important suit, and great accuracy was imperative. Having all things arranged, I called Turkey, Nippers, and Ginger Nut from the next room, meaning to place the four copies in the hands of my four clerks, while I should read from the original. Accordingly, Turkey, Nippers, and Ginger Nut had taken their seats in a row, each with his document in his hand, when I called to Bartleby to join this interesting group.

"Bartleby! quick, I am waiting."

I heard a slow scrape of his chair legs on the uncarpeted floor, and soon he appeared standing at the entrance of his hermitage.

"What is wanted?" said he, mildly.

"The copies, the copies," said I, hurriedly. "We are going to examine them. There—" and I held towards him the fourth quadruplicate.

"I would prefer not to," he said, and gently disappeared behind the screen.

For a few moments I was turned into a pillar of salt, standing at the head of my seated column of clerks. Recovering myself, I advanced towards the screen, and demanded the reason for such extraordinary conduct.

"*Why* do you refuse?"

"I would prefer not to."

With any other man I should have flown outright into a dreadful passion, scorned all further words, and thrust him ignominiously from my presence. But there was something about Bartleby that not only strangely disarmed me, but in a wonderful manner, touched and disconcerted me. I began to reason with him.

"These are your own copies we are about to examine. It is labor saving to you, because one examination will answer for your four papers. It is common usage. Every copyist is bound to help examine his copy. Is it not so? Will you not speak? Answer!"

"I prefer not to," he replied in a flutelike tone. It seemed to me that, while I had been addressing him, he carefully revolved every statement that I made; fully comprehended the meaning; could not gainsay the irresistible conclusion; but, at the same time, some paramount consideration prevailed with him to reply as he did.

"You are decided, then, not to comply with my request—a request made according to common usage and common sense?"

He briefly gave me to understand, that on that point my judgment was sound. Yes: his decision was irreversible.

It is not seldom the case that, when a man is browbeaten in some unprecedented and violently unreasonable way, he begins to stagger in his own plainest faith. He begins, as it were, vaguely to surmise that, wonderful as it may be, all the justice and all the reason is on the other side. Accordingly, if any disinterested persons are present, he turns to them for some reinforcement of his own faltering mind.

"Turkey," said I, "what do you think of this? Am I not right?"

"With submission, sir," said Turkey, in his blandest tone, "I think that you are."

"Nippers," said I, "what do *you* think of it?"

"I think I should kick him out of the office."

(The reader, of nice perceptions, will here perceive that, it being morning, Turkey's answer is couched in polite and tranquil terms, but Nippers replies in ill-tempered ones. Or, to repeat a previous sentence, Nippers's ugly mood was on duty, and Turkey's off.)

"Ginger Nut," said I, willing to enlist the smallest suffrage in my behalf, "what do *you* think of it?"

"I think, sir, he's a little *luny*," replied Ginger Nut, with a grin.

"You hear what they say," said I, turning towards the screen, "come forth and do your duty."

But he vouchsafed no reply. I pondered a moment in sore perplexity. But once more business hurried me. I determined again to postpone the consideration of this dilemma to my future leisure. With a little trouble we made out to examine the papers without Bartleby, though at every page or two Turkey deferentially dropped his opinion, that this proceeding was quite out of the common; while Nippers, twitching in his chair with a dyspeptic nervousness, ground out, between his set teeth, occasional hissing maledictions against the stubborn oaf behind the screen. And for his (Nippers's) part, this was the first and the last time he would do another man's business without pay.

Meanwhile Bartleby sat in his hermitage, oblivious to everything but his own peculiar business there.

Some days passed, the scrivener being employed upon another lengthy work. His late remarkable conduct led me to regard his ways narrowly. I observed that he never went to dinner; indeed, that he never went anywhere. As yet I had never, of my personal knowledge, known him to be outside of my office. He was a perpetual sentry in the corner. At about eleven o'clock though, in the morning, I noticed that Ginger Nut would advance toward the opening in Bartleby's screen, as if silently beckoned thither by a gesture invisible to me where I sat. The boy would then leave the office, jingling a few pence, and reappear with a handful of ginger-nuts, which he delivered in the hermitage, receiving two of the cakes for his trouble.

He lives, then, on ginger-nuts, thought I; never eats a dinner, properly speaking; he must be a vegetarian, then; but no; he never eats even vegetables; he eats nothing but ginger-nuts. My mind then ran on in reveries concerning the probable effects upon the human constitution of living entirely on ginger-nuts. Ginger-nuts are so called, because they contain ginger as one of their peculiar constituents, and the final flavoring one. Now, what was ginger? A hot, spicy thing. Was Bartleby hot and spicy? Not at all. Ginger, then, had no effect upon Bartleby. Probably he preferred it should have none.

Nothing so aggravates an earnest person as a passive resistance. If the individual so resisted be of a not inhumane temper, and the resisting one perfectly harmless in his passivity, then, in the better moods of the former, he will endeavor charitably to construe to his imagination what proves impossible to be solved by his judgment. Even so, for the most part, I regarded Bartleby and his ways. Poor fellow! thought I, he means no mischief; it is plain he intends no insolence; his aspect sufficiently evinces that his eccentricities are involuntary. He is useful to me. I can get along with him. If I turn him away, the chances are he will fall in with some less-indulgent employer, and then he will be rudely treated, and perhaps driven forth miserably to starve. Yes. Here I can cheaply purchase a delicious self-approval. To befriend Bartleby; to humor him in his strange willfulness, will cost me little or nothing, while I lay up in my soul what will eventually prove a sweet morsel for my conscience. But this mood was not invariable with me. The passiveness of Bartleby sometimes irritated me. I felt strangely goaded on to encounter him in new opposition—to elicit some angry spark from him answerable to my own. But, indeed, I might as well have essayed to strike fire with my knuckles against a bit of Windsor soap. But one afternoon the evil impulse in me mastered me, and the following little scene ensued:

"Bartleby," said I, "when those papers are all copied, I will compare them with you."

"I would prefer not to."

"How? Surely you do not mean to persist in that mulish vagary?"

No answer.

I threw open the folding-doors near by, and, turning upon Turkey and Nippers, exclaimed:

"Bartleby a second time says, he won't examine his papers. What do you think of it, Turkey?"

It was afternoon, be it remembered. Turkey sat glowing like a brass boiler; his bald head steaming; his hands reeling among his blotted papers.

"Think of it?" roared Turkey; "I think I'll just step behind his screen, and black his eyes for him!"

So saying, Turkey rose to his feet and threw his arms into a pugilistic position. He was hurrying away to make good his promise, when I detained him, alarmed at the effect of incautiously rousing Turkey's combativeness after dinner.

"Sit down, Turkey," said I, "and hear what Nippers has to say. What do you think of it, Nippers? Would I not be justified in immediately dismissing Bartleby?"

"Excuse me, that is for you to decide, sir. I think his conduct quite unusual, and, indeed, unjust, as regards Turkey and myself. But it may only be a passing whim."

"Ah," exclaimed I, "you have strangely changed your mind, then—you speak very gently of him now."

"All beer," cried Turkey; "gentleness is effects of beer—Nippers and I dined together to-day. You see how gentle *I* am, sir. Shall I go and black his eyes?"

"You refer to Bartleby, I suppose. No, not to-day, Turkey," I replied; "pray, put up your fists."

I closed the doors, and again advanced towards Bartleby. I felt additional incentives tempting me to my fate. I burned to be rebelled against again. I remembered that Bartleby never left the office.

"Bartleby," said I, "Ginger Nut is away; just step around to the Post Office, won't you? (it was but a three minutes' walk), and see if there is anything for me."

"I would prefer not to."

"You *will* not?"

"I *prefer* not."

I staggered to my desk, and sat there in a deep study. My blind inveteracy returned. Was there any other thing in which I could procure myself to be ignominiously repulsed by this lean, penniless wight?—my hired clerk? What added thing is there, perfectly reasonable, that he will be sure to refuse to do?

"Bartleby!"

No answer.

"Bartleby," in a louder tone.

No answer.

"Bartleby," I roared.

Like a very ghost, agreeably to the laws of magical invocation, at the third summons, he appeared at the entrance of his hermitage.

"Go to the next room, and tell Nippers to come to me."

"I prefer not to," he respectfully and slowly said and mildly disappeared.

"Very good, Bartleby," said I, in a quiet sort of serenely-severe, self-possessed tone, intimating the unalterable purpose of some terrible retribution very close at hand. At the moment I half intended something of the kind. But upon the whole, as it was drawing towards my dinner-hour, I thought it best to put on my hat and walk home for the day, suffering much from perplexity and distress of mind.

Shall I acknowledge it? The conclusion of this whole business was, that it soon became a fixed fact of my chambers, that a pale young scrivener, by the name of Bartleby, had a desk there; that he copied for me at the usual rate of four cents a folio (one hundred words); but he was permanently exempt from examining the work done by him, that duty being transferred to Turkey and Nippers, out of compliment, doubtless, to their superior acuteness; moreover, said Bartleby was never, on any account, to be dispatched on the most trivial errand of any sort; and that even if entreated to take upon him such a matter, it was generally understood that he would "prefer not to"—in other words, that he would refuse point-blank.

As days passed on, I became considerably reconciled to Bartleby. His steadiness, his freedom from all dissipation, his incessant industry (except when he chose to throw himself into a standing revery behind his screen), his great stillness, his unalterableness of demeanor under all circumstances, made him a valuable acquisition. One prime thing was this—*he was always there*—first in the morning, continually through the day, and the last at night. I had a singular confidence in his honesty. I felt my most precious papers perfectly safe in his hands. Sometimes, to be sure, I could not, for the very soul of me, avoid falling into sudden spasmodic passions with him. For it was exceeding difficult to bear in mind all the time those strange peculiarities, privileges, and unheard of exemptions, forming the tacit stipulations on Bartleby's part under which he remained in my office. Now and then, in the eagerness of dispatching pressing business, I would inadvertently summon Bartleby, in a short, rapid tone, to put his finger, say, on the incipient tie of a bit of red tape with which I was about compressing some papers. Of course, from behind the screen the usual answer, "I prefer not to," was sure to come; and then, how could a human creature, with the common infirmities of our nature, refrain from bitterly exclaiming upon such perverseness—such unreasonableness. However, every added repulse of this sort which I received only tended to lessen the probability of my repeating the inadvertence.

Here it must be said, that according to the custom of most legal gentlemen occupying chambers in densely-populated law buildings, there were several keys to my door. One was kept by a woman residing in the attic, which person weekly scrubbed and daily swept and dusted my apartments. Another was kept by Turkey for convenience sake. The third I sometimes carried in my own pocket. The fourth I knew not who had.

Now, one Sunday morning I happened to go to Trinity Church, to hear a celebrated preacher, and finding myself rather early on the ground I thought I would walk around to my chambers for a while. Luckily I had my key with me; but upon applying it to the lock, I found it resisted by something inserted from the inside. Quite surprised, I called out; when to my consternation a key was turned from within; and thrusting his lean visage at me, and holding the door ajar, the apparition of Bartleby appeared, in his shirt sleeves, and otherwise in a strangely tattered *déshabillé,* saying quietly that he was sorry, but he was deeply engaged just then, and—preferred not admitting me at present. In a brief word or two, he moreover added, that perhaps I had better walk around the block two or three times, and by that time he would probably have concluded his affairs.

Now, the utterly unsurmised appearance of Bartleby, tenanting my law-chambers of a Sunday morning, with his cadaverously gentlemanly *nonchalance,* yet withal firm and self-possessed, had such a strange effect upon me, that incontinently I slunk away from my own door, and did as desired. But not without sundry twinges of impotent rebellion against the mild effrontery of this unaccountable scrivener. Indeed, it was his wonderful mildness chiefly, which not only disarmed me, but unmanned me as it were. For I consider that one, for the time, is somehow unmanned when he tranquilly permits his hired clerk to dictate to him, and order him away from his own premises. Furthermore, I was full of uneasiness as to what Bartleby could possibly be doing in my office in his shirt sleeves, and in an otherwise dismantled condition of a Sunday morning. Was anything amiss going on? Nay, that was out of the question. It was not to be thought of for a moment that Bartleby was an immoral person. But what could he be doing there?—copying? Nay again, whatever might be his eccentricities, Bartleby was an eminently decorous person. He would be the last man to sit down to his desk in any state approaching to nudity. Besides, it was Sunday; and there was something about Bartleby that forbade the supposition that he would by any secular occupation violate the proprieties of the day.

Nevertheless, my mind was not pacified; and full of a restless curiosity, at last I returned to the door. Without hindrance I inserted my key, opened it, and entered. Bartleby was not to be seen. I looked round anxiously, peeped behind his screen; but it was very plain that he was gone. Upon more closely examining the place, I surmised that for an indefinite period Bartleby must have eaten, dressed, and slept in my office, and that, too, without plate, mirror, or bed. The cushioned seat of a rickety old sofa in one corner bore the faint impress of a lean, reclining form. Rolled away under his desk, I found a blanket; under the empty grate, a blacking box and brush; on a chair, a tin basin, with soap and a ragged towel; in a newspaper a few crumbs of ginger-nuts and a morsel of cheese. Yes, thought I, it is evident enough that Bartleby has been making his home here, keeping bachelor's hall all by himself. Immediately then the thought came sweeping across me, what miserable friendlessness and loneliness are here revealed! His poverty is great; but his solitude, how horrible! Think of it. Of a Sunday, Wall Street is deserted as Petra, and every night of every day it is an emptiness. This building, too, which of week-days hums with industry and life, at nightfall echoes with sheer vacancy, and all through Sunday is forlorn. And here Bartleby makes his home; sole spectator of a solitude which he has seen all populous—a sort of innocent and transformed Marius brooding among the ruins of Carthage!

For the first time in my life a feeling of over-powering stinging melancholy seized me. Before, I had never experienced aught but a not unpleasing sadness. The bond of a common humanity now drew me irresistibly to gloom. A fraternal melancholy! For both I and Bartleby were sons of Adam. I remembered the bright silks and sparkling faces I had seen that day, in gala trim, swan-like sailing down the Mississippi of Broadway; and I contrasted them with the pallid copyist, and thought to myself, Ah, happiness courts the light, so we deem the world is gay; but misery hides aloof, so we deem that misery there is none. These sad fancyings—chimeras, doubtless, of a sick and silly brain—led on to other and more special thoughts, concerning the eccentricities of Bartleby. Presentiments of strange discoveries hovered round me. The scrivener's pale form appeared to me laid out, among uncaring strangers, in its shivering winding sheet.

Suddenly I was attracted by Bartleby's closed desk, the key in open sight left in the lock.

I mean no mischief, seek the gratification of no heartless curiosity, thought I; besides, the desk is mine, and its contents, too, so I will make bold to look within. Everything was methodically arranged, the papers smoothly placed. The pigeon holes were deep, and removing the files of documents, I groped into their recesses. Presently I felt something there, and dragged it out. It was an old bandanna handkerchief, heavy and knotted. I opened it, and saw it was a savings bank.

I now recalled all the quiet mysteries which I had noted in the man. I remembered that he never spoke but to answer; that, though at intervals he had considerable time to himself, yet I had never seen him reading—no, not even a newspaper; that for long periods he would stand looking out, at his pale window behind the screen, upon the dead brick wall; I was quite sure he never visited any refectory or eating house; while his pale face clearly indicated that he never drank beer like Turkey, or tea and coffee even, like other men; that he never went anywhere in particular that I could learn; never went out for a walk, unless, indeed, that was the case at present; that he had declined telling who he was, or whence he came, or whether he had any relatives in the world; that though so thin and pale, he never complained of ill health. And more than all, I remembered a certain unconscious air of pallid—how shall I call it?—of pallid haughtiness, say, or rather an austere reserve about him, which had positively awed me into my tame compliance with his eccentricities, when I had feared to ask him to do the slightest incidental thing for me, even though I might know, from his long-continued motionlessness, that behind his screen he must be standing in one of those dead-wall reveries of his.

Revolving all these things, and coupling them with the recently discovered fact, that he made my office his constant abiding place and home, and not forgetful of his morbid moodiness; revolving all these things, a prudential feeling began to steal over me. My first emotions had been those of pure melancholy and sincerest pity; but just in proportion as the forlornness of Bartleby grew and grew to my imagination, did that same melancholy merge into fear, that pity into repulsion. So true it is, and so terrible, too, that up to a certain point the thought or sight of misery enlists our best affections; but, in certain special cases, beyond that point it does not. They err who would assert that invariably this is owing to the inherent selfishness of the human heart. It rather proceeds from a certain hopelessness of remedying excessive and organic ill. To a sensitive being, pity is not seldom pain. And when at last it is perceived that such pity cannot lead to effectual succor, common sense bids the soul be rid of it. What I saw that morning persuaded me that the scrivener was the victim of innate and incurable disorder. I might give alms to his body; but his body did not pain him; it was his soul that suffered, and his soul I could not reach.

I did not accomplish the purpose of going to Trinity Church that morning. Somehow, the things I had seen disqualified me for the time from churchgoing. I walked homeward, thinking what I would do with Bartleby. Finally, I resolved upon this—I would put certain calm questions to him the next morning, touching his history, etc., and if he declined to answer them openly and unreservedly (and I supposed he would prefer not), then to give him a twenty dollar bill over and above whatever I might owe him, and tell him his services were no longer required; but that if in any other way I could assist him, I would be happy to do so, especially if he desired to return to his native place, wherever that might be, I would willingly help to defray the expenses. Moreover, if, after reaching home, he found himself at any time in want of aid, a letter from him would be sure of a reply.

The next morning came.

"Bartleby," said I, gently calling to him behind his screen.

No reply.

"Bartleby," said I, in a still gentler tone, "come here; I am not going to ask you to do anything you would prefer not to do—I simply wish to speak to you."

Upon this he noiselessly slid into view.

"Will you tell me, Bartleby, where you were born?"

"I would prefer not to."

"Will you tell me *anything* about yourself?"

"I would prefer not to."

"But what reasonable objection can you have to speak to me? I feel friendly towards you."

He did not look at me while I spoke, but kept his glance fixed upon my bust of Cicero, which, as I then sat, was directly behind me, some six inches above my head.

"What is your answer, Bartleby," said I, after waiting a considerable time for a reply, during which his countenance remained immovable, only there was the faintest conceivable tremor of the white attenuated mouth.

"At present I prefer to give no answer," he said, and retired into his hermitage.

It was rather weak in me I confess, but his manner, on this occasion, nettled me. Not only did there seem to lurk in it a certain calm disdain, but his perverseness seemed ungrateful, considering the undeniable good usage and indulgence he had received from me.

Again I sat ruminating what I should do. Mortified as I was at his behavior, and resolved as I had been to dismiss him when I entered my office, nevertheless I strangely felt something superstitious knocking at my heart, and forbidding me to carry out my purpose, and denouncing me for a villain if I dared to breathe one bitter word against this forlornest of mankind. At last, familiarly drawing my chair behind his screen, I sat down and said: "Bartleby, never mind, then, about revealing your history; but let me entreat you, as a friend, to comply as far as may be with the usages of this office. Say now, you will help to examine papers to-morrow or next day: in short, say now, that in a day or two you will begin to be a little reasonable:—say so, Bartleby."

"At present I would prefer not to be a little reasonable," was his mildly cadaverous reply.

Just then the folding-doors opened, and Nippers approached. He seemed suffering from an unusually bad night's rest, induced by severer indigestion than common. He overheard those final words of Bartleby.

"*Prefer not*, eh?" gritted Nippers—"I'd *prefer* him, if I were you, sir," addressing me—"I'd *prefer* him; I'd give him preferences, the stubborn mule! What is it, sir, pray, that he *prefers* not to do now?"

Bartleby moved not a limb.

"Mr. Nippers," said I, "I'd prefer that you would withdraw for the present."

Somehow, of late, I had got into the way of involuntarily using this word "prefer" upon all sorts of not exactly suitable occasions. And I trembled to think that my contact with the scrivener had already and seriously affected me in a mental way. And what further and deeper aberration might it not yet produce? This apprehension had not been without efficacy in determining me to summary measures.

As Nippers, looking very sour and sulky, was departing, Turkey blandly and deferentially approached.

"With submission, sir," said he, "yesterday I was thinking about Bartleby here, and I think that if he would but prefer to take a quart of good ale every day, it would do much towards mending him, and enabling him to assist in examining his papers."

"So you have got the word, too," said I, slightly excited.

"With submission, what word, sir," asked Turkey, respectfully crowding himself into the contracted space behind the screen, and by so doing, making me jostle the scrivener. "What word, sir?"

"I would prefer to be left alone here," said Bartleby, as if offended at being mobbed in his privacy.

"*That's* the word, Turkey," said I—"*that's* it."

"Oh, *prefer?* oh yes—queer word. I never use it myself. But, sir, as I was saying, if he would but prefer—"

"Turkey," interrupted I, "you will please withdraw."

"Oh certainly, sir, if you prefer that I should."

As he opened the folding-door to retire, Nippers at his desk caught a glimpse of me, and asked whether I would prefer to have a certain paper copied on blue paper or white. He did not in the least roguishly accent the word prefer. It was plain that it involuntarily rolled from his tongue. I thought to myself, surely I must get rid of a demented man, who already has in some degree turned the tongues, if not the heads of myself and clerks. But I thought it prudent not to break the dismission at once.

The next day I noticed that Bartleby did nothing but stand at his window in his dead-wall revery. Upon asking him why he did not write, he said that he had decided upon doing no more writing.

"Why, how now? what next?" exclaimed I, "do no more writing?"

"No more."

"And what is the reason?"

"Do you not see the reason for yourself," he indifferently replied.

I looked steadfastly at him, and perceived that his eyes looked dull and glazed. Instantly it occurred to me, that his unexampled diligence in copying by his dim window for the first few weeks of his stay with me might have temporarily impaired his vision.

I was touched. I said something in condolence with him. I hinted that of course he did wisely in abstaining from writing for a while; and urged him to embrace that opportunity of taking wholesome exercise in the open air. This, however, he did not do. A few days after this, my other clerks being absent, and being in a great hurry to dispatch certain letters by the mail, I thought that, having nothing else earthly to do, Bartleby would surely be less inflexible than usual, and carry these letters to the post-office. But he blankly declined. So, much to my inconvenience, I went myself.

Still added days went by. Whether Bartleby's eyes improved or not, I could not say. To all appearance I thought they did. But when I asked him if they did, he vouchsafed no answer. At all events, he would do no copying. At last, in reply to my urgings, he informed me that he had permanently given up copying.

"What!" exclaimed I; "suppose your eyes should get entirely well—better than ever before—would you not copy then?"

"I have given up copying," he answered, and slid aside.

He remained as ever, a fixture in my chamber. Nay—if that were possible—he became still more of a fixture than before. What was to be done? He would do nothing in the office; why should he stay there? In plain fact, he had now become a millstone to me, not only useless as a necklace, but afflictive to bear. Yet I was sorry for him. I speak less than truth when I say that, on his own account, he occasioned me uneasiness. If he would but have named a single relative or friend, I would instantly have written, and urged their taking the poor fellow away to some convenient retreat. But he seemed alone, absolutely alone in the universe. A bit of wreck in the mid Atlantic. At length, necessities connected with my business tyrannized over all other considerations. Decently as I could, I told Bartleby that in six days time he must unconditionally leave the office. I warned him to take measures, in the interval, for procuring some other abode. I offered to assist him in his endeavor, if he himself would but take the first step towards a removal. "And when you finally quit me, Bartleby," added I, "I shall see that you go not away entirely unprovided. Six days from this hour, remember."

At the expiration of that period, I peeped behind the screen, and lo! Bartleby was there.

I buttoned up my coat, balanced myself; advanced slowly towards him, touched his shoulder, and said, "The time has come; you must quit this place; I am sorry for you; here is money; but you must go."

"I would prefer not," he replied, with his back still towards me.

"You *must.*"

He remained silent.

Now I had an unbounded confidence in this man's common honesty. He had frequently restored to me sixpences and shillings carelessly dropped upon the floor, for I am apt to be very reckless in such shirt-button affairs. The proceeding, then, which followed will not be deemed extraordinary.

"Bartleby," said I, "I owe you twelve dollars on account; here are thirty-two; the odd twenty are yours—Will you take it?" and I handed the bills towards him.

But he made no motion.

"I will leave them here, then," putting them under a weight on the table. Then taking my hat and cane and going to the door, I tranquilly turned and added—"After you have removed your things from these offices, Bartleby, you will of course lock the door—since every one is now gone for the day but you—and if you please, slip your key underneath the mat, so that I may have it in the morning. I shall not see you again; so good-by to you. If, hereafter, in your new place of abode, I can be of any service to you, do not fail to advise me by letter. Good-by, Bartleby, and fare you well."

But he answered not a word; like the last column of some ruined temple, he remained standing mute and solitary in the middle of the otherwise deserted room.

As I walked home in a pensive mood, my vanity got the better of my pity. I could not but highly plume myself on my masterly management in getting rid of Bartleby. Masterly I call it, and such it must appear to any dispassionate thinker. The beauty of my procedure seemed to consist in its perfect quietness. There was no vulgar bullying, no bravado of any sort, no choleric hectoring, and striding to and fro across the apartment, jerking out vehement commands for Bartleby to bundle himself off with his beggarly traps. Nothing of the kind. Without loudly bidding Bartleby depart—as an inferior genius might have done—I *assumed* the ground that depart he must; and upon that assumption built all I had to say. The more I thought over my procedure, the more I was charmed with it. Nevertheless, next morning, upon awakening, I had my doubts—I had somehow slept off the fumes of vanity. One of the coolest and wisest hours a man has, is just after he awakes in the morning. My procedure seemed as sagacious as ever—but only in theory. How it would prove in practice—there was the rub. It was truly a beautiful thought to have assumed Bartleby's departure; but, after all, that assumption was simply my own, and none of Bartleby's. The great point was, not whether I had assumed that he would quit me, but whether he would prefer so to do. He was more a man of preferences than assumptions.

After breakfast, I walked down town, arguing the probabilities *pro* and *con*. One moment I thought it would prove a miserable failure, and Bartleby would be found all alive at my office as usual; the next moment it seemed certain that I should find his chair empty. And so I kept veering about. At the corner of Broadway and Canal Street, I saw quite an excited group of people standing in earnest conversation.

"I'll take odds he doesn't," said a voice as I passed.

"Doesn't go?—done!" said I; "put up your money."

I was instinctively putting my hand in my pocket to produce my own, when I remembered that this was an election day. The words I had overheard bore no reference to Bartleby, but to the success or non-success of some candidate for the mayoralty. In my intent frame of mind, I had, as it were, imagined that all Broadway shared in my excitement, and were debating the same question with me. I passed on, very thankful that the uproar of the street screened my momentary absent-mindedness.

As I had intended, I was earlier than usual at my office door. I stood listening for a moment. All was still. He must be gone. I tried the knob. The door was locked. Yes, my procedure had worked to a charm; he indeed must be vanished. Yet a certain melancholy mixed with this: I was almost sorry for my brilliant success. I was fumbling under the door mat for the key, which Bartleby was to have left there for me, when accidentally my knee knocked against a panel, producing a summoning sound, and in response a voice came to me from within—"Not yet; I am occupied."

It was Bartleby.

I was thunderstruck. For an instant I stood like the man who, pipe in mouth, was killed one cloudless afternoon long ago in Virginia, by summer lightning; at his own warm open window he was killed, and remained leaning out there upon the dreamy afternoon, till some one touched him, when he fell.

"Not gone!" I murmured at last. But again obeying that wondrous ascendancy which the inscrutable scrivener had over me, and from which ascendancy, for all my chafing, I could not completely escape, I slowly went down stairs and out into the street, and while walking round the block, considered what I should next do in this unheard-of perplexity. Turn the man out by an actual thrusting I could not; to drive him away by calling him hard names would not do; calling in the police was an unpleasant idea; and yet, permit him to enjoy his cadaverous triumph over me—this, too, I could not think of. What was to be done? or, if nothing could be done, was there anything further that I could *assume* in the matter? Yes, as before I had prospectively assumed that Bartleby would depart, so now I might retrospectively assume that departed he was. In the legitimate carrying out of this assumption, I might enter my office in a great hurry, and pretending not to see Bartleby at all, walk straight against him as if he were air. Such a proceeding would in a singular degree have the appearance of a home-thrust. It was hardly possible that Bartleby could withstand such an application of the doctrine of assumptions. But upon second thoughts the success of the plan seemed rather dubious. I resolved to argue the matter over with him again.

"Bartleby," said I, entering the office, with a quietly severe expression, "I am seriously displeased. I am pained, Bartleby. I had thought better of you. I had imagined you of such a gentlemanly organization, that in any delicate dilemma a slight hint would suffice—in short, an assumption. But it appears I am deceived. Why," I added, unaffectedly starting, "you have not even touched that money yet," pointing to it, just where I had left it the evening previous.

He answered nothing.

"Will you, or will you not, quit me?" I now demanded in a sudden passion, advancing close to him.

"I would prefer *not* to quit you," he replied, gently emphasizing the *not*.

"What earthly right have you to stay here? Do you pay any rent? Do you pay my taxes? Or is this property yours?"

He answered nothing.

"Are you ready to go on and write now? Are your eyes recovered? Could you copy a small paper for me this morning? or help examine a few lines? or step round to the post-office? In a word, will you do anything at all, to give a coloring to your refusal to depart the premises?"

He silently retired into his hermitage.

I was now in such a state of nervous resentment that I thought it but prudent to check myself at present from further demonstrations. Bartleby and I were alone. I remembered the tragedy of the unfortunate Adams and the still more unfortunate Colt in the solitary office of the latter; and how poor Colt, being dreadfully incensed by Adams, and imprudently permitting himself to get wildly excited, was at unawares hurried into his fatal act—an act which certainly no man could possibly deplore more than the actor himself. Often it had occurred to me in my ponderings upon the subject, that had that altercation taken place in the public street, or at a private residence, it would not have terminated as it did. It was the circumstance of being alone in a solitary office, up stairs, of a building entirely unhallowed by humanizing domestic associations—an uncarpeted office, doubtless, of a dusty, haggard sort of appearance—this it must have been, which greatly helped to enhance the irritable desperation of the hapless Colt.

But when this old Adam of resentment rose in me and tempted me concerning Bartleby, I grappled him and threw him. How? Why, simply by recalling the divine injunction: "A new commandment give I unto you, that ye love one another." Yes, this it was that saved me. Aside from higher considerations, charity often operates as a vastly wise and prudent principle—a great safeguard to its possessor. Men have committed murder for jealousy's sake, and anger's sake, and hatred's sake, and selfishness' sake, and spiritual pride's sake; but no man, that ever I heard of, ever committed a diabolical murder for sweet charity's sake. Mere self-interest, then, if no better motive can be enlisted, should, especially with high-tempered men, prompt all beings to charity and philanthropy. At any rate, upon the occasion in question, I strove to drown my exasperated feelings towards the scrivener by benevolently construing his conduct. Poor fellow, poor fellow! thought I, he don't mean anything; and besides, he has seen hard times, and ought to be indulged.

I endeavored, also, immediately to occupy myself, and at the same time to comfort my despondency. I tried to fancy, that in the course of the morning, at such time as might prove agreeable to him, Bartleby, of his own free accord, would emerge from his hermitage and take up some decided line of march in the direction of the door. But no. Half-past twelve o'clock came; Turkey began to glow in the face, overturn his inkstand, and become generally obstreperous; Nippers abated down into quietude and courtesy; Ginger Nut munched his noon apple; and Bartleby remained standing at his window in one of his profoundest dead-wall reveries. Will it be credited? Ought I to acknowledge it? That afternoon I left the office without saying one further word to him.

Some days now passed, during which, at leisure intervals I looked a little into "Edwards on the Will," and "Priestley on Necessity." Under the circumstances, those books induced a salutary feeling. Gradually I slid into the persuasion that these troubles of mine, touching the scrivener, had been all predestinated from eternity, and Bartleby was billeted upon me for some mysterious purpose of an all-wise Providence, which it was not for a mere mortal like me to fathom. Yes, Bartleby, stay there behind your screen, thought I; I shall persecute you no more; you are harmless and noiseless as any of these old chairs; in short, I never feel so private as when I know you are here. At last I see it, I feel it; I penetrate to the predestinated purpose of my life. I am content. Others may have loftier parts to enact; but my mission in this world, Bartleby, is to furnish you with office-room for such period as you may see fit to remain.

I believe that this wise and blessed frame of mind would have continued with me, had it not been for the unsolicited and uncharitable remarks obtruded upon me by my professional friends who visited the rooms. But thus it often is, that the constant friction of illiberal minds wears out at last the best resolves of the more generous. Though to be sure, when I reflected upon it, it was not strange that people entering my office should be struck by the peculiar aspect of the unaccountable Bartleby, and so be tempted to throw out some sinister observations concerning him. Sometimes an attorney, having business with me, and calling at my office, and finding no one but the scrivener there, would undertake to obtain some sort of precise information from him touching my whereabouts; but without heeding his idle talk, Bartleby would remain standing immovable in the middle of the room. So after contemplating him in that position for a time, the attorney would depart, no wiser than he came.

Also, when a reference was going on, and the room full of lawyers and witnesses, and business driving fast, some deeply-occupied legal gentleman present, seeing Bartleby wholly unemployed, would request him to run round to his (the legal gentleman's) office and fetch some papers for him. Thereupon, Bartleby would tranquilly decline, and yet remain idle as before. Then the lawyer would give a great stare, and turn to me. And what could I say? At last I was made aware that all through the circle of my professional acquaintance, a whisper of wonder was running round, having reference to the strange creature I kept at my office. This worried me very much. And as the idea came upon me of his possibly turning out a long-lived man, and keep occupying my chambers, and denying my authority; and perplexing my visitors; and scandalizing my professional reputation; and casting a general gloom over the premises; keeping soul and body together to the last upon his savings (for doubtless he spent but half a dime a day), and in the end perhaps outlive me, and claim possession of my office by right of his perpetual occupancy: as all these dark anticipations crowded upon me more and more, and my friends continually intruded their relentless remarks upon the apparition in my room; a great change was wrought in me. I resolved to gather all my faculties together, and forever rid me of this intolerable incubus.

Ere revolving any complicated project, however, adapted to this end, I first simply suggested to Bartleby the propriety of his permanent departure. In a calm and serious tone, I commended the idea to his careful and mature consideration. But, having taken three days to mediate upon it, he apprised me, that his original determination remained the same; in short, that he still preferred to abide with me.

What shall I do? I now said to myself, buttoning up my coat to the last button. What shall I do? what ought I to do? what does conscience say I *should* do with this man, or, rather, ghost. Rid myself of him, I must; go, he shall. But how? You will not thrust him, the poor, pale, passive mortal—you will not thrust such a helpless creature out of your door? you will not dishonor yourself by such cruelty? No, I will not, I cannot do that. Rather would I let him live and die here, and then mason up his remains in the wall. What, then, will you do? For all your coaxing, he will not budge. Bribes he leaves under your own paper-weight on your table; in short, it is quite plain that he prefers to cling to you.

Then something severe, something unusual must be done. What! surely you will not have him collared by a constable, and commit his innocent pallor to the common jail? And upon what ground could you procure such a thing to be done?— a vagrant, is he? What! he a vagrant, a wanderer, who refuses to budge? It is because he will *not* be a vagrant, then, that you seek to count him *as* a vagrant. This is too absurd. No visible means of support: there I have him. Wrong again: for indubitably he *does* support himself, and that is the only unanswerable proof that any man can show of his possessing the means so to do. No more, then. Since he will not quit me, I must quit him. I will change my offices; I will move elsewhere, and give him fair notice, that if I find him on my new premises I will then proceed against him as a common trespasser.

Acting accordingly, next day I thus addressed him: "I find these chambers too far from the City Hall; the air is unwholesome. In a word, I propose to remove my offices next week, and shall no longer require your services. I tell you this now, in order that you may seek another place."

He made no reply; and nothing more was said.

On the appointed day I engaged carts and men, proceeded to my chambers, and, having but little furniture, everything was removed in a few hours. Throughout, the scrivener remained standing behind the screen, which I directed to be removed the last thing. It was withdrawn; and, being folded up like a huge folio, left him the motionless occupant of a naked room. I stood in the entry watching him a moment, while something from within me upbraided me.

I re-entered, with my hand in my pocket—and—and my heart in my mouth.

"Good-by, Bartleby; I am going—good-by, and God some way bless you; and take that," slipping something in his hand. But it dropped upon the floor, and then—strange to say—I tore myself from him whom I had so longed to be rid of.

Established in my new quarters, for a day or two I kept the door locked, and started at every footfall in the passages. When I returned to my rooms, after any little absence, I would pause at the threshold for an instant, and attentively listen, ere applying my key. But these fears were needless. Bartleby never came nigh me.

I thought all was going well, when a perturbed-looking stranger visited me, inquiring whether I was the person who had recently occupied rooms at No. ____ Wall Street.

Full of forebodings, I replied that I was.

"Then, sir," said the stranger, who proved a lawyer, "you are responsible for the man you left there. He refuses to do any copying; he refuses to do anything; he says he prefers not to; and he refuses to quit the premises."

"I am very sorry, sir," said I, with assumed tranquillity, but an inward tremor, "but, really, the man you allude to is nothing to me—he is no relation or apprentice of mine, that you should hold me responsible for him."

"In mercy's name, who is he?"

"I certainly cannot inform you. I know nothing about him. Formerly I employed him as a copyist; but he has done nothing for me now for some time past."

"I shall settle him, then—good morning, sir."

Several days passed, and I heard nothing more; and, though I often felt a charitable prompting to call at the place and see poor Bartleby, yet a certain squeamishness, of I know not what, withheld me.

All is over with him, by this time, thought I, at last, when, through another week, no further intelligence reached me. But, coming to my room the day after, I found several persons waiting at my door in a high state of nervous excitement.

"That's the man—here he comes," cried the foremost one, whom I recognized as the lawyer who had previously called upon me alone.

"You must take him away, sir, at once," cried a portly person among them, advancing upon me, and whom I knew to be the landlord of No.____ Wall Street. "These gentlemen, my tenants, cannot stand it any longer; Mr. B——," pointing to the lawyer, "has turned him out of his room, and he now persists in haunting the building generally, sitting upon the banisters of the stairs by day, and sleeping in the entry by night. Everybody is concerned; clients are leaving the offices; some fears are entertained of a mob; something you must do, and that without delay."

Aghast at this torrent, I fell back before it, and would fain have locked myself in my new quarters. In vain I persisted that Bartleby was nothing to me—no more than to any one else. In vain—I was the last person known to have anything to do with him, and they held me to the terrible account. Fearful, then, of being exposed in the papers (as one person present obscurely threatened), I considered the matter, and, at length, said, that if the lawyer would give me a confidential interview with the scrivener, in his (the lawyer's) own room, I would, that afternoon, strive my best to rid them of the nuisance they complained of.

Going up stairs to my old haunt, there was Bartleby silently sitting upon the banister at the landing.

"What are you doing here, Bartleby?" said I.

"Sitting upon the banister," he mildly replied.

I motioned him into the lawyer's room, who then left us.

"Bartleby," said I, "are you aware that you are the cause of great tribulation to me, by persisting in occupying the entry after being dismissed from the office?"

No answer.

"Now one of two things must take place. Either you must do something, or something must be done to you. Now what sort of business would you like to engage in? Would you like to re-engage in copying for some one?"

"No; I would prefer not to make any change."

"Would you like a clerkship in a dry-goods store?"

"There is too much confinement about that. No, I would not like a clerkship; but I am not particular."

"Too much confinement," I cried, "why you keep yourself confined all the time!"

"I would prefer not to take a clerkship," he rejoined, as if to settle that little item at once.

"How would a bar-tender's business suit you? There is no trying of the eye-sight in that."

"I would not like it at all; though, as I said before, I am not particular."

His unwonted wordiness inspirited me. I returned to the charge.

"Well, then, would you like to travel through the country collecting bills for the merchants? That would improve your health."

"No, I would prefer to be doing something else."

"How, then, would going as a companion to Europe, to entertain some young gentleman with your conversation—how would that suit you?"

"Not at all. It does not strike me that there is anything definite about that. I like to be stationary. But I am not particular."

"Stationary you shall be, then," I cried, now losing all patience, and, for the first time in all my exasperating connection with him, fairly flying into a passion. "If you do not go away from these premises before night, I shall feel bound—indeed, I *am* bound—to—to—to quit the premises myself!" I rather absurdly concluded, knowing not with what possible threat to try to frighten his immobility into compliance. Despairing of all further efforts, I was precipitately leaving him, when a final thought occurred to me—one which had not been wholly unindulged before.

"Bartleby," said I, in the kindest tone I could assume under such exciting circumstances, "will you go home with me now—not to my office, but my dwelling—and remain there till we can conclude upon some convenient arrangement for you at our leisure? Come, let us start now, right away."

"No: at present I would prefer not to make any change at all."

I answered nothing; but, effectually dodging every one by the suddenness and rapidity of my flight, rushed from the building, ran up Wall Street towards Broadway, and, jumping into the first omnibus, was soon removed from pursuit. As soon as tranquility returned, I distinctly perceived that I had now done all that I possibly could, both in respect to the demands of the landlord and his tenants, and with regard to my own desire and sense of duty, to benefit Bartleby, and shield him from rude persecution. I now strove to be entirely care-free and quiescent; and my conscience justified me in the attempt; though, indeed, it was not so successful as I could have wished. So fearful was I of being again hunted out by the incensed landlord and his exasperated tenants, that, surrendering my business to Nippers, for a few days, I drove about the upper part of the town and through the suburbs, in my rockaway; crossed over to Jersey City and Hoboken, and paid fugitive visits to Manhattanville and Astoria. In fact, I almost lived in my rockaway for the time.

When again I entered my office, lo, a note from the landlord lay upon the desk. I opened it with trembling hands. It informed me that the writer had sent to the police, and had Bartleby removed to the Tombs as a vagrant. Moreover, since I knew more about him than any one else, he wished me to appear at that place, and make a suitable statement of the facts. These tidings had a conflicting effect upon me. At first I was indignant; but, at last, almost approved. The landlord's energetic, summary disposition, had led him to adopt a procedure which I do not think I would have decided upon myself; and yet, as a last resort, under such peculiar circumstances, it seemed the only plan.

As I afterwards learned, the poor scrivener, when told that he must be conducted to the Tombs, offered not the slightest obstacle, but, in his pale, unmoving way, silently acquiesced.

Some of the compassionate and curious bystanders joined the party; and headed by one of the constables arm in arm with Bartleby, the silent procession filed its way through all the noise, and heat, and joy of the roaring thoroughfares at noon.

The same day I received the note, I went to the Tombs, or, to speak more properly, the Halls of Justice. Seeking the right officer, I stated the purpose of my call, and was informed that the individual I described was, indeed, within. I then assured the functionary that Bartleby was a perfectly honest man, and greatly to be compassionated, however unaccountably eccentric. I narrated all I knew, and closed by suggesting the idea of letting him remain in as indulgent confinement as possible, till something less harsh might be done—though, indeed, I hardly knew what. At all events, if nothing else could be decided upon, the alms-house must receive him. I then begged to have an interview.

Being under no disgraceful charge, and quite serene and harmless in all his ways, they had permitted him freely to wander about the prison, and, especially, in the inclosed grass-platted yards thereof. And so I found him there, standing all alone in the quietest of the yards, his face towards a high wall, while all around, from the narrow slits of the jail windows, I thought I saw peering out upon him the eyes of murderers and thieves.

"Bartleby!"

"I know you," he said, without looking round—"and I want nothing to say to you."

"It was not I that brought you here, Bartleby," said I, keenly pained at his implied suspicion. "And to you, this should not be so vile a place. Nothing reproachful attaches to you by being here. And see, it is not so sad a place as one might think. Look, there is the sky, and here is the grass."

"I know where I am," he replied, but would say nothing more, and so I left him.

As I entered the corridor again, a broad meat-like man, in an apron, accosted me, and, jerking his thumb over his shoulder, said—"Is that your friend?"

"Yes."

"Does he want to starve? If he does, let him live on the prison fare, that's all."

"Who are you?" asked I, not knowing what to make of such an unofficially speaking person in such a place.

"I am the grub-man. Such gentlemen as have friends here, hire me to provide them with something good to eat."

"Is this so?" said I, turning to the turnkey.

He said it was.

"Well, then," said I, slipping some silver into the grub-man's hands (for so they called him), "I want you to give particular attention to my friend there; let him have the best dinner you can get. And you must be as polite to him as possible."

"Introduce me, will you?" said the grub-man, looking at me with an expression which seemed to say he was all impatience for an opportunity to give a specimen of his breeding.

Thinking it would prove of benefit to the scrivener, I acquiesced; and, asking the grub-man his name, went up with him to Bartleby.

"Bartleby, this is a friend; you will find him very useful to you."

"Your sarvant, sir, your sarvant," said the grub-man, making a low salutation behind his apron. "Hope you find it pleasant here, sir; nice grounds—cool apartments—hope you'll stay with us sometime—try to make it agreeable. What will you have for dinner to-day?"

"I prefer not to dine to-day," said Bartleby, turning away. "It would disagree with me; I am unused to dinners." So saying, he slowly moved to the other side of the inclosure, and took up a position fronting the dead-wall.

"How's this?" said the grub-man, addressing me with a stare of astonishment. "He's odd, ain't he?"

"I think he is a little deranged," said I, sadly.

"Deranged? deranged is it? Well, now, upon my word, I thought that friend of yourn was a gentleman forger; they are always pale and genteel-like, them forgers. I can't help pity 'em—can't help it, sir. Did you know Monroe Edwards?" he added, touchingly, and paused. Then, laying his hand piteously on my shoulder, sighed, "He died of consumption at Sing-Sing. So you weren't acquainted with Monroe?"

"No, I was never socially acquainted with any forgers. But I cannot stop longer. Look to my friend yonder. You will not lose by it. I will see you again."

Some few days after this, I again obtained admission to the Tombs, and went through the corridors in quest of Bartleby; but without finding him.

"I saw him coming from his cell not long ago," said a turnkey, "may be he's gone to loiter in the yards."

So I went in that direction.

"Are you looking for the silent man?" said another turnkey, passing me. "Yonder he lies—sleeping in the yard there. 'Tis not twenty minutes since I saw him lie down."

The yard was entirely quiet. It was not accessible to the common prisoners. The surrounding walls of amazing thickness, kept off all sounds behind them. The Egyptian character of the masonry weighed upon me with its gloom. But a soft imprisoned turf grew under foot. The heart of the eternal pyramids, it seemed, wherein, by some strange magic, through the clefts, grass-seed, dropped by birds, had sprung.

Strangely huddled at the base of the wall, his knees drawn up, and lying on his side, his head touching the cold stones, I saw the wasted Bartleby. But nothing stirred. I paused; then went close up to him; stooped over, and saw that his dim eyes were open; otherwise he seemed profoundly sleeping. Something prompted me to touch him. I felt his hand, when a tingling shiver ran up my arm and down my spine to my feet.

The round face of the grub-man peered upon me now. "His dinner is ready. Won't he dine to-day, either? Or does he live without dining?"

"Lives without dining," said I, and closed the eyes.

"Eh!—He's asleep, ain't he?"

"With kings and counselors," murmured I.

There would seem little need for proceeding further in this history. Imagination will readily supply the meagre recital of poor Bartleby's interment. But, ere parting with the reader, let me say, that if this little narrative has sufficiently interested him, to awaken curiosity as to who Bartleby was, and what manner of life he led prior to the present narrator's making his acquaintance, I can only reply, that in such curiosity I fully share, but am wholly unable to gratify it. Yet here I hardly know whether I should divulge one little item of rumor, which came to my ear a few months after the scrivener's decease. Upon what basis it rested, I could never ascertain; and hence, how true it is I cannot now tell. But, inasmuch as this vague report has not been without a certain suggestive interest to me, however sad, it may prove the same with some others; and so I will briefly mention it. The report was this: that Bartleby had been a subordinate clerk in the Dead Letter Office at Washington, from which he had been suddenly removed by a change in the administration. When I think over this rumor, hardly can I express the emotions which seize me. Dead letters! does it not sound like dead men? Conceive a man by nature and misfortune prone to a pallid hopelessness, can any business seem more fitted to heighten it than that of continually handling these dead letters, and assorting them for the flames? For by the cart-load they are annually burned. Some times from out the folded paper the pale clerk takes a ring—the finger it was meant for, perhaps, moulders in the grave; a bank-note sent in swiftest charity—he whom it would relieve, nor eats nor hungers any more; pardon for those who died despairing; hope for those who died unhoping; good tidings for those who died stifled by unrelieved calamities. On errands of life, these letters speed to death.

Ah, Bartleby! Ah, humanity!

Questions for Discussion

1. How effectively does the opening paragraph build our interest in Bartleby?

2. Because the story ostensibly concerns Bartleby, what is the purpose of the descriptions of Turkey, Nippers, and Ginger Nut?

3. What kind of person is the narrator? List some characteristics.

4. "Nothing so aggravates an earnest person as a passive resistance," observes the narrator. To what extent do you agree with him?

5. How does the narrator's attitude toward Bartleby change?

Suggestions for Writing

1. Write an essay that attempts to justify and explain Bartleby's behavior.

2. Write an essay that compares and contrasts Melville's story of Wall Street with the motion picture *Wall Street.*

3. Write a journal entry about a circumstance when you engaged in passive resistance.

4. Write sketches of coworkers.

5. Write an essay that analyzes the narrator's reactions to Bartleby throughout the story.

The Necklace

GUY DE MAUPASSANT

She was one of those pretty and charming girls who are sometimes, as if by a mistake of destiny, born in a family of clerks. She had no dowry, no expectations, no means of being known, understood, loved, wedded by any rich and distinguished man; and she let herself be married to a little clerk at the Ministry of Public Instruction.

She dressed plainly because she could not dress well, but she was as unhappy as though she had really fallen from her proper station, since with women there is neither caste nor rank: and beauty, grace, and charm act instead of family and birth. Natural fineness, instinct for what is elegant, suppleness of wit, are the sole hierarchy, and make from women of the people the equals of the very greatest ladies.

She suffered ceaselessly, feeling herself born for all the delicacies and all the luxuries. She suffered from the poverty of her dwelling, from the wretched look of the walls, from the worn-out chairs, from the ugliness of the curtains. All those things, of which another woman of her rank would never even have been conscious, tortured her and made her angry. The sight of the little Breton peasant who did her humble housework aroused in her regrets which were despairing, and distracted dreams. She thought of the silent antechambers hung with Oriental tapestry, lit by tall bronze candelabra, and of the two great footmen in knee breeches who sleep in the big armchairs, made drowsy by the heavy warmth of the hot-air stove. She thought of the long *salons* fitted up with ancient silk, of the delicate furniture carrying priceless curiosities, and of the coquettish perfumed boudoirs made for talks at five o'clock with intimate friends, with men famous and sought after, whom all women envy and whose attention they all desire.

When she sat down to dinner, before the round table covered with a tablecloth three days old, opposite her husband, who uncovered the soup tureen and declared with an enchanted air, "Ah, the good *pot-au-feu!* I don't know anything better than that," she thought of dainty dinners, of shining silverware, of tapestry which peopled the walls with ancient personages and with strange birds flying in the midst of a fairy forest; and she thought of delicious dishes served on marvelous plates, and of the whispered gallantries which you listen to with a sphinxlike smile, while you are eating the pink flesh of a trout or the wings of a quail.

She had no dresses, no jewels, nothing. And she loved nothing but that; she felt made for that. She would so have liked to please, to be envied, to be charming, to be sought after.

She had a friend, a former schoolmate at the convent, who was rich, and whom she did not like to go and see any more, because she suffered so much when she came back.

But one evening, her husband returned home with a triumphant air, and holding a large envelope in his hand.

"There," said he. "Here is something for you."

She tore the paper sharply, and drew out a printed card which bore these words:

"The Minister of Public Instruction and Mme. Georges Ramponneau request the honor of M. and Mme. Loisel's company at the palace of the Ministry on Monday evening, January eighteenth."

Instead of being delighted, as her husband hoped, she threw the invitation on the table with disdain, murmuring:

"What do you want me to do with that?"

"But, my dear, I thought you would be glad. You never go out, and this is such a fine opportunity. I had awful trouble to get it. Everyone wants to go; it is very select, and they are not giving many invitations to clerks. The whole official world will be there."

She looked at him with an irritated glance, and said, impatiently:

"And what do you want me to put on my back?"

He had not thought of that; he stammered:

"Why, the dress you go to the theater in. It looks very well, to me."

He stopped, distracted, seeing his wife was crying. Two great tears descended slowly from the corners of her eyes toward the corners of her mouth. He stuttered:

"What's the matter? What's the matter?"

But, by violent effort, she had conquered her grief, and she replied, with a calm voice, while she wiped her wet cheeks:

"Nothing. Only I have no dress and therefore I can't go to this ball. Give your card to some colleague whose wife is better equipped than I."

He was in despair. He resumed:

"Come, let us see, Mathilde. How much would it cost, a suitable dress, which you could use on other occasions, something very simple?"

She reflected several seconds, making her calculations and wondering also what sum she could ask without drawing on herself an immediate refusal and a frightened exclamation from the economical clerk.

Finally, she replied, hesitatingly:

"I don't know exactly, but I think I could manage it with four hundred francs."

He had grown a little pale, because he was laying aside just that amount to buy a gun and treat himself to a little shooting next summer on the plain of Nanterre, with several friends who went to shoot larks down there, of a Sunday.

But he said:

"All right. I will give you four hundred francs. And try to have a pretty dress."

The day of the ball drew near, and Mme. Loisel seemed sad, uneasy, anxious. Her dress was ready, however. Her husband said to her one evening:

"What is the matter? Come, you've been so queer these last three days."

And she answered:

"It annoys me not to have a single jewel, not a single stone, nothing to put on. I shall look like distress. I should almost rather not go at all."

He resumed:

"You might wear natural flowers. It's very stylish at this time of the year. For ten francs you can get two or three magnificent roses."

She was not convinced.

"No; there's nothing more humiliating than to look poor among other women who are rich."

But her husband cried:

"How stupid you are! Go look up your friend Mme. Forestier, and ask her to lend you some jewels. You're quite thick enough with her to do that."

She uttered a cry of joy:

"It's true. I never thought of it."

The next day she went to her friend and told of her distress.

Mme. Forestier went to a wardrobe with a glass door, took out a large jewel-box, brought it back, opened it, and said to Mme. Loisel:

"Choose, my dear."

She saw first of all some bracelets, then a pearl necklace, then a Venetian cross, gold and precious stones of admirable workmanship. She tried on the ornaments before the glass, hestitated, could not make up her mind to part with them, to give them back. She kept asking:

"Haven't you any more?"

"Why, yes. Look. I don't know what you like."

All of a sudden she discovered, in a black satin box, a superb necklace of diamonds, and her heart began to beat with an immoderate desire. Her hands trembled as she took it. She fastened it around her throat, outside her high-necked dress, and remained lost in ecstasy at the sight of herself.

Then she asked, hesitating, filled with anguish:

"Can you lend me that, only that?"

"Why, yes, certainly."

She sprang upon the neck of her friend, kissed her passionately, then fled with her treasure.

The day of the ball arrived. Mme. Loisel made a great success. She was prettier than them all, elegant, gracious, smiling, and crazy with joy. All the men looked at her, asked her name, endeavored to be introduced. All the attachés of the Cabinet wanted to waltz with her. She was remarked by the minister himself.

She danced with intoxication, with passion, made drunk by pleasure, forgetting all, in the triumph of her beauty, in the glory of her success, in a sort of cloud of happiness composed of all this homage, of all this admiration, of all these awakened desires, and of that sense of complete victory which is so sweet to a woman's heart.

She went away about four o'clock in the morning. Her husband had been sleeping since midnight, in a little deserted anteroom, with three other gentlemen whose wives were having a very good time. He threw over her shoulders the wraps which he had brought, modest wraps of common life, whose poverty contrasted with the elegance of the ball dress. She felt this, and wanted to escape so as not to be remarked by the other women, who were enveloping themselves in costly furs.

Loisel held her back.

"Wait a bit. You will catch cold outside. I will go and call a cab."

But she did not listen to him, and rapidly descended the stairs. When they were in the street they did not find a carriage; and they began to look for one, shouting after the cabmen whom they saw passing by at a distance.

They went down toward the Seine, in despair, shivering with cold. At last they found on the quay one of those ancient noctambulant coupés which, exactly as if they were ashamed to show their misery during the day, are never seen round Paris until after nightfall.

It took them to their door in the Rue des Martyrs, and once more, sadly, they climbed up homeward. All was ended, for her. And as to him, he reflected that he must be at the Ministry at ten o'clock.

She removed the wraps which covered her shoulders, before the glass, so as once more to see herself in all her glory. But suddenly she uttered a cry. She no longer had the necklace around her neck!

Her husband, already half undressed, demanded:

"What is the matter with you?"

She turned madly towards him:

"I have—I have—I've lost Mme. Forestier's necklace."

He stood up, distracted.

"What!—how?—impossible!"

And they looked in the folds of her dress, in the folds of her cloak, in her pockets, everywhere. They did not find it.

He asked:

"You're sure you had it on when you left the ball?"

"Yes, I felt it in the vestibule of the palace."

"But if you had lost it in the street we should have heard it fall. It must be in the cab."

"Yes. Probably. Did you take his number?"

"No. And you, didn't you notice it?"

"No."

They looked, thunderstruck, at one another. At last Loisel put on his clothes.

"I shall go back on foot," said he, "over the whole route which we have taken to see if I can find it."

And he went out. She sat waiting on a chair in her ball dress, without strength to go to bed, overwhelmed, without fire, without a thought.

Her husband came back about seven o'clock. He had found nothing.

He went to Police Headquarters, to the newspaper offices, to offer a reward; he went to the cab companies—everywhere, in fact, whither he was urged by the least suspicion of hope.

She waited all day, in the same condition of mad fear before this terrible calamity.

Loisel returned at night with a hollow, pale face; he had discovered nothing.

"You must write to your friend," said he, "that you have broken the clasp of her necklace and that you are having it mended. That will give us time to turn round."

She wrote at his dictation.

At the end of a week they had lost all hope.

And Loisel, who had aged five years, declared:

"We must consider how to replace that ornament."

The next day they took the box which had contained it, and they went to the jeweler whose name was found within. He consulted his books.

"It was not I, madame, who sold that necklace; I must simply have furnished the case."

Then they went from jeweler to jeweler, searching for a necklace like the other, consulting their memories, sick both of them with chagrin and anguish.

They found, in a shop at the Palais Royal, a string of diamonds which seemed to them exactly like the one they looked for. It was worth forty thousand francs. They could have it for thirty-six.

So they begged the jeweler not to sell it for three days yet. And they made a bargain that he should buy it back for thirty-four thousand francs, in case they found the other one before the end of February.

Loisel possessed eighteen thousand francs which his father had left him. He would borrow the rest.

He did borrow, asking a thousand francs of one, five hundred of another, five louis here, three louis there. He gave notes, took up ruinous obligations, dealt with usurers and all the race of lenders. He compromised all the rest of his life, risked his signature without even knowing if he could meet it; and, frightened by the pains yet to come, by the black misery which was about to fall upon him, by the prospect of all the physical privation and of all the moral tortures which he was to suffer, he went to get the new necklace, putting down upon the merchant's counter thirty-six thousand francs.

When Mme. Loisel took back the necklace, Mme. Forestier said to her, with a chilly manner:

"You should have returned it sooner; I might have needed it."

She did not open the case, as her friend had so much feared. If she had detected the substitution, what would she have thought, what would she have said? Would she not have taken Mme. Loisel for a thief?

Mme. Loisel now knew the horrible existence of the needy. She took her part, moreover, all of a sudden, with heroism. That dreadful debt must be paid. She would pay it. They dismissed their servant; they changed their lodgings; they rented a garret under the roof.

She came to know what heavy housework meant and the odious cares of the kitchen. She washed the dishes, using her rosy nails on the greasy pots and pans. She washed the dirty linen, the shirts, and the dishcloths, which she dried upon a line; she carried the slops down to the street every morning, and carried up the water, stopping for breath at every landing. And, dressed like a woman of the people, she went to the fruiterer, the grocer, the butcher, her basket on her arm, bargaining, insulted, defending her miserable money sou by sou.

Each month they had to meet some notes, renew others, obtain more time.

Her husband worked in the evening making a fair copy of some tradesman's accounts, and late at night he often copied manuscript for five sous a page.

And this life lasted for ten years.

At the end of ten years, they had paid everything, everything, with the rates of usury, and the accumulations of the compound interest.

Mme. Loisel looked old now. She had become the woman of impoverished households—strong and hard and rough. With frowsy hair, skirts askew, and red hands, she talked loud while washing the floor with great swishes of water. But sometimes, when her husband was at the office, she sat down near the window, and she thought of that gay evening of long ago, of that ball where she had been so beautiful and so fêted.

What would have happened if she had not lost that necklace? Who knows? Who knows? How life is strange and changeful! How little a thing is needed for us to be lost or to be saved!

But, one Sunday, having gone to take a walk in the Champs Elysées to refresh herself from the labor of the week, she suddenly perceived a woman who was leading a child. It was Mme. Forestier, still young, still beautiful, still charming.

Mme. Loisel felt moved. Was she going to speak to her? Yes, certainly. And now that she had paid, she was going to tell her all about it. Why not?

She went up.

"Good-day, Jeanne."

The other, astonished to be familiarly addressed by this plain goodwife, did not recognize her at all, and stammered:

"But—madam!—I do not know—You must be mistaken."

"No. I am Mathilde Loisel."

Her friend uttered a cry.

"Oh, my poor Mathilde! How you are changed!"

"Yes, I have had days hard enough, since I have seen you, days wretched enough—and that because of you!"

"Of me! How so?"

"Do you remember that diamond necklace which you lent me to wear at the ministerial ball?"

"Yes. Well?"

"Well, I lost it."

"What do you mean? You brought it back."

"I brought you back another just like it. And for this we have been ten years paying. You can understand that it was not easy for us, us who had nothing. At last it is ended, and I am very glad."

Mme. Forestier had stopped.

"You say that you bought a necklace of diamonds to replace mine?"

"Yes. You never noticed it, then! They were very like."

And she smiled with a joy which was proud and naïve at once.

Mme. Forestier, strongly moved, took her two hands.

"Oh, my poor Mathilde! Why, my necklace was paste. It was worth at most five hundred francs!"

Questions for Discussion

1. To what extent do you sympathize with Mathilde Loisel? That is, to what extent do you believe she got what she deserved, and to what extent do you believe she was excessively victimized?

2. What would you have done if you had lost the necklace?

3. Was Mathilde wrong to be obsessed with having more material goods? Why or why not?

4. Should de Maupassant have given us Mathilde's reaction at the news about the necklace's being paste? Why or why not?

Suggestions for Writing

1. Write an essay about "character and fate" in "The Necklace," attempting to show which element you believe plays a greater role in Mathilde's actions. In the essay you may want to say what part "social pressures" play in fate and character.

2. De Maupassant deliberately neglects to give us Mathilde's response at the end of the story. Write a paragraph—or just a sentence—describing her response as you envisage it.

3. Write a story about a character who wants something that brings social or material status with it.

4. Write an entry in your journal or notebook that analyzes the narrator's attitude toward Mathilde specifically and to different social classes in general.

Bezhin Meadow

IVAN   TURGENEV

It was a splendid day in July, one of those days which occur only during a long spell of good weather. Since earliest morning the sky is clear; the dawn glow does not flare like a conflagration—it diffuses itself like a gentle blush. The sun is not fire, is not incandescent, as it is during a sultry drought, nor is it a dull purple, as before a storm, but bright and affably radiant; it floats upward peacefully from under a narrow and lengthy cloud, sends its fresh radiance through it, and then plunges into its lilac haze. The thin upper rim of the distended cloudlet begins to coruscate with little snakes of light: their gleam is like the gleam of wrought silver. But now the playful beams have again gushed forth—and blithely and majestically, as if it were winging upward, the mighty luminary comes up.

About noontime a host of round, lofty clouds appears, aureately gray, rimmed with soft whiteness. Like islands scattered over a river in infinite flood that runs around them in deeply transparent channels, they hardly budge; farther on, toward the sky's rim, they move near to one another, they huddle; there is no longer any blue to be seen between them, but they themselves are of the same azure as the sky; all of them are shot through and through with light and warmth. The hue of the horizon, ethereal, pale lilac, does not change throughout the day and is uniform all around; nowhere is there a thunderstorm darkling, gathering, save that here and there streaks of pale blue may extend downward: a barely noticeable drizzle, this, being sown upon the earth. Toward evening these clouds vanish; the last of them, rather black and of indeterminate form, like smoke, lie down in roseate swirls against the setting sun; at the spot where it has set, as calmly as it had risen in the sky, a ruby-red aura lingers for a brief while over the darkened earth and, gently flickering, like a candle solicitously borne along, the evening star will come to a soft glow against it.

On such days all pigments are softened, they are bright yet not vivid; an impression of some touching mildness lies upon all things. On such days the heat can, at times, be quite intense—occasionally it even steams along the slopes of the fields: but the wind scatters, sunders the accumulated sultriness, and whirlwinds (an indubitable sign of a long spell of good weather) wander in towering white pillars on their rounds over the roads, across plowed land. The dry pure air is filled with the odors of wormwood, of reaped rye, of buckwheat; even at the hour before nightfall you feel no dampness. It is weather such as this that the husbandman longs for to gather in his grain.

It was on just such a day that I happened to be hunting grouse in the Chernov district of the Tula province. I had come across and had shot quite a lot of game; the full gamebag was cutting into my shoulder mercilessly; but it was only when the evening glow had already died out and the chill shadows were already beginning to grow denser and to spread through the air, which was still full of light although no longer lit by the rays of the set sun, that I at last decided to turn homeward. With long strides I traversed an extensive stretch of brushwood, clambered up on a knoll—and, instead of the familiar plain I expected, with a small oak grove to the right and a squat little church in the distance, beheld an altogether different locality which was unknown to me. A narrow dale stretched away at my feet; directly opposite me a thick copse of aspens rose in a steep wall. I halted in perplexity and looked about me.

"Eh!" I reflected. "I haven't hit on the right spot at all—I've gone too far to the right." And, wondering at my own mistake, I quickly descended the knoll. An unpleasant, stagnant dampness enveloped me at once, just as though I had stepped into a cellar; wet grass, thick and high, looked as white and even as a tablecloth at the bottom of the dale; one felt somehow creepy walking on it. I clambered out as quickly as I could on the other side and went on, heading to the left along the copse of aspens. Bats, mysteriously circling and quivering against the dimly clear sky, were already flitting over the slumbering treetops; a young hawk, belated, flew past, hastening to its nest.

"There," I kept thinking, "as soon as I come out at that end I'll hit on the road at once. But, just the same, I must have gone almost a mile out of my way!"

I finally managed to reach the end of the woods, but there was no road of any sort there: some kind of untouched low bushes spread far and wide before me, while beyond them, ever so far off, one could glimpse a desertlike field. I stopped again.

"What is all this! Come, where am I, after all?"

I started in recalling which way I had been going and where I had been during the course of the day.

"Why, this is the Parahin stretch of brushwood!" I exclaimed at last. "Sure enough—that must be the Sindeiev copse over there. Yes, but how did I ever get here, as far as all this? That's odd! Now I'll have to turn to the right."

I started off toward the right, through the bushes. In the meanwhile the night was nearing and spreading, like a thundercloud; darkness seemed to be rising everywhere with the evening vapors, and even pouring down from on high. I came across a little-used, grass-grown path; I set out along it, peering ahead. Everything around me was darkling fast and quieting down; the quail alone were calling out at infrequent intervals. Some small night bird, darting low and without a sound of its soft wings, almost flew against me and then swooped to one side in fright. I came out on the edge of the brushwood and walked along the boundary line between two fields. By now I could make out objects in the distance only with difficulty: the field was glimmering whitely all around; beyond it, advancing with every moment in enormous swirls, somber murk was rising fast. My steps echoed dully in the congealing air. The sky, which had grown wan, had again begun to turn blue—but now it was the blue of night. The little stars had started twinkling, had started stirring in it.

That which I had taken for a copse turned out to be a dark and rounded mound. "Come, where am I, after all?" I repeated aloud, stopped for the third time, and looked questioningly at my yellow-spotted bitch Dianka, who was of an

English breed, absolutely the cleverest of all four-legged creatures. But the cleverest of all four-legged creatures merely kept wagging her bit of a tail, blinked her tired little eyes dismally, and offered me no sound advice whatsoever. I became ashamed before her and desperately hastened onward, as though I had suddenly conjectured which way I ought to go, skirted the mound, and discovered I was in a shallow valley that had been plowed everywhere. At once a strange feeling took possession of me. This valley looked almost like a regular caldron with sloping sides; at its bottom several huge white stones were standing up on end—it seemed as if they had crept together there for a secret council—and so voiceless and forsaken was everything in that valley, and so flat, and so despondently did the sky hang over it, that my heart shrank within me. Some tiny beast emitted a faint and plaintive squeak among the stones. I lost no time in clambering back up on the mound. Up to now I still hadn't abandoned hope of finding the way home, but at this point I became definitely convinced that I had gone completely astray and, no longer making the least attempt to recognize my surroundings, by now almost sunk in gloom, I went straight ahead, following the stars—and trusting to luck.

For something like half an hour did I walk thus, shifting my feet with difficulty. It seemed to me as if I had never been in such a deserted locality in all my born days: not a light, no matter how small, glimmered anywhere, nor was there a sound of any sort to be heard. One sloping knoll succeeded another, field stretched endlessly after field, the bushes seemed to spring up unexpectedly out of the ground before my very nose. I kept on walking, and was just about to lie down somewhere until morning when I suddenly found myself above a frightful chasm.

I quickly drew my lifted foot back and, through the barely transparent dusk of night, saw an enormous plain far below me. A broad river curved around it, receding from me in a semicircle; steely reflections on the water, glimmering indistinctly and intermittently, marked its current. The knoll on which I found myself went down in an abrupt, almost perpendicular precipice; its enormous outlines stood out darkly from the bluish ethereal void and, directly beneath me, in the angle formed by that precipice and the plain, near the river which at that spot, under the steepest part of the knoll, was an unmoving dark mirror, two small fires were flaming redly and smoking close to each other. People were bustling and shadows were swaying around them; now and then the forepart of some small curly head would become vividly lit.

I recognized, at last, the place I had come to. This meadow is celebrated throughout our parts under the name of Bezhin Meadow. However, there was no possibility whatsoever of turning homeward then, especially in the nighttime; my legs were caving in under me from fatigue. I decided to walk over to the fires and to bide the coming of the dawn in the company of those people, whom I took to be drovers. I came down safely, but hardly had I let go of the last branch I had seized when two great, white shaggy dogs suddenly threw themselves upon me with vicious barking. Children's voices were raised around the fires; two or three boys quickly got up from the ground. I answered their hails. They ran up, immediately called off their dogs, who had been particularly overcome when my Dianka had put in her appearance, and I came over to them.

I had erred in taking those sitting around the fires for drovers. They were simply peasant urchins from a village close by, tending a drove of horses. During the hot spells of summer the horses in our parts are driven out to graze at night; in the daytime the flies and gadflies would give them no rest. To bring out the drove toward evening and to bring it back at morning glow is a great and festal affair for peasant boys. Bareheaded, in old sheepskin jackets, astride the liveliest of the little nags, they race along with gay whoops and shouts, their arms and legs threshing about, their laughter ringing as they bounce high. The light dust rises and races along the road in a yellow pillar; the beat of hoofs pounding in unison spreads far and wide; the horses run with their ears cocked; at their very head, with his tail straight up and constantly changing stride, gallops some russet-colored shaggy stallion with cockleburs in his tangled mane.

I told the boys that I had lost my way and sat down near them. They asked me where I had come from, were silent for a while, and made room for me. We talked a little. I lay down under a small bush that had been nibbled clean and began looking about me. The picture was a wondrous one: a round, reddish reflection quivered near the fires and seemed to poise in midair, leaning against the darkness; the flames, flaring up, would cast occasional fleeting glints beyond the limits of that ringed reflection; a slender tongue of light would lick the bare boughs of the willow bushes and momentarily vanish; long pointed shadows impetuously intruding for an instant, in their turn darted up to the very embers: murk contending with light.

Now and then, when the flame burned fainter, and the ring of light contracted, out of the advancing darkness a horse's head would emerge suddenly—a sorrel head, with a winding scar, or one all white; it would regard you attentively and stolidly, champing the high grass in an expert fashion and, lowering itself again, would promptly disappear. All one could hear was its continued champing and its snorts. When one sits where it is light, it is hard to make out what is going on in the dark, and therefore everything near at hand seemed to have an almost black curtain drawn over it; but farther on, toward the horizon, one could glimpse the knolls and woods dimly, lying in long blotches. The dark clear sky in all its mysterious splendor was austere and unencompassably high above us. One's chest felt a delectable pressure as it breathed in that unique, stirring, and fresh fragrance—the fragrance of a Russian night in summer. All around us there was hardly a noise of any sort to be heard. Only at infrequent intervals, in the river close by, some large fish would plash with abrupt loudness, and the bankside reeds, barely stirred by some suddenly risen wave, would break into faint soughing. . . . All was quiet, save for the crackling, ever so low, of the small campfires.

The boys were sitting around them; here, too, squatted those dogs who had been so eager to devour me. For a long time they could not become reconciled to my presence and, drowsily puckering up their eyes against the fire and watching it askance, kept growling every so often with an extraordinary sense of their own dignity; they would growl at first, and then whine a little, as though regretting the impossibility of fulfilling their desire. There were five boys in all: Fedya, Pavlusha, Iliusha, Kostya, and Vanya. (I picked up their names from their conversations, and it is my intention to acquaint the reader with these boys right now.)

Fedya, the first and the oldest among them, one would judge to be fourteen. A well-built boy, this, with handsome and fine features, somewhat small, hair flaxen and curly, clear eyes and a steady smile, half merry, half absent-minded. By all the signs he belonged to a well-to-do family and had ridden out into the field not out of any necessity but just so, for the fun of the thing. He had on a shirt of brightly patterned calico, hemmed with yellow; his small, new overcoat, thrown over his narrow little shoulders, perched there precariously; a comb dangled from his belt of pale-blue leather. His boots, with low tops, were his own sure enough, and no hand-me-downs from his father.

Pavlusha, the second boy, had black tousled hair, gray eyes, broad cheekbones, a face pale, pockmarked, a mouth wide yet regular; his whole head was huge, big as a beer vat, as they say; his body was squat, unwieldy. None too good-looking a youngster—what's the use of talking!—but just the same I took a liking to him; his looks were very intelligent and forthright, and in his voice, too, there was the ring of strength. He could hardly have shown off with his clothes: they consisted, all in all, of a common linen shirt and much-patched breeches.

The face of the third, Iliusha, was rather insignificant: hump-nosed, long-drawn, purblind, it bore an expression of some dull, sickly care; his pursed lips did not move, his knit eyebrows did not relax—he seemed to be puckering his eyes from the firelight all the time. His yellow, almost white hair stuck out in pointed tufts like little pigtails from under his rather low, small felt cap, which he was forever shoving down over his ears with both hands. He had on new bast sandals and foot clouts; a stout rope, wound thrice about his waist, snugly girded his neat, black, short overcoat. Both he and Pavlusha looked no more than twelve.

The fourth, Kostya, a boy of ten, aroused my curiosity by his stare of melancholy and deep thought. His whole face was none too big; it was thin, sprinkled with freckles, sharply pointed toward the chin, like a squirrel's; one could barely make out his lips; but it was his eyes—big, dark, gleaming with a fluid gleam—which created a strange impression: they wanted to say something, it seemed, something for which language (his language, at least) had no words. He was short, of a puny build, and was dressed rather poorly.

The last, Vanya, I had at first actually failed to notice: he was lying on the ground, curled up ever so peacefully under stiff matting, and only at rare intervals did he thrust out his flaxen, curly head from under it. This boy was no more than seven.

And so, I was lying off to one side under a small bush and looking at the boys from time to time. A small kettle was hanging over one of the fires, with "spuds" cooking therein. Pavlusha was keeping an eye on them, standing on his knees and thrusting a piece of kindling wood into the water, which was coming to a boil. Fedya was lying propped up on one elbow and with the skirts of his overcoat spread out. Iliusha was sitting alongside of Kostya and puckering his eyes as intently as before. Kostya had let his head droop a little and was looking somewhere off into the distance. Vanya did not stir under his matting. I pretended to be asleep. Little by little the boys got to talking again.

At first they chatted a bit about this and that, abut the work they would have to face on the morrow, about horses—when Fedya suddenly turned to Iliusha and, as though he were resuming an interrupted conversation, asked him:

"Well, now, and did you see the hobgoblin for fair?"

"No, see him I didn't, and besides you can't see him," Iliusha answered in a hoarse and weak voice, the sound of which could not possibly have been more in keeping with the expression on his face. "But I did hear him. And I weren't the only one that did."

"And whereabouts in your place does he keep himself?" asked Pavlusha.

"In the old rolling room."

"Why, do you people go to the paper mill?"

"Sure, why not? My brother Avdiushka and me work there as glossers."

"So that's how. You're factory hands!"

"Well, how come you to hear him?" asked Fedya.

"Why, this is how. It so happened that my brother Avdiushka and me, and Fedor Mihievsky, and Ivashka Kossoi, and also another Ivashka, the one from Red Knolls, and still another Ivashka, by the name of Suhorukii, and there was other lads there, too—there must have been ten boys of us altogether—the whole shift, for the matter of that—well, it so happened we had to pass the night in that rolling room; that is, we didn't really have to, only Nazarov, the overseer, forbade us to go home: 'What's the use of you boys traipsing home,' says he, 'there's a lot of work tomorrow, so don't you go home, lads.' So we stayed on there, and we was lying together, all of us, and Avdiushka he gets to talking: 'Well, now, lads, what if the hobgoblin was to come?' And hardly had he done saying this—Avdei, I mean—when all of a sudden somebody starts walking around over our heads; we was lying down below, see, but he starts walking around up there, near the wheel. We hear him walking around, the boards simply bending, simply cracking under him; there, he'd passed right over our heads—when all of a sudden the water starts making a noise, and what a noise! going over the wheel; the wheel begins knocking, knocking, and turning—and yet the gates to the castle, now, was all lowered. So we wondered who could ever have raised them, so that the water had started flowing. However, that wheel turned and turned a while, and then stopped.

"Then he began walking about again, making for the door upstairs, and then he started down the stairs, and he was coming down them stairs like he weren't in no hurry at all; the steps was just simply groaning under him. Well, he walked right up to our door, hung around and hung around there for a bit—and then all of a sudden that door pops right open. All startled, we was; then we look—and there's nothing there. Suddenly, when we give another look, there was the form at one of the vats moving, rising, dipping; it kept going like that for a while through the air, as if someone was rinsing it, and then got back to its place again. Then at another vat the hook took off of its nail and fell back on the nail again; after that it seemed like somebody had walked over toward the door, and all of a sudden he got such a coughing spell, such a sneezing fit, like a sheep or something, and that so loud and all. We just tumbled down in a heap, all of us, trying to crawl under one another. Lord, but we was plenty scared that time!"

"So that's how it was!" Pavel commented. "But what made him go off in a coughing spell like that?"

"Don't know; maybe it was the damp."

They were all silent for a space.

"Well, now, is them spuds cooked yet?" asked Fedya.

Pavlusha prodded them:

"No; they're still hard. Listen to that splash!" he added, turning his face toward the river. "Must be a pike. And look at that little star rolling down the sky—"

"Well, now, fellows, here's something I'm going to tell you," Kostya began in a piping voice. "You just listen to what my dad was telling us the other day, whilst I happened to be there—"

"All right, we're listening," said Fedya with a patronizing air.

"Guess you know Gavrila, the carpenter in that big village near town?"

"Well, yes, we know him."

"But do you know why he's always down in the mouth like that, never saying anything? Do you know why? Here's why he's such a glum fellow; he once went, says my dad—he once went, brothers of mine, into the forest, after nuts. Well, so he went into the forest, after nuts, and he ups and loses his way; he went ever so far out of his way—God knows how far out of his way he went. And he walked, and he walked, brothers of mine—but he couldn't find the right path, no how! And it was already night out. So then he sat him down under a tree: 'There, now, let's wait for morning here'; he sat him down and dozed off. There, he'd dozed off, and all of a sudden he heard someone calling him. He looked—there was no one around. He dozed off again, and again he heard someone calling him. He looked and he looked—and right before him there was a nixie, perched on a bough; she was swinging there and calling him to come to her, whilst she herself was laughing, laughing fit to kill. And the moon, now—the moon was shining ever so bright, plain as plain; you could see everything, brothers of mine. There, she was calling him to come to her, and she herself, this water creature, was such a shining little thing, for all the world like she were some small dace, or a minnow—there's also a carp like that, all sort of white, silverlike. Gavrila the carpenter, he were plumb scared to death, brothers of mine; but all she knew was to laugh out loud, and all the time she kept beckoning to him with her hand to come over to her—like this. Gavrila, he'd already gotten up on his feet, actually; he was all set by then to heed that water fairy, brothers of mine, but I guess the Lord Himself must have sent him some sense: he did contrive to make the sign of the cross over himself. And how hard it was for him by then to be making that sign, brothers of mine! 'My hand,' said he later, 'was like stone, for fair; couldn't even turn it. Ah, hang it all!'

"Well, soon as he'd made that sign, brothers of mine, that there little nixie she plumb stopped laughing—and all of a sudden started in to weep! My! She was weeping, brothers of mine, wiping her eyes with her hair—and her hair was all green, now, green as hemp. So Gavrila he looked and looked at her, and he started in for to question her: 'What are you weeping about, you evil forest creature?' But the nixie, she spoke up to him: 'You oughtn't to be crossing yourself,' said she, 'you that was born of woman, but ought to be living with me in blitheness to the end of your days; and the reason I'm weeping, killing myself for grief, is because you made the sign of the cross over yourself; however, I won't be the only one killing myself for grief: kill yourself with grief also, to the end of your days.' And right then and there, brothers of mine, she vanished; and as for Gavrila, everything at once became clear to him—how he was to get out of the forest, that is. Only thing is, since that time he walks about the way you see him, always down at the mouth."

"There!" Fedya got out after a brief silence. "But could such a foul forest creature ever spoil a human soul—after all, he had paid her no heed."

"And yet, there it is!" said Kostya. "And Gavrila was also telling us that her voice, now, was ever so high, ever so pitiful, like a toad's."

"Was it your old man himself who told this story?" Fedya persisted.

"He himself. I was lying on the ledge atop the oven; I heard everything."

"It sure is a queer business! Still, why should he be down at the mouth? Well, I guess he must have been to her liking, seeing as how she was calling him."

"Yes, was he to her liking?" Iliusha chimed in quickly.

"Guess again! She was after tickling him to death, that's what she was after. That's what they do, those nixies, now."

"Why, I guess there must be nixies right around here, too," Fedya remarked.

"No," answered Kostya, "this place is clean, right out in the open. The only thing is, the river is close by."

They all fell silent. Suddenly, somewhere in the distance, a long-drawn, ringing, almost moaning sound arose, one of those incomprehensible night sounds which sometimes spring up amid profound silence; they soar, linger in the air, and at last spread slowly, as if dying away. Hearken closely—and it is as though there were no sound, and yet there is a ringing in the air. It sounded as if someone had emitted a long, long cry, under the very rim of the sky, as if some other had responded in the forest with high-pitched, piercing laughter, and a faint, sibilant whistle had then sped over the river. The boys exchanged looks, shuddered. . . .

"The power of the Cross be with us!" Ilya got out in a whisper.

"Oh, you crows!" Pavel called out. "What did you get all up in the air about? Look, now, them spuds is all cooked." They all moved up to the small kettle and began eating the steaming potatoes; Vanya alone did not stir. "Say, what about you?" Pavel asked him, but Vanya did not crawl out from under his matting. It was not long before the kettle was empty.

"But have you heard, fellows," Iliusha spoke up, "about what happened the other day in our Varnavitzy?"

"On the dam, now?" Fedya wanted to know.

"Yes, yes, on the dam—the one that the water broke through. Now *there's* an unclean place that's really unclean, and ever so forsaken. There's all them ravines and gullies roundabout, and the gullies is all full of snakes."

"Well, what happened there? Go ahead and tell us."

"Why, here's what happened. Maybe you don't know it, Fedya, but we've got a drowned man buried there, and he drowned himself ever so long ago, when the millpond was still deep; however, you can still see his small grave, although you can hardly make it out, at that—it's just a little mound. Well, a few days ago our clerk calls Ermila, the kennel keeper: 'You go and fetch the mail, now, Ermil,' he tells him. Our Ermil always goes after the mail, for he'd done all his hounds to death—they don't live under his care, somehow, and they never did, if it comes to that, yet he's a good man with dogs, in all ways. So this Ermil, now, he started off on a horse for the mail, but he hung around a little too long in town, and when he was driving back he was already tipsy. And it was night by then, a light night—the moon was shining. Well, so there was Ermil, riding across the dam. That was the road he'd happened to take. So there he was, riding along like that, this Ermil the kennel keeper, and what does he see but a little woolly lamb on the drowned man's grave—a white little thing, its wool all curly—a pretty little thing, ambling about. So Ermil, he thought to himself: 'Might as well take it along—what's the use of its getting lost, all for nothing,' and he got off of his horse and took that little lamb in his arms. And the lamb, now, it don't mind at all. So then Ermil he goes toward his horse—but the horse backs away from him, breathing hard, tossing its head; just the same, he quieted it down, got up on it together with the lamb, and rode on, holding the lamb in front of him. He looks at it, and the lamb just stares him right in the eye. He felt uncanny, did this Ermil the kennel keeper. 'I disremember,' he kept thinking, 'about any rams staring anyone in the eye like that.' However, it weren't so bad; he fell to stroking its wool, like that, and talking to it: 'There, little lamby, there!' But that there little ram, it bares its teeth, all of a sudden, and comes right back at him: 'There, little lamb, there!' "

Hardly had the narrator uttered the last word when both dogs suddenly rose up as one, dashed away from the fire with convulsive barking, and vanished in the dark. All the boys were thoroughly frightened. Vanya jumped out from under his matting. Pavlusha, shouting, rushed off after the dogs. Their barking was rapidly receding. One could hear the uneasy trampling of the startled drove. "Here, Gray! Here, Beetle!" Pavlusha was loudly calling. In a few moments the barking quieted down; by now Pavel's voice was coming from afar. A little more time passed; the boys were looking at one another in perplexity, as though waiting for what would happen next. Suddenly there came the hoofbeats of a galloping horse; it stopped short near the fire, and holding tight to its mane, Pavlusha sprang down nimbly from its back. Both dogs in their turn leaped within the ring of light and immediately squatted on their haunches, letting their red tongues loll.

"What happened there? What's up?" asked the boys.

"Nothing," answered Pavel, taking a swipe at the horse. "The dogs must have scented something, that's all. I thought it might be a wolf," he added in an indifferent voice, breathing quickly with all his chest heaving.

I involuntarily took an admiring look at Pavlusha. He was very fine at that moment. His homely face, animated from the fast ride, glowed with derring-do and firm resolve. Without as much as a dry twig in his hand, at night, he had without the least hesitation dashed off against a wolf all by himself. "What a splendid boy!" I reflected as I looked at him.

"But has anybody seen them, now—the wolves, I mean?" asked Kostya, the little poltroon.

"There's always plenty of them around here," Pavel answered. "But it's only in winter that they're troublesome."

He again snuggled down before the fire. As he had been about to sit down on the ground he let his hand drop on the shaggy neck of one of the dogs, and the animal, thus gladdened, would not turn its head for a long time, glancing out of the corner of its eye at Pavlusha with appreciative pride.

Vanya again burrowed deep under his matting.

"My, Iliusha, what dreadful things you were telling us," began Fedya, upon whom, as the son of a well-to-do peasant, it devolved to start the talk going. (He himself spoke little, as though wary of lowering his dignity.) "Then, too, the Restless One had to egg on the dogs to start barking. But it's true enough—I've heard tell your place is haunted."

"The Varnavitzy? I should say so! And how! They've seen our old master there more than once. He walks about in a long-skirted coat, they say, and all the time he keeps oh'ing, like this, looking for something on the ground. Grandpa Trophimych met up with him once. 'What, now, may it be your pleasure to be seeking for on the ground, Ivan Ivanych, father of mine?' "

"He asked him that?" the astonished Fedya interrupted him.

"Yes, he did."

"Well, I must say Trophimych is a brave fellow after that. Well, and what did the other have to say?"

" 'It's loose-all grass I'm looking for,' said he. And he said it in such a stifled voice, ever so stifled. 'And what would you be wanting loose-all grass for, Ivan Ivanych, father of mine?'—'My grave is crushing me,' said the other, 'it's crushing me, Trophimych; I want to get out of it, I want to get out—' "

"So that's the sort he is!" remarked Fedya. "Guess he hadn't lived long enough."

"That sure is a great wonder!" Kostya commented. "I thought you can see the departed only on a Parental Sabbath."

"You can see the departed at any time," Iliusha chimed in with assurance—he, as far as I could observe, knew all the local superstitions better than the others. "But then, on a Parental Sabbath you can see even the living departed—those whose turn has come to die that year, I mean. All you've got to do is to sit down on the church porch at night, and keep watching the road. And those people will start marching past you along the road—those, that is, who are to die that year. There was Uliana, now, one of our womenfolk—she went to the church porch at night last year."

"Well, and did she see anybody?" Kostya asked with curiosity.

"I should say so! First off, she sat there a long, long while, without seeing or hearing anybody—only all the time it sounded like there was a little dog starting in to bark, sort of, starting in to bark somewheres. All of a sudden she gives a look, and there's a little boy walking along the road, in nothing but a little shift. She looked more closely: it was Ivashka Theodosiev walking along—"

"The one that died this spring?" Fedya cut in.

"The very same. He was walking along, and didn't even raise his little head, but Uliana recognized him. And then she looked again, and there was a countrywoman coming along. Uliana, she looked more closely and—the Lord be with us!—if it weren't her own self walking along that road . . . Uliana, her own self."

"Her own self, for sure?" asked Fedya.

"Her own self, by God!"

"Well, what of it? For she hasn't died yet, has she?"

"Yes, but the year ain't over yet. Just the same, you take a look at her: it's a wonder how she keeps body and soul together."

They all fell silent again. Pavel threw a handful of dry branches into the fire. They showed sharply black against the instantaneous flare-up of the flames, began to crackle, to smoke, and then to buckle, lifting up their charred ends. The reflection of the light, fitfully quivering, spurted in all directions, especially upward. Suddenly, coming from none knows where, a white pigeon flew straight against this reflection, timorously circled a while in one spot, all bathed in the warm glow, and vanished, beating its wings resoundingly.

"Guess it's lost its way home," Pavel remarked. "Now it'll keep on flying until it strikes against something, and wherever it strikes, that's where it'll stay through the night until dawn."

"Well, now, Pavlusha," Kostya spoke up, "weren't that some righteous soul winging its way to heaven, eh?"

Pavel threw another handful of dead branches into the fire.

"Could be," he let drop at last.

"But tell me, Pavlusha, do," Fedya began, "were you Shalamovo folks, too, able to see the heavenly prevision?" That is what our muzhiks call a solar eclipse.

"You mean when you couldn't see the sun any more? I should say so!"

"Guess your folks got plenty scared, too?"

"Why, we wasn't the only ones. Our master, now, even though he made it clear to us beforehand, telling us: 'You're going to have a prevision,' got scared himself as pretty as you please, they say, soon as it turned dark. And in the servants' quarters, I heard tell, the old woman that does the cooking, soon as it started turning dark in the middle of the day, why, she took and smashed all the pots with an oven fork: 'Who'd be eating now,' said she, 'when the Day of Judgment is upon us!' There was rivers of cabbage soup all over the place. And, brother, what rumors there were going around in our village! That there would be white wolves, now running over the land, that they would be devouring folks, that there would be flights of birds of prey, and that folks might even behold Trishka himself."

"What Trishka is that?" asked Kostya.

"Why, don't you know?" Iliusha chimed in ardently. "Why, brother, where do you come from that you don't know about Trishka? They sure must be a lot of sticks-in-the-mud in your village, that's what, just sticks-in-the-mud! Trishka, he's a certain amazing man who will come, and he'll come, this amazing man, in such a way that you won't be able as much as to lay hands on him, and there's nary a thing you'll be able to do to him; that's the sort of amazing man he will be. Suppose, for instance, the peasants want to take him; they'll come out against him with oaken staves, and will throw a ring around him, but he'll just pull the wool over their eyes, in such a way that they themselves will beat up one another. They may put him in prison, for instance, so he'll beg for a drink of water out of a dipper; they'll bring him the dipper, but he'll dive right into it—and that's the last they'll ever see of him. They'll put him in chains, but he'll just clasp his hands together, and those chains will fall right off of him. Well, then, this Trishka will be going about through the hamlets and the towns, and this Trishka will be tempting

Christian folks—and yet there'll be nary a thing you can do to him. For that's the sort of amazing, crafty man he will be."

"Well, yes," Pavel resumed after this interruption, "that's what he's like. The old folks was saying, now, that as soon as the heavenly prevision would begin, why, Trishka would come. And so the prevision began. All the folks poured out of doors, into the fields, waiting for what would come. And, as you know, our place is such that you can see everything—there's plenty of room. There they were, watching, when all of a sudden, coming down the hill from the big village near town, there's some sort of a man walking along, queer as can be, the head on him so amazing—they all just let out one yell: 'Oh, Trishka's coming! Oh, Trishka's coming!' and each one lit out for himself, every which way. Our elder, he crawled into a ditch; the elder's wife, she got stuck under a gate, screaming for all she was worth, scaring her own yard dog so that it tore loose off of its chain, and over the wattle fence it went, and kept on into the woods, whilst Dorotheich—Kuzka's father, that is—dived into a field of oats, squatted there, and started calling like a quail, figuring that, who knows, maybe the Enemy, the Destroyer of Souls, might spare a bird, at least. That's how upset they all was! But the man that was walking along, now, was none other than our own cooper, Vavila; he'd bought himself a new tub with handles, and had put that tub on his head, so's to carry it the better."

All the boys broke into laughter and again fell silent for a moment, as is so often the case when people are talking out of doors. I looked around me: night was all about us, silent and majestic; the damp freshness of late evening had been replaced by the crisp warmth of midnight, and for a long while yet was it to lie in a soft pall upon the fields that had fallen into slumber; still a long time remained to the first bird song, to the first dewdrops of dawn. There was no moon in the sky—at that period it rose late. The innumerable golden stars were trying to outtwinkle one another, were flowing along, it seemed, in the same direction as the Milky Way; and, watching them, you yourself seemed to feel vaguely the impetuous, never-ceasing course of the earth. . . . A strange, grating, pained scream broke out over the river, twice in succession, and a few seconds later was repeated, this time farther off.

Kostya shuddered: "What was that?"

"That's a crane calling," Pavel replied calmly.

"A crane," Kostya repeated. "But there was something I heard yesterday," he added after a short silence. "Maybe you know—"

"What was it you heard?"

"Well, here's what. I was walking from Stony Ridge to Shashkino, and at first I kept close to our hazel bushes, then started going along a little meadow—you know, there where it comes out at a sharp turn from the gully, there's a deep water hole left after the spring freshets, you must know it, why, it's even all grown over with reeds—well, then, I started going past this water hole, brothers of mine, when all of a sudden somebody in that there water hole starts in to moan—and that so pitifully, so pitifully: *Oo-oo . . . oo-oo . . . oo-oo!* What a scare came over me then, brothers of mine! The time was so late, and the voice was full of such pain. Why, you felt you'd be starting in to cry yourself right then and there. What might that have been? Eh?"

"Last year some thieves drowned Akim the forester in that water hole," Pavlusha remarked, "so maybe it were his soul, complaining, like."

"Well, come to think of it, brothers of mine, that may be the very thing," Kostya spoke up, opening wide his eyes, which were enormous enough even without that. "And I didn't even know that they'd drowned Akim in that water hole—if I had, I'd have been scared still worse!"

"Then, too, they say there's a kind of tiny frogs," Pavel went on, "that have a way of croaking so pitifully."

"Frogs? Well, no, that weren't no frogs; how could it have been—" At this point the crane again sent forth its call over the river. "Eh, damn her!" Kostya said involuntarily. "Screeching like a forest fiend!"

"A forest fiend don't screech—he's mute," Iliusha caught him up. "All he does is clap his hands and cackle—"

"Why, did you ever lay eyes on him, by any chance—on a forest fiend, that is?" Fedya cut him short mockingly.

"No, I never did, and may God save me from seeing him, but there's others as has. There, just the other day he got around one of our muzhiks; he led him about and about, through the woods, and kept him going in circles over a certain meadow. It was all he could do to reach home just as it was getting light."

"Well, and did he see the forest fiend?"

"He did that. Ever so big, he was, big as big, says he, all dark, muffled up, just like he was behind a tree or something—no making him out well, like he were hiding from the moon, and he stares and stares at you with those huge eyes of his, now, and he keeps on blinking them, and blinking them—"

"Oh, my!" Fedya cried out, with a slight shudder and his shoulders jerking, and spat in disgust.

"And why have these foul things come upon this world in such numbers?" Pavel remarked. "Really, now!"

"Stop calling names," Ilya remarked in his turn. "Watch out, he may hear you."

There was another silence.

"Just look, lads, just look!" Vanya's childish voice suddenly broke the silence. "Just look at God's little stars; they're swarming like bees!"

He thrust out his fresh little face from under the matting, propped his head on one tiny fist, and slowly raised his big, gentle eyes. The eyes of all the boys were raised toward the heavens, and it was some time before they lowered them again.

"Well, Vanya," Fedya began kindly, "how is your sister Aniutka? Is she all right?"

"She is," Vanya answered, lisping a little.

"You ask her, why don't she come to us?"

"I don't know."

"You tell her to come."

"I will."

"You tell her I'll give her a present."

"And will you give me one, too?"

"And you, too."

Vanya sighed. "Well, no, I don't need it. Better give it to her; our Aniutka is such a kind little thing."

And Vanya again laid his head on the ground. Pavel got up and picked up the small kettle, now empty.

"Where are you going?" Fedya asked him.

"To the river, to dip up some water; I feel like having a drink."

The dogs got up and followed him.

"Watch out; don't fall into the river," Iliusha called after him.

"Why should he fall in?" asked Fedya. "He'll be careful."

"Yes, he'll be careful. But there's all sorts of things can happen. There, he may lean over, start dipping up the water—and the water fiend will grab a holt of his hand and begin pulling him in. Later on they'll be saying: 'The little boy tumbled into the water, now.' Tumbled, me eye! The-ere, he's climbed in amongst the reeds," he added, listening intently.

Sure enough: the reeds, as they parted, were rustling.

"But is it true," Kostya asked, "that Akulina has been a little innocent ever since that time she'd been under water?"

"From that very time. And what she looks like now! And yet they say she used to be a beauty. The water fiend ruined her. Guess he weren't expecting they would pull her out so soon. Well, it was he that ruined her there, in his place at the bottom of the river."

(I myself had more than once come across this Akulina. Covered with tatters, frightful, gaunt, with a face black as coal, with a bewildered gaze and her teeth perpetually bared, she would stomp for hours on the same spot, somewhere on the road, with her bony hands pressed hard to her breast, and slowly shifting from foot to foot, just like some wild beast in its cage. She understood nothing, no matter what you said to her, and merely laughed loudly and spasmodically every now and then.)

"Still, they do be saying," Kostya went on, "that Akulina threw herself into the river for no other reason than that her lover deceived her."

"That's the very reason."

"And do you remember Vassya?" Kostya added sadly.

"What Vassya is that?" asked Fedya.

"Why, the one that drowned in this very river," answered Kostya. "What a fine lad he was, what a lad! His mother, Theklista, now—oh, how she loved him, how she loved this Vassya! And it was as though she felt, this Theklista, now, that he would come to his end because of water. Whenever that same Vassya would go with us in the summertime to swim in the river—why, she'd get all in a fluster. The other womenfolk, going by with their washtubs, waddling along, why, they don't pay no mind to their children; but Theklista, she'd put down her tub on the ground and start calling him: 'Come back, now, my little sun! Oh, come back, my young falcon!' And the Lord only knows how he come to drown! He was playing on the bank, and his mother was right there, raking the hay, when all of a sudden she hears a sound like someone was letting bubbles in the water. She looks, and there's nothing there but Vassya's little cap floating on the water. And it's from that very time that Theklista ain't in her right mind; she'll come and lie down at the spot where he drowned; she'll lie down, brothers of mine, and start singing a long-drawn little song—you remember, Vassya, now, always used to sing a song like that; well, that's the very song she'll start singing, and she'll cry, and cry, complaining bitterly to God—"

"There, Pavlusha is coming," Fedya remarked.

Pavel walked up to the fire, lugging the filled kettle.

"Well, lads," he began after a short silence, "it's a bad business."

"Why, what's up?" Kostya asked hastily.

"I heard Vassya's voice."

All of them plainly shuddered.

"What are you saying, what are you saying?" babbled Kostya.

"I did hear it, by God! No sooner did I start bending over the water when all of a sudden I heard someone calling me, like it was in Vassya's little voice, and just as if it was coming from under the water: 'Pavlusha, oh, Pavlusha—come here.' I walked a little ways off. I did draw some water, though."

"Oh, Lordy! Oh, Lordy!" the boys managed to say, crossing themselves.

"Why, that was a water fiend calling you, Pavel," Fedya added. "And we was just talking about him—about Vassya, that is—"

"Ah, that is a bad sign," Iliusha uttered, stopping at every word.

"Well, it don't matter—let come what may!" Pavel declared resolutely and resumed his seat. "No man can get around his fate."

The boys quieted down. It was evident that Pavel's words had made a deep impression on them. They began bedding down before the fire, as if preparing for sleep.

"What's that?" Kostya asked abruptly, raising his head.

Pavel listened attentively. "Those are snipe, calling as they fly."

"But where are they flying to?"

"Why, to the place where there's no winter, they say."

"And is there such a land?"

"There is."

"Far away?"

"Far, far away, beyond the warm seas."

Kostya sighed and closed his eyes.

More than three hours had passed since I had joined the boys. The crescent moon rose at last; I did not notice it at once, so small was it and so slender. This practically moonless night was, it seemed, still as magnificent as before. But many stars that only a short while ago had been high in heaven had already inclined to the earth's dark rim; all about us everything had become perfectly stilled, as it usually does only toward morning; everything was sleeping the unbroken, motionless sleep that comes before dawn. The air was no longer so fraught with night odors; dampness seemed to be spreading through it anew. Not long do the nights of summer last! The talk of the boys was dying down together with the fires. Even the dogs were dozing; the horses, as far as I could make out in the barely glimmering, faintly flowing light of the stars, were also lying down, with their heads drooping. A slight drowsiness overcame me; it passed into dozing.

A stream of fresh air sped across my face. I opened my eyes: morning was being engendered. As yet the flush of the dawn glow was nowhere to be seen, but already something was showing white in the east. Everything had become visible, even though only dimly visible, all about me. The pale-gray sky was growing light, chill, blue; the stars now twinkled with a faint light, now vanished; the earth had had its fill of dampness, the leaves had broken into a sweat, living sounds began to spring up here and there, and voices, and the tenuous early breeze was already wandering and fluttering over the earth. My body responded to it by a light, joyous shiver. I got up quickly enough and went over toward the boys. They were all sleeping as if they had been slain; Pavel alone raised himself halfway and looked at me intently. I nodded to him and went my way along the river, now smoky with mist.

I had hardly gone a little over a mile when torrents of young, hot light came pouring down all around me—over the far-spreading wet meadow, and ahead of me, over the now newly green knolls, from forest to forest, and behind me, over the long, dusty road, over the sparkling, encrimsoned bushes, and over the river, diffidently showing its blue from under its now thinning mist—torrents of light, at first ruby-red, then red, and golden. . . . Everything began to stir, everything awoke, broke into song, into sound. Everywhere, in rayey gems, great drops of dew burst into glow; pure and clear, as though they too had been laved by the morning coolness, the peals of bells came floating toward me, and suddenly, urged on by the boys whom I now knew, the rested drove of horses raced by. . . .

I must add, to my regret, that in the same year Pavel was no longer among the living. He did not drown; he was killed in a fall off a horse. A pity; he was a fine lad!

Questions for Discussion

1. Characterize the voice of this first-person narrator. What adjectives would you use to describe it? How would you characterize his attitude toward the boys?

2. What are the similarities among the tales the boys tell over the campfire?

3. To what extent does having listened to the boys' tales seem to affect the way the narrator responds to (and describes) dawn?

4. At the end of the story the narrator reports Pavel's death. What is the significance of his reporting this event, and why does he take pains to tell us *how* Pavel died?

Suggestions for Writing

1. Write an essay about the importance (or unimportance) of plot in "Bezhin Meadow." In your "prewriting," outline the "plot" of the story.

2. Write an essay about the perception of nature that the boys' tales in "Bezhin Meadow" reveal.

3. Write a story that springs from your own experience hunting or from another experience in nature.

The Death of Iván Ilych

LEO TOLSTOY

1

During an interval in the Melvínski trial in the large building of the Law Courts the members and public prosecutor met in Iván Egórovich Shébek's private room, where the conversation turned on the celebrated Krasóvski case. Fëdor Vasílievich warmly maintained that it was not subject to their jurisdiction, Iván Egórovich maintained the contrary, while Peter Ivánovich, not having entered into the discussion at the start, took no part in it but looked through the *Gazette* which had just been handed in.

"Gentlemen," he said, "Iván Ilych has died!"

"You don't say!"

"Here, read it yourself," replied Peter Ivánovich, handing Fëdor Vasílievich the paper still damp from the press. Surrounded by a black border were the words: "Praskóvya Fëdorovna Goloviná, with profound sorrow, informs relatives and friends of the demise of her beloved husband Iván Ilych Golovín, Member of the Court of Justice, which occurred on February the 4th of this year 1882. The funeral will take place on Friday at one o'clock in the afternoon."

Iván Ilych had been a colleague of the gentlemen present and was liked by them all. He had been ill for some weeks with an illness said to be incurable. His post had been kept open for him, but there had been conjectures that in case of his death Alexéev might receive his appointment, and that either Vínnikov or Shtábel would succeed Alexéev. So on receiving the news of Iván Ilych's death the first thought of each of the gentlemen in that private room was of the changes and promotions it might occasion among themselves or their acquaintances.

"I shall be sure to get Shtábel's place or Vínnikov's," thought Fëdor Vasílievich. "I was promised that long ago, and the promotion means an extra eight hundred rubles a year for me besides the allowance."

"Now I must apply for my brother-in-law's transfer from Kalúga," thought Peter Ivánovich. "My wife will be very glad, and then she won't be able to say that I never do anything for her relations."

"I thought he would never leave his bed again," said Peter Ivánovich aloud. "It's very sad."

"But what really was the matter with him?"

"The doctors couldn't say—at least they could, but each of them said something different. When last I saw him I thought he was getting better."

"And I haven't been to see him since the holidays. I always meant to go."

"Had he any property?"

"I think his wife had a little—but something quite trifling."

"We shall have to go to see her, but they live so terribly far away."

"Far away from you, you mean. Everything's far away from your place."

"You see, he never can forgive my living on the other side of the river," said Peter Ivánovich, smiling at Shébek. Then, still talking of the distances between different parts of the city, they returned to the Court.

Besides considerations as to the possible transfers and promotions likely to result from Iván Ilych's death, the mere fact of the death of a near acquaintance aroused, as usual, in all who heard of it the complacent feeling that, "it is he who is dead and not I."

Each one thought or felt, "Well, he's dead but I'm alive!" But the more intimate of Iván Ilych's acquaintances, his so-called friends, could not help thinking also that they would now have to fulfil the very tiresome demands of propriety by attending the funeral service and paying a visit of condolence to the widow.

Fëdor Vasílievich and Peter Ivánovich had been his nearest acquaintances. Peter Ivánovich had studied law with Iván Ilych and had considered himself to be under obligations to him.

Having told his wife at dinner-time of Iván Ilych's death, and of his conjecture that it might be possible to get her brother transferred to their circuit, Peter Ivánovich sacrificed his usual nap, put on his evening clothes, and drove to Iván Ilych's house.

At the entrance stood a carriage and two cabs. Leaning against the wall in the hall downstairs near the cloak-stand was a coffin-lid covered with cloth of gold, ornamented with gold cord and tassels, that had been polished up with metal powder. Two ladies in black were taking off their fur cloaks. Peter Ivánovich recognized one of them as Iván Ilych's sister, but the other was a stranger to him. His colleague Schwartz was just coming downstairs, but on seeing Peter Ivánovich enter he stopped and winked at him, as if to say: "Iván Ilych has made a mess of things—not like you and me."

Schwartz's face with his Piccadilly whiskers, and his slim figure in evening dress, had as usual an air of elegant solemnity which contrasted with the playfulness of his character and had a special piquancy here, or so it seemed to Peter Ivánovich.

Peter Ivánovich allowed the ladies to precede him and slowly followed them upstairs. Schwartz did not come down but remained where he was, and Peter Ivánovich understood that he wanted to arrange where they should play bridge that evening. The ladies went upstairs to the widow's room, and Schwartz with seriously compressed lips but a playful look in his eyes, indicated by a twist of his eyebrows the room to the right where the body lay.

Peter Ivánovich, like everyone else on such occasions, entered feeling uncertain what he would have to do. All he knew was that at such times it is always safe to cross oneself. But he was not quite sure whether one should make obeisances while doing so. He therefore adopted a middle course. On entering the room he began crossing himself and made a slight movement resembling a bow. At the same time, as far as the motion of his head and arm allowed, he surveyed the room. Two young men—apparently nephews, one of whom was a high-school pupil—were leaving the room, crossing themselves as they did so. An old woman was standing motionless, and a lady with strangely arched eyebrows was saying something to her in a whisper. A vigorous, resolute Church Reader, in a frock-coat, was reading something in a loud voice with an expression that precluded any contradiction. The butler's assistant, Gerásim, stepping lightly in front of Peter Ivánovich, was strewing something on the floor. Noticing this, Peter Ivánovich was immediately aware of a faint odour of a decomposing body.

The last time he had called on Iván Ilych, Peter Ivánovich had seen Gerásim in the study. Iván Ilych had been particularly fond of him and he was performing the duty of a sick nurse.

Peter Ivánovich continued to make the sign of the cross slightly inclining his head in an intermediate direction between the coffin, the Reader, and the icons on the table in a corner of the room. Afterwards, when it seemed to him that this movement of his arm in crossing himself had gone on too long, he stopped and began to look at the corpse.

The dead man lay, as dead men always lie, in a specially heavy way, his rigid limbs sunk in the soft cushions of the coffin, with the head forever bowed on the pillow. His yellow waxen brow with bald patches over his sunken temples was thrust up in the way peculiar to the dead, the protruding nose seeming to press on the upper lip. He was much changed and had grown even thinner since Peter Ivánovich had last seen him, but, as is always the case with the dead, his face was handsomer and above all more dignified than when he was alive. The expression on the face said that what was necessary had been accomplished, and accomplished rightly. Besides this there was in that expression a reproach and a warning to the living. This warning seemed to Peter Ivánovich out of place, or at least not applicable to him. He felt a certain discomfort and so he hurriedly crossed himself once more and turned and went out of the door—too hurriedly and too regardless of propriety, as he himself was aware.

Schwartz was waiting for him in the adjoining room with legs spread wide apart and both hands toying with his top-hat behind his back. The mere sight of that playful, well-groomed, and elegant figure refreshed Peter Ivánovich. He felt that Schwartz was above all these happenings and would not surrender to any depressing influences. His very look said that this incident of a church service for Iván Ilych could not be a sufficient reason for infringing the order of the session—in other words, that it would certainly not prevent his unwrapping a new pack of cards and shuffling them that evening while a footman placed four fresh candles on the table: in fact, that there was no reason for supposing that this incident would hinder their spending the evening agreeably. Indeed he said this in a whisper as Peter Ivánovich passed him, proposing that they should meet for a game at Fëdor Vasílievich's. But apparently Peter Ivánovich was not destined to play bridge that evening. Praskóvya Fëdorovna (a short, fat woman who despite all efforts to the contrary had continued to broaden steadily from her shoulders downwards and who had the same extraordinary arched eyebrows as the lady who had been standing by the coffin), dressed all in black, her head covered with lace, came out of her own room with some other ladies, conducted them to the room where the dead body lay, and said: "The service will begin immediately. Please go in."

Schwartz, making an indefinite bow, stood still, evidently neither accepting nor declining this invitation. Praskóvya Fëdorovna recognizing Peter Ivánovich, sighed, went close up to him, took his hand, and said: "I know you were a true friend to Iván Ilych . . ." and looked at him awaiting some suitable response. And

Peter Ivánovich knew that, just as it had been the right thing to cross himself in that room, so what he had to do here was to press her hand, sigh, and say, "Believe me. . . ." So he did all this and as he did it felt that the desired result had been achieved: that both he and she were touched.

"Come with me. I want to speak to you before it begins," said the widow. "Give me your arm."

Peter Ivánovich gave her his arm and they went to the inner rooms, passing Schwartz, who winked at Peter Ivánovich compassionately.

"That does for our bridge! Don't object if we find another player. Perhaps you can cut in when you do escape," said his playful look.

Peter Ivánovich sighed still more deeply and despondently, and Praskóvya Fëdorovna pressed his arm gratefully. When they reached the drawing-room, upholstered in pink cretonne and lighted by a dim lamp, they sat down at the table—she on a sofa and Peter Ivánovich on a low pouffe, the springs of which yielded spasmodically under his weight. Praskóvya Fëdorovna had been on the point of warning him to take another seat, but felt that such a warning was out of keeping with her present condition and so changed her mind. As he sat down on the pouffe Peter Ivánovich recalled how Iván Ilych had arranged this room and had consulted him regarding this pink cretonne with green leaves. The whole room was full of furniture and knick-knacks, and on her way to the sofa the lace of the widow's black shawl caught on the carved edge of the table. Peter Ivánovich rose to detach it, and the springs of the pouffe, relieved of his weight, rose also and gave him a push. The widow began detaching her shawl herself, and Peter Ivánovich again sat down, suppressing the rebellious springs of the pouffe under him. But the widow had not quite freed herself and Peter Ivánovich got up again, and again the pouffe rebelled and even creaked. When this was all over she took out a clean cambric handkerchief and began to weep. The episode with the shawl and the struggle with the pouffe had cooled Peter Ivánovich's emotions and he sat there with a sullen look on his face. This awkward situation was interrupted by Sokolóv, Iván Ilych's butler, who came to report that the plot in the cemetery that Praskóvya Fëdorovna had chosen would cost two hundred rubles. She stopped weeping and, looking at Peter Ivánovich with the air of a victim, remarked in French that it was very hard for her. Peter Ivánovich made a silent gesture signifying his full conviction that it must indeed be so.

"Please smoke," she said in a magnanimous yet crushed voice, and turned to discuss with Sokolóv the price of the plot for the grave.

Peter Ivánovich while lighting his cigarette heard her inquiring very circumstantially into the prices of different plots in the cemetery and finally decide which she would take. When that was done she gave instructions about engaging the choir. Sokolóv then left the room.

"I look after everything myself," she told Peter Ivánovich, shifting the albums that lay on the table; and noticing that the table was endangered by his cigarette-ash, she immediately passed him an ash-tray, saying as she did so: "I consider it an affectation to say that my grief prevents my attending to practical affairs. On the contrary, if anything can—I won't say console me, but—distract me, it is seeing to everything concerning him." She again took out her handkerchief as if preparing to cry, but suddenly, as if mastering her feeling, she shook herself and began to speak calmly. "But there is something I want to talk to you about."

Peter Ivánovich bowed, keeping control of the springs of the pouffe, which immediately began quivering under him.

"He suffered terribly the last few days."

"Did he?" said Peter Ivánovich.

"Oh, terribly! He screamed unceasingly, not for minutes but for hours. For the last three days he screamed incessantly. It was unendurable. I cannot understand how I bore it; you could hear him three rooms off. Oh, what I have suffered!"

"Is it possible that he was conscious all that time?" asked Peter Ivánovich.

"Yes," she whispered. "To the last moment. He took leave of us a quarter of an hour before he died, and asked us to take Volódya away."

The thought of the sufferings of this man he had known so intimately, first as a merry little boy, then as a school-mate, and later as a grown-up colleague, suddenly struck Peter Ivánovich with horror, despite an unpleasant consciousness of his own and this woman's dissimulation. He again saw that brow, and that nose pressing down on the lip, and felt afraid for himself.

"Three days of frightful suffering and then death! Why, that might suddenly, at any time, happen to me," he thought, and for a moment felt terrified. But—he did not himself know how—the customary reflection at once occurred to him that this had happened to Iván Ilych and not to him, and that it should not and could not happen to him, and that to think that it could would be yielding to depression which he ought not to do, as Schwartz's expression plainly showed. After which reflection Peter Ivánovich felt reassured, and began to ask with interest about the details of Iván Ilych's death, as though death was an accident natural to Iván Ilych but certainly not to himself.

After many details of the really dreadful physical sufferings Iván Ilych had endured (which details he learnt only from the effect those sufferings had produced on Praskóvya Fëdorovna's nerves) the widow apparently found it necessary to get to business.

"Oh, Peter Ivánovich, how hard it is! How terribly, terribly hard!" and she again began to weep.

Peter Ivánovich sighed and waited for her to finish blowing her nose. When she had done so he said, "Believe me . . ." and she again began talking and brought out what was evidently her chief concern with him—namely, to question him as to how she could obtain a grant of money from the government on the occasion of her husband's death. She made it appear that she was asking Peter Ivánovich's advice about her pension, but he soon saw that she already knew about that to the minutest detail, more even than he did himself. She knew how much could be got out of the government in consequence of her husband's death, but wanted to find out whether she could not possibly extract something more. Peter Ivánovich tried to think of some means of doing so, but after reflecting for a while and, out of propriety, condemning the government for its niggardliness, he said he thought that nothing more could be got. Then she sighed and evidently began to devise means of getting rid of her visitor. Noticing this, he put out his cigarette, rose, pressed her hand, and went out into the anteroom.

In the dining-room where the clock stood that Iván Ilych had liked so much and had bought at an antique shop, Peter Ivánovich met a priest and a few acquaintances who had come to attend the service, and he recognized Iván Ilych's daughter, a handsome young woman. She was in black and her slim figure appeared slimmer than ever. She had a gloomy, determined, almost angry expression, and bowed to Peter Ivánovich as though he were in some way to blame. Behind her, with the same offended look, stood a wealthy young man, an examining magistrate, whom Peter Ivánovich also knew and who was her fiancé, as he had heard. He bowed mournfully to them and was about to pass into the death-chamber, when from under the stairs appeared the figure of Iván Ilych's schoolboy son, who was extremely like his father. He seemed a little Iván Ilych, such as Peter Ivánovich remembered when they studied law together. His tear-stained eyes had in them the look that is seen in the eyes of boys of thirteen or fourteen who are not pure-minded. When he saw Peter Ivánovich he scowled morosely and shamefacedly. Peter Ivánovich nodded to him and entered the death-chamber. The service began: candles, groans, incense, tears, and sobs. Peter Ivánovich stood looking gloomily down at his feet. He did not look once at the dead man, did not yield to any depressing influence, and was one of the first to leave the room. There was no one in the anteroom, but Gerásim darted out of the dead man's room, rummaged with his strong hands among the fur coats to find Peter Ivánovich's and helped him on with it.

"Well, friend Gerásim," said Peter Ivánovich, so as to say something. "It's a sad affair, isn't it?"

"It's God's will. We shall all come to it some day," said Gerásim, displaying his teeth—the even, white teeth of a healthy peasant—and, like a man in the thick of urgent work, he briskly opened the front door, called the coachman, helped Peter Ivánovich into the sledge, and sprang back to the porch as if in readiness for what he had to do next.

Peter Ivánovich found the fresh air particularly pleasant after the smell of incense, the dead body, and carbolic acid.

"Where to, sir?" asked the coachman.

"It's not too late even now. . . . I'll call round on Fëdor Vasílievich."

He accordingly drove there and found them just finishing the first rubber, so that it was quite convenient for him to cut in.

2

Iván Ilych's life had been most simple and most ordinary and therefore most terrible.

He had been a member of the Court of Justice, and died at the age of forty-five. His father had been an official who after serving in various ministries and departments in Petersburg had made the sort of career which brings men to positions from which by reason of their long service they cannot be dismissed, though they are obviously unfit to hold any responsible position, and for whom therefore posts are specially created, which though fictitious carry salaries of from six to ten thousand rubles that are not fictitious and in receipt of which they live on to a great age.

Such was the Privy Councillor and superfluous member of various superfluous institutions, Ilya Epímovich Golovín.

He had three sons, of whom Iván Ilych was the second. The eldest son was following in his father's footsteps only in another department, and was already approaching that stage in the service at which a similar sinecure would be reached. The third son was a failure. He had ruined his prospects in a number of positions and was now serving in the railway department. His father and brothers, and still more their wives, not merely disliked meeting him, but avoided remembering his existence unless compelled to do so. His sister had married Baron Greff, a Petersburg official of her father's type. Iván Ilych was *le phénix de la famille* as people said. He was neither as cold and formal as his elder brother nor as wild as the younger, but was a happy mean between them—an intelligent, polished, lively and agreeable man. He had studied with his younger brother at the School of Law, but the latter had failed to complete the course and was expelled when he was in the fifth class. Iván Ilych finished the course well. Even when he was at the School of Law he was just what he remained for the rest of his life: a capable, cheerful, good-natured, and sociable man, though strict in the fulfilment of what he considered to be his duty: and he considered his duty to be what was so considered by those in authority. Neither as a boy nor as a man was he a toady, but from early youth was by nature attracted to people of high station as a fly is drawn to the light, assimilating their ways and views of life and establishing friendly relations with them. All the enthusiasms of childhood and youth passed without leaving much trace on him; he succumbed to sensuality, to vanity, and latterly among the highest classes to liberalism, but always within limits which his instinct unfailingly indicated to him as correct.

At school he had done things which had formerly seemed to him very horrid and made him feel disgusted with himself when he did them; but when later on he saw that such actions were done by people of good position and that they did not regard them as wrong, he was able not exactly to regard them as right, but to forget about them entirely or not be at all troubled at remembering them.

Having graduated from the School of Law and qualified for the tenth rank of the civil service, and having received money from his father for his equipment, Iván Ilych ordered himself clothes at Scharmer's, the fashionable tailor, hung a medallion inscribed *respice finem* on his watch-chain, took leave of his professor and the prince who was patron of the school, had a farewell dinner with his comrades at Donon's first-class restaurant, and with his new and fashionable portmanteau, linen, clothes, shaving and other toilet appliances, and a travelling rug, all purchased at the best shops, he set off for one of the provinces where, through his father's influence, he had been attached to the governor as an official for special service.

In the province Iván Ilych soon arranged as easy and agreeable a position for himself as he had had at the School of Law. He performed his official tasks, made his career, and at the same time amused himself pleasantly and decorously. Occasionally he paid official visits to country districts, where he behaved with dignity both to his superiors and inferiors, and performed the duties entrusted to him, which related chiefly to the sectarians, with an exactness and incorruptible honesty of which he could not but feel proud.

In official matters, despite his youth and taste for frivolous gaiety, he was exceedingly reserved, punctilious, and even severe; but in society he was often amusing and witty, and always good-natured, correct in his manner, and *bon enfant,* as the governor and his wife—with whom he was like one of the family—used to say of him.

In the province he had an affair with a lady who made advances to the elegant young lawyer, and there was also a milliner; and there were carousals with aides-de-camp who visited the district, and after-supper visits to a certain outlying street of doubtful reputation; and there was too some obsequiousness to his chief and even to his chief's wife, but all this was done with such a tone of good breeding that no hard names could be applied to it. It all came under the heading of the French saying: *"Il faut que jeunesse se passe."* It was all done with clean hands, in clean linen, with French phrases, and above all among people of the best society and consequently with the approval of people of rank.

So Iván Ilych served for five years and then came a change in his official life. The new and reformed judicial institutions were introduced, and new men were needed. Iván Ilych became such a new man. He was offered the post of Examining Magistrate, and he accepted it though the post was in another province and obliged him to give up the connexions he had formed and to make new ones. His friends met to give him a send-off; they had a group-photograph taken and presented him with a silver cigarette-case, and he set off to his new post.

As examining magistrate Iván Ilych was just as *comme il faut* and decorous a man, inspiring general respect and capable of separating his official duties from his private life, as he had been when acting as an official on special service. His duties now as examining magistrate were far more interesting and attractive than before. In his former position it had been pleasant to wear an undress uniform made by Scharmer, and to pass through the crowd of petitioners and officials who were timorously awaiting an audience with the governor, and who envied him as with free and easy gait he went straight into his chief's private room to have a cup of tea and a cigarette with him. But not many people had then been directly dependent on him—only police officials and the sectarians when he went on special missions—and he liked to treat them politely, almost as comrades, as if he were letting them feel that he who had the power to crush them was treating them in this simple, friendly way. There were then but few such people. But now, as an examining magistrate, Iván Ilych felt that everyone without exception, even the most important and self-satisfied, was in his power, and that he need only write a few words on a sheet of paper with a certain heading, and this or that important, self-satisfied person would be brought before him in the role of an accused person or a witness, and if he did not choose to allow him to sit down, would have to stand before him and answer his questions. Iván Ilych never abused his power; he tried on the contrary to soften its expression, but the consciousness of it and of the possibility of softening its effect, supplied the chief interest and attraction of his office. In his work itself, especially in his examinations, he very soon acquired a method of eliminating all considerations irrelevant to the legal aspect of the case, and reducing even the most complicated case to a form in which it would be presented on paper only in its externals, completely excluding his personal opinion of the matter, while above all observing every prescribed formality. The work was new and Iván Ilych was one of the first men to apply the new Code of 1864.

On taking up the post of examining magistrate in a new town, he made new acquaintances and connexions, placed himself on a new footing, and assumed a somewhat different tone. He took up an attitude of rather dignified aloofness towards the provincial authorities, but picked out the best circle of legal gentlemen and wealthy gentry living in the town and assumed a tone of slight dissatisfaction with the government of moderate liberalism, and of enlightened citizenship. At the same time, without at all altering the elegance of his toilet, he ceased shaving his chin and allowed his beard to grow as it pleased.

Iván Ilych settled down very pleasantly in this new town. The society there, which inclined towards opposition to the governor, was friendly, his salary was larger, and he began to play *vint* [a form of bridge], which he found added not a little to the pleasure of life, for he had a capacity for cards, played good-humouredly, and calculated rapidly and astutely, so that he usually won.

After living there for two years he met his future wife, Praskóvya Fëdorovna Míkhel, who was the most attractive, clever, and brilliant girl of the set in which he moved, and among other amusements and relaxations from his labours as examining magistrate, Iván Ilych established light and playful relations with her.

While he had been an official on special service he had been accustomed to dance, but now as an examining magistrate it was exceptional for him to do so. If he danced now, he did it as if to show that though he served under the reformed order of things, and had reached the fifth official rank, yet when it came to dancing he could do it better than most people. So at the end of an evening he sometimes danced with Praskóvya Fëdorovna, and it was chiefly during these dances that he captivated her. She fell in love with him. Iván Ilych had at first no definite intention of marrying, but when the girl fell in love with him he said to himself: "Really, why shouldn't I marry?"

Praskóvya Fëdorovna came of a good family, was not bad looking, and had some little property. Iván Ilych might have aspired to a more brilliant match, but even this was good. He had his salary, and she, he hoped, would have an equal income. She was well connected, and was a sweet, pretty, and thoroughly correct young woman. To say that Iván Ilych married because he fell in love with Praskóvya Fëdorovna and found that she sympathized with his views of life would be as incorrect as to say that he married because his social circle approved of the match. He was swayed by both these considerations: the marriage gave him personal satisfaction, and at the same time it was considered the right thing by the most highly placed of his associates.

So Iván Ilych got married.

The preparations for marriage and the beginning of married life, with its conjugal caresses, the new furniture, new crockery, and new linen, were very pleasant until his wife became pregnant—so that Iván Ilych had begun to think that marriage would not impair the easy, agreeable, gay, and always decorous character of his life, approved of by society and regarded by himself as natural, but would even improve it. But from the first months of his wife's pregnancy, something new, unpleasant, depressing, and unseemly, and from which there was no way of escape, unexpectedly showed itself.

His wife, without any reason—*de gaieté de coeur* as Iván Ilych expressed it to himself — began to disturb the pleasure and propriety of their life. She began to be jealous without any cause, expected him to devote his whole attention to her, found fault with everything, and made coarse and ill-mannered scenes.

At first Iván Ilych hoped to escape from the unpleasantness of this state of affairs by the same easy and decorous relation to life that had served him heretofore: he tried to ignore his wife's disagreeable moods, continued to live in his usual easy and pleasant way, invited friends to his house for a game of cards, and also tried going out to his club or spending his evenings with friends. But one day his wife began upbraiding him so vigorously, using such coarse words, and continued to abuse him every time he did not fulfil her demands, so resolutely and with such evident determination not to give way till he submitted—that is, till he stayed at home and was bored just as she was—that he became alarmed. He now realized that matrimony—at any rate with Praskóvya Fëdorovna—was not always conducive to the pleasures and amenities of life, but on the contrary often infringed both comfort and propriety, and that he must therefore entrench himself against such infringement. And Iván Ilych began to seek for means of doing so. His official duties were the one thing that imposed upon Praskóvya Fëdorovna, and by means of his official work and the duties attached to it he began struggling with his wife to secure his own independence.

With the birth of their child, the attempts to feed it and the various failures in doing so, and with the real and imaginary illnesses of mother and child, in which Iván Ilych's sympathy was demanded but about which he understood nothing, the need of securing for himself an existence outside his family life became still more imperative.

As his wife grew more irritable and exacting and Iván Ilych transferred the centre of gravity of his life more and more to his official work, so did he grow to like his work better and became more ambitious than before.

Very soon, within a year of his wedding, Iván Ilych had realized that marriage, though it may add some comforts to life, is in fact a very intricate and difficult affair towards which in order to perform one's duty, that is, to lead a decorous life approved of by society, one must adopt a definite attitude just as towards one's official duties.

And Iván Ilych evolved such an attitude towards married life. He only required of it those conveniences—dinner at home, housewife, and bed—which it could give him, and above all that propriety of external forms required by public opinion. For the rest he looked for light-hearted pleasure and propriety, and was very thankful when he found them, but if he met with antagonism and querulousness he at once retired into his separate fenced-off world of official duties, where he found satisfaction.

Iván Ilych was esteemed a good official, and after three years was made Assistant Public Prosecutor. His new duties, their importance, the possibility of indicting and imprisoning anyone he chose, the publicity his speeches received, and the success he had in all these things, made his work still more attractive.

More children came. His wife became more and more querulous and ill-tempered, but the attitude Iván Ilych had adopted towards his home life rendered him almost impervious to her grumbling.

After seven years' service in that town he was transferred to another province as Public Prosecutor. They moved, but were short of money and his wife did not like the place they moved to. Though the salary was higher the cost of living was greater, besides which two of their children died and family life became still more unpleasant for him.

Praskóvya Fëdorovna blamed her husband for every inconvenience they encountered in their new home. Most of the conversations between husband and wife, especially as to the children's education, led to topics which recalled former disputes, and those disputes were apt to flare up again at any moment. There remained only those rare periods of amorousness which still came to them at times but did not last long. These were islets at which they anchored for a while and then again set out upon that ocean of veiled hostility which showed itself in their aloofness from one another. This aloofness might have grieved Iván Ilych had he considered that it ought not to exist, but he now regarded the position as normal, and even made it the goal at which he aimed in family life. His aim was to free himself more and more from those unpleasantnesses and to give them a semblance of harmlessness and propriety. He attained this by spending less and less time with his family, and when obliged to be at home he tried to safeguard his position by the presence of outsiders. The chief thing however was that he had his official duties. The whole interest of his life now centered in the official world and that interest absorbed him. The consciousness of his power, being able to ruin anybody he wished to ruin, the importance, even the external dignity of his entry into court, or meetings with his subordinates, his success with superiors and inferiors, and above all his masterly handling of cases, of which he was conscious—all this gave him pleasure and filled his life, together with chats with his colleagues, dinners, and bridge. So that on the whole Iván Ilych's life continued to flow as he considered it should do—pleasantly and properly.

So things continued for another seven years. His eldest daughter was already sixteen, another child had died, and only one son was left, a schoolboy and a subject of dissensions. Iván Ilych wanted to put him in the School of Law, but to spite him Praskóvya Fëdorovna entered him at the High School. The daughter had been educated at home and had turned out well; the boy did not learn badly either.

3

So Iván Ilych lived for seventeen years after his marriage. He was already a Public Prosecutor of long standing, and had declined several proposed transfers while awaiting a more desirable post, when an unanticipated and unpleasant occurrence quite upset the peaceful course of his life. He was expecting to be offered the post of presiding judge in a University town, but Happe somehow came to the front and obtained the appointment instead. Iván Ilych became irritable, reproached Happe, and quarrelled both with him and his immediate superiors—who became colder to him and again passed him over when other appointments were made.

This was in 1880, the hardest year of Iván Ilych's life. It was then that it became evident on the one hand that his salary was insufficient for them to live on, and on the other that he had been forgotten, and not only this, but that what was for him the greatest and most cruel injustice appeared to others a quite ordinary occurrence. Even his father did not consider it his duty to help him. Iván Ilych felt himself abandoned by everyone, and that they regarded his position with a salary of 3,500 rubles as quite normal and even fortunate. He alone knew that with the consciousness of the injustices done him, with his wife's incessant nagging, and with the debts he had contracted by living beyond his means, his position was far from normal.

In order to save money that summer he obtained leave of absence and went with his wife to live in the country at her brother's place.

In the country, without this work, he experienced *ennui* for the first time in his life, and not only *ennui* but intolerable depression, and he decided that it was impossible to go on living like that, and that it was necessary to take energetic measures.

Having passed a sleepless night pacing up and down the veranda, he decided to go to Petersburg and bestir himself, in order to punish those who had failed to appreciate him and to get transferred to another ministry.

Next day, despite many protests from his wife and her brother, he started for Petersburg with the sole object of obtaining a post with a salary of five thousand rubles a year. He was no longer bent on any particular department, or tendency, or kind of activity. All he now wanted was an appointment to another post with a salary of five thousand rubles, in one of the Empress Márya's Institutions, or even in the customs—but it had to carry with it a salary of five thousand rubles and be in a ministry other than that in which they had failed to appreciate him.

And this quest of Iván Ilych's was crowned with remarkable and unexpected success. At Kursk an acquaintance of his, F. I. Ilyín, got into the first-class carriage, sat down beside Iván Ilych, and told him of a telegram just received by the governor of Kursk announcing that a change was about to take place in the ministry: Peter Ivánovich was to be superseded by Iván Semënovich.

The proposed change, apart from its significance for Russia, had a special significance for Iván Ilych, because by bringing forward a new man, Peter Petróvich, and consequently his friend Zachár Ivánovich, it was highly favourable for Iván Ilych, since Zachár Ivánovich was a friend and colleague of his.

In Moscow this news was confirmed, and on reaching Petersburg Iván Ilych found Zachár Ivánovich and received a definite promise of an appointment in his former department of Justice.

A week later he telegraphed to his wife: "Zachár in Miller's place. I shall receive appointment on presentation of report."

Thanks to this change of personnel, Iván Ilych had unexpectedly obtained an appointment in his former ministry which placed him two stages above his former colleagues besides giving him five thousand rubles salary and three thousand five hundred rubles for expenses connected with his removal. All his ill humour towards his former enemies and the whole department vanished, and Iván Ilych was completely happy.

He returned to the country more cheerful and contented than he had been for a long time. Praskóvya Fëdorovna also cheered up and a truce was arranged between them. Iván Ilych told of how he had been fêted by everybody in Petersburg, how all those who had been his enemies were put to shame and now fawned on him, how envious they were of his appointment, and how much everybody in Petersburg had liked him.

Praskóvya Fëdorovna listened to all this and appeared to believe it. She did not contradict anything, but only made plans for their life in the town to which they were going. Iván Ilych saw with delight that these plans were his plans, that he and his wife agreed, and that, after a stumble, his life was regaining its due and natural character of pleasant lightheartedness and decorum.

Iván Ilych had come back for a short time only, for he had to take up his new duties on the 10th of September. Moreover, he needed time to settle into the new place, to move all his belongings from the province, and to buy and order many additional things: in a word, to make such arrangements as he had resolved on, which were almost exactly what Praskóvya Fëdorovna too had decided on.

Now that everything had happened so fortunately, and that he and his wife were at one in their aims and moreover saw so little of one another they got on together better than they had done since the first years of marriage. Iván Ilych had thought of taking his family away with him at once, but the insistence of his wife's brother and her sister-in-law, who had suddenly become particularly amiable and friendly to him and his family, induced him to depart alone.

So he departed, and the cheerful state of mind induced by his success and by the harmony between his wife and himself, the one intensifying the other, did not leave him. He found a delightful house, just the thing both he and his wife had dreamt of. Spacious, lofty reception rooms in the old style, a convenient and dignified study, rooms for his wife and daughter, a study for his son—it might have been specially built for them. Iván Ilych himself superintended the arrangements, chose the wallpapers, supplemented the furniture (preferably with antiques which he considered particularly *comme il faut*), and supervised the upholstering. Everything progressed and progressed and approached the ideal he had set himself: even when things were only half completed they exceeded his expectations. He saw what a refined and elegant character, free from vulgarity, it would all have when it was ready. On falling asleep he pictured to himself how the reception-room would look. Looking at the yet unfurnished drawing-room he could see the fireplace, the screen, the what-not, the little chairs dotted here and there, the dishes and plates on the walls, and the bronzes, as they would be when everything was in place. He was pleased by the thought of how his wife and daughter, who shared his taste in this matter, would be impressed by it. They were certainly not expecting as much. He had been particularly successful in finding, and buying cheaply, antiques which gave a particularly aristocratic character to the whole place. But in his letters he intentionally understated everything in order to be able to surprise them. All this so absorbed him that his new duties—though he liked his official work—interested him less than he had expected. Sometimes he even had moments of absent-mindedness during the Court Sessions, and would consider whether he should have straight or curved cornices for his curtains. He was so interested in it all that he often did things himself, rearranging the furniture, or rehanging the curtains. Once when mounting a step-ladder to show the upholsterer, who did not understand, how he wanted the hangings draped, he made a false step and slipped, but being a strong and agile man he clung on and only knocked his side against the knob of the window frame. The bruised place was painful but the pain soon passed, and he felt particularly bright and well just then. He wrote: "I feel fifteen years younger." He thought he would have everything ready by September, but it dragged on til mid-October. But the result was charming not only in his eyes but to everyone who saw it.

In reality it was just what is usually seen in the houses of people of moderate means who want to appear rich, and therefore succeed only in resembling others like themselves: there were damasks, dark wood, plants, rugs, and dull and polished bronzes—all the things people of a certain class have in order to resemble other people of that class. His house was so like the others that it would never have been noticed, but to him it all seemed to be quite exceptional. He was very happy when he met his family at the station and brought them to the newly furnished house all lit up, where a footman in a white tie opened the door into the hall decorated with plants, and when they went on into the drawing-room and the study uttering exclamations of delight. He conducted them everywhere, drank in their praises eagerly, and beamed with pleasure. At tea that evening, when Praskóvya Fëdorovna among other things asked him about his fall, he laughed, and showed them how he had gone flying and had frightened the upholsterer.

"It's a good thing I'm a bit of an athlete. Another man might have been killed, but I merely knocked myself, just here; it hurts when it's touched, but it's passing off already—it's only a bruise."

So they began living in their new home—in which, as always happens when they got thoroughly settled in they found they were just one room short—and with the increased income, which as always was just a little (some five hundred rubles) too little, but it was all very nice.

Things went particularly well at first, before everything was finally arranged and while something had still to be done; this thing bought, that thing ordered, another thing moved, and something else adjusted. Though there were some disputes between husband and wife, they were both so well satisfied and had so much to do that it all passed off without any serious quarrels. When nothing was left to arrange it became rather dull and something seemed to be lacking, but they were then making acquaintances, forming habits, and life was growing fuller.

Iván Ilych spent his mornings at the law court and came home to dinner, and at first he was generally in a good humour, though he occasionally became irritable just on account of his house. (Every spot on the tablecloth or the upholstery, and every broken window-blind string, irritated him. He had devoted so much trouble to arranging it all that every disturbance of it distressed him.) But on the whole his life ran its course as he believed life should do: easily, pleasantly, and decorously.

He got up at nine, drank his coffee, read the paper, and then put on his undress uniform and went to the law courts. There the harness in which he worked had already been stretched to fit him and he donned it without a hitch: petitioners, inquiries at the chancery, the chancery itself, and the sittings public and administrative. In all this the thing was to exclude everything fresh and vital, which always disturbs the regular course of official business, and to admit only official relations with people, and then only on official grounds. A man would come, for instance, wanting some information. Iván Ilych, as one in whose sphere the matter did not lie, would have nothing to do with him: but if the man had some business with him in his official capacity, something that could be expressed on officially stamped paper, he would do everything, positively everything he could within the limits of such relations, and in doing so would maintain the semblance of friendly human relations, that is, would observe the courtesies of life. As soon as the official relations ended, so did everything else. Iván Ilych possessed this capacity to separate his real life from the official side of affairs and not mix the two, in the highest degree, and by long practice and natural aptitude had brought it to such a pitch that sometimes, in the manner of a virtuoso, he would even allow himself to let the human and official relations mingle. He let himself do this just because he felt that he could at any time he chose resume the strictly official attitude again and drop the human relation. And he did it all easily, pleasantly, correctly, and even artistically. In the intervals between the sessions he smoked, drank tea, chatted a little about politics, a little about general topics, a little about cards, but most of all about official appointments. Tired, but with the feelings of a virtuoso—one of the first violins who has played his part in an orchestra with precision— he would return home to find that his wife and daughter had been out paying calls, or had a visitor, and that his son had been to school, had done his homework with his tutor, and was duly learning what is taught in High Schools. Everything was as it should be. After dinner, if they had no visitors, Iván Ilych sometimes read a book that was being much discussed at the time, and in the evening settled down to work, that is, read official papers, compared the depositions of witnesses, and noted paragraphs of the Code applying to them. This was neither dull nor amusing. It was dull when he might have been playing bridge, but if no bridge was available it was at any rate better than doing nothing or sitting with his wife. Iván Ilych's chief pleasure was giving little dinners to which he invited men and women of good social position, and just as his drawing-room resembled all other drawing-rooms so did his enjoyable little parties resemble all other such parties.

Once they even gave a dance. Iván Ilych enjoyed it and everything went off well, except that it led to a violent quarrel with his wife about the cakes and sweets. Praskóvya Fëdorovna had made her own plans, but Iván Ilych insisted on getting everything from an expensive confectioner and ordered too many cakes, and the quarrel occurred because some of those cakes were left over and the confectioner's bill came to forty-five rubles. It was a great and disagreeable quarrel. Praskóvya Fëdorovna called him "a fool and an imbecile," and he clutched at his head and made angry allusions to divorce.

But the dance itself had been enjoyable. The best people were there, and Iván Ilych had danced with Princess Trúfonova, a sister of the distinguished founder of the Society "Bear my Burden."

The pleasures connected with his work were pleasures of ambition; his social pleasures were those of vanity; but Iván Ilych's greatest pleasure was playing bridge. He acknowledged that whatever disagreeable incident happened in his life, the pleasure that beamed like a ray of light above everything else was to sit down to bridge with good players, not noisy partners, and of course to four-handed bridge (with five players it was annoying to have to stand out, though one pretended not to mind), to play a clever and serious game (when the cards allowed it) and then to have supper and drink a glass of wine. After a game of bridge, especially if he had won a little (to win a large sum was unpleasant), Iván Ilych went to bed in specially good humour.

So they lived. They formed a circle of acquaintances among the best people and were visited by people of importance and by young folk. In their views as to their acquaintances, husband, wife, and daughter were entirely agreed, and tacitly and unanimously kept at arm's length and shook off the various shabby friends and relations who, with much show of affection, gushed into the drawing-room with its Japanese plates on the walls. Soon these shabby friends ceased to obtrude themselves and only the best people remained in the Golovíns' set.

Young men made up to Lisa, and Petríschhev, an examining magistrate and Dmítri Ivánovich Petríschhev's son and sole heir, began to be so attentive to her that Iván Ilych had already spoken to Praskóvya Fëdorovna about it, and considered whether they should not arrange a party for them, or get up some private theatricals.

So they lived, and all went well, without change, and life flowed pleasantly.

4

They were all in good health. It could not be called ill health if Iván Ilych sometimes said that he had a queer taste in his mouth and felt some discomfort in his left side.

But this discomfort increased and, though not exactly painful, grew into a sense of pressure in his side accompanied by ill humour. And his irritability became worse and worse and began to mar the agreeable, easy, and correct life that had established itself in the Golovín family. Quarrels between husband and wife became more and more frequent, and soon the ease and amenity disappeared and even the decorum was barely maintained. Scenes again became frequent, and very few of those islets remained on which husband and wife could meet without an explosion. Praskóvya Fëdorovna now had good reason to say that her husband's temper was trying. With characteristic exaggeration she said he had always had a dreadful temper, and that it had needed all her good nature to put up with it for twenty years. It was true that now the quarrels were started by him. His bursts of temper always came just before dinner, often just as he began to eat his soup. Sometimes he noticed that a plate or dish was chipped, or the food was not done right, or his son put his elbow on the table, or his daughter's hair was not done as he liked it, and for all this he blamed Praskóvya Fëdorovna. At first she retorted and said disagreeable things to him, but once or twice he fell into such a rage at the beginning of dinner that she realized it was due to some physical derangement brought on by taking food, and so she restrained herself and did not answer, but only hurried to get the dinner over. She regarded this self-restraint as highly praiseworthy. Having come to the conclusion that her husband had a dreadful temper and made her life miserable, she began to feel sorry for herself, and the more she pitied herself the more she hated her husband. She began to wish he would die; yet she did not want him to die because then his salary would cease. And this irritated her against him still more. She considered herself dreadfully unhappy just because not even his death could save her, and though she concealed her exasperation, that hidden exasperation of hers increased his irritation also.

After one scene in which Iván Ilych had been particularly unfair and after which he had said in explanation that he certainly was irritable but that it was due to his not being well, she said that if he was ill it should be attended to, and insisted on his going to see a celebrated doctor.

He went. Everything took place as he had expected and as it always does. There was the usual waiting and the important air assumed by the doctor, with which he was so familiar (resembling that which he himself assumed in court), and the sounding and listening, and the questions which called for answers that were foregone conclusions and were evidently unnecessary, and the look of importance which implied that "if only you put yourself in our hands we will arrange everything—we know indubitably how it has to be done, always in the same way for everybody alike." It was all just as it was in the law courts. The doctor put on just the same air towards him as he himself put on towards an accused person.

The doctor said that so-and-so indicated that there was so-and-so inside the patient, but if the investigation of so-and-so did not confirm this, then he must assume that and that. If he assumed that and that, then . . . and so on. To Iván Ilych only one question was important: was his case serious or not? But the doctor ignored that inappropriate question. From his point of view it was not the one under consideration, the real question was to decide between a floating kidney, chronic catarrh, or appendicitis. It was not a question of Iván Ilych's life or death, but one between a floating kidney and appendicitis. And that question the doctor solved brilliantly, as it seemed to Iván Ilych, in favour of the appendix, with the reservation that should an examination of the urine give fresh indications the matter would be reconsidered. All this was just what Iván Ilych had himself brilliantly accomplished a thousand times in dealing with men on trial. The doctor summed up just as brilliantly, looking over his spectacles triumphantly and even gaily at the accused. From the doctor's summing up Iván Ilych concluded that things were bad, but that for the doctor, and perhaps for everybody else, it was a matter of indifference, though for him it was bad. And this conclusion struck him painfully, arousing in him a great feeling of pity for himself and of bitterness towards the doctor's indifference to a matter of such importance.

He said nothing of this, but rose, placed the doctor's fee on the table, and remarked with a sigh: "We sick people probably often put inappropriate questions. But tell me, in general, is this complaint dangerous, or not? . . ."

The doctor looked at him sternly over his spectacles with one eye, as if to say: "Prisoner, if you will not keep to the questions put to you, I shall be obliged to have you removed from the court."

"I have already told you what I consider necessary and proper. The analysis may show something more." And the doctor bowed.

Iván Ilych went out slowly, seated himself disconsolately in his sledge, and drove home. All the way home he was going over what the doctor had said, trying to translate those complicated, obscure, scientific phrases into plain language and find in them an answer to the question: "Is my condition bad? Is it very bad? Or is there as yet nothing much wrong?" And it seemed to him that the meaning of what the doctor had said was that it was very bad. Everything in the streets seemed depressing. The cabmen, the houses, the passers-by, and the shops, were dismal. His ache, this dull gnawing ache that never ceased for a moment, seemed to have acquired a new and more serious significance from the doctor's dubious remarks. Iván Ilych now watched it with a new and oppressive feeling.

He reached home and began to tell his wife about it. She listened, but in the middle of his account his daughter came in with her hat on, ready to go out with her mother. She sat down reluctantly to listen to this tedious story, but could not stand it long, and her mother too did not hear him to the end.

"Well, I am very glad," she said. "Mind now to take your medicine regularly. Give me the prescription and I'll send Gerásim to the chemist's." And she went to get ready to go out.

While she was in the room Iván Ilych had hardly taken time to breathe, but he sighed deeply when she left it.

"Well," he thought, "perhaps it isn't so bad after all."

He began taking his medicine and following the doctor's directions, which had been altered after the examination of the urine. But then it happened that there was a contradiction between the indications drawn from the examination of the urine and the symptoms that showed themselves. It turned out that what was happening differed from what the doctor had told him, and that he had either forgotten, or blundered, or hidden something from him. He could not, however, be blamed for that, and Iván Ilych still obeyed his orders implicitly and at first derived some comfort from doing so.

From the time of his visit to the doctor, Iván Ilych's chief occupation was the exact fulfilment of the doctor's instructions regarding hygiene and the taking of medicine, and the observation of his pain and his excretions. His chief interests came to be people's ailments and people's health. When sickness, deaths, or recoveries were mentioned in his presence, especially when the illness resembled his own, he listened with agitation which he tried to hide, asked questions, and applied what he heard to his own case.

The pain did not grow less, but Iván Ilych made efforts to force himself to think that he was better. And he could do this so long as nothing agitated him. But as soon as he had any unpleasantness with his wife, any lack of success in his official work, or held bad cards at bridge, he was at once acutely sensible of his disease. He had formerly borne such mischances, hoping soon to adjust what was wrong, to master it and attain success, or make a grand slam. But now every mischance upset him and plunged him into despair. He would say to himself:

"There now, just as I was beginning to get better and the medicine had begun to take effect, comes this accursed misfortune, or unpleasantness. . . . And he was furious with the mishap, or with the people who were causing the unpleasantness and killing him, for he felt that this fury was killing him but could not restrain it. One would have thought that it should have been clear to him that this exasperation with circumstances and people aggravated his illness, and that he ought therefore to ignore unpleasant occurrences. But he drew the very opposite conclusion: he said that he needed peace, and he watched for everything that might disturb it and became irritable at the slightest infringement of it. His condition was rendered worse by the fact that he read medical books and consulted doctors. The progress of his disease was so gradual that he could deceive himself when comparing one day with another—the difference was so slight. But when he consulted the doctors it seemed to him that he was getting worse, and even very rapidly. Yet despite this he was continually consulting them.

That month he went to see another celebrity, who told him almost the same as the first had done but put his questions rather differently, and the interview with this celebrity only increased Iván Ilych's doubts and fears. A friend of a friend of his, a very good doctor, diagnosed his illness again quite differently from the others, and though he predicted recovery, his questions and suppositions bewildered Iván Ilych still more and increased his doubts. A homoeopathist diagnosed the disease in yet another way, and prescribed medicine which Iván Ilych took secretly for a week. But after a week, not feeling any improvement and having lost confidence both in the former doctor's treatment and in this one's, he became still more despondent. One day a lady acquaintance mentioned a cure effected by a wonder-working icon. Iván Ilych caught himself listening attentively and beginning to believe that it had occurred. This incident alarmed him. "Has my mind really weakened to such an extent?" he asked himself. "Nonsense! It's all rubbish. I mustn't give way to nervous fears but having chosen a doctor must keep strictly to his treatment. That is what I will do. Now it's all settled. I won't think about it, but will follow the treatment seriously till summer, and then we shall see. From now there must be no more of this wavering!" This was easy to say but impossible to carry out. The pain in his side oppressed him and seemed to grow worse and more incessant, while the taste in his mouth grew stranger and stranger. It seemed to him that his breath had a disgusting smell, and he was conscious of a loss of appetite and strength. There was no deceiving himself: something terrible, new, and more important than anything before in his life, was taking place within him of which he alone was aware. Those about him did not understand or would not understand it, but thought everything in the world was going on as usual. That tormented Iván Ilych more than anything. He saw that his household, especially his wife and daughter, who were in a perfect whirl of visiting, did not understand anything of it and were annoyed that he was so depressed and so exacting, as if he were to blame for it. Though they tried to disguise it he saw that he was an obstacle in their path, and that his wife had adopted a definite line in regard to his illness and kept to it regardless of anything he said or did. Her attitude was this: "You know," she would say to her friends, "Iván Ilych can't do as other people do, and keep to the treatment prescribed for him. One day he'll take his drops and keep strictly to his diet and go to bed in good time, but the next day unless I watch him he'll suddenly forget his medicine, eat sturgeon—which is forbidden—and sit up playing cards till one o'clock in the morning."

"Oh, come, when was that?" Iván Ilych would ask in vexation. "Only once at Peter Ivánovich's."

"And yesterday with Shébek."

"Well, even if I hadn't stayed up, this pain would have kept me awake."

"Be that as it may you'll never get well like that, but will always make us wretched."

Praskóvya Fëdorovna's attitude to Iván Ilych's illness, as she expressed it both to others and to him, was that it was his own fault and was another of the annoyances he caused her. Iván Ilych felt that this opinion escaped her involuntarily—but that did not make it easier for him.

At the law courts too, Iván Ilych noticed, or thought he noticed, a strange attitude towards himself. It sometimes seemed to him that people were watching him inquisitively as a man whose place might soon be vacant. Then again, his friends would suddenly begin to chaff him in a friendly way about his low spirits, as if the awful, horrible, and unheard-of thing that was going on within him, incessantly gnawing at him and irresistibly drawing him away, was a very agreeable subject for jests. Schwartz in particular irritated him by his jocularity, vivacity, and *savoir-faire*, which reminded him of what he himself had been ten years ago.

Friends came to make up a set and they sat down to cards. They dealt, bending the new cards to soften them, and he sorted the diamonds in his hand and found he had seven. His partner said "No trumps" and supported him with two diamonds. What more could be wished for? It ought to be jolly and lively. They would make a grand slam. But suddenly Iván Ilych was conscious of that gnawing pain, that taste in his mouth, and it seemed ridiculous that in such circumstances he should be pleased to make a grand slam.

He looked at his partner Mikháil Mikháylovich, who rapped the table with his strong hand and instead of snatching up the tricks pushed the cards courteously and indulgently towards Iván Ilych that he might have the pleasure of gathering them up without the trouble of stretching out his hand for them. "Does he think I am too weak to stretch out my arm?" thought Iván Ilych, and forgetting what he was doing he over-trumped his partner, missing the grand slam by three tricks. And what was most awful of all was that he saw how upset Mikháil Mikháylovich was about it but did not himself care. And it was dreadful to realize why he did not care.

They all saw that he was suffering, and said: "We can stop if you are tired. Take a rest." Lie down? No, he was not at all tired, and he finished the rubber. All were gloomy and silent. Iván Ilych felt that he had diffused this gloom over them and could not dispel it. They had supper and went away, and Iván Ilych was left alone with the consciousness that his life was poisoned and was poisoning the lives of others, and that this poison did not weaken but penetrated more and more deeply into his whole being.

With this consciousness, and with physical pain besides the terror, he must go to bed, often to lie awake the greater part of the night. Next morning he had to get up again, dress, go to the law courts, speak, and write; or if he did not go out, spend at home those twenty-four hours a day each of which was a torture. And he had to live thus all alone on the brink of an abyss, with no one who understood or pitied him.

5

So one month passed and then another. Just before the New Year his brother-in-law came to town and stayed at their house. Iván Ilych was at the law courts and Praskóvya Fёdorovna had gone shopping. When Iván Ilych came home and entered his study he found his brother-in-law there—a healthy, florid man—unpacking his portmanteau himself. He raised his head on hearing Iván Ilych's footsteps and looked up at him for a moment without a word. That stare told Iván Ilych everything. His brother-in-law opened his mouth to utter an exclamation of surprise but checked himself, and that action confirmed it all.

"I have changed, eh?"

"Yes, there is a change."

And after that, try as he would to get his brother-in-law to return to the subject of his looks, the latter would say nothing about it. Praskóvya Fёdorovna came home and her brother went out to her. Iván Ilych locked the door and began to examine himself in the glass, first full face, then in profile. He took up a portrait of himself taken with his wife, and compared it with what he saw in the glass. The change in him was immense. Then he bared his arms to the elbow, looked at them, drew the sleeves down again, sat down on an ottoman, and grew blacker than night.

"No, no, this won't do!" he said to himself, and jumped up, went to the table, took up some law papers and began to read them, but could not continue. He unlocked the door and went into the reception-room. The door leading to the drawing-room was shut. He approached it on tiptoe and listened.

"No, you are exaggerating!" Praskóvya Fёdorovna was saying.

"Exaggerating! Don't you see it? Why, he's a dead man! Look at his eyes—there's no light in them. But what is it that is wrong with him?"

"No one knows. Nilolа́evich [that was another doctor] said something, but I don't know what. And Leshchetítsky [this was the celebrated specialist] said quite the contrary. . . ."

Iván Ilych walked away, went to his own room, lay down, and began musing: "The kidney, a floating kidney." He recalled all the doctors had told him of how it detached itself and swayed about. And by an effort of imagination he tried to catch that kidney and arrest it and support it. So little was needed for this, it seemed to him. "No, I'll go to see Peter Ivánovich again." [That was the friend whose friend was a doctor.] He rang, ordered the carriage, and got ready to go.

"Where are you going, Jean?" asked his wife, with a specially sad and exceptionally kind look.

This exceptionally kind look irritated him. He looked morosely at her.

"I must go to see Peter Ivánovich."

He went to see Peter Ivánovich, and together they went to see his friend, the doctor. He was in, and Iván Ilych had a long talk with him.

Reviewing the anatomical and physiological details of what in the doctor's opinion was going on inside him, he understood it all.

There was something, a small thing, in the vermiform appendix. It might all come right. Only stimulate the energy of one organ and check the activity of another, then absorption would take place and everything would come right. He got home rather late for dinner, ate his dinner, and conversed cheerfully, but could not for a long time bring himself to go back to work in his room. At last, however, he went to his study and did what was necessary, but the consciousness that he had put something aside—an important, intimate matter which he would revert to when his work was done—never left him. When he had finished his work he remembered that this intimate matter was the thought of his vermiform appendix. But he did not give himself up to it, and went to the drawing-room for tea. There were callers there, including the examining magistrate who was a desirable match for his daughter, and they were conversing, playing the piano, and singing. Iván Ilych, as Praskóvya Fëdorovna remarked, spent that evening more cheerfully than usual, but he never for a moment forgot that he had postponed the important matter of the appendix. At eleven o'clock he said good-night and went to his bedroom. Since his illness he had slept alone in a small room next to his study. He undressed and took up a novel by Zola, but instead of reading it he fell into thought, and in his imagination that desired improvement in the vermiform appendix occurred. There was the absorption and evacuation and the re-establishment of normal activity. "Yes, that's it!" he said to himself. "One need only assist nature, that's all." He remembered his medicine, rose, took it, and lay down on his back watching for the beneficent action of the medicine and for it to lessen the pain. "I need only take it regularly and avoid all injurious influences. I am already feeling better, much better." He began touching his side: it was not painful to the touch. "There, I really don't feel it. It's much better already." He put out the light and turned on his side. . . . "The appendix is getting better, absorption is occurring." Suddenly he felt the old, familiar, dull, gnawing pain, stubborn and serious. There was the same familiar loathsome taste in his mouth. His heart sank and he felt dazed. "My God! My God!" he muttered. "Again, again! And it will never cease." And suddenly the matter presented itself in a quite different aspect. "Vermiform appendix! Kidney!" he said to himself. "It's not a question of appendix or kidney, but of life and . . . death. Yes, life was there and now it is going, going and I cannot stop it. Yes. Why deceive myself? Isn't it obvious to everyone but me that I'm dying, and that it's only a question of weeks, days . . . it may happen this moment. There was light and now there is darkness. I was here and now I'm going there! Where?" A chill came over him, his breathing ceased, and he felt only the throbbing of his heart.

"When I am not, what will there be? There will be nothing. Then where shall I be when I am no more? Can this be dying? No, I don't want to!" He jumped up and tried to light the candle, felt for it with trembling hands, dropped candle and candlestick on the floor, and fell back on his pillow.

"What's the use? It makes no difference," he said to himself, staring with wide-open eyes into the darkness. "Death. Yes, death. And none of them know or wish to know it, and they have no pity for me. Now they are playing." (He heard through the door the distant sound of a song and its accompaniment.) "It's all the same to them, but they will die too! Fools! I first, and they later, but it will be the same for them. And now they are merry . . . the beasts!"

Anger choked him and he was agonizingly, unbearably miserable. "It is impossible that all men have been doomed to suffer this awful horror!" He raised himself.

"Something must be wrong. I must calm myself—must think it all over from the beginning." And he again began thinking. "Yes, the beginning of my illness: I knocked my side, but I was still quite well that day and the next. It hurt a little, then rather more. I saw the doctors, then followed despondency and anguish, more doctors, and I drew nearer to the abyss. My strength grew less and I kept coming nearer and nearer, and now I have wasted away and there is no light in my eyes. I think of the appendix—but this is death! I think of mending the appendix, and all the while here is death! Can it really be death?" Again terror seized him and he gasped for breath. He leant down and began feeling for the matches, pressing with his elbow on the stand beside the bed. It was in his way and hurt him, he grew furious with it, pressed on it still harder, and upset it. Breathless and in despair he fell on his back, expecting death to come immediately.

Meanwhile the visitors were leaving. Praskóvya Fëdorovna was seeing them off. She heard something fall and came in.

"What has happened?"

"Nothing. I knocked it over accidentally."

She went out and returned with a candle. He lay there panting heavily, like a man who has run a thousand yards, and stared upwards at her with a fixed look.

"What is it, Jean?"

"No . . . o . . . thing. I upset it." ("Why speak of it? She won't understand," he thought.)

And in truth she did not understand. She picked up the stand, lit his candle, and hurried away to see another visitor off. When she came back he still lay on his back, looking upwards.

"What is it? Do you feel worse?"

"Yes."

She shook her head and sat down.

"Do you know, Jean, I think we must ask Leshchetítsky to come and see you here."

This meant calling in the famous specialist, regardless of expense. He smiled malignantly and said "No." She remained a little longer and then went up to him and kissed his forehead.

While she was kissing him he hated her from the bottom of his soul and with difficulty refrained from pushing her away.

"Good-night. Please God you'll sleep."

"Yes."

6

Iván Ilych saw that he was dying, and he was in continual despair.

In the depth of his heart he knew he was dying, but not only was he not accustomed to the thought, he simply did not and could not grasp it.

The syllogism he had learned from Kiezewetter's Logic: "Caius is a man, men are mortal, therefore Caius is mortal," had always seemed to him correct as applied to Caius, but certainly not as applied to himself. That Caius—man in the abstract—was mortal, was perfectly correct, but he was not Caius, not an abstract man, but a creature quite, quite separate from all others. He had been little Ványa, with a mamma and a papa, with Mítya and Volódya, with the toys, a coachman and a nurse, afterwards with Kátenka and with all the joys, griefs, and delights of childhood, boyhood, and youth. What did Caius know of the smell of that striped leather ball Ványa had been so fond of? Had Caius kissed his mother's hand like that, and did the silk of her dress rustle so for Caius? Had he rioted like that at school when the pastry was bad? Had Caius been in love like that? Could Caius preside at a session as he did? Caius really was mortal, and it was right for him to die; but for me, little Ványa, Iván Ilych, with all my thoughts and emotions, it's altogether a different matter. It cannot be that I ought to die. That would be too terrible.

Such was his feeling.

"If I had to die like Caius I should have known it was so. An inner voice would have told me so, but there was nothing of the sort in me and I and all my friends felt that our case was quite different from that of Caius. And now here it is!" he said to himself. "It can't be. It's impossible! But here it is. How is this? How is one to understand it?"

He could not understand it, and tried to drive this false, incorrect, morbid thought away and to replace it by other proper and healthy thoughts. But that thought, and not the thought only but the reality itself, seemed to come and confront him.

And to replace that thought he called up a succession of others, hoping to find in them some support. He tried to get back into the former current of thoughts that had once screened the thought of death from him. But strange to say, all that had formerly shut off, hidden, and destroyed, his consciousness of death, no longer had that effect. Iván Ilych now spent most of his time in attempting to re-establish that old current. He would say to himself: "I will take up my duties again—after all I used to live by them." And banishing all doubts he would go to the law courts, enter into conversation with his colleagues, and sit carelessly as was his wont, scanning the crowd with a thoughtful look and leaning both his emaciated arms on the arms of his oak chair; bending over as usual to a colleague and drawing his papers nearer he would interchange whispers with him, and then suddenly raising his eyes and sitting erect would pronounce certain words and open the proceedings. But suddenly in the midst of those proceedings the pain in his side, regardless of the stage the proceedings had reached, would begin its own gnawing work. Iván Ilych would turn his attention to it and try to drive the thought of it away, but without success. *It* would come and stand before him and look at him, and he would be petrified and the light would die out of his eyes, and he would again begin asking himself whether *It* alone was true. And his colleagues and subordinates would see with surprise and distress that he, the brilliant and subtle judge, was becoming confused and making mistakes. He would shake himself, try to pull himself together, manage somehow to bring the sitting to a close, and return home with the sorrowful consciousness that his judicial labours could not as formerly hide from him what he wanted them to hide, and could not deliver him from *It*. And what was worst of all was that *It* drew his attention to itself not in order to make him take some action but only that he should look at *It*, look it straight in the face: look at it without doing anything, suffer inexpressibly.

And to save himself from this condition Iván Ilych looked for consolations—new screens—and new screens were found and for a while seemed to save him, but then they immediately fell to pieces or rather became transparent, as if *It* penetrated them and nothing could veil *It*.

In these latter days he would go into the drawing-room he had arranged—that drawing-room where he had fallen and for the sake of which (how bitterly ridiculous it seemed) he had sacrificed his life—for he knew that his illness originated with that knock. He would enter and see that something had scratched the polished table. He would look for the cause of this and find that it was the bronze ornamentation of an album, that had got bent. He would take up the expensive album which he had lovingly arranged, and feel vexed with his daughter and her friends for their untidiness—for the album was torn here and there and some of the photographs turned upside down. He would put it carefully in order and bend the ornamentation back into position. Then it would occur to him to place all those things in another corner of the room, near the plants. He would call the footman, but his daughter or wife would come to help him. They would not agree, and his wife would contradict him, and he would dispute and grow angry. But that was all right, for then he did not think about *It*. *It* was invisible.

But then, when he was moving something himself, his wife would say: "Let the servants do it. You will hurt yourself again." And suddenly *It* would flash through the screen and he would see it. It was just a flash, and he hoped it would disappear, but he would involuntarily pay attention to his side. "It sits there as before, gnawing just the same!" And he could no longer forget *It*, but could distinctly see it looking at him from behind the flowers. "What is it all for?"

"It really is so! I lost my life over that curtain as I might have done when storming a fort. Is that possible? How terrible and how stupid. It can't be true! It can't, but it is."

He would go to his study, lie down, and again be alone with *It*: face to face with *It*. And nothing could be done with *It* except to look at it and shudder.

7

How it happened it is impossible to say because it came about step by step, unnoticed, but in the third month of Iván Ilych's illness, his wife, his daughter, his son, his acquaintances, the doctors, the servants, and above all he himself, were aware that the whole interest he had for other people was whether he would soon vacate his place, and at last release the living from the discomfort caused by his presence and be himself released from his sufferings.

He slept less and less. He was given opium and hypodermic injections of morphine, but this did not relieve him. The dull depression he experienced in a somnolent condition at first gave him a little relief, but only as something new, afterwards it became as distressing as the pain itself or even more so.

Special foods were prepared for him by the doctors' orders, but all those foods became increasingly distasteful and disgusting to him.

For his excretions also special arrangements had to be made, and this was a torment to him every time—a torment from the uncleanliness, the unseemliness, and the smell, and from knowing that another person had to take part in it.

But just through this most unpleasant matter, Iván Ilych obtained comfort. Gerásim, the butler's young assistant, always came in to carry the things out. Gerásim was a clean, fresh peasant lad, grown stout on town food and always cheerful and bright. At first the sight of him, in his clean Russian peasant costume, engaged on that disgusting task embarrassed Iván Ilych.

Once when he got up from the commode too weak to draw up his trousers, he dropped into a soft armchair and looked with horror at his bare, enfeebled thighs with the muscles so sharply marked on them.

Gerásim with a firm light tread, his heavy boots emitting a pleasant smell of tar and fresh winter air, came in wearing a clean Hessian apron, the sleeves of his print shirt tucked up over his strong bare young arms; and refraining from looking at his sick master out of consideration for his feelings, and restraining the joy of life that beamed from his face, he went up to the commode.

"Gerásim!" said Iván Ilych in a weak voice.

Gerásim started, evidently afraid he might have committed some blunder, and with a rapid movement turned his fresh, kind, simple young face which just showed the first downy signs of a beard.

"Yes, sir?"

"That must be very unpleasant for you. You must forgive me. I am helpless."

"Oh, why, sir," and Gerásim's eyes beamed and he showed his glistening white teeth, "what's a little trouble? It's a case of illness with you, sir."

And his deft strong hands did their accustomed task, and he went out of the room stepping lightly. Five minutes later he as lightly returned.

Iván Ilych was still sitting in the same position in the armchair.

"Gerásim," he said when the latter had replaced the freshly-washed utensil. "Please come here and help me." Gerásim went up to him. "Lift me up. It is hard for me to get up, and I have sent Dmítri away."

Gerásim went up to him, grasped his master with his strong arms deftly but gently, in the same way that he stepped—lifted him, supported him with one hand, and with the other drew up his trousers and would have set him down again, but Iván Ilych asked to be led to the sofa. Gerásim, without an effort and without apparent pressure, led him, almost lifting him, up to the sofa and placed him on it.

"Thank you. How easily and well you do it all!"

Gerásim smiled again and turned to leave the room. But Iván Ilych felt his presence such a comfort that he did not want to let him go.

"One thing more, please move up that chair. No, the other one—under my feet. It is easier for me when my feet are raised."

Gerásim brought the chair, set it down gently in place, and raised Iván

Ilych's legs on to it. It seemed to Iván Ilych that he felt better while Gerásim was holding up his legs.

"It's better when my legs are higher," he said. "Place that cushion under them."

Gerásim did so. He again lifted the legs and placed them, and again Iván Ilych felt better while Gerásim held his legs. When he set them down Iván Ilych fancied he felt worse.

"Gerásim," he said. "Are you busy now?"

"Not at all, sir," said Gerásim, who had learnt from the townsfolk how to speak to gentlefolk.

"What have you still to do?"

"What have I to do? I've done everything except chopping the logs for to-morrow."

"Then hold my legs up a bit higher, can you?"

"Of course I can. Why not?" And Gerásim raised his master's legs higher and Iván Ilych thought that in that position he did not feel any pain at all.

"And how about the logs?"

"Don't trouble about that, sir. There's plenty of time."

Iván Ilych told Gerásim to sit down and hold his legs, and began to talk to him. And strange to say it seemed to him that he felt better while Gerásim held his legs up.

After that Iván Ilych would sometimes call Gerásim and get him to hold his legs on his shoulders, and he liked talking to him. Gerásim did it all easily, willingly, simply, and with a good nature that touched Iván Ilych. Health, strength, and vitality in other people were offensive to him, but Gerásim's strength and vitality did not mortify but soothed him.

What touched Iván Ilych most was the deception, the lie, which for some reason they all accepted, that he was not dying but was simply ill, and that he only need keep quiet and undergo a treatment and then something very good would result. He however knew that do what they would nothing would come of it, only still more agonizing suffering and death. This deception tortured him—their not wishing to admit what they all knew and what he knew, but wanting to lie to him concerning his terrible condition, and wishing and forcing him to participate in that lie. Those lies—lies enacted over him on the eve of his death and destined to degrade this awful, solemn act to the level of their visitings, their curtains, their sturgeon for dinner—were a terrible agony for Iván Ilych. And strangely enough, many times when they were going through their antics over him he had been within a hairbreadth of calling out to them: "Stop lying! You know and I know that I am dying. Then at least stop lying about it!" But he had never had the spirit to do it. The awful, terrible act of his dying was, he could see, reduced by those about him to the level of a casual, unpleasant, and almost indecorous incident (as if someone entered a drawing-room diffusing an unpleasant odour) and this was done by that very decorum which he had served all his life long. He saw that no one felt for him, because no one even wished to grasp his position. Only Gerásim recognized and pitied him. And so Iván Ilych felt at ease only with him. He felt comforted when Gerásim supported his legs (sometimes all night long) and refused to go to bed, saying: "Don't you worry, Iván Ilych. I'll get sleep enough later on," or when he suddenly became familiar and exclaimed: "If you weren't sick it would be another matter, but as it is, why should I grudge a little trouble?" Gerásim alone did not lie; everything showed that he alone understood the facts of the case and did not consider it necessary to disguise them, but simply felt sorry for his emaciated and enfeebled master. Once when Iván Ilych was sending him away he even said straight out: "We shall all of us die, so why should I grudge a little trouble?"—expressing the fact that he did not think his work burdensome, because he was doing it for a dying man and hoped someone would do the same for him when his time came.

Apart from this lying, or because of it, what most tormented Iván Ilych was that no one pitied him as he wished to be pitied. At certain moments after prolonged suffering he wished most of all (though he would have been ashamed to confess it) for someone to pity him as a sick child is pitied. He longed to be petted and comforted. He knew he was an important functionary, that he had a beard turning grey, and that therefore what he longed for was impossible, but still he longed for it. And in Gerásim's attitude towards him there was something akin to what he wished for, and so that attitude comforted him. Iván Ilych wanted to weep, wanted to be petted and cried over, and then his colleague Shébek would come, and instead of weeping and being petted, Iván Ilych would assume a serious, severe, and profound air, and by force of habit would express his opinion on a decision of the Court of Cassation and would stubbornly insist on that view. This falsity around him and within him did more than anything else to poison his last days.

8

It was morning. He knew it was morning because Gerásim had gone, and Peter the footman had come and put out the candles, drawn back one of the curtains, and begun quietly to tidy up. Whether it was morning or evening, Friday or Sunday, made no difference, it was all just the same: the gnawing, unmitigated, agonizing pain, never ceasing for an instant, the consciousness of life inexorably waning but not yet extinguished, the approach of that ever dreaded and hateful Death which was the only reality, and always the same falsity. What were days, weeks, hours, in such a case?

"Will you have some tea, sir?"

"He wants things to be regular, and wishes the gentlefolk to drink tea in the morning," thought Iván Ilych, and only said "No."

"Wouldn't you like to move onto the sofa, sir?"

"He wants to tidy up the room, and I'm in the way. I am uncleanliness and disorder," he thought, and said only:

"No, leave me alone."

The man went on bustling about. Iván Ilych stretched out his hand. Peter came up, ready to help.

"What is it, sir?"

"My watch."

Peter took the watch which was close at hand and gave it to his master.

"Half-past eight. Are they up?"

"No sir, except Vladímir Ivánovich," (the son) "who has gone to school. Praskóvya Fëdorovna ordered me to wake her if you asked for her. Shall I do so?"

"No, there's no need to." "Perhaps I'd better have some tea," he thought, and added aloud: "Yes, bring me some tea."

Peter went to the door, but Iván Ilych dreaded being left alone. "How can I keep him here? Oh yes, my medicine." "Peter, give me my medicine." "Why not? Perhaps it may still do me some good." He took a spoonful and swallowed it. "No, it won't help. It's all tomfoolery, all deception," he decided as soon as he became aware of the familiar, sickly, hopeless taste. "No, I can't believe in it any longer. But the pain, why this pain? If it would only cease just for a moment!" And he moaned. Peter turned towards him. "It's all right. Go and fetch me some tea."

Peter went out. Left alone Iván Ilych groaned not so much with pain, terrible though that was, as from mental anguish. Always and forever the same, always these endless days and nights. If only it would come quicker! If only *what* would come quicker? Death, darkness? . . . No, no! Anything rather than death!

When Peter returned with the tea on a tray, Iván Ilych stared at him for a time in perplexity, not realizing who and what he was. Peter was disconcerted by that look and his embarrassment brought Iván Ilych to himself.

"Oh, tea! All right, put it down. Only help me to wash and put on a clean shirt."

And Iván Ilych began to wash. With pauses for rest, he washed his hands and then his face, cleaned his teeth, brushed his hair, and looked in the glass. He was terrified by what he saw, especially by the limp way in which his hair clung to his pallid forehead.

While his shirt was being changed he knew that he would be still more frightened at the sight of his body, so he avoided looking at it. Finally he was ready. He drew on a dressing-gown, wrapped himself in a plaid, and sat down in the armchair to take his tea. For a moment he felt refreshed, but as soon as he began to drink the tea he was again aware of the same taste, and the pain also returned. He finished it with an effort, and then lay down stretching out his legs, and dismissed Peter.

Always the same. Now a spark of hope flashes up, then a sea of despair rages, and always pain: always pain, always despair, and always the same. When alone he had a dreadful and distressing desire to call someone, but he knew beforehand that with others present it would be still worse. "Another dose of morphine—to lose consciousness. I will tell him, the doctor, that he must think of something else. It's impossible, impossible, to go on like this."

An hour and another pass like that. But now there is a ring at the door bell. Perhaps it's the doctor? It is. He comes in fresh, hearty, plump, and cheerful, with that look on his face that seems to say: "There now, you're in a panic about something, but we'll arrange it all for you directly!" The doctor knows this expression is out of place here, but he has put it on once for all and can't take it off—like a man who has put on a frock-coat in the morning to pay a round of calls.

The doctor rubs his hands vigorously and reassuringly.

"Brr! How cold it is! There's such a sharp frost; just let me warm myself!" he says, as if it were only a matter of waiting till he was warm, and then he would put everything right.

"Well now, how are you?"

Iván Ilych feels that the doctor would like to say: "Well, how are our affairs?" but that even he feels that this would not do, and says instead: "What sort of a night have you had?"

Iván Ilych looks at him as much as to say: "Are you really never ashamed of lying?" But the doctor does not wish to understand this question, and Iván Ilych says: "Just as terrible as ever. The pain never leaves me and never subsides. If only something . . ."

"Yes, you sick people are always like that. . . . There, now I think I'm warm enough. Even Praskóvya Fëdorovna, who is so particular, could find no fault with my temperature. Well, now I can say good-morning," and the doctor presses his patient's hand.

Then, dropping his former playfulness, he begins with a most serious face to examine the patient, feeling his pulse and taking his temperature, and then begins the sounding and auscultation.

Iván Ilych knows quite well and definitely that all this is nonsense and pure deception, but when the doctor, getting down on his knee, leans over him, putting his ear first higher then lower, and performs various gymnastic movements over him with a significant expression on his face, Iván Ilych submits to it all as he used to submit to the speeches of the lawyers, though he knew very well that they were all lying and why they were lying.

The doctor, kneeling on the sofa, is still sounding him when Praskóvya Fëdorovna's silk dress rustles at the door and she is heard scolding Peter for not having let her know of the doctor's arrival.

She comes in, kisses her husband, and at once proceeds to prove that she has been up a long time already, and only owing to a misunderstanding failed to be there when the doctor arrived.

Iván Ilych looks at her, scans her all over, sets against her the whiteness and plumpness and cleanness of her hands and neck, the gloss of her hair, and the sparkle of her vivacious eyes. He hates her with his whole soul. And the thrill of hatred he feels for her makes him suffer from her touch.

Her attitude towards him and his disease is still the same. Just as the doctor had adopted a certain relation to his patient which he could not abandon, so had she formed one towards him—that he was not doing something he ought to do and was himself to blame, and that she reproached him lovingly for this—and she could not now change that attitude.

"You see he doesn't listen to me and doesn't take his medicine at the proper time. And above all he lies in a position that is no doubt bad for him—with his legs up."

She described how he made Gerásim hold his legs up.

The doctor smiled with a contemptuous affability that said: "What's to be done? These sick people do have foolish fancies of that kind, but we must forgive them."

When the examination was over the doctor looked at his watch, and then Praskóvya Fëdorovna announced to Iván Ilych that it was of course as he pleased, but she had sent to-day for a celebrated specialist who would examine him and have a consultation with Michael Danílovich (their regular doctor).

"Please don't raise any objections. I am doing this for my own sake," she said ironically, letting it be felt that she was doing it all for his sake and only said this to leave him no right to refuse. He remained silent, knitting his brows. He felt that he was so surrounded and involved in a mesh of falsity that it was hard to unravel anything.

Everything she did for him was entirely for her own sake, and she told him she was doing for herself what she actually was doing for herself, as if that was so incredible that he must understand the opposite.

At half-past eleven the celebrated specialist arrived. Again the sounding began and the significant conversations in his presence and in another room, about the kidneys and the appendix, and the questions and answers, with such an air of importance that again, instead of the real question of life and death which now alone confronted him, the question arose of the kidney and the appendix which were not behaving as they ought to and would now be attacked by Michael Danílovich and the specialist and forced to amend their ways.

The celebrated specialist took leave of him with a serious though not hopeless look, and in reply to the timid question Iván Ilych, with eyes glistening with fear and hope, put to him as to whether there was a chance of recovery, said that he could not vouch for it but there was a possibility. The look of hope with which Iván Ilych watched the doctor out was so pathetic that Praskóvya Fëdorovna, seeing it, even wept as she left the room to hand the doctor his fee.

The gleam of hope kindled by the doctor's encouragement did not last long. The same room, the same pictures, curtains, wall-paper, medicine bottles, were all there, and the same aching suffering body, and Iván Ilych began to moan. They gave him a subcutaneous injection and he sank into oblivion.

It was twilight when he came to. They brought him his dinner and he swallowed some beef tea with difficulty, and then everything was the same again and night was coming on.

After dinner, at seven o'clock, Praskóvya Fëdorovna came into the room in evening dress, her full bosom pushed up by her corset, and with traces of powder on her face. She had reminded him in the morning that they were going to the theatre. Sarah Bernhardt was visiting the town and they had a box, which he had insisted on their taking. Now he had forgotten about it and her toilet offended him, but he concealed his vexation when he remembered that he had himself insisted on their securing a box and going because it would be an instructive and aesthetic pleasure for the children.

Praskóvya Fëdorovna came in, self-satisfied but yet with a rather guilty air. She sat down and asked how he was, but, as he saw, only for the sake of asking and not in order to learn about it, knowing that there was nothing to learn—and then went on to what she really wanted to say: that she would not on any account have gone but that the box had been taken and Helen and their daughter were going, as well as Petríschhev (the examining magistrate, their daughter's fiancé) and that it was out of the question to let them go alone; but that she would have much preferred to sit with him for a while; and he must be sure to follow the doctor's orders while she was away.

"Oh, and Fëdor Petróvich" (the fiancé) "would like to come in. May he? And Lisa?"

"All right."

Their daughter came in in full evening dress, her fresh young flesh exposed (making a show of that very flesh which in his own case caused so much suffering), strong, healthy, evidently in love, and impatient with illness, suffering, and death, because they interfered with her happiness.

Fëdor Petróvich came in too, in evening dress, his hair curled *á la Capoul,* a tight stiff collar round his long sinewy neck, an enormous white shirt-front and narrow black trousers tightly stretched over his strong thighs. He had one white glove tightly drawn on, and was holding his opera hat in his hand.

Following him the schoolboy crept in unnoticed, in a new uniform, poor little fellow, and wearing gloves. Terribly dark shadows showed under his eyes, the meaning of which Iván Ilych knew well.

His son had always seemed pathetic to him, and now it was dreadful to see the boy's frightened look of pity. It seemed to Iván Ilych that Vásya was the only one besides Gerásim who understood and pitied him.

They sat down and again asked how he was. A silence followed. Lisa asked her mother about the opera-glasses, and there was an altercation between mother and daughter as to who had taken them and where they had been put. This occasioned some unpleasantness.

Fëdor Petróvich inquired of Iván Ilych whether he had ever seen Sarah Bernhardt. Iván Ilych did not at first catch the question, but then replied: "No, have you seen her before?"

"Yes, in *Adrienne Lecouvreur.*"

Praskóvya Fëdorovna mentioned some rôles in which Sarah Bernhardt was particularly good. Her daughter disagreed. Conversation sprang up as to the elegance and realism of her acting—the sort of conversation that is always repeated and is always the same.

In the midst of the conversation Fëdor Petróvich glanced at Iván Ilych and became silent. The others also looked at him and grew silent. Iván Ilych was staring with glittering eyes straight before him, evidently indignant with them. This had to be rectified, but it was impossible to do so. The silence had to be broken, but for a time no one dared to break it and they all became afraid that the conventional deception would suddenly become obvious and the truth become plain to all. Lisa was the first to pluck up courage and break that silence, but by trying to hide what everybody was feeling, she betrayed it.

"Well, if we are going it's time to start," she said, looking at her watch, a present from her father, and with a faint and significant smile at Fëdor Petróvich relating to something known only to them. She got up with a rustle of her dress.

They all rose, said good-night, and went away.

When they had gone it seemed to Iván Ilych that he felt better; the falsity had gone with them. But the pain remained—that same pain and that same fear that made everything monotonously alike, nothing harder and nothing easier. Everything was worse.

Again minute followed minute and hour followed hour. Everything remained the same and there was no cessation. And the inevitable end of it all became more and more terrible.

"Yes, send Gerásim here," he replied to a question Peter asked.

9

His wife returned late at night. She came in on tiptoe, but he heard her, opened his eyes, and made haste to close them again. She wished to send Gerásim away and to sit with him herself, but he opened his eyes and said: "No, go away."

"Are you in great pain?"

"Always the same."

"Take some opium."

He agreed and took some. She went away.

Till about three in the morning he was in a state of stupefied misery. It seemed to him that he and his pain were being thrust into a narrow, deep black sack, but though they were pushed further and further in they could not be pushed to the bottom. And this, terrible enough in itself, was accompanied by suffering. He was frightened yet wanted to fall through the sack, he struggled but yet co-operated. And suddenly he broke through, fell, and regained consciousness. Gerásim was sitting at the foot of the bed dozing quietly and patiently, while he himself lay with his emaciated stockinged legs resting on Gerásim's shoulders; the same shaded candle was there and the same unceasing pain.

"Go away, Gerásim," he whispered.

"It's all right, sir. I'll stay a while."

"No. Go away."

He removed his legs from Gerásim's shoulders, turned side ways onto his arm, and felt sorry for himself. He only waited till Gerásim had gone into the next room and then restrained himself no longer but wept like a child. He wept on account of his helplessness, his terrible loneliness, the cruelty of man, the cruelty of God, and the absence of God.

"Why hast Thou done all this? Why hast Thou brought me here? Why dost Thou torment me so terribly?"

He did not expect an answer and yet wept because there was no answer and could be none. The pain again grew more acute, but he did not stir and did not call. He said to himself: "Go on! Strike me! But what is it for? What have I done to Thee? What is it for?"

Then he grew quiet and not only ceased weeping but even held his breath and became all attention. It was as though he were listening not to an audible voice but to a voice of his soul, to the current of thoughts arising within him.

"What is it you want?" was the first clear conception capable of expression in words, that he heard.

"What do you want? What do you want? he repeated to himself.

"What do I want? To live and not to suffer," he answered.

And again he listened with such concentrated attention that even his pain did not distract him.

"To live? How?" asked his inner voice.

"Why, to live as I used to—well and pleasantly."

"As you lived before, well and pleasantly?" the voice repeated.

And in imagination he began to recall the best moments of his pleasant life.

But strange to say none of those best moments of his pleasant life now seemed at all what they had then seemed—none of them except the first recollections of childhood. There, in childhood, there had been something really pleasant with which it would be possible to live if it could return. But the child who had experienced that happiness existed no longer, it was like a reminiscence of somebody else.

As soon as the period began which had produced the present Iván Ilych, all that had then seemed joys now melted before his sight and turned into something trivial and often nasty.

And the further he departed from childhood and the nearer he came to the present the more worthless and doubtful were the joys. This began with the School of Law. A little that was really good was still found there—there was light-heartedness, friendship, and hope. But in the upper classes there had already been fewer of such good moments. Then during the first years of his official career, when he was in the service of the Governor, some pleasant moments again occurred: they were the memories of love for a woman. Then all became confused and there was still less of what was good; later on again there was still less that was good, and the further he went the less there was. His marriage, a mere accident, then the disenchantment that followed it, his wife's bad breath and the sensuality and hypocrisy: then the deadly official life and those preoccupations about money, a year of it, and two, and ten, and twenty, and always the same thing. And the longer it lasted the more deadly it became. "It is as if I had been going downhill while I imagined I was going up. And that is really what it was. I was going up in public opinion, but to the same extent life was ebbing away from me. And now it is all done and there is only death."

"Then what does it mean? Why? It can't be that life is so senseless and horrible. But if it really has been so horrible and senseless, why must I die and die in agony? There is something wrong!"

"Maybe I did not live as I ought to have done," it suddenly occurred to him. "But how could that be, when I did everything properly?" he replied, and immediately dismissed from his mind this, the sole solution of all the riddles of life and death, as something quite impossible.

"Then what do you want now? To live? Live how? Live as you lived in the law courts when the usher proclaimed 'The judge is coming!' The judge is coming, the judge!" he repeated to himself. "Here he is, the judge. But I am not guilty!" he exclaimed angrily. "What is it for?" And he ceased crying, but turning his face to the wall continued to ponder on the same question: Why, and for what purpose, is there all this horror? But however much he pondered he found no answer. And whenever the thought occurred to him, as it often did, that it all resulted from his not having lived as he ought to have done, he at once recalled the correctness of his whole life, and dismissed so strange an idea.

10

Another fortnight passed. Iván Ilych now no longer left his sofa. He would not lie in bed but lay on the sofa, facing the wall nearly all the time. He suffered ever the same unceasing agonies and in his loneliness pondered always on the same insoluble question: "What is this? Can it be that it is Death?" And the inner voice answered: "Yes, it is Death."

"Why these sufferings?" And the voice answered, "For no reason—they just are so." Beyond and besides this there was nothing.

From the very beginning of his illness, ever since he had first been to see the doctor, Iván Ilych's life had been divided between two contrary and alternating moods: now it was despair and the expectation of this uncomprehended and terrible death, and now hope and an intently interested observation of the functioning of his organs. Now before his eyes there was only a kidney or an intestine that temporarily evaded its duty, and now only that incomprehensible and dreadful death from which it was impossible to escape.

These two states of mind had alternated from the very beginning of his illness, but the further it progressed the more doubtful and fantastic became the conception of the kidney, and the more real the sense of impending death.

He had but to call to mind what he had been three months before and what he was now, to call to mind with what regularity he had been going downhill, for every possibility of hope to be shattered.

Latterly during that loneliness in which he found himself as he lay facing the back of the sofa, a loneliness in the midst of a populous town and surrounded by numerous acquaintances and relations but that yet could not have been more complete anywhere—either at the bottom of the sea or under the earth—during that terrible loneliness Iván Ilych had lived only in memories of the past. Pictures of his past rose before him one after another. They always began with what was nearest in time and then went back to what was most remote—to his childhood—and rested there. If he thought of the stewed prunes that had been offered him that day, his mind went back to the raw shrivelled French plums of his childhood, their peculiar flavour and the flow of saliva when he sucked their stones, and along with the memory of that taste came a whole series of memories of those days: his nurse, his brother, and their toys. "No, I mustn't think of that. . . . It is too painful," Iván Ilych said to himself, and brought himself back to the present—to the button on the back of the sofa and the creases in its morocco. "Morocco is expensive, but it does not wear well; there had been a quarrel about it. It was a different kind of quarrel and a different kind of morocco that time when we tore father's portfolio and were punished, and mamma brought us some tarts. . . ." And again his thoughts dwelt on his childhood, and again it was painful and he tried to banish them and fix his mind on something else.

Then again together with that chain of memories another series passed through his mind—of how his illness had progressed and grown worse. There also the further back he looked the more life there had been. There had been more of what was good in life and more of life itself. The two merged together. "Just as the pain went on getting worse and worse, so my life grew worse and worse," he thought. "There is one bright spot there at the back, at the beginning of life, and afterwards all becomes blacker and blacker and proceeds more and more rapidly—in inverse ratio to the square of the distance from death," thought Iván Ilych. And the example of a stone falling downwards with increasing velocity entered his mind. Life, a series of increasing sufferings, flies further and further towards its end—the most terrible suffering. "I am flying. . . ." He shuddered, shifted himself, and tried to resist, but was already aware that resistance was impossible, and again with eyes weary of gazing but unable to cease seeing what was before them, he stared at the back of the sofa and waited—awaiting that dreadful fall and shock and destruction.

"Resistance is impossible!" he said to himself. "If I could only understand what it is all for! But that too is impossible. An explanation would be possible if it could be said that I have not lived as I ought to. But it is impossible to say that," and he remembered all the legality, correctitude, and propriety of his life. "That at any rate can certainly not be admitted," he thought, and his lips smiled ironically as if someone could see that smile and be taken in by it. "There is no explanation! Agony, death. . . . What for?"

11

Another two weeks went by in this way and during that fortnight an event occurred that Iván Ilych and his wife had desired. Petríshchev formally proposed. It happened in the evening. The next day Praskóvya Fëdorovna came into her husband's room considering how best to inform him of it, but that very night there had been a fresh change for the worse in his condition. She found him still lying on the sofa but in a different position. He lay on his back, groaning and staring fixedly straight in front of him.

She began to remind him of his medicines, but he turned his eyes towards her with such a look that she did not finish what she was saying; so great an animosity, to her in particular, did that look express.

"For Christ's sake let me die in peace!" he said.

She would have gone away, but just then their daughter came in and went up to say good morning. He looked at her as he had done at his wife, and in reply to her inquiry about his health said dryly that he would soon free them all of himself. They were both silent and after sitting with him for a while went away.

"Is it our fault?" Lisa said to her mother. "It's as if we were to blame! I am sorry for papa, but why should we be tortured?"

The doctor came at his usual time. Iván Ilych answered "Yes" and "No," never taking his angry eyes from him, and at last said: "You know you can do nothing for me, so leave me alone."

"We can ease your sufferings."

"You can't even do that. Let me be."

The doctor went into the drawing-room and told Praskóvya Fëdorovna that the case was very serious and that the only resource left was opium to allay her husband's sufferings, which must be terrible.

It was true, as the doctor said, that Iván Ilych's physical sufferings were terrible, but worse than the physical sufferings were his mental sufferings which were his chief torture.

His mental sufferings were due to the fact that that night, as he looked at Gerásim's sleepy, good-natured face with its prominent cheek-bones, the question suddenly occurred to him: "What if my whole life has really been wrong?"

It occurred to him that what had appeared perfectly impossible before, namely that he had not spent his life as he should have done, might after all be true. It occurred to him that his scarcely perceptible attempts to struggle against what was considered good by the most highly placed people, those scarcely noticeable impulses which he had immediately suppressed, might have been the real thing, and all the rest false. And his professional duties and the whole arrangement of his life and of his family, and all his social and official interests, might all have been false. He tried to defend all those things to himself and suddenly felt the weakness of what he was defending. There was nothing to defend.

"But if that is so," he said to himself, "and I am leaving this life with the consciousness that I have lost all that was given me and it is impossible to rectify it—what then?"

He lay on his back and began to pass his life in review in quite a new way. In the morning when he saw first his footman, then his wife, then his daughter, and then the doctor, their every word and movement confirmed to him the awful truth that had been revealed to him during the night. In them he saw himself—all that for which he had lived—and saw clearly that it was not real at all, but a terrible and huge deception which had hidden both life and death. This consciousness intensified his physical suffering tenfold. He groaned and tossed about, and pulled at his clothing which choked and stifled him. And he hated them on that account.

He was given a large dose of opium and became unconscious, but at noon his sufferings began again. He drove everybody away and tossed from side to side.

His wife came to him and said:

"Jean, my dear, do this for me. It can't do any harm and often helps. Healthy people often do it."

He opened his eyes wide.

"What? Take communion? Why? It's unnecessary! However . . ."

She began to cry.

"Yes, do, my dear. I'll send for our priest. He is such a nice man."

"All right. Very well," he muttered.

When the priest came and heard his confession, Iván Ilych was softened and seemed to feel a relief from his doubts and consequently from his sufferings, and for a moment there came a ray of hope. He again began to think of the vermiform appendix and the possibility of correcting it. He received the sacrament with tears in his eyes.

When they laid him down again afterwards he felt a moment's ease, and the hope that he might live awoke in him again. He began to think of the operation that had been suggested to him. "To live! I want to live!" he said to himself.

His wife came in to congratulate him after his communion, and when uttering the usual conventional words she added:

"You feel better, don't you?"

Without looking at her he said "Yes."

Her dress, her figure, the expression of her face, the tone of her voice, all revealed the same thing. "This is wrong, it is not as it should be. All you have lived for and still live for is falsehood and deception, hiding life and death from you." And as soon as he admitted that thought, his hatred and his agonizing physical suffering again sprang up, and with that suffering a consciousness of the unavoidable, approaching end. And to this was added a new sensation of grinding shooting pain and a feeling of suffocation.

The expression of his face when he uttered that "yes" was dreadful. Having uttered it, he looked her straight in the eyes, turned on his face with a rapidity extraordinary in his weak state and shouted:

"Go away! Go away! and leave me alone!"

12

From that moment the screaming began that continued for three days, and was so terrible that one could not hear it through two closed doors without horror. At the moment he answered his wife he realized that he was lost, that there was no return, that the end had come, the very end, and his doubts were still unsolved and remained doubts.

"Oh! Oh! Oh!" he cried in various intonations. He had begun by screaming "I won't!" and continued screaming on the letter "o."

For three whole days, during which time did not exist for him, he struggled in that black sack into which he was being thrust by an invisible, resistless force. He struggled as a man condemned to death struggles in the hands of the executioner, knowing that he cannot save himself. And every moment he felt that despite all his efforts he was drawing nearer and nearer to what terrified him. He felt that his agony was due to his being thrust into that black hole and still more to his not being able to get right into it. He was hindered from getting into it by his conviction that his life had been a good one. That very justification of his life held him fast and prevented his moving forward, and it caused him most torment of all.

Suddenly some force struck him in the chest and side, making it still harder to breathe, and he fell through the hole and there at the bottom was a light. What had happened to him was like the sensation one sometimes experiences in a railway carriage when one thinks one is going backwards while one is really going forwards and suddenly becomes aware of the real direction.

"Yes, it was all not the right thing," he said to himself, "but that's no matter. It can be done. But what *is* the right thing?" he asked himself, and suddenly grew quiet.

This occurred at the end of the third day, two hours before his death. Just then his schoolboy son had crept softly in and gone up to the bedside. The dying man was still screaming desperately and waving his arms. His hand fell on the boy's head, and the boy caught it, pressed it to his lips, and began to cry.

At that very moment Iván Ilych fell through and caught sight of the light, and it was revealed to him that though his life had not been what it should have been, this could still be rectified. He asked himself, "What *is* the right thing?" and grew still, listening. Then he felt that someone was kissing his hand. He opened his eyes, looked at his son, and felt sorry for him. His wife came up to him and he glanced at her. She was gazing at him open-mouthed, with undried tears on her nose and cheek and a despairing look on her face. He felt sorry for her too.

"Yes, I am making them wretched," he thought. "They are sorry, but it will be better for them when I die." He wished to say this but had not the strength to utter it. "Besides, why speak? I must act," he thought. With a look at his wife he indicated his son and said: "Take him away . . . sorry for him . . . sorry for you too. . . ." He tried to add, "forgive me," but said "forego" and waved his hand, knowing that He whose understanding mattered would understand.

And suddenly it grew clear to him that what had been oppressing him and would not leave him was all dropping away at once from two sides, from ten sides, and from all sides. He was sorry for them, he must act so as not to hurt them: release them and free himself from these sufferings. "How good and how simple!" he thought. "And the pain?" he asked himself. "What has become of it? Where are you, pain?"

He turned his attention to it.

"Yes, here it is. Well, what of it? Let the pain be."

"And death . . . where is it?"

He sought his former accustomed fear of death and did not find it. "Where is it? What death?" There was no fear because there was no death.

In place of death there was light.

"So that's what it is!" he suddenly exclaimed aloud. "What joy!"

To him all this happened in a single instant, and the meaning of that instant did not change. For those present his agony continued for another two hours. Something rattled in his throat, his emaciated body twitched, then the gasping and rattle became less and less frequent.

"It is finished!" said someone near him.

He heard these words and repeated them in his soul.

"Death is finished," he said to himself. "It is no more!"

He drew in a breath, stopped in the midst of a sigh, stretched out, and died.

Translated by Louise and Aylmer Maude

Questions for Discussion

1. Describe Peter Ivánovich's responses to the death of Iván Ilych. Do the same for the widow's response.

2. In your view, what are the chief differences in tone, purpose, and point of view between each numbered section in the story?

3. What kind of person was Iván Ilych (personally, socially, politically)? Speculate about Tolstoy's reasons for focusing on the death of this kind of person.

4. After Ivan experiences *ennui* and depression for the first time, what motives begin to drive him in his life?

5. How does Ivan react to his family and friends in the last months, days, and hours of his life?

Suggestions for Writing

1. Write an essay about the role of Peter Ivánovich in Tolstoy's story.

2. Many colleges and universities now have courses in "Death and Dying." If you have taken one of these courses, write an essay about "The Death of Iván Ilych" in light of the nonfiction about death and dying that you have read.

3. How *universal* are the responses to Iván Ilych's death by his family and friends? Write an essay that attempts to answer this question.

4. " 'The Death of Iván Ilych' is depressing and morbid. Fiction should entertain us and let us escape from such emotions and 'facts of life.' " Write a journal entry in response to these statements. To what extent should fiction involve "negative" or "depressing" subjects?

Gooseberries

ANTON CHEKHOV

T he sky had been overcast since early morning; it was a still day, not hot, but tedious, as it usually is when the weather is gray and dull, when clouds have been hanging over the fields for a long time, and you wait for the rain that does not come. Ivan Ivanych, a veterinary, and Burkin, a high school teacher, were already tired with walking, and the plain seemed endless to them. Far ahead were the scarcely visible windmills of the village of Mironositzkoe; to the right lay a range of hills that disappeared in the distance beyond the village, and both of them knew that over there were the river, and fields, green willows, homesteads, and if you stood on one of the hills, you could see from there another vast plain, telegraph poles, and a train that from afar looked like a caterpillar crawling, and in clear weather you could even see the town. Now, when it was still and when nature seemed mild and pensive, Ivan Ivanych and Burkin were filled with love for this plain, and both of them thought what a beautiful land it was.

"Last time when we were in Elder Prokofy's barn," said Burkin, "you were going to tell me a story."

"Yes; I wanted to tell you about my brother."

Ivan Ivanych heaved a slow sigh and lit his pipe before beginning his story, but just then it began to rain. And five minutes later there was a downpour, and it was hard to tell when it would be over. The two men halted, at a loss; the dogs, already wet, stood with their tails between their legs and looked at them feelingly.

"We must find shelter somewhere," said Burkin. "Let's go to Alyohin's; it's quite near."

"Let's."

They turned aside and walked across a mown meadow, now going straight ahead, now bearing to the right, until they reached the road. Soon poplars came into view, a garden, then the red roofs of barns; the river gleamed, and the view opened on a broad expanse of water with a mill and a white bathing-cabin. That was Sofyino, Alyohin's place.

The mill was going, drowning out the sound of the rain; the dam was shaking. Wet horses stood near the carts, their heads drooping, and men were walking about, their heads covered with sacks. It was damp, muddy, dreary; and the water looked cold and unkind. Ivan Ivanych and Burkin felt cold and messy and uncomfortable through and through; their feet were heavy with mud and when, having crossed the dam, they climbed up to the barns, they were silent as though they were cross with each other.

The noise of a winnowing-machine came from one of the barns, the door was open, and clouds of dust were pouring from within. On the threshold stood Alyohin himself, a man of forty, tall and rotund, with long hair, looking more like a professor or an artist than a gentleman farmer. He was wearing a white blouse, badly in need of washing, that was belted with a rope, and drawers, and his high boots were plastered with mud and straw. His eyes and nose were black with dust. He recognized Ivan Ivanych and Burkin and was apparently very glad to see them.

"Please go up to the house, gentlemen," he said, smiling; "I'll be there directly, in a moment."

It was a large structure of two stories. Alyohin lived downstairs in what was formerly the stewards' quarters: two rooms that had arched ceilings and small windows; the furniture was plain, and the place smelled of rye bread, cheap vodka, and harness. He went into the showy rooms upstairs only rarely, when he had guests. Once in the house, the two visitors were met by a chambermaid, a young woman so beautiful that both of them stood still at the same moment and glanced at each other.

"You can't imagine how glad I am to see you, gentlemen," said Alyohin, joining them in the hall. "What a surprise! Pelageya," he said, turning to the chambermaid, "give the guests a change of clothes. And, come to think of it, I will change, too. But I must go and bathe first, I don't think I've had a wash since spring. Don't you want to go into the bathing-cabin? In the meanwhile things will be got ready here."

The beautiful Pelageya, with her soft, delicate air, brought them bath towels and soap, and Alyohin went to the bathing-cabin with his guests.

"Yes, it's a long time since I've bathed," he said, as he undressed. "I've an excellent bathing-cabin, as you see—it was put up by my father—but somehow I never find time to use it." He sat down on the steps and lathered his long hair and neck, and the water around him turned brown.

"I say—" observed Ivan Ivanych significantly, looking at his head.

"I haven't had a good wash for a long time," repeated Alyohin, embarrassed, and soaped himself once more; the water about him turned dark-blue, the color of ink.

Ivan Ivanych came out of the cabin, plunged into the water with a splash and swam in the rain, thrusting his arms out wide; he raised waves on which white lilies swayed. He swam out to the middle of the river and dived and a minute later came up in another spot and swam on and kept diving, trying to touch bottom. "By God!" he kept repeating delightedly, "by God!" He swam to the mill, spoke to the peasants there, and turned back and in the middle of the river lay floating, exposing his face to the rain. Burkin and Alyohin were already dressed and ready to leave, but he kept on swimming and diving. "By God!" he kept exclaiming. "Lord, have mercy on me."

"You've had enough!" Burkin shouted to him.

They returned to the house. And only when the lamp was lit in the big drawing room upstairs, and the two guests, in silk dressing-gowns and warm slippers, were lounging in armchairs, and Alyohin himself, washed and combed, wearing a new jacket, was walking about the room, evidently savoring the warmth, the cleanliness, the dry clothes and light footwear, and when pretty Pelageya, stepping noiselessly across the carpet and smiling softly, brought in a tray with tea and jam, only then did Ivan Ivanych begin his story, and it was as though not only Burkin and Alyohin were listening, but also the ladies, old and young, and the military men who looked down upon them, calmly and severely, from their gold frames.

"We are two brothers," he began, "I, Ivan Ivanych, and my brother, Nikolay Ivanych, who is two years my junior. I went in for a learned profession and became a veterinary; Nikolay at nineteen began to clerk in a provincial branch of the Treasury. Our father was a *kantonist,*[1] but he rose to be an officer and so a nobleman, a rank that he bequeathed to us together with a small estate. After his death there was a lawsuit and we lost the estate to creditors, but be that as it may, we spent our childhood in the country. Just like peasant children we passed days and nights in the fields and the woods, herded horses, stripped bast from the trees, fished, and so on. And, you know, whoever even once in his life has caught a perch or seen thrushes migrate in the autumn, when on clear, cool days they sweep in flocks over the village, will never really be a townsman and to the day of his death will have a longing for the open. My brother was unhappy in the government office. Years passed, but he went on warming the same seat, scratching away at the same papers, and thinking of one and the same thing: how to get away to the country. And little by little this vague longing turned into a definite desire, into a dream of buying a little property somewhere on the banks of a river or a lake.

"He was a kind and gentle soul and I loved him, but I never sympathized with his desire to shut himself up for the rest of his life on a little property of his own. It is a common saying that a man needs only six feet of earth. But six feet is what a corpse needs, not a man. It is also asserted that if our educated class is drawn to the land and seeks to settle on farms, that's a good thing. But these farms amount to the same six feet of earth. To retire from the city, from the struggle, from the hubbub, to go off and hide on one's own farm—that's not life, it is selfishness, sloth, it is a kind of monasticism, but monasticism without works. Man needs not six feet of earth, not a farm, but the whole globe, all of Nature, where unhindered he can display all the capacities and peculiarities of his free spirit.

"My brother Nikolay, sitting in his office, dreamed of eating his own *shchi,* which would fill the whole farmyard with a delicious aroma, of picnicking on the green grass, of sleeping in the sun, of sitting for hours on the seat by the gate gazing at field and forest. Books on agriculture and the farming items in almanacs were his joy, the delight of his soul. He liked newspapers too, but the only things he read in them were advertisements of land for sale, so many acres of tillable land and pasture, with house, garden, river, mill, and millpond. And he pictured to himself garden paths, flowers, fruit, bird-houses with starlings in them, crucians in the pond, and all that sort of thing, you know. These imaginary pictures varied with the advertisements he came upon, but somehow gooseberry bushes figured in every one of them. He could not picture to himself a single country-house, a single rustic nook, without gooseberries.

---

1.   The son of a private, registered at birth in the army and trained in a military school.

" 'Country life has its advantages,' he used to say. 'You sit on the veranda having tea, and your ducks swim in the pond, and everything smells delicious and—the gooseberries are ripening.'

"He would draw a plan of his estate and invariably it would contain the following features: a) the master's house; b) servants' quarters; c) kitchen-garden; d) a gooseberry patch. He lived meagerly: he deprived himself of food and drink; he dressed God knows how, like a beggar, but he kept on saving and salting money away in the bank. He was terribly stingy. It was painful for me to see it, and I used to give him small sums and send him something on holidays, but he would put that away too. Once a man is possessed by an idea, there is no doing anything with him.

"Years passed. He was transferred to another province, he was already past forty, yet he was still reading newspaper advertisements and saving up money. Then I heard that he was married. Still for the sake of buying a property with a gooseberry patch he married an elderly, homely widow, without a trace of affection for her, but simply because she had money. After marrying her he went on living parsimoniously, keeping her half-starved, and he put her money in the bank in his own name. She had previously been the wife of a postmaster, who had got her used to pies and cordials. This second husband did not even give her enough black bread. She began to sicken, and some three years later gave up the ghost. And, of course, it never for a moment occurred to my brother that he was to blame for her death. Money, like vodka, can do queer things to a man. Once in our town a merchant lay on his deathbed; before he died, he ordered a plateful of honey and he ate up all his money and lottery tickets with the honey, so that no one should get it. One day when I was inspecting a drove of cattle at a railway station, a cattle dealer fell under a locomotive and it sliced off his leg. We carried him in to the infirmary, the blood was gushing from the wound—a terrible business, but he kept begging us to find his leg and was very anxious about it: he had twenty rubles in the boot that was on that leg, and he was afraid they would be lost."

"That's a tune from another opera," said Burkin.

Ivan Ivanych paused a moment and then continued:

"After his wife's death, my brother began to look around for a property. Of course, you may scout about for five years and in the end make a mistake, and buy something quite different from what you have been dreaming of. Through an agent my brother bought a mortgaged estate of three hundred acres with a house, servants' quarters, a park, but with no orchard, no gooseberry patch, no duckpond. There was a stream, but the water in it was the color of coffee, for on one of its banks there was a brickyard and on the other a glue factory. But my brother was not at all disconcerted: he ordered a score of gooseberry bushes, planted them, and settled down to the life of a country gentleman.

"Last year I paid him a visit. I thought I would go and see how things were with him. In his letter to me my brother called his estate 'Chumbaroklov Waste, or Himalaiskoe' (our surname was Chimsha-Himalaisky). I reached the place in the afternoon. It was hot. Everywhere there were ditches, fences, hedges, rows of fir trees, and I was at a loss as to how to get to the yard and where to leave my horse. I made my way to the house and was met by a fat dog with reddish hair that looked like a pig. It wanted to bark, but was too lazy. The cook, a fat, barelegged woman, who also looked like a pig, came out of the kitchen and said that the master was resting after dinner. I went in to see my brother, and found him sitting up in bed, with a quilt over his knees. He had grown older, stouter, flabby; his cheeks, his nose, his lips jutted out: it looked as though he might grunt into the quilt at any moment.

"We embraced and dropped tears of joy and also of sadness at the thought that the two of us had once been young, but were now gray and nearing death. He got dressed and took me out to show me his estate.

" 'Well, how are you getting on here?' I asked.

" 'Oh, all right, thank God. I am doing very well.'

"He was no longer the poor, timid clerk he used to be but a real landowner, a gentleman. He had already grown used to his new manner of living and developed a taste for it. He ate a great deal, steamed himself in the bathhouse, was growing stout, was already having a lawsuit with the village commune and the two factories and was very much offended when the peasants failed to address him as 'Your Honor.' And he concerned himself with his soul's welfare too in a substantial, upper-class manner, and performed good deeds not simply, but pompously. And what good works! He dosed the peasants with bicarbonate and castor oil for all their ailments and on his name day he had a thanksgiving service celebrated in the center of the village, and then treated the villagers to a gallon of vodka, which he thought was the thing to do. Oh, those horrible gallons of vodka! One day a fat landowner hauls the peasants up before the rural police officer for trespassing, and the next, to mark a feast day, treats them to a gallon of vodka, and they drink and shout 'Hurrah' and when they are drunk bow down at his feet. A higher standard of living, overeating and idleness develop the most insolent self-conceit in a Russian. Nikolay Ivanych, who when he was a petty official was afraid to have opinions of his own even if he kept them to himself, now uttered nothing but incontrovertible truths and did so in the tone of a minister of state: 'Education is necessary, but the masses are not ready for it; corporal punishment is generally harmful, but in some cases it is useful and nothing else will serve.'

" 'I know the common people, and I know how to deal with them,' he would say. 'They love me. I only have to raise my little finger, and they will do anything I want.'

"And all this, mark you, would be said with a smile that bespoke kindness and intelligence. Twenty times over he repeated: 'We, of the gentry,' 'I, as a member of the gentry.' Apparently he no longer remembered that our grandfather had been a peasant and our father just a private. Even our surname, 'Chimsha-Himalaisky,' which in reality is grotesque, seemed to him sonorous, distinguished, and delightful.

"But I am concerned now not with him, but with me. I want to tell you about the change that took place in me during the few hours that I spent on his estate. In the evening when we were having tea, the cook served a plateful of gooseberries. They were not bought, they were his own gooseberries, the first ones picked since the bushes were planted. My brother gave a laugh and for a minute looked at the gooseberries in silence, with tears in his eyes—he could not speak for excitement. Then he put one berry in his mouth, glanced at me with the triumph of a child who has at last been given a toy he was longing for and said: 'How tasty!' And he ate the gooseberries greedily, and kept repeating: 'Ah, how delicious! Do taste them!'

"They were hard and sour, but as Pushkin has it,

The falsehood that exalts we cherish more
Than meaner truths that are a thousand strong.

I saw a happy man, one whose cherished dream had so obviously come true, who had attained his goal in life, who had got what he wanted, who was satisfied with his lot and with himself. For some reason an element of sadness had always mingled with my thoughts of human happiness, and now at the sight of a happy man I was assailed by an oppressive feeling bordering on despair. It weighed on me particularly at night. A bed was made up for me in a room next to my brother's bedroom, and I could hear that he was wakeful, and that he would get up again and again, go to the plate of gooseberries and eat one after another. I said to myself: how many contented, happy people there really are! What an overwhelming force they are! Look at life: the insolence and idleness of the strong, the ignorance and brutishness of the weak, horrible poverty everywhere, overcrowding, degeneration, drunkenness, hypocrisy, lying—Yet in all the houses and on all the streets there is peace and quiet; of the fifty thousand people who live in our town there is not one who would cry out, who would vent his indignation aloud. We see the people who go to market, eat by day, sleep by night, who babble nonsense, marry, grow old, good-naturedly drag their dead to the cemetery, but we do not see or hear those who suffer, and what is terrible in life goes on somewhere behind the scenes. Everything is peaceful and quiet and only mute statistics protest: so many people gone out of their minds, so many gallons of vodka drunk, so many children dead from malnutrition—And such a state of things is evidently necessary; obviously the happy man is at ease only because the unhappy ones bear their burdens in silence, and if there were not this silence, happiness would be impossible. It is a general hypnosis. Behind the door of every contented, happy man there ought to be someone standing with a little hammer and continually reminding him with a knock that there are unhappy people, that however happy he may be, life will sooner or later show him its claws, and trouble will come to him—illness, poverty, losses, and then no one will see or hear him, just as now he neither sees nor hears others. But there is no man with a hammer. The happy man lives at his ease, faintly fluttered by small daily cares, like an aspen in the wind—and all is well."

"That night I came to understand that I too had been contented and happy," Ivan Ivanych continued, getting up. "I too over the dinner table or out hunting would hold forth on how to live, what to believe, the right way to govern the people. I too would say that learning was the enemy of darkness, that education was necessary but that for the common people the three R's were sufficient for the time being. Freedom is a boon, I used to say, it is as essential as air, but we must wait awhile. Yes, that's what I used to say, and now I ask: Why must we wait?" said Ivan Ivanych, looking wrathfully at Burkin. "Why must we wait, I ask you? For what reason? I am told that nothing can be done all at once, that every idea is realized gradually, in its own time. But who is it that says so? Where is the proof that it is just? You cite the natural order of things, the law governing all phenomena, but is there law, is there order in the fact that I, a living, thinking man, stand beside a ditch and wait for it to close up of itself or fill up with silt, when I could jump over it or throw a bridge across it? And again, why must we wait? Wait, until we have no strength to live, and yet we have to live and are eager to live!

"I left my brother's place early in the morning, and ever since then it has become intolerable for me to stay in town. I am oppressed by the peace and the quiet, I am afraid to look at the windows, for there is nothing that pains me more than the spectacle of a happy family sitting at table having tea. I am an old man now and unfit for combat, I am not even capable of hating. I can only grieve inwardly, get irritated, worked up, and at night my head is ablaze with the rush of ideas and I cannot sleep. Oh, if I were young!"

Ivan Ivanych paced up and down the room excitedly and repeated, "If I were young!"

He suddenly walked up to Alyohin and began to press now one of his hands, now the other.

"Pavel Konstantinych," he said imploringly, "don't quiet down, don't let yourself be lulled to sleep! As long as you are young, strong, alert, do not cease to do good! There is no happiness and there should be none, and if life has a meaning and a purpose, that meaning and purpose is not our happiness but something greater and more rational. Do good!"

All this Ivan Ivanych said with a pitiful, imploring smile, as though he were asking a personal favor.

Afterwards all three of them sat in armchairs in different corners of the drawing room and were silent. Ivan Ivanych's story satisfied neither Burkin nor Alyohin. With the ladies and generals looking down from the golden frames, seeming alive in the dim light, it was tedious to listen to the story of the poor devil of a clerk who ate gooseberries. One felt like talking about elegant people, about women. And the fact that they were sitting in a drawing room where everything—the chandelier under its cover, the armchairs, the carpets under-foot—testified that the very people who were now looking down from the frames had once moved about here, sat and had tea, and the fact that lovely Pelageya was noiselessly moving about—that was better than any story.

Alyohin was very sleepy; he had gotten up early, before three o'clock in the morning, to get some work done, and now he could hardly keep his eyes open, but he was afraid his visitors might tell an interesting story in his absence, and he would not leave. He did not trouble to ask himself if what Ivan Ivanych had just said was intelligent or right. The guests were not talking about groats, or hay, or tar, but about something that had no direct bearing on his life, and he was glad of it and wanted them to go on.

"However, it's bedtime," said Burkin, rising. "Allow me to wish you good night."

Alyohin took leave of his guests and went downstairs to his own quarters, while they remained upstairs. They were installed for the night in a big room in which stood two old wooden beds decorated with carvings and in the corner was an ivory crucifix. The wide cool beds which had been made by the lovely Pelageya gave off a pleasant smell of clean linen.

Ivan Ivanych undressed silently and got into bed.

"Lord forgive us sinners!" he murmured, and drew the bedclothes over his head.

His pipe, which lay on the table, smelled strongly of burnt tobacco, and Burkin, who could not sleep for a long time, kept wondering where the unpleasant odor came from.

The rain beat against the window panes all night.

Questions for Discussion

1. Summarize Ivan Ivanych's reaction to the way his brother has changed. In what ways has his brother changed? To what extent do you sympathize with Ivan's reaction? Explain.

2. Ivan observes, ". . . obviously the happy man is at ease only because the unhappy ones bear the burdens in silence, and if there were not this silence, happiness would be impossible." In your view, how accurate is this observation, and how applicable is it nowadays?

3. The narrator observes that Burkin and Alyohin are not satisfied with Ivan's story, and that the ambience of the drawing room "was better than any story." Explain why Ivan's story is "unsatisfying" to these men, and explain how their reaction might be taken as Chekhov's ironic comment on his own fiction.

4. Explain the possible significance of the story's last two images: the unpleasant-smelling pipe and the rain beating on the windowpanes. Two what extent are these symbols?

5. Compare and contrast the way Turgenev uses descriptions of weather to begin his story with the way Chekhov uses them to begin "Gooseberries."

Suggestions for Writing

1. In your journal, write about a relative or friend who, like Ivan's brother, has changed in ways that puzzle or dissatisfy you.

2. The fourth question for discussion concerns two key images in "Gooseberries." Write an essay that interprets these and other images in Chekhov's story.

3. Write an essay about Burkin's and Alyohin's response to Ivan and his story.

4. Since Chekhov is regarded as one precursor of the modern fiction writer, write an essay that explains the "modernness" of "Gooseberries." You many want to compare and contrast it with a specific contemporary story.

5. Write a story that features a character who tells a story to other characters—a "story within a story," that is.

The Pupil

HENRY JAMES

I

The poor young man hesitated and procrastinated: it cost him such an effort to broach the subject of terms, to speak of money to a person who spoke only of feelings and, as it were, of the aristocracy. Yet he was unwilling to take leave, treating his engagement as settled, without some more conventional glance in that direction that he could find an opening for in the manner of the large, affable lady who sat there drawing a pair of soiled *gants de Suède* through a fat, jewelled hand and, at once pressing and gliding, repeated over and over everything but the thing he would have liked to hear. He would have liked to hear the figure of his salary; but just as he was nervously about to sound that note the little boy came back—the little boy Mrs. Moreen had sent out of the room to fetch her fan. He came back without the fan, only with the casual observation that he couldn't find it. As he dropped this cynical confession he looked straight and hard at the candidate for the honour of taking his education in hand. This personage reflected, somewhat grimly, that the first thing he should have to teach his little charge would be to appear to address himself to his mother when he spoke to her—especially not to make her such an improper answer as that.

When Mrs. Moreen bethought herself of this pretext for getting rid of their companion, Pemberton supposed it was precisely to approach the delicate subject of his remuneration. But it had been only to say some things about her son which it was better that a boy of eleven shouldn't catch. They were extravagantly to his advantage, save when she lowered her voice to sigh, tapping her left side familiarly: "And all overclouded by *this,* you know—all at the mercy of a weakness—!" Pemberton gathered that the weakness was in the region of the heart. He had known the poor child was not robust: this was the basis on which he had been invited to treat, through an English lady, an Oxford acquaintance, then at Nice, who happened to know both his needs and those of the amiable American family looking out for something really superior in the way of a resident tutor.

The young man's impression of his prospective pupil, who had first come into the room, as if to see for himself, as soon as Pemberton was admitted, was not quite the soft solicitation the visitor had taken for granted. Morgan Moreen was, somehow, sickly without being delicate, and that he looked intelligent (it is true Pemberton wouldn't have enjoyed his being stupid), only added to the suggestion that, as with his big mouth and big ears he really couldn't be called pretty, he might be unpleasant. Pemberton was modest—he was even timid; and the chance that his small scholar might prove cleverer than himself had quite figured, to his nervousness, among the dangers of an untried experiment. He reflected, however, that these were risks one had to run when one accepted a position, as it was called, in a private family; when as yet one's University honours had, pecuniarily speaking, remained barren. At any rate, when Mrs. Moreen got up as if to intimate that, since it was understood he would enter upon his duties within the week she would let him off now, he succeeded, in spite of the presence of the child, in squeezing out a phrase about the rate of payment. It was not the fault of the conscious smile which seemed a reference to the lady's expensive identity, if the allusion did not sound rather vulgar. This was exactly because she became still more gracious to reply: "Oh! I can assure you that all that will be quite regular."

Pemberton only wondered, while he took up his hat, what "all that" was to amount to—people had such different ideas. Mrs. Moreen's words, however, seemed to commit the family to a pledge definite enough to elicit from the child a strange little comment, in the shape of the mocking, foreign ejaculation, "Oh, là-là!"

Pemberton, in some confusion, glanced at him as he walked slowly to the window with his back turned, his hands in his pockets and the air in his elderly shoulders of a boy who didn't play. The young man wondered if he could teach him to play, though his mother had said it would never do and that this was why school was impossible. Mrs. Moreen exhibited no discomfiture; she only continued blandly: "Mr. Moreen will be delighted to meet your wishes. As I told you, he has been called to London for a week. As soon as he comes back you shall have it out with him."

This was so frank and friendly that the young man could only reply, laughing as his hostess laughed: "Oh! I don't imagine we shall have much of a battle."

"They'll give you anything you like," the boy remarked unexpectedly, returning from the window. "We don't mind what anything costs—we live awfully well."

"My darling, you're too quaint!" his mother exclaimed, putting out to caress him a practiced but ineffectual hand. He slipped out of it, but looked with intelligent, innocent eyes at Pemberton, who had already had time to notice that from one moment to the other his small satiric face seemed to change its time of life. At this moment it was infantine; yet it appeared also to be under the influence of curious intuitions and knowledges. Pemberton rather disliked precocity, and he was disappointed to find gleams of it in a disciple not yet in his teens. Nevertheless he divined on the spot that Morgan wouldn't prove a bore. He would prove on the contrary a kind of excitement. This idea held the young man, in spite of a certain repulsion.

"You pompous little person! We're not extravagant!" Mrs. Moreen gayly protested, making another unsuccessful attempt to draw the boy to her side. "You must know what to expect," she went on to Pemberton.

"The less you expect the better!" her companion interposed. "But we *are* people of fashion."

"Only so far as *you* make us so!" Mrs. Moreen mocked, tenderly. "Well, then, on Friday—don't tell me you're superstitious—and mind you don't fail us. Then you'll see us all. I'm so sorry the girls are out. I guess you'll like the girls. And, you know, I've another son, quite different from this one."

"He tries to imitate me," said Morgan to Pemberton.

"He tries? Why, he's twenty years old!" cried Mrs. Moreen.

"You're very witty," Pemberton remarked to the child—a proposition that his mother echoed with enthusiasm, declaring that Morgan's sallies were the delight of the house. The boy paid no heed to this; he only inquired abruptly of the visitor, who was surprised afterwards that he hadn't struck him as offensively forward: "Do you *want* very much to come?"

"Can you doubt it, after such a description of what I shall hear?" Pemberton replied. Yet he didn't want to come at all; he was coming because he had to go somewhere, thanks to the collapse of his fortune at the end of a year abroad, spent on the system of putting his tiny patrimony into a single full wave of experience. He had had his full wave, but he couldn't pay his hotel bill. Moreover, he had caught in the boy's eyes the glimpse of a far-off appeal.

"Well, I'll do the best I can for you," said Morgan; with which he turned away again. He passed out of one of the long windows; Pemberton saw him go and lean on the parapet of the terrace. He remained there while the young man took leave of his mother, who, on Pemberton's looking as if he expected a farewell from him, interposed with: "Leave him, leave him; he's so strange!" Pemberton suspected she was afraid of something he might say. "He's a genius—you'll love him," she added. "He's much the most interesting person in the family." And before he could invent some civility to oppose to this, she wound up with: "But we're all good, you know!"

"He's a genius—you'll love him!" were words that recurred to Pemberton before the Friday, suggesting, among other things that geniuses were not invariably lovable. However, it was all the better if there was an element that would make tutorship absorbing: he had perhaps taken too much for granted that it would be dreary. As he left the villa after his interview, he looked up at the balcony and saw the child leaning over it. "We shall have great larks!" he called up.

Morgan hesitated a moment; then he answered, laughing: "By the time you come back I shall have thought of something witty!"

This made Pemberton say to himself: "After all he's rather nice."

II

On the Friday he saw them all, as Mrs. Moreen had promised, for her husband had come back and the girls and the other son were at home. Mr. Moreen had a white moustache, a confiding manner and, in his buttonhole, the ribbon of a foreign order—bestowed, as Pemberton eventually learned, for services. For what services he never clearly ascertained: this was a point—one of a large number—that Mr. Moreen's manner never confided. What it emphatically did confide was that he was a man of the world. Ulick, the firstborn, was in visible training for the same profession—under the disadvantage as yet, however, of a buttonhole only feebly floral and a moustache with no pretensions to type. The girls had hair and figures and manners and small fat feet, but had never been out alone. As for Mrs. Moreen, Pemberton saw on a nearer view that her elegance was intermittent and her parts didn't always match. Her husband, as she had promised, met with enthusiasm Pemberton's ideas in regard to a salary. The young man had endeavoured to make them modest, and Mr. Moreen confided to him that *he* found them positively meagre. He further assured him that he aspired to be intimate with his children, to be their best friend, and that he was always looking out for them. That was what he went off for, to London and other places—to look out; and this vigilance was the theory of life, as well as the real occupation, of the whole family. They all looked out, for they were very frank on the subject of its being necessary. They desired it to be understood that they were earnest people, and also that their fortune, though quite adequate for earnest people, required the most careful administration. Mr. Moreen, as the parent bird, sought sustenance for the nest. Ulick found sustenance mainly at the club, where Pemberton guessed that it was usually served on green cloth. The girls used to do up their hair and their frocks themselves, and our young man felt appealed to be glad, in regard to Morgan's education, that, though it must naturally be of the best, it didn't cost too much. After a little he *was* glad, forgetting at times his own needs in the interest inspired by the child's nature and education and the pleasure of making easy terms for him.

During the first weeks of their acquaintance Morgan had been as puzzling as a page in an unknown language—altogether different from the obvious little Anglo-Saxons who had misrepresented childhood to Pemberton. Indeed the whole mystic volume in which the boy had been bound demanded some practice in translation. To-day, after a considerable interval, there is something phantasma-goric, like a prismatic reflection or a serial novel, in Pemberton's memory of the queerness of the Moreens. If it were not for a few tangible tokens—a lock of Morgan's hair, cut by his own hand, and the half-dozen letters he got from him when they were separated—the whole episode and the figures peopling it would seem too inconsequent for anything but dreamland. The queerest thing about them was their success (as it appeared to him for a while at the time), for he had never seen a family so brilliantly equipped for failure. Wasn't it success to have kept him so hatefully long? Wasn't it success to have drawn him in that first morning at *déjeuner,* the Friday he came—it was enough to *make* one superstitious—so that he utterly committed himself, and this not by calculation or a *mot d' ordre,* but by a happy instinct which made them, like a band of gypsies, work so neatly together? They amused him as much as if they had really been a band of gypsies. He was still young and had not seen much of the world—his English years had been intensely usual; therefore the reversed conventions of the Moreens (for they had their standards), struck him as topsy-turvy. He had encountered nothing like them at Oxford; still less had any such note been struck to his younger American ear during the four years at Yale in which he had richly supposed himself to be reacting against Puritanism. The reaction of the Moreens, at any rate, went ever so much further. He had thought himself very clever that first day in hitting them all off in his mind with the term "cosmopolite." Later, it seemed feeble and colourless enough—confessedly, helplessly provisional.

However, when he first applied it to them he had a degree of joy—for an instructor he was still empirical—as if from the apprehension that to live with them would really be to see life. Their sociable strangeness was an intimation of that—their chatter of tongues, their gaiety and good humour, their infinite dawdling (they were always getting themselves up, but it took forever, and Pemberton had once found Mr. Moreen shaving in the drawing-room), their

French, their Italian and, in the spiced fluency, their cold, tough slices of American. They lived on macaroni and coffee (they had these articles prepared in perfection), but they knew recipes for a hundred other dishes. They overflowed with music and song, were always humming and catching each other up, and had a kind of professional acquaintance with continental cities. They talked of "good places" as if they had been strolling players. They had at Nice a villa, a carriage, a piano and a banjo, and they went to official parties. They were a perfect calendar of the "days" of their friends, which Pemberton knew them, when they were indisposed, to get out of bed to go to, and which made the week larger than life when Mrs. Moreen talked of them with Paula and Amy. Their romantic initiations gave their new inmate at first an almost dazzling sense of culture. Mrs. Moreen had translated something, at some former period—an author whom it made Pemberton feel *borné* never to have heard of. They could imitate Venetian and sing Neapolitan, and when they wanted to say something very particular they communicated with each other in an ingenious dialect of their own—a sort of spoken cipher, which Pemberton at first took for Volapuk, but which he learned to understand as he would not have understood Volapuk.

"It's the family language—Ultramoreen," Morgan explained to him drolly enough; but the boy rarely condescended to use it himself, though he attempted colloquial Latin as if he had been a little prelate.

Among all the "days" with which Mrs. Moreen's memory was taxed she managed to squeeze in one of her own, which her friends sometimes forgot. But the house derived a frequented air from the number of fine people who were freely named there and from several mysterious men with foreign titles and English clothes whom Morgan called the princes and who, on sofas with the girls, talked French very loud, as if to show they were saying nothing improper. Pemberton wondered how the princes could ever propose in that tone and so publicly: he took for granted cynically that this was what was desired of them. Then he acknowledged that even for the chance of such an advantage Mrs. Moreen would never allow Paula and Amy to receive alone. These young ladies were not at all timid, but it was just the safeguards that made them so graceful. It was a houseful of Bohemians who wanted tremendously to be Philistines.

In one respect, however, certainly, they achieved no rigour—they were wonderfully amiable and ecstatic about Morgan. It was a genuine tenderness, an artless admiration, equally stong in each. They even praised his beauty, which was small, and were rather afraid of him, as if they recognized that he was of a finer clay. They called him a little angel and a little prodigy and pitied his want of health effusively. Pemberton feared at first that their extravagance would make him hate the boy, but before this happened he had become extravagant himself. Later, when he had grown rather to hate the others, it was a bribe to patience for him that they were at any rate nice about Morgan, going on tiptoe if they fancied he was showing symptoms, and even giving up somebody's "day" to procure him a pleasure. But mixed with this was the oddest wish to make him independent, as if they felt that they were not good enough for him. They passed him over to Pemberton very much as if they wished to force a constructive adoption on the obliging bachelor and shirk altogether a responsibility. They were delighted when they perceived that Morgan liked his preceptor, and could think of no higher praise for the young man. It was strange how they contrived to reconcile the appearance, and indeed the essential fact, of adoring the child with their eagerness to wash their hands of him. Did they want to get rid of him before he should find them out? Pemberton was finding them out month by month. At any rate, the boy's relations turned their backs with exaggerated delicacy, as if to escape the charge of interfering. Seeing in time how little he had in common with them (it was by *them* he first observed it—they proclaimed it with complete humility), his preceptor was moved to speculate on the mysteries of transmission, the far jumps of heredity. Where his detachment from most of the things they represented had come from was more than an observer could say—it certainly had burrowed under two or three generations.

As for Pemberton's own estimate of his pupil, it was a good while before he got the point of view, so little had he been prepared for it by the smug young barbarians to whom the tradition of tutorship, as hitherto revealed to him, had been adjusted. Morgan was scrappy and surprising, deficient in many properties supposed common to the *genus* and abounding in others that were the portion only of the supernaturally clever. One day Pemberton made a great stride: it cleared up the question to perceive that Morgan *was* supernaturally clever and that, though the formula was temporarily meagre, this would be the only assumption on which one could successfully deal with him. He had the general quality of a child for whom life had not been simplified by school, a kind of homebred sensibility which might have been bad for himself but was charming for others, and a whole range of refinement and perception—little musical vibrations as taking as picked-up airs—begotten by wandering about Europe at the tail of his migratory tribe. This might not have been an education to recommend in advance, but its results with Morgan were as palpable as a fine texture. At the same time he had in his composition a sharp spice of stoicism, doubtless the fruit of having had to begin early to bear pain, which produced the impression of pluck and made it of less consequence that he might have been thought at school rather a polyglot little beast. Pemberton indeed quickly found himself rejoicing that school was out of the question: in any million of boys it was probably good for all but one, and Morgan was that millionth. It would have made him comparative and superior—it might have made him priggish. Pemberton would try to be school himself—a bigger seminary than five hundred grazing donkeys; so that, winning no prizes, the boy would remain unconscious and irresponsible and amusing—amusing, because, though life was already intense in his childish nature, freshness still made there a strong draught for jokes. It turned out that even in the still air of Morgan's various disabilities jokes flourished greatly. He was a pale, lean, acute, undeveloped little cosmopolite, who liked intellectual gymnastics and who, also, as regards the behaviour of mankind, had noticed more things than you might suppose, but who nevertheless had his proper playroom of superstitions, where he smashed a dozen toys a day.

III

At Nice once, towards evening, as the pair sat resting in the open air after a walk, looking over the sea at the pink western lights, Morgan said suddenly to his companion: "Do you like it—you know, being with us all in this intimate way?"

"My dear fellow, why should I stay if I didn't?"

"How do I know you will stay? I'm almost sure you won't, very long."

"I hope you don't mean to dismiss me," said Pemberton.

Morgan considered a moment, looking at the sunset. "I think if I did right I ought to."

"Well, I know I'm supposed to instruct you in virtue; but in that case don't do right."

"You're very young—fortunately," Morgan went on, turning to him again.

"Oh yes, compared with you!"

"Therefore, it won't matter so much if you do lose a lot of time."

"That's the way to look at it," said Pemberton accommodatingly.

They were silent a minute; after which the boy asked: "Do you like my father and mother very much?"

"Dear me, yes. They're charming people."

Morgan received this with another silence; then, unexpectedly, familiarly, but at the same time affectionately, he remarked: "You're a jolly old humbug!"

For a particular reason the words made Pemberton change colour. The boy noticed in an instant that he had turned red, whereupon he turned red himself and the pupil and the master exchanged a longish glance in which there was a consciousness of many more things than are usually touched upon, even tacitly, in such a relation. It produced for Pemberton an embarrassment; it raised, in a shadowy form, a question (this was the first glimpse of it), which was destined to play as singular and, as he imagined, owing to the altogether peculiar conditions, an unprecedented part in his intercourse with his little companion. Later, when he found himself talking with this small boy in a way in which few small boys could ever have been talked with, he thought of that clumsy moment on the bench at Nice as the dawn of an understanding that had broadened. What had added to the clumsiness then was that he thought it his duty to declare to Morgan that he might abuse him (Pemberton) as much as he liked, but must never abuse his parents. To this Morgan had the easy reply that he hadn't dreamed of abusing them; which appeared to be true: it put Pemberton in the wrong.

"Then why am I a humbug for saying *I* think them charming?" the young man asked, conscious of a certain rashness.

"Well—they're not *your* parents."

"They love you better than anything in the world—never forget that," said Pemberton.

"Is that why you like them so much?"

"They're very kind to me," Pemberton replied, evasively.

"You *are* a humbug!" laughed Morgan, passing an arm into his tutor's. He leaned against him, looking off at the sea again and swinging his long, thin legs.

"Don't kick my shins," said Pemberton, while he reflected: "Hang it, I can't complain of them to the child!"

"There's another reason, too," Morgan went on, keeping his legs still.

"Another reason for what?"

"Besides their not being your parents."

"I don't understand you," said Pemberton.

"Well, you will before long. All right!"

Pemberton did understand, fully, before long; but he made a fight even with himself before he confessed it. He thought it the oddest thing to have a struggle with the child about. He wondered he didn't detest the child for launching him in such a struggle. But by the time it began the resource of detesting the child was closed to him. Morgan was a special case, but to know him was to accept him on his own odd terms. Pemberton had spent his aversion to special cases before arriving at knowledge. When at last he did arrive he felt that he was in an extreme predicament. Against every interest he had attached himself. They would have to meet things together. Before they went home that evening, at Nice, the boy had said, clinging to his arm:

"Well, at any rate you'll hang on to the last."

"To the last?"

"Till you're fairly beaten."

"*You* ought to be fairly beaten!" cried the young man, drawing him closer.

IV

A year after Pemberton had come to live with them Mr. and Mrs. Moreen suddenly gave up the villa at Nice. Pemberton had got used to suddenness, having seen it practiced on a considerable scale during two jerky little tours—one in Switzerland the first summer, and the other late in the winter, when they all ran down to Florence and then, at the end of ten days, liking it much less than they had intended, straggled back in mysterious depression. They had returned to Nice "for ever," as they said; but this didn't prevent them from squeezing, one rainy, muggy May night, into a second-class railway-carriage—you could never tell by which class they would travel—where Pemberton helped them to stow away a wonderful collection of bundles and bags. The explanation of this manoeuvre was that they had determined to spend the summer "in some bracing place;" but in Paris they dropped into a small furnished apartment—a fourth floor in a third-rate avenue, where there was a smell on the staircase and the *portier* was hateful—and passed the next four months in blank indigence.

The better part of this baffled sojourn was for the preceptor and his pupil, who, visiting the Invalides and Notre Dame, the Conciergerie and all the museums, took a hundred remunerative rambles. They learned to know their Paris, which was useful, for they came back another year for a longer stay, the general character of which in Pemberton's memory to-day mixes pitiably and confusedly with that of the first. He sees Morgan's shabby knickerbockers—the everlasting pair that didn't match his blouse and that as he grew longer could only grow faded. He remembers the particular holes in his three or four pair of coloured stockings.

Morgan was dear to his mother, but he never was better dressed than was absolutely necessary—partly, no doubt, by his own fault, for he was as indifferent to his appearance as a German philosopher. "My dear fellow, you *are* coming to pieces," Pemberton would say to him in sceptical remonstrance; to which the child would reply, looking at him serenely up and down: "My dear fellow, so are you! I don't want to cast you in the shade." Pemberton could have no rejoinder for this—the assertion so closely represented the fact. If however the deficiencies of his own wardrobe were a chapter by themselves he didn't like his little charge to look too poor. Later he used to say: "Well, if we are poor, why, after all, shouldn't we look it?" and he consoled himself with thinking there was something rather elderly and gentlemanly in Morgan's seediness—it differed from the untidiness of the urchin who plays and spoils his things. He could trace perfectly the degrees by which, in proportion as her little son confined himself to his tutor for society, Mrs. Moreen shrewdly forbore to renew his garments. She did nothing that didn't show, neglected him because he escaped notice, and then, as he illustrated this clever policy, discouraged at home his public appearances. Her position was logical enough—those members of her family who did show had to be showy.

During this period and several others Pemberton was quite aware of how he and his comrade might strike people; wandering languidly through the Jardin des Plantes as if they had nowhere to go, sitting, on the winter days, in the galleries of the Louvre, so splendidly ironical to the homeless, as if for the advantage of the *calorifère*. They joked about it sometimes: it was the sort of joke that was perfectly within the boy's compass. They figured themselves as part of the vast, vague, hand-to-mouth multitude of the enormous city and pretended they were proud of their position in it—it showed them such a lot of life and made them conscious of a sort of democratic brotherhood. If Pemberton could not feel a sympathy in destitution with his small companion (for after all Morgan's fond parents would never have let him really suffer), the boy would at least feel it with him, so it came to the same thing. He used sometimes to wonder what people would think they were—fancy they were looked askance at, as if it might be a suspected case of kidnapping. Morgan wouldn't be taken for a young patrician with a preceptor—he wasn't smart enough; though he might pass for his companion's sickly little brother. Now and then he had a five-franc piece, and except once, when they bought a couple of lovely neckties, one of which he made Pemberton accept, they laid it out scientifically in old books. It was a great day, always spent on the quays, rummaging among the dusty boxes that garnish the parapets. These were occasions that helped them to live, for their books ran low very soon after the beginning of their acquaintance. Pemberton had a good many in England, but he was obliged to write to a friend and ask him kindly to get some fellow to give him something for them.

If the bracing climate was untasted that summer the young man had an idea that at the moment they were about to make a push the cup had been dashed from their lips by a movement of his own. It had been his first blow-out, as he called it, with his patrons; his first successful attempt (though there was little other success about it), to bring them to a consideration of his impossible position. As the ostensible eve of a costly journey the moment struck him as a good one to put in a signal protest—to present an ultimatum. Ridiculous as it sounded he had never yet been able to compass an uninterrupted private interview with the elder pair or with either of them singly. They were always flanked by their elder children, and poor Pemberton usually had his own little charge at his side. He was conscious of its being a house in which the surface of one's delicacy got rather smudged; nevertheless he had kept the bloom of his scruple against announcing to Mr. and Mrs. Moreen with publicity that he couldn't go on longer without a little money. He was still simple enough to suppose Ulick and Paula and Amy might not know that since his arrival he had only had a hundred and forty francs; and he was magnanimous enough to wish not to compromise their parents in their eyes. Mr. Moreen now listened to him, as he listened to every one and to everything, like a man of the world, and seemed to appeal to him—though not of course too grossly—to try and be a little more of one himself. Pemberton recognised the importance of the character from the advantage it gave Mr. Moreen. He was not even confused, whereas poor Pemberton was more so than there was any reason for. Neither was he surprised—at least any more than a gentleman had to be who freely confessed himself a little shocked, though not, strictly, at Pemberton.

"We must go into this, mustn't we, dear?" he said to his wife. He assured his young friend that the matter should have his very best attention; and he melted into space as elusively as if, at the door, he were taking an inevitable but deprecatory precedence. When, the next moment, Pemberton found himself alone with Mrs. Moreen it was to hear her say: "I see, I see," stroking the roundness of her chin and looking as if she were only hesitating between a dozen easy remedies. If they didn't make their push Mr. Moreen could at least disappear for several days. During his absence his wife took up the subject again spontaneously, but her contribution to it was merely that she had thought all the while they were getting on so beautifully. Pemberton's reply to this revelation was that unless they immediately handed him a substantial sum he would leave them for ever. He knew she would wonder how he would get away, and for a moment expected her to inquire. She didn't, for which he was almost grateful to her, so little was he in a position to tell.

"You won't, you know you won't—you're too interested," she said. "You *are* interested, you know you are, you dear, kind man!" She laughed, with almost condemnatory archness, as if it were a reproach (but she wouldn't insist), while she flirted a soiled pocket-handkerchief at him.

Pemberton's mind was fully made up to quit the house the following week. This would give him time to get an answer to a letter he had despatched to England. If he did nothing of the sort—that is, if he stayed another year and then went away only for three months—it was not merely because before the answer to his letter came (most unsatisfactory when it did arrive), Mr. Moreen generously presented him—again with all the precautions of a man of the world—three hundred francs. He was exasperated to find that Mrs. Moreen was right, that he couldn't bear to leave the child. This stood out clearer for the very reason that, the night of his desperate appeal to his patrons, he had seen fully for the first time where he was. Wasn't it another proof of the success with which those patrons practiced their arts that they had managed to avert for so long the illuminating flash? It descended upon Pemberton with a luridness which perhaps would have struck a spectator as comically excessive, after he had returned to his little servile room, which looked into a close court where a bare, dirty opposite wall took, with the sound of shrill clatter, the reflection of lighted back-windows. He had simply given himself away to a band of adventurers. The idea, the word itself, had a sort of romantic horror for him—he had always lived on such safe lines. Later it assumed a more interesting, almost a soothing, sense: it pointed a moral, and Pemberton could enjoy a moral. The Moreens were adventurers not merely because they didn't pay their debts, because they lived on society, but because their whole view of life, dim and confused and instinctive, like that of clever colour-blind animals, was speculative and rapacious and mean. Oh! they were "respectable," and that only made them more *immondes*. The young man's analysis of them put it at last very simply—they were adventurers because they were abject snobs. That was the completest account of them—it was the law of their being. Even when this truth became vivid to their ingenious inmate he remained unconscious of how much his mind had been prepared for it by the extraordinary little boy who had now become such a complication in his life. Much less could he then calculate on the information he was still to owe to the extraordinary little boy.

V

But it was during the ensuing time that the real problem came up—the problem of how far it was excusable to discuss the turpitude of parents with a child of twelve, of thirteen, of fourteen. Absolutely inexcusable and quite impossible it of course at first appeared; and indeed the question didn't press for a while after Pemberton had received his three hundred francs. They produced a sort of lull, a relief from the sharpest pressure. Pemberton frugally amended his wardrobe and even had a few francs in his pocket. He thought the Moreens looked at him as if he were almost too smart, as if they ought to take care not to spoil him. If Mr. Moreen hadn't been such a man of the world he would perhaps have said something to him about his neckties. But Mr. Moreen was always enough a man of the world to let things pass—he had certainly shown that. It was singular how Pemberton guessed that Morgan, though saying nothing about it, knew something had happened. But three hundred francs, especially when one owed money, couldn't last for ever; and when they were gone—the boy knew when they were gone—Morgan did say something. The party had returned to Nice at the beginning of the winter, but not to the charming villa. They went to an hotel, where they stayed three months, and then they went to another hotel, explaining that they had left the first because they had waited and waited and couldn't get the rooms they wanted. These apartments, the rooms they wanted, were generally very splendid; but fortunately they never *could* get them—fortunately, I mean, for Pemberton, who reflected always that if they had got them there would have been still less for educational expenses. What Morgan said at last was said suddenly, irrelevantly, when the moment came, in the middle of a lesson, and consisted of the apparently unfeeling words: "You ought to *filer*, you know—you really ought."

Pemberton stared. He had learnt enough French slang from Morgan to know that to *filer* meant to go away. "Ah, my dear fellow, don't turn me off!"

Morgan pulled a Greek lexicon toward him (he used a Greek-German), to look out a word, instead of asking it of Pemberton. "You can't go on like this, you know."

"Like what, my boy?"

"You know they don't pay you up," said Morgan, blushing and turning his leaves.

"Don't pay me?" Pemberton stared again and feigned amazement. "What on earth put that into your head?"

"It has been there a long time," the boy replied, continuing his search.

Pemberton was silent, then he went on: "I say, what are you hunting for? They pay me beautifully."

"I'm hunting for the Greek for transparent fiction," Morgan dropped.

"Find that rather for gross impertinence, and disabuse your mind. What do I want of money?"

"Oh, that's another question!"

Pemberton hesitated—he was drawn in different ways. The severely correct thing would have been to tell the boy that such a matter was none of his business and bid him go on with his lines. But they were really too intimate for that; it was not the way he was in the habit of treating him; there had been no reason it should be. On the other hand Morgan had quite lighted on the truth—he really shouldn't be able to keep it up much longer; therefore why not let him know one's real motive for forsaking him? At the same time it wasn't decent to abuse to one's pupil the family of one's pupil; it was better to misrepresent than to do that. So in reply to Morgan's last exclamation he just declared, to dismiss the subject, that he had received several payments.

"I say—I say!" the boy ejaculated, laughing.

"That's all right," Pemberton insisted. "Give me your written rendering."

Morgan pushed a copybook across the table, and his companion began to read the page, but with something running in his head that made it no sense. Looking up after a minute or two he found the child's eyes fixed on him, and he saw something strange in them. Then Morgan said: "I'm not afraid of the reality."

"I haven't yet seen the thing that you *are* afraid of—I'll do you that justice!"

This came out with a jump (it was perfectly true), and evidently gave Morgan pleasure. "I've thought of it a long time," he presently resumed.

"Well, don't think of it any more."

The child appeared to comply, and they had a comfortable and even an amusing hour. They had a theory that they were very thorough, and yet they seemed always to be in the amusing part of lessons, the intervals between the tunnels, where there were waysides and views. Yet the morning was brought to a violent end by Morgan's suddenly leaning his arms on the table, burying his head in them and bursting into tears. Pemberton would have been startled at any rate; but he was doubly startled because, as it then occurred to him, it was the first time he had ever seen the boy cry. It was rather awful.

The next day, after much thought, he took a decision and, believing it to be just, immediately acted upon it. He cornered Mr. and Mrs. Moreen again and informed them that if, on the spot, they didn't pay him all they owed him, he would not only leave their house, but would tell Morgan exactly what had brought him to it.

"Oh, you *haven't* told him?" cried Mrs. Moreen, with a pacifying hand on her well-dressed bosom.

"Without warning you? For what do you take me?"

Mr. and Mrs. Moreen looked at each other, and Pemberton could see both that they were relieved and that there was a certain alarm in their relief. "My dear fellow," Mr. Moreen demanded, "what use *can* you have, leading the quiet life we all do, for such a lot of money?"—an inquiry to which Pemberton made no answer, occupied as he was in perceiving that what passed in the mind of his patrons was something like: "Oh, then, if we've felt that the child, dear little angel, has judged us and how he regards us, and we haven't been betrayed, he must have guessed—and, in short, it's *general!*" an idea that rather stirred up Mr. and Mrs. Moreen, as Pemberton had desired that it should. At the same time, if he had thought that his threat would do something towards bringing them round, he was disappointed to find they had taken for granted (how little they appreciated his delicacy!) that he had already given them away to his pupil. There was a mystic uneasiness in their parental breasts, and that was the way they had accounted for it. None the less his threat did touch them; for if they had escaped it was only to meet a new danger. Mr. Moreen appealed to Pemberton, as usual, as a man of the world; but his wife had recourse, for the first time since the arrival of their inmate, to a fine *hauteur,* reminding him that a devoted mother, with her child, had arts that protected her against gross misrepresentation.

"I should misrepresent you grossly if I accused you of common honesty!" the young man replied; but as he closed the door behind him sharply, thinking he had not done himself much good, while Mr. Moreen lighted another cigarette, he heard Mrs. Moreen shout after him, more touchingly:

"Oh, you do, you *do,* put the knife to one's throat!"

The next morning, very early, she came to his room. He recognized her knock, but he had no hope that she brought him money; as to which he was wrong, for she had fifty francs in her hand. She squeezed forward in her dressing-gown and he received her in his own, between his bath-tub and his bed. He had been tolerably schooled by this time to the "foreign ways" of his hosts. Mrs. Moreen was zealous, and when she was zealous she didn't care what she did; so she now sat down on his bed, his clothes being on the chairs, and, in her preoccupation, forgot, as she glanced round, to be ashamed of giving him such a nasty room. What Mrs. Moreen was zealous about on this occasion was to persuade him that in the first place she was very good-natured to bring him fifty francs, and, in the second, if he would only see it, he was really too absurd to expect to be *paid.* Wasn't he paid enough, without perpetual money—wasn't he paid by the comfortable, luxurious home that he enjoyed with them all, without a care, an anxiety, a solitary want? Wasn't he sure of his position, and wasn't that everything to a young man like him, quite unknown, with singularly little to show, the ground of whose exorbitant pretensions it was not easy to discover? Wasn't he paid, above all, by the delightful relation he had established with Morgan— quite ideal, as from master to pupil—and by the simple privilege of knowing and living with so amazingly gifted a child, than whom really—she meant literally what she said—there was no better company in Europe? Mrs. Moreen herself took to appealing to him as a man of the world; she said "Voyons, mon cher," and "My dear sir, look here now;" and urged him to be reasonable, putting it before him that it was really a chance for him. She spoke as if, according as he *should* be reasonable, he would prove himself worthy to be her son's tutor and of the extraordinary confidence they had placed in him.

After all, Pemberton reflected, it was only a difference of theory, and the theory didn't matter much. They had hitherto gone on that of remunerated, as now they would go on that of gratuitous, service; but why should they have so many words about it? Mrs. Moreen, however, continued to be convincing; sitting there with her fifty francs she talked and repeated, as women repeat, and bored and irritated him, while he leaned against the wall with his hands in the pockets of his wrapper, drawing it together round his legs and looking over the head of his visitor at the grey negations of his window. She wound up with saying: "You see I bring you a definite proposal."

"A definite proposal?"

"To make our relations regular, as it were—to put them on a comfortable footing."

"I see—it's a system," said Pemberton. "A kind of blackmail."

Mrs. Moreen bounded up, which was what the young man wanted.

"What do you mean by that?"

"You practice on one's fears—one's fears about the child if one should go away."

"And, pray, what would happen to him in that event?" demanded Mrs. Moreen, with majesty.

"Why, he'd be alone with *you*."

"And pray, with whom *should* a child be but with those whom he loves most?"

"If you think that, why don't you dismiss me?"

"Do you pretend that he loves you more than he loves *us?*" cried Mrs. Moreen.

"I think he ought to. I make sacrifices for him. Though I've heard of those *you* make, I don't see them."

Mrs. Moreen stared a moment; then, with emotion, she grasped Pemberton's hand. "*Will* you make it—the sacrifice?"

Pemberton burst out laughing. "I'll see—I'll do what I can—I'll stay a little longer. Your calculation is just—I *do* hate intensely to give him up; I'm fond of him and he interests me deeply, in spite of the inconvenience I suffer. You know my situation perfectly; I haven't a penny in the world, and, occupied as I am with Morgan, I'm unable to earn money."

Mrs. Moreen tapped her undressed arm with her folded bank-note. "Can't you write articles? Can't you translate, as *I* do?"

"I don't know about translating; it's wretchedly paid."

"I am glad to earn what I can," said Mrs. Moreen virtuously, with her head high.

"You ought to tell me who you do it for." Pemberton paused a moment, and she said nothing; so he added: "I've tried to turn off some little sketches, but the magazines won't have them—they're declined with thanks."

"You see then you're not such a phoenix—to have such pretensions," smiled his interlocutress.

"I haven't time to do things properly," Pemberton went on. Then as it came over him that he was almost abjectly good-natured to give these explanations he added: "If I stay on longer it must be on one condition—that Morgan shall know distinctly on what footing I am."

Mrs. Moreen hesitated. "Surely you don't want to show off to a child?"

"To show *you* off, do you mean?"

Again Mrs. Moreen hesitated, but this time it was to produce a still finer flower. "And *you* talk of blackmail!"

"You can easily prevent it," said Pemberton.

"And *you* talk of practicing on fears," Mrs. Moreen continued.

"Yes, there's no doubt I'm a great scoundrel."

His visitor looked at him a moment—it was evident that she was sorely bothered. Then she thrust out her money at him. "Mr. Moreen desired me to give you this on account."

"I'm much obliged to Mrs. Moreen; but we have no account."

"You won't take it?"

"That leaves me more free," said Pemberton.

"To poison my darling's mind?" groaned Mrs. Moreen.

"Oh, your darling's mind!" laughed the young man.

She fixed him a moment, and he thought she was going to break out tormentedly, pleadingly. "For God's sake, tell me what *is* in it!" But she checked this impulse—another was stronger. She pocketed the money—the crudity of the alternative was comical—and swept out of the room with the desperate concession: "You may tell him any horror you like!"

VI

A couple of days after this, during which Pemberton had delayed to profit by Mrs. Moreen's permission to tell her son any horror, the two had been for a quarter of an hour walking together in silence when the boy became sociable again with the remark: "I'll tell you how I know it; I know it through Zénobie."

"Zénobie? Who in the world is *she?*"

"A nurse I used to have—ever so many years ago. A charming woman. I liked her awfully, and she liked me."

"There's no accounting for tastes. What is it you know through her?"

"Why, what their idea is. She went away because they didn't pay her. She did like me awfully, and she stayed two years. She told me all about it—that at last she could never get her wages. As soon as they saw how much she liked me they stopped giving her anything. They thought she'd stay for nothing, out of devotion. And she did stay ever so long—as long as she could. She was only a poor girl. She used to send money to her mother. At last she couldn't afford it any longer, and she went away in a fearful rage one night—I mean of course in a rage against *them*. She cried over me tremendously, she hugged me nearly to death. She told me all about it," Morgan repeated. "She told me it was their idea. So I guessed, ever so long ago, that they have had the same idea with you."

"Zénobie was very shrewd," said Pemberton. "And she made you so."

"Oh, that wasn't Zénobie; that was nature. And experience!" Morgan laughed.

"Well, Zénobie was a part of your experience."

"Certainly I was a part of hers, poor dear!" the boy exclaimed. "And I'm a part of yours."

"A very important part. But I don't see how you know that I've been treated like Zénobie."

"Do you take me for an idiot?" Morgan asked. "Haven't I been conscious of what we've been through together?"

"What we've been through?"

"Our privations—our dark days."

"Oh, our days have been bright enough."

Morgan went on in silence for a moment. Then he said: "My dear fellow, you're a hero!"

"Well, you're another!" Pemberton retorted.

"No, I'm not; but I'm not a baby. I won't stand it any longer. You must get some occupation that pays. I'm ashamed, I'm ashamed!" quavered the boy in a little passionate voice that was very touching to Pemberton.

"We ought to go off and live somewhere together," said the young man.

"I'll go like a shot if you'll take me."

"I'd get some work that would keep us both afloat," Pemberton continued.

"So would I. Why shouldn't I work? I ain't such a *crétin!*"

"The difficulty is that your parents wouldn't hear of it," said Pemberton. "They would never part with you; they worship the ground you tread on. Don't you see the proof of it? They don't dislike me; they wish me no harm; they're very amiable people; but they're perfectly ready to treat me badly for your sake."

The silence in which Morgan received this graceful sophistry struck Pemberton somehow as expressive. After a moment Morgan repeated: "You *are* a hero!" Then he added: "They leave me with you altogether. You've all the responsibility. They put me off on you from morning till night. Why, then, should they object to my taking up with you completely? I'd help you."

"They're not particularly keen about my being helped, and they delight in thinking of you as *theirs*. They're tremendously proud of you."

"I'm not proud of them. But you know *that*," Morgan returned.

"Except for the little matter we speak of they're charming people," said Pemberton, not taking up the imputation of lucidity, but wondering greatly at the child's own, and especially at this fresh reminder of something he had been conscious of from the first—the strangest thing in the boy's large little composition, a temper, a sensibility, even a sort of ideal, which made him privately resent the general quality of his kinsfolk. Morgan had in secret a small loftiness which begot an element of reflection, a domestic scorn not imperceptible to his companion (though they never had any talk about it), and absolutely anomalous in a juvenile nature, especially when one noted that it had not made this nature "old-fashioned," as the word is of children—quaint or wizened or offensive. It was as if he had been a little gentleman and had paid the penalty by discovering that he was the only such person in the family. This comparison didn't make him vain; but it could make him melancholy and a trifle austere. When Pemberton guessed at these young dimnesses he saw him serious and gallant, and was partly drawn on and partly checked, as if with a scruple, by the charm of attempting to sound the little cool shallows which were quickly growing deeper. When he tried to figure to himself the morning twilight of childhood, so as to deal with it safely, he perceived that it was never fixed, never arrested, that ignorance, at the instant one touched it, was already flushing faintly into knowledge, that there was nothing that at a given moment you could say a clever child didn't know. It seemed to him that *he* both knew too much to imagine Morgan's simplicity and too little to disembroil his tangle.

The boy paid no heed to his last remark; he only went on: "I should have spoken to them about their idea, as I call it, long ago, if I hadn't been sure what they would say."

"And what would they say?"

"Just what they said about what poor Zénobie told me—that it was a horrid, dreadful story, that they had paid her every penny they owed her."

"Well, perhaps they had," said Pemberton.

"Perhaps they've paid you!"

"Let us pretend they have, and *n'en parlons plus.*"

"They accused her of lying and cheating," Morgan insisted perversely. "That's why I don't want to speak to them."

"Lest they should accuse me, too?"

To this Morgan made no answer, and his companion, looking down at him (the boy turned his eyes, which had filled, away), saw that he couldn't have trusted himself to utter.

"You're right. Don't squeeze them," Pemberton pursued. "Except for that, they *are* charming people."

"Except for *their* lying and *their* cheating?"

"I say—I say!" cried Pemberton, imitating a little tone of the lad's which was itself an imitation.

"We must be frank, at the last; we *must* come to an understanding," said Morgan, with the importance of the small boy who lets himself think he is arranging great affairs—almost playing at shipwreck or at Indians. "I know all about everything," he added.

"I daresay your father has his reasons," Pemberton observed, too vaguely, as he was aware.

"For lying and cheating?"

"For saving and managing and turning his means to the best account. He has plenty to do with his money. You're an expensive family."

"Yes, I'm very expensive," Morgan rejoined, in a manner which made his preceptor burst out laughing.

"He's saving for *you*," said Pemberton. "They think of you in everything they do."

"He might save a little—" The boy paused. Pemberton waited to hear what. Then Morgan brought out oddly: "A little reputation."

"Oh, there's plenty of that. That's all right!"

"Enough of it for the people they know, no doubt. The people they know are awful."

"Do you mean the princes? We mustn't abuse the princes."

"Why not? They haven't married Paula—they haven't married Amy. They only clean out Ulick."

"You *do* know everything!" Pemberton exclaimed.

"No, I don't, after all. I don't know what they live on, or how they live, or *why* they live! What have they got and how did they get it? Are they rich, are they poor, or have they a *modeste aisance?* Why are they always chiveying about—living one year like ambassadors and the next like paupers? Who are they, any way, and what are they? I've thought of all that—I've thought of a lot of things. They're so beastly worldly. That's what I hate most—oh, I've *seen* it! All they care about is to make an appearance and to pass for something or other. What do they want to pass for? What *do* they, Mr. Pemberton?"

"You pause for a reply," said Pemberton, treating the inquiry as a joke, yet wondering too, and greatly struck with the boy's intense, if imperfect, vision. "I haven't the least idea."

"And what good does it do? Haven't I seen the way people treat them—the 'nice' people, the ones they want to know? They'll take anything from them—they'll lie down and be trampled on. The nice ones hate that—they just sicken them. You're the only really nice person we know."

"Are you sure? They don't lie down for me!"

"Well, you shan't lie down for them. You've got to go—that's what you've got to do." said Morgan.

"And what will become of you?"

"Oh, I'm growing up. I shall get off before long. I'll see you later."

"You had better let me finish you," Pemberton urged, lending himself to the child's extraordinarily competent attitude.

Morgan stopped in their walk, looking up at him. He had to look up much less than a couple of years before—he had grown, in his loose leanness, so long and high. "Finish me?" he echoed.

"There are such a lot of jolly things we can do together yet. I want to turn you out—I want you to do me credit."

Morgan continued to look at him. "To give you credit—do you mean?"

"My dear fellow, you're too clever to live."

"That's just what I'm afraid you think. No, no; it isn't fair—I can't endure it. We'll part next week. The sooner it's over the sooner to sleep."

"If I hear of anything—any other chance, I promise to go," said Pemberton.

Morgan consented to consider this. "But you'll be honest," he demanded; "you won't pretend you haven't heard?"

"I'm much more likely to pretend I have."

"But what can you hear of, this way, stuck in a hole with us? You ought to be on the spot, to go to England—you ought to go to America."

"One would think you were *my* tutor!" said Pemberton.

Morgan walked on, and after a moment he began again: "Well, now that you know that I know and that we look at the facts and keep nothing back—it's much more comfortable, isn't it?"

"My dear boy, it's so amusing, so interesting, that it surely will be quite impossible for me to forego such hours as these."

This made Morgan stop once more. "You *do* keep something back. Oh, you're not straight—*I* am!"

"Why am I not straight?"

"Oh, you've got your idea!"

"My idea?"

"Why, that I probably sha'nt live, and that you can stick it out till I'm removed."

"You *are* too clever to live!" Pemberton repeated.

"I call it a mean idea," Morgan pursued. "But I shall punish you by the way I hang on."

"Look out or I'll poison you!" Pemberton laughed.

"I'm stronger and better every year. Haven't you noticed that there hasn't been a doctor near me since you came?"

"*I'm* your doctor," said the young man, taking his arm and drawing him on again.

Morgan proceeded, and after a few steps he gave a sigh of mingled weariness and relief. "Ah, now that we look at the facts, it's all right!"

VII

They looked at the facts a good deal after this; and one of the first consequences of their doing so was that Pemberton stuck it out, as it were, for the purpose. Morgan made the facts so vivid and so droll, and at the same time so bald and so ugly, that there was fascination in talking them over with him, just as there would have been heartlessness in leaving him alone with them. Now that they had such a number of perceptions in common it was useless for the pair to pretend that they didn't judge such people; but the very judgment, and the exchange of perceptions, created another tie. Morgan had never been so interesting as now that he himself was made plainer by the sidelight of these confidences. What came out in it most was the soreness of his characteristic pride. He had plenty of that, Pemberton felt—so much that it was perhaps well it should have had to take some early bruises. He would have liked his people to be gallant, and he had waked up too soon to the sense that they were perpetually swallowing humble-pie. His mother would consume any amount, and his father would consume even more than his mother. He had a theory that Ulick had wriggled out of an "affair" at Nice: there had once been a flurry at home, a regular panic, after which they all went to bed and took medicine, not to be accounted for an any other supposition. Morgan had a romantic imagination, fed by poetry and history, and he would have liked those who "bore his name" (as he used to say to Pemberton with the humour that made his sensitiveness manly), to have a proper spirit. But their one idea was to get in with people who didn't want them and to take snubs as if they were honourable scars. Why people didn't want them more he didn't know—that was people's own affair; after all they were not superficially repulsive—they were a hundred times cleverer than most of the dreary grandees, the "poor swells" they rushed about Europe to catch up with. "After all, they *are* amusing—they are!" Morgan used to say, with the wisdom of the ages. To which Pemberton always replied: "Amusing—the great Moreen troupe? Why, they're altogether delightful; and if it were not for the hitch that you and I (feeble performers!) make in the *ensemble,* they would carry everything before them."

What the boy couldn't get over was that this particular blight seemed, in a tradition of self-respect, so undeserved and so arbitrary. No doubt people had a right to take the line they liked; but why should *his* people have liked the line of pushing and toadying and lying and cheating? What had their forefathers—all decent folk, so far as he knew—done to them, or what had *he* done to them? Who had poisoned their blood with the fifth-rate social ideal, the fixed idea of making smart acquaintances and getting into the *monde chic,* especially when it was foredoomed to failure and exposure? They showed so what they were after; that was what made the people they wanted not want *them.* And never a movement of dignity, never a throb of shame at looking each other in the face, never any independence or resentment or disgust. If his father or his brother would only knock some one down once or twice a year! Clever as they were they never guessed how they appeared. They were good-natured, yes—as good-natured as Jews at the doors of clothing-shops! But was that the model one wanted one's family to follow? Morgan had dim memories of an old grandfather, the maternal, in New York, whom he had been taken across the ocean to see, at the age of five: a gentleman with a high neckcloth and a good deal of pronunciation, who wore a dress-coat in the morning, which made one wonder what he wore in the evening, and had, or was supposed to have, "property" and something to do with the Bible Society. It couldn't have been but that *he* was a good type. Pemberton himself remembered Mrs. Clancy, a widowed sister of Mr. Moreen's, who was as irritating as a moral tale and had paid a fortnight's visit to the family at Nice shortly after he came to live with them. She was "pure and refined," as Amy said, over the banjo, and had the air of not knowing what they meant and of keeping something back. Pemberton judged that what she kept back was an approval of many of their ways; therefore it was to be supposed that she too was of a good type, and that Mr. and Mrs. Moreen and Ulick and Paula and Amy might easily have been better if they would.

But that they wouldn't was more and more perceptible from day to day. They continued to "chivey," as Morgan called it, and in due time became aware of a variety of reasons for proceeding to Venice. They mentioned a great many of them—they were always strikingly frank, and had the brightest friendly chatter, at the late foreign breakfast in especial, before the ladies had made up their faces, when they learned their arms on the table, had something to follow the *demi-tasse,* and, in the heat of familiar discussion as to what they "really ought" to do, fell inevitably into the languages in which they could *tutoyer.* Even Pemberton liked them, then; he could endure even Ulick when he heard him give his little flat voice for the "sweet sea-city." That was what made him have a sneaking kindness for them—that they were so out of the workaday world and kept him so out of it. The summer had waned when, with cries of ecstasy, they all passed out on the balcony that overhung the Grand Canal; the sunsets were splendid—the Dorringtons had arrived. The Dorringtons were the only reason they had not talked of at breakfast; but the reasons that they didn't talk of at breakfast always came out in the end. The Dorringtons, on the other hand, came out very little; or else, when they did, they stayed—as was natural—for hours, during which periods Mrs. Moreen and the girls sometimes called at their hotel (to see if they had returned) as many as three times running. The gondola was for the ladies; for in Venice too there were "days," which Mrs. Moreen knew in their order an hour after she arrived. She immediately took one herself, to which the Dorringtons never came, though on a certain occasion when Pemberton and his pupil were together at St. Mark's— where, taking the best walks they had ever had and haunting a hundred churches, they spent a great deal of time—they saw the old lord turn up with Mr. Moreen and Ulick, who showed him the dim basilica as if it belonged to them. Pemberton noted how much less, among its curiosities, Lord Dorrington carried himself as a man of the world; wondering too whether, for such services, his companions took a fee from him. The autumn, at any rate, waned, the Dorringtons departed, and Lord Verschoyle, the eldest son, had proposed neither for Amy nor for Paula.

One sad November day, while the wind roared round the old palace and the rain lashed the lagoon, Pemberton, for exercise and even somewhat for warmth (the Moreens were horribly frugal about fires—it was a cause of suffering to their inmate), walked up and down the big bare *sala* with his pupil. The scagliola floor was cold, the high battered casements shook in the storm, and the stately decay of the place was unrelieved by a particle of furniture. Pemberton's spirits were low, and it came over him that the fortune of the Moreens was now even lower. A blast of desolation, a prophecy of disaster and disgrace, seemed to draw through the comfortless hall. Mr. Moreen and Ulick were in the Piazza, looking out for something, strolling drearily, in mackintoshes, under the arcades; but still, in spite of mackintoshes, unmistakable men of the world. Paula and Amy were in bed—it might have been thought they were staying there to keep warm. Pemberton looked askance at the boy at his side, to see to what extent he was conscious of these portents. But Morgan, luckily for him, was now mainly conscious of growing taller and stronger and indeed of being in his fifteenth year. This fact was intensely interesting to him—it was the basis of a private theory (which, however, he had imparted to his tutor) that in a little while he should stand on his own feet. He considered that the situation would change—that, in short, he should be "finished," grown up, producible in the world of affairs and ready to prove himself of sterling ability. Sharply as he was capable, at times, of questioning his circumstances, there were happy hours when he was as superficial as a child; the proof of which was his fundamental assumption that he should presently go to Oxford, to Pemberton's college, and, aided and abetted by Pemberton, do the most wonderful things. It vexed Pemberton to see how little, in such a project, he took account of ways and means: on other matters he was so sceptical about them. Pemberton tried to imagine the Moreens at Oxford, and fortunately failed; yet unless they were to remove there as a family there would be no *modus vivendi* for Morgan. How could he live without an allowance, and where was the allowance to come from? He (Pemberton) might live on Morgan; but how could Morgan live on him? What was to become of him anyhow? Somehow, the fact that he was a big boy now, with better prospects of health, made the question of his future more difficult. So long as he was frail the consideration that he inspired seemed enough of an answer to it. But at the bottom of Pemberton's heart was the recognition of his probably being strong enough to live and not strong enough to thrive. He himself, at any rate, was in a period of natural, boyish rosiness about all this, so that the beating of the tempest seemed to him only the voice of life and the challenge of fate. He had on his shabby little overcoat, with the collar up, but he was enjoying his walk.

It was interrupted at last by the appearance of his mother at the end of the *sala*. She beckoned to Morgan to come to her, and while Pemberton saw him, complacent, pass down the long vista, over the damp false marble, he wondered what was in the air. Mrs. Moreen said a word to the boy and made him go into the room she had quitted. Then, having closed the door after him, she directed her steps swiftly to Pemberton. There *was* something in the air, but his wildest flight of fancy wouldn't have suggested what it proved to be. She signified that she had made a pretext to get Morgan out of the way, and then she inquired—without hesitation—if the young man could lend her sixty francs. While, before bursting into a laugh, he stared at her with surprise, she declared that she was awfully pressed for the money; she was desperate for it—it would save her life.

"Dear lady, *c'est trop fort!*" Pemberton laughed. "Where in the world do you suppose I should get sixty francs, *du train dont vous allez?*"

"I thought you worked—wrote things; don't they pay you?"

"Not a penny."

"Are you such a fool as to work for nothing?"

"You ought surely to know that."

Mrs. Moreen stared an instant, then she coloured a little. Pemberton saw she had quite forgotten the terms—if "terms" they could be called—that he had ended by accepting from herself; they had burdened her memory as little as her conscience. "Oh, yes, I see what you mean—you have been very nice about that; but why go back to it so often?" She had been perfectly urbane with him ever since the rough scene of explanation in his room, the morning he made her accept *his* "terms"—the necessity of his making his case known to Morgan. She had felt no resentment, after seeing that there was no danger of Morgan's taking the matter up with her. Indeed, attributing this immunity to the good taste of his influence with the boy, she had once said to Pemberton: "My dear fellow; it's an immense comfort you're a gentleman." She repeated this, in substance, now. "Of course you're a gentleman—that's a bother the less!" Pemberton reminded her that he had not "gone back" to anything; and she also repeated her prayer that, somewhere and somehow, he would find her sixty francs. He took the liberty of declaring that if he could find them it wouldn't be to lend them to *her*—as to which he consciously did himself injustice, knowing that if he had them he would certainly place them in her hand. He accused himself, at bottom and with some truth, of a fantastic, demoralised sympathy with her. If misery made strange bedfellows it also made strange sentiments. It was moreover a part of the demoralisation and of the general bad effect of living with such people that one had to make rough retorts, quite out of the tradition of good manners. "Morgan, Morgan, to what pass have I come for you?" he privately exclaimed, while Mrs. Moreen floated voluminously down the *sala* again, to liberate the boy; groaning, as she went, that everything was too odious.

Before the boy was liberated there came a thump at the door communicating with the staircase, followed by the apparition of a dripping youth who poked in his head. Pemberton recognised him as the bearer of a telegram and recognized the telegram as addressed to himself. Morgan came back as, after glancing at the signature (that of a friend in London), he was reading the words: "Found jolly job for you—engagement to coach opulent youth on own terms. Come immediately." The answer, happily, was paid, and the messenger waited. Morgan, who had drawn near, waited too, and looked hard at Pemberton; and Pemberton, after a moment, having met his look, handed him the telegram. It was really by wise looks (they knew each other so well), that, while the telegraph-boy, in his waterproof cape, made a great puddle on the floor, the thing was settled between them. Pemberton wrote the answer with a pencil against the frescoed wall, and the messenger departed. When he had gone Pemberton said to Morgan:

"I'll make a tremendous charge; I'll earn a lot of money in a short time, and we'll live on it."

"Well, I hope the opulent youth will be stupid—he probably will—" Morgan parenthesised, "and keep you a long time."

"Of course, the longer he keeps me the more we shall have for our old age."

"But suppose *they* don't pay you!" Morgan awfully suggested.

"Oh, there are not two such—!" Pemberton paused, he was on the point of using an invidious term. Instead of this he said "two such chances."

Morgan flushed—the tears came to his eyes. *"Dites toujours,* two such rascally crews!" Then, in a different tone, he added: "Happy opulent youth!"

"Not if he's stupid!"

"Oh, they're happier then. But you can't have everything, can you?" the boy smiled.

Pemberton held him, his hands on his shoulders. "What will become of *you,* what will you do?" He thought of Mrs. Moreen, desperate for sixty francs.

"I shall turn into a man." And then, as if he recognised all the bearings of Pemberton's allusion: "I shall get on with them better when you're not here."

"Ah, don't say that—it sounds as if I set you against them!"

"You do—the sight of you. It's all right; you know what I mean. I shall be beautiful. I'll take their affairs in hand; I'll marry my sisters."

"You'll marry yourself!" joked Pemberton; as high, rather tense pleasantry would evidently be the right, or the safest, tone for their separation.

It was, however, not purely in this strain that Morgan suddenly asked: "But I say—how will you get to your jolly job? You'll have to telegraph to the opulent youth for money to come on."

Pemberton bethought himself. "They won't like that, will they?"

"Oh, look out for them!"

Then Pemberton brought out his remedy. "I'll go to the American Consul; I'll borrow some money of him—just for the few days, on the strength of the telegram."

Morgan was hilarious. "Show him the telegram—then stay and keep the money!"

Pemberton entered into the joke enough to reply that, for Morgan, he was really capable of that; but the boy, growing more serious, and to prove that he hadn't meant what he said, not only hurried him off to the Consulate (since he was to start that evening, as he had wired to his friend), but insisted on going with him. They splashed through the tortuous perforations and over the humpbacked bridges, and they passed through the Piazza, where they saw Mr. Moreen and Ulick go into a jeweller's shop. The Consul proved accommodating (Pemberton said it wasn't the letter, but Morgan's grand air), and on their way back they went into St. Mark's for a hushed ten minutes. Later they took up and kept up the fun of it to the very end; and it seemed to Pemberton a part of that fun that Mrs. Moreen, who was very angry when he had announced to her his intention, should charge him, grotesquely and vulgarly, and in reference to the loan she had vainly endeavored to effect, with bolting lest they should "get something out" of him. On the other hand he had to do Mr. Moreen and Ulick the justice to recognise that when, on coming in, *they* heard the cruel news, they took it like perfect men of the world.

VIII

When Pemberton got at work with the opulent youth, who was to be taken in hand for Balliol, he found himself unable to say whether he was really an idiot or it was only, on his own part, the long association with an intensely living little mind that made him seem so. From Morgan he heard half-a-dozen times: the boy wrote charming young letters, a patchwork of tongues, with indulgent postscripts in the family Volapuk and, in little squares and rounds and crannies of the text, the drollest illustrations—letters that he was divided between the impulse to show his present disciple, as a kind of wasted incentive, and the sense of something in them that was profanable by publicity. The opulent youth went up, in due course, and failed to pass; but it seemed to add to the presumption that brilliancy was not expected of him all at once that his parents, condoning the lapse, which they good-naturedly treated as little as possible as if it were Pemberton's, should have sounded the rally again, begged the young coach to keep his pupil in hand another year.

The young coach was now in a position to lend Mrs. Moreen sixty francs, and he sent her a post-office order for the amount. In return for his favour he received a frantic, scribbled line from her: "Implore you to come back instantly—Morgan dreadfully ill." They were on the rebound, once more in Paris—often as Pemberton had seen them depressed he had never seen them crushed—and communication was therefore rapid. He wrote to the boy to ascertain the state of his health, but he received no answer to his letter. Accordingly he took an abrupt leave of the opulent youth and, crossing the Channel, alighted at the small hotel, in the quarter of the Champs Elysées, of which Mrs. Moreen had given him the address. A deep if dumb dissatisfaction with this lady and her companions bore him company: they couldn't be vulgarly honest, but they could live at hotels, in velvety *entresols,* amid a smell of burnt pastilles, in the most expensive city in Europe. When he had left them, in Venice, it was with an irrepressible suspicion that something was going to happen; but the only thing that had happened was that they succeeded in getting away. "How is he? where is he?" he asked of Mrs. Moreen; but before she could speak, these questions were answered by the pressure round his neck of a pair of arms, in shrunken sleeves, which were perfectly capable of an effusive young foreign squeeze.

"Dreadfully ill—I don't see it!" the young man cried. And then, to Morgan: "Why on earth didn't you relieve me? Why didn't you answer my letter?"

Mrs. Moreen declared that when she wrote he was very bad, and Pemberton learned at the same time from the boy that he had answered every letter he had received. This led to the demonstration that Pemberton's note had been intercepted. Mrs. Moreen was prepared to see the fact exposed, as Pemberton perceived, the moment he faced her, that she was prepared for a good many other things. She was prepared above all to maintain that she had acted from a sense of duty, that she was enchanted she had got him over, whatever they might say; and that it was useless of him to pretend that he didn't *know,* in all his bones, that his place at such a time was with Morgan. He had taken the boy away from them, and now he had no right to abandon him. He had created for himself the gravest responsibilities; he must at least abide by what he had done.

"Taken him away from you?" Pemberton exclaimed indignantly.

"Do it—do it, for pity's sake; that's just what I want. I can't stand *this*—and such scenes. They're treacherous!" These words broke from Morgan, who had intermitted his embrace, in a key which made Pemberton turn quickly to him, to see that he suddenly seated himself, was breathing with evident difficulty and was very pale.

"*Now* do you say he's not ill—my precious pet?" shouted his mother, dropping on her knees before him with clasped hands, but touching him no more than if he had been a gilded idol. "It will pass—it's only for an instant; but don't say such dreadful things!"

"I'm all right—all right," Morgan panted to Pemberton, whom he sat looking up at with a strange smile, his hands resting on either side of the sofa.

"Now do you pretend I've been treacherous—that I've deceived?" Mrs. Moreen flashed at Pemberton as she got up.

"It isn't *he* says it, it's I!" the boy returned, apparently easier, but sinking back against the wall; while Pemberton, who had sat down beside him, taking his hand, bent over him.

"Darling child, one does what one can; there are so many things to consider," urged Mrs. Moreen. "It's his *place*—his only place. You see *you* think it is now."

"Take me away—take me away," Morgan went on, smiling to Pemberton from his white face.

"Where shall I take you, and how—oh, *how,* my boy?" the young man stammered, thinking of the rude way in which his friends in London held that, for his convenience, and without a pledge of instantaneous return, he·had thrown them over; of the just resentment with which they would already have called in a successor, and of the little help as regarded finding fresh employment that resided for him in the flatness of his having failed to pass his pupil.

"Oh, we'll settle that. You used to talk about it," said Morgan. "If we can only go, all the rest's a detail."

"Talk about it as much as you like, but don't think you can attempt it. Mr. Moreen would never consent—it would be so precarious," Pemberton's hostess explained to him. Then to Morgan she explained: "It would destroy our peace, it would break our hearts. Now that he's back it will be all the same again. You'll have your life, your work and your freedom, and we'll all be happy as we used to be. You'll bloom and grow perfectly well, and we won't have any more silly experiments, will we? They're too absurd. It's Mr. Pemberton's place—every one in his place. You in yours, your papa in his, me in mine—*n'est-ce pas, chéri?* We'll all forget how foolish we've been, and we'll have lovely times."

She continued to talk and to surge vaguely about the little draped, stuffy *salon,* while Pemberton sat with the boy, whose colour gradually came back; and she mixed up her reasons, dropping that there were going to be changes, that the other children might scatter (who knew?—Paula had her ideas), and that then it might be fancied how much the poor old parent-birds would want the little nestling. Morgan looked at Pemberton, who wouldn't let him move; and Pemberton knew exactly how he felt at hearing himself called a little nestling. He admitted that he had had one or two bad days, but he protested afresh against the iniquity of his mother's having made them the ground of an appeal to poor Pemberton. Poor Pemberton could laugh now, apart from the comicality of Mrs. Moreen's producing so much philosophy for her defence (she seemed to shake it out of her agitated petticoats, which knocked over the light gilt chairs), so little did the sick boy strike him as qualified to repudiate any advantage.

He himself was in for it, at any rate. He should have Morgan on his hands again indefinitely; though indeed he saw the lad had a private theory to produce which would be intended to smooth this down. He was obliged to him for it in advance; but the suggested amendment didn't keep his heart from sinking a little, any more than it prevented him from accepting the prospect on the spot, with some confidence moreover that he would do so even better if he could have a little supper. Mrs. Moreen threw out more hints about the changes that were to be looked for, but she was such a mixture of smiles and shudders (she confessed she was very nervous), that he couldn't tell whether she were in high feather or only in hysterics. If the family were really at last going to pieces why shouldn't she recognise the necessity of pitching Morgan into some sort of lifeboat? This presumption was fostered by the fact that they were established in luxurious quarters in the capital of pleasure; that was exactly where they naturally *would* be established in view of going to pieces. Moreover didn't she mention that Mr. Moreen and the others were enjoying themselves at the opera with Mr. Granger, and wasn't *that* also precisely where one would look for them on the eve of a smash? Pemberton gathered that Mr. Granger was a rich, vacant American—a big bill with a flourishy heading and no items; so that one of Paula's "ideas" was probably that this time she had really done it, which was indeed an unprecedented blow to the general cohesion. And if the cohesion was to terminate what was to become of poor Pemberton? He felt quite enough bound up with them to figure, to his alarm, as a floating spar in case of a wreck.

It was Morgan who eventually asked if no supper had been ordered for him; sitting with him below, later, at the dim, delayed meal, in the presence of a great deal of corded green plush, a plate of ornamental biscuit and a languor marked on the part of the waiter. Mrs. Moreen had explained that they had been obliged to secure a room for the visitor out of the house; and Morgan's consolation (he offered it while Pemberton reflected on the nastiness of lukewarm sauces), proved to be, largely, that this circumstance would facilitate their escape. He talked of their escape (recurring to it often afterwards), as if they were making up a "boy's book" together. But he likewise expressed his sense that there was something in the air, that the Moreens couldn't keep it up much longer. In point of fact, as Pemberton was to see, they kept it up for five or six months. All the while, however, Morgan's contention was designed to cheer him. Mr. Moreen and Ulick, whom he had met the day after his return, accepted that return like perfect men of the world. If Paula and Amy treated it even with less formality an allowance was to be made for them, inasmuch as Mr. Granger had not come to the opera after all. He had only placed his box at their service, with a bouquet for each of the party; there was even one apiece, embittering the thought of his profusion, for Mr. Moreen and Ulick. "They're all like that," was Morgan's comment; "at the very last, just when we think we've got them fast, we're chucked!"

Morgan's comments, in these days, were more and more free; they even included a large recognition of the extraordinary tenderness with which he had been treated while Pemberton was away. Oh, yes, they couldn't do enough to be nice to him, to show him they had him on their mind and make up for his loss. That was just what made the whole thing so sad, and him so glad, after all, of Pemberton's return—he had to keep thinking of their affection less, had less sense of obligation. Pemberton laughed out at this last reason, and Morgan blushed and said: "You know what I mean." Pemberton knew perfectly what he meant; but there were a good many things it didn't make any clearer. This episode of his second sojourn in Paris stretched itself out wearily, with their resumed readings and wanderings and maunderings, their potterings on the quays, their hauntings of the museums, their occasional lingerings in the Palais Royal, when the first sharp weather came on and there was a comfort in warm emanations, before Chevet's wonderful succulent window. Morgan wanted to hear a great deal about the opulent youth—he took an immense interest in him. Some of the details of his opulence—Pemberton could spare him none of them—evidently intensified the boy's appreciation of all his friend had given up to come back to him; but in addition to the greater reciprocity established by such a renunciation he had always his little brooding theory, in which there was a frivolous gaiety too, that their long probation was drawing to a close. Morgan's conviction that the Moreens couldn't go on much longer kept pace with the unexpended impetus with which, from month to month, they did go on. Three weeks after Pemberton had rejoined them they went on to another hotel, a dingier one than the first; but Morgan rejoiced that his tutor had at least still not sacrificed the advantage of a room outside. He clung to the romantic utility of this when the day, or rather the night, should arrive for their escape.

For the first time, in this complicated connection, Pemberton felt sore and exasperated. It was, as he had said to Mrs. Moreen in Venice, *trop fort*— everything was *trop fort*. He could neither really throw off his blighting burden nor find in it the benefit of a pacified conscience or of a rewarded affection. He had spent all the money that he had earned in England, and he felt that his youth was going and that he was getting nothing back for it. It was all very well for Morgan to seem to consider that he would make up to him for all inconveniences by settling himself upon him permanently—there was an irritating flaw in such a view. He saw what the boy had in his mind; the conception that as his friend had had the generosity to come back to him he must show his gratitude by giving him his life. But the poor friend didn't desire the gift—what could he do with Morgan's life? Of course at the same time that Pemberton was irritated he remembered the reason, which was very honourable to Morgan and which consisted simply of the fact that he was perpetually making one forget that he was after all only a child. If one dealt with him on a different basis one's misadventures were one's own fault. So Pemberton waited in a queer confusion of yearning and alarm for the catastrophe which was held to hang over the house of Moreen, of which he certainly at moments felt the symptoms brush his cheek and as to which he wondered much in what form it would come.

Perhaps it would take the form of dispersal—a frightened *sauve qui peut,* a scuttling into selfish corners. Certainly they were less elastic than of yore; they were evidently looking for something they didn't find. The Dorringtons hadn't reappeared, the princes had scattered; wasn't that the beginning of the end? Mrs. Moreen had lost her reckoning of the famous "days"; her social calendar was blurred—it had turned its face to the wall. Pemberton suspected that the great, the cruel, discomfiture had been the extraordinary behaviour of Mr. Granger, who seemed not to know what he wanted, or, what was much worse, what *they* wanted. He kept sending flowers, as if to bestrew the path of his retreat, which was never the path of return. Flowers were all very well, but—Pemberton could complete the proposition. It was now positively conspicuous that in the long run the Moreens were a failure; so that the young man was almost grateful the run had not been short. Mr. Moreen, indeed, was still occasionally able to get away on business, and, what was more surprising, he was also able to get back. Ulick had no club, but you could not have discovered it from his appearance, which was as much as ever that of a person looking at life from the window of such an institution; therefore Pemberton was doubly astonished at an answer he once heard him make to his mother, in the desperate tone of a man familiar with the worst privations. Her question Pemberton had not quite caught; it appeared to be an appeal for a suggestion as to whom they could get to take Amy. "Let the devil take her!" Ulick snapped; so that Pemberton could see that not only they had lost their amiability, but had ceased to believe in themselves. He could also see that if Mrs. Moreen was trying to get people to take her children she might be regarded as closing the hatches for the storm. But Morgan would be the last she would part with.

One winter afternoon—it was a Sunday—he and the boy walked far together in the Bois de Boulogne. The evening was so splendid, the cold lemon-coloured sunset so clear, the stream of carriages and pedestrians so amusing and the fascination of Paris so great, that they stayed out later than usual and became aware that they would have to hurry home to arrive in time for dinner. They hurried accordingly, arm-in-arm, good-humoured and hungry, agreeing that there was nothing like Paris after all and that after all, too, that had come and gone they were not yet sated with innocent pleasures. When they reached the hotel they found that, though scandalously late, they were in time for all the dinner they were likely to sit down to. Confusion reigned in the apartments of the Moreens (very shabby ones this time, but the best in the house), and before the interrupted service of the table (with objects displaced almost as if there had been a scuffle, and a great wine stain from an overturned bottle), Pemberton could not blink the fact that there had been a scene of proprietary mutiny. The storm had come—they were all seeking refuge. The hatches were down—Paula and Amy were invisible (they had never tried the most casual art upon Pemberton, but he felt that they had enough of an eye to him not to wish to meet him as young ladies whose frocks had been confiscated), and Ulick appeared to have jumped overboard. In a word, the host and his staff had ceased to "go on" at the pace of their guests, and the air of embarrassed detention, thanks to a pile of gaping trunks in the passage, was strangely commingled with the air of indignant withdrawal.

When Morgan took in all this—and he took it in very quickly—he blushed to the roots of his hair. He had walked, from his infancy, among difficulties and dangers, but he had never seen a public exposure. Pemberton noticed, in a second glance at him, that the tears had rushed into his eyes and that they were tears of bitter shame. He wondered for an instant, for the boy's sake, whether he might successfully pretend not to understand. Not successfully, he felt, as Mr. and Mrs. Moreen, dinnerless by their extinguished hearth, rose before him in their little dishonoured *salon,* considering apparently with much intensity what lively capital would be next on their list. They were not prostrate, but they were very pale, and Mrs. Moreen had evidently been crying. Pemberton quickly learned however that her grief was not for the loss of her dinner, much as she usually enjoyed it, but on account of a necessity much more tragic. She lost no time in laying this necessity bare, in telling him how the change had come, the bolt had fallen, and how they would all have to turn themselves about. Therefore cruel as it was to them to part with their darling she must look to him to carry a little further the influence he had so fortunately acquired with the boy—to induce his young charge to follow him into some modest retreat. They depended upon him, in a word, to take their delightful child temporarily under his protection—it would leave Mr. Moreen and herself so much more free to give the proper attention (too little, alas! had been given), to the readjustment of their affairs.

"We trust you—we feel that we can," said Mrs. Moreen, slowly rubbing her plump white hands and looking, with compunction, hard at Morgan, whose chin, not to take liberties, her husband stroked with a tentative paternal forefinger.

"Oh, yes; we feel that we can. We trust Mr. Pemberton fully, Morgan," Mr. Moreen conceded.

Pemberton wondered again if he might pretend not to understand; but the idea was painfully complicated by the immediate perception that Morgan had understood.

"Do you mean that he may take me to live with him—for ever and ever?" cried the boy. "Away, away, anywhere he likes?"

"For ever and ever? *Comme vous-y-allez!*" Mr. Moreen laughed indulgently. "For as long as Mr. Pemberton may be so good."

"We've struggled, we've suffered," his wife went on; "but you've made him so your own that we've already been through the worst of the sacrifice."

Morgan had turned away from his father—he stood looking at Pemberton with a light in his face. His blush had died out, but something had come that was brighter and more vivid. He had a moment of boyish joy, scarcely mitigated by the reflection that, with this unexpected consecration of his hope—too sudden and too violent; the thing was a good deal less like a boy's book—the "escape" was left on their hands. The boyish joy was there for an instant, and Pemberton was almost frightened at the revelation of gratitude and affection that shone through his humiliation. When Morgan stammered "My dear fellow, what do you say to *that?*" he felt that he should say something enthusiastic. But he was still more frightened at something else that immediately followed and that made the lad sit down quickly on the nearest chair. He had turned very white and had raised his hand to his left side. They were all three looking at him, but Mrs. Moreen was the first to bound forward. "Ah, his darling little heart!" she broke out; and this time, on her knees before him and without respect for the idol, she caught him ardently in her arms. "You walked him too far, you hurried him too fast!" she tossed over her shoulder at Pemberton. The boy made no protest, and the next instant his mother, still holding him, sprang up with her face convulsed and with the terrified cry "Help, help! he's going, he's gone!" Pemberton saw, with equal horror, by Morgan's own stricken face, that he *was* gone. He pulled him half out of his mother's hands, and for a moment, while they held him together, they looked, in their dismay, into each other's eyes. "He couldn't stand it, with his infirmity," said Pemberton— "The shock, the whole scene, the violent emotion."

"But I thought he *wanted* to go to you!" wailed Mrs. Moreen.

"I *told* you he didn't, my dear," argued Mr. Moreen. He was trembling all over, and he was, in his way, as deeply affected as his wife. But, after the first, he took his bereavement like a man of the world.

Questions for Discussion

1. What do we learn about the conflicts of the story just in the first paragraph?

2. What kind of family are the Moreens?

3. How would you describe the relationship between Pemberton and Morgan?

4. Who is responsible for Morgan's death? To what extent is it possible to place responsibility for the death with the family, with Pemberton, and with Morgan himself? Explain.

5. James was one of the first writers to emphasize "showing" versus "telling," to avoid what came to be called "authorial intrusion." Find at least two scenes in "The Pupil" that show us certain emotions or conflicts but that do so without telling us explicitly. How does James use dialogue, imagery, and setting to achieve the "showing"?

Suggestions for Writing

1. Write an essay about the character of Pemberton. Is he admirable or not? Is he greedy? Compassionate? Naive?

2. Write an essay about the relationship between Pemberton and Morgan. What is the basis of the friendship? Why do they like each other?

3. Write an essay that analyzes the psychological issues, problems, and patterns that James's story represents.

The Story of an Hour

KATE CHOPIN

Knowing that Mrs. Mallard was afflicted with a heart trouble, great care was taken to break to her as gently as possible the news of her husband's death.

It was her sister Josephine who told her, in broken sentences; veiled hints that revealed in half concealing. Her husband's friend Richards was there, too, near her. It was he who had been in the newspaper office when intelligence of the railroad disaster was received, with Brently Mallard's name leading the list of "killed." He had only taken the time to assure himself of its truth by a second telegram, and had hastened to forestall any less careful, less tender friend in bearing the sad message.

She did not hear the story as many women have heard the same, with a paralyzed inability to accept its significance. She wept at once, with sudden, wild abandonment, in her sister's arms. When the storm of grief had spent itself she went away to her room alone. She would have no one follow her.

There stood, facing the open window, a comfortable, roomy armchair. Into this she sank, pressed down by a physical exhaustion that haunted her body and seemed to reach into her soul.

She could see in the open square before her house the tops of trees that were all aquiver with the new spring life. The delicious breath of rain was in the air. In the street below a peddler was crying his wares. The notes of a distant song which some one was singing reached her faintly, and countless sparrows were twittering in the eaves.

There were patches of blue sky showing here and there through the clouds that had met and piled one above the other in the west facing her window.

She sat with her head thrown back upon the cushion of the chair, quite motionless, except when a sob came up into her throat and shook her, as a child who has cried itself to sleep continues to sob in its dreams.

She was young, with a fair, calm face, whose lines bespoke repression and even a certain strength. But now there was a dull stare in her eyes, whose gaze was fixed away off yonder on one of those patches of blue sky. It was not a glance of reflection, but rather indicated a suspension of intelligent thought.

There was something coming to her and she was waiting for it, fearfully. What was it? She did not know; it was too subtle and elusive to name. But she felt it, creeping out of the sky, reaching toward her through the sounds, the scents, the color that filled the air.

Now her bosom rose and fell tumultuously. She was beginning to recognize this thing that was approaching to possess her, and she was striving to beat it back with her will—as powerless as her two white slender hands would have been.

When she abandoned herself a little whispered word escaped her slightly parted lips. She said it over and over under her breath: "free, free, free!" The vacant stare and the look of terror that had followed it went from her eyes. They stayed keen and bright. Her pulses beat fast, and the coursing blood warmed and relaxed every inch of her body.

She did not stop to ask if it were or were not a monstrous joy that held her. A clear and exalted perception enabled her to dismiss the suggestion as trivial.

She knew that she would weep again when she saw the kind, tender hands folded in death; the face that had never looked save with love upon her, fixed and gray and dead. But she saw beyond that bitter moment a long procession of years to come that would belong to her absolutely. And she opened and spread her arms out to them in welcome.

There would be no one to live for her during those coming years; she would live for herself. There would be no powerful will bending hers in that blind persistence with which men and women believe they have a right to impose a private will upon a fellow-creature. A kind intention or a cruel intention made the act seem no less a crime as she looked upon it in that brief moment of illumination.

And yet she had loved him—sometimes. Often she had not. What did it matter! What could love, the unsolved mystery, count for in face of this possession of self-assertion which she suddenly recognized as the strongest impulse of her being!

"Free! Body and soul free!" she kept whispering.

Josephine was kneeling before the closed door with her lips to the keyhole, imploring for admission. "Louise, open the door! I beg; open the door—you will make yourself ill. What are you doing, Louise? For heaven's sake open the door."

"Go away. I am not making myself ill." No; she was drinking in a very elixir of life through that open window.

Her fancy was running riot along those days ahead of her. Spring days, and summer days, and all sorts of days that would be her own. She breathed a quick prayer that life might be long. It was only yesterday she had thought with a shudder that life might be long.

She rose at length and opened the door to her sister's importunities. There was a feverish triumph in her eyes, and she carried herself unwittingly like a goddess of Victory. She clasped her sister's waist, and together they descended the stairs. Richards stood waiting for them at the bottom.

Some one was opening the front door with a latchkey. It was Brently Mallard who entered, a little travel-stained, composedly carrying his grip-sack and umbrella. He had been far from the scene of the accident, and did not even know there had been one. He stood amazed at Josephine's piercing cry; at Richards' quick motion to screen him from the view of his wife.

But Richards was too late.

When the doctors came they said she had died of heart disease—of joy that kills.

Questions for Discussion

1. Describe Louise's reaction to the news of her husband's death. To what extent do you sympathize with her response?

2. Paragraph 14 of the story concerns "the will." Louise believes that it is a crime "to impose a private will on a fellow creature." What does this belief have to do with her response to her husband's death?

3. Louise dies "of joy that kills." What is your interpretation of this statement?

Suggestions for Writing

1. Write a response in your journal to paragraph 14.

2. Write an essay about "what really kills" Louise Mallard.

3. Write a story that concerns "imposition of a private will on a fellow creature."

The Yellow Wallpaper

CHARLOTTE PERKINS GILMAN

It is very seldom that mere ordinary people like John and myself secure ancestral halls for the summer.

A colonial mansion, a hereditary estate, I would say a haunted house and reach the height of romantic felicity—but that would be asking too much of fate!

Still I will proudly declare that there is something queer about it.

Else, why should it be let so cheaply? And why have stood so long untenanted?

John laughs at me, of course, but one expects that.

John is practical in the extreme. He has no patience with faith, an intense horror of superstition, and he scoffs openly at any talk of things not to be felt and seen and put down in figures.

John is a physician, and *perhaps*—(I would not say it to a living soul, of course, but this is dead paper and a great relief to my mind)—*perhaps* that is one reason I do not get well faster.

You see, he does not believe I am sick! And what can one do?

If a physician of high standing, and one's own husband, assures friends and relatives that there is really nothing the matter with one but temporary nervous depression—a slight hysterical tendency—what is one to do?

My brother is also a physician, and also of high standing, and he says the same thing.

So I take phosphates or phosphites—whichever it is—and tonics, and air and exercise, and journeys, and am absolutely forbidden to "work" until I am well again.

Personally, I disagree with their ideas.

Personally, I believe that congenial work, with excitement and change, would do me good.

But what is one to do?

I did write for a while in spite of them; but it *does* exhaust me a good deal—having to be so sly about it, or else meet with heavy opposition.

I sometimes fancy that in my condition, if I had less opposition and more society and stimulus—but John says the very worst thing I can do is to think about my condition, and I confess it always makes me feel bad.

So I will let it alone and talk about the house.

The most beautiful place! It is quite alone, standing well back from the road, quite three miles from the village. It makes me think of English places that you read about, for there are hedges and walls and gates that lock, and lots of separate little houses for the gardeners and people.

There is a *delicious* garden! I never saw such a garden—large and shady, full of box-bordered paths, and lined with long grape-covered arbors with seats under them.

There were greenhouses, but they are all broken now.

There was some legal trouble, I believe, something about the heirs and co-heirs; anyhow, the place has been empty for years.

That spoils my ghostliness, I am afraid, but I don't care—there is something strange about the house—I can feel it.

I even said so to John one moonlight evening, but he said what I felt was a draught, and shut the window.

I get unreasonably angry with John sometimes. I'm sure I never used to be so sensitive. I think it is due to this nervous condition.

But John says if I feel so I shall neglect proper self-control; so I take pains to control myself—before him, at least, and that makes me very tired.

I don't like our room a bit. I wanted one downstairs that opened onto the piazza and had roses all over the window, and such pretty old-fashioned chintz hangings! But John would not hear of it.

He said there was only one window and not room for two beds, and no near room for him if he took another.

He is very careful and loving, and hardly lets me stir without special direction.

I have a schedule prescription for each hour in the day; he takes all care from me, and so I feel basely ungrateful not to value it more.

He said he came here solely on my account, that I was to have perfect rest and all the air I could get. "Your exercise depends on your strength, my dear," said he, "and your food somewhat on your appetite; but air you can absorb all the time." So we took the nursery at the top of the house.

It is a big, airy room, the whole floor nearly, with windows that look all ways, and air and sunshine galore. It was nursery first, and then playroom and gymnasium, I should judge, for the windows are barred for little children, and there are rings and things in the walls.

The paint and paper look as if a boys' school had used it. It is stripped off—the paper—in great patches all around the head of my bed, about as far as I can reach, and in a great place on the other side of the room low down. I never saw a worse paper in my life. One of those sprawling, flamboyant patterns committing every artistic sin.

It is dull enough to confuse the eye in following, pronounced enough constantly to irritate and provoke study, and when you follow the lame uncertain curves for a little distance they suddenly commit suicide—plunge off at outrageous angles, destroy themselves in unheard-of contradictions.

The color is repellant, almost revolting: a smouldering unclean yellow, strangely faded by the slow-turning sunlight. It is a dull yet lurid orange in some places, a sickly sulphur tint in others.

No wonder the children hated it! I should hate it myself if I had to live in this room long.

There comes John, and I must put this away—he hates to have me write a word.

We have been here two weeks, and I haven't felt like writing before, since that first day.

I am sitting by the window now, up in this atrocious nursery, and there is nothing to hinder my writing as much as I please, save lack of strength.

John is away all day, and even some nights when his cases are serious.

I am glad my case is not serious!

But these nervous troubles are dreadfully depressing.

John does not know how much I really suffer. He knows there is no reason to suffer, and that satisfies him.

Of course it is only nervousness. It does weigh on me so not to do my duty in any way!

I meant to be such a help to John, such a real rest and comfort, and here I am a comparative burden already!

Nobody would believe what an effort it is to do what little I am able —to dress and entertain, and order things.

It is fortunate Mary is so good with the baby. Such a dear baby!

And yet I *cannot* be with him, it makes me so nervous.

I suppose John never was nervous in his life. He laughs at me so about this wallpaper!

At first he meant to repaper the room, but afterward he said that I was letting it get the better of me, and that nothing was worse for a nervous patient than to give way to such fancies.

He said that after the wallpaper was changed it would be the heavy bedstead, and then the barred windows, and then that gate at the end of the stairs, and so on.

"You know the place is doing you good," he said, "and really, dear, I don't care to renovate the house just for a three months' rental."

"Then do let us go downstairs," I said. "There are such pretty rooms there."

Then he took me in his arms and called me a blessed little goose, and said he would go down cellar, if I wished, and have it whitewashed into the bargain.

But he is right enough about the beds and windows and things.

It is as airy and comfortable a room as anyone need wish, and, of course, I would not be so silly as to make him uncomfortable just for a whim.

I'm really getting quite fond of the big room, all but that horrid paper.

Out of one window I can see the garden—those mysterious deep-shaded arbors, the riotous old-fashioned flowers, and bushes and gnarly trees.

Out of another I get a lovely view of the bay and a little private wharf belonging to the estate. There is a beautiful shaded lane that runs down there from the house. I always fancy I see people walking in these numerous paths and arbors, but John has cautioned me not to give way to fancy in the least. He says that with my imaginative power and habit of story-making, a nervous weakness like mine is sure to lead to all manner of excited fancies, and that I ought to use my will and good sense to check the tendency. So I try.

I think sometimes that if I were only well enough to write a little it would relieve the press of ideas and rest me.

But I find I get pretty tired when I try.

It is so discouraging not to have any advice and companionship about my work. When I get really well, John says we will ask Cousin Henry and Julia down for a long visit; but he says he would as soon put fireworks in my pillow-case as to let me have those stimulating people about now.

I wish I could get well faster.

But I must not think about that. This paper looks to me as if it *knew* what a vicious influence it had!

There is a recurrent spot where the pattern lolls like a broken neck and two bulbous eyes stare at you upside down.

I get positively angry with the impertinence of it and the everlastingness. Up and down and sideways they crawl, and those absurd unblinking eyes are everywhere. There is one place where two breadths didn't match, the eyes go all up and down the line, one a little higher than the other.

I never saw so much expression in an inanimate thing before, and we all know how much expression they have! I used to lie awake as a child and get more entertainment and terror out of blank walls and plain furniture than most children could find in a toy-store.

I remember what a kindly wink the knobs of our big old bureau used to have, and there was one chair that always seemed like a strong friend.

I used to feel that if any of the other things looked too fierce I could always hop into that chair and be safe.

The furniture in this room is no worse than inharmonious, however, for we had to bring it all from downstairs. I suppose when this was used as a playroom they had to take the nursery things out, and no wonder! I never saw such ravages as the children have made here.

The wallpaper, as I said before, is torn off in spots, and it sticketh closer than a brother—they must have had perseverance as well as hatred.

Then the floor is scratched and gouged and splintered, the plaster itself is dug out here and there, and this great heavy bed, which is all we found in the room, looks as if it had been through the wars.

But I don't mind it a bit—only the paper.

There comes John's sister. Such a dear girl as she is, and so careful of me! I must not let her find me writing.

She is a perfect and enthusiastic housekeeper, and hopes for no better profession. I verily believe she thinks it is the writing which made me sick!

But I can write when she is out, and see her a long way off from these windows.

There is one that commands the road, a lovely shaded winding road, and one that just looks off over the country. A lovely country, too, full of great elms and velvet meadows.

This wallpaper has a kind of sub-pattern in a different shade, a particularly irritating one, for you can only see it in certain lights, and not clearly then.

But in the places where it isn't faded and where the sun is just so—I can see a strange, provoking, formless sort of figure that seems to skulk about behind that silly and conspicuous front design.

There's sister on the stairs!

Well, the Fourth of July is over! The people are all gone, and I am tired out. John thought it might do me good to see a little company, so we just had Mother and Nellie and the children down for a week.

Of course I didn't do a thing. Jennie sees to everything now.

But it tired me all the same.

John says if I don't pick up faster he shall send me to Weir Mitchell in the fall.

But I don't want to go there at all. I had a friend who was in his hands once, and she says he is just like John and my brother, only more so!

Besides, it is such an undertaking to go so far.

I don't feel as if it was worthwhile to turn my hand over for anything, and I'm getting dreadfully fretful and querulous.

I cry at nothing, and cry most of the time.

Of course I don't when John is here, or anybody else, but when I am alone.

And I am alone a good deal just now. John is kept in town very often by serious cases, and Jennie is good and lets me alone when I want her to.

So I walk a little in the garden or down that lovely lane, sit on the porch under the roses, and lie down up here a good deal.

I'm getting really fond of the room in spite of the wallpaper. Perhaps *because* of the wallpaper.

It dwells in my mind so!

I lie here on this great immovable bed—it is nailed down, I believe—and follow that pattern about by the hour. It is as good as gymnastics, I assure you. I start, we'll say, at the bottom, down in the corner over there where it has not been touched, and I determine for the thousandth time that I *will* follow that pointless pattern to some sort of a conclusion.

I know a little of the principle of design, and I know this thing was not arranged on any laws of radiation, or alternation, or repetition, or symmetry, or anything else that I ever heard of.

It is repeated, of course, by the breadths, but not otherwise.

Looked at in one way, each breadth stands alone; the bloated curves and flourishes—a kind of "debased Romanesque" with delirium tremens go waddling up and down in isolated columns of fatuity.

But, on the other hand, they connect diagonally, and the sprawling outlines run off in great slanting waves of optic horror, like a lot of wallowing sea-weeds in full chase.

The whole thing goes horizontally, too, at least it seems so, and I exhaust myself trying to distinguish the order of its going in that direction.

They have used a horizontal breadth for a frieze, and that adds wonderfully to the confusion.

There is one end of the room where it is almost intact, and there, when the crosslights fade and the low sun shines directly upon it, I can almost fancy radiation after all—the interminable grotesque seems to form around a common center and rush off in headlong plunges of equal distraction.

It makes me tired to follow it. I will take a nap, I guess.

I don't know why I should write this.

I don't want to.

I don't feel able.

And I know John would think it absurd. But I *must* say what I feel and think in some way—it is such a relief!

But the effort is getting to be greater than the relief.

Half the time now I am awfully lazy, and lie down ever so much. John says I mustn't lose my strength, and has me take cod liver oil and lots of tonics and things, to say nothing of ale and wine and rare meat.

Dear John! He loves me very dearly, and hates to have me sick. I tried to have a real earnest reasonable talk with him the other day, and tell him how I wish he would let me go and make a visit to Cousin Henry and Julia.

But he said I wasn't able to go, nor able to stand it after I got there; and I did not make out a very good case for myself, for I was crying before I had finished.

It is getting to be a great effort for me to think straight. Just this nervous weakness, I suppose.

And dear John gathered me up in his arms, and just carried me upstairs and laid me on the bed, and sat by me and read to me till it tired my head.

He said I was his darling and his comfort and all he had, and that I must take care of myself for his sake, and keep well.

He says no one but myself can help me out of it, that I must use my will and self-control and not let any silly fancies run away with me.

There's one comfort—the baby is well and happy, and does not have to occupy this nursery with the horrid wallpaper.

If we had not used it, that blessed child would have! What a fortunate escape! Why, I wouldn't have a child of mine, an impressionable little thing, live in such a room for worlds.

I never thought of it before, but it is lucky that John kept me here after all; I can stand it so much easier than a baby, you see.

Of course I never mention it to them any more—I am too wise—but I keep watch for it all the same.

There are things in that wallpaper that nobody knows about but me, or ever will.

Behind that outside pattern the dim shapes get clearer every day.

It is always the same shape, only very numerous.

And it is like a woman stooping down and creeping about behind that pattern. I don't like it a bit. I wonder—I began to think—I wish John would take me away from here!

It is so hard to talk with John about my case, because he is so wise, and because he loves me so.

But I tried it last night.

It is moonlight. The moon shines in all around just as the sun does.

I hate to see it sometimes, it creeps so slowly, and always comes in by one window or another.

John was asleep and I hated to waken him, so I kept still and watched the moonlight on that undulating wallpaper till I felt creepy.

The faint figure behind seemed to shake the pattern, just as if she wanted to get out.

I got up softly and went to feel and see if the paper *did* move, and when I came back John was awake.

"What is it, little girl?" he said. "Don't go walking about like that—you'll get cold."

I thought it was a good time to talk, so I told him that I really was not gaining here, and that I wished he would take me away.

"Why, darling!" said he. "Our lease will be up in three weeks, and I can't see how to leave before.

"The repairs are not done at home, and I cannot possibly leave town just now. Of course, if you were in any danger, I could and would, but you really are better, dear, whether you can see it or not. I am a doctor, dear, and I know. You are gaining flesh and color, your appetite is better, I feel really much easier about you."

"I don't weigh a bit more," said I, "nor as much; and my appetite may be better in the evening when you are here but it is worse in the morning when you are away!"

"Bless her little heart!" said he with a big hug. "She shall be as sick as she pleases! But now let's improve the shining hours by going to sleep, and talk about it in the morning!"

"And you won't go away?" I asked gloomily.

"Why, how can I, dear? It is only three weeks more and then we will take a nice little trip of a few days while Jennie is getting the house ready. Really, dear, you are better!"

"Better in body perhaps—" I began, and stopped short, for he sat up straight and looked at me with such a stern, reproachful look that I could not say another word.

"My darling," said he, "I beg of you, for my sake and for our child's sake, as well as for your own, that you will never for one instant let that idea enter your mind! There is nothing so dangerous, so fascinating, to a temperament like yours. It is a false and foolish fancy. Can you not trust me as a physician when I tell you so?"

So of course I said no more on that score, and we went to sleep before long. He thought I was asleep first, but I wasn't, and lay there for hours trying to decide whether that front pattern and the back pattern really did move together or separately.

On a pattern like this, by daylight, there is a lack of sequence, a defiance of law, that is a constant irritant to a normal mind.

The color is hideous enough, and unreliable enough, and infuriating enough, but the pattern is torturing.

You think you have mastered it, but just as you get well under way in following, it turns a back-somersault and there you are. It slaps you in the face, knocks you down, and tramples upon you. It is like a bad dream.

The outside pattern is a florid arabesque, reminding one of a fungus. If you can imagine a toadstool in joints, an interminable string of toadstools, budding and sprouting in endless convolutions—why, that is something like it.

That is, sometimes!

There is one marked peculiarity about this paper, a thing nobody seems to notice but myself, and that is that it changes as the light changes.

When the sun shoots in through the east window—I always watch for that first long, straight ray—it changes so quickly that I never can quite believe it.

That is why I watch it always.

By moonlight—the moon shines in all night when there is a moon—I wouldn't know it was the same paper.

At night in any kind of light, in twilight, candlelight, lamplight, and worst of all by moonlight, it becomes bars! The outside pattern, I mean, and the woman behind it is as plain as can be.

I didn't realize for a long time what the thing was that showed behind, that dim sub-pattern, but now I am quite sure it is a woman.

By daylight she is subdued, quiet. I fancy it is the pattern that keeps her so still. It is so puzzling. It keeps me quiet by the hour.

I lie down ever so much now. John says it is good for me, and to sleep all I can.

Indeed he started the habit by making me lie down for an hour after each meal.

It is a very bad habit, I am convinced, for you see, I don't sleep.

And that cultivates deceit, for I don't tell them I'm awake—oh, no!

The fact is I am getting a little afraid of John.

He seems very queer sometimes, and even Jennie has an inexplicable look.

It strikes me occasionally, just as a scientific hypothesis, that perhaps it is the paper!

I have watched John when he did not know I was looking, and come into the room suddenly on the most innocent excuses, and I've caught him several times *looking at the paper!* And Jennie too. I caught Jennie with her hand on it once.

She didn't know I was in the room, and when I asked her in a quiet, a very quiet voice, with the most restrained manner possible, what she was doing with the paper, she turned around as if she had been caught stealing, and looked quite angry—asked me why I should frighten her so!

Then she said that the paper stained everything it touched, that she had found yellow smooches on all my clothes and John's and she wished we would be more careful!

Did not that sound innocent? But I know she was studying that pattern, and I am determined that nobody shall find it out but myself!

Life is very much more exciting now than it used to be. You see, I have something more to expect, to look forward to, to watch. I really do eat better, and am more quiet than I was.

John is so pleased to see me improve! He laughed a little the other day, and said I seemed to be flourishing in spite of my wallpaper.

I turned it off with a laugh. I had no intention of telling him it was *because* of the wallpaper—he would make fun of me. He might even want to take me away.

I don't want to leave now until I have found it out. There is a week more, and I think that will be enough.

I'm feeling so much better!

I don't sleep much at night, for it is so interesting to watch developments; but I sleep a good deal during the daytime.

In the daytime it is tiresome and perplexing.

There are always new shoots on the fungus, and new shades of yellow all over it. I cannot keep count of them, though I have tried conscientiously.

It is the strangest yellow, that wallpaper! It makes me think of all the yellow things I ever saw—not beautiful ones like buttercups, but old, foul, bad yellow things.

But there is something else about that paper—the smell! I noticed it the moment we came into the room, but with so much air and sun it was not bad. Now we have had a week of fog and rain, and whether the windows are open or not, the smell is here.

It creeps all over the house.

I find it hovering in the dining-room, skulking in the parlor, hiding in the hall, lying in wait for me on the stairs.

It gets into my hair.

Even when I go to ride, if I turn my head suddenly and surprise it—there is that smell!

Such a peculiar odor, too! I have spent hours in trying to analyze it, to find what it smelled like.

It is not bad—at first—and very gentle, but quite the subtlest, most enduring odor I ever met.

In this damp weather it is awful. I wake up in the night and find it hanging over me.

It used to disturb me at first. I thought seriously of burning the house—to reach the smell.

But now I am used to it. The only thing I can think of that it is like the *color* of the paper! A yellow smell.

There is a very funny mark on this wall, low down, near the mopboard. A streak that runs round the room. It goes behind every piece of furniture, except the bed, a long, straight, even *smooch,* as if it had been rubbed over and over.

I wonder how it was done and who did it, and what they did it for. Round and round and round—round and round and round—it makes me dizzy!

I really have discovered something at last.

Through watching so much at night, when it changes so, I have finally found out.

The front pattern *does* move—and no wonder! The woman behind shakes it!

Sometimes I think there are a great many women behind, and sometimes only one, and she crawls around fast, and her crawling shakes it all over.

Then in the very bright spots she keeps still, and in the very shady spots she just takes hold of the bars and shakes them hard.

And she is all the time trying to climb through. But nobody could climb through that pattern—it strangles so; I think that is why it has so many heads.

They get through and then the pattern strangles them off and turns them upside down, and makes their eyes white!

If those heads were covered or taken off it would not be half so bad.

I think that woman gets out in the daytime!

And I'll tell you why—privately—I've seen her!

I can see her out of every one of my windows!

It is the same woman, I know, for she is always creeping, and most women do not creep by daylight.

I see her in that long shaded lane, creeping up and down. I see her in those dark grape arbors, creeping all around the garden.

I see her on that long road under the trees, creeping along, and when a carriage comes she hides under the blackberry vines.

I don't blame her a bit. It must be very humiliating to be caught creeping by daylight!

I always lock the door when I creep by daylight. I can't do it at night, for I know John would suspect something at once.

And John is so queer now that I don't want to irritate him. I wish he would take another room! Besides, I don't want anybody to get that woman out at night but myself.

I often wonder if I could see her out of all the windows at once.

But, turn as fast as I can, I can only see out of one at a time.

And though I always see her, she *may* be able to creep faster than I can turn! I have watched her sometimes away off in the open country, creeping as fast as a cloud shadow in a wind.

If only that top pattern could be gotten off from the under one! I mean to try it, little by little.

I have found out another funny thing, but I shan't tell this time! It does not do to trust people too much.

There are only two more days to get this paper off, and I believe John is beginning to notice. I don't like the look in his eyes.

And I heard him ask Jennie a lot of professional questions about me. She had a very good report to give.

She said I slept a good deal in the daytime.

John knows I don't sleep very well at night, for all I'm so quiet!

He asked me all sorts of questions, too, and pretended to be very loving and kind.

As if I couldn't see through him!

Still, I don't wonder he acts so, sleeping under this paper for three months.

It only interests me, but I feel sure John and Jennie are affected by it.

Hurray! This is the last day, but it is enough. John is to stay in town over night, and won't be out until this evening.

Jennie wanted to sleep with me—the sly thing; but I told her I should undoubtedly rest better for a night all alone.

That was clever, for really I wasn't alone a bit! As soon as it was moonlight and that poor thing began to crawl and shake the pattern, I got up and ran to help her.

I pulled and she shook. I shook and she pulled, and before morning we had peeled off yards of that paper.

A strip about as high as my head and half around the room.

And then when the sun came and that awful pattern began to laugh at me, I declared I would finish it today!

We go away tomorrow, and they are moving all my furniture down again to leave things as they were before.

Jennie looked at the wall in amazement, but I told her merrily that I did it out of pure spite at the vicious thing.

She laughed and said she wouldn't mind doing it herself, but I must not get tired.

How she betrayed herself that time!

But I am here, and no person touches this paper but Me—not *alive!*

She tried to get me out of the room—it was too patent! But I said it was so quiet and empty and clean now that I believed I would lie down again and sleep all I could, and not to wake me even for dinner—I would call when I woke.

So now she is gone, and the servants are gone, and the things are gone, and there is nothing left but that great bedstead nailed down, with the canvas mattress we found on it.

We shall sleep downstairs tonight, and take the boat home tomorrow.

I quite enjoy the room, now it is bare again.

How those children did tear about here!

This bedstead is fairly gnawed!

But I must get to work.

I have locked the door and thrown the key down into the front path.

I don't want to go out, and I don't want to have anybody come in, till John comes.

I want to astonish him.

I've got a rope up here that even Jennie did not find. If that woman does get out, and tries to get away, I can tie her!

But I forgot I could not reach far without anything to stand on!

This bed will *not* move!

I tried to lift and push it until I was lame, and then I got so angry I bit off a little piece at one corner—but it hurt my teeth.

Then I peeled off all the paper I could reach standing on the floor. It sticks horribly and the pattern just enjoys it! All those strangled heads and bulbous eyes and waddling fungus growths just shriek with derision!

I am getting angry enough to do something desperate. To jump out of the window would be admirable exercise, but the bars are too strong even to try.

Besides I wouldn't do it. Of course not. I know well enough that a step like that is improper and might be misconstrued.

I don't like to *look* out of the windows even—there are so many of those creeping women, and they creep so fast.

I wonder if they all come out of that wallpaper as I did?

But I am securely fastened now by my well-hidden rope—you don't get *me* out in the road there!

I suppose I shall have to get back behind the pattern when it comes night, and that is hard!

It is so pleasant to be out in this great room and creep around as I please!

I don't want to go outside. I won't, even if Jennie asks me to.

For outside you have to creep on the ground, and everything is green instead of yellow.

But here I can creep smoothly on the floor, and my shoulder just fits in that long smooch around the wall, so I cannot lose my way.

Why, there's John at the door!

It is no use, young man, you can't open it!

How he does call and pound!

Now he's crying to Jennie for an axe.

It would be a shame to break down that beautiful door!

"John, dear!" said I in the gentlest voice. "The key is down by the front steps, under a plantain leaf!"

That silenced him for a few moments.

Then he said, very quietly indeed, "Open the door, my darling!"

"I can't," said I. "The key is down by the front door under a plantain leaf!" And then I said it again, several times, very gently and slowly, and said it so often that he had to go and see, and he got it of course, and came in. He stopped short by the door.

"What is the matter?" he cried. "For God's sake, what are you doing?"

I kept on creeping just the same, but I looked at him over my shoulder.

"I've got out at last," said I, "in spite of you and Jane. And I've pulled off most of the paper, so you can't put me back."

Now why should that man have fainted? But he did, and right across my path by the wall, so that I had to creep over him every time!

Questions for Discussion

1. What does Gilman gain by telling the story in first person rather than third?

2. Describe John. What kind of husband is he? How does he treat her? Why doesn't he like her to write?

3. Give examples of how Gilman increases the sense of the woman's madness gradually.

4. What does the wallpaper come to symbolize for the woman?

Suggestions for Writing

1. Write an essay in which you compare and contrast "The Yellow Wallpaper" with "The Story of an Hour."

2. Write an essay in which you contrast Gilman's depiction of madness with Poe's in "The Tell-Tale Heart."

3. Write a one-page monologue from John's point of view in which you summarize the events of the story. Then explain who you think is more reliable as a narrator—the "John" you've created or Gilman's "I" narrator.

A Scandal in Bohemia

ARTHUR   CONAN   DOYLE

To Sherlock Holmes she is always *the* woman. I have seldom heard him mention her under any other name. In his eyes she eclipses and predominates the whole of her sex. It was not that he felt any emotion akin to love for Irene Adler. All emotions, and that one particularly, were abhorrent to his cold, precise but admirably balanced mind. He was, I take it, the most perfect reasoning and observing machine that the world has seen, but as a lover he would have placed himself in a false position. He never spoke of the softer passions, save with a gibe and a sneer. They were admirable things for the observer—excellent for drawing the veil from men's motives and actions. But for the trained reasoner to admit such intrusions into his own delicate and finely adjusted temperament was to introduce a distracting factor which might throw a doubt upon all his mental results. Grit in a sensitive instrument, or a crack in one of his own high-power lenses, would not be more disturbing than a strong emotion in a nature such as his. And yet there was but one woman to him, and that woman was the late Irene Adler, of dubious and questionable memory.

I had seen little of Holmes lately. My marriage had drifted us away from each other. My own complete happiness, and the home-centred interests which rise up around the man who first finds himself master of his own establishment, were sufficient to absorb all my attention, while Holmes, who loathed every form of society with his whole Bohemian soul, remained in our lodgings in Baker Street, buried among his old books, and alternating from week to week between cocaine and ambition, the drowsiness of the drug, and the fierce energy of his own keen nature. He was still, as ever, deeply attracted by the study of crime, and occupied his immense faculties and extraordinary powers of observation in following out those clues, and clearing up those mysteries which had been abandoned as hopeless by the official police. From time to time I heard some vague account of his doings: of his summons to Odessa in the case of the Trepoff murder, of his clearing up of the singular tragedy of the Atkinson brothers at Trincomalee, and finally of the mission which he had accomplished so delicately and successfully for the reigning family of Holland. Beyond these signs of his activity, however, which I merely shared with all the readers of the daily press, I knew little of my former friend and companion.

One night—it was on the twentieth of March, 1888—I was returning from a journey to a patient (for I had now returned to civil practice), when my way led me through Baker Street. As I passed the well-remembered door, which must always be associated in my mind with my wooing, and with the dark incidents of the *Study in Scarlet*, I was seized with a keen desire to see Holmes again, and to know how he was employing his extraordinary powers. His rooms were brilliantly lit, and, even as I looked up, I saw his tall, spare figure pass twice in a dark silhouette against the blind. He was pacing the room swiftly, eagerly, with his head sunk upon his chest and his hands clasped behind him. To me, who knew his every mood and habit, his attitude and manner told their own story. He was at work again. He had risen out of his drug-created dreams and was hot upon the scent of some new problem. I rang the bell and was shown up to the chamber which had formerly been in part my own.

His manner was not effusive. It seldom was; but he was glad, I think, to see me. With hardly a word spoken, but with a kindly eye, he waved me to an armchair, threw across his case of cigars, and indicated a spirit case and a gasogene in the corner. Then he stood before the fire and looked me over in his singular introspective fashion.

"Wedlock suits you," he remarked. "I think, Watson, that you have put on seven and a half pounds since I saw you."

"Seven!" I answered.

"Indeed, I should have thought a little more. Just a trifle more, I fancy, Watson. And in practice again, I observe. You did not tell me that you intended to go into harness."

"Then, how do you know?"

"I see it, I deduce it. How do I know that you have been getting yourself very wet lately, and that you have a most clumsy and careless servant girl?"

"My dear Holmes," said I, "this is too much. You would certainly have been burned, had you lived a few centuries ago. It is true that I had a country walk on Thursday and came home in a dreadful mess, but as I have changed my clothes I can't imagine how you deduce it. As to Mary Jane, she is incorrigible, and my wife has given her notice; but there, again, I fail to see how you work it out."

He chuckled to himself and rubbed his long, nervous hands together.

"It is simplicity itself," said he; "my eyes tell me that on the inside of your left shoe, just where the firelight strikes it, the leather is scored by six almost parallel cuts. Obviously they have been caused by someone who has very carelessly scraped round the edges of the sole in order to remove crusted mud from it. Hence, you see, my double deduction that you had been out in vile weather, and that you had a particularly malignant boot-slitting specimen of the London slavey. As to your practice, if a gentleman walks into my rooms smelling of iodoform, with a black mark of nitrate of silver upon his right forefinger, and a bulge on the right side of his top-hat to show where he has secreted his stethoscope, I must be dull, indeed, if I do not pronounce him to be an active member of the medical profession."

I could not help laughing at the ease with which he explained his process of deduction. "When I hear you give your reasons," I remarked, "the thing always appears to me to be so ridiculously simple that I could easily do it myself, though at each successive instance of your reasoning I am baffled until you explain your process. And yet I believe that my eyes are as good as yours."

"Quite so," he answered, lighting a cigarette, and throwing himself down into an armchair. "You see, but you do not observe. The distinction is clear. For example, you have frequently seen the steps which lead up from the hall to this room."

"Frequently."

"How often?"

"Well, some hundreds of times."

"Then how many are there?"

"How many? I don't know."

"Quite so! You have not observed. And yet you have seen. That is just my point. Now, I know that there are seventeen steps, because I have both seen and observed. By the way, since you are interested in these little problems, and since you are good enough to chronicle one or two of my trifling experiences, you may be interested in this." He threw over a sheet of thick, pink-tinted note-paper which had been lying open upon the table. "It came by the last post," said he. "Read it aloud."

The note was undated, and without either signature or address.

There will call upon you to-night, at a quarter to eight o'clock [it said], a gentleman who desires to consult you upon a matter of the very deepest moment. Your recent services to one of the royal houses of Europe have shown that you are one who may safely be trusted with matters which are of an importance which can hardly be exaggerated. This account of you we have from all quarters received. Be in your chamber then at that hour, and do not take it amiss if your visitor wear a mask.

"This is indeed a mystery," I remarked. "What do you imagine that it means?"

"I have no data yet. It is a capital mistake to theorize before one has data. Insensibly one begins to twist facts to suit theories, instead of theories to suit facts. But the note itself. What do you deduce from it?"

I carefully examined the writing, and the paper upon which it was written.

"The man who wrote it was presumably well to do," I remarked, endeavouring to imitate my companion's processes. "Such paper could not be bought under half a crown a packet. It is peculiarly strong and stiff."

"Peculiar—that is the very word," said Holmes. "It is not an English paper at all. Hold it up to the light."

I did so, and saw a large "*E*" with a small "*g*," a "*P*," and a large "*G*" with a small "*t*" woven into the texture of the paper.

"What do you make of that?" asked Holmes.

"The name of the maker, no doubt; or his monogram, rather."

"Not at all. The '*G*' with the small '*t*' stands for '*Gesellschaft*,' which is the German for 'Company.' It is a customary contraction like our 'Co.' '*P*,' of course, stands for 'Papier.' Now for the '*Eg*.' Let us glance at our Continental Gazetteer." He took down a heavy brown volume from his shelves. "Eglow, Eglonitz—here we are, Egria. It is in a German-speaking country—in Bohemia, not far from Carlsbad. 'Remarkable as being the scene of the death of Wallenstein, and for its numerous glass-factories and paper-mills.' Ha, ha, my boy, what do you make of that?" His eyes sparkled, and he sent up a great blue triumphant cloud from his cigarette.

"The paper was made in Bohemia," I said.

"Precisely. And the man who wrote the note is a German. Do you note the peculiar construction of the sentence—'This account of you we have from all quarters received.' A Frenchman or Russian could not have written that. It is the German who is so uncourteous to his verbs. It only remains, therefore, to discover what is wanted by this German who writes upon Bohemian paper and prefers wearing a mask to showing his face. And here he comes, if I am not mistaken, to resolve all our doubts."

As he spoke there was the sharp sound of horses' hoofs and grating wheels against the curb, followed by a sharp pull at the bell. Holmes whistled.

"A pair, by the sound," said he. "Yes," he continued, glancing out of the window. "A nice little brougham and a pair of beauties. A hundred and fifty guineas apiece. There's money in this case, Watson, if there is nothing else."

"I think that I had better go, Holmes."

"Not a bit, Doctor. Stay where you are. I am lost without my Boswell. And this promises to be interesting. It would be a pity to miss it."

"But your client——"

"Never mind him. I may want your help, and so may he. Here he comes. Sit down in that armchair, Doctor, and give us your best attention."

A slow and heavy step, which had been heard upon the stairs and in the passage, paused immediately outside the door. Then there was a loud and authoritative tap.

"Come in!" said Holmes.

A man entered who could hardly have been less than six feet six inches in height, with the chest and limbs of a Hercules. His dress was rich with a richness which would, in England, be looked upon as akin to bad taste. Heavy bands of astrakhan were slashed across the sleeves and fronts of his double-breasted coat, while the deep blue cloak which was thrown over his shoulders was lined with flame-coloured silk and secured at the neck with a brooch which consisted of a single flaming beryl. Boots which extended halfway up his calves, and which were trimmed at the tops with rich brown fur, completed the impression of barbaric opulence which was suggested by his whole appearance. He carried a broad-brimmed hat in his hand, while he wore across the upper part of his face, extending down past the cheekbones, a black vizard mask, which he had apparently adjusted that very moment, for his hand was still raised to it as he entered. From the lower part of the face he appeared to be a man of strong character, with a thick, hanging lip, and a long, straight chin suggestive of resolution pushed to the length of obstinacy.

"You had my note?" he asked with a deep harsh voice and a strongly marked German accent. "I told you that I would call." He looked from one to the other of us, as if uncertain which to address.

"Pray take a seat," said Holmes. "This is my friend and colleague, Dr. Watson, who is occasionally good enough to help me in my cases. Whom have I the honour to address?"

"You may address me as the Count Von Kramm, a Bohemian nobleman. I understand that this gentleman, your friend, is a man of honour and discretion, whom I may trust with a matter of the most extreme importance. If not, I should much prefer to communicate with you alone."

I rose to go, but Holmes caught me by the wrist and pushed me back into my chair. "It is both, or none," said he. "You may say before this gentleman anything which you may say to me."

The Count shrugged his broad shoulders. "Then I must begin," said he, "by binding you both to absolute secrecy for two years; at the end of that time the matter will be of no importance. At present it is not too much to say that it is of such weight it may have an influence upon European history."

"I promise," said Holmes.

"And I."

"You will excuse this mask," continued our strange visitor. "The august person who employs me wishes his agent to be unknown to you, and I may confess at once that the title by which I have just called myself is not exactly my own."

"I was aware of it," said Holmes drily.

"The circumstances are of great delicacy, and every precaution has to be taken to quench what might grow to be an immense scandal and seriously compromise one of the reigning families of Europe. To speak plainly, the matter implicates the great House of Ormstein, hereditary kings of Bohemia."

"I was also aware of that," murmured Holmes, settling himself down in his armchair and closing his eyes.

Our visitor glanced with some apparent surprise at the languid, lounging figure of the man who had been no doubt depicted to him as the most incisive reasoner and most energetic agent in Europe. Holmes slowly reopened his eyes and looked impatiently at his gigantic client.

"If your Majesty would condescend to state your case," he remarked, "I should be better able to advise you."

The man sprang from his chair and paced up and down the room in uncontrollable agitation. Then, with a gesture of desperation, he tore the mask from his face and hurled it upon the ground. "You are right," he cried; "I am the King. Why should I attempt to conceal it?"

"Why, indeed?" murmured Holmes. "Your Majesty had not spoken before I was aware that I was addressing Wilhelm Gottsreich Sigismond von Ormstein, Grand Duke of Cassel-Felstein, and hereditary King of Bohemia."

"But you can understand," said our strange visitor, sitting down once more and passing his hand over his high white forehead, "you can understand that I am not accustomed to doing such business in my own person. Yet the matter was so delicate that I could not confide it to an agent without putting myself in his power. I have come incognito from Prague for the purpose of consulting you."

"Then, pray consult," said Holmes, shutting his eyes once more.

"The facts are briefly these: Some five years ago, during a lengthy visit to Warsaw, I made the acquaintance of the well-known adventuress, Irene Adler. The name is no doubt familiar to you."

"Kindly look her up in my index, Doctor," murmured Holmes without opening his eyes. For many years he had adopted a system of docketing all paragraphs concerning men and things, so that it was difficult to name a subject or a person on which he could not at once furnish information. In this case I found her biography sandwiched in between that of a Hebrew rabbi and that of a staff-commander who had written a monograph upon the deep-sea fishes.

"Let me see!" said Holmes. "Hum! Born in New Jersey in the year 1858. Contralto—hum! La Scala, hum! Prima donna Imperial Opera of Warsaw—yes! Retired from operatic stage—ha! Living in London—quite so! Your Majesty, as I understand, became entangled with this young person, wrote her some compromising letters, and is now desirous of getting those letters back."

"Precisely so. But how——"

"Was there a secret marriage?"

"None."

"No legal papers or certificates?"

"None."

"Then I fail to follow your Majesty. If this young person should produce her letters for blackmailing or other purposes, how is she to prove their authenticity?"

"There is the writing."

"Pooh, pooh! Forgery."

"My private note-paper."

"Stolen."

"My own seal."

"Imitated."

"My photograph."

"Bought."

"We were both in the photograph."

"Oh, dear! That is very bad! Your Majesty has indeed committed an indiscretion."

"I was mad—insane."

"You have compromised yourself seriously."

"I was only Crown Prince then. I was young. I am but thirty now."

"It must be recovered."

"We have tried and failed."

"Your Majesty must pay. It must be bought."

"She will not sell."

"Stolen, then."

"Five attempts have been made. Twice burglars in my pay ransacked her house. Once we diverted her luggage when she travelled. Twice she has been waylaid. There has been no result."

"No sign of it?"

"Absolutely none."

Holmes laughed. "It is quite a pretty little problem," said he.

"But a very serious one to me," returned the King reproachfully.

"Very, indeed. And what does she propose to do with the photograph?"

"To ruin me."

"But how?"

"I am about to be married."

"So I have heard."

"To Clotilde Lothman von Saxe-Meningen, second daughter of the King of Scandinavia. You may know the strict principles of her family. She is herself the very soul of delicacy. A shadow of a doubt as to my conduct would bring the matter to an end."

"And Irene Adler?"

"Threatens to send them the photograph. And she will do it. I know that she will do it. You do not know her, but she has a soul of steel. She has the face of the most beautiful of women, and the mind of the most resolute of men. Rather than I should marry another woman, there are no lengths to which she would not go—none."

"You are sure that she has not sent it yet?"

"I am sure."

"And why?"

"Because she has said that she would send it on the day when the betrothal was publicly proclaimed. That will be next Monday."

"Oh, then we have three days yet," said Holmes with a yawn. "That is very fortunate, as I have one or two matters of importance to look into just at present. Your Majesty will, of course, stay in London for the present?"

"Certainly. You will find me at the Langham under the name of the Count Von Kramm."

"Then I shall drop you a line to let you know how we progress."

"Pray do so. I shall be all anxiety."

"Then, as to money?"

"You have carte blanche."

"Absolutely?"

"I tell you that I would give one of the provinces of my kingdom to have that photograph."

"And for present expenses?"

The King took a heavy chamois leather bag from under his cloak and laid it on the table.

"There are three hundred pounds in gold and seven hundred in notes," he said.

Holmes scribbled a receipt upon a sheet of his note-book and handed it to him.

"And Mademoiselle's address?" he asked.

"Is Briony Lodge, Serpentine Avenue, St. John's Wood."

Holmes took a note of it. "One other question," said he. "Was the photograph a cabinet?"

"It was."

"Then, good-night, your Majesty, and I trust that we shall soon have some good news for you. And good-night, Watson," he added, as the wheels of the royal brougham rolled down the street. "If you will be good enough to call to-morrow afternoon at three o'clock I should like to chat this little matter over with you."

2

At three o'clock precisely I was at Baker Street, but Holmes had not yet returned. The landlady informed me that he had left the house shortly after eight o'clock in the morning. I sat down beside the fire, however, with the intention of awaiting him, however long he might be. I was already deeply interested in his inquiry, for, though it was surrounded by none of the grim and strange features which were associated with the two crimes which I have already recorded,[1] still, the nature of the case and the exalted station of his client gave it a character of its own. Indeed, apart from the nature of the investigation which my friend had on hand, there was something in his masterly grasp of a situation, and his keen, incisive reasoning, which made it a pleasure to me to study his system of work, and to follow the quick, subtle methods by which he disentangled the most inextricable mysteries. So accustomed was I to his invariable success that the very possibility of his failing had ceased to enter into my head.

It was close upon four before the door opened, and a drunken-looking groom, ill-kempt and side-whiskered, with an inflamed face and disreputable clothes, walked into the room. Accustomed as I was to my friend's amazing powers in the use of disguises, I had to look three times before I was certain that it was indeed he. With a nod he vanished into the bedroom, whence he emerged in five minutes tweed-suited and respectable, as of old. Putting his hands into his pockets, he stretched out his legs in front of the fire and laughed heartily for some minutes.

"Well, really!" he cried, and then he choked and laughed again until he was obliged to lie back, limp and helpless, in the chair.

"What is it?"

"It's quite too funny. I am sure you could never guess how I employed my morning, or what I ended by doing."

"I can't imagine. I suppose that you have been watching the habits, and perhaps the house, of Miss Irene Adler."

"Quite so; but the sequel was rather unusual. I will tell you, however. I left the house a little after eight o'clock this morning in the character of a groom out of work. There is a wonderful sympathy and freemasonry among horsy men. Be one of them, and you will know all that there is to know. I soon found Briony Lodge. It is a *bijou* villa, with a garden at the back, but built out in front right up to the road, two stories. Chubb lock to the door. Large sitting-room on the right side, well furnished, with long windows almost to the floor, and those preposterous English window fasteners which a child could open. Behind there was nothing remarkable, save that the passage window could be reached from the top of the coach-house. I walked round it and examined it closely from every point of view, but without noting anything else of interest.

---

1. Watson refers here to other crimes "recorded" in other stories he has written about Holmes. [Editor]

"I then lounged down the street and found, as I expected, that there was a mews in a lane which runs down by one wall of the garden. I lent the ostlers a hand in rubbing down their horses, and received in exchange two pence, a glass of half and half, two fills of shag tobacco, and as much information as I could desire about Miss Adler, to say nothing of half a dozen other people in the neighbourhood in whom I was not in the least interested, but whose biographies I was compelled to listen to."

"And what of Irene Adler?" I asked.

"Oh, she has turned all the men's heads down in that part. She is the daintiest thing under a bonnet on this planet. So say the Serpentine-mews, to a man. She lives quietly, sings at concerts, drives out at five every day, and returns at seven sharp for dinner. Seldom goes out at other times, except when she sings. Has only one male visitor, but a good deal of him. He is dark, handsome, and dashing, never calls less than once a day, and often twice. He is a Mr. Godfrey Norton, of the Inner Temple. See the advantages of a cabman as a confidant. They had driven him home a dozen times from Serpentine-mews, and knew all about him. When I had listened to all they had to tell, I began to walk up and down near Briony Lodge once more, and to think over my plan of campaign.

"This Godfrey Norton was evidently an important factor in the matter. He was a lawyer. That sounded ominous. What was the relation between them, and what the object of his repeated visits? Was she his client, his friend, or his mistress? If the former, she had probably transferred the photograph to his keeping. If the latter, it was less likely. On the issue of this question depended whether I should continue my work at Briony Lodge, or turn my attention to the gentleman's chambers in the Temple. It was a delicate point, and it widened the field of my inquiry. I fear that I bore you with these details, but I have to let you see my little difficulties, if you are to understand the situation."

"I am following you closely," I answered.

"I was still balancing the matter in my mind when a hansom cab drove up to Briony Lodge, and a gentleman sprang out. He was a remarkably handsome man, dark, aquiline, and moustached—evidently the man of whom I had heard. He appeared to be in a great hurry, shouted to the cabman to wait, and brushed past the maid who opened the door with the air of a man who was thoroughly at home.

"He was in the house about half an hour, and I could catch glimpses of him in the windows of the sitting-room, pacing up and down, talking excitedly, and waving his arms. Of her I could see nothing. Presently he emerged, looking even more flurried than before. As he stepped up to the cab, he pulled a gold watch from his pocket and looked at it earnestly, 'Drive like the devil,' he shouted, 'first to Gross & Hankey's in Regent Street, and then to the Church of St. Monica in the Edgeware Road. Half a guinea if you do it in twenty minutes!'

"Away they went, and I was just wondering whether I should not do well to follow them when up the lane came a neat little landau, the coachman with his coat only half-buttoned, and his tie under his ear, while all the tags of his harness were sticking out of the buckles. It hadn't pulled up before she shot out of the hall door and into it. I only caught a glimpse of her at the moment, but she was a lovely woman, with a face that a man might die for.

"'The Church of St. Monica, John,' she cried, 'and half a sovereign if you reach it in twenty minutes.'

"This was quite too good to lose, Watson. I was just balancing whether I should run for it, or whether I should perch behind her landau when a cab came through the street. The driver looked twice at such a shabby fare, but I jumped in before he could object. 'The Church of St. Monica,' said I, 'and half a sovereign if you reach it in twenty minutes.' It was twenty-five minutes to twelve, and of course it was clear enough what was in the wind.

"My cabby drove fast. I don't think I ever drove faster, but the others were there before us. The cab and the landau with their steaming horses were in front of the door when I arrived. I paid the man and hurried into the church. There was not a soul there save the two whom I had followed and a surpliced clergyman, who seemed to be expostulating with them. They were all three standing in a knot in front of the altar. I lounged up the side aisle like any other idler who has dropped into a church. Suddenly, to my surprise, the three at the altar faced round to me, and Godfrey Norton came running as hard as he could towards me.

"'Thank God,' he cried. 'You'll do. Come! Come!'

"'What then?' I asked.

"'Come, man, come, only three minutes, or it won't be legal.'

"I was half-dragged up to the altar, and before I knew where I was I found myself mumbling responses which were whispered in my ear, and vouching for things of which I knew nothing, and generally assisting in the secure tying up of Irene Adler, spinster, to Godfrey Norton, bachelor. It was all done in an instant, and there was the gentleman thanking me on the one side and the lady on the other, while the clergyman beamed on me in front. It was the most preposterous position in which I ever found myself in my life, and it was the thought of it that started me laughing just now. It seems that there had been some informality about their license, that the clergyman absolutely refused to marry them without a witness of some sort, and that my lucky appearance saved the bridegroom from having to sally out into the streets in search of a best man. The bride gave me a sovereign, and I mean to wear it on my watch-chain in memory of the occasion."

"This is a very unexpected turn of affairs," said I; "and what then?"

"Well, I found my plans very seriously menaced. It looked as if the pair might take an immediate departure, and so necessitate very prompt and energetic measures on my part. At the church door, however, they separated, he driving back to the Temple, and she to her own house. 'I shall drive out in the park at five as usual,' she said as she left him. I heard no more. They drove away in different directions, and I went off to make my own arrangements."

"Which are?"

"Some cold beef and a glass of beer," he answered, ringing the bell. "I have been too busy to think of food, and I am likely to be busier still this evening. By the way, Doctor, I shall want your coöperation."

"I shall be delighted."

"You don't mind breaking the law?"

"Not in the least."

"Nor running a chance of arrest?"

"Not in a good cause."

"Oh, the cause is excellent!"

"Then I am your man."

"I was sure that I might rely on you."

"But what is it you wish?"

"When Mrs. Turner has brought in the tray I will make it clear to you. Now," he said as he turned hungrily on the simple fare that our landlady had provided, "I must discuss it while I eat, for I have not much time. It is nearly five now. In two hours we must be on the scene of action. Miss Irene, or Madame, rather, returns from her drive at seven. We must be at Briony Lodge to meet her."

"And what then?"

"You must leave that to me. I have already arranged what is to occur. There is only one point on which I must insist. You must not interfere, come what may. You understand?"

"I am to be neutral?"

"To do nothing whatever. There will probably be some small unpleasantness. Do not join in it. It will end in my being conveyed into the house. Four or five minutes afterwards the sitting-room window will open. You are to station yourself close to that open window."

"Yes."

"You are to watch me, for I will be visible to you."

"Yes."

"And when I raise my hand—so—you will throw into the room what I give you to throw, and will, at the same time, raise the cry of fire. You quite follow me?"

"Entirely."

"It is nothing very formidable," he said, taking a long cigar-shaped roll from his pocket. "It is an ordinary plumber's smoke-rocket, fitted with a cap at either end to make it self-lighting. Your task is confined to that. When you raise your cry of fire, it will be taken up by quite a number of people. You may then walk to the end of the street, and I will rejoin you in ten minutes. I hope that I have made myself clear?"

"I am to remain neutral, to get near the window, to watch you, and at the signal to throw in this object, then to raise the cry of fire, and to wait for you at the corner of the street."

"Precisely."

"Then you may entirely rely on me."

"That is excellent. I think, perhaps, it is almost time that I prepare for the new rôle I have to play."

He disappeared into his bedroom and returned in a few minutes in the character of an amiable and simple-minded Nonconformist clergyman. His broad black hat, his baggy trousers, his white tie, his sympathetic smile, and general look of peering and benevolent curiosity were such as Mr. John Hare alone could have equalled. It was not merely that Holmes changed his costume. His expression, his manner, his very soul seemed to vary with every fresh part that he assumed. The stage lost a fine actor, even as science lost an acute reasoner, when he became a specialist in crime.

It was a quarter past six when we left Baker Street, and it still want d ten minutes to the hour when we found ourselves in Serpentine Avenue. It was already dusk, and the lamps were just being lighted as we paced up and down in front of Briony Lodge, waiting for the coming of its occupant. The house was just such as I had pictured it from Sherlock Holmes's succinct description, but the locality appeared to be less private than I expected. On the contrary, for a small street in a quiet neighbourhood, it was remarkably animated. There was a group of shabbily dressed men smoking and laughing in a corner, a scissors-grinder with his wheel, two guardsmen who were flirting with a nurse-girl, and several well-dressed young men who were lounging up and down with cigars in their mouths.

"You see," remarked Holmes, as we paced to and fro in front of the house, "this marriage rather simplifies matters. The photograph becomes a double-edged weapon now. The chances are that she would be as averse to its being seen by Mr. Godfrey Norton, as our client is to its coming to the eyes of his princess. Now the question is, Where are we to find the photograph?"

"Where, indeed?"

"It is most unlikely that she carries it about with her. It is cabinet size. Too large for easy concealment about a woman's dress. She knows that the King is capable of having her waylaid and searched. Two attempts of the sort have already been made. We may take it, then, that she does not carry it about with her."

"Where, then?"

"Her banker or her lawyer. There is that double possibility. But I am inclined to think neither. Women are naturally secretive, and they like to do their own secreting. Why should she hand it over to anyone else? She could trust her own guardianship, but she could not tell what indirect or political influence might be brought to bear upon a business man. Besides, remember that she had resolved to use it within a few days. It must be where she can lay her hands upon it. It must be in her own house."

"But it has twice been burgled."

"Pshaw! They did not know how to look."

"But how will you look?"

"I will not look."

"What then?"

"I will get her to show me."

"But she will refuse."

"She will not be able to. But I hear the rumble of wheels. It is her carriage. Now carry out my orders to the letter."

As he spoke the gleam of the side-lights of a carriage came round the curve of the avenue. It was a smart little landau which rattled up to the door of Briony Lodge. As it pulled up, one of the loafing men at the corner dashed forward to open the door in the hope of earning a copper, but was elbowed away by another loafer, who had rushed up with the same intention. A fierce quarrel broke out, which was increased by the two guardsmen, who took sides with one of the loungers, and by the scissors-grinder, who was equally hot upon the other side. A blow was struck, and in an instant the lady, who had stepped from her carriage, was the centre of a little knot of flushed and struggling men, who struck savagely at each other with their fists and sticks. Holmes dashed into the crowd to protect the lady; but just as he reached her he gave a cry and dropped to the ground, with the blood running freely down his face. At his fall the guardsmen took to their heels in one direction and the loungers in the other, while a number of better-dressed people, who had watched the scuffle without taking part in it, crowded in to help the lady and to attend to the injured man. Irene Adler, as I will still call her, had hurried up the steps; but she stood at the top with her superb figure outlined against the lights of the hall, looking back into the street.

"Is the poor gentleman much hurt?" she asked.

"He is dead," cried several voices.

"No, no, there's life in him!" shouted another. "But he'll be gone before you can get him to hospital."

"He's a brave fellow," said a woman. "They would have had the lady's purse and watch if it hadn't been for him. They were a gang, and a rough one, too. Ah, he's breathing now."

"He can't lie in the street. May we bring him in, marm?"

"Surely. Bring him into the sitting-room. There is a comfortable sofa. This way, please!"

Slowly and solemnly he was borne into Briony Lodge and laid out in the principal room, while I still observed the proceedings from my post by the window. The lamps had been lit, but the blinds had not been drawn, so that I could see Holmes as he lay upon the couch. I do not know whether he was seized with compunction at that moment for the part he was playing, but I know that I never felt more heartily ashamed of myself in my life than when I saw the beautiful creature against whom I was conspiring, or the grace and kindliness with which she waited upon the injured man. And yet it would be the blackest treachery to Holmes to draw back now from the part which he had intrusted to me. I hardened my heart, and took the smoke-rocket from under my ulster. After all, I thought, we are not injuring her. We are but preventing her from injuring another.

Holmes had sat up upon the couch, and I saw him motion like a man who is in need of air. A maid rushed across and threw open the window. At the same instant I saw him raise his hand, and at the signal I tossed my rocket into the room with a cry of "Fire!" The word was no sooner out of my mouth than the whole crowd of spectators, well dressed and ill—gentlemen, ostlers, and servant-maids—joined in a general shriek of "Fire!" Thick clouds of smoke curled through the room and out at the open window. I caught a glimpse of rushing figures, and a moment later the voice of Holmes from within assuring them that it was a false alarm. Slipping through the shouting crowd I made my way to the corner of the street, and in ten minutes was rejoiced to find my friend's arm in mine, and to get away from the scene of uproar. He walked swiftly and in silence for some few minutes until we had turned down one of the quiet streets which lead towards the Edgeware Road.

"You did it very nicely, Doctor," he remarked. "Nothing could have been better. It is all right."

"You have the photograph?"

"I know where it is."

"And how did you find out?"

"She showed me, as I told you she would."

"I am still in the dark."

"I do not wish to make a mystery," said he, laughing. "The matter was perfectly simple. You, of course, saw that everyone in the street was an accomplice. They were all engaged for the evening."

"I guessed as much."

"Then, when the row broke out, I had a little moist red paint in the palm of my hand. I rushed forward, fell down, clapped my hand to my face, and became a piteous spectacle. It is an old trick."

"That also I could fathom."

"Then they carried me in. She was bound to have me in. What else could she do? And into her sitting-room, which was the very room which I suspected. It lay between that and her bedroom, and I was determined to see which. They laid me on a couch, I motioned for air, they were compelled to open the window, and you had your chance."

"How did that help you?"

"It was all-important. When a woman thinks that her house is on fire, her instinct is at once to rush to the thing which she values most. It is a perfectly overpowering impulse, and I have more than once taken advantage of it. In the case of the Darlington substitution scandal it was of use to me, and also in the Arnsworth Castle business. A married woman grabs at her baby; an unmarried one reaches for her jewel-box. Now it was clear to me that our lady of to-day had nothing in the house more precious to her than what we are in quest of. She would rush to secure it. The alarm of fire was admirably done. The smoke and shouting were enough to shake nerves of steel. She responded beautifully. The photograph is in a recess behind a sliding panel just above the right bell-pull. She was there in an instant, and I caught a glimpse of it as she half-drew it out. When I cried out that it was a false alarm, she replaced it, glanced at the rocket, rushed from the room, and I have not seen her since. I rose, and, making my excuses, escaped from the house. I hesitated whether to attempt to secure the photograph at once; but the coachman had come in, and as he was watching me narrowly it seemed safer to wait. A little over-precipitance may ruin all."

"And now?" I asked.

"Our quest is practically finished. I shall call with the King to-morrow, and with you, if you care to come with us. We will be shown into the sitting-room to wait for the lady, but it is probable that when she comes she may find neither us nor the photograph. It might be a satisfaction to his Majesty to regain it with his own hands."

"And when will you call?"

"At eight in the morning. She will not be up, so that we shall have a clear field. Besides, we must be prompt, for this marriage may mean a complete change in her life and habits. I must wire to the King without delay."

We had reached Baker Street and had stopped at the door. He was searching his pockets for the key when someone passing said:

"Good-night, Mister Sherlock Holmes."

There were several people on the pavement at the time, but the greeting appeared to come from a slim youth in an ulster who had hurried by.

"I've heard that voice before," said Holmes, staring down the dimly lit street. "Now, I wonder who the deuce that could have been."

3

I slept at Baker Street that night, and we were engaged upon our toast and coffee in the morning when the King of Bohemia rushed into the room.

"You have really got it!" he cried, grasping Sherlock Holmes by either shoulder and looking eagerly into his face.

"Not yet."

"But you have hopes?"

"I have hopes."

"Then, come. I am all impatience to be gone."

"We must have a cab."

"No, my brougham is waiting."

"Then that will simplify matters." We descended and started off once more for Briony Lodge.

"Irene Adler is married," remarked Holmes.

"Married! When?"

"Yesterday."

"But to whom?"

"To an English lawyer named Norton."

"But she could not love him."

"I am in hopes that she does."

"And why in hopes?"

"Because it would spare your Majesty all fear of future annoyance. If the lady loves her husband, she does not love your Majesty. If she does not love your Majesty, there is no reason why she should interfere with your Majesty's plan."

"It is true. And yet—— Well! I wish she had been of my own station! What a queen she would have made!" He relapsed into a moody silence, which was not broken until we drew up in Serpentine Avenue.

The door of Briony Lodge was open, and an elderly woman stood upon the steps. She watched us with a sardonic eye as we stepped from the brougham.

"Mr. Sherlock Holmes, I believe?" said she.

"I am Mr. Holmes," answered my companion, looking at her with a questioning and rather startled gaze.

"Indeed! My mistress told me that you were likely to call. She left this morning with her husband by the 5:15 train from Charing Cross for the Continent."

"What!" Sherlock Holmes staggered back, white with chagrin and surprise. "Do you mean that she has left England?"

"Never to return."

"And the papers?" asked the King hoarsely. "All is lost."

"We shall see." He pushed past the servant and rushed into the drawing-room, followed by the King and myself. The furniture was scattered about in every direction, with dismantled shelves and open drawers, as if the lady had hurriedly ransacked them before her flight. Holmes rushed at the bell-pull, tore back a small sliding shutter, and, plunging in his hand, pulled out a photograph and a letter. The photograph was of Irene Adler herself in evening dress, the letter was superscribed to "Sherlock Holmes, Esq. To be left till called for." My friend tore it open, and we all three read it together. It was dated at midnight of the preceding night and ran in this way:

MY DEAR MR. SHERLOCK HOLMES:

You really did it very well. You took me in completely. Until after the alarm of fire, I had not a suspicion. But then, when I found how I had betrayed myself, I began to think. I had been warned against you months ago. I had been told that if the King employed an agent it would certainly be you. And your address had been given me. Yet, with all this, you made me reveal what you wanted to know. Even after I became suspicious, I found it hard to think evil of such a dear, kind old clergyman. But, you know, I have been trained as an actress myself. Male costume is nothing new to me. I often take advantage of the freedom which it gives. I sent John, the coachman, to watch you, ran upstairs, got into my walking-clothes, as I call them, and came down just as you departed.

Well, I followed you to your door, and so made sure that I was really an object of interest to the celebrated Mr. Sherlock Holmes. Then I, rather imprudently, wished you good-night, and started for the Temple to see my husband.

We both thought the best resource was flight, when pursued by so formidable an antagonist; so you will find the nest empty when you call to-morrow. As to the photograph, your client may rest in peace. I love and am loved by a better man than he. The King may do what he will without hindrance from one whom he has cruelly wronged. I keep it only to safeguard myself, and to preserve a weapon which will always secure me from any steps which he might take in the future. I leave a photograph which he might care to possess; and I remain, dear Mr. Sherlock Holmes,

Very truly yours,

IRENE NORTON, *née* ADLER.

"What a woman—oh, what a woman!" cried the King of Bohemia, when we had all three read this epistle. "Did I not tell you how quick and resolute she was? Would she not have made an admirable queen? Is it not a pity that she was not on my level?"

"From what I have seen of the lady she seems indeed to be on a very different level to your Majesty," said Holmes coldly. "I am sorry that I have not been able to bring your Majesty's business to a more successful conclusion."

"On the contrary, my dear sir," cried the King; "nothing could be more successful. I know that her word is inviolate. The photograph is now as safe as if it were in the fire."

"I am glad to hear your Majesty say so."

"I am immensely indebted to you. Pray tell me in what way I can reward you. This ring—" He slipped an emerald snake ring from his finger and held it out upon the palm of his hand.

"Your Majesty has something which I should value even more highly," said Holmes.

"You have but to name it."

"This photograph!"

The King stared at him in amazement.

"Irene's photograph!" he cried. "Certainly, if you wish it."

"I thank your Majesty. Then there is no more to be done in the matter. I have the honour to wish you a very good-morning." He bowed, and, turning away without observing the hand which the King had stretched out to him, he set off in my company for his chambers.

And that was how a great scandal threatened to affect the kingdom of Bohemia, and how the best plans of Mr. Sherlock Holmes were beaten by a woman's wit. He used to make merry over the cleverness of women, but I have not heard him do it of late. And when he speaks of Irene Adler, or when he refers to her photograph, it is always under the honourable title of *the* woman.

Questions for Discussion

1. On the basis of this story, how would you characterize Dr. Watson? What sort of person is he? What is his relationship with Holmes?

2. From reading this story, how would you characterize Holmes? Is he as likable as Dr. Watson? Why or why not?

3. Contrast Holmes with other detectives with whom you are familiar, either from literature or from film and television.

4. In what ways is Irene Adler a stereotypical character? In what ways is she a particular character?

5. From this story alone, list as many characteristics of a detective story as you can. What does a detective story *have* to have to be a detective story?

Suggestions for Writing

1. "It was not that he felt any emotion akin to love for Irene Adler. All emotions, and that one particularly, were abhorrent to his cold, precise but admirably balanced mind." Write a journal entry (or a short essay) about the extent to which you agree with this characterization of Holmes's mind by Watson. Are all emotions abhorrent to Holmes? Is his mind "admirably balanced"?

2. Read several more Sherlock Holmes stories and then write an essay about them. Possible topics: (1) Dr. Watson as narrator. (2) What drives Sherlock Holmes? (3) Why is Sherlock Holmes the most popular detective ever?

3. Write an essay about "the detective story" as a subgenre. Why is it attractive to so many readers? What different kinds are there? Should we automatically regard it as less significant than other kinds of literature— why or why not? Consider these and other questions.

4. Write your own detective story. You might want to begin by creating the detective (amateur or professional), by creating an interesting crime, or by establishing an unusual setting before you actually create the plot.

The Gift of the Magi

O. HENRY

One dollar and eighty-seven cents. That was all. And sixty cents of it was in pennies. Pennies saved one and two at a time by bulldozing the grocer and the vegetable man and the butcher until one's cheeks burned with the silent imputation of parsimony that such close dealing implied. Three times Della counted it. One dollar and eighty-seven cents. And the next day would be Christmas.

There was clearly nothing to do but flop down on the shabby little couch and howl. So Della did it. Which instigates the moral reflection that life is made up of sobs, sniffles, and smiles, with sniffles predominating.

While the mistress of the home is gradually subsiding from the first stage to the second, take a look at the home. A furnished flat at $8 per week. It did not exactly beggar description, but it certainly had that word on the lookout for the mendicancy squad.

In the vestibule below was a letter-box into which no letter would go, and an electric button from which no mortal finger could coax a ring. Also appertaining thereunto was a card bearing the name "Mr. James Dillingham Young."

The "Dillingham" had been flung to the breeze during a former period of prosperity when its possessor was being paid $30 per week. Now, when the income was shrunk to $20, the letters of "Dillingham" looked blurred, as though they were thinking seriously of contracting to a modest and unassuming D. But whenever Mr. James Dillingham Young came home and reached his flat above he was called "Jim" and greatly hugged by Mrs. James Dillingham Young, already introduced to you as Della. Which is all very good.

Della finished her cry and attended to her cheeks with the powder rag. She stood by the window and looked out dully at a gray cat walking a gray fence in a gray backyard. To-morrow would be Christmas Day, and she had only $1.87 with which to buy Jim a present. She had been saving every penny she could for months, with this result. Twenty dollars a week doesn't go far. Expenses had been greater than she had calculated. They always are. Only $1.87 to buy a present for Jim. Her Jim. Many a happy hour she had spent planning for something nice for him. Something fine and rare and sterling—something just a little bit near to being worthy of the honour of being owned by Jim.

There was a pier-glass between the windows of the room. Perhaps you have seen a pier-glass in an $8 flat. A very thin and very agile person may, by observing his reflection in a rapid sequence of longitudinal strips, obtain a fairly accurate conception of his looks. Della, being slender, had mastered the art.

Suddenly she whirled from the window and stood before the glass. Her eyes were shining brilliantly, but her face had lost its colour within twenty seconds. Rapidly she pulled down her hair and let it fall to its full length.

Now, there were two possessions of the James Dillingham Youngs in which they both took a mighty pride. One was Jim's gold watch that had been his father's and his grandfather's. The other was Della's hair. Had the Queen of Sheba lived in the flat across the airshaft, Della would have let her hair hang out the window some day to dry just to depreciate Her Majesty's jewels and gifts. Had King Solomon been the janitor, with all his treasures piled up in the basement, Jim would have pulled out his watch every time he passed, just to see him pluck at his beard from envy.

So now Della's beautiful hair fell about her, rippling and shining like a cascade of brown waters. It reached below her knee and made itself almost a garment for her. And then she did it up again nervously and quickly. Once she faltered for a minute and stood still while a tear or two splashed on the worn red carpet.

On went her old brown jacket; on went her old brown hat. With a whirl of skirts and with the brilliant sparkle still in her eyes, she fluttered out the door and down the stairs to the street.

Where she stopped the sign read: "Mme. Sofronie. Hair Goods of All Kinds." One flight up Della ran, and collected herself, panting. Madame, large, too white, chilly, hardly looked the "Sofronie."

"Will you buy my hair?" asked Della.

"I buy hair," said Madame. "Take yer hat off and let's have a sight at the looks of it."

Down rippled the brown cascade.

"Twenty dollars," said Madame, lifting the mass with a practised hand.

"Give it to me quick," said Della.

Oh, and the next two hours tripped by on rosy wings. Forget the hashed metaphor. She was ransacking the stores for Jim's present.

She found it at last. It surely had been made for Jim and no one else. There was no other like it in any of the stores, and she had turned all of them inside out. It was a platinum fob chain simple and chaste in design, properly proclaiming its value by substance alone and not by meretricious ornamentation—as all good things should do. It was even worthy of The Watch. As soon as she saw it she knew that it must be Jim's. It was like him. Quietness and value—the description applied to both. Twenty-one dollars they took from her for it, and she hurried home with the 87 cents. With that chain on his watch Jim might be properly anxious about the time in any company. Grand as the watch was, he sometimes looked at it on the sly on account of the old leather strap that he used in place of a chain.

When Della reached home her intoxication gave way a little to prudence and reason. She got out her curling irons and lighted the gas and went to work repairing the ravages made by generosity added to love. Which is always a tremendous task, dear friends—a mammoth task.

Within forty minutes her head was covered with tiny, close-lying curls that made her look wonderfully like a truant schoolboy. She looked at her reflection in the mirror long, carefully, and critically.

"If Jim doesn't kill me," she said to herself, "before he takes a second look at me, he'll say I look like a Coney Island chorus girl. But what could I do—oh! what could I do with a dollar and eighty-seven cents?"

At 7 o'clock the coffee was made and the frying-pan was on the back of the stove hot and ready to cook the chops.

Jim was never late. Della doubled the fob chain in her hand and sat on the corner of the table near the door that he always entered. Then she heard his step on the stair away down on the first flight, and she turned white for just a moment. She had a habit of saying little silent prayers about the simplest everyday things, and now she whispered: "Please God, make him think I am still pretty."

The door opened and Jim stepped in and closed it. He looked thin and very serious. Poor fellow, he was only twenty-two—and to be burdened with a family! He needed a new overcoat and he was without gloves.

Jim stopped inside the door, as immovable as a setter at the scent of quail. His eyes were fixed upon Della, and there was an expression in them that she could not read, and it terrified her. It was not anger, nor surprise, nor disapproval, nor horror, nor any of the sentiments that she had been prepared for. He simply stared at her fixedly with that peculiar expression on his face.

Della wriggled off the table and went for him.

"Jim, darling," she cried, "don't look at me that way. I had my hair cut off and sold it because I couldn't have lived through Christmas without giving you a present. It'll grow out again—you won't mind, will you? I just had to do it. My hair grows awfully fast. Say 'Merry Christmas!' Jim, and let's be happy. You don't know what a nice—what a beautiful, nice gift I've got for you."

"You've cut off your hair?" asked Jim, laboriously, as if he had not arrived at that patent fact yet even after the hardest mental labour.

"Cut it off and sold it," said Della. "Don't you like me just as well, anyhow? I'm me without my hair, ain't I?"

Jim looked about the room curiously.

"You say your hair is gone?" he said, with an air almost of idiocy.

"You needn't look for it," said Della. "It's sold, I tell you—sold and gone, too. It's Christmas Eve, boy. Be good to me, for it went for you. Maybe the hairs of my head were numbered," she went on with a sudden serious sweetness, "but nobody could ever count my love for you. Shall I put the chops on, Jim?"

Out of his trance Jim seemed quickly to wake. He enfolded his Della. For ten seconds let us regard with discreet scrutiny some inconsequential object in the other direction. Eight dollars a week or a million a year—what is the difference? A mathematician or a wit would give you the wrong answer. The magi brought valuable gifts, but that was not among them. This dark assertion will be illuminated later on.

Jim drew a package from his overcoat pocket and threw it upon the table.

"Don't make any mistake, Dell," he said, "about me. I don't think there's anything in the way of a haircut or a shave or a shampoo that could make me like my girl any less. But if you'll unwrap that package you may see why you had me going a while at first."

White fingers and nimble tore at the string and paper. And then an ecstatic scream of joy; and then, alas! a quick feminine change to hysterical tears and wails, necessitating the immediate employment of all the comforting powers of the lord of the flat.

For there lay The Combs—the set of combs, side and back, that Della had worshipped for long in a Broadway window. Beautiful combs, pure tortoise shell, with jewelled rims—just the shade to wear in the beautiful vanished hair. They were expensive combs, she knew, and her heart had simply craved and yearned over them without the least hope of possession. And now, they were hers, but the tresses that should have adorned the coveted adornments were gone.

But she hugged them to her bosom, and at length she was able to look up with dim eyes and a smile and say: "My hair grows so fast, Jim!"

And then Della leaped up like a little singed cat and cried, "Oh, oh!"

Jim had not yet seen his beautiful present. She held it out to him eagerly upon her open palm. The dull precious metal seemed to flash with a reflection of her bright and ardent spirit.

"Isn't it a dandy, Jim? I hunted all over town to find it. You'll have to look at the time a hundred times a day now. Give me your watch. I want to see how it looks on it."

Instead of obeying, Jim tumbled down on the couch and put his hands under the back of his head and smiled.

"Dell," said he, "let's put our Christmas presents away and keep 'em a while. They're too nice to use just at present. I sold the watch to get the money to buy your combs. And now suppose you put the chops on."

The magi, as you know, were wise men—wonderfully wise men—who brought gifts to the Babe in the manger. They invented the art of giving Christmas presents. Being wise, their gifts were no doubt wise ones, possibly bearing the privilege of exchange in case of duplication. And here I have lamely related to you the uneventful chronicle of two foolish children in a flat who most unwisely sacrificed for each other the greatest treasures of their house. But in a last word to the wise of these days let it be said that of all who give gifts these two were the wisest. Of all who give and receive gifts, such as they are wisest. Everywhere they are wisest. They are the magi.

Questions for Discussion

1. Characterize the attitude of the narrator at the beginning of the story and throughout.

2. To what extent does O. Henry's narrator tell us how to interpret the story?

3. In your view, what is more important in this story—the characters or the plot? Explain.

4. If you were recommending excellent stories to a friend, would you recommend O. Henry's? Why or why not?

Suggestions for Writing

1. Write an essay that compares and contrasts O. Henry's use of plot to that of another writer in this section.

2. Write a story that has a "twist" plot and a clear moral.

3. Write a parody of a story that has a "twist" plot and a clear moral.

4. Write a story in which "giving and receiving" are more complicated, more uncertain matters than they are in this O. Henry story.

On Account of a Hat

SHOLOM ALEICHEM

"**D**id I hear you say absent-minded? Now, in our town, that is, in Kasrilevke, we've really got someone for you—do you hear what I say? His name is Sholem Shachnah, but we call him Sholem Shachnah Rattlebrain, and is he absentminded, is this a distracted creature, Lord have mercy on us! The stories they tell about him, about this Sholem Shachnah—bushels and baskets of stories—I tell you, whole crates full of stories and anecdotes! It's too bad you're in such a hurry on account of the Passover, because what I could tell you, Mr. Sholom Aleichem—do you hear what I say?—you could go on writing it down forever. But if you can spare a moment I'll tell you a story about what happened to Sholem Shachnah on a Passover eve—a story about a hat, a true story, I should live so, even if it does sound like someone made it up."

These were the words of a Kasrilevke merchant, a dealer in stationery, that is to say, snips of paper. He smoothed out his beard, folded it down over his neck, and went on smoking his thin little cigarettes, one after the other.

I must confess that this true story, which he related to me, does indeed sound like a concocted one, and for a long time I couldn't make up my mind whether or not I should pass it on to you. But I thought it over and decided that if a respectable merchant and dignitary of Kasrilevke, who deals in stationery and is surely no *litterateur*—if he vouches for a story, it must be true. What would he be doing with fiction? Here it is in his own words. I had nothing to do with it.

This Sholem Shachnah I'm telling you about, whom we call Sholem Shachnah Rattlebrain, is a real-estate broker—you hear what I say? He's always with landowners, negotiating transactions. Transactions? Well, at least he hangs around the landowners. So what's the point? I'll tell you. Since he hangs around the landed gentry, naturally some of their manner has rubbed off on him, and he always has a mouth full of farms, homesteads, plots, acreage, soil, threshing machines, renovations, woods, timber, and other such terms having to do with estates.

One day God took pity on Sholem Shachnah, and for the first time in his career as a real-estate broker—are you listening?—he actually worked out a deal. That is to say, the work itself, as you can imagine, was done by others, and when the time came to collect the fee, the big rattler turned out to be not Sholem Shachnah Rattlebrain, but Drobkin, a Jew from Minsk province, a great big fearsome rattler, a real-estate broker from way back—he and his two brothers, also brokers and also big rattlers. So you can take my word for it, there was quite a to-do. A Jew has contrived and connived and has finally, with God's help, managed to cut himself in—so what do they do but come along and cut him out!

Where's Justice? Sholem Shachnah wouldn't stand for it—are you listening to me? He set up such a holler and an outcry—"Look what they've done to me!"—that at last they gave in to shut him up, and good riddance it was too.

When he got his few cents Sholem Shachnah sent the greater part of it home to his wife, so she could pay off some debts, shoo the wolf from the door, fix up new outfits for the children, and make ready for the Passover holidays. And as for himself, he also needed a few things, and besides he had to buy presents for his family, as was the custom.

Meanwhile the time flew by, and before he knew it, it was almost Passover. So Sholem Shachnah—now listen to this—ran to the telegraph office and sent home a wire: *Arriving home Passover without fail.* It's easy to say "arriving" and "without fail" at that. But you just try it! Just try riding out our way on the new train and see how fast you'll arrive. Ah, what a pleasure! Did they do us a favor! I tell you, Mr. Sholem Aleichem, for a taste of Paradise such as this you'd gladly forsake your own grandchildren! You see how it is: until you get to Zlodievka there isn't much you can do about it, so you just lean back and ride. But at Zlodievka the fun begins, because that's where you have to change, to get onto the new train, which they did us such a favor by running out to Kasrilevke. But not so fast. First, there's the little matter of several hours' wait, exactly as announced in the schedule—provided, of course, that you don't pull in after the Kasrilevke train has left. And at what time of night may you look forward to this treat? The very middle, thank you, when you're dead tired and disgusted, without a friend in the world except sleep—and there's not one single place in the whole station where you can lay your head, not one. When the wise men of Kasrilevke quote the passage from the Holy Book, *"Tov shem meshemon tov,"* they know what they're doing. I'll translate it for you: We were better off without the train.

To make a long story short, when our Sholem Shachnah arrived in Zlodievka with his carpetbag he was half dead; he had already spent two nights without sleep. But that was nothing at all to what was facing him—he still had to spend the whole night waiting in the station. What shall he do? Naturally he looked around for a place to sit down. Whoever heard of such a thing? Nowhere. Nothing. No place to sit. The walls of the station were covered with soot, the floor was covered with spit. It was dark, it was terrible. He finally discovered one miserable spot on a bench where he had just room enough to squeeze in, and no more than that, because the bench was occupied by an official of some sort in a uniform full of buttons, who was lying there all stretched out and snoring away to beat the band. Who this Buttons was, whether he was coming or going, he hadn't the vaguest idea, Sholem Shachnah, that is. But he could tell that Buttons was no dime-a-dozen official. This was plain by his cap, a military cap with a red band and a visor. He could have been an officer or a police official. Who knows? But surely he had drawn up to the station with a ringing of bells, had staggered in, full to the ears with meat and drink, laid himself out on the bench, as in his father's vineyard, and worked up a glorious snoring.

It's not such a bad life to be a gentile, and an official one at that, with buttons, thinks he, Sholem Shachnah, that is, and he wonders, dare he sit next to this Buttons, or hadn't he better keep his distance? Nowadays you never can tell whom you're sitting next to. If he's no more than a plain inspector, that's still all right. But what if he turns out to be a district inspector? Or a provincial commander? Or even higher than that? And supposing this is even Purishkevitch himself, the famous anti-Semite, may his name perish? Let someone else deal with him and Sholem Shachnah turns cold at the mere thought of falling into such a fellow's hands. But then he says to himself—now listen to this—Buttons, he says, who the hell is Buttons? And who gives a hang for Purishkevitch? Don't I pay my fare the same as Purishkevitch? So why should he have all the comforts of life and I none? If Buttons is entitled to a delicious night's sleep, then doesn't he, Sholem Shachnah that is, at least have a nap coming? After all, he's human too, and besides, he's already gone two nights without a wink. And so he sits down, on a corner of the bench, and leans his head back, not, God forbid, to sleep, but just like that, to snooze. But all of a sudden he remembers—he's supposed to be home for Passover, and tomorrow is Passover eve! What if, God have mercy, he should fall asleep and miss his train? But that's why he's got a Jewish head on his shoulders—are you listening to me or not?—so he figures out the answer to that one too, Sholem Shachnah, that is, and goes looking for the porter, a certain Yeremei, he knows him well, to make a deal with him. Whereas he, Sholem Shachnah, is already on his third sleepless night and is afraid, God forbid, that he may miss his train, therefore let him, Yeremei, that is, in God's name, be sure to wake him, Sholem Shachnah, because tomorrow night is a holiday, Passover. "Easter," he says to him in Russian and lays a coin in Yeremei's mitt. "Easter, Yeremei, do you understand, *goyisher kop?* Our Easter." The peasant pockets the coin, no doubt about that, and promises to wake him at the first sign of the train—he can sleep soundly and put his mind at rest. So Sholem Shachnah sits down in his corner of the bench, gingerly, pressed up against the wall, with his carpetbag curled around him so that no one should steal it. Little by little he sinks back, makes himself comfortable, and half shuts his eyes—no more than forty winks, you understand. But before long he's got one foot propped up on the bench and then the other; he stretches out and drifts off to sleep. Sleep? I'll say sleep, like God commanded us: with his head thrown back and his hat rolling away on the floor, Sholem Shachnah is snoring like an eight-day wonder. After all, a human being, up two nights in a row—what would you have him do?

He had a strange dream. He tells this himself, that is, Sholem Shachnah does. He dreamed that he was riding home for Passover—are you listening to me?—but not on the train, in a wagon, driven by a thievish peasant, Ivan Zlodi we call him. The horses were terribly slow, they barely dragged along. Sholem Shachnah was impatient, and he poked the peasant between the shoulders and cried, "May you only drop dead, Ivan darling! Hurry up, you lout! Passover is coming, our Jewish Easter!" Once he called out to him, twice, three times. The thief paid him no mind. But all of a sudden he whipped his horses to a gallop and they went whirling away, up hill and down, like demons. Sholem Shachnah lost his hat. Another minute of this and he would have lost God knows what. "Whoa, there, Ivan old boy! Where's the fire? Not so fast!" cried Sholem Shachnah. He covered his head with his hands—he was worried, you see, over his lost hat. How can he drive into town bareheaded? But for all the good it did him, he could have been hollering at a post. Ivan the Thief was racing the horses as if forty devils were after him. All of a sudden—tppprrru!—they came to a dead stop, right in the middle of the field—you hear me?—a dead stop. What's the matter? Nothing. "Get up," said Ivan, "time to get up."

Time? What time? Sholem Shachnah is all confused. He wakes up, rubs his eyes, and is all set to step out of the wagon when he realizes he has lost his hat. Is he dreaming or not? And what's he doing here? Sholem Shachnah finally comes to his senses and recognizes the peasant—this isn't Ivan Zlodi at all but Yeremei the porter. So he concludes that he isn't on the high road after all, but in the station at Zlodievka, on the way home for Passover, and that if he means to get there he'd better run to the window for a ticket, but fast. Now what? No hat. The carpetbag is right where he left it, but his hat? He pokes around under the bench, reaching all over, until he comes up with a hat—not his own, to be sure, but the official's, with the red band and the visor. But Sholem Shachnah has no time for details and he rushes off to buy a ticket. The ticket window is jammed, everybody and his cousins are crowding in. Sholem Shachnah thinks he won't get to the window in time, perish the thought, and he starts pushing forward, carpetbag and all. The people see the red band and the visor and they make way for him. "Where to, Your Excellency?" asks the ticket agent. What's this Excellency, all of a sudden? wonders Sholem Shachnah, and he rather resents it. Some joke, a gentile poking fun at a Jew. All the same he says, Sholem Shachnah, that is, "Kasrilevke." "Which class, Your Excellency?" The ticket agent is looking straight at the red band and the visor. Sholem Shachnah is angrier than ever. I'll give him an Excellency, so he'll know how to make fun of a poor Jew! But then he thinks, Oh, well, we Jews are in Diaspora—do you hear what I say?—let it pass. And he asks for a ticket third class. "Which class?" The agent blinks at him, very much surprised. This time Sholem Shachnah gets good and sore and he really tells him off. "Third!" says he. All right, thinks the agent, third is third.

In short, Sholem Shachnah buys his ticket, takes up his carpetbag, runs out onto the platform, plunges into the crowd of Jews and gentiles, no comparison intended, and goes looking for the third-class carriage. Again the red band and the visor work like a charm, everyone makes way for the official. Sholem Shachnah is wondering, What goes on here? But he runs along the platform till he meets a conductor carrying a lantern. "Is this third class?" asks Sholem Shachnah, putting one foot on the stairs and shoving his bag into the door of the compartment. "Yes, Your Excellency," says the conductor, but he holds him back. "If you please, sir, it's packed full, as tight as your fist. You couldn't squeeze a needle into that crowd." And he takes Sholem Shachnah's carpetbag—you hear what I'm saying?—and sings out, "Right this way, Your Excellency, I'll find you a seat." "What the Devil!" cries Sholem Shachnah. "Your Excellency and Your Excellency!" But he hasn't much time for the fine points; he's worried about his carpetbag. He's afraid, you see, that with all these Excellencies he'll be swindled out of his belongings. So he runs after the conductor with the lantern, who leads him into a second-class carriage. This is also packed to the rafters, no room even to yawn in there. "This way please, Your Excellency!" And again the conductor grabs the bag and Sholem Shachnah lights out after him. "Where in blazes is he taking me?" Sholem Shachnah is racking his brains over this Excellency business, but meanwhile he keeps his eye on the main thing—the carpetbag. They enter the first-class carriage, the conductor sets down the bag, salutes, and backs away, bowing. Sholem Shachnah bows right back. And there he is, alone at last.

Left alone in the carriage, Sholem Shachnah looks around to get his bearings—you hear what I say? He has no idea why all these honors have suddenly been heaped on him—first class, salutes, Your Excellency. Can it be on account of the real-estate deal he just closed? That's it! But wait a minute. If his own people, Jews, that is, honored him for this, it would be understandable. But gentiles! The conductor! The ticket agent! What's it to them? Maybe he's dreaming. Sholem Shachnah rubs his forehead, and while passing down the corridor glances into the mirror on the wall. It nearly knocks him over! He sees not himself but the official with the red band. That's who it is! "All my bad dreams on Yeremei's head and on his hands and feet, that lug! Twenty times I tell him to wake me and I even give him a tip, and what does he do, that dumb ox, may he catch cholera in his face, but wake the official instead! And me he leaves asleep on the bench! Tough luck, Sholem Shachnah old boy, but this year you'll spend Passover in Zlodievka, not at home."

Now get a load of this. Sholem Shachnah scoops up his carpetbag and rushes off once more, right back to the station where he is sleeping on the bench. He's going to wake himself up before the locomotive, God forbid, lets out a blast and blasts his Passover to pieces. And so it was. No sooner had Sholem Shachnah leaped out of the carriage with his carpetbag than the locomotive did let go with a blast—do you hear me?—one followed by another, and then, good night!

The paper dealer smiled as he lit a fresh cigarette, thin as a straw. "And would you like to hear the rest of the story? The rest isn't so nice. On account of being such a rattlebrain, our dizzy Sholem Shachnah had a miserable Passover, spending both Seders among strangers in the house of a Jew in Zlodievka. But this was nothing—listen to what happened afterward. First of all, he has a wife, Sholem Shachnah, that is, and his wife—how shall I describe her to you? *I* have a wife, *you* have a wife, we all have wives, we've had a taste of Paradise, we know what it means to be married. All I can say about Sholem Shachnah's wife is that she's A Number One. And did she give him a royal welcome! Did she lay into him! Mind you, she didn't complain about his spending the holiday away from home, and she said nothing about the red band and the visor. She let that stand for the time being; she'd take it up with him later. The only thing she complained about was—the telegram! And not so much the telegram—you hear what I say?—as the one short phrase, *without fail*. What possessed him to put that into the wire: *Arriving home Passover without fail.* Was he trying to make the telegraph company rich? And besides, how dare a human being say "without fail" in the first place? It did him no good to answer and explain. She buried him alive. Oh, well, that's what wives are for. And not that she was altogether wrong—after all, she had been waiting so anxiously. But this was nothing compared with what he caught from the town, Kasrilevke, that is. Even before he returned the whole town—you hear what I say?—knew all about Yeremei and the official and the red band and the visor and the conductor's Your Excellency—the whole show. He himself, Sholem Shachnah, that is, denied everything and swore up and down that the Kasrilevke smart-alecks had invented the entire story for lack of anything better to do. It was all very simple—the reason he came home late, after the holidays, was that he had made a special trip to inspect a wooded estate. Woods? Estate? Not a chance—no one bought *that!* They pointed him out in the streets and held their sides, laughing. And everybody asked him, 'How does it feel, Reb Sholem Shachnah, to wear a cap with a red band and a visor?' 'And tell us,' said others, 'what's it like to travel first class?' As for the children, this was made to order for them—you hear what I say? Wherever he went they trooped after him, shouting, 'Your Excellency! Your excellent Excellency! Your most excellent Excellency!'

"You think it's so easy to put one over on Kasrilevke?"

Questions for Discussion

1. Who narrates this story? Who does most of the storytelling? Who is the main character?

2. What sort of person is Sholem Shachnah? To what extent do you sympathize with him?

3. Why is the accident of the hat somehow an *appropriate* one to happen to Shachnah?

4. Describe Kasrilevke's storytelling style.

Suggestions for Writing

1. In a journal response, discuss the elements of oral storytelling that Aleichem captures.

2. Write a comic story involving a character who makes a promise he or she cannot keep.

3. Write an essay about "On Account of a Hat" in which you focus on Sholem Shachnah's vanity.

The Blue Hotel

STEPHEN CRANE

1

The Palace Hotel at Fort Romper was painted a light blue, a shade that is on the legs of a kind of heron, causing the bird to declare its position against any background. The Palace Hotel, then, was always screaming and howling in a way that made the dazzling winter landscape of Nebraska seem only a grey swampish hush. It stood alone on the prairie, and when the snow was falling the town two hundred yards away was not visible. But when the traveller alighted at the railway station he was obliged to pass the Palace Hotel before he could come upon the company of low clapboard houses which composed Fort Romper, and it was not to be thought that any traveller could pass the Palace Hotel without looking at it. Pat Scully, the proprietor, had proved himself a master of strategy when he chose his paints. It is true that on clear days, when the great transcontinental expresses, long lines of swaying Pullmans, swept through Fort Romper, passengers were overcome at the sight, and the cult that knows the brown-reds and the subdivisions of the dark greens of the East expressed shame, pity, horror, in a laugh. But to the citizens of this prairie town and to the people who would naturally stop there, Pat Scully had performed a feat. With this opulence and splendour, these creeds, classes, egotisms, that streamed through Romper on the rails day after day, they had no colour in common.

As if the displayed delights of such a blue hotel were not sufficiently enticing, it was Scully's habit to go every morning and evening to meet the leisurely trains that stopped at Romper and work his seductions upon any man that he might see wavering, gripsack in hand.

One morning, when a snow-crusted engine dragged its long string of freight cars and its one passenger coach to the station, Scully performed the marvel of catching three men. One was a shaky and quick-eyed Swede, with a great shining cheap valise; one was a tall bronzed cowboy, who was on his way to a ranch near the Dakota line; one was a little silent man from the East, who didn't look it, and didn't announce it. Scully practically made them prisoners. He was so nimble and merry and kindly that each probably felt it would be the height of brutality to try to escape. They trudged off over the creaking board sidewalks in the wake of the eager little Irishman. He wore a heavy fur cap squeezed tightly down on his head. It caused his two red ears to stick out stiffly, as if they were made of tin.

At last, Scully, elaborately, with boisterous hospitality, conducted them through the portals of the blue hotel. The room which they entered was small. It seemed to be merely a proper temple for an enormous stove, which, in the centre, was humming with godlike violence. At various points on its surface the iron had become luminous and glowed yellow from the heat. Beside the stove Scully's son Johnnie was playing High-Five with an old farmer who had whiskers both grey and sandy. They were quarreling. Frequently the old farmer turned his face toward a box of sawdust—coloured brown from tobacco juice—that was behind the stove, and spat with an air of great impatience and irritation. With a loud flourish of words, Scully destroyed the game of cards, and bustled his son upstairs with part of the baggage of the new guests. He himself conducted them to three basins of the coldest water in the world. The cowboy and the Easterner burnished themselves fiery red with this water, until it seemed to be some kind of metal-polish. The Swede, however, merely dipped his fingers gingerly and with trepidation. It was notable that throughout this series of small ceremonies the three travellers were made to feel that Scully was very benevolent. He was conferring great favours upon them. He handed the towel from one to another with an air of philanthropic impulse.

Afterward they went to the first room, and, sitting about the stove, listened to Scully's officious clamour at his daughters, who were preparing the midday meal. They reflected in the silence of experienced men who tread carefully amid new people. Nevertheless, the old farmer, stationary, invincible in his chair near the warmest part of the stove, turned his face from the sawdust-box frequently and addressed a glowing commonplace to the strangers. Usually he was answered in short but adequate sentences by either the cowboy or the Easterner. The Swede said nothing. He seemed to be occupied in making furtive estimates of each man in the room. One might have thought that he had the sense of silly suspicion which comes to guilt. He resembled a badly frightened man.

Later, at dinner, he spoke a little, addressing his conversation entirely to Scully. He volunteered that he had come from New York, where for ten years he had worked as a tailor. These facts seemed to strike Scully as fascinating, and afterward he volunteered that he had lived at Romper for fourteen years. The Swede asked about the crops and the price of labour. He seemed barely to listen to Scully's extended replies. His eyes continued to rove from man to man.

Finally, with a laugh and a wink, he said that some of these Western communities were very dangerous; and after his statement he straightened his legs under the table, tilted his head, and laughed again, loudly. It was plain that the demonstration had no meaning to the others. They looked at him wondering and in silence.

2

As the men trooped heavily back into the front room, the two little windows presented views of a turmoiling sea of snow. The huge arms of the wind were making attempts—mighty, circular, futile—to embrace the flakes as they sped. A gate-post like a still man with a blanched face stood aghast amid this profligate fury. In a hearty voice Scully announced the presence of a blizzard. The guests of the blue hotel, lighting their pipes, assented with grunts of lazy masculine contentment. No island of the sea could be exempt in the degree of this little room with its humming stove. Johnnie, son of Scully, in a tone which defined his opinion of his ability as a card-player, challenged the old farmer of both grey and sandy whiskers to a game of High-Five. The farmer agreed with a contemptuous and bitter scoff. They sat close to the stove, and squared their knees under a wide board. The cowboy and the Easterner watched the game with interest. The Swede remained near the window, aloof, but with a countenance that showed signs of an inexplicable excitement.

The play of Johnnie and the grey-beard was suddenly ended by another quarrel. The old man arose while casting a look of heated scorn at his adversary. He slowly buttoned his coat, and then stalked with fabulous dignity from the room. In the discreet silence of all other men the Swede laughed. His laughter rang somehow childish. Men by this time had begun to look at him askance, as if they wished to inquire what ailed him.

A new game was formed jocosely. The cowboy volunteered to become the partner of Johnnie, and they all then turned to ask the Swede to throw in his lot with the little Easterner. He asked some questions about the game, and, learning that it wore many names, and that he had played it when it was under an alias, he accepted the invitation. He strode toward the men nervously, as if he expected to be assaulted. Finally, seated, he gazed from face to face and laughed shrilly. This laugh was so strange that the Easterner looked up quickly, the cowboy sat intent and with his mouth open, and Johnnie paused, holding the cards with still fingers.

Afterward there was a short silence. Then Johnnie said, "Well, let's get at it. Come on now!" They pulled their chairs forward until their knees were bunched under the board. They began to play, and their interest in the game caused the others to forget the manner of the Swede.

The cowboy was a board-whacker. Each time that he held superior cards he whanged them, one by one, with exceeding force, down upon the improvised table, and took the tricks with a glowing air of prowess and pride that sent thrills of indignation into the hearts of his opponents. A game with a board-whacker in it is sure to become intense. The countenances of the Easterner and the Swede were miserable whenever the cowboy thundered down his aces and kings, while Johnnie, his eyes gleaming with joy, chuckled and chuckled.

Because of the absorbing play none considered the strange ways of the Swede. They paid strict heed to the game. Finally, during a lull caused by a new deal, the Swede suddenly addressed Johnnie: "I suppose there have been a good many men killed in this room." The jaws of the others dropped and they looked at him.

"What in hell are you talking about?" said Johnnie.

The Swede laughed again his blatant laugh, full of a kind of false courage and defiance. "Oh, you know what I mean all right," he answered.

"I'm a liar if I do!" Johnnie protested. The card was halted, and the men stared at the Swede. Johnnie evidently felt that as the son of the proprietor he should make a direct inquiry. "Now, what might you be drivin' at, mister?" he asked. The Swede winked at him. It was a wink full of cunning. His fingers shook on the edge of the board. "Oh, maybe you think I have been to nowheres. Maybe you think I'm a tenderfoot?"

"I don't know nothin' about you," answered Johnnie, "and I don't give a damn where you've been. All I got to say is that I don't know what you're driving at. There hain't never been nobody killed in this room."

The cowboy, who had been steadily gazing at the Swede, then spoke: "What's wrong with you, mister?"

Apparently it seemed to the Swede that he was formidably menaced. He shivered and turned white near the corners of his mouth. He sent an appealing glance in the direction of the little Easterner. During these moments he did not forget to wear his air of advanced pot-valour. "They say they don't know what I mean," he remarked mockingly to the Easterner.

The latter answered after prolonged and cautious reflection. "I don't understand you," he said, impassively.

The Swede made a movement then which announced that he thought he had encountered treachery from the only quarter where he had expected sympathy, if not help. "Oh, I see you are all against me. I see——"

The cowboy was in a state of deep stupefaction. "Say," he cried, as he tumbled the deck violently down upon the board, "say, what are you gittin' at, hey?"

The Swede sprang up with the celerity of a man escaping from a snake on the floor. "I don't want to fight!" he shouted. "I don't want to fight!"

The cowboy stretched his long legs indolently and deliberately. His hands were in his pockets. He spat into the sawdust-box. "Well, who the hell thought you did?" he inquired.

The Swede backed rapidly toward a corner of the room. His hands were out protectingly in front of his chest, but he was making an obvious struggle to control his fright. "Gentlemen," he quavered, "I suppose I am going to be killed before I can leave this house! I suppose I am going to be killed before I can leave this house!" In his eyes was the dying-swan look. Through the windows could be seen the snow turning blue in the shadow of dusk. The wind tore at the house, and some loose thing beat regularly against the clap-boards like a spirit tapping.

A door opened, and Scully himself entered. He paused in surprise as he noted the tragic attitude of the Swede. Then he said, "What's the matter here?"

The Swede answered him swiftly and eagerly: "These men are going to kill me."

"Kill you!" ejaculated Scully. "Kill you! What are you talkin'?"

The Swede made the gesture of a martyr.

Scully wheeled sternly upon his son. "What is this, Johnnie?"

The lad had grown sullen. "Damned if I know," he answered. "I·can't make no sense to it." He began to shuffle the cards, fluttering them together with an angry snap. "He says a good many men have been killed in this room, or something like that. And he says he's goin' to be killed here too. I don't know what ails him. He's crazy, I shouldn't wonder."

Scully then looked for explanation to the cowboy, but the cowboy simply shrugged his shoulders.

"Kill you?" said Scully again to the Swede. "Kill you? Man, you're off your nut."

"Oh, I know," burst out the Swede. "I know what will happen. Yes, I'm crazy—yes. Yes, of course, I'm crazy—yes. But I know one thing——" There was a sort of sweat of misery and terror upon his face. "I know I won't get out of here alive."

The cowboy drew a deep breath, as if his mind was passing into the last stages of dissolution. "Well, I'm doggoned," he whispered to himself.

Scully wheeled suddenly and faced his son. "You've been troublin' this man!"

Johnnie's voice was loud with its burden of grievance. "Why, good Gawd, I ain't done nothin' to 'im."

The Swede broke in. "Gentlemen, do not disturb yourselves. I will leave this house. I will go away, because"—he accused them dramatically with his glance—"because I do not want to be killed."

Scully was furious with his son. "Will you tell me what is the matter, you young divil? What's the matter, anyhow? Speak out!"

"Blame it!" cried Johnnie in despair, "don't I tell you I don't know? He—he says we want to kill him, and that's all I know. I can't tell what ails him."

The Swede continued to repeat: "Never mind, Mr. Scully; never mind. I will leave this house. I will go away, because I do not wish to be killed. Yes, of course, I am crazy—yes. But I know one thing! I will go away. I will leave this house. Never mind, Mr. Scully; never mind. I will go away."

"You will not go 'way," said Scully. "You will not go 'way until I hear the reason of this business. If anybody has troubled you I will take care of him. This is my house. You are under my roof, and I will not allow any peaceable man to be troubled here." He cast a terrible eye upon Johnnie, the cowboy, and the Easterner.

"Never mind, Mr. Scully; never mind. I will go away. I do not wish to be killed." The Swede moved toward the door which opened upon the stairs. It was evidently his intention to go at once for his baggage.

"No, no," shouted Scully peremptorily; but the white-faced man slid by him and disappeared. "Now," said Scully severely, "what does this mean?"

Johnnie and the cowboy cried together: "Why, we didn't do nothin' to 'im!"

Scully's eyes were cold. "No," he said, "you didn't?"

Johnnie swore a deep oath. "Why, this is the wildest loon I ever see. We didn't do nothin' at all. We were jest sittin' here playin' cards, and he——"

The father suddenly spoke to the Easterner. "Mr. Blanc," he asked, "what has these boys been doin'?"

The Easterner reflected again. "I didn't see anything wrong at all," he said at last, slowly.

Scully began to howl. "But what does it mane?" He stared ferociously at his son. "I have a mind to lather you for this, me boy."

Johnnie was frantic. "Well, what have I done?" he bawled at his father.

3

"I think you are tongue-tied," said Scully finally to his son, the cowboy, and the Easterner; and at the end of this scornful sentence he left the room.

Upstairs the Swede was swiftly fastening the straps of his great valise. Once his back happened to be half turned toward the door, and, hearing a noise there, he wheeled and sprang up, uttering a loud cry. Scully's wrinkled visage showed grimly in the light of the small lamp he carried. This yellow effulgence, streaming upward, coloured only his prominent features, and left his eyes, for instance, in mysterious shadow. He resembled a murderer.

"Man! man!" he exclaimed, "have you gone daffy?"

"Oh, no! Oh, no!" rejoined the other. "There are people in this world who know pretty nearly as much as you do—understand?"

For a moment they stood gazing at each other. Upon the Swede's deathly pale cheeks were two spots brightly crimson and sharply edged, as if they had been carefully painted. Scully placed the light on the table and sat himself on the edge of the bed. He spoke ruminatively. "By cracky, I never heard of such a thing in my life. It's a complete muddle. I can't, for the soul of me, think how you ever got this idea into your head." Presently he lifted his eyes and asked: "And did you sure think they were going to kill you?"

The Swede scanned the old man as if he wished to see into his mind. "I did," he said at last. He obviously suspected that this answer might precipitate an outbreak. As he pulled on a strap his whole arm shook, the elbow wavering like a bit of paper.

Scully banged his hand impressively on the footboard of the bed. "Why, man, we're goin' to have a line of ilictric street-cars in this town next spring."

" 'A line of electric street-cars,' " repeated the Swede, stupidly.

"And," said Scully, "there's a new railroad goin' to be built down from Broken Arm to here. Not to mention the four churches and the smashin' big brick schoolhouse. Then there's the big factory, too. Why, in two years Romper'll be a met-tro-*pol*-is."

Having finished the preparation of his baggage, the Swede straightened himself. "Mr. Scully," he said, with sudden hardihood, "how much do I owe you?"

"You don't owe me anythin'," said the old man, angrily.

"Yes, I do," retorted the Swede. He took seventy-five cents from his pocket and tendered it to Scully; but the latter snapped his fingers in disdainful refusal. However, it happened that they both stood gazing in a strange fashion at three silver pieces on the Swede's open palm.

"I'll not take your money," said Scully at last. "Not after what's been goin' on here." Then a plan seemed to strike him. "Here," he cried, picking up his lamp and moving toward the door. "Here! Come with me a minute."

"No," said the Swede, in overwhelming alarm.

"Yes," urged the old man. "Come on! I want you to come and see a picter—just across the hall—in my room."

The Swede must have concluded that his hour was come. His jaw dropped and his teeth showed like a dead man's. He ultimately followed Scully across the corridor, but he had the step of one hung in chains.

Scully flashed the light high on the wall of his own chamber. There was revealed a ridiculous photograph of a little girl. She was leaning against a balustrade of gorgeous decoration, and the formidable bang to her hair was prominent. The figure was as graceful as an upright sled-stake, and withal, it was of the hue of lead. "There," said Scully, tenderly, "that's the picter of my little girl that died. Her name was Carrie. She had the purtiest hair you ever saw! I was that fond of her, she——"

Turning then, he saw that the Swede was not contemplating the picture at all, but, instead, was keeping keen watch on the gloom in the rear.

"Look man!" cried Scully, heartily. "That's the picter of my little gal that died. Her name was Carrie. And then here's the picter of my oldest boy, Michael.

He's a lawyer in Lincoln, an' doin' well. I gave that boy a grand eddication, and I'm glad for it now. He's a fine boy. Look at 'im now. Ain't he bold as blazes, him there in Lincoln, an honoured an' respicted gintleman! An honoured and respicted gintleman," concluded Scully with a flourish. And, so saying, he smote the Swede jovially on the back.

The Swede faintly smiled.

"Now," said the old man, "there's only one more thing." He dropped suddenly to the floor and thrust his head beneath the bed. The Swede could hear his muffled voice. "I'd keep it under my piller if it wasn't for that boy Johnnie. Then there's the old woman—— Where is it now? I never put it twice in the same place. Ah, now come out with you!"

Presently he backed clumsily from under the bed, dragging with him an old coat rolled into a bundle. "I've fetched him," he muttered. Kneeling on the floor, he unrolled the coat and extracted from its heart a large yellow-brown whisky-bottle.

His first manœuvre was to hold the bottle up to the light. Reassured, apparently, that nobody had been tampering with it, he thrust it with a generous movement toward the Swede.

The weak-kneed Swede was about to eagerly clutch this element of strength, but he suddenly jerked his hand away and cast a look of horror upon Scully.

"Drink," said the old man affectionately. He had risen to his feet, and now stood facing the Swede.

There was a silence. Then again Scully said: "Drink!"

The Swede laughed wildly. He grabbed the bottle, put it to his mouth; and as his lips curled absurdly around the opening and his throat worked, he kept his glance, burning with hatred, upon the old man's face.

4

After the departure of Scully the three men, with the cardboard still upon their knees, preserved for a long time an astounded silence. Then Johnnie said: "That's the dod-dangedest Swede I ever see."

"He ain't no Swede," said the cowboy scornfully.

"Well, what is he then?" cried Johnnie. "What is he then?"

"It's my opinion," replied the cowboy deliberately, "he's some kind of a Dutchman." It was a venerable custom of the country to entitle as Swedes all light-haired men who spoke with a heavy tongue. In consequence the idea of the cowboy was not without its daring. "Yes, sir," he repeated. "It's my opinion this feller is some kind of a Dutchman."

"Well, he says he's a Swede, anyhow," muttered Johnnie, sulkily. He turned to the Easterner: "What do you think, Mr. Blanc?"

"Oh, I don't know," replied the Easterner.

"Well, what do you think makes him act that way?" asked the cowboy.

"Why, he's frightened." The Easterner knocked his pipe against a rim of the stove. "He's clear frightened out of his boots."

"What at?" cried Johnnie and the cowboy together.

The Easterner reflected over his answer.

"What at?" cried the others again.

"Oh, I don't know, but it seems to me this man has been reading dime novels, and he thinks he's right out in the middle of it—the shootin' and stabbin' and all."

"But," said the cowboy, deeply scandalized, "this ain't Wyoming, ner none of them places. This is Nebrasker."

"Yes," added Johnnie, "an' why don't he wait till he gits *out West?*"

The travelled Easterner laughed. "It isn't different there even—not in these days. But he thinks he's right in the middle of hell."

Johnnie and the cowboy mused along.

"It's awful funny," remarked Johnnie at last.

"Yes," said the cowboy. "This is a queer game. I hope we don't get snowed in, because then we'd have to stand this here man bein' around with us all the time. That wouldn't be no good."

"I wish pop would throw him out," said Johnnie.

Presently they heard a loud stamping on the stairs, accompanied by ringing jokes in the voice of old Scully, and laughter, evidently from the Swede. The men around the stove stared vacantly at each other. "Gosh!" said the cowboy. The door flew open, and old Scully, flushed and anecdotal, came into the room. He was jabbering at the Swede, who followed him, laughing bravely. It was the entry of two roisterers from a banquet hall.

"Come now," said Scully sharply to the three seated men, "move up and give us a chance at the stove." The cowboy and the Easterner obediently sidled their chairs to make room for the new-comers. Johnnie, however, simply arranged himself in a more indolent attitude, and then remained motionless.

"Come! Git over, there," said Scully.

"Plenty of room on the other side of the stove," said Johnnie.

"Do you think we want to sit in the draught?" roared the father.

But the Swede had interposed with a grandeur of confidence. "No, no. Let the boy sit where he likes," he cried in a bullying voice to the father.

"All right! All right!" said Scully, deferentially. The cowboy and the Easterner exchanged glances of wonder.

The five chairs were formed in a crescent about one side of the stove. The Swede began to talk; he talked arrogantly, profanely, angrily. Johnnie, the cowboy, and the Easterner maintained a morose silence, while old Scully appeared to be receptive and eager, breaking in constantly with sympathetic ejaculations.

Finally, the Swede announced that he was thirsty. He moved in his chair, and said that he would go for a drink of water.

"I'll git it for you," cried Scully at once.

"No," said the Swede, contemptuously. "I'll get it for myself." He arose and stalked with the air of an owner off into the executive parts of the hotel.

As soon as the Swede was out of hearing Scully sprang to his feet and whispered intensely to the others: "Upstairs he thought I was tryin' to poison 'im."

"Say," said Johnnie, "this makes me sick. Why don't you throw 'im out in the snow?"

"Why, he's all right now," declared Scully. "It was only that he was from the East, and he thought this was a tough place. That's all. He's all right now."

The cowboy looked with admiration upon the Easterner. "You were straight," he said. "You were on to that there Dutchman."

"Well," said Johnnie to his father, "he may be all right now, but I don't see it. Other time he was scared, but now he's too fresh."

Scully's speech was always a combination of Irish brogue and idiom, Western twang and idiom, and scraps of curiously formal diction taken from the story-books and newspapers. He now hurled a strange mass of language at the head of his son. "What do I keep? What do I keep? What do I keep?" he demanded, in a voice of thunder. He slapped his knee impressively, to indicate that he himself was going to make reply, and that all should heed. "I keep a hotel," he shouted. "A hotel, do you mind? A guest under my roof has sacred privileges. He is to be intimidated by none. Not one word shall he hear that would prijudice him in favour of goin' away. I'll not have it. There's no place in this here town where they can say they iver took in a guest of mine because he was afraid to stay here." He wheeled suddenly upon the cowboy and the Easterner, "Am I right?"

"Yes, Mr. Scully," said the cowboy, "I think you're right."

"Yes, Mr. Scully," said the Easterner, "I think you're right."

5

At six-o'clock supper, the Swede fizzed like a fire-wheel. He sometimes seemed on the point of bursting into riotous song, and in all his madness he was encouraged by old Scully. The Easterner was encased in reserve; the cowboy sat in wide-mouthed amazement, forgetting to eat, while Johnnie wrathily demolished great plates of food. The daughters of the house, when they were obliged to replenish the biscuits, approached as warily as Indians, and, having succeeded in their purpose, fled with ill-concealed trepidation. The Swede domineered the whole feast, and he gave it the appearance of a cruel bacchanal. He seemed to have grown suddenly taller; he gazed, brutally disdainful, into every face. His voice rang through the room. Once when he jabbed out harpoon-fashion with his fork to pinion a biscuit, the weapon nearly impaled the hand of the Easterner, which had been stretched quietly out for the same biscuit.

After supper, as the men filed toward the other room, the Swede smote Scully ruthlessly on the shoulder. "Well, old boy, that was a good, square meal." Johnnie looked hopefully at his father; he knew that shoulder was tender from an old fall; and, indeed, it appeared for a moment as if Scully was going to flame out over the matter, but in the end he smiled a sickly smile and remained silent. The others understood from his manner that he was admitting his responsibility for the Swede's new view-point.

Johnnie, however, addressed his parent in an aside. "Why don't you license somebody to kick you downstairs?" Scully scowled darkly by way of reply.

When they were gathered about the stove, the Swede insisted on another game of High-Five. Scully gently deprecated the plan at first, but the Swede turned a wolfish glare upon him. The old man subsided, and the Swede canvassed the others. In his tone there was always a great threat. The cowboy and the

Easterner both remarked indifferently that they would play. Scully said that he would presently have to go to meet the 6.58 train, and so the Swede turned menacingly upon Johnnie. For a moment their glances crossed like blades, and then Johnnie smiled and said, "Yes, I'll play."

They formed a square, with the little board on their knees. The Easterner and the Swede were again partners. As the play went on, it was noticeable that the cowboy was not board-whacking a usual. Meanwhile, Scully, near the lamp, had put on his spectacles and, with an appearance curiously like an old priest, was reading a newspaper. In time he went out to meet the 6.58 train, and, despite his precautions, a gust of polar wind whirled into the room as he opened the door. Besides scattering the cards, it chilled the players to the marrow. The Swede cursed frightfully. When Scully returned, his entrance disturbed a cosy and friendly scene. The Swede again cursed. But presently they were once more intent, their heads bent forward and their hands moving swiftly. The Swede had adopted the fashion of board-whacking.

Scully took up his paper and for a long time remained immersed in matters which were extraordinarily remote from him. The lamp burned badly, and once he stopped to adjust the wick. The newspaper, as he turned from page to page, rustled with a slow and comfortable sound. Then suddenly he heard three terrible words: "You are cheatin'!"

Such scenes often prove that there can be little of dramatic import in environment. Any room can present a tragic front; any room can be comic. This little den was now hideous as a torture-chamber. The new faces of the men themselves had changed it upon the instant. The Swede held a huge fist in front of Johnnie's face, while the latter looked steadily over it into the blazing orbs of his accuser. The Easterner had grown pallid; the cowboy's jaw had dropped in that expression of bovine amazement which was one of his important mannerisms. After the three words, the first sound in the room was made by Scully's paper as it floated forgotten to his feet. His spectacles had also fallen from his nose, but by a clutch he had saved them in air. His hand, grasping the spectacles, now remained poised awkwardly and near his shoulder. He stared at the cardplayers.

Probably the silence was while a second elapsed. Then, if the floor had been suddenly twitched out from under the men they could not have moved quicker. The five had projected themselves headlong toward a common point. It happened that Johnnie, in rising to hurl himself upon the Swede, had stumbled slightly because of his curiously instinctive care for the cards and the board. The loss of the moment allowed time for the arrival of Scully, and also allowed the cowboy time to give the Swede a great push which sent him staggering back. The men found tongue together, and hoarse shouts of rage, appeal, or fear burst from every throat. The cowboy pushed and jostled feverishly at the Swede, and the Easterner and Scully clung widly to Johnnie; but through the smoky air, above the swaying bodies of the peace-compellers, the eyes of the two warriors ever sought each other in glances of challenge that were at once hot and steely.

Of course the board had been overturned, and now the whole company of cards was scattered over the floor, where the boots of the men trampled the fat and painted kings and queens as they gazed with their silly eyes at the war that was waging above them.

Scully's voice was dominating the yells. "Stop now! Stop, I say! Stop, now——"

Johnnie, as he struggled to burst through the rank formed by Scully and the Easterner, was crying, "Well, he says I cheated! He says I cheated! I won't allow no man to say I cheated! If he says I cheated, he's a—— —— !"

The cowboy was telling the Swede, "Quit now! Quit, d'ye hear——"

The screams of the Swede never ceased: "He did cheat! I saw him! I saw him——"

As for the Easterner, he was importuning in a voice that was not heeded: "Wait a moment, can't you? Oh, wait a moment. What's the good of a fight over a game of cards? Wait a moment——"

In this tumult no complete sentences were clear. "Cheat"—"Quit"—"He says"—these fragments pierced the uproar and rang out sharply. It was remarkable that, whereas Scully undoubtedly made the most noise, he was the least heard of any of the riotous band.

Then suddenly there was a great cessation. It was as if each man had paused for breath; and although the room was still lighted with the anger of men, it could be seen that there was no danger of immediate conflict, and at once Johnnie, shouldering his way forward, almost succeeded in confronting the Swede. "What did you say I cheated for? What did you say I cheated for? I don't cheat, and I won't let no man say I do!"

The Swede said, "I saw you! I saw you!"

"Well," cried Johnnie, "I'll fight any man what says I cheat!"

"No, you won't," said the cowboy. "Not here."

"Ah, be still, can't you?" said Scully, coming between them.

The quiet was sufficient to allow the Easterner's voice to be heard. He was repeating, "Oh, wait a moment, can't you? What's the good of a fight over a game of cards? Wait a moment!"

Johnnie, his red face appearing above his father's shoulder, hailed the Swede again. "Did you say I cheated?"

The Swede showed his teeth. "Yes."

"Then," said Johnnie, "we must fight."

"Yes, fight," roared the Swede. He was like a demoniac. "Yes, fight! I'll show you what kind of a man I am! I'll show you who you want to fight! Maybe you think I can't fight! Maybe you think I can't! I'll show you, you skin, you card-sharp! Yes, you cheated! You cheated! You cheated!"

"Well, let's go at it, then, mister," said Johnnie, coolly.

The cowboy's brow was beaded with sweat from his efforts in intercepting all sorts of raids. He turned in despair to Scully. "What are you goin' to do now?"

A change had come over the Celtic visage of the old man. He now seemed all eagerness; his eyes glowed.

"We'll let them fight," he answered, stalwartly. "I can't put up with it any longer. I've stood this damned Swede till I'm sick. We'll let them fight."

6

The men prepared to go out of doors. The Easterner was so nervous that he had great difficulty in getting his arms into the sleeves of his new leather coat.

As the cowboy drew his fur cap down over his ears his hands trembled. In fact, Johnnie and old Scully were the only ones who displayed no agitation. These preliminaries were conducted without words.

Scully threw open the door. "Well, come on," he said. Instantly a terrific wind caused the flame of the lamp to struggle at its wick, while a puff of black smoke sprang from the chimmey-top. The stove was in mid-current of the blast, and its voice swelled to equal the roar of the storm. Some of the scarred and bedabbled cards were caught up from the floor and dashed helplessly against the farther wall. The men lowered their heads and plunged into the tempest as into a sea.

No snow was falling, but great whirls and clouds of flakes, swept up from the ground by the frantic winds, were streaming southward with the speed of bullets. The covered land was blue with the sheen of an unearthly satin, and there was no other hue save where, at the low, black railway station—which seemed incredibly distant—one light gleamed like a tiny jewel. As the men floundered into a thigh-deep drift, it was known that the Swede was bawling out something. Scully went to him, put a hand on his shoulder, and projected an ear. "What's that you say?" he shouted.

"I say," bawled the Swede again, "I won't stand much show against this gang. I know you'll all pitch on me."

Scully smote him reproachfully on the arm. "Tut, man!" he yelled. The wind tore the words from Scully's lips and scattered them far alee.

"You are all a gang of——" boomed the Swede, but the storm also seized the remainder of this sentence.

Immediately turning their backs upon the wind, the men had swung around a corner to the sheltered side of the hotel. It was the function of the little house to preserve here, amid this great devastation of snow, an irregular V-shape of heavily encrusted grass, which crackled beneath the feet. One could imagine the great drifts piled against the windward side. When the party reached the comparative peace of this spot it was found that the Swede was still bellowing.

"Oh, I know what kind of a thing this is! I know you'll all pitch on me. I can't lick you all!"

Scully turned upon him panther-fashion. "You'll not have to whip all of us. You'll have to whip my son Johnnie. An' the man what troubles you durin' that time will have me to dale with."

The arrangements were swiftly made. The two men faced each other, obedient to the harsh commands of Scully, whose face, in the subtly luminous gloom, could be seen set in the austere impersonal lines that are pictured on the countenances of the Roman veterans. The Easterner's teeth were chattering, and he was hopping up and down like a mechanical toy. The cowboy stood rock-like.

The contestants had not stripped off any clothing. Each was in his ordinary attire. Their fists were up, and they eyed each other in a calm that had the elements of leonine cruelty in it.

During this pause, the Easterner's mind, like a film, took lasting impressions of three men—the iron-nerved master of the ceremony; the Swede, pale, motionless, terrible; and Johnnie, serene yet ferocious, brutish yet heroic. The entire prelude had in it a tragedy greater than the tragedy of action, and this aspect was accentuated by the long, mellow cry of the blizzard, as it sped the tumbling and wailing flakes into the black abyss of the south.

"Now!" said Scully.

The two combatants leaped forward and crashed together like bullocks. There was heard the cusioned sound of blows, and of a curse squeezing out from between the tight teeth of one.

As for the spectators, the Easterner's pent-up breath exploded from him with a pop of relief, absolute relief from the tension of the preliminaries. The cowboy bounded into the air with a yowl. Scully was immovable as from supreme amazement and fear at the fury of the fight which he himself had permitted and arranged.

For a time the encounter in the darkness was such a perplexity of flying arms that it presented no more detail than would a swiftly revolving wheel. Occasionally a face, as if illumined by a flash of light, would shine out, ghastly and marked with pink spots. A moment later, the men might have been known as shadows, if it were not for the involuntary utterance of oaths that came from them in whispers.

Suddenly a holocaust of warlike desire caught the cowboy, and he bolted forward with the speed of a broncho. "Go it, Johnnie! Go it! Kill him! Kill him!"

Scully confronted him. "Kape back," he said; and by his glance the cowboy could tell that this man was Johnnie's father.

To the Easterner there was a monotony of unchangeable fighting that was an abomination. This confused mingling was eternal to his sense, which was concentrated in a longing for the end, the priceless end. Once the fighters lurched near him, and as he scrambled hastily backward he heard them breathe like men on the rack.

"Kill him, Johnnie! Kill him! Kill him! Kill him!" The cowboy's face was contorted like one of those agony masks in museums.

"Keep still," said Scully, icily.

Then there was a sudden loud grunt, incomplete, cut short, and Johnnie's body swung away from the Swede and fell with sickening heaviness to the grass. The cowboy was barely in time to prevent the mad Swede from flinging himself upon his prone adversary. "No, you don't," said the cowboy, interposing an arm. "Wait a second."

Scully was at his son's side. "Johnnie! Johnnie, me boy!" His voice had a quality of melancholy tenderness. "Johnnie! Can you go on with it?" He looked anxiously down into the bloody, pulpy face of his son.

There was a moment of silence, and then Johnnie answered in his ordinary voice, "Yes, I—it—yes."

Assisted by his father he struggled to his feet. "Wait a bit now till you git your wind," said the old man.

A few paces away the cowboy was lecturing the Swede. "No, you don't! Wait a second!"

The Easterner was plucking at Scully's sleeve. "Oh, this is enough," he pleaded. "This is enough! Let it go as it stands. This is enough!"

"Bill," said Scully, "git out of the road." The cowboy stepped aside. "Now." The combatants were actuated by a new caution as they advanced toward collision. They glared at each other, and then the Swede aimed a lightning blow that carried with it his entire weight. Johnnie was evidently half stupid from weakness, but he miraculously dodged, and his fist sent the over-balanced Swede sprawling.

The cowboy, Scully, and the Easterner burst into a cheer that was like a chorus of triumphant soldiery, but before its conclusion the Swede had scuffled agilely to his feet and come in berserk abandon at his foe. There was another perplexity of flying arms, and Johnnie's body again swung away and fell, even as a bundle might fall from the roof. The Swede instantly staggered to a little wind-waved tree and leaned upon it, breathing like an engine, while his savage and flamelit eyes roamed from face to face as the men bent over Johnnie. There was a splendour of isolation in his situation at this time which the Easterner felt once when, lifting his eyes from the man on the ground, he beheld that mysterious and lonely figure, waiting.

"Are you any good yet, Johnnie?" asked Scully in a broken voice.

The son gasped and opened his eyes languidly. After a moment he answered, "No—I ain't—any good—any—more." Then, from shame and bodily ill, he began to weep, the tears furrowing down through the blood-stains on his face. "He was too—too—too heavy for me."

Scully straightened and addressed the waiting figure. "Stranger," he said, evenly, "it's all up with our side." Then his voice changed into that vibrant huskiness which is commonly the tone of the most simple and deadly announcements. "Johnnie is whipped."

Without replying, the victor moved off on the route to the front door of the hotel.

The cowboy was formulating new and unspellable blasphemies. The Easterner was startled to find that they were out in a wind that seemed to come direct from the shadowed arctic floes. He heard again the wail of the snow as it was flung to its grave in the south. He knew now that all this time the cold had been sinking into him deeper and deeper, and he wondered that he had not perished. He felt indifferent to the condition of the vanquished man.

"Johnnie, can you walk?" asked Scully.

"Did I hurt—hurt him any?" asked the son.

"Can you walk, boy? Can you walk?"

Johnnie's voice was suddenly strong. There was a robust impatience in it. "I asked you whether I hurt him any!"

"Yes, yes, Johnnie," answered the cowboy, consolingly; "he's hurt a good deal."

They raised him from the ground, and as soon as he was on his feet he went tottering off, rebuffing all attempts at assistance. When the party rounded the corner they were fairly blinded by the pelting of the snow. It burned their faces like fire. The cowboy carried Johnnie through the drift to the door. As they entered, some cards again rose from the floor and beat against the wall.

The Easterner rushed to the stove. He was so profoundly chilled that he almost dared to embrace the glowing iron. The Swede was not in the room. Johnnie sank into a chair and, folding his arms on his knees, buried his face in them. Scully, warming one foot and then the other at a rim of the stove, muttered to himself with Celtic mournfulness. The cowboy had removed his fur cap, and with a dazed and rueful air he was running one hand through his tousled locks. From overhead they could hear the creaking of boards, as the Swede tramped here and there in his room.

The sad quiet was broken by the sudden flinging open of a door that led toward the kitchen. It was instantly followed by an inrush of women. They precipitated themselves upon Johnnie amid a chorus of lamentation. Before they carried their prey off to the kitchen, there to be bathed and harangued with that mixture of sympathy and abuse which is a feat of their sex, the mother straightened herself and fixed old Scully with an eye of stern reproach. "Shame be upon you, Patrick Scully!" she cried. "Your own son, too. Shame be upon you!"

"There, now! Be quiet, now!" said the old man, weakly.

"Shame be upon you, Patrick Scully!" The girls, rallying to this slogan, sniffed disdainfully in the direction of those trembling accomplices, the cowboy and the Easterner. Presently they bore Johnnie away, and left the three men to dismal reflection.

"I'd like to fight this here Dutchman myself," said the cowboy; breaking a long silence.

Scully wagged his head sadly. "No, that wouldn't do. It wouldn't be right. It wouldn't be right."

"Well, why wouldn't it?" argued the cowboy. "I don't see no harm in it."

"No," answered Scully, with mournful heroism. "It wouldn't be right. It was Johnnie's fight, and now we mustn't whip the man just because he whipped Johnnie."

"Yes, that's true enough," said the cowboy; "but—he better not get fresh with me, because I couldn't stand no more of it."

"You'll not say a word to him," commanded Scully, and even then they heard the tread of the Swede on the stairs. His entrance was made theatric. He swept the door back with a bang and swaggered to the middle of the room. No one looked at him. "Well," he cried, insolently, at Scully, "I s'pose you'll tell me now how much I owe you!"

The old man remained stolid. "You don't owe me nothin'."

"Huh!" said the Swede, "huh! Don't owe 'im nothin'."

The cowboy addressed the Swede. "Stranger, I don't see how you come to be so gay around here."

Old Scully was instantly alert. "Stop!" he shouted, holding his hand forth, fingers upward. "Bill, you shut up!"

The cowboy spat carelessly into the sawdust-box. "I didn't say a word, did I?" he asked.

"Mr. Scully," called the Swede, "how much do I owe you?" It was seen that he was attired for departure, and that he had his valise in his hand.

"You don't owe me nothin'," repeated Scully in the same imperturbable way.

"Huh!" said the Swede. "I guess you're right. I guess if it was any way at all, you'd owe me somethin'. That's what I guess." He turned to the cowboy. " 'Kill him! Kill him! Kill him!' " he mimicked, and then guffawed victoriously. " 'Kill him!' " He was convulsed with ironical humour.

But he might have been jeering the dead. The three men were immovable and silent, staring with glassy eyes at the stove.

The Swede opened the door and passed into the storm, giving one derisive glance backward at the still group.

As soon as the door was closed, Scully and the cowboy leaped to their feet and began to curse. They trampled to and fro, waving their arms and smashing into the air with their fists. "Oh, but that was a hard minute!" wailed Scully. "That was a hard minute! Him there leerin' and scoffin'! One bang at his nose was worth forty dollars to me that minute! How did you stand it, Bill?"

"How did I stand it?" cried the cowboy in a quivering voice. "How did I stand it? Oh!"

The old man burst into sudden brogue. "I'd loike to take that Swade," he wailed, "and hould 'im down on a shtone flure and bate 'im to a jelly wid a shtick!"

The cowboy groaned in sympathy. "I'd like to git him by the neck and ha-ammer him"—he brought his hand down on a chair with a noise like a pistol-shot—"hammer that there Dutchman until he couldn't tell himself from a dead coyote!"

"I'd bate 'im until he——"

"I'd show *him* some things——"

And then together they raised a yearning, fanatic cry—"Oh-o-oh! if we only could——"

"Yes!"

"Yes!"

"And then I'd——"

"O-o-oh!"

8

The Swede, tightly gripping his valise, tacked across the face of the storm as if he carried sails. He was following a line of little naked, gasping trees which, he knew, must mark the way of the road. His face, fresh from the pounding of Johnnie's fists, felt more pleasure than pain in the wind and the driving snow. A number of square shapes loomed upon him finally, and he knew them as the houses of the main body of the town. He found a street and made travel along it, leaning heavily upon the wind whenever, at a corner, a terrific blast caught him.

He might have been in a deserted village. We picture the world as thick with conquering and elate humanity, but here, with the bugles of the tempest pealing, it was hard to imagine a peopled earth. One viewed the existence of man then as a marvel, and conceded a glamour of wonder to these lice which were caused to cling to a whirling, fire-smitten, ice-locked, disease-stricken, space-lost bulb. The conceit of man was explained by this storm to be the very engine of life. One was a coxcomb not to die in it. However, the Swede found a saloon.

In front of it an indomitable red light was burning, and the snowflakes were made blood-colour as they flew through the circumscribed territory of the lamp's shining. The Swede pushed open the door of the saloon and entered. A sanded expanse was before him, and at the end of it four men sat about a table drinking.

Down one side of the room extended a radiant bar, and its guardian was leaning upon his elbows listening to the talk of the men at the table. The Swede dropped his valise upon the floor and, smiling fraternally upon the barkeeper, said, "Gimme some whisky, will you?" The man placed a bottle, a whisky-glass, and a glass of ice-thick water upon the bar. The Swede poured himself an abnormal portion of whisky and drank it in three gulps. "Pretty bad night," remarked the bartender, indifferently. He was making the pretension of blindness which is usually a distinction of his class; but it could have been seen that he was furtively studying the half-erased blood-stains on the face of the Swede. "Bad night," he said again.

"Oh, it's good enough for me," replied the Swede, hardily, as he poured himself some more whisky. The barkeeper took his coin and manœuvred it through its reception by the highly nickelled cash-machine. A bell rang; a card labelled "20 cts." had appeared.

"No," continued the Swede, "this isn't too bad weather. It's good enough for me."

"So?" murmured the barkeeper, languidly.

The copious drams made the Swede's eyes swim, and he breathed a trifle heavier. "Yes, I like this weather. I like it. It suits me." It was apparently his design to impart a deep significance to these words.

"So?" murmured the bartender again. He turned to gaze dreamily at the scroll-like birds and bird-like scrolls which had been drawn with soap upon the mirrors in back of the bar.

"Well, I guess I'll take another drink," said the Swede, presently. "Have something?"

"No, thanks; I'm not drinkin'," answered the bartender. Afterwards he asked, "How did you hurt your face?"

The Swede immediately began to boast loudly. "Why, in a fight. I thumped the soul out of a man down here at Scully's hotel."

The interest of the four men at the table was at last aroused.

"Who was it?" said one.

"Johnnie Scully," blustered the Swede. "Son of the man what runs it. He will be pretty near dead for some weeks, I can tell you. I made a nice thing of him, I did. He couldn't get up. They carried him in the house. Have a drink?"

Instantly the men in some subtle way encased themselves in reserve. "No, thanks," said one. The group was of curious formation. Two were prominent local business men; one was the district attorney; and one was a professional gambler of the kind known as "square." But a scrutiny of the group would not have enabled an observer to pick the gambler from the men of more reputable pursuits. He was, in fact, a man so delicate in manner, when among people of fair class, and so judicious in his choice of victims, that in the strictly masculine part of the town's life he had come to be explicitly trusted and admired. People called him a thoroughbred. The fear and contempt with which his craft was regarded were undoubtedly the reason why his quiet dignity shone conspicuous above the quiet dignity of men who might be merely hatters, billiard-markers, or grocery clerks. Beyond an occasional unwary traveller who came by rail, this gambler was supposed to prey solely upon reckless and senile farmers, who, when flush with good crops, drove into town in all the pride and confidence of an absolutely invulnerable stupidity. Hearing at times in circuitous fashion of the despoilment of such a farmer, the important men of Romper invariably laughed in contempt of the victim, and if they thought of the wolf at all, it was with a kind of pride at the knowledge that he would never dare think of attacking their wisdom and courage. Besides, it was popular that this gambler had a real wife and two real children in a neat cottage in a suburb, where he led an exemplary home life; and when any one even suggested a discrepancy in his character, the crowd immediately vociferated descriptions of this virtuous family circle. Then men who led exemplary home lives, and men who did not lead exemplary home lives, all subsided in a bunch, remarking that there was nothing more to be said.

However, when a restriction was placed upon him—as, for instance, when a strong clique of members of the new Pollywog Club refused to permit him, even as a spectator, to appear in the rooms of the organization—the candour and gentleness with which he accepted the judgment disarmed many of his foes and made his friends more desperately partisan. He invariably distinguished between himself and a respectable Romper man so quickly and frankly that his manner actually appeared to be a continual broadcast compliment.

And one must not forget to declare the fundamental fact of his entire position in Romper. It is irrefutable that in all affairs outside his business, in all matters that occur eternally and commonly between man and man, this thieving card-player was so generous, so just, so moral, that, in a contest, he could have put to flight the consciences of nine-tenths of the citizens of Romper.

And so it happened that he was seated in this saloon with the two prominent local merchants and the district attorney.

The Swede continued to drink raw whisky, meanwhile babbling at the barkeeper and trying to induce him to indulge in potations. "Come on. Have a drink. Come on. What—no? Well, have a little one, then. By gawd, I've whipped a man to-night, and I want to celebrate. I whipped him good, too. Gentlemen," the Swede cried to the men at the table, "have a drink?"

"Ssh!" said the barkeeper.

The group at the table, although furtively attentive, had been pretending to be deep in talk, but now a man lifted his eyes toward the Swede and said, shortly, "Thanks. We don't want any more."

At this reply the Swede ruffled out his chest like a rooster. "Well," he exploded, "it seems I can't get anybody to drink with me in this town. Seems so, don't it? Well!"

"Ssh!" said the barkeeper.

"Say," snarled the Swede, "don't you try to shut me up. I won't have it. I'm a gentleman, and I want people to drink with me. And I want 'em to drink with me now. *Now*—do you understand?" He rapped the bar with his knuckles.

Years of experience had calloused the bartender. He merely grew sulky. "I hear you," he answered.

"Well," cried the Swede, "listen hard then. See those men over there? Well, they're going to drink with me, and don't you forget it. Now you watch."

"Hi!" yelled the barkeeper, "this won't do!"

"Why won't it?" demanded the Swede. He stalked over to the table, and by chance laid his hand upon the shoulder of the gambler. "How about this?" he asked wrathfully. "I asked you to drink with me."

The gambler simply twisted his head and spoke over his shoulder. "My friend, I don't know you."

"Oh, hell!" answered the Swede, "come and have a drink."

"Now, my boy," advised the gambler, kindly, "take your hand off my shoulder and go 'way and mind your own business." He was a little, slim man, and it seemed strange to hear him use this tone of heroic patronage to the burly Swede. The other men at the table said nothing.

"What! You won't drink with me, you little dude? I'll make you, then! I'll make you!" The Swede had grasped the gambler frenziedly at the throat, and was dragging him from his chair. The other men sprang up. The barkeeper dashed around the corner of his bar. There was a great tumult, and then was seen a long blade in the hand of the gambler. It shot forward, and a human body, this citadel of virtue, wisdom, power, was pierced as easily as if it had been a melon. The Swede fell with a cry of supreme astonishment.

The prominent merchants and the district attorney must have at once tumbled out of the place backward. The bartender found himself hanging limply to the arm of a chair and gazing into the eyes of a murderer.

"Henry," said the latter, as he wiped his knife on one of the towels that hung beneath the bar rail, "you tell 'em where to find me. I'll be home, waiting for 'em." Then he vanished. A moment afterward the barkeeper was in the street dinning through the storm for help and, moreover, companionship.

The corpse of the Swede, alone in the saloon, had its eyes fixed upon a dreadful legend that dwelt atop of the cash-machine: "This registers the amount of your purchase."

9

Months later, the cowboy was frying pork over the stove of a little ranch near the Dakota line, when there was a quick thud of hoofs outside, and presently the Easterner entered with the letters and the papers.

"Well," said the Easterner at once, "the chap that killed the Swede has got three years. Wasn't much, was it?"

"He has? Three years?" The cowboy poised his pan of pork, while he ruminated upon the news. "Three years. That ain't much."

"No. It was a light sentence," replied the Easterner as he unbuckled his spurs. "Seems there was a good deal of sympathy for him in Romper."

"If the bartender had been any good," observed the cowboy, thoughtfully, "he would have gone in and cracked that there Dutchman on the head with a bottle in the beginnin' of it and stopped all this here murderin'."

"Yes, a thousand things might have happened," said the Easterner, tartly.

The cowboy returned his pan of pork to the fire, but his philosophy continued. "It's funny, ain't it? If he hadn't said Johnnie was cheatin' he'd be alive this minute. He was an awful fool. Game played for fun, too. Not for money. I believe he was crazy."

"I feel sorry for that gambler," said the Easterner.

"Oh, so do I," said the cowboy. "He don't deserve none of it for killin' who he did."

"The Swede might not have been killed if everything had been square."

"Might not have been killed?" exclaimed the cowboy. "Everythin' square? Why, when he said that Johnnie was cheatin' and acted like such a jackass? And then in the saloon he fairly walked up to git hurt?" With these arguments the cowboy browbeat the Easterner and reduced him to rage.

"You're a fool!" cried the Easterner, viciously. "You're a bigger jackass than the Swede by a million majority. Now let me tell you one thing. Let me tell you something. Listen! Johnnie *was* cheating!"

" 'Johnnie,' " said the cowboy, blankly. There was a minute of silence, and then he said, robustly, "Why, no. The game was only for fun."

"Fun or not," said the Easterner, "Johnnie was cheating. I saw him. I know it. I saw him. And I refused to stand up and be a man. I let the Swede fight it out alone. And you—you were simply puffing around the place and wanting to fight. And then old Scully himself! We are all in it! This poor gambler isn't even a noun. He is kind of an adverb. Every sin is the result of a collaboration. We, five of us, have collaborated in the murder of this Swede. Usually there are from a dozen to forty women really involved in every murder, but in this case it seems to be only five men—you, I, Johnnie, old Scully; and that fool of an unfortunate gambler came merely as a culmination, the apex of a human movement, and gets all the punishment."

The cowboy, injured and rebellious, cried out blindly into this fog of mysterious theory: "Well, I didn't do anythin', did I?"

Questions for Discussion

1. How is the Swede portrayed immediately as a mysterious, important character?

2. In what ways does the Swede both predict and create his fate?

3. Describing the storm, the narrator says, "The conceit of man was explained by this storm to be the very engine of life." Interpret this statement, not just in connection with the storm but with the Swede's fate.

4. How does the narrator use the Swede to comment on the general behavior of the town?

5. How does the information at the end of the story alter our sense of who is responsible for the Swede's death? Who is responsible, in your view, and why?

Suggestions for Writing

1. Write an essay about the causes of the Swede's death. To what extent is it his fault? The gambler's? The bartender's? The rest of the town's? To what extent does the story deliberately complicate this issue?

2. How do setting and atmosphere (the hotel, the town, the storm, the region) influence the conflicts and themes of this story? Write a response in your notebook or journal to this question.

3. Write a story in which a disliked person is treated badly, but in which this treatment is ultimately not seen as just.

The Secret Sharer

JOSEPH CONRAD

I

On my right hand there were lines of fishing stakes resembling a mysterious system of half-submerged bamboo fences, incomprehensible in its division of the domain of tropical fishes, and crazy of aspect as if abandoned forever by some nomad tribe of fishermen now gone to the other end of the ocean; for there was no sign of human habitation as far as the eye could reach. To the left a group of barren islets, suggesting ruins of stone walls, towers, and blockhouses, had its foundations set in a blue sea that itself looked solid, so still and stable did it lie below my feet; even the track of light from the westering sun shone smoothly, without that animated glitter which tells of an imperceptible ripple. And when I turned my head to take a parting glance at the tug which had just left us anchored outside the bar, I saw the straight line of the flat shore joined to the stable sea, edge to edge, with a perfect and unmarked closeness, in one leveled floor half brown, half blue under the enormous dome of the sky. Corresponding in their insignificance to the islets of the sea, two small clumps of trees, one on each side of the only fault in the impeccable joint, marked the mouth of the river Meinam we had just left on the first preparatory stage of our homeward journey; and, far back on the inland level, a larger and loftier mass, the grove surrounding the great Paknam pagoda, was the only thing on which the eye could rest from the vain task of exploring the monotonous sweep of the horizon. Here and there gleams as of a few scattered pieces of silver marked the windings of the great river; and on the nearest of them, just within the bar, the tug steaming right into the land became lost to my sight, hull and funnel and masts, as though the impassive earth had swallowed her up without an effort, without a tremor. My eye followed the light cloud of her smoke, now here, now there, above the plain, according to the devious curves of the stream, but always fainter and farther away, till I lost it at last behind the miter-shaped hill of the great pagoda. And then I was left alone with my ship, anchored at the head of the Gulf of Siam.

She floated at the starting point of a long journey, very still in an immense stillness, the shadows of her spars flung far to the eastward by the setting sun. At that moment I was alone on her decks. There was not a sound in her—and around us nothing moved, nothing lived, not a canoe on the water, not a bird in the air, not a cloud in the sky. In this breathless pause at the threshold of a long passage we seemed to be measuring our fitness for a long and arduous enterprise, the appointed task of both our existences to be carried out, far from all human eyes, with only sky and sea for spectators and for judges.

There must have been some glare in the air to interfere with one's sight, because it was only just before the sun left us that my roaming eyes made out beyond the highest ridge of the principal islet of the group something which did away with the solemnity of perfect solitude. The tide of darkness flowed on swiftly; and with tropical suddenness a swarm of stars came out above the shadowy earth, while I lingered yet, my hand resting lightly on my ship's rail as if on the shoulder of a trusted friend. But, with all that multitude of celestial bodies staring down at one, the comfort of quiet communion with her was gone for good. And there were also disturbing sounds by this time—voices, footsteps forward; the steward flitted along the main deck, a busily ministering spirit; a hand bell tinkled urgently under the poop deck. . . .

I found my two officers waiting for me near the supper table, in the lighted cuddy. We sat down at once, and as I helped the chief mate, I said:

"Are you aware that there is a ship anchored inside the islands? I saw her mastheads above the ridge as the sun went down."

He raised sharply his simple face, overcharged by a terrible growth of whisker, and emitted his usual ejaculations: "Bless my soul, sir! You don't say so!"

My second mate was a sound-cheeked, silent young man, grave beyond his years, I thought; but as our eyes happened to meet I detected a slight quiver on his lips. I looked down at once. It was not my part to encourage sneering on board my ship. It must be said, too, that I knew very little of my officers. In consequence of certain events of no particular significance, except to myself, I had been appointed to the command only a fortnight before. Neither did I know much of the hands forward. All these people had been together for eighteen months or so, and my position was that of the only stranger on board. I mention this because it has some bearing on what is to follow. But what I felt most was my being a stranger to the ship; and if truth must be told, I was somewhat of a stranger to myself. The youngest man on board (barring the second mate), and untried as yet by a position of the fullest responsibility, I was willing to take the adequacy of the others for granted. They had simply to be equal to their tasks: but I wondered how far I should turn out faithful to that ideal conception of one's own personality every man sets up for himself secretly.

Meantime the chief mate, with an almost visible effect of collaboration on the part of his round eyes and frightful whiskers, was trying to evolve a theory of the anchored ship. His dominant trait was to take all things into earnest consideration. He was of a painstaking turn of mind. As he used to say, he "liked to account to himself" for practically everything that came in his way, down to a miserable scorpion he had found in his cabin a week before. The why and the wherefore of that scorpion—how it got on board and came to select his room rather than the pantry (which was a dark place and more what a scorpion would be partial to), and how on earth it managed to drown itself in the inkwell of his writing desk—had exercised him infinitely. The ship within the islands was much more easily accounted for; and just as we were about to rise from the table he made his pronouncement. She was, he doubted not, a ship from home lately arrived. Probably she drew too much water to cross the bar except at the top of spring tides. Therefore she went into that natural harbor to wait for a few days in preference to remaining in an open roadstead.

"That's so," confirmed the second mate, suddenly, in his slightly hoarse voice. "She draws over twenty feet. She's the Liverpool ship *Sephora* with a cargo of coal. Hundred and twenty-three days from Cardiff."

We looked at him in surprise.

"The tugboat skipper told me when he came on board for your letters, sir," explained the young man. "He expects to take her up the river the day after tomorrow."

After thus overwhelming us with the extent of his information he slipped out of the cabin. The mate observed regretfully that he "could not account for that young fellow's whims." What prevented him telling us all about it at once, he wanted to know.

I detained him as he was making a move. For the last two days the crew had had plenty of hard work, and the night before they had very little sleep. I felt painfully that I—a stranger—was doing something unusual when I directed him to let all hands turn in without setting an anchor watch. I proposed to keep on deck myself till one o'clock or thereabouts. I would get the second mate to relieve me at that hour.

"He will turn out the cook and the steward at four," I concluded, "and then give you a call. Of course at the lightest sign of any sort of wind we'll have the hands up and make a start at once."

He concealed his astonishment. "Very well, sir." Outside the cuddy he put his head in the second mate's door to inform him of my unheard-of caprice to take a five hours' anchor watch on myself. I heard the other raise his voice incredulously: "What? The captain himself?" Then a few more murmurs, a door closed, then another. A few moments later I went on deck.

My strangeness, which had made me sleepless, had prompted that unconventional arrangement, as if I had expected in those solitary hours of the night to get on terms with the ship of which I knew nothing, manned by men of whom I knew very little more. Fast alongside a wharf, littered like any ship in port with a tangle of unrelated things, invaded by unrelated shore people, I had hardly seen her yet properly. Now, as she lay cleared for sea, the stretch of her main deck seemed to me very fine under the stars. Very fine, very roomy for her size, and very inviting. I descended the poop and paced the waist, my mind picturing to myself the coming passage through the Malay Archipelago, down the Indian Ocean, and up the Atlantic. All its phases were familiar enough to me, every characteristic, all the alternatives which were likely to face me on the high seas—everything! . . . except the novel responsibility of command. But I took heart from the reasonable thought that the ship was like other ships, the men like other men, and that the sea was not likely to keep any special surprises expressly for my discomfiture.

Arrived at that comforting conclusion, I bethought myself of a cigar and went below to get it. All was still down there. Everybody at the after end of the ship was sleeping profoundly. I came out again on the quarter-deck, agreeably at ease in my sleeping suit on that warm breathless night, barefooted, a glowing cigar in my teeth, and, going forward, I was met by the profound silence of the fore end of the ship. Only as I passed the door of the forecastle I heard a deep, quiet, trustful sigh of some sleeper inside. And suddenly I rejoiced in the great security of the sea as compared with the unrest of the land, in my choice of that untempted life presenting no disquieting problems, invested with an elementary moral beauty by the absolute straightforwardness of its appeal and by the singleness of its purpose.

The riding light in the fore-rigging burned with a clear, untroubled, as if symbolic, flame, confident and bright in the mysterious shades of the night. Passing on my way aft along the other side of the ship, I observed that the rope side ladder, put over, no doubt, for the master of the tug when he came to fetch away our letters, had not been hauled in as it should have been. I became annoyed at this, for exactitude in small matters is the very soul of discipline. Then I reflected that I had myself peremptorily dismissed my officers from duty, and by my own act had prevented the anchor watch being formally set and things properly attended to. I asked myself whether it was wise ever to interfere with the established routine of duties even from the kindest of motives. My action might have made me appear eccentric. Goodness only knew how that absurdly whiskered mate would "account" for my conduct, and what the whole ship thought of that informality of their new captain. I was vexed with myself.

Not from compunction certainly, but, as it were mechanically, I proceeded to get the ladder in myself. Now a side ladder of that sort is a light affair and comes in easily, yet my vigorous tug, which should have brought it flying on board, merely recoiled upon my body in a totally unexpected jerk. What the devil! . . . I was so astounded by the immovableness of that ladder that I remained stock-still, trying to account for it to myself like that imbecile mate of mine. In the end, of course, I put my head over the rail.

The side of the ship made an opaque belt of shadow on the darkling glassy shimmer of the sea. But I saw at once something elongated and pale floating very close to the ladder. Before I could form a guess a faint flash of phosphorescent light, which seemed to issue suddenly from the naked body of a man, flickered in the sleeping water with the elusive, silent play of summer lightning in a night sky. With a gasp I saw revealed to my stare a pair of feet, the long legs, a broad livid back immersed right up to the neck in a greenish cadaverous glow. One hand, awash, clutched the bottom rung of the ladder. He was complete but for the head. A headless corpse! The cigar dropped out of my gaping mouth with a tiny plop and a short hiss quite audible in the absolute stillness of all things under heaven. At that I suppose he raised up his face, a dimly pale oval in the shadow of the ship's side. But even then I could only barely make out down there the shape of his black-haired head. However, it was enough for the horrid, frost-bound sensation which had gripped me about the chest to pass off. The moment of vain exclamations was past, too. I only climbed on the spare spar and leaned over the rail as far as I could, to bring my eyes nearer to that mystery floating alongside.

As he hung by the ladder, like a resting swimmer, the sea lightning played about his limbs at every stir; and he appeared in it ghastly, silvery, fishlike. He remained as mute as a fish, too. He made no motion to get out of the water, either. It was inconceivable that he should not attempt to come on board, and strangely troubling to suspect that perhaps he did not want to. And my first words were prompted by just that troubled incertitude.

"What's the matter?" I asked in my ordinary tone, speaking down to the face upturned exactly under mine.

"Cramp," it answered, no louder. Then slightly anxious, "I say, no need to call anyone."

"I was not going to," I said.

"Are you alone on deck?"

"Yes."

I had somehow the impression that he was on the point of letting go the ladder to swim away beyond my ken—mysterious as he came. But, for the moment, this being appearing as if he had risen from the bottom of the sea (it was certainly the nearest land to the ship) wanted only to know the time. I told him. And he, down there, tentatively:

"I suppose your captain's turned in?"

"I am sure he isn't," I said.

He seemed to struggle with himself, for I heard something like the low, bitter murmur of doubt. "What's the good?" His next words came out with a hestitating effort.

"Look here, my man. Could you call him out quietly?"

I thought the time had come to declare myself.

"*I* am the captain."

I heard a "By Jove!" whispered at the level of the water. The phosphorescence flashed in the swirl of the water all about his limbs, his other hand seized the ladder.

"My name's Leggatt."

The voice was calm and resolute. A good voice. The self-possession of that man had somehow induced a corresponding state in myself. It was very quietly that I remarked:

"You must be a good swimmer."

"Yes, I've been in the water practically since nine o'clock. The question for me now is whether I am to let go this ladder and go on swimming till I sink from exhaustion, or—to come on board here."

I felt this was no mere formula of desperate speech, but a real alternative in the view of a strong soul. I should have gathered from this that he was young; indeed, it is only the young who are ever confronted by such clear issues. But at this time it was pure intuition on my part. A mysterious communication was established already between us two—in the face of that silent darkened tropical sea. I was young, too; young enough to make no comment. The man in the water began suddenly to climb up the ladder, and I hastened away from the rail to fetch some clothes.

Before entering the cabin I stood still, listening in the lobby at the foot of the stairs. A faint snore came through the closed door of the chief mate's room. The second mate's door was on the hook, but the darkness in there was absolutely soundless. He, too, was young and could sleep like a stone. Remained the steward, but he was not likely to wake up before he was called. I got a sleeping suit out of my room and, coming back on deck, saw the naked man from the sea sitting on the main hatch, glimmering white in the darkness, his elbows on his knees and his head in his hands. In a moment he had concealed his damp body in a sleeping suit of the same gray-stripe pattern as the one I was wearing and followed me like my double on the poop. Together we moved right aft, barefooted, silent.

"What is it?" I asked in a deadened voice, taking the lighted lamp out of the binnacle, and raising it to his face.

"An ugly business."

He had rather regular features; a good mouth; light eyes under somewhat heavy, dark eyebrows; a smooth, square forehead; no growth on his cheeks; a small, brown mustache, and a well-shaped, round chin. His expression was concentrated, meditative, under the inspecting light of the lamp I held up to his face; such as a man thinking hard in solitude might wear. My sleeping suit was just right for his size. A well-knit young fellow of twenty-five at most. He caught his lower lip with the edge of white, even teeth.

"Yes," I said, replacing the lamp in the binnacle. The warm, heavy tropical night closed upon his head again.

"There's a ship over there," he murmured.

"Yes, I know. The *Sephora*. Did you know of us?"

"Hadn't the slightest idea. I am the mate of her—" He paused and corrected himself. "I should say I was."

"Aha! Something wrong?"

"Yes. Very wrong indeed. I've killed a man."

"What do you mean? Just now?"

"No, on the passage. Weeks ago. Thirty-nine south. When I say a man—"

"Fit of temper," I suggested, confidently.

The shadowy, dark head, like mine, seemed to nod imperceptibly above the ghostly gray of my sleeping suit. It was, in the night, as though I had been faced by my own reflection in the depths of a somber and immense mirror.

"A pretty thing to have to own up to for a Conway boy," murmured my double, distinctly.

"You're a Conway boy?"

"I am," he said, as if startled. Then, slowly . . . "Perhaps you too—"

It was so; but being a couple of years older I had left before he joined. After a quick interchange of dates a silence fell; and I thought suddenly of my absurd mate with his terrific whiskers and the "Bless my soul—you don't say so" type of intellect. My double gave me an inkling of his thoughts by saying:

"My father's a parson in Norfolk. Do you see me before a judge and jury on that charge? For myself I can't see the necessity. There are fellows that an angel from heaven—And I am not that. He was one of those creatures that are just simmering all the time with a silly sort of wickedness. Miserable devils that have no business to live at all. He wouldn't do his duty and wouldn't let anybody else do theirs. But what's the good of talking! You know well enough the sort of ill-conditioned snarling cur—"

He appealed to me as if our experiences had been as identical as our clothes. And I knew well enough the pestiferous danger of such a character where there are no means of legal repression. And I knew well enough also that my double there was no homicidal ruffian. I did not think of asking him for details, and he told me the story roughly in brusque, disconnected sentences. I needed no more. I saw it all going on as though I were myself inside that other sleeping suit.

"It happened while we were setting a reefed foresail, at dusk. Reefed foresail! You understand the sort of weather. The only sail we had left to keep the ship running; so you may guess what it had been like for days. Anxious sort of job, that. He gave me some of his cursed insolence at the sheet. I tell you I was overdone with this terrific weather that seemed to have no end to it. Terrific, I tell you—and a deep ship. I believe the fellow himself was half crazed with funk. It was no time for gentlemanly reproof, so I turned round and felled him like an ox. He up and at me. We closed just as an awful sea made for the ship. All hands saw it coming and took to the rigging, but I had him by the throat, and went on shaking him like a rat, the men above us yelling, 'Look out! look out!' Then a crash as if the sky had fallen on my head. They say that for over ten minutes hardly anything was to be seen of the ship—just the three masts and a bit of the forecastle head and of the poop all awash driving along in a smother of foam. It was a miracle that they found us, jammed together behind the forebits. It's clear that I meant business, because I was holding him by the throat still when they picked us up. He was black in the face. It was too much for them. It seems they rushed us aft together, gripped as we were, screaming 'Murder!' like a lot of lunatics, and broke into the cuddy. And the ship running for her life, touch and go all the time, any minute her last in a sea fit to turn your hair gray only a-looking at it. I understand that the skipper, too, started raving like the rest of them. The man had been deprived of sleep for more than a week, and to have this sprung on him at the height of a furious gale nearly drove him out of his mind. I wonder they didn't fling me overboard after getting the carcass of their precious shipmate out of my fingers. They had rather a job to separate us, I've been told. A sufficiently fierce story to make an old judge and a respectable jury sit up a bit. The first thing I heard when I came to myself was the maddening howling of that endless gale, and on that the voice of the old man. He was hanging on to my bunk, staring into my face out of his sou'wester.

"'Mr. Leggatt, you have killed a man. You can act no longer as chief mate of this ship.'"

His care to subdue his voice made it sound monotonous. He rested a hand on the end of the skylight to steady himself with, and all that time did not stir a limb, so far as I could see. "Nice little tale for a quiet tea party," he concluded in the same tone.

One of my hands, too, rested on the end of the skylight; neither did I stir a limb, so far as I knew. We stood less than a foot from each other. It occurred to me that if old "Bless my soul—you don't say so" were to put his head up the companion and catch sight of us, he would think he was seeing double, or imagine himself come upon a scene of weird witchcraft; the strange captain having a quiet confabulation by the wheel with his own gray ghost. I became very much concerned to prevent anything of the sort. I heard the other's soothing undertone.

"My father's a parson in Norfolk," it said. Evidently he had forgotten he had told me this important fact before. Truly a nice little tale.

"You had better slip down into my stateroom now," I said, moving off stealthily. My double followed my movements; our bare feet made no sound; I let him in, closed the door with care, and, after giving a call to the second mate, returned on deck for my relief.

"Not much sign of any wind yet," I remarked when he approached.

'No, sir. Not much," he assented, sleepily, in his hoarse voice, with just enough deference, no more, and barely suppressing a yawn.

"Well, that's all you have to look out for. You have got your orders."

"Yes, sir."

I paced a turn or two on the poop and saw him take up his position face forward with his elbow in the rat-lines of the mizzen-rigging before I went below. The mate's faint snoring was still going on peacefully. The cuddy lamp was burning over the table on which stood a vase with flowers, a polite attention from the ships' provision merchant—the last flowers we should see for the next three months at the very least. Two bunches of bananas hung from the beam symmetrically, one on each side of the rudder casing. Everything was as before in the ship—except that two of her captain's sleeping suits were simultaneously in use, one motionless in the cuddy, the other keeping very still in the captain's stateroom.

It must be explained here that my cabin had the form of the capital letter L, the door being within the angle and opening into the short part of the letter. A couch was to the left, the bed-place to the right; my writing desk and the chronometers' table faced the door. But anyone opening it, unless he stepped right inside, had no view of what I call the long (or vertical) part of the letter. It contained some lockers surmounted by a bookcase; and a few clothes, a thick jacket or two, caps, oilskin coat, and such like, hung on hooks. There was at the bottom of that part a door opening into my bathroom, which could be entered also directly from the saloon. But that way was never used.

The mysterious arrival had discovered the advantage of this particular shape. Entering my room, lighted strongly by a big bulkhead lamp swung on gimbals above my writing desk, I did not see him anywhere till he stepped out quietly from behind the coats hung in the recessed part.

"I heard somebody moving about, and went in there at once," he whispered.

I, too, spoke under my breath.

"Nobody is likely to come in here without knocking and getting permission."

He nodded. His face was thin and the sunburn faded, as though he had been ill. And no wonder. He had been, I heard presently, kept under arrest in his cabin for nearly seven weeks. But there was nothing sickly in his eyes or in his expression. He was not a bit like me, really; yet, as we stood leaning over my bed-place, whispering side by side, with our dark heads together and our backs to the door, anybody bold enough to open it stealthily would have been treated to the uncanny sight of a double captain busy talking in whispers with his other self.

"But all this doesn't tell me how you came to hang on to our side ladder," I inquired, in the hardly audible murmurs we used, after he had told me something more of the proceedings on board the *Sephora* once the bad weather was over.

"When we sighted Java Head I had had time to think all those matters out several times over. I had six weeks of doing nothing else, and with only an hour or so every evening for a tramp on the quarter-deck."

He whispered, his arms folded on the side of my bed-place, staring through the open port. And I could imagine perfectly the manner of this thinking out—a stubborn if not a steadfast operation; something of which I should have been perfectly incapable.

"I reckoned it would be dark before we closed with the land," he continued, so low that I had to strain my hearing, near as we were to each other, shoulder touching shoulder almost. "So I asked to speak to the old man. He always seemed very sick when he came to see me—as if he could not look me in the face. You know, that foresail saved the ship. She was too deep to have run long under bare poles. And it was I that managed to set it for him. Anyway, he came. When I had him in my cabin—he stood by the door looking at me as if I had the halter around my neck already—I asked him right away to leave my cabin door unlocked at night while the ship was going through Sunda Straits. There would be the Java coast within two or three miles, off Angier Point. I wanted nothing more. I've had a prize for swimming my second year in the Conway."

"I can believe it," I breathed out.

"God only knows why they locked me in every night. To see some of their faces you'd have thought they were afraid I'd go about at night strangling people. Am I a murdering brute? Do I look it? By Jove! if I had been he wouldn't have trusted himself like that into my room. You'll say I might have chucked him aside and bolted out, there and then—it was dark already. Well, no. And for the same reason I wouldn't think of trying to smash the door. There would have been a rush to stop me at the noise, and I did not mean to get into a confounded scrimmage. Somebody else might have got killed—for I would not have broken out only to get chucked back, and I did not want any more of that work. He refused, looking more sick than ever. He was afraid of the men, and also of that old second mate of his who had been sailing with him for years—a gray-headed old humbug; and his steward, too, had been with him devil knows how long—seventeen years or more—a dogmatic sort of loafer who hated me like poison, just because I was the chief mate. No chief mate ever made more than one voyage in the *Sephora*, you know. Those two old chaps ran the ship. Devil only knows what the skipper wasn't afraid of (all his nerve went to pieces altogether in that hellish spell of bad weather we had)—of what the law would do to him—of his wife, perhaps. Oh, yes! she's on board. Though I don't think she would have meddled. She would have been only too glad to have me out of the ship in any way. The 'brand of Cain' business, don't you see. That's all right. I was ready enough to go off wandering on the face of the earth—and that was price enough to pay for an Abel of that sort. Anyhow, he wouldn't listen to me. 'This thing must take its course. I represent the law here.' He was shaking life a leaf. 'So you won't?' 'No!' 'Then I hope you will be able to sleep on that,' I said, and turned my back on him. 'I wonder that you can,' cries he, and locks the door.

"Well, after that, I couldn't. Not very well. That was three weeks ago. We have had a slow passage through the Java Sea; drifted about Carimata for ten days. When we anchored here they thought, I suppose, it was all right. The nearest land (and that's five miles) is the ship's destination; the consul would soon set about catching me; and there would have been no object in bolting to these islets there. I don't suppose there's a drop of water on them. I don't know how it was, but tonight that steward, after bringing me my supper, went out to let me eat it, and left the door unlocked. And I ate it—all there was, too. After I had finished I strolled out on the quarter-deck. I don't know that I meant to do anything. A breath of fresh air was all I wanted, I believe. Then a sudden temptation came over me. I kicked off my slippers and was in the water before I had made up my mind fairly. Somebody heard the splash and they raised an awful hullabaloo. 'He's gone! Lower the boats! He's committed suicide! No, he's swimming.' Certainly I was swimming. It's not so easy for a swimmer like me to commit suicide by drowning. I landed on the nearest islet before the boat left the ship's side. I heard them pulling about in the dark, hailing, and so on, but after a bit they gave up. Everything quieted down and the anchorage became as still as death. I sat down on a stone and began to think. I felt certain they would start searching for me at daylight. There was no place to hide on those stony things—and if there had been, what would have been the good? But now I was clear of that ship, I was not going back. So after a while I took off all my clothes, tied them up in a bundle with a stone inside, and dropped them in the deep water on the outer side of the islet. That was suicide enough for me. Let them think what they liked, but I didn't mean to drown myself. I meant to swim till I sank—but that's not the same thing. I struck out for another of these little islands, and it was from that one that I first saw your riding light. Something to swim for. I went on easily, and on the way I came upon a flat rock a foot or two above water. In the daytime, I dare say, you might make it out with a glass from your poop. I scrambled up on it and rested myself for a bit. Then I made another start. That last spell must have been over a mile."

His whisper was getting fainter and fainter, and all the time he stared straight out through the porthole, in which there was not even a star to be seen. I had not interrupted him. There was something that made comment impossible in his narrative, or perhaps in himself; a sort of feeling, a quality, which I can't find a name for. And when he ceased, all I found was a futile whisper: "So you swam for our light?"

"Yes—straight for it. It was something to swim for. I couldn't see any stars low down because the coast was in the way, and I couldn't see the land, either. The water was like glass. One might have been swimming in a confounded thousand-feet deep cistern with no place for scrambling out anywhere; but what I didn't like was the notion of swimming round and round like a crazed bullock before I gave out; and as I didn't mean to go back . . . No. Do you see me being hauled back, stark naked, off one of these little islands by the scruff of the neck and fighting like a wild beast? Somebody would have got killed for certain, and I did not want any of that. So I went on. Then your ladder—"

"Why didn't you hail the ship?" I asked, a little louder.

He touched my shoulder lightly. Lazy footsteps came right over our heads and stopped. The second mate had crossed from the other side of the poop and might have been hanging over the rail, for all we knew.

"He couldn't hear us talking—could he?" My double breathed into my very ear, anxiously.

His anxiety was an answer, a sufficient answer, to the question I had put to him. An answer containing all the difficulty of that situation. I closed the porthole quietly, to make sure. A louder word might have been overheard.

"Who's that?" he whispered then.

"My second mate. But I don't know much more of the fellow than you do."

And I told him a little about myself. I had been appointed to take charge while I least expected anything of the sort, not quite a fortnight ago. I didn't know either the ship or the people. Hadn't had the time in port to look about me or size anybody up. And as to the crew, all they knew was that I was appointed to take the ship home. For the rest, I was almost as much of a stranger on board as himself, I said. And at the moment I felt it most acutely. I felt that it would take very little to make me a suspect person in the eyes of the ship's company.

He had turned about meantime; and we, the two strangers in the ship, faced each other in identical attitudes.

"Your ladder—" he murmured, after a silence. "Who'd have thought of finding a ladder hanging over at night in a ship anchored out here! I felt just then a very unpleasant faintness. After the life I've been leading for nine weeks, anybody would have got out of condition. I wasn't capable of swimming round as far as your rudder chains. And, lo and behold! there was a ladder to get hold of. After I gripped it I said to myself, 'What's the good?' When I saw a man's head looking over I thought I would swim away presently and leave him shouting—in whatever language it was. I didn't mind being looked at. I—I liked it. And then you speaking to me so quietly—as if you had expected me —made me hold on a little longer. It had been a confounded lonely time—I don't mean while swimming. I was glad to talk a little to somebody that didn't belong to the *Sephora*. As to asking for the captain, that was a mere impulse. It could have been no use, with all the ship knowing about me and the other people pretty certain to be round here in the morning. I don't know—I wanted to be seen, to talk with somebody, before I went on. I don't know what I would have said. . . . 'Fine night, isn't it?' or something of the sort."

"Do you think they will be round here presently?" I asked with some incredulity.

"Quite likely," he said, faintly.

He looked extremely haggard all of a sudden. His head rolled on his shoulders.

"H'm. We shall see then. Meantime get into that bed," I whispered. "Want help? There."

It was a rather high bed-place with a set of drawers underneath. This amazing swimmer really needed the lift I gave him by seizing his leg. He tumbled in, rolled over on his back, and flung one arm across his eyes. And then, with his face nearly hidden, he must have looked exactly as I used to look in that bed. I gazed upon my other self for a while before drawing across carefully the two green serge curtains which ran on a brass rod. I thought for a moment of pinning them together for greater safety, but I sat down on the couch, and once there I felt unwilling to rise and hunt for a pin. I would do it in a moment. I was extremely tired, in a peculiarly intimate way, by the strain of stealthiness, by the effort of whispering and the general secrecy of this excitement. It was three o'clock by now and I had been on my feet since nine, but I was not sleepy; I could not have gone to sleep. I sat there, fagged out, looking at the curtains, trying to clear my mind of the confused sensation of being in two places at once, and greatly bothered by an exasperating knocking in my head. It was a relief to discover suddenly that it was not in my head at all, but on the outside of the door. Before I could collect myself the words "Come in" were out of my mouth, and the steward entered with a tray, bringing in my morning coffee. I had slept, after all, and I was so frightened that I shouted, "This way! I am here, steward," as though he had been miles away. He put down the tray on the table next the couch and only then said, very quietly, "I can see you are here, sir." I felt him give me a keen look, but I dared not meet his eyes just then. He must have wondered why I had drawn the curtains of my bed before going to sleep on the couch. He went out, hooking the door open as usual.

I heard the crew washing decks above me. I knew I would have been told at once if there had been any wind. Calm, I thought, and I was doubly vexed. Indeed, I felt dual more than ever. The steward reappeared suddenly in the doorway. I jumped up from the couch so quickly that he gave a start.

"What do you want here?"

"Close your port, sir—they are washing decks."

"It is closed," I said, reddening.

"Very well, sir." But he did not move from the doorway and returned my stare in an extraordinary, equivocal manner for a time. Then his eyes wavered, all his expression changed, and in a voice unusually gentle, almost coaxingly:

"May I come in to take the empty cup away, sir?"

"Of course!" I turned my back on him while he popped in and out. Then I unhooked and closed the door and even pushed the bolt. This sort of thing could not go on very long. The cabin was as hot as an oven, too. I took a peep at my double, and discovered that he had not moved, his arm was still over his eyes; but his chest heaved; his hair was wet; his chin glistened with perspiration. I reached over him and opened the port.

"I must show myself on deck," I reflected.

Of course, theoretically, I could do what I liked, with no one to say nay to me within the whole circle of the horizon; but to lock my cabin door and take the key away I did not dare. Directly I put my head out of the companion I saw the group of my two officers, the second mate barefooted, the chief mate in long india-rubber boots, near the break of the poop, and the steward halfway down the poop ladder talking to them eagerly. He happened to catch sight of me and dived, the second ran down on the main deck shouting some order or other, and the chief mate came to meet me, touching his cap.

There was a sort of curiosity in his eye that I did not like. I don't know whether the steward had told them that I was "queer" only, or downright drunk, but I know the man meant to have a good look at me. I watched him coming with a smile which, as he got into point-blank range, took effect and froze his very whiskers. I did not give him time to open his lips.

"Square the yards by lifts and braces before the hands go to breakfast."

It was the first particular order I had given on board that ship; and I stayed on deck to see it executed, too. I had felt the need of asserting myself without loss of time. That sneering young cub got taken down a peg or two on that occasion, and I also seized the opportunity of having a good look at the face of every foremast man as they filed past me to go to the after braces. At breakfast time, eating nothing myself, I presided with such frigid dignity that the two mates were only too glad to escape from the cabin as soon as decency permitted; and all the time the dual working of my mind distracted me almost to the point of insanity. I was constantly watching myself, my secret self, as dependent on my actions as my own personality, sleeping in that bed, behind that door which faced me as I sat at the head of the table. It was very much like being mad, only it was worse because one was aware of it.

I had to shake him for a solid minute, but when at last he opened his eyes it was in the full possession of his senses, with an inquiring look.

"All's well so far," I whispered. "Now you must vanish into the bathroom."

He did so, as noiseless as a ghost, and I then rang for the steward, and facing him boldly, directed him to tidy up my stateroom while I was having my bath—"and be quick about it." As my tone admitted of no excuses, he said, "Yes, sir," and ran off to fetch his dustpan and brushes. I took a bath and did most of my dressing, splashing, and whistling softly for the steward's edification, while the secret sharer of my life stood drawn up bolt upright in that little space, his face looking very sunken in daylight, his eyelids lowered under the stern, dark line of his eyebrows drawn together by a slight frown.

When I left him there to go back to my room the steward was finished dusting. I sent for the mate and engaged him in some insignificant conversation. It was, as it were, trifling with the terrific character of whiskers; but my object was to give him an opportunity for a good look at my cabin. And then I could at last shut, with a clear conscience, the door of my stateroom and get my double back into the recessed part. There was nothing else for it. He had to sit still on a small folding stool, half smothered by the heavy coats hanging there. We listened to the steward going into the bathroom out of the saloon, filling the water bottles there, scrubbing the bath, setting things to rights, whisk, bang, clatter—out again into the saloon—turn the key—click. Such was my scheme for keeping my second self invisible. Nothing better could be contrived under the circumstances. And there we sat; I at my writing desk ready to appear busy with some papers, he behind me, out of sight of the door. It would not have been prudent to talk in daytime; and I could not have stood the excitement of that queer sense of whispering to myself. Now and then, glancing over my shoulder, I saw him far back there, sitting rigidly on the low stool, his bare feet close together, his arms folded, his head hanging on his breast—and perfectly still. Anybody would have taken him for me.

I was fascinated by it myself. Every moment I had to glance over my shoulder. I was looking at him when a voice outside the door said:

"Beg pardon, sir."

"Well!" . . . I kept my eyes on him, and so, when the voice outside the door announced, "There's a ship's boat coming our way, sir," I saw him give a start—the first movement he had made for hours. But he did not raise his bowed head.

"All right. Get the ladder over."

I hesitated. Should I whisper something to him? But what? His immobility seemed to have been never disturbed. What could I tell him he did not know already? . . . Finally I went on deck.

II

The skipper of the *Sephora* had a thin red whisker all round his face, and the sort of complexion that goes with hair of that color; also the particular, rather smeary shade of blue in the eyes. He was not exactly a showy figure; his shoulders were high, his stature but middling—one leg slightly more bandy than the other. He shook hands, looking vaguely around. A spiritless tenacity was his main characteristic, I judged. I behaved with a politeness which seemed to disconcert him. Perhaps he was shy. He mumbled to me as if he were ashamed of what he was saying; gave his name (it was something like Archbold—but at this distance of years I hardly am sure), his ship's name, and a few other particulars of that sort, in the manner of a criminal making a reluctant and doleful confession. He had had terrible weather on the passage out—terrible—terrible—wife aboard, too.

By this time we were seated in the cabin and the steward brought in a tray with a bottle and glasses. "Thanks! No." Never took liquor. Would have some water, though. He drank two tumblerfuls. Terrible thirsty work. Ever since daylight had been exploring the islands round his ship.

"What was that for—fun?" I asked, with an appearance of polite interest.

"No!" He sighed. "Painful duty."

As he persisted in his mumbling and I wanted my double to hear every word, I hit upon the notion of informing him that I regretted to say I was hard of hearing.

"Such a young man, too!" he nodded, keeping his smeary blue, unintelligent eyes fastened upon me. What was the cause of it—some disease? he inquired, without the least sympathy and as if he thought that, if so, I'd got no more than I deserved.

"Yes; disease," I admitted in a cheerful tone which seemed to shock him. But my point was gained, because he had to raise his voice to give me his tale. It is not worth while to record that version. It was just over two months since all this had happened, and he had thought so much about it that he seemed completely muddled as to its bearings, but still immensely impressed.

"What would you think of such a thing happening on board your own ship? I've had the *Sephora* for these fifteen years. I am a well-known shipmaster."

He was densely distressed—and perhaps I should have sympathized with him if I had been able to detach my mental vision from the unsuspected sharer of my cabin as though he were my second self. There he was on the other side of the bulkhead, four or five feet from us, no more, as we sat in the saloon. I looked politely at Captain Archbold (if that was his name), but it was the other I saw, in a gray sleeping suit, seated on a low stool, his bare feet close together, his arms folded, and every word said between us falling into the ears of his dark head bowed on his chest.

"I have been at sea now, man and boy, for seven-and-thirty years, and I've never heard of such a thing happening in an English ship. And that it should be my ship. Wife on board, too."

I was hardly listening to him.

"Don't you think," I said, "that the heavy sea which, you told me, came aboard just then might have killed the man? I have seen the sheer weight of a sea kill a man very neatly, by simply breaking his neck."

"Good God!" he uttered, impressively, fixing his smeary blue eyes on me. "The sea! No man killed by the sea ever looked like that." He seemed positively scandalized at my suggestion. And as I gazed at him, certainly not prepared for anything original on his part, he advanced his head close to mine and thrust his tongue out at me so suddenly that I couldn't help starting back.

After scoring over my calmness in this graphic way he nodded wisely. If I had seen the sight, he assured me, I would never forget it as long as I lived. The weather was too bad to give the corpse a proper sea burial. So next day at dawn they took it up on the poop, covering its face with a bit of bunting; he read a short prayer, and then, just as it was, in its oilskins and long boots, they launched it amongst those mountainous seas that seemed ready every moment to swallow up the ship herself and the terrified lives on board of her.

"That reefed foresail saved you," I threw in.

"Under God—it did," he exclaimed fervently. "It was by a special mercy, I firmly believe, that it stood some of those hurricane squalls."

"It was the setting of that sail which—" I began.

"God's own hand in it," he interrupted me. "Nothing less could have done it. I don't mind telling you that I hardly dared give the order. It seemed impossible that we could touch anything without losing it, and then our last hope would have been gone."

The terror of that gale was on him yet. I let him go on for a bit, then said, casually—as if returning to a minor subject:

"You were very anxious to give up your mate to the shore people, I believe?"

He was. To the law. His obscure tenacity on that point had in it something incomprehensible and a little awful; something, as it were, mystical, quite apart from his anxiety that he should not be suspected of "countenancing any doings of that sort." Seven-and-thirty virtuous years at sea, of which over twenty of immaculate command, and the last fifteen in the *Sephora,* seemed to have laid him under some pitiless obligation.

"And you know," he went on, groping shamefacedly amongst his feelings, "I did not engage that young fellow. His people had some interest with my owners. I was in a way forced to take him on. He looked very smart, very gentlemanly, and all that. But do you know—I never liked him, somehow. I am a plain man. You see, he wasn't exactly the sort for the chief mate of a ship like the *Sephora.*"

I had become so connected in thoughts and impressions with the secret sharer of my cabin that I felt as if I, personally, were being given to understand that I, too, was not the sort that would have done for the chief mate of a ship like the *Sephora*. I had no doubt of it in my mind.

"Not at all the style of man. You understand," he insisted, superfluously, looking hard at me.

I smiled urbanely. He seemed at a loss for a while.

"I suppose I must report a suicide."

"Beg pardon?"

"Sui-cide! That's what I'll have to write to my owners directly I get in."

"Unless you manage to recover him before tomorrow," I assented, dispassionately. . . . "I mean, alive."

He mumbled something which I really did not catch, and I turned my ear to him in a puzzled manner. He fairly bawled:

"The land—I say, the mainland is at least seven miles off my anchorage."

"About that."

My lack of excitement, of curiosity, of surprise, of any sort of pronounced interest, began to arouse his distrust. But except for the felicitous pretense of deafness I had not tried to pretend anything. I had felt utterly incapable of playing the part of ignorance properly, and therefore was afraid to try. It is also certain that he had brought some ready-made suspicions with him, and that he viewed my politeness as a strange and unnatural phenomenon. And yet how else could I have received him? Not heartily! That was impossible for psychological reasons, which I need not state here. My only object was to keep off his inquiries. Surlily? Yes, but surliness might have provoked a point-blank question. From its novelty to him and from its nature, punctilious courtesy was the manner best calculated to restrain the man. But there was the danger of his breaking through my defense bluntly. I could not, I think, have met him by a direct lie, also for psychological (not moral) reasons. If he had only known how afraid I was of his putting my feeling of identity with the other to the test! But, strangely enough—(I thought of it only afterward)—I believe that he was not a little disconcerted by the reverse side of that weird situation, by something in me that reminded him of the man he was seeking—suggested a mysterious similitude to the young fellow he had distrusted and disliked from the first.

However that might have been, the silence was not very prolonged. He took another oblique step.

"I reckon I had no more than a two-mile pull to your ship. Not a bit more."

"And quite enough, too, in this awful heat," I said.

Another pause full of mistrust followed. Necessity, they say, is mother of invention, but fear, too, is not barren of ingenious suggestions. And I was afraid he would ask me point-blank for news of my other self.

"Nice little saloon, isn't it?" I remarked, as if noticing for the first time the way his eyes roamed from one closed door to the other. "And very well fitted out, too. Here, for instance," I continued reaching over the back of my seat negligently and flinging the door open, "is my bathroom."

He made an eager movement, but hardly gave it a glance. I got up, shut the door of the bathroom, and invited him to have a look round, as if I were very proud of my accommodation. He had to rise and be shown round, but he went through the business without any raptures whatever.

"And now we'll have a look at my stateroom," I declared, in a voice as loud as I dared to make it, crossing the cabin to the starboard side with purposely heavy steps.

He followed me in and gazed around. My intelligent double had vanished. I played my part.

"Very convenient—isn't it?"

"Very nice. Very comf . . ." He didn't finish, and went out brusquely as if to escape from some unrighteous wiles of mine. But it was not to be. I had been too frightened not to feel vengeful; I felt I had him on the run, and I meant to keep him on the run. My polite insistence must have had something menacing in it, because he gave in suddenly. And I did not let him off a single item; mate's room, pantry, storerooms, the very sail locker which was also under the poop—he had to look into them all. When at last I showed him out on the quarter-deck he drew a long, spiritless sigh, and mumbled dismally that he must really be going back to his ship now. I desired my mate, who had joined us, to see to the captain's boat.

The man of whiskers gave a blast on the whistle which he used to wear hanging round his neck, and yelled, "*Sephora* away!" My double down there in my cabin must have heard, and certainly could not feel more relieved than I. Four fellows came running out from somewhere forward and went over the side, while my own men, appearing on deck too, lined the rail. I escorted my visitor to the gangway ceremoniously, and nearly overdid it. He was a tenacious beast. On the very ladder he lingered, and in that unique, guiltily conscientious manner of sticking to the point:

"I say . . . you . . . you don't think that—"

I covered his voice loudly:

"Certainly not. . . . I am delighted. Good-by."

I had an idea of what he meant to say, and just saved myself by the privilege of defective hearing. He was too shaken generally to insist, but my mate, close witness of that parting, looked mystified and his face took on a thoughtful cast. As I did not want to appear as if I wished to avoid all communication with my officers, he had the opportunity to address me.

"Seems a very nice man. His boat's crew told our chaps a very extraordinary story, if what I am told by the steward is true. I suppose you had it from the captain, sir?"

"Yes. I had a story from the captain."

"A very horrible affair—isn't it, sir?"

"It is."

"Beats all these tales we hear about murders in Yankee ships."

"I don't think it beats them. I don't think it resembles them in the least."

"Bless my soul—you don't say so! But of course I've no acquaintance whatever with American ships, not I, so I couldn't go against your knowledge. It's horrible enough for me. . . . But the queerest part is that these fellows seemed to have some idea the man was hidden aboard here. They had really. Did you ever hear of such a thing?"

"Preposterous—isn't it?"

We were walking to and fro athwart the quarter-deck. No one of the crew forward could be seen (the day was Sunday), and the mate pursued:

"There was some little dispute about it. Our chaps took offense. 'As if we would harbor a thing like that,' they said. 'Wouldn't you like to look for him in our coal hole?' Quite a tiff. But they made it up in the end. I suppose he did drown himself. Don't you, sir?"

"I don't suppose anything."

"You have no doubt in the matter, sir?"

"None whatever."

I left him suddenly. I felt I was producing a bad impression, but with my double down there it was most trying to be on deck. And it was almost as trying to be below. Altogether a nerve-trying situation. But on the whole I felt less torn in two when I was with him. There was no one in the whole ship whom I dared take into my confidence. Since the hands had got to know his story, it would have been impossible to pass him off for anyone else, and an accidental discovery was to be dreaded now more than ever. . . .

The steward being engaged in laying the table for dinner, we could talk only with our eyes when I first went down. Later in the afternoon we had a cautious try at whispering. The Sunday quietness of the ship was against us; the stillness of air and water around her was against us; the elements, the men were against us—everything was against us in our secret partnership; time itself—for this could not go on forever. The very trust in Providence was, I suppose, denied to his guilt. Shall I confess that this thought cast me down very much? And as to the chapter of accidents which counts for so much in the book of success, I could only hope that it was closed. For what favorable accident could be expected?

"Did you hear everything?" were my first words as soon as we took up our position side by side, leaning over my bed-place.

He had. And the proof of it was his earnest whisper, "The man told you he hardly dared to give the order."

I understood the reference to be to that saving foresail.

"Yes. He was afraid of it being lost in the setting."

"I assure you he never gave the order. He may think he did, but he never gave it. He stood there with me on the break of the poop after the main topsail blew away, and whimpered about our last hope—positively whimpered about it and nothing else—and the night coming on! To hear one's skipper go on like that in such weather was enough to drive any fellow out of his mind. It worked me up into a sort of desperation. I just took it into my hands and went away from him, boiling, and—But what's the use telling you? *You* know! . . . Do you think that if I had not been pretty fierce with them I should have got the men to do anything? Not it! The bosun perhaps? Perhaps! It wasn't a heavy sea—it was a sea gone mad! I suppose the end of the world will be something like that; and a man may have the heart to see it coming once and be done with it—but to have to face it day after day—I don't blame anybody. I was precious little better than the rest. Only—I was an officer of that old coal-wagon, anyhow—"

"I quite understand," I conveyed that sincere assurance into his ear. He was out of breath with whispering; I could hear him pant slightly. It was all very simple. The same strung-up force which had given twenty-four men a chance, at least, for their lives, had, in a sort of recoil, crushed an unworthy mutinous existence.

But I had no leisure to weigh the merits of the matter—footsteps in the saloon, a heavy knock. "There's enough wind to get under way with, sir." Here was the call of a new claim upon my thoughts and even upon my feelings.

"Turn the hands up," I cried through the door. "I'll be on deck directly."

I was going out to make the acquaintance of my ship. Before I left the cabin our eyes met—the eyes of the only two strangers on board. I pointed to the recessed part where the little campstool awaited him and laid my finger on my lips. He made a gesture—somewhat vague—a little mysterious, accompanied by a faint smile, as if of regret.

This is not the place to enlarge upon the sensations of a man who feels for the first time a ship move under his feet to his own independent word. In my case they were not unalloyed. I was not wholly alone with my command; for there was that stranger in my cabin. Or rather, I was not completely and wholly with her. Part of me was absent. That mental feeling of being in two places at once affected me physically as if the mood of secrecy had penetrated my very soul. Before an hour had elapsed since the ship had begun to move, having occasion to ask the mate (he stood by my side) to take a compass bearing of the Pagoda, I caught myself reaching up to his ear in whispers. I say I caught myself, but enough had escaped to startle the man. I can't describe it otherwise than by saying that he shied. A grave, preoccupied manner, as though he were in possesion of some perplexing intelligence, did not leave him henceforth. A little later I moved away from the rail to look at the compass with such a stealthy gait that the helmsman noticed it—and I could not help noticing the unusual roundness of his eyes. These are trifling instances, though it's to no commander's advantage to be suspected of ludicrous eccentricities. But I was also more seriously affected. There are to a seaman certain words, gestures, that should in given conditions come as naturally, as instinctively as the winking of a menaced eye. A certain order should spring on to his lips without thinking; a certain sign should get itself made, so to speak, without reflection. But all unconscious alertness had abandoned me. I had to make an effort of will to recall myself back (from the cabin) to the conditions of the moment. I felt that I was appearing an irresolute commander to those people who were watching me more or less critically.

And, besides, there were the scares. On the second day out, for instance, coming off the deck in the afternoon (I had straw slippers on my bare feet) I stopped at the open pantry door and spoke to the steward. He was doing something there with his back to me. At the sound of my voice he nearly jumped out of his skin, as the saying is, and incidentally broke a cup.

"What on earth's the matter with you?" I asked, astonished.

He was extremely confused. "Beg your pardon, sir. I made sure you were in your cabin."

"You see I wasn't."

"No, sir. I could have sworn I had heard you moving in there not a moment ago. It's most extraordinary . . . very sorry, sir."

I passed on with an inward shudder. I was so identified with my secret double that I did not even mention the fact in those scanty, fearful whispers we exchanged. I suppose he had made some slight noise of some kind or other. It would have been miraculous if he hadn't at one time or another. And yet, haggard as he appeared, he looked always perfectly self-controlled, more than calm—almost invulnerable. On my suggestion he remained almost entirely in the bathroom, which, upon the whole, was the safest place. There could be really no shadow of an excuse for anyone ever wanting to go in there, once the steward had done with it. It was a very tiny place. Sometimes he reclined on the floor, his legs bent, his head sustained on one elbow. At others I would find him on the campstool, sitting in his gray sleeping suit and with his cropped dark hair like a patient, unmoved convict. At night I would smuggle him into my bed-place, and we would whisper together, with the regular foot-falls of the officer of the watch passing and repassing over our heads. It was an infinitely miserable time. It was lucky that some tins of fine preserves were stowed in a locker in my stateroom; hard bread I could always get hold of; and so he lived on stewed chicken, paté de foie gras, asparagus, cooked oysters, sardines—on all sorts of abominable sham delicacies out of tins. My early morning coffee he always drank; and it was all I dared do for him in that respect.

Every day there was the horrible maneuvering to go through so that my room and then the bathroom should be done in the usual way. I came to hate the sight of the steward, to abhor the voice of that harmless man. I felt that it was he who would bring on the disaster of discovery. It hung like a sword over our heads.

The fourth day out, I think (we were working down the east side of the Gulf of Siam, tack for tack, in light winds and smooth water)—the fourth day, I say, of this miserable juggling with the unavoidable, as we sat at our evening meal, that man, whose slightest movement I dreaded, after putting down the dishes ran up on deck busily. This could not be dangerous. Presently he came down again; and then it appeared that he had remembered a coat of mine which I had thrown over a rail to dry after having been wetted in a shower which had passed over the ship in the afternoon. Sitting stolidly at the head of the table I became terrified at the sight of the garment on his arm. Of course he made for my door. There was no time to lose.

"Steward," I thundered. My nerves were so shaken that I could not govern my voice and conceal my agitation. This was the sort of thing that made my terrifically whiskered mate tap his forehead with his forefinger. I had detected him using that gesture while talking on deck with a confidential air to the carpenter. It was too far to hear a word, but I had no doubt that this pantomime could only refer to the strange new captain.

"Yes, sir," the pale-faced steward turned resignedly to me. It was this maddening course of being shouted at, checked without rhyme or reason, arbitrarily chased out of my cabin, suddenly called into it, sent flying out of his pantry on incomprehensible errands, that accounted for the growing wretchedness of his expression.

"Where are you going with that coat?"

"To your room, sir."

"Is there another shower coming?"

"I'm sure I don't know, sir. Shall I go up again and see, sir?"

"No! never mind."

My object was attained, as of course my other self in there would have heard everything that passed. During this interlude my two officers never raised their eyes off their respective plates; but the lip of that confounded cub, the second mate, quivered visibly.

I expected the steward to hook my coat on and come out at once. He was very slow about it; but I dominated my nervousness sufficiently not to shout after him. Suddenly I became aware (it could be heard plainly enough) that the fellow for some reason or other was opening the door of the bathroom. It was the end. The place was literally not big enough to swing a cat in. My voice died in my throat and I went stony all over. I expected to hear a yell of surprise and terror, and made a movement, but had not the strength to get on my legs. Everything remained still. Had my second self taken the poor wretch by the throat? I don't know what I would have done next moment if I had not seen the steward come out of my room, close the door, and then stand quietly by the sideboard.

Saved, I thought. But, no! Lost! Gone! He was gone!

I laid my knife and fork down and leaned back in my chair. My head swam. After a while, when sufficiently recovered to speak in a steady voice, I instructed my mate to put the ship round at eight o'clock himself.

"I won't come on deck," I went on. "I think I'll turn in, and unless the wind shifts I don't want to be disturbed before midnight. I feel a bit seedy."

"You did look middling bad a little while ago," the chief mate remarked without showing any great concern.

They both went out, and I stared at the steward clearing the table. There was nothing to be read on that wretched man's face. But why did he avoid my eyes I asked myself. Then I thought I should like to hear the sound of his voice.

"Steward!"

"Sir!" Startled as usual.

"Where did you hang up that coat?"

"In the bathroom, sir." The usual anxious tone. "It's not quite dry yet, sir."

For some time longer I sat in the cuddy. Had my double vanished as he had come? But of his coming there was an explanation, whereas his disappearance would be inexplicable. . . . I went slowly into my dark room, shut the door, lighted the lamp, and for a time dared not turn round. When at last I did I saw him standing bolt upright in the narrow recessed part. I would not be true to say I had a shock, but an irresistible doubt of his bodily existence flitted through my mind. Can it be, I asked myself, that he is not visible to other eyes than mine? It was like being haunted. Motionless, with a grave face, he raised his hands slightly at me in a gesture which meant clearly, "Heavens! what a narrow escape!" Narrow indeed. I think I had come creeping quietly as near insanity as any man who has not actually gone over the border. That gesture restrained me, so to speak.

The mate with the terrific whiskers was now putting the ship on the other tack. In the moment of profound silence which follows upon the hands going to their stations I heard on the poop his raised voice: "Hard alee!" and the distant shout of the order repeated on the maindeck. The sails, in that light breeze, made but a faint fluttering noise. It ceased. The ship was coming round slowly; I held my breath in the renewed stillness of expectation; one wouldn't have thought that there was a single living soul on her decks. A sudden brisk shout, "Mainsail haul!"

broke the spell, and in the noisy cries and rush overhead of the men running away with the main brace we two, down in my cabin, came together in our usual position by the bed-place.

He did not wait for my question. "I heard him fumbling here and just managed to squat myself down in the bath," he whispered to me. "The fellow only opened the door and put his arm in to hang the coat up. All the same—"

"I never thought of that," I whispered back, even more appalled than before at the closeness of the shave, and marveling at that something unyielding in his character which was carrying him through so finely. There was no agitation in his whisper. Whoever was being driven distracted, it was not he. He was sane. And the proof of his sanity was continued when he took up the whispering again.

"It would never do for me to come to life again."

It was something that a ghost might have said. But what he was alluding to was his old captain's reluctant admission of the theory of suicide. It would obviously serve his turn—if I had understood at all the view which seemed to govern the unalterable purpose of his action.

"You must maroon me as soon as ever you can get amongst these islands off the Cambodje shore," he went on.

"Maroon you! We are not living in a boy's adventure tale," I protested. His scornful whispering took me up.

"We aren't indeed! There's nothing of a boy's tale in this. But there's nothing else for it. I want no more. You don't suppose I am afraid of what can be done to me? Prison or gallows or whatever they may please. But you don't see me coming back to explain such things to an old fellow in a wig and twelve respectable tradesmen, do you? What can they know whether I am guilty or not—or of *what* I am guilty, either? That's my affair. What does the Bible say? 'Driven off the face of the earth.' Very well. I am off the face of the earth now. As I came at night so I shall go."

"Impossible!" I murmured. "You can't."

"Can't? . . . Not naked like a soul on the Day of Judgment. I shall freeze on to this sleeping suit. The Last Day is not yet—and . . . you have understood thoroughly. Didn't you?"

I felt suddenly ashamed of myself. I may say truly that I understood—and my hesitation in letting that man swim away from my ship's side had been a mere sham sentiment, a sort of cowardice.

"It can't be done now till next night," I breathed out. "The ship is on the offshore tack and the wind may fail us."

"As long as I know that you understand," he whispered. "But of course you do. It's a great satisfaction to have got somebody to understand. You seem to have been there on purpose." And in the same whisper, as if we two whenever we talked had to say things to each other which were not fit for the world to hear, he added, "It's very wonderful."

We remained side by side talking in our secret way—but sometimes silent or just exchanging a whispered word or two at long intervals. And as usual he stared through the port. A breath of wind came now and again into our faces. The ship might have been moored in dock, so gently and on an even keel she slipped through the water, that did not murmur even at our passage, shadowy and silent like a phantom sea.

At midnight I went on deck, and to my mate's great surprise put the ship round on the other tack. His terrible whiskers flitted round me in silent criticism. I certainly should not have done it if it had been only a question of getting out of that sleepy gulf as quickly as possible. I believe he told the second mate, who relieved him, that it was a great want of judgment. The other only yawned. That intolerable cub shuffled about so sleepily and lolled against the rails in such a slack, improper fashion that I came down on him sharply.

"Aren't you properly awake yet?"

"Yes, sir! I am awake."

"Well, then, be good enough to hold yourself as if you were. And keep a lookout. If there's any current we'll be closing with some islands before daylight."

The east side of the gulf is fringed with islands, some solitary, others in groups. On the blue background of the high coast they seem to float on silvery patches of calm water, arid and gray, or dark green and rounded like clumps of evergreen bushes, with the larger ones, a mile or two long, showing the outlines of ridges, ribs of gray rock under the dark mantle of matted leafage. Unknown to trade, to travel, almost to geography, the manner of life they harbor is an unsolved secret. There must be villages—settlements of fishermen at least—on the largest of them, and some communication with the world is probably kept up by native craft. But all forenoon, as we headed for them, fanned along by the faintest of breezes, I saw no sign of man or canoe in the field of the telescope I kept on pointing at the scattered group.

At noon I gave no orders for a change of course, and the mate's whiskers became much concerned and seemed to be offering themselves unduly to my notice. At last I said:

"I am going to stand right in. Quite in—as far as I can take her."

The stare of extreme surprise imparted an air of ferocity also to his eyes, and he looked truly terrific for a moment.

"We're not doing well in the middle of the gulf," I continued, casually. "I am going to look for the land breezes tonight."

"Bless my soul! Do you mean, sir, in the dark amongst the lot of all them islands and reefs and shoals?"

"Well—if there are any regular land breezes at all on this coast one must get close inshore to find them, mustn't one?"

"Bless my soul!" he exclaimed again under his breath. All that afternoon he wore a dreamy, contemplative appearance which in him was a mark of perplexity. After dinner I went into my stateroom as if I meant to take some rest. There we two bent our dark heads over a half-unrolled chart lying on my bed.

"There," I said. "It's got to be Koh-ring. I've been looking at it ever since sunrise. It has got two hills and a low point. It must be inhabited. And on the coast opposite there is what looks like the mouth of a biggish river—with some town, no doubt, not far up. It's the best chance for you that I can see.

"Anything. Koh-ring let it be."

He looked thoughtfully at the chart as if surveying chances and distances from a lofty height—and following with his eyes his own figure wandering on the blank land of Cochin China, and then passing off that piece of paper clean out of sight into uncharted regions. And it was as if the ship had two captains to plan her course for her. I had been so worried and restless running up and down that I had not had the patience to dress that day. I had remained in my sleeping suit, with straw slippers and a soft floppy hat. The closeness of the heat in the gulf had been most oppressive, and the crew were used to see me wandering in that airy attire.

"She will clear the south point as she heads now," I whispered into his ear. "Goodness only knows when, though, but certainly after dark. I'll edge her in to half a mile, as far as I may be able to judge in the dark—"

"Be careful," he murmured, warningly—and I realized suddenly that all my future, the only future for which I was fit, would perhaps go irretrievably to pieces in any mishap to my first command.

I could not stop a moment longer in the room. I motioned him to get out of sight and made my way on the poop. That unplayful cub had the watch. I walked up and down for a while thinking things out, then beckoned him over.

"Send a couple of hands to open the two quarter-deck ports," I said, mildly.

He actually had the impudence, or else so forgot himself in his wonder at such an incomprehensible order, as to repeat:

"Open the quarter-deck ports! What for, sir?"

"The only reason you need concern yourself about is because I tell you to do so. Have them open wide and fastened properly."

He reddened and went off, but I believe made some jeering remark to the carpenter as to the sensible practice of ventilating a ship's quarter-deck. I know he popped into the mate's cabin to impart the fact to him because the whiskers came on deck, as it were by chance, and stole glances at me from below—for signs of lunacy or drunkenness, I suppose.

A little before supper, feeling more restless than ever, I rejoined, for a moment, my second self. And to find him sitting so quietly was surprising, like something against nature, inhuman.

I developed my plan in a hurried whisper.

"I shall stand in as close as I dare and then put her round. I shall presently find means to smuggle you out of here into the sail locker, which communicates with the lobby. But there is an opening, a sort of square for hauling the sails out, which gives straight on the quarter-deck and which is never closed in fine weather, so as to give air to the sails. When the ship's way is deadened in stays and all the hands are aft at the main braces you shall have a clear road to slip out and get overboard through the open quarter-deck port. I've had them both fastened up. Use a rope's end to lower yourself into the water so as to avoid a splash—you know. It could be heard and cause some beastly complication."

He kept silent for a while, then whispered, "I understand."

"I won't be there to see you go," I began with an effort. "The rest . . . I only hope I have understood, too."

"You have. From first to last," and for the first time there seemed to be a faltering, something strained in his whisper. He caught hold of my arm, but the ringing of the supper bell made me start. He didn't, though; he only released his grip.

After supper I didn't come below again till well past eight o'clock. The faint, steady breeze was loaded with dew; and the wet, darkened sails held all there was of propelling power in it. The night, clear and starry, sparkled darkly, and the opaque, lightless patches shifting slowly against the low stars were the drifting islets. On the port bow there was a big one more distant and shadowily imposing by the great space of sky it eclipsed.

On opening the door I had a back view of my very own self looking at a chart. He had come out of the recess and was standing near the table.

"Quite dark enough," I whispered.

He stepped back and leaned against my bed with a level, quiet glance. I sat on the couch. We had nothing to say to each other. Over our heads the officer of the watch moved here and there. Then I heard him move quickly. I knew what that meant. He was making for the companion; and presently his voice was outside my door.

"We are drawing in pretty fast, sir. Land looks rather close."

"Very well," I answered. "I am coming on deck directly."

I waited till he was gone out of the cuddy, then rose. My double moved too. The time had come to exchange our last whispers, for neither of us was ever to hear each other's natural voice.

"Look here!" I opened a drawer and took out three sovereigns. "Take this, anyhow. I've got six and I'd give you the lot, only I must keep a little money to buy some fruit and vegetables for the crew from native boats as we go through Sunda Straits."

He shook his head.

"Take it," I urged him, whispering desperately. "No one can tell what—"

He smiled and slapped meaningly the only pocket of the sleeping jacket. It was not safe, certainly. But I produced a large old silk handkerchief of mine, and tying the three pieces of gold in a corner, pressed it on him. He was touched, I suppose, because he took it at last and tied it quickly round his waist under the jacket, on his bare skin.

Our eyes met; several seconds elapsed, till, our glances still mingled, I extended my hand and turned the lamp out. Then I passed through the cuddy, leaving the door of my room wide open. . . . "Steward!"

He was still lingering in the pantry in the greatness of his zeal, giving a rub-up to a plated cruet stand the last thing before going to bed. Being careful not to wake up the mate, whose room was opposite, I spoke in an undertone.

He looked round anxiously. "Sir!"

"Can you get me a little hot water from the galley?"

"I am afraid, sir, the galley fire's been out for some time now."

"Go and see."

He fled up the stairs.

"Now," I whispered, loudly, into the saloon—too loudly, perhaps, but I was afraid I couldn't make a sound. He was by my side in an instant—the double captain slipped past the stairs—through the tiny dark passage . . . a sliding door. We were in the sail locker, scrambling on our knees over the sails. A sudden thought struck me. I saw myself wandering barefooted, bareheaded, the sun beating on my dark poll. I snatched off my floppy hat and tried hurriedly in the dark to ram it on my other self. He dodged and fended off silently. I wonder what he thought had come to me before he understood and suddenly desisted. Our hands met gropingly, lingered united in a steady, motionless clasp for a second. . . . No word was breathed by either of us when they separated.

I was standing quietly by the pantry door when the steward returned.

"Sorry, sir. Kettle barely warm. Shall I light the spirit lamp?"

"Never mind."

I came out on deck slowly. It was now a matter of conscience to shave the land as close as possible—for now he must go overboard whenever the ship was put in stays. Must! There could be no going back for him. After a moment I walked over to leeward and my heart flew into my mouth at the nearness of the land on the bow. Under any other circumstances I would not have held on a minute longer. The second mate had followed me anxiously.

I looked on till I felt I could command my voice.

"She will weather," I said then in a quiet tone.

"Are you going to try that, sir?" he stammered out incredulously.

I took no notice of him and raised my tone just enough to be heard by the helmsman.

"Keep her good full."

"Good full, sir."

The wind fanned my cheek, the sails slept, the world was silent. The strain of watching the dark loom of the land grow bigger and denser was too much for me. I had shut my eyes—because the ship must go closer. She must! The stillness was intolerable. Were we standing still?

When I opened my eyes the second view started my heart with a thump. The black southern hill of Koh-ring seemed to hang right over the ship like a towering fragment of the everlasting night. On that enormous mass of blackness there was not a gleam to be seen, not a sound to be heard. It was gliding irresistibly toward us and yet seemed already within reach of the hand. I saw the vague figures of the watch grouped in the waist, gazing in awed silence.

"Are you going on, sir?" inquired an unsteady voice at my elbow. I ignored it. I had to go on.

"Keep her full. Don't check her way. That won't do now," I said warningly.

"I can't see the sails very well," the helmsman answered me, in strange, quavering tones.

Was she close enough? Already she was, I won't say in the shadow of the land, but in the very blackness of it, already swallowed up as it were, gone too close to be recalled, gone from me altogether.

"Give the mate a call," I said to the young man who stood at my elbow still as death. "And turn all hands up."

My tone had a borrowed loudness reverberated from the height of the land. Several voices cried out together: "We are all on deck, sir."

Then stillness again, with the great shadow gliding closer, towering higher, without a light, without a sound. Such a hush had fallen on the ship that she might have been a bark of the dead floating in slowly under the very gate of Erebus.

"My God! Where are we?"

It was the mate moaning at my elbow. He was thunderstruck, and as it were deprived of the moral support of his whiskers. He clapped his hands and absolutely cried out, "Lost!"

"Be quiet," I said sternly.

He lowered his tone, but I saw the shadowy gesture of his despair. "What are we doing here?"

"Looking for the land wind."

He made as if to tear his hair, and addressed me recklessly.

"She will never get out. You have done it, sir. I knew it'd end in something like this. She will never weather, and you are too close now to stay. She'll drift ashore before she's round. O my God!"

I caught his arm as he was raising it to batter his poor devoted head, and shook it violently.

"She's ashore already," he wailed, trying to tear himself away.

"Is she? . . . Keep good full there!"

"Good full, sir," cried the helmsman in a frightened, thin, childlike voice.

I hadn't let go the mate's arm and went on shaking it. "Ready about, do you hear? You go forward"—shake—"and stop there"—shake—"and hold your noise"—shake—"and see these head sheets properly overhauled"—shake, shake—shake.

And all the time I dared not look toward the land lest my heart should fail me. I released my grip at last and he ran forward as if fleeing for dear life.

I wondered what my double there in the sail locker thought of this commotion. He was able to hear everything—and perhaps he was able to understand why, on my conscience, it had to be thus close—no less. My first order "Hard alee!" re-echoed ominously under the towering shadow of Koh-ring as if I had shouted in a mountain gorge. And then I watched the land intently. In that smooth water and light wind it was impossible to feel the ship coming-to. No! I could not feel her. And my second self was making now ready to slip out and lower himself overboard. Perhaps he was gone already . . . ?

The great black mass brooding over our very mastheads began to pivot away from the ship's side silently. And now I forgot the secret stranger ready to depart, and remembered only that I was a total stranger to the ship. I did not know her. Would she do it? How was she to be handled?

I swung the mainyard and waited helplessly. She was perhaps stopped, and her very fate hung in the balance, with the black mass of Koh-ring like the gate of the everlasting night towering over her taffrail. What would she do now? Had she way on her yet? I stepped to the side swiftly, and on the shadowy water I could see nothing except a faint phosphorescent flash revealing the glassy smoothness of the sleeping surface. It was impossible to tell—and I had not learned yet the feel of my ship. Was she moving? What I needed was something easily seen, a piece of paper, which I could throw overboard and watch. I had nothing on me. To run down for it I didn't dare. There was no time. All at once my strained, yearning stare distinguished a white object floating within a yard of the ship's side. White on the black water. A phosphorescent flash passed under it. What was that thing? . . . I recognized my own floppy hat. It must have fallen off his head . . . and he didn't bother. Now I had what I wanted—the saving mark for my eyes. But I hardly thought of my other self, now gone from the ship, to be hidden forever from all friendly faces, to be a fugitive and a vagabond on the earth, with no brand of the curse on his sane forehead to stay a slaying hand . . . too proud to explain.

And I watched the hat—the expression of my sudden pity for his mere flesh. It had been meant to save his homeless head from the dangers of the sun. And now—behold—it was saving the ship, by serving me for a mark to help out the ignorance of my strangeness. Ha! It was drifting forward, warning me just in time that the ship had gathered sternway.

"Shift the helm," I said in a low voice to the seaman standing still like a statue.

The man's eyes glistened wildly in the binnacle light as he jumped round to the other side and spun round the wheel.

I walked to the break of the poop. On the overshadowed deck all hands stood by the forebraces waiting for my order. The stars ahead seemed to be gliding from right to left. And all was so still in the world that I heard the quiet remark "She's round," passed in a tone of intense relief between two seamen.

"Let go and haul."

The foreyards ran round with a great noise, amidst cheery cries. And now the frightful whiskers made themselves heard giving various orders. Already the ship was drawing ahead. And I was alone with her. Nothing! no one in the world should stand now between us, throwing a shadow on the way of silent knowledge and mute affection, the perfect communion of a seaman with his first command.

Walking to the taffrail, I was in time to make out, on the very edge of a darkness thrown by a towering black mass like the very gateway of Erebus—yes, I was in time to catch an evanescent glimpse of my white hat left behind to mark the spot where the secret sharer of my cabin and of my thoughts, as though he were my second self, had lowered himself into the water to take his punishment: a free man, a proud swimmer striking out for a new destiny.

Questions for Discussion

1. Why is the narrator (the captain) nervous? What about him makes his crew nervous?

2. List as much evidence as you can to establish that Leggatt actually exists. Then list the evidence suggesting that Leggatt is created by the captain's imagination.

3. In your view, is the captain right to protect Leggatt? Why or why not?

4. Is the narrator a reliable one? That is, do you always believe him? Why or why not?

Suggestions for Writing

1. Write a page (or so) spoken by an unreliable narrator and let the reader know *gradually* that the narrator is untrustworthy.

2. Write an essay about the conflict between personality and authority in Conrad's story. You might think of this conflict as one between "self-image" and an image of "the captain" that needs to be projected publicly.

3. Read Conrad's *Heart of Darkness* and then write an essay that compares and contrasts the captain and Marlowe.

4. "We're not supposed to know for sure whether Leggatt really exists." Write an essay that either supports or refutes this thesis.

Overview: Additional Questions for Discussion and Suggestions for Writing

1. Of these 15 stories, which ones seem anchored most specifically to their historical context? Which ones seem least anchored to their historical context?

2. With regard to subject matter and/or style, which of these 15 stories seems most dated or old-fashioned? Why?

3. Assuming that your knowledge of the nineteenth century came only from these 15 stories, list several generalizations you might make about that century. Think in terms of politics, social customs, preoccupations, and so forth.

4. From your knowledge of the nineteenth century—in North America or Europe—what subjects are conspicuously absent here among these 15 stories?

5. Which of these stories best demonstrates an awareness of social conflict?

6. If Sherlock Holmes were to be "adapted" to the twentieth century, what would Doyle need to change about him?

7. What do the stories by Chopin and Gilman tell us about the lives of middle-class American women in the 1800s?

8. Generalize: what do the stories by the three Russian writers—Turgenev, Tolstoy, and Chekhov—contribute to the history of short fiction? Which of these three stories seems most significant to you?

Suggestions for Writing

1. Using the stories by Poe, Gilman, Hawthorne, Conrad, and Melville, write an essay about depictions of madness and/or alienation.

2. Using the stories by Aleichem, Poe, Gilman, and Conrad, write an essay about different kinds of unreliable narration.

3. Write an essay about depictions of women in the stories by Hawthorne, de Maupassant, Tolstoy, James, Gilman, Chopin, Doyle, and O. Henry.

4. Make a checklist of important novels that were written by these authors.

5. Write an essay in which you compare and contrast the ways Poe, Turgenev, Tolstoy, James, Chopin, Crane, and Conrad write about death.

6. Write an essay in which you compare and contrast the ways Melville, de Maupassant, Tolstoy, Chekhov, James, O. Henry, and Aleichem write about economic/financial predicaments.

7. Using several of these stories, write about the various uses (and redefinitions) of "plot."

8. "_____ is the most 'modern' of these 15 stories." Fill in the blank and then write an essay that defends your choice—and that explains what *you* mean by "modern."

Part Two

Modern Voices

Introduction to Modern Voices

MODERNISM

Modernism is one of those ism words that can frighten people, and with good reason: critics use the word often and just as often disagree about what it means. It's too important a concept to ignore but often too inclusive and complicated to seem useful.

Perhaps we should begin with a simple clarification, therefore: When applied to art and literature, *Modern* (with a capital *M*) refers to a specific time period and does not mean merely "current" or "recent" or "new."

"On or about December 1910," the British writer Virginia Woolf once remarked only somewhat jokingly, "human character changed." The Modern period of art and literature is generally considered to begin when Woolf noticed this change, though the period is often said to begin nearer the time of World War I (1914–1918). In fact, the nature of that war and the changes in society that it caused are themselves important features of modernism. As Paul Fussell has remarked in his book *The Great War and Modern Memory,* World War I was more brutal and devastating than any previous conflict. It introduced chemical warfare, trench warfare, and artillery on such a scale that European civilization seemed to be devouring itself.

This war was not the only major event out of which modernism materialized, of course, and one should be careful to note that some origins of modernism arose decades earlier. The spread of factory-based economies, the growth of cities, the impact of Marx's ideas of conflict between social classes, the influence of Freud's ideas about human psychology, Darwin's revision of biological concepts, and Einstein's revision of physical "laws" are six of many phenomena we now point to as the roots of modernism.

In sum these redefinitions of "the world" and "humanity" amounted to a dramatic break with conventional thinking in nearly every aspect of human endeavor. Also, as noted above, many of these redefinitions took shape well before 1914, so any date we choose for the beginning of modernism is to some degree arbitrary.

But what *is* modernism? To a great extent, it is *an artistic response* to the Great War and these other phenomena, some of which belong to the late nineteenth century. The world about which writers wrote seemed "changed, changed utterly," to borrow from a poem by a modernist poet, William Butler Yeats. Such severe changes forced art to change.

The world is always changing, of course, but the kinds and degree of change at this time were unprecedented. Many artists responded in extreme ways to extreme events, and extremity is one characteristic of modernist writing.

In a book called *The Dehumanization of Art,* the scholar Ortega y Gassett identified a seven-point "credo" to describe the extremity of modernist art. According to Ortega, modernists dehumanized art, avoided "living" forms, saw a work of art only as a work of art, considered art as play, relied on irony, preferred clarity of image over "statements" of any kind, and considered art as a thing of no transcending consequence. Any such list is bound to be controversial and is certainly too schematic to apply to all specific works of art. Nonetheless, the list gives us the flavor of the modernist movement, and it gives us characteristics that many of the stories in this section exhibit.

ALIENATION

For example, at this time more writers than ever before thought of themselves as outsiders, as voices in a kind of intellectual wilderness that had few connections with mainstream society. After all, during the 1920s many American writers, painters, and musicians exiled themselves to Europe and other parts of the globe, physically and spiritually removing themselves from their own culture. (The expatriates to France in the 1920s are now known as "the Lost Generation"; the term was invented by the writer Gertrude Stein, a contemporary of Hemingway's and one who influenced his experiments with style). Furthermore, even while abroad they sought a life in contrast to middle-class values, and they often thought of themselves as participating in an *avant-garde*—a group that was leading the way in redefining art, or "making it new," to borrow a phrase from the modernist poet Ezra Pound.

Such artists *alienated* themselves, socially and artistically, because alienation seemed an appropriate response to what was going on. In other ways the world alienated them. One product of this alienation was a deliberate attempt to make dramatic changes in the way music was composed, paintings were painted, and literature was written.

EXPERIMENTATION

In music "making it new" included the "atonal" music of Stravinsky and Schönberg; in art it included cubism and abstract expressionism; in writing it included surrealism and stream of consciousness. These experiments quickly became more than experiments; they became defining movements, and they share several basic characteristics.

First, they spring from a self-conscious plan to alter and even reject many conventions (or "rules") of art forms. Second, they symptomize an aggressive attitude toward "the audience" for art. Instead of writing or painting or composing what would predictably please an audience, these writers, painters, and composers experimented at will and let the audience decide whether it would go along with the experimentation or not. (The infamous "Armory Show," which introduced Americans to abstract painting in 1913, inflamed its audience.) Third, the experiments were often involved in redefining perception and form. For instance, a painting by Picasso and a stream-of-consciousness passage by Joyce ask the viewer and reader to see reality differently and to shed traditional concepts of "good art"; these artists also deliberately introduce *dis*continuity and fragmentation into the form of their art.

Listen to a piece of music by Schönberg; read a few pages of *Ulysses* or *Finnegans Wake;* look at reprints of paintings by Dali or Picasso. Even such brief encounters with examples of modernism will suggest how dramatically art was changing, give you concrete examples of Ortega y Gassett's list of modernist tenets, and introduce you to a deeper study of modernist art and literature. They will also illuminate the kinds of experimentation to be found in stories by Kafka, Hemingway, Lawrence, and others.

MODERN VOICES OF THE SHORT STORY

The effects of modernism on poetry and the novel were profound and obvious. For example, T. S. Eliot's long poem *The Waste Land,* James Joyce's novel *Ulysses* (both published in 1922), and William Faulkner's *As I Lay Dying* (1930) present astonishing new artistic forms, including the "stream-of-consciousness" technique.

The effects of modernism on the short story are less easy to describe, and it is somewhat more difficult to find a key example of a modernist short story that equals Eliot's poem or Joyce's novel. Joyce himself wrote short stories, of course, but his experiments with form in that genre are comparatively less dramatic than those in the novel. Nonetheless, his work offers a good starting point for discussing "modern voices of the short story."

James Joyce

Joyce's *Dubliners* (1914) remains a landmark book for several reasons. It presents a remarkable vision of the modern city, its disconnectedness and hopelessness. Also, the stories in the volume to some extent perpetuate the "revolt against plot" that is often ascribed to Chekhov. In Joyce's stories the external action is unsensational and muted, and yet the revelations that spring from such action can be shattering. In fact, Joyce invented a term for such revelations: *epiphany,* which refers to a moment of unexpected insight into one's life, one's city, even one's culture. In "Araby," for example, the young narrator's naïveté and a series of seemingly inconsequential disappointments collide and produce an epiphany whereby the young man will *never* be the same again. His vanity—and a certain unyielding despair—are revealed to him with brutal finality.

Although Joyce's experiments with form are less extreme in his stories than in his novels, his short stories are nonetheless one touchstone of modernism. They force us to revise our ideas of plot, action, and character; they are painstakingly observant and sometimes transform the most ordinary images into extraordinary symbols; and they are filled with despair, alienation, and a sense of fragmented experience—the bleak spirit of modernism.

D. H. Lawrence and Ernest Hemingway

Two other key "modern voices" of the short story are Lawrence and Hemingway. Lawrence was able to make remarkable achievements in three genres—fiction, short fiction, and poetry—as well as in literary criticism. He is probably best known as an aggressive critic of modern life and middle-class values, and he was especially incensed by the forces in modern industrial life that seemed to smother sexuality, passion, and instinct. His most famous, if not his best, novel is *Lady Chatterly's Lover* (1928), which explored sexuality directly and scandalized many readers.

"The Horse Dealer's Daughter" represents a similar impulse to reveal "society" to be a sterilizing, deadening force. The brief emotional life the two lovers share ends when they give it a label and when they start to think of social conventions and obligations. Lawrence is a modernist, then, not so much because of his experiments with form but because of his perspective on mainstream manners and behavior.

Stylistic experimentation is the major reason for Ernest Hemingway's stature as a short-story writer. "The Hemingway hero" and subjects of war and expatriate experience are important to Hemingway's work, but they pale in comparison to the significance of the prose style he created. It is lean and spare; it avoids ornament; and it often appears to be as simple as the prose of children's books. The style often creates a flat, detached, even "frigid" tone, and for this reason it has been compared to the prose of newspaper writing and of hard-boiled-detective fiction as practiced by "the big three" of that fiction, Dashiell Hammett, Ross MacDonald, and Raymond Chandler. (A Chandler story appears in this part of the anthology.)

One of Hemingway's responses to a brutal, alienating world, then, was to create a style that was nearly transparent in its simplicity and that seemed to replicate a mood of alienation with a fictional tone of detachment. Of course, the style is related to what is now known as "the Hemingway hero," a person who maintains "grace" and "toughness" under the most dire circumstances. However, the influence of the prose style has been more far-reaching than "the Hemingway hero."

Franz Kafka

If we consider only short-story writers, Franz Kafka may be the "purest" example of a modernist, though he has been somewhat less influential than Joyce,

Hemingway, and Lawrence. He wrote stories that applied the simplicity of parables to absurd and extreme situations, such as a man waking up one day to find that he has changed into a cockroach, or, as in "The Hunger Artist," that a person has made an "art" out of denying an "appetite."

His stories remain astonishingly original, and they still seem to strike at the heart of alienation and despair, so much so that Kafka is often regarded as the preeminent "absurdist" writer. That is, the situations in his fiction often do not "make sense"; but of course, that's the point.

Although his style is often simple, it is less easy to label than Hemingway's (particularly when it comes to us in translation), and even though he was a perceptive observer of human experience, his "social criticism," if it exists, is far more oblique than Lawrence's.

Because Kafka deliberately explores irrational and absurd experiences, his stories are among the most fascinating and the most difficult to interpret from this or any period. Both in terms of experiment and alienation, furthermore, his writing remains a key example of modernism. He found striking ways to dramatize the psychological and social confusion of his time.

William Faulkner

We can draw a rough parallel between William Faulkner and James Joyce by saying that Faulkner also was less experimental in his short fiction than he was in his novels, in which, like Joyce, he used the stream-of-consciousness technique in a variety of successful ways.

Nonetheless, even as a short-fiction writer, Faulkner's is an important Modern voice because he captures the South as it moves from one age into another and because he achieves the nearly impossible task of fiercely remaining a regionalist and yet creating a fictional world that appeals to readers everywhere. "A Rose for Emily" shows these qualities and also demonstrates how rich Faulkner's prose style is in contrast to that of many of his contemporaries.

Faulkner is also important because of his writing style, which is as rich and full of rhetorical devices as Hemingway's style is spare. "A Rose for Emily," for instance, begins with a series of elaborate descriptions of the neighborhood in which Emily lives and uses a formal level of diction.

Frank O'Connor, Luigi Pirandello, Tadeusz Borowski, Aya Koda

As we have said, responses to the first world war account for one source of the Modern period of art and literature. Responses to the second world war form the opposite bookend to the period several decades later, and they show that, as horrible as the Great War was, human society could actually do worse.

In the stories by O'Connor, Pirandello, Borowski, and Koda we find four widely different depictions of war early in the century and at mid-century. Borowski's story may be the most brutal one in this volume; it presents an unadulterated glimpse of the Holocaust. It is a story that is impossible to forget. O'Connor's "Guests of the Nation" presents a brutal view of civil war and the confusion of values and loyalties such wars inevitably produce. Although Pirandello's and Koda's stories are more indirect in their treatment of war, they are no less effective in showing the degree to which war has reached every corner of the globe in this century, and the degree to which war shaped modernism.

Sherwood Anderson, Ralph Ellison, Langston Hughes, Zora Neale Hurston, Katherine Ann Porter, John Steinbeck, Eudora Welty, Willa Cather

Taken as a group, these eight writers provide an important lesson about trying to label literary periods. For in different ways, these writers resist the label *modernism,* or at least force us to stretch the term until it becomes very problematic.

Although he was a contemporary of Hemingway's for example, Sherwood Anderson is in many ways Hemingway's opposite, even though the young Hemingway once sought advice on writing from Anderson. He is most famous for his painstaking fictional analysis of small-town, midwestern American life (in the work *Winesburg, Ohio,* published in 1919). Although his perspective on this life is deeply ironic and in this sense Modern, the style and form of his stories are comparatively conventional, though "The Egg" possesses a highly complicated scheme of point of view.

Like Anderson, Eudora Welty, John Steinbeck, Katherine Ann Porter, and Willa Cather write fiction that is more or less rooted in specific regions and more or less conventional in its form. In a sense, such regionalism is one expression of how young America still is; these writers were not just depicting regions but defining them as the regions matured and even changed dramatically. Katherine Anne Porter's work, including "The Jilting of Granny Weatherall," provides an interesting bridge between modernism and regionalism, for although Porter's interests are regionally grounded, her technique reflects the influence of modernism, as the stream-of-consciousness quality of the Weatherall story suggests.

Steinbeck and Welty both explore the plight of unsophisticated rural women, although Steinbeck's depiction is sympathetic whereas Welty's is nearly satiric in its ingenious replication of "beauty shop" gossip.

No writer in this section has a career that is any more "American" than Willa Cather's. Cather is best know for her novels concerning the Nebraska frontier (such as *My Antonia,* 1918), but as "Paul's Case" and much of her other writing indicates, she was also capable of confronting characters and conflicts we might consider "urban." With ties to the Great Plains, Virginia, and New York, Cather in many ways represents an America poised between a rural, agrarian century and an urban, industrial one.

The stories of the above-mentioned writers demonstrate that the concerns of modernists like Eliot, Joyce, and Kafka were not the only concerns of writers at that time. Modernism was a powerful movement, but it did not account for all of the enduring writing that would emerge in the first half of the twentieth century. Nor did its assumptions necessarily appeal to all writers.

African-American Writers

The assumptions of modernism also did not necessarily appeal to writers such as Ellison, Hughes, and Hurston, who present three other original perspectives on experience, and who also present three perspectives on the experience of African-Americans. To some extent, these writers express a kind of expatriotism that is forced on groups of people, an outsider status that is inflicted, not chosen. (Ralph Ellison's 1952 novel *The Invisible Man* expresses this predicament with overwhelming force.) The alienation of such writers springs from different social and economic sources and necessarily results in a different literary expression.

The situation is even more complicated with a writer like Zora Neale Hurston, whose story "Sweat" concerns a woman who is doubly oppressed—as an African-American and as a woman. Consequently, we should recognize that while it is useful to make some generalizations about these stories on the basis of ethnic background, it is also important to explore the differences in subject matter and style these stories exhibit. There is no single kind of "African-American" short story, as the selections by these writers demonstrate.

Raymond Chandler

With Raymond Chandler's story, we are able to see one direction in which detective fiction developed after Arthur Conan Doyle invented Sherlock Holmes. This particular story comes from the 1950s, but it exhibits all of the elements of the hard-boiled style that Chandler and others perfected by writing for the pulp magazines of the 1930s. The story also features Chandler's famous detective Philip Marlowe, who along with Hammett's Sam Spade and MacDonald's Lew Archer, is one of an immortal trio of "tough guy" detectives.

As in much modern detective fiction, the boundaries between the investigator and the criminal are less clear in Chandler's stories than in Conan Doyle's; Los Angeles of the twentieth century is a meaner, more violent place than London of the late nineteenth century (and a great many Holmes tales take place outside of London). Nonetheless, like Holmes, Marlowe remains an essentially "good" person and one who accepts money but solves crimes for other "purer" reasons.

Chandler's style resembles Hemingway's in its spareness, though it depends more on flashy similes and metaphors and on the central voice of Marlowe's detective. Indeed, the invention of the first-person tough-guy voice is the other major innovation Chandler (along with Dashiell Hammett and Ross

MacDonald) brought to detective fiction; in this context it is useful to remember that Conan Doyle "reported" Holmes's exploits through the voice of a peripheral narrator, Watson.

Yasunari Kawabata and Katherine Mansfield

In some ways, no two writers could be more different than Yasunari Kawabata and Katherine Mansfield, and yet their careers both demonstrate how quickly the "reinvented" short story of the nineteenth century traveled beyond Europe and America. Many readers associate Mansfield with English modernists like John Middleton Murry (the editor and writer Mansfield married) and D. H. Lawrence, and indeed she was of that generation. Mansfield is actually a New Zealand writer, however, and her lasting contribution to short fiction anticipated the enormous contribution New Zealander and Australian writers would make to the genre as the century progressed. "The Fly" is a representative Mansfield story: vivid, tough, unsentimental, highly compressed.

Kawabata's symbolic, psychological tale "The Mole" suggests that symbol and psychology were not the sole property of Western writers. Also, like Mansfield's career, Kawabata's shows the extent to which barriers between Eastern and Western cultures were reduced during the Modern period. (The modernist ideas of Pound and Yeats owe a great deal to Eastern thought, or at least to their "reading" of such thought.)

CAREERS AND TRANSLATION

Two phenomena that deserve mention are the extent to which short fiction established the careers of some writers and the extent to which translation began to change the history and tradition of short fiction. The careers of at least four writers in this section depend almost exclusively on short fiction: Frank O'Connor, Katherine Mansfield, Katherine Anne Porter, and Franz Kafka. This circumstance is one measure of how important the genre had become in the literary world and how useful it had become as a medium for interpreting the Modern age.

Translation of short stories also enhanced the importance of the genre and began to connect literary traditions more intricately. The stories by Pirandello, Borowski, Kawabata, and Koda (translated from Italian, Polish, and Japanese) are but four examples of how significant the role of translation is in our conception of short fiction. The Modern period was in many ways a fragmented era, but it was also an era in which the literary world was becoming more diverse in healthy ways, thanks in part to an increased availability of translations.

SUMMARY

Although it is difficult to arrive at an exhaustive definition of modernism, we can at least point to a specific time period (roughly, 1910–1945), we can point to specific historical events and intellectual responses to those events, and we can point to a kind of revolution in the world of art.

Further, we can point to the enormous extent to which these writers addressed alienation, confusion, and upheaval in cultures worldwide. Taking but two representative stories from this section—Kafka's "A Hunger Artist" and Hemingway's "A Clean, Well-Lighted Place"—we see that writers turned away from the so-called advances of the industrial society and examined a world that seemed plagued with discontinuity and disintegrated spirituality.

At the same time, we must be careful not to force the label *modernist* on writers. Gender, region, ethnic background, and even individual temperament exert their own influence on the stories in this section, and the influence often goes against the grain of modernism.

Furthermore, as we discuss the despair, alienation, and discontinuity associated with modernism, we must not forget the richness and affirmation in many of these stories, which are as much about survival as they are about dissolution.

"Modern Voices" includes but is not limited to writers who belong to the artistic revolutions of the movement known as modernism, and it includes an astonishing range of contributors to the art of short fiction. Between 1914 and the late 1940s, the world in general and consequently the world of short fiction became more complicated and more difficult to understand but also richer and more diverse.

Araby

JAMES JOYCE

Northr Richmond Street, being blind, was a quiet street except at the hour when the Christian Brothers' School set the boys free. An uninhabited house of two storeys stood at the blind end, detached from its neighbours in a square ground. The other houses of the street, conscious of decent lives within them, gazed at one another with brown imperturbable faces.

The former tenant of our house, a priest, had died in the back drawing-room. Air, musty from having been long enclosed, hung in all the rooms, and the waste room behind the kitchen was littered with old useless papers. Among these I found a few paper-covered books, the pages of which were curled and damp: *The Abbot,* by Walter Scott, *The Devoit Communicant* and *The Memoirs of Vidocq.* I liked the last best because its leaves were yellow. The wild garden behind the house contained a central apple-tree and a few straggling bushes under one of which I found the late tenant's rusty bicycle-pump. He had been a very charitable priest; in his will he had left all his money to institutions and the furniture of his house to his sister.

When the short days of winter came dusk fell before we had well eaten our dinners. When we met in the street the houses had grown sombre. The space of sky above us was the colour of ever-changing violet and towards it the lamps of the street lifted their feeble lanterns. The cold air stung us and we played till our bodies glowed. Our shouts echoed in the silent street. The career of our play brought us through the dark muddy lanes behind the houses where we ran the gauntlet of the rough tribes from the cottages, to the back doors of the dark dripping gardens where odours arose from the ashpits, to the dark odorous stables where a coachman smoothed and combed the horse or shook music from the buckled harness. When we returned to the street light from the kitchen windows had filled the areas. If my uncle was seen turning the corner we hid in the shadow until we had seen him safely housed. Or if Mangan's sister came out on the doorstep to call her brother in to his tea we watched her from our shadow peer up and down the street. We waited to see whether she would remain or go in and, if she remained, we left our shadow and walked up to Mangan's steps resignedly. She was waiting for us, her figure defined by the light from the half-opened door. Her brother always teased her before he obeyed and I stood by the railings looking at her. Her dress swung as she moved her body and the soft rope of her hair tossed from side to side.

Every morning I lay on the floor in the front parlour watching her door. The blind was pulled down to within an inch of the sash so that I could not be seen. When she came out on the doorstep my heart leaped. I ran to the hall, seized my books and followed her. I kept her brown figure always in my eye, and, when we came near the point at which our ways diverged, I quickened my pace and passed her. This happened morning after morning. I had never spoken to her, except for a few casual words, and yet her name was like a summons to all my foolish blood.

Her image accompanied me even in places the most hostile to romance. On Saturday evenings when my aunt went marketing I had to go to carry some of the parcels. We walked through the flaring streets, jostled by drunken men and bargaining women, amid the curses of labourers, the shrill litanies of shop-boys who stood on guard by the barrels of pigs' cheeks, the nasal chanting of street-singers, who sang a *come-all-you* about O'Donovan Rossa, or a ballad about the troubles in our native land. These noises converged in a single sensation of life for me: I imagined that I bore my chalice safely through a throng of foes. Her name sprang to my lips at moments in strange prayers and praises which I myself did not understand. My eyes were often full of tears (I could not tell why) and at times a flood from my heart seemed to pour itself out into my bosom. I thought little of the future. I did not know whether I would ever speak to her or not or, if I spoke to her, how I could tell her of my confused adoration. But my body was like a harp and her words and gestures were like fingers running upon the wires.

One evening I went into the back drawing-room in which the priest had died. It was a dark rainy evening and there was no sound in the house. Through one of the broken panes I heard the rain impinge upon the earth, the fine incessant needles of water playing in the sodden beds. Some distant lamp or lighted window gleamed below me. I was thankful that I could see so little. All my senses seemed to desire to veil themselves and, feeling that I was about to slip from them, I pressed the palms of my hands together until they trembled, murmuring: *"O love! O love!"* many times.

At last she spoke to me. When she addressed the first words to me I was so confused that I did not know what to answer. She asked me was I going to *Araby.* I forgot whether I answered yes or no. It would be a splendid bazaar, she said she would love to go.

"And why can't you?" I asked.

While she spoke she turned a silver bracelet round and round her wrist. She could not go, she said, because there would be a retreat that week in her convent. Her brother and two other boys were fighting for their caps and I was alone at the railings. She held one of the spikes, bowing her head towards me. The light from the lamp opposite our door caught the white curve of her neck, lit up her hair that rested there and, falling, lit up the hand upon the railing. It fell over one side of her dress and caught the white border of a petticoat, just visible as she stood at ease.

"It's well for you," she said.

"If I go," I said, "I will bring you something."

What innumerable follies laid waste my waking and sleeping thoughts after that evening! I wished to annihilate the tedious intervening days. I chafed against the work of school. At night in my bedroom and by day in the classroom her image came between me and the page I strove to read. The syllables of the word *Araby* were called to me through the silence in which my soul luxuriated and cast an Eastern enchantment over me. I asked for leave to go to the bazaar on Saturday night. My aunt was surprised and hoped it was not some Freemason affair. I answered few questions in class. I watched my master's face pass from amiability to sternness; he hoped I was not beginning to idle. I could not call my wandering thoughts together. I had hardly any patience with the serious work of life which, now that it stood between me and my desire, seemed to me child's play, ugly monotonous child's play.

On Saturday morning I reminded my uncle that I wished to go to the bazaar in the evening. He was fussing at the hallstand, looking for the hat-brush, and answered curtly:

"Yes, boy, I know."

As he was in the hall I could not go into the front parlour and lie at the window. I left the house in bad humour and walked slowly towards the school. The air was pitilessly raw and already my heart misgave me.

When I came home to dinner my uncle had not yet been home. Still it was early. I sat staring at the clock for some time and, when its ticking began to irritate me, I left the room. I mounted the staircase and gained the upper part of the house. The high cold empty gloomy rooms liberated me and I went from room to room singing. From the front window I saw my companions playing below in the street. Their cries reached me weakened and indistinct and, leaning my forehead against the cool glass, I looked over at the dark house where she lived. I may have stood there for an hour, seeing nothing but the brown-clad figure cast by my imagination, touched discreetly by the lamplight at the curved neck, at the hand upon the railings and at the border below the dress.

When I came downstairs again I found Mrs. Mercer sitting at the fire. She was an old garrulous woman, a pawnbroker's widow, who collected used stamps for some pious purpose. I had to endure the gossip of the tea-table. The meal was prolonged beyond an hour and still my uncle did not come. Mrs. Mercer stood up to go: she was sorry she couldn't wait any longer, but it was after eight o'clock and she did not like to be out late, as the night air was bad for her. When she had gone I began to walk up and down the room, clenching my fists. My aunt said:

"I'm afraid you may put off your bazaar for this night of Our Lord."

At nine o'clock I heard my uncle's latchkey in the halldoor. I heard him talking to himself and heard the hallstand rocking when it had received the weight of his overcoat. I could interpret these signs. When he was midway through his dinner I asked him to give me the money to go to the bazaar. He had forgotten.

"The people are in bed and after their first sleep now," he said.

I did not smile. My aunt said to him energetically:

"Can't you give him the money and let him go? You've kept him late enough as it is."

My uncle said he was very sorry he had forgotten. He said he believed in the old saying: "All work and no play makes Jack a dull boy." He asked me where I was going and, when I had told him a second time he asked me did I know *The Arab's Farewell to his Steed.* When I left the kitchen he was about to recite the opening lines of the piece to my aunt.

I held a florin tightly in my hand as I strode down Buckingham Street towards the station. The sight of the streets thronged with buyers and glaring with gas recalled to me the purpose of my journey. I took my seat in a third-class carriage of a deserted train. After an intolerable delay the train moved out of the station slowly. It crept onward among ruinous houses and over the twinkling river. At Westland Row Station a crowd of people pressed to the carriage doors; but the porters moved them back, saying that it was a special train for the bazaar. I remained alone in the bare carriage. In a few minutes the train drew up beside an improvised wooden platform. I passed out on to the road and saw by the lighted dial of a clock that it was ten minutes to ten. In front of me was a large building which displayed the magical name.

I could not find any sixpenny entrance and, fearing that the bazaar would be closed, I passed in quickly through a turnstile, handing a shilling to a weary-looking man. I found myself in a big hall girdled at half its height by a gallery. Nearly all the stalls were closed and the greater part of the hall was in darkness. I recognised a silence like that which pervades a church after a service. I walked into the center of the bazaar timidly. A few people were gathered about the stalls which were still open. Before a curtain, over which the words *Café Chantant* were written in coloured lamps, two men were counting money on a salver. I listened to the fall of the coins.

Remembering with difficulty why I had come I went over to one of the stalls and examined porcelain vases and flowered tea-sets. At the door of the stall a young lady was talking and laughing with two young gentlemen. I remarked their English accents and listened vaguely to their conversation.

"O, I never said such a thing!"

"Oh, but you did!"

"Oh, but I didn't!"

"Didn't she say that?"

"Yes. I heard her."

"Oh, there's a . . . fib!"

Observing me the young lady came over and asked me did I wish to buy anything. The tone of her voice was not encouraging; she seemed to have spoken to me out of a sense of duty. I looked humbly at the great jars that stood like eastern guards at either side of the dark entrance to the stall and murmured:

"No, thank you."

The young lady changed the position of one of the vases and went back to the two young men. They began to talk of the same subject. Once or twice the young lady glanced at me over her shoulder.

I lingered before her stall, though I knew my stay was useless, to make my interest in her wares seem the more real. Then I turned away slowly and walked down the middle of the bazaar. I allowed the two pennies to fall against the sixpence in my pocket. I heard a voice call from one end of the gallery that the light was out. The upper part of the hall was now completely dark.

Gazing up into the darkness I saw myself as a creature driven and derided by vanity; and my eyes burned with anguish and anger.

Questions for Discussion

1. Characterize the young man's attitude toward Mangan's sister.

2. What is the function of the uncle in the story?

3. Apply Joyce's concept of "epiphany" (see glossary) to this story. Is there an epiphany, and if so, where does it occur?

4. What causes the young man's disillusionment? What illusions are taken from him?

Suggestions for Writing

1. Write an essay about Joyce's use of imagery in "Araby."

2. " 'Araby' is an overly sentimental, nostalgic story." Take issue with this "devil's advocate" sentence and explain the extent to which Joyce avoids sentimentality and nostalgia.

3. Read *Dubliners,* the collection of stories from which "Araby" is taken, and write an essay about several of the stories.

4. Read "The Dead," also from *Dubliners,* and view the film version of the story from 1988. Write an essay about either the story or the film or both.

5. Write a sketch of a neighborhood in which you once lived.

6. Write a story about young and unrequited love.

The Horse Dealer's Daughter

D .   H .   L A W R E N C E

"**W**ell, Mabel, and what are you going to do with yourself?" asked Joe, with foolish flippancy. He felt quite safe himself. Without listening for an answer, he turned aside, worked a grain of tobacco to the tip of his tongue, and spat it out. He did not care about anything, since he felt safe himself.

The three brothers and the sister sat round the desolate breakfast table, attempting some sort of desultory consultation. The morning's post had given the final tap to the family fortune, and all was over. The dreary dining-room itself, with its heavy mahogany furniture, looked as if it were waiting to be done away with.

But the consultation amounted to nothing. There was a strange air of ineffectuality about the three men, as they sprawled at table, smoking and reflecting vaguely on their own condition. The girl was alone, a rather short, sullen-looking young woman of twenty-seven. She did not share the same life as her brothers. She would have been good-looking, save for the impassive fixity of her face, "bull-dog," as her brothers called it.

There was a confused tramping of horses' feet outside. The three men all sprawled round in their chairs to watch. Beyond the dark hollybushes that separated the strip of lawn from the high-road, they could see a cavalcade of shire horses swinging out of their own yard, being taken for exercise. This was the last time. These were the last horses that would go through their hands. The young men watched with critical, callous look. They were all frightened at the collapse of their lives, and the sense of disaster in which they were involved left them no inner freedom.

Yet they were three fine, well-set fellows enough. Joe, the eldest, was a man of thirty-three, broad and handsome in a hot, flushed way. His face was red, he twisted his black moustache over a thick finger, his eyes were shallow and restless. He had a sensual way of uncovering his teeth when he laughed, and his bearing was stupid. Now he watched the horses with a glazed look of helplessness in his eyes, a certain stupor of downfall.

The great draught-horses swung past. They were tied head to tail, four of them, and they heaved along to where a lane branched off from the high-road, planting their great hoofs floutingly in the fine black mud, swinging their great rounded haunches sumptuously, and trotting a few sudden steps as they were led into the lane, round the corner. Every movement showed a massive, slumbrous strength, and stupidity which held them in subjection. The groom at the head looked back, jerking the leading rope. And the cavalcade moved out of sight up the lane, the tail of the last horse bobbed up tight and stiff, held out taut from the swinging great haunches as they rocked behind the hedges in a motion like sleep.

Joe watched with glazed hopeless eyes. The horses were almost like his own body to him. He felt he was done for now. Luckily he was engaged to a woman as old as himself, and therefore her father, who was steward of a neighbouring estate, would provide him with a job. He would marry and go into harness. His life was over, he would be a subject animal now.

He turned uneasily aside, the retreating steps of the horses echoing in his ears. Then, with foolish restlessness, he reached for the scraps of bacon-rind from the plates, and making a faint whistling sound, flung them to the terrier that lay against the fender. He watched the dog swallow them, and waited till the creature looked into his eyes. Then a faint grin came on his face, and in a high, foolish voice he said:

"You won't get much more bacon, shall you, you little bitch?"

The dog faintly and dismally wagged its tail, then lowered its haunches, circled round, and lay down again.

There was another helpless silence at the table. Joe sprawled uneasily in his seat, not willing to go till the family conclave was dissolved. Fred Henry, the second brother, was erect, clean-limbed, alert. He had watched the passing of the horses with more sangfroid. If he was an animal, like Joe, he was an animal which controls, not one which is controlled. He was master of any horse, and he carried himself with a well-tempered air of mastery. But he was not master of the situations of life. He pushed his coarse brown moustache upwards, off his lip, and glanced irritably at his sister, who sat impassive and inscrutable.

"You'll go and stop with Lucy for a bit, shan't you?" he asked. The girl did not answer.

"I don't see what else you can do," persisted Fred Henry.

"Go as a skivvy," Joe interpolated laconically.

The girl did not move a muscle.

"If I was her, I should go in for training for a nurse," said Malcolm, the youngest of them all. He was the baby of the family, a young man of twenty-two, with a fresh, jaunty *museau*.

But Mabel did not take any notice of him. They had talked at her and round her for so many years, that she hardly heard them at all.

The marble clock on the mantelpiece softly chimed the half-hour, the dog rose uneasily from the hearthrug and looked at the party at the breakfast table. But still they sat on in ineffectual conclave.

"Oh, all right," said Joe suddenly, apropos of nothing. "I'll get a move on."

He pushed back his chair, straddled his knees with a downward jerk, to get them free, in horsey fashion, and went to the fire. Still he did not go out of the room; he was curious to know what the others would do or say. He began to charge his pipe, looking down at the dog and saying, in a high, affected voice:

"Going wi' me? Going wi' me are ter? Tha'rt goin' further than tha counts on just now, dost hear?"

The dog faintly wagged its tail, the man stuck out his jaw and covered his pipe with his hands, and puffed intently, losing himself in the tobacco, looking down all the while at the dog with an absent brown eye. The dog looked up at him in mournful distrust. Joe stood with his knees stuck out, in real horsey fashion.

"Have you had a letter from Lucy?" Fred Henry asked of his sister.

"Last week," came the neutral reply.

"And what does she say?"

There was no answer.

"Does she *ask* you to go and stop there?" persisted Fred Henry.

"She says I can if I like."

"Well, then, you'd better. Tell her you'll come on Monday."

This was received in silence.

"That's what you'll do then, is it?" said Fred Henry, in some exasperation.

But she made no answer. There was a silence of futility and irritation in the room. Malcolm grinned fatuously.

"You'll have to make up your mind between now and next Wednesday," said Joe loudly, "or else find yourself lodgings on the kerbstone."

The face of the young woman darkened, but she sat on immutable.

"Here's Jack Fergusson!" exclaimed Malcolm, who was looking aimlessly out of the window.

"Where?" exclaimed Joe, loudly.

"Just gone past."

"Coming in?"

Malcolm craned his neck to see the gate.

"Yes," he said.

There was a silence. Mabel sat on like one condemned, at the head of the table. Then a whistle was heard from the kitchen. The dog got up and barked sharply. Joe opened the door and shouted:

"Come on."

After a moment a young man entered. He was muffled up in overcoat and a purple woollen scarf, and his tweed cap, which he did not remove, was pulled down on his head. He was of medium height, his face was rather long and pale, his eyes looked tired.

"Hello, Jack! Well, Jack!" exclaimed Malcolm and Joe. Fred Henry merely said, "Jack."

"What's doing?" asked the newcomer, evidently addressing Fred Henry.

"Same. We've got to be out by Wednesday. Got a cold?"

"I have—got it bad, too."

"Why don't you stop in?"

"*Me* stop in? When I can't stand on my legs, perhaps I shall have a chance." The young man spoke huskily. He had a slight Scotch accent.

"It's a knock-out, isn't it?" said Joe, boisterously, "if a doctor goes round croaking with a cold. Looks bad for the patients, doesn't it?"

The young doctor looked at him slowly.

"Anything the matter with *you*, then?" he asked sarcastically.

"Not as I know of. Damn your eyes, I hope not. Why?"

"I thought you were very concerned about the patients, wondered if you might be one yourself."

"Damn it, no, I've never been patient to no flaming doctor, and hope I never shall be," returned Joe.

At this point Mabel rose from the table, and they all seemed to become aware of her existence. She began putting the dishes together. The young doctor looked at her, but did not address her. He had not greeted her. She went out of the room with the tray, her face impassive and unchanged.

"When are you off then, all of you?" asked the doctor.

"I'm catching the eleven-forty," replied Malcolm. "Are you goin' down wi' th' trap, Joe?"

"Yes, I've told you I am going down wi' th' trap, haven't I?"

"We'd better be getting her in then. So long, Jack, if I don't see you before I go," said Malcolm, shaking hands.

He went out, followed by Joe, who seemed to have his tail between his legs.

"Well, this is the devil's own," exclaimed the doctor, when he was left alone with Fred Henry. "Going before Wednesday, are you."

"That's the orders," replied the other.

"Where, to Northampton?"

"That's it."

"The devil!" exclaimed Fergusson, with quiet chagrin.

And there was silence between the two.

"All settled up, are you?" asked Fergusson.

"About."

There was another pause.

"Well, I shall miss yer, Freddy, boy," said the young doctor.

"And I shall miss thee, Jack," returned the other.

"Miss you like hell," mused the doctor.

Fred Henry turned aside. There was nothing to say. Mabel came in again, to finish clearing the table.

"What are *you* to do, then, Miss Pervin?" asked Fergusson. "Going to your sister's, are you?"

Mabel looked at him with her steady, dangerous eyes, that always made him uncomfortable, unsettling his superficial ease.

"No," she said.

"Well, what in the name of fortune are *you* going to do? Say what you mean to do," cried Fred Henry, with futile intensity.

But she only averted her head, and continued her work. She folded the white tablecloth, and put on the chenile cloth.

"The sulkiest bitch that ever trod!" muttered her brother.

But she finished her task with perfectly impassive face, the young doctor watching her interestedly all the while. Then she went out.

Fred Henry stared after her, clenching his lips, his blue eyes fixing in sharp antagonism, as he made a grimace of sour exasperation.

"You could bray her into bits, and that's all you'd get out of her," he said in a small, narrowed tone.

The doctor smiled faintly.

"What's she *going* to do, then?" he asked.

"Strike me if I know!" returned the other.

There was a pause. Then the doctor stirred.

"I'll be seeing you to-night, shall I?" he said to his friend.

"Ay—where's it to be? Are we going over to Jessdale?"

"I don't know. I've got such a cold on me. I'll come round to the Moon and Stars, anyway."

"Let Lizzie and May miss their night for once, eh?"

"That's it—if I feel as I do now."

"All's one—"

The two young men went through the passage and down to the back door together. The house was large, but it was servantless now, and desolate. At the back was a small bricked house-yard, and beyond that a big square, gravelled fine and red, and having stables on two sides. Sloping, dank, winter-dark fields stretched away on the open sides.

But the stables were empty. Joseph Pervin, the father of the family, had been a man of no education, who had become a fairly large horse dealer. The stables had been full of horses, there was a great turmoil and come-and-go of horses and of dealers and grooms. Then the kitchen was full of servants. But of late things had declined. The old man had married a second time, to retrieve his fortunes. Now he was dead and everything was gone to the dogs, there was nothing but debt and threatening.

For months, Mabel had been servantless in the big house, keeping the home together in penury for her ineffectual brothers. She had kept house for ten years. But previously it was with unstinted means. Then, however brutal and coarse everything was, the sense of money had kept her proud, confident. The men might be foul-mouthed, the women in the kitchen might have bad reputations, her brothers might have illegitimate children. But so long as there was money, the girl felt herself established and brutally proud, reserved.

No company came to the house, save dealers and coarse men. Mabel had no associates of her own sex, after her sister went away. But she did not mind. She went regularly to church, she attended to her father. And she lived in the memory of her mother, who had died when she was fourteen, and whom she had loved. She had loved her father, too, in a different way, depending upon him, and feeling secure in him, until at the age of fifty-four he married again. And then she had set hard against him. Now he had died and left them all hopelessly in debt.

She had suffered badly during the period of poverty. Nothing, however, could shake the curious sullen, animal pride that dominated each member of the family. Now, for Mabel, the end had come. Still she would not cast about her. She would follow her own way just the same. She would always hold the keys of her own situation. Mindless and persistent, she endured from day to day. What should she think? Why should she answer anybody? It was enough that this was the end and there was no way out. She need not pass any more darkly along the main street of the small town, avoiding every eye. She need not demean herself any more, going into the shops and buying the cheapest food. This was at an end. She thought of nobody, not even of herself. Mindless and persistent, she seemed in a sort of ecstasy to be coming nearer to her fulfilment, her own glorification, approaching her dead mother, who was glorified.

In the afternoon she took a little bag, with shears and sponge and a small scrubbing brush, and went out. It was a grey, wintry day, with saddened, dark green fields and an atmosphere blackened by the smoke of foundries not far off. She went quickly, darkly along the causeway, heeding nobody, through the town to the churchyard.

There she always felt secure, as if no one could see her, although as a matter of fact she was exposed to the stare of every one who passed along under the churchyard wall. Nevertheless, once under the shadow of the great looming church, among the graves, she felt immune from the world, reserved within the thick churchyard wall as in another country.

Carefully she clipped the grass from the grave, and arranged the pinky white, small chrysanthemums in the tin cross. When this was done, she took an empty jar from a neighbouring grave, brought water, and carefully, most scrupulously sponged the marble head-stone and the coping-stone.

It gave her sincere satisfaction to do this. She felt in immediate contact with the world of her mother. She took minute pains, went through the park in a state bordering on pure happiness, as if in performing this task she came into a subtle, intimate connection with her mother. For the life she followed here in the world was far less real than the world of death she inherited from her mother.

The doctor's house was just by the church. Fergusson, being a mere hired assistant, was slave to the country-side. As he hurried now to attend to the out-patients in the surgery, glancing across the graveyard with his quick eye, he saw the girl at her task at the grave. She seemed so intent and remote, it was like looking into another world. Some mystical element was touched in him. He slowed down as he walked, watching her as if spell-bound.

She lifted her eyes, feeling him looking. Their eyes met. And each looked away again at once, each feeling, in some way, found out by the other. He lifted his cap and passed on down the road. There remained distinct in his consciousness, like a vision, the memory of her face, lifted from the tombstone in the churchyard, and looking at him with slow, large, portentous eyes. It *was* portentous, her face. It seemed to mesmerize him. There was a heavy power in her eyes which laid hold of his whole being, as if he had drunk some powerful drug. He had been feeling weak and done before. Now the life came back into him, he felt delivered from his own fretted, daily self.

He finished his duties at the surgery as quickly as might be, hastily filling up the bottle of the waiting people with cheap drugs. Then, in perpetual haste, he set off again to visit several cases in another part of his round, before tea-time. At all times he preferred to walk if he could, not particularly when he was not well. He fancied the motion restored him.

The afternoon was falling. It was grey, deadened, and wintry, with a slow, moist, heavy coldness sinking in and deadening all the faculties. But why should he think or notice? He hastily climbed the hill and turned across the dark green fields, following the black cinder-track. In the distance, across a shallow dip in the country, the small town was clustered like smouldering ash, a tower, a spire, a heap of low, raw, extinct houses. And on the nearest fringe of the town, sloping into the dip, was Oldmeadow, the Pervins' house. He could see the stables and the outbuildings distinctly, as they lay towards him on the slope. Well, he would not go there many more times! Another resource would be lost to him, another place gone: the only company he cared for in the alien, ugly little town he was losing. Nothing but work, drudgery, constant hastening from dwelling to dwelling among the colliers and the ironworkers. It wore him out, but at the same time he had a craving for it. It was a stimulant to him to be in the homes of the working people, moving as it were through the innermost body of their life. His nerves were excited and gratified. He could come so near, into the very lives of the rough, inarticulate, powerfully emotional men and women. He grumbled, he said he hated the hellish hole. But as a matter of fact it excited him, the contact with the rough, strongly-feeling people was a stimulant applied direct to his nerves.

Below Oldmeadow, in the green, shallow, soddened hollow of fields lay a square, deep pond. Roving across the landscape, the doctor's quick eye detected a figure in black passing through the gate of the field, down towards the pond. He looked again. It would be Mabel Pervin. His mind suddenly became alive and attentive.

Why was she going down there? He pulled up on the path on the slope above, and stood staring. He could just make sure of the small black figure moving in the hollow of the failing day. He seemed to see her in the midst of such obscurity, that he was like a clairvoyant, seeing rather with the mind's eye than with ordinary sight. Yet he could see her positively enough, whilst he kept his eye attentive. He felt, if he looked away from her, in the thick, ugly falling dusk, he would lose her altogether.

He followed her minutely as she moved, direct and intent, like something transmitted rather than stirring in voluntary activity, straight down the field towards the pond. There she stood on the bank for a moment. She never raised her head. Then she waded slowly into the water.

He stood motionless as the small black figure walked slowly and deliberately towards the centre of the pond, very slowly, gradually moving deeper into the motionless water, and still moving forward as the water got up to her breast. Then he could see her no more in the dusk of the dead afternoon.

"There!" he exclaimed. "Would you believe it?"

And he hastened straight down, running over the wet, soddened fields, pushing through the hedges, down into the depression of callous wintry obscurity. It took him several minutes to come to the pond. He stood on the bank, breathing heavily. He could see nothing. His eyes seemed to penetrate the dead water. Yes, perhaps that was the dark shadow of her black clothing beneath the surface of the water.

He slowly ventured into the pond. The bottom was deep, soft clay, he sank in, and the water clasped dead cold round his legs. As he stirred he could smell the cold, rotten clay that fouled up into the water. It was objectionable in his lungs. Still, repelled and yet not heeding, he moved deeper into the pond. The cold water rose over his thighs, over his loins, upon his abdomen. The lower part of his body was all sunk in the hideous cold element. And the bottom was so deeply soft and uncertain, he was afraid of pitching with his mouth underneath. He could not swim, and was afraid.

He crouched a little, spreading his hands under the water and moving them round, trying to feel for her. The dead cold pond swayed upon his chest. He moved again, a little deeper, and again, with his hands underneath, he felt all around the water. And he touched her clothing. But it evaded his fingers. He made a desperate effort to grasp it.

And so doing he lost his balance and went under, horribly, suffocating in the foul earthy water, struggling madly for a few moments. At last, after what seemed an eternity, he got his footing, rose again into the air and looked around. He gasped, and knew he was in the world. Then he looked at the water. She had risen near him. He grasped her clothing, and drawing her nearer, turned to take his way to land again.

He went very slowly, carefully, absorbed in the slow progress. He rose higher, climbing out of the pond. The water was now only about his legs; he was thankful, full of relief to be out of the clutches of the pond. He lifted her and staggered on to the bank, out of the horror of wet, grey clay.

He laid her down on the bank. She was quite unconscious and running with water. He made the water come from her mouth, he worked to restore her. He did not have to work very long before he could feel the breathing begin again in her; she was breathing naturally. He worked a little longer. He could feel her live beneath his hands; she was coming back. He wiped her face, wrapped her in his overcoat, looked round into the dim, dark grey world, then lifted her and staggered down the bank and across the fields.

It seemed an unthinkably long way, and his burden so heavy he felt he would never get to the house. But at last he was in the stable-yard, and then in the house-yard. He opened the door and went into the house. In the kitchen he laid her down on the hearth-rug, and called. The house was empty. But the fire was burning in the grate.

Then again he kneeled to attend to her. She was breathing regularly, her eyes were wide open and as if conscious, but there seemed something missing in her look. She was conscious in herself, but unconscious of her surroundings.

He ran upstairs, took blankets from a bed, and put them before the fire to warm. Then he removed her saturated, earthy-smelling clothing, rubbed her dry with a towel, and wrapped her naked in the blankets. Then he went into the dining-room, to look for spirits. There was a little whisky. He drank a gulp himself, and put some into her mouth.

The effect was instantaneous. She looked full into his face, as if she had been seeing him for some time, and yet had only just become conscious of him.

"Dr. Fergusson?" she said.

"What?" he answered.

He was divesting himself of his coat, intending to find some dry clothing upstairs. He could not bear the smell of the dead, clayey water, and he was mortally afraid for his own health.

"What did I do?" she asked.

"Walked into the pond," he replied. He had begun to shudder like one sick, and could hardly attend to her. Her eyes remained full on him, he seemed to be going dark in his mind, looking back at her helplessly. The shuddering became quieter in him, his life came back in him, dark and unknowing, but strong again.

"Was I out of my mind?" she asked, while her eyes were fixed on him all the time.

"Maybe, for the moment," he replied. He felt quiet, because his strength had come back. The strange fretful strain had left him.

"Am I out of my mind now?" she asked.

"Are you?" he reflected a moment. "No," he answered truthfully. "I don't see that you are." He turned his face aside. He was afraid now, because he felt dazed, and felt dimly that her power was stronger than his, in this issue. And she continued to look at him fixedly all the time. "Can you tell me where I shall find some dry things to put on?" he asked.

"Did you dive into the pond for me?" she asked.

"No," he answered. "I walked in. But I went in overhead as well."

There was a silence for a moment. He hesitated. He very much wanted to go upstairs to get into dry clothing. But there was another desire in him. And she seemed to hold him. His will seemed to have gone to sleep, and left him, standing there slack before her. But he felt warm inside himself. He did not shudder at all, though his clothes were sodden on him.

"Why did you?" she asked.

"Because I didn't want you to do such a foolish thing," he said.

"It wasn't foolish," she said, still gazing at him as she lay on the floor, with a sofa cushion under her head. "It was the right thing to do. *I* knew best, then."

"I'll go and shift these wet things," he said. But still he had not the power to move out of her presence, until she sent him. It was as if she had the life of his body in her hands, and he could not extricate himself. Or perhaps he did not want to.

Suddenly she sat up. Then she became aware of her own immediate condition. She felt the blankets about her, she knew her own limbs. For a moment it seemed as if her reason were going. She looked round, with wild eyes, as if seeking something. He stood still with fear. She saw her clothing lying scattered.

"Who undressed me?" she asked, her eyes resting full and inevitable on his face.

"I did," he replied, "to bring you round."

For some moments she sat and gazed at him awfully, her lips parted.

"Do you love me, then?" she asked.

He only stood and stared at her, fascinated. His soul seemed to melt.

She shuffled forward on her knees, and put her arms around him, round his legs, as he stood there, pressing her breasts against his knees and thighs, clutching him with strange, convulsive certainty, pressing his thighs against her, drawing him to her face, her throat, as she looked up at him with flaring, humble eyes of transfiguration, triumphant in first possession.

"You love me," she murmured, in strange transport, yearning and triumphant and confident. "You love me. I know you love me, I know."

And she was passionately kissing his knees, through the wet clothing, passionately and indiscriminately kissing his knees, his legs, as if unaware of everything.

He looked down at the tangled wet hair, the wild, bare, animal shoulders. He was amazed, bewildered, and afraid. He had never thought of loving her. He had never wanted to love her. When he rescued her and restored her, he was a doctor, and she was a patient. He had had no single personal thought of her. Nay, this introduction of the personal element was very distasteful to him, a violation of his professional honour. It was horrible to have her there embracing his knees. It was horrible. He revolted from it, violently. And yet—and yet—he had not the power to break away.

She looked at him again, with the same supplication of powerful love, and that same transcendent, frightening light of triumph. In view of the delicate flame which seemed to come from her face like a light, he was powerless. And yet he had never intended to love her. He had never intended. And something stubborn in him could not give way.

"You love me," she repeated, in a murmur of deep rhapsodic assurance. "You love me."

Her hands were drawing him, drawing him down to her. He was afraid, even a little horrified. For he had, really, no intention of loving her. Yet her hands were drawing him towards her. He put out his hand quickly to steady himself, and grasped her bare shoulder. A flame seemed to burn the hand that grasped her soft shoulder. He had no intention of loving her: his whole will was against his yielding. It was horrible. And yet wonderful was the touch of her shoulders, beautiful the shining of her face. Was she perhaps mad? He had a horror of yielding to her. Yet something in him ached also.

He had been staring away at the door, away from her. But his hand remained on her shoulder. She had gone suddenly very still. He looked down at her. Her eyes were now wide with fear, and doubt, the light was dying from her face, a shadow of terrible greyness was returning. He could not bear the touch of her eyes' question upon him, and the look of death behind the question.

With an inward groan he gave way, and let his heart yield towards her. A sudden gentle smile came on his face. And her eyes, which never left his face, slowly, slowly filled with tears. He watched the strange water rise in her eyes, like some slow fountain coming up. And his heart seemed to burn and melt away in his breast.

He could not bear to look at her any more. He dropped on his knees and caught her head with his arms and pressed her face against his throat. She was very still. His heart, which seemed to have broken, was burning with a kind of agony in his breast. And he felt her slow, hot tears wetting his throat. But he could not move.

He felt the hot tears wet his neck and the hollows of his neck, and he remained motionless, suspended through one of man's eternities. Only now it had become indispensable to him to have her face pressed close to him; he could never let her go again. He could never let her head go away from the close clutch of his arm. He wanted to remain like that for ever, with his heart hurting him in a pain that was also life to him. Without knowing, he was looking down on her damp, soft brown hair.

Then, as it were suddenly, he smelt the horrid stagnant smell of that water. And at the same moment she drew away from him and looked at him. Her eyes were wistful and unfathomable. He was afraid of them, and he fell to kissing her, not knowing what he was doing. He wanted her eyes not to have that terrible, wistful, unfathomable look.

When she turned her face to him again, a faint delicate flush was glowing, and there was again dawning that terrible shining of joy in her eyes, which really terrified him, and yet which he now wanted to see, because he feared the look of doubt still more.

"You love me?" she said, rather faltering.

"Yes." The word cost him a painful effort. Not because it wasn't true. But because it was too newly true, the *saying* seemed to tear open again his newly-torn heart. And he hardly wanted it to be true, even now.

She lifted her face to him, and he bent forward and kissed her on the mouth, gently, with the one kiss that is an eternal pledge. And as he kissed her his heart strained again in his breast. He never intended to love her. But now it was over. He had crossed over the gulf to her, and all that he had left behind had shrivelled and become void.

After the kiss, her eyes again slowly filled with tears. She sat still, away from him, with her face drooped aside, and her hands folded in her lap. The tears fell very slowly. There was complete silence. He too sat there motionless and silent on the hearthrug. The strange pain of his heart that was broken seemed to consume him. That he should love her? That this was love! That he should be ripped open in this way! Him, a doctor! How they would all jeer if they knew! It was agony to him to think they might know.

In the curious naked pain of the thought he looked again to her. She was sitting there drooped into a muse. He saw a tear fall, and his heart flared hot. He saw for the first time that one of her shoulders was quite uncovered, one arm bare, he could see one of her small breasts; dimly, because it had become almost dark in the room.

"Why are you crying?" he asked, in an altered voice.

She looked at him, and behind her tears the consciousness of her situation for the first time brought a dark look of shame to her eyes.

"I'm not crying, really," she said, watching him half frightened.

He reached his hand, and softly closed it on her bare arm.

"I love you! I love you!" he said in a soft, low vibrating voice, unlike himself.

She shrank, and dropped her head. The soft, penetrating grip of his hand on her arm distressed her. She looked up at him.

"I want to go," she said. "I want to go and get you some dry things."

"Why?" he said. "I'm all right."

"But I want to go," she said. "And I want you to change your things."

He released her arm, and she wrapped herself in the blanket, looking at him rather frightened. And still she did not rise.

"Kiss me," she said wistfully.

He kissed her, but briefly, half in anger.

Then, after a second, she rose nervously, all mixed up in the blanket. He watched her in her confusion, as she tried to extricate herself and wrap herself up so that she could walk. He watched her relentlessly, as she knew. And as she went, the blanket trailing, and as he saw a glimpse of her feet and her white leg, he tried to remember her as she was when he had wrapped her in the blanket. But then he didn't want to remember, because she had been nothing to him then, and his nature revolted from remembering her as she was when she was nothing to him.

A tumbling, muffled noise from within the dark house startled him. Then he heard her voice:—"There are clothes." He rose and went to the foot of the stairs, and gathered up the garments she had thrown down. Then he came back to the fire, to rub himself down and dress. He grinned at his own appearance when he had finished.

The fire was sinking, so he put on coal. The house was now quite dark, save for the light of a street-lamp that shone in faintly from beyond the holly trees. He lit the gas with matches he found on the mantelpiece. Then he emptied the pockets of his own clothes, and threw all his wet things in a heap into the scullery. After which he gathered up her sodden clothes, gently, and put them in a separate heap on the copper-top in the scullery.

It was six o'clock on the clock. His own watch had stopped. He ought to go back to the surgery. He waited, and still she did not come down. So he went to the foot of the stairs and called:

"I shall have to go."

Almost immediately he heard her coming down. She had on her best dress of black voile, and her hair was tidy, but still damp. She looked at him—and in spite of herself, smiled.

"I don't like you in those clothes," she said.

"Do I look a sight?" he answered.

They were shy of one another.

"I'll make you some tea," she said.

"No, I must go."

"Must you?" And she looked at him again with the wide, strained, doubtful eyes. And again, from the pain of his breast, he knew how he loved her. He went and bent to kiss her, gently, passionately, with his heart's painful kiss.

"And my hair smells so horrible," she murmured in distraction. "And I'm so awful. I'm so awful! Oh, no, I'm too awful." And she broke into bitter, heartbroken sobbing. "You can't want to love me, I'm horrible."

"Don't be silly, don't be silly," he said, trying to comfort her, kissing her, holding her in his arms. "I want you, I want to marry you, we're going to be married, quickly, quickly—tomorrow if I can."

But she only sobbed terribly, and cried:

"I feel awful. I feel awful. I feel I'm horrible to you."

"No, I want you, I want you," was all he answered, blindly, with that terrible intonation which frightened her almost more than her horror lest he should *not* want her.

Questions for Discussion

1. How do the first several paragraphs suggest the themes of sexuality and liberation that the meeting between Jack and Mabel emphasizes later?

2. What is the point of view of the story?

3. How should we interpret the two most striking episodes of the story—the scene at the pond and the scene back at the house?

Suggestions for Writing

1. Write an essay in which you explain how this story "comments" on "modern" relationships and concepts of romantic love.

2. " 'The Horse Dealer's Daughter' is a weird story, especially the scene at the pond." Write a paragraph in which you argue against this "devil's advocate" sentence; justify the importance of the scene at the pond, showing how the scene may be more than simply "weird."

3. Write an interpretive essay about this story that includes an analysis of symbolism. For example, are the horses and the pond more than horses and a pond; do they symbolize something more?

4. See the motion picture *The Priest of Love,* which is about D. H. Lawrence, and write a review of it.

5. Read *Women in Love* and/or *Lady Chatterley's Lover* and write an essay about the connections between the novel(s) and "The Horse Dealer's Daughter."

A Clean, Well-Lighted Place

ERNEST HEMINGWAY

It was late and every one had left the café except an old man who sat in the shadow the leaves of the tree made against the electric light. In the day time the street was dusty, but at night the dew settled the dust and the old man liked to sit late because he was deaf and now at night it was quiet and he felt the difference. The two waiters inside the café knew that the old man was a little drunk, and while he was a good client they knew that if he became too drunk he would leave without paying, so they kept watch on him.

"Last week he tried to commit suicide," one waiter said.

"Why?"

"He was in despair."

"What about?"

"Nothing."

"How do you know it was nothing?"

"He has plenty of money."

They sat together at a table that was close against the wall near the door of the café and looked at the terrace where the tables were all empty except where the old man sat in the shadow of the leaves of the tree that moved slightly in the wind. A girl and a soldier went by in the street. The street light shone on the brass number on his collar. The girl wore no head covering and hurried beside him.

"The guard will pick him up," one waiter said.

"What does it matter if he gets what he's after?"

"He had better get off the street now. The guard will get him. They went by five minutes ago."

The old man sitting in the shadow rapped on his saucer with his glass. The younger waiter went over to him.

"What do you want?"

The old man looked at him. "Another brandy," he said.

"You'll be drunk," the waiter said. The old man looked at him. The waiter went away.

"He'll stay all night," he said to his colleague. "I'm sleepy now. I never get into bed before three o'clock. He should have killed himself last week."

The waiter took the brandy bottle and another saucer from the counter inside the café and marched out to the old man's table. He put down the saucer and poured the glass full of brandy.

"You should have killed yourself last week," he said to the deaf man. The old man motioned with his finger. "A little more," he said. The waiter poured on into the glass so that the brandy slopped over and ran down the stem into the top saucer of the pile. "Thank you," the old man said. The waiter took the bottle back inside the café. He sat down at the table with his colleague again.

"He's drunk now," he said.

"He's drunk every night."

"What did he want to kill himself for?"

"How should I know."

"How did he do it?"

"He hung himself with a rope."

"Who cut him down?"

"His niece."

"Why did they do it?"

"Fear for his soul."

"How much money has he got?"

"He's got plenty."

"He must be eighty years old."

"Anyway I should say he was eighty."

"I wish he would go home. I never get to bed before three o'clock. What kind of hour is that to go to bed?"

"He stays up because he likes it."

"He's lonely. I'm not lonely. I have a wife waiting in bed for me."

"He had a wife once too."

"A wife would be no good to him now."

"You can't tell. He might be better with a wife."

"His niece looks after him. You said she cut him down."

"I know."

"I wouldn't want to be that old. An old man is a nasty thing."

"Not always. This old man is clean. He drinks without spilling. Even now, drunk. Look at him."

"I don't want to look at him. I wish he would go home. He has no regard for those who must work."

The old man looked from his glass across the square, then over at the waiters.

"Another brandy," he said, pointing to his glass. The waiter who was in a hurry came over.

"Finished," he said, speaking with that omission of syntax stupid people employ when talking to drunken people or foreigners. "No more tonight. Close now."

"Another," said the old man.

"No. Finished." The waiter wiped the edge of the table with a towel and shook his head.

The old man stood up, slowly counted the saucers, took a leather coin purse from his pocket and paid for the drinks, leaving half a peseta tip.

The waiter watched him go down the street, a very old man walking unsteadily but with dignity.

"Why didn't you let him stay and drink?" the unhurried waiter asked. They were putting up the shutters. "It is not half-past two."

"I want to go home to bed."

"What is an hour?"

"More to me than to him."

"An hour is the same."

"You talk like an old man yourself. He can buy a bottle and drink at home."

"It's not the same."

"No, it is not," agreed the waiter with a wife. He did not wish to be unjust. He was only in a hurry.

"And you? You have no fear of going home before your usual hour?"

"Are you trying to insult me?"

"No, hombre, only to make a joke."

"No," the waiter who was in a hurry said, rising from pulling down the metal shutters. "I have confidence. I am all confidence."

"You have youth, confidence, and a job," the older waiter said. "You have everything."

"And what do you lack?"

"Everything but work."

"You have everything I have."

"No. I have never had confidence and I am not young."

"Come on. Stop talking nonsense and lock up."

"I am of those who like to stay late at the café," the older waiter said. "With all those who do not want to go to bed. With all those who need a light for the night."

"I want to go home and into bed."

"We are of two different kinds," the older waiter said. He was now dressed to go home. "It is not only a question of youth and confidence although those things are very beautiful. Each night I am reluctant to close up because there may be some one who needs the café."

"Hombre, there are bodegas open all night long."

"You do not understand. This is a clean and pleasant café. It is well lighted. The light is very good and also, now, there are shadows of the leaves."

"Good night," said the younger waiter.

"Good night," the other said. Turning off the electric light he continued the conversation with himself. It is the light of course but it is necessary that the place be clean and pleasant. You do not want music. Certainly you do not want music. Nor can you stand before a bar with dignity although that is all that is provided for these hours. What did he fear? It was not fear or dread. It was a nothing that he knew too well. It was all a nothing and a man was nothing too. It was only that and light was all it needed and a certain cleanness and order. Some lived in it and never felt it but he knew it all was nada y pues nada y nada y pues nada. Our nada who art in nada, nada be the name thy kingdom nada thy will be nada in nada as it is in nada. Give us this nada our daily nada and nada us our nada as we nada our nadas and nada us not into nada but deliver us from nada; pues nada. Hail nothing full of nothing, nothing is with thee. He smiled and stood before a bar with a shining steam pressure coffee machine.

"What's yours?" asked the barman.

"Nada."

"Otro loco más," said the barman and turned away.

"A little cup," said the waiter.

The barman poured it for him.

"The light is very bright and pleasant but the bar is unpolished," the waiter said.

The barman looked at him but did not answer. It was too late at night for conversation.

"You want another copita?" the barman asked.

"No, thank you," said the waiter and went out. He disliked bars and bodegas. A clean, well-lighted café was a very different thing. Now, without thinking further, he would go home to his room. He would lie in the bed and finally, with daylight, he would go to sleep. After all, he said to himself, it is probably only insomnia. Many must have it.

Questions for Discussion

1. What do the first several lines reveal about the waiters and their attitude toward the old man?

2. Why does "a clean, well-lighted place" seem so important to the older waiter?

3. Contrast the younger and older waiters.

4. How should we interpret the older waiter's version of the Lord's Prayer?

Suggestions for Writing

1. If you have read about or taken a course in existential philosophy, write an essay that discusses the extent to which Hemingway's story expresses this philosophy.

2. In your notebook, write a one-page description of a public place and try to imitate the style of Hemingway's story.

3. Read W. B. Yeats's poem "Sailing to Byzantium" and write an essay that compares and contrasts it with "A Clean, Well-Lighted Place."

A Hunger Artist

FRANZ KAFKA

During these last decades the interest in professional fasting has markedly diminished. It used to pay very well to stage such great performances under one's own management, but today that is quite impossible. We live in a different world now. At one time the whole town took a lively interest in the hunger artist; from day to day of his fast the excitement mounted; everybody wanted to see him at least once a day; there were people who bought season tickets for the last few days and sat from morning till night in front of his small barred cage; even in the nighttime there were visiting hours, when the whole effect was heightened by torch flares; on fine days the cage was set out in the open air, and then it was the children's special treat to see the hunger artist; for their elders he was often just a joke that happened to be in fashion, but the children stood openmouthed, holding each other's hands for greater security, marveling at him as he sat there pallid in black tights, with his ribs sticking out so prominently, not even on a seat but down among straw on the ground, sometimes giving a courteous nod, answering questions with a constrained smile, or perhaps stretching an arm through the bars so that one might feel how thin it was, and then again withdrawing deep into himself, paying no attention to anyone or anything, not even to the all-important striking of the clock that was the only piece of furniture in his cage, but merely staring into vacancy with half-shut eyes, now and then taking a sip from a tiny glass of water to moisten his lips.

Besides casual onlookers there were also relays of permanent watchers selected by the public, usually butchers, strangely enough, and it was their task to watch the hunger artist day and night, three of them at a time, in case he should have some secret recourse to nourishment. This was nothing but a formality, instituted to reassure the masses, for the initiates knew well enough that during his fast the artist would never in any circumstances, not even under forcible compulsion, swallow the smallest morsel of food; the honor of his profession forbade it. Not every watcher, of course, was capable of understanding this, there were often groups of night watchers who were very lax in carrying out their duties and deliberately huddled together in a retired corner to play cards with great absorption, obviously intending to give the hunger artist the chance of a little refreshment, which they supposed he could draw from some private hoard. Nothing annoyed the artist more than such watchers; they made him miserable; they made his fast seem unendurable; sometimes he mastered his feebleness sufficiently to sing during their watch for as long as he could keep going, to show them how unjust their suspicions were. But that was of little use; they only wondered at his cleverness in being able to fill his mouth even while singing. Much more to his taste were the watchers who sat close up to the bars, who were not content with the dim night lighting of the hall but focused him in the full glare of the electric pocket torch given them by the impresario. The harsh light did not trouble him at all, in any case he could never sleep properly, and he could always drowse a little, whatever the light, at any hour, even when the hall was thronged with noisy onlookers. He was quite happy at the prospect of spending a sleepless night with such watchers; he was ready to exchange jokes with them, to tell them stories out of his nomadic life, anything at all to keep them awake and demonstrate to them again that he had no eatables in his cage and that he was fasting as not one of them could fast. But his happiest moment was when the morning came and an enormous breakfast was brought them, at his expense, on which they flung themselves with the keen appetite of healthy men after a weary night of wakefulness. Of course there were people who argued that this breakfast was an unfair attempt to bribe the watchers, but that was going rather too far, and when they were invited to take on a night's vigil without a breakfast, merely for the sake of the cause, they made themselves scarce, although they stuck stubbornly to their suspicions.

Such suspicions, anyhow, were a necessary accompaniment to the profession of fasting. No one could possibly watch the hunger artist continuously, day and night, and so no one could produce first-hand evidence that the fast had really been rigorous and continuous; only the artist himself could know that, he was therefore bound to be the sole completely satisfied spectator of his own fast. Yet for other reasons he was never satisfied; it was not perhaps mere fasting that had brought him to such skeleton thinness that many people had regretfully to keep away from his exhibitions, because the sight of him was too much for them, perhaps it was dissatisfaction with himself that had worn him down. For he alone knew, what no other initiate knew, how easy it was to fast. It was the easiest thing in the world. He made no secret of this, yet people did not believe him, at the best they set him down as modest; most of them, however, thought he was out for publicity or else was some kind of cheat who found it easy to fast because he had discovered a way of making it easy, and then had the impudence to admit the fact, more or less. He had to put up with all that, and in the course of time had got used to it, but his inner dissatisfaction always rankled, and never yet, after any term of fasting—this must be granted to his credit—had he left the cage of his own free will. The longest period of fasting was fixed by his impresario at forty days, beyond that term he was not allowed to go, not even in great cities, and there was good reason for it, too. Experience had proved that for about forty days the interest of the public could be stimulated by a steadily increasing pressure of advertisement, but after that the town began to lose interest, sympathetic support began notably to fall off; there were of course local variations as between one town and another or one country and another, but as a general rule forty days marked the limit. So on the fortieth day the flower-bedecked cage was opened, enthusiastic spectators filled the hall, a military band played, two doctors entered the cage to measure the results of the fast, which were announced through a megaphone, and finally two young ladies appeared, blissful at having been selected for the honor, to help the hunger artist down the few steps leading to a small table on which was spread a carefully chosen invalid repast. And at this very moment the artist always turned stubborn. True, he would entrust his bony arms to the outstretched helping hands of the ladies bending over him, but stand up he would not. Why stop fasting at this particular moment, after forty days of it? He had held out for a long time, an illimitably long time; why stop now, when he was in his best fasting form, or rather, not yet quite in his best fasting form? Why should he be cheated of the fame he would get for fasting longer, for being not only the record hunger artist of all time, which presumably he was already, but for beating his own record by a performance beyond human imagination, since he felt that there were no limits to his capacity for fasting? His public pretended to admire him so much, why should it have so little patience with him; if he could endure fasting longer, why shouldn't the public endure it? Besides, he was tired, he was comfortable sitting in the straw, and now he was supposed to lift himself to his full height and go down to a meal the very thought of which gave him a nausea that only the presence of the ladies kept him from betraying, and even that with an effort. And he looked up into the eyes of the ladies who were apparently so friendly and in reality so cruel, and shook his head, which felt too heavy on its strengthless neck. But then there happened yet again what always happened. The impresario came forward, without a word—for the band made speech impossible—lifted his arms in the air above the artist, as if inviting Heaven to look down upon its creature here in the straw, this suffering martyr, which indeed he was, although in quite another sense; grasped him around the emaciated waist, with exaggerated caution, so that the frail condition he was in might be appreciated; and committed him to the care of the blenching ladies, not without secretly giving him a shaking so that his legs and body tottered and swayed. The artist now submitted completely; his head lolled on his breast as if it had landed there by chance; his body was hollowed out; his legs in a spasm of self-preservation clung close to each other at the knees, yet scraped on the ground as if it were not really solid ground, as if they were only trying to find solid ground; and the whole weight of his body, a featherweight after all, relapsed onto one of the ladies, who, looking around for help and panting a little—this post of honor was not at all what she had expected it to be—first stretched her neck as far as she could to keep her face at least free from contact with the artist, then finding this impossible, and her more fortunate companion not coming to her aid but merely holding extended in her own trembling hand the little bunch of knucklebones that was the artist's, to the great delight of the spectators burst into tears and had to be replaced by an attendant who had long been stationed in readiness. Then came the food, a little of which the impresario managed to get between the artist's lips, while he sat in a kind of half-fainting trance, to the accompaniment of cheerful patter designed to distract the public's attention from the artist's condition; after that, a toast was drunk to the public, supposedly prompted by a whisper from the artist in the impresario's ear; the band confirmed it with a mighty flourish, the spectators melted away, and no one had any cause to be dissatisfied with the proceedings, no one except the hunger artist himself, he only, as always.

So he lived for many years, with small regular intervals of recuperation, in visible glory, honored by the world, yet in spite of that troubled in spirit, and all the more troubled because no one would take his trouble seriously. What comfort could he possibly need? What more could he possibly wish for? And if some good-natured person, feeling sorry for him, tried to console him by pointing out that his melancholy was probably caused by fasting, it could happen, especially when he had been fasting for some time, that he reacted with an outburst of fury and to the general alarm began to shake the bars of his cage like a wild animal. Yet the impresario had a way of punishing these outbreaks which he rather enjoyed putting into operation. He would apologize publicly for the artist's behavior, which was only to be excused, he admitted, because of the irritability caused by fasting; a condition hardly to be understood by well-fed people; then by natural transition he went on to mention the artist's equally incomprehensible boast that he could fast for much longer than he was doing; he praised the high ambition, the good will, the great self-denial undoubtedly implicit in such a statement; and then quite simply countered it by bringing out photographs, which were also on sale to the public, showing the artist on the fortieth day of a fast lying in bed almost dead from exhaustion. This perversion of the truth, familiar to the artist though it was, always unnerved him afresh and proved too much for him. What was a consequence of the premature ending of his fast was here presented as the cause of it! To fight against this lack of understanding, against a whole world of nonunderstanding, was impossible. Time and again in good faith he stood by the bars listening to the impresario, but as soon as the photographs appeared he always let go and sank with a groan back onto his straw, and the reassured public could once more come close and gaze at him.

A few years later when the witnesses of such scenes called them to mind, they often failed to understand themselves at all. For meanwhile the aforementioned change in public interest had set in; it seemed to happen almost overnight; there may have been profound causes for it, but who was going to bother about that; at any rate the pampered hunger artist suddenly found himself deserted one fine day by the amusement-seekers, who went streaming past him to other more-favored attractions. For the last time the impresario hurried him over half Europe to discover whether the old interest might still survive here and there; all in vain; everywhere, as if by secret agreement, a positive revulsion from professional fasting was in evidence. Of course it could not really have sprung up so suddenly as all that, and many premonitory symptoms which had not been sufficiently remarked or suppressed during the rush and glitter of success now came retrospectively to mind, but it was now too late to take any countermeasures. Fasting would surely come into fashion again at some future date, yet that was no comfort for those living in the present. What, then, was the hunger artist to do? He had been applauded by thousands in his time and could hardly come down to showing himself in a street booth at village fairs, and as for adopting another profession, he was not only too old for that but too fanatically devoted to fasting. So he took leave of the impresario, his partner in an unparalleled career, and hired himself to a large circus; in order to spare his own feelings he avoided reading the conditions of his contract.

A large circus with its enormous traffic in replacing and recruiting men, animals, and apparatus can always find a use for people at any time, even for a hunger artist, provided of course that he does not ask too much, and in this particular case anyhow it was not only the artist who was taken on but his famous and long-known name as well, indeed considering the peculiar nature of his performance, which was not impaired by advancing age, it could not be objected that here was an artist past his prime, no longer at the height of his professional skill, seeking a refuge in some quiet corner of a circus; on the contrary, the hunger artist averred that he could fast as well as ever, which was entirely credible, he even alleged that if he were allowed to fast as he liked, and this was at once promised him without more ado, he could astound the world by establishing a record never yet achieved, a statement that certainly provoked a smile among the other professionals, since it left out of account the change in public opinion, which the hunger artist in his zeal conveniently forgot.

He had not, however, actually lost his sense of the real situation and took it as a matter of course that he and his cage should be stationed, not in the middle of the ring as a main attraction, but outside, near the animal cages, on a site that was after all easily accessible. Large and gaily painted placards made a frame for the cage and announced what was to be seen inside it. When the public came thronging out in the intervals to see the animals, they could hardly avoid passing the hunger artist's cage and stopping there for a moment, perhaps they might even have stayed longer had not those pressing behind them in the narrow gangway, who did not understand why they should be held up on their way toward the excitements of the menagerie, made it impossible for anyone to stand gazing quietly for any length of time. And that was the reason why the hunger artist, who had of course been looking forward to these visiting hours as the main achievement of his life, began instead to shrink from them. At first he could hardly wait for the intervals; it was exhilarating to watch the crowds come streaming his way, until only too soon—not even the most obstinate self-deception, clung to almost consciously, could hold out against the fact—the conviction was borne in upon him that these people, most of them, to judge from their actions, again and again, without exception, were all on their way to the menagerie. And the first sight of them from the distance remained the best. For when they reached his cage he was at once deafened by the storm of shouting and abuse that arose from the two contending factions, which renewed themselves continuously, of those who wanted to stop and stare at him—he soon began to dislike them more than the others—not out of real interest but only out of obstinate self-assertiveness, and those who wanted to go straight on to the animals. When the first great rush was past, the stragglers came along, and these, whom nothing could have prevented from stopping to look at him as long as they had breath, raced past with long strides, hardly even glancing at him, in their haste to get to the menagerie in time. And all too rarely did it happen that he had a stroke of luck, when some father of a family fetched up before him with his children, pointed a finger at the hunger artist, and explained at length what the phenomenon meant, telling stories of earlier years when he himself had watched similar but much more thrilling performances, and the children, still rather uncomprehending, since neither inside nor outside school had they been sufficiently prepared for this lesson—what did they care about fasting?—yet showed by the brightness of their intent eyes that new and better times might be coming. Perhaps, said the hunger artist to himself many a time, things would be a little better if his cage were set not quite so near the menagerie. That made it too easy for people to make their choice, to say nothing of what he suffered from the stench of the menagerie, the animals' restlessness by night, the carrying past of raw lumps of flesh for the beasts of prey, the roaring at feeding times, which depressed him continually. But he did not dare to lodge a complaint with the management; after all, he had the animals to thank for the troops of people who passed his cage, among whom there might always be one here and there to take an interest in him, and who could tell where they might seclude him if he called attention to his existence and thereby to the fact that, strictly speaking, he was only an impediment on the way to the menagerie.

A small impediment, to be sure, one that grew steadily less. People grew familiar with the strange idea that they could be expected, in times like these, to take an interest in a hunger artist, and with this familiarity the verdict went out against him. He might fast as much as he could, and he did so; but nothing could save him now, people passed him by. Just try to explain to anyone the art of fasting! Anyone who has no feeling for it cannot be made to understand it. The fine placards grew dirty and illegible, they were torn down; the little notice board telling the number of fast days achieved, which at first was changed carefully every day, had long stayed at the same figure, for after the first few weeks even this small task seemed pointless to the staff; and so the artist simply fasted on and on, as he had once dreamed of doing, and it was no trouble to him, just as he had always foretold, but no one counted the days, no one, not even the artist himself, knew what records he was already breaking, and his heart grew heavy. And when once in a while some leisurely passer-by stopped, made merry over the old figure on the board, and spoke of swindling, that was in its way the stupidest lie ever invented by indifference and inborn malice, since it was not the hunger artist who was cheating, he was working honestly, but the world was cheating him of his reward.

Many more days went by, however, and that too came to an end. An overseer's eye fell on the cage one day and he asked the attendants why this perfectly good cage should be left standing there unused with dirty straw inside it; nobody knew, until one man, helped out by the notice board, remembered about the hunger artist. They poked into the straw with sticks and found him in it. "Are you still fasting?" asked the overseer, "when on earth do you mean to stop?" "Forgive me, everybody," whispered the hunger artist; only the overseer, who had his ear to the bars, understood him. "Of course," said the overseer, and tapped his forehead with a finger to let the attendants know what state the man was in, "we forgive you." "I always wanted you to admire my fasting," said the hunger artist. "We do admire it," said the overseer, affably. "But you shouldn't admire it," said the hunger artist. "Well then we don't admire it," said the overseer, "but why shouldn't we admire it?" "Because I have to fast, I can't help it," said the hunger artist. "What a fellow you are," said the overseer, "and why can't you help it?" "Because," said the hunger artist, lifting his head a little and speaking, with his lips pursed, as if for a kiss, right into the overseer's ear, so that no syllable might be lost, "because I couldn't find the food I liked. If I had found it, believe me, I should have made no fuss and stuffed myself like you or anyone else." These were his last words, but in his dimming eyes remained the firm though no longer proud persuasion that he was still continuing to fast.

"Well, clear this out now!" said the overseer, and they buried the hunger artist, straw and all. Into the cage they put a young panther. Even the most insensitive felt it refreshing to see this wild creature leaping around the cage that had so long been dreary. The panther was all right. The food he liked was brought him without hesitation by the attendants; he seemed not even to miss his freedom; his noble body, furnished almost to the bursting point with all that it needed, seemed to carry freedom around with it too; somewhere in his jaws it seemed to lurk; and the joy of life streamed with such ardent passion from his throat that for the onlookers it was not easy to stand the shock of it. But they braced themselves, crowded around the cage, and did not want ever to move away.

Translated by Willa and Edwin Muir

Questions for Discussion

1. Draw a parallel between the hunger artist and certain performers today who attract attention by means of unusual, even perverse, "art."

2. Where and when does the story take place?

3. Describe the narrative voice in this story. What is the narrator's attitude toward the hunger artist?

4. In the hunger artist has Kafka created a symbol of certain kinds of human behavior? What does the hunger artist represent?

Suggestions for Writing

1. Write an essay in which you interpret the hunger artist as a symbolic figure.

2. "The situation in Kafka's story is unbelievable, absurd, and silly because there are no 'hunger artists.' " In your journal, defend Kafka's story from this charge.

3. Write an essay in which you compare and contrast Bartleby and the hunger artist.

A Rose for Emily

WILLIAM FAULKNER

1

When Miss Emily Grierson died, our whole town went to her funeral: the men through a sort of respectful affection for a fallen monument, the women mostly out of curiosity to see the inside of her house, which no one save an old manservant—a combined gardener and cook—had seen in at least ten years.

It was a big, squarish frame house that had once been white, decorated with cupolas and spires and scrolled balconies in the heavily lightsome style of the seventies, set on what had once been our most select street. But garages and cotton gins had encroached and obliterated even the august names of that neighborhood; only Miss Emily's house was left, lifting its stubborn and coquettish decay above the cotton wagons and the gasoline pumps—an eyesore among eyesores. And now Miss Emily had gone to join the representatives of those august names where they lay in the cedar-bemused cemetery among the ranked and anonymous graves of Union and Confederate soldiers who fell at the battle of Jefferson.

Alive, Miss Emily had been a tradition, a duty, and a care; a sort of hereditary obligation upon the town, dating from that day in 1894 when Colonel Sartoris, the mayor—he who fathered the edict that no Negro woman should appear on the streets without an apron—remitted her taxes, the dispensation dating from the death of her father on into perpetuity. Not that Miss Emily would have accepted charity. Colonel Sartoris invented an involved tale to the effect that Miss Emily's father had loaned money to the town, which the town, as a matter of business, preferred this way of repaying. Only a man of Colonel Sartoris' generation and thought could have invented it, and only a woman could have believed it.

When the next generation, with its more modern ideas, became mayors and aldermen, this arrangement created some little dissatisfaction. On the first of the year they mailed her a tax notice. February came, and there was no reply. They wrote her a formal letter, asking her to call at the sheriff's office at her convenience. A week later the mayor wrote her himself, offering to call or to send his car for her, and received in reply a note on paper of an archaic shape, in a thin, flowing calligraphy in faded ink, to the effect that she no longer went out at all. The tax notice was also enclosed, without comment.

They called a special meeting of the Board of Aldermen. A deputation waited upon her, knocked at the door through which no visitor had passed since she ceased giving china-painting lessons eight or ten years earlier. They were admitted by the old Negro into a dim hall from which a stairway mounted into still more shadow. It smelled of dust and disuse—a close, dank smell. The Negro led them into the parlor. It was furnished in heavy, leather-covered furniture. When the Negro opened the blinds of one window, they could see that the leather was cracked; and when they sat down, a faint dust rose sluggishly about their thighs, spinning with slow motions in the single sunray. On a tarnished gilt easel before the fireplace stood a crayon portrait of Miss Emily's father.

They rose when she entered—a small, fat woman in black, with a thin gold chain descending to her waist and vanishing into her belt, leaning on an ebony cane with a tarnished gold head. Her skeleton was small and spare; perhaps that was why what would have been merely plumpness in another was obesity in her. She looked bloated, like a body long submerged in motionless water, and of that pallid hue. Her eyes, lost in the fatty ridges of her face, looked like two small pieces of coal pressed into a lump of dough as they moved from one face to another while the visitors stated their errand.

She did not ask them to sit. She just stood in the door and listened quietly until the spokesman came to a stumbling halt. Then they could hear the invisible watch ticking at the end of the gold chain.

Her voice was dry and cold. "I have no taxes in Jefferson. Colonel Sartoris explained it to me. Perhaps one of you can gain access to the city records and satisfy yourselves."

"But we have. We are the city authorities, Miss Emily. Didn't you get a notice from the sheriff, signed by him?"

"I received a paper, yes," Miss Emily said. "Perhaps he considers himself the sheriff . . . I have no taxes in Jefferson."

"But there is nothing on the books to show that, you see. We must go by the—"

"See Colonel Sartoris." (Colonel Sartoris had been dead almost ten years.) "I have no taxes in Jefferson. Tobe!" The Negro appeared. "Show these gentlemen out."

2

So she vanquished them, horse and foot, just as she had vanquished their fathers thirty years before about the smell. That was two years after her father's death and a short time after her sweetheart—the one we believed would marry her—had deserted her. After her father's death she went out very little; after her sweetheart went away, people hardly saw her at all. A few of the ladies had the temerity to call, but were not received, and the only sign of life about the place was the Negro man—a young man then—going in and out with a market basket.

"Just as if a man—any man—could keep a kitchen properly," the ladies said; so they were not surprised when the smell developed. It was another link between the gross, teeming world and the high and mighty Griersons.

A neighbor, a woman, complained to the mayor, Judge Stevens, eighty years old.

"But what will you have me do about it, madam?" he said.

"Why, send her word to stop it," the woman said. "Isn't there a law?"

"I'm sure that won't be necessary," Judge Stevens said. "It's probably just a snake or a rat that nigger of hers killed in the yard. I'll speak to him about it."

The next day he received two more complaints, one from a man who came in diffident deprecation. "We really must do something about it, Judge. I'd be the last one in the world to bother Miss Emily, but we've got to do something." That night the Board of Aldermen met—three graybeards and one younger man, a member of the rising generation.

"It's simple enough," he said. "Send her word to have her place cleaned up. Give her a certain time to do it in, and if she don't . . ."

"Dammit, sir," Judge Stevens said, "will you accuse a lady to her face of smelling bad?"

So the next night, after midnight, four men crossed Miss Emily's lawn and slunk about the house like burglars, sniffing along the base of the brickwork and at the cellar openings while one of them performed a regular sowing motion with his hand out of a sack slung from his shoulder. They broke open the cellar door and sprinkled lime there, and in all the outbuildings. As they recrossed the lawn, a window that had been dark was lighted and Miss Emily sat in it, the light behind her, and her upright torso motionless as that of an idol. They crept quietly across the lawn and into the shadow of the locusts that lined the street. After a week or two the smell went away.

That was when people had begun to feel really sorry for her. People in our town, remembering how old lady Wyatt, her great-aunt, had gone completely crazy at last, believed that the Griersons held themselves a little too high for what they really were. None of the young men were quite good enough for Miss Emily and such. We had long thought of them as a tableau, Miss Emily a slender figure in white in the background, her father a spraddled silhouette in the foreground, his back to her and clutching a horsewhip, the two of them framed by the back-flung front door. So when she got to be thirty and was still single, we were not pleased exactly, but vindicated; even with insanity in the family she wouldn't have turned down all of her chances if they had really materialized.

When her father died, it got about that the house was all that was left to her; and in a way, people were glad. At last they could pity Miss Emily. Being left alone, and a pauper, she had become humanized. Now she too would know the old thrill and the old despair of a penny more or less.

The day after his death all the ladies prepared to call at the house and offer condolence and aid, as is our custom. Miss Emily met them at the door, dressed as usual and with no trace of grief on her face. She told them that her father was not dead. She did that for three days, with the ministers calling on her, and the doctors, trying to persuade her to let them dispose of the body. Just as they were about to resort to law and force, she broke down, and they buried her father quickly.

We did not say she was crazy then. We believed she had to do that. We remembered all the young men her father had driven away, and we knew that with nothing left, she would have to cling to that which had robbed her, as people will.

3

She was sick for a long time. When we saw her again, her hair was cut short, making her look like a girl, with a vague resemblance to those angels in colored church windows—sort of tragic and serene.

The town had just let the contracts for paving the sidewalks, and in the summer after her father's death they began the work. The construction company came with niggers and mules and machinery, and a foreman named Homer Barron, a Yankee—a big, dark, ready man, with a big voice and eyes lighter than his face. The little boys would follow in groups to hear him cuss the niggers, and the niggers singing in time to the rise and fall of picks. Pretty soon he knew everybody in town. Whenever you heard a lot of laughing anywhere about the square, Homer Barron would be in the center of the group. Presently we began to see him and Miss Emily on Sunday afternoons driving in the yellow-wheeled buggy and the matched team of bays from the livery stable.

At first we were glad that Miss Emily would have an interest, because the ladies all said, "Of course a Grierson would not think seriously of a Northerner, a day laborer." But there were still others, older people, who said that even grief could not cause a real lady to forget *noblesse oblige*—without calling it *noblesse oblige*. They just said, "Poor Emily. Her kinsfolk should come to her." She had some kin in Alabama; but years ago her father had fallen out with them over the estate of old lady Wyatt, the crazy woman, and there was no communication between the two families. They had not even been represented at the funeral.

And as soon as the old people said, "Poor Emily," the whispering began. "Do you suppose it's really so?" they said to one another. "Of course it is. What else could . . ." This behind their hands; rustling of craned silk and satin behind jalousies closed upon the sun of Sunday afternoon as the thin, swift clop-clop-clop of the matched team passed: "Poor Emily."

She carried her head high enough—even when we believed that she was fallen. It was as if she demanded more than ever the recognition of her dignity as the last Grierson; as if it had wanted that touch of earthiness to reaffirm her imperviousness. Like when she bought the rat poison, the arsenic. That was over a year after they had begun to say "Poor Emily," and while the two female cousins were visiting her.

"I want some poison," she said to the druggist. She was over thirty then, still a slight woman, though thinner than usual, with cold, haughty black eyes in a face the flesh of which was strained across the temples and about the eye-sockets as you imagine a lighthouse-keeper's face ought to look. "I want some poison," she said.

"Yes, Miss Emily. What kind? For rats and such? I'd recom—"

"I want the best you have. I don't care what kind."

The druggist named several. "They'll kill anything up to an elephant. But what you want is—"

"Arsenic," Miss Emily said. "Is that a good one?"

"Is . . . arsenic? Yes, ma'am. But what you want—"

"I want arsenic."

The druggist looked down at her. She looked back at him, erect, her face like a strained flag. "Why, of course," the druggist said. "If that's what you want. But the law requires you to tell what you are going to use it for."

Miss Emily just stared at him, her head tilted back in order to look him eye for eye, until he looked away and went and got the arsenic and wrapped it up. The Negro delivery boy brought her the package; the druggist didn't come back. When she opened the package at home there was written on the box, under the skull and bones: "For rats."

4

So the next day we all said, "She will kill herself"; and we said it would be the best thing. When she had first begun to be seen with Homer Barron, we had said, "She will marry him." Then we said, "She will persuade him yet," because Homer himself had remarked—he liked men, and it was known that he drank with the younger men in the Elks' Club—that he was not a marrying man. Later we said, "Poor Emily" behind the jalousies as they passed on Sunday afternoon in the glittering buggy, Miss Emily with her head high and Homer Barron with his hat cocked and a cigar in his teeth, reins and whip in a yellow glove.

Then some of the ladies began to say that it was a disgrace to the town and a bad example to the young people. The men did not want to interfere, but at last the ladies forced the Baptist minister—Miss Emily's people were Episcopal—to call upon her. He would never divulge what happened during that interview, but he refused to go back again. The next Sunday they again drove about the streets, and the following day the minister's wife wrote to Miss Emily's relations in Alabama.

So she had blood-kin under her roof again and we sat back to watch developments. At first nothing happened. Then we were sure that they were to be married. We learned that Miss Emily had been to the jeweler's and ordered a man's toilet set in silver, with the letters H. B. on each piece. Two days later we learned that she had bought a complete outfit of men's clothing, including a nightshirt, and we said, "They are married." We were really glad. We were glad because the two female cousins were even more Grierson than Miss Emily had ever been.

So we were not surprised when Homer Barron—the streets had been finished some time since—was gone. We were a little disappointed that there was not a public blowing-off, but we believed that he had gone on to prepare for Miss Emily's coming, or to give her a chance to get rid of the cousins. (By that time it was a cabal, and we were all Miss Emily's allies to help circumvent the cousins.) Sure enough, after another week they departed. And, as we had expected all along, within three days Homer Barron was back in town. A neighbor saw the Negro man admit him at the kitchen door at dusk one evening.

And that was the last we saw of Homer Barron. And of Miss Emily for some time. The Negro man went in and out with the market basket, but the front door remained closed. Now and then we would see her at a window for a moment, as the men did that night when they sprinkled the lime, but for almost six months she did not appear on the streets. Then we knew that this was to be expected too; as if that quality of her father which had thwarted her woman's life so many times had been too virulent and too furious to die.

When we next saw Miss Emily, she had grown fat and her hair was turning gray. During the next few years it grew grayer and grayer until it attained an even pepper-and-salt iron-gray, when it ceased turning. Up to the day of her death at seventy-four it was still that vigorous iron-gray, like the hair of an active man.

From that time on her front door remained closed, save for a period of six or seven years, when she was about forty, during which she gave lessons in china-painting. She fitted up a studio in one of the downstairs rooms, where the daughters and granddaughters of Colonel Sartoris' contemporaries were sent to her with the same regularity and in the same spirit that they were sent to church on Sundays with a twenty-five-cent piece for the collection plate. Meanwhile her taxes had been remitted.

Then the newer generation became the backbone and the spirit of the town, and the painting pupils grew up and fell away and did not send their children to her with boxes of color and tedious brushes and pictures cut from the ladies' magazines. The front door closed upon the last one and remained closed for good. When the town got free postal delivery, Miss Emily alone refused to let them fasten the metal numbers above her door and attach a mailbox to it. She would not listen to them.

Daily, monthly, yearly we watched the Negro grow grayer and more stooped, going in and out with the market basket. Each December we sent her a tax notice, which would be returned by the post office a week later, unclaimed. Now and then we would see her in one of the downstairs windows—she had evidently shut up the top floor of the house—like the carven torso of an idol in a niche, looking or not looking at us, we could never tell which. Thus she passed from generation to generation—dear, inescapable, impervious, tranquil, and perverse.

And so she died. Fell ill in the house filled with dust and shadows, with only a doddering Negro man to wait on her. We did not even know she was sick; we had long since given up trying to get any information from the Negro. He talked to no one, probably not even to her, for his voice had grown harsh and rusty, as if from disuse.

She died in one of the downstairs rooms, in a heavy walnut bed with a curtain, her gray head propped on a pillow yellow and moldy with age and lack of sunlight.

5

The Negro met the first of the ladies at the front door and let them in, with their hushed, sibilant voices and their quick, curious glances, and then he disappeared. He walked right through the house and out the back and was not seen again.

The two female cousins came at once. They held the funeral on the second day, with the town coming to look at Miss Emily beneath a mass of bought flowers, with the crayon face of her father musing profoundly above the bier and the ladies sibilant and macabre; and the very old men—some in their brushed Confederate uniforms—on the porch and the lawn, talking of Miss Emily as if she had been a contemporary of theirs, believing that they had danced with her and courted her perhaps, confusing time with its mathematical progression, as the old do, to whom all the past is not a diminishing road but, instead, a huge meadow which no winter ever quite touches, divided from them now by the narrow bottle-neck of the most recent decade of years.

Already we knew that there was one room in that region above stairs which no one had seen in forty years, and which would have to be forced. They waited until Miss Emily was decently in the ground before they opened it.

The violence of breaking down the door seemed to fill this room with pervading dust. A thin, acrid pall as of the tomb seemed to lie everywhere upon this room decked and furnished as for a bridal: upon the valance curtains of faded rose color, upon the rose-shaded lights, upon the dressing table, upon the delicate array of crystal and the man's toilet things backed with tarnished silver, silver so tarnished that the monogram was obscured. Among them lay a collar and tie, as if they had just been removed, which, lifted, left upon the surface a pale crescent in the dust. Upon a chair hung the suit, carefully folded; beneath it the two mute shoes and the discarded socks.

The man himself lay in the bed.

For a long while we just stood there, looking down at the profound and fleshless grin. The body had apparently once lain in the attitude of an embrace, but now the long sleep that outlasts love, that conquers even the grimace of love, had cuckolded him. What was left of him, rotted beneath what was left of the nightshirt, had become inextricable from the bed in which he lay; and upon him and upon the pillow beside him lay that even coating of the patient and biding dust.

Then we noticed that in the second pillow was the indentation of a head. One of us lifted something from it, and leaning forward, that faint and invisible dust dry and acrid in the nostrils, we saw a long strand of iron-gray hair.

Questions for Discussion

1. Who narrates the story? What is the effect of this narrative voice?

2. Identify and assess the figurative language (metaphors, similes, figurative verbs, possible symbols) in the story's first section. Find as many examples of this language as you can, and look for "buried" metaphors as well as obvious ones.

3. What does the description about the neighborhood and the house tell us about how the South has changed?

4. Describe Homer Barron. What qualities of his attract Emily? What qualities of his represent a culture much different from hers?

5. Interpret Miss Emily as a symbolic character. What larger issues and events does she represent?

Suggestions for Writing

1. Write an essay that interprets Emily and Homer as symbolic characters.

2. Write a journal or notebook entry about the use of the "we" narration and the effects it creates.

3. If you were filming "A Rose for Emily," how would you film the opening moments of the movie? How would you get across the sense of the "we" narration? Write in your notebook about these questions.

4. Write a story that makes symbolic use of a house and/or a neighborhood.

Guests of the Nation

FRANK O'CONNOR

1

At dusk the big Englishman, Belcher, would shift his long legs out of the ashes and say "Well, chums, what about it?" and Noble or me would say "All right, chum" (for we had picked up some of their curious expressions), and the little Englishman, Hawkins', would light the lamp and bring out the cards. Sometimes Jeremiah Donovan would come up and supervise the game and get excited over Hawkins's cards, which he always played badly, and shout at him as if he was one of our own, "Ah, you divil, you, why didn't you play the tray?"

But ordinarily Jeremiah was a sober and contented poor devil like the big Englishman, Belcher, and was looked up to only because he was a fair hand at documents, though he was slow enough even with them. He wore a small cloth hat and big gaiters over his long pants, and you seldom saw him with his hands out of his pockets. He reddened when you talked to him, tilting from toe to heel and back, and looking down all the time at his big farmer's feet. Noble and me used to make fun of his broad accent, because we were from the town.

I couldn't at the time see the point of me and Noble guarding Belcher and Hawkins at all, for it was my belief that you could have planted that pair down anywhere from this to Claregalway and they'd have taken root there like a native weed. I never in my short experience seen two men to take to the country as they did.

They were handed on to us by the Second Battalion when the search for them became too hot, and Noble and myself, being young, took over with a natural feeling of responsibility, but Hawkins made us look like fools when he showed that he knew the country better than we did.

"You're the bloke they calls Bonaparte," he says to me. "Mary Brigid O'Connell told me to ask you what you done with the pair of her brother's socks you borrowed."

For it seemed, as they explained it, that the Second used to have little evenings, and some of the girls of the neighborhood turned in, and, seeing they were such decent chaps, our fellows couldn't leave the two Englishmen out of them. Hawkins learned to dance "The Walls of Limerick," "The Siege of Ennis," and "The Waves of Tory" as well as any of them, though, naturally, we couldn't return the compliment, because our lads at that time did not dance foreign dances on principle.

So whatever privileges Belcher and Hawkins had with the Second they just naturally took with us, and after the first day or two we gave up all pretense of keeping a close eye on them. Not that they could have got far, for they had accents you could cut with a knife and wore khaki tunics and overcoats with civilian pants and boots. But it's my belief that they never had any idea of escaping and were quite content to be where they were.

It was a treat to see how Belcher got off with the old woman of the house where we were staying. She was a great warrant to scold, and cranky even with us, but before ever she had a chance of giving our guests, as I may call them, a lick of her tongue, Belcher had made her his friend for life. She was breaking sticks, and Belcher, who hadn't been more than ten minutes in the house, jumped up from his seat and went over to her.

"Allow me, madam," he says, smiling his queer little smile, "please allow me"; and he takes the bloody hatchet. She was struck too paralytic to speak, and after that, Belcher would be at her heels, carrying a bucket, a basket, or a load of turf, as the case might be. As Noble said, he got into looking before she leapt, and hot water, or any little thing she wanted, Belcher would have it ready for her. For such a huge man (and though I am five foot ten myself I had to look up at him) he had an uncommon shortness—or should I say lack?—of speech. It took us some time to get used to him, walking in and out, like a ghost, without a word. Especially because Hawkins talked enough for a platoon, it was strange to hear big Belcher with his toes in the ashes come out with a solitary "Excuse me, chum," or "That's right, chum." His one and only passion was cards, and I will say for him that he was a good cardplayer. He could have fleeced myself and Noble, but whatever we lost to him Hawkins lost to us, and Hawkins played with the money Belcher gave him.

Hawkins lost to us because he had too much old gab, and we probably lost to Belcher for the same reason. Hawkins and Noble would spit at one another about religion into the early hours of the morning, and Hawkins worried the soul out of Noble, whose brother was a priest, with a string of questions that would puzzle a cardinal. To make it worse, even in treating of holy subjects, Hawkins had a deplorable tongue. I never in all my career met a man who could mix such a variety of cursing and bad language into an argument. He was a terrible man, and a fright to argue. He never did a stroke of work, and when he had no one else to talk to, he got stuck in the old woman.

He met his match in her, for one day when he tried to get her to complain profanely of the drought, she gave him a great come-down by blaming it entirely on Jupiter Pluvius (a deity neither Hawkins nor I had ever heard of, though Noble said that among the pagans it was believed that he had something to do with the rain). Another day he was swearing at the capitalists for starting the German war when the old lady laid down her iron, puckered up her little crab's mouth, and said: "Mr. Hawkins, you can say what you like about the war, and think you'll deceive me because I'm only a simple poor countrywoman, but I know what started the war. It was the Italian Count that stole the heathen divinity out of the temple in Japan. Believe me, Mr. Hawkins, nothing but sorrow and want can follow the people that disturb the hidden powers."

A queer old girl, all right.

2

We had our tea one evening, and Hawkins lit the lamp and we all sat into cards. Jeremiah Donovan came in too, and sat down and watched us for a while, and it suddenly struck me that he had no great love for the two Englishmen. It came as a great surprise to me, because I hadn't noticed anything about him before.

Late in the evening a really terrible argument blew up between Hawkins and Noble, about capitalists and priests and love of your country.

"The capitalists," says Hawkins with an angry gulp, "pay the priests to tell you about the next world so you won't notice what the bastards are up to in this."

"Nonsense, man!" says Noble, losing his temper. "Before ever a capitalist was thought of, people believed in the next world."

Hawkins stood up as though he was preaching a sermon.

"Oh, they did, did they?" he says with a sneer. "They believed all the things you believe, isn't that what you mean? And you believe that God created Adam, and Adam created Shem, and Shem created Jehoshaphat. You believe all that silly old fairytale about Eve and Eden and the apple. Well, listen to me, chum. If you're entitled to hold a silly belief like that, I'm entitled to hold my silly belief—which is that the first thing your God created was a bleeding capitalist, with morality and Rolls-Royce complete. Am I right, chum?" he says to Belcher.

"You're right, chum," says Belcher with his amused smile, and got up from the table to stretch his long legs into the fire and stroke his moustache. So, seeing that Jeremiah Donovan was going, and that there was no knowing when the argument about religion would be over, I went out with him. We strolled down to the village together, and then he stopped and started blushing and mumbling and saying I ought to be behind, keeping guard on the prisoners. I didn't like the tone he took with me, and anyway I was bored with life in the cottage, so I replied by asking him what the hell he wanted guarding them at all for. I told him I'd talked it over with Noble, and that we'd both rather be out with a fighting column.

"What use are those fellows to us?" says I.

He looked at me in surprise and said: "I thought you knew we were keeping them as hostages."

"Hostages?" I said.

"The enemy have prisoners belonging to us," he says, "and now they're talking of shooting them. If they shoot our prisoners, we'll shoot theirs."

"Shoot them?" I said.

"What else did you think we were keeping them for?" he says.

"Wasn't it very unforeseen of you not to warn Noble and myself of that in the beginning?" I said.

"How was it?" says he. "You might have known it."

"We couldn't know it, Jeremiah Donovan," says I. "How could we when they were on our hands so long?"

"The enemy have our prisoners as long and longer," says he.

"That's not the same thing at all," says I.

"What difference is there?" says he.

I couldn't tell him, because I knew he wouldn't understand. If it was only an old dog that was going to the vet's, you'd try and not get too fond of him, but Jeremiah Donovan wasn't a man that would ever be in danger of that.

"And when is this thing going to be decided?" says I.

"We might hear tonight," he says. "Or tomorrow or the next day at latest. So if it's only hanging round here that's a trouble to you, you'll be free soon enough."

It wasn't the hanging round that was a trouble to me at all by this time. I had worse things to worry about. When I got back to the cottage the argument was still on. Hawkins was holding forth in his best style, maintaining that there was no next world, and Noble as maintaining that there was; but I could see that Hawkins had had the best of it.

"Do you know what, chum?" he was saying with a saucy smile. "I think you're just as big a bleeding unbeliever as I am. You say you believe in the next world, and you know just as much about the next world as I do, which is sweet damn-all. What's heaven? You don't know. Where's heaven? You don't know. You know sweet damn-all! I ask you again, do they wear wings?"

"Very well, then," says Noble, "they do. Is that enough for you? They do wear wings."

"Where do they get them, then? Who makes them? Have they a factory for wings? Have they a sort of store where you hands in your chit and takes your bleeding wings?"

"You're an impossible man to argue with," says Noble. "Now, listen to me—" And they were off again.

It was long after midnight when we locked up and went to bed. As I blew out the candle I told Noble what Jeremiah Donovan was after telling me. Noble took it very quietly. When we'd been in bed about an hour he asked me did I think we ought to tell the Englishmen. I didn't think we should, because it was more than likely that the English wouldn't shoot our men, and even if they did, the brigade officers, who were always up and down with the Second Battalion and knew the Englishmen well, wouldn't be likely to want them plugged. "I think so too," says Noble. "It would be great cruelty to put the wind up them now."

"It was very unforeseen of Jeremiah Donovan anyhow," says I.

It was next morning that we found it so hard to face Belcher and Hawkins. We went about the house all day scarcely saying a word. Belcher didn't seem to notice; he was stretched into the ashes as usual, with his usual look of waiting in quietness for something unforeseen to happen, but Hawkins noticed and put it down to Noble's being beaten in the argument of the night before.

"Why can't you take a discussion in the proper spirit?" he says severely. "You and your Adam and Eve! I'm a Communist, that's what I am. Communist or anarchist, it all comes to much the same thing." And for hours he went round the house, muttering when the fit took him. "Adam and Eve! Adam and Eve! Nothing better to do with their time than picking bleeding apples!"

3

I don't know how we got through that day, but I was very glad when it was over, the tea things were cleared away, and Belcher said in his peaceable way:

"Well, chums, what about it?" We sat round the table and Hawkins took out the cards, and just then I heard Jeremiah Donovan's footstep on the path and a dark presentiment crossed my mind. I rose from the table and caught him before he reached the door.

"What do you want?" I asked.

"I want those two soldier friends of yours," he says, getting red.

"Is that the way, Jeremiah Donovan?" I asked.

"That's the way. There were four of our lads shot this morning, one of them a boy of sixteen."

"That's bad," I said.

At that moment Noble followed me out, and the three of us walked down the path together, talking in whispers. Feeney, the local intelligence officer, was standing by the gate.

"What are you going to do about it?" I asked Jeremiah Donovan.

"I want you and Noble to get them out; tell them they're being shifted again; that'll be the quietest way."

"Leave me out of that," says Noble under his breath.

Jeremiah Donovan looks at him hard.

"All right," he says. "You and Feeney get a few tools from the shed and dig a hole by the far end of the bog. Bonaparte and myself will be after you. Don't let anyone see you with the tools. I wouldn't like it to go beyond ourselves."

We saw Feeney and Noble go round to the shed and went in ourselves. I left Jeremiah Donovan to do the explanations. He told them that he had orders to send them back to the Second Batallion. Hawkins let out a mouthful of curses, and you could see that though Belcher didn't say anything, he was a bit upset too. The old woman was for having them stay in spite of us, and she didn't stop advising them until Jeremiah Donovan lost his temper and turned on her. He had a nasty temper, I noticed. It was pitch-dark in the cottage by this time, but no one thought of lighting the lamp, and in the darkness the two Englishmen fetched their topcoats and said good-bye to the old woman.

"Just as a man makes a home of a bleeding place, some bastard at headquarters thinks you're too cushy and shunts you off," says Hawkins, shaking her hand.

"A thousand thanks, madam," says Belcher. "A thousand thanks for everything"—as though he'd made it up.

"We went round to the back of the house and down towards the bog. It was only then that Jeremiah Donovan told them. He was shaking with excitement.

"There were four of our fellows shot in Cork this morning and now you're to be shot as a reprisal."

"What are you talking about?" snaps Hawkins. "It's bad enough being mucked about as we are without having to put up with your funny jokes."

"It isn't a joke," says Donovan. "I'm sorry, Hawkins, but it's true," and begins on the usual rigmarole about duty and how unpleasant it is.

I never noticed that people who talk a lot about duty find it much of a trouble to them.

"Oh, cut it out!" says Hawkins.

"Ask Bonaparte," says Donovan, seeing that Hawkins isn't taking him seriously. "Isn't it true, Bonaparte?"

"It is," I say, and Hawkins stops.

"Ah, for Christ's sake, chum."

"I mean it, chum," I say.

"You don't sound as if you mean it."

"If he doesn't mean it, I do," says Donovan, working himself up.

"What have you against me, Jeremiah Donovan?"

"I never said I had anything against you. But why did your people take out four of our prisoners and shoot them in cold blood?"

He took Hawkins by the arm and dragged him on, but it was impossible to make him understand that we were in earnest. I had the Smith and Wesson in my pocket and I kept fingering it and wondering what I'd do if they put up a fight for it or ran, and wishing to God they'd do one or the other. I knew if they did run for it, that I'd never fire on them. Hawkins wanted to know was Noble in it, and when we said yes, he asked why Noble wanted to plug him. Why did any of us want to plug him? What had he done to us? Weren't we all chums? Didn't we understand him and didn't he understand us? Did we imagine for an instant that he'd shoot us for all the so-and-so officers in the so-and-so British Army?

By this time we'd reached the bog, and I was so sick I couldn't even answer him. We walked along the edge of it in the darkness, and every now and then Hawkins would call a halt and begin all over again, as if he was wound up, about our being chums, and I knew that nothing but the sight of the grave would convince him that we had to do it. And all the time I was hoping that something would happen; that they'd run for it or that Noble would take over the responsibility from me. I had the feeling that it was worse on Noble than on me.

4

At last we saw the lantern in the distance and made towards it. Noble was carrying it, and Feeney was standing somewhere in the darkness behind him, and the picture of them so still and silent in the bogland brought it home to me that we were in earnest, and banished the last bit of hope I had.

Belcher, on recognizing Noble, said: "Hallo, chum," in his quiet way, but Hawkins flew at him at once, and the argument began all over again, only this time Noble had nothing to say for himself and stood with his head down, holding the lantern between his legs.

It was Jeremiah Donovan who did the answering. For the twentieth time, as though it was haunting his mind, Hawkins asked if anybody thought he'd shoot Noble.

"Yes, you would," says Jeremiah Donovan.

"No, I wouldn't, damn you!"

"You would, because you'd know you'd be shot for not doing it."

"I wouldn't, not if I was to be shot twenty time over. I wouldn't shoot a pal. And Belcher wouldn't—isn't that right, Belcher?"

"That's right, chum," Belcher said, but more by way of answering the question than of joining in the argument. Belcher sounded as though whatever unforeseen thing he'd always been waiting for had come at last.

"Anyway, who says Noble would be shot if I wasn't? What do you think I'd do if I was in his place, out in the middle of a blasted bog?"

"What would you do?" asks Donovan.

"I'd go with him wherever he was going, of course. Share my last bob with him and stick by him through thick and thin. No one can ever say of me that I let down a pal."

"We had enough of this," says Jeremiah Donovan, cocking his revolver. "Is there any message you want to send?"

"No, there isn't."

"Do you want to say your prayers?"

Hawkins came out with a cold-blooded remark that even shocked me and turned on Noble again.

"Listen to me, Noble," he says. "You and me are chums. You can't come over to my side, so I'll come over to your side. That show you I mean what I say? Give me a rifle and I'll go along with you and the other lads."

Nobody answered him. We knew that was no way out.

"Hear what I'm saying?" he says. "I'm through with it. I'm a deserter or anything else you like. I don't believe in your stuff, but it's no worse than mine. That satisfy you?"

Noble raised his head, but Donovan began to speak and he lowered it again without replying.

"For the last time, have you any messages to send?" says Donovan in a cold, excited sort of voice.

"Shut up, Donovan! You don't understand me, but these lads do. They're not the sort to make a pal and kill a pal. They're not the tools of any capitalist."

I alone of the crowd saw Donovan raise his Webley to the back of Hawkins's neck, and as he did so I shut my eyes and tried to pray. Hawkins had begun to say something else when Donovan fired, and as I opened my eyes at the bang, I saw Hawkins stagger at the knees and lie out flat at Noble's feet, slowly and as quiet as a kid falling asleep, with the lantern-light on his lean legs and bright farmer's boots. We all stood very still, watching him settle out in the last agony.

Then Belcher took out a handkerchief and began to tie it about his own eyes (in our excitement we'd forgotten to do the same for Hawkins), and, seeing it wasn't big enough, turned and asked for the loan of mine. I gave it to him and he knotted the two together and pointed with his foot at Hawkins.

"He's not quite dead," he says. "Better give him another."

Sure enough, Hawkins's left knee is beginning to rise. I bend down and put my gun to his head; then, recollecting myself, I get up again. Belcher understands what's in my mind.

"Give him his first," he says. "I don't mind. Poor bastard, we don't know what's happening to him now."

I knelt and fired. By this time I didn't seem to know what I was doing. Belcher, who was fumbling a bit awkwardly with the handkerchiefs, came out with a laugh as he heard the shot. It was the first time I heard him laugh and it sent a shudder down my back; it sounded so unnatural.

"Poor bugger!" he said quietly. "And last night he was so curious about it all. It's very queer, chums, I always think. Now he knows as much about it as they'll ever let him know, and last night he was all in the dark."

Donovan helped him to tie the handkerchiefs about his eyes. "Thanks, chum," he said. Donovan asked if there were any messages he wanted sent.

"No, chum," he says. "Not for me. If any of you would like to write to Hawkins's mother, you'll find a letter from her in his pocket. He and his mother were great chums. But my missus left me eight years ago. Went away with another fellow and took the kid with her. I like the feeling of a home, as you may have noticed, but I couldn't start again after that."

It was an extraordinary thing, but in those few minutes Belcher said more than in all the weeks before. It was just as if the sound of the shot had started a flood of talk in him and he could go on the whole night like that, quite happily, talking about himself. We stood round like fools now that he couldn't see us any longer. Donovan looked at Noble, and Noble shook his head. Then Donovan raised his Webley, and at that moment Belcher gives his queer laugh again. He may have thought we were talking about him, or perhaps he noticed the same thing I'd noticed and couldn't understand it.

"Excuse me, chums," he says. "I feel I'm talking the hell of a lot, and so silly, about my being so handy about a house and things like that. But this thing came on me suddenly. You'll forgive me, I'm sure."

"You don't want to say a prayer?" asked Donovan.

"No, chum," he says. "I don't think it would help. I'm ready, and you boys want to get it over."

"You understand that we're only doing our duty?" says Donovan.

Belcher's head was raised like a blind man's, so that you could only see his chin and the tip of his nose in the lantern-light.

"I never could make out what duty was myself," he said. "I think you're all good lads, if that's what you mean. I'm not complaining."

Noble, just as if he couldn't bear any more of it, raised his fist at Donovan, and in a flash Donovan raised his gun and fired. The big man went over like a sack of meal, and this time there was no need of a second shot.

I don't remember much about the burying, but that it was worse than all the rest because we had to carry them to the grave. It was all made lonely with nothing but a patch of lantern-light between ourselves and the dark, and birds hooting and screeching all round, disturbed by the guns. Noble went through Hawkins's belongings to find the letter from his mother, and then joined his hands together. He did the same with Belcher. Then, when we'd filled in the grave, we separated from Jeremiah Donovan and Feeney and took our tools back to the shed. All the way we didn't speak a word. The kitchen was dark and cold as we'd left it, and the old woman was sitting over the hearth, saying her beads. We walked past her into the room, and Noble struck a match to light the lamp. She rose quietly and came to the doorway with all her cantankerousness gone.

"What did ye do with them?" she asked in a whisper, and Noble started so that the match went out in his hand.

"What's that?" he asked without turning round.

"I heard ye," she said.

"What did you hear?" asked Noble.

"I heard ye. Do ye think I didn't hear ye, putting the spade back in the houseen?"

Noble struck another match and this time the lamp lit for him.

"Was that what ye did to them?" she asked.

Then, by God, in the very doorway, she fell on her knees and began praying, and after looking at her for a minute or two Noble did the same by the fireplace. I pushed my way out past her and left them at it. I stood at the door, watching the stars and listening to the shrieking of the birds dying out over the bogs. It is so strange what you feel at times like that you can't describe it. Noble says he saw everything ten times the size, as though there were nothing in the whole world but that little patch of bog with the two Englishmen stiffening into it, but with me it was as if the patch of bog where the Englishmen were was a million miles away, and even Noble and the old woman, mumbling behind me, and the birds and the bloody stars were all far away, and I was somehow very small and very lost and lonely like a child astray in the snow. And anything that happened to me afterwards, I never felt the same about again.

Questions for Discussion

1. Characterize the relationship between the Irishmen and the Englishmen early in the story. How does the first section establish that relationship?

2. Describe Hawkins and Belcher, the Englishmen. In what ways are they different? In what ways do they react to their executions differently?

3. Describe the narrator's attitude toward duty and his attitude toward those who speak frequently of duty.

4. What role does the old woman play in the story? What is the significance of her remark at the end of section one?

Suggestions for Writing

1. Find a history of modern Ireland and read about the civil war that is the background for O'Connor's story. In your journal summarize the causes of the civil war.

2. Write an essay about O'Connor's story in which you assess the narrator's attitude toward duty in general and his attitude toward his particular duty in the story.

War

LUIGI PIRANDELLO

The passengers who had left Rome by the night express had had to stop until dawn at the small station of Fabriano in order to continue their journey by the small old-fashioned local joining the main line with Sulmona.

At dawn, in a stuffy and smoky second-class carriage in which five people had already spent the night, a bulky woman in deep mourning was hoisted in—almost like a shapeless bundle. Behind her—puffing and moaning, followed her husband—a tiny man, thin and weakly, his face death-white, his eyes small and bright and looking shy and uneasy.

Having at last taken a seat he politely thanked the passengers who had helped his wife and who had made room for her; then he turned round to the woman trying to pull down the collar of her coat and politely inquired:

"Are you all right, dear?"

The wife, instead of answering, pulled up her collar again to her eyes, so as to hide her face.

"Nasty world," muttered the husband with a sad smile.

And he felt it his duty to explain to his traveling companions that the poor woman was to be pitied for the war was taking away from her her only son, a boy of twenty to whom both had devoted their entire life, even breaking up their home at Sulmona to follow him to Rome, where he had to go as a student, then allowing him to volunteer for war with an assurance, however, that at least for six months he would not be sent to the front and now, all of a sudden, receiving a wire saying that he was due to leave in three days' time and asking them to go and see him off.

The woman under the big coat was twisting and wriggling, at times growling like a wild animal, feeling certain that all those explanations would not have aroused even a shadow of sympathy from those people who—most likely—were in the same plight as herself. One of them, who had been listening with particular attention, said:

"You should thank God that your son is only leaving now for the front. Mine has been sent there the first day of the war. He has already come back twice wounded and been sent back again to the front."

"What about me? I have two sons and three nephews at the front," said another passenger.

"Maybe, but in our case it is our *only* son," ventured the husband.

"What difference can it make? You may spoil your only son with excessive attentions, but you cannot love him more than you would all your other children if you had any. Paternal love is not like bread that can be broken into pieces and split amongst the children in equal shares. A father gives *all* his love to each one of his children without discrimination, whether it be one or ten, and if I am suffering now for my two sons, I am not suffering half for each of them but double . . ."

"True . . . true . . ." sighed the embarrassed husband, "but suppose (of course we all hope it will never be your case) a father has two sons at the front and he loses one of them, there is still one left to console him . . . while . . ."

"Yes," answered the other, getting cross, "a son left to console him but also a son left for whom he must survive, while in the case of the father of an only son if the son dies the father can die too and put an end to his distress. Which of the two positions is the worse? Don't you see how my case would be worse than yours?"

"Nonsense," interrupted another traveler, a fat, red-faced man with bloodshot eyes of the palest gray.

He was panting. From his bulging eyes seemed to spurt inner violence of an uncontrolled vitality which his weakened body could hardly contain.

"Nonsense," he repeated, trying to cover his mouth with his hand so as to hide the two missing front teeth. "Nonsense. Do we give life to our children for our own benefit?"

The other travelers stared at him in distress. The one who had had his son at the front since the first day of the war sighed: "You are right. Our children do not belong to us, they belong to the Country. . . ."

"Bosh," retorted the fat traveler. "Do we think of the Country when we give life to our children? Our sons are born because . . . well, because they must be born and when they come to life they take our own life with them. This is the truth. We belong to them but they never belong to us. And when they reach twenty they are exactly what we were at their age. We too had a father and mother, but there were so many other things as well . . . girls, cigarettes, illusions, new ties . . . and the Country, of course, whose call we would have answered—when we were twenty—even if father and mother had said no. Now, at our age, the love of our Country is still great, of course, but stronger than it is the love for our children. Is there any one of us here who wouldn't gladly take his son's place at the front if he could?"

There was a silence all round, everybody nodding as to approve.

"Why then," continued the fat man, "shouldn't we consider the feelings of our children when they are twenty? Isn't it natural that at their age they should consider the love for their Country (I am speaking of decent boys, of course) even greater than the love for us? Isn't it natural that it should be so, as after all they must look upon us as upon old boys who cannot move any more and must stay at home? If Country exists, if Country is a natural necessity, like bread, of which each of us must eat in order not to die of hunger, somebody must go to defend it. And our sons go, when they are twenty, and they don't want tears, because if they die, they die inflamed and happy (I am speaking, of course, of decent boys). Now, if one dies young and happy, without having the ugly sides of life, the boredom of it, the pettiness, the bitterness of disillusion . . . what more can we ask for him? Everyone should stop crying; everyone should laugh, as I do . . . or at least thank God—as I do—because my son, before dying, sent me a message saying that he was dying satisfied at having ended his life in the best way he could have wished. That is why, as you see, I do not even wear mourning. . . .”

He shook his light fawn coat as to show it; his livid lip over his missing teeth was trembling, his eyes were watery and motionless, and soon after he ended with a shrill laugh which might well have been a sob.

“Quite so . . . quite so . . .” agreed the others.

The woman who, bundled in a corner under her coat, had been sitting and listening had—for the last three months—tried to find in the words of her husband and her friends something to console her in her deep sorrow, something that might show her how a mother should resign herself to send her son not even to death but to a probable danger of life. Yet not a word had she found amongst the many which had been said . . . and her grief had been greater in seeing that nobody—as she thought—could share her feelings.

But now the words of the traveler amazed and almost stunned her. She suddenly realized that it wasn’t the others who were wrong and could not understand her but herself who could not rise up to the same height of those fathers and mothers willing to resign themselves, without crying, not only to the departure of their sons but even to their death.

She lifted her head, she bent over from her corner trying to listen with great attention to the details which the fat man was giving to his companions about the way his son had fallen as a hero, for his King and his Country, happy and without regrets. It seemed to her that she had stumbled into a world she had never dreamt of, a world so far unknown to her and she was so pleased to hear everyone joining in congratulating that brave father who could so stoically speak of his child’s death.

Then suddenly, just as if she had heard nothing of what had been said and almost as if waking up from a dream, she turned to the old man, asking him:

“Then . . . is your son really dead?”

Everybody stared at her. The old man, too, turned to look at her, fixing his great, bulging, horribly watery light gray eyes, deep in her face. For some little time he tried to answer, but words failed him. He looked and looked at her, almost as if only then—at that silly, incongruous question—he had suddenly realized at last that his son was really dead—gone for ever—for ever. His face contracted, became horribly distorted, then he snatched in haste a handkerchief from his pocket and, to the amazement of everyone, broke into harrowing, heart-rending, uncontrollable sobs.

Questions for Discussion

1. What is your reaction to the debate between the travelers about love of children and love of country?

2. List as many images as you can from the story and be able to discuss your view of their importance.

3. In what ways is the ending of the story ironic?

4. What significance (if any) is there to the fact that it is a woman, a mother, who asks the "devastating" question?

Suggestions for Writing

1. Write an essay in which you compare and contrast Pirandello's story with other stories about war, either from this anthology or from other sources.

2. A "short-short story" like Pirandello's places extraordinary demands on a writer. In your journal write about the techniques Pirandello uses to compress the conflict and theme into such a brief piece of fiction.

3. Write a story about war, but write about it only within a context with which you are familiar. That is, if you consider your experience of war distant or indirect or removed, do not try to compensate for that fact; instead, write a story that makes use of such distance and indirection.

4. Write an essay about Pirandello's story that takes into account Italy's role in the Great War. Whose side was Italy on? Why? How many Italians died in the war? Where was "the front" to which the story refers?

The Supper

TADEUSZ BOROWSKI

We waited patiently for the darkness to fall. The sun had already slipped far beyond the hills. Deepening shadows, permeated with the evening mist, lay over the freshly ploughed hillsides and valleys, still covered with occasional patches of dirty snow; but here and there, along the sagging underbelly of the sky, heavy with rain clouds, you could still see a few rose-coloured streaks of sunlight.

A dark, gusty wind, heavy with the smells of the thawing, sour earth, tossed the clouds about and cut through your body like a blade of ice. A solitary piece of tar-board, torn by a stronger gust, rattled monotonously on a rooftop; a dry but penetrating chill was moving in from the fields. In the valley below, wheels clattered against rails and locomotives whined mournfully. Dusk was falling; our hunger was growing more and more terrible; the traffic along the highway had died down almost completely, only now and then the wind would waft a fragment of conversation, a coachman's call, or the occasional rumble of a cow-drawn cart; the cows dragged their hooves lazily along the gravel. The clatter of wooden sandals on the pavement and the guttural laughter of the peasant girls hurrying to a Saturday night dance at the village were slowly fading in the distance.

The darkness thickened at last and a soft rain began to fall. Several bluish lamps, swaying to and fro on top of high lamp-posts, threw a dim light over the black, tangled tree branches reaching out over the road, the shiny sentry-shack roofs, and the empty pavement that glistened like a wet leather strap. The soldiers marched under the circle of lights and then disappeared again in the dark. The sound of their footsteps on the road was coming nearer.

And then the camp Kommandant's driver threw a searchlight beam on a passage between two blockhouses. Twenty Russian soldiers in camp stripes, their arms tied with barbed-wire behind their backs, were being led out of the washroom and driven down the embankment. The Block Elders lined them up along the pavement facing the crowd that had been standing there for many silent hours, motionless, bareheaded, hungry. In the strong glare, the Russians' bodies stood out incredibly clearly. Every fold, bulge or wrinkle in their clothing; the cracked soles in their worn-out boots; the dry lumps of brown clay stuck to the edges of their trousers; the thick seams along their crotches; the white thread showing on the blue stripe of their prison suits; their sagging buttocks; their stiff hands and bloodless fingers twisted in pain, with drops of dry blood at the joints; their swollen wrists where the skin had started turning blue from the rusty wire cutting into the flesh; their naked elbows, pulled back unnaturally and tied with another piece of wire—all this emerged out of the surrounding blackness as if carved in ice. The elongated shadows of the men fell across the road and the barbed-wire fences glittering with tiny drops of water, and were lost on the hillside covered with dry, rustling grasses.

The Kommandant, a greying, sunburned man, who had come from the village especially for the occasion, crossed the lighted area with a tired but firm step and, stopping at the edge of the darkness, decided that the two rows of Russians were indeed a proper distance apart. From then on matters proceeded quickly, though maybe not quite quickly enough for the freezing body and the empty stomach that had been waiting seventeen hours for a pint of soup, still kept hot perhaps in the kettles at the barracks. "This is a serious matter!" cried a very young Camp Elder, stepping out from behind the Kommandant. He had one hand under the lapel of his "custom made," fitted black jacket, and in the other hand he was holding a willow crop which he kept tapping rhythmically against the top of his high boots.

"These men—they are criminals! I reckon I don't have to explain . . . They are Communists! Herr Kommandant says to tell you that they are going to be punished properly, and what the Herr Kommandant says . . . Well boys, I tell you, you too had better be careful, eh?"

"*Los, los,* we have no time to waste," interrupted the Kommandant, turning to an officer in an unbuttoned top-coat. He was leaning against the fender of his small Skoda automobile and slowly removing his gloves.

"This certainly shouldn't take long," said the officer in the unbuttoned top-coat. He snapped his fingers, a smile at the corner of his mouth.

"*Ja,* and tonight the entire camp will go without dinner!" shouted the young Camp Elder. "The Block Elders will carry the soup back to the kitchen and . . . if even one cup is missing, you'll have to answer to me. Understand, boys?"

A long, deep sigh went through the crowd. Slowly, slowly, the rear rows began pushing forward; the crowd near the road grew denser and a pleasant warmth spread along your back from the breath of the men pressing behind you, preparing to jump forward.

The Kommandant gave a signal and out of the darkness emerged a long line of S.S. men with rifles in their hands. They placed themselves neatly behind the Russians, each behind one man. You could no longer tell that they had returned from the labour Kommandos with us. They had had time to eat, to change to fresh, gala uniforms, and even to have a manicure. Their fingers were clenched tightly around their rifle butts and their fingernails looked neat and pink; apparently they were planning to join the local girls at the village dance. They cocked their rifles sharply, leaned the rifle butts on their hips and pressed the muzzles up against the clean-shaven napes of the Russians.

"*Achtung! Bereit, Feuer!*" said the Kommandant without raising his voice. The rifles barked, the soldiers jumped back a step to keep from being splattered by the shattered heads. The Russians seemed to quiver on their feet for an instant and then fell to the ground like heavy sacks, splashing the pavement with blood and scattered chunks of brain. Throwing their rifles over their shoulders, the soldiers marched off quickly. The corpses were dragged temporarily under the fence. The Kommandant and his retinue got into the Skoda; it backed up to the gate, snorting loudly.

No sooner was the greying, sunburned Kommandant out of sight than the silent crowd, pressing forward more and more persistently, burst into a shrieking roar, and fell in an avalanche on the blood-spattered pavement, swarming over it noisily. Then, dispersed by the Block Elders and the barracks chiefs called in for help from the camp, they scattered and disappeared one by one inside the blocks. I had been standing some distance away from the place of execution so I could not reach the road. But the following day, when we were again driven out to work, a "Muslimized" Jew from Estonia who was helping me haul steel bars tried to convince me all day that human brains are, in fact, so tender you can eat them absolutely raw.

Questions for Discussion

1. What does this brief story show us about the German soldiers in charge of the death camps?

2. Describe the attitude of the narrator.

3. What does the story show us about the effects of this existence on the surviving prisoners?

4. What is the value of such a brutal story?

Suggestions for Writing

1. Write about this story in your journal.

2. Read other stories, poems, and books about the Holocaust and write a paper based on your reading. You might consider such authors as Primo Levi, Elie Wiesel, and William Styron. You may also want to view all or parts of the documentary, *Shoah.*

The Black Kimono

AYA KŌDA

Chiyo quivered in the intensity of her resolve, all the resolve of the sixteen-year-old. For the first time she was going out among people as her mother's representative—it was to her uncle's funeral—and she meant to perform all the adult duties that went with being a representative. The resolve growing as she stepped off the streetcar, she marched off toward the temple with her head high and her shoulders back.

She had taken great pains to tone down her clothes. The kimono was much too somber for her age, the stockings were white, strips of black cloth were wound around the thongs of the sandals. But even so the discomfiture of not having a real funeral kimono lay over her spirits like dust. "What does it matter? I'm still in school, after all," she had said, very much the self-sufficient child reared by but one parent, as she threw off her mother's objections and left the house; but now she saw with some uneasiness how badly put together her funeral dress really was.

She stopped short in astonishment at the temple gate. It appeared that an earlier funeral was not yet over. Under awnings along either side of the granite walk stretched white-covered tables, and three gentlemen, at ease in shirt sleeves and striped trousers, were quietly at work on something. At the main hall, straight ahead, three workmen faced this way and that as they worried over a confused mass of real and artificial flowers. The temple under the hot sun of rainless late July, was aloof and undisturbed. It was just after eleven, and the funeral was to begin at two. Chiyo had meant to be there in time to help get ready for the hearse, and it had not occurred to her that there might be another funeral in the morning. She was far too early. What was to be done? And then her eyes fell on a sign under the awning: "Funeral of the Late—." It was not a stranger's funeral after all. It was her uncle's. But would her uncle be having such an elaborate funeral? Chiyo flushed. Her uncle's funeral was several grades above what she had pictured, and she had been wanting imagination.

But what was still more embarrassing was the way the men under the awning stared at her. She reddened by the second. There was a barrier gate to be gone through, however, and she would have to announce herself. Her sandals pattered off in the direction of the three men almost before she knew what was happening. She had quite lost her head.

"It is good of all of you to help us today. My mother should be here, but unfortunately she is not well, and I have come in her place to work in the kitchen or wherever you think I may be of use. And I must ask you to forgive me for not having a funeral kimono." She could feel the perspiration streaming over her face, but she was sure that it would only be worse if she tried to wipe it away. The men stood there stiffly. Chiyo had done her best, and they only fidgeted. They were as embarrassed as she was.

A handsome head bowed into the scene from beside her. "You are most kind. Since it is still a little early, however, suppose you come this way and rest a bit." He had on a cool black summer kimono and a crisp black overskirt. They started around the tables. "Damn!" The carefully composed features collapsed, leaving behind only a very approachable youthfulness. "I forgot to ask your name."

Chiyo was at ease again. "I'm Chiyo from Ushigome."

"Ushigome? Uncle Jirō's?"

"That's right."

"Well, then." He was outraged. "Why did you have to make that speech?"

"It came out just as Mother told me."

"As a matter of fact I had some coaching myself last night. But yours was much better. I was overcome." The young man left her at the door, and, as she took off her sandals it came to her that she had not thought to ask his name.

Presently Sakai, who was married to the oldest daughter of the dead uncle, drove up. Chiyo, all by herself in the big anteroom, had only the formal speech her mother had taught her with which to be polite—she had thought of nothing for herself. Sakai answered with equal formality, however, and she was glad she had made the speech again. The son of a well-to-do provincial family, Sakai had left his father, still sound and healthy, to take care of the family interests, and had come to live and work in Tokyo. He was actually closer to his father-in-law than to his father. He was intelligent, his taste was good, he was efficient in business and honest in his personal relations, and he was easily the most respected of the men who had married into the family—it was he who was noticed beyond all the nephews and nieces. And it was he who would manage the funeral.

"You'll help us, will you, Chiyo? What can you do?"

Chiyo was abashed. She had no skills.

"I think I could take care of serving the tea."

"Fine. We'll put you in charge of the tea." Much relieved, Chiyo went out among the women.

Relatives began arriving well in advance of the funeral, and Chiyo was busy with her tea. Unfortunately, however, most of the tea she poured so carefully went untouched. She would give a cup to a new arrival, and there it would sit. As the guests moved about to exchange greetings, the tea stayed behind. Presently it began to get in the way. Someone would knock a cup over, no one would be sure which was his, it would be left to gather dust. This bothered Chiyo. She was managing things badly. She must do something, and as she studied the problem she came upon the secret of timing. If the timing was skillful, the guest would put the cup to his lips immediately, and now and then someone even returned an empty cup with a word of praise. Chiyo was pleased. Sakai was busier as the guests gathered. He was always speaking to someone or being spoken to by someone, and often he was carrying on as many as three conferences at once. It was to him that all the problems came, and it was from him that the orders went, so constant a stream of them that one had to feel sorry for him. The young man at the gate, evidently awed by Sakai, called him "Uncle" and answered to the name Kō. Sakai, thought Chiyo, probably needed a cup of tea more than anyone else.

"Good," he said with gusto. "Another cup." This was the point, Chiyo saw—to be where you were needed. She felt even brisker.

The hearse arrived at the main hall, and the relatives withdrew to the anteroom. The heat and the confusion flowed over, the excitement engulfed them like a whirlpool. Since even Sakai was in danger of being carried under, the unpracticed Chiyo was of course lost immediately. Quite forgetting that she was at a funeral and should be sad, she concentrated like a lunatic on the one problem of keeping the water hot. She poured tea into empty cups, and she did not notice that in the course of time she had become the center about which the other tea pourers worked.

Presently word came that they were to go into the main hall. Back from the tea department and in her place as a niece of the deceased, Chiyo knelt among all her cousins. The unmarried cousins, as if by arrangement, wore purple kimonos and white obis, and the adults were an elegant wave of black. Well enough prepared by now, Chiyo was untroubled at the inadequacy of her own funeral dress. But for slight misgivings about the dirt on her socks and the perspiration on her face, she was quite comfortable. She could view things calmly, knowing that she had worked well. Flowers and birds painted on the roof panels, a sandalwood canopy and under it the dark altar recess, a cloth of gold over the coffin, the altar platform, heaped baskets of funeral offerings, sometimes a ribbon bearing the name of the giver, tall green branches, two or three on either side . . . and an overflow of flowers and funeral guests. Presently the sadness of the funeral, the sadness of the parting, swept through the room, and the voices of the priests chanting sutras in unison made it more intense. Here and there a low sobbing set off an epidemic of tears. Chiyo, perhaps the most sentimental of all, sat dry-eyed, looking at the floor. The funeral was rather different from what funerals had always been, and, for some reason, it seemed a last affectionate duty to find out why.

Chiyo and Kō stayed to help after the funeral. The strain of those seven or eight hours was beginning to tell, and the night wind was cool as they departed. The one went left and the other right. She had not even learned his family name.

The hundred days of mourning passed, and, in late autumn, there was a letter from Sakai's wife Keiko. She was having a dinner for the people who had been especially helpful at the funeral. All the other guests were members of the Sakai family living in Tokyo—Kō among them, and a woman who had helped Chiyo with the tea. Chiyo saw that the funeral had been managed not by blood relatives of her uncle but rather by Sakai's family. She was introduced again to them all. Kō's name, as she had suspected, was Sakai. He had just finished school and gone to work, and he too had been helping at his first funeral.

"You caught us off guard, though. A face like a judge, and then that speech. I was so surprised that my own speech rolled out before I had time to think." She was just a little annoyed, and she wanted to tell him to stop. And yet she had to smile at the light-hearted exaggeration. "All of those people, and some of them in everyday clothes, and you were the only one who apologized. I'll remember it every time I dress up for a funeral. 'I must ask you to forgive me for not having a funeral kimono.' You were wonderful. As a matter of fact my own clothes were borrowed from my uncle."

"But I said what my mother told me to, and if anyone is wonderful I suppose it must be Mother. I'm sure she'll be pleased to hear how you praised her."

Whether by design or not, Kō had taken it upon himself to make the conversation lively. Chiyo was afraid, since she was his chief subject, that she might find herself listening too carefully to what was after all only amusing. Even an occasional touch of sharpness passed smoothly along in the flow. The *saké* was having its effect, and Kō was soon lost in his burlesque, complete now with inflection and gestures, of Chiyo's performance. At a brisk warning from Sakai, he was suddenly tame—and then almost immediately he was chattering away again, as if to demonstrate that he was perfectly capable of managing his liquor. The table talk, with its touch of vaudeville, was memorable indeed for a girl used to dining alone with her mother. She was happy at her honored place between the host and hostess, and at all the dishes before her, and most especially at the way in which she, the lone outsider, had been taken into the family.

"It's really nothing, Chiyo, but Sakai says I am to give you this to remember the occasion by." The corridor was cold as they went into the bedroom, and it seemed very late. There was a casual arrangement of yellow chrysanthemums in the alcove.

"Don't let that Kō bother you," said Sakai. "He's a little too lively for his own good. But we all think you did very well indeed, and we're most grateful for your help." That directness was something she would know for only a little while longer. It would be a warm memory, as the years passed, of when she was very young. "Shall we say then that this is something to make you remember how it was to be sixteen?"

The present was a cut-glass powder jar, and Chiyo's initials were engraved on the lid—no doubt that was Keiko's touch. And so, Chiyo thought, her uncle's funeral, which had somehow gone on and on, was over at last.

It was only the first of Chiyo's funerals. There were aunts and uncles on her father's side and aunts and uncles on her mother's side, and there were nearly fifty cousins. With the families they had married into and with their children, they made a vast clan indeed. Something was always happening in one branch or another. One could overlook happy events, perhaps, but sad events demanded a show of sympathy. Spring came—or rather the New Year's festivities were barely over—and her father's brother-in-law died. Chiyo's mother had always done the funeral chores, but Chiyo had passed her test and was immediately sent off to the wake.

"So here we are again. And so soon, too." That "so soon" had a strange ring to it. With Sakai and Keiko away on their New Year's visit to the provinces, Kō had come as their representative, and he could not take his leave with the perfunctory condolences that would ordinarily have been enough. Having offered to help, he was happily showing how helpful he could be. The relatives of the dead man were of course there, but the widow, always a forceful woman, was so aroused to the crisis that the balance of power had turned sharply away from her husband's family. That was not as it should be. The dissatisfaction clear in the manner of those who had to work under her cast a shadow over the wake.

"We'll have to do something to make them feel better," said Kō. Very much the adult, he gave Chiyo another warning at about eight: "We should think about leaving. If we're too formal, we may find ourselves in trouble, though. It might be better just to say good-bye to some of the younger ones."

It was only six months since the last funeral, but Kō's way of thinking and speaking had matured astonishingly. Chiyo was left hopelessly behind. He was trying to protect her, and in fact it might have been best to do as he suggested; but, as she faced this grown-up Kō, the thought of the directness that would make her remember her youth came back to annoy her. She stayed until ten as her mother had instructed, and she was careful to say good-bye to her aunt before she left. At this funeral there was no barrier gate, and of course there were no apologies for dress. Kō was more friendly to Chiyo's relatives than before. Perhaps he would come and help in Sakai's place at the next funeral too, someone suggested.

The remark proved to be no joke. Soon there was a third funeral. Funerals came in waves, as though to mark off a phase in the family's destinies. This time it was the oldest son of the senior branch of the family, a man to whom Chiyo had never been particularly close. The difference in their ages had made him more like an uncle than a cousin. With this second funeral, of little concern to her, Chiyo quite mastered a woman's funeral duties. As she worked away at her tea, she picked up all the miscellaneous funeral lore: how to address the widow and the family, how to manage the people who came with condolences, how to help in the kitchen, how to serve the food.

None of the work was especially difficult, but a lack of system made the waste extreme.

"Go ahead, tell them so," laughed Kō. "That's the schoolgirl way of doing things, they'll say. They manage to ignore everything young people suggest."

Presently Chiyo finished school.

"It seems that I am to be a specialist in funerals. Why don't you give me a funeral kimono for graduation?"

"But people don't have funeral kimonos made unless there's a reason. I've never heard of getting a funeral kimono for graduation."

Chiyo won after a mild battle. She even brushed aside her mother's suggestion that the kimono be purple rather than black, and ordered good material that would last a lifetime.

"But I've never heard of such a thing." Her mother was unconvinced to the end.

It almost seemed that the new kimono had been made especially for the funeral of Sakai's younger brother. They knew of course that the brother had come to Tokyo in search of a good doctor and that he was living quietly in the suburbs, but Chiyo's mother did not miss her opportunity: "See what you've brought us with your new kimono?" Chiyo, pretending she did not hear, passed her hand over the glowing black silk. It was fine and caressing when she put it on. What pleasure new clothes gave, even funeral clothes! "Clothes are to enjoy while you're young. It's out of place to say so, I suppose, but the black is very becoming." This from her mother, the objector. The rich rustle of the black skirt!

Kō, who had long since had his own formal clothes, was his usual self: "Well,

Chiyo, and aren't you going to announce this time that fortunately you have a funeral kimono? You look wiser than ever in black."

The funeral proper was to be held in the provinces, and the memorial services were quiet and lonely. Chiyo worked furiously, as though to fight off the loneliness. She had met the dead man no more than five or six times, and then only briefly; and yet the sorrow was far keener than at any of her earlier funerals. Had she caught something of Sakai's sadness for this invalid brother, or was she sad rather for the unfortunate man himself? In any case it was clear, even from her short experience, that there were all sorts of funerals.

A little over a week later two picture postcards, each a snow scene, came from Kō. The one was a continuation of the other. It was her first letter from him.

"The funeral is tomorrow. There are all sorts of relatives I have to look up to, and it's almost impossible not to do something wrong. I feel smothered. And country women, now that I've been away, seem so slow that I feel like giving them all a shove. The cousin I have to work with is the worst of all—a genius at slowness. She is more of a load than a help, and I would do better by myself. I know that if this were Tokyo I would have someone who would be a real help, and that is as a matter of fact why I am writing. I am sure we will work together at a funeral again some time, and when we do I mean to be more grateful."

Before they met at their next funeral, however, Chiyo heard from Keiko of Kō's wedding. She wondered whether he had worn his funeral coat. Her mother sent a present.

Chiyo went to work. Her mother, worried at first because working women have trouble finding husbands, gradually learned to live on the new income and stopped insisting that the girl resign. Spring moved into fall, one year to another. The marriageable years went by, and a sadly fresh young woman was left behind. As a woman passes twenty-five, the light inside grows stronger, but the color of youth begins to leave the line of the back and the shoulders. Age comes on from the places that do not show in the mirror, decay makes its way from the corners one does not notice. And in those years black is the best of all colors. Chiyo's beauty was clearer each time she put on her mourning kimono. The natural sadness had its effect, the words of condolence and the offering of incense took on smoothness from long practice, one spot of black silk seemed to give off a special glow there among the mourning women. Probably Chiyo seemed more bereaved than the chief mourner. At work she came to be called "the black princess," and it was she who always set out when her company had to have its representative. Wherever she went she was a help. At a funeral, the smallest incident left behind an impression, which sometimes grew into a new friendship. The gossip was a nuisance. "Aren't women lucky? All the capital they need is a funeral kimono. Go to a funeral and find someone who's susceptible, and you're taken care of for life."

Chiyo, who had always been proper almost to the point of fussiness, began to withdraw into herself. Sorry to see that happen, Keiko let fall a secret: "There was a time, you know, when Kō wanted to marry you, but Sakai wouldn't have it. He's always disliked that playfulness, and he said it would take someone with more substance to make you happy. He wouldn't interfere if the two of you made up your own minds to it, he said, but he would not be a go-between. But Kō is doing beautifully. He's already head of a department in his company, and he's making all sorts of money in a business he started on his own. I feel a little sorry we didn't have him marry you."

Chiyo was not especially pleased. She knew how perceptive Sakai could be, and she was left with doubts about Kō. "I haven't seen him for a long time. I suppose that means there have been no funerals for a long time."

"That's true, isn't it? But you may have a chance to meet soon. Eiko is much worse."

Eiko was Keiko's younger sister. She had not been well since her marriage (to a member of the Sakai family), and whenever they visited her they found her in and out of bed in a little round-windowed room.

Kō was stouter, and almost too thoroughly the gentleman. The charm and talkativeness were as they had always been, however.

"I know this is hardly the place for it, but I have all sorts of things to congratulate you for. You're married, you have two children, you're the head of a department, your own business is doing well—five congratulations piled on top of each other."

"You know everything, don't you?" The strong white teeth showed as he smiled.

"Everything. Big things and little things, good things and bad things."

For just a fraction of a second there was a suggestion of confusion. Not long enough really to be sure.

"Oh?" The gaze was firm again, almost shamelessly so. "I'm sure you don't know about my unhappiness."

"And are you unhappy?"

"Very. I can't settle down. I'm bored."

"Because you've been too lucky. Isn't it fine to be bored from being too lucky."

"Don't be sarcastic. But then you always have been. You remember you said I was a good man with sugar needles?"

Chiyo did remember it. She had meant that he was good at picking people's faults, compressing them to mustard seeds, adding a coat of sugar with sharp corners, and serving them up, pleasant to the taste, for everyone to enjoy.

" 'Forgive me for not having a funeral kimono'—I'll never be the talker you are."

Here we are again, thought Chiyo. She smiled and moved away. Keiko had told her that Sakai was most displeased with Kō these days, and that Kō was becoming increasingly evasive. But Kō bustled about the funeral with all the old energy, and he seemed to be holding back the self-satisfaction that went with success.

"And won't we be having to congratulate you too, Chiyo?" he asked. What a talent the man had! Chiyo had decided only the day before that she would be married, and she had not even told her mother.

At first blissfully happy, Chiyo's marriage was in the end a failure. Her happiness had been dammed up through the unmarried years, and it burst through explosively. Her husband was a weak, good-natured man who had little talent for making his way in the world. After about two years, when their child was born, he found that he was no longer well matched with his "talented wife." Love faded on both sides, and yet something remained, and with it regrets, and bickering. The family resources wasted away. Chiyo rose to the challenge. She worked herself thin trying to win back the losses, and, ashamed of her poverty, she avoided her relatives and friends—or rather, she quite cut herself off from them through those ten years. Quarrels, despair, poverty—they were like ten years in a stockade. And all that they left for a keepsake was the black kimono. It would bring almost nothing at the used-clothes stores. How many times had she thought of cutting it down into a cloak? And then, at her husband's funeral, she felt the black silk at her shoulders again—for the first time in how many years? The dark married life which she had not been able to break off thus came to a natural end, and as she put on the kimono she thought to mark the end yet more clearly with a black curtain. But the tears trickled down over her face—why should that have been?—as they had at no other funeral.

Her mother bewailed the decay: "It's the same old black kimono, but there's nothing left of the old effect."

A year later, she was able to wear the kimono again. The doctor who had treated her husband died. Her husband had had a strange ailment with a long German name, and, since the doctor had done his best, Chiyo felt deeply indebted. The funeral was held at the doctor's university. The line of mourners wound across the heavily wooded campus, through the trees, around the lake, and up the sidewalk. It was a quiet, impressive funeral.

Chiyo had offered her incense and started out to take a streetcar when she saw Kō. He had a brand-new morning coat and his own automobile. "I saw you and waited," he said. She suspected from the fact that he asked nothing about her life these last years that he knew everything. "We've only been together at one really pleasant party," he said in the few minutes he was seeing her home. "At dinner after Aunt Keiko's father died. Funerals were fun in those days. They didn't seem to have much to do with me personally."

With an aging mother and a daughter, a tired Chiyo eked out a meager living as the defeat came in sight, the desire to live weakened, the days went by somehow bodiless and fleeting. Presently the air raids began and everywhere there were seared wastes. Those who had escaped only waited for the fire to come to them too. As they waited, a certain greed took hold of them, all the more distasteful for their inability to be rid of it. At dawn one morning the siren sounded again. In the middle of the raid, it was Kō who came calling. Sakai had been injured, and Chiyo was to go with Kō immediately. Because of his work, Sakai had taken refuge in a neighboring prefecture. He had decided that that was too dangerous, however, and he was today going back to his home in the provinces. A message had just come saying that he had been caught in the incendiary raid the night before. Urged out of the house whether she would go or not, Chiyo noted that Kō had an army automobile, an army cap, and a yellowish uniform she took to be that of a civilian army employee. She found it hard to look at him as he leaned over into the front seat and prodded the driver to go faster.

The seaside town was in ruins. Near the outskirts, in what had once been a lumber warehouse, Sakai lay on a bare floor with only an army blanket over him. Keiko was holding his hand. Chiyo and Kō arrived in time, but barely in time, to see him die. Chiyo could only have described the scene as appalling. The nose was proud and high on the miraculously unburned face, however, and only the thick eyebrows, never known to show dismay, were scorched.

Kō worked as if possessed, and somehow managed to put together a funeral. A wake was of course out of the question—even the funeral offerings came from their rations. There were many pines about the place, and the most they could do was bring pine branches in place of flowers. Since cremation was not the custom of the district, the lone crematory oven was some distance away, on a pine-covered hill.

All of them, Keiko and the rest, climbed into a truck with the body. A wild-haired old woman came out to meet them. "You men can carry it to the oven." Chiyo took a corner of the coffin and worked along with the men from the Sakai family, and the pain was pleasant. No one lived there but the old woman. They sat uncomfortably on the veranda of her cottage while they waited. The wind sang in the pines, the sun began to go down, and after a time the old woman told them the ashes were ready.

She pulled the iron tray out with a clatter, and, transferring it to a sort of handcar, wheeled it roughly out through the darkness into an open space. Flames that could hardly be called embers blazed up with the breeze, and the scene suggested nothing so much as the old hag who pulls the fire carriage in pictures of hell. Kō said something. The old woman turned a red face on him.

"Don't be a fool. I'm just being good to you. Do you think these women could see without the fire? I could myself, but then I'm used to it."

Keiko was taken away almost unconscious when she had made but a token gesture toward gathering ashes. Only Chiyo and Kō and one other stayed behind. Since the chopsticks, like thick wires, heated up immediately, they were long in finishing. The old woman, who sat on a pine root watching suddenly laughed to herself. "That man and that woman aren't married. I smell something funny."

Kō cast a sidelong glance at Chiyo, who had stiffened and put down her chopsticks. He went on gathering ashes, a red demon in the firelight.

When they had finished, the old woman brushed together the last of the embers and threw water over them. A cloud of white steam rose with a hiss. "How much do you want besides the usual price? I'll give you whatever you say." Chiyo gritted her teeth and tried to concentrate on the high wind in the pines, but somehow her eyes were fixed on Kō's back.

For a time Chiyo took to her bed. There was nothing really the matter with her, but she could not sleep and she had no appetite. The sight and the smell of that cremation came to her, fight though she would to keep them off. She had a note from Keiko, who had gone back to Sakai's home in the provinces. The year ended, presently Hiroshima was destroyed. On the last day of the war, Chiyo was chief mourner at a funeral in her own house, unbombed among the ruins. It was her mother's funeral. Chiyo thought Kō might come, but she had told no one except the people in the neighborhood. Though she still had a summer mourning kimono, she thought it enough to wear the black cotton bloomers that had become uniform during the war—to say a prayer, offer a bit of incense, and mourn her mother and country at the same time.

Keiko came back to Tokyo three years after Sakai's death.

"Did you hear about Kō? A terrible thing. He's disappeared." Investigation since the war had uncovered what was probably at the root of Sakai's growing aloofness in his last years. Keiko listed all the crimes. "And the more you hear, the worse they seem, the things he had planned. Remember how extravagant he used to be?"

Sensing the end, Kō had moved about to avoid arrest, and finally, at a cliff on the seacoast near the family home, he had disappeared. He had always known how to drive, but where had he found the car, and what had he had in mind? Kō had been the driver, there could be no doubt about that. The car was found with the front wheels almost over the cliff, and marks to show that he had jammed on the brakes at the last minute. But what had happened to him after that close escape? Chiyo, listening to the story, could hear the scream of the brakes and feel the seat against the small of her back as the rear wheels leaped into the air. Concluding that Kō had drowned himself, the police had gone on with the search, as had the Sakai family at its own expense. There was still no trace of him, but what he had done after he stopped the car seemed clearer than what exactly his crimes had been. A wave of horror and sorrow swept over Chiyo.

"And so they haven't had the funeral yet," said Keiko.

Today was the funeral of her last uncle. Chiyo started dressing forty minutes early. It would take her ten minutes to wash and dress. An easy twenty minutes on the way, and she would have ten minutes to spare—it was a more leisurely schedule than she usually allowed herself. The habit of looking closely at herself in the mirror had left her, she did not know when. She no longer insisted that her face and her hair had to be right. The mirror had come to give off a faint shadow, and she dressed herself with a vague lack of interest. She only knelt in front of the mirror these days, even when there was a cushion for her to sit on.

She slipped the black funeral kimono on over a white under-kimono, passed a cord about the waist, straightened the neck, tied the obi, and fastened it in place with a black cord; and her funeral dress was ready. She could tell better from the feel of that familiar kimono than from looking in a mirror. Just to make very sure, however, she knelt down again to glance at the neck, and twisted to see that the line of the back was as it should be. As she rose to one knee, ready to leave, a blur passed over the crisp white of the new stocking.

The hem had worn through and the wadding, a dirty gray, hung down like a sagging bridge.

The old housekeeper tried to ward off a little of the scolding she knew would come. "I just noticed it. Saki had been taking care of your clothes, and I hadn't noticed before. And I couldn't find time to mend it."

No doubt the old woman was telling the truth, but something had to be done. "How many minutes?"

"I beg your pardon?"

"The time. How many minutes do I have?"

"Shall I go see?" Prod the old woman though you would, you could not hurry her. But Chiyo had allowed ten minutes for dressing, and she knew the time well enough already.

"Never mind. Bring me a pair of scissors. Scissors. Can I do it in three minutes?"

"I beg your pardon?"

"The scissors. Hurry."

"There, in the dresser drawer."

"But those are fingernail scissors. Bring me the shears."

"I beg your pardon? You're going to cut it?"

"Just bring me the scissors and the sewing box." Chiyo undid her obi as she spoke, and knelt down intently in the white under-kimono.

The black kimono lay like a great bat. The scissors opened and bit into the skirt.

"But do you have to be so rough with it?"

The cloth sang out its resistance.

"What else can I do? And do you have to shout at me?" The scissors, the kimono, even the sound of the cutting seemed to resist as she came to the hemmed edge, but she forced her way on. "Don't just sit there. Run a black thread through the needle. I have no time."

The strip of black cloth and the wadding inside trailed across the mat like a dead snake. Chiyo snatched the needle and thread from the confused old woman. She had to have her glasses, however. She reached furiously for them, even though she was not as angry as she seemed. Neither sewing nor basting, she brought the front and the lining together, and passed a hot iron over them. The old silk protested all the while.

"How many minutes has it been?" But there was no point in worrying over that. She could have taken no more than three minutes. As she pulled the kimono over her shoulders and straightened the front, the warmth at the skirt passed through to her feet. "I'm a little late. Call a taxi."

The old woman, back from the telephone, sat down solidly on her heels.

"Is something the matter?" Chiyo thought she saw tears. "What's the matter?"

She knelt down and looked into the old woman's eyes. There were indeed tears.

"It's nothing. It just came to me, that's all."

"What did?"

"But you're on your way out. I'll tell you later."

Chiyo knelt tying her obi. "I don't know what your trouble is, but I'll worry about it until I come back. Did I do something wrong?"

"It's nothing. But won't you have a new kimono made, please?"

"Why?"

"I can't tell you how I felt when I saw you cutting at it. To cut a kimono that's all made up—I could never have done it myself." The old woman toyed with that dark snake, its insides dangling out. "I know I'm being foolish, but I couldn't help thinking when I saw you that you would be having a new kimono made for my own funeral, and I started crying. You'll take care of everything for me when the time comes, won't you?"

At her age, the old woman might well be right. And no doubt it had been too much for the brittle old nerves to see the younger woman brandishing her scissors at the black funeral skirt. In her impatience to be on time, Chiyo had made a woman see her own funeral—the callousness of one who lived alone had shown itself.

"I may very well have a new one made. But let's promise that we'll neither of us have a funeral for a while yet."

Snatching up her handbag, she ran for the taxi. The old woman bowed in the doorway. Sunlight flooded in through the wide windows. But what a problem a woman's funeral kimono was! A man could have formal clothes made just as well for a happy occasion. Kō—this was one of the days on which she would have seen him. And what had happened to that trim morning coat? Her black kimono, now that she looked at it, was badly worn indeed. Should she have a new one made? And if she did, at whose funeral would she wear it? This uncle was the last of the old generation. There were only cousins left, plenty of cousins, but all fairly young. Someone outside the family, then? But there was no limit to people outside the family. It came to her that she was seeing off the last of the line today. That was the truth—she had finally seen them all off. She had been rough with the black kimono, but if she had it mended and gave it better care, it might last for years—it might outlast Chiyo herself. The life of the funeral kimono and the life of the woman, one might say, were roughly the same.

"No, you must have a new one. There's still one more important event. You'll have to look good at your own funeral." That was the sort of joke Kō would have made. I don't suppose anyone will come to my funeral—but then it is just possible he might. Kō. Will he joke about it, as usual? It will make me happy if he will only be serious. I'll be able to give him his final marks then. He has done many unpleasant things, I suppose, but they have all been to other people. Not to me. My friend—my funeral friend.

The taxi entered a residential district, and even in the city the early summer air was clean. Chiyo felt more and more that she wanted her funeral friend to be a good friend. They met for two or three days, he and she, when there was a death; they worked together to manage the funeral; and afterwards they were friends who heard nothing of each other. And now Chiyo was left alone. All of her funerals, from sixteen to fifty, passed through her mind. Perhaps it told what the age had been for the Japanese woman, the fact that a man and a woman could see each other only at funerals.

"We're on time, lady. Two minutes to spare."

"Thank you very much. You needn't wait." She wrapped a little money in paper. "Buy yourself some tobacco." But it seemed to her that being on time no longer made a difference.

The son of a cousin was standing with the mourners' register as she went in through the open back gate.

"Am I on time?"

"What!"

"Don't be so absent-minded. Am I on time for the funeral?"

"Oh, that." The cuffs were immaculate under the dark blue sleeves. "You're just on time, as usual. No, they've been after me these last few days to see that everything was ready on time. Everything had to be ready on time. And you caught me by surprise. I thought you were something else I had to have ready on time." The boy stretched and took a deep breath. "This is the first funeral I've worked at. Funerals are full of things that have to be ready on time. Everything has to be ready. No—that's not it. Funerals are full of things that aren't ready on time. That's it."

How young you are, Chiyo wanted to say. Even there outside the kitchen, with its splashing water and clattering dishes, a tranquil freedom from household cares seemed to radiate from the boy.

A breeze came in through the deep green of the wide garden, and rustled at the hastily mended black kimono. Someone had died, and a calm—a funeral calm—was falling over the house.

Translated by E. G. Seidensticker

Questions for Discussion

1. When does the action of the story take place? How do we know?

2. Describe the relationship between Chiyo and Kō.

3. How do Chiyo's attitudes toward funerals—and toward her role in them—change?

4. Is this a war story? Why or why not?

Suggestions for Writing

1. Write an essay about the role of ritual in this story. Analyze the way in which Chiyo responds to ritual.

2. Write a story that makes use of private or cultural rituals.

3. Write an essay about the relationship between Chiyo and Kō.

The Egg

SHERWOOD ANDERSON

My father was, I am sure, intended by nature to be a cheerful, kindly man. Until he was thirty-four years old he worked as a farm-hand for a man named Thomas Butterworth whose place lay near the town of Bidwell, Ohio. He had then a horse of his own and on Saturday evenings drove into town to spend a few hours in social intercourse with other farm-hands. In town he drank several glasses of beer and stood about in Ben Head's saloon—crowded on Saturday evenings with visiting farm-hands. Songs were sung and glasses thumped on the bar. At ten o'clock father drove home along a lonely country road, made his horse comfortable for the night and himself went to bed, quite happy in his position in life. He had at that time no notion of trying to rise in the world.

It was in the spring of his thirty-fifth year that father married my mother, then a country school-teacher, and in the following spring I came wriggling and crying into the world. Something happened to the two people. They became ambitious. The American passion for getting up in the world took possession of them.

It may have been that mother was responsible. Being a school-teacher she had no doubt read books and magazines. She had, I presume, read of how Garfield, Lincoln, and other Americans rose from poverty to fame and greatness and as I lay beside her—in the days of her lying-in—she may have dreamed that I would some day rule men and cities. At any rate she induced father to give up his place as a farm-hand, sell his horse and embark on an independent enterprise of his own. She was a tall silent woman with a long nose and troubled grey eyes. For herself she wanted nothing. For father and myself she was incurably ambitious.

The first venture into which the two people went turned out badly. They rented ten acres of poor stony land on Grigg's Road, eight miles from Bidwell, and launched into chicken raising. I grew into boyhood on the place and got my first impressions of life there. From the beginning they were impressions of disaster and if, in my turn, I am a gloomy man inclined to see the darker side of life, I attribute it to the fact that what should have been for me the happy joyous days of childhood were spent on a chicken farm.

One unversed in such matters can have no notion of the many and tragic things that can happen to a chicken. It is born out of an egg, lives for a few weeks as a tiny fluffy thing such as you will see pictured on Easter cards, then becomes hideously naked, eats quantities of corn and meal bought by the sweat of your father's brow, gets diseases called pip, cholera, and other names, stands looking with stupid eyes at the sun, becomes sick and dies. A few hens and now and then a rooster, intended to serve God's mysterious ends, struggle through to maturity.

The hens lay eggs out of which come other chickens and the dreadful cycle is thus made complete. It is all unbelievably complex. Most philosophers must have been raised on chicken farms. One hopes for so much from a chicken and is so dreadfully disillusioned. Small chickens, just setting out on the journey of life, look so bright and alert and they are in fact so dreadfully stupid. They are so much like people they mix one up in one's judgments of life. If disease does not kill them they wait until your expectations are thoroughly aroused and then walk under the wheels of a wagon—to go squashed and dead back to their maker. Vermin infest their youth, and fortunes must be spent for curative powders. In later life I have seen how a literature has been built up on the subject of fortunes to be made out of the raising of chickens. It is intended to be read by the gods who have just eaten of the tree of the knowledge of good and evil. It is a hopeful literature and declares that much may be done by simple ambitious people who own a few hens. Do not be led astray by it. It was not written for you. Go hunt for gold on the frozen hills of Alaska, put your faith in the honesty of a politician, believe if you will that the world is daily growing better and that good will triumph over evil, but do not read and believe the literature that is written concerning the hen. It was not written for you.

I, however, digress. My tale does not primarily concern itself with the hen. If correctly told it will center on the egg. For ten years my father and mother struggled to make our chicken farm pay and then they gave up that struggle and began another. They moved into the town of Bidwell, Ohio, and embarked in the restaurant business. After ten years of worry with incubators that did not hatch, and with tiny—and in their own way lovely—balls of fluff that passed on into semi-naked pullethood and from that into dead henhood, we threw all aside and packing our belongings on a wagon drove down Grigg's Road toward Bidwell, a tiny caravan of hope looking for a new place from which to start on our upward journey through life.

We must have been a sad looking lot, not, I fancy, unlike refugees fleeing from a battlefield. Mother and I walked in the road. The wagon that contained our goods had been borrowed for the day from Mr. Albert Griggs, a neighbor. Out of its sides stuck the legs of cheap chairs and at the back of the pile of beds, tables, and boxes filled with kitchen utensils was a crate of live chickens, and on top of that the baby carriage in which I had been wheeled about in my infancy. Why we stuck to the baby carriage I don't know. It was unlikely other children would be born and the wheels were broken. People who have few possessions cling tightly to those they have. That is one of the facts that make life so discouraging.

Father rode on top of the wagon. He was then a bald-headed man of forty-five, a little fat and from long association with mother and the chickens he had become habitually silent and discouraged. All during our ten years on the chicken farm he had worked as a laborer on neighboring farms and most of the money he had earned had been spent for remedies to cure chicken diseases, on Wilmer's White Wonder Cholera Cure or Professor Bidlow's Egg Producer or some other preparations that mother found advertised in the poultry papers. There were two little patches of hair on father's head just above his ears. I remember that as a child I used to sit looking at him when he had gone to sleep in a chair before the stove on Sunday afternoons in the winter. I had at that time already begun to read books and have notions of my own and the bald path that led over the top of his head was, I fancied, something like a broad road, such a road as Caesar might have made on which to lead his legions out of Rome and into the wonders of an unknown world. The tufts of hair that grew above father's ears were, I thought, like forests. I fell into a half-sleeping, half-waking state and dreamed I was a tiny thing going along the road into a far beautiful place where there were no chicken farms and where life was a happy eggless affair.

One might write a book concerning our flight from the chicken farm into town. Mother and I walked the entire eight miles—she to be sure that nothing fell from the wagon and I to see the wonders of the world. On the seat of the wagon beside father was his greatest treasure. I will tell you of that.

On a chicken farm where hundreds and even thousands of chickens come out of eggs surprising things sometimes happen. Grotesques are born out of eggs as out of people. The accident does not often occur—perhaps once in a thousand births. A chicken is, you see, born that has four legs, two pairs of wings, two heads or what not. The things do not live. They go quickly back to the hand of their maker that has for a moment trembled. The fact that the poor little things could not live was one of the tragedies of life to father. He had some sort of notion that if he could but bring into henhood or roosterhood a five-legged hen or a two-headed rooster his fortune would be made. He dreamed of taking the wonder about to county fairs and of growing rich by exhibiting it to other farm-hands.

At any rate he saved all the little monstrous things that had been born on our chicken farm. They were preserved in alcohol and put each in its own glass bottle. These he had carefully put into a box and on our journey into town it was carried on the wagon seat beside him. He drove the horses with one hand and with the other clung to the box. When we got to our destination the box was taken down at once and the bottles removed. All during our days as keepers of a restaurant in the town of Bidwell, Ohio, the grotesques in their little glass bottles sat on a shelf back of the counter. Mother sometimes protested but father was a rock on the subject of his treasure. The grotesques were, he declared, valuable. People, he said, liked to look at strange and wonderful things.

Did I say that we embarked in the restaurant business in the town of Bidwell, Ohio? I exaggerated a little. The town itself lay at the foot of a low hill and on the shore of a small river. The railroad did not run through the town and the station was a mile away to the north at a place called Pickleville. There had been a cider mill and pickle factory at the station, but before the time of our coming they had both gone out of business. In the morning and in the evening busses came down to the station along a road called Turner's Pike from the hotel on the main street of Bidwell. Our going to the out of the way place to embark in the restaurant business was mother's idea. She talked of it for a year and then one day went off and rented an empty store building opposite the railroad station. It was her idea that the restaurant would be profitable. Travelling men, she said, would be always waiting around to take trains out of town and town people would come to the station to await incoming trains. They would come to the restaurant to buy pieces of pie and drink coffee. Now that I am older I know that she had another motive in going. She was ambitious for me. She wanted me to rise in the world, to get into a town school and become a man of the towns.

At Pickleville father and mother worked hard as they always had done. At first there was the necessity of putting our place into shape to be a restaurant. That took a month. Father built a shelf on which he put tins of vegetables. He painted a sign on which he put his name in large red letters. Below his name was the sharp command—"EAT HERE "—that was so seldom obeyed. A show case was bought and filled with cigars and tobacco. Mother scrubbed the floor and the walls of the room. I went to school in the town and was glad to be away from the farm and from the presence of the discouraged, sad-looking chickens. Still I was not very joyous. In the evening I walked home from school along Turner's Pike and remembered the children I had seen playing in the town school yard. A troop of little girls had gone hopping about and singing. I tried that. Down along the frozen road I went hopping solemnly on one leg. "Hippity Hop To The Barber Shop," I sang shrilly. Then I stopped and looked doubtfully about. I was afraid of being seen in my gay mood. It must have seemed to me that I was doing a thing that should not be done by one who, like myself, had been raised on a chicken farm where death was a daily visitor.

Mother decided that our restaurant should remain open at night. At ten in the evening a passenger train went north past our door followed by a local freight. The freight crew had switching to do in Pickleville and when the work was done they came to our restaurant for hot coffee and food. Sometimes one of them ordered a fried egg. In the morning at four they returned north-bound and again visited us. Our little trade began to grow up. Mother slept at night and during the day tended the restaurant and fed our boarders while father slept. He slept in the same bed mother had occupied during the night and I went off to the town of Bidwell and to school. During the long nights, while mother and I slept, father cooked meats that were to go into sandwiches for the lunch baskets of our boarders. Then an idea in regard to getting up in the world came into his head. The American spirit took hold of him. He also became ambitious.

In the long nights when there was little to do father had time to think. That was his undoing. He decided that he had in the past been an unsuccessful man because he had not been cheerful enough and that in the future he would adopt a cheerful outlook on life. In the early morning he came upstairs and got into bed with mother. She woke and the two talked. From my bed in the corner I listened.

It was father's idea that both he and mother should try to entertain the people who came to eat at our restaurant. I cannot now remember his words, but he gave the impression of one about to become in some obscure way a kind of public entertainer. When people, particularly young people from the town of Bidwell, came into our place, as on very rare occasions they did, bright entertaining conversation was to be made. From father's words I gathered that something of the jolly inn-keeper effect was to be sought. Mother must have been doubtful from the first, but she said nothing discouraging. It was father's notion that a passion for the company of himself and mother would spring up in the breasts of the younger people of the town of Bidwell. In the evening bright happy groups would come singing down Turner's Pike. They would troop shouting with joy and laughter into our place. There would be song and festivity. I do not mean to give the impression that father spoke so elaborately of the matter. He was as I have said an uncommunicative man. "They want some place to go. I tell you they want some place to go," he said over and over. That was as far as he got. My own imagination has filled in the blanks.

For two or three weeks this notion of father's invaded our house. We did not talk much, but in our daily lives tried earnestly to make smiles take the place of glum looks. Mother smiled at the boarders and I, catching the infection, smiled at our cat. Father became a little feverish in his anxiety to please. There was no doubt, lurking somewhere in him, a touch of the spirit of the showman. He did not waste much of his ammunition on the railroad men he served at night but seemed to be waiting for a young man or woman from Bidwell to come in to show what he could do. On the counter in the restaurant there was a wire basket kept always filled with eggs, and it must have been before his eyes when the idea of being entertaining was born in his brain. There was something pre-natal about the way eggs kept themselves connected with the development of his idea. At any rate an egg ruined his new impulse in life. Late one night I was awakened by a roar of anger coming from father's throat. Both mother and I sat upright in our beds. With trembling hands she lighted a lamp that stood on a table by her head. Downstairs the front door of our restaurant went shut with a bang and in a few minutes father tramped up the stairs. He held an egg in his hand and his hand trembled as though he were having a chill. There was a half insane light in his eyes. As he stood glaring at us I was sure he intended throwing the egg at either mother or me. Then he laid it gently on the table beside the lamp and dropped on his knees beside mother's bed. He began to cry like a boy and I, carried away by his grief, cried with him. The two of us filled the little upstairs room with our wailing voices. It is ridiculous, but of the picture we made I can remember only the fact that mother's hand continually stroked the bald path that ran across the top of his head. I have forgotten what mother said to him and how she induced him to tell her of what had happened downstairs. His explanation also has gone out of my mind. I remember only my own grief and fright and the shiny path over father's head glowing in the lamp light as he knelt by the bed.

As to what happened downstairs. For some unexplainable reason I know the story as well as though I had been a witness to my father's discomfiture. One in time gets to know many unexplainable things. On that evening young Joe Kane, son of a merchant of Bidwell, came to Pickleville to meet his father, who was expected on the ten o'clock evening train from the South. The train was three hours late and Joe came into our place to loaf about and to wait for its arrival. The local freight train came in and the freight crew were fed. Joe was left alone in the restaurant with father.

From the moment he came into our place the Bidwell young man must have been puzzled by my father's actions. It was his notion that father was angry at him for hanging around. He noticed that the restaurant keeper was apparently disturbed by his presence and he thought of going out. However, it began to rain and he did not fancy the long walk to town and back. He bought a five-cent cigar and ordered a cup of coffee. He had a newspaper in his pocket and took it out and began to read. "I'm waiting for the evening train. It's late," he said apologetically.

For a long time father, whom Joe Kane had never seen before, remained silently gazing at his visitor. He was no doubt suffering from an attack of stage fright. As so often happens in life he had thought so much and so often of the situation that now confronted him that he was somewhat nervous in its presence.

For one thing, he did not know what to do with his hands. He thrust one of them nervously over the counter and shook hands with Joe Kane. "How-de-do," he said. Joe Kane put his newspaper down and stared at him. Father's eye lighted on the basket of eggs that sat on the counter and he began to talk. "Well," he began hesitatingly, "well, you have heard of Christopher Columbus, eh?" He seemed to be angry. "That Christopher Columbus was a cheat," he declared emphatically. "He talked of making an egg stand on its end. He talked, he did, and then he went and broke the end of the egg."

My father seemed to his visitor to be beside himself at the duplicity of Christopher Columbus. He muttered and swore. He declared it was wrong to teach children that Christopher Columbus was a great man when, after all, he cheated at the critical moment. He had declared he would make an egg stand on end and then when his bluff had been called he had done a trick. Still grumbling at Columbus, father took an egg from the basket on the counter and began to walk up and down. He rolled the egg between the palms of his hands. He smiled genially. He began to mumble words regarding the effect to be produced on an egg by the electricity that comes out of the human body. He declared that without breaking its shell and by virtue of rolling it back and forth in his hands he could stand the egg on its end. He explained that the warmth of his hands and the gentle rolling movement he gave the egg created a new center of gravity, and Joe Kane was mildly interested. "I have handled thousands of eggs," father said. "No one knows more about eggs than I do."

He stood the egg on the counter and it fell on its side. He tried the trick again and again, each time rolling the egg between the palms of his hands and saying the words regarding the wonders of electricity and the laws of gravity. When after a half hour's effort he did succeed in making the egg stand for a moment he looked up to find that his visitor was no longer watching. By the time he had succeeded in calling Joe Kane's attention to the success of his effort the egg had again rolled over and lay on its side.

Afire with the showman's passion and at the same time a good deal disconcerted by the failure of his first effort, father now took the bottles containing the poultry monstrosities down from their place on the shelf and began to show them to his visitor. "How would you like to have seven legs and two heads like this fellow?" he asked, exhibiting the most remarkable of his treasures. A cheerful smile played over his face. He reached over the counter and tried to slap Joe Kane on the shoulder as he had seen men do in Ben Head's saloon when he was a young farm-hand and drove to town on Saturday evenings. His visitor was made a little ill by the sight of the body of the terribly deformed bird floating in the alcohol in the bottle and got up to go. Coming from behind the counter father took hold of the young man's arm and led him back to his seat. He grew a little angry and for a moment had to turn his face away and force himself to smile. Then he put the bottles back on the shelf. In an outburst of generosity he fairly compelled Joe Kane to have a fresh cup of coffee and another cigar at his expense. Then he took a pan and filling it with vinegar, taken from a jug that sat beneath the counter, he declared himself about to do a new trick. "I will heat this egg in this pan of vinegar," he said. "Then I will put it through the neck of a bottle without breaking the shell. When the egg is inside the bottle it will resume its normal shape and the shell will become hard again. Then I will give the bottle with the egg in it to you. You can take it about with you wherever you go. People will want to know how you got the egg in the bottle. Don't tell them. Keep them guessing. That is the way to have fun with this trick."

Father grinned and winked at his visitor. Joe Kane decided that the man who confronted him was mildly insane but harmless. He drank the cup of coffee that had been given him and began to read his paper again. When the egg had been heated in vinegar father carried it on a spoon to the counter and going into a back room got an empty bottle. He was angry because his visitor did not watch him as he began to do his trick, but nevertheless went cheerfully to work. For a long time he struggled, trying to get the egg to go through the neck of the bottle. He put the pan of vinegar back on the stove, intending to reheat the egg, then picked it up and burned his fingers. After a second bath in the hot vinegar the shell of the egg had been softened a little but not enough for his purpose. He worked and worked and a spirit of desperate determination took possession of him. When he thought that at last the trick was about to be consummated the delayed train came in at the station and Joe Kane started to go nonchalantly out at the door. Father made a last desperate effort to conquer the egg and make it do the thing that would establish his reputation as one who knew how to entertain guests who came into his restaurant. He worried the egg. He attempted to be somewhat rough with it. He swore and the sweat stood out on his forehead. The egg broke under his hand. When the contents spurted over his clothes, Joe Kane, who had stopped at the door, turned and laughed.

A roar of anger rose from my father's throat. He danced and shouted a string of inarticulate words. Grabbing another egg from the basket on the counter, he threw it, just missing the head of the young man as he dodged through the door and escaped.

Father came upstairs to mother and me with an egg in his hand. I do not know what he intended to do. I imagine he had some idea of destroying it, of destroying all eggs, and that he intended to let mother and me see him begin. When, however, he got into the presence of mother something happened to him. He laid the egg gently on the table and dropped on his knees by the bed as I have already explained. He later decided to close the restaurant for the night and to come upstairs and get into bed. When he did so he blew out the light and after much muttered conversation both he and mother went to sleep. I suppose I went to sleep also, but my sleep was troubled. I awoke at dawn and for a long time looked at the egg that lay on the table. I wondered why eggs had to be and why from the egg came the hen who again laid the egg. The question got into my blood. It has stayed there, I imagine, because I am the son of my father. At any rate, the problem remains unsolved in my mind. And that, I conclude, is but another evidence of the complete and final triumph of the egg—at least as far as my family is concerned.

Questions for Discussion

1. Speculate: Is it "character" or "fate" that drives the father to do what he does?

2. What is the son's attitude toward what happens to his father?

3. Would you characterize the story as mainly comic or mainly tragic?

4. What does "the egg" symbolize, both for the narrator and for us?

Suggestions for Writing

1. Write an essay that interprets the egg symbolically.

2. Write an essay that interprets the events of "The Egg" as peculiarly *American* expressions of ambition (and of misguided ambition). What is characteristically American about the characters and action?

3. Write a story about someone who is driven to try various ventures that are destined to fail.

The Jilting of Granny Weatherall

KATHERINE ANNE PORTER

She flicked her wrist neatly out of Doctor Harry's pudgy careful fingers and pulled the sheet up to her chin. The brat ought to be in knee breeches. Doctoring around the country with spectacles on his nose! "Get along now, take your schoolbooks and go. There's nothing wrong with me."

Doctor Harry spread a warm paw like a cushion on her forehead where the forked green vein danced and made her eyelids twitch. "Now, now, be a good girl, and we'll have you up in no time."

"That's no way to speak to a woman nearly eighty years old just because she's down. I'd have you respect your elders, young man."

"Well, Missy, excuse me." Doctor Harry patted her cheek. "But I've got to warn you, haven't I? You're a marvel, but you must be careful or you're going to be good and sorry."

"Don't tell me what I'm going to be. I'm on my feet now, morally speaking. It's Cornelia. I had to go to bed to get rid of her."

Her bones felt loose, and floated around in her skin, and Doctor Harry floated like a balloon around the foot of the bed. He floated and pulled down his waistcoat and swung his glasses on a cord. "Well, stay where you are, it certainly can't hurt you."

"Get along and doctor your sick," said Granny Weatherall. "Leave a well woman alone. I'll call for you when I want you. . . . Where were you forty years ago when I pulled through milk-leg and double pneumonia? You weren't even born. Don't let Cornelia lead you on," she shouted, because Doctor Harry appeared to float up to the ceiling and out. "I pay my own bills, and I don't throw my money away on nonsense!"

She meant to wave good-by, but it was too much trouble. Her eyes closed of themselves, it was like a dark curtain drawn around the bed. The pillow rose and floated under her, pleasant as a hammock in a light wind. She listened to the leaves rustling outside the window. No, somebody was swishing newspapers: no, Cornelia and Doctor Harry were whispering together. She leaped broad awake, thinking they whispered in her ear.

"She was never like this, *never* like this!" "Well, what can we expect?" "Yes, eighty years old. . . ."

Well, and what if she was? She still had ears. It was like Cornelia to whisper around doors. She always kept things secret in such a public way. She was always being tactful and kind. Cornelia was dutiful; that was the trouble with her. Dutiful and good: "So good and dutiful," said Granny, "that I'd like to spank her." She saw herself spanking Cornelia and making a fine job of it.

"What'd you say, Mother?"

Granny felt her face tying up in hard knots.

"Can't a body think, I'd like to know?"

"I thought you might want something."

"I do. I want a lot of things. First off, go away and don't whisper."

She lay and drowsed, hoping in her sleep that the children would keep out and let her rest a minute. It had been a long day. Not that she was tired. It was always pleasant to snatch a minute now and then. There are always so much to be done, let me see: tomorrow.

Tomorrow was far away and there was nothing to trouble about. Things were finished somehow when the time came; thank God there was always a little margin over for peace: then a person could spread out the plan of life and tuck in the edges orderly. It was good to have everything clean and folded away, with the hair brushes and tonic bottles sitting straight on the white embroidered linen: the day started without fuss and the pantry shelves laid out with rows of jelly glasses and brown jugs and white stone-china jars with blue whirligigs and words painted on them: coffee, tea, sugar, ginger, cinnamon, allspice: and the bronze clock with the lion on top nicely dusted off. The dust that lion could collect in twenty-four hours! The box in the attic with all those letters tied up, well she'd have to go through that tomorrow. All those letters—George's letters and John's letters and her letters to them both—lying around for the children to find afterwards made her uneasy. Yes, that would be tomorrow's business. No use to let them know how silly she had been once.

While she was rummaging around she found death in her mind and it felt clammy and unfamiliar. She had spent so much time preparing for death there was no need for bringing it up again. Let it take care of itself now. When she was sixty she had felt very old, finished, and went around making farewell trips to see her children and grandchildren, with a secret in her mind: This is the very last of your mother, children! Then she made her will and came down with a long fever. That was all just a notion like a lot of other things, but it was lucky too, for she had once and for all got over the idea of dying for a long time. Now she couldn't be worried. She hoped she had better sense now. Her father had lived to be one hundred and two years old and had drunk a noggin of strong hot toddy on his last birthday. He told the reporters it was his daily habit, and he owed his long life to that. He had made quite a scandal and was very pleased about it. She believed she'd just plague Cornelia a little.

"Cornelia! Cornelia!" No footsteps, but a sudden hand on her cheek. "Bless you, where have you been?"

"Here, mother."

"Well, Cornelia, I want a noggin of hot toddy."

"Are you cold, darling?"

"I'm chilly, Cornelia. Lying in bed stops the circulation. I must have told you that a thousand times."

Well, she could just hear Cornelia telling her husband that Mother was getting childish and they'd have to humor her. The thing that most annoyed her was that Cornelia thought she was deaf, dumb, and blind. Little hasty glances and tiny gestures tossed around her and over her head saying, "Don't cross her, let her have her way, she's eighty years old," and she sitting there as if she lived in a thin glass cage. Sometimes Granny almost made up her mind to pack up and move back to her own house where nobody could remind her every minute that she was old. Wait, wait, Cornelia, till your own children whisper behind your back!

In her day she had kept a better house and had got more work done. She wasn't too old yet for Lydia to be driving eighty miles for advice when one of the children jumped the track, and Jimmy still dropped in and talked things over: "Now, Mammy, you've a good business head, I want to know what you think of this? . . ." Old Cornelia couldn't change the furniture around without asking. Little things, little things! They had been so sweet when they were little. Granny wished the old days were back again with the children young and everything to be done over. It had been a hard pull, but not too much for her. When she thought of all the food she had cooked, and all the clothes she had cut and sewed, and all the gardens she had made—well, the children showed it. There they were, made out of her, and they couldn't get away from that. Sometimes she wanted to see John again and point to them and say, Well, I didn't do so badly, did I? But that would have to wait. That was for tomorrow. She used to think of him as a man, but now all the children were older than their father, and he would be a child beside her if she saw him now. It seemed strange and there was something wrong in the idea. Why, he couldn't possibly recognize her. She had fenced in a hundred acres once, digging the post holes herself and clamping the wires with just a negro boy to help. That changed a woman. John would be looking for a young woman with the peaked Spanish comb in her hair and the painted fan. Digging post holes changed a woman. Riding country roads in the winter when women had their babies was another thing: sitting up nights with sick horses and sick negroes and sick children and hardly ever losing one. John, I hardly ever lost one of them! John would see that in a minute, that would be something he could understand, she wouldn't have to explain anything!

It made her feel like rolling up her sleeves and putting the whole place to rights again. No matter if Cornelia was determined to be everywhere at once, there were a great many things left undone on this place. She would start tomorrow and do them. It was good to be strong enough for everything, even if all you made melted and changed and slipped under your hands, so that by the time you finished you almost forgot what you were working for. What was it I set out to do? she asked herself intently, but she could not remember. A fog rose over the valley, she saw it marching across the creek swallowing the trees and moving up the hill like an army of ghosts. Soon it would be at the near edge of the orchard, and then it was time to go in and light the lamps. Come in, children, don't stay out in the night air.

Lighting the lamps had been beautiful. The children huddled up to her and breathed like little calves waiting at the bars in the twilight. Their eyes followed the match and watched the flame rise and settle in a blue curve, then they moved away from her. The lamp was lit, they didn't have to be scared and hang on to mother any more. Never, never, never more. God, for all my life I thank Thee. Without Thee, my God, I could never have done it. Hail, Mary, full of grace.

I want you to pick all the fruit this year and see that nothing is wasted. There's always someone who can use it. Don't let good things rot for want of using. You waste life when you waste good food. Don't let things get lost. It's bitter to lose things. Now, don't let me get to thinking, not when I am tired and taking a little nap before supper. . . .

The pillow rose about her shoulders and pressed against her heart and the memory was being squeezed out of it: oh, push down the pillow, somebody: it would smother her if she tried to hold it. Such a fresh breeze blowing and such a green day with no threats in it. But he had not come, just the same. What does a woman do when she has put on the white veil and set out the white cake for a man and he doesn't come? She tried to remember. No, I swear he never harmed me but in that. He never harmed me but in that . . . and what if he did? There was the day, the day, but a whirl of dark smoke rose and covered it, crept up and over into the bright field where everything was planted so carefully in orderly rows. That was hell, she knew hell when she saw it. For sixty years she had prayed against remembering him and against losing her soul in the deep pit of hell, and now the two things were mingled in one and the thought of him was a smoky cloud from hell that moved and crept in her head when she had just got rid of Doctor Harry and was trying to rest a minute. Wounded vanity, Ellen, said a sharp voice in the top of her mind. Don't let your wounded vanity get the upper hand of you. Plenty of girls get jilted. You were jilted, weren't you? Then stand up to it. Her eyelids wavered and let in streamers of blue-gray light like tissue paper over her eyes. She must get up and pull the shades down or she'd never sleep. She was in bed again and the shades were not down. How could that happen? Better turn over, hide from the light, sleeping in the light gave you nightmares. "Mother, how do you feel now?" and a stinging wetness on her forehead. But I don't like having my face washed in cold water!

Hapsy? George? Lydia? Jimmy? No, Cornelia, and her features were swollen and full of little puddles. "They're coming, darling, they'll all be here soon." Go wash your face, child, you look funny.

Instead of obeying, Cornelia knelt down and put her head on the pillow. She seemed to be talking but there was no sound. "Well, are you tongue-tied? Whose birthday is it? Are you going to give a party?"

Cornelia's mouth moved urgently in strange shapes. "Don't do that, you bother me, daughter."

"Oh, no, Mother. Oh, no. . . ."

Nonsense. It was strange about children. They disputed your every word. "No what, Cornelia?"

"Here's Doctor Harry."

"I won't see that boy again. He just left five minutes ago."

"That was this morning, Mother. It's night now. Here's the nurse."

"This is Doctor Harry, Mrs. Weatherall. I never saw you look so young and happy!"

"Ah, I'll never be young again—but I'd be happy if they'd let me lie in peace and get rested."

She thought she spoke up loudly, but no one answered. A warm weight on her forehead, a warm bracelet on her wrist, and a breeze went on whispering, trying to tell her something. A shuffle of leaves in the everlasting hand of God. He blew on them and they danced and rattled. "Mother, don't mind, we're going to give you a little hypodermic." "Look here, daughter, how do ants get in this bed? I saw sugar ants yesterday." Did you send for Hapsy too?

It was Hapsy she really wanted. She had to go a long way back through a great many rooms to find Hapsy standing with a baby on her arm. She seemed to herself to be Hapsy also, and the baby on Hapsy's arm was Hapsy and himself and herself, all at once, and there was no surprise in the meeting. Then Hapsy melted from within and turned flimsy as gray gauze and the baby was a gauzy shadow, and Hapsy came up close and said, "I thought you'd never come," and looked at her very searchingly and said, "You haven't changed a bit!" They leaned forward to kiss, when Cornelia began whispering from a long way off, "Oh, is there anything you want to tell me? Is there anything I can do for you?"

Yes, she had changed her mind after sixty years and she would like to see George. I want you to find George. Find him and be sure to tell him I forgot him. I want him to know I had my husband just the same and my children and my house like any other woman. A good house too and a good husband that I loved and fine children out of him. Better than I hoped for even. Tell him I was given back everything he took away and more. Oh, no, oh, God, no, there was something else besides the house and the man and the children. Oh, surely they were not all? What was it? Something not given back. . . . Her breath crowded down under her ribs and grew into a monstrous frightening shape with cutting edges; it bored up into her head, and the agony was unbelievable: Yes, John, get the doctor now, no more talk, my time has come.

When this one was born it should be the last. The last. It should have been born first, for it was the one she had truly wanted. Everything came in good time. Nothing left out, left over. She was strong, in three days she would be as well as ever. Better. A woman needed milk in her to have her full health.

"Mother, do you hear me?"

"I've been telling you—"

"Mother, Father Connolly's here."

"I went to Holy Communion only last week. Tell him I'm not so sinful as all that."

"Father just wants to speak to you."

He could speak as much as he pleased. It was like him to drop in and inquire about her soul as if it were a teething baby, and then stay on for a cup of tea and a round of cards and gossip. He always had a funny story of some sort, usually about an Irishman who made his little mistakes and confessed them, and the point lay in some absurd thing he would blurt out in the confessional showing his struggles between native piety and original sin. Granny felt easy about her soul. Cornelia, where are your manners? Give Father Connolly a chair. She had her secret comfortable understanding with a few favorite saints who cleared a straight road to God for her. All as surely signed and sealed as the papers for the new Forty Acres. Forever . . . heirs and assigns forever. Since the day the wedding cake was not cut, but thrown out and wasted. The whole bottom dropped out of the world, and there she was blind and sweating with nothing under her feet and the walls falling away. His hand had caught her under the breast, she had not fallen, there was the freshly polished floor with the green rug on it, just as before.

He had cursed like a sailor's parrot and said, "I'll kill him for you." Don't lay a hand on him, for my sake leave something to God. "Now, Ellen, you must believe what I tell you. . . ."

So there was nothing, nothing to worry about any more, except sometimes in the night one of the children screamed in a nightmare, and they both hustled out shaking and hunting for the matches and calling, "There, wait a minute, here we are!" John, get the doctor now, Hapsy's time has come. But there was Hapsy standing by the bed in a white cap. "Cornelia, tell Hapsy to take off her cap. I can't see her plain."

Her eyes opened very wide and the room stood out like a picture she had seen somewhere. Dark colors with the shadows rising towards the ceiling in long angles. The tall black dresser gleamed with nothing on it but John's picture, enlarged from a little one, with John's eyes very black when they should have been blue. You never saw him, so how do you know how he looked? But the man insisted the copy was perfect, it was very rich and handsome. For a picture, yes, but it's not my husband. The table by the bed had a linen cover and a candle and a crucifix. The light was blue from Cornelia's silk lampshades. No sort of light at all, just frippery. You had to live forty years with kerosene lamps to appreciate honest electricity. She felt very strong and she saw Doctor Harry with a rosy nimbus around him.

"You look like a saint, Doctor Harry, and I vow that's as near as you'll ever come to it."

"She's saying something."

"I heard you, Cornelia. What's all this carrying-on?"

"Father Connolly's saying—"

Cornelia's voice staggered and bumped like a cart in a bad road. It rounded corners and turned back again and arrived nowhere. Granny stepped up in the cart very lightly and reached for the reins, but a man sat beside her and she knew him by his hands, driving the cart. She did not look in his face, for she knew without seeing, but looked instead down the road where the trees leaned over and bowed to each other and a thousand birds were singing a Mass. She felt like singing too, but she put her hand in the bosom of her dress and pulled out a rosary, and Father Connolly murmured Latin in a very solemn voice and tickled her feet. My God, will you stop that nonsense? I'm a married woman. What if he did run away and leave me to face the priest by myself? I found another a whole world better. I wouldn't have exchanged my husband for anybody except St. Michael himself, and you may tell him that for me with a thank you in the bargain.

Light flashed on her closed eyelids, and a deep roaring shook her. Cornelia, is that lightning? I hear thunder. There's going to be a storm. Close all the windows. Call the children in. . . . "Mother, here we are, all of us." "Is that you, Hapsy?" "Oh no, I'm Lydia. We drove as fast as we could." Their faces drifted above her, drifted away. The rosary fell out of her hands and Lydia put it back. Jimmy tried to help, their hands fumbled together, and Granny closed two fingers around Jimmy's thumb. Beads wouldn't do, it must be something alive. She was so amazed her thoughts ran round and round. So, my dear Lord, this is my death and I wasn't even thinking about it. My children have come to see me die. But I can't, it's not time. Oh, I always hated surprises. I wanted to give Cornelia the amethyst set—Cornelia, you're to have the amethyst set, but Hapsy's to wear it when she wants, and, Doctor Harry, do shut up. Nobody sent for you. Oh, my dear Lord, do wait a minute. I meant to do something about the Forty Acres, Jimmy doesn't need it and Lydia will later on, with that worthless husband of hers. I meant to finish the altar cloth and send six bottles of wine to Sister Borgia for her dyspepsia. I want to send six bottles of wine to Sister Borgia, Father Connolly, now don't let me forget.

Cornelia's voice made short turns and tilted over and crashed. "Oh, Mother, oh, Mother, oh, Mother. . . ."

"I'm not going, Cornelia. I'm taken by surprise. I can't go."

You'll see Hapsy again. What about her? "I thought you'd never come." Granny made a long journey outward, looking for Hapsy. What if I don't find her? What then? Her heart sank down and down, there was no bottom to death, she couldn't come to the end of it. The blue light from Cornelia's lampshade drew into a tiny point in the center of her brain, it flickered and winked like an eye, quietly it fluttered and dwindled. Granny lay curled down within herself, amazed and watchful, staring at the point of light that was herself; her body was now only a deeper mass of shadow in an endless darkness and this darkness would curl around the light and swallow it up. God, give a sign!

For the second time there was no sign. Again no bridegroom and the priest in the house. She could not remember any other sorrow because this grief wiped them all away. Oh, no, there's nothing more cruel than this—I'll never forgive it. She stretched herself with a deep breath and blew out the light.

Questions for Discussion

1. What does the opening paragraph reveal about Granny Weatherall's personality?

2. Interpret the name "Weatherall."

3. What is the connection between the jilting that Granny cannot forget and her death?

4. In what ways does Porter suggest Granny's mental dissolution? How effective is the suggestion?

Suggestions for Writing

1. Write an essay about the connection between religious faith and romantic love in this story.

2. Are you sympathetic toward Granny? Write a journal entry in response to this question.

3. Write a monologue (which may eventually become a story) from the point of view of someone who is in an extreme mental or physical state (in great pain, about to die, shocked about some event, or so on).

The Chrysanthemums

JOHN STEINBECK

The high grey-flannel fog of winter closed off the Salinas Valley from the sky and from all the rest of the world. On every side it sat like a lid on the mountains and made of the great valley a closed pot. On the broad, level land floor the gang plows bit deep and left the black earth shining like metal where the shares had cut. On the foothill ranches across the Salinas River, the yellow stubble fields seemed to be bathed in pale cold sunshine, but there was no sunshine in the valley now in December. The thick willow scrub along the river flamed with sharp and positive yellow leaves.

It was a time of quiet and of waiting. The air was cold and tender. A light wind blew up from the southwest so that the farmers were mildly hopeful of a good rain before long; but fog and rain do not go together.

Across the river, on Henry Allen's foothill ranch there was little work to be done, for the hay was cut and stored and the orchards were plowed up to receive the rain deeply when it should come. The cattle on the higher slopes were becoming shaggy and rough-coated.

Elisa Allen, working in her flower garden, looked down across the yard and saw Henry, her husband, talking to two men in business suits. The three of them stood by the tractor shed, each man with one foot on the side of the little Fordson. They smoked cigarettes and studied the machine as they talked.

Elisa watched them for a moment and then went back to her work. She was thirty-five. Her face was lean and strong and her eyes were as clear as water. Her figure looked blocked and heavy in her gardening costume, a man's black hat pulled low down over her eyes, clod-hopper shoes, a figured print dress almost completely covered by a big corduroy apron with four big pockets to hold the snips, the trowel and scratcher, the seeds and the knife she worked with. She wore heavy leather gloves to protect her hands while she worked.

She was cutting down the old year's chrysanthemum stalks with a pair of short and powerful scissors. She looked down toward the men by the tractor shed now and then. Her face was eager and mature and handsome; even her work with the scissors was over-eager, over-powerful. The chrysanthemum stems seemed too small and easy for her energy.

She brushed a cloud of hair out of her eyes with the back of her glove, and left a smudge of earth on her cheek in doing it. Behind her stood the neat white farm house with red geraniums close-banked around it as high as the windows. It was a hard-swept looking little house with hard-polished windows, and a clean mud-mat on the front steps.

Elisa cast another glance toward the tractor shed. The strangers were getting into their Ford coupe. She took off a glove and put her strong fingers down into the forest of new green chrysanthemum sprouts that were growing around the old roots. She spread the leaves and looked down among the close-growing stems. No aphids were there, no sowbugs or snails or cutworms. Her terrier fingers destroyed such pests before they could get started.

Elisa started at the sound of her husband's voice. He had come near quietly, and he leaned over the wire fence that protected her flower garden from cattle and dogs and chickens.

"At it again," he said. "You've got a strong new crop coming."

Elisa straightened her back and pulled on the gardening glove again. "Yes. They'll be strong this coming year." In her tone and on her face there was a little smugness.

"You've got a gift with things," Henry observed. "Some of those yellow chrysanthemums you had this year were ten inches across. I wish you'd work out in the orchard and raise some apples that big."

Her eyes sharpened. "Maybe I could do it, too. I've a gift with things, all right. My mother had it. She could stick anything in the ground and make it grow. She said it was having planters' hands that knew how to do it."

"Well, it sure works with flowers," he said.

"Henry, who were those men you were talking to?"

"Why, sure, that's what I came to tell you. They were from the Western Meat Company. I sold those thirty head of three-year-old steers. Got nearly my own price, too."

"Good," she said. "Good for you."

"And I thought," he continued, "I thought how it's Saturday afternoon, and we might go into Salinas for dinner at a restaurant, and then to a picture show—to celebrate, you see."

"Good," she repeated. "Oh, yes. That will be good."

Henry put on his joking tone. "There's fights tonight. How'd you like to go to the fights?"

"Oh, no," she said breathlessly. "No, I wouldn't like fights."

"Just fooling, Elisa. We'll go to a movie. Let's see. It's two now. I'm going to take Scotty and bring down those steers from the hill. It'll take us maybe two hours. We'll go in town about five and have dinner at the Cominos Hotel. Like that?"

"Of course I'll like it. It's good to eat away from home."

"All right, then. I'll go get up a couple of horses."

She said, "I'll have plenty of time to transplant some of these sets, I guess."

She heard her husband calling Scotty down by the barn. And a little later she saw the two men ride up the pale yellow hillside in search of the steers.

There was a little square sandy bed kept for rooting the chrysanthemums. With her trowel she turned the soil over and over, and smoothed it and patted it firm. Then she dug ten parallel trenches to receive the sets. Back at the chrysanthemum bed she pulled out the little crisp shoots, trimmed off the leaves of each one with her scissors and laid it on a small orderly pile.

A squeak of wheels and plod of hoofs came from the road. Elisa looked up. The country road ran along the dense bank of willows and cottonwoods that bordered the river, and up this road came a curious vehicle, curiously drawn. It was an oid spring-wagon, with a round canvas top on it like the corner of a prairie schooner. It was drawn by an old bay horse and a little grey-and-white burro. A big stubble-bearded man sat between the cover flaps and drove the crawling team. Underneath the wagon, between the hind wheels, a lean and rangy mongrel dog walked sedately. Words were painted on the canvas, in clumsy, crooked letters. "Pots, pans, knives, sisors, lawn mores, Fixed." Two rows of articles, and the triumphantly definitive "Fixed" below. The black paint had run down in little sharp points beneath each letter.

Elisa, squatting on the ground, watched to see the crazy, loose-jointed wagon pass by. But it didn't pass. It turned into the farm road in front of her house, crooked old wheels skirling and squeaking. The rangy dog darted from between the wheels and ran ahead. Instantly the two ranch shepherds flew out at him. Then all three stopped, and with stiff and quivering tails, with taut straight legs, with ambassadorial dignity, they slowly circled, sniffing daintily. The caravan pulled up to Elisa's wire fence and stopped. Now the newcomer dog, feeling out-numbered, lowered his tail and retired under the wagon with raised hackles and bared teeth.

The man on the wagon seat called out, "That's a bad dog in a fight when he gets started."

Elisa laughed. "I see he is. How soon does he generally get started?"

The man caught up her laughter and echoed it heartily. "Sometimes not for weeks and weeks," he said. He climbed stiffly down, over the wheel. The horse and the donkey drooped like unwatered flowers.

Elisa saw that he was a very big man. Although his hair and beard were greying, he did not look old. His worn black suit was wrinkled and spotted with grease. The laughter had disappeared from his face and eyes the moment his laughing voice ceased. His eyes were dark, and they were full of the brooding that gets in the eyes of teamsters and of sailors. The calloused hands he rested on the wire fence were cracked, and every crack was a black line. He took off his battered hat.

"I'm off my general road, ma'am," he said. "Does this dirt road cut over across the river to the Los Angeles highway?"

Elisa stood up and shoved the thick scissors in her apron pocket. "Well, yes, it does, but it winds around and then fords the river. I don't think your team could pull through the sand."

He replied with some asperity, "It might surprise you what them beasts can pull through."

"When they get started?" she asked.

He smiled for a second. "Yes. When they get started."

"Well," said Elisa, "I think you'll save time if you go back to the Salinas road and pick up the highway there."

He drew a big finger down the chicken wire and made it sing. "I ain't in any hurry, ma'am. I go from Seattle to San Diego and back every year. Takes all my time. About six months each way. I aim to follow nice weather."

Elisa took off her gloves and stuffed them in the apron pocket with the scissors. She touched the under edge of her man's hat, searching for fugitive hairs. "That sounds like a nice kind of a way to live," she said.

He leaned confidentially over the fence. "Maybe you noticed the writing on my wagon. I mend pots and sharpen knives and scissors. You got any of them things to do?"

"Oh, no," she said, quickly. "Nothing like that." Her eyes hardened with resistance.

"Scissors is the worst thing," he explained. "Most people just ruin scissors trying to sharpen 'em, but I know how. I got a special tool. It's a little bobbit kind of thing, and patented. But it sure does the trick."

"No. My scissors are all sharp."

"All right, then. Take a pot," he continued earnestly, "a bent pot, or a pot with a hole. I can make it like new so you don't have to buy no new ones. That's a saving for you."

"No," she said shortly. "I tell you I have nothing like that for you to do."

His face fell to an exaggerated sadness. His voice took on a whining undertone. "I ain't had a thing to do today. Maybe I won't have no supper tonight. You see I'm off my regular road. I know folks on the highway clear from Seattle to San Diego. They save their things for me to sharpen up because they know I do it so good and save them money."

"I'm sorry," Elisa said irritably. "I haven't anything for you to do."

His eyes left her face and fell to searching the ground. They roamed about until they came to the chrysanthemum bed where she had been working. "What's them plants, ma'am?"

The irritation and resistance melted from Elisa's face. "Oh, those are chrysanthemums, giant whites and yellows. I raise them every year, bigger than anybody around here."

"Kind of a long-stemmed flower? Looks like a quick puff of colored smoke?" he asked.

"That's it. What a nice way to describe them."

"They smell kind of nasty till you get used to them," he said.

"It's a good bitter smell," she retorted, "not nasty at all."

He changed his tone quickly. "I like the smell myself."

"I had ten-inch blooms this year," she said.

The man leaned farther over the fence. "Look. I know a lady down the road a piece, has got the nicest garden you ever seen. Got nearly every kind of flower but no chrysanthemums. Last time I was mending a copper-bottom washtub for her (that's a hard job but I do it good), she said to me, 'If you ever run acrost some nice chrysanthemums I wish you'd try to get me a few seeds.' That's what she told me."

Elisa's eyes grew alert and eager. "She couldn't have known much about chrysanthemums. You *can* raise them from seed, but it's much easier to root the little sprouts you see there."

"Oh," he said. "I s'pose I can't take none to her, then."

"Why yes you can," Elisa cried. "I can put some in damp sand, and you can carry them right along with you. They'll take root in the pot if you keep them damp. And then she can transplant them."

"She'd sure like to have some, ma'am. You say they're nice ones?"

"Beautiful," she said. "Oh, beautiful." Her eyes shone. She tore off the battered hat and shook out her dark pretty hair. "I'll put them in a flower pot, and you can take them right with you. Come into the yard."

While the man came through the picket gate Elisa ran excitedly along the geranium-bordered path to the back of the house. And she returned carrying a big red flower pot. The gloves were forgotten now. She kneeled on the ground by the starting bed and dug up the sandy soil with her fingers and scooped it into the bright new flower pot. Then she picked up the little pile of shoots she had prepared. With her strong fingers she pressed them into the sand and tamped around them with her knuckles. The man stood over her. "I'll tell you what to do," she said. "You remember so you can tell the lady."

"Yes, I'll try to remember."

"Well, look. These will take root in about a month. Then she must set them out, about a foot apart in good rich earth like this, see?" She lifted a handful of dark soil for him to look at. "They'll grow fast and tall. Now remember this: In July tell her to cut them down, about eight inches from the ground."

"Before they bloom?" he asked.

"Yes, before they bloom." Her face was tight with eagerness. "They'll grow right up again. About the last of September the buds will start."

She stopped and seemed perplexed. "It's the budding that takes the most care," she said hesitantly. "I don't know how to tell you." She looked deep into his eyes, searchingly. Her mouth opened a little, and she seemed to be listening. "I'll try to tell you," she said. "Did you ever hear of planting hands?"

"Can't say I have, ma'am."

"Well, I can only tell you what it feels like. It's when you're picking off the buds you don't want. Everything goes right down into your fingertips. You watch your fingers work. They do it themselves. You can feel how it is. They pick and pick the buds. They never make a mistake. They're with the plant. Do you see? Your fingers and the plant. You can feel that, right up your arm. They know. They never make a mistake. You can feel it. When you're like that you can't do anything wrong. Do you see that? Can you understand that?"

She was kneeling on the ground looking up at him. Her breast swelled passionately.

The man's eyes narrowed. He looked away self-consciously. "Maybe I know," he said. "Sometimes in the night in the wagon there—"

Elisa's voice grew husky. She broke in on him, "I've never lived as you do, but I know what you mean. When the night is dark—why, the stars are sharp-pointed, and there's quiet. Why, you rise up and up! Every pointed star gets driven into your body. It's like that. Hot and sharp and—lovely."

Kneeling there, her hand went out toward his legs in the greasy black trousers. Her hesitant fingers almost touched the cloth. Then her hand dropped to the ground. She crouched low like a fawning dog.

He said, "It's nice, just like you say. Only when you don't have no dinner, it ain't."

She stood up then, very straight, and her face was ashamed. She held the flower pot out to him and placed it gently in his arms. "Here. Put it in your wagon, on the seat, where you can watch it. Maybe I can find something for you to do."

At the back of the house she dug in the can pile and found two old and battered aluminum saucepans. She carried them back and gave them to him. "Here, maybe you can fix these."

His manner changed. He became professional. "Good as new I can fix them." At the back of his wagon he set a little anvil, and out of an oily tool box dug a small machine hammer. Elisa came through the gate to watch him while he pounded out the dents in the kettles. His mouth grew sure and knowing. At a difficult part of the work he sucked his under-lip.

"You sleep right in the wagon?" Elisa asked.

"Right in the wagon, ma'am. Rain or shine I'm dry as a cow in there."

"It must be nice," she said. "It must be very nice. I wish women could do such things."

"It ain't the right kind of a life for a woman."

Her upper lip raised a little, showing her teeth. "How do you know? How can you tell?" she said.

"I don't know, ma'am," he protested. "Of course I don't know. Now here's your kettles, done. You don't have to buy no new ones."

"How much?"

"Oh, fifty cents'll do. I keep my prices down and my work good. That's why I have all them satisfied customers up and down the highway."

Elisa brought him a fifty-cent piece from the house and dropped it in his hand. "You might be surprised to have a rival some time. I can sharpen scissors, too. And I can beat the dents out of little pots. I could show you what a woman might do."

He put his hammer back in the oily box and shoved the little anvil out of sight. "It would be a lonely life for a woman, ma'am, and a scarey life, too, with animals creeping under the wagon all night." He climbed over the singletree, steadying himself with a hand on the burro's white rump. He settled himself in the seat, picked up the lines. "Thank you kindly, ma'am," he said. "I'll do like you told me; I'll go back and catch the Salinas road."

"Mind," she called, "if you're long in getting there, keep the sand damp."

"Sand, ma'am? . . . Sand? Oh, sure. You mean around the chrysanthemums. Sure I will." He clucked his tongue. The beasts leaned luxuriously into their collars. The mongrel dog took his place between the back wheels. The wagon turned and crawled out the entrance road and back the way it had come, along the river.

Elisa stood in front of her wire fence watching the slow progress of the caravan. Her shoulders were straight, her head thrown back, her eyes half-closed, so that the scene came vaguely into them. Her lips moved silently, forming the words "Good-bye—good-bye." Then she whispered, "That's a bright direction. There's a glowing there." The sound of her whisper startled her. She shook herself free and looked about to see whether anyone had been listening. Only the dogs had heard. They lifted their heads toward her from their sleeping in the dust, and then stretched out their chins and settled asleep again. Elisa turned and ran hurriedly into the house.

In the kitchen she reached behind the stove and felt the water tank. It was full of hot water from the noonday cooking. In the bathroom she tore off her soiled clothes and flung them into the corner. And then she scrubbed herself with a little block of pumice, legs and thighs, loins and chest and arms, until her skin was scratched and red. When she had dried herself she stood in front of a mirror in her bedroom and looked at her body. She tightened her stomach and threw out her chest. She turned and looked over her shoulder at her back.

After a while she began to dress, slowly. She put on her newest underclothing and her nicest stockings and the dress which was the symbol of her prettiness. She worked carefully on her hair, penciled her eyebrows and rouged her lips.

Before she was finished she heard the little thunder of hoofs and the shouts of Henry and his helper as they drove the red steers into the corral. She heard the gate bang shut and set herself for Henry's arrival.

His step sounded on the porch. He entered the house calling, "Elisa, where are you?"

"In my room, dressing. I'm not ready. There's hot water for your bath. Hurry up. It's getting late."

When she heard him splashing in the tub, Elisa laid his dark suit on the bed, and shirt and socks and tie beside it. She stood his polished shoes on the floor beside the bed. Then she went to the porch and sat primly and stiffly down. She looked toward the river road where the willow-line was still yellow with frosted leaves so that under the high grey fog they seemed a thin band of sunshine. This was the only color in the grey afternoon. She sat unmoving for a long time. Her eyes blinked rarely.

Henry came banging out of the door, shoving his tie inside his vest as he came. Elisa stiffened and her face grew tight. Henry stopped short and looked at her. "Why—why, Elisa. You look so nice!"

"Nice? You think I look nice? What do you mean by 'nice'?"

Henry blundered on. "I don't know. I mean you look different, strong and happy."

"I am strong? Yes, strong. What do you mean 'strong'?"

He looked bewildered. "You're playing some kind of a game," he said helplessly. "It's a kind of a play. You look strong enough to break a calf over your knee, happy enough to eat it like a watermelon."

For a second she lost her rigidity. "Henry! Don't talk like that. You didn't know what you said." She grew complete again. "I'm strong," she boasted. "I never knew before how strong."

Henry looked down toward the tractor shed, and when he brought his eyes back to her, they were his own again. "I'll get out the car. You can put on your coat while I'm starting."

Elisa went into the house. She heard him drive to the gate and idle down his motor, and then she took a long time to put on her hat. She pulled it here and pressed it there. When Henry turned the motor off she slipped into her coat and went out.

The little roadster bounced along on the dirt road by the river, raising the birds and driving the rabbits into the brush. Two cranes flapped heavily over the willow-line and dropped into the river-bed.

Far ahead on the road Elisa saw a dark speck. She knew.

She tried not to look as they passed it, but her eyes would not obey. She whispered to herself sadly, "He might have thrown them off the road. That wouldn't have been much trouble, not very much. But he kept the pot," she explained, "He had to keep the pot. That's why he couldn't get them off the road."

The roadster turned a bend and she saw the caravan ahead. She swung full around toward her husband so she could not see the little covered wagon and the mismatched team as the car passed them.

In a moment it was over. The thing was done. She did not look back.

She said loudly, to be heard above the motor, "It will be good, tonight, a good dinner."

"Now you're changed again," Henry complained. He took one hand from the wheel and patted her knee. "I ought to take you in to dinner oftener. It would be good for both of us. We get so heavy out on the ranch."

"Henry," she asked, "could we have wine at dinner?"

"Sure we could. Say! That will be fine."

She was silent for a while; then she said, "Henry, at those prize fights, do the men hurt each other very much?"

"Sometimes a little, not often. Why?"

"Well, I've read how they break noses, and blood runs down their chests. I've read how the fighting gloves get heavy and soggy with blood."

He looked around at her. "What's the matter, Elisa? I didn't know you read things like that." He brought the car to a stop, then turned to the right over the Salinas River bridge.

"Do any women ever go to the fights?" she asked.

"Oh, sure, some. What's the matter, Elisa? Do you want to go? I don't think you'd like it, but I'll take you if you really want to go."

She relaxed limply in the seat. "Oh, no. No. I don't want to go. I'm sure I don't." Her face was turned away from him. "It will be enough if we can have wine. It will be plenty." She turned up her coat collar so he could not see that she was crying weakly—like an old woman.

Questions for Discussion

1. What do we find out about Henry and Elisa in the scenes before the tinker arrives?

2. What is it about Elisa's character and situation that makes her vulnerable?

3. Why doesn't she tell Henry what happened to her?

4. How important is the setting to this story?

Suggestions for Writing

1. Write an essay in which you compare and contrast Elisa with the women characters in the stories by Chopin, Gilman, or Hurston.

2. Read *East of Eden,* a novel by Steinbeck set in California's Salinas Valley, and write an essay that assesses its use of setting.

3. Assuming that "The Chrysanthemums" is a regional story, what elements in it appeal to readers unfamiliar with the region? In other words, what is universal about this story? Write a response to these questions in your journal.

Petrified Man

EUDORA   WELTY

"Reach in my purse and git me a cigarette without no powder in it if you kin, Mrs. Fletcher, honey," said Leota to her ten o'clock shampoo-and-set customer. "I don't like no perfumed cigarettes."

Mrs. Fletcher gladly reached over to the lavender shelf under the lavender-framed mirror, shook a hair net loose from the clasp of the patent-leather bag, and slapped her hand down quickly on a powder puff which burst out when the purse was opened.

"Why, look at the peanuts, Leota!" said Mrs. Fletcher in her marvelling voice.

"Honey, them goobers has been in my purse a week if they's been in it a day. Mrs. Pike bought them peanuts."

"Who's Mrs. Pike?" asked Mrs. Fletcher, settling back. Hidden in this den of curling fluid and henna packs, separated by a lavender swing-door from the other customers, who were being gratified in other booths, she could give her curiosity its freedom. She looked expectantly at the black part in Leota's yellow curls as she bent to light the cigarette.

"Mrs. Pike is this lady from New Orleans," said Leota, puffing, and pressing into Mrs. Fletcher's scalp with strong red-nailed fingers. "A friend, not a customer. You see, like maybe I told you last time, me and Fred and Sal and Joe all had us a fuss, so Sal and Joe up and moved out, so we didn't do a thing but rent out their room. So we rented it to Mrs. Pike. And Mr. Pike." She flicked an ash into the basket of dirty towels. "Mrs. Pike is a very decided blonde. *She* bought me the peanuts."

"She must be cute," said Mrs. Fletcher.

"Honey, 'cute' ain't the word for what she is. I'm tellin' you, Mrs. Pike is attractive. She has her a good time. She's got a sharp eye out, Mrs. Pike has."

She dashed the comb through the air, and paused dramatically as a cloud of Mrs. Fletcher's hennaed hair floated out of the lavender teeth like a small storm-cloud.

"Hair fallin'."

"Aw, Leota."

"Uh-huh, commencin' to fall out," said Leota, combing again, and letting fall another cloud.

"Is it any dandruff in it?" Mrs. Fletcher was frowning, her hair-line eyebrows diving down toward her nose, and her wrinkled, beady-lashed eyelids batting with concentration.

"Nope." She combed again. "Just fallin' out."

"Bet it was that last perm'nent you gave me that did it," Mrs. Fletcher said cruelly. "Remember you cooked me fourteen minutes."

"You had fourteen minutes comin' to you," said Leota with finality.

"Bound to be somethin'," persisted Mrs. Fletcher. "Dandruff, dandruff. I couldn't of caught a thing like that from Mr. Fletcher, could I?"

"Well," Leota answered at last, "you know what I heard in here yestiddy, one of Thelma's ladies was settin' over yonder in Thelma's booth gittin' a machineless, and I don't mean to insist or insinuate or anything, Mrs. Fletcher, but Thelma's lady just happ'med to throw out—I forgotten what she was talkin' about at the time—that you was p-r-e-g., and lots of times that'll make your hair do awful funny, fall out and God knows what all. It just ain't our fault, is the way I look at it."

There was a pause. The women stared at each other in the mirror.

"Who was it?" demanded Mrs. Fletcher.

"Honey, I really couldn't say," said Leota. "Not that you look it."

"Where's Thelma? I'll get it out of her," said Mrs. Fletcher.

"Now, honey, I wouldn't go and git mad over a little thing like that," Leota said, combing hastily, as though to hold Mrs. Fletcher down by the hair. "I'm sure it was somebody didn't mean no harm in the world. How far gone are you?"

"Just wait," said Mrs. Fletcher, and shrieked for Thelma, who came in and took a drag from Leota's cigarette.

"Thelma, honey, throw your mind back to yestiddy if you kin," said Leota, drenching Mrs. Fletcher's hair with a thick fluid and catching the overflow in a cold wet towel at her neck.

"Well, I got my lady half wound for a spiral," said Thelma doubtfully.

"This won't take but a minute," said Leota. "Who is it you got in there, old Horse Face? Just cast your mind back and try to remember who your lady was yestiddy who happ'm to mention that my customer was pregnant, that's all. She's dead to know."

Thelma drooped her blood-red lips and looked over Mrs. Fletcher's head into the mirror. "Why, honey, I ain't got the faintest," she breathed. "I really don't recollect the faintest. But I'm sure she meant no harm. I declare, I forgot my hair finally got combed and thought it was a stranger behind me."

"Was it that Mrs. Hutchinson?" Mrs. Fletcher was tensely polite.

"Mrs. Hutchinson? Oh, Mrs. Hutchinson." Thelma batted her eyes. "Naw, precious, she come in Thursday and didn't ev'm mention your name. I doubt if she ev'm knows you're on the way."

"Thelma!" cried Leota staunchly.

"All I know is, whoever it is 'll be sorry some day. Why, I just barely knew it myself!" cried Mrs. Fletcher. "Just let her wait!"

"Why? What're you gonna do to her?"

It was a child's voice, and the women looked down. A little boy was making tents with aluminum wave pinchers on the floor under the sink.

"Billy Boy, hon, mustn't bother nice ladies," Leota smiled. She slapped him brightly and behind her back waved Thelma out of the booth. "Ain't Billy Boy a sight? Only three years old and already just nuts about the beauty-parlor business."

"I never saw him here before," said Mrs. Fletcher, still unmollified.

"He ain't been here before, that's how come," said Leota. "He belongs to Mrs. Pike. She got her a job but it was Fay's Millinery. He oughtn't to try on those ladies' hats, they come down over his eyes like I don't know what. They just git to look ridiculous, that's what, an' of course he's gonna put 'em on: hats. They tole Mrs. Pike they didn't appreciate him hangin' around there. Here, he couldn't hurt a thing."

"Well! I don't like children that much," said Mrs. Fletcher.

"Well!" said Leota moodily.

"Well! I'm almost tempted not to have this one," said Mrs. Fletcher. "That Mrs. Hutchinson! Just looks straight through you when she sees you on the street and then spits at you behind your back."

"Mr. Fletcher would beat you on the head if you didn't have it now," said Leota reasonably. "After going this far."

Mrs. Fletcher sat up straight. "Mr. Fletcher can't do a thing with me."

"He can't!" Leota winked at herself in the mirror.

"No, siree, he can't. If he so much as raises his voice against me, he knows good and well I'll have one of my sick headaches, and then I'm just not fit to live with. And if I really look that pregnant already—"

"Well, now, honey, I just want you to know—I habm't told any of my ladies and I ain't goin' to tell 'em—even that you're losin' your hair. You just get you one of those Stork-a-Lure dresses and stop worryin'. What people don't know don't hurt nobody, as Mrs. Pike says."

"Did you tell Mrs. Pike?" asked Mrs. Fletcher sulkily.

"Well, Mrs. Fletcher, look, you ain't ever goin' to lay eyes on Mrs. Pike or her lay eyes on you, so what diffunce does it make in the long run?"

"I knew it!" Mrs. Fletcher deliberately nodded her head so as to destroy a ringlet Leota was working on behind her ear. "Mrs. Pike!"

Leota sighed. "I reckon I might as well tell you. It wasn't any more Thelma's lady tole me you was pregnant than a bat."

"Not Mrs. Hutchinson?"

"Naw, Lord! It was Mrs. Pike."

"Mrs. Pike!" Mrs. Fletcher could only sputter and let curling fluid roll into her ear. "How could Mrs. Pike possibly know I was pregnant or otherwise, when she doesn't even know me? The nerve of some people!"

"Well, here's how it was. Remember Sunday?"

"Yes," said Mrs. Fletcher.

"Sunday, Mrs. Pike an' me was all by ourself. Mr. Pike and Fred had gone over to Eagle Lake, sayin' they was goin' to catch 'em some fish, but they didn't a course. So we was settin' in Mrs. Pike's car, it's a 1939 Dodge—"

"1939, eh," said Mrs. Fletcher.

"—An' we was gettin' us a Jax beer apiece—that's the beer that Mrs. Pike says is made right in N.O., so she won't drink no other kind. So I seen you drive up to the drugstore an' run in for just a secont, leavin' I reckon Mr. Fletcher in the car, an' come runnin' out with looked like a perscription. So I says to Mrs. Pike, just to be makin' talk, 'Right yonder's Mrs. Fletcher, and I reckon that's Mr. Fletcher—she's one of my regular customers," I says.

"I had on a figured print," said Mrs. Fletcher tentatively.

"You sure did," agreed Leota. "So Mrs. Pike, she give you a good look—she's very observant, a good judge of character, cute as a minute, you know—and she says, 'I bet you another Jax that lady's three months on the way.' "

"What gall!" said Mrs. Fletcher. "Mrs. Pike!"

"Mrs. Pike ain't goin' to bite you," said Leota. "Mrs. Pike is a lovely girl, you'd be crazy about her, Mrs. Fletcher. But she can't sit still a minute. We went to the travellin' freak show yestiddy after work. I got through early—nine o'clock. In the vacant store next door. What, you ain't been?"

"No, I despise freaks," declared Mrs. Fletcher.

"Aw. Well, honey, talkin' about bein' pregnant an' all, you ought to see those twins in a bottle, you really owe it to yourself."

"What twins?" asked Mrs. Fletcher out of the side of her mouth.

"Well, honey, they got these two twins in a bottle, see? Born joined plumb together—dead a course." Leota dropped her voice into a soft lyrical hum. "They was about this long—pardon—must of been full time, all right, wouldn't you say?—an' they had these two heads an' two faces an' four arms an' four legs, all kind of joined *here*. See, this face looked this-a-way, and the other face looked that-a-way, over their shoulder, see. Kinda pathetic."

"Glah!" said Mrs. Fletcher disapprovingly.

"Well, ugly? Honey, I mean to tell you—their parents was first cousins and all like that. Billy Boy, git me a fresh towel from off Teeny's stack—this 'n's wringin' wet—an' quit ticklin' my ankles with that curler. I declare! He don't miss nothin'."

"Me and Mr. Fletcher aren't one speck of kin, or he could never of had me," said Mrs. Fletcher placidly.

"Of course not!" protested Leota. "Neither is me an' Fred, not that we know of. Well, honey, what Mrs. Pike liked was the pygmies. They've got these pygmies down there, too, an' Mrs. Pike was just wild about 'em. You know, the teeniest men in the universe? Well, honey, they can just rest back on their little bohunkus an' roll around an' you can't hardly tell if they're sittin' or standin'. That'll give you some idea. They're about forty-two years old. Just suppose it was your husband!"

"Well, Mr. Fletcher is five foot nine and one half," said Mrs. Fletcher quickly.

"Fred's five foot ten," said Leota, "but I tell him he's still a shrimp, account of I'm so tall." She made a deep wave over Mrs. Fletcher's other temple with the comb. "Well, these pygmies are a kind of a dark brown, Mrs. Fletcher. Not bad-lookin' for what they are, you know."

"I wouldn't care for them," said Mrs. Fletcher. "What does that Mrs. Pike see in them?"

"Aw, I don't know," said Leota. "She's just cute, that's all. But they got this man, this petrified man, that ever'thing ever since he was nine years old, when it goes through his digestion, see, somehow Mrs. Pike says it goes to his joints and has been turning to stone."

"How awful!" said Mrs. Fletcher.

"He's forty-two too. That looks like a bad age."

"Who said so, that Mrs. Pike? I bet she's forty-two," said Mrs. Fletcher.

"Naw," said Leota. "Mrs. Pike's thirty-three, born in January, an Aquarian. He could move his head—like this. A course his head and mind ain't a joint, so to speak, and I guess his stomach ain't, either—not yet, anyways. But see—his food, he eats it, and it goes down, see, and then he digests it"—Leota rose on her toes for an instant—"and it goes out to his joints and before you can say 'Jack Robinson,' it's stone—pure stone. He's turning to stone. How'd you like to be married to a guy like that? All he can do, he can move his head just a quarter of an inch. A course he *looks* just *terrible*."

"I should think he would," said Mrs. Fletcher frostily. "Mr. Fletcher takes bending exercises every night of the world. I make him."

"All Fred does is lay around the house like a rug. I wouldn't be surprised if he woke up some day and couldn't move. The petrified man just sat there moving his quarter of an inch though," said Leota reminiscently.

"Did Mrs. Pike like the petrified man?" asked Mrs. Fletcher.

"Not as much as she did the others," said Leota deprecatingly. "And then she likes a man to be a good dresser, and all that."

"Is Mr. Pike a good dresser?" asked Mrs. Fletcher sceptically.

"Oh, well, yeah," said Leota, "but he's twelve or fourteen years older'n her. She ast Lady Evangeline about him."

"Who's Lady Evangeline?" asked Mrs. Fletcher.

"Well, it's this mind reader they got in the freak show," said Leota. "Was real good. Lady Evangeline is her name, and if I had another dollar I wouldn't do a thing but have my other palm read. She had what Mrs. Pike said was the 'sixth mind' but she had the worst manicure I ever saw on a living person."

"What did she tell Mrs. Pike?" asked Mrs. Fletcher.

"She told her Mr. Pike was as true to her as he could be and besides, would come into some money."

"Humph!" said Mrs. Fletcher. "What does he do?"

"I can't tell," said Leota, "because he don't work. Lady Evangeline didn't tell me enough about my nature or anything. And I would like to go back and find out some more about this boy. Used to go with this boy until he got married to this girl. Oh, shoot, that was about three and a half years ago, when you was still goin' to the Robert E. Lee Beauty Shop in Jackson. He married her for her money. Another fortune-teller tole me that at the time. So I'm not in love with him any more, anyway, besides being married to Fred, but Mrs. Pike thought, just for the hell of it, see, to ask Lady Evangeline was he happy."

"Does Mrs. Pike know everything about you already?" asked Mrs. Fletcher unbelievingly. "Mercy!"

"Oh, yeah, I tole her ever'thing about ever'thing, from now on back to I don't know when—to when I first started goin' out," said Leota. "So I ast Lady

Evangeline for one of my questions, was he happily married, and she says, just like she was glad I ask her, 'Honey,' she says, 'naw, he idn't. You write down this day, March 8, 1941,' she says, 'and mock it down: three years from today him and her won't be occupyin' the same bed.' There it is, up on the wall with them other dates—see, Mrs. Fletcher? And she says, 'Child, you ought to be glad you didn't git him, because he's so mercenary.' So I'm glad I married Fred. He sure ain't mercenary, money don't mean a thing to him. But I sure would like to go back and have my other palm read."

"Did Mrs. Pike believe in what the fortune-teller said?" asked Mrs. Fletcher in a superior tone of voice.

"Lord, yes, she's from New Orleans. Ever'body in New Orleans believes ever'thing spooky. One of 'em in New Orleans before it was raided says to Mrs. Pike one summer she was goin' to go from State to State and meet some grey-headed men, and, sure enough, she says she went on a beautician convention up to Chicago. . . ."

"Oh!" said Mrs. Fletcher. "Oh, is Mrs. Pike a beautician too?"

"Sure she is," protested Leota. "She's a beautician. I'm going to git her in here if I can. Before she married. But it don't leave you. She says sure enough, there was three men who was a very large part of making her trip what it was, and they all three had grey in their hair and they went in six States. Got Christmas cards from 'em. Billy Boy, go see if Thelma's got any dry cotton. Look how Mrs. Fletcher's a-drippin'."

"Where did Mrs. Pike meet Mr. Pike?" asked Mrs. Fletcher primly.

"On another train," said Leota.

"I met Mr. Fletcher, or rather he met me, in a rental library," said Mrs. Fletcher with dignity, as she watched the net come down over her head.

"Honey, me an' Fred, we met in a rumble seat eight months ago and we was practically on what you might call the way to the altar inside of half an hour," said Leota in a guttural voice, and bit a bobby pin open. "Course it don't last. Mrs. Pike says nothin' like that ever lasts."

"Mr. Fletcher and myself are as much in love as the day we married," said Mrs. Fletcher belligerently as Leota stuffed cotton into her ears.

"Mrs. Pike says it don't last," repeated Leota in a louder voice. "Now go git under the dryer. You can turn yourself on, can't you? I'll be back to comb you out. Durin' lunch I promised to give Mrs. Pike a facial. You know—free. Her bein' in the business, so to speak."

"I bet she needs one," said Mrs. Fletcher, letting the swing-door fly back against Leota. "Oh, pardon me."

A week later, on time for her appointment, Mrs. Fletcher sank heavily into Leota's chair after first removing a drug-store rental book, called *Life Is Like That,* from the seat. She stared in a discouraged way into the mirror.

"You can tell it when I'm sitting down, all right," she said.

Leota seemed preoccupied and stood shaking out a lavender cloth. She began to pin it around Mrs. Fletcher's neck in silence.

"I said you sure can tell it when I'm sitting straight on and coming at you this way," Mrs. Fletcher said.

"Why, honey, naw you can't," said Leota gloomily. "Why, I'd never know. If somebody was to come up to me on the street and say, 'Mrs. Fletcher is pregnant!' I'd say, 'Heck, she don't look it to me.' "

"If a certain party hadn't found it out and spread it around, it wouldn't be too late even now," said Mrs. Fletcher frostily, but Leota was almost choking her with the cloth, pinning it so tight, and she couldn't speak clearly. She paddled her hands in the air until Leota wearily loosened her.

"Listen, honey, you're just a virgin compared to Mrs. Montjoy," Leota was going on, still absent-minded. She bent Mrs. Fletcher back in the chair and, sighing, tossed liquid from a teacup on to her head and dug both hands into her scalp. "You know Mrs. Montjoy—her husband's that premature-gray-headed fella?"

"She's in the Trojan Garden Club, is all I know," said Mrs. Fletcher.

"Well, honey," said Leota, but in a weary voice, "she come in here not the week before and not the day before she had her baby—she come in here the very selfsame day, I mean to tell you. Child, we was all plumb scared to death. There she was! Come for her shampoo an' set. Why, Mrs. Fletcher, in an hour an' twenty minutes she was layin' up there in the Babtist Hospital with a seb'm-pound son. It was that close a shave. I declare, if I hadn't been so tired I would of drank up a bottle of gin that night."

"What gall," said Mrs. Fletcher. "I never knew her at all well."

"See, her husband was waitin' outside in the car, and her bags was all packed an' in the back seat, an' she was all ready, 'cept she wanted her shampoo an' set. An havin' one pain right after another. Her husband kep' comin' in here, scared-like, but couldn't do nothin' with her a course. She yelled bloody murder, too, but she always yelled her head off when I give her a perm'nent."

"She must of been crazy," said Mrs. Fletcher. "How did she look?"

"Shoot!" said Leota.

"Well, I can guess," said Mrs. Fletcher. "Awful."

"Just wanted to look pretty while she was havin' her baby, is all," said Leota airily. "Course, we was glad to give the lady what she was after—that's our motto—but I bet a hour later she wasn't payin' no mind to them little end curls. I bet she wasn't thinkin' about she ought to have on a net. It wouldn't of done her no good if she had."

"No, I don't suppose it would," said Mrs. Fletcher.

"Yeah man! She was a-yellin'. Just like when I give her her perm'nent."

"Her husband ought to make her behave. Don't it seem that way to you?" asked Mrs. Fletcher. "He ought to put his foot down."

"Ha," said Leota. "A lot he could do. Maybe some women is soft."

"Oh, you mistake me, I don't mean for her to get soft—far from it! Women have to stand up for themselves, or there's just no telling. But now you take me—I ask Mr. Fletcher's advice now and then, and he appreciates it, especially on something important, like is it time for a permanent—not that I've told him about the baby. He says, 'Why, dear, go ahead!' Just ask their *advice.*"

"Huh! If I ever ast Fred's advice we'd be floatin' down the Yazoo River on a houseboat or somethin' by this time," said Leota. "I'm sick of Fred. I told him to go over to Vicksburg."

"Is he going?" demanded Mrs. Fletcher.

"Sure. See, the fortune-teller—I went back and had my other palm read, since we've got to rent the room agin—said my lover was goin' to work in Vicksburg, so I don't know who she could mean, unless she meant Fred. And Fred ain't workin' here—that much is so."

"Is he going to work in Vicksburg?" asked Mrs. Fletcher. "And—"

"Sure. Lady Evangeline said so. Said the future is going to be brighter than the present. He don't want to go, but I ain't gonna put up with nothin' like that. Lays around the house an' bulls—did bull—with that good-for-nothin' Mr. Pike. He says if he goes who'll cook, but I says I never get to eat anyway—not meals. Billy Boy, take Mrs. Grover that *Screen Secrets* and leg it."

Mrs. Fletcher heard stamping feet go out the door.

"Is that that Mrs. Pike's little boy here again?" she asked, sitting up gingerly.

"Yeah, that's still him." Leota stuck out her tongue.

Mrs. Fletcher could hardly believe her eyes. "Well! How's Mrs. Pike, your attractive new friend with the sharp eyes who spreads it around town that perfect strangers are pregnant?" she asked in a sweetened tone.

"Oh, Mizziz Pike." Leota combed Mrs. Fletcher's hair with heavy strokes.

"You act like you're tired," said Mrs. Fletcher.

"Tired? Feel like it's four o'clock in the afternoon, already," said Leota. "I ain't told you the awful luck we had, me and Fred? It's the worst thing you ever heard of. Maybe *you* think Mrs. Pike's got sharp eyes. Shoot, there's a limit! Well, you know, we rented out our room to this Mr. and Mrs. Pike from New Orleans when Sal an' Joe Fentress got mad at us 'cause they drank up some home-brew we had in the closet—Sal an' Joe did. So, a week ago Sat'day Mr. and Mrs. Pike moved in. Well, I kinda fixed up the room, you know—put a sofa pillow on the couch and picked some ragged robbins and put in a vase, but they never did say they appreciated it. Anyway, then I put some old magazines on the table."

"I think that was lovely," said Mrs. Fletcher.

"Wait. So, come night 'fore last, Fred and this Mr. Pike, who Fred just took up with, was back from they said they was fishin', bein' as neither one of 'em has got a job to his name, and we was all settin' around in their room. So Mrs. Pike was settin' there readin' a old *Startling G-Men Tales* that was mine, mind you, I'd bought it myself, and all of a sudden she jumps!—into the air—you'd 'a' thought she'd set on a spider—an' says, 'Canfield'—ain't that silly, that's Mr. Pike—'Canfield, my God A'mighty,' she says, 'honey,' she says, 'we're rich, and you won't have to work.' Not that he turned one hand anyway. Well, me and Fred rushes over to her, and Mr. Pike, too, and there she sets, pointin' her finger at a photo in my copy of *Startling G-Man*. 'See that man?' yells Mrs. Pike. 'Remember him, Canfield?' 'Never forget a face,' says Mr. Pike. 'It's Mr. Petrie, that we stayed with him in the apartment next to ours in Toulouse Street in N.O. for six weeks. Mr. Petrie.' 'Well,' says Mrs. Pike, like she can't hold out one secont longer, 'Mr. Petrie is wanted for five hundred dollars cash, for rapin' four women in California, and I know where he is.'"

"Mercy!" said Mrs. Fletcher. "Where was he?"

At some time Leota had washed her hair and now she yanked her up by the back locks and sat her up.

"Know where he was?"

"I certainly don't," Mrs. Fletcher said. Her scalp hurt all over.

Leota flung a towel around the top of her customer's head. "Nowhere else but in that freak show! I saw him just as plain as Mrs. Pike. *He* was the petrified man!"

"Who would ever have thought that?" cried Mrs. Fletcher sympathetically.

"So Mr. Pike says, 'Well whatta you know about that,' an' he looks real hard at the photo and whistles. And she starts dancin' and singin' about their good luck. She meant our bad luck! I made a point of tellin' that fortune-teller the next time I saw her. I said, 'Listen, that magazine was layin' around the house for a month, and there was the freak show runnin' night an' day, not two steps away from my own beauty parlor, with Mr. Petrie just settin' there waitin'. An' it had to be Mr. and Mrs. Pike, almost perfect strangers.' "

"What gall," said Mrs. Fletcher. She was only sitting there, wrapped in a turban, but she did not mind.

"Fortune-tellers don't care. And Mrs. Pike, she goes around actin' like she thinks she was Mrs. God," said Leota. "So they're goin' to leave tomorrow, Mr. and Mrs. Pike. And in the meantime I got to keep that mean, bad little ole kid here, gettin' under my feet ever' minute of the day an' talkin' back too."

"Have they gotten the five hundred dollars' reward already?" asked Mrs. Fletcher.

"Well," said Leota, "at first Mr. Pike didn't want to do anything about it. Can you feature that? Said he kinda liked that ole bird and said he was real nice to 'em, lent 'em money or somethin'. But Mrs. Pike simply tole him he could just go to hell, and I can see her point. She says, 'You ain't worked a lick in six months, and here I make five hundred dollars in two seconts, and what thanks do I get for it? You go to hell, Canfield,' she says. "So," Leota went on in a despondent voice, "they called up the cops and they caught the ole bird, all right, right there in the freak show where I saw him with my own eyes, thinkin' he was petrified. He's the one. Did it under his real name—Mr. Petrie. Four women in California, all in the month of August. So Mrs. Pike gits five hundred dollars. And my magazine, and right next door to my beauty parlor. I cried all night, but Fred said it wasn't a bit of use and to go to sleep, because the whole thing was just a sort of coincidence—you know: can't do nothin' about it. He says it put him clean out of the notion of goin' to Vicksburg for a few days till we rent out the room again—no tellin' who we'll git this time."

"But can you imagine anybody knowing this old man, that's raped four women?" persisted Mrs. Fletcher, and she shuddered audibly. "Did Mrs. Pike *speak* to him when she met him in the freak show?"

Leota had begun to comb Mrs. Fletcher's hair. "I says to her, I says, 'I didn't notice you fallin' on his neck when he was the petrified man—don't tell me you didn't recognize your fine friend?' And she says, 'I didn't recognize him with that white powder all over his face. He just looked familiar.' Mrs. Pike says, 'and lots of people look familiar.' But she says that ole petrified man did put her in mind of somebody. She wondered who it was! Kep' her awake, which man she'd ever knew it reminded her of. So when she seen the photo, it all come to her. Like a flash. Mr. Petrie. The way he'd turn his head and look at her when she took him in his breakfast."

"Took him in his breakfast!" shrieked Mrs. Fletcher. "Listen—don't tell me. I'd a' felt something."

"Four women. I guess those women didn't have the faintest notion at the time they'd be worth a hundred an' twenty-five bucks a piece some day to Mrs. Pike. We ast her how old the fella was then, an' she says he musta had one foot in the grave, at least. Can you beat it?"

"Not really petrified at all, of course," said Mrs. Fletcher meditatively. She drew herself up. "I'd a' felt something," she said proudly.

"Shoot! I did feel somethin'," said Leota. "I tole Fred when I got home I felt so funny. I said, 'Fred, that ole petrified man sure did leave me with a funny feelin'.'" He says, 'Funny-haha or funny-peculiar?' and I says, 'Funny-peculiar.'" She pointed her comb into the air emphatically.

"I'll bet you did," said Mrs. Fletcher.

They both heard a crackling noise.

Leota screamed. "Billy Boy! What you doin' in my purse?"

"Aw, I'm just eatin' these ole stale peanuts up," said Billy Boy.

"You come here to me!" screamed Leota, recklessly flinging down the comb, which scattered a whole ashtray full of bobby pins and knocked down a row of Coca-Cola bottles. "This is the last straw!"

"I caught him! I caught him!" giggled Mrs. Fletcher. "I'll hold him on my lap. You bad, bad boy, you! I guess I better learn how to spank little old bad boys," she said.

Leota's eleven o'clock customer pushed open the swing-door upon Leota paddling him heartily with the brush, while he gave angry but belittling screams which penetrated beyond the booth and filled the whole curious beauty parlor. From everywhere ladies began to gather round to watch the paddling. Billy Boy kicked both Leota and Mrs. Fletcher as hard as he could, Mrs. Fletcher with her new fixed smile.

Billy Boy stomped through the group of wildhaired ladies and went out the door, but flung back the words, "If you're so smart, why ain't you rich?"

Questions for Discussion

1. How does Welty achieve the effect of dialect without necessarily overwhelming the reader?

2. How and why do Mrs. Fletcher's and Leota's attitudes toward Mrs. Pike change?

3. What is the effect of Billy Boy's getting in the last word?

Suggestions for Writing

1. Write an essay about Welty's story in which you discuss the ways Mrs. Fletcher and Leota are "petrified."

2. Write an essay about the images of women we find in this story.

3. Write a story that consists chiefly of dialogue between two characters and also features a story within a story.

Paul's Case
A Study in Temperament

WILLA CATHER

It was Paul's afternoon to appear before the faculty of the Pittsburgh High School to account for his various misdemeanors. He had been suspended a week ago, and his father had called at the Principal's office and confessed his perplexity about his son. Paul entered the faculty room suave and smiling. His clothes were a trifle outgrown, and the tan velvet on the collar of his open overcoat was frayed and worn; but for all that there was something of the dandy about him, and he wore an opal pin in his neatly knotted black four-in-hand, and a red carnation in his buttonhole. This latter adornment the faculty somehow felt was not properly significant of the contrite spirit befitting a boy under the ban of suspension.

Paul was tall for his age and very thin, with high, cramped shoulders and a narrow chest. His eyes were remarkable for a certain hysterical brilliancy, and he continually used them in a conscious, theatrical sort of way, peculiarly offensive in a boy. The pupils were abnormally large, as though he were addicted to belladonna, but there was a glassy glitter about them which that drug does not produce.

When questioned by the Principal as to why he was there Paul stated, politely enough, that he wanted to come back to school. This was a lie, but Paul was quite accustomed to lying; found it, indeed, indispensable for overcoming friction. His teachers were asked to state their respective charges against him, which they did with such a rancor and aggrievedness as evinced that this was not a usual case. Disorder and impertinence were among the offenses named, yet each of his instructors felt that it was scarcely possible to put into words the real cause of the trouble, which lay in a sort of hysterically defiant manner of the boy's; in the contempt which they all knew he felt for them, and which he seemingly made not the least effort to conceal. Once, when he had been making a synopsis of a paragraph at the blackboard, his English teacher had stepped to his side and attempted to guide his hand. Paul had started back with a shudder and thrust his hands violently behind him. The astonished woman could scarcely have been more hurt and embarrassed had he struck at her. The insult was so involuntary and definitely personal as to be unforgettable. In one way and another he had made all his teachers, men and women alike, conscious of the same feeling of physical aversion. In one class he habitually sat with his hand shading his eyes; in another he always looked out of the window during the recitation; in another he made a running commentary on the lecture, with humorous intention.

His teachers felt this afternoon that his whole attitude was symbolized by his shrug and his flippantly red carnation flower, and they fell upon him without mercy, his English teacher leading the pack. He stood through it smiling, his pale lips parted over his white teeth. (His lips were continually twitching, and he had a habit of raising his eyebrows that was contemptuous and irritating to the last degree.) Older boys than Paul had broken down and shed tears under that baptism of fire, but his set smile did not once desert him, and his only sign of discomfort was the nervous trembling of the fingers that toyed with the buttons of his overcoat, and an occasional jerking of the other hand that held his hat. Paul was always smiling, always glancing about him, seeming to feel that people might be watching him and trying to detect something. This conscious expression, since it was as far as possible from boyish mirthfulness, was usually attributed to insolence or "smartness."

As the inquisition proceeded one of his instructors repeated an impertinent remark of the boy's, and the Principal asked him whether he thought that a courteous speech to have made a woman. Paul shrugged his shoulders slightly and his eyebrows twitched.

"I don't know," he replied. "I didn't mean to be polite or impolite, either. I guess it's a sort of way I have of saying things regardless."

The Principal, who was a sympathetic man, asked him whether he didn't think that a way it would be well to get rid of. Paul grinned and said he guessed so. When he was told that he could go he bowed gracefully and went out. His bow was but a repetition of the scandalous red carnation.

His teachers were in despair, and his drawing master voiced the feeling of them all when he declared there was something about the boy which none of them understood. He added: "I don't really believe that smile of his comes altogether from insolence; there's something sort of haunted about it. The boy is not strong, for one thing. I happen to know that he was born in Colorado, only a few months before his mother died out there of a long illness. There is something wrong about the fellow."

The drawing master had come to realize that, in looking at Paul, one saw only his white teeth and the forced animation of his eyes. One warm afternoon the boy had gone to sleep at his drawing board, and his master had noted with amazement what a white, blueveined face it was; drawn and wrinkled like an old man's about the eyes, the lips twitching even in his sleep, and stiff with a nervous tension that drew them back from his teeth.

His teachers left the building dissatisfied and unhappy; humiliated to have felt so vindictive toward a mere boy, to have uttered this feeling in cutting terms, and to have set each other on, as it were, in the gruesome game of intemperate reproach. Some of them remembered having seen a miserable street cat set at bay by a ring of tormentors.

As for Paul, he ran down the hill whistling the "Soldiers' Chorus" from *Faust,* looking wildly behind him now and then to see whether some of his teachers were not there to writhe under his lightheartedness. As it was now late in the afternoon and Paul was on duty that evening as usher at Carnegie Hall, he decided that he would not go home to supper. When he reached the concert hall the doors were not yet open and, as it was chilly outside, he decided to go up into the picture gallery—always deserted at this hour—where there were some of Raffelli's gay studies of Paris streets and an airy blue Venetian scene or two that always exhilarated him. He was delighted to find no one in the gallery but the old guard, who sat in one corner, a newspaper on his knee, a black patch over one eye and the other closed. Paul possessed himself of the place and walked confidently up and down, whistling under his breath. After a while he sat down before a blue Rico and lost himself. When he bethought him to look at his watch, it was after seven o'clock, and he rose with a start and ran downstairs, making a face at Augustus, peering out from the cast room, and an evil gesture at the Venus de Milo as he passed her on the stairway.

When Paul reached the ushers' dressing room half a dozen boys were there already, and he began excitedly to tumble into his uniform. It was one of the few that at all approached fitting, and Paul thought it very becoming—though he knew that the tight, straight coat accentuated his narrow chest, about which he was exceedingly sensitive. He was always considerably excited while he dressed, twanging all over to the tuning of the strings and the preliminary flourishes of the horns in the music room; but tonight he seemed quite beside himself, and he teased and plagued the boys until, telling him that he was crazy, they put him down on the floor and sat on him.

Somewhat calmed by his suppression, Paul dashed out to the front of the house to seat the early comers. He was a model usher; gracious and smiling he ran up and down the aisles; nothing was too much trouble for him; he carried messages and brought programs as though it were his greatest pleasure in life, and all the people in his section thought him a charming boy, feeling that he remembered and admired them. As the house filled, he grew more and more vivacious and animated, and the color came to his cheeks and lips. It was very much as though this were a great reception and Paul were the host. Just as the musicians came out to take their places, his English teacher arrived with checks for the seats which a prominent manufacturer had taken for the season. She betrayed some embarrassment when she handed Paul the tickets, and a hauteur which subsequently made her feel very foolish. Paul was startled for a moment, and had the feeling of wanting to put her out; what business had she here among all these fine people and gay colors? He looked her over and decided that she was not appropriately dressed and must be a fool to sit downstairs in such togs. The tickets had probably been sent her out of kindness, he reflected as he put down a seat for her, and she had about as much right to sit there as he had.

When the symphony began Paul sank into one of the rear seats with a long sigh of relief, and lost himself, as he had done before the Rico. It was not that symphonies, as such, meant anything in particular to Paul, but the first sigh of the instruments seemed to free some hilarious and potent spirit within him; something that struggled there like the genie in the bottle found by the Arab fisherman. He felt a sudden zest of life; the lights danced before his eyes and the concert hall blazed into unimaginable splendor. When the soprano soloist came on Paul forgot even the nastiness of his teacher's being there and gave himself up to the peculiar stimulus such personages always had for him. The soloist chanced to be a German woman, by no means in her first youth, and the mother of many children; but she wore an elaborate gown and tiara, and above all she had that indefinable air of achievement, that world-shine upon her, which, in Paul's eyes, made her a veritable queen of Romance.

After a concert was over Paul was always irritable and wretched until he got to sleep, and tonight he was even more than usually restless. He had the feeling of not being able to let down, of its being impossible to give up this delicious excitement which was the only thing that could be called living at all. During the last number he withdrew and, after hastily changing his clothes in the dressing room, slipped out to the side door where the soprano's carriage stood. Here he began pacing rapidly up and down the walk, waiting to see her come out.

Over yonder, the Schenley, in its vacant stretch, loomed big and square through the fine rain, the windows of its twelve stories glowing like those of a lighted cardboard house under a Christmas tree. All the actors and singers of the better class stayed there when they were in the city, and a number of the big manufacturers of the place lived there in the winter. Paul had often hung about the hotel, watching the people go in and out, longing to enter and leave schoolmasters and dull care behind him forever.

At last the singer came out, accompanied by the conductor, who helped her into her carriage and closed the door with a cordial *auf wiedersehen* which set Paul to wondering whether she were not an old sweetheart of his. Paul followed the carriage over to the hotel, walking so rapidly as not to be far from the entrance when the singer alighted, and disappeared behind the swinging glass doors that were opened by a Negro in a tall hat and a long coat. In the moment that the door was ajar it seemed to Paul that he, too, entered. He seemed to feel himself go after her up the steps, into the warm, lighted building, into an exotic, tropical world of shiny, glistening surfaces and basking ease. He reflected upon the mysterious dishes that were brought into the dining room, the green bottles in buckets of ice, as he had seen them in the supper party pictures of the *Sunday World* supplement. A quick gust of wind brought the rain down with sudden vehemence, and Paul was startled to find that he was still outside in the slush of the gravel driveway; that his boots were letting in the water and his scanty overcoat was clinging wet about him; that the lights in front of the concert hall were out and that the rain was driving in sheets between him and the orange glow of the windows above him. There it was, what he wanted—tangibly before him, like the fairy world of a Christmas pantomime—but mocking spirits stood guard at the doors, and, as the rain beat in his face, Paul wondered whether he were destined always to shiver in the black night outside, looking up at it.

He turned and walked reluctantly toward the car tracks. The end had to come sometime; his father in his nightclothes at the top of the stairs, explanations that did not explain, hastily improvised fictions that were forever tripping him up, his upstairs room and its horrible yellow wallpaper, the creaking bureau with the greasy plush collarbox, and over his painted wooden bed the pictures of George Washington and John Calvin, and the framed motto, "Feed my Lambs," which had been worked in red worsted by his mother.

Half an hour later Paul alighted from his car and went slowly down one of the side streets off the main thoroughfare. It was a highly respectable street, where all the houses were exactly alike, and where businessmen of moderate means begot and reared large families of children, all of whom went to Sabbath school and learned the shorter catechism, and were interested in arithmetic; all of whom were as exactly alike as their homes, and of a piece with the monotony in which they lived. Paul never went up Cordelia Street without a shudder of loathing. His home was next to the house of the Cumberland minister. He approached it tonight with the nerveless sense of defeat, the hopeless feeling of sinking back forever into ugliness and commonness that he had always had when he came home. The moment he turned into Cordelia Street he felt the waters close above his head. After each of these orgies of living he experienced all the physical depression which follows a debauch; the loathing of respectable beds, of common food, of a house penetrated by kitchen odors; a shuddering repulsion for the flavorless, colorless mass of everyday existence; a morbid desire for cool things and soft lights and fresh flowers.

The nearer he approached the house, the more absolutely unequal Paul felt to the sight of it all: his ugly sleeping chamber; the cold bathroom with the grimy zinc tub, the cracked mirror, the dripping spigots; his father, at the top of the stairs, his hairy legs sticking out from his nightshirt, his feet thrust into carpet slippers. He was so much later than usual that there would certainly be inquiries and reproaches. Paul stopped short before the door. He felt that he could not be accosted by his father tonight; that he could not toss again on that miserable bed. He would not go in. He would tell his father that he had no carfare and it was raining so hard he had gone home with one of the boys and stayed all night.

Meanwhile, he was wet and cold. He went around to the back of the house and tried one of the basement windows, found it open, raised it cautiously, and scrambled down the cellar wall to the floor. There he stood, holding his breath, terrified by the noise he had made, but the floor above him was silent, and there was no creak on the stairs. He found a soapbox, and carried it over to the soft ring of light that streamed from the furnace door, and sat down. He was horribly afraid of rats, so he did not try to sleep, but sat looking distrustfully at the dark, still terrified lest he might have awakened his father. In such reactions, after one of the experiences which made days and nights out of the dreary blanks of the calendar, when his senses were deadened, Paul's head was always singularly clear. Suppose his father had heard him getting in at the window and had come down and shot him for a burglar? Then, again, suppose his father had come down, pistol in hand, and he had cried out in time to save himself, and his father had been horrified to think how nearly he had killed him? Then, again, suppose a day should come when his father would remember that night, and wish there had been no warning cry to stay his hand? With this last supposition Paul entertained himself until daybreak.

The following Sunday was fine; the sodden November chill was broken by the last flash of autumnal summer. In the morning Paul had to go to church and Sabbath school, as always. On seasonable Sunday afternoons the burghers of Cordelia Street always sat out on their front stoops and talked to their neighbors on the next stoop, or called to those across the street in neighborly fashion. The men usually sat on gay cushions placed upon the steps that led down to the sidewalk, while the women, in their Sunday "waists," sat in rockers on the cramped porches, pretending to be greatly at their ease. The children played in the streets; there were so many of them that the place resembled the recreation grounds of a kindergarten. The men on the steps—all in their shirt sleeves, their vests unbuttoned—sat with their legs well apart, their stomachs comfortably protruding, and talked of the prices of things, or told anecdotes of the sagacity of their various chiefs and overlords. They occasionally looked over the multitude of squabbling children, listened affectionately to their high-pitched, nasal voices, smiling to see their own proclivities reproduced in their offspring, and interspersed their legends of the iron kings with remarks about their sons' progress at school, their grades in arithmetic, and the amounts they had saved in their toy banks.

On this last Sunday of November Paul sat all the afternoon on the lowest step of his stoop, staring into the street, while his sisters, in their rockers, were talking to the minister's daughters next door about how many shirtwaists they had made in the last week, and how many waffles someone had eaten at the last church supper. When the weather was warm, and his father was in a particularly jovial frame of mind, the girls made lemonade, which was always brought out in a red-glass pitcher, ornamented with forget-me-nots in blue enamel. This the girls thought very fine, and the neighbors always joked about the suspicious color of the pitcher.

Today Paul's father sat on the top step, talking to a young man who shifted a restless baby from knee to knee. He happened to be the young man who was daily held up to Paul as a model, and after whom it was his father's dearest hope that he would pattern. This young man was of a ruddy complexion, with a compressed, red mouth, and faded, nearsighted eyes, over which he wore thick spectacles, with gold bows that curved about his ears. He was clerk to one of the magnates of a great steel corporation, and was looked upon in Cordelia Street as a young man with a future. There was a story that, some five years ago—he was now barely twenty-six—he had been a trifle dissipated, but in order to curb his appetites and save the loss of time and strength that a sowing of wild oats might have entailed, he had taken his chief's advice, oft reiterated to his employees, and at twenty-one had married the first woman whom he could persuade to share his fortunes. She happened to be an angular schoolmistress, much older than he, who also wore thick glasses, and who had now borne him four children, all nearsighted, like herself.

The young man was relating how his chief, now cruising in the Mediterranean, kept in touch with all the details of the business, arranging his office hours on his yacht just as though he were at home, and "knocking off work enough to keep two stenographers busy." His father told, in turn, the plan his corporation was considering, of putting in an electric railway plant in Cairo. Paul snapped his teeth; he had an awful apprehension that they might spoil it all before he got there. Yet he rather liked to hear these legends of the iron kings that were told and retold on Sundays and holidays; these stories of palaces in Venice, yachts on the Mediterranean, and high play at Monte Carlo appealed to his fancy, and he was interested in the triumphs of these cash boys who had become famous, though he had no mind for the cash-boy stage.

After supper was over and he had helped to dry the dishes, Paul nervously asked his father whether he could go to George's to get some help in his geometry, and still more nervously asked for carfare. This latter request he had to repeat, as his father, on principle, did not like to hear requests for money, whether much or little. He asked Paul whether he could not go to some boy who lived nearer, and told him that he ought not to leave his schoolwork until Sunday; but he gave him the dime. He was not a poor man, but he had a worthy ambition to come up in the world. His only reason for allowing Paul to usher was that he thought a boy ought to be earning a little.

Paul bounded upstairs, scrubbed the greasy odor of the dishwater from his hands with the ill-smelling soap he hated, and then shook over his fingers a few drops of violet water from the bottle he kept hidden in his drawer. He left the house with his geometry conspicuously under his arm, and the moment he got out of Cordelia Street and boarded a downtown car, he shook off the lethargy of two deadening days and began to live again.

The leading juvenile of the permanent stock company which played at one of the downtown theaters was an acquaintance of Paul's, and the boy had been invited to drop in at the Sunday-night rehearsals whenever he could. For more than a year Paul had spent every available moment loitering about Charley Edwards's dressing room. He had won a place among Edwards's following not only because the young actor, who could not afford to employ a dresser, often found him useful, but because he recognized in Paul something akin to what churchmen term "vocation."

It was at the theater and at Carnegie Hall that Paul really lived; the rest was but a sleep and a forgetting. This was Paul's fairy tale, and it had for him all the allurement of a secret love. The moment he inhaled the gassy, painty, dusty odor behind the scenes, he breathed like a prisoner set free, and felt within him the possibility of doing or saying splendid, brilliant, poetic things. The moment the cracked orchestra beat out the overture from *Martha,* or jerked at the serenade from *Rigoletto,* all stupid and ugly things slid from him, and his senses were deliciously, yet delicately fired.

Perhaps it was because, in Paul's world, the natural nearly always wore the guise of ugliness, that a certain element of artificiality seemed to him necessary in beauty. Perhaps it was because his experience of life elsewhere was so full of Sabbath-school picnics, petty economies, wholesome advice as to how to succeed in life, and the inescapable odors of cooking, that he found this existence so alluring, these smartly clad men and women so attractive, that he was so moved by these starry apple orchards that bloomed perennially under the limelight.

It would be difficult to put it strongly enough how convincingly the stage entrance of that theater was for Paul the actual portal of Romance. Certainly none of the company ever suspected it, least of all Charley Edwards. It was very like the old stories that used to float about London of fabulously rich Jews, who had subterranean halls there, with palms, and fountains, and soft lamps and richly appareled women who never saw the disenchanting light of London day. So, in the midst of that smoke-palled city, enamored of figures and grimy toil, Paul had his secret temple, his wishing carpet, his bit of blue-and-white Mediterranean shore bathed in perpetual sunshine.

Several of Paul's teachers had a theory that his imagination had been perverted by garish fiction but the truth was that he scarcely ever read at all. The books at home were not such as would either tempt or corrupt a youthful mind, and as for reading the novels that some of his friends urged upon him—well, he got what he wanted much more quickly from music; any sort of music, from an orchestra to a barrel organ. He needed only the spark, the indescribable thrill that made his imagination master of his senses, and he could make plots and pictures enough of his own. It was equally true that he was not stagestruck—not, at any rate, in the usual acceptation of that expression. He had no desire to become an actor, any more than he had to become a musician. He felt no necessity to do any of these things; what he wanted was to see, to be in the atmosphere, float on the wave of it, to be carried out, blue league after blue league, away from everything.

After a night behind the scenes Paul found the schoolroom more than ever repulsive; the bare floors and naked walls; the prosy men who never wore frock coats, or violets in their buttonholes; the women with their dull gowns, shrill voices, and pitiful seriousness about prepositions that govern the dative. He could not bear to have the other pupils think, for a moment, that he took these people seriously; he must convey to them that he considered it all trivial, and was there only by way of a jest, anyway. He had autographed pictures of all the members of the stock company which he showed his classmates, telling them the most incredible stories of his familiarity with these people, of his acquaintance with the soloists who came to Carnegie Hall, his suppers with them and the flowers he sent them. When these stories lost their effect, and his audience grew listless, he became desperate and would bid all the boys goodbye, announcing that he was going to travel for a while; going to Naples, to Venice, to Egypt. Then, next Monday, he would slip back, conscious and nervously smiling; his sister was ill, and he should have to defer his voyage until spring.

Matters went steadily worse with Paul at school. In the itch to let his instructors know how heartily he despised them and their homilies, and how thoroughly he was appreciated elsewhere, he mentioned once or twice that he had no time to fool with theorems; adding—with a twitch of the eyebrows and a touch of that nervous bravado which so perplexed them—that he was helping the people down at the stock company; they were old friends of his.

The upshot of the matter was that the Principal went to Paul's father, and Paul was taken out of school and put to work. The manager at Carnegie Hall was told to get another usher in his stead; the doorkeeper at the theater was warned not to admit him to the house; and Charley Edwards remorsefully promised the boy's father not to see him again.

The members of the stock company were vastly amused when some of Paul's stories reached them—especially the women. They were hard-working women, most of them supporting indigent husbands or brothers, and they laughed rather bitterly at having stirred the boy to such fervid and florid inventions. They agreed with the faculty and with his father that Paul's was a bad case.

The eastbound train was plowing through a January snowstorm; the dull dawn was beginning to show gray when the engine whistled a mile out of Newark. Paul started up from the seat where he had lain curled in uneasy slumber, rubbed the breath-misted window glass with his hand, and peered out. The snow was whirling in curling eddies above the white bottom lands, and the drifts lay already deep in the fields and along the fences, while here and there the long dead grass and dried weed stalks protruded black above it. Lights shone from the scattered houses, and a gang of laborers who stood beside the track waved their lanterns.

Paul had slept very little, and he felt grimy and uncomfortable. He had made the all-night journey in a day coach, partly because he was ashamed, dressed as he was, to go into a Pullman, and partly because he was afraid of being seen there by some Pittsburgh businessman, who might have noticed him in Denny & Carson's office. When the whistle awoke him, he clutched quickly at his breast pocket, glancing about him with an uncertain smile. But the little, clay-bespattered Italians were still sleeping, the slatternly women across the aisle were in open-mouthed oblivion, and even the crumby, crying babies were for the nonce stilled. Paul settled back to struggle with his impatience as best he could.

When he arrived at the Jersey City station he hurried through his breakfast, manifestly ill at ease and keeping a sharp eye about him. After he reached the Twenty-third Street station, he consulted a cabman and had himself driven to a men's-furnishings establishment that was just opening for the day. He spent upward of two hours, buying with endless reconsidering and great care. His new street suit he put on in the fitting room; the frock coat and dress clothes he had bundled into the cab with his linen. Then he drove to a hatter's and a shoe house. His next errand was at Tiffany's, where he selected his silver and a new scarf pin. He would not wait to have his silver marked, he said. Lastly, he stopped at a trunk shop on Broadway and had his purchases packed into various traveling bags.

It was a little after one o'clock when he drove up to the Waldorf, and after settling with the cabman, went into the office. He registered from Washington; said his mother and father had been abroad, and that he had come down to await the arrival of their steamer. He told his story plausibly and had no trouble, since he volunteered to pay for them in advance, in engaging his rooms; a sleeping room, sitting room, and bath.

Not once, but a hundred times, Paul had planned this entry into New York. He had gone over every detail of it with Charley Edwards, and in his scrapbook at home there were pages of description about New York hotels, cut from the Sunday papers. When he was shown to his sitting room on the eighth floor he saw at a glance that everything was as it should be; there was but one detail in his mental picture that the place did not realize, so he rang for the bellboy and sent him down for flowers. He moved about nervously until the boy returned, putting away his new linen and fingering it delightedly as he did so. When the flowers came he put them hastily into water, and then tumbled into a hot bath. Presently he came out of his white bathroom, resplendent in his new silk underwear, and playing with the tassels of his red robe. The snow was whirling so fiercely outside his windows that he could scarcely see across the street, but within the air was deliciously soft and fragrant. He put the violets and jonquils on the taboret beside the couch, and threw himself down, with a long sigh, covering himself with a Roman blanket. He was thoroughly tired; he had been in such haste, he had stood up to such a strain, covered so much ground in the last twenty-four hours, that he wanted to think how it had all come about. Lulled by the sound of the wind, the warm air, and the cool fragrance of the flowers, he sank into deep, drowsy retrospection.

It had been wonderfully simple; when they had shut him out of the theater and concert hall, when they had taken away his bone, the whole thing was virtually determined. The rest was a mere matter of opportunity. The only thing that at all surprised him was his own courage—for he realized well enough that he had always been tormented by fear, a sort of apprehensive dread that, of late years, as the meshes of the lies he had told closed about him, had been pulling the muscles of his body tighter and tighter. Until now he could not remember the time when he had not been dreading something. Even when he was a little boy it was always there—behind him, or before, or on either side. There had always been the shadowed corner, the dark place into which he dared not look, but from which something seemed always to be watching him—and Paul had done things that were not pretty to watch, he knew.

But now he had a curious sense of relief, as though he had at last thrown down the gauntlet to the thing in the corner.

Yet it was but a day since he had been sulking in the traces; but yesterday afternoon that he had been sent to the bank with Denny & Carson's deposit, as usual—but this time he was instructed to leave the book to be balanced. There was above two thousand dollars in checks, and nearly a thousand in the bank notes which he had taken from the book and quietly transferred to his pocket. At the bank he had made out a new deposit slip. His nerves had been steady enough to permit of his returning to the office, where he had finished his work and asked for a full day's holiday tomorrow, Saturday, giving a perfectly reasonable pretext. The bankbook, he knew, would not be returned before Monday or Tuesday, and his father would be out of town for the next week. From the time he slipped the bank notes into his pocket until he boarded the night train for New York, he had not known a moment's hesitation. It was not the first time Paul had steered through treacherous waters.

How astonishingly easy it had all been; here he was, the thing done; and this time there would be no awakening, no figure at the top of the stairs. He watched the snowflakes whirling by his window until he fell asleep.

When he awoke, it was three o'clock in the afternoon. He bounded up with a start; half of one of his precious days gone already! He spent more than an hour in dressing, watching every stage of his toilet carefully in the mirror. Everything was quite perfect; he was exactly the kind of boy he had always wanted to be.

When he went downstairs Paul took a carriage and drove up Fifth Avenue toward the Park. The snow had somewhat abated; carriages and tradesmen's wagons were hurrying soundlessly to and fro in the winter twilight; boys in woolen mufflers were shoveling off the doorsteps; the avenue stages made fine spots of color against the white street. Here and there on the corners were stands, with whole flower gardens blooming under glass cases, against the sides of which the snowflakes stuck and melted; violets, roses, carnations, lilies of the valley— somehow vastly more lovely and alluring that they blossomed thus unnaturally in the snow. The Park itself was a wonderful stage winterpiece.

When he returned, the pause of the twilight had ceased and the tune of the streets had changed. The snow was falling faster, lights streamed from the hotels that reared their dozen stories fearlessly up into the storm, defying the raging Atlantic winds. A long, black stream of carriages poured down the avenue, intersected here and there by other streams, tending horizontally. There were a score of cabs about the entrance of this hotel, and his driver had to wait. Boys in livery were running in and out of the awning stretched across the sidewalk, up and down the red velvet carpet laid from the door to the street. Above, about, within it all was the rumble and roar, the hurry and toss of thousands of human beings as hot for pleasure as himself, and on every side of him towered the glaring affirmation of the omnipotence of wealth.

The boy set his teeth and drew his shoulders together in a spasm of realization; the plot of all dramas, the text of all romances, the nerve-stuff of all sensations was whirling about him like the snowflakes. He burnt like a faggot in a tempest.

When Paul went down to dinner the music of the orchestra came floating up the elevator shaft to greet him. His head whirled as he stepped into the thronged corridor, and he sank back into one of the chairs against the wall to get his breath. The lights, the chatter, the perfumes, the bewildering medley of color—he had, for a moment, the feeling of not being able to stand it. But only for a moment; these were his own people, he told himself. He went slowly about the corridors, through the writing rooms, smoking rooms, reception rooms, as though he were exploring the chambers of an enchanted palace, built and peopled for him alone.

When he reached the dining room he sat down at a table near a window. The flowers, the white linen, the many-colored wineglasses, the gay toilettes of the women, the low popping of corks, the undulating repetitions of the *Blue Danube* from the orchestra, all flooded Paul's dream with bewildering radiance. When the roseate tinge of his champagne was added—that cold, precious, bubbling stuff that creamed and foamed in his glass—Paul wondered that there were honest men in the world at all. This was what all the world was fighting for, he reflected; this was what all the struggle was about. He doubted the reality of his past. Had he ever known a place called Cordelia Street, a place where fagged-looking businessmen got on the early car; mere rivets in a machine they seemed to Paul,—sickening men, with combings of children's hair always hanging to their coats, and the smell of cooking in their clothes. Cordelia Street—Ah, that belonged to another time and country; had he not always been thus, had he not sat here night after night, from as far back as he could remember, looking pensively over just such shimmering textures and slowly twirling the stem of a glass like this one between his thumb and middle finger? He rather thought he had.

He was not in the least abashed or lonely. He had no especial desire to meet or to know any of these people; all he demanded was the right to look on and conjecture, to watch the pageant. The mere stage properties were all he contended for. Nor was he lonely later in the evening, in his lodge at the Metropolitan. He was now entirely rid of his nervous misgivings, of his forced aggressiveness, of the imperative desire to show himself different from his surroundings. He felt now that his surroundings explained him. Nobody questioned the purple; he had only to wear it passively. He had only to glance down at his attire to reassure himself that here it would be impossible for anyone to humiliate him.

He found it hard to leave his beautiful sitting room to go to bed that night, and sat long watching the raging storm from his turret window. When he went to sleep it was with the lights turned on in his bedroom; partly because of his old timidity, and partly so that, if he should wake in the night, there would be no wretched moment of doubt, no horrible suspicion of yellow wallpaper, or of Washington and Calvin above his bed.

Sunday morning the city was practically snowbound. Paul breakfasted late, and in the afternoon he fell in with a wild San Francisco boy, a freshman at Yale, who said he had run down for a "little flyer" over Sunday. The young man offered to show Paul the night side of the town, and the two boys went out together after dinner, not returning to the hotel until seven o'clock the next morning. They had started out in the confiding warmth of a champagne friendship, but their parting in the elevator was singularly cool. The freshman pulled himself together to make his train, and Paul went to bed. He awoke at two o'clock in the afternoon, very thirsty and dizzy, and rang for ice-water, coffee, and the Pittsburgh papers.

On the part of the hotel management, Paul excited no suspicion. There was this to be said for him, that he wore his spoils with dignity and in no way made himself conspicuous. Even under the glow of his wine he was never boisterous, though he found the stuff like a magician's wand for wonder-building. His chief greediness lay in his ears and eyes, and his excesses were not offensive ones. His dearest pleasures were the gray winter twilights in his sitting room; his quiet enjoyment of his flowers, his clothes, his wide divan, his cigarette, and his sense of power. He could not remember a time when he had felt so at peace with himself. The mere release from the necessity of petty lying, lying every day and every day, restored his self-respect. He had never lied for pleasure, even at school; but to be noticed and admired, to assert his difference from other Cordelia Street boys; and he felt a good deal more manly, more honest, even, now that he had no need for boastful pretensions, now that he could, as his actor friends used to say, "dress the part." It was characteristic that remorse did not occur to him. His golden days went by without a shadow, and he made each as perfect as he could.

On the eighth day after his arrival in New York he found the whole affair exploited in the Pittsburgh papers, exploited with a wealth of detail which indicated that local news of a sensational nature was at a low ebb. The firm of Denny & Carson announced that the boy's father had refunded the full amount of the theft and that they had no intention of prosecuting. The Cumberland minister had been interviewed, and expressed his hope of yet reclaiming the motherless lad, and his Sabbath-school teacher declared that she would spare no effort to that end. The rumor had reached Pittsburgh that the boy had been seen in a New York hotel, and his father had gone East to find him and bring him home.

Paul had just come in to dress for dinner; he sank into a chair, weak to the knees, and clasped his head in his hands. It was to be worse than jail, even; the tepid waters of Cordelia Street were to close over him finally and forever. The gray monotony stretched before him in hopeless, unrelieved years; Sabbath school, Young People's Meeting, the yellow-papered room, the damp dish-towels; it all rushed back upon him with a sickening vividness. He had the old feeling that the orchestra had suddenly stopped, the sinking sensation that the play was over. The sweat broke out on his face, and he sprang to his feet, looked about him with his white, conscious smile, and winked at himself in the mirror. With something of the old childish belief in miracles with which he had so often gone to class, all his lessons unlearned, Paul dressed and dashed whistling down the corridor to the elevator.

conflict

He had no sooner entered the dining room and caught the measure of the music than his remembrance was lightened by his old elastic power of claiming the moment, mounting with it, and finding it all-sufficient. The glare and glitter about him, the mere scenic accessories had again, and for the last time, their old potency. He would show himself that he was game, he would finish the thing splendidly. He doubted, more than ever, the existence of Cordelia Street, and for the first time he drank his wine recklessly. Was he not, after all, one of those fortunate beings born to the purple, was he not still himself and in his own place? He drummed a nervous accompaniment to the Pagliacci music and looked about him, telling himself over and over that it had paid.

He reflected drowsily, to the swell of the music and the chill sweetness of his wine, that he might have done it more wisely. He might have caught an outbound steamer and been well out of their clutches before now. But the other side of the world had seemed too far away and too uncertain then; he could not have waited for it; his need had been too sharp. If he had to choose over again, he would do the same thing tomorrow. He looked affectionately about the dining room, now gilded with a soft mist. Ah, it had paid indeed!

Paul was awakened next morning by a painful throbbing in his head and feet. He had thrown himself across the bed without undressing, and had slept with his shoes on. His limbs and hands were lead heavy, and his tongue and throat were parched and burnt. There came upon him one of those fateful attacks of clearheadedness that never occurred except when he was physically exhausted and his nerves hung loose. He lay still, closed his eyes, and let the tide of things wash over him.

His father was in New York; "stopping at some joint or other," he told himself. The memory of successive summers on the front stoop fell upon him like a weight of black water. He had not a hundred dollars left; and he knew now, more than ever, that money was everything, the wall that stood between all he loathed and all he wanted. The thing was winding itself up; he had thought of that on his first glorious day in New York, and had even provided a way to snap the thread. It lay on his dressing table now; he had got it out last night when he came blindly up from dinner, but the shiny metal hurt his eyes, and he disliked the looks of it.

He rose and moved about with a painful effort, succumbing now and again to attacks of nausea. It was the old depression exaggerated; all the world had become Cordelia Street. Yet somehow he was not afraid of anything, was absolutely calm; perhaps because he had looked into the dark corner at last and knew. It was bad enough, what he saw there, but somehow not so bad as his long fear of it had been. He saw everything clearly now. He had a feeling that he had made the best of it, that he had lived the sort of life he was meant to live, and for half an hour he sat staring at the revolver. But he told himself that was not the way, so he went downstairs and took a cab to the ferry.

When Paul arrived in Newark he got off the train and took another cab, directing the driver to follow the Pennsylvania tracks out of the town. The snow lay heavy on the roadways and had drifted deep in the open fields. Only here and there the dead grass or dried weed stalks projected, singularly black, above it. Once well into the country, Paul dismissed the carriage and walked, floundering along the tracks, his mind a medley of irrelevant things. He seemed to hold in his brain an actual picture of everything he had seen that morning. He remembered every feature of both his drivers, of the toothless old woman from whom he had bought the red flowers in his coat, the agent from whom he had got his ticket, and all of his fellow passengers on the ferry. His mind, unable to cope with vital matters near at hand, worked feverishly and deftly at sorting and grouping these images. They made for him a part of the ugliness of the world, of the ache in his head, and the bitter burning on his tongue. He stooped and put a handful of snow into his mouth as he walked, but that, too, seemed hot. When he reached a little hillside, where the tracks ran through a cut some twenty feet below him, he stopped and sat down.

The carnations in his coat were drooping with the cold, he noticed, their red glory all over. It occurred to him that all the flowers he had seen in the glass cases that first night must have gone the same way, long before this. It was only one splendid breath they had, in spite of their brave mockery at the winter outside the glass; and it was a losing game in the end, it seemed, this revolt against the homilies by which the world is run. Paul took one of the blossoms carefully from his coat and scooped a little hole in the snow, where he covered it up. Then he dozed awhile, from his weak condition, seemingly insensible to the cold.

The sound of an approaching train awoke him, and he started to his feet, remembering only his resolution, and afraid lest he should be too late. He stood watching the approaching locomotive, his teeth chattering, his lips drawn away from them in a frightened smile; once or twice he glanced nervously sidewise, as though he were being watched. When the right moment came, he jumped. As he fell, the folly of his haste occurred to him with merciless clearness, the vastness of what he had left undone. There flashed through his brain, clearer than ever before, the blue of Adriatic water, the yellow of Algerian sands.

He felt something strike his chest, and that his body was being thrown swiftly through the air, on and on, immeasurably far and fast, while his limbs were gently relaxed. Then, because the picture-making mechanism was crushed, the disturbing visions flashed into black, and Paul dropped back into the immense design of things.

Questions for Discussion

1. What do the descriptions of Paul in the first paragraph reveal about his character?

2. Summarize Paul's behavior. Why does he do what he does?

3. Describe the tone of the narrator.

4. How does the carnation function in the story? To what extent is it a symbol?

Suggestions for Writing

1. Write an essay in which you describe Paul's "case" and explain how relevant it is to the lives of young persons today.

2. Write a journal response to the ending of the story. How did the ending affect you? To what extent is it an appropriate and/or believable ending?

3. Write a sketch of a friend or acquaintance whose "case" is similar to Paul's. Speculate about the causes of this person's aimlessness, dishonesty, or rebellion.

King of the Bingo Game

RALPH ELLISON

T he woman in front of him was eating roasted peanuts that smelled so good that he could barely contain his hunger. He could not even sleep and wished they'd hurry and begin the bingo game. There, on his right, two fellows were drinking wine out of a bottle wrapped in a paper bag, and he could hear soft gurgling in the dark. His stomach gave a low, gnawing growl. "If this was down South," he thought, "all I'd have to do is lean over and say, 'Lady, gimme a few of those peanuts, please ma'm,' and she'd pass me the bag and never think nothing of it." Or he could ask the fellows for a drink in the same way. Folks down South stuck together that way; they didn't even have to know you. But up here it was different. Ask somebody for something, and they'd think you were crazy. Well, I ain't crazy. I'm just broke, 'cause I got no birth certificate to get a job, and Laura 'bout to die 'cause we got no money for a doctor. But I ain't crazy. And yet a pinpoint of doubt was focused in his mind as he glanced toward the screen and saw the hero stealthily entering a dark room and sending the beam of a flashlight along a wall of bookcases. This is where he finds the trapdoor, he remembered. The man would pass abruptly through the wall and find the girl tied to a bed, her legs and arms spread wide, and her clothing torn to rags. He laughed softly to himself. He had seen the picture three times, and this was one of the best scenes.

On his right the fellow whispered wide-eyed to his companion. "Man, look a-yonder!"

"Damn!"

"Wouldn't I like to have her tied up like that . . ."

"Hey! That fool's letting her loose!"

"Aw, man, he loves her."

"Love or no love!"

The man moved impatiently beside him, and he tried to involve himself in the scene. But Laura was on his mind. Tiring quickly of watching the picture he looked back to where the white beam filtered from the projection room above the balcony. It started small and grew large, specks of dust dancing in its whiteness as it reached the screen. It was strange how the beam always landed right on the screen and didn't mess up and fall somewhere else. But they had it all fixed. Everything was fixed. Now suppose when they showed that girl with her dress torn the girl started taking off the rest of her clothes, and when the guy came in he didn't untie her but kept her there and went to taking off his own clothes? *That* would be something to see. If a picture got out of hand like that those guys up there would go nuts. Yeah, and there'd be so many folks in here you couldn't find a seat for nine months! A strange sensation played over his skin. He shuddered.

Yesterday he'd seen a bedbug on a woman's neck as they walked out into the bright street. But exploring his thigh through a hole in his pocket he found only goose pimples and old scars.

The bottle gurgled again. He closed his eyes. Now a dreamy music was accompanying the film and train whistles were sounding in the distance, and he was a boy again walking along a railroad trestle down South, and seeing the train coming, and running back as fast as he could go, and hearing the whistle blowing, and getting off the trestle to solid ground just in time, with the earth trembling beneath his feet, and feeling relieved as he ran down the cinder-strewn embankment onto the highway, and looking back and seeing with terror that the train had left the track and was following him right down the middle of the street, and all the white people laughing as he ran screaming . . .

"Wake up there, buddy! What the hell do you mean hollering like that! Can't you see we trying to enjoy this here picture?"

He stared at the man with gratitude.

"I'm sorry, old man," he said. "I musta been dreaming."

"Well, here, have a drink. And don't be making no noise like that, damn!"

His hands trembled as he tilted his head. It was not wine, but whiskey. Cold rye whiskey. He took a deep swoller, decided it was better not to take another, and handed the bottle back to its owner.

"Thanks, old man," he said.

Now he felt the cold whiskey breaking a warm path straight through the middle of him, growing hotter and sharper as it moved. He had not eaten all day, and it made him light-headed. The smell of the peanuts stabbed him like a knife, and he got up and found a seat in the middle aisle. But no sooner did he sit than he saw a row of intense-faced young girls, and got up again, thinking, "You chicks musta been Lindy-hopping somewhere." He found a seat several rows ahead as the lights came on, and he saw the screen disappear behind a heavy red and gold curtain; then the curtain rising, and the man with the microphone and a uniformed attendant coming on the stage.

He felt for his bingo cards, smiling. The guy at the door wouldn't like it if he knew about his having *five* cards. Well, not everyone played the bingo game; and even with five cards he didn't have much of a chance. For Laura, though, he had to have faith. He studied the cards, each with its different numerals, punching the free center hole in each and spreading them neatly across his lap; and when the lights faded he sat slouched in his seat so that he could look from his cards to the bingo wheel with but a quick shifting of his eyes.

Ahead, at the end of the darkness, the man with the microphone was pressing a button attached to a long cord and spinning the bingo wheel and calling out the number each time the wheel came to rest. And each time the voice rang out his finger raced over the cards for the number. With five cards he had to move fast. He became nervous; there were too many cards, and the man went too fast with his grating voice. Perhaps he should just select one and throw the others away. But he was afraid. He became warm. Wonder how much Laura's doctor would cost? Damn that, watch the cards! And with despair he heard the man call three in a row which he missed on all five cards. This way he'd never win . . .

When he saw the row of holes punched across the third card, he sat paralyzed and heard the man call three more numbers before he stumbled forward, screaming.

"Bingo! Bingo!"

"Let that fool up there," someone called.

"Get up there, man!"

He stumbled down the aisle and up the steps to the stage into a light so sharp and bright that for a moment it blinded him, and he felt that he had moved into the spell of some strange, mysterious power. Yet it was as familiar as the sun, and he knew it was the perfectly familiar bingo.

The man with the microphone was saying something to the audience as he held out his card. A cold light flashed from the man's finger as the card left his hand. His knees trembled. The man stepped closer, checking the card against the numbers chalked on the board. Suppose he had made a mistake? The pomade on the man's hair made him feel faint, and he backed away. But the man was checking the card over the microphone now, and he had to stay. He stood tense, listening.

"Under the O, forty-four," the man chanted. "Under the I, seven. Under the G, three. Under the B, ninety-six. Under the N, thirteen!"

His breath came easier as the man smiled at the audience.

"Yessir, ladies and gentlemen, he's one of the chosen people!"

The audience rippled with laughter and applause.

"Step right up to the front of the stage."

He moved slowly forward, wishing that the light was not so bright.

"To win tonight's jackpot of $36.90 the wheel must stop between the double zero, understand?"

He nodded, knowing the ritual from the many days and nights he had watched the winners march across the stage to press the button that controlled the spinning wheel and receive the prizes. And now he followed the instructions as though he'd crossed the slippery stage a million prize-winning times.

The man was making some kind of a joke, and he nodded vacantly. So tense had he become that he felt a sudden desire to cry and shook it away. He felt vaguely that his whole life was determined by the bingo wheel; not only that which would happen now that he was at last before it, but all that had gone before, since his birth, and his mother's birth and the birth of his father. It had always been there, even though he had not been aware of it, handing out the unlucky cards and numbers of his days. The feeling persisted, and he started quickly away. I better get down from here before I make a fool of myself, he thought.

"Here, boy," the man called. "You haven't started yet."

Someone laughed as he went hesitantly back.

"Are you all reet?"

He grinned at the man's jive talk, but no words would come, and he knew it was not a convincing grin. For suddenly he knew that he stood on the slippery brink of some terrible embarrassment.

"Where are you from, boy?" the man asked.

"Down South."

"He's from down South, ladies and gentlemen," the man said. "Where from? Speak right into the mike."

"Rocky Mont," he said. "Rock' Mont, North Car'lina."

"So you decided to come down off that mountain to the U.S.," the man laughed. He felt that the man was making a fool of him, but then something cold was placed in his hand, and the lights were no longer behind him.

Standing before the wheel he felt alone, but that was somehow right, and he remembered his plan. He would give the wheel a short quick twirl. Just a touch of the button. He had watched it many times, and always it came close to double zero when it was short and quick. He steeled himself; the fear had left, and he felt a profound sense of promise, as though he were about to be repaid for all the things he'd suffered all his life. Trembling, he pressed the button. There was a whirl of lights, and in a second he realized with finality that though he wanted to, he could not stop. It was as though he held a high-powered line in his naked hand. His nerves tightened. As the wheel increased its speed it seemed to draw him more and more into its power, as though it held his fate; and with it came a deep need to submit, to whirl, to lose himself in its swirl of color. He could not stop it now, he knew. So let it be.

The button rested snugly in his palm where the man had placed it. And now he became aware of the man beside him, advising him through the microphone, while behind the shadowy audience hummed with noisy voices. He shifted his feet. There was still that feeling of helplessness within him, making part of him desire to turn back, even now that the jackpot was right in his hand. He squeezed the button until his fist ached. Then, like the sudden shriek of a subway whistle, a doubt tore through his head. Suppose he did not spin the wheel long enough? What could he do, and how could he tell? And then he knew, even as he wondered, that as long as he pressed the button, he could control the jackpot. He and only he could determine whether or not it was to be his. Not even the man with the microphone could do anything about it now. He felt drunk. Then, as though he had come down from a high hill into a valley of people, he heard the audience yelling.

"Come down from there, you jerk!"

"Let somebody else have a chance . . ."

"Ole Jack thinks he done found the end of the rainbow . . ."

The last voice was not unfriendly, and he turned and smiled dreamily into the yelling mouths. Then he turned his back squarely on them.

"Don't take too long, boy," a voice said.

He nodded. They were yelling behind him. Those folks did not understand what had happened to him. They had been playing the bingo game day in and night out for years, trying to win rent money or hamburger change. But not one of those wise guys had discovered this wonderful thing. He watched the wheel whirling past the numbers and experienced a burst of exaltation: This is God! This is the really truly God! He said it aloud, "This is God!"

He said it with such absolute conviction that he feared he would fall fainting into the footlights. But the crowd yelled so loud that they could not hear. Those fools, he thought. I'm here trying to tell them the most wonderful secret in the world, and they're yelling like they gone crazy. A hand fell upon his shoulder.

"You'll have to make a choice now, boy. You've taken too long."

He brushed the hand violently away.

"Leave me alone, man. I know what I'm doing!"

The man looked surprised and held on to the microphone for support. And because he did not wish to hurt the man's feelings he smiled, realizing with a sudden pang that there was no way of explaining to the man just why he had to stand there pressing the button forever.

"Come here," he called tiredly.

The man approached, rolling the heavy microphone across the stage.

"Anybody can play this bingo game, right?" he said.

"Sure, but . . ."

He smiled, feeling inclined to be patient with this slick looking white man with his blue sport shirt and his sharp gabardine suit.

"That's what I thought," he said. "Anybody can win the jackpot as long as they get the lucky number, right?"

"That's the rule, but after all . . ."

"That's what I thought," he said. "And the big prize goes to the man who knows how to win it?"

The man nodded speechlessly.

"Well then, go on over there and watch me win like I want to. I ain't going to hurt nobody," he said, "and I'll show you how to win. I mean to show the whole world how it's got to be done."

And because he understood, he smiled again to let the man know that he held nothing against him for being white and impatient. Then he refused to see the man any longer and stood pressing the button, the voices of the crowd reaching him like sounds in distant streets. Let them yell. All the Negroes down there were just ashamed because he was black like them. He smiled inwardly, knowing how it was. Most of the time he was ashamed of what Negroes did himself. Well, let them be ashamed for something this time. Like him. He was like a long thin black wire that was being stretched and wound upon the bingo wheel; wound until he wanted to scream; wound, but this time himself controlling the winding and the sadness and the shame, and because he did, Laura would be all right. Suddenly the lights flickered. He staggered backwards. Had something gone wrong? All this noise. Didn't they know that although he controlled the wheel, it also controlled him, and unless he pressed the button forever and forever and ever it would stop, leaving him high and dry, dry and high on this hard high slippery hill and Laura dead? There was only one chance; he had to do whatever the wheel demanded. And gripping the button in despair, he discovered with surprise that it imparted a nervous energy. His spine tingled. He felt a certain power.

Now he faced the raging crowd with defiance, its screams penetrating his eardrums like trumpets shrieking from a jukebox. The vague faces glowing in the bingo lights gave him a sense of himself that he had never known before. He was running the show, by God! They had to react to him, for he was their luck. This is *me,* he thought. Let the bastards yell. Then someone was laughing inside him, and he realized that somehow he had forgotten his own name. It was a sad, lost feeling to lose your name, and a crazy thing to do. That name had been given him by the white man who had owned his grandfather a long lost time ago down South. But maybe those wise guys knew his name.

"Who am I?" he screamed.

"Hurry up and bingo, you jerk!"

They didn't know either, he thought sadly. They didn't even know their own names, they were all poor nameless bastards. Well, he didn't need that old name; he was reborn. For as long as he pressed the button he was The-man-who-pressed-the-button-who-held-the-prize-who-was-the-King-of-Bingo. That was the way it was, and he'd have to press the button even if nobody understood, even though Laura did not understand.

"Live!" he shouted.

The audience quieted like the dying of a huge fan.

"Live, Laura, baby. I got holt of it now, sugar. Live!"

He screamed it, tears streaming down his face. "I got nobody but YOU!"

The screams tore from his very guts. He felt as though the rush of blood to his head would burst out in baseball seams of small red droplets, like a head beaten by police clubs. Bending over he saw a trickle of blood splashing the toe of his shoe. With his free hand he searched his head. It was his nose. God, suppose something has gone wrong? He felt that the whole audience had somehow entered him and was stamping its feet in his stomach, and he was unable to throw them out. They wanted the prize, that was it. They wanted the secret for themselves. But they'd never get it; he would keep the bingo wheel whirling forever, and Laura would be safe in the wheel. But would she? It had to be, because if she were not safe the wheel would cease to turn; it could not go on. He had to get away, *vomit* all, and his mind formed an image of himself running with Laura in his arms down the tracks of the subway just ahead of an A train, running desperately *vomit* with people screaming for him to come out but knowing no way of leaving the tracks because to stop would bring the train crushing down upon him and to attempt to leave across the other tracks would mean to run into a hot third rail as high as his waist which threw blue sparks that blinded his eyes until he could hardly see.

He heard singing and the audience was clapping its hands.

> *Shoot the liquor to him, Jim, boy!*
> *Clap-clap-clap*
> *Well a-calla the cop*
> *He's blowing his top!*
> *Shoot the liquor to him, Jim, boy!*

Bitter anger grew within him at the singing. They think I'm crazy. Well let 'em laugh. I'll do what I got to do.

He was standing in an attitude of intense listening when he saw that they were watching something on the stage behind him. He felt weak. But when he turned he saw no one. If only his thumb did not ache so. Now they were applauding. And for a moment he thought that the wheel had stopped. But that was impossible, his thumb still pressed the button. Then he saw them. Two men in uniform beckoned from the end of the stage. They were coming toward him, walking in step, slowly, like a tap-dance team returning for a third encore. But their shoulders shot forward, and he backed away, looking wildly about. There was nothing to fight them with. He had only the long black cord which led to a plug somewhere back stage, and he couldn't use that because it operated the bingo wheel. He backed slowly, fixing the men with his eyes as his lips stretched over his teeth in a tight, fixed grin; moved toward the end of the stage and realizing that he couldn't go much further, for suddenly the cord became taut and he couldn't afford to break the cord. But he had to do something. The audience was howling. Suddenly he stopped dead, seeing the men halt, their legs lifted as in an interrupted step of a slow-motion dance. There was nothing to do but run in the other direction and he dashed forward, slipping and sliding. The men fell back, surprised. He struck out violently going past.

"Grab him!"

He ran, but all too quickly the cord tightened, resistingly, and he turned and ran back again. This time he slipped them, and discovered by running in a circle before the wheel he could keep the cord from tightening. But this way he had to flail his arms to keep the men away. Why couldn't they leave a man alone? He ran, circling.

"Ring down the curtain," someone yelled. But they couldn't do that. If they did the wheel flashing from the projection room would be cut off. But they had him before he could tell them so, trying to pry open his fist, and he was wrestling and trying to bring his knees into the fight and holding on to the button, for it was his life. And now he was down, seeing a foot coming down, crushing his wrist cruelly, down, as he saw the wheel whirling serenely above.

"I can't give it up," he screamed. Then quietly, in a confidential tone, "Boys, I really can't give it up."

It landed hard against his head. And in the blank moment they had it away from him, completely now. He fought them trying to pull him up from the stage as he watched the wheel spin slowly to a stop. Without surprise he saw it rest at double zero.

"You see," he pointed bitterly.

"Sure, boy, sure, it's O.K.," one of the men said smiling.

And seeing the man bow his head to someone he could not see, he felt very, very happy; he would receive what all the winners received.

But as he warmed in the justice of the man's tight smile he did not see the man's slow wink, nor see the bow-legged man behind him step clear of the swiftly descending curtain and set himself for a blow. He only felt the dull pain exploding in his skull, and he knew even as it slipped out of him that his luck had run out on the stage.

Questions for Discussion

1. What methods does Ellison use to show us how desperate the main character is? What circumstances have made him desperate?

2. What does the bingo wheel come to represent to the main character? To what extent is the wheel an illusion?

3. To what extent is the title of the story ironic?

Suggestions for Writing

1. Write an essay about this story, focusing the wheel as a symbol of power and fate.

2. Read Ellison's novel *The Invisible Man* and write an essay that compares and contrasts the novel with "King of the Bingo Game."

3. Write a story that makes use of a game of chance.

4. Read several essays by James Baldwin in books such as *Notes of a Native Son, Nobody Knows My Name,* or *The Fire Next Time* and write an essay about Ellison's story in the context of Baldwin's ideas concerning American society.

On the Road

LANGSTON HUGHES

He was not interested in the snow. When he got off the freight, one early evening during the depression, Sargeant never even noticed the snow. But he must have felt it seeping down his neck, cold, wet, sopping in his shoes. But if you had asked him, he wouldn't have known it was snowing. Sargeant didn't see the snow, not even under the bright lights of the main street, falling white and flaky against the night. He was too hungry, too sleepy, too tired.

The Reverend Mr. Dorset, however, saw the snow when he switched on his porch light, opened the front door of his parsonage, and found standing there before him a big black man with snow on his face, a human piece of night with snow on his face—obviously unemployed.

Said the Reverend Mr. Dorset before Sargeant even realized he'd opened his mouth: "I'm sorry. No! Go right on down this street four blocks and turn to your left, walk up seven and you'll see the Relief Shelter. I'm sorry. No!" He shut the door.

Sargeant wanted to tell the holy man that he had already been to the Relief Shelter, been to hundreds of relief shelters during the depression years, the beds were always gone and supper was over, the place was full, and they drew the color line anyhow. But the minister said, "No," and shut the door. Evidently he didn't want to hear about it. And he *had* a door to shut.

The big black man turned away. And even yet he didn't see the snow, walking right into it. Maybe he sensed it, cold, wet, sticking to his jaws, wet on his black hands, sopping in his shoes. He stopped and stood on the sidewalk hunched over—hungry, sleepy, cold—looking up and down. Then he looked right where he was—in front of a church. Of course! A church! Sure, right next to a parsonage, certainly a church.

It had *two* doors.

Broad white steps in the night all snowy white. Two high arched doors with slender stone pillars on either side. And way up, a round lacy window with a stone crucifix in the middle and Christ on the crucifix in stone. All this was pale in the street lights, solid and stony pale in the snow.

Sargeant blinked. When he looked up, the snow fell into his eyes. For the first time that night he *saw* the snow. He shook his head. He shook the snow from his coat sleeves, felt hungry, felt lost, felt not lost, felt cold. He walked up the steps of the church. He knocked at the door. No answer. He tried the handle. Locked. He put his shoulder against the door and his long black body slanted like a ramrod. He pushed. With loud rhythmic grunts, like the grunts in a chain-gang song, he pushed against the door.

"I'm tired . . . Huh! . . . Hongry . . . Uh! . . . I'm sleepy . . . Huh! I'm cold . . . I got to sleep somewheres," Sargeant said. "This here is a church, ain't it? Well, uh!"

He pushed against the door.

Suddenly, with an undue cracking and screaking, the door began to give way to the tall black Negro who pushed ferociously against it.

By now two or three white people had stopped in the street, and Sargeant was vaguely aware of some of them yelling at him concerning the door. Three or four more came running, yelling at him.

"Hey!" they said. "Hey!"

"Uh-huh," answered the big tall Negro, "I know it's a white folks' church, · but I got to sleep somewhere." He gave another lunge at the door. "Huh!"

And the door broke open.

But just when the door gave way, two white cops arrived in a car, ran up the steps with their clubs, and grabbed Sargeant. But Sargeant for once had no intention of being pulled or pushed away from the door.

Sargeant grabbed, but not for anything so weak as a broken door. He grabbed for one of the tall stone pillars beside the door, grabbed at it and caught it. And held it. The cops pulled and Sargeant pulled. Most of the people in the street got behind the cops and helped them pull.

"A big black unemployed Negro holding onto our church!" thought the people. "The idea!"

The cops began to beat Sargeant over the head, and nobody protested. But he held on.

And then the church fell down.

Gradually, the big stone front of the church fell down, the walls and the rafters, the crucifix and the Christ. Then the whole thing fell down, covering the cops and the people with bricks and stones and debris. The whole church fell down in the snow.

Sargeant got out from under the church and went walking on up the street with the stone pillar on his shoulder. He was under the impression that he had buried the parsonage and the Reverend Mr. Dorset who said, "No!" So he laughed, and threw the pillar six blocks up the street and went on.

Sargeant thought he was alone, but listening to the *crunch, crunch, crunch* on the snow of his own footsteps, he heard other footsteps, too, doubling his own. He looked around, and there was Christ walking along beside him, the same Christ that had been on the cross on the church—still stone with a rough stone surface, walking along beside him just like he was broken off the cross when the church fell down.

"Well, I'll be dogged," said Sargeant. "This here's the first time I ever seed you off the cross."

"Yes," said Christ, crunching his feet in the snow. "You had to pull the church down to get me off the cross."

"You glad?" said Sargeant.

"I sure am," said Christ

They both laughed.

"I'm a hell of a fellow, ain't I?" said Sargeant. "Done pulled the church down!"

"You did a good job," said Christ. "They have kept me nailed on a cross for nearly two thousand years."

"Whee-ee-e!" said Sargeant. "I know you are glad to get off."

"I sure am," said Christ.

They walked on in the snow. Sargeant looked at the man of stone.

"And you have been up there two thousand years?"

"I sure have," said Christ.

"Well, if I had a little cash," said Sargeant, "I'd show you around a bit."

"I been around," said Christ.

"Yeah, but that was a long time ago."

"All the same," said Christ, "I've been around."

They walked on in the snow until they came to the railroad yards. Sargeant was tired, sweating and tired.

"Where you goin'?" Sargeant said, stopping by the tracks. He looked at Christ. Sargeant said, "I'm just a bum on the road. How about you? Where you goin'?"

"God knows," Christ said, "but I'm leavin' here."

They saw the red and green lights of the railroad yard half veiled by the snow that fell out of the night. Away down the track they saw a fire in a hobo jungle.

"I can go there and sleep," Sargeant said.

"You can?"

"Sure," said Sargeant. "That place ain't got no doors."

Outside the town, along the tracks, there were barren trees and bushes below the embankment, snow-gray in the dark. And down among the trees and bushes there were makeshift houses made out of boxes and tin and old pieces of wood and canvas. You couldn't see them in the dark, but you knew they were there if you'd ever been on the road, if you had ever lived with the homeless and hungry in a depression.

"I'm side-tracking," Sargeant said. "I'm tired."

"I'm gonna make it on to Kansas City," said Christ.

"O.K.," Sargeant said. "So long!"

He went down into the hobo jungle and found himself a place to sleep. He never did see Christ no more. About 6:00 A.M. a freight came by. Sargeant scrambled out of the jungle with a dozen or so more hobos and ran along the track, grabbing at the freight. It was dawn, early dawn, cold and gray.

"Wonder where Christ is by now?" Sargeant thought. "He musta gone on way on down the road. He didn't sleep in this jungle."

Sargeant grabbed the train and started to pull himself up into a moving coal car, over the edge of a wheeling coal car. But strangely enough, the car was full of cops. The nearest cop rapped Sargeant soundly across the knuckles with his night stick. Wham! Rapped his big black hands for clinging to the top of the car. Wham! But Sargeant did not turn loose. He clung on and tried to pull himself into the car. He hollered at the top of his voice, "Damn it, lemme in this car!"

"Shut up," barked the cop. "You crazy coon!" He rapped Sargeant across the knuckles and punched him in the stomach. "You ain't out in no jungle now. This ain't no train. You in jail."

Wham! across his bare black fingers clinging to the bars of his cell. Wham! between the steel bars low down against his shins.

Suddenly Sargeant realized that he really was in jail. He wasn't on no train. The blood of the night before had dried on his face, his head hurt terribly, and a cop outside in the corridor was hitting him across the knuckles for holding onto the door, yelling and shaking the cell door.

"They musta took me to jail for breaking down the door last night," Sargeant thought, "that church door."

Sargeant went over and sat on a wooden bench against the cold stone wall. He was emptier than ever. His clothes were wet, clammy cold wet, and shoes sloppy with snow water. It was just about dawn. There he was, locked up behind a cell door, nursing his bruised fingers.

The bruised fingers were his, but not the *door.*

Not the *club,* but the fingers.

"You wait," mumbled Sargeant, black against the jail wall. "I'm gonna break down this door, too."

"Shut up—or I'll paste you one," said the cop.

"I'm gonna break down this door," yelled Sargeant as he stood up in his cell.

Then he must have been talking to himself because he said, "I wonder where Christ's gone? I wonder if he's gone to Kansas City?"

Questions for Discussion

1. To what extent do "snow" and "doors" take on symbolic meaning in the story?

2. Assuming that Sargeant's dream of Christ *is* a dream, what does it say about the connection between Christ and the church that Sargeant tries to enter?

3. This story is over thirty years old. To what extent is it still relevant to today's problems of homelessness, poverty, and racism in America?

Suggestions for Writing

1. Write an essay about Hughes's story that focuses on the relationships between, race, religion, poverty, and social justice.

2. Write an essay that contrasts Hughes's "On the Road" with Jack Kerouac's *On the Road*.

3. Write a story concerning poverty or racism or both.

Sweat

ZORA NEALE HURSTON

It was eleven o'clock of a Spring night in Florida. It was Sunday. Any other night, Delia Jones would have been in bed for two hours by this time. But she was a washwoman, and Monday morning meant a great deal to her. So she collected the soiled clothes on Saturday when she returned the clean things. Sunday night after church, she sorted them and put the white things to soak. It saved her almost a half day's start. A great hamper in the bedroom held the clothes that she brought home. It was so much neater than a number of bundles lying around.

She squatted in the kitchen floor beside the great pile of clothes, sorting them into small heaps according to color, and humming a song in a mournful key, but wondering through it all where Sykes, her husband, had gone with her horse and buckboard.

Just then something long, round, limp and black fell upon her shoulders and slithered to the floor beside her. A great terror took hold of her. It softened her knees and dried her mouth so that it was a full minute before she could cry out or move. Then she saw that it was the big bull whip her husband liked to carry when he drove.

She lifted her eyes to the door and saw him standing there bent over with laughter at her fright. She screamed at him.

"Sykes, what you throw dat whip on me like dat? You know it would skeer me—looks like a snake, an' you knows how skeered Ah is of snakes."

"Course Ah knowed it! That's how come Ah done it." He slapped his leg with his hand and almost rolled on the ground in his mirth. "If you such a big fool dat you got to have a fit over a earth worm or a string, Ah don't keer how bad Ah skeer you."

"You aint got no business doing it. Gawd knows it's a sin. Some day Ah'm gointuh drop dead from some of yo' foolishness. 'Nother thing, where you been wid mah rig? Ah feeds dat pony. He aint fuh you to be drivin' wid no bull whip."

"You sho is one aggravatin' nigger woman!" he declared and stepped into the room. She resumed her work and did not answer him at once. "Ah done tole you time and again to keep them white folks' clothes outa dis house."

He picked up the whip and glared down at her. Delia went on with her work. She went out into the yard and returned with a galvanized tub and set it on the washbench. She saw that Sykes had kicked all of the clothes together again, and now stood in her way truculently, his whole manner hoping, *praying,* for an argument. But she walked calmly around him and commenced to re-sort the things.

"Next time, Ah'm gointer kick 'em outdoors," he threatened as he struck a match along the leg of his corduroy breeches.

Delia never looked up from her work, and her thin, stooped shoulders sagged further.

"Ah aint for no fuss t'night, Sykes. Ah just come from taking sacrament at the church house."

He snorted scornfully. "Yeah, you just come from de church house on a Sunday night, but heah you is gone to work on them clothes. You aint nothing but a hypocrite. One of them amen-corner Christians—sing, whoop, and shout, then come home and wash white folks' clothes on the Sabbath."

He stepped roughly upon the whitest pile of things, kicking them helter-skelter as he crossed the room. His wife gave a little scream of dismay, and quickly gathered them together again.

"Sykes, you quit grindin' dirt into these clothes! How can Ah git through by Sat'day if Ah don't start on Sunday?"

"Ah don't keer if you never git through. Anyhow, Ah done promised Gawd and a couple of other men, Ah aint gointer have it in mah house. Don't gimme no lip neither, else Ah'll throw 'em out and put mah fist up side yo' head to boot."

Delia's habitual meekness seemed to slip from her shoulders like a blown scarf. She was on her feet; her poor little body, her bare knuckly hands bravely defying the strapping hulk before her.

"Looka heah, Sykes, you done gone too fur. Ah been married to you fur fifteen years, and Ah been takin' in washin' fur fifteen years, Sweat, sweat, sweat! Work and sweat, cry and sweat, pray and sweat!"

"What's that got to do with me?" he asked brutally.

"What's it got to do with you, Sykes? Mah tub of suds is filled yo' belly with vittles more times than yo' hands is filled it. Mah sweat is done paid for this house and Ah reckon Ah kin keep on sweatin' in it."

She seized the iron skillet from the stove and struck a defensive pose, which act surprised him greatly, coming from her. It cowed him and he did not strike her as he usually did.

"Naw you won't," she panted, "that ole snaggle-toothed black woman you runnin' with aint comin' heah to pile up on *mah* sweat and blood. You aint paid for nothin' on this place, and Ah'm gointer stay right heah till Ah'm toted out foot foremost."

"Well, you better quit gittin' me riled up, else they'll be totin' you out sooner than you expect. Ah'm so tired of you Ah don't know whut to do. Gawd! how Ah hates skinny wimmen!"

A little awed by his new Delia, he sidled out of the door and slammed the back gate after him. He did not say where he had gone, but she knew too well. She knew very well that he would not return until nearly daybreak also. Her work over, she went on to bed but not to sleep at once. Things had come to a pretty pass!

She lay awake, gazing upon the debris that cluttered their matrimonial trail. Not an image left standing along the way. Anything like flowers had long ago been drowned in the salty stream that had been pressed from her heart. Her tears, her sweat, her blood. She had brought love to the union and he had brought a longing after the flesh. Two months after the wedding, he had given her the first brutal beating. She had the memory of his numerous trips to Orlando with all of his wages when he had returned to her penniless, even before the first year had passed. She was young and soft then, but now she thought of her knotty, muscled limbs, her harsh knuckly hands, and drew herself up into an unhappy little ball in the middle of the big feather bed. Too late now to hope for love, even if it were not Bertha it would be someone else. This case differed from the others only in that she was bolder than the others. Too late for everything except her little home. She had built it for her old days, and planted one by one the trees and flowers there. It was lovely to her, lovely.

Somehow, before sleep came, she found herself saying aloud: "Oh well, whatever goes over the Devil's back, is got to come under his belly. Sometime or ruther, Sykes, like everybody else, is gointer reap his sowing." After that she was able to build a spiritual earthworks against her husband. His shells could no longer reach her. *Amen.* She went to sleep and slept until he announced his presence by kicking her feet and rudely snatching the covers away.

"Gimme some kivah heah, an' git yo' damn foots over on yo' own side! Ah oughter mash you in yo' mouf fuh drawing dat skillet on me."

Delia went clear to the rail without answering him. A triumphant indifference to all that he was or did.

The week was full of work for Delia as all other weeks, and Saturday found her behind her little pony, collecting and delivering clothes.

It was a hot, hot day near the end of July. The village men on Joe Clarke's porch even chewed cane listlessly. They did not hurl the caneknots as usual. They let them dribble over the edge of the porch. Even conversation had collapsed under the heat.

"Heah come Delia Jones," Jim Merchant said, as the shaggy pony came 'round the bend of the road toward them. The rusty buckboard was heaped with baskets of crisp, clean laundry.

"Yep," Joe Lindsay agreed. "Hot or col', rain or shine, jes ez reg'lar ez de weeks roll roun' Delia carries 'em an' fetches 'em on Sat'day."

"She better if she wanter eat," said Moss. "Syke Jones aint wuth de shot an' powder hit would tek tuh kill 'em. Not to *huh* he aint."

"He sho' aint," Walter Thomas chimed in. "It's too bad, too, cause she wuz a right pritty lil trick when he got huh. Ah'd uh mah'ied huh mahseff if he hadnter beat me to it."

Delia nodded briefly at the men as she drove past.

"Too much knockin' will ruin *any* 'oman. He done beat huh 'nough tuh kill three women, let 'lone change they looks," said Elijah Moseley. "How Syke kin stommuck dat big black greasy Mogul he's layin' roun' wid, gits me. Ah swear dat eight-rock couldn't kiss a sardine can Ah done thowed out de back do' 'way las' yeah."

"Aw, she's fat, thass how come. He's allus been crazy 'bout fat women," put in Merchant. "He'd a' been tied up wid one long time ago if he could a' found one tuh have him. Did Ah tell yuh 'bout him come sidlin' in' roun' *mah* wife—bringin' her a basket uh peecans outa his yard fuh a present? Yessir, mah wife! She tol' him tuh take em right straight back home, cause Delia works so hard ovah dat wash tub she reckon everything on de place taste lak sweat an' soapsuds. Ah jus' wisht

Ah'd a caught 'im 'roun' dere! Ah'd a' made his hips ketch on fiah down dat shell road."

"Ah know he done it, too. Ah sees 'im grinnin' at every 'oman dat passes," Walter Thomas said. "But even so, he useter eat some mighty big hunks uh humble pie tuh git dat lil' 'oman he got. She wuz ez pritty ez a speckled pup! Dat wuz fifteen yeahs ago. He useter be so skeered uh losin' huh, she could make him do some parts of a husband's duty. Dey never wuz de same in de mind."

"There oughter be a law about him," said Lindsay. "He aint fit tuh carry guts tuh a bear."

Clarke spoke for the first time. "Taint no law on earth dat kin make a man be decent if it aint in 'im. There's plenty men dat takes a wife lak dey do a joint uh sugar-cane. It's round, juicy an' sweet when dey gits it. But dey squeeze an' grind, squeeze an' grind an' wring tell dey wring every drop uh pleasure dat's in 'em out. When dey's satisfied dat dey is wrung dry, dey treats 'em jes lak dey do a cane-chew. Dey throws 'em away. Dey knows whut dey is doin' while dey is at it, an' hates theirselves fuh it but they keeps on hangin' after huh tell she's empty. Den dey hates huh fuh bein' a cane-chew an' in de way."

"We oughter take Syke an' dat stray 'oman uh his'n down in Lake Howell swamp an' lay on de rawhide till they cain't say Lawd a' mussy.' He allus wuz uh ovahbearin' niggah, but since dat white 'oman from up north done teached 'im how to run a automobile, he done got too biggety to live—an' we oughter kill 'im." Old man Anderson advised.

A grunt of approval went around the porch. But the heat was melting their civic virtue and Elijah Moseley began to bait Joe Clarke.

"Come on, Joe, git a melon outa dere an' slice it up for yo' customers. We'se all sufferin' wid de heat. De bear's done got *me!*"

"Thass right, Joe, a watermelon is jes' whut Ah needs tuh cure de eppizudicks," Walter Thomas joined forces with Moseley. "Come on dere, Joe. We all is steady customers an' you aint set us up in a long time. Ah chooses dat long, bowlegged Floridy favorite."

"A god, an' be dough. You all gimme twenty cents and slice way." Clarke retorted. "Ah needs a col' slice m'self. Heah, everybody chip in. Ah'll lend y'll mah meat knife."

The money was quickly subscribed and the huge melon brought forth. At that moment, Sykes and Bertha arrived. A determined silence fell on the porch and the melon was put away again.

Merchant snapped down the blade of his jackknife and moved toward the store door.

"Come on in, Joe, an' gimme a slab uh sow belly an' uh pound uh coffee—almost fuhgot 'twas Sat'day. Got to git on home." Most of the men left also.

Just then Delia drove past on her way home, as Sykes was ordering magnificently for Bertha. It pleased him for Delia to see.

"Git whutsoever yo' heart desires, Honey. Wait a minute, Joe. Give huh two bottles uh strawberry soda-water, uh quart uh parched ground-peas, an' a block uh chewin' gum."

With all this they left the store, with Sykes reminding Bertha that this was his town and she could have it if she wanted it.

The men returned soon after they left, and held their watermelon feast.

"Where did Syke Jones git da 'oman from nohow?" Lindsay asked.

"Ovah Apopka. Guess dey musta been cleanin' out de town when she lef'. She don't look lak a thing but a hunk uh liver wid hair on it."

"Well, she sho' kin squall," Dave Carter contributed. "When she gits ready tuh laff, she jes' opens huh mouf an' latches it back tuh de las' notch. No ole grandpa alligator down in Lake Bell aint got nothin' on huh."

Bertha had been in town three months now. Sykes was still paying her room rent at Della Lewis'—the only house in town that would have taken her in. Sykes took her frequently to Winter Park to "stomps." He still assured her that he was the swellest man in the state.

"Sho' you kin have dat lil' ole house soon's Ah kin git dat 'oman outa dere. Everything b'longs tuh me an' you sho' kin have it. Ah sho' 'bominates uh skinny 'oman. Lawdy, you sho' is got one portly shape on you! You kin git *anything* you wants. Dis is *mah* town an' you sho' kin have it."

Delia's work-worn knees crawled over the earth in Gethsemane and up the rocks of Calvary many, many times during these months. She avoided the villagers and meeting places in her efforts to be blind and deaf. But Bertha nullified this to a degree, by coming to Delia's house to call Sykes out to her at the gate.

Delia and Sykes fought all the time now with no peaceful interludes. They slept and ate in silence. Two or three times Delia had attempted a timid friendliness, but she was repulsed each time. It was plain that the breaches must remain agape.

The sun had burned July to August. The heat streamed down like a million hot arrows, smiting all things living upon the earth. Grass withered, leaves browned, snakes went blind in shedding and men and dogs went mad. Dog days!

Delia came home one day and found Sykes there before her. She wondered, but started to go on into the house without speaking, even though he was standing in the kitchen door and she must either stoop under his arm or ask him to move. He made no room for her. She noticed a soap box beside the steps, but paid no particular attention to it, knowing that he must have brought it there. As she was stooping to pass under his outstretched arm, he suddenly pushed her backward, laughingly.

"Look in de box dere Delia, Ah done brung yuh somethin'!"

She nearly fell upon the box in her stumbling, and when she saw what it held, she all but fainted outright.

"Syke! Syke, mah Gawd! You take dat rattlesnake 'way from heah! You *gottuh*. Oh, Jesus, have mussy!"

"Ah aint gut tuh do nuthin' uh de kin'—fact is Ah aint got tuh do nothin' but die. Taint no use uh you puttin' on airs makin' out lak you skeered uh dat snake—he's gointer stay right heah tell he die. He wouldn't bite me cause Ah knows how tuh handle 'im. Nohow he wouldn't risk breakin' out his fangs 'gin *yo'* skinny laigs."

"Naw, now Syke, don't keep dat thing 'roun' heah tuh skeer me tuh death. You knows Ah'm even feared uh earth worms. Thass de biggest snake Ah evah did see. Kill 'im Syke, please."

"Doan ast me tuh do nothin' fuh yuh. Goin' 'roun' tryin' tuh be so damn asterperious. Naw, Ah aint gonna kill it. Ah think uh damn sight mo' uh him dan you! Dat's a nice snake an' anybody doan lak 'im kin jes' hit de grit."

The village soon heard that Sykes had the snake, and came to see and ask questions.

"How de hen-fire did you ketch dat six-foot rattler, Syke?" Thomas asked.

"He's full uh frogs so he caint hardly move, thass how Ah eased up on 'm. But Ah'm a snake charmer an' knows how tuh handle 'em. Shux, dat aint nothin'. Ah could ketch one eve'y day if Ah so wanted tuh."

"Whut he needs is a heavy hick'ry club leaned real heavy on his head. Dat's de bes' way tuh charm a rattlesnake."

"Naw, Walt, y'll jes' don't understand dese diamon' backs lak Ah do," said Sykes in a superior tone of voice.

The village agreed with Walter, but the snake stayed on. His box remained by the kitchen door with its screen wire covering. Two or three days later it had digested its meal of frogs and literally came to life. It rattled at every movement in the kitchen or the yard. One day as Delia came down the kitchen steps she saw his chalky-white fangs curved like scimitars hung in the wire meshes. This time she did not run away with averted eyes as usual. She stood for a long time in the doorway in a red fury that grew bloodier for every second that she regarded the creature that was her torment.

That night she broached the subject as soon as Sykes sat down to the table.

"Syke, Ah wants you tuh take dat snake 'way fum heah. You done starved me an' Ah put up widcher, you done beat me an Ah took dat, but you done kilt all mah insides bringin' dat varmint heah."

Sykes poured out a saucer full of coffee and drank it deliberately before he answered her.

"A whole lot Ah keer 'bout how you feels inside uh out. Dat snake aint goin' no damn wheah till Ah gits ready fuh 'im tuh go. So fur as beatin' is concerned, yuh aint took near all dat you gointer take ef yuh stay 'roun' *me.*"

Delia pushed back her plate and got up from the table. "Ah hates you, Sykes," she said calmly. "Ah hates you tuh de same degree dat Ah useter love yuh. Ah done took an' took till mah belly is full up tuh mah neck. Dat's de reason Ah got mah letter fum de church an' moved mah membership tuh Woodbridge—so Ah don't haftuh take no sacrament wid yuh. Ah don't wantuh see yuh 'roun' me atall. Lay 'roun' wid dat 'oman all yuh wants tuh, but gwan 'way fum me an' mah house. Ah hates yuh lak uh suck-egg dog."

Sykes almost let the huge wad of corn bread and collard greens he was chewing fall out of his mouth in amazement. He had a hard time whipping himself up to the proper fury to try to answer Delia.

"Well, Ah'm glad you does hate me. Ah'm sho' tiahed uh you hangin' ontuh me. Ah don't want yuh. Look at yuh stringey ole neck! Yo' rawbony laigs an' arms is enough tuh cut uh man tuh death. You looks jes' lak de devvul's doll-baby tuh *me.* You cain't hate me no worse dan Ah hates you. Ah been hatin' *you* fuh years."

"Yo' ole black hide don't look lak nothin' tuh me, but uh passle uh wrinkled up rubber, wid yo' big ole yeahs flappin' on each side lak uh paih uh buzzard wings. Don't think Ah'm gointuh be run 'way fum mah house neither. Ah'm goin' tuh de white folks bout *you,* mah young man, de very nex' time you lay yo' han's on me. Mah cup is done run ovah."

Delia said this with no signs of fear and Sykes departed from the house, threatening her, but made not the slightest move to carry out any of them.

That night he did not return at all, and the next day being Sunday, Delia was glad she did not have to quarrel before she hitched up her pony and drove the four miles to Woodbridge.

She stayed to the night service—"love feast"—which was very warm and full of spirit. In the emotional winds her domestic trials were borne far and wide so that she sang as she drove homeward,

> "Jurden water, black an' col'
> Chills de body, not de soul
> An' Ah wantah cross Jurden in uh calm time."

She came from the barn to the kitchen door and stopped.

"Whut's de mattah, ol' satan, you aint kickin' up yo' racket?" She addressed the snake's box. Complete silence. She went on into the house with a new hope in its birth struggles. Perhaps her threat to go to the white folks had frightened Sykes! Perhaps he was sorry! Fifteen years of misery and suppression had brought Delia to the place where she would hope *anything* that looked towards a way over or through her wall of inhibitions.

She felt in the match safe behind the stove at once for a match. There was only one there.

"Dat niggah wouldn't fetch nothin' heah tuh save his rotten neck, but he kin run thew whut Ah brings quick enough. Now he done toted off nigh on tuh haff uh box uh matches. He done had dat 'oman heah in mah house too."

Nobody but a woman could tell how she knew this even before she struck the match. But she did and it put her into a new fury.

Presently she brought in the tubs to put the white things to soak. This time she decided she need not bring the hamper out of the bedroom: she would go in there and do the sorting. She picked up the pot-bellied lamp and went in. The room was small and the hamper stood hard by the foot of the white iron bed. She could sit and reach through the bedposts—resting as she worked.

"Ah wantah cross Jurden in uh calm time." She was singing again. The mood of the "love feast" had returned. She threw back the lid of the basket almost gaily. Then, moved by both horror and terror, she sprang back toward the door. *There lay the snake in the basket!* He moved sluggishly at first, but even as she turned round and round, jumped up and down in an insanity of fear, he began to stir vigorously. She saw him pouring his awful beauty from the basket upon the bed, then she seized the lamp and ran as fast as she could to the kitchen. The wind from the open door blew out the light and the darkness added to her terror. She sped to the darkness of the yard, slamming the door after her before she thought to set down the lamp. She did not feel safe even on the ground, so she climbed up in the hay barn.

There for an hour or more she lay sprawled upon the hay a gibbering wreck.

Finally she grew quiet, and after that, coherent thought. With this, stalked through her a cold, bloody rage. Hours of this. A period of introspection, a space of retrospection, then a mixture of both. Out of this an awful calm.

"Well, Ah done de bes' Ah could. If things aint right, Gawd knows taint mah fault."

She went to sleep—a twitch sleep—and woke up to a faint gray sky. There was a loud hollow sound below. She peered out. Sykes was at the wood-pile, demolishing a wire-covered box.

He hurried to the kitchen door, but hung outside there some minutes before he entered, and stood some minutes more inside before he closed it after him.

The gray in the sky was spreading. Delia descended without fear now, and crouched beneath the low bedroom window. The drawn shade shut out the dawn, shut in the night. But the thin walls held back no sound.

"Dat ol' scratch is woke up now!" She mused at the tremendous whirr inside, which every woodsman knows, is one of the sound illusions. The rattler is a ventriloquist. His whirr sounds to the right, to the left, straight ahead, behind, close under foot—everywhere but where it is. Woe to him who guesses wrong unless he is prepared to hold up his end of the argument! Sometimes he strikes without rattling at all.

Inside, Sykes heard nothing until he knocked a pot lid off the stove while trying to reach the match safe in the dark. He had emptied his pockets at Bertha's.

The snake seemed to wake up under the stove and Sykes made a quick leap into the bedroom. In spite of the gin he had had, his head was clearing now.

"Mah Gawd!" he chattered, "ef Ah could on'y strack uh light!"

The rattling ceased for a moment as he stood paralyzed. He waited. It seemed that the snake waited also.

"Oh, fuh de light! Ah thought he'd be too sick"—Sykes was muttering to himself when the whirr began again, closer, right underfoot this time. Long before this, Sykes' ability to think had been flattened down to primitive instinct and he leaped—onto the bed.

Outside Delia heard a cry that might have come from a maddened chimpanzee, a stricken gorilla. All the terror, all the horror, all the rage that man possibly could express, without a recognizable human sound.

A tremendous stir inside there, another series of animal screams, the intermittent whirr of the reptile. The shade torn violently down from the window, letting in the red dawn, a huge brown hand seizing the window stick, great dull blows upon the wooden floor punctuating the gibberish of sound long after the rattle of the snake had abruptly subsided. All this Delia could see and hear from her place beneath the window, and it made her ill. She crept over to the four-o'clocks and stretched herself on the cool earth to recover.

She lay there. "Delia, Delia!" She could hear Sykes calling in a most despairing tone as one who expected no answer. The sun crept on up, and he called. Delia could not move—her legs were gone flabby. She never moved, he called, and the sun kept rising.

"Mah Gawd!" She heard him moan, "Mah Gawd fum Heben!" She heard him stumbling about and got up from her flower-bed. The sun was growing warm. As she approached the door she heard him call out hopefully, "Delia, is dat you Ah heah?"

She saw him on his hands and knees as soon as she reached the door. He crept an inch or two toward her—all that he was able, and she saw his horribly swollen neck and his one open eye shining with hope. A surge of pity too strong to support bore her away from that eye that must, could not, fail to see the tubs. He would see the lamp. Orlando with its doctors was too far. She could scarcely reach the Chinaberry tree, where she waited in the growing heat while inside she knew the cold river was creeping up and up to extinguish that eye which must know by now that she knew.

Questions for Discussion

1. In what ways does the first scene between Delia and Sykes foreshadow what is to come in the story?

2. Characterize Sykes. What kind of person is he?

3. If you were to interpret the rattlesnake as a symbol, what larger significance would you attribute to it?

4. Analyze Delia's response to Sykes's death.

Suggestions for Writing

1. Write a paragraph about how the community reacts to the conflict between Sykes and Delia.

2. Compare and contrast "Sweat" with "The Story of an Hour." How is the plight of each woman different? The same? What socioeconomic background does each woman come from? Contrast the resolutions of each story.

3. Write a story about two people in an ostensibly intimate relationship that has actually become a struggle for power.

Wrong Pigeon

RAYMOND CHANDLER

He was a slightly fat man with a dishonest smile that pulled the corners of his mouth out half an inch leaving the thick lips tight and his eyes bleak. For a fattish man he had a slow walk. Most fat men are brisk and light on their feet. He wore a gray herringbone suit and a hand-painted tie with part of a diving girl visible on it. His shirt was clean, which comforted me, and his brown loafers, as wrong as the tie for his suit, shone from a recent polishing.

He sidled past me as I held the door between the waiting room and my thinking parlor. Once inside, he took a quick look around. I'd have placed him as a mobster, second grade, if I had been asked. For once I was right. If he carried a gun, it was inside his pants. His coat was too tight to hide the bulge of an underarm holster.

He sat down carefully and I sat opposite and we looked at each other. His face had a sort of foxy eagerness. He was sweating a little. The expression on my face was meant to be interested but not clubby. I reached for a pipe and the leather humidor in which I kept my Pearce's tobacco. I pushed cigarettes at him.

"I don't smoke." He had a rusty voice. I didn't like it any more than I liked his clothes, or his face. While I filled the pipe he reached inside his coat, prowled in a pocket, came out with a bill, glanced at it and dropped it across the desk in front of me. It was a nice bill and clean and new. One thousand dollars.

"Ever save a guy's life?"

"Once in a while, maybe."

"Save mine."

"What goes?"

"I heard you levelled with the customers, Marlowe."

"That's why I stay poor."

"I still got two friends. You make it three and you'll be out of the red. You got five grand coming if you pry me loose."

"From what?"

"You're talkative as hell this morning. Don't you pipe who I am?"

"Nope."

"Never been east, huh?"

"Sure—but I wasn't in your set."

"What set would that be?"

I was getting tired of it. "Stop being so goddam cagey or pick up your grand and be missing."

"I'm Ikky Rosenstein. I'll be missing but good unless you can figure some out. Guess."

"I've already guessed. You tell me and tell me quick. I don't have all day to watch you feeding me with an eye-dropper."

"I ran out on the Outfit. The high boys don't go for that. To them it means you got info you figure you can peddle, or you got independent ideas, or you lost your moxie. Me, I lost my moxie. I had it up to here." He touched his Adam's apple with the forefinger of a stretched hand. "I done bad things. I scared and hurt guys. I never killed nobody. That's nothing to the Outfit. I'm out of line. So they pick up the pencil and they draw a line. I got the word. The operators are on the way. I made a bad mistake. I tried to hole up in Vegas. I figured they'd never expect me to lie up in their own joint. They outfigured me. What I did's been done before, but I didn't know it. When I took the plane to LA there must have been somebody on it. They know where I live."

"Move."

"No good now. I'm covered." I knew he was right.

"Why haven't they taken care of you already?"

"They don't do it that way. Always specialists. Don't you know how it works?"

"More or less. A guy with a nice hardware store in Buffalo. A guy with a small dairy in KC. Always a good front. They report back to New York or somewhere. When they mount the plane west or wherever they're going, they have guns in their briefcases. They're quiet and well-dressed, and they don't sit together. They could be a couple of lawyers or income tax sharpies—anything at all that's well-mannered and inconspicuous. All sorts of people carry briefcases. Including women."

"Correct as hell. And when they land they'll be steered to me, but not from the airfield. They got ways. If I go to the cops, somebody will know about me. They could have a couple Mafia boys right on the City Council for all I know. It's been done. The cops will give me twenty-fours to leave town. No use. Mexico? Worse than here. Canada? Better but still no good. Connections there too."

"Australia?"

"Can't get a passport. I been here twenty-five years—illegal. They can't deport me unless they can prove a crime on me. The Outfit would see they didn't. Suppose I got tossed into the freezer. I'm out on a writ in twenty-four hours. And my nice friends got a car waiting to take me home—only not home."

I had my pipe lit and going well. I frowned down at the grand note. I could use it very nicely. My checking account could kiss the sidewalk without stooping.

"Let's stop horsing," I said. "Suppose—just suppose—I could figure an out for you. What's your next move?"

"I know a place—if I could get there without bein' tailed. I'd leave my car here and take a rent car. I'd turn it in just short of the county line and buy a secondhand job. Halfway to where I'm going I trade it on a new last's model, a leftover. This is just the right time of year. Good discount, new models out soon. Not to save money—less show off. Where I'd go is a good-sized place but still pretty clean."

"Uh-huh," I said. "Wichita, last I heard. But it may have changed."

He scowled at me. "Get smart, Marlowe, but not too damn smart."

"I'll get as smart as I want to. Don't try to make rules for me. If I take this on, there aren't any rules. I take it for this grand and the rest if I bring it off. Don't cross me. I might leak information. If I get knocked off, put just one red rose on my grave. I don't like cut flowers. I like to see them growing. But I could take one, because you're such a sweet character. When's the plane in?"

"Sometime today. It's nine hours from New York. Probably come in about 5:30 p.m."

"Might come by San Diego and switch or by San Francisco and switch. A lot of planes from Dago and Frisco. I need a helper."

"Goddam you, Marlowe—"

"Hold it. I know a girl. Daughter of a chief of police who got broken for honesty. She wouldn't leak under torture."

"You got no right to risk her," Ikky said angrily.

I was so astonished my jaw hung halfway to my waist. I closed it slowly and swallowed.

"Good God, the man's got a heart."

"Women ain't built for the rough stuff," he said, grudgingly.

I picked up the thousand dollar note and snapped it. "Sorry. No receipt," I said. "I can't have my name in your pocket. And there won't be any rough stuff if I'm lucky. They'd have me outclassed. There's only one way to work it. Now give me your address and all the dope you can think of, names, descriptions of any operators you have ever seen in the flesh."

He did. He was a pretty good observer. Trouble was the Outfit would know what he had seen. The operators would be strangers to him.

He got up silently and put his hand out. I had to shake it, but what he had said about women made it easier. His hand was moist. Mine would have been in his spot. He nodded and went out silently.

It was a quiet street in Bay City, if there are any quiet streets in this beatnik generation when you can't get through a meal without some male or female stomach singer belching out a kind of love that is as old-fashioned as a bustle or some Hammond organ jazzing it up in the customer's soup.

The little one story house was as neat as a fresh pinafore. The front lawn was cut lovingly and very green. The smooth composition driveway was free of grease spots from standing cars, and the hedge that bordered it looked as though the barber came every day.

The white door had a knocker with a tiger's head, a go-to-hell window and a dingus that let someone inside talk to someone outside without even opening the little window.

I'd have given a mortgage on my left leg to live in a house like that. I didn't think I ever would.

The bell chimed inside and after a while she opened the door in a pale blue sports shirt and white shorts that were short enough to be friendly. She had gray-blue eyes, dark red hair and fine bones in her face. There was usually a trace of bitterness in the gray-blue eyes. She couldn't forget that her father's life had been destroyed by the crooked power of a gambling ship mobster, that her mother had died too. She was able to suppress the bitterness when she wrote nonsense about young love for the shiny magazines, but this wasn't her life. She didn't really have a life. She had an existence without much pain and enough oil money to make it safe. But in a tight spot she was as cool and resourceful as a good cop. Her name was Anne Riordan.

She stood to one side and I passed her pretty close. But I have rules too. She shut the door and parked herself on a davenport and went through the cigarette routine, and here was one doll who had the strength to light her own cigarette.

I stood looking around. There were a few changes, not many.

"I need your help," I said.

"That's the only time I ever see you."

"I've got a client who is an ex-hood; used to be a trouble-shooter for the Outfit, the Syndicate, the big mob, or whatever name you want to use for it. You know damn well it exists and is as rich as Rockefeller. You can't beat it because not enough people want to, especially the million-a-year lawyers that work for it, and the bar associations that seem more anxious to protect other lawyers than their own country."

"My God, are you running for office somewhere? I never knew you to sound so pure."

She moved her legs around, not provocatively—she wasn't the type—but it made it difficult for me to think straight just the same.

"Stop moving your legs around," I said. "Or else put a pair of slacks on."

"Damn you, Marlowe. Can't you think of anything else?"

"I'll try. I like to think that I know at least one pretty and charming female who doesn't have round heels." I swallowed and went on. "The man's name is Ikky Rosenstein. He's not beautiful and he's not anything that I like—except one. He got mad when I said I needed a girl helper. He said women were not made for the rough stuff. That's why I took the job. To a real mobster, a woman means no more than a sack of flour. They use women in the usual way, but if it's advisable to get rid of them, they do it without a second thought."

"So far you've told me a whole lot of nothing. Perhaps you need a cup of coffee or a drink."

"You're sweet but I don't in the morning—except sometimes and this isn't one of them. Coffee later. Ikky has been pencilled."

"Now what's that?"

"You have a list. You draw a line through a name with a pencil. The guy is as good as dead. The Outfit has reasons. They don't do it just for kicks any more. They don't get any kick. It's just bookkeeping to them."

"What on earth can I do? I might even have said, what can *you* do?"

"I can try. What you can do is help me spot their plane and see where they go—the operators assigned to the job."

"How can you do anything?"

"I said I could try. If they took a night plane they are already here. If they took a morning plane they can't be here before five or so. Plenty of time to get set. You know what they look like."

"Oh sure. I meet killers everyday. I have them in for whiskey sours and caviare on hot toast." She grinned. While she was grinning I took four long steps across the tan figured rug and lifted her and put a kiss on her mouth. She didn't fight me but she didn't go all trembly either. I went back and sat down.

"They'll look like anybody who's in a quiet well-run business or profession. They'll have quiet clothes and they'll be polite—when they want to be. They'll have briefcases with guns in them that have changed hands so often they can't possibly be traced. When and if they do the job, they'll drop the guns. They'll probably use revolvers, but they could use automatics. They won't use silencers because silencers can jam a gun and the weight makes it hard to shoot accurately. They won't sit together on the plane, but once off of it they may pretend to know each other and simply not have noticed during the flight. They may shake hands with appropriate smiles and walk away and get in the same taxi. I think they'll go to a hotel first. But very soon they will move into something from which they can watch Ikky's movements and get used to his schedule. They won't be in a hurry unless Ikky makes a move. That would tip them off that Ikky has been tipped off. He has a couple of friends left—he says."

"Will they shoot him from this room or apartment across the street—assuming there is one?"

"No. They'll shoot him from three feet away. They'll walk up behind him and say, 'Hello, Ikky.' He'll either freeze or turn. They'll fill him with lead, drop the guns, and hop into the car they have waiting. Then they'll follow the crash car off the scene."

"Who'll drive the crash car?"

"Some well-fixed and blameless citizen who hasn't been rapped. He'll drive his own car. He'll clear the way, even if he has to accidentally on purpose crash somebody, even a police car. He'll be so goddam sorry he'll cry all the way down his monogrammed shirt. And the killers will be long gone."

"Good heavens," Anne said. "How can you stand your life? If you did bring it off, they'll send operators to you."

"I don't think so. They don't kill a legit. The blame will go to the operators. Remember, these top mobsters are businessmen. They want lots and lots of money. They only get really tough when they figure they have to get rid of somebody, and they don't crave that. There's always a chance of a slip-up. Not much of a chance. No gang killing has ever been solved here or anywhere else except two or three times. Lepke Buchalter fried. Remember Anastasia? He was awful big and awful tough. Too big, too tough. Pencil."

She shuddered a little. "I think I need a drink myself."

I grinned at her. "You're right in the atmosphere, darling. I'll weaken."

She brought a couple of Scotch highballs. When we were drinking them I said: "If you spot them or think you spot them, follow to where they go—if you can do it safely. Not otherwise. If it's a hotel—and ten to one it will be—check in and keep calling me until you get me."

She knew my office number and I was still on Yucca Avenue. She knew that too.

"You're the damnedest guy," she said. "Women do anything you want them to. How come I'm still a virgin at twenty-eight?"

"We need a few like you. Why don't you get married?"

"To what? Some cynical chaser who has nothing left but technique? I don't know any really nice men—except you. I'm no pushover for white teeth and a gaudy smile."

I went over and pulled her to her feet. I kissed her long and hard. "I'm honest," I almost whispered. "That's something. But I'm too shop-soiled for a girl like you. I've thought of you. I've wanted you, but that sweet clear look in your eyes tells me to lay off."

"Take me," she said softly. "I have dreams too."

"I couldn't. It's not the first time it's happened to me. I've had too many women to deserve one like you. We have to save a man's life. I'm going."

She stood up and watched me leave with a grave face.

The women you get and the women you don't get—they live in different worlds. I don't sneer at either world. I live in both myself.

At Los Angeles International Airport you can't get close to the planes unless you're leaving on one. You see them land, if you happen to be in the right place, but you have to wait at a barrier to get a look at the passengers. The airport buildings don't make it any easier. They are strung out from here to breakfast time, and you can get calluses walking from TWA to American.

I copied an arrival schedule off the boards and prowled around like a dog that has forgotten where he put his bone. Planes came in, planes took off, porters carried luggage, passengers sweated and scurried, children whined, the loud-speaker overrode all the other noises.

I passed Anne a number of times. She took no notice of me.

At 5:45 they must have come.

Anne disappeared. I gave it half an hour, just in case she had some other reason for fading. No. She was gone for good. I went out to my car and drove some long crowded miles to Hollywood and my office. I had a drink and sat. At 6:45 the phone rang.

"I think so," she said. "Beverly-Western Hotel. Room 410. I couldn't get any names. You know the clerks don't leave registration cards lying around these days. I didn't like to ask any questions. But I rode up in the elevator with them and spotted their room. I walked right on past them when the bellman put a key in their door, and walked down to the mezzanine and then downstairs with a bunch of women from the tea room. I didn't bother to take a room."

"What were they like?"

"They came up the ramp together but I didn't hear them speak. Both had briefcases, both wore quiet suits, nothing flashy. White shirts, starched, one blue tie, one black striped with gray. Black shoes. A couple of businessmen from the East Coast. They could be publishers, lawyers, doctors, account executives—no, cut the last; they weren't gaudy enough. You wouldn't look at them twice."

"Look at them twice. Faces."

"Both medium brown hair, one a bit darker than the other. Smooth faces, rather expressionless. One had gray eyes; the one with the lighter hair had blue eyes. Their eyes were interesting. Very quick to move, very observant, watching everything near them. That might have been wrong. They should have been a bit preoccupied with what they came out for or interested in California. They seemed more occupied with faces. It's a good thing I spotted them and not you. You don't look like a cop, but you don't look like a man who is not a cop. You have marks on you."

"Phooey. I'm a damn good looking heart wrecker."

"Their features were strictly assembly line. Neither looked Italian. Each picked up a flight suitcase. One suitcase was gray with two red and white stripes up and down, about six or seven inches from the ends, the other a blue and white tartan. I didn't know there was such a tartan."

"There is, but I forget the name of it."

"I thought you knew everything."

"Just almost everything. Run along home now."

"Do I get a dinner and maybe a kiss?"

"Later, and if you're not careful you'll get more than you want."

"A rapist, eh? I'll carry a gun. You'll take over and follow them?"

"If they're the right men, they'll follow me. I already took an apartment across the street from Ikky. That block on Poynter and the two on each side of it have about six lowlife apartment houses to the block. I'll bet the incidence of chippies is very high."

"It's high everywhere these days."

"So long, Anne. See you."

"When you need help."

She hung up. I hung up. She puzzled me. Too wise to be so nice. I guess all nice women are wise too. I called Ikky. He was out. I had a drink from the office bottle, smoked for half an hour and called again. This time I got him.

I told him the score up to then, and said I hoped Anne had picked the right men. I told him about the apartment I had taken.

"Do I get expenses?" I asked.

"Five grand ought to cover the lot."

"If I earn it and get it. I heard you had a quarter of a million," I said at a wild venture.

"Could be, pal; but how do I get at it? The high boys know where it is. It'll have to cool a long time."

I said that was all right. I had cooled a long time myself. Of course I didn't expect to get the four thousand, even if I brought the job off. Men like Ikky Rosenstein would steal their mother's gold teeth. There seemed to be a little good in him somewhere—but little was the operative word.

I spent the next half hour trying to think of a plan. I couldn't think of one that looked promising. It was almost eight o'clock and I needed food. I didn't think the boys would move that night. Next morning they would drive past Ikky's place and scout the neighborhood.

I was ready to leave the office when the buzzer sounded from the door of my waiting room. I opened the communicating door. A small tight-looking man was standing in the middle of the floor rocking on his heels with his hands behind his back. He smiled at me, but he wasn't good at it. He walked towards me.

"You Marlowe?"

"Who else? What can I do for you?"

He was close now. He brought his right hand around fast with a gun in it. He stuck the gun in my stomach.

"You can lay off Ikky Rosenstein," he said in a voice that matched his face, "or you can get your belly full of lead."

He was an amateur. If he had stayed four feet away, he might have had something. I reached up and took the cigarette out of my mouth and held it carelessly.

"What makes you think I know any Ikky Rosenstein?"

He laughed a high-pitched laugh and pushed his gun into my stomach.

"Wouldn't you like to know?" The cheap sneer, the empty triumph of power when you hold a fat gun in a small hand.

"It would be fair to tell me."

As his mouth opened for another crack, I dropped the cigarette and swept a hand. I can be fast when I have to. There are boys that are faster, but they don't stick guns in your stomach. I got my thumb behind the trigger and my hand over his. I kneed him in the groin. He bent over with a whimper. I twisted his arm to the right and I had his gun. I hooked a heel behind his heel and he was on the floor. He lay there blinking with surprise and pain, his knees drawn up against his stomach. He rolled from side to side groaning. I reached down and grabbed his left hand and yanked him to his feet. I had six inches and forty pounds on him. They ought to have sent a bigger, better trained messenger.

"Let's go into my thinking parlor," I said. "We could have a chat and you could have a drink to pick you up. Next time don't get near enough to a prospect for him to get your gun hand. I'll just see if you have any more iron on you."

He hadn't. I pushed him through the door and into a chair. His breath wasn't quite so rasping. He grabbed out a handkerchief and mopped at his face.

"Next time," he said between his teeth. "Next time."

"Don't be an optimist. You don't look the part."

I poured him a drink of Scotch in a paper cup, set it down in front of him. I broke his 38 and dumped the cartridges into the desk drawer. I clicked the chamber back and laid the gun down.

"You can have it when you leave—if you leave."

"That's a dirty way to fight," he said, still gasping.

"Sure. Shooting a man is so much cleaner. Now, how did you get here?"

"Screw yourself."

"Don't be a crumb. I have friends. Not many, but some. I can get you for armed assault, and you know what would happen then. You'd be out on a writ or on bail and that's the last anyone would hear of you. The biggies don't go for failures. Now who sent you and how did you know where to come?"

"Ikky was covered," he said sullenly. "He's dumb. I trailed him here without no trouble at all. Why would he go see a private eye? People want to know."

"More."

"Go to hell."

"Come to think of it, I don't have to get you for armed assault. I can smash it out of you right here and now."

I got up from the chair and he put a flat hand out.

"If I get knocked about, a couple of real tough monkeys will drop around. If I don't report back, same thing. You ain't holding no real high cards. They just look high," he said.

"You haven't anything to tell. If this Ikky guy came to see me, you don't know why, nor whether I took him on. If he's a mobster, he's not my type of client."

"He come to get you to try to save his hide."

"Who from?"

"That'd be talking."

"Go right ahead. Your mouth seems to work fine. And tell the boys any time I front for a hood, that will be the day."

You have to lie a little once in a while in my business. I was lying a little. "What's Ikky done to get himself disliked? Or would that be talking?"

"You think you're a lot of man," he sneered, rubbing the place where I had kneed him. "In my league you wouldn't make pinch runner."

I laughed in his face. Then I grabbed his right wrist and twisted it behind his back. He began to squawk. I reached into his breast pocket with my left hand and hauled out a wallet. I let him go. He reached for his gun on the desk and I bisected his upper arm with a hard cut. He fell into the customer's chair and grunted.

"You can have your gun," I told him. "When I give it to you. Now be good or I'll have to bounce you just to amuse myself."

In the wallet I found a driver's license made out to Charles Hickon. It did me no good at all. Punks of his type always have slangy pseudonyms. They probably called him Tiny, or Slim, or Marbles, or even just 'you'. I tossed the wallet back to him. It fell to the floor. He couldn't even catch it.

"Hell," I said, "there must be an economy campaign on, if they sent you to do more than pick up cigarette butts."

"Screw yourself."

"All right, mug. Beat it back to the laundry. Here's your gun."

He took it, made a business of shoving it into his waistband, stood up, gave me as dirty a look as he had in stock, and strolled to the door, nonchalant as a hustler with a new mink stole. He turned at the door and gave me the beady eye.

"Stay clean, tinhorn. Tin bends easy."

With this blinding piece of repartee he opened the door and drifted out.

After a little while I locked my other door, cut the buzzer, made the office dark, and left. I saw no one who looked like a lifetaker. I drove to my house, packed a suitcase, drove to a service station where they were almost fond of me, stored my car and picked up a Hertz Chevrolet. I drove this to Poynter Street, dumped my suitcase in the sleazy apartment I had rented early in the afternoon, and went to dinner at Victor's. It was nine o'clock, too late to drive to Bay City and take Anne to dinner. She'd have cooked her own long ago.

I ordered a double Gibson with fresh limes and drank it, and I was as hungry as a schoolboy.

On the way back to Poynter Street I did a good deal of weaving in and out and circling blocks and stopping, with a gun on the seat beside me. As far as I could tell, no one was trying to tail me.

I stopped on Sunset at a service station and made two calls from the box. I caught Bernie Ohls just as he was leaving to go home.

"This is Marlowe, Bernie. We haven't had a fight in years. I'm getting lonely."

"Well, get married. I'm chief investigator for the Sheriff's Office now. I rank acting-captain until I pass the exam. I don't hardly speak to private eyes."

"Speak to this one. I could need help. I'm on a ticklish job where I could get killed."

"And you expect me to interfere with the course of nature?"

"Come off it, Bernie. I haven't been a bad guy. I'm trying to save an ex-mobster from a couple of executioners."

"The more they mow each other down, the better I like it."

"Yeah. If I call you, come running or send a couple of good boys. You'll have had time to teach them."

We exchanged a couple of mild insults and hung up. I dialed Ikky Rosenstein. His rather unpleasant voice said: "Okay, talk."

"Marlowe. Be ready to move out about midnight. We've spotted your boy friends and they are holed up at the Beverly-Western. They won't move to your street tonight. Remember, they don't know you've been tipped."

"Sounds chancy."

"Good God, it wasn't meant to be a Sunday School picnic. You've been careless, Ikky. You were followed to my office. That cuts the time we have."

He was silent for a moment. I heard him breathing. "Who by?" he asked.

"Some little tweezer who stuck a gun in my belly and gave me the trouble of taking it away from him. I can only figure why they sent a punk on the theory that they don't want me to know too much, in case I don't know it already."

"You're in for trouble, friend."

"When not? I'll come over to your place about midnight. Be ready. Where's your car?"

"Out front."

"Get it on a side street and make a business of locking it up. Where's the back door of your flop?"

"In back. Where would it be? On the alley."

"Leave your suitcase there. We walk out together and go to your car. We drive the alley and pick up the suitcase or cases."

"Suppose some guy steals them?"

"Yeah. Suppose you get dead. Which do you like better?"

"Okay," he grunted. "I'm waiting. But we're taking big chances."

"So do race drivers. Does that stop them? There's no way to get out but fast. Douse your lights about ten and rumple the bed well. It would be good if you could leave some baggage behind. Wouldn't look so planned."

He grunted another okay and I hung up. The telephone box was well lighted outside. They usually are, at service stations. I took a good long gander around while I pawed over the collection of give away maps inside the station. I saw nothing to worry me. I took a map of San Diego just for the hell of it and got into my rent car.

On Poynter I parked around the corner and went up to my second floor sleazy apartment and sat in the dark watching from my window. I saw nothing to worry about. A couple of medium-class chippies came out of Ikky's apartment house and were picked up in a late model car. A man about Ikky's height and build went into the apartment house. Various people came and went. The street was fairly quiet. Since they put in the Hollywood Freeway nobody much uses the off-the-boulevard streets unless they live in the neighborhood.

It was a nice fall night—or as nice as they get in Los Angeles' spoiled climate—clearish but not even crisp. I don't know what's happened to the weather in our overcrowded city but it's not the weather I knew when I came to it.

It seemed like a long time to midnight. I couldn't spot anybody watching anything, and no couple of quiet-suited men paged any of the six apartment houses available. I was pretty sure they'd try mine first when they came, and if Anne had picked the right men, and if anybody had come at all, and if the tweezer's message back to his bosses had done me any good or otherwise. In spite of the hundred ways Anne could be wrong, I had a hunch she was right. The killers had no reason to be cagey if they didn't know Ikky had been warned. No reason but one. He had come to my office and been tailed there. But the Outfit, with all its arrogance of power, might laugh at the idea he had been tipped off or come to me for help. I was so small they would hardly be able to see me.

At midnight I left the apartment, walked two blocks watching for a tail, crossed the street and went into Ikky's dive. There was no locked door, and no elevator. I climbed steps to the third floor and looked for his apartment. I knocked lightly. He opened the door with a gun in his hand. He probably looked scared.

There were two suitcases by the door and another against the far wall. I went over and lifted it. It was heavy enough. I opened it. It was unlocked.

"You don't have to worry," he said. "It's got everything a guy could need for three-four nights, and nothing except some clothes that I couldn't glom off in any ready to wear place."

I picked up one of the other suitcases. "Let's stash this by the back door."

"We can leave by the alley too."

"We leave by the front door. Just in case we're covered—though I don't think so—we're just two guys going out together. Just one thing. Keep both hands in your coat pockets and the gun in your right. If anybody calls out your name behind you, turn fast and shoot. Nobody but a lifetaker will do it. I'll do the same."

"I'm scared," he said in his rusty voice.

"Me too, if it helps any. But we have to do it. If you're braced, they'll have guns in their hands. Don't bother asking them questions. They wouldn't answer in words. If it's just my small friend, we'll cool him and dump him inside the door. Got it?"

He nodded, licking his lips. We carried the suitcases down and put them outside the back door. I looked along the alley. Nobody, and only a short distance to the side street. We went back in and along the hall to the front. We walked out on Poynter Street with all the casualness of a wife buying her husband a birthday tie.

Nobody made a move. The street was empty. We walked around the corner to Ikky's rent car. He unlocked it. I went back with him for the suitcases. Not a stir. We put the suitcases in the car and started up and drove to the next street.

A traffic light not working, a boulevard stop or two, the entrance to the Freeway. There was plenty of traffic on it even at midnight. California is loaded with people going places and making speed to get there. If you don't drive eighty miles an hour, everybody passes you. If you do, you have to watch the rear-view mirror for highway patrol cars. It's the rat race of rat races.

Ikky did a quiet seventy. We reached the junction to Route 66 and he took it. So far nothing. I stayed with him to Pomona.

"This is far enough for me," I said. "I'll grab a bus back if there is one, or park myself in a motor court. Drive to a service station and we'll ask for the bus stop. It should be close to the Freeway. Take us towards the business section."

He did that and stopped midway of a block. He reached out his pocketbook, and held out four thousand-dollar bills to me.

"I don't really feel I've earned all that. It was too easy."

He laughed with a kind of wry amusement on his pudgy face. "Don't be a sap. I have it made. You didn't know what you was walking into. What's more, your troubles are just beginning. The Outfit has eyes and ears everywhere. Perhaps I'm safe if I'm damn careful. Perhaps I ain't as safe as I think I am. Either way, you did what I asked. Take the dough. I got plenty."

I took it and put it away. He drove to an all-night service station and we were told where to find the bus stop. "There's a cross-country Greyhound at 2:25 a.m.," the attendant said, looking at a schedule. "They'll take you, if they got room."

Ikky drove to the bus stop. We shook hands and he went gunning down the road towards the Freeway. I looked at my watch and found a liquor store still open and bought a pint of Scotch. Then I found a bar and ordered a double with water.

My troubles were just beginning, Ikky had said. He was so right.

I got off at the Hollywood bus station, grabbed a taxi and drove to my office. I asked the driver to wait a few moments. At that time of night he was glad to. The colored night man let me into the building.

"You work late, Mr. Marlowe. But you always did, didn't you?"

"It's that sort of a business," I said. "Thanks, Jasper."

Up in my office I pawed the floor for mail and found nothing but a longish narrowish box, Special Delivery, with a Glendale postmark.

I opened it. It contained nothing at all but a new freshly-sharpened yellow pencil, the mobster's mark of death.

I didn't take it too hard. When they mean it, they don't send it to you. I took it as a sharp warning to lay off. There might be a beating arranged. From their point of view, that would be good discipline. "When we pencil a guy, any guy that tries to help him is in for a smashing." That could be the message.

I thought of going to my house on Yucca Avenue. Too lonely. I thought of going to Anne's place in Bay City. Worse. If they got wise to her, real hoods would think nothing of raping her and then beating her up.

It was the Poynter Street flop for me. Easily the safest place now. I went down to the waiting taxi and had him drive me to within three blocks of the so-called apartment house. I went upstairs, undressed and slept raw. Nothing bothered me but a broken spring. That bothered my back. I lay until 3:30 pondering the situation with my massive brain. I went to sleep with a gun under the pillow, which is a bad place to keep a gun when you have one pillow as thick and soft as a typewriter pad. It bothered me so I transferred it to my right hand. Practice had taught me to keep it there even in sleep.

I woke up with the sun shining. I felt like a piece of spoiled meat. I struggled into the bathroom and doused myself with cold water and wiped off with a towel you couldn't have seen if you held it sideways. This was a really gorgeous apartment. All it needed was a set of Chippendale furniture to graduate it into the slum class.

There was nothing to eat and if I went out, Miss-Nothing Marlowe might miss something. I had a pint of whiskey. I looked at it and smelled it, but I couldn't take it for breakfast, on an empty stomach, even if I could reach my stomach, which was floating around near the ceiling. I looked into the closets in case a previous tenant might have left a crust of bread in a hasty departure. Nope. I wouldn't have liked it anyhow, not even with whiskey on it. So I sat at the window. An hour of that and I was ready to bite a piece off a bellhop.

I dressed and went around the corner to the rent car and drove to an eatery. The waitress was sore too. She swept a cloth over the counter in front of me and let me have the last customer's crumbs in my lap.

"Look, sweetness," I said, "don't be so generous. Save the crumbs for a rainy day. All I want is two eggs three minutes—no more—a slice of your famous concrete toast, a tall glass of tomato juice with a dash of Lea & Perrins, a big happy smile, and don't give anybody else any coffee. I might need it all."

"I got a cold," she said. "Don't push me around. I might crack you one on the kisser."

"I had a rough night too."

She gave me a half-smile and went through the swing door sideways. It showed more of her curves, which were ample, even excessive. But I got the eggs the way I liked them. The toast had been painted with melted butter past its bloom.

"No Lea & Perrins," she said, putting down the tomato juice. "How about a little Tabasco? We're fresh out of arsenic too."

I used two drops of Tabasco, swallowed the eggs, drank two cups of coffee and was about to leave the toast for a tip, but I went soft and left a quarter instead. That really brightened her. It was a joint where you left a dime or nothing. Mostly nothing.

Back on Poynter nothing had changed. I got to my window again and sat. At about 8:30 the man I had seen go into the apartment house across the way—the one with the same sort of height and build as Ikky—came out with a small briefcase and turned east. Two men got out of a dark blue sedan. They were of the same height and very quietly dressed and had soft hats pulled low over their foreheads. Each jerked out a revolver.

"Hey, Ikky!" one of them called out.

The man turned. "So long, Ikky," the other man said. Gunfire racketed between the houses. The man crumpled and lay motionless. The two men rushed for their car and were off, going west. Halfway down the block I saw a Caddy pull out and start ahead of them.

In no time at all they were completely gone.

It was a nice swift clean job. The only thing wrong with it was that they hadn't given it enough time for preparation.

They had shot the wrong man.

I got out of there fast, almost as fast as the two killers. There was a smallish crowd grouped around the dead man. I didn't have to look at him to know he was dead—the boys were pros. Where he lay on the sidewalk on the other side of the street I couldn't see him; people were in the way. But I knew just how he would look and I already heard sirens in the distance. It could have been just the routine shrieking from Sunset, but it wasn't. So somebody had telephoned. It was too early for the cops to be going to lunch.

I strolled around the corner with my suitcase and jammed into the rent car and went away from there. The neighborhood was not my piece of shortcake any more. I could imagine the questions.

"Just what took you over there, Marlowe? You got a flop of your own, ain't you?"

"I was hired by an ex-mobster in trouble with the Outfit. They'd sent killers after him."

"Don't tell us he was trying to go straight."

"I don't know. But I liked his money."

"Didn't do much to earn it, did you?"

"I got him away last night. I don't know where he is now. I don't want to know."

"You got him away?"

"That's what I said."

"Yeah—only he's in the morgue with multiple bullet wounds. Try something better. Or somebody's in the morgue."

And on and on. Policeman's dialogue. It comes out of an old shoe box. What they say doesn't mean anything, what they ask doesn't mean anything. They just keep boring in until you are so exhausted you flip on some detail. Then they smile happily and rub their hands, and say: "Kind of careless there, weren't you? Let's start all over again."

The less I had of that, the better. I parked in my usual parking slot and went up to the office. It was full of nothing but stale air. Every time I went into the dump it felt more and more tired. Why the hell hadn't I got myself a government job ten years ago? Make it fifteen years. I had brains enough to get a mail-order law degree. The country's full of lawyers that couldn't write a complaint without the book.

So I sat in my office chair and disadmired myself. After a while I remembered the pencil. I made certain arrangements with a forty-five gun, more gun than I ever carry—too much weight. I dialed the Sheriff's Office and asked for Bernie Ohls. I got him. His voice was sour.

"Marlowe. I'm in trouble—real trouble."

"Why tell me?" he growled. "You must be used to it by now."

"This kind of trouble you don't get used to. I'd like to come over and tell you."

"You in the same office?"

"The same."

"Have to go over that way. I'll drop in."

He hung up. I opened two windows. The gentle breeze wafted a smell of coffee and stale fat to me from Joe's Eats next door. I hated it. I hated myself. I hated everything.

Ohls didn't bother with my elegant waiting room. He rapped on my own door and I let him in. He scowled his way to the customer's chair.

"Okay. Give."

"Ever hear of a character named Ikky Rosenstein?"

"Why would I? Record?"

"An ex-mobster who got disliked by the mob. They put a pencil through his name and sent the usual two tough boys on a plane. He got tipped and hired me to help him get away."

"Nice clean work."

"Cut it out, Bernie." I lit a cigarette and blew smoke in his face. In retaliation he began to chew a cigarette. He never lit one.

"Look," I went on. "Suppose the man wants to go straight and suppose he doesn't. He's entitled to his life as long as he hasn't killed anyone. He told me he hadn't."

"And you believed the hood, huh? When do you start teaching Sunday School?"

"I neither believed him nor disbelieved him. I took him on. There was no reason not to. A girl I know and I watched the planes yesterday. She spotted the boys and tailed them to a hotel. She was sure of what they were. They looked it right down to their black shoes. They got off the plane separately and then pretended to know each other and not to have noticed on the plane. This girl—"

"Would she have a name?"

"Only for you."

"I'll buy, if she hasn't cracked any laws."

"Her name is Anne Riordan. She lives in Bay City. Her father was once Chief of Police there. And don't say that makes him a crook, because he wasn't."

"Uh-huh. Let's have the rest. Make a little time too."

"I took an apartment opposite Ikky. The killers were still at the hotel. At midnight I got Ikky out and drove with him as far as Pomona. He went on in his rent car and I came back by Greyhound. I moved into the apartment on Poynter Street, right across from his dump."

"Why—if he was already gone?"

I opened the middle desk drawer and took out the nice sharp pencil. I wrote my name on a piece of paper and ran the pencil through it.

"But because someone sent me this. I didn't think they'd kill me, but I thought they planned to give me enough of a beating to warn me off any more pranks."

"They knew you were in on it?"

"Ikky was tailed here by a little squirt who later came around and stuck a gun in my stomach. I knocked him around a bit, but I had to let him go. I thought Poynter Street was safer after that. I live lonely."

"I get around," Bernie Ohls said. "I hear reports. So they gunned the wrong guy."

"Same height, same build, same general appearance. I saw them gun him.

I couldn't tell if it was the two guys from the Beverly-Western. I'd never seen them. It was just two guys in dark suits with hats pulled down. They jumped into a blue Pontiac sedan, about two years old, and lammed off, with a big Caddy running crash for them."

Bernie stood up and stared at me for a long moment. "I don't think they'll bother with you now," he said. "They've hit the wrong guy. The mob will be very quiet for a while. You know something? This town is getting to be almost as lousy as New York, Brooklyn and Chicago. We could end up real corrupt."

"We've made a hell of a good start."

"You haven't told me anything that makes me take action, Phil. I'll talk to the city homicide boys. I don't guess you're in any trouble. But you saw the shooting. They'll want that."

"I couldn't identify anybody, Bernie. I didn't know the man who was shot. How did *you* know it was the wrong man?"

"You told me, stupid."

"I thought perhaps the city boys had a make on him."

"They wouldn't tell me, if they had. Besides, they ain't hardly had time to go out for breakfast. He's just a stiff in the morgue to them until the ID comes up with something. But they'll want to talk to you, Phil. They just love their tape recorders."

He went out and the door whooshed shut behind him. I sat there wondering whether I had been a dope to talk to him. Or to take Ikky's troubles on. Five thousand green men said no. But they can be wrong too.

Somebody banged on my door. It was a uniform holding a telegram. I receipted for it and tore it loose.

It said: "On my way to Flagstaff. Mirador Motor Court. Think I've been spotted. Come fast."

I tore the wire into small pieces and burned them in my big ash tray.

I called Anne Riordan.

"Funny thing happened," I told her, and told her about the funny thing.

"I don't like the pencil," she said. "And I don't like the wrong man being killed, probably some poor bookkeeper in a cheap business or he wouldn't be living in that neighborhood. You should never have touched it, Phil."

"Ikky had a life. Where he's going he might make himself decent. He can change his name. He must be loaded or he wouldn't have paid me so much."

"I said I didn't like the pencil. You'd better come down here for a while. You can have your mail re-addressed—if you get any mail. You don't have to work right away anyhow. And LA is oozing with private eyes."

"You don't get the point. I'm not through with the job. The city dicks have to know where I am, and if they do, all the crime beat reporters will know too. The cops might even decide to make me a suspect. Nobody who saw the shooting is going to put out a description that means anything. The American people know better than to be witnesses to gang killings."

"All right, loud brain. But my offer stands."

The buzzer sounded in the outside room. I told Anne I had to hang up. I opened the communicating door and a well-dressed—I might say elegantly dressed—middle-aged man stood six feet inside the outer door. He had a pleasantly dishonest smile on his face. He wore a white Stetson and one of those narrow ties that go through an ornamental buckle. His cream-colored flannel suit was beautifully tailored.

He lit a cigarette with a gold lighter and looked at me over the first puff of smoke.

"Mr. Marlowe?"

I nodded.

"I'm Foster Grimes from Las Vegas. I run the Rancho Esperanza on South Fifth. I hear you got a little involved with a man named Ikky Rosenstein."

"Won't you come in?"

He strolled past me into my office. His appearance told me nothing. A prosperous man who liked or felt it good business to look a bit western. You see them by the dozen in the Palm Springs winter season. His accent told me he was an eastener, but not New England. New York or Baltimore, likely. Long Island, the Berkshires—no, too far from the city.

I showed him the customer's chair with a flick of the wrist and sat down in my antique swivel-squeaker. I waited.

"Where is Ikky now, if you know?"

"I don't know, Mr. Grimes."

"How come you messed with him?"

"Money."

"A damned good reason." he smiled. "How far did it go?"

"I helped him leave town. I'm telling you this, although I don't know who the hell you are, because I've already told an old friend-enemy of mine, a top man in the Sheriff's Office."

"What's a friend-enemy?"

"Law men don't go around kissing me, but I've known him for years, and we are as much friends as a private star can be with a law man."

"I told you who I was. We have a unique set-up in Vegas. We own the place except for one lousy newspaper editor who keeps climbing our backs and the backs of our friends. We let him live because letting him live makes us look better than knocking him off. Killings are not good business any more."

"Like Ikky Rosenstein."

"That's not a killing. It's an execution. Ikky got out of line."

"So your gun boys had to rub the wrong guy. They could have hung around a little to make sure."

"They would have, if you'd kept your nose where it belonged. They hurried. We don't appreciate that. We want cool efficiency."

"Who's this great big fat 'we' you keep talking about?"

"Don't go juvenile on me, Marlowe."

"Okay. Let's say I know."

"Here's what we want." He reached into his pocket and drew out a loose bill. He put it on the desk on his side. "Find Ikky and tell him to get back in line and everything is oke. With an innocent bystander gunned, we don't want any trouble or any extra publicity. It's that simple. You get this now," he nodded at the bill. It was a grand. Probably the smallest bill they had. "And another when you find Ikky and give him the message. If he holds out—curtains."

"Suppose I say take your goddam grand and blow your nose with it?"

"That would be unwise." He flipped out a Colt Woodsman with a short silencer on it. A Colt Woodsman will take one without jamming. He was fast too, fast and smooth. The genial expression on his face didn't change.

"I never left Vegas," he said calmly. "I can prove it. You're dead in your office chair and nobody knows anything. Just another private eye that tried the wrong pitch. Put your hands on the desk and think a little. Incidentally, I'm a crack shot even with this damned silencer."

"Just to sink a little lower in the social scale, Mr. Grimes, I ain't putting no hands on no desk. But tell me about this."

I flipped the nicely sharpened pencil across to him. He grabbed for it after a swift change of the gun to his left hand—very swift. He held the pencil up so that he could look at it without taking his eyes off me.

I said: "It came to me by Special Delivery mail. No message, no return address. Just the pencil. Think I've never heard about the pencil, Mr. Grimes?"

He frowned and tossed the pencil down. Before he could shift his long lithe gun back to his right hand I dropped mine under the desk and grabbed the butt of the .45 and put my finger hard on the trigger.

"Look under the desk, Mr. Grimes. You'll see a .45 in an open-end holster. It's fixed there and it's pointing at your belly. Even if you could shoot me through the heart the .45 would still go off from a convulsive movement of my hand. And your belly would be hanging by a shred and you would be knocked out of that chair. A .45 slug can throw you back six feet. Even the movies learned that at last.

"Looks like a Mexican stand-off," he said quietly. He holstered his gun. He grinned. "Nice smooth work, Marlowe. We could use you. But it's a long long time for you and no time at all to us. Find Ikky and don't be a drip. He'll listen to reason. He doesn't really want to be on the run for the rest of his life. We'd trace him eventually."

"Tell me something, Mr. Grimes. Why pick on me? Apart from Ikky, what did I ever do to make you dislike me?"

Not moving, he thought a moment, or pretended to. "The Larsen case. You helped send one of our boys to the gas chamber. That we don't forget. We had you in mind as a fall guy for Ikky. You'll always be a fall guy, unless you play it our way. Something will hit you when you least expect it."

"A man in my business is always a fall guy Mr. Grimes. Pick up your grand and drift out quietly. I might decide to do it your way, but I have to think. As for the Larsen case, the cops did all the work. I just happened to know where he was. I don't guess you miss him terribly."

"We don't like interference." He stood up. He put the grand note casually back in his pocket. While he was doing it I let go of the .45 and jerked out my Smith and Wesson five-inch .38.

He looked at it contemptuously. "I'll be in Vegas, Marlowe. In fact I never left Vegas. You can catch me at the Esperanza. No, we don't give a damn about Larsen personally. Just another gun handler. They come in gross lots. We *do* give a damn that some punk private eye fingered him."

He nodded and went out by my office door.

I did some pondering. I knew Ikky wouldn't go back to the Outfit. He wouldn't trust them enough if he got the chance. But there was another reason now. I called Anne Riordan again.

"I'm going to look for Ikky. I have to. If I don't call you in three days, get hold of Bernie Ohls. I'm going to Flagstaff, Arizona. Ikky says he will be there."

"You're a fool," she wailed. "It's some sort of trap."

"A Mr. Grimes of Vegas visited me with a silenced gun. I beat him to the punch, but I won't always be that lucky. If I find Ikky and report to Grimes, the mob will let me alone."

"You'd condemn a man to death?" Her voice was sharp and incredulous.

"No. He won't be there when I report. He'll have to hop a plane to Montreal, buy forged papers—Montreal is almost as crooked as we are—and plane to Europe. He may be fairly safe there. But the Outfit has long arms and Ikky will have a damned dull life staying alive. He hasn't any choice. For him it's either hide or get the pencil."

"So clever of you, darling. What about your own pencil?"

"If they meant it, they wouldn't have sent it. Just a bit of scare technique."

"And you don't scare, you wonderful handsome brute."

"I scare. But it doesn't paralyze me. So long. Don't take any lovers until I get back."

"Damn you, Marlowe!"

She hung up on me. I hung up on myself.

Saying the wrong thing is one of my specialties.

I beat it out of town before the homicide boys could hear about me. It would take them quite a while to get a lead. And Bernie Ohls wouldn't give a city dick a used paper bag. The Sheriff's men and the City Police co-operate about as much as two tomcats on a fence.

I made Phoenix by evening and parked myself in a motor court on the outskirts. Phoenix was damned hot. The motor court had a dining room so I had dinner. I collected some quarters and dimes from the cashier and shut myself in a phone booth and started to call the Mirador in Flagstaff. How silly could I get? Ikky might be registered under any name from Cohen to Cordileone, from Watson to Woichehovski. I called anyway and got nothing but as much of a smile as you can get on the phone. So I asked for a room the following night. Not a chance unless someone checked out, but they would put me down for a cancellation or something. Flagstaff is too near the Grand Canyon. Ikky must have arranged in advance. That was something to ponder too.

I bought a paperback and read it. I set my alarm watch for 6:30. The paperback scared me so badly that I put two guns under my pillow. It was about a guy who bucked the hoodlum boss of Milwaukee and got beaten up every fifteen minutes. I figured that his head and face would be nothing but a piece of bone with a strip of skin hanging from it. But in the next chapter he was as gay as a meadow lark. Then I asked myself why I was reading this drivel when I could have been memorizing The Brothers Karamasov. Not knowing any good answers, I turned the light out and went to sleep. At 6:30 I shaved and showered and had breakfast and took off for Flagstaff. I got there by lunchtime, and there was Ikky in the reastaurant eating mountain trout. I sat down across from him. He looked surprised to see me.

I ordered mountain trout and ate it from the outside in, which is the proper way. Boning spoils it a little.

"What gives?" he asked me with his mouth full. A delicate eater.

"You read the papers?"

"Just the sporting section."

"Let's go to your room and talk about it. There's more than that."

We paid for our lunches and went along to a nice double. The motor courts are getting so good that they make a lot of hotels look cheap. We sat down and lit cigarettes.

"The two hoods got up too early and went over to Poynter Street. They parked outside your apartment house. They hadn't been briefed carefully enough. They shot a guy who looked a little like you."

"That's a hot one," he grinned. "But the cops will find out, and the Outfit will find out. So the tag for me stays on."

"You must think I'm dumb," I said. "I am."

"I thought you did a first class job, Marlowe. What's dumb about that?"

"What job did I do?"

"You got me out of there pretty slick."

"Anything about it you couldn't have done yourself?"

"With luck—no. But it's nice to have a helper."

"You mean sucker."

His face tightened. And his rusty voice growled. "I don't catch. And give me back some of that five grand, will you? I'm shorter than I thought."

"I'll give it back to you when you find a hummingbird in a salt shaker."

"Don't be like that," he almost sighed, and flicked a gun into his hand. I didn't have to flick. I was holding one in my side pocket.

"I oughtn't to have boobed off," I said. "Put the heater away. It doesn't pay any more than a Vegas slot machine."

"Wrong. Them machines pay the jackpot every so often. Otherwise—no customers."

"Every so seldom, you mean. Listen, and listen good."

He grinned. His dentist was tired waiting for him.

"The set-up intrigued me," I went on, debonair as Milo Vance in a Van Dyne story and a lot brighter in the head. "First off, could it be done? Second, if it could be done, where would I be? But gradually I saw the little touches that flaw the picture. Why would you come to me at all? The Outfit isn't that naive. Why would they send a little punk like this Charles Hickon or whatever name he uses on Thursdays? Why would an old hand like you let anybody trail you to a dangerous connection?"

"You slay me, Marlowe. You're so bright I could find you in the dark. You're so dumb you couldn't see a red white and blue giraffe. I bet you were back there in your unbrain emporium playing with that five grand like a cat with a bag of catnip. I bet you were kissing the notes."

"Not after you handled them. They why the pencil that was sent to me? Big dangerous threat. It re-inforced the rest. But like I told your choir boy from Vegas, they don't send them when they mean them. By the way, he had a gun too. A Woodsman .22 with a silencer. I had to make him put it away. He was nice about that. He started waving grands at me to find out where you were and tell him. A well-dressed, nice looking front man for a pack of dirty rats. The Women's Christian Temperance Association and some bootlicking politicians gave them the money to be big, and they learned how to use it and make it grow. Now they're pretty well unstoppable. But they're still a pack of dirty rats. And they're always where they can't make a mistake. That's inhuman. Any man has a right to a few mistakes. Not the rats. They have to be perfect all the time. Or else they get stuck with *you*."

"I don't know what the hell you're talking about. I just know it's too long."

"Well, allow me to put it in English. Some poor jerk from the East Side gets involved with the lower echelons of a mob. You know what an echelon is, Ikky?"

"I been in the Army," he sneered.

"He grows up in the mob, but he's not all rotten. He's not rotten enough. So he tries to break loose. He comes out here and gets himself a cheap job of some sort and changes his name or names and lives quietly in a cheap apartment house. But the mob by now has agents in many places. Somebody spots him and recognizes him. It might be a pusher, a front man for a bookie joint, a night girl, even a cop that's on the take. So the mob, or call them the Outfit, say through their cigar smoke: 'Ikky can't do this to us. It's a small operation because he's small. But it annoys us. Bad for discipline. Call a couple of boys and have them pencil him.' But what boys do they call? A couple they're tired of. Been around too long. Might make a mistake or get chilly toes. Perhaps they like killing. That's bad too. That makes recklessness. The best boys are the ones that don't care either way. So although they don't know it, the boys they call are on their way out. But it would be kind of cute to frame a guy they already don't like, for fingering a hood named Larsen. One of these puny little jokes the Outfit takes big. 'Look guys, we even got time to play footies with a private eye. Jesus, we can do anything. We could even suck our thumbs.' So they send a ringer."

"The Torri brothers ain't ringers. They're real hard boys. They proved it—even if they did make a mistake."

Mistake nothing. They got Ikky Rosenstein. You're just a singing commercial in this deal. And as of now you're under arrest for murder. You're worse off than that. The Outfit will habeas corpus you out of the clink and blow you down. You've served your purpose and you failed to finger me into a patsy."

His finger tightened on the trigger. I shot the gun out of his hand. My gun in my coat pocket was small, but at that distance accurate. And it was one of my days to be accurate myself.

He made a faint moaning sound and sucked at his hand. I went over and kicked him hard in the chest. Being nice to killers is not part of my repertoire. He went over backwards and sideways and stumbled four or five steps. I picked up his gun and held it on him while I tapped all the places—not just pockets or holsters—where a man could stash a second gun. He was clean—that way anyhow.

"What are you trying to do to me?" he said whiningly. "I paid you. You're clear. I paid you damn well."

"We both have problems there. Yours is to stay alive." I took a pair of cuffs out of my pocket and wrestled his hands behind him and snapped them on. His hand was bleeding. I tied his show handkerchief around it. I went to the telephone.

Flagstaff was big enough to have a police force. The DA might even have his office there. This was Arizona, a poor state, relatively. The cops might even be honest.

I had to stick around for a few days, but I didn't mind that as long as I could have trout caught eight or nine thousand feet up. I called Anne and Bernie Ohls. I called my answering service. The Arizona DA was a young keen-eyed man and the Chief of Police was one of the biggest men I ever saw.

I got back to LA in time and took Anne to Romanoff's for dinner and champagne.

"What I can't see," she said over a third glass of bubbly, "is why they dragged you into it, why they set up the fake Ikky Rosenstein. Why didn't they just let the two lifetakers do their job?"

"I couldn't really say. Unless the big boys feel so safe they're developing a sense of humor. And unless this Larsen guy that went to the gas chamber was bigger than he seemed to be. Only three or four important mobsters have made the electric chair or the rope or the gas chamber. None that I know of in the life-imprisonment states like Michigan. If Larsen was bigger than anyone thought, they might have had my name on a waiting list."

"But why wait?" she asked me. "They'd go after you quickly."

"They can afford to wait. Who's going to bother them—Kefauver? He did his best, but do you notice any change in the set-up—except when they make one themselves?"

"Costello?"

"Income tax rap—like Capone. Capone may have had several hundred men killed, and killed a few of them himself, personally. But it took the Internal Revenue boys to get him. The Outfit won't make that mistake often."

"What I like about you, apart from your enormous personal charm is that when you don't know an answer you make one up."

"The money worries me," I said. "Five grand of their dirty money. What do I do with it?"

"Don't be a jerk all your life. You earned the money and you risked your life for it. You can buy Series E Bonds. They'll make the money clean. And to me that would be part of the joke."

"*You* tell *me* one good reason why they pulled the switch."

"You have more of a reputation than you realize. And how would it be if the false Ikky pulled the switch? He sounds like one of these overclever types that can't do anything simple."

"The Outfit will get him for making his own plans—if you're right."

"If the DA doesn't. And I couldn't care less about what happens to him. More champagne, please."

They extradited "Ikky" and he broke under pressure and named the two gunmen—after I had already named them, the Torri brothers. But nobody could find them. They never went home. And you can't prove conspiracy on one man. The law couldn't even get him for accessory after the fact. They couldn't prove he knew the real Ikky had been gunned.

They could have got him for some trifle, but they had a better idea. They left him to his friends. They turned him loose.

Where is he now? My hunch says nowhere.

Anne Riordan was glad it was all over and I was safe. Safe—that isn't a word you use in my trade.

Questions for Discussion

1. What kind of person is Marlowe? Is he likable? Honest? Explain. (If you have read the Sherlock Holmes story in the first section, contrast Marlowe with Holmes.)

2. With Dashiell Hammett and Ross MacDonald, Chandler is considered to be an early master of the "hard-boiled" style of detective fiction. Judging from this story, what are the characteristics of that style? List as many as you can.

3. Judging from this story, what's more important to detective fiction, the plot or the character of the detective? Explain.

4. What motivates Marlowe? Why is he a detective, and why does he take this case?

Suggestions for Writing

1. Write a one-page imitation of the hard-boiled-detective fiction.

2. Write an essay in which you compare and contrast Sherlock Holmes and Philip Marlowe.

3. Write an essay in which you analyze the use of dialogue to advance the plot in detective fiction.

4. "Detective fiction is less serious and significant than mainstream fiction; it is merely for entertainment." In your journal, respond to this statement and develop your own sense of this particular subgenre of short fiction.

The Fly

KATHERINE MANSFIELD

"**Y**ou are very snug in here," piped old Mr. Woodifield, and he peered out of the great, green leather armchair by his friend the boss's desk as a baby peers out of its pram. His talk was over; it was time for him to be off. But he did not want to go. Since he had retired, since his . . . stroke, the wife and the girls kept him boxed up in the house every day of the week except Tuesday. On Tuesday he was dressed up and brushed and allowed to cut back to the City for the day. Though what he did there the wife and girls couldn't imagine. Made a nuisance of himself to his friends, they supposed . . . Well, perhaps so. All the same, we cling to our last pleasures as the tree clings to its last leaves. So there sat old Woodifield, smoking a cigar and staring almost greedily at the boss, who rolled in his office chair, stout, rosy, five years older than he, and still going strong, still at the helm. It did one good to see him.

Wistfully, admiringly, the old voice added, "It's snug in here, upon my word!"

"Yes, it's comfortable enough," agreed the boss, and he flipped the *Financial Times* with a paper-knife. As a matter of fact he was proud of his room; he liked to have it admired, especially by old Woodifield. It gave him a feeling of deep, solid satisfaction to be planted there in the midst of it in full view of that frail old figure in the muffler.

"I've had it done up lately," he explained, as he had explained for the past—how many?—weeks. "New carpet," and he pointed to the bright red carpet with a pattern of large white rings. "New furniture," and he nodded towards the massive bookcase and the table with legs like twisted treacle. "Electric heating!" He waved almost exultantly towards the five transparent, pearly sausages glowing so softly in the tilted copper pan.

But he did not draw old Woodifield's attention to the photograph over the table of a grave-looking boy in uniform standing in one of those spectral photographers' parks with photographers' storm-clouds behind him. It was not new. It had been there for over six years.

"There was something I wanted to tell you," said old Woodifield, and his eyes grew dim remembering. "Now what was it? I had it in my mind when I started out this morning." His hands began to tremble, and patches of red showed above his beard.

Poor old chap, he's on his last pins, thought the boss. And, feeling kindly, he winked at the old man, and said jokingly, "I tell you what. I've got a little drop of something here that'll do you good before you go out into the cold again. It's beautiful stuff. It wouldn't hurt a child." He took a key off his watch-chain, unlocked a cupboard below his desk, and drew forth a dark, squat bottle. "That's the medicine," said he. "And the man from whom I got it told me on the strict Q.T. it came from the cellars at Windsor Cassel."

Old Woodifield's mouth fell open at the sight. He couldn't have looked more surprised if the boss had produced a rabbit.

"It's whisky, ain't it?" he piped, feebly.

The boss turned the bottle and lovingly showed him the label. Whisky it was.

"D'you know," said he, peering up at the boss wonderingly, "they won't let me touch it at home." And he looked as though he was going to cry.

"Ah, that's where we know a bit more than the ladies," cried the boss, swooping across for two tumblers that stood on the table with the waterbottle, and pouring a generous finger into each. "Drink it down. It'll do you good. And don't put any water with it. It's sacrilege to tamper with stuff like this. Ah!" He tossed off his, pulled out his handkerchief, hastily wiped his moustaches, and cocked an eye at old Woodifield, who was rolling his in his chaps.

The old man swallowed, was silent a moment, and then said faintly, "It's nutty!"

But it warmed him; it crept into his chill old brain—he remembered.

"That was it," he said, heaving himself out of his chair. "I thought you'd like to know. The girls were in Belgium last week having a look at poor Reggie's grave, and they happened to come across your boy's. They're quite near each other, it seems."

Old Woodifield paused, but the boss made no reply. Only a quiver in his eyelids showed that he heard.

"The girls were delighted with the way the place is kept," piped the old voice. "Beautifully looked after. Couldn't be better if they were at home. You've not been across, have yer?"

"No, no!" For various reasons the boss had not been across.

"There's miles of it," quavered old Woodifield, "and it's all as neat as a garden. Flowers growing on all the graves. Nice broad paths." It was plain from his voice how much he liked a nice broad path.

The pause came again. Then the old man brightened wonderfully.

"D'you know what the hotel made the girls pay for a pot of jam?" he piped. "Ten francs! Robbery, I call it. It was a little pot, so Gertrude says, no bigger than a half-crown. And she hadn't taken more than a spoonful when they charged her ten francs. Gertrude brought the pot away with her to teach 'em a lesson. Quite right, too; it's trading on our feelings. They think because we're over there having a look around we're ready to pay anything. That's what it is." And he turned towards the door.

"Quite right, quite right!" cried the boss, though what was quite right he hadn't the least idea. He came round by his desk, followed the shuffling footsteps to the door, and saw the old fellow out. Woodifield was gone.

For a long moment the boss stayed, staring at nothing, while the grey-haired office messenger, watching him, dodged in and out of his cubbyhole like a dog that expects to be taken for a run. Then: "I'll see nobody for half an hour, Macey," said the boss. "Understand? Nobody at all."

"Very good, sir."

The door shut, the firm heavy steps recrossed the bright carpet, the fat body plumped down in the spring chair, and leaning forward, the boss covered his face with his hands. He wanted, he intended, he had arranged to weep . . .

It had been a terrible shock to him when old Woodifield sprang that remark upon him about the boy's grave. It was exactly as though the earth had opened and he had seen the boy lying there with Woodifield's girls staring down at him. For it was strange. Although over six years had passed away, the boss never thought of the boy except as lying unchanged, unblemished in his uniform, asleep for ever. "My son!" groaned the boss. But no tears came yet. In the past, in the first months and even years after the boy's death, he had only to say those words to be overcome by such grief that nothing short of a violent fit of weeping could relieve him. Time, he had declared then, he had told everybody, could make no difference. Other men perhaps might recover, might live their loss down, but not he. How was it possible? His boy was an only son. Ever since his birth the boss had worked at building up this business for him; it had no other meaning if it was not for the boy. Life itself had come to have no other meaning. How on earth could he have slaved, denied himself, kept going all those years without the promise for ever before him of the boy's stepping into his shoes and carrying on where he left off?

And that promise had been so near being fulfilled. The boy had been in the office learning the ropes for a year before the war. Every morning they had started off together; they had come back by the same train. And what congratulations he had received as the boy's father! No wonder; he had taken to it marvellously. As to his popularity with the staff, every man jack of them down to old Macey couldn't make enough of the boy. And he wasn't in the least spoilt. No, he was just his bright, natural self, with the right word for everybody, with that boyish look and his habit of saying, "Simply splendid!"

But all that was over and done with as though it never had been. The day had come when Macey had handed him the telegram that brought the whole place crashing about his head. "Deeply regret to inform you . . ." And he had left the office a broken man, with his life in ruins.

Six years ago, six years . . . How quickly time passed! It might have happened yesterday. The boss took his hands from his face; he was puzzled. Something seemed to be wrong with him. He wasn't feeling as he wanted to feel. He decided to get up and have a look at the boy's photograph. But it wasn't a favorite photograph of his; the expression was unnatural. It was cold, even stern-looking. The boy had never looked like that.

At that moment the boss noticed that a fly had fallen into his broad inkpot, and was trying feebly but desperately to clamber out again. Help! help! said those struggling legs. But the sides of the inkpot were wet and slippery; it fell back again and began to swim. The boss took up a pen, picked the fly out of the ink, and shook it on to a piece of blotting-paper. For a fraction of a second it lay still on the dark patch that oozed round it. Then the front legs waved, took hold, and, pulling its small sodden body up it began the immense task of cleaning the ink from its wings. Over and under, over and under, went a leg along a wing, as the stone goes over and under the scythe. Then there was a pause, while the fly, seeming to stand on the tips of its toes, tried to expand first one wing and then the other.

It succeeded at last, and, sitting down, it began, like a minute cat, to clean its face. Now one could imagine that the little front legs rubbed against each other lightly, joyfully. The horrible danger was over; it had escaped; it was ready for life again.

But just then the boss had an idea. He plunged his pen back into the ink, leaned his thick wrist on the blotting paper, and as the fly tried its wings down came a great heavy blot. What would it make of that? What indeed! The little beggar seemed absolutely cowed, stunned, and afraid to move because of what would happen next. But then, as if painfully, it dragged itself forward. The front legs waved, caught hold, and, more slowly this time, the task began from the beginning.

He's a plucky little devil, thought the boss, and he felt a real admiration for the fly's courage. That was the way to tackle things; that was the right spirit. Never say die; it was only a question of . . . But the fly had again finished its laborious task, and the boss had just time to refill his pen, to shake fair and square on the new-cleaned body yet another dark drop. What about it this time? A painful moment of suspense followed. But behold, the front legs were again waving; the boss felt a rush of relief. He leaned over the fly and said to it tenderly, "You artful little b . . ." And he actually had the brilliant notion of breathing on it to help the drying process. All the same, there was something timid and weak about its efforts now, and the boss decided that this time should be the last, as he dipped the pen into the inkpot.

It was. The last blot on the soaked blotting-paper, and the draggled fly lay in it and did not stir. The back legs were stuck to the body; the front legs were not to be seen.

"Come on," said the boss. "Look sharp!" And he stirred it with his pen—in vain. Nothing happened or was likely to happen. The fly was dead.

The boss lifted the corpse on the end of the paper-knife and flung it into the waste-paper basket. But such a grinding feeling of wretchedness seized him that he felt positively frightened. He started forward and pressed the bell for Macey.

"Bring me some fresh blotting-paper," he said, sternly, "and look sharp about it." And while the old dog padded away he fell to wondering what it was he had been thinking about before. What was it? It was . . . He took out his handkerchief and passed it inside his collar. For the life of him he could not remember.

Questions for Discussion

1. Speculate: What is the purpose of the shift in point of view from the older man to "the boss"?

2. How do you react to and interpret the boss's behavior toward the fly? Would you call it a fairly typical human response or something out of the ordinary?

3. What does this story suggest about the nature of human grief and of human emotions in general?

Suggestions for Writing

1. Write an essay concerning what Mansfield's story reveals about human nature.

2. In a journal entry defend the man's behavior toward the fly.

3. In your journal describe an instance when you were cruel to an animal and try to assess your motivation.

4. Write a story that focuses on an emotional response that might be regarded as "inappropriate."

The Mole

YASUNARI KAWABATA

Last night I dreamed about that mole.

I need only write the word. You must know what I mean. That mole—how many times have I been scolded by you because of it?

It is on my right shoulder, or perhaps I should say high on my back.

"It's already bigger than a bean. Go on playing with it and it will be sending out shoots one of these days."

You used to tease me about it. But as you said, it was large for a mole, large and wonderfully round and swollen.

As a child I used to lie in bed and play with that mole; How ashamed I was when you first noticed it!

I even wept, and I remember your surprise.

"Stop it, Sayoko. The more you touch it the bigger it gets." My mother scolded me too. I was still a child, and afterwards I kept the habit to myself. It persisted after I had all but forgotten about it.

When you first noticed it, I was still more child than wife. I wonder if you, a man, can imagine how ashamed I was. But it was more than shame. This is dreadful, I thought to myself. Being married to you seemed a fearful thing indeed.

I felt as though all my secrets had been discovered—as though you had bared secret after secret of which I was not even conscious myself—as though I had no refuge left.

You went off happily to sleep. Sometimes I felt relieved, and a little lonely, and sometimes I pulled myself up with a start as my hand traveled to the mole again.

"I can't even touch my mole any more," I thought of writing to my mother, but even as I thought of it I felt my face go fiery red.

"But what nonsense to worry about a mole," you once said. I was happy, and I nodded, but looking back now, I wonder if you should not have learned to love my unfortunate habit a little more.

I did not worry very much about the mole. Surely people do not go about looking down women's necks for moles. Sometimes the expression "unspoiled as a locked room" is used to describe a deformed girl. But a mole, no matter how large it is, can hardly be called a deformity.

Why do you suppose I fell into the habit of playing with that mole?

And why did the habit annoy you so?

"Stop it," you would say. "Stop it." I do not know how many hundred times you scolded me.

"Do you have to use your left hand?" you asked once in a fit of irritation.

"My left hand?" I was startled by the question.

It was true. I had not noticed before, but I always used my left hand.

"It's on your right shoulder. You should use your right hand."

"Oh?" I raised my right hand. "But it's strange."

"It's not a bit strange."

"But it's more natural with my left hand."

"The right hand is nearer."

"It's backwards with my right hand."

"Backwards?"

"Yes. It's a choice between bringing my arm in front of my neck or reaching around in back like this." I was no longer agreeing meekly with everything you said. Even as I answered you, however, it came to me that when I brought my left arm around it was as though I were warding you off, as though I were embracing myself. "I have been cruel to him," I thought.

I asked gently: "But what is wrong with using my left hand?"

"Left hand or right hand, it's a bad habit."

"I know."

"Haven't I told you time and time again to go to a doctor and have the thing removed?"

"But I couldn't. I'd be ashamed to."

"It would be a very simple matter."

"Who would go to a doctor to have a mole removed?"

"A great many people seem to."

"For moles in the middle of the face, maybe. I doubt if anyone goes to have a mole removed from the neck. The doctor would laugh. He would know I was there because my husband had complained."

"You could tell him it was because you had a habit of playing with it."

"Really. Something as insignificant as a mole, in a place where you can't even see it. Why should it bother you so?"

"I wouldn't mind the mole if you wouldn't play with it."

"I don't mean to."

"You are stubborn, though. I could go on talking forever, and you would make no effort to change yourself."

"I do try. I even tried wearing a high-necked nightgown so that I wouldn't touch it."

"Not for long."

"But is it so wrong for me to touch it?" I suppose I must have seemed to be fighting back.

"It's not wrong, especially. I only ask you to stop because I don't like it."

"But why do you dislike it so?"

"There's no need to go into the reasons. You don't need to play with that mole, and it's a bad habit, and I wish you would stop."

"I've never said I won't stop."

"And when you touch it you always get that strange, absent-minded expression on your face."

You were probably right—something made the remark go straight to my heart, and I wanted to nod my agreement.

"Next time you see me doing it, slap my hand. Slap my face even."

"But doesn't it bother you that even though you've been trying for years you haven't been able to cure a trivial little habit like that by yourself?"

I did not answer. I was thinking of what you had said.

That pose, with my left arm drawn up around my neck—it must look somehow dreary, forlorn. I would hesitate to use a grand word like "solitary." Shabby, rather, and mean, the pose of a woman concerned only with protecting her own small self. And the expression on my face must be just as you described it, "strange, absent-minded."

Did it seem a sign that I had not really given myself to you, that a space lay between us? And did my true feelings come out on my face when I touched the mole and gave myself up to reverie, as I had done since I was a child?

But it must have been because you were already dissatisfied with me that you made so much of that one small habit. If you had been pleased with me you would have smiled and thought no more of it.

That was the frightening thought. I trembled when it came to me that there might be men who would find the habit charming.

It was your love for me that first made you notice. I do not doubt that even now. But it is just this sort of small annoyance, as it grows and becomes distorted, that drives its roots down into a marriage. To a real husband and wife personal eccentricities have stopped mattering, and I suppose that on the other hand there are husbands and wives who find themselves at odds on everything. I do not say that those who accommodate themselves to each other necessarily love each other, and that those who constantly disagree hate each other. I do think, though, and I cannot get over thinking, that it would have been better if you had brought yourself to overlook my habit of playing with the mole.

You actually came to beat me and to kick me. I wept and asked why you could not be a little less violent, why I had to suffer because I touched my mole. That was only the surface. "How can we cure it?" you said, your voice trembling, and I quite understood how you felt and did not resent what you did. If I had told anyone of this, I could have made you seem like an abusive husband. But since we had reached a point where the most trivial matter added to the tension between us, your hitting me actually brought a sudden feeling of release.

"I will never get over it, never. Tie up my hands." I brought my hands together and thrust them at your chest, as though I were giving myself to you.

You looked confused, your anger seemed to have left you limp and drained of emotion. You took the cord from my sash and tied my hands with it.

I was happy when I saw the look in your eyes, watching me try to smooth my hair with my bound hands. This time the long habit might be cured, I said to myself.

But I do not know what dangerous thoughts I would have had even then if anyone had mentioned the mole.

And was it because the habit came back afterwards that the last of your affection for me died? Did you mean to tell me that you had given up and that I could very well do as I pleased? When I played with the mole, you pretended you did not see, and you said nothing.

Then a strange thing happened. The habit which scolding and beating had done nothing to cure—was it not gone? None of the extreme remedies worked. It left of its own accord.

"What do you know—I'm not playing with the mole any more." I said it as though I had only that moment noticed. You grunted, and looked as if you did not care.

If it mattered so little to you, why did you have to scold me so, I wanted to ask; and I suppose that you for your part wanted to ask why, if the habit was to be cured so easily, I had not been able to cure it earlier. But you would not even talk to me.

A habit that makes no difference, that is neither medicine nor poison—go ahead and indulge yourself all day long if it pleases you. That is what the expression on your face seemed to say. I felt dejected. Just to annoy you, I thought of touching the mole again there in front of you, but, strangely, my hand refused to move.

I felt lonely. And I felt angry.

I thought too of touching it when you were not around. But somehow that seemed shameful, repulsive, and again my hand refused to move.

I looked at the floor, and I bit my lip.

"What's happened to your mole?" I was waiting for you to say, but after that the word "mole" disappeared from our conversation.

And perhaps many other things disappeared with it.

Why could I do nothing in the days when I was being scolded by you? Surely I am the most worthless of women.

Back at home again, away from you, I took a bath with my mother.

"You're not as good-looking as you once were, Sayoko," she said. "You can't fight age, I suppose."

I looked at her, startled. She was as she had always been, plump and fresh-skinned.

"And that mole used to be rather attractive."

I have really suffered because of that mole—but I could not say that to my mother. What I did say was: "They say it's no trouble for a doctor to remove a mole."

"Oh? For a doctor . . . but there would be a scar." How calm and easygoing my mother is! "We used to laugh about it. We said that Sayoko was probably still playing with that mole even now that she was married."

"I was playing with it."

"We thought you would be."

"It was a bad habit. When did I start?"

"When do children begin to have moles, I wonder. You don't seem to see them on babies."

"My children have none."

"Oh? But they begin to come out as you grow up, and they never disappear. It's not often you see one this size, though. You must have had it when you were very small." Mother looked at my shoulder and laughed.

I remembered how, when I was very young, my mother and my sisters sometimes poked at the mole, a charming little spot then. And was that not why I had fallen into the habit of playing with it myself?

I lay in bed fingering the mole and trying to remember how it had been when I was a child and a young woman.

It was a very long time since I had last played with it. How many years, I wonder.

Back in the house where I was born, I could play with it as I liked. No one would stop me.

But it was no good.

As my finger touched the mole, cold tears came to my eyes.

I meant to think of long ago, when I was young, but when I touched the mole all I thought of was you.

I have been damned as a bad wife, and perhaps I shall be divorced; but it would not have occurred to me that here in bed at home again I would have only these thoughts of you.

I turned my damp pillow—and I even dreamed of the mole.

I could not tell after I awoke where the room might have been, but you were there, and some other woman seemed to be with us. I had been drinking. Indeed I was drunk. I kept pleading with you about something.

My bad habit came out again. I reached around with my left hand, my arm across my breast as always. But the mole—did it not come off between my fingers? It came off painlessly, quite as though that were the most natural thing in the world. Between my fingers it felt exactly like roasted bean.

Like a spoiled child I asked you to put my mole in the pit of that mole beside your nose.

I pushed my mole at you. I cried and clamored, I clutched at your sleeve and your chest.

When I awoke the pillow was still wet. I was still weeping.

I felt tired through and through. And at the same time I felt light, as though I had laid down a burden.

I lay smiling for a time, wondering if the mole had really disappeared. I had trouble bringing myself to touch it.

That is all there is to the story of my mole.

I can still feel it like a black bean between my fingers.

I have never thought much about that little mole beside your nose, and I have never spoken of it, and yet I suppose I have always had it on my mind.

What a fine fairy story it would make if your mole really were to swell up because you put mine in it.

And how happy I would be if I thought you in your turn had dreamed of my mole.

I have forgotten one thing.

You complained of the expression on my face, and so well did I understand that I even thought the remark a sign of your affection for me. I thought that all the meanest things in me came out when I fingered the mole.

I wonder, however, if a fact of which I have already spoken does not redeem me: it was perhaps because of the way my mother and sisters petted me that I first fell into the habit of fingering the mole.

"I suppose you used to scold me when I played with the mole," I said to my mother, "long ago."

"I did—but it wasn't so long ago."

"Why did you scold me?"

"Why? It's bad habit, that's all."

"But how did you feel when you saw me playing with the mole?"

"Well." My mother cocked her head to one side. "It wasn't becoming."

"That's true. But how did it look? Were you sorry for me? Or did I seem dirty and mean?"

"I didn't really think about it much. It just seemed that you ought to leave it alone. And that sleepy expression on your face."

"You were annoyed?"

"It seemed a little as though something might be weighing on your mind."

"And you and the others used to poke at the mole to tease me?"

"I suppose we did."

If that is true, then wasn't I fingering the mole in that absent way to remember the love my mother and sisters had for me when I was young?

Wasn't I doing it to think of the people I loved?

This is what I must say to you.

Weren't you mistaken from beginning to end about my mole?

Could I have been thinking of anyone else when I was with you?

Over and over I ask myself whether the gesture you so disliked might not have been a confession of a love that I could not put into words.

My habit of playing with the mole is a small thing, and I do not mean to make excuses for it; but might not all of the other things that turned me into a bad wife have begun in the same way? Might they not have been in the beginning expressions of my love for you, turned to unwifeliness only by your refusal to see what they were?

Even as I write I wonder if I do not sound like a bad wife trying to seem wronged. Still there are these things that I must say to you.

Translated by E. G. Seidensticker

Questions for Discussion

1. Assuming the mole is a symbol, what does it symbolize?

2. To whom does the narrator speak? What is the effect of this rhetorical situation?

3. Characterize the relationship between the speaker and her husband.

Suggestions for Writing

1. Write an essay in which you compare and contrast Poe's "The Tell-Tale Heart" with Kawabata's "The Mole."

2. Write an essay that analyzes the symbol of the mole in detail.

3. Write a story in which something as superficial as a mole comes to represent much more.

Overview: Additional Questions for Discussion and Suggestions for Writing

Questions for Discussion

1. "Alienation" is often cited as a key preoccupation of modernist writers. Identify as many kinds of alienation as you can in the stories that you have read from this section. What patterns of alienation can you detect? What kinds of alienation are you most sympathetic to? What is your definition of "alienation"?

2. Of the stories you have read from this section, which ones deserve to be considered "classics" and why? Which ones are overrated and why? Try to move beyond mere personal preference in this question and come up with a variety of criteria for your judgments.

3. Discuss the variety of narrative techniques you encounter in the stories from this section. Consider the "detached" voice of Hemingway and Borowski, the ironic narrator of Anderson's story, and the "we" narration of Faulkner's story as you begin thinking about this question. Then you may want to generalize about the differences and similarities in narrative technique between the stories in this section and those in the first section.

4. Apply Joyce's concept of "epiphany" to other stories in this section. Consult the glossary for a basic working definition but also begin to formulate your own idea of Joyce's important term. What is the nature of the epiphany in "Araby"? What other stories seem to contain similar moments?

5. Which of these stories seems most aware of the social or political issues that shaped the world of the early twentieth century? You may want to begin answering this question by listing several key issues.

6. What do these stories tell us about the nature of relationships between men and women, about how certain authors perceive these relationships in significant new ways, and about the ways in which these relationships were changing in the early part of the century?

7. Of the stories you have read in this section, which ones seem to rely least on their social or historical context? How does a story's relationship to these contexts affect your assessment of the story?

8. Discontinuity, fragmentation, aburdity: these are all qualities associated

with modernist literature. Which stories in this section significantly exhibit such qualities? What challenges do these qualities create for the reader?

9. Compare and contrast the stories written by American, European, and Asian writers. To what extent is the culture reflected in the story? To what extent is nationality *not* important?

Suggestions for Writing

1. Write an essay about women in several stories from this section. You might write about women characters in stories by men, women characters in stories by women, or some combination thereof. You might also add another variable, such as social class, nationality, or ethnic background. Authors to consider include Lawrence, Joyce, Steinbeck, Hurston, Welty, Faulkner, Porter, Koda, and Kawabata.

2. Write an essay about small-town or rural life as depicted in stories by Anderson, Steinbeck, Porter, Faulkner, Welty.

3. Write an essay about the stories that spring in part from the experience of African-Americans: Hurston, Hughes, Ellison.

4. Write an essay that concerns the stories about war (stories by Pirandello, Borowski, Koda, and O'Connor).

5. Write an essay about a novel that was written by one of these writers. Possibilities include *Portrait of the Artist as a Young Man* by James Joyce, *Light in August* by William Faulkner, *Women in Love* by D. H. Lawrence, *Ship of Fools* by Katherine Anne Porter, *The Sun Also Rises* by Ernest Hemingway, *Invisible Man* by Ralph Ellison, *The Grapes of Wrath* by John Steinbeck, *Farewell, My Lovely* by Raymond Chandler, *My Antonia* by Willa Cather.

6. Of all the stories in this section, which one most inspired you in your own fiction and why? Write in your journal or notebook about this question.

7. Of all the stories in this section, which one springs from an experience, a background, or a region that is most similar to your life? Write in your notebook about this story and your response to it.

8. The American writers in this section include Hemingway, Steinbeck, Faulkner, Welty, Hurston, Porter, Anderson, Hughes, Chandler, and Ellison. What preoccupations seem particularly American to you in some or all of these stories? Write an essay on this question.

Part Three

Contemporary Voices

Introduction to Contemporary Voices

POSTMODERNISM

The term *post-Modern* is sometimes applied to literature and other arts that have been created since the 1940s. It is easy to see why this term might be even more frustrating than the complicated term *modernism,* because *postmodernism* implies a kind of surrender. It suggests that a distinct definition of the period has eluded those who define culture, because it is a term that, on the surface at least, merely states the obvious: "Post-Modern follows Modern."

THE HOLOCAUST AND THE NUCLEAR AGE

Before we try to scratch beneath this obvious surface, it might help to sketch a reminder of what has gone on in America and the world since 1945 (or so). If the events that helped create modernist art were dramatic, the occurrences of the last four or five decades sometimes defy comprehension. At least two events are unique in history; consequently, they have challenged our very notions of "history," they have put the future in question, and they have forced us to reexamine—constantly—the nature of human beings. The events: Germany's attempted extermination of Jews—the Holocaust, the extent of which was not widely known until after the war—and America's use of nuclear weapons against Japan.

These events wrought such widespread destruction and were of such enormous implication that they have defined the age in which we live. The causes of each event were different, but the scope was not. The nature of the human spirit, the existence of God, the potential annihilation of civilization and the planet itself—these are among the issues that the Holocaust and the nuclear age force us to confront in a new context. They are events that stir controversy, at the very least, and that resist attempts at understanding or explanation. Often literature of the post-Modern era reveals a frustrated attempt to understand these events, or—more indirectly—reveals a deep alienation springing from these massive events.

GLOBAL TUMULT

These decades have also been marked by revolution and counterrevolution on an unprecedented scale. Some countries and cultures have continued to shed the domination of European colonialism; others have been smothered by militaristic, totalitarian rule. In this period America and Russia have often seemed to divide the world between them, empires of colossal dimensions. But simultaneously, a "world" beyond Europe and America—peoples of Africa, the Caribbean, India, the Middle East, the South Pacific, and Latin America—has asserted its various cultural identities and political influences. Also, recent events in Europe have begun dramatically to redefine the polarity between Russia and America and their allies. The earth has not for one moment been free of armed conflict during this period, and with the omnipresent threat of nuclear war, "minor" crises have ceased to exist, as evidenced by the Cuban missile crisis of 1962.

This post-Modern world, then, has been one darkened by the shadow of total destruction and kept in a state of near-chaos by political, cultural, and economic conflict.

To complicate matters, it has also been a period of astonishing achievement: a period that has seen medicine eradicate heretofore "unconquerable" diseases; one that has seen us walk on the moon and peer at the far reaches of the universe; and one that has seen the technology of global travel and communication shrink the planet to the size of a soccer ball.

AMERICA SINCE 1945

World War II thrust America into the complicated "superpower" status it now possesses. Since 1945 it has been perceived (and has perceived itself) sometimes as the defender of freedom everywhere and sometimes as the global bully: ethnocentric, selfish, greedy. For America this period has brought the Cold War, in which America defined itself almost exclusively in relation to one other nation, Russia. Changes in Eastern Europe have begun to alter that definition, as mentioned above.

The period has also brought the Korean and Vietnam wars, in which stalemate and defeat undermined Americans' sense of invincibility and divided them bitterly, and which forced a debate about America's role in the world. That debate persists to this moment. (The Iran-Contra scandal and other recent episodes of foreign policy are linked ideologically to these earlier conflicts.)

The period brought the civil rights movement and the women's movement, in which Rosa Parks, Betty Friedan, Malcolm X, Martin Luther King, Jr., and thousands of others challenged America to use the ideals of the Declaration of Independence and the Constitution to dismantle barriers of color and gender. It brought rock and roll and it saw television proliferate—phenomena that changed popular culture here and abroad forever; it brought the Flower Generation, chiefly middle-class white youths who thwarted their parents' conventionality but who also had more expendable income than any comparable generation ever; it brought beatniks and hippies, yippies and yuppies; it brought race riots and war protests, lynchings and church bombings; it brought underground political organizations, political kidnappings, assassinations, cults, gurus, psychedelic drugs, a deposed president, and the age of the computer. It made a Hollywood actor president, and it brought pictures of war to the dinner table. It transformed names like McCarthy, Elvis, the Beatles, Woodstock, Birmingham, Kent State, Haight-Ashbury, Watergate, Saigon, Dealey Plaza, the Berlin Wall, and Tiananmen Square into icons of sorts.

Charles Dickens was thinking of the French Revolution when he wrote, "It was the best of times; it was the worst of times" *(A Tale of Two Cities),* but his indelible sentence applies as well to the post-Modern period and to America after 1945. If anything, the opposites of worst and best have become more extreme than at any time in human history.

Updike, Cheever, Frame, Munro, Beattie

Considering the first five stories in this section, one might wonder whether the tumult of the post-Modern world has had any impact on the short story. For these five stories essentially carry on the work of Chekhov, who applied a magnifying glass to the private agonies of the middle class. It is true that John Updike's "A & P" contains one allusion to the Cold War and has a hint of the adolescent rebellion that marked the 1950s and 1960s in America. But the tale of Sammy's mild protest, sparked chiefly by infatuation, is a universal coming-of-age story. It is a classic Updike piece, set in New England, rich with contemporary lingo, and abundant with the sharp imagery that has characterized his work from the first.

John Cheever's "Goodbye, My Brother" also springs from a middle-class New England world similar to Updike's. But in many ways it is a darker, more complex story in which the bleak Puritanism of one brother elicits violence from another.

The stories by Janet Frame, Alice Munro, and Ann Beattie take place in middle-class settings, too, and each one deals in a different way with the illusion of security in such a setting. In "Insulation," the New Zealander writer Frame constructs a story of astonishing lyricism from the seemingly unlyrical subject of a man who loses his job and decides to try to sell insulation to his neighbors. The Canadian writer Munro tells the story of a woman for whom a drowning witnessed in childhood and a near-drowning of a child force her to revise her ideas of "accident," "responsibility," and "safety." And finally, Ann Beattie explores the "necessary, small adjustments" a middle-class couple must make after their daughter dies.

Collectively, these five writers represent a highly polished, stylish form of the short story and one that is strongly associated with the *New Yorker* magazine. These writers indirectly still pay homage to the example of Chekhov, Henry

James, and de Maupassant by concentrating on psychological crises and emphasizing well-wrought, highly imagistic scenes.

Yamamoto, Yates, Ozick

The stories by Hisaye Yamamoto, Richard Yates, and Cynthia Ozick at first seem like an unlikely grouping, and yet they are similar insofar as they depict "the outsider" in America. They are also stories that make deft and clever use of point of view. Yamamoto's story is in part a coming-of-age story, but it is also the tale of an Asian-American farm family and the difficulties it must confront in a nation dominated by Christianity. Richard Yates's story concerns the initiation of a young working-class orphan into a middle-class school. And Cynthia Ozick's story, which begins with a tour-de-force meditation on ancient cities, captures the essence of the American midsize city—its absence of texture and history, and the way it can confound those whose ethnic background is tied to a history of enormous depth. All three stories reveal a spirit of survival—an assertion of identity—which teaches us that "the outsider" does not merely want to be "inside" but wants to question, critique, and redefine what is "mainstream America."

"Yoneko's Earthquake," "Doctor Jack-o'-lantern," and "The Butterfly and the Traffic Light" also give us a glimpse of how varied the landscape of short fiction (and literature in general) becomes in this post-Modern era, particularly in America. In one sense such stories are "classically" American because they repeat the necessary but unanswerable questions of "What is America?" and "What is an American?" Contrasted with earlier stories, however, they also give us narrators we may sense we have not heard before—highly original voices and perspectives.

O'Connor, O'Brien, Atwood, Bradbury

Flannery O'Connor's "Everything That Rises Must Converge" and Tim O'Brien's "The Things They Carried" spring from two of the most crucial, divisive, and defining episodes in American history since 1945: the civil rights movement and the Vietnam War. Each story approaches its subject from an unusual angle.

Point of view is everything in O'Connor's story because she narrates through the consciousness not just of a southern white racist, but of a young man whose racism is complicated and therefore even more dangerous. For Julian believes he is enlightened about the plight of blacks, and he uses his supposed enlightenment as a way to exact revenge on his domineering but simple-minded mother. O'Connor's use of a public bus for the crucial scene resonates because of how important "the bus" has been in the civil rights conflict. The bus is where Rosa Parks quietly and nonviolently challenged segregation; it symbolizes one public meeting place where blacks and whites confronted racism daily; and it represents one method of desegregation that was sufficiently controversial to not just divide communities but also influence presidential elections. (A major platform of George Wallace's campaigns for the White House was his opposition to busing.)

The denouement is quintessential O'Connor, one of the most unflinching writers of the century; it is tragic, brutal, even garish in its view of the consequences of smug racism.

Tim O'Brien immerses us in America's most difficult and most tragic war via the apparently mundane: He makes lists of what soldiers carried in the fields and jungles of Vietnam. The mundane quickly becomes the extraordinary in the story, however, and the result is an original, poignant, but unsentimental picture not just of the Vietnam War but of war in general. The story also shows how, some twenty years later, America is still trying to come to terms with the war in Southeast Asia.

"Rape Fantasies," by the Canadian writer Margaret Atwood, gives us one glimpse of how the women's movement has influenced the short story (and all literature) in North America and Europe. To some extent, writing by contemporary women has been an act of redefinition: redefining specific perspectives, such as those about rape, but also redefining gender itself—erasing stereotypes, questioning limits, and claiming authority for a feminist point of view. Atwood's simple, unassuming narrator discovers—almost in spite of herself—a profound reexamination of a loaded term, *rape fantasy*.

Science fiction is often classified as "escape" fiction, and Ray Bradbury's classic sci-fi story, "2002: Night Meeting," provides a momentary escape from the topics of war, racism, and rape. It is not a frivolous, shallow story, however. Indeed, it uses the medium or "angle" of science fiction to speculate about central questions that are at once scientific and philosophical, for example, What are time and space? Much science fiction either transplants "action adventure" to space or feasts on technological gadgetry. Bradbury's brand speculates about key issues of perception, good, and evil, and in so doing leaps beyond the confines of the subgenre.

Fuentes, Gustafsson, Malamud

The stories of Carlos Fuentes, Bernard Malamud, and Lars Gustafsson give us some sense of how inventive and bold postmodernist writing has been. Fuentes returns to the ancient topic of "eternal youth," mixing Gothic elements with fantastic ones, employing the rare second-person narrative voice, and blending arcane history with the erotic. The result is "Aura," a superb example of the "fantastical realism" that Fuentes, Jorge Luis Borges, Gabriel Garcia Marquez, and other Latin American writers have given the world. It is an approach to writing that combines the playful and the profound in daring ways.

Bernard Malamud may be best known to general readers as the author of *The Natural,* the novel (and subsequently a film) that yoked myth, ritual, rural America, and baseball. Malamud is no less inventive in "The Jewbird," which explores anti-Semitism with the fable form, a raven far more articulate than Poe's, and the Yiddish humor of Shalom Aleichem.

Lars Gustafsson brings us Uncle Sven, a befuddled Swedish engineer and an unlikely but convincing spokesperson for a "Third World" perspective that has had to negotiate the arrogance of superpowers like Germany, America, and (more recently) China. Along the way, such dissimilar items as table tennis, propeller blades, roses, Asian painting, and telescopes suddenly seem quite logically associated.

Indeed, it is the joining together of unlikely, surprising elements (in form and subject) and the blurring of the comic and the serious that make these three stories distinctively post-Modern.

Böll, Barthelme, Oates, Valenzuela, Brautigan

These five authors exhibit the bold inventiveness and experimentation of Fuentes, Malamud, and Gustafsson, and in some cases go them one better. In addition, these stories also explore various kinds of alienation in startling ways, and in several instances this alienation springs from a preoccupation with the arbitrary, soulless, and massive power of "the modern state." Hence, Heinrich Böll gives us a man living in a police state that arrests citizens for (among other things) having a happy face, or a melancholy one, or both, or neither. His only solution is to become No One—to have no face.

"Metafiction—or fiction exploring the fiction-making process—is a key form of postmodernist art, and Donald Barthelme's story, "The Author" exemplifies this kind of writing. With characteristic wit and playfulness, Barthelme gives us a story that thwarts conventional notions of authorship and fiction and a narrator whose story seems to tell *him* what to do and say.

Absurdity, characterize, and paranoia characterize in Joyce Carol Oates's "Murder," a story that sets the subgenre of crime fiction on its head, explores the psychosexual drama of political assassination, and warps fictional conventions. Like Böll's "My Melancholy Face," Oates's "Murder" owes something to the examples of Poe and Kafka, masters of the horrific and the absurd.

While the form of Luisa Valenzuela's "The Censors" is simpler and more accessible than that of the Böll, Barthelme, and Oates stories, her concern with the terrors and paranoia of power is no less profound. In fact, the almost fairy-tale simplicity of her narrative adds to the force of her political and psychological statement. It also shows that political awareness is one other gift that Latin American writers have offered to the world's literary forum.

Richard Brautigan's small story, "The Ghost Children of Tacoma," may seem out of place with these other darker, more complex narratives, but his wit is not so different from Barthelme's, Böll's, or Valenzuela's. He gives us a wry, tongue-in-cheek piece that is more memoir than fiction, but there is a sad, bluesy, elegiac undertone here, too. Above all, Brautigan shows that fiction of the late 1960s and early 1970s was not always full of protest, confusion, rage, and paranoia—that it added a self-deprecating, wise, and funny voice to the chorus.

Walker and Oz

The American Alice Walker and the Israeli writer Amos Oz might at first seem like an unlikely pair, but their stories depict forms of agrarian life in the late twentieth century, albeit in different corners of the globe. Walker's "Everyday Use" investigates one black American family's internal debate about "heritage," whereas Oz's story probes the psyche and self-image of an Israeli soldier home on leave. Both writers have earned enormous reputations in their own countries and abroad. Walker's novel *The Color Purple* won the Pulitzer Prize and attracted a larger audience to her work; Oz's fiction has been read worldwide.

Raymond Carver

Some critics have called Carver "the American Chekhov," partly because of his deceptively artful and complicated short stories, and partly because, like Chekhov, he explored the everyday agonies of working-class and middle-class people. It is appropriate, then, that one of Carver's last published stories is about Chekhov's final hours. Carver's stories often seem unadorned in their uncanny replication of contemporary American speech and behavior, and his unpretentious style has been compared with Hemingway's. A closer study of Carver's work reveals a broader range of subject and style than one might at first believe, however, and "Errand" clearly shows that Carver's imagination was not linked solely to the harsh, impoverished life of the western United States that he experienced and about which he wrote extensively.

Shirley Jackson

The section includes what may well be *the* most famous and most anthologized story of the postwar period, Shirley Jackson's unique story, "The Lottery." The story is so original and so disturbing, even after many readings, that to read it is more like visiting a strange island than experiencing fiction. It is not about a totalitarian state, or the Holocaust, or the nuclear age—but its examination of evil and acquiescence to evil and its yoking of the folksy and the terrible are so powerful that it remains one of the most important works of postmodernist literature. Its power also fulfills the promise of early voices like Hawthorne's, Poe's, Chopin's, and Chekhov's: the promise that the short story would become an art form second to none.

SUMMARY

The world after "the Second War" is one that has had to confront incessant political turmoil and also one in which two events of overwhelming consequence dominate: the Holocaust and the birth of the nuclear age. America after the war has had to struggle with a changing, sometimes confused, sometimes contradictory identity and place in the world. Within its borders America has experienced significant social change as a result of the civil rights movement, the Vietnam War, and the women's movement, among many other social and political phenomena.

Some of the stories from this period still operate well within the conventions established by nineteenth-century American, English, French, and Russian writers, exploring private conflicts of ordinary peoplé, many of whom lead middle-class lives. Other stories, though, are distinctly post-Modern: They distort or ignore realistic conventions, including those of plot, character, and resolution. They use highly inventive and challenging narrative structure. They are unabashedly eclectic in the use of language, in linking unlikely subjects and images, in blending characteristics of different subgenres, and in projecting unfamiliar voices and characters. With the post-Modern story, the unconventional becomes the conventional, as the stories by Barthelme, Ozick, Malamud, Oates, O'Brien, and Fuentes (among others) suggest.

Whether they use conventional techniques or announce themselves as postmodernist, many of these stories immerse themselves in the paranoia, irrationality, evil, and confusion of the times, deliberately confronting—one might even say absorbing—absurdity and despair, much of which is linked to the arbitrary and coercive power of a community or a state. (We might think especially of the stories by Heinrich Böll and Shirley Jackson in this regard.) Finally, the landscape of the contemporary literary world is marvelously diverse, full of voices from every part of the globe and every stratum of society. With regard to gender, race, nationality, global region, and ethnic background, the world of the short story after 1945 becomes richer and more varied in almost every conceivable way.

A & P

JOHN UPDIKE

In walks these three girls in nothing but bathing suits. I'm in the third checkout slot, with my back to the door, so I don't see them until they're over by the bread. The one that caught my eye first was the one in the plaid green two-piece. She was a chunky kid, with a good tan and a sweet broad soft-looking can with those two crescents of white just under it, where the sun never seems to hit, at the top of the backs of her legs. I stood there with my hand on a box of HiHo crackers trying to remember if I rang it up or not. I ring it up again and the customer starts giving me hell. She's one of these cash-register-watchers, a witch about fifty with rouge on her cheekbones and no eyebrows, and I know it made her day to trip me up. She'd been watching cash registers for fifty years and probably never seen a mistake before.

By the time I got her feathers smoothed and her goodies into a bag—she gives me a little snort in passing, if she'd been born at the right time they would have burned her over in Salem—by the time I get her on her way the girls had circled around the bread and were coming back, without a pushcart, back my way along the counters, in the aisle between the checkouts and the Special bins. They didn't even have shoes on. There was this chunky one, with the two-piece—it was bright green and the seams on the bra were still sharp and her belly was still pretty pale so I guessed she just got it (the suit)—there was this one, with one of those chubby berry-faces, the lips all bunched together under her nose, this one, and a tall one, with black hair that hadn't quite frizzed right, and one of these sunburns right across under the eyes, and a chin that was too long—you know, the kind of girl other girls think is very "striking" and "attractive" but never quite makes it, as they very well know, which is why they like her so much—and then the third one, that wasn't quite so tall. She was the queen. She kind of led them, the other two peeking around and making their shoulders round. She didn't look around, not this queen, she just walked straight on slowly, on these long white primadonna legs. She came down a little hard on her heels, as if she didn't walk in bare feet that much, putting down her heels and then letting the weight move along to her toes as if she was testing the floor with every step, putting a little deliberate extra action into it. You never know for sure how girls' minds work (do you really think it's a mind in there or just a little buzz like a bee in a glass jar?) but you got the idea she had talked the other two into coming in here with her, and now she was showing them how to do it, walk slow and hold yourself straight.

She had on a kind of dirty-pink—beige maybe, I don't know—bathing suit with a little nubble all over it and, what got me, the straps were down. They were off her shoulders looped loose around the cool tops of her arms, and I guess as a result the suit had slipped a little on her, so all around the top of the cloth there was this shining rim. If it hadn't been there you wouldn't have known there could have been anything whiter than those shoulders. With the straps pushed off, there was nothing between the top of the suit and the top of her head except just *her,* this clean bare plane of the top of her chest down from the shoulder bones like a dented sheet of metal tilted in the light. I mean, it was more than pretty.

She had a sort of oaky hair that the sun and salt had bleached, done up in a bun that was unravelling, and a kind of prim face. Walking into the A & P with your straps down, I suppose it's the only kind of face you *can* have. She held her head so high her neck, coming up out of those white shoulders, looked kind of stretched, but I didn't mind. The longer her neck was, the more of her there was.

She must have felt in the corner of her eye me and over my shoulder Stokesie in the second slot watching, but she didn't tip. Not this queen. She kept her eyes moving across the racks, and stopped, and turned so slow it made my stomach rub the inside of my apron, and buzzed to the other two, who kind of huddled against her for relief, and then they all three of them went up the cat-and-dog-food-breakfast-cereal-macaroni-rice-raisins-seasonings-spreads-spa-ghetti-soft-drinks-crackers-and-cookies aisle. From the third slot I look straight up this aisle to the meat counter, and I watched them all the way. The fat one with the tan sort of fumbled with the cookies, but on second thought she put the package back. The sheep pushing their carts down the aisle—the girls were walking against the usual traffic (not that we have one-way signs or anything)—were pretty hilarious. You could see them, when Queenie's white shoulders dawned on them, kind of jerk, or hop, or hiccup, but their eyes snapped back to their own baskets and on they pushed. I bet you could set off dynamite in an A & P and the people would by and large keep reaching and checking oatmeal off their lists and muttering "Let me see, there was a third thing, began with A, asparagus, no, ah, yes, applesauce!" or whatever it is they do mutter. But there was no doubt, this jiggled them. A few houseslaves in pin curlers even looked around after pushing their carts past to make sure what they had seen was correct.

You know, it's one thing to have a girl in a bathing suit down on the beach, where what with the glare nobody can look at each other much anyway, and another thing in the cool of the A & P, under the fluorescent lights, against all those stacked packages, with her feet paddling along naked over our checker-board green-and-cream rubber-tile floor.

"Oh Daddy," Stokesie said beside me. "I feel so faint."

"Darling," I said. "Hold me tight." Stokesie's married, with two babies chalked up on his fuselage already, but as far as I can tell that's the only difference. He's twenty-two, and I was nineteen this April.

"Is it done?" he asks, the responsible married man finding his voice. I forgot to say he thinks he's going to be manager some sunny day, maybe in 1990 when it's called the Great Alexandrov and Petrooshki Tea Company or something.

What he meant was, our town is five miles from a beach, with a big summer colony out on the Point, but we're right in the middle of town, and the women generally put on a shirt or shorts or something before they get out of the car into the street. And anyway these are usually women with six children and varicose veins mapping their legs and nobody, including them, could care less. As I say, we're right in the middle of town, and if you stand at our front doors you can see two banks and the Congregational church and the newspaper store and three real-estate offices and about twenty-seven old freeloaders tearing up Central Street because the sewer broke again. It's not as if we're on the Cape, we're north of Boston and there's people in this town haven't seen the ocean for twenty years.

The girls had reached the meat counter and were asking McMahon something. He pointed, they pointed, and they shuffled out of sight behind a pyramid of Diet Delight peaches. All that was left for us to see was old McMahon patting his mouth and looking after them sizing up their joints. Poor kids, I began to feel sorry for them, they couldn't help it.

Now here comes the sad part of the story, at least my family says it's sad, but I don't think it's so sad myself. The store's pretty empty, it being Thursday afternoon, so there was nothing much to do except lean on the register and wait for the girls to show up again. The whole store was like a pinball machine and I didn't know which tunnel they'd come out of. After a while they come around out of the far aisle, around the light bulbs, records at discount of the Caribbean Six or Tony Martin Sings or some such gunk you wonder they waste the wax on, six-packs of candy bars, and plastic toys done up in cellophane that fall apart when a kid looks at them anyway. Around they come, Queenie still leading the way, and holding a little gray jar in her hand. Slots Three through Seven are unmanned and I could see her wondering between Stokes and me, but Stokesie with his usual luck draws an old party in baggy gray pants who stumbles up with four giant cans of pineapple juice (what do these bums *do* with all that pineapple juice? I've often asked myself) so the girls come to me. Queenie puts down the jar and I take it into my fingers icy cold. Kingfish Fancy Herring Snacks in Pure Sour Cream: 49¢. Now her hands are empty, not a ring or a bracelet, bare as God made them, and I wonder where the money's coming from. Still with that prim look she lifts a folded dollar bill out of the hollow at the center of her nubbled pink top. The jar went heavy in my hand. Really, I thought that was so cute.

Then everybody's luck begins to run out. Lengel comes in from haggling with a truck full of cabbages on the lot and is about to scuttle into that door marked MANAGER behind which he hides all day when the girls touch his eye. Lengel's pretty dreary, teaches Sunday school and the rest, but he doesn't miss that much. He comes over and says, "Girls, this isn't the beach."

Queenie blushes, though maybe it's just a brush of sunburn I was noticing for the first time, now that she was so close. "My mother asked me to pick up a jar of herring snacks." Her voice kind of startled me, the way voices do when you see the people first, coming out so flat and dumb yet kind of tony, too, the way it ticked over "pick up" and "snacks." All of a sudden I slid right down her voice into her living room. Her father and the other men were standing around in ice-cream coats and bow ties and the women were in sandals picking up herring snacks on toothpicks off a big glass plate and they were all holding drinks the color of water with olives and sprigs of mint in them. When my parents have somebody over they get lemonade and if it's a real racy affair Schlitz in tall glasses with "They'll Do It Every Time" cartoons stencilled on.

"That's all right," Lengel said. "But this isn't the beach." His repeating this struck me as funny, as if it had just occurred to him, and he had been thinking all these years the A & P was a great big dune and he was the head lifeguard. He didn't like my smiling—as I say he doesn't miss much—but he concentrates on giving the girls that sad Sunday-school-superintendent state.

Queenie's blush is no sunburn now, and the plump one in plaid, that I liked better from the back—a really sweet can—pipes up, "We weren't doing any shopping. We just came in for the one thing."

"That makes no difference," Lengel tells her, and I could see from the way his eyes went that he hadn't noticed she was wearing a two-piece before. "We want you decently dressed when you come in here."

"We *are* decent," Queenie says suddenly, her lower lip pushing, getting sore now that she remembers her place, a place from which the crowd that runs the A & P must look pretty crummy. Fancy Herring Snacks flashed in her very blue eyes.

"Girls, I don't want to argue with you. After this come in here with your shoulders covered. It's our policy." He turns his back. That's policy for you. Policy is what the kingpins want. What the others want is juvenile delinquency.

All this while, the customers had been showing up with their carts but, you know, sheep, seeing a scene, they had all bunched up on Stokesie, who shook open a paper bag as gently as peeling a peach, not wanting to miss a word. I could feel in the silence everybody getting nervous, most of all Lengel, who asks me, "Sammy, have you rung up their purchase?"

I thought and said "No" but it wasn't about that I was thinking. I go through the punches, 4, 9, GROC, TOT—it's more complicated than you think, and after you do it often enough, it begins to make a little song, that you hear words to, in my case "Hello (*bing*) there, you (*gung*) hap-py *pee*-pul (*splat*)!"—the *splat* being the drawer flying out. I uncrease the bill, tenderly as you may imagine, it just having come from between the two smoothest scoops of vanilla I had ever known there were, and pass a half and a penny into her narrow pink palm, and nestle the herrings in a bag and twist its neck and hand it over, all the time thinking.

The girls, and who'd blame them, are in a hurry to get out, so I say "I quit" to Lengel quick enough for them to hear, hoping they'll stop and watch me, their unsuspected hero. They keep right on going, into the electric eye; the door flies open and they flicker across the lot to their car, Queenie and Plaid and Big Tall Goony-Goony (not that as raw material she was so bad), leaving me with Lengel and a kink in his eyebrow.

"Did you say something, Sammy?"

"I said I quit."

"I thought you did."

"You didn't have to embarrass them."

"It was they who were embarrassing us."

I started to say something that came out "Fiddle-de-do." It's a saying of my grandmother's, and I know she would have been pleased.

"I don't think you know what you're saying," Lengel said.

"I know you don't," I said. "But I do." I pull the bow at the back of my apron and start shrugging it off my shoulders. A couple of customers that had been heading for my slot begin to knock against each other, like scared pigs in a chute.

Lengel sighs and begins to look very patient and old and gray. He's been a friend of my parents for years. "Sammy, you don't want to do this to your Mom and Dad," he tells me. It's true, I don't. But it seems to me that once you begin a gesture it's fatal not to go through with it. I fold the apron, "Sammy" stitched in red on the pocket, and put it on the counter, and drop the bow tie on top of it. The bow tie is theirs, if you've ever wondered. "You'll feel this for the rest of your life," Lengel says, and I know that's true, too, but remembering how he made that pretty girl blush makes me so scrunchy inside I punch the No Sale tab and the machine whirs "pee-pul" and the drawer splats out. One advantage to this scene taking place in summer, I can follow this up with a clean exit, there's no fumbling around getting your coat and galoshes, I just saunter into the electric eye in my white shirt that my mother ironed the night before, and the door heaves itself open, and outside the sunshine is skating around on the asphalt.

I look around for my girls, but they're gone, of course. There wasn't anybody but some young married screaming with her children about some candy they didn't get by the door of a powder-blue Falcon station wagon. Looking back in the big windows, over the bags of peat moss and aluminum lawn furniture stacked on the pavement, I could see Lengel in my place in the slot, checking the sheep through. His face was dark gray and his back stiff, as if he's just had an injection of iron, and my stomach kind of fell as I felt how hard the world was going to be to me hereafter.

Questions for Discussion

1. Describe Sammy's personality as created by the first-person narration. What sort of person is he?

2. What personal and social conflicts are suggested by the appearance of Queenie in the store, by the turmoil this creates, and by Sammy's actions? *Is* there a sense of conflict between social classes in the story? Explain.

3. Do you sympathize with Sammy's decision to quit? Why or why not? In your view, why does he quit?

4. What do Lengel and Stokesie represent for Sammy?

5. What concrete images do you remember from Updike's depiction of the store, the young women, and the customers? What do these add to the story?

Suggestions for Writing

1. Write an essay about Sammy's attitude toward women, as revealed by his responses to different customers and, of course, to Queenie.

2. Write an essay about Sammy's quitting, discussing it as an act of protest. Is quitting a justified act of protest in this case? Is it effective? Explain.

3. Write a story set in a specific workplace with which you are familiar.

4. Write a journal entry about the methods Updike uses to create Sammy's "voice." Consider vocabulary, speech rhythm, implied values, and so forth.

Goodbye, My Brother

JOHN   CHEEVER

We are a family that has always been very close in spirit. Our father was drowned in a sailing accident when we were young, and our mother had always stressed the fact that our familial relationships have a kind of permanence that we will never meet with again. I don't think about the family much, but when I remember its members and the coast where they lived and the sea salt that I think is in our blood, I am happy to recall that I am a Pommeroy—that I have the nose, the coloring, and the promise of longevity—and that while we are not a distinguished family, we enjoy the illusion, when we are together, that the Pommeroys are unique. I don't say any of this because I'm interested in family history or because this sense of uniqueness is deep or important to me but in order to advance the point that we are loyal to one another in spite of our differences, and that any rupture in this loyalty is a source of confusion and pain.

We are four children; there is my sister Diana and the three men—Chaddy, Lawrence, and myself. Like most families in which the children are out of their twenties, we have been separated by business, marriage, and war. Helen and I live on Long Island now, with our four children. I teach in a secondary school, and I am past the age where I expect to be made headmaster—or principal, as we say—but I respect the work. Chaddy, who has done better than the rest of us, lives in Manhattan, with Odette and their children. Mother lives in Philadelphia, and Diana, since her divorce, has been living in France, but she comes back to the States in the summer to spend a month at Laud's Head. Laud's Head is a summer place on the shore of one of the Massachusetts islands. We used to have a cottage there, and in the twenties our father built the big house. It stands on a cliff above the sea and, excepting St. Tropez and some of the Apennine villages, it is my favorite place in the world. We each have an equity in the place and we contribute some money to help keep it going.

Our youngest brother, Lawrence, who is a lawyer, got a job with a Cleveland firm after the war, and none of us saw him for four years. When he decided to leave Cleveland and go to work for a firm in Albany, he wrote Mother that he would, between jobs, spend ten days at Laud's Head, with his wife and their two children. This was when I had planned to take my vacation—I had been teaching summer school—and Helen and Chaddy and Odette and Diana were all going to be there, so the family would be together. Lawrence is the member of the family with whom the rest of us have least in common. We have never seen a great deal of him, and I suppose that's why we still call him Tifty—a nickname he was given when he was a child, because when he came down the hall toward the dining room for breakfast, his slippers made a noise that sounded like "Tifty, tifty, tifty." That's what Father called him, and so did everyone else. When he grew older, Diana sometimes used to call him Little Jesus, and Mother often called him the Croaker. We had disliked Lawrence, but we looked forward to his return with a mixture of apprehension and loyalty, and with some of the joy and delight of reclaiming a brother.

Lawrence crossed over from the mainland on the four-o'clock boat one afternoon late in the summer, and Chaddy and I went down to meet him. The arrivals and departures of the summer ferry have all the outward signs that suggest a voyage—whistles, bells, hand trucks, reunions, and the smell of brine—but it is a voyage of no import, and when I watched the boat come into the blue harbor that afternoon and thought that it was completing a voyage of no import, I realized that I had hit on exactly the kind of observation that Lawrence would have made. We looked for his face behind the windshields as the cars drove off the boat, and we had no trouble in recognizing him. And we ran over and shook his hand and clumsily kissed his wife and the children. "Tifty!" Chaddy shouted. "Tifty!" It is difficult to judge changes in the appearance of a brother, but both Chaddy and I agreed, as we drove back to Laud's Head, that Lawrence still looked very young. He got to the house first, and we took the suitcases out of his car. When I came in, he was standing in the living room, talking with Mother and Diana. They were in their best clothes and all their jewelry, and they were welcoming him extravagantly, but even then, when everyone was endeavoring to seem most affectionate and at a time when these endeavors come easiest, I was aware of a faint tension in the room. Thinking about this as I carried Lawrence's heavy suitcases up the stairs, I realized that our dislikes are as deeply ingrained as our better passions, and I remembered that once, twenty-five years ago, when I had hit Lawrence on the head with a rock, he had picked himself up and gone directly to our father to complain.

I carried the suitcases up to the third floor, where Ruth, Lawrence's wife, had begun to settle her family. She is a thin girl, and she seemed very tired from the journey, but when I asked her if she didn't want me to bring a drink upstairs to her, she said she didn't think she did.

When I got downstairs, Lawrence wasn't around, but the others were all ready for cocktails, and we decided to go ahead. Lawrence is the only member of the family who has never enjoyed drinking. We took our cocktails onto the terrace, so that we could see the bluffs and the sea and the islands in the east, and the return of Lawrence and his wife, their presence in the house, seemed to refresh our responses to the familiar view; it was as if the pleasure they would take in the sweep and the color of that coast, after such a long absence, had been imparted to us. While we were there, Lawrence came up the path from the beach.

"Isn't the beach fabulous, Tifty?" Mother asked. "Isn't it fabulous to be back? Will you have a Martini?"

"I don't care," Lawrence said. "Whiskey, gin—I don't care what I drink. Give me a little rum."

"We don't have any *rum*," Mother said. It was the first note of asperity. She had taught us never to be indecisive, never to reply as Lawrence had. Beyond this, she is deeply concerned with the propriety of her house, and anything irregular by her standards, like drinking straight rum or bringing a beer can to the dinner table, excites in her a conflict that she cannot, even with her capacious sense of humor, surmount. She sensed the asperity and worked to repair it. "Would you like some Irish, Tifty dear?" she said. "Isn't Irish what you've always liked? There's some Irish on the sideboard. Why don't you get yourself some Irish?" Lawrence said that he didn't care. He poured himself a Martini, and then Ruth came down and we went in to dinner.

In spite of the fact that we had, through waiting for Lawrence, drunk too much before dinner, we were all anxious to put our best foot forward and to enjoy a peaceful time. Mother is a small woman whose face is still a striking reminder of how pretty she must have been, and whose conversation is unusually light, but she talked that evening about a soil-reclamation project that is going on up-island. Diana is as pretty as Mother must have been; she is an animated and lovely woman who likes to talk about the dissolute friends that she had made in France, but she talked that night about the school in Switzerland where she had left her two children. I could see that the dinner had been planned to please Lawrence. It was not too rich, and there was nothing to make him worry about extravagance.

After supper, when we went back onto the terrace, the clouds held that kind of light that looks like blood, and I was glad that Lawrence had such a lurid sunset for his homecoming. When we had been out there a few minutes, a man named Edward Chester came to get Diana. She had met him in France, or on the boat home, and he was staying for ten days at the inn in the village. He was introduced to Lawrence and Ruth, and then he and Diana left.

"Is that the one she's sleeping with now?" Lawrence asked.

"What a horrid thing to say!" Helen said.

"You ought to apologize for that, Tifty," Chaddy said.

"I don't know," Mother said tiredly. "I don't know, Tifty. Diana is in a position to do whatever she wants, and I don't ask sordid questions. She's my only daughter. I don't see her often."

"Is she going back to France?"

"She's going back the week after next."

Lawrence and Ruth were sitting at the edge of the terrace, not in the chairs, not in the circle of chairs. With his mouth set, my brother looked to me then like a Puritan cleric. Sometimes, when I try to understand his frame of mind, I think of the beginnings of our family in this country, and his disapproval of Diana and her lover reminded me of this. The branch of the Pommeroys to which we belong was founded by a minister who was eulogized by Cotton Mather for his untiring abjuration of the Devil. The Pommeroys were ministers until the middle of the nineteenth century, and the harshness of their thought—man is full of misery, and all earthly beauty is lustful and corrupt—has been preserved in books and sermons. The temper of our family changed somewhat and became more lighthearted, but when I was of school age, I can remember a cousinage of old men and women who seemed to hark back to the dark days of the ministry and to be animated by perpetual guilt and the deification of the scourge. If you are raised in this atmosphere—and in a sense we were—I think it is a trial of the spirit to reject its habits of guilt, self-denial, taciturnity, and penitence, and it seemed to me to have been a trial of the spirit in which Lawrence had succumbed.

"Is that Cassiopeia?" Odette asked.

"No, dear," Chaddy said. "That isn't Cassiopeia."

"Who was Cassiopeia?" Odette said.

"She was the wife of Cepheus and the mother of Andromeda," I said.

"The cook is a Giants fan," Chaddy said. "She'll give you even money that they win the pennant."

It had grown so dark that we could see the passage of light through the sky from the lighthouse at Cape Heron. In the dark below the cliff, the continual detonations of the surf sounded. And then, as she often does when it is getting dark and she has drunk too much before dinner, Mother began to talk about the improvements and additions that would someday be made on the house, the wings and bathrooms and gardens.

"This house will be in the sea in five years," Lawrence said.

"Tifty the Croaker," Chaddy said.

"Don't call me Tifty," Lawrence said.

"Little Jesus," Chaddy said.

"The sea wall is badly cracked," Lawrence said. "I looked at it this afternoon. You had it repaired four years ago, and it cost eight thousand dollars. You can't do that every four years".

"Please, Tifty," Mother said.

"Facts are facts," Lawrence said, "and it's a damned-fool idea to build a house at the edge of the cliff on a sinking coastline. In my lifetime, half the garden has washed away and there's four feet of water where we used to have a bathhouse."

"Let's have a very *general* conversation," Mother said bitterly. "Let's talk about politics or the boat-club dance."

"As a matter of fact," Lawrence said, "the house is probably in some danger now. If you had an unusually high sea, a hurricane sea, the wall would crumble and the house would go. We could all be drowned."

"I can't *bear* it," Mother said. She went into the pantry and came back with a full glass of gin.

I have grown too old now to think that I can judge the sentiments of others, but I was conscious of the tension between Lawrence and Mother, and I knew some of the history of it. Lawrence couldn't have been more than sixteen years old when he decided that Mother was frivolous, mischievous, destructive, and overly strong. When he had determined this, he decided to separate himself from her. He was at boarding school then, and I remember that he did not come home for Christmas. He spent Christmas with a friend. He came home very seldom after he had made his unfavorable judgment on Mother, and when he did come home, he always tried, in his conversation, to remind her of his estrangement. When he married Ruth, he did not tell Mother. He did not tell her when his children were born. But in spite of these principled and lengthy exertions he seemed, unlike the rest of us, never to have enjoyed any separation, and when they are together, you feel at once a tension, an unclearness.

And it was unfortunate, in a way, that Mother should have picked that night to get drunk. It's her privilege, and she doesn't get drunk often, and fortunately she wasn't bellicose, but we were all conscious of what was happening. As she quietly drank her gin, she seemed sadly to be parting from us; she seemed to be in the throes of travel. Then her mood changed from travel to injury, and the few remarks she made were petulant and irrelevant. When her glass was nearly empty, she stared angrily at the dark air in front of her nose, moving her head a little, like a fighter. I knew that there was not room in her mind then for all the injuries that were crowding into it. Her children were stupid, her husband was drowned, her servants were thieves, and the chair she sat in was uncomfortable. Suddenly she put down her empty glass and interrupted Chaddy, who was talking about baseball. "I know one *thing,*" she said hoarsely. "I know that if there is an afterlife, I'm going to have a very different kind of family. I'm going to have nothing but fabulously rich, witty, and enchanting children." She got up and, starting for the door, nearly fell. Chaddy caught her and helped her up the stairs. I could hear their tender good-nights, and then Chaddy came back. I thought that Lawrence by now would be tired from his journey and his return, but he remained on the terrace, as if he were waiting to see the final malfeasance, and the rest of us left him there and went swimming in the dark.

When I woke the next morning, or half woke, I could hear the sound of someone rolling the tennis court. It is a fainter and a deeper sound than the iron buoy bells off the point—an unrhythmic iron chiming—that belongs in my mind to the beginnings of a summer day, a good portent. When I went downstairs, Lawrence's two kids were in the living room, dressed in ornate cowboy suits. They are frightened and skinny children. They told me their father was rolling the tennis court but that they did not want to go out because they had seen a snake under the doorstep. I explained to them that their cousins—all the other children—ate breakfast in the kitchen and that they'd better run along in there. At this announcement, the boy began to cry. Then his sister joined him. They cried as if to go in the kitchen and eat would destroy their most precious rights. I told them to sit down with me. Lawrence came in, and I asked him if he wanted to play some tennis. He said no, thanks, although he thought he might play some singles with Chaddy. He was in the right here, because both he and Chaddy play better tennis than I, and he did play some singles with Chaddy after breakfast, but later on, when the others came down to play family doubles, Lawrence disappeared. This made me cross—unreasonably so, I suppose—but we play darned interesting family doubles and he could have played in a set for the sake of courtesy.

Late in the morning, when I came up from the court alone, I saw Tifty on the terrace, prying up a shingle from the wall with his jackknife. "What's the matter, Lawrence?" I said. "Termites?" There are termites in the wood and they've given us a lot of trouble.

He pointed out to me, at the base of each row of shingles, a faint blue line of carpenter's chalk. "This house is about twenty-two years old," he said. "These shingles are about two hundred years old. Dad must have bought shingles from all the farms around here when he built the place, to make it look venerable. You can still see the carpenter's chalk put down where these antiques were nailed into place."

It was true about the shingles, although I had forgotten it. When the house was built, our father, or his architect, had ordered it covered with lichened and weather-beaten shingles. I didn't follow Lawrence's reasons for thinking that this was scandalous.

"And look at these doors," Lawrence said. "Look at these doors and window frames." I followed him over to a big Dutch door that opens onto the terrace and looked at it. It was a relatively new door, but someone had worked hard to conceal its newness. The surface had been deeply scored with some metal implement, and white paint had been rubbed into the incisions to imitate brine, lichen, and weather rot. "Imagine spending thousands of dollars to make a sound house look like a wreck," Lawrence said. "Imagine the frame of mind this implies. Imagine wanting to live so much in the past that you'll pay men carpenters' wages to disfigure your front door." Then I remembered Lawrence's sensitivity to time and his sentiments and opinions about our feelings for the past. I had heard him say, years ago, that we and our friends and our part of the nation, finding ourselves unable to cope with the problems of the present, had, like a wretched adult, turned back to what we supposed was a happier and a simpler time, and that our taste for reconstruction and candlelight was a measure of this irremediable failure. The faint blue line of chalk had reminded him of these ideas, the scarified door had reinforced them, and now clue after clue presented itself to him—the stern light at the door, the bulk of the chimney, the width of the floorboards and the pieces set into them to resemble pegs. While Lawrence was lecturing me on these frailties, the others came up from the court. As soon as Mother saw Lawrence, she responded, and I saw that there was little hope of any rapport between the matriarch and the changeling. She took Chaddy's arm. "Let's go swimming and have Martinis on the beach," she said. "Let's have a *fabulous* morning."

The sea that morning was a solid color, like verd stone. Everyone went to the beach but Tifty and Ruth. "I don't mind *him*," Mother said. She was excited, and she tipped her glass and spilled some gin into the sand. "I don't mind *him*. It doesn't matter to me how *rude* and *horrid* and *gloomy* he is, but what I can't bear are the faces of his wretched little children, those fabulously unhappy little children." With the height of the cliff between us, everyone talked wrathfully about Lawrence; about how he had grown worse instead of better, how unlike the rest of us he was, how he endeavored to spoil every pleasure. We drank our gin; the abuse seemed to reach a crescendo, and then, one by one, we went swimming in the solid green water. But when we came out no one mentioned Lawrence unkindly; the line of abusive conversation had been cut, as if swimming had the cleansing force claimed for baptism. We dried our hands and lighted cigarettes, and if Lawrence was mentioned, it was only to suggest, kindly, something that might please him. Wouldn't he like to sail to Barin's cove, or go fishing?

And now I remember that while Lawrence was visiting us, we went swimming oftener than we usually do, and I think there was a reason for this. When the irritability that accumulated as a result of his company began to lessen our patience, not only with Lawrence but with one another, we would all go swimming and shed our animus in the cold water. I can see the family now, smarting from Lawrence's rebukes as they sat on the sand, and I can see them wading and diving and surface-diving and hear in their voices the restoration of patience and the rediscovery of inexhaustible good will. If Lawrence noticed this change—this illusion of purification—I suppose that he would have found in the vocabulary of psychiatry, or the mythology of the Atlantic, some circumspect name for it, but I don't think he noticed the change. He neglected to name the curative powers of the open sea, but it was one of the few chances for diminution that he missed.

The cook we had that year was a Polish woman named Anna Ostrovick, a summer cook. She was first-rate—a big, fat, hearty, industrious woman who took her work seriously. She liked to cook and to have the food she cooked appreciated and eaten, and whenever we saw her, she always urged us to eat. She cooked hot bread—crescents and brioches—for breakfast two or three times a week, and she would bring these into the dining room herself and say, "Eat, eat, eat!" When the maid took the serving dishes back into the pantry, we could sometimes hear Anna, who was standing there, say, "Good! They eat." She fed the garbage man, the milkman, and the gardener. "Eat!" she told them. "Eat, eat!" On Thursday afternoons, she went to the movies with the maid, but she didn't enjoy the movies, because the actors were all so thin. She would sit in the dark theatre for an hour and a half watching the screen anxiously for the appearance of someone who had enjoyed his food. Bette Davis merely left with Anna the impression of a woman who has not eaten well. "They are all so skinny," she would say when she left the movies. In the evenings, after she had gorged all of us, and washed the pots and pans, she would collect the table scraps and go out to feed the creation. We had a few chickens that year, and although they would have roosted by then, she would dump food into their troughs and urge the sleeping fowl to eat. She fed the songbirds in the orchard and the chipmunks in the yard. Her appearance at the edge of the garden and her urgent voice—we could hear her calling "Eat, eat, eat"—had become, like the sunset gun at the boat club and the passage of light from Cape Heron, attached to that hour. "Eat, eat, eat," we could hear Anna say. "Eat, eat . . ." Then it would be dark.

When Lawrence had been there three days, Anna called me into the kitchen. "You tell your mother," she said, "that *he* doesn't come into my kitchen. If *he* comes into my kitchen all the time, I go. *He* is always coming into my kitchen to tell me what a sad woman I am. He is always telling me that I work too hard and that I don't get paid enough and that I should belong to a union with vacations. Ha! He is so skinny but he is always coming into my kitchen when I am busy to pity me, but I am as good as him, I am as good as *anybody,* and I do not have to have people like that getting into my way all the time and feeling sorry for me. I am a famous and a wonderful cook and I have jobs everywhere and the only reason I come here to work this summer is because I was never before on an island, but I can have other jobs tomorrow, and if he is always coming into my kitchen to pity me, you tell your mother I am going. I am as good as *anybody* and I do not have to have that skinny all the time telling how poor I am."

I was pleased to find that the cook was on our side, but I felt that the situation was delicate. If Mother asked Lawrence to stay out of the kitchen, he would make a grievance out of the request. He could make a grievance out of anything, and it sometimes seemed that as he sat darkly at the dinner table, every word of disparagement, wherever it was aimed, came home to him. I didn't mention the cook's complaint to anyone, but somehow there wasn't any more trouble from that quarter.

The next cause for contention that I had from Lawrence came over our backgammon games.

When we are at Laud's Head, we play a lot of backgammon. At eight o'clock, after we have drunk our coffee, we usually get out the board. In a way, it is one of our pleasantest hours. The lamps in the room are still unlighted, Anna can be seen in the dark garden, and in the sky above her head there are continents of shadow and fire. Mother turns on the light and rattles the dice as a signal. We usually play three games apiece, each with the others. We play for money, and you can win or lose a hundred dollars on a game, but the stakes are usually much lower. I think that Lawrence used to play—I can't remember—but he doesn't play any more. He doesn't gamble. This is not because he is poor or because he has any principles about gambling but because he thinks the game is foolish and a waste of time. He was ready enough, however, to waste his time watching the rest of us play. Night after night, when the game began, he pulled a chair up beside the board, and watched the checkers and the dice. His expression was scornful, and yet he watched carefully. I wondered why he watched us night after night, and, through watching his face, I think that I may have found out.

Lawrence doesn't gamble, so he can't understand the excitement of winning and losing money. He has forgotten how to play the game, I think, so that its complex odds can't interest him. His observations were bound to include the facts that backgammon is an idle game and a game of chance, and that the board, marked with points, was a symbol of our worthlessness. And since he doesn't understand gambling or the odds of the game, I thought that what interested him must be the members of his family. One night when I was playing with Odette—I had won thirty-seven dollars from Mother and Chaddy—I think I saw what was going on in his mind.

Odette has black hair and black eyes. She is careful never to expose her white skin to the sun for long, so the striking contrast of blackness and pallor is not changed in the summer. She needs and deserves admiration—it is the element that contents her—and she will flirt, unseriously, with any man. Her shoulders were bare that night, her dress was cut to show the division of her breasts and to show her breasts when she leaned over the board to play. She kept losing and flirting and making her losses seem like a part of the flirtation. Chaddy was in the other room. She lost three games, and when the third game ended, she fell back on the sofa and, looking at me squarely, said something about going out on the dunes to settle the score. Lawrence heard her. I looked at Lawrence. He seemed shocked and gratified at the same time, as if he had suspected all along that we were not playing for anything so insubstantial as money. I may be wrong, of course, but I think that Lawrence felt that in watching our backgammon he was observing the progress of a mordant tragedy in which the money we won and lost served as a symbol for more vital forfeits. It is like Lawrence to try to read significance and finality into every gesture that we make, and it is certain of Lawrence that when he finds the inner logic to our conduct, it will be sordid.

Chaddy came in to play with me. Chaddy and I have never liked to lose to each other. When we were younger, we used to be forbidden to play games together, because they always ended in a fight. We think we know each other's mettle intimately. I think he is prudent; he thinks I am foolish. There is always bad blood when we play anything—tennis or backgammon or softball or bridge—and it does seem at times as if we were playing for the possession of each other's liberties. When I lose to Chaddy, I can't sleep. All this is only half the truth of our competitive relationship, but it was the half-truth that would be discernible to Lawrence, and his presence at the table made me so self-conscious that I lost two games. I tried not to seem angry when I got up from the board. Lawrence was watching me. I went out onto the terrace to suffer there in the dark the anger I always feel when I lose to Chaddy.

When I came back into the room, Chaddy and Mother were playing. Lawrence was still watching. By his lights, Odette had lost her virtue to me, I had lost my self-esteem to Chaddy, and now I wondered what he saw in the present match. He watched raptly, as if the opaque checkers and the marked board served for an exchange of critical power. How dramatic the board, in its ring of light, and the quiet players and the crash of the sea outside must have seemed to him! Here was spiritual cannibalism made visible; here, under his nose, were the symbols of the rapacious use human beings make of one another.

Mother plays a shrewd, an ardent, and an interfering game. She always has her hands in her opponent's board. When she plays with Chaddy, who is her favorite, she plays intently. Lawrence would have noticed this. Mother is a sentimental woman. Her heart is good and easily moved by tears and frailty, a characteristic that, like her handsome nose, has not been changed at all by age. Grief in another provokes her deeply, and she seems at times to be trying to divine in Chaddy some grief, some loss, that she can succor and redress, and so re-establish the relationship that she enjoyed with him when he was sickly and young. She loves defending the weak and the childlike, and now that we are old, she misses it. The world of debts and business, men and war, hunting and fishing has on her an exacerbating effect. (When Father drowned, she threw away his fly rods and his guns.) She has lectured us all endlessly on self-reliance, but when we come back to her for comfort and for help—particularly Chaddy—she seems to feel most like herself. I suppose Lawrence thought that the old woman and her son were playing for each other's soul.

She lost. "Oh *dear,*" she said. She looked stricken and bereaved, as she always does when she loses. "Get me my glasses, get me my checkbook, get me something to drink." Lawrence got up at last and stretched his legs. He looked at us all bleakly. The wind and the sea had risen, and I thought that if he heard the waves, he must hear them only as a dark answer to all his dark questions; that he would think that the tide had expunged the embers of our picnic fires. The company of a lie is unbearable, and he seemed like the embodiment of a lie. I couldn't explain to him the simple and intense pleasures of playing for money, and it seemed to me hideously wrong that he should have sat at the edge of the board and concluded that we were playing for one another's soul. He walked restlessly around the room two or three times and then, as usual, gave us a parting shot. "I should think you'd go crazy," he said, "cooped up with one another like this, night after night. Come on, Ruth. I'm going to bed."

That night, I dreamed about Lawrence. I saw his plain face magnified into ugliness, and when I woke in the morning, I felt sick, as if I had suffered a great spiritual loss while I slept, like the loss of courage and heart. It was foolish to let myself be troubled by my brother. I needed a vacation. I needed to relax. At school, we live in one of the dormitories, we eat at the house table, and we never get away. I not only teach English winter and summer but I work in the principal's office and fire the pistol at track meets. I needed to get away from this and from every other form of anxiety, and I decided to avoid my brother. Early that day, I took Helen and the children sailing, and we stayed out until suppertime. The next day, we went on a picnic. Then I had to go to New York for a day, and when I got back, there was the costume dance at the boat club. Lawrence wasn't going to this, and it's a party where I always have a wonderful time.

The invitations that year said to come as you wish you were. After several conversations, Helen and I had decided what to wear. The thing she most wanted to be again, she said, was a bride, and so she decided to wear her wedding dress. I thought this was a good choice—sincere, light-hearted, and inexpensive. Her choice influenced mine, and I decided to wear an old football uniform. Mother decided to go as Jenny Lind, because there was an old Jenny Lind costume in the attic. The others decided to rent costumes, and when I went to New York, I got the clothes. Lawrence and Ruth didn't enter into any of this.

Helen was on the dance committee, and she spent most of Friday decorating the club. Diana and Chaddy and I went sailing. Most of the sailing that I do these days is in Manhasset, and I am used to setting a homeward course by the gasoline barge and the tin roofs of the boat shed, and it was a pleasure that afternoon, as we returned, to keep the bow on a white church spire in the village and to find even the inshore water green and clear. At the end of our sail, we stopped at the club to get Helen. The committee had been trying to give a submarine appearance to the ballroom, and the fact that they had nearly succeeded in accomplishing this illusion made Helen very happy. We drove back to Laud's Head. It had been a brilliant afternoon, but on the way home we could smell the east wind—the dark wind, as Lawrence would have said—coming in from the sea.

My wife, Helen, is thirty-eight, and her hair would be gray, I guess, if it were not dyed, but it is dyed an unobtrusive yellow—a faded color—and I think it becomes her. I mixed cocktails that night while she was dressing, and when I took a glass upstairs to her, I saw her for the first time since our marriage in her wedding dress. There would be no point in saying that she looked to me more beautiful than she did on our wedding day, but because I have grown older and have, I think, a greater depth of feeling, and because I could see in her face that night both youth and age, both her devotion to the young woman that she had been and the positions that she had yielded graciously to time, I think I have never been so deeply moved. I had already put on the football uniform, and the weight of it, the heaviness of the pants and the shoulder guards, had worked a change in me, as if in putting on these old clothes I had put off the reasonable anxieties and troubles of my life. It felt as if we had both returned to the years before our marriage, the years before the war.

The Collards had a big dinner party before the dance, and our family—excepting Lawrence and Ruth—went to this. We drove over to the club, through the fog, at about half past nine. The orchestra was playing a waltz. While I was checking my raincoat, someone hit me on the back. It was Chucky Ewing, and the funny thing was that Chucky had on a football uniform. This seemed comical as hell to both of us. We were laughing when we went down the hall to the dance floor. I stopped at the door to look at the party, and it was beautiful. The committee had hung fish nets around the sides and over the high ceiling. The nets on the ceiling were filled with colored balloons. The light was soft and uneven, and the people—our friends and neighbors—dancing in the soft light to "Three O'Clock in the Morning" made a pretty picture. Then I noticed the number of women dressed in white, and I realized that they, like Helen, were wearing wedding dresses. Patsy Hewitt and Mrs. Gear and the Lackland girl waltzed by, dressed as brides. Then Pep Talcott came over to where Chucky and I were standing. He was dressed to be Henry VIII, but he told us that the Auerbach twins and Henry Barrett and Dwight MacGregor were all wearing football uniforms, and that by the last count there were ten brides on the floor.

This coincidence, this funny coincidence, kept everybody laughing, and made this one of the most lighthearted parties we've ever had at the club. At first I thought that the women had planned with one another to wear wedding dresses, but the ones that I danced with said it was a coincidence and I'm sure that Helen had made her decision alone. Everything went smoothly for me until a little before midnight. I saw Ruth standing at the edge of the floor. She was wearing a long red dress. It was all wrong. It wasn't the spirit of the party at all. I danced with her, but no one cut in, and I was darned if I'd spend the rest of the night dancing with her and I asked her where Lawrence was. She said he was out on the dock, and I took her over to the bar and left her and went out to get Lawrence.

The east fog was thick and wet, and he was alone on the dock. He was not in costume. He had not even bothered to get himself up as a fisherman or a sailor. He looked particularly saturnine. The fog blew around us like a cold smoke. I wished that it had been a clear night, because the easterly fog seemed to play into my misanthropic brother's hands. And I knew that the buoys—the groaners and bells that we could hear then—would sound to him like half-human, half-drowned cries, although every sailor knows that buoys are necessary and reliable fixtures, and I knew that the foghorn at the lighthouse would mean wanderings and losses to him and that he could misconstrue the vivacity of the dance music. "Come on in, Tifty," I said, "and dance with your wife or get her some partners."

"Why should I?" he said. "Why should I?" And he walked to the window and looked in at the party. "Look at it," he said. "Look at that . . ."

Chucky Ewing had got hold of a balloon and was trying to organize a scrimmage line in the middle of the floor. The others were dancing a samba. And I knew that Lawrence was looking bleakly at the party as he had looked at the weather-beaten shingles on our house, as if he saw here an abuse and a distortion of time; as if in wanting to be brides and football players we exposed the fact that, the lights of youth having been put out in us, we had been unable to find other lights to go by and, destitute of faith and principle, had become foolish and sad. And that he was thinking this about so many kind and happy and generous people made me angry, made me feel for him such an unnatural abhorrence that I was ashamed, for he is my brother and a Pommeroy. I put my arm around his shoulders and tried to force him to come in, but he wouldn't.

I got back in time for the Grand March, and after the prizes had been given out for the best costumes, they let the balloons down. The room was hot, and someone opened the big doors onto the dock, and the easterly wind circled the room and went out, carrying across the dock and out onto the water most of the balloons. Chucky Ewing went running out after the balloons, and when he saw them pass the dock and settle on the water, he took off his football uniform and dove in. Then Eric Auerbach dove in and Lew Phillips dove in and I dove in, and you know how it is at a party after midnight when people start jumping into the water. We recovered most of the balloons and dried off and went on dancing, and we didn't get home until morning.

The next day was the day of the flower show. Mother and Helen and Odette all had entries. We had a pickup lunch, and Chaddy drove the women and children over to the show. I took a nap, and in the middle of the afternoon I got some trunks and a towel and, on leaving the house, passed Ruth in the laundry. She was washing clothes. I don't know why she should seem to have so much more work to do than anyone else, but she is always washing or ironing or mending clothes. She may have been taught, when she was young, to spend her time like this, or she may be at the mercy of an expiatory passion. She seems to scrub and iron with a penitential fervor, although I can't imagine what it is that she thinks she's done wrong. Her children were with her in the laundry. I offered to take them to the beach, but they didn't want to go.

It was late in August, and the wild grapes that grow profusely all over the island made the land wind smell of wine. There is a little grove of holly at the end of the path, and then you climb the dunes, where nothing grows but that coarse grass. I could hear the sea, and I remember thinking how Chaddy and I used to talk mystically about the sea. When we were young, we had decided that we could never live in the West because we would miss the sea. "It is very nice here," we used to say politely when we visited people in the mountains, "but we miss the Atlantic." We used to look down our noses at people from Iowa and Colorado who had been denied this revelation, and we scorned the Pacific. Now I could hear the waves, whose heaviness sounded like a reverberation, like a tumult, and it pleased me as it had pleased me when I was young, and it seemed to have a purgative force, as if it had cleared my memory of, among other things, the penitential image of Ruth in the laundry.

But Lawrence was on the beach. There he sat. I went in without speaking. The water was cold, and when I came out, I put on a shirt. I told him that I was going to walk up to Tanners Point, and he said that he would come with me. I tried to walk beside him. His legs are no longer than mine, but he always likes to stay a little ahead of his companion. Walking along behind him, looking at his bent head and his shoulders, I wondered what he could make of that landscape.

There were the dunes and cliffs, and then, where they declined, there were some fields that had begun to turn from green to brown and yellow. The fields were used for pasturing sheep, and I guess Lawrence would have noticed that the soil was eroded and that the sheep would accelerate this decay. Beyond the fields there are a few coastal farms, with square and pleasant buildings, but Lawrence could have pointed out the hard lot of an island farmer. The sea, at our other side, was the open sea. We always tell guests that there, to the east, lies the coast of Portugal, and for Lawrence it would be an easy step from the coast of Portugal to the tyranny in Spain. The waves broke with a noise like a "hurrah, hurrah, hurrah," but to Lawrence they would say *"Vale, vale."* I suppose it would have occurred to his baleful and incisive mind that the coast was terminal moraine, the edge of the prehistoric world, and it must have occurred to him that we walked along the edge of the known world in spirit as much as in fact. If he should otherwise have overlooked this, there were some Navy planes bombing an uninhabited island to remind him.

That beach is a vast and preternaturally clean and simple landscape. It is like a piece of the moon. The surf had pounded the floor solid, so it was easy walking, and everything left on the sand had been twice changed by the waves. There was the spine of a shell, a broomstick, part of a bottle and part of a brick, both of them milled and broken until they were nearly unrecognizable, and I suppose Lawrence's sad frame of mind—for he kept his head down—went from one broken thing to another. The company of his pessimism began to infuriate me, and I caught up with him and put a hand on his shoulder. "It's only a summer day, Tifty," I said. "It's only a summer day. What's the matter? Don't you like it here?"

"I don't like it here," he said blandly, without raising his eyes. "I'm going to sell my equity in the house to Chaddy. I didn't expect to have a good time. The only reason I came back was to say goodbye."

I let him get ahead again and I walked behind him, looking at his shoulders and thinking of all the goodbyes he had made. When Father drowned, he went to church and said goodbye to Father. It was only three years later that he concluded that Mother was frivolous and said goodbye to her. In his freshman year at college, he had been very good friends with his roommate, but the man drank too much, and at the beginning of the spring term Lawrence changed roommates and said goodbye to his friend. When he had been in college for two years, he concluded that the atmosphere was too sequestered and he said goodbye to Yale. He enrolled at Columbia and got his law degree there, but he found his first employer dishonest, and at the end of six months he said goodbye to a good job. He married Ruth in City Hall and said goodbye to the Protestant Episcopal Church; they went to live on a back street in Tuckahoe and said goodbye to the middle class. In 1938, he went to Washington to work as a government lawyer, saying goodbye to private enterprise, but after eight months in Washington he concluded that the Roosevelt administration was sentimental and he said goodbye to it. They left Washington for a suburb of Chicago, where he said goodbye to his neighbors, one by one, on counts of drunkenness, boorishness, and stupidity. He said goodbye to Chicago and went to Kansas; he said goodbye to Kansas and went to Cleveland. Now he had said goodbye to Cleveland and come East again, stopping at Laud's Head long enough to say goodbye to the sea.

It was elegiac and it was bigoted and narrow, it mistook circumspection for character, and I wanted to help him. "Come out of it," I said. "Come out of it, Tifty."

"Come out of what?"

"Come out of this gloominess. Come out of it. It's only a summer day. You're spoiling your own good time and you're spoiling everyone else's. We need a vacation, Tifty. I need one. I need to rest. We all do. And you've made everything tense and unpleasant. I only have two weeks in the year. Two weeks. I need to have a good time and so do all the others. We need to rest. You think that your pessimism is an advantage, but it's nothing but an unwillingness to grasp realities."

"What are the realities?" he said. "Diana is a foolish promiscuous woman. So is Odette. Mother is an alcoholic. If she doesn't discipline herself, she'll be in a hospital in a year or two. Chaddy is dishonest. He always has been. The house is going to fall into the sea." He looked at me and added, as an afterthought, "You're a fool."

"You're a gloomy son of a bitch," I said. "You're a gloomy son of a bitch."

"Get your fat face out of mine," he said. He walked along.

Then I picked up a root and, coming at his back—although I have never hit a man from the back before—I swung the root, heavy with sea water, behind me, and the momentum sped my arm and I gave him, my brother, a blow on the head that forced him to his knees on the sand, and I saw the blood come out and begin to darken his hair. Then I wished that he was dead, dead and about to be buried, not buried but about to be buried, because I did not want to be denied ceremony and decorum in putting him away, in putting him out of my consciousness, and I saw the rest of us—Chaddy and Mother and Diana and Helen—in mourning in the house on Belvedere Street that was torn down twenty years ago, greeting our guests and our relatives at the door and answering their mannerly condolences with mannerly grief. Nothing decorous was lacking so that even if he had been murdered on a beach, one would feel before the tiresome ceremony ended that he had come into the winter of his life and that it was a law of nature, and a beautiful one, that Tifty should be buried in the cold, cold ground.

He was still on his knees. I looked up and down. No one had seen us. The naked beach, like a piece of the moon, reached to invisibility. The spill of a wave, in a glancing run, shot up to where he knelt. I would still have liked to end him, but now I had begun to act like two men, the murderer and the Samaritan. With a swift roar, like hollowness made sound, a white wave reached him and encircled him, boiling over his shoulders, and I held him against the undertow. Then I led him to a higher place. The blood had spread all through his hair, so that it looked black. I took off my shirt and tore it to bind up his head. He was conscious, and I didn't think he was badly hurt. He didn't speak. Neither did I. Then I left him there.

I walked a little way down the beach and turned to watch him, and I was thinking of my own skin then. He had got to his feet and he seemed steady. The daylight was still clear, but on the sea wind fumes of brine were blowing in like a light fog, and when I had walked a little way from him, I could hardly see his dark figure in this obscurity. All down the beach I could see the heavy salt air blowing in. Then I turned my back on him, and as I got near the house, I went swimming again, as I seem to have done after every encounter with Lawrence that summer.

When I got to the house, I lay down on the terrace. The others came back.

I could hear Mother defaming the flower arrangements that had won prizes. None of ours had won anything. Then the house quieted, as it always does at that hour. The children went into the kitchen to get supper and the others went upstairs to bathe. Then I heard Chaddy making cocktails, and the conversation about the flower show judges was resumed. Then Mother cried, "Tifty! Tifty! Oh, Tifty!"

He stood in the door, looking half dead. He had taken off the bloody bandage and he held it in his hand. "My brother did this," he said. "My brother did it. He hit me with a stone—something—on the beach." His voice broke with self-pity. I thought he was going to cry. No one else spoke. "Where's Ruth?" he cried. "Where's Ruth? Where in hell is Ruth? I want her to start packing. I don't have any more time to waste here. I have important things to do. I have *important* things to do." And he went up the stairs.

They left for the mainland the next morning, taking the six-o'clock boat. Mother got up to say goodbye, but she was the only one, and it is a harsh and an easy scene to imagine—the matriarch and the changeling, looking at each other with a dismay that would seem like the powers of love reversed. I heard the children's voices and the car go down the drive, and I got up and went to the window, and what a morning that was! Jesus, what a morning! The wind was northerly. The air was clear. In the early heat, the roses in the garden smelled like strawberry jam. While I was dressing, I heard the boat whistle, first the warning signal and then the double blast, and I could see the good people on the top deck drinking coffee out of fragile paper cups, and Lawrence at the bow, saying to the sea, *"Thalassa, thalassa,"* while his timid and unhappy children watched the creation from the encirclement of their mother's arms. The buoys would toll mournfully for Lawrence, and while the grace of the light would make it an exertion not to throw out your arms and swear exultantly, Lawrence's eyes would trace the black sea as it fell astern; he would think of the bottom, dark and strange, where full fathom five our father lies.

Oh, what can you do with a man like that? What can you do? How can you dissuade his eye in a crowd from seeking out the cheek with acne, the infirm hand; how can you teach him to respond to the inestimable greatness of the race, the harsh surface beauty of life; how can you put his finger for him on the obdurate truths before which fear and horror are powerless? The sea that morning was iridescent and dark. My wife and my sister were swimming—Diana and Helen—and I saw their uncovered heads, black and gold in the dark water. I saw them come out and I saw that they were naked, unshy, beautiful, and full of grace, and I watched the naked women walk out of the sea.

Questions for Discussion

1. "We enjoy the illusion," says the narrator, "when we are together, that the Pommeroys are unique." To what extent is this statement true of all families? To what extent is it true of your family?

2. At one point early in the story the narrator observes that the light in the evening sky is like blood. What is the significance of this image, beyond the merely descriptive?

3. The narrator claims that his brother Lawrence mistakes "circumspection" for "character." What do you think he means by this? What is the difference, in your view, between circumspection and character?

4. Are you sympathetic to the narrator at the end of the story? Was he justified in doing what he did? Explain.

5. Characterize Lawrence. What sort of person is he? What are the key details the narrator gives us to explain Lawrence's personality?

Suggestions for Writing

1. In a journal entry, take Lawrence's side and try to justify why he behaves the way he does.

2. In a journal entry, explain the significance of the father having drowned and its influence on the family.

3. In a handbook of Greek and Roman mythology, look up the figures Diana and Helen, and then apply the information to the last scene of the story, writing a brief analysis in your notebook or journal.

4. Write an essay that interprets the conflict of this story as a conflict not so much between brothers but between extremely different worldviews.

5. Write a story that is based on a relative of yours who, like Lawrence, is the odd person out. Do not merely base the story on "actual events"; fictionalize significantly.

Insulation

JANET FRAME

In the summer days when the lizards come out and the old ewes, a rare generation, a gift of the sun, gloat at us from the television screen, and the country, skull in hand, recites To kill or not to kill, and tomatoes and grapes ripen in places unused to such lingering light and warmth, then the people of Stratford, unlike the 'too happy happy tree' of the poem, do remember the 'drear-nighted' winter. They order coal and firewood, they mend leaks in the spouting and roof, they plant winter savoys, swedes, a last row of parsnips.

The country is not as rich as it used to be. The furniture in the furniture store spills out on the footpath and stays unsold. The seven varieties of curtain rail with their seven matching fittings stay on display, useless extras in the new education of discernment and necessity. The dazzling bathroom ware, the chrome and fur and imitation marble are no longer coveted and bought. For some, though, the time is not just a denial of gluttony, of the filling of that worthy space in the heart and the imagination with assorted satisfied cravings. Some have lost their jobs, their life-work, a process described by one factory-manager as 'shedding'.

'Yes, we have been shedding some of our workers.'

'Too happy happy tree?'

The leaves fall as if from other places, only they fall here. They are brittle in the sun. Shedding, severing, pruning. God's country, the garden of Eden and the conscientious gardeners.

Some find work again. Some who have never had work advertise in the local newspaper. There was that advertisement which appeared every day for two weeks, full of the hope of youth, sweet and sad with unreal assumptions about the world.

'Sixteen-year-old girl with one thousand hours training at hairdressing College seeks work.' The *one thousand hours* was in big dark print. It made the reader gasp as if with a sudden visitation of years so numerous they could scarcely be imagined, as if the young girl had undergone, like an operation, a temporal insertion which made her in some way older and more experienced than anyone else. And there was the air of pride with which she flaunted her thousand hours. She was pleading, using her richness of time as her bargain. In another age she might have recorded such time in her Book of Hours.

And then there was the boy, just left school. 'Boy, sixteen, would like to join pop group as vocalist fulltime'—the guileless advertisement of a dream. Did anyone answer either advertisement? Sometimes I imagine they did (I too have unreal assumptions about the world), that the young girl has found a place in the local Salon Paris, next to the Manhattan Takeaway, where she is looked at with admiration and awe (one thousand hours!) and I think that somewhere, maybe, say, in Hamilton (which is to other cities what round numbers are to numbers burdened by decimal points), there's a pop group with a new young vocalist fulltime, appearing, perhaps, on *Opportunity Knocks,* the group playing their instruments, the young man running up and down the stairs, being sexy with his microphone and singing in the agony style.

But my real story is just an incident, a passing glance at insulation and one of those who were pruned, shed, severed, and in the curious mixture of political metaphor, irrationally rationalized, with a sinking lid fitted over his sinking heart. I don't know his name. I only know he lost his job and he couldn't get other work and he was a man used to working with never a thought of finding himself jobless. Like the others he had ambled among the seven varieties of curtain rail and matching fittings, and the fancy suites with showwood arms and turned legs, and the second circular saw. He was into wrought iron, too, and there was a wishing well in his garden and his wife had leaflets about a swimming-pool. And somewhere, at the back of his mind, he had an internal stairway to the basement rumpus. Then one day, suddenly, although there had been rumours, he was pruned from the dollar-flowering tree.

He tried to get other work but there was nothing. Then he thought of spending his remaining money on a franchise to sell insulation. It was a promising district with the winters wet and cold and frosty. The price of electricity had gone up, the government was giving interest-free loans—why, everyone would be insulating. At first, having had a number of leaflets printed, he was content to distribute them in letter boxes, his two school-age children helping. His friends were sympathetic and optimistic. They too said, Everyone will be wanting insulation. And after this drought you can bet on a cold winter. Another thing, there was snow on Egmont at Christmas, and that's a sign.

He sat at home waiting for the orders to come in. None came. He tried random telephoning, still with no success. Finally, he decided to sell from door to door.

'I'm going from door to door,' he told his wife.

She was young and able. She had lost her job in the local clothing factory, and was thinking of buying a knitting-machine and taking orders. On TV when they demonstrated knitting-machines the knitter (it was always a she, with the he demonstrating) simply moved her hands to and fro as if casting a magic spell and the machine did the rest. To and fro, to and fro, a fair-isle sweater knitted in five hours, and fair-isle was coming back, people said. Many of her friends had knitting-machines, in the front room, near the window, to catch the light, where, in her mother's day, the piano always stood, and when she walked by her friends' houses she could see them sitting in the light moving their hands magically to and fro, making fair-isle and bulky knit, intently reading the pattern.

'Yes, door to door.'

The words horrified her. Not in her family, surely! Not door to door. Her father, a builder, had once said that if a man had to go door to door to advertise his work there was something wrong with it.

'If you're reputable,' he said, 'you don't advertise. People just come to you through word of mouth, through your own work standing up to the test.' Well, it wasn't like that now, she knew. Even Smart and Rogers had a full-page advertisement in the latest edition of the local paper. All the same, door to door!

'Oh no,' she said plaintively.

'It can't be helped. I have to look for custom.'

He put on his work clothes, a red checkered shirt, jeans, and he carried a bundle of leaflets, and even before he had finished both sides of one street he was tired and he had begun to look worried and shabby.

This is how I perceived him when he came to my door. I saw a man in his thirties wearing a work-used shirt and jeans yet himself looking the picture of disuse, that is, severed, shed, rationalized, with a great lid sinking over his life, putting out the flame.

'I thought you might like to insulate your house,' he said, thrusting a leaflet into my hand.

I was angry. Interrupted in my work, brought to the door for nothing! Why, the electrician had said my house was well insulated with its double ceilings. Besides, I'd had experience of that stuff they blow into the ceiling and every time there's a wind it all comes out making snowfall in the garden, drifting over to the neighbours too.

'No, I'm not interested,' I said. 'I tried that loose-fill stuff once and it snowed everywhere, every time the wind blew.'

'There's a government loan, you know.'

'I'm really not interested,' I said.

'But it's new. New. Improved.'

'Can't afford it, anyway.'

'Read about it, then, and let me know.'

'Sorry,' I said.

My voice was brisk and dismissing. He looked as if he were about to plead with me, then he changed his mind. He pointed to the red print stamped on the leaflet. There was pride in his pointing, like that of the girl with the thousand hours.

'That's my name and phone number, if you change your mind.'

'Thank you, but I don't think I will.'

He walked away and I shut the door quickly. Insulation, I said to myself with no special meaning or tone. How lovely the summer is, how cosy this house is. The people here before me had carpets that will last for ever, the ceiling is double, there are no cracks in the corners, that is, unless the place decides to shift again on its shaky foundations. How well insulated I am! How solid the resistance of this house against the searching penetrating winds of Stratford. The hunted safe from the hunter, the fleeing from the pursuer, the harmed from the harmer.

'How well insulated I am!'

That night I had a curious ridiculous dream. I dreamed of a land like a vast forest 'in green felicity' where the leaves had started to fall, not by nature, for the forest was evergreen, but under the influence of a season that came to the land from within it and had scarcely been recognized, and certainly not ruled against. Now how could that have been? At first I thought I was trapped in a legend of far away and long ago, for the characters of long ago were there. I could see a beggar walking among the fallen leaves. He was the beggar of other times and other countries, and yet he was not, he was new, and he was ashamed. I saw a cottage in the forest and a young woman at the window combing her hair and—a young man with a—lute? No, a guitar—surely that was the prince?—and with the guitar plugged in to nowhere he began to play and sing and as he sang he sparkled—why, it was Doug Dazzle—and he was singing,

> *One thousand hours of cut and set*
> *my showwood arms will hold you yet*
> *baby baby insulate,*
> *apprentice and certificate*
> *God of nations at thy feet*
> *in our bonus bonds we meet*
> *lest we forget lest we forget*
> *one thousand hours of cut and set. . .*

The girl at the window listened and smiled and then she turned to the knitting-machine by the window and began to play it as if from a 90 per cent worsted, 10 per cent acrylic score. I could see the light falling on her hands as they moved to and fro, to and fro in a leisurely saraband of fair-isle. Then the beggar appeared. He was carrying a sack that had torn and was leaking insulation, faster and faster, until it became a blizzard, vermiculite falling like snow, endlessly, burying everything, the trees and their shed leaves, the cottage, the beggar, the prince, and the princess of the thousand hours.

The next morning I found the leaflet and telephoned the number on it.
    'I'd like to be insulated,' I said.
    The man was clearly delighted.
    'I'll come at once and measure.'
    We both knew we were playing a game, he trying to sell what he didn't possess, and I imagining I could ever install it, to deaden the world. All the same, he measured the house and he put in the loose-fill insulation, and following the Stratford custom, although it was summer, I ordered my firewood against the other 'drear-nighted' winter.

Questions for Discussion

1. What is the significance of the allusion to *Hamlet* in the first paragraph? What does it have to do with the narrator's description of the season?

2. How does Frame connect seasonal change with the changes in the local economy? What are the symptoms of harsh economic times?

3. Interpret the dream the narrator has. How does it transform what has gone on already in the story?

4. Why does she finally order the insulation?

5. What figurative meaning does "insulation" take on in the story?

Suggestions for Writing

1. Write an essay that explores the ways in which Frame attempts to connect nature, literature, and economics in this story.

2. Write an "economic" story—one that involves work or economic ills or obsession with material goods.

3. Midway through the story Frame presents "symptoms" of economic well-being—the things the couple purchased before he lost his job. In your notebook, make a list of things that someone you know owns, and select the list in such a way that a reader will be able to interpret the economic status of the person.

4. To some extent, the narrator recognizes a kinship between herself and the man who has lost his job and who now tries to sell insulation. Write a story that expresses such a moment of recognition between a narrator and an unfortunate person whom the main character first wants to dismiss.

Miles City, Montana

ALICE   MUNRO

My father came across the field, carrying the body of the boy who had been drowned. There were several men together, returning from the search, but he was the one carrying the body. The men were muddy and exhausted, and walked with their heads down, as if they were ashamed. Even the dogs were dispirited, dripping from the cold river. When they all set out, hours before, the dogs were nervy and yelping, the men tense and determined, and there was a constrained, unspeakable excitement about the whole scene. It was understood that they might find something horrible.

The boy's name was Steve Gauley. He was eight years old. His hair and clothes were mud-colored now and carried some bits of dead leaves, twigs, and grass. He was like a heap of refuse that had been left out all winter. His face was turned in to my father's chest, but I could see a nostril, an ear, plugged up with greenish mud.

I don't think I really saw all this. Perhaps I saw my father carrying him, and the other men coming with him, and the dogs, but I would not have been allowed to get close enough to see something like mud in his nostril. I must have heard someone talking about that and imagined that I saw it. I see his face unaltered except for the mud—Steve Gauley's familiar, sharp-honed, sneaky-looking face—and it wouldn't have been like that; it would have been bloated and changed and perhaps muddied all over after so many hours in the water.

To have to bring back such news, such evidence, to a waiting family, particularly a mother, would have made searchers move heavily, but what was happening here was worse. It seemed a worse shame (to hear people talk) that there was no mother, no woman at all—no grandmother or aunt, or even a sister—to receive Steve Gauley and give him his due of grief. His father was a hired man, a drinker but not a drunk, an erratic man without being entertaining, not friendly but not exactly a troublemaker. His fatherhood seemed accidental, and the fact that the child had been left with him when the mother went away, and that they continued living together, seemed accidental. They lived in a steep-roofed, gray-shingled hillbilly sort of house that was just a bit better than a shack—the father fixed the roof and put supports under the porch, just enough and just in time—and their life was held together in a similar manner; that is, just well enough to keep the Children's Aid at bay. They didn't eat meals together or cook for each other, but there was food. Sometimes the father would give Steve money to buy food at the store, and Steve was seen to buy quite sensible things, such as pancake mix and macaroni dinner.

I had known Steve Gauley fairly well. I had not liked him more often that I had liked him. He was two years older than I was. He would hang around our place on Saturdays, scornful of whatever I was doing but unable to leave me alone. I couldn't be on the swing without him wanting to try it, and if I wouldn't give it up he came and pushed me so that I went crooked. He teased the dog. He got me into trouble—deliberately and maliciously, it seemed to me afterward—by daring me to do things I wouldn't have thought of on my own: digging up the potatoes to see how big they were, when they were still only the size of marbles, and pushing over the stacked firewood to make a pile we could jump off. At school we never spoke to each other. He was solitary, though not tormented. But on Saturday mornings when I saw his thin, self-possessed figure sliding through the cedar hedge I knew I was in for something, and he would decide what. Sometimes it was all right. We pretended we were cowboys who had to tame wild horses. We played in the pasture by the river, not far from the place where Steve drowned. We were horses and riders both, screaming and neighing and bucking and waving whips of tree branches beside a little nameless river that flows into the Saugeen, in southern Ontario.

The funeral was held in our house. There was not enough room at Steve's father's place for the large crowd that was expected, because of the circumstances. I have a memory of the crowded room but no picture of Steve in his coffin, or of the minister, or of wreaths of flowers. I remember that I was holding one flower, a white narcissus, which must have come from a pot somebody forced indoors, because it was too early for even the forsythia bush or the trilliums and marsh marigolds in the woods. I stood in a row of children, each of us holding a narcissus. We sang a children's hymn, which somebody played on our piano: "When He Cometh, When He Cometh, to Make Up His Jewels." I was wearing white ribbed stockings, which were disgustingly itchy and which wrinkled at the knees and ankles. The feeling of these stockings on my legs is mixed up with another feeling in my memory. It is hard to describe. It had to do with my parents. Adults in general but my parents in particular. My father, who had carried Steve's body from the river, and my mother, who must have done most of the arranging of this funeral. My father in his dark-blue suit and my mother in her brown velvet dress with the creamy satin collar. They stood side by side opening and closing their mouths for the hymn, and I stood removed from them, in the row of children, watching. I felt a furious, and sickening, disgust. Children sometimes have an access of disgust concerning adults. The size, the lumpy shapes, the bloated power. The breath, the coarseness, the hairiness, the horrid secretions. But this was more. And the accompanying anger had nothing sharp and self-respecting about it. There was no release, as when I would finally bend and pick up a stone and throw it at Steve Gauley. It could not be understood or expressed, though it died down after a while into a heaviness, then just a taste, an occasional taste—a thin, familiar misgiving.

Twenty years or so later, in 1961, my husband, Andrew, and I got a brand-new car, our first—that is, our first brand-new. It was a Morris Oxford, oyster-colored (the dealer had some fancier name for the color)—a big small car, with plenty of room for us and our two children. Cynthia was six and Meg three and a half.

Andrew took a picture of me standing beside the car. I was wearing white pants, a black turtleneck, and sunglasses. I lounged against the car door, canting my hips to make myself look slim.

"Wonderful," Andrew said. "Great. You look like Jackie Kennedy." All over this continent probably, dark-haired, reasonably slender young women were told, when they were stylishly dressed or getting their pictures taken, that they looked like Jackie Kennedy.

Andrew took a lot of pictures of me, and of the children, our house, our garden, our excursions and possessions. He got copies made, labeled them carefully, and sent them back to his mother and his aunt and uncle, in Ontario. He got copies for me to send to my father, who also lived in Ontario, and I did so, but less regularly than he sent his. When he saw pictures he thought I had already sent lying around the house, Andrew was perplexed and annoyed. He liked to have this record go forth.

That summer we were presenting ourselves, not pictures. We were driving back from Vancouver, where we lived, to Ontario, which we still called "home," in our new car. Five days to get there, ten days there, five days back. For the first time, Andrew had three weeks' holiday. He worked in the legal department at B. C. Hydro.

On a Saturday morning we loaded suitcases, two thermos bottles—one filled with coffee and one with lemonade—some fruit and sandwiches, picture books and coloring books, crayons, drawing pads, insect repellent, sweaters (in case it got cold in the mountains), and our two children into the car. Andrew locked the house and Cynthia said ceremoniously, "Good-bye, house."

Meg said, "Good-bye, house." Then she said, "Where will we live now?"

"It's not good-bye forever," said Cynthia. "We're coming back. Mother! Meg thought we weren't ever coming back!"

"I did not," said Meg, kicking the back of my seat.

Andrew and I put on our sunglasses and we drove away, over the Lions Gate Bridge and through the main part of Vancouver. We shed our house, the neighborhood, the city, and—at the crossing point between Blaine, Washington, and British Columbia—our country. We were driving east across the United States, taking the most northerly route, and would cross into Canada again at Sarnia, Ontario. I don't know if we chose this route because the Trans-Canada Highway was not completely finished at the time or if we just wanted the feeling of driving through a foreign, a very slightly foreign, country—that extra bit of interest and adventure.

We were both in high spirits. Andrew congratulated the car several times. He said he felt so much better driving it than our old car, a 1951 Austin that slowed down dismally on the hills and had a fussy-old-lady image. So Andrew said now.

"What kind of image does this one have?" said Cynthia. She listened to us carefully and liked to try out new words such as "image." Usually she got them right.

"Lively," I said. "Slightly sporty. It's not show-off."

"It's sensible, but it has class," Andrew said. "Like my image."

Cynthia thought that over and said with a cautious pride, "That means like you think you want to be, Daddy?"

As for me, I was happy because of the shedding. I loved taking off. In my own house, I seemed to be often looking for a place to hide—sometimes from the children but more often from the jobs to be done and the phone ringing and the sociability of the neighborhood. I wanted to hide so that I could get busy at my real work, which was a sort of wooing of distant parts of myself. I lived in a state of siege, always losing just what I wanted to hold on to. But on trips there was no difficulty. I could be talking to Andrew, talking to the children and looking at whatever they wanted me to look at—a pig on a sign, a pony in a field, a Volkswagen on a revolving stand—and pouring lemonade into plastic cups, and all the time those bits and pieces would be flying together inside me. The essential composition would be achieved. This made me hopeful and lighthearted. It was being a watcher that did it. A watcher, not a keeper.

We turned east at Everett and climbed into the Cascades. I showed Cynthia our route on the map. First I showed her the map of the whole United States, which showed also the bottom part of Canada. Then I turned to the separate maps of each of the states we were going to pass through. Washington, Idaho, Montana, North Dakota, Minnesota, Wisconsin. I showed her the dotted line across Lake Michigan, which was the route of the ferry we would take. Then we would drive across Michigan to the bridge that linked the United States and Canada, at Sarnia. Ontario. Home.

Meg wanted to see, too.

"You won't understand," said Cynthia. But she took the road atlas into the backseat.

"Sit back," she said to Meg. "Sit still. I'll show you."

I could hear her tracing the route for Meg, very accurately, just as I had done it for her. She looked up all the states' maps, knowing how to find them in alphabetical order.

"You know what that line is?" she said. "It's the road. That line is the road we're driving on. We're going right along this line."

Meg did not say anything.

"Mother, show me where we are right this minute," said Cynthia.

I took the atlas and pointed out the road through the mountains, and she took it back and showed it to Meg. "See where the road is all wiggly?" she said. "It's wiggly because there are so many turns in it. The wiggles are the turns." She flipped some pages and waited a moment. "Now," she said, "show me where we are." Then she called to me, "Mother, she understands! She pointed to it! Meg understands maps!"

It seems to me now that we invented characters for our children. We had them firmly set to play their parts. Cynthia was bright and diligent, sensitive, courteous, watchful. Sometimes we teased her for being too conscientious, too eager to be what we in fact depended on her to be. Any reproach or failure, any rebuff, went terribly deep with her. She was fair-haired, fair-skinned, easily showing the effects of the sun, raw winds, pride, or humiliation. Meg was more solidly built, more reticent—not rebellious but stubborn sometimes, mysterious. Her silences seemed to us to show her strength of character, and her negatives were taken as signs of an imperturbable independence. Her hair was brown, and we cut it in straight bangs. Her eyes were a light hazel, clear and dazzling.

We were entirely pleased with these characters, enjoying the contradictions as well as the confirmations of them. We disliked the heavy, the uninventive, approach to being parents. I had a dread of turning into a certain kind of mother—the kind whose body sagged and ripened, who moved in a woolly-smelling, milky-smelling fog, solemn with trivial burdens. I believed that all the attention these mothers paid, their need to be burdened, was the cause of colic, bedwetting, asthma. I favored another approach—the mock desperation, the inflated irony of the professional mothers who wrote for magazines. In those magazine pieces the children were splendidly self-willed, hard-edged, perverse, indomitable. So were the mothers, through their wit, indomitable. The other mothers I warmed to were the sort who would phone up and say, "Is my embryo Hitler by any chance over at your house?" They cackled clear above the milky fog.

We saw a dead deer strapped across the front of a pickup truck.

"Somebody shot it," Cynthia said. "Hunters shoot the deer."

"It's not hunting season yet," Andrew said. "They may have hit it on the road. See the sign for deer crossing?"

"I would cry if we hit one," Cynthia said sternly.

I had made peanut-butter-and-marmalade sandwiches for the children and salmon-and-mayonnaise for us. But I had not put any lettuce in, and Andrew was disappointed.

"I didn't have any," I said.

"Couldn't you have got some?"

"I'd have had to buy a whole head of lettuce just to get enough for sandwiches, and I decided it wasn't worth it."

This was a lie. I had forgotten.

"They're a lot better with lettuce."

"I didn't think it made that much difference." After a silence I said, "Don't be mad."

"I'm not mad. I like lettuce on sandwiches."

"I just didn't think it mattered that much."

"How would it be if I didn't bother to fill up the gas tank?"

"That's not the same thing."

"Sing a song," said Cynthia. She started to sing:

Five little ducks went out one day,
Over the hills and far away.
One little duck went
"Quack-quack-quack."
Four little ducks came swimming back.

Andrew squeezed my hand and said, "Let's not fight."

"You're right. I should have got lettuce."

"It doesn't matter that much."

I wished that I could get my feelings about Andrew to come together into serviceable and dependable feeling. I had even tried writing two lists, one of things I liked about him, one of things I disliked—in the cauldron of intimate life, things I loved and things I hated—as if I hoped by this to prove something, to come to a conclusion one way or the other. But I gave it up when I saw that all it proved was what I already knew—that I had violent contradictions. Sometimes the very sound of his footsteps seemed to me tyrannical, the set of his mouth smug and mean, his hard, straight body a barrier interposed—quite consciously, even dutifully, and with a nasty pleasure in its masculine authority—between me and whatever joy or lightness I could get in life. Then, with not much warning, he became my good friend and most essential companion. I felt the sweetness of his light bones and serious ideas, the vulnerability of his love, which I imagined to be much purer and more straightforward than my own. I could be greatly moved by an inflexibility, a harsh propriety, that at other times I scorned. I would think how humble he was, really, taking on such a ready-made role of husband, father, breadwinner, and how I myself in comparison was really a secret monster of egotism. Not so secret, either—not from him.

At the bottom of our fights we served up what we thought were the ugliest truths. "I know there is something basically selfish and basically untrustworthy about you," Andrew once said. "I've always known it. I also know that that is why I fell in love with you."

"Yes," I said, feeling sorrowful but complacent.

"I know that I'd be better off without you."

"Yes. You would."

"You'd be happier without me."

"Yes."

And finally—finally—racked and purged, we clasped hands and laughed, laughed at those two benighted people, ourselves. Their grudges, their grievances, their self-justification. We leapfrogged over them. We declared them liars. We would have wine for dinner, or decide to give a party.

I haven't seen Andrew for years, don't know if he is still thin, has gone completely gray, insists on lettuce, tells the truth, or is hearty and disappointed.

We stayed the night in Wenatchee, Washington, where it hadn't rained for weeks. We ate dinner in a restaurant built about a tree—not a sapling in a tub but a tall, sturdy cottonwood. In the early-morning light we climbed out of the irrigated valley, up dry, rocky, very steep hillsides that would seem to lead to more hills, and there on the top was a wide plateau, cut by the great Spokane and Columbia rivers. Grainland and grassland, mile after mile. There were straight roads here, and little farming towns with grain elevators. In fact, there was a sign announcing that this county we were going through, Douglas County, had one of the highest wheat yields of any county in the United States. The towns had planted shade trees. At least, I thought they had been planted, because there were no such big trees in the countryside.

All this was marvelously welcome to me. "Why do I love it so much?" I said to Andrew. "Is it because it isn't scenery?"

"It reminds you of home," said Andrew. "A bout of severe nostalgia." But he said this kindly.

When we said "home" and meant Ontario, we had very different places in mind. My home was a turkey farm, where my father lived as a widower, and though it was the same house my mother had lived in, had papered, painted, cleaned, furnished, it showed the effects now of neglect and of some wild sociability. A life went on in it that my mother could not have predicted or condoned. There were parties for the turkey crew, the gutters and pluckers, and sometimes one or two of the young men would be living there temporarily, inviting their own friends and having their own impromptu parties. This life, I thought, was better for my father than being lonely, and I did not disapprove, had certainly no right to disapprove. Andrew did not like to go there, naturally enough, because he was not the sort who could sit around the kitchen table with the turkey crew, telling jokes. They were intimidated by him and contemptuous of him, and it seemed to me that my father, when they were around, had to be on their side. And it wasn't only Andrew who had trouble. I could manage those jokes, but it was an effort.

I wished for the days when I was little, before we had the turkeys. We had cows, and sold the milk to the cheese factory. A turkey farm is nothing like as pretty as a dairy farm or a sheep farm. You can see that the turkeys are on a straight path to becoming frozen carcasses and table meat. They don't have the pretense of a life of their own, a browsing idyll, that cattle have, or pigs in the dappled orchard. Turkey barns are long, efficient buildings—tin sheds. No beams or hay or warm stables. Even the smell of guano seems thinner and more offensive than the usual smell of stable manure. No hints of hay coils and rail fences and songbirds and the flowering hawthorn. The turkeys were all let out into one long field, which they picked clean. They didn't look like great birds there but like fluttering laundry.

Once, shortly after my mother died and I was married—in fact, I was packing to join Andrew in Vancouver—I was at home alone for a couple of days with my father. There was a freakishly heavy rain all night. In the early light we saw that the turkey field was flooded. At least, the low-lying parts of it were flooded—it was like a lake with many islands. The turkeys were huddled on these islands. Turkeys are very stupid. (My father would say, "You know a chicken? You know how stupid a chicken is? Well, a chicken is an Einstein compared with a turkey.") But they had managed to crowd to higher ground and avoid drowning. Now they might push each other off, suffocate each other, get cold and die. We couldn't wait for the water to go down. We went out in an old rowboat we had. I rowed and my father pulled the heavy, wet turkeys into the boat and we took them to the barn. It was still raining a little. The job was difficult and absurd and very uncomfortable. We were laughing. I was happy to be working with my father. I felt close to all hard, repetitive, appalling work, in which the body is finally worn out, the mind sunk (though sometimes the spirit can stay marvelously light), and I was homesick in advance for this life and this place. I thought that if Andrew could see me there in the rain, redhanded, muddy, trying to hold on to turkey legs and row the boat at the same time, he would only want to get me out of there and make me forget about it. This raw life angered him. My attachment to it angered him. I thought that I shouldn't have married him. But who else? One of the turkey crew?

And I didn't want to stay there. I might feel bad about leaving, but I would feel worse if somebody made me stay.

Andrew's mother lived in Toronto, in an apartment building looking out on

Muir Park. When Andrew and his sister were both at home, his mother slept in the living room. Her husband, a doctor, had died when the children were still too young to go to school. She took a secretarial course and sold her house at Depression prices, moved to this apartment, managed to raise her children, with some help from relatives—her sister Caroline, her brother-in-law Roger. Andrew and his sister went to private schools and to camp in the summer.

"I suppose that was courtesy of the Fresh Air Fund?" I said once, scornful of his claim that he had been poor. To my mind, Andrew's urban life had been sheltered and fussy. His mother came home with a headache from working all day in the noise, the harsh light of a department-store office, but it did not occur to me that hers was a hard or admirable life. I don't think she herself believed that she was admirable—only unlucky. She worried about her work in the office, her clothes, her cooking, her children. She worried most of all about what Roger and Caroline would think.

Caroline and Roger lived on the east side of the park, in a handsome stone house. Roger was a tall man with a bald, freckled head, a fat, firm stomach. Some operation on his throat had deprived him of his voice—he spoke in a rough whisper. But everybody paid attention. At dinner once in the stone house—where all the dining-room furniture was enormous, darkly glowing, palatial—I asked him a question. I think it had to do with Whittaker Chambers, whose story was then appearing in *The Saturday Evening Post.* The question was mild in tone, but he guessed its subversive intent and took to calling me Mrs. Gromyko, referring to what he alleged to be my "sympathies." Perhaps he really craved an adversary, and could not find one. At that dinner I saw Andrew's hand tremble as he lit his mother's cigarette. His Uncle Roger had paid for Andrew's education, and was on the board of directors of several companies.

"He is just an opinionated old man," Andrew said to me later. "What is the point of arguing with him?"

Before we left Vancouver, Andrew's mother had written, "Roger seems quite intrigued by the idea of your buying a small car!" Her exclamation mark showed apprehension. At that time, particularly in Ontario, the choice of a small, European car over a large, American car could be seen as some sort of declaration—a declaration of tendencies Roger had been sniffing after all along.

"It isn't that small a car," said Andrew huffily.

"That's not the point," I said. "The point is, it isn't any of his business!"

"He's bored."

We spent the second night in Missoula. We had been told in Spokane, at a gas station, that there was a lot of repair work going on along Highway 2, and that we were in for a very hot, dusty drive, with long waits, so we turned onto the interstate, and drove through Cur d'Alene and Kellogg into Montana. After Missoula we turned south, toward Butte, but detoured to see Helena, the state capital. In the car we played Who Am I?

Cynthia was somebody dead, and an American, and a girl. Possibly a lady. She was not in a story. She had not been seen on television. Cynthia had not read about her in a book. She was not anybody who had come to the kindergarten, or a relative of any of Cynthia's friends.

"Is she human?" said Andrew, with a sudden shrewdness.

"No! That's what you forgot to ask!"

"An animal," I said reflectively.

"Is that a question? Sixteen questions!"

"No, it is not a question. I'm thinking. A dead animal."

"It's the deer," said Meg, who hadn't been playing.

"That's not fair! said Cynthia. "She's not playing!"

"What deer?" said Andrew.

I said, "Yesterday."

"The day before," said Cynthia. "Meg wasn't playing. Nobody got it."

"The deer on the truck," said Andrew.

"It was a lady deer, because it didn't have antlers, and it was an American and it was dead," Cynthia said.

Andrew said, "I think it's kind of morbid, being a dead deer."

"I got it," said Meg.

Cynthia said, "I think I know what morbid is. It's depressing."

Helena, an old silver-mining town, looked forlorn to us even in the morning sunlight. Then Bozeman and Billings, not forlorn in the slightest—energetic, strung-out towns, with miles of blinding tinsel fluttering over used-car lots. We got too tired and hot even to play Who Am I? These busy, prosaic cities reminded me of similar places in Ontario, and I thought about what was really waiting there—the great tombstone furniture of Roger and Caroline's dining room, the dinners for which I must iron the children's dresses and warn them about forks, and then the other table a hundred miles away, the jokes of my father's crew. The pleasures I had been thinking of—looking at the countryside or drinking a Coke in an old-fashioned drugstore with fans and a high, pressed-tin ceiling—would have to be snatched in between.

"Meg's asleep," Cynthia said. "She's so hot. She makes me hot in the same seat with her."

"I hope she isn't feverish," I said, not turning around.

What are we doing this for, I thought, and the answer came—to show off. To give Andrew's mother and my father the pleasure of seeing their grandchildren. That was our duty. But beyond that we wanted to show them something. What strenuous children we were, Andrew and I, what relentless seekers of approbation. It was as if at some point we had received an unforgettable, indigestible message—that we were far from satisfactory, and that the most commonplace success in life was probably beyond us. Roger dealt out such messages, of course—that was his style—but Andrew's mother, my own mother and father couldn't have meant to do so. All they meant to tell us was "Watch out. Get along." When I was in high school my father teased me that I was getting to think I was so smart I would never find a boyfriend. He would have forgotten that in a week. I never forgot it. Andrew and I didn't forget things. We took umbrage.

"I wish there was a beach," said Cynthia.

"There probably is one," Andrew said. "Right around the next curve."

"There isn't any curve," she said, sounding insulted.

"That's what I mean."

"I wish there was some more lemonade."

"I will just wave my magic wand and produce some," I said. "O.K., Cynthia? Would you rather have grape juice? Will I do a beach while I'm at it?"

She was silent, and soon I felt repentant. "Maybe in the next town there might be a pool," I said. I looked at the map. "In Miles City. Anyway, there'll be something cool to drink."

"How far is it?" Andrew said.

"Not so far," I said. "Thirty miles, about."

"In Miles City," said Cynthia, in the tones of an incantation, "there is a beautiful blue swimming pool for children, and a park with lovely trees."

Andrew said to me, "You could have started something."

But there was a pool. There was a park, too, though not quite the oasis of Cynthia's fantasy. Prairie trees—cottonwoods and poplars—worn grass, and a high wire fence around the pool. Within this fence, a wall, not yet completed, of cement blocks. Nobody was around. There were no shouts or splashes. Over the entrance I saw a sign that said the pool was closed every day from noon until two o'clock. It was then twenty-five after twelve.

Nevertheless I called out, "Is anybody there?" I though somebody must be around, because there was a small truck parked near the entrance. On the side of the truck were these words: "We have Brains, to fix your Drains. (We have Roto-Rooter too.)"

A girl came out, wearing a red lifeguard's shirt over her bathing suit. "Sorry, we're closed."

"We were just driving through," I said.

"We close every day from twelve until two. It's on the sign." She was eating a sandwich.

"I saw the sign," I said. "But this is the first water we've seen for so long, and the children are awfully hot, and I wondered if they could just dip in and out—just five minutes. We'd watch them."

A boy came into sight behind her. He was wearing jeans and a T-shirt with the words "Roto-Rooter" on it.

I was going to say that we were driving from British Columbia to Ontario, but I remembered that Canadian place names usually meant nothing to Americans. "We're driving right across the country," I said. "We haven't time to wait for the pool to open. We were just hoping the children could get cooled off."

Cynthia came running up barefoot behind me. "Mother. Mother, where is my bathing suit?" Then she stopped, sensing the serious adult negotiations. Meg was climbing out of the car—just wakened, with her top pulled up and her shorts pulled down, showing her pink stomach.

"Is it just those two?" the girl said.

"Just the two. We'll watch them."

"I can't let any adults in. If it's just the two, I guess I could watch them. I'm having my lunch." She said to Cynthia, "Do you want to come in the pool?"

"Yes, please," said Cynthia firmly.

Meg looked at the ground.

"Just a short time, because the pool is really closed," I said. "We appreciate this very much," I said to the girl.

"Well, I can eat my lunch out there, if it's just the two of them." She looked toward the car as if she thought I might try to spring some more children on her.

When I found Cynthia's bathing suit, she took it into the changing room. She would not permit anybody, even Meg, to see her naked. I changed Meg, who stood on the front seat of the car. She had a pink cotton bathing suit with straps that crossed and buttoned. There were ruffles across the seat.

"She *is* hot," I said. "But I don't think she's feverish."

I loved helping Meg to dress or undress, because her body still had the solid unself-consciousness, the sweet indifference, something of the milky smell, of a baby's body. Cynthia's body had long ago been pared down, shaped and altered, into Cynthia. We all liked to hug Meg, press and nuzzle her. Sometimes she would scowl and beat us off, and this forthright independence, this ferocious bashfulness, simply made her more appealing, more apt to be teased and tickled in the way of family love.

Andrew and I sat in the car with the windows open. I could hear a radio playing, and thought it must belong to the girl or her boyfriend. I was thirsty, and got out of the car to look for a concession stand, or perhaps a softdrink machine, somewhere in the park. I was wearing shorts, and the backs of my legs were slick with sweat. I saw a drinking fountain at the other side of the park and was walking toward it in a roundabout way, keeping to the shade of the trees. No place became real till you got out of the car. Dazed with the heat, with the sun on the blistered houses, the pavement, the burned grass, I walked slowly. I paid attention to a poor thin leaf, ground a Popsicle stick under the heel of my sandal, squinted at a trash can strapped to a tree that I would never see again.

Where are the children?

I turned around and moved quickly, not quite running, to a part of the fence beyond which the cement wall was not completed. I could see some of the pool. I saw Cynthia, standing about waist-deep in the water, fluttering her hands on the surface and discreetly watching something at the end of the pool, which I could not see. I thought by her pose, her discretion, the look on her face that she must be watching some byplay between the lifeguard and her boyfriend. I couldn't see Meg, but I thought she must be playing in the shallower water—both the shallow and the deep ends of the pool were out of my sight.

"Cynthia!" I had to call twice before she knew where my voice was coming from. "Cynthia! Where's Meg?"

It always seems to me, when I recall this scene, that Cynthia turns very gracefully toward me, then turns all around in the water—making me think of a ballerina on point—then spreads her arms in a gesture of the stage. "Dis-ap-peared!"

Cynthia was naturally graceful, and she did take dancing lessons, so these movements may have been as I have described. She did say "Disappeared," after looking all around the pool, but the strangely artificial style of speech and gesture, the lack of urgency, is more likely my invention. The fear I felt instantly when I couldn't see Meg—even while I was telling myself she must be in the shallower water—must have made Cynthia's movements seem unbearably slow and inappropriate to me, and the tone in which she could say "Disappeared" before the implications struck her (or was she covering, at once, some ever-ready guilt?) was heard by me as quite exquisitely, monstrously self-possessed.

I cried out for Andrew, and the lifeguard came into view. She was pointing toward the deep end of the pool, saying, "What's that?"

There, just within my view, a cluster of pink ruffles appeared, a bouquet, beneath the surface of the water. Why would a lifeguard stop and point, why would she ask what that was, why didn't she just dive into the water and swim to it? She didn't swim, she ran all the way around the edge of the pool. But by this time Andrew was over the fence. So many things seemed not quite plausible— Cynthia's behavior, then the lifeguard's—and now I had the impression that Andrew jumped with one bound over the fence, which seemed about seven feet high. He must have climbed it very quickly, getting a grip on the wire.

I could not jump or climb it, so I ran to the entrance, where there was a sort of latticed gate, locked. It was not very high, and I did pull myself over it. I ran through the cement corridors, through the disinfectant pool for your feet, and came out on the edge of the pool.

The drama was over.

Andrew had got to Meg first, and had pulled her out of the water. He just had to reach over and grab her, because she was swimming somehow, with her head underwater—she was moving toward the edge of the pool. He was carrying her now, and the lifeguard was trotting along behind. Cynthia had climbed out of the water and was running to meet them. The only person aloof from the situation was the boyfriend, who had stayed on the bench at the shallow end, drinking a milkshake. He smiled at me, and I thought that unfeeling of him, even though the danger was past. He may have meant it kindly. I noticed that he had not turned the radio off, just down.

Meg had not swallowed any water. She hadn't even scared herself. Her hair was plastered to her head and her eyes were wide open, golden with amazement.

"I was getting the comb," she said. "I didn't know it was deep."

Andrew said, "She was swimming! She was swimming by herself. I saw her bathing suit in the water and then I saw her swimming."

"She nearly drowned," Cynthia said. "Didn't she? Meg nearly drowned."

"I don't know how it could have happened," said the lifeguard. "One moment she was there, and the next she wasn't."

What had happened was that Meg had climbed out of the water at the shallow end and run along the edge of the pool toward the deep end. She saw a comb that somebody had dropped lying on the bottom. She crouched down and reached in to pick it up, quite deceived as to the depth of the water. She went over the edge and slipped into the pool, making such a light splash that nobody heard—not the lifeguard, who was kissing her boyfriend, nor Cynthia, who was watching them. That must have been the moment under the trees when I thought, Where are the children? It must have been the same moment. At that moment Meg was slipping, surprised, into the treacherously clear blue water.

"It's O.K.," I said to the lifeguard, who was nearly crying. "She can move pretty fast." (Though that wasn't what we usually said about Meg at all. We said she thought everything over and took her time.)

"You swam, Meg," said Cynthia, in a congratulatory way. (She told us about the kissing later.)

"I didn't know it was deep," Meg said. "I didn't drown."

We had lunch at a takeout place, eating hamburgers and fries at a picnic table not far from the highway. In my excitement I forgot to get Meg a plain hamburger, and had to scrape off the relish and mustard with plastic spoons, then wipe the meat with a paper napkin, before she would eat it. I took advantage of the trash can there to clean out the car. Then we resumed driving east, with the car windows open in front. Cynthia and Meg fell asleep in the backseat.

Andrew and I now talked quietly about what had happened. Suppose I hadn't had the impulse just at that moment to check on the children? Suppose we had gone uptown to get drinks, as we had thought of doing? How had Andrew got over the fence? Did he jump or climb? (He couldn't remember.) How had he reached Meg so quickly? And think of the lifeguard not watching. And Cynthia, taken up with the kissing. Not seeing anything else. Not seeing Meg drop over the edge.

Disappeared.

But she swam. She held her breath and came up swimming.

What a chain of lucky links.

That was all we spoke about—luck. But I was compelled to picture the opposite. At this moment we could have been filling out forms. Meg removed from us, Meg's body being prepared for shipment. To Vancouver—where we had never noticed such a thing as a graveyard—or to Ontario? The scribbled drawings she had made this morning would be still in the backseat of the car. How could this be borne all at once, how did people bear it? The plump, sweet shoulders and hands and feet, the fine brown hair, the rather satisfied, secretive expression—all exactly the same as when she had been alive. The most ordinary tragedy. A child drowned in a swimming pool at noon on a sunny day. Things tidied up quickly. The pool open as usual at two o'clock. The lifeguard is a bit shaken up and gets the afternoon off. She drives away with her boyfriend in the Roto-Rooter truck. The body sealed away in some kind of shipping coffin. Sedatives, phone calls, arrangements. Such a sudden vacancy, a blind sinking and shifting. Waking up groggy from the pills, thinking for a moment it wasn't true. Thinking if only we hadn't stopped, if only we hadn't taken this route, if only they hadn't let us use the pool. Probably no one would ever have known about the comb.

There's something trashy about this kind of imagining, isn't there? Something shameful. Laying your finger on the wire to get the safe shock, feeling a bit of what it's like, then pulling back. I believed that Andrew was more scrupulous than I about such things, and that at this moment he was really trying to think about something else.

When I stood apart from my parents at Steve Gauley's funeral and watched them, and had this new, unpleasant feeling about them, I thought that I was understanding something about them for the first time. It was a deadly serious thing. I was understanding that they were implicated. Their big, stiff, dressed-up bodies did not stand between me and sudden death, or any kind of death. They gave consent. So it seemed. They gave consent to the death of children and to my death not by anything they said or thought but by the very fact that they had made children—they had made me. They had made me, and for that reason my death—however grieved they were, however they carried on—would seem to them anything but impossible or unnatural. This was a fact, and even then I knew they were not to blame.

But I did blame them. I charged them with effrontery, hypocrisy. And not just on my own behalf. On Steve Gauley's behalf, and on behalf of all children, who knew that by rights they should have sprung up free, to live a new, superior kind of life, not to be caught in the snares of grownups, with their sex and funerals.

Steve Gauley drowned, people said, because he was next thing to an orphan and was let run free. If he had been warned enough and given chores to do and kept in check, he wouldn't have fallen from an untrustworthy tree branch into a a spring pond, a full gravel pit near the river—he wouldn't have drowned. He was neglected, he was free, so he drowned. And his father took it as an accident, such as might happen to a dog. He didn't have a good suit for the funeral, and he didn't bow his head for the prayers. But he was the only grownup that I let off the hook. He was the only one I didn't see giving consent. He couldn't prevent anything, but he wasn't implicated in anything, either—not like the others, saying the Lord's Prayer in their unnaturally weighted voices, oozing religion and dishonor.

At Glendive, not far from the North Dakota border, we had a choice—either to continue on the Interstate or head northeast, toward Williston, taking Route 16, then some secondary roads that would get us back to Highway 2.

We agreed that the Interstate would be faster, and that it was important for us not to spend too much time—that is, money—on the road. Nevertheless, we decided to cut back to Highway 2.

"I just like the idea of it better," I said.

Andrew said, "That's because it's what we planned to do in the beginning."

"We missed seeing Kalispell and Havre. And Wolf Point. I like the names."

"We'll see them on the way back."

Andrew's saying "on the way back" in such an easy tone was a surprising pleasure to me. Of course, I had believed that we would be coming back, with our car and our lives and our family intact, having covered all that distance, having dealt somehow with those loyalties and problems, held ourselves up for inspection in such a foolhardy way. But it was a relief to hear him say it.

"What I can't get over," said Andrew, "is how you got the signal. It's got to be some kind of extra sense that mothers have."

Partly I wanted to believe that, to bask in my extra sense. Partly I wanted to warn him—to warn everybody—never to count on it.

"What I can't understand," I said, "is how you got over that fence."

"Neither can I."

So we went on, with the two in the backseat trusting us, because of no choice, and we ourselves trusting to be forgiven in time what first had to be seen and condemned by those children: whatever was flippant, arbitrary, careless, callous—all our natural, and particular, mistakes.

Questions for Discussion

1. What is visually memorable about the opening images of the story? Why is it ultimately significant that the narrator's father is the one carrying the drowned boy?

2. Characterize Steve Gauley. What is his relationship with the narrator like?

3. Describe the narrator's reaction to the funeral. What does she dislike about the adults? To what extent do you sympathize with her response?

4. This is a story with two distinct "halves" or sections. What connects them? How effective is the connection? What does the car trip teach us about the characters? Evaluate the structure of the story.

5. What does the story suggest about "accident" and "responsibility" in connection with death? How do the drowning of Steve Gauley and the near-drowning of the narrator's daughter change the narrator's attitude toward accident and responsibility?

Suggestions for Writing

1. Write an essay that analyzes the connections between the death of Steve Gauley and the near-death of the narrator's daughter, especially as these connections are expressed and/or suggested by the narrator.

2. The narrator defends Steve Gauley's father, or at least sympathizes with his perspective. To what extent do you agree with her? Write about this question in your journal.

3. Write an essay about the roles of the fathers in this story: the narrator's father, Steve Gauley's father, and the narrator's husband.

4. Write a story that springs from memories of an unusual childhood acquaintance or friend.

In The White Night

ANN   BEATTIE

"**D**on't think about a cow," Matt Brinkley said. "Don't think about a river, don't think about a car, don't think about snow. . . ."

Matt was standing in the doorway, hollering after his guests. His wife, Gaye, gripped his arm and tried to tug him back into the house. The party was over. Carol and Vernon turned to wave good-bye, calling back their thanks, whispering to each other to be careful. The steps were slick with snow; an icy snow had been falling for hours, frozen granules mixed in with lighter stuff, and the instant they moved out from under the protection of the Brinkleys' porch the cold froze the smiles on their faces. The swirls of snow blowing against Carol's skin reminded her—an odd thing to remember on a night like this—of the way sand blew up at the beach, and the scratchy pain it caused.

"Don't think about an apple!" Matt hollered. Vernon turned his head, but he was left smiling at a closed door.

In the small, bright areas under the streetlights, there seemed for a second to be some logic to all the swirling snow. If time itself could only freeze, the snowflakes could become the lacy filigree of a valentine. Carol frowned. Why had Matt conjured up the image of an apple? Now she saw an apple where there was no apple, suspended in midair, transforming the scene in front of her into a silly surrealist painting.

It was going to snow all night. They had heard that on the radio, driving to the Brinkleys'. The Don't-Think-About-Whatever game had started as a joke, something long in the telling and startling to Vernon, to judge by his expression as Matt went on and on. When Carol crossed the room near midnight to tell Vernon that they should leave, Matt had quickly whispered the rest of his joke or story—whatever he was saying—into Vernon's ear, all in a rush. They looked like two children, the one whispering madly and the other with his head bent, but something about the inclination of Vernon's head let you know that if you bent low enough to see, there would be a big, wide grin on his face. Vernon and Carol's daughter, Sharon, and Matt and Gaye's daughter, Becky, had sat side by side, or kneecap to kneecap, and whispered that way when they were children—a privacy so rushed that it obliterated anything else. Carol, remembering that scene now, could not think of what passed between Sharon and Becky without thinking of sexual intimacy. Becky, it turned out, had given the Brinkleys a lot of trouble. She had run away from home when she was thirteen, and, in a family-counseling session years later, her parents found out that she had had an abortion at fifteen. More recently, she had flunked out of college. Now she was working in a bank in Boston and taking a night-school course in poetry. Poetry or pottery? The apple that reappeared as the windshield wipers slushed snow off the glass metamorphosed for Carol into a red bowl, then again became an apple, which grew rounder as the car came to a stop at the intersection.

She had been weary all day. Anxiety always made her tired. She knew the party would be small (the Brinkleys' friend Mr. Graham had just had his book accepted for publication, and of course much of the evening would be spent talking about that); she had feared that it was going to be a strain for all of them. The Brinkleys had just returned from the Midwest, where they had gone for Gaye's father's funeral. It didn't seem a time to carry through with plans for a party. Carol imagined that not canceling it had been Matt's idea, not Gaye's. She turned toward Vernon now and asked how the Brinkleys had seemed to him. Fine, he said at once. Before he spoke, she knew how he would answer. If people did not argue in front of their friends, they were not having problems; if they did not stumble into walls, they were not drunk. Vernon tried hard to think positively, but he was never impervious to real pain. His reflex was to turn aside something serious with a joke, but he was just as quick to wipe the smile off his face and suddenly put his arm around a person's shoulder. Unlike Matt, he was a warm person, but when people unexpectedly showed him affection it embarrassed him. The same counselor the Brinkleys had seen had told Carol—Vernon refused to see the man, and she found that she did not want to continue without him—that it was possible that Vernon felt uncomfortable with expressions of kindness because he blamed himself for Sharon's death: he couldn't save her, and when people were kind to him now he felt it was undeserved. But Vernon was the last person who should be punished. She remembered him in the hospital, pretending to misunderstand Sharon when she asked for her barrette, on her bedside table, and picking it up and clipping the little yellow duck into the hair above his own ear. He kept trying to tickle a smile out of her—touching some stuffed animal's button nose to the tip of her nose and then tapping it on her earlobe. At the moment when Sharon died, Vernon had been sitting on her bed (Carol was backed up against the door, for some reason), surrounded by a battlefield of pastel animals.

They passed safely through the last intersection before their house. The car didn't skid until they turned onto their street. Carol's heart thumped hard, once, in the second when she felt the car becoming light, but they came out of the skid easily. He had been driving carefully, and she said nothing, wanting to appear casual about the moment. She asked if Matt had mentioned Becky. No, Vernon said, and he hadn't wanted to bring up a sore subject.

Gaye and Matt had been married for twenty-five years; Carol and Vernon had been married twenty-two. Sometimes Vernon said, quite sincerely, that Matt and Gaye were their alter egos, who absorbed and enacted crises, saving the two of them from having to experience such chaos. It frightened Carol to think that some part of him believed that. Who could really believe that there was some way to find protection in this world—or someone who could offer it? What happened happened at random, and one horrible thing hardly precluded the possibility of others happening next. There had been that fancy internist who hospitalized Vernon later in the same spring when Sharon died, and who looked up at him while drawing blood and observed almost offhandedly that it would be an unbearable irony if Vernon also had leukemia. When the test results came back, they showed that Vernon had mononucleosis. There was the time when the Christmas tree caught fire, and she rushed toward the flames, clapping her hands like cymbals, and Vernon pulled her away just in time, before the whole tree became a torch, and she with it. When Hobo, their dog, had to be put to sleep, during their vacation in Maine, that awful woman veterinarian, with her cold green eyes, issued the casual death sentence with one manicured hand on the quivering dog's fur and called him "Bobo," as though their dog were like some circus clown.

"Are you crying?" Vernon said. They were inside their house now, in the hallway, and he had just turned toward her, holding out a pink padded coat hanger.

"No," she said. "The wind out there is fierce." She slipped her jacket onto the hanger he held out and went into the downstairs bathroom, where she buried her face in a towel. In time, she looked at herself in the mirror. She had pressed the towel hard against her eyes, and for a few seconds she had to blink herself into focus. She was reminded of the kind of camera they had had when Sharon was young. There were two images when you looked through the finder, and you had to make the adjustment yourself so that one superimposed itself upon the other and the figure suddenly leaped into clarity. She patted the towel to her eyes again and held her breath. If she couldn't stop crying, Vernon would make love to her. When she was very sad, he sensed that his instinctive optimism wouldn't work; he became tongue-tied, and when he couldn't talk he would reach for her. Through the years, he had knocked over wineglasses shooting his hand across the table to grab hers. She had found herself suddenly hugged from behind in the bathroom; he would even follow her in there if he suspected that she was going to cry—walk in to grab her without even having bothered to knock.

She opened the door now and turned toward the hall staircase, and then realized—felt it before she saw it, really—that the light was on in the living room.

Vernon lay stretched out on the sofa, with his legs crossed; one foot was planted on the floor and his top foot dangled in the air. Even when he was exhausted, he was always careful not to let his shoes touch the sofa. He was very tall, and couldn't stretch out on the sofa without resting his head on the arm. For some reason, he had not hung up her jacket. It was spread like a tent over his head and shoulders, rising and falling with his breathing. She stood still long enough to be sure that he was really asleep, and then came into the room. The sofa was too narrow to curl up on with him. She didn't want to wake him. Neither did she want to go to bed alone. She went back to the hall closet and took out his overcoat—the long, elegant camel's-hair coat he had not worn tonight because he thought it might snow. She slipped off her shoes and went quietly over to where he lay and stretched out on the floor beside the sofa, pulling the big blanket of the coat up high, until the collar touched her lips. Then she drew her legs up into the warmth.

Such odd things happened. Very few days were like the ones before. Here they were, in their own house with four bedrooms, ready to sleep in this peculiar double-decker fashion, in the largest, coldest room of all. What would anyone think?

She knew the answer to that question, of course. A person who didn't know them would mistake this for a drunken collapse, but anyone who was a friend would understand exactly. In time, each of the two of them had learned to stop passing judgment on how they coped with the inevitable sadness that set in, always unexpectedly but so real that it was met with the instant acceptance one gave to a snowfall. In the white night world outside, their daughter might be drifting past like an angel, and she would see this tableau, for the second that she hovered, as a necessary small adjustment.

Questions for Discussion

1. What thoughts and emotions does Matt Brinkley's game of "Don't think about . . ." trigger in Carol?

2. Characterize Vernon. What kind of person is he? What details of his personality and behavior are most memorable?

3. Characterize the way Carol and Vernon grieve. To what extent does the story suggest that no act of grief is *the* appropriate way to grieve?

4. How does Beattie's use of imagery—the snow, the apple, the white night, the daughter-as-angel—express the emotion of the story? Explain your own emotional response to these or other images that the story creates in your mind.

Suggestions for Writing

1. Write an essay about Beattie's use of imagery in this story. You may want to begin by listing images that seem particularly significant, memorable, or vivid.

2. Take the last three words of the story—"necessary small adjustments"— and write an essay that explores the way Carol and Vernon make such adjustments throughout the story.

3. Write a story involving some aspect of grief.

Yoneko's Earthquake

HISAYE   YAMAMOTO

Y oneko Hosoume became a free-thinker on the night of March 10, 1933, only a few months after her first actual recognition of God. Ten years old at the time, of course she had heard rumors about God all along, long before Marpo came. Her cousins who lived in the city were all Christians, living as they did right next door to a Baptist church exclusively for Japanese people. These city cousins, of whom there were several, had been baptized en masse and were very proud of their condition. Yoneko was impressed when she heard of this and thereafter was given to referring to them as "my cousins, the Christians." She, too, yearned at times after Christianity, but she realized the absurdity of her whim, seeing that there was no Baptist church for Japanese in the rural community she lived in. Such a church would have been impractical, moreover, since Yoneko, her father, her mother, and her little brother Seigo were the only Japanese thereabouts. They were the only ones, too, whose agriculture was so diverse as to include blackberries, cabbages, rhubarb, potatoes, cucumbers, onions, and canteloupes. The rest of the countryside there was like one vast orange grove.

Yoneko had entered her cousins' church once, but she could not recall the sacred occasion without mortification. It had been one day when the cousins had taken her and Seigo along with them to Sunday school. The church was a narrow wooden building, mysterious-looking because of its unusual bluish-gray paint and its steeple, but the basement schoolroom inside had been disappointingly ordinary, with desks, a blackboard, and erasers. They had all sung "Let Us Gather at the River" in Japanese. This goes:

> *Mamonaku kanata no*
> *Nagare no soba de*
> *Tanoshiku ai-masho*
> *Mata tomodachi to*
>
> *Mamonaku ai-masho*
> *Kirei-na, kirei-na kawa de*
> *Tanoshiku ai-masho*
> *Mata tomodachi to.*

Yoneko had not known the words at all, but always clever in such situations, she had opened her mouth and grimaced nonchalantly to the rhythm. What with everyone else singing at the top of his lungs, no one had noticed that she was not making a peep. Then everyone had sat down again and the man had suggested, "Let us pray." Her cousins and the rest had promptly curled their arms on the desks to make nests for their heads, and Yoneko had done the same. But not Seigo. Because when the room had become so still that one was aware of the breathing, the creaking, and the chittering in the trees outside, Seigo, sitting with her, had suddenly flung his arm around her neck and said with concern, "Sis, what are you crying for? Don't cry." Even the man had laughed and Yoneko had been terribly ashamed that Seigo should thus disclose them to be interlopers. She had pinched him fiercely and he had begun to cry, so she had had to drag him outside, which was a fortunate move, because he had immediately wet his pants. But he had been only three then, so it was not very fair to expect dignity of him.

So it remained for Marpo to bring the word of God to Yoneko—Marpo with the face like brown leather, the thin mustache like Edmund Lowe's, and the rare, breathtaking smile like white gold. Marpo, who was twenty-seven years old, was a Filipino and his last name was lovely, something like Humming Wing, but no one ever ascertained the spelling of it. He ate principally rice, just as though he were Japanese, but he never sat down to the Hosoume table, because he lived in the bunkhouse out by the barn and cooked on his own kerosene stove. Once Yoneko read somewhere that Filipinos trapped wild dogs, starved them for a time, then, feeding them mountains of rice, killed them at the peak of their bloatedness, thus insuring themselves meat ready to roast, stuffing and all, without further ado. This, the book said, was considered a delicacy. Unable to hide her disgust and her fascination, Yoneko went straightway to Marpo and asked, "Marpo, is it true that you eat dogs?", and he, flashing that smile, answered, "Don't be funny, honey!" This caused her no end of amusement, because it was a poem, and she completely forgot about the wild dogs.

Well, there seemed to be nothing Marpo could not do. Mr. Hosoume said Marpo was the best hired man he had ever had, and he said this often, because it was an irrefutable fact among Japanese in general that Filipinos in general were an indolent lot. Mr. Hosoume ascribed Marpo's industry to his having grown up in Hawaii, where there is known to be considerable Japanese influence. Marpo had gone to a missionary school there and he owned a Bible given him by one of his teachers. This had black leather covers that gave as easily as cloth, golden edges, and a slim purple ribbon for a marker. He always kept it on the little table by his bunk, which was not a bed with springs but a low, three-plank shelf with a mattress only. On the first page of the book, which was stiff and black, his teacher had written in large swirls of white ink, "As we draw near to God, He will draw near to us."

What, for instance, could Marpo do? Why, it would take an entire, leisurely evening to go into his accomplishments adequately, because there was not only Marpo the Christian and Marpo the best hired man, but Marpo the athlete, Marpo the musician (both instrumental and vocal), Marpo the artist, and Marpo the radio technician:

(1) As an athlete, Marpo owned a special pair of black shoes, equipped with sharp nails on the soles, which he kept in shape with the regular application of neatsfoot oil. Putting these on, he would dash down the dirt road to the highway, a distance of perhaps half a mile, and back again. When he first came to work for the Hosoumes, he undertook this sprint every evening before he went to get his supper, but as time went on he referred to these shoes less and less and in the

end, when he left, he had not touched them for months. He also owned a muscle-builder sent him by Charles Atlas which, despite his unassuming size, he could stretch the length of his outspread arms; his teeth gritted then and his whole body became temporarily victim to a jerky vibration. (2) As an artist, Marpo painted larger-than-life water colors of his favorite movie stars, all of whom were women and all of whom were blonde, like Ann Harding and Jean Harlow, and tacked them up on his walls. He also made for Yoneko a folding contraption of wood holding two pencils, one with lead and one without, with which she, too, could obtain double-sized likenesses of any picture she wished. It was a fragile instrument, however, and Seigo splintered it to pieces one day when Yoneko was away at school. He claimed he was only trying to copy Boob McNutt from the funny paper when it failed. (3) As a musician, Marpo owned a violin for which he had paid over one hundred dollars. He kept this in a case whose lining was red velvet, first wrapping it gently in a brilliant red silk scarf. This scarf, which weighed nothing, he tucked under his chin when he played, gathering it up delicately by the center and flicking it once to unfurl it—a gesture Yoneko prized. In addition to this, Marpo was a singer, with a soft tenor which came out in professional quavers and rolled r's when he applied a slight pressure to his Adam's apple with thumb and forefinger. His violin and vocal repertoire consisted of the same numbers, mostly hymns and Irish folk airs. He was especially addicted to "The Rose of Tralee" and the "Londonderry Air." (4) Finally, as a radio technician who had spent two previous winters at a specialists' school in the city, Marpo had put together a bulky table-size radio which brought in equal proportions of static and entertainment. He never got around to building a cabinet to house it and its innards of metal and glass remained public throughout its lifetime. This was just as well, for not a week passed without Marpo's deciding to solder one bit or another. Yoneko and Seigo became a part of the great listening audience with such fidelity that Mr. Hosoume began remarking the fact that they dwelt more with Marpo than with their own parents. He eventually took a serious view of the matter and bought the naked radio from Marpo, who thereupon put away his radio manuals and his soldering iron in the bottom of his steamer trunk and divided more time among his other interests.

However, Marpo's versatility was not revealed, as it is here, in a lump. Yoneko uncovered it fragment by fragment every day, by dint of unabashed questions, explorations among his possessions, and even silent observation, although this last was rare. In fact, she and Seigo visited with Marpo at least once a day and both of them regularly came away amazed with their findings. The most surprising thing was that Marpo was, after all this, a rather shy young man meek to the point of speechlessness in the presence of Mr. and Mrs. Hosoume. With Yoneko and Seigo, he was somewhat more self-confident and at ease.

It is not remembered now just how Yoneko and Marpo came to open their protracted discussion on religion. It is sufficient here to note that Yoneko was an ideal apostle, adoring Jesus, desiring Heaven and fearing Hell. Once Marpo had enlightened her on these basics, Yoneko never questioned their truth. The questions she put up to him, therefore, sought neither proof of her exegeses nor balm for her doubts, but simply additional color to round out her mental images. For example, who did Marpo suppose was God's favorite movie star? Or, what sound did Jesus' laughter have (it must be like music, she added, nodding sagely, answering herself to her own satisfaction), and did Marpo suppose that God's sense of humor would have appreciated the delicious chant she had learned from friends at school today:

> *There ain't no bugs on us,*
> *There ain't no bugs on us,*
> *There may be bugs on the rest of you mugs,*
> *But there ain't no bugs on us?*

Or did Marpo believe Jesus to have been exempt from stinging eyes when he shampooed that long, naturally wavy hair of his?

To shake such faith, there would have been required a most monstrous upheaval of some sort, and it might be said that this is just what happened. For early on the evening of March 10, 1933, a little after five o'clock this was, as Mrs. Hosoume was getting supper, as Marpo was finishing up in the fields alone because Mr. Hosoume had gone to order some chicken fertilizer, and as Yoneko and Seigo were listening to Skippy, a tremendous roar came out of nowhere and the Hosoume house began shuddering violently as though some giant had seized it in his two hands and was giving it a good shaking. Mrs. Hosoume, who remembered similar, although milder experiences from her childhood in Japan, screamed, *"Jishin, jishin!"* before she ran and grabbed Yoneko and Seigo each by a hand and dragged them outside with her. She took them as far as the middle of the rhubarb patch near the house, and there they all crouched, pressed together, watching the world about them rock and sway. In a few minutes, Marpo, stumbling in from the fields, joined them, saying, "Earthquake, earthquake!" and he gathered them all in his arms, as much to protect them as to support himself.

Mr. Hosoume came home later that evening in a stranger's car, with another stranger driving the family Reo. Pallid, trembling, his eyes wildly staring, he could have been mistaken for a drunkard, except that he was famous as a teetotaler. It seemed that he had been on the way home when the first jolt came, that the old green Reo had been kissed by a broken live wire dangling from a suddenly leaning pole. Mr. Hosoume, knowing that the end had come by electrocution, had begun to writhe and kick and this had been his salvation. His hands had flown from the wheel, the car had swerved into a ditch, freeing itself from the sputtering wire. Later it was found that he was left permanently inhibited about driving automobiles and permanently incapable of considering electricity with calmness. He spent the larger part of his later life weakly, wandering about the house or fields and lying down frequently to rest because of splitting headaches and sudden dizzy spells.

So it was Marpo who went back into the house as Yoneko screamed, "No, Marpo, no!" and brought out the Hosoumes' kerosene stove, the food, the blankets, while Mr. Hosoume huddled on the ground near his family.

The earth trembled for days afterwards. The Hosoumes and Marpo Humming Wing lived during that time on a natural patch of Bermuda grass between the house and the rhubarb patch, remembering to take three meals a day and retire at night. Marpo ventured inside the house many times despite Yoneko's protests and reported the damage slight: a few dishes had been broken; a gallon jug of mayonnaise had fallen from the top pantry shelf and splattered the kitchen floor with yellow blobs and pieces of glass.

Yoneko was in constant terror during this experience. Immediately on learning what all the commotion was about, she began praying to God to end this violence. She entreated God, flattered Him, wheedled Him, commanded Him, but He did not listen to her at all—inexorably, the earth went on rumbling. After three solid hours of silent, desperate prayer, without any results whatsoever, Yonkeo began to suspect that God was either powerless, callous, downright cruel, or nonexistent. In the murky night, under a strange moon wearing a pale ring of light, she decided upon the last as the most plausible theory. "Ha," was one of the things she said tremulously to Marpo, when she was not begging him to stay out of the house, "you and your God!"

The others soon oriented themselves to the catastrophe with philosophy, saying how fortunate they were to live in the country where the peril was less than in the city and going so far as to regard the period as a sort of vacation from work, with their enforced alfresco existence a sort of camping trip. They tried to bring Yoneko to partake of this pleasant outlook, but she, shivering with each new quiver, looked on them as dreamers who refused to see things as they really were. Indeed, Yoneko's reaction was so notable that the Hosoume household thereafter spoke of the event as "Yoneko's earthquake."

After the earth subsided and the mayonnaise was mopped off the kitchen floor, life returned to normal, except that Mr. Hosoume stayed at home most of the time. Sometimes if he had a relatively painless day, he would have supper on the stove when Mrs. Hosoume came in from the fields. Mrs. Hosoume and Marpo did all the field labor now, except on certain overwhelming days when several Mexicans were hired to assist them. Marpo did most of the driving, too, and it was now he and Mrs. Hosoume who went into town on the weekly trip for groceries. In fact Marpo became indispensable and both Mr. and Mrs. Hosoume often told each other how grateful they were for Marpo.

When summer vacation began and Yoneko stayed at home, too, she found the new arrangement rather inconvenient. Her father's presence cramped her style: for instance, once when her friends came over and it was decided to make fudge, he would not permit them, saying fudge used too much sugar and that sugar was not a plaything; once when they were playing paper dolls, he came along and stuck his finger up his nose and pretended he was going to rub some snot off onto the dolls. Things like that. So on some days, she was very much annoyed with her father.

Therefore when her mother came home breathless from the fields one day and pushed a ring at her, a gold-colored ring with a tiny glasslike stone in it, saying, "Look, Yoneko, I'm going to give you this ring. If your father asks where you got it, say you found it on the street." Yoneko was perplexed but delighted both by the unexpected gift and the chance to have some secret revenge on her father, and she said, certainly, she was willing to comply with her mother's request. Her mother went back to the fields then and Yoneko put the pretty ring on her middle finger, taking up the loose space with a bit of newspaper. It was similar to the rings found occasionally in boxes of Crackerjack, except that it appeared a bit more substantial.

Mr. Hosoume never asked about the ring; in fact, he never noticed she was wearing one. Yoneko thought he was about to, once, but he only reproved her for the flamingo nail polish she was wearing, which she had applied from a vial brought over by Yvonne Fournier, the French girl two orange groves away. "You look like a Filipino," Mr. Hosoume said sternly, for it was another irrefutable fact among Japanese in general that Filipinos in general were a gaudy lot. Mrs. Hosoume immediately came to her defense, saying that in Japan, if she remembered correctly, young girls did the same thing. In fact she remembered having gone to elaborate lengths to tint her fingernails: she used to gather, she said, the petals of the red *tsubobana* or the purple *kogane* (which grows on the underside of stones), grind them well, mix them with some alum powder, then cook the mixture and leave it to stand overnight in an envelope of either persimmon or taro leaves (both very strong leaves). The second night, just before going to bed, she used to obtain threads by ripping a palm leaf (because real thread was dear) and tightly bind the paste to her fingernails under shields of persimmon or taro leaves. She would be helpless for the night, the fingertips bound so well that they were alternately numb or aching; but she would grit her teeth and tell herself that the discomfort indicated the success of the operation. In the morning, finally releasing her fingers, she would find the nails shining with a translucent red-orange color.

Yoneko was fascinated, because she usually thought of her parents as having been adults all their lives. She thought that her mother must have been a beautiful child, with or without bright fingernails, because, though surely past thirty, she was even yet a beautiful person. When she herself was younger, she remembered she had at times been so struck with her mother's appearance that she had dropped to her knees and mutely clasped her mother's legs in her arms. She had left off this habit as she learned to control her emotions, because at such times her mother had usually walked away, saying, "My, what a clinging child you are. You've got to learn to be a little more independent." She also remembered she had once heard someone comparing her mother to "a dewy, half-opened rosebud."

Mr. Hosoume, however, was irritated. "That's no excuse for Yoneko to begin using paint on her fingernails," he said. "She's only ten."

"Her Japanese age is eleven, and we weren't much older," Mrs. Hosoume said.

"Look," Mr. Hosoume said, "if you're going to contradict every piece of advice I give the children, they'll end up disobeying us both and doing what they very well please. Just because I'm ill just now is no reason for them to start being disrespectful."

"When have I ever contradicted you before?" Mrs. Hosoume said.

"Countless times," Mr. Hosoume said.

"Name one instance," Mrs. Hosoume said.

Certainly there had been times, but Mr. Hosoume could not happen to mention the one requested instance on the spot and he became quite angry. "That's quite enough of your insolence," he said. Since he was speaking in

Japanese, his exact accusation was that she was *nama-iki,* which is a shade more revolting than being merely insolent.

"*Nama-iki, nama-iki?*" said Mrs. Hosoume. "How dare you? I'll not have anyone calling me *nama-iki!*"

At that, Mr. Hosoume went up to where his wife was ironing and slapped her smartly on the face. It was the first time he had ever laid hands on her. Mrs. Hosoume was immobile for an instant, but she resumed her ironing as though nothing had happened, although she glanced over at Marpo, who happened to be in the room reading a newspaper. Yoneko and Seigo forgot they were listening to the radio and stared at their parents, thunderstruck.

"Hit me again," said Mrs. Hosoume quietly, as she ironed. "Hit me all you wish."

Mr. Hosoume was apparently about to, but Marpo stepped up and put his hand on Mr. Hosoume's shoulder. "The children are here," said Marpo, "the children."

"Mind your own business," said Mr. Hosoume in broken English. "Get out of here!"

Marpo left, and that was about all. Mrs. Hosoume went on ironing, Yoneko and Seigo turned back to the radio, and Mr. Hosoume muttered that Marpo was beginning to forget his place. Now that he thought of it, he said, Marpo had been increasingly impudent towards him since his illness. He said just because he was temporarily an invalid was no reason for Marpo to start being disrespectful. He added that Marpo had better watch his step or that he might find himself jobless one of these fine days.

And something of the sort must have happened. Marpo was here one day and gone the next, without even saying good-bye to Yoneko and Seigo. That was also the day the Hosoume family went to the city on a weekday afternoon, which was most unusual. Mr. Hosoume, who now avoided driving as much as possible, handled the cumbersome Reo as though it were a nervous stallion, sitting on the edge of the seat and hugging the steering wheel. He drove very fast and about halfway to the city struck a beautiful collie which had dashed out barking from someone's yard. The car jerked with the impact, but Mr. Hosoume drove right on and Yoneko, wanting suddenly to vomit, looked back and saw the collie lying very still at the side of the road.

When they arrived at the Japanese hospital, which was their destination, Mr. Hosoume cautioned Yoneko and Seigo to be exemplary children and wait patiently in the car. It seemed hours before he and Mrs. Hosoume returned, she walking with very small, slow steps and he assisting her. When Mrs. Hosoume got in the car, she leaned back and closed her eyes. Yoneko inquired as to the source of her distress, for she was obviously in pain, but she only answered that she was feeling a little under the weather and that the doctor had administered some necessarily astringent treatment. At that Mr. Hosoume turned around and advised Yoneko and Seigo that they must tell no one of coming to the city on a weekday afternoon, absolutely no one, and Yoneko and Seigo readily assented. On the way home they passed the place of the encounter with the collie, and Yoneko looked up and down the stretch of road but the dog was nowhere to be seen.

Not long after that the Hosoumes got a new hired hand, an old Japanese man who wore his gray hair in a military cut and who, unlike Marpo, had no particular interests outside working, eating, sleeping, and playing an occasional game of *goh* with Mr. Hosoume. Before he came Yoneko and Seigo played sometimes in the empty bunkhouse and recalled Marpo's various charms together. Privately, Yoneko was wounded more than she would admit even to herself that Marpo should have subjected her to such an abrupt desertion. Whenever her indignation became too great to endure gracefully, she would console herself by telling Seigo that, after all, Marpo was a mere Filipino, an eater of wild dogs.

Seigo never knew about the disappointing new hired man, because he suddenly died in the night. He and Yoneko had spent the hot morning in the nearest orange grove, she driving him to distraction by repeating certain words he could not bear to hear: she had called him Serge, a name she had read somewhere, instead of Seigo; and she had chanted off the name of the tires they were rolling around like hoops as Goodrich Silver-TO-town, Goodrich Silver-TO-town, instead of Goodrich Silvertown. This had enraged him, and he had chased her around the trees most of the morning. Finally she had taunted him from several trees away by singing "You're a Yellow-streaked Coward," which was one of several small songs she had composed. Seigo had suddenly grinned and shouted, "Sure!" and walked off leaving her, as he intended, with a sense of emptiness. In the afternoon they had perspired and followed the potato-digging machine and the Mexican workers—both hired for the day—around the field, delighting in unearthing marble-sized, smooth-skinned potatoes that both the machine and the men had missed. Then in the middle of the night Seigo began crying, complaining of a stomach ache. Mrs. Hosoume felt his head and sent her husband for the doctor, who smiled and said Seigo would be fine in the morning. He said it was doubtless the combination of green oranges, raw potatoes, and the July heat. But as soon as the doctor left, Seigo fell into a coma and a drop of red blood stood out on his underlip, where he had evidently bit it. Mr. Hosoume again fetched the doctor, who was this time very grave and wagged his head, saying several times, "It looks very bad." So Seigo died at the age of five.

Mrs. Hosoume was inconsolable and had swollen eyes in the morning for weeks afterwards. She now insisted on visiting the city relatives each Sunday, so that she could attend church services with them. One Sunday she stood up and accepted Christ. It was through accompanying her mother to many of these services that Yoneko finally learned the Japanese words to "Let Us Gather at the River." Mrs. Hosoume also did not seem interested in discussing anything but God and Seigo. She was especially fond of reminding visitors how adorable Seigo had been as an infant, how she had been unable to refrain from dressing him as a little girl and fixing his hair in bangs until he was two. Mr. Hosoume was very gentle with her and when Yoneko accidentally caused her to giggle once, he nodded and said, "Yes, that's right, Yoneko, we must make your mother laugh and forget about Seigo." Yoneko herself did not think about Seigo at all. Whenever the thought of Seigo crossed her mind, she instantly began composing a new song, and this worked very well.

One evening, when the new hired man had been with them awhile, Yoneko was helping her mother with the dishes when she found herself being examined with such peculiarly intent eyes that, with a start of guilt, she began searching in her mind for a possible crime she had lately committed. But Mrs. Hosoume only said, "Never kill a person, Yoneko, because if you do, God will take from you someone you love."

"Oh, that," said Yoneko quickly, "I don't believe in that, I don't believe in God." And her words tumbling pell-mell over one another, she went on eagerly to explain a few of her reasons why. If she neglected to mention the test she had given God during the earthquake, it was probably because she was a little upset. She had believed for a moment that her mother was going to ask about the ring (which, alas, she had lost already, somewhere in the flumes along the canteloupe patch).

Questions for Discussion

1. At first glance the events of the story—the visit to church, Marpo's arrival, Mr. Hosoume's physical abuse of his wife, the earthquake, the death of the collie, the death of Seigo—may seem unrelated. In terms of their impact on Yoneko, however, to what extent are the events similar? In what other ways are they similar?

2. How is the "reporting" done by the narrator influenced by the consciousness of the young girl Yoneko? You may want to isolate one example, such as the list of Marpo's achievements.

3. How do the earthquake and the other occurrences influence Yoneko's attitude toward God?

4. How sympathetic are you to Yoneko's attitude?

5. How does Marpo deflate the racist ideas of Mr. Hosoume, which Yoneko repeats to him? Why does Marpo leave? What is the role of his character in the story, from your viewpoint?

Suggestions for Writing

1. "This is a sacrilegious story, an attack on Christianity." Write a journal entry in response to this observation, supporting your view with concrete examples from the story.

2. Interpret this story as an "initiation" or "coming-of-age" story. What crucial "lessons" does Yoneko learn during the course of the story? How do these change her? What does she learn about her family? In what ways does "earthquake" refer to more than just the actual earthquake that hits the area?

3. Write a story about your early encounters with a religion or belief.

4. Write a story that springs from an "earthquake" or "formative" period in your life, and feel free to fictionalize and create a main character who may be quite different from you.

5. Write an essay in which you compare and contrast Yoneko with Vincent Sabella in "Doctor Jack-o'-lantern" by Richard Yates.

Doctor Jack-o'-lantern

R I C H A R D   Y A T E S

All Miss Price had been told about the new boy was that he'd spent most of his life in some kind of orphanage, and that the gray-haired "aunt and uncle" with whom he now lived were really foster parents, paid by the Welfare Department of the City of New York. A less dedicated or less imaginative teacher might have pressed for more details, but Miss Price was content with the rough outline. It was enough, in fact, to fill her with a sense of mission that shone from her eyes, as plain as love, from the first morning he joined the fourth grade.

He arrived early and sat in the back row—his spine very straight, his ankles crossed precisely under the desk and his hands folded on the very center of its top, as if symmetry might make him less conspicuous—and while the other children were filing in and settling down, he received a long, expressionless stare from each of them.

"We have a new classmate this morning," Miss Price said, laboring the obvious in a way that made everybody want to giggle. "His name is Vincent Sabella and he comes from New York City. I know we'll all do our best to make him feel at home."

This time they all swung around to stare at once, which caused him to duck his head slightly and shift his weight from one buttock to the other. Ordinarily, the fact of someone's coming from New York might have held a certain prestige, for to most of the children the city was an awesome, adult place that swallowed up their fathers every day, and which they themselves were permitted to visit only rarely, in their best clothes, as a treat. But anyone could see at a glance that Vincent Sabella had nothing whatever to do with skyscrapers. Even if you could ignore his tangled black hair and gray skin, his clothes would have given him away: absurdly new corduroys, absurdly old sneakers and a yellow sweatshirt, much too small, with the shredded remains of a Mickey Mouse design stamped on its chest. Clearly, he was from the part of New York that you had to pass through on the train to Grand Central—the part where people hung bedding over their windowsills and leaned out on it all day in a trance of boredom, and where you got vistas of straight, deep streets, one after another, all alike in the clutter of their sidewalks and all swarming with gray boys at play in some desperate kind of ball game.

The girls decided that he wasn't very nice and turned away, but the boys lingered in their scrutiny, looking him up and down with faint smiles. This was the kind of kid they were accustomed to thinking of as "tough," the kind whose stares had made all of them uncomfortable at one time or another in unfamiliar neighborhoods; here was a unique chance for retaliation.

"What would you like us to call you, Vincent?" Miss Price inquired. "I mean, do you prefer Vincent, or Vince, or—or what?" (It was purely an academic question; even Miss Price knew that the boys would call him "Sabella" and that the girls wouldn't call him anything at all.)

"Vinny's okay," he said in a strange, croaking voice that had evidently yelled itself hoarse down the ugly streets of his home.

"I'm afraid I didn't hear you," she said, craning her pretty head forward and to one side so that a heavy lock of hair swung free of one shoulder. "Did you say 'Vince'?"

"Vinny, I said," he said again, squirming.

"Vincent, is it? All right, then, Vincent." A few of the class giggled, but nobody bothered to correct her; it would be more fun to let the mistake continue.

"I won't take time to introduce you to everyone by name, Vincent," Miss Price went on, "because I think it would be simpler just to let you learn the names as we go along, don't you? Now, we won't expect you to take any real part in the work for the first day or so; just take your time, and if there's anything you don't understand, why, don't be afraid to ask."

He made an unintelligible croak and smiled fleetingly, just enough to show that the roots of his teeth were green.

"Now then," Miss Price said, getting down to business. "This is Monday morning, and so the first thing on the program is reports. Who'd like to start off?"

Vincent Sabella was momentarily forgotten as six or seven hands went up, and Miss Price drew back in mock confusion. "Goodness, we do have a lot of reports this morning," she said. The idea of the reports—a fifteen-minute period every Monday in which the children were encouraged to relate their experiences over the weekend—was Miss Price's own, and she took a pardonable pride in it. The principal had commended her on it at a recent staff meeting, pointing out that it made a splendid bridge between the worlds of school and home, and that it was a fine way for children to learn poise and assurance. It called for intelligent supervision—the shy children had to be drawn out and the show-offs curbed—but in general, as Miss Price had assured the principal, it was fun for everyone. She particularly hoped it would be fun today, to help put Vincent Sabella at ease, and that was why she chose Nancy Parker to start off; there was nobody like Nancy for holding an audience.

The others fell silent as Nancy moved gracefully to the head of the room; even the two or three girls who secretly despised her had to feign enthrallment when she spoke (she was that popular), and every boy in the class, who at recess liked nothing better than to push her shrieking into the mud, was unable to watch her without an idiotically tremulous smile.

"Well—" she began, and then she clapped a hand over her mouth while everyone laughed.

"Oh, *Nancy*," Miss Price said. "You *know* the rule about starting a report with 'well.'"

Nancy knew the rule; she had only broken it to get the laugh. Now she let her fit of giggles subside, ran her fragile forefingers down the side seams of her skirt, and began again in the proper way. "On Friday my whole family went for a ride in my brother's new car. My brother bought this new Pontiac last week, and he wanted to take us all for a ride—you know, to try it out and everything? So we went into White Plains and had dinner in a restaurant there, and then we all wanted to go see this movie, 'Doctor Jekyll and Mr. Hyde,' but my brother said it was too horrible and everything, and I wasn't old enough to enjoy it—oh, he made me so mad! And then, let's see. On Saturday I stayed home all day and helped my mother make my sister's wedding dress. My sister's engaged to be married, you see, and my mother's making this wedding dress for her? So we did that, and then on Sunday this friend of my brother's came over for dinner, and then they both had to get back to college that night, and I was allowed to stay up late and say goodbye to them and everything, and I guess that's all." She always had a sure instinct for keeping her performance brief—or rather, for making it seem briefer than it really was.

"Very good, Nancy," Miss Price said. "Now, who's next?"

Warren Berg was next, elaborately hitching up his pants as he made his way down the aisle. "On Saturday I went over to Bill Stringer's house for lunch," he began in his direct, man-to-man style, and Bill Stringer wriggled bashfully in the front row. Warren Berg and Bill Stringer were great friends, and their reports often overlapped. "And then after lunch we went into White Plains, on our bikes. Only we *saw* 'Doctor Jekyll and Mr. Hyde.' " Here he nodded his head in Nancy's direction, and Nancy got another laugh by making a little whimper of envy. "It was real good, too," he went on, with mounting excitement. "It's all about this guy who—"

"About *a man* who," Miss Price corrected.

"About a man who mixes up this chemical, like, that he drinks? And whenever he drinks this chemical, he changes into this real monster, like? You see him drink this chemical, and then you see his hands start to get all scales all over them, like a reptile and everything, and then you see his face start to change into this real horrible-looking face—with fangs and all? Sticking out of his mouth?"

All the girls shuddered in pleasure. "Well," Miss Price said, "I think Nancy's brother was probably wise in not wanting her to see it. What did you do *after* the movie, Warren?"

There was a general *"Aw-w-w!"* of disappointment—everyone wanted to hear more about the scales and fangs—but Miss Price never liked to let the reports degenerate into accounts of movies. Warren continued without much enthusiasm: all they had done after the move was fool around Bill Stringer's yard until suppertime. "And then on Sunday," he said, brightening again, "Bill Stringer came over to *my* house, and my dad helped us rig up this old tire on this long rope? From a tree? There's this steep hill down behind my house, you see—this ravine, like?—and we hung this tire so that what you do is, you take the tire and run a little ways and then lift your feet, and you go swinging way, way out over the ravine and back again."

"That sounds like fun," Miss Price said, glancing at her watch.

"Oh, it's *fun,* all right," Warren conceded. But then he hitched up his pants again and added, with a puckering of his forehead, " 'Course, it's pretty dangerous. You let go of that tire or anything, you'd get a bad fall. Hit a rock or anything, you'd probably break your leg, or your spine. But my dad said he trusted us both to look out for our own safety."

"Well, I'm afraid that's all we'll have time for, Warren," Miss Price said. "Now, there's just time for one more report. Who's ready? Arthur Cross?"

There was a soft groan, because Arthur Cross was the biggest dope in class and his reports were always a bore. This time it turned out to be something tedious about going to visit his uncle on Long Island. At one point he made a slip—he said "botormoat" instead of "motorboat"—and everyone laughed with the particular edge of scorn they reserved for Arthur Cross. But the laughter died abruptly when it was joined by a harsh, dry croaking from the back of the room. Vincent Sabella was laughing too, green teeth and all, and they all had to glare at him until he stopped.

When the reports were over, everyone settled down for school. It was recess time before any of the children thought much about Vincent Sabella again, and then they thought of him only to make sure he was left out of everything. He wasn't in the group of boys that clustered around the horizontal bar to take turns at skinning-the-cat, or the group that whispered in a far corner of the playground, hatching a plot to push Nancy Parker in the mud. Nor was he in the larger group, of which even Arthur Cross was a member, that chased itself in circles in a frantic variation of the game of tag. He couldn't join the girls, of course, or the boys from other classes, and so he joined nobody. He stayed on the apron of the playground, close to school, and for the first part of the recess he pretended to be very busy with the laces of his sneakers. He would squat to undo and retie them, straighten up and take a few experimental steps in a springy, athletic way, and then get down and go to work on them again. After five minutes of this he gave it up, picked up a handful of pebbles and began shying them at an invisible target several yards away. That was good for another five minutes, but then there were still five minutes left, and he could think of nothing to do but stand there, first with his hands in his pockets, then with his hands on his hips, and then with his arms folded in a manly way across his chest.

Miss Price stood watching all this from the doorway, and she spent the full recess wondering if she ought to go out and do something about it. She guessed it would be better not to.

She managed to control the same impulse at recess the next day, and every other day that week, though every day it grew more difficult. But one thing she could not control was a tendency to let her anxiety show in class. All Vincent Sabella's errors in schoolwork were publicly excused, even those having nothing to do with his newness, and all his accomplishments were singled out for special mention. Her campaign to build him up was painfully obvious, and never more so than when she tried to make it subtle; once, for instance, in explaining an arithmetic problem, she said, "Now, suppose Warren Berg and Vincent Sabella went to the store with fifteen cents each, and candy bars cost ten cents. How many candy bars would each boy have?" By the end of the week he was well on the way to becoming the worst possible kind of teacher's pet, a victim of the teacher's pity.

On Friday she decided the best thing to do would be to speak to him privately, and try to draw him out. She could say something about the pictures he had painted in art class—that would do for an opening—and she decided to do it at lunchtime.

The only trouble was that lunchtime, next to recess, was the most trying part of Vincent Sabella's day. Instead of going home for an hour as the other children did, he brought his lunch to school in a wrinkled paper bag and ate it in the classroom, which always made for a certain amount of awkwardness. The last children to leave would see him still seated apologetically at his desk, holding his paper bag, and anyone who happened to straggle back later for a forgotten hat or sweater would surprise him in the middle of his meal—perhaps shielding a hard-boiled egg from view or wiping mayonnaise from his mouth with a furtive hand. It was a situation that Miss Price did not improve by walking up to him while the room was still half full of children and sitting prettily on the edge of the desk beside his, making it clear that she was cutting her own lunch hour short in order to be with him.

"Vincent," she began, "I've been meaning to tell you how much I enjoyed those pictures of yours. They're really very good."

He mumbled something and shifted his eyes to the cluster of departing children at the door. She went right on talking and smiling, elaborating on her praise of the pictures; and finally, after the door had closed behind the last child, he was able to give her his attention. He did so tentatively at first; but the more she talked, the more he seemed to relax, until she realized she was putting him at ease. It was as simple and as gratifying as stroking a cat. She had finished with the pictures now and moved on, triumphantly, to broader fields of praise. "It's never easy," she was saying, "to come to a new school and adjust yourself to the—well, the new work, and new working methods, and I think you've done a splendid job so far. I really do. But tell me, do you think you're going to like it here?"

He looked at the floor just long enough to make his reply—"It's awright"—and then his eyes stared into hers again.

"I'm so glad. Please don't let me interfere with your lunch, Vincent. Do go ahead and eat, that is, if you don't mind my sitting here with you." But it was now abundantly clear that he didn't mind at all, and he began to unwrap a bologna sandwich with what she felt sure was the best appetite he'd had all week. It wouldn't even have mattered very much now if someone from the class had come in and watched, though it was probably just as well that no one did.

Miss Price sat back more comfortably on the desk top, crossed her legs and allowed one slim stockinged foot to slip part of the way out of its moccasin. "Of course," she went on, "it always does take a little time to sort of get your bearings in a new school. For one thing, well, it's never too easy for the new member of the class to make friends with the other members. What I mean is, you mustn't mind if the others seem a little rude to you at first. Actually, they're just as anxious to make friends as you are, but they're shy. All it takes is a little time, and a little effort on your part as well as theirs. Not too much, of course, but a little. Now for instance, these reports we have Monday mornings—they're a fine way for people to get to know one another. A person never feels he has to make a report; it's just a thing he can do if he wants to. And that's only one way of helping others to know the kind of person you are; there are lots and lots of ways. The main thing to remember is that making friends is the most natural thing in the world, and it's only a question of time until you have all the friends you want. And in the meantime, Vincent, I hope you'll consider *me* your friend, and feel free to call on me for whatever advice or anything you might need. Will you do that?"

He nodded, swallowing.

"Good." She stood up and smoothed her skirt over her long thighs. "Now I must go or I'll be late for *my* lunch. But I'm glad we had this little talk, Vincent, and I hope we'll have others."

It was probably a lucky thing that she stood up when she did, for if she'd stayed on that desk a minute longer Vincent Sabella would have thrown his arms around her and buried his face in the warm gray flannel of her lap, and that might have been enough to confuse the most dedicated and imaginative of teachers.

At report time on Monday morning, nobody was more surprised than Miss Price when Vincent Sabella's smudged hand was among the first and most eager to rise. Apprehensively she considered letting someone else start off, but then, for fear of hurting his feelings, she said, "All right, Vincent," in as matter-of-fact a way as she could manage.

There was a suggestion of muffled titters from the class as he walked confidently to the head of the room and turned to face his audience. He looked, if anything, too confident: there were signs, in the way he held his shoulders and the way his eyes shone, of the terrible poise of panic.

"Saturday I seen that pitcha," he announced.

"Saw, Vincent," Miss Price corrected gently.

"That's what I mean," he said; "I sore that pitcha. 'Doctor Jack-o'-lantern and Mr. Hide.' "

There was a burst of wild, delighted laughter and a chorus of correction: "Doctor *Jekyll!*"

He was unable to speak over the noise. Miss Price was on her feet, furious. "It's a *perfectly natural mistake!*" she was saying. "There's no reason for any of you to be so rude. Go on, Vincent, and please excuse this very silly interruption." The laughter subsided, but the class continued to shake their heads derisively from side to side. It hadn't, of course, been a perfectly natural mistake at all; for one thing it proved that he was a hopeless dope, and for another it proved that he was lying.

"That's what I mean," he continued. " 'Doctor Jackal and Mr. Hide.' I got it a little mixed up. Anyways, I seen all about where his teet' start comin' outa his mout' and all like that, and I thought it was very good. And then on Sunday my mudda and fodda come out to see me in this car they got. This Buick. My fodda siz, 'Vinny, wanna go for a little ride?' I siz, 'Sure, where yiz goin'?' He siz, 'Anyplace ya like.' So I siz, 'Let's go out in the country a ways, get on one of them big roads and make some time.' So we go out—oh, I guess fifty, sixty miles—and we're cruisin' along this highway, when this cop starts tailin' us? My fodda siz, 'Don't worry, we'll shake him,' and he steps on it, see? My mudda's gettin' pretty scared, but my fodda siz, 'Don't worry, dear.' He's tryin' to make this turn, see, so he can get off the highway and shake the cop? But just when he's makin' the turn, the cop opens up and starts shootin', see?"

By this time the few members of the class who could bear to look at him at all were doing so with heads on one side and mouths partly open, the way you look at a broken arm or a circus freak.

"We just barely made it," Vincent went on, his eyes gleaming, "and this one bullet got my fodda in the shoulder. Didn't hurt him bad—just grazed him, like—so my mudda bandaged it up for him and all, but he couldn't do no more drivin' after that, and we had to get him to a doctor, see? So my fodda siz, 'Vinny, think you can drive a ways?' I siz, 'Sure, if you show me how.' So he showed me how to work the gas and the brake, and all like that, and I drove to the doctor. My mudda siz, 'I'm prouda you, Vinny, drivin' all by yourself.' So anyways, we got to the doctor, got my fodda fixed up and all, and then he drove us back home." He was breathless. After an uncertain pause he said, "And that's all." Then he walked quickly back to his desk, his stiff new corduroy pants whistling faintly with each step.

"Well, that was very—entertaining, Vincent," Miss Price said, trying to act as if nothing had happened. "Now, who's next?" But nobody raised a hand.

Recess was worse than usual for him that day; at least it was until he found a place to hide—a narrow concrete alley, blind except for several closed fire-exit doors, that cut between two sections of the school building. It was reassuringly dismal and cool in there—he could stand with his back to the wall and his eyes guarding the entrance, and the noises of recess were as remote as the sunshine. But when the bell rang he had to go back to class, and in another hour it was lunchtime.

Miss Price left him alone until her own meal was finished. Then, after standing with one hand on the doorknob for a full minute to gather courage, she went in and sat beside him for another little talk, just as he was trying to swallow the last of a pimento-cheese sandwich.

"Vincent," she began, "we all enjoyed your report this morning, but I think we would have enjoyed it more—a great deal more—if you'd told us something about your real life instead. I mean," she hurried on, "for instance, I noticed you were wearing a nice new windbreaker this morning. It *is* new, isn't it? And did your aunt buy it for you over the weekend?"

He did not deny it.

"Well then, why couldn't you have told us about going to the store with your aunt, and buying the windbreaker, and whatever you did afterwards. That would have made a perfectly good report." She paused, and for the first time looked steadily into his eyes. "You do understand what I'm trying to say, don't you, Vincent?"

He wiped crumbs of bread from his lips, looked at the floor, and nodded.

"And you'll remember next time, won't you?"

He nodded again. "Please may I be excused, Miss Price?"

"Of course you may."

He went to the boys' lavatory and vomited. Afterwards he washed his face and drank a little water, and then he returned to the classroom. Miss Price was busy at her desk now, and didn't look up. To avoid getting involved with her again, he wandered out to the cloakroom and sat on one of the long benches, where he picked up someone's discarded overshoe and turned it over and over in his hands.

In a little while he heard the chatter of returning children, and to avoid being discovered there, he got up and went to the fire-exit door. Pushing it open, he found that it gave onto the alley he had hidden in that morning, and he slipped outside. For a minute or two he just stood there, looking at the blankness of the concrete wall; then he found a piece of chalk in his pocket and wrote out all the dirty words he could think of, in block letters a foot high. He had put down four words and was trying to remember a fifth when he heard a shuffling at the door behind him. Arthur Cross was there, holding the door open and reading the words with wide eyes. "Boy," he said in an awed half-whisper. "Boy, you're gonna get it. You're really gonna *get* it."

Startled, and then suddenly calm, Vincent Sabella palmed his chalk, hooked his thumbs in his belt and turned on Arthur Cross with a menacing look. "Yeah?" he inquired. "Who's gonna squeal on me?"

"Well, nobody's gonna *squeal* on you," Arthur Cross said uneasily, "but you shouldn't go around writing—"

"Arright," Vincent said, advancing a step. His shoulders were slumped, his head thrust forward and his eyes narrowed, like Edward G. Robinson. "Arright. That's all I wanna know. I don't like squealers, unnastand?"

While he was saying this, Warren Berg and Bill Stringer appeared in the doorway—just in time to hear it and to see the words on the wall before Vincent turned on them. "And that goes fa you too, unnastand?" he said. "Both a yiz."

And the remarkable thing was that both their faces fell into the same foolish, defensive smile that Arthur Cross was wearing. It wasn't until they had glanced at each other that they were able to meet his eyes with the proper degree of contempt, and by then it was too late. "Think you're pretty smart, don'tcha, Sabella?" Bill Stringer said.

"Never mind what I think," Vincent told him. "You heard what I said. Now let's get back inside."

And they could do nothing but move aside to make way for him, and follow him dumfounded into the cloakroom.

It was Nancy Parker who squealed—although, of course, with someone like Nancy Parker you didn't think of it as squealing. She had heard everything from the cloakroom; as soon as the boys came in she peeked into the alley, saw the words and, setting her face in a prim frown, went straight to Miss Price. Miss Price was just about to call the class to order for the afternoon when Nancy came up and whispered in her ear. They both disappeared into the cloakroom—from which, after a moment, came the sound of the fire-exit door being abruptly slammed—and when they returned to class Nancy was flushed with righteousness, Miss Price very pale. No announcement was made. Classes proceeded in the ordinary way all afternoon, though it was clear that Miss Price was upset, and it wasn't until she was dismissing the children at three o'clock that she brought the thing into the open. "Will Vincent Sabella please remain seated?" She nodded at the rest of the class. "That's all."

While the room was clearing out she sat at her desk, closed her eyes and massaged the frail bridge of her nose with thumb and forefinger, sorting out half-remembered fragments of a book she had once read on the subject of seriously disturbed children. Perhaps, after all, she should never have undertaken the responsibility of Vincent Sabella's loneliness. Perhaps the whole thing called for the attention of a specialist. She took a deep breath.

"Come over here and sit beside me, Vincent," she said, and when he had settled himself, she looked at him. "I want you to tell me the truth. Did you write those words on the wall outside?"

He stared at the floor.

"Look at me," she said, and he looked at her. She had never looked prettier: her cheeks slightly flushed, her eyes shining and her sweet mouth pressed into a self-conscious frown. "First of all," she said, handing him a small enameled basin streaked with poster paint, "I want you to take this to the boys' room and fill it with hot water and soap."

He did as he was told, and when he came back, carrying the basin carefully to keep the suds from spilling, she was sorting out some old rags in the bottom drawer of her desk. "Here," she said, selecting one and shutting the drawer in a businesslike way. "This will do. Soak this up." She led him back to the fire exit and stood in the alley watching him, silently, while he washed off all the words.

When the job had been done, and the rag and basin put away, they sat down at Miss Price's desk again. "I suppose you think I'm angry with you, Vincent," she said. "Well, I'm not. I almost wish I could be angry—that would make it much easier—but instead I'm hurt. I've tried to be a good friend to you, and I thought you wanted to be my friend too. But this kind of thing—well, it's very hard to be friendly with a person who'd do a thing like that."

She saw, gratefully, that there were tears in his eyes. "Vincent, perhaps I understand some things better than you think. Perhaps I understand that sometimes, when a person does a thing like that, it isn't really because he wants to hurt anyone, but only because he's unhappy. He knows it isn't a good thing to do, and he even knows it isn't going to make him any happier afterwards, but he goes ahead and does it anyway. Then when he finds he's lost a friend, he's terribly sorry, but it's too late. The thing is done."

She allowed this somber note to reverberate in the silence of the room for a little while before she spoke again. "I won't be able to forget this, Vincent. But perhaps, just this once, we can still be friends—as long as I understand that you didn't mean to hurt me. But you must promise me that you won't forget it either. Never forget that when you do a thing like that, you're going to hurt people who want very much to like you, and in that way you're going to hurt yourself. Will you promise me to remember that, dear?"

The "dear" was as involuntary as the slender hand that reached out and held the shoulder of his sweatshirt; both made his head hang lower than before.

"All right," she said. "You may go now."

He got his windbreaker out of the cloakroom and left, avoiding the tired uncertainty of her eyes. The corridors were deserted, and dead silent except for the hollow, rhythmic knocking of a janitor's push-broom against some distant wall. His own rubber-soled tread only added to the silence; so did the lonely little noise made by the zipping-up of his windbreaker, and so did the faint mechanical sigh of the heavy front door. The silence made it all the more startling when he found, several yards down the concrete walk outside, that two boys were walking beside him: Warren Berg and Bill Stringer. They were both smiling at him in an eager, almost friendly way.

"What'd she do to ya, anyway?" Bill Stringer asked.

Caught off guard, Vincent barely managed to put on his Edward G. Robinson face in time. "Nunnya business," he said, and walked faster.

"No, listen—wait up, hey," Warren Berg said, as they trotted to keep up with him. "What'd she do, anyway? She bawl ya out, or what? Wait up, hey, Vinny."

The name made him tremble all over. He had to jam his hands in his windbreaker pockets and force himself to keep on walking; he had to force his voice to be steady when he said "Nunnya *business,* I told ya. Lea' me alone."

But they were right in step with him now. "Boy, she must of given you the works," Warren Berg persisted. "What'd she say, anyway? C'mon, tell us, Vinny."

This time the name was too much for him. It overwhelmed his resistance and made his softening knees slow down to a slack, conversational stroll. "She din say nothin' " he said at last; and then after a dramatic pause he added, "She let the ruler do her talkin' for her."

"The *ruler?* Ya mean she used a *ruler* on ya?" Their faces were stunned, either with disbelief or admiration, and it began to look more and more like admiration as they listened.

"On the knuckles," Vincent said through tightening lips. "Five times on each hand. She siz, 'Make a fist. Lay it out here on the desk.' Then she takes the ruler and *Whop! Whop! Whop!* Five times. Ya think that don't hurt, you're crazy."

Miss Price, buttoning her polo coat as the front door whispered shut behind her, could scarcely believe her eyes. This couldn't be Vincent Sabella—this perfectly normal, perfectly happy boy on the sidewalk ahead of her, flanked by attentive friends. But it was, and the scene made her want to laugh aloud with pleasure and relief. He was going to be all right, after all. For all her well-intentioned groping in the shadows she could never have predicted a scene like this, and certainly could never have caused it to happen. But it was happening, and it just proved, once again, that she would never understand the ways of children.

She quickened her graceful stride and overtook them, turning to smile down at them as she passed. "Goodnight, boys," she called, intending it as a kind of cheerful benediction; and then, embarrassed by their three startled faces, she smiled even wider and said, "Goodness, it *is* getting colder, isn't it? That windbreaker of yours looks nice and warm, Vincent. I envy you." Finally they nodded bashfully at her; she called goodnight again, turned, and continued on her way to the bus stop.

She left a profound silence in her wake. Staring after her, Warren Berg and Bill Stringer waited until she had disappeared around the corner before they turned on Vincent Sabella.

"Ruler, my eye!" Bill Stringer said. "Ruler, my eye!" He gave Vincent a disgusted shove that sent him stumbling against Warren Berg, who shoved him back.

"Jeez, you lie about *everything,* don'tcha, Sabella? You lie about *everything!*"

Jostled off balance, keeping his hands tight in the windbreaker pockets, Vincent tried in vain to retain his dignity. "Think *I* care if yiz believe me?" he said, and then because he couldn't think of anything else to say, he said it again. "Think *I* care if yiz believe me?"

But he was walking alone. Warren Berg and Bill Stringer were drifting away across the street, walking backwards in order to look back on him with furious contempt. "Just like the lies you told about the policeman shooting your father," Bill Stringer called.

"Even *movies* he lies about," Warren Berg put in; and suddenly doubling up with artificial laughter he cupped both hands to his mouth and yelled, "Hey, Doctor Jack-o'-lantern!"

It wasn't a very good nickname, but it had an authentic ring to it—the kind of a name that might spread around, catch on quickly, and stick. Nudging each other, they both took up the cry:

"What's the matter, Doctor Jack-o'-lantern?"

"Why don'tcha run on home with Miss Price, Doctor Jack-o'-lantern?"

"So long, Doctor Jack-o'-lantern!"

Vincent Sabella went on walking, ignoring them, waiting until they were out of sight. Then he turned and retraced his steps all the way back to school, around through the playground and back to the alley, where the wall was still dark in spots from the circular scrubbing of his wet rag.

Choosing a dry place, he got out his chalk and began to draw a head with great care, in profile, making the hair long and rich and taking his time over the face, erasing it with moist fingers and reworking it until it was the most beautiful face he had ever drawn: a delicate nose, slightly parted lips, an eye with lashes that curved as gracefully as a bird's wing. He paused to admire it with a lover's solemnity; then from the lips he drew a line that connected with a big speech balloon, and in the balloon he wrote, so angrily that the chalk kept breaking in his fingers, every one of the words he had written that noon. Returning to the head, he gave it a slender neck and gently sloping shoulders, and then, with bold strikes, he gave it the body of a naked woman: great breasts with hard little nipples, a trim waist, a dot for a navel, wide hips and thighs that flared around a triangle of fiercely scribbled pubic hair. Beneath the picture he printed its title: "Miss Price."

He stood there looking at it for a while, breathing hard, and then he went home.

Questions for Discussion

1. This story is over thirty years old. To what extent does it's depiction of how a new pupil is greeted remain accurate? How would you characterize the greeting Vincent Sabella receives?

2. Give the point of view of this story some consideration: Through what character's (or characters') mind(s) is the story told? How effective is the point of view Yates chooses?

3. Why does Vincent lie?

4. Why does Vincent do what he does at the end of the story? To what extent are you sympathetic to his action?

5. Speculate: Given what we know about Vincent already, what will happen to him during the rest of the school year?

6. What is the significance of all the confusion about Vincent's name (Vinny, Vince, Vincent)? Why does he react so strongly at the end of the story to being called Vinny, and what is the significance of what his nickname will be?

Suggestions for Writing

1. Write an essay in which you analyze the relationship between Miss Price and Vincent Sabella. What motivates her to behave the way she does? What motivates Vincent? To whom are you more sympathetic and why?

2. Write an autobiographical sketch that describes a time when you and fellow classmates were cruel to a new student, or write one that describes a time when you were new to a school or when you were excluded from a group.

3. In your notebook list all the images, actions, and other concrete details Yates gives us to demonstrate how much of an outsider Vincent is. In your view, which of these details is most convincing and effective? Why?

4. Write an essay in which you compare and contrast Sammy's "rebellion" in "A & P" with Vincent's in Yates's story.

The Butterfly and the Traffic Light

CYNTHIA OZICK

. . . the moth for the star.
—*Shelley*

Jerusalem, that phoenix city, is not known by its street-names. Neither is Baghdad, Copenhagen, Rio de Janeiro, Camelot, or Athens; nor Peking, Florence, Babylon, St. Petersburg. These fabled capitals rise up ready-spired, story-domed and filigreed; they come to us at the end of a plain, behind hill or cloud, walled and moated by myths and antique rumors. They are built of copper, silver, and gold; they are founded on milkwhite stone; the bright thrones of ideal kings jewel them. Balconies, parks, little gates, columns and statuary, carriage-houses and stables, attics, kitchens, gables, tiles, yards, rubied steeples, brilliant roofs, peacocks, lapdogs, grand ladies, beggars, towers, bowers, harbors, barbers, wigs, judges, courts, and wines of all sorts fill them. Yet, though we see the shimmer of the smallest pebble beneath the humblest foot in all the great seats of legend, still not a single street is celebrated. The thoroughfares of beautiful cities are somehow obscure, unless, of course, we count Venice: but a canal is not really the same as a street. The ways, avenues, plazas, and squares of old cities are lost to us, we do not like to think of them, they move like wicked scratches upon the smooth enamel of our golden towns; we have forgotten most of them. There is no beauty in cross-section—we take our cities, like our wishes, whole.

It is different with places of small repute or where time has not yet deigned to be an inhabitant. It is different especially in America. They tell us that Boston is our Jerusalem; but, as anyone who has ever lived there knows, Boston owns only half a history. Honor, pomp, hallowed scenes, proud families, the Athenaeum and the Symphony are Boston's; but Boston has no tragic tradition. Boston has never wept. No Bostonian has ever sung, mourning for his city, "If I do not remember thee, let my tongue cleave to the roof of my mouth"—for, to manage his accent, the Bostonian's tongue is already in that position. We hear of Beacon Hill and Back Bay, of Faneuil market and State Street: it is all cross-section, all map. And the State House with its gilt dome (it counts for nothing that Paul Revere supplied the bottommost layer of gold leaf: he was businessman, not horseman, then) throws back furious sunsets garishly, boastfully, as no power-rich Carthage, for shame, would dare. There is no fairy mist in Boston. True, its street-names are notable: Boylston, Washington, Commonwealth, Marlborough, Tremont, Beacon; and then the Squares, Kenmore, Copley,

Louisburg, and Scollay—evidence enough that the whole, unlike Jerusalem, has not transcended its material parts. Boston has a history of neighborhoods. Jerusalem has a history of histories.

The other American towns are even less fortunate. It is not merely that they lack rudimentary legends, that their names are homely and unimaginative, half ending in -burg and half in -ville, or that nothing has ever happened in them. Unlike the ancient capitals, they are not infixed in our vision, we are not born knowing them, as though, in some earlier migration, we had been dwellers there: for no one is a stranger to Jerusalem. And unlike even Boston, most cities in America have no landmarks, no age-enshrined graveyards (although death is famous everywhere), no green park to show a massacre, poet's murder, or high marriage. The American town, alas, has no identity hinting at immortality; we recognize it only by its ubiquitous street-names: sometimes Main Street, sometimes High Street, and frequently Central Avenue. Grandeur shuns such streets. It is all ambition and aspiration there, and nothing to look back at. Cicero said that men who know nothing of what has gone before them are like children. But Main, High, and Central have no past; rather, their past is now. It is not the fault of the inhabitants that nothing has gone before them. Nor are they to be condemned if they make their spinal streets conspicuous, and confer egregious luster and false acclaim on Central, High, or Main, and erect minarets and marquees indeed as though their city were already in dream and fable. But it is where one street in particular is regarded as the central life, the high spot, the main drag, that we know the city to be a prenatal trace only. The kiln of history bakes out these prides and these divisions. When the streets have been forgotten a thousand years, the divine city is born.

In the farm-village where the brewer Buldenquist had chosen to establish his Mighty College, the primitive commercial artery was called, not surprisingly, "downtown," and then, more respectably, Main Street, and then, rather covetously looking to civic improvement, Buldenquist Road. But the Sacred Bull had dedicated himself to the foundation and perpetuation of scientific farming, and had a prejudice against putting money into pavements and other citifications. So the town fathers (for by that time the place *was* a town, swollen by the boarding houses and saloons frequented by crowds of young farm students)—the town fathers scratched their heads for historical allusions embedded in local folklore, but found nothing except two or three old family scandals, until one day a traveling salesman named Rogers sold the mayor an "archive"—a wrinkled, torn, doused, singed, and otherwise quite ancient-looking holographic volume purporting to hold the records and diaries of one Colonel Elihu Bigghe. This rather obscure officer had by gratifying coincidence passed through the neighborhood during the war with a force of two hundred, the document claimed, encountering a skirmish with the enemy on the very spot of the present firehouse—the "war" being, according to some, the Civil War, and in the positive authority of others, one of the lesser Indian Wars—in his private diary Bigghe was not, after all, expected to drop hints. At any rate, the skirmish was there in detail—one hundred or more of the enemy dead; not one of ours; ninety-seven of theirs wounded; our survivors all hale but three; the bravery of our side; the cowardice and brutality of the foe; and further pious and patriotic remarks on Country, Creator, and Christian Charity. A decade or so after this remarkable discovery the mayor heard of Rogers' arrest, somewhere in the East, for forgery, and in his secret heart began to wonder whether he might not have been taken in: but by then the Bigghe diaries were under glass in the antiseptic-smelling lobby of the town hall, school children were being herded regularly by their teachers to view it, boring Fourth of July speeches had been droned before the firehouse in annual commemoration, and most people had forgotten that Bigghe Road had ever been called after the grudging brewer. And who could blame the inhabitants if, after half a hundred years, they began to spell it Big Road? For by then the town had grown into a city, wide and clamorous.

For Fishbein it was an imitation of a city. He claimed (not altogether correctly) that he had seen all the capitals of Europe, and yet had never come upon anything to match Big Road in name or character. He liked to tell how the streets of Europe were "employed," as he put it: he would people them with beggars and derelicts—"they keep their cash and their beds in the streets"; and with crowds assembled for riot or amusement or politics—"in Moscow they filled, the revolutionaries I mean, three troikas with White Russians and shot them, the White Russians I mean, and let them run wild in the street, the horses I mean, to spill all the corpses" (but he had never been to Moscow); and with travelers determined on objective and destination—"they use the streets there to go from one place to another, the original design of streets, *n'est-ce pas?*" Fishbein considered that, while a city exists for its own sake, a street is utilitarian. The uses of Big Road, on the contrary, were plainly secondary. In Fishbein's view Big Road had come into being only that the city might have a conscious center—much as the nucleus of a cell demonstrates the cell's character and maintains its well-being ("although," Fishbein argued, "in the cell it is a moot question whether the nucleus exists for the sake of the cell or the cell for the sake of the nucleus: whereas it is clear that a formless city such as this requires a centrality from which to learn the idea of form"). But if the city were to have modeled itself after Big Road, it would have grown long, like a serpent, and unreliable in its sudden coilings. This had not happened. Big Road crept, toiled, and ran, but the city nibbled at this farmhouse and that, and spread and spread with no pattern other than exuberance and greed. And if Fishbein had to go to biology or botany or history for his analogies, the city was proud that it had Big Road to stimulate such comparisons.

Big Road was different by day and by night, weekday and weekend. Daylight, sunlight, and even rainlight gave everything its shadow, winter and summer, so that every person and every object had its Doppelgänger, persistent and hopeless. There was a kind of doubleness that clung to the street, as though one remembered having seen this and this and this before. The stores, hung with signs, had it, the lazy-walking old women had it (all of them uniformly rouged in the geometric centers of their cheeks like victims of some senile fever already dangerously epidemic), the traffic lights suspended from their wires had it, the air dense with the local accent had it.

This insistent sense of recognition was the subject of one of Fishbein's favorite lectures to his walking companion. "It's America repeating itself!

Imitating its own worst habits! Haven't I seen the same thing everywhere? It's a simultaneous urbanization all over, you can almost hear the coxswain crow 'Now all together, boys!'—This lamppost, I saw it years ago in Birmingham, that same scalloped bowl teetering on a wrought-iron stick. At least in Europe the lampposts look different in each place, they have individual characters. And this traffic light! There's no cross-street there, so what do they want it for in such a desert? I'll tell you: they put it up to pretend they're a real city—to tease the transients who might be naïve enough to stop for it. And that click and buzz, that flash and blink, why do they all do that in just the same way? Repeat and repeat, nothing meaningful by itself. . . ."

"I don't mind them, they're like abstract statues," Isabel once replied to this. "As though we were strangers from another part of the world and thought them some kind of religious icon with a red and a green eye. The ones on poles especially."

He recognized his own fancifulness, coarsened, labored, and made literal. He had taught her to think like this. But she had a distressing disinclination to shake off logic; she did not know how to ride her intuition.

"No, no," he objected, "then you don't know what an icon is! A traffic light could never be anything but a traffic light. —What kind of religion would it be which had only one version of its deity—a whole row of identical icons in every city?"

She considered rapidly. "An advanced religion. I mean a monotheistic one."

"And what makes you certain that monotheism is 'advanced'? On the contrary, little dear! It's as foolish to be fixed on one God as it is to be fixed on one idea, isn't that plain? The index of advancement is flexibility. Human temperaments are so variable, how could one God satisfy them all? The Greeks and Romans had a god for every personality, the way the Church has a saint for every mood. Savages, Hindus, and Roman Catholics understand all that. It's only the Jews and their imitators who insist on a rigid unitarian God—I can't think of anything more unfortunate for history: it's the narrow way, like God imposing his will on Job. The disgrace of the fable is that Job didn't turn to another god, one more germane to his illusions. It's what any sensible man would have done. And then wouldn't the boils have gone away of their own accord?—the Bible states clearly that they were simply a psychogenic nervous disorder—isn't that what's meant by 'Satan'? There's no disaster that doesn't come of missing an imagination: I've told you that before, little dear. Now the Maccabean War for instance, for an altogether unintelligible occasion! All Antiochus the Fourth intended—he was Emperor of Syria at the time—was to set up a statue of Zeus on the altar of the Temple of Jerusalem, a harmless affair—who would be hurt by it? It wasn't that Antiochus cared anything for Zeus himself—he was nothing if not an agnostic: a philosopher, anyway—the whole movement was only to symbolize the Syrian hegemony. It wasn't worth a war to get rid of the thing! A little breadth of vision, you see, a little imagination, a little *flexibility,* I mean—there ought to be room for Zeus *and* God under one roof. . . . That's why traffic lights won't do for icons! They haven't been conceived in a pluralistic spirit, they're all exactly alike. Icons ought to differ from one another, don't you see? An icon's only a mask, that's the point, a representational mask which stands for an idea."

"In that case," Isabel tried it, "if a traffic light were an icon it would stand for two ideas, stop and go—"

"Stop and go, virtue and vice, logic and law!—Why are you always on the verge of moralizing, little dear, when it's a fever, not morals, that keeps the world spinning! Are masks only for showing the truth? But no, they're for hiding, they're for misleading, too. . . . It's a maxim, you see: one mask reveals, another conceals."

"Which kind is better?"

"Whichever you happen to be wearing at the moment," he told her.

Often he spoke to her in this manner among night crowds on Big Road. Sometimes, too argumentative to be touched, she kept her hands in her pockets and, unexpectedly choosing a corner to turn, he would wind a rope of hair around his finger and draw her leashed after him. She always went easily; she scarcely needed to be led. Among all those night walkers the two of them seemed obscure, dimmed-out, and under a heat-screened autumn moon, one of those shimmering country-moons indigenous to midwestern America, he came to a kind of truce with the street. It was no reconcilement, nothing so friendly as that, not even a cessation of warfare, only of present aggression. To come to terms with Big Road would have been to come to terms with America. And since this was impossible, he dallied instead with masks, and icons, and Isabel's long brown hair.

After twilight on the advent of the weekend the clutter of banners, the parades, the caravans of curiously outfitted convertibles vanished, and the students came out to roam. They sought each other with antics and capers, brilliantly tantalizing in the beginning darkness. Voices hung in the air, shot upward all along the street, and celebrated the Friday madness. It was a grand posture of relief: the stores already closed but the display-windows still lit, and the mannequins leaning forward from their glass cages with leers of painted horror and malignant eyeballs; and then the pirate movie letting out (this is 1949, my hearties), and the clusters of students flowing in gleaming rows, like pearls on a string, past posters raging with crimson seas and tall-masted ships and black-haired beauties shrieking, out of the scented palace into drugstores and ice cream parlors. Sweet, sweet, it was all sweet there before the shops and among the crawling automobiles and under the repetitious street lamps and below the singular moon. On the sidewalks the girls sprouted like tapestry blossoms, their heads rising from slender necks like woven petals swaying on the stems. They wore thin dresses, and short capelike coats over them; they wore no stockings, and their round bare legs moved boldly through an eddy of rainbow skirts; the swift white bone of ankle cut into the breath of the wind. A kind of greed drove Fishbein among them. "See that one," he would say, consumed with yearning, turning back in the wake of the young lasses to observe their gait, and how the filaments of their dresses seemed to float below their arms caught in a gesture, and how the dry sparks of their eyes flickered with the sheen of spiders.

And he would halt until Isabel too had looked. "Are you envious?" he asked, "because you are not one of them? Then console yourself." But he saw that she studied his greed and read his admiration. "Take comfort," he said again. "They are not free to become themselves. They are different from you." "Yes," Isabel answered, "they are prettier." "They will grow corrupt. Time will overwhelm them. They have only their one moment, like the butterflies." "Looking at butterflies gives pleasure." "Yes, it is a kind of joy, little dear, but full of poison. It belongs to the knowledge of rapid death. The butterfly lures us not only because he is beautiful, but because he is transitory. The caterpillar is uglier, but in him we can regard the better joy of becoming. The caterpillar's fate is bloom. The butterfly's is waste."

They stopped, and around them milled and murmured the girls in their wispy dresses and their little cut-off capes, and their yellow hair, whitish hair, tan hair, hair of brown-and-pink. The lithe, O the ladies young! It was all sweet there among the tousled bevies wormy with ribbon streamers and sashes, mock-tricked with make-believe gems, gems pinned over the breast, on the bar of a barrette, aflash even in the rims of their glasses. The alien gaiety took Fishbein in; he rocked in their strong sea-wave. From a record shop came a wild shiver of jazz, eyes unwound like coils of silk and groped for other eyes: the street churned with the laughter of girls. And Fishbein, arrested in the heart of the whirlpool, was all at once plunged again into war with the street and with America, where everything was illusion and all illusion led to disillusion. What use was it then for him to call O lyric ladies, what use to chant O languorous lovely November ladies, O lilting, lolling, lissome ladies—while corrosion sat waiting in their ears, he saw the maggots breeding in their dissolving jewels?

Meanwhile Isabel frowned with logic. "But it's only that the caterpillar's future is longer and his fate farther off. In the end he will die too." "Never, never, never," said Fishbein; "it is only the butterfly who dies, and then he has long since ceased to be a caterpillar. The caterpillar never dies.—Neither to die nor to be immortal, it is the enviable state, little dear, to live always at the point of beautiful change! That is what it means to be extraordinary—when did I tell you that?—" He bethought himself. "The first day, of course. It's always best to begin with the end—with the image of what is desired. If I had begun with the beginning I would have bored you, you would have gone away. . . . In my ideal kingdom, little dear, everyone, even the very old, will be passionately in the process of guessing at and preparing for his essential self. Boredom will be unnatural, like a curse, or unhealthy, like a plague. Everyone will be extraordinary."

"But if the whole population were extraordinary," Isabel objected, "then nobody would be extraordinary."

"Ssh, little dear, why must you insist on dialectics? Nothing true is ever found by that road. There are millions of caterpillars, and not one of them is intended to die, and they are all of them extraordinary. *Your* aim," he admonished, as they came into the darkened neighborhood beyond Big Road, "is to avoid growing into a butterfly. Come," he said, and took her hand, "let us live for that."

Questions for Discussion

1. In some respects the opening section of the story reads like an essay rather than a conventional story. Discuss the effect this has on you. Also, to what extent do you agree with the author's discussion of cities and of the contrast she establishes between older cities and American cities?

2. Summarize the "argument" about streets and their roles in different kinds of cities.

3. The story gives us a brief history of an American farm village that becomes a city. How does this history reveal certain typical features of American culture? To what extent does the history mirror that of a city or large town with which you are familiar?

4. What are Fishbein's reasons for describing the young girls on the street as "butterflies"?

5. Characterize Fishbein's attitude toward Isabel and her opinions. Toward which character are you more sympathetic, Fishbein or Isabel?

6. What does the discussion of butterflies and caterpillars have to do with the preceding discussions of cities, streets, Big Road, and traffic lights? How do all of these discussions relate to America and Fishbein's struggle to come to terms with America?

Suggestions for Writing

1. Write an essay in which you assess the effectiveness of this story's "critique" (analysis) of American culture.

2. Write an essay that assesses all of the "things" the narrator and Fishbein interpret as cultural symbols: streets, roads, town histories, traffic lights, caterpillars, and butterflies.

3. Write a story that, for better or worse, springs from the "culture" and "character" of a town or city with which you are familiar.

4. If you have been to a large European, Asian, or South American city, write an entry in your journal that gives your perspective not just on your

experience there but also on the nature of the city itself. If you are a fiction writer, build on this journal entry and try to develop a story.

5. Ozick uses streets as an entry point for analyzing cities in general. Choose another element of cities and develop an analysis from that entry point. Write the analysis in an informal journal or notebook entry or in a more formal essay.

Everything That Rises Must Converge

FLANNERY O'CONNOR

Her doctor had told Julian's mother that she must lose twenty pounds on account of her blood pressure, so on Wednesday nights Julian had to take her downtown on the bus for a reducing class at the Y. The reducing class was designed for working girls over fifty, who weighed from 165 to 200 pounds. His mother was one of the slimmer ones, but she said ladies did not tell their age or weight. She would not ride the buses by herself at night since they had been integrated, and because the reducing class was one of her few pleasures, necessary for her health, and *free,* she said Julian could at least put himself out to take her, considering all she did for him. Julian did not like to consider all she did for him, but every Wednesday night he braced himself and took her.

She was almost ready to go, standing before the hall mirror, putting on her hat, while he, his hands behind him, appeared pinned to the door frame, waiting like Saint Sebastian for the arrows to begin piercing him. The hat was new and had cost her seven dollars and a half. She kept saying, "Maybe I shouldn't have paid that for it. No, I shouldn't have. I'll take it off and return it tomorrow. I shouldn't have bought it."

Julian raised his eyes to heaven. "Yes, you should have bought it," he said. "Put it on and let's go." It was a hideous hat. A purple velvet flap came down on one side of it and stood up on the other; the rest of it was green and looked like a cushion with the stuffing out. He decided it was less comical than jaunty and pathetic. Everything that gave her pleasure was small and depressed him.

She lifted the hat one more time and set it down slowly on top of her head. Two wings of gray hair protruded on either side of her florid face, but her eyes, sky-blue, were as innocent and untouched by experience as they must have been when she was ten. Were it not that she was a widow who had struggled fiercely to feed and clothe and put him through school and who was supporting him still, "until he got on his feet," she might have been a little girl that he had to take to town.

"It's all right, it's all right," he said. "Let's go." He opened the door himself and started down the walk to get her going. The sky was a dying violet and the houses stood out darkly against it, bulbous liver-colored monstrosities of a uniform ugliness though no two were alike. Since this had been a fashionable neighborhood forty years ago, his mother persisted in thinking they did well to have an apartment in it. Each house had a narrow collar of dirt around it in which sat, usually, a grubby child. Julian walked with his hands in his pockets, his head down and thrust forward and his eyes glazed with the determination to make himself completely numb during the time he would be sacrificed to her pleasure.

The door closed and he turned to find the dumpy figure, surmounted by the atrocious hat, coming toward him. "Well," she said, "you only live once and paying a little more for it, I at least won't meet myself coming and going."

"Some day I'll start making money," Julian said gloomily—he knew he never would—"and you can have one of those jokes whenever you take the fit." But first they would move. He visualized a place where the nearest neighbors would be three miles away on either side.

"I think you're doing fine," she said, drawing on her gloves. "You've only been out of school a year. Rome wasn't built in a day."

She was one of the few members of the Y reducing class who arrived in hat and gloves and who had a son who had been to college. "It takes time," she said, "and the world is in such a mess. This hat looked better on me than any of the others, though when she brought it out I said, 'Take that thing back. I wouldn't have it on my head,' and she said, 'Now wait till you see it on,' and when she put it on me, I said, 'we-ull,' and she said, 'If you ask me, that hat does something for you and you do something for that hat, and besides,' she said, 'with that hat, you won't meet yourself coming and going.'"

Julian thought he could have stood his lot better if she had been selfish, if she had been an old hag who drank and screamed at him. He walked along, saturated in depression, as if in the midst of his martyrdom he had lost his faith. Catching sight of his long, hopeless, irritated face, she stopped suddenly with a grief-stricken look, and pulled back on his arm. "Wait on me," she said. "I'm going back to the house and take this thing off and tomorrow I'm going to return it. I was out of my head. I can pay the gas bill with the seven-fifty."

He caught her arm in a vicious grip. "You are not going to take it back," he said. "I like it."

"Well," she said, "I don't think I ought . . ."

"Shut up and enjoy it," he muttered, more depressed than ever.

"With the world in the mess it's in," she said, "it's a wonder we can enjoy anything. I tell you, the bottom rail is on the top."

Julian sighed.

"Of course," she said, "if you know who you are, you can go anywhere." She said this every time he took her to the reducing class. "Most of them in it are not our kind of people," she said, "but I can be gracious to anybody. I know who I am."

"They don't give a damn for your graciousness," Julian said savagely. "Knowing who you are is good for one generation only. You haven't the foggiest idea where you stand now or who you are."

She stopped and allowed her eyes to flash at him. "I most certainly do know who I am," she said, "and if you don't know who you are, I'm ashamed of you."

"Oh hell," Julian said.

"Your great-grandfather was a former governor of this state," she said. "Your grandfather was a prosperous landowner. Your grandmother was a Godhigh."

"Will you look around you," he said tensely, "and see where you are now?" and he swept his arm jerkily out to indicate the neighborhood, which the growing darkness at least made less dingy.

"You remain what you are," she said. "Your great-grandfather had a plantation and two hundred slaves."

"There are no more slaves," he said irritably.

"They were better off when they were," she said. He groaned to see that she was off on that topic. She rolled onto it every few days like a train on an open track. He knew every stop, every junction, every swamp along the way, and knew the exact point at which her conclusion would roll majestically into the station: "It's ridiculous. It's simply not realistic. They should rise, yes, but on their own side of the fence."

"Let's skip it," Julian said.

"The ones I feel sorry for," she said, "are the ones that are half white. They're tragic."

"Will you skip it?"

"Suppose we were half white. We would certainly have mixed feelings."

"I have mixed feelings now," he groaned.

"Well let's talk about something pleasant," she said. "I remember going to Grandpa's when I was a little girl. Then the house had double stairways that went up to what was really the second floor—all the cooking was done on the first. I used to like to stay down in the kitchen on account of the way the walls smelled. I would sit with my nose pressed against the plaster and take deep breaths. Actually the place belonged to the Godhighs but your grandfather Chestny paid the mortgage and saved it for them. They were in reduced circumstances," she said, "but reduced or not, they never forgot who they were."

"Doubtless that decayed mansion reminded them," Julian muttered. He never spoke of it without contempt or thought of it without longing. He had seen it once when he was a child before it had been sold. The double stairways had rotted and been torn down. Negroes were living in it. But it remained in his mind as his mother had known it. It appeared in his dreams regularly. He would stand on the wide porch, listening to the rustle of oak leaves, then wander through the high-ceilinged hall into the parlor that opened onto it and gaze at the worn rugs and faded draperies. It occurred to him that it was he, not she, who could have appreciated it. He preferred its threadbare elegance to anything he could name and it was because of it that all the neighborhoods they had lived in had been a torment to him—whereas she had hardly known the difference. She called her insensitivity "being adjustable."

"And I remember the old darky who was my nurse, Caroline. There was no better person in the world. I've always had a great respect for my colored friends," she said. "I'd do anything in the world for them and they'd . . ."

"Will you for God's sake get off that subject?" Julian said. When he got on a bus by himself, he made it a point to sit down beside a Negro, in reparation as it were for his mother's sins.

"You're mighty touchy tonight," she said. "Do you feel all right?"

"Yes I feel all right," he said. "Now lay off."

She pursed her lips. "Well, you certainly are in a vile humor," she observed. "I just won't speak to you at all."

They had reached the bus stop. There was no bus in sight and Julian, his hands still jammed in his pockets and his head thrust forward, scowled down the empty street. The frustration of having to wait on the bus as well as ride on it began to creep up his neck like a hot hand. The presence of his mother was borne in upon him as she gave a pained sigh. He looked at her bleakly. She was holding herself very erect under the preposterous hat, wearing it like a banner of her imaginary dignity. There was in him an evil urge to break her spirit. He suddenly unloosened his tie and pulled it off and put it in his pocket.

She stiffened. "Why must you look like *that* when you take me to town?" she said. "Why must you deliberately embarrass me?"

"If you'll never learn where you are," he said, "you can at least learn where I am."

"You look like a—thug," she said.

"Then I must be one," he murmured.

"I'll just go home," she said. "I will not bother you. If you can't do a little thing like that for me . . ."

Rolling his eyes upward, he put his tie back on. "Restored to my class," he muttered. He thrust his face toward her and hissed, "True culture is in the mind, the *mind,* " he said, and tapped his head, "the mind."

"It's in the heart," she said, "and in how you do things and how you do things is because of who you *are.*"

"Nobody in the damn bus cares who you are."

"I care who I am," she said icily.

The lighted bus appeared on top of the next hill and as it approached, they moved out into the street to meet it. He put his hand under her elbow and hoisted her up on the creaking step. She entered with a little smile, as if she were going into a drawing room where everyone had been waiting for her. While he put in the tokens, she sat down on one of the broad front seats for three which faced the aisle. A thin woman with protruding teeth and long yellow hair was sitting on the end of it. His mother moved up beside her and left room for Julian beside herself. He sat down and looked at the floor across the aisle where a pair of thin feet in red and white canvas sandals were planted.

His mother immediately began a general conversation meant to attract anyone who felt like talking. "Can it get any hotter?" she said and removed from her purse a folding fan, black with a Japanese scene on it, which she began to flutter before her.

"I reckon it might could," the woman with the protruding teeth said, "but I know for a fact my apartment couldn't get no hotter."

"It must get the afternoon sun," his mother said. She sat forward and looked up and down the bus. It was half filled. Everybody was white. "I see we have the bus to ourselves," she said. Julian cringed.

"For a change," said the woman across the aisle, the owner of the red and white canvas sandals. "I come on one the other day and they were thick as fleas—up front and all through."

"The world is in a mess everywhere," his mother said. "I don't know how we've let it get in this fix."

"What gets my goat is all those boys from good families stealing automobile tires," the woman with the protruding teeth said. "I told my boy, I said you may not be rich but you been raised right and if I ever catch you in any such mess, they can send you on to the reformatory. Be exactly where you belong."

"Training tells," his mother said. "Is your boy in high school?"

"Ninth grade," the woman said.

"My son just finished college last year. He wants to write but he's selling typewriters until he gets started," his mother said.

The woman leaned forward and peered at Julian. He threw her such a malevolent look that she subsided against the seat. On the floor across the aisle there was an abandoned newspaper. He got up and got it and opened it out in front of him. His mother discreetly continued the conversation in a lower tone but the woman across the aisle said in a loud voice, "Well that's nice. Selling typewriters is close to writing. He can go right from one to the other."

"I tell him," his mother said, "that Rome wasn't built in a day."

Behind the newspaper Julian was withdrawing into the inner compartment of his mind where he spent most of his time. This was a kind of mental bubble in which he established himself when he could not bear to be a part of what was going on around him. From it he could see out and judge but in it he was safe from any kind of penetration from without. It was the only place where he felt free of the general idiocy of his fellows. His mother had never entered it but from it he could see her with absolute clarity.

The old lady was clever enough and he thought that if she had started from any of the right premises, more might have been expected of her. She lived according to the laws of her own fantasy world, outside of which he had never seen her set foot. The law of it was to sacrifice herself for him after she had first created the necessity to do so by making a mess of things. If he had permitted her sacrifices, it was only because her lack of foresight had made them necessary. All of her life had been a struggle to act like a Chestny without the Chestny goods, and to give him everything she thought a Chestny ought to have; but since, said she, it was fun to struggle, why complain? And when you had won, as she had won, what fun to look back on the hard times! He could not forgive her that she had enjoyed the struggle and that she thought *she* had won.

What she meant when she said she had won was that she had brought him up successfully and had sent him to college and that he had turned out so well—good looking (her teeth had gone unfilled so that his could be straightened), intelligent (he realized he was too intelligent to be a success), and with a future ahead of him (there was of course no future ahead of him). She excused his gloominess on the grounds that he was still growing up and his radical ideas on his lack of practical experience. She said he didn't yet know a thing about "life," that he hadn't even entered the real world—when already he was as disenchanted with it as a man of fifty.

The further irony of all this was that in spite of her, he had turned out so well. In spite of going to only a third-rate college, he had, on his own initiative, come out with a first-rate education; in spite of growing up dominated by a small mind, he had ended up with a large one; in spite of all her foolish views, he was free of prejudice and unafraid to face facts. Most miraculous of all, instead of being blinded by love for her as she was for him, he had cut himself emotionally free of her and could see her with complete objectivity. He was not dominated by his mother.

The bus stopped with a sudden jerk and shook him from his meditation. A woman from the back lurched forward with little steps and barely escaped falling in his newspaper as she righted herself. She got off and a large Negro got on. Julian kept his paper lowered to watch. It gave him a certain satisfaction to see injustice in daily operation. It confirmed his view that with a few exceptions there was no one worth knowing within a radius of three hundred miles. The Negro was well dressed and carried a briefcase. He looked around and then sat down on the other end of the seat where the woman with the red and white canvas sandals was sitting. He immediately unfolded a newspaper and obscured himself behind it. Julian's mother's elbow at once prodded insistently into his ribs. "Now you see why I won't ride on these buses by myself," she whispered.

The woman with the red and white canvas sandals had risen at the same time the Negro sat down and had gone further back in the bus and taken the seat of the woman who had got off. His mother leaned forward and cast her an approving look.

Julian rose, crossed the aisle, and sat down in the place of the woman with the canvas sandals. From this position, he looked serenely across at his mother. Her face had turned an angry red. He stared at her, making his eyes the eyes of a stranger. He felt his tension suddenly lift as if he had openly declared war on her.

He would have liked to get in conversation with the Negro and to talk with him about art or politics or any subject that would be above the comprehension of those around them, but the man remained entrenched behind his paper. He was either ignoring the change of seating or had never noticed it. There was no way for Julian to convey his sympathy.

His mother kept her eyes fixed reproachfully on his face. The woman with the protruding teeth was looking at him avidly as if he were a type of monster new to her.

"Do you have a light?" he asked the Negro.

Without looking away from his paper, the man reached in his pocket and handed him a packet of matches.

"Thanks," Julian said. For a moment he held the matches foolishly. A NO SMOKING sign looked down upon him from over the door. This alone would not have deterred him; he had no cigarettes. He had quit smoking some months before because he could not afford it. "Sorry," he muttered and handed back the matches. The Negro lowered the paper and gave him an annoyed look. He took the matches and raised the paper again.

His mother continued to gaze at him but she did not take advantage of his momentary discomfort. Her eyes retained their battered look. Her face seemed to be unnaturally red, as if her blood pressure had risen. Julian allowed no glimmer of sympathy to show on his face. Having got the advantage, he wanted desperately to keep it and carry it through. He would have liked to teach her a lesson that would last her a while, but there seemed no way to continue the point. The Negro refused to come out from behind his paper.

Julian folded his arms and looked stolidly before him, facing her but as if he did not see her, as if he had ceased to recognize her existence. He visualized a scene in which, the bus having reached their stop, he would remain in his seat and when she said, "Aren't you going to get off?" he would look at her as at a stranger who had rashly addressed him. The corner they got off on was usually deserted, but it was well lighted and it would not hurt her to walk by herself the four blocks to the Y. He decided to wait until the time came and then decide whether or not he would let her get off by herself. He would have to be at the Y at ten to bring her back, but he could leave her wondering if he was going to show up. There was no reason for her to think she could always depend on him.

He retired again into the high-ceilinged room sparsely settled with large pieces of antique furniture. His soul expanded momentarily but then he became aware of his mother across from him and the vision shriveled. He studied her coldly. Her feet in little pumps dangled like a child's and did not quite reach the floor. She was training on him an exaggerated look of reproach. He felt completely detached from her. At that moment he could with pleasure have slapped her as he would have slapped a particularly obnoxious child in his charge.

He began to imagine various unlikely ways by which he could teach her a lesson. He might make friends with some distinguished Negro professor or lawyer and bring him home to spend the evening. He would be entirely justified but her blood pressure would rise to 300. He could not push her to the extent of making her have a stroke, and moreover, he had never been successful at making any Negro friends. He had tried to strike up an acquaintance on the bus with some of the better types, with ones that looked like professors or ministers or lawyers. One morning he had sat down next to a distinguished-looking dark brown man who had answered his questions with a sonorous solemnity but who had turned out to be an undertaker. Another day he had sat down beside a cigar-smoking Negro with a diamond ring on his finger, but after a few stilted pleasantries, the Negro had rung the buzzer and risen, slipping two lottery tickets into Julian's hand as he climbed over him to leave.

He imagined his mother lying desperately ill and his being able to secure only a Negro doctor for her. He toyed with that idea for a few minutes and then dropped it for a momentary vision of himself participating as a sympathizer in a sit-in demonstration. This was possible but he did not linger with it. Instead, he approached the ultimate horror. He brought home a beautiful suspiciously Negroid woman. Prepare yourself, he said. There is nothing you can do about it. This is the woman I've chosen. She's intelligent, dignified, even good, and she's suffered and she hasn't thought it *fun*. Now persecute us, go ahead and persecute us. Drive her out of here, but remember, you're driving me too. His eyes were narrowed and through the indignation he had generated, he saw his mother across the aisle, purple-faced, shrunken to the dwarf-like proportions of her moral nature, sitting like a mummy beneath the ridiculous banner of her hat.

He was tilted out of his fantasy again as the bus stopped. The door opened with a sucking hiss and out of the dark a large, gaily dressed, sullen-looking colored woman got on with a little boy. The child, who might have been four, had on a short plaid suit and a Tyrolean hat with a blue feather in it. Julian hoped that he would sit down beside him and that the woman would push in beside his mother. He could think of no better arrangement.

As she waited for her tokens, the woman was surveying the seating possibilities—he hoped with the idea of sitting where she was least wanted. There was something familiar-looking about her but Julian could not place what it was. She was a giant of a woman. Her face was set not only to meet opposition but to seek it out. The downward tilt of her large lower lip was like a warning sign: DON'T TAMPER WITH ME. Her bulging figure was encased in a green crepe dress and her feet overflowed in red shoes. She had on a hideous hat. A purple velvet flap came down on one side of it and stood up on the other; the rest of it was green and looked like a cushion with the stuffing out. She carried a mammoth red pocketbook that bulged throughout as if it were stuffed with rocks.

To Julian's disappointment, the little boy climbed up on the empty seat beside his mother. His mother lumped all children, black and white, into the common category, "cute," and she thought little Negroes were on the whole cuter than little white children. She smiled at the little boy as he climbed on the seat.

Meanwhile the woman was bearing down upon the empty seat beside Julian. To his annoyance, she squeezed herself into it. He saw his mother's face change as the woman settled herself next to him and he realized with satisfaction that this was more objectionable to her than it was to him. Her face seemed almost gray and there was a look of dull recognition in her eyes, as if suddenly she had sickened at some awful confrontation. Julian saw that it was because she and the woman had, in a sense, swapped sons. Though his mother would not realize the symbolic significance of this, she would feel it. His amusement showed plainly on his face.

The woman next to him muttered something unintelligible to herself. He was conscious of a kind of bristling next to him, muted growling like that of an angry cat. He could not see anything but the red pocketbook upright on the bulging green thighs. He visualized the woman as she had stood waiting for her tokens—the ponderous figure, rising from the red shoes upward over the solid hips, the mammoth bosom, the haughty face, to the green and purple hat.

His eyes widened.

The vision of the two hats, identical, broke upon him with the radiance of a brilliant sunrise. His face was suddenly lit with joy. He could not believe that Fate had thrust upon his mother such a lesson. He gave a loud chuckle so that she would look at him and see that he saw. She turned her eyes on him slowly. The blue in them seemed to have turned a bruised purple. For a moment he had an uncomfortable sense of her innocence, but it lasted only a second before principle rescued him. Justice entitled him to laugh. His grin hardened until it said to her as plainly as if he were saying aloud: Your punishment exactly fits your pettiness. This should teach you a permanent lesson.

Her eyes shifted to the woman. She seemed unable to bear looking at him and to find the woman preferable. He became conscious again of the bristling presence at his side. The woman was rumbling like a volcano about to become active. His mother's mouth began to twitch slightly at one corner. With a sinking heart, he saw incipient signs of recovery on her face and realized that this was going to strike her suddenly as funny and was going to be no lesson at all. She kept her eyes on the woman and an amused smile came over her face as if the woman were a monkey that had stolen her hat. The little Negro was looking up at her with large fascinated eyes. He had been trying to attract her attention for some time.

"Carver!" the woman said suddenly. "Come heah!"

When he saw that the spotlight was on him at last, Carver drew his feet up and turned himself toward Julian's mother and giggled.

"Carver!" the woman said. "You heah me? Come heah!"

Carver slid down from the seat but remained squatting with his back against the base of it, his head turned slyly around toward Julian's mother, who was smiling at him. The woman reached a hand across the aisle and snatched him to her. He righted himself and hung backwards on her knees, grinning at Julian's mother. "Isn't he cute?" Julian's mother said to the woman with the protruding teeth.

"I reckon he is," the woman said without conviction.

The Negress yanked him upright but he eased out of her grip and shot across the aisle and scrambled, giggling wildly, onto the seat beside his love.

"I think he likes me," Julian's mother said, and smiled at the woman. It was the smile she used when she was being particularly gracious to an inferior. Julian saw everything lost. The lesson had rolled off her like rain on a roof.

The woman stood up and yanked the little boy off the seat as if she were snatching him from contagion. Julian could feel the rage in her at having no weapon like his mother's smile. She gave the child a sharp slap across his leg. He howled once and then thrust his head into her stomach and kicked his feet against her shins. "Behave," she said vehemently.

The bus stopped and the Negro who had been reading the newspaper got off. The woman moved over and set the little boy down with a thump between herself and Julian. She held him firmly by the knee. In a moment he put his hands in front of his face and peeped at Julian's mother through his fingers.

"I see yoooooooo!" she said and put her hand in front of her face and peeped at him.

The woman slapped his hand down. "Quit yo' foolishness," she said, "before I knock the living Jesus out of you!"

Julian was thankful that the next stop was theirs. He reached up and pulled the cord. The woman reached up and pulled it at the same time. Oh my God, he thought. He had the terrible intuition that when they got off the bus together, his mother would open her purse and give the little boy a nickel. The gesture would be as natural to her as breathing. The bus stopped and the woman got up and lunged to the front, dragging the child, who wished to stay on, after her. Julian and his mother got up and followed. As they neared the door, Julian tried to relieve her of her pocketbook.

"No," she murmured, "I want to give the little boy a nickel."

"No!" Julian hissed. "No!"

She smiled down at the child and opened her bag. The bus door opened and the woman picked him up by the arm and descended with him, hanging at her hip. Once in the street she set him down and shook him.

Julian's mother had to close her purse while she got down the bus step but as soon as her feet were on the ground, she opened it again and began to rummage inside. "I can't find but a penny," she whispered, "but it looks like a new one."

"Don't do it!" Julian said fiercely between his teeth. There was a streetlight on the corner and she hurried to get under it so that she could better see into her pocketbook. The woman was heading off rapidly down the street with the child still hanging backward on her hand.

"Oh little boy!" Julian's mother called and took a few quick steps and caught up with them just beyond the lamppost. "Here's a bright new penny for you," and she held out the coin, which shone bronze in the dim light.

The huge woman turned and for a moment stood, her shoulders lifted and her face frozen with frustrated rage, and stared at Julian's mother. Then all at once she seemed to explode like a piece of machinery that had been given one ounce of pressure too much. Julian saw the black fist swing out with the red pocketbook. He shut his eyes and cringed as he heard the woman shout, "He don't take nobody's pennies!" When he opened his eyes, the woman was disappearing down the street with the little boy staring wide-eyed over her shoulder. Julian's mother was sitting on the sidewalk.

"I told you not to do that," Julian said angrily. "I told you not to do that!"

He stood over her for a minute, gritting his teeth. Her legs were stretched out in front of her and her hat was on her lap. He squatted down and looked her in the face. It was totally expressionless. "You got exactly what you deserved," he said. "Now get up."

He picked up her pocketbook and put what had fallen out back in it. He picked the hat up off her lap. The penny caught his eye on the sidewalk and he picked that up and let it drop before her eyes into the purse. Then he stood up and leaned over and held his hands out to pull her up. She remained immobile. He sighed. Rising above them on either side were black apartment buildings, marked with irregular rectangles of light. At the end of the block a man came out of a door and walked off in the opposite direction. "All right," he said, "suppose somebody happens by and wants to know why you're sitting on the sidewalk?"

She took the hand and, breathing hard, pulled heavily up on it and then stood for a moment, swaying slightly as if the spots of light in the darkness were circling around her. Her eyes, shadowed and confused, finally settled on his face. He did not try to conceal his irritation. "I hope this teaches you a lesson," he said. She leaned forward and her eyes raked his face. She seemed trying to determine his identity. Then, as if she found nothing familiar about him, she started off with a headlong movement in the wrong direction.

"Aren't you going on to the Y?" he asked.

"Home," she muttered.

"Well, are we walking?"

For answer she kept going. Julian followed along, his hands behind him. He saw no reason to let the lesson she had had go without backing it up with an explanation of its meaning. She might as well be made to understand what had happened to her. "Don't think that was just an uppity Negro woman," he said. "That was the whole colored race which will no longer take your condescending pennies. That was your black double. She can wear the same hat as you, and to be sure," he added gratuitously (because he thought it was funny), "it looked better on her than it did on you. What all this means," he said, "is that the old world is gone. The old manners are obsolete and your graciousness is not worth a damn." He thought bitterly of the house that had been lost for him. "You aren't who you think you are," he said.

She continued to plow ahead, paying no attention to him. Her hair had come undone on one side. She dropped her pocketbook and took no notice. He stopped and picked it up and handed it to her but she did not take it.

"You needn't act as if the world had come to an end," he said, "because it hasn't. From now on you've got to live in a new world and face a few realities for a change. Buck up," he said, "it won't kill you."

She was breathing fast.

"Let's wait on the bus," he said.

"Home," she said thickly.

"I hate to see you behave like this," he said. "Just like a child. I should be able to expect more of you." He decided to stop where he was and make her stop and wait for a bus. "I'm not going any farther," he said, stopping. "We're going on the bus."

She continued to go on as if she had not heard him. He took a few steps and caught her arm and stopped her. He looked into her face and caught his breath. He was looking into a face he had never seen before. "Tell Grandpa to come get me," she said.

He stared, stricken.

"Tell Caroline to come get me," she said.

Stunned, he let her go and she lurched forward again, walking as if one leg were shorter than the other. A tide of darkness seemed to be sweeping her from him. "Mother!" he cried. "Darling, sweetheart, wait!" Crumpling, she fell to the pavement. He dashed forward and fell at her side, crying, "Mamma, Mamma!" He turned her over. Her face was fiercely distorted. One eye, large and staring, moved slightly to the left as if it had become unmoored. The other remained fixed on him, raked his face again, found nothing and closed.

"Wait here, wait here!" he cried and jumped up and began to run for help toward a cluster of lights he saw in the distance ahead of him. "Help, help!" he shouted, but his voice was thin, scarcely a thread of sound. The lights drifted farther away the faster he ran and his feet moved numbly as if they carried him nowhere. The tide of darkness seemed to sweep him back to her, postponing from moment to moment his entry into the world of guilt and sorrow.

Questions for Discussion

1. What does the opening scene tell and show us about the relationship between Julian and his mother?

2. Describe the mother's treatment of the young man on the bus.

3. Describe Julian's thoughts and actions on the bus. Are you sympathetic to Julian? Why or why not?

4. What do the hats symbolize for Julian?

5. Why does the woman strike Julian's mother and how does this resolution to the story affect Julian? To what extent is this ending a form of dramatic irony?

Suggestions for Writing

1. Write a monologue from the woman's point of view about her experience on the bus and her sense of Julian and his mother.

2. Write an essay that elaborates on the significance of "the bus" in a story that touches on the era and the issues of civil rights. (You may want to begin by finding articles about Rosa Parks.)

3. Who is least sympathetic to you: Julian or his mother? Why? Write a paragraph in response to these questions in your notebook or journal.

The Things They Carried

TIM O'BRIEN

First Lieutenant Jimmy Cross carried letters from a girl named Martha, a junior at Mount Sebastian College in New Jersey. They were not love letters, but Lieutenant Cross was hoping, so he kept them folded in plastic at the bottom of his rucksack. In the late afternoon, after a day's march, he would dig his foxhole, wash his hands under a canteen, unwrap the letters, hold them with the tips of his fingers, and spend the last hour of light pretending. He would imagine romantic camping trips into the White Mountains in New Hampshire. He would sometimes taste the envelope flaps, knowing her tongue had been there. More than anything, he wanted Martha to love him as he loved her, but the letters were mostly chatty, elusive on the matter of love. She was a virgin, he was almost sure. She was an English major at Mount Sebastian, and she wrote beautifully about her professors and roommates and midterm exams, about her respect for Chaucer and her great affection for Virginia Woolf. She often quoted lines of poetry; she never mentioned the war, except to say, Jimmy, take care of yourself. The letters weighed ten ounces. They were signed "Love, Martha," but Lieutenant Cross understood that Love was only a way of signing and did not mean what he sometimes pretended it meant. At dusk, he would carefully return the letters to his rucksack. Slowly, a bit distracted, he would get up and move among his men, checking the perimeter, then at full dark he would return to his hole and watch the night and wonder if Martha was a virgin.

The things they carried were largely determined by necessity. Among the necessities or near-necessities were P-38 can openers, pocket knives, heat tabs, wristwatches, dog tags, mosquito repellent, chewing gum, candy, cigarettes, salt tablets, packets of Kool-Aid, lighters, matches, sewing kits, Military Payment Certificates, C rations, and two or three canteens of water. Together, these items weighed between fifteen and twenty pounds, depending upon a man's habits or rate of metabolism. Henry Dobbins, who was a big man, carried extra rations; he was especially fond of canned peaches in heavy syrup over pound cake. Dave Jensen, who practiced field hygiene, carried a toothbrush, dental floss, and several hotel-size bars of soap he'd stolen on R&R in Sydney, Australia. Ted Lavender, who was scared, carried tranquilizers until he was shot in the head outside the village of Than Khe in mid-April. By necessity, and because it was SOP, they all carried steel helmets that weighed five pounds including the liner and camouflage cover. They carried the standard fatigue jackets and trousers. Very few carried underwear. On their feet they carried jungle boots—2.1 pounds—and Dave Jensen carried three pairs of socks and a can of Dr. Scholl's foot powder as a precaution against trench foot. Until he was shot, Ted Lavender carried six or seven ounces of premium dope, which for him was a necessity.

Mitchell Sanders, the RTO, carried condoms. Norman Bowker carried a diary. Rat Kiley carried comic books. Kiowa, a devout Baptist, carried an illustrated New Testament that had been presented to him by his father, who taught Sunday school in Oklahoma City, Oklahoma. As a hedge against bad times, however, Kiowa also carried his grandmother's distrust of the white man, his grandfather's old hunting hatchet. Necessity dictated. Because the land was mined and booby-trapped, it was SOP for each man to carry a steel-centered, nylon-covered flak jacket, which weighed 6.7 pounds, but which on hot days seemed much heavier. Because you could die so quickly, each man carried at least one large compress bandage, usually in the helmet band for easy access. Because the nights were cold, and because the monsoons were wet, each carried a green plastic poncho that could be used as a raincoat or groundsheet or makeshift tent. With its quilted liner, the poncho weighed almost two pounds, but it was worth every ounce. In April, for instance, when Ted Lavender was shot, they used his poncho to wrap him up, then to carry him across the paddy, then to lift him into the chopper that took him away.

They were called legs or grunts.

To carry something was to "hump" it, as when Lieutenant Jimmy Cross humped his love for Martha up the hills and through the swamps. In its intransitive form, "to hump" meant "to walk," or "to march," but it implied burdens far beyond the intransitive.

Almost everyone humped photographs. In his wallet, Lieutenant Cross carried two photographs of Martha. The first was a Kodachrome snapshot signed "Love," though he knew better. She stood against a brick wall. Her eyes were gray and neutral, her lips slightly open as she stared straight-on at the camera. At night, sometimes, Lieutenant Cross wondered who had taken the picture, because he knew she had boyfriends, because he loved her so much, and because he could see the shadow of the picture taker spreading out against the brick wall. The second photograph had been clipped from the 1968 Mount Sebastian yearbook. It was an action shot—women's volleyball—and Martha was bent horizontal to the floor, reaching, the palms of her hands in sharp focus, the tongue taut, the expression frank and competitive. There was no visible sweat. She wore white gym shorts. Her legs, he thought, were almost certainly the legs of a virgin, dry and without hair, the left knee cocked and carrying her entire weight, which was just over one hundred pounds. Lieutenant Cross remembered touching that left knee. A dark theater, he remembered, and the movie was *Bonnie and Clyde,* and Martha wore a tweed skirt, and during the final scene, when he touched her knee, she turned and looked at him in a sad, sober way that made him pull his hand back, but he would always remember the feel of the tweed skirt and the knee beneath it and the sound of the gunfire that killed Bonnie and Clyde, how embarrassing it was, how slow and oppressive. He remembered kissing her goodnight at the dorm door. Right then, he thought, he should've done something brave. He should've carried her up the stairs to her room and tied her to the bed and touched that left knee all night long. He should've risked it. Whenever he looked at the photographs, he thought of new things he should've done.

What they carried was partly a function of rank, partly of field specialty.

As a first lieutenant and platoon leader, Jimmy Cross carried a compass, maps, code books, binoculars, and a .45-caliber pistol that weighed 2.9 pounds fully loaded. He carried a strobe light and the responsibility for the lives of his men.

As an RTO, Mitchell Sanders carried the PRC-25 radio, a killer, twenty-six pounds with its battery.

As a medic, Rat Kiley carried a canvas satchel filled with morphine and plasma and malaria tablets and surgical tape and comic books and all the things a medic must carry, including M&M's for especially bad wounds, for a total weight of nearly twenty pounds.

As a big man, therefore a machine gunner, Henry Dobbins carried the M-60, which weighed twenty-three pounds unloaded, but which was almost always loaded. In addition, Dobbins carried between ten and fifteen pounds of ammunition draped in belts across his chest and shoulders.

As PFCs or Spec 4s, most of them were common grunts and carried the standard M-16 gas-operated assault rifle. The weapon weighed 7.5 pounds unloaded, 8.2 pounds with its full twenty-round magazine. Depending on numerous factors, such as topography and psychology, the riflemen carried anywhere from twelve to twenty magazines, usually in cloth bandoliers, adding on another 8.4 pounds at minimum, fourteen pounds at maximum. When it was available, they also carried M-16 maintenance gear—rods and steel brushes and swabs and tubes of LSA oil—all of which weighed about a pound. Among the grunts, some carried the M-79 grenade launcher, 5.9 pounds unloaded, a reasonably light weapon except for the ammunition, which was heavy. A single round weighed ten ounces. The typical load was twenty-five rounds. But Ted Lavender, who was scared, carried thirty-four rounds when he was shot and killed outside Than Khe, and he went down under an exceptional burden, more than twenty pounds of ammunition, plus the flak jacket and helmet and rations and water and toilet paper and tranquilizers and all the rest, plus the unweighed fear. He was dead weight. There was no twitching or flopping. Kiowa, who saw it happen, said it was like watching a rock fall, or a big sandbag or something—just boom, then down—not like the movies where the dead guy rolls around and does fancy spins and goes ass over teakettle—not like that, Kiowa said, the poor bastard just flat-fuck fell. Boom. Down. Nothing else. It was a bright morning in mid-April. Lieutenant Cross felt the pain. He blamed himself. They stripped off Lavender's canteens and ammo, all the heavy things, and Rat Kiley said the obvious, the guy's dead, and Mitchell Sanders used his radio to report one U.S. KIA and to request a chopper. Then they wrapped Lavender in his poncho. They carried him out to a dry paddy, established security, and sat smoking the dead man's dope until the chopper came. Lieutenant Cross kept to himself. He pictured Martha's smooth young face, thinking he loved her more than anything, more than his men, and now Ted Lavender was dead because he loved her so much and could not stop thinking about her. When the dust-off arrived, they carried Lavender aboard. Afterward they burned Than Khe. They marched until dusk, then dug their holes, and that night Kiowa kept explaining how you had to be there, how fast it was, how the poor guy just dropped like so much concrete. Boom-down, he said. Like cement.

In addition to the three standard weapons—the M-60, M-16, and M-79—they carried whatever presented itself, or whatever seemed appropriate as a means of killing or staying alive. They carried catch-as-catch-can. At various times, in various situations, they carried M-14s and CAR-15s and Swedish Ks and grease guns and captured AK-47s and Chi-Coms and RPGs and Simonov carbines and black-market Uzis and .38-caliber Smith & Wesson handguns and 66 mm LAWs and shotguns and silencers and blackjacks and bayonets and C-4 plastic explosives. Lee Strunk carried a slingshot; a weapon of last resort, he called it. Mitchell Sanders carried brass knuckles. Kiowa carried his grandfather's feathered hatchet. Every third or fourth man carried a Claymore antipersonnel mine—3.5 pounds with its firing device. They all carried fragmentation grenades—fourteen ounces each. They all carried at least one M-18 colored smoke grenade—twenty-four ounces. Some carried CS or tear-gas grenades. Some carried white-phosphorus grenades. They carried all they could bear, and then some, including a silent awe for the terrible power of the things they carried.

In the first week of April, before Lavender died, Lieutenant Jimmy Cross received a good-luck charm from Martha. It was a simple pebble, an ounce at most. Smooth to the touch, it was a milky-white color with flecks of orange and violet, oval-shaped, like a miniature egg. In the accompanying letter, Martha wrote that she had found the pebble on the Jersey shoreline, precisely where the land touched water at high tide, where things came together but also separated. It was this separate-but-together quality, she wrote, that had inspired her to pick up the pebble and to carry it in her breast pocket for several days, where it seemed weightless, and then to send it through the mail, by air, as a token of her truest feelings for him. Lieutenant Cross found this romantic. But he wondered what her truest feelings were, exactly, and what she meant by separate-but-together. He wondered how the tides and waves had come into play on that afternoon along the Jersey shoreline when Martha saw the pebble and bent down to rescue it from geology. He imagined bare feet. Martha was a poet, with the poet's sensibilities, and her feet would be brown and bare, the toenails unpainted, the eyes chilly and somber like the ocean in March, and though it was painful, he wondered who had been with her that afternoon. He imagined a pair of shadows moving along the strip of sand where things came together but also separated. It was phantom jealousy, he knew, but he couldn't help himself. He loved her so much. On the march, through the hot days of early April, he carried the pebble in his mouth, turning it with his tongue, tasting sea salts and moisture. His mind wandered. He had difficulty keeping his attention on the war. On occasion he would yell at his men to spread out the column, to keep their eyes open, but then he would slip away into daydreams, just pretending, walking barefoot along the Jersey shore, with Martha, carrying nothing. He would feel himself rising. Sun and waves and gentle winds, all love and lightness.

What they carried varied by mission.

When a mission took them to the mountains, they carried mosquito netting, machetes, canvas tarps, and extra bug juice.

If a mission seemed especially hazardous, or if it involved a place they knew to be bad, they carried everything they could. In certain heavily mined AOs, where the land was dense with Toe Poppers and Bouncing Betties, they took turns humping a twenty-eight-pound mine detector. With its headphones and big sensing plate, the equipment was a stress on the lower back and shoulders, awkward to handle, often useless because of the shrapnel in the earth, but they carried it anyway, partly for safety, partly for the illusion of safety.

On ambush, or other night missions, they carried peculiar little odds and ends. Kiowa always took along his New Testament and a pair of moccasins for silence. Dave Jensen carried night-sight vitamins high in carotin. Lee Strunk carried his slingshot; ammo, he claimed, would never be a problem. Rat Kiley carried brandy and M&M's. Until he was shot, Ted Lavender carried the starlight scope, which weighed 6.3 pounds with its aluminum carrying case. Henry Dobbins carried his girlfriend's panty hose wrapped around his neck as a comforter. They all carried ghosts. When dark came, they would move out single file across the meadows and paddies to their ambush coordinates, where they would quietly set up the Claymores and lie down and spend the night waiting.

Other missions were more complicated and required special equipment. In mid-April, it was their mission to search out and destroy the elaborate tunnel complexes in the Than Khe area south of Chu Lai. To blow the tunnels, they carried one-pound blocks of pentrite high explosives, four blocks to a man, sixty-eight pounds in all. They carried wiring, detonators, and battery-powered clackers. Dave Jensen carried earplugs. Most often, before blowing the tunnels, they were ordered by higher command to search them, which was considered bad news, but by and large they just shrugged and carried out orders. Because he was a big man, Henry Dobbins was excused from tunnel duty. The others would draw numbers. Before Lavender died there were seventeen men in the platoon, and whoever drew the number seventeen would strip off his gear and crawl in headfirst with a flashlight and Lieutenant Cross's .45-caliber pistol. The rest of them would fan out as security. They would sit down or kneel, not facing the hole, listening to the ground beneath them, imagining cobwebs and ghosts, whatever was down there—the tunnel walls squeezing in—how the flashlight seemed impossibly heavy in the hand and how it was tunnel vision in the very strictest sense, compression in all ways, even time, and how you had to wiggle in—ass and elbows—a swallowed-up feeling—and how you found yourself worrying about odd things—will your flashlight go dead? Do rats carry rabies? If you screamed, how far would the sound carry? Would your buddies hear it? Would they have the courage to drag you out? In some respects, though not many, the waiting was worse than the tunnel itself. Imagination was a killer.

On April 16, when Lee Strunk drew the number seventeen, he laughed and muttered something and went down quickly. The morning was hot and very still. Not good, Kiowa said. He looked at the tunnel opening, then out across a dry paddy toward the village of Than Khe. Nothing moved. No clouds or birds or people. As they waited, the men smoked and drank Kool-Aid, not talking much, feeling sympathy for Lee Strunk but also feeling the luck of the draw. You win some, you lose some, said Mitchell Sanders, and sometimes you settle for a rain check. It was a tired line and no one laughed.

Henry Dobbins ate a tropical chocolate bar. Ted Lavender popped a tranquilizer and went off to pee.

After five minutes, Lieutenant Jimmy Cross moved to the tunnel, leaned down, and examined the darkness. Trouble, he thought—a cave-in maybe. And then suddenly, without willing it, he was thinking about Martha. The stresses and fractures, the quick collapse, the two of them buried alive under all that weight. Dense, crushing love. Kneeling, watching the hole, he tried to concentrate on Lee Strunk and the war, all the dangers, but his love was too much for him, he felt paralyzed, he wanted to sleep inside her lungs and breathe her blood and be smothered. He wanted her to be a virgin and not a virgin, all at once. He wanted to know her. Intimate secrets—why poetry? Why so sad? Why that grayness in her eyes? Why so alone? Not lonely, just alone—riding her bike across campus or sitting off by herself in the cafeteria. Even dancing, she danced alone—and it was the aloneness that filled him with love. He remembered telling her that one evening. How she nodded and looked away. And how, later, when he kissed her, she received the kiss without returning it, her eyes wide open, not afraid, not a virgin's eyes, just flat and uninvolved.

Lieutenant Cross gazed at the tunnel. But he was not there. He was buried with Martha under the white sand at the Jersey shore. They were pressed together, and the pebble in his mouth was her tongue. He was smiling. Vaguely, he was aware of how quiet the day was, the sullen paddies, yet he could not bring himself to worry about matters of security. He was beyond that. He was just a kid at war, in love. He was twenty-two years old. He couldn't help it.

A few moments later Lee Strunk crawled out of the tunnel. He came up grinning, filthy but alive. Lieutenant Cross nodded and closed his eyes while the others clapped Strunk on the back and made jokes about rising from the dead.

Worms, Rat Kiley said. Right out of the grave. Fuckin' zombie.

The men laughed. They all felt great relief.

Spook City, said Mitchell Sanders.

Lee Strunk made a funny ghost sound, a kind of moaning, yet very happy, and right then, when Strunk made that high happy moaning sound, when he went *Ahhooooo,* right then Ted Lavender was shot in the head on his way back from peeing. He lay with his mouth open. The teeth were broken. There was a swollen black bruise under his left eye. The cheekbone was gone. Oh shit, Rat Kiley said, the guy's dead. The guy's dead, he kept saying, which seemed profound—the guy's dead. I mean really.

The things they carried were determined to some extent by superstition. Lieutenant Cross carried his good-luck pebble. Dave Jensen carried a rabbit's foot. Norman Bowker, otherwise a very gentle person, carried a thumb that had been presented to him as a gift by Mitchell Sanders. The thumb was dark brown, rubbery to the touch, and weighed four ounces at most. It had been cut from a VC corpse, a boy of fifteen or sixteen. They'd found him at the bottom of an irrigation ditch, badly burned, flies in his mouth and eyes. The boy wore black shorts and sandals. At the time of his death he had been carrying a pouch of rice, a rifle, and three magazines of ammunition.

You want my opinion, Mitchell Sanders said, there's a definite moral here.

He put his hand on the dead boy's wrist. He was quiet for a time, as if counting a pulse, then he patted the stomach, almost affectionately, and used Kiowa's hunting hatchet to remove the thumb.

Henry Dobbins asked what the moral was.

Moral?

You know. *Moral.*

Sanders wrapped the thumb in toilet paper and handed it across to Norman Bowker. There was no blood. Smiling, he kicked the boy's head, watched the flies scatter, and said, It's like with that old TV show—Paladin. Have gun, will travel.

Henry Dobbins thought about it.

Yeah, well, he finally said. I don't see no moral.

There it *is,* man.

Fuck off.

They carried USO stationery and pencils and pens. They carried Sterno, safety pins, trip flares, signal flares, spools of wire, razor blades, chewing tobacco, liberated joss sticks and statuettes of the smiling Buddha, candles, grease pencils, *The Stars and Stripes,* fingernail clippers, Psy Ops leaflets, bush hats, bolos, and much more. Twice a week, when the resupply choppers came in, they carried hot chow in green Mermite cans and large canvas bags filled with iced beer and soda pop. They carried plastic water containers, each with a two-gallon capacity. Mitchell Sanders carried a set of starched tiger fatigues for special occasions. Henry Dobbins carried Black Flag insecticide. Dave Jensen carried empty sandbags that could be filled at night for added protection. Lee Strunk carried tanning lotion. Some things they carried in common. Taking turns, they carried the big PRC-77 scrambler radio, which weighed thirty pounds with its battery. They shared the weight of memory. They took up what others could no longer bear. Often, they carried each other, the wounded or weak. They carried infections. They carried chess sets, basketballs, Vietnamese-English dictionaries, insignia of rank, Bronze Stars and Purple Hearts, plastic cards imprinted with the Code of Conduct. They carried diseases, among them malaria and dysentery. They carried lice and ringworm and leeches and paddy algae and various rots and molds. They carried the land itself—Vietnam, the place, the soil—a powdery orange-red dust that covered their boots and fatigues and faces. They carried the sky. The whole atmosphere, they carried it, the humidity, the monsoons, the stink of fungus and decay, all of it, they carried gravity. They moved like mules. By daylight they took sniper fire, at night they were mortared, but it was not battle, it was just the endless march, village to village, without purpose, nothing won or lost. They marched for the sake of the march. They plodded along slowly, dumbly, leaning forward against the heat, unthinking, all blood and bone, simple grunts, soldiering with their legs, toiling up the hills and down into the paddies and across the rivers and up again and down, just humping, one step and then the next and then another, but no volition, no will, because it was automatic, it was anatomy, and the war was entirely a matter of posture and carriage, the hump was everything, a kind of inertia, a kind of emptiness, a dullness of desire and intellect and conscience and hope and human sensibility. Their principles were in their feet. Their calculations were biological. They had no sense of strategy or mission. They searched the villages without knowing what to look for, not caring, kicking over jars of rice, frisking children and old men, blowing tunnels, sometimes setting fires and sometimes not, then forming up and moving on to the next village, then other villages, where it would always be the same. They carried their own lives. The pressures were enormous. In the heat of early afternoon, they would remove their helmets and flak jackets, walking bare, which was dangerous but which helped ease the strain. They would often discard things along the route of march. Purely for comfort, they would throw away rations, blow their Claymores and grenades, no matter, because by nightfall the resupply choppers would arrive with more of the same, then a day or two later still more, fresh watermelons and crates of ammunition and sunglasses and woolen sweaters—the resources were stunning—sparklers for the Fourth of July, colored eggs for Easter. It was the great American war chest—the fruits of science, the smokestacks, the canneries, the arsenals at Hartford, the Minnesota forests, the machine shops, the vast fields of corn and wheat—they carried like freight trains; they carried it on their backs and shoulders—and for all the ambiguities of Vietnam, all the mysteries and unknowns, there was at least the single abiding certainty that they would never be at a loss for things to carry.

After the chopper took Lavender away, Lieutenant Jimmy Cross led his men into the village of Than Khe. They burned everything. They shot chickens and dogs, they trashed the village well, they called in artillery and watched the wreckage, then they marched for several hours through the hot afternoon, and then at dusk, while Kiowa explained how Lavender died, Lieutenant Cross found himself trembling.

He tried not to cry. With his entrenching tool, which weighed five pounds, he began digging a hole in the earth.

He felt shame. He hated himself. He had loved Martha more than his men, and as a consequence Lavender was now dead, and this was something he would have to carry like a stone in his stomach for the rest of the war.

All he could do was dig. He used his entrenching tool like an ax, slashing, feeling both love and hate, and then later, when it was full dark, he sat at the bottom of his foxhole and wept. It went on for a long while. In part, he was grieving for Ted Lavender, but mostly it was for Martha, and for himself, because she belonged to another world, which was not quite real, and because she was a junior at Mount Sebastian College in New Jersey, a poet and a virgin and uninvolved, and because he realized she did not love him and never would.

Like cement, Kiowa whispered in the dark. I swear to God—boom-down. Not a word.

I've heard this, said Norman Bowker.

A pisser, you know? Still zipping himself up. Zapped while zipping.

All right, fine. That's enough.

Yeah, but you had to see it, the guy just—

I *heard,* man. Cement. So why not shut the fuck *up?*

Kiowa shook his head sadly and glanced over at the hole where Lieutenant Jimmy Cross sat watching the night. The air was thick and wet. A warm, dense fog had settled over the paddies and there was the stillness that precedes rain.

After a time Kiowa sighed.

One thing for sure, he said. The Lieutenant's in some deep hurt. I mean that crying jag—the way he was carrying on—it wasn't fake or anything, it was real heavy-duty hurt. The man cares.

Sure, Norman Bowker said.

Say what you want, the man does care.

We all got problems.

Not Lavender.

No, I guess not, Bowker said. Do me a favor, though.

Shut up?

That's a smart Indian. Shut up.

Shrugging, Kiowa pulled off his boots. He wanted to say more, just to lighten up his sleep, but instead he opened his New Testament and arranged it beneath his head as a pillow. The fog made things seem hollow and unattached. He tried not to think about Ted Lavender, but then he was thinking how fast it was, no drama, down and dead, and how it was hard to feel anything except surprise. It seemed unchristian. He wished he could find some great sadness, or even anger, but the emotion wasn't there and he couldn't make it happen. Mostly he felt pleased to be alive. He liked the smell of the New Testament under his cheek, the leather and ink and paper and glue, whatever the chemicals were. He liked hearing the sounds of night. Even his fatigue, it felt fine, the stiff muscles and the prickly awareness of his own body, a floating feeling. He enjoyed not being dead. Lying there, Kiowa admired Lieutenant Jimmy Cross's capacity for grief. He wanted to share the man's pain, he wanted to care as Jimmy Cross cared. And yet when he closed his eyes, all he could think was Boom-down, and all he could feel was the pleasure of having his boots off and the fog curling in around him and the damp soil and the Bible smells and the plush comfort of night.

After a moment Norman Bowker sat up in the dark.

What the hell, he said. You want to talk, *talk.* Tell it to me.

Forget it.

No, man, go on. One thing I hate, it's a silent Indian.

For the most part they carried themselves with poise, a kind of dignity. Now and then, however, there were times of panic, when they squealed or wanted to squeal but couldn't, when they twitched and made moaning sounds and covered their heads and said Dear Jesus and flopped around on the earth and fired their weapons blindly and cringed and sobbed and begged for the noise to stop and went wild and made stupid promises to themselves and to God and to their mothers and fathers, hoping not to die. In different ways, it happened to all of them. Afterward, when the firing ended, they would blink and peek up. They would touch their bodies, feeling shame, then quickly hiding it. They would force themselves to stand. As if in slow motion, frame by frame, the world would take on the old logic—absolute silence, then the wind, then sunlight, then voices. It was the burden of being alive. Awkwardly, the men would reassemble themselves, first in private, then in groups, becoming soldiers again. They would repair the leaks in their eyes. They would check for casualties, call in dust-offs, light cigarettes, try to smile, clear their throats and spit and begin cleaning their weapons. After a time someone would shake his head and say, No lie, I almost shit my pants, and someone else would laugh, which meant it was bad, yes, but the guy had obviously not shit his pants, it wasn't that bad, and in any case nobody would ever do such a thing and then go ahead and talk about it. They would squint into the dense, oppressive sunlight. For a few moments, perhaps, they would fall silent, lighting a joint and tracking its passage from man to man, inhaling, holding in the humiliation. Scary stuff, one of them might say. But then someone else would grin or flick his eyebrows and say, Roger-dodger, almost cut me a new asshole, *almost.*

There were numerous such poses. Some carried themselves with a sort of wistful resignation, others with pride or stiff soldierly discipline or good humor or macho zeal. They were afraid of dying but they were even more afraid to show it.

They found jokes to tell.

They used a hard vocabulary to contain the terrible softness. *Greased,* they'd say. *Offed, lit up, zapped while zipping.* It wasn't cruelty, just stage presence. They were actors and the war came at them in 3-D. When someone died, it wasn't quite dying, because in a curious way it seemed scripted, and because they had their lines mostly memorized, irony mixed with tragedy, and because they called it by other names, as if to encyst and destroy the reality of death itself. They kicked corpses. They cut off thumbs. They talked grunt lingo. They told stories about Ted Lavender's supply of tranquilizers, how the poor guy didn't feel a thing, how incredibly tranquil he was.

There's a moral here, said Mitchell Sanders.

They were waiting for Lavender's chopper, smoking the dead man's dope.

The moral's pretty obvious, Sanders said, and winked. Stay away from drugs. No joke, they'll ruin your day every time.

Cute, said Henry Dobbins.

Mind-blower, get it? Talk about wiggy—nothing left, just blood and brains.

They made themselves laugh.

There it is, they'd say, over and over, as if the repetition itself were an act of poise, a balance between crazy and almost crazy, knowing without going. There it is, which meant be cool, let it ride, because oh yeah, man, you can't change what can't be changed, there it is, there it absolutely and positively and fucking well *is.*

They were tough.

They carried all the emotional baggage of men who might die. Grief, terror, love, longing—these were intangibles, but the intangibles had their own mass and specific gravity, they had tangible weight. They carried shameful memories. They carried the common secret of cowardice barely restrained, the instinct to run or freeze or hide, and in many respects this was the heaviest burden of all, for it could never be put down, it required perfect balance and perfect posture. They carried their reputations. They carried the soldier's greatest fear, which was the fear of blushing. Men killed, and died, because they were embarrassed not to. It was what had brought them to the war in the first place, nothing positive, no dreams of glory or honor, just to avoid the blush of dishonor. They died so as not to die of embarrassment. They crawled into tunnels and walked point and advanced under fire. Each morning, despite the unknowns, they made their legs move. They endured. They kept humping. They did not submit to the obvious alternative, which was simply to close the eyes and fall. So easy, really. Go limp and tumble to the ground and let the muscles unwind and not speak and not budge until your buddies picked you up and lifted you into the chopper that would roar and dip its nose and carry you off to the world. A mere matter of falling, yet no one ever fell. It was not courage, exactly; the object was not valor. Rather, they were too frightened to be cowards.

By and large they carried these things inside, maintaining the masks of composure. They sneered at sick call. They spoke bitterly about guys who had found release by shooting off their own toes or fingers. Pussies, they'd say. Candyasses. It was fierce, mocking talk, with only a trace of envy or awe, but even so, the image played itself out behind their eyes.

They imagined the muzzle against flesh. They imagined the quick, sweet pain, then the evacuation to Japan, then a hospital with warm beds and cute geisha nurses.

They dreamed of freedom birds.

At night, on guard, staring into the dark, they were carried away by jumbo jets. They felt the rush of takeoff. *Gone!* they yelled. And then velocity, wings, and engines, a smiling stewardess—but it was more than a plane, it was a real bird, a big sleek silver bird with feathers and talons and high screeching. They were flying. The weights fell off, there was nothing to bear. They laughed and held on tight, feeling the cold slap of wind and altitude, soaring, thinking *It's over, I'm gone!*—they were naked, they were light and free—it was all lightness, bright and fast and buoyant, light as light, a helium buzz in the brain, a giddy bubbling in the lungs as they were taken up over the clouds and the war, beyond duty, beyond gravity and mortification and global entanglements—*Sin loi!* they yelled, *I'm sorry, motherfuckers, but I'm out of it, I'm goofed, I'm on a space cruise, I'm gone!*—and it was a restful, disencumbered sensation, just riding the light waves, sailing that big silver freedom bird over the mountains and oceans, over America, over the farms and great sleeping cities and cemeteries and highways and the Golden Arches of McDonald's. It was flight, a kind of fleeing, a kind of falling, falling higher and higher, spinning off the edge of the earth and beyond the sun and through the vast, silent vacuum where there were no burdens and where everything weighed exactly nothing. *Gone!* they screamed, *I'm sorry but I'm gone!* And so at night, not quite dreaming, they gave themselves over to lightness, they were carried, they were purely borne.

On the morning after Ted Lavender died, First Lieutenant Jimmy Cross crouched at the bottom of his foxhole and burned Martha's letters. Then he burned the two photographs. There was a steady rain falling, which made it difficult, but he used heat tabs and Sterno to build a small fire, screening it with his body, holding the photographs over the tight blue flame with the tips of his fingers.

He realized it was only a gesture. Stupid, he thought. Sentimental, too, but mostly just stupid.

Lavender was dead. You couldn't burn the blame.

Besides, the letters were in his head. And even now, without photographs, Lieutenant Cross could see Martha playing volleyball in her white gym shorts and yellow T-shirt. He could see her moving in the rain.

When the fire died out, Lieutenant Cross pulled his poncho over his shoulders and ate breakfast from a can.

There was no great mystery, he decided.

In those burned letters Martha had never mentioned the war, except to say, Jimmy, take care of yourself. She wasn't involved. She signed the letters "Love," but it wasn't love, and all the fine lines and technicalities did not matter.

The morning came up wet and blurry. Everything seemed part of everything else, the fog and Martha and the deepening rain.

It was a war, after all.

Half smiling, Lieutenant Jimmy Cross took out his maps. He shook his head hard, as if to clear it, then bent forward and began planning the day's march. In ten minutes, or maybe twenty, he would rouse the men and they would pack up and head west, where the maps showed the country to be green and inviting. They would do what they had always done. The rain might add some weight, but otherwise it would be one more day layered upon all the other days.

He was realistic about it. There was that new hardness in his stomach.

No more fantasies, he told himself.

Henceforth, when he thought about Martha, it would be only to think that she belonged elsewhere. He would shut down the daydreams. This was not Mount Sebastian, it was another world, where there were no pretty poems or midterm exams, a place where men died because of carelessness and gross stupidity. Kiowa was right. Boom-down, and you were dead, never partly dead.

Briefly, in the rain, Lieutenant Cross saw Martha's gray eyes gazing back at him.

He understood.

It was very sad, he thought. The things men carried inside. The things men did or felt they had to do.

He almost nodded at her, but didn't.

Instead he went back to his maps. He was now determined to perform his duties firmly and without negligence. It wouldn't help Lavender, he knew that, but from this point on he would comport himself as a soldier. He would dispose of his good-luck pebble. Swallow it, maybe, or use Lee Strunk's slingshot, or just drop it along the trail. On the march he would impose strict field discipline. He would be careful to send out flank security, to prevent straggling or bunching up, to keep his troops moving at the proper pace and at the proper interval. He would insist on clean weapons. He would confiscate the remains of Lavender's dope. Later in the day, perhaps, he would call the men together and speak to them plainly. He would accept the blame for what had happened to Ted Lavender. He would be a man about it. He would look them in the eyes, keeping his chin level, and he would issue the new SOPs in a calm, impersonal tone of voice, an officer's voice, leaving no room for argument or discussion. Commencing immediately, he'd tell them, they would no longer abandon equipment along the route of march. They would police up their acts. They would get their shit together, and keep it together, and maintain it neatly and in good working order.

He would not tolerate laxity. He would show strength, distancing himself.

Among the men there would be grumbling, of course, and maybe worse, because their days would seem longer and their loads heavier, but Lieutenant Cross reminded himself that his obligation was not to be loved but to lead. He would dispense with love; it was not now a factor. And if anyone quarreled or complained, he would simply tighten his lips and arrange his shoulders in the correct command posture. He might give a curt little nod. Or he might not. He might just shrug and say Carry on, then they would saddle up and form into a column and move out toward the villages west of Than Khe.

Questions for Discussion

1. How does O'Brien use a topic that might appear to be peripheral to the war (what soldiers carried) to address central issues of war and being a soldier?

2. Describe the structure of this story. How is it different from the structures of other short stories?

3. In a story preoccupied by "things," how does O'Brien convey people? That is, how does he give us a sense of the personalities of these men? How do the things show us the people?

4. How would you describe the soldiers' responses to Lavender's being killed? How would you describe the narrator's attitude toward death and fear?

5. In what ways does this story enlarge or change your view of the Vietnam War and of war in general?

6. O'Brien speaks of the harsh and sometimes encoded language the soldiers used, and he says that it was a product of "stage presence." Elaborate on what you think he means by this assessment.

Suggestions for Writing

1. Write an essay in which you analyze the structure of O'Brien's story—the way in which he organizes the material, the nature of his "lists," how the lists change, and the effect of the structure on the reader.

2. Write an essay in which you compare and contrast O'Brien's view of what it means to be a soldier with a more popularized view, such as the one we get from the "Rambo" movies.

3. Write a journal entry that explores your definition of "hero" and "heroism" and that discusses the extent to which the soldiers in O'Brien's story are heroes, as well as the extent to which the story altered your notion of heroism.

Rape Fantasies

MARGARET ATWOOD

The way they're going on about it in the magazines you'd think it was just invented, and not only that but it's something terrific, like a vaccine for cancer. They put it in capital letters on the front cover, and inside they have these questionnaires like the ones they used to have about whether you were a good enough wife or an endomorph or an ectomorph, remember that? with the scoring upside down on page 73, and then these numbered do-it-yourself dealies, you know? RAPE, TEN THINGS TO DO ABOUT IT, like it was ten new hairdos or something. I mean, what's so new about it?

So at work they all have to talk about it because no matter what magazine you open, there it is, staring you right between the eyes, and they're beginning to have it on the television, too. Personally I'd prefer a June Allyson movie anytime but they don't make them any more and they don't even have them that much on the Late Show. For instance, day before yesterday, that would be Wednesday, thank god it's Friday as they say, we were sitting around in the women's lunch room—the *lunch* room, I mean you'd think you could get some peace and quiet in there—and Chrissy closes up the magazine she's been reading and says, "How about it, girls, do you have rape fantasies?"

The four of us were having our game of bridge the way we always do, and I had a bare twelve points counting the singleton with not that much of a bid in anything. So I said one club, hoping Sondra would remember about the one club convention, because the time before when I used that she thought I really meant clubs and she bid us up to three, and all I had was four little ones with nothing higher than a six, and we went down two and on top of that we were vulnerable. She is not the world's best bridge player. I mean, neither am I but there's a limit.

Darlene passed but the damage was done, Sondra's head went round like it was on ball bearings and she said, *"What* fantasies?"

"Rape fantasies," Chrissy said. She's a receptionist and she looks like one; she's pretty but cool as a cucumber, like she's been painted all over with nail polish, if you know what I mean. Varnished. "It says here all women have rape fantasies."

"For Chrissake, I'm eating an egg sandwich," I said, "and I bid one club and Darlene passed."

"You mean, like some guy jumping you in an alley or something," Sondra said. She was eating her lunch, we all eat our lunches during the game, and she bit into a piece of that celery she always brings and started to chew away on it with this thoughtful expression in her eyes and I knew we might as well pack it in as far as the game was concerned.

"Yeah, sort of like that," Chrissy said. She was blushing a little, you could see it even under her makeup.

"I don't think you should go out alone at night," Darlene said, "you put yourself in a position," and I may have been mistaken but she was looking at me. She's the oldest, she's forty-one though you wouldn't know it and neither does she, but I looked it up in the employees' file. I like to guess a person's age and then look it up to see if I'm right. I let myself have an extra pack of cigarettes if I am, though I'm trying to cut down. I figure it's harmless as long as you don't tell. I mean, not everyone has access to that file, it's more or less confidential. But it's all right if I tell you, I don't expect you'll ever meet her, though you never know, it's a small world. Anyway.

"For *heaven's* sake, it's only *Toronto,*" Greta said. She worked in Detroit for three years and she never lets you forget it, it's like she thinks she's a war hero or something, we should all admire her just for the fact that she's still walking this earth, though she was really living in Windsor the whole time, she just worked in Detroit. Which for me doesn't really count. It's where you sleep, right?

"Well, do you?" Chrissy said. She was obviously trying to tell us about hers but she wasn't about to go first, she's cautious, that one.

"I certainly don't," Darlene said, and she wrinkled up her nose, like this, and I had to laugh. "I think it's disgusting." She's divorced, I read that in the file too, she never talks about it. It must've been years ago anyway. She got up and went over to the coffee machine and turned her back on us as though she wasn't going to have anything more to do with it.

"Well," Greta said. I could see it was going to be between her and Chrissy. They're both blondes, I don't mean that in a bitchy way but they do try to outdress each other. Greta would like to get out of Filing, she'd like to be a receptionist too so she could meet more people. You don't meet much of anyone in Filing except other people in Filing. Me, I don't mind it so much, I have outside interests.

"Well," Greta said, "I sometimes think about, you know my apartment? It's got this little balcony, I like to sit out there in the summer and I have a few plants out there. I never bother that much about locking the door to the balcony, it's one of those sliding glass ones, I'm on the eighteenth floor for heaven's sake, I've got a good view of the lake and the CN Tower and all. But I'm sitting around one night in my housecoat, watching TV with my shoes off, you know how you do, and I see this guy's feet, coming down past the window, and the next thing you know he's standing on the balcony, he's let himself down by a rope with a hook on the end of it from the floor above, that's the nineteenth, and before I can even get up off the chesterfield he's inside the apartment. He's all dressed in black with black gloves on"—I knew right away what show she got the black gloves off because I saw the same one—"and then he, well, you know."

"You know what?" Chrissy said, but Greta said, "And afterwards he tells me that he goes all over the outside of the apartment building like that, from one floor to another, with his rope and his hook . . . and then he goes out to the balcony and tosses his rope, and he climbs up it and disappears."

"Just like Tarzan," I said, but nobody laughed.

"Is that all?" Chrissy said. "Don't you ever think about, well, I think about being in the bathtub, with no clothes on . . ."

"So who takes a bath in their clothes?" I said, you have to admit it's stupid when you come to think of it, but she just went on, ". . . with lots of bubbles, what I use is Vitabath, it's more expensive but it's so relaxing, and my hair pinned up, and the door opens and this fellow's standing there. . . ."

"How'd he get in?" Greta said.

"Oh, I don't know, through a window or something. Well, I can't very well get out of the bathtub, the bathroom's too small and besides he's blocking the doorway, so I just *lie* there, and he starts to very slowly take his own clothes off, and then he gets into the bathtub with me."

"Don't you scream or anything?" said Darlene. She'd come back with her cup of coffee, she was getting really interested. "I'd scream like bloody murder."

"Who'd hear me?" Chrissy said. "Besides, all the articles say it's better not to resist, that way you don't get hurt."

"Anyway you might get bubbles up your nose," I said, "from the deep breathing," and I swear all four of them looked at me like I was in bad taste, like I'd insulted the Virgin Mary or something. I mean, I don't see what's wrong with a little joke now and then. Life's too short, right?

"Listen," I said, "those aren't *rape* fantasies. I mean, you aren't getting *raped,* it's just some guy you haven't met formally who happens to be more attractive than Derek Cummins"—he's the Assistant Manager, he wears elevator shoes or at any rate they have these thick soles and he has this funny way of talking, we call him Derek Duck—"and you have a good time. Rape is when they've got a knife or something and you don't want to."

"So what about you, Estelle," Chrissy said, she was miffed because I laughed at her fantasy, she thought I was putting her down. Sondra was miffed too, by this time she'd finished her celery and she wanted to tell about hers, but she hadn't got in fast enough.

"All right, let me tell you one," I said. "I'm walking down this dark street at night and this fellow comes up and grabs my arm. Now it so happens that I have a plastic lemon in my purse, you know how it always says you should carry a plastic lemon in your purse? I don't really do it, I tried it once but the darn thing leaked all over my chequebook, but in this fantasy I have one, and I say to him, "You're intending to rape me, right?" and he nods, so I open my purse to get the plastic lemon, and I can't find it! My purse is full of all this junk, Kleenex and cigarettes and my change purse and my lipstick and my driver's licence, you know the kind of stuff; so I ask him to hold out his hands, like this, and I pile all this junk into them and down at the bottom there's the plastic lemon, and I can't get the top off. So I hand it to him and he's very obliging, he twists the top off and hands it back to me, and I squirt him in the eye."

I hope you don't think that's too vicious. Come to think of it, it is a bit mean, especially when he was so polite and all.

"*That's* your rape fantasy?" Chrissy says. "I don't believe it."

"She's a card," Darlene says, she and I are the ones that've been here the longest and she never will forget the time I got drunk at the office party and insisted I was going to dance under the table instead of on top of it, I did a sort of Cossack number but then I hit my head on the bottom of the table—actually it was a desk—when I went to get up, and I knocked myself out cold. She's decided that's the mark of an original mind and she tells everyone new about it and I'm not sure that's fair. Though I did do it.

"I'm being totally honest," I say. I always am and they know it. There's no point in being anything else, is the way I look at it, and sooner or later the truth will out so you might as well not waste the time, right? "You should hear the one about the Easy-Off Oven Cleaner."

But that was the end of the lunch hour, with one bridge game shot to hell, and the next day we spent most of the time arguing over whether to start a new game or play out the hands we had left over from the day before, so Sondra never did get a chance to tell about her rape fantasy.

It started me thinking though, about my own rape fantasies. Maybe I'm abnormal or something, I mean I have fantasies about handsome strangers coming in through the window too, like Mr. Clean, I wish one would, please god somebody without flat feet and big sweat marks on his shirt, and over five feet five, believe me being tall is a handicap though it's getting better, tall guys are starting to like someone whose nose reaches higher than their belly button. But if you're being totally honest you can't count those as rape fantasies. In a real rape fantasy, what you should feel is this anxiety, like when you think about your apartment building catching on fire and whether you should use the elevator or the stairs or maybe just stick your head under a wet towel, and you try to remember everything you've read about what to do but you can't decide.

For instance, I'm walking along this dark street at night and this short, ugly fellow comes up and grabs my arm, and not only is he ugly, you know, with a sort of puffy nothing face, like those fellows you have to talk to in the bank when your account's overdrawn—of course I don't mean they're all like that—but he's absolutely covered in pimples. So he gets me pinned against the wall, he's short but he's heavy, and he starts to undo himself and the zipper gets stuck. I mean, one of the most significant moments in a girl's life, it's almost like getting married or having a baby or something, and he sticks the zipper.

So I say, kind of disgusted, "Oh for Chrissake," and he starts to cry. He tells me he's never been able to get anything right in his entire life, and this is the last straw, he's going to go jump off a bridge.

"Look," I say, I feel so sorry for him, in my rape fantasies I always end up feeling sorry for the guy, I mean there has to be something *wrong* with them, if it was Clint Eastwood it'd be different but worse luck it never is. I was the kind of little girl who buried dead robins, know what I mean? It used to drive my mother nuts, she didn't like me touching them, because of the germs I guess. So I say, "Listen, I know how you feel. You really should do something about those pimples, if you got rid of them you'd be quite good looking, honest; then you wouldn't have to go around doing stuff like this. I had them myself once," I say, to comfort him, but in fact I did, and it ends up I give him the name of my old dermatologist, the one I had in high school, that was back in Leamington, except I used to go to St. Catharine's for the dermatologist. I'm telling you, I was really lonely when I first came here; I thought it was going to be such a big adventure and all, but it's a lot harder to meet people in a city. But I guess it's different for a guy.

Or I'm lying in bed with this terrible cold, my face is all swollen up, my eyes are red and my nose is dripping like a leaky tap, and this fellow comes in through the window and *he* has a terrible cold too, it's a new kind of flu that's been going around. So he says, "I'b goig do rabe you"—I hope you don't mind me holding my nose like this but that's the way I imagine it—and he lets out this terrific sneeze, which slows him down a bit, also I'm no object of beauty myself, you'd have to be some kind of pervert to want to rape someone with a cold like mine, it'd be like raping a bottle of LePage's mucilage the way my nose is running. He's looking wildly around the room, and I realize it's because he doesn't have a piece of Kleenex! "Id's ride here," I say, and I pass him the Kleenex, god knows why he even bothered to get out of bed, you'd think if you were going to go around climbing in windows you'd wait till you were healthier, right? I mean, that takes a certain amount of energy. So I ask him why doesn't he let me fix him a NeoCitran and scotch, that's what I always take, you still have the cold but you don't feel it, so I do and we end up watching the Late Show together. I mean, they aren't all sex maniacs, the rest of the time they must lead a normal life. I figure they enjoy watching the Late Show just like anybody else.

I do have a scarier one though . . . where the fellow says he's hearing angel voices that're telling him he's got to kill me, you know, you read about things like that all the time in the papers. In this one I'm not in the apartment where I live now, I'm back in my mother's house in Leamington and the fellow's been hiding in the cellar, he grabs my arm when I go downstairs to get a jar of jam and he's got hold of the axe too, out of the garage, that one is really scary. I mean, what do you say to a nut like that?

So I start to shake but after a minute I get control of myself and I say, is he sure the angel voices have got the right person, because I hear the same angel voices and they've been telling me for some time that I'm going to give birth to the reincarnation of St. Anne who in turn has the Virgin Mary and right after that comes Jesus Christ and the end of the world, and he wouldn't want to interfere with that, would he? So he gets confused and listens some more, and then he asks for a sign and I show him my vaccination mark, you can see it's sort of an odd-shaped one, it got infected because I scratched the top off, and that does it, he apologizes and climbs out the coal chute again, which is how he got in in the first place, and I say to myself there's some advantage in having been brought up a Catholic even though I haven't been to church since they changed the service into English, it just isn't the same, you might as well be a Protestant. I must write to Mother and tell her to nail up that coal chute, it always has bothered me. Funny, I couldn't tell you at all what this man looks like but I know exactly what kind of shoes he's wearing, because that's the last I see of him, his shoes going up the coal chute, and they're the old-fashioned kind that lace up the ankles, even though he's a young fellow. That's strange, isn't it?

Let me tell you though I really sweat until I see him safely out of there and I go upstairs right away and make myself a cup of tea. I don't think about that one much. My mother always said you shouldn't dwell on unpleasant things and I generally agree with that, I mean, dwelling on them doesn't make them go away. Though not dwelling on them doesn't make them go away either, when you come to think of it.

Sometimes I have these short ones where the fellow grabs my arm but I'm really a Kung-Fu expert, can you believe it, in real life I'm sure it would just be a conk on the head and that's that, like getting your tonsils out, you'd wake up and it would be all over except for the sore places, and you'd be lucky if your neck wasn't broken or something. I could never even hit the volleyball in gym and a volleyball is fairly large, you know?—and I just go *zap* with my fingers into his eyes and that's it, he falls over, or I flip him against a wall or something. But I could never really stick my fingers in anyone's eyes, could you? It would feel like hot jello and I don't even like cold jello, just thinking about it gives me the creeps. I feel a bit guilty about that one, I mean how would you like walking around knowing someone's been blinded for life because of you?

But maybe it's different for a guy.

The most touching one I have is when the fellow grabs my arm and I say, sad and kind of dignified, "You'd be raping a corpse." That pulls him up short and I explain that I've just found out I have leukaemia and the doctors have only given me a few months to live. That's why I'm out pacing the streets alone at night, I need to think, you know, come to terms with myself. I don't really have leukaemia but in the fantasy I do, I guess I chose that particular disease because a girl in my grade four class died of it, the whole class sent her flowers when she was in the hospital. I didn't understand then that she was going to die and I wanted to have leukaemia too so I could get flowers. Kids are funny, aren't they? Well, it turns out that he has leukaemia himself, and *he* only has a few months to live, that's why he's going around raping people, he's very bitter because he's so young and his life is being taken from him before he's really lived it. So we walk along gently under the street lights, it's spring and sort of misty, and we end up going for coffee, we're happy we've found the only other person in the world who can understand what we're going through, it's almost like fate, and after a while we just sort of look at each other and our hands touch, and he comes back with me and moves into my apartment and we spend our last months together before we die, we just sort of don't wake up in the morning, though I've never decided which one of us gets to die first. If it's him I have to go on and fantasize about the funeral, if it's me I don't have to worry about that, so it just about depends on how tired I am at the time. You may not believe this but sometimes I even start crying. I cry at the ends of movies, even the ones that aren't all that sad, so I guess it's the same thing. My mother's like that too.

The funny thing about these fantasies is that the man is always someone I don't know, and the statistics in the magazines, well, most of them anyway, they say it's often someone you do know, at least a little bit, like your boss or something—I mean, it wouldn't be *my* boss, he's over sixty and I'm sure he couldn't rape his way out of a paper bag, poor old thing, but it might be someone like Derek Duck, in his elevator shoes, perish the thought—or someone you just met, who invites you up for a drink, it's getting so you can hardly be sociable any more, and how are you supposed to meet people if you can't trust them even that basic amount? You can't spend your whole life in the Filing Department or cooped up in your own apartment with all the doors and windows locked and the shades down. I'm not what you would call a drinker but I like to go out now and then for a drink or two in a nice place, even if I am by myself, I'm with Women's Lib on that even though I can't agree with a lot of the other things they say. Like here for instance, the waiters all know me and if anyone, you know, bothers me . . . I don't know why I'm telling you all this, except I think it helps you get to know a person, especially at first, hearing some of the things they think about. At work they call me the office worry wart, but it isn't so much like worrying, it's more like figuring out what you should do in an emergency, like I said before.

Anyway, another thing about it is that there's a lot of conversation, in fact I spend most of my time, in the fantasy that is, wondering what I'm going to say and what he's going to say, I think it would be better if you could get a conversation going. Like, how could a fellow do that to a person he's just had a long conversation with, once you let them know you're human, you have a life too, I don't see how they could go ahead with it, right? I mean, I know it happens but I just don't understand it, that's the part I really don't understand.

Questions for Discussion

1. In what ways does the story define (or redefine) for us the term *rape fantasy?*

2. To some extent, the narrator Atwood has created is naïve. That is, Atwood has created a speaker who seems somewhat unaware of how her story will strike the listener. What effect does this narrator have on you, and how does such a narrator shape the perspective on rape that this story provides?

3. To what extent does the story attempt to deal with "date rape" or "acquaintance rape"?

4. How would you characterize the "rape" fantasies of the narrator's coworkers? Are they really about rape? Explain.

5. What is your overall assessment of how this story deals with the topic of rape?

Suggestions for Writing

1. Write an essay about the perspective on rape that this story conveys, both directly and indirectly.

2. Write an essay about the nature and function of the narrator in "Rape Fantasies."

3. Collect several articles or books on "date rape" or "acquaintance rape" and then write an essay that assesses the extent to which Atwood's story presents an accurate perspective on these kinds of rapes.

4. In your journal write an entry about your own attitudes toward rape and how rape is viewed in both your college community and society at large.

5. In your journal, write an entry in which you consider the potential problems fiction writers might encounter if they chose to write stories concerning rape. Also consider different problems and prejudices writers of different genders might encounter in writing fiction about this topic.

August 2002: Night Meeting

RAY   BRADBURY

Before going on up into the blue hills, Tomás Gomez stopped for gasoline at the lonely station.

"Kind of alone out here, aren't you, Pop?" said Tomás.

The old man wiped off the windshield of the small truck. "Not bad."

"How do you like Mars, Pop?"

"Fine. Always something new. I made up my mind when I came here last year I wouldn't expect nothing, nor ask nothing, nor be surprised at nothing. We've got to forget Earth and how things were. We've got to look at what we're in here, and how *different* it is. I get a hell of a lot of fun out of just the weather here. It's *Martian* weather. Hot as hell daytimes, cold as hell nights. I get a big kick out of the different flowers and different rain. I came to Mars to retire and I wanted to retire in a place where everything is different. An old man needs to have things different. Young people don't want to talk to him, other old people bore hell out of him. So I thought the best thing for me is a place so different that all you got to do is open your eyes and you're entertained. I got this gas station. If business picks up too much, I'll move on back to some other old highway that's not so busy, where I can earn just enough to live on and still have time to feel the *different* things here."

"You got the right idea, Pop," said Tomás, his brown hands idly on the wheel. He was feeling good. He had been working in one of the new colonies for ten days straight and now he had two days off and was on his way to a party.

"I'm not surprised at anything any more," said the old man. "I'm just looking. I'm just experiencing. If you can't take Mars for what she is, you might as well go back to Earth. Everything's crazy up here, the soil, the air, the canals, the natives (I never saw any yet, but I hear they're around), the clocks. Even my clock acts funny. Even *time* is crazy up here. Sometimes I feel I'm here all by myself, no one else on the whole damn planet. I'd take bets on it. Sometimes I feel about eight years old, my body squeezed up and everything else tall. Jesus, it's just the place for an old man. Keeps me alert and keeps me happy. You know what Mars is? It's like a thing I got for Christmas seventy years ago—don't know if you ever had one—they called them kaleidoscopes, bits of crystal and cloth and beads and pretty junk. You held it up to the sunlight and looked in through at it, and it took your breath away. All the patterns! Well, that's Mars. Enjoy it. Don't ask it to be nothing else but what it is. Jesus, you know that highway right there, built by the Martians, is over sixteen centuries old and still in good condition? That's one dollar and fifty cents, thanks and good night."

Tomás drove off down the ancient highway, laughing quietly.

It was a long road going into darkness and hills and he held to the wheel, now and again reaching into his lunch bucket and taking out a piece of candy. He had been driving steadily for an hour, with no other car on the road, no light, just the road going under, the hum, the roar, and Mars out there, so quiet. Mars was always quiet, but quieter tonight than any other. The deserts and empty seas swung by him, and the mountains against the stars.

There was a smell of Time in the air tonight. He smiled and turned the fancy in his mind. There was a thought. What did Time smell like? Like dust and clocks and people. And if you wondered what Time sounded like it sounded like water running in a dark cave and voices crying and dirt dropping down upon hollow box lids, and rain. And, going further, what did Time *look* like? Time looked like snow dropping silently into a black room or it looked like a silent film in an ancient theater, one hundred billion faces falling like those New Year balloons, down and down into nothing. That was how Time smelled and looked and sounded. And tonight—Tomás shoved a hand into the wind outside the truck—tonight you could almost *touch* Time.

He drove the truck between hills of Time. His neck prickled and he sat up, watching ahead.

He pulled into a little dead Martian town, stopped the engine, and let the silence come in around him. He sat, not breathing, looking out at the white buildings in the moonlight. Uninhabited for centuries. Perfect, faultless, in ruins, yes, but perfect, nevertheless.

He started the engine and drove on another mile or more before stopping again, climbing out, carrying his lunch bucket, and walking to a little promontory where he could look back at that dusty city. He opened his thermos and poured himself a cup of coffee. A night bird flew by. He felt very good, very much at peace.

Perhaps five minutes later there was a sound. Off in the hills, where the ancient highway curved, there was a motion, a dim light, and then a murmur.

Tomás turned slowly with the coffee cup in his hand.

And out of the hills came a strange thing.

It was a machine like a jade-green insect, a praying mantis, delicately rushing through the cold air, indistinct, countless green diamonds winking over its body, and red jewels that glittered with multifaceted eyes. Its six legs fell upon the ancient highway with the sounds of a sparse rain which dwindled away, and from the back of the machine a Martian with melted gold for eyes looked down at Tomás as if he were looking into a well.

Tomás raised his hand and thought Hello! automatically but did not move his lips, for this *was* a Martian. But Tomás had swum in blue rivers on Earth, with strangers passing on the road, and eaten in strange houses with strange people, and his weapon had always been his smile. He did not carry a gun. And he did not feel the need of one now, even with the little fear that gathered about his heart at this moment.

The Martian's hands were empty too. For a moment they looked across the cool air at each other.

It was Tomás who moved first.

"Hello!" he called.

"Hello!" called the Martian in his own language.

They did not understand each other.

"Did you say hello?" they both asked.

"What did you say?" they said, each in a different tongue.

They scowled.

"Who are you?" said Tomás in English.

"What are you doing here?" In Martian; the stranger's lips moved.

"Where are you going?" they said, and look bewildered.

"I'm Tomás Gomez."

"I'm Muhe Ca."

Neither understood, but they tapped their chests with the words and then it became clear.

And then the Martian laughed. "Wait!" Tomás felt his head touched, but no hand had touched him. "There!" said the Martian in English. "That is better!"

"You learned my language, so quick!"

"Nothing at all!"

They looked, embarrassed with a new silence, at the steaming coffee he had in one hand.

"Something different?" said the Martian, eying him and the coffee, referring to them both, perhaps.

"May I offer you a drink?" said Tomás.

"Please."

The Martian slid down from his machine.

A second cup was produced and filled, steaming. Tomás held it out.

Their hands met and—like mist—fell through each other.

"Jesus Christ!" cried Tomás, and dropped the cup.

"Name of the Gods!" said the Martian in his own tongue.

"Did you see what happened?" they both whispered.

They were very cold and terrified.

The Martian bent to touch the cup but could not touch it.

"Jesus!" said Tomás.

"Indeed." The Martian tried again and again to get hold of the cup, but could not. He stood up and thought for a moment, then took a knife from his belt. "Hey!" cried Tomás. "You misunderstand, catch!" said the Martian, and tossed it. Tomás cupped his hands. The knife fell through his flesh. It hit the ground. Tomás bent to pick it up but could not touch it, and he recoiled, shivering.

Now he looked at the Martian against the sky.

"The stars!" he said.

"The stars!" said the Martian, looking, in turn, at Tomás.

The stars were white and sharp beyond the flesh of the Martian, and they were sewn into his flesh like scintillas swallowed into the thin, phosphorescent membrane of a gelatinous sea fish. You could see stars flickering like violet eyes in the Martian's stomach and chest, and through his wrists, like jewelry.

"I can see through you!" said Tomás.

"And I through you!" said the Martian, stepping back.

Tomás felt his own body and, feeling the warmth, was reassured. *I* am real, he thought.

The Martian touched his own nose and lips. *"I have flesh,"* he said, half aloud. *"I am alive."*

Tomás stared at the stranger. "And if *I* am real, then you must be dead."

"No, you!"

"A ghost!"

"A phantom!"

They pointed at each other, with starlight burning in their limbs like daggers and icicles and fireflies, and then fell to judging their limbs again, each finding himself intact, hot, excited, stunned, awed, and the other, ah yes, that other over there, unreal, a ghostly prism flashing the accumulated light of distant worlds.

I'm drunk, thought Tomás. I won't tell anyone of this tomorrow, no, no.

They stood there on the ancient highway, neither of them moving.

"Where are you from?" asked the Martian at last.

"Earth."

"What is that?"

"There." Tomás nodded to the sky.

"When?"

"We landed over a year ago, remember?"

"No."

"And all of you were dead, all but a few. You're rare, don't you *know* that?"

"That's not true."

"Yes, dead. I saw the bodies. Black, in the rooms, in the houses, dead. Thousands of them."

"That's ridiculous. We're *alive!*"

"Mister, you're invaded, only you don't know it. You must have escaped."

"I haven't escaped; there was nothing to escape. What do you mean? I'm on my way to a festival now at the canal, near the Eniall Mountains. I was there last night. Don't you see the city there?" The Martian pointed.

Tomás looked and saw the ruins. "Why, that city's been dead thousands of years."

The Martian laughed. "Dead. I slept there yesterday!"

"And I was in it a week ago and the week before that, and I just drove through it now, and it's a heap. See the broken pillars?"

"Broken? Why, I see them perfectly. The moonlight helps. And the pillars are upright."

"There's dust in the streets," said Tomás.

"The streets are clean!"

"The canals are empty right there!"

"The canals are full of lavender wine!"

"It's dead."

"It's alive!" protested the Martian, laughing more now. "Oh, you're quite wrong. See all the carnival lights? There are beautiful boats as slim as women, beautiful women as slim as boats, women the color of sand, women with fire flowers in their hands. I can see them, small, running in the streets there. That's where I'm going now, to the festival; we'll float on the waters all night long; we'll sing, we'll drink, we'll make love. Can't you *see* it?"

"Mister, that city is dead as a dried lizard. Ask any of our party. Me, I'm on my way to Green City tonight; that's the new colony we just raised over near Illinois Highway. You're mixed up. We brought in a million board feet of Oregon lumber and a couple dozen tons of good steel nails and hammered together two of the nicest little villages you ever saw. Tonight we're warming one of them. A couple rockets are coming in from Earth, bringing our wives and girl friends. There'll be barn dances and whisky—"

The Martian was now disquieted. "You say it is over *that* way?"

"There are the rockets." Tomás walked him to the edge of the hill and pointed down. "See?"

"No."

"Damn it, there they *are!* Those long silver things."

"No."

Now Tomás laughed. "You're blind!"

"I see very well. You are the one who does not see."

"But you see the new *town,* don't you?"

"I see nothing but an ocean, and water at low tide."

"Mister, that water's been evaporated for forty centuries."

"Ah, now, now, that *is* enough."

"It's true, I tell you."

The Martian grew very serious. "Tell me again. You do not see the city the way I describe it? The pillars very white, the boats very slender, the festival lights—oh, I see them *clearly!* And listen! I can hear them singing. It's no space away at all."

Tomás listened and shook his head. "No."

"And I, on the other hand," said the Martian, "cannot see what you describe. Well."

Again they were cold. An ice was in their flesh.

"Can it be. . .?"

"What?"

"You say 'from the sky'?"

"Earth."

"Earth, a name, nothing," said the Martian. "*But. . .* as I came up the pass an hour ago. . . ." He touched the back of his neck. "I felt . . ."

"Cold?"

"Yes."

"And now?"

"Cold again. Oddly. There was a thing to the light, to the hills, the road," said the Martian. "I felt the strangeness, the road, the light, and for a moment I felt as if I were the last man alive on this world . . . ."

"So did I!" said Tomás, and it was like talking to an old and dear friend, confiding, growing warm with the topic.

The Martian closed his eyes and opened them again. "This can only mean one thing. It has to do with Time. Yes. You are a figment of the Past!"

"No, you are from the Past," said the Earth Man, having had time to think of it now.

"You are so *certain*. How can you prove who is from the Past, who from the Future? What year is it?"

"Two thousand and one!"

"What does that mean to *me?*"

Tomás considered and shrugged. "Nothing."

"It is as if I told you that it is the year 4462853 s.e.c. It is nothing and more than nothing! Where is the clock to show us how the stars stand?"

"But the ruins prove it! They prove that *I* am the Future, *I* am alive, *you* are dead!"

"Everything in me denies this. My heart beats, my stomach hungers, my mouth thirsts. No, no, not dead, not alive, either of us. More alive than anything else. Caught between is more like it. Two strangers passing in the night, that is it. Two strangers passing. Ruins, you say?"

"Yes. You're afraid?"

"Who wants to see the Future, who *ever* does? A man can face the Past, but to think—the pillars *crumbled,* you say? And the sea empty, and the canals dry, and the maidens dead, and the flowers withered?" The Martian was silent, but then he looked on ahead. "But there they *are*. I *see* them. Isn't that enough for me? They wait for me now, no matter *what* you say."

And for Tomás the rockets, far away, waiting for *him,* and the town and the women from Earth. "We can never agree," he said.

"Let us agree to disagree," said the Martian. "What does it matter who is Past or Future, if we are both alive, for what follows will follow, tomorrow or in ten thousand years. How do you know that those temples are not the temples of your own civilization one hundred centuries from now, tumbled and broken? You do not know. Then don't ask. But the night is very short. There go the festival fires in the sky, and the birds."

Tomás put out his hand. The Martian did likewise in imitation.

Their hands did not touch; they melted through each other.

"Will we meet again?"

"Who knows? Perhaps some other night."

"I'd like to go with you to that festival."

"And I wish I might come to your new town, to see this ship you speak of, to see these men, to hear all that has happened."

"Good-by," said Tomás.

"Good night."

The Martian rode his green metal vehicle quietly away into the hills. The Earth Man turned his truck and drove it silently in the opposite direction.

"Good lord, what a dream that was," sighed Tomás, his hands on the wheel, thinking of the rockets, the women, the raw whisky, the Virginia reels, the party.

How strange a vision was that, thought the Martian, rushing on, thinking of the festival, the canals, the boats, the women with golden eyes, and the songs.

The night was dark. The moons had gone down. Starlight twinkled on the empty highway where now there was not a sound, no car, no person, nothing. And it remained that way all the rest of the cool dark night.

Questions for Discussion

1. To what extent is Tomás an unusual or atypical science fiction character?

2. What is the conflict between Tomás and the Martian? Is it a conflict that applies to our own everyday experience or not? Explain.

3. How does Bradbury make the abstraction "Time" concrete?

4. As a science fiction tale, how is this story different from the science fiction "tales" of the cinema, such as the *Star Wars* films?

Suggestions for Writing

1. Write an essay that explains and assesses this story's depiction of "Time."

2. Write an essay in which you compare and contrast Bradbury's story with other kinds of science fiction stories or novels that you have read. You may want to attempt to classify certain kinds of science fiction.

3. Write an essay in which you compare and contrast the way Faulkner depicts the passage of time in "A Rose for Emily" with the way Bradbury depicts it in this story.

4. Write a science fiction story in which an "ordinary" earthling like Tomás is transported to an extraordinary place or time.

5. Write a paragraph of your own that gives concrete attributes to the abstraction "Time" (see Bradbury's paragraph midway through the story).

Aura

CARLOS   FUENTES

Man hunts and struggles.
Woman intrigues and dreams;
she is the mother of fantasy,
the mother of the gods.
She has second sight,
the wings that enable her to fly
to the infinite of
desire and the imagination . . .
The gods are like men:
they are born and they die
on a woman's breast . . .

Jules Michelet

I

You're reading the advertisement: an offer like this isn't made every day. You read it and reread it. It seems to be addressed to you and nobody else. You don't even notice when the ash from your cigarette falls into the cup of tea you ordered in this cheap, dirty café. You read it again. "Wanted, young historian, conscientious, neat. Perfect knowledge colloquial French." Youth . . . knowledge of French, preferably after living in France for a while . . . "Four thousand pesos a month, all meals, comfortable bedroom-study." All that's missing is your name. The advertisement should have two more words, in bigger, blacker type: Felipe Montero. Wanted, Felipe Montero, formerly on scholarship at the Sorbonne, historian full of useless facts, accustomed to digging among yellowed documents, part-time teacher in private schools, nine hundred pesos a month. But if you read that, you'd be suspicious, and take it as a joke. "Address, Donceles 815." No telephone. Come in person.

You leave a tip, reach for your brief case, get up. You wonder if another young historian, in the same situation you are, has seen the same advertisement, has got ahead of you and taken the job already. You walk down to the corner, trying to forget this idea. As you wait for the bus, you run over the dates you must have on the tip of your tongue so that your sleepy pupils will respect you. The bus is coming now, and you're staring at the tips of your black shoes. You've got to be prepared. You put your hand in your pocket, search among the coins, and finally take out thirty centavos. You've got to be prepared. You grab the handrail—the bus slows down but doesn't stop—and jump aboard. Then you shove your way forward, pay the driver the thirty centavos, squeeze yourself in among the passengers already standing in the aisle, hang onto the overhead rail, press your brief case tighter under your left arm, and automatically put your left hand over the back pocket where you keep your billfold.

This day is just like any other day, and you don't remember the advertisement until the next morning, when you sit down in the same café and order breakfast and open your newspaper. You come to the advertising section and there it is again: *young historian*. The job is still open. You reread the advertisement, lingering over the final words: four thousand pesos.

It's surprising to know that anyone lives on Donceles Street. You always thought that nobody lived in the old center of the city. You walk slowly, trying to pick out the number *815* in that conglomeration of old colonial mansions, all of them converted into repair shops, jewelry shops, shoe stores, drugstores. The numbers have been changed, painted over, confused. A *13* next to a *200*. An old plaque reading *47* over a scrawl in blurred charcoal: *Now 924*. You look up at the second stories. Up there, everything is the same as it was. The jukeboxes don't disturb them. The mercury streetlights don't shine in. The cheap merchandise on sale along the street doesn't have any effect on that upper level; on the baroque harmony of the carved stones; on the battered stone saints with pigeons clustering on their shoulders; on the latticed balconies, the copper gutters, the sandstone gargoyles; on the greenish curtains that darken the long windows; on that window from which someone draws back when you look at it. You gaze at the fanciful vines carved over the doorway, then lower your eyes to the peeling wall and discover *815, formerly 69.*

You rap vainly with the knocker, that copper head of a dog, so worn and smooth that it resembles the head of a canine foetus in a museum of natural science. It seems as if the dog is grinning at you and you let go of the cold metal. The door opens at the first light push of your fingers, but before going in you give a last look over your shoulder, frowning at the long line of stalled cars that growl, honk, and belch out the unhealthy fumes of their impatience. You try to retain some single image of that indifferent outside world.

You close the door behind you and peer into the darkness of a roofed alleyway. It must be a patio of some sort, because you can smell the mold, the dampness of the plants, the rotting roots, the thick drowsy aroma. There isn't any light to guide you, and you're searching in your coat pocket for the box of matches when a sharp, thin voice tells you, from a distance: "No, it isn't necessary. Please. Walk thirteen steps forward and you'll come to a stairway at your right. Come up, please. There are twenty-two steps. Count them."

Thirteen. To the right. Twenty-two.

The dank smell of the plants is all around you as you count out your steps, first on the paving-stones, then on the creaking wood, spongy from the dampness. You count to twenty-two in a low voice and then stop, with the matchbox in your hand, and the brief case under your arm. You knock on a door that smells of old pine. There isn't any knocker. Finally you push it open. Now you can feel a carpet under your feet, a thin carpet, badly laid. It makes you trip and almost fall. Then you notice the grayish filtered light that reveals some of the humps.

"Señora," you say, because you seem to remember a woman's voice. "Señora . . ."

"Now turn to the left. The first door. Please be so kind."

You push the door open: you don't expect any of them to be latched, you know they all open at a push. The scattered lights are braided in your eyelashes, as if you were seeing them through a silken net. All you can make out are the dozens of flickering lights. At last you can see that they're votive lights, all set on brackets or hung between unevenly spaced panels. They cast a faint glow on the silver objects, the crystal flasks, the gilt-framed mirrors. Then you see the bed in the shadows beyond, and the feeble movement of a hand that seems to be beckoning to you.

But you can't see her face until you turn your back on that galaxy of religious lights. You stumble to the foot of the bed, and have to go around it in order to get to the head of it. A tiny figure is almost lost in its immensity. When you reach out your hand, you don't touch another hand, you touch the ears and thick fur of a creature that's chewing silently and steadily, looking up at you with its glowing red eyes. You smile and stroke the rabbit that's crouched beside her hand. Finally you shake hands, and her cold fingers remain for a long while in your sweating palm.

"I'm Felipe Montero. I read your advertisement."

"Yes, I know. I'm sorry, there aren't any chairs."

"That's all right. Don't worry about it."

"Good. Please let me see your profile. No, I can't see it well enough. Turn toward the light. That's right. Excellent."

"I read your advertisement . . ."

"Yes, of course. Do you think you're qualified? *Avez-vous fait des études?*"

"*A Paris, madame.*"

"*Ah, oui, ça me fait plaisir, toujours, toujours, d'entendre . . . oui . . . vous savez . . . on était tellement habitué . . . et après . . .*"

You move aside so that the light from the candles and the reflections from the silver and crystal show you the silk coif that must cover a head of very white hair, and that frames a face so old it's almost childlike. Her whole body is covered by the sheets and the feather pillows and the high, tightly buttoned white collar, all except for her arms, which are wrapped in a shawl, and her pallid hands resting on her stomach. You can only stare at her face until a movement of the rabbit lets you glance furtively at the crusts and bits of bread scattered on the worn-out red silk of the pillows.

"I'll come directly to the point. I don't have many years ahead of me, Se-ñor Montero, and therefore I decided to break a life-long rule and place an advertisement in the newspaper."

"Yes, that's why I'm here."

"Of course. So you accept."

"Well, I'd like to know a little more."

"Yes. You're wondering."

She sees you glance at the night table, the different-colored bottles, the glasses, the aluminum spoons, the row of pillboxes, the other glasses —all stained with whitish liquids—on the floor within reach of her hand. Then you notice that the bed is hardly raised above the level of the floor. Suddenly the rabbit jumps down and disappears in the shadows.

"I can offer you four thousand pesos."

"Yes, that's what the advertisement said today."

"Ah, then it came out."

"Yes, it came out."

"It has to do with the memoirs of my husband, General Llorente. They must be put in order before I die. I want them to be published. I decided that a short time ago."

"But the General himself? Wouldn't he be able to . . ."

"He died sixty years ago, Señor. They're his unfinished memoirs. They have to be completed before I die."

"But . . ."

"I can tell you everything. You'll learn to write in my husband's own style. You'll only have to arrange and read his manuscripts to become fascinated by his style . . . his clarity . . . his . . ."

"Yes, I understand."

"Saga, Saga. Where are you? *Ici,* Saga!"

"Who?"

"My companion."

"The rabbit?"

"Yes. She'll come back."

When you raise your eyes, which you've been keeping lowered, her lips are closed but you can hear her words again—"She'll come back"—as if the old lady were pronouncing them at that instant. Her lips remain still. You look in back of you and you're almost blinded by the gleam from the religious objects. When you look at her again you see that her eyes have opened very wide, and that they're clear, liquid, enormous, almost the same color as the yellowish whites around them, so that only the black dots of the pupils mar that clarity. It's lost a moment later in the heavy folds of her lowered eyelids, as if she wanted to protect that glance which is now hiding at the back of its dry cave.

"Then you'll stay here. Your room is upstairs. It's sunny there."

"It might be better if I didn't trouble you, Señora. I can go on living where I am and work on the manuscripts there."

"My conditions are that you have to live here. There isn't much time left."

"I don't know if . . ."

"Aura . . ."

The old woman moves for the first time since you entered her room. As she reaches out her hand again, you sense that agitated breathing beside you, and another hand reaches out to touch the Señora's fingers. You look around and a girl is standing there, a girl whose whole body you can't see because she's standing so close to you and her arrival was so unexpected, without the slightest sound—not even those sounds that can't be heard but are real anyway because they're remembered immediately afterwards, because in spite of everything they're louder than the silence that accompanies them.

"I told you she'd come back."

"Who?"

"Aura. My companion. My niece."

"Good afternoon."

The girl nods and at the same instant the old lady imitates her gesture.

"This is Señor Montero. He's going to live with us."

You move a few steps so that the light from the candles won't blind you. The girl keeps her eyes closed, her hands at her sides. She doesn't look at you at first, then little by little she opens her eyes as if she were afraid of the light. Finally you can see that those eyes are sea green and that they surge, break to foam, grow calm again, then surge again like a wave. You look into them and tell yourself it isn't true, because they're beautiful green eyes just like all the beautiful green eyes you've ever known. But you can't deceive yourself: those eyes do surge, do change, as if offering you a landscape that only you can see and desire.

"Yes. I'm going to live with you."

II

The old woman laughs sharply and tells you that she is grateful for your kindness and that the girl will show you to your room. You're thinking about the salary of four thousand pesos, and how the work should be pleasant because you like these jobs of careful research that don't include physical effort or going from one place to another or meeting people you don't want to meet. You're thinking about this as you follow her out of the room, and you discover that you've got to follow her with your ears instead of your eyes: you follow the rustle of her skirt, the rustle of taffeta, and you're anxious now to look into her eyes again. You climb the stairs behind that sound in the darkness, and you're still unused to the obscurity. You remember it must be about six in the afternoon, and the flood of light surprises you when Aura opens the door to your bedroom—another door without a latch—and steps aside to tell you: "This is your room. We'll expect you for supper in an hour."

She moves away with that same faint rustle of taffeta, and you weren't able to see her face again.

You close the door and look up at the skylight that serves as a roof. You smile when you find that the evening light is blinding compared with the darkness in the rest of the house, and smile again when you try out the mattress on the gilded metal bed. Then you glance around the room: a red wool rug, olive and gold wallpaper, an easy chair covered in red velvet, an old walnut desk with a green leather top, an old Argand lamp with its soft glow for your nights of research, and a bookshelf over the desk in reach of your hand. You walk over to the other door, and on pushing it open you discover an outmoded bathroom: a four-legged bathtub with little flowers painted on the porcelain, a blue hand basin, an old-fashioned toilet. You look at yourself in the large oval mirror on the door of the wardrobe—it's also walnut—in the bathroom hallway. You move your heavy, eyebrows and wide thick lips, and your breath fogs the mirror. You close your black eyes, and when you open them again the mirror has cleared. You stop holding your breath and run your hand through your dark, limp hair; you touch your fine profile, your lean cheeks; and when your breath hides your face again you're repeating her name: "Aura."

After smoking two cigarettes while lying on the bed, you get up, put on your jacket, and comb your hair. You push the door open and try to remember the route you followed coming up. You'd like to leave the door open so that the lamplight could guide you, but that's impossible because the springs close it behind you. You could enjoy playing with that door, swinging it back and forth. You don't do it. You could take the lamp down with you. You don't do it. This house will always be in darkness, and you've got to learn it and relearn it by touch. You grope your way like a blind man, with your arms stretched out wide, feeling your way along the wall, and by accident you turn on the light-switch. You stop and blink in the bright middle of that long, empty hall. At the end of it you can see the bannister and the spiral staircase.

You count the stairs as you go down: another custom you've got to learn in Señora Llorente's house. You take a step backward when you see the reddish eyes of the rabbit, which turns its back on you and goes hopping away.

You don't have time to stop in the lower hallway because Aura is waiting for you at a half-open stained-glass door, with a candelabra in her hand. You walk toward her, smiling, but you stop when you hear the painful yowling of a number of cats—yes, you stop to listen, next to Aura, to be sure that they're cats—and then follow her to the parlor.

"It's the cats," Aura tells you. "There are lots of rats in this part of the city."

You go through the parlor: furniture upholstered in faded silk; glass-fronted cabinets containing porcelain figurines, musical clocks, medals, glass balls; carpets with Persian designs; pictures of rustic scenes; green velvet curtains. Aura is dressed in green.

"Is your room comfortable?"

"Yes. But I have to get my things from the place where . . ."

"It won't be necessary. The servant has already gone for them."

"You shouldn't have bothered."

You follow her into the dining room. She places the candelabra in the middle of the table. The room feels damp and cold. The four walls are paneled in dark wood, carved in Gothic style, with fretwork arches and large rosettes. The cats have stopped yowling. When you sit down, you notice that four places have been set. There are two large, covered plates and an old, grimy bottle.

Aura lifts the cover from one of the plates. You breathe in the pungent odor of the liver and onions she serves you, then you pick up the old bottle and fill the cut-glass goblets with that thick red liquid. Out of curiosity you try to read the label on the wine bottle, but the grime has obscured it. Aura serves you some whole broiled tomatoes from the other plate.

"Excuse me," you say, looking at the two extra places, the two empty chairs, "but are you expecting someone else?"

Aura goes on serving the tomatoes. "No. Señora Consuelo feels a little ill tonight. She won't be joining us."

"Señora Consuelo? Your aunt?"

"Yes. She'd like you to go in and see her after supper."

You eat in silence. You drink that thick wine, occasionally shifting your glance so that Aura won't catch you in the hypnotized stare that you can't control. You'd like to fix the girl's features in your mind. Every time you look away you forget them again, and an irresistible urge forces you to look at her once more. As usual, she has her eyes lowered. While you're searching for the pack of cigarettes in your coat pocket, you run across that big key, and remember, and say to Aura: "Ah! I forgot that one of the drawers in my desk is locked. I've got my papers in it."

And she murmurs: "Then you want to go out?" She says it as a reproach.

You feel confused, and reach out your hand to her with the key dangling from one finger.

"It isn't important. The servant can go for them tomorrow."

But she avoids touching your hand, keeping her own hands on her lap. Finally she looks up, and once again you question your senses, blaming the wine for your bewilderment, for the dizziness brought on by those shining, clear green eyes, and you stand up after Aura does, running your hand over the wooden back of the Gothic chair, without daring to touch her bare shoulder or her motionless head.

You make an effort to control yourself, diverting your attention away from her by listening to the imperceptible movement of a door behind you—it must lead to the kitchen—or by separating the two different elements that make up the room: the compact circle of light around the candelabra, illuminating the table and one carved wall, and the larger circle of darkness surrounding it. Finally you have the courage to go up to her, take her hand, open it, and place your key-ring in her smooth palm as a token.

She closes her hand, looks up at you, and murmurs, "Thank you." Then she rises and walks quickly out of the room.

You sit down in Aura's chair, stretch your legs, and light a cigarette, feeling a pleasure you've never felt before, one that you knew was part of you but that only now you're experiencing fully, setting it free, bringing it out because this time you know it'll be answered and won't be lost . . . And Señora Consuelo is waiting for you, as Aura said. She's waiting for you after supper . . .

You leave the dining room, and with the candelabra in your hand you walk through the parlor and the hallway. The first door you come to is the old lady's. You rap on it with your knuckles, but there isn't any answer. You knock again. Then you push the door open because she's waiting for you, You enter cautiously, murmuring: "Señora . . . Señora . . ."

She doesn't hear you, for she's kneeling in front of that wall of religious objects, with her head resting on her clenched fists. You see her from a distance: she's kneeling there in her coarse woolen nightgown, with her head sunk into her narrow shoulders; she's thin, even emaciated, like a medieval sculpture; her legs are like two sticks, and they're inflamed with erysipelas. While you're thinking of the continual rubbing of that rough wool against her skin, she suddenly raises her fists and strikes feebly at the air, as if she were doing battle against the images you can make out as you tiptoe closer: Christ, the Virgin, St. Sebastian, St. Lucia, the Archangel Michael, and the grinning demons in an old print, the only happy figures in that iconography of sorrow and wrath, happy because they're jabbing their pitchforks into the flesh of the damned, pouring cauldrons of boiling water on them, violating the women, getting drunk, enjoying all the liberties forbidden to the saints. You approach that central image, which is surrounded by the tears of Our Lady of Sorrows, the blood of Our Crucified Lord, the delight of Lucifer, the anger of the Archangel, the viscera preserved in bottles of alcohol, the silver heart: Señora Consuelo, kneeling, threatens them with her fists, stammering the words you can hear as you move even closer: "Come, City of God! Gabriel, sound your trumpet! Ah, how long the world takes to die!"

She beats her breast until she collapses in front of the images and candles in a spasm of coughing. You raise her by the elbow, and as you gently help her to the bed you're surprised at her smallness: she's almost a little girl, bent over almost double. You realize that without your assistance she would have had to get back to bed on her hands and knees. You help her into that wide bed with its bread crumbs and old feather pillows, and cover her up, and wait until her breathing is back to normal, while the involuntary tears run down her parchment cheeks.

"Excuse me . . . excuse me, Señor Montero. Old ladies have nothing left but . . . the pleasures of devotion . . . Give me my handkerchief, please."

"Señorita Aura told me . . ."

"Yes, of course. I don't want to lose any time. We should . . . we should begin working as soon as possible. Thank you."

"You should try to rest."

"Thank you . . . Here . . ."

The old lady raises her hand to her collar, unbuttons it, and lowers her head to remove the frayed purple ribbon that she hands to you. It's heavy because there's a copper key hanging from it.

"Over in that corner . . . Open that trunk and bring me the papers at the right, on top of the others. . . They're tied with a yellow ribbon."

"I can't see very well . . ."

"Ah, yes . . . it's just that I'm so accustomed to the darkness. To my right . . . Keep going till you come to the trunk. They've walled us in, Señor Montero. They've built up all around us and blocked off the light. They've tried to force me to sell, but I'll die first. This house is full of memories for us. They won't take me out of here till I'm dead! Yes, that's it. Thank you. You can begin reading this part. I will give you the others later. Goodnight, Señor Montero. Thank you. Look, the candelabra has gone out. Light it outside the door, please. No, no, you can keep the key. I trust you."

"Señora, there's a rat's nest in that corner."

"Rats? I never go over there."

"You should bring the cats in here."

"The cats? What cats? Goodnight. I'm going to sleep. I'm very tired."

"Goodnight."

III

That same evening you read those yellow papers written in mustard-colored ink, some of them with holes where a careless ash had fallen, others heavily flyspecked. General Llorente's French doesn't have the merits his wife attributed to it. You tell yourself you can make considerable improvements in the style, can tighten up his rambling account of past events: his childhood on a hacienda in Oaxaca, his military studies in France, his friendship with the duc de Morny and the intimates of Napoleon III, his return to Mexico on the staff of Maximilian, the imperial ceremonies and gatherings, the battles, the defeat in 1867, his exile in France. Nothing that hasn't been described before. As you undress you think of the old lady's distorted notions, the value she attributes to these memoirs. You smile as you get into bed, thinking of the four thousand pesos.

You sleep soundly until a flood of light wakes you up at six in the morning: that glass roof doesn't have any curtain. You bury your head under the pillow and try to go back to sleep. Ten minutes later you give it up and walk into the bathroom, where you find all your things neatly arranged on a table and your few clothes hanging in the wardrobe. Just as you finish shaving the early morning silence is broken by that painful, desperate yowling.

You try to find out where it's coming from: you open the door to the hallway, but you can't hear anything from there: those cries are coming from up above, from the skylight. You jump up on the chair, from the chair onto the desk, and by supporting yourself on the bookshelf you can reach the skylight. You open one of the windows and pull yourself up to look out at that side garden, that square of yew trees and brambles where five, six, seven cats—you can't count them, can't hold yourself up there for more than a second—are all twined together, all writhing in flames and giving off a dense smoke that reeks of burnt fur. As you get down again you wonder if you really saw it: perhaps you only imagined it from those dreadful cries that continue, grow less, and finally stop.

You put on your shirt, brush off your shoes with a piece of paper, and listen to the sound of a bell that seems to run through passageways of the house until it arrives at your door. You look out into the hallway. Aura is walking along it with a bell in her hand. She turns her head to look at you and tells you that breakfast is ready. You try to detain her but she goes down the spiral staircase, still ringing that black-painted bell as if she were trying to wake up a whole asylum, a whole boarding-school.

You follow her in your shirt-sleeves, but when you reach the downstairs hallway you can't find her. The door of the old lady's bedroom opens behind you and you see a hand that reaches out from behind the partly-opened door, sets a chamberpot in the hallway and disappears again, closing the door.

In the dining room your breakfast is already on the table, but this time only one place has been set. You eat quickly, return to the hallway, and knock at Señora Consuelo's door. Her sharp, weak voice tells you to come in. Nothing has changed: the perpetual shadows, the glow of the votive lights and the silver objects.

"Good morning, Señor Montero. Did you sleep well?"

"Yes. I read till quite late."

The old lady waves her hand as if in a gesture of dismissal. "No, no, no. Don't give me your opinion. Work on those pages and when you've finished I'll give you the others."

"Very well, Señora, would I be able to go into the garden?"

"What garden, Señor Montero?"

"The one that's outside my room."

"This house doesn't have any garden. We lost our garden when they built up all around us."

"I think I could work better outdoors."

"This house has only got that dark patio where you came in. My niece is growing some shade plants there. But that's all."

"It's all right, Señora."

"I'd like to rest during the day. But come to see me tonight."

"Very well, Señora."

You spend all morning working on the papers, copying out the passages you intend to keep, rewriting the ones you think are especially bad, smoking one cigarette after another and reflecting that you ought to space your work so that the job lasts as long as possible. If you can manage to save at least twelve thousand pesos, you can spend a year on nothing but your own work, which you've postponed and almost forgotten. Your great, inclusive work on the Spanish discoveries and conquests in the New World. A work that sums up all the scattered chronicles, makes them intelligible, and discovers the resemblances among all the undertakings and adventures of Spain's Golden Age, and all the human prototypes and major accomplishments of the Renaissance. You end up by putting aside the General's tedious pages and starting to compile the dates and summaries of your own work. Time passes and you don't look at your watch until you hear the bell again. Then you put on your coat and go down to the dining room.

Aura is already seated. This time Señora Llorente is at the head of the table, wrapped in her shawl and nightgown and coif, hunching over her plate. But the fourth place has also been set. You note it in passing. It doesn't bother you any more. If the price of your future creative liberty is to put up with all the manias of this old woman, you can pay it easily. As you watch her eating her soup you try to figure out her age. There's a time after which it's impossible to detect the passing of the years, and Señora Consuelo crossed that frontier a long time ago. The General hasn't mentioned her in what you've already read of the memoirs. But if the General was 42 at the time of the French invasion, and died in 1901, forty years later, he must have died at the age of 82. He must have married the Señora after the defeat at Querétaro and his exile. But she would only have been a girl at that time . . .

The dates escape you because now the Señora is talking in that thin, sharp voice of hers, that bird-like chirping. She's talking to Aura and you listen to her as you eat, hearing her long list of complaints, pains, suspected illnesses, more complaints about the cost of medicines, the dampness of the house and so forth. You'd like to break in on this domestic conversation to ask about the servant who went for your things yesterday, the servant you've never even glimpsed and who never waits on table. You're going to ask about him but you're suddenly surprised to realize that up to this moment Aura hasn't said a word and is eating with a sort of mechanical fatality, as if she were waiting for some outside impulse before picking up her knife and fork, cutting a piece of liver—yes, it's liver again, apparently the favorite dish in this house—and carrying it to her mouth. You glance quickly from the aunt to the niece, but at that moment the Señora becomes motionless, and at the same moment Aura puts her knife on her plate and also becomes motionless, and you remember that the Señora put down her knife only a fraction of a second earlier.

There are several minutes of silence: you finish eating while they sit there rigid as statues, watching you. At last the Señora says, "I'm very tired. I ought not to eat at the table. Come, Aura, help me to my room."

The Señora tries to hold your attention: she looks directly at you so that you'll keep looking at her, although what she's saying is aimed at Aura. You have to make an effort in order to evade that look, which once again is wide, clear, and yellowish, free of the veils and wrinkles that usually obscure it. Then you look at Aura, who is staring fixedly at nothing and silently moving her lips. She gets up with a motion like those you associate with dreaming, takes the arm of the bent old lady, and slowly helps her from the dining room.

Alone now, you help yourself to the coffee that has been there since the beginning of the meal, the cold coffee you sip as you wrinkle your brow and ask yourself if the Señora doesn't have some secret power over her niece: if the girl, your beautiful Aura in her green dress, isn't kept in this dark old house against her will. But it would be so easy for her to escape while the Señora was asleep in her shadowy room. You tell yourself that her hold over the girl must be terrible. And you consider the way out that occurs to your imagination: perhaps Aura is waiting for you to release her from the chains in which the perverse, insane old lady, for some unknown reason, has bound her. You remember Aura as she was a few moments ago, spiritless, hypnotized by her terror, incapable of speaking in front of the tyrant, moving her lips in silence as if she were silently begging you to set her free; so enslaved that she imitated every gesture of the Señora, as if she were permitted to do only what the Señora did.

You rebel against this tyranny. You walk toward the other door, the one at the foot of the staircase, the one next to the old lady's room: that's where Aura must live, because there's no other room in the house. You push the door open and go in. This room is dark also, with whitewashed walls, and the only decoration is an enormous black Christ. At the left there's a door that must lead into the widow's bedroom. You go up to it on tiptoe, put your hands against it, then decide not to open it: you should talk with Aura alone.

And if Aura wants your help she'll come to your room. You go up there for a while, forgetting the yellowed manuscripts and your own notebooks, thinking only about the beauty of your Aura. And the more you think about her, the more you make her yours, not only because of her beauty and your desire, but also because you want to set her free: you've found a moral basis for your desire, and you feel innocent and self-satisfied. When you hear the bell again you don't go down to supper because you can't bear another scene like the one at the middle of the day. Perhaps Aura will realize it, and come to look for you after supper.

You force yourself to go on working on the papers. When you're bored with them you undress slowly, get into bed, and fall asleep at once, and for the first time in years you dream, dream of only one thing, of a fleshless hand that comes toward you with a bell, screaming that you should go away, everyone should go away; and when that face with its empty eye-sockets comes close to yours, you wake up with a muffled cry, sweating, and feel those gentle hands caressing your face, those lips murmuring in a low voice, consoling you and asking you for affection. You reach out your hands to find that other body, that naked body with a key dangling from its neck, and when you recognize the key you recognize the woman who is lying over you, kissing you, kissing your whole body. You can't see her in the black of the starless night, but you can smell the fragrance of the patio plants in her hair, can feel her smooth, eager body in your arms; you kiss her again and don't ask her to speak.

When you free yourself, exhausted, from her embrace, you hear her first whisper: "You're my husband." You agree. She tells you it's daybreak, then leaves you, saying that she'll wait for you that night in her room. You agree again, and then fall asleep, relieved, unburdened, emptied of desire, still feeling the touch of Aura's body, her trembling, her surrender.

It's hard for you to wake up. There are several knocks on the door, and at last you get out of bed, groaning and still half-asleep. Aura, on the other side of the door, tells you not to open it: she says that Señora Consuelo wants to talk with you, is waiting for you in her room.

Ten minutes later you enter the widow's sanctuary. She's propped up against the pillows, motionless, her eyes hidden by those drooping, wrinkled, dead-white lids; you notice the puffy wrinkles under her eyes, the utter weariness of her skin.

Without opening her eyes she asks you, "Did you bring the key to the trunk?"

"Yes, I think so . . . Yes, here it is."

"You can read the second part. It's in the same place. It's tied with a blue ribbon."

You go over to the trunk, this time with a certain disgust: the rats are swarming around it, peering at you with their glittering eyes from the cracks in the rotted floorboards, galloping toward the holes in the rotted walls. You open the trunk and take out the second batch of papers, then return to the foot of the bed. Señora Consuelo is petting her white rabbit. A sort of croaking laugh emerges from her buttoned-up throat, and she asks you, "Do you like animals?"

"No, not especially. Perhaps because I've never had any."

"They're good friends. Good companions. Above all when you're old and lonely."

"Yes, they must be."

"They're always themselves, Señor Montero. They don't have any pretensions."

"What did you say his name is?"

"The rabbit? She's Saga. She's very intelligent. She follows her instincts. She's natural and free."

"I thought it was a male rabbit."

"Oh? Then you still can't tell the difference."

"Well, the important thing is that you don't feel all alone."

"They want us to be alone, Señor Montero, because they tell us that solitude is the only way to achieve saintliness. They forget that in solitude the temptation is even greater."

"I don't understand, Señora."

"Ah, it's better that you don't. Get back to work now, please."

You turn your back on her, walk to the door, leave her room. In the hallway you clench your teeth. Why don't you have courage enough to tell her that you love the girl? Why don't you go back and tell her, once and for all, that you're planning to take Aura away with you when you finish the job? You approach the door again and start pushing it open, still uncertain, and through the crack you see Señora Consuelo standing up, erect, transformed, with a military tunic in her arms: a blue tunic with gold buttons, red epaulettes, bright medals with crowned eagles—a tunic the old lady bites ferociously, kisses tenderly, drapes over her shoulders as she performs a few teetering dance steps. You close the door.

"She was fifteen years old when I met her," you read in the second part of the memoirs. *"Elle avait quinze ans lorsque je l'ai connue et, si j'ose le dire, ce sont ses yeux verts qui ont fait ma perdition."* Consuelo's green eyes, Consuelo who was only fifteen in 1867, when General Llorente married her and took her with him into exile in Paris. *"Ma jeune poupée,"* he wrote in a moment of inspiration, *"ma juene poupée aux yeux verts; je t'ai comblée d'amour."* He described the house they lived in, the outings, the dances, the carriages, the world of the Second Empire, but all in a dull enough way. *"J'ai même supporté ta haine des chats, moi qu' aimais tellement les jolies bêtes . . ."* One day he found her torturing a cat: she had it clasped between her legs, with her crinoline skirt pulled up, and he didn't know how to attract her attention because it seemed to him that *"tu faisais ça d'une façon si innocent, par pur enfantillage,"* and in fact it excited him so much that if you can believe what he wrote, he made love to her that night with extraordinary passion, *"parce que tu m'avais dit que torturer les chats était ta manière a toi de rendre notre amour favorable, par un sacrifice symbolique . . ."* You've figured it up: Señora Consuelo must be 109. Her husband died fifty-nine years ago. *"Tu sais si bien t'habiller, ma douce Consuelo, toujours drappé dans de velours verts, verts comme tes yeux. Je pense que tu seras toujours belle," même dans cent ans . . ."* Always dressed in green. Always beautiful, even after a hundred years. *"Tu es si fière de ta beauté; que no ferais-tu pas pour rester toujours jeune?"*

IV

Now you know why Aura is living in this house: to perpetuate the illusion of youth and beauty in that poor, crazed old lady. Aura, kept here like a mirror, like one more icon on that votive wall with its clustered offerings, preserved hearts, imagined saints and demons.

You put the manuscript aside and go downstairs, suspecting there's only one place Aura could be in the morning—the place that greedy old woman has assigned to her.

Yes, you find her in the kitchen, at the moment she's beheading a kid: the vapor that rises from the open throat, the smell of spilt blood, the animal's glazed eyes, all give you nausea. Aura is wearing a ragged, blood-stained dress and her hair is disheveled; she looks at you without recognition and goes on with her butchering.

You leave the kitchen: this time you'll really speak to the old lady, really throw her greed and tyranny in her face. When you push open the door she's standing behind the veil of lights, performing a ritual with the empty air, one hand stretched out and clenched, as if holding something up, and the other clasped around an invisible object, striking again and again at the same place. Then she wipes her hands against her breast, sighs, and starts cutting the air again, as if—yes, you can see it clearly—as if she were skinning an animal . . .

You run through the hallway, the parlor, the dining room, to where Aura is slowly skinning the kid, absorbed in her work, heedless of your entrance or your words, looking at you as if you were made of air.

You climb up to your room, go in, and brace yourself against the door as if you were afraid someone would follow you: panting, sweating, victim of your horror, of your certainty. If something or someone should try to enter, you wouldn't be able to resist, you'd move away from the door, you'd let it happen. Frantically you drag the armchair over to that latchless door, push the bed up against it, then fall onto the bed, exhausted, drained of your willpower, with your eyes closed and your arms wrapped around your pillow—the pillow that isn't yours. Nothing is yours.

You fall into a stupor, into the depths of a dream that's your only escape, your only means of saying No to insanity. "She's crazy, she's crazy," you repeat again and again to make yourself sleepy, and you can see her again as she skins the imaginary kid with an imaginary knife. "She's crazy, she's crazy . . ."

in the depths of the dark abyss, in your silent dream with its mouths opening in silence, you see her coming toward you from the blackness of the abyss, you see her crawling toward you.

in silence,

moving her fleshless hand, coming toward you until her face touches yours and you see the old lady's bloody gums, her toothless gums, and you scream and she goes away again, moving her hand, sowing the abyss with the yellow teeth she carries in her blood-stained apron:

your scream is an echo of Aura's, she's standing in front of you in your dream, and she's screaming because someone's hands have ripped her green taffeta skirt in two, and then

she turns her head toward you

with the torn folds of the skirt in her hands, turns toward you and laughs silently, with the old lady's teeth superimposed on her own, while her legs, her naked legs, shatter into bits and fly toward the abyss . . .

There's a knock at the door, then the sound of the bell, the supper bell. Your head aches so much that you can't make out the hands on the clock, but you know it must be late: above your head you can see the night clouds beyond the skylight. You get up painfully, dazed and hungry. You hold the glass pitcher under the faucet, wait for the water to run, fill the pitcher, then pour it into the basin. You wash your face, brush your teeth with your worn toothbrush that's clogged with greenish paste, dampen your hair—you don't notice you're doing all this in the wrong order—and comb it meticulously in front of the oval mirror on the walnut wardrobe. Then you tie your tie, put on your jacket and go down to the empty dining room, where only one place has been set—yours.

Beside your plate, under your napkin, there's an object you start caressing with your fingers: a clumsy little rag doll, filled with a powder that trickles from its badly-sewn shoulder; its face is drawn with India ink, and its body is naked, sketched with a few brush strokes. You eat the cold supper—liver, tomatoes, wine—with your right hand while holding the doll in your left.

You eat mechanically, without noticing at first your own hypnotized attitude, but later you glimpse a reason for your oppressive sleep, your nightmare, and finally identify your sleep-walking movements with those of Aura and the old lady. You're suddenly disgusted by that horrible little doll, in which you begin to suspect a secret illness, a contagion. You let it fall to the floor. You wipe your lips with the napkin, look at your watch, and remember that Aura is waiting for you in her room.

You go cautiously up to Señora Consuelo's door, but there isn't a sound from within. You look at your watch again: it's barely nine o'clock. You decide to feel your way down to that dark, roofed patio you haven't been in since you came through it, without seeing anything, on the day you arrived here.

You touch the damp, mossy walls, breathe the perfumed air, and try to isolate the different elements you're breathing, to recognize the heavy, sumptuous aromas that surround you. The flicker of your match lights up the narrow, empty patio, where various plants are growing on each side in the loose, reddish earth. You can make out the tall, leafy forms that cast their shadows on the walls in the light of the match. But it burns down, singeing your fingers, and you have to light another one to finish seeing the flowers, fruits and plants you remember reading about in old chronicles, the forgotten herbs that are growing here so fragrantly and drowsily: the long, broad, downy leaves of the henbane; the twining stems with flowers that are yellow outside, red inside; the pointed, heart-shaped leaves of the nightshade; the ash-colored down of the grape-mullein with its clustered flowers; the bushy gatheridge with its white blossoms; the belladonna. They come to life in the flare of your match, swaying gently with their shadows, while you recall the uses of these herbs that dilate the pupils, alleviate pain, reduce the pangs of childbirth, bring consolation, weaken the will, induce a voluptuous calm.

You're all alone with the perfumes when the third match burns out. You go up to the hallway slowly, listen again at Señora Consuelo's door, then tiptoe on to Aura's. You push it open without knocking and go into that bare room, where a circle of light reveals the bed, the huge Mexican crucifix, and the woman who comes toward you when the door is closed. Aura is dressed in green, in a green taffeta robe from which, as she approaches, her moonpale thighs reveal themselves. The woman, you repeat as she comes close, the woman, not the girl of yesterday: the girl of yesterday—you touch Aura's fingers, her waist—couldn't have been more than twenty; the woman of today—you caress her loose black hair, her pallid cheeks—seems to be forty. Between yesterday and today, something about her green eyes has turned hard; the red of her lips has strayed beyond their former outlines, as if she wanted to fix them in a happy grimace, a troubled smile; as if, like that plant in the patio, her smile combined the taste of honey and the taste of gall. You don't have time to think of anything more.

"Sit down on the bed, Felipe."

"Yes."

"We're going to play. You don't have to do anything. Let me do everything myself."

Sitting on the bed, you try to make out the source of that diffuse, opaline light that hardly lets you distinguish the objects in the room, and the presence of Aura, from the golden atmosphere that surrounds them. She sees you looking up, trying to find where it comes from. You can tell from her voice that she's kneeling down in front of you.

"The sky is neither high nor low. It's over us and under us at the same time."

She takes off your shoes and socks and caresses your bare feet.

You feel the warm water that bathes the soles of your feet, while she washes them with a heavy cloth, now and then casting furtive glances at that Christ carved from black wood. Then she dries your feet, takes you by the hand, fastens a few violets in her loose hair, and begins to hum a melody, a waltz, to which you dance with her, held by the murmur of her voice, gliding around to the slow, solemn rhythm she's setting, very different from the light movements of her hands, which unbutton your shirt, caress your chest, reach around to your back and grasp it. You also murmur that wordless song, that melody rising naturally from your throat: you glide around together, each time closer to the bed, until you muffle the song with your hungry kisses on Aura's mouth, until you stop the dance with your crushing kisses on her shoulders and breasts.

You're holding the empty robe in your hands. Aura, squatting on the bed, places an object against her closed thighs, caressing it, summoning you with her hand. She caresses that thin wafer, breaks it against her thighs, oblivious of the crumbs that roll down her hips: she offers you half of the wafer and you take it, place it in your mouth at the same time she does, and swallow it with difficulty. Then you fall on Aura's naked body, you fall on her naked arms, which are stretched out from one side of the bed to the other like the arms of the crucifix hanging on the wall, the black Christ with that scarlet silk wrapped around his thighs, his spread knees, his wounded side, his crown of thorns set on a tangled black wig with silver spangles. Aura opens up like an altar.

You murmur her name in her ear. You feel the woman's full arms against your back. You hear her warm voice in your ear: "Will you love me forever?"

"Forever, Aura. I'll love you forever."

"Forever? Do you swear it?"

"I swear it."

"Even though I grow old? Even though I lose my beauty? Even though my hair turns white?"

"Forever, my love, forever."

"Even if I die, Felipe? Will you love me forever, even if I die?"

"Forever, forever. I swear it. Nothing can separate us."

"Come, Felipe, come . . ."

When you wake up, you reach out to touch Aura's shoulder, but you only touch the still-warm pillow and the white sheet that covers you.

You murmur her name.

You open your eyes and see her standing at the foot of the bed, smiling but not looking at you. She walks slowly toward the corner of the room, sits down on the floor, places her arms on the knees that emerge from the darkness you can't peer into, and strokes the wrinkled hand that comes forward from the lessening darkness: she's sitting at the feet of the old lady, of Señora Consuelo, who is seated in an armchair you hadn't noticed earlier: Señora Consuelo smiles at you, nodding her head, smiling at you along with Aura, who moves her head in rhythm with the old lady's: they both smile at you, thanking you. You lie back, without any will, thinking that the old lady has been in the room all the time;

> *you remember her movements, her voice, her dance,*
> *though you keep telling yourself she wasn't there.*

The two of them get up at the same moment, Consuelo from the chair, Aura from the floor. Turning their backs on you, they walk slowly toward the door that leads to the widow's bedroom, enter that room where the lights are forever trembling in front of the images, close the door behind them, and leave you to sleep in Aura's bed.

V

Your sleep is heavy and unsatisfying. In your dreams you had already felt the same vague melancholy, the weight on your diaphragm, the sadness that won't stop oppressing your imagination. Although you're sleeping in Aura's room, you're sleeping all alone, far from the body you believe you've possessed.

When you wake up, you look for another presence in the room, and realize it's not Aura who disturbs you but rather the double presence of something that was engendered during the night. You put your hands on your forehead, trying to calm your disordered senses: that dull melancholy is hinting to you in a low voice, the voice of memory and premonition, that you're seeking your other half, that the sterile conception last night engendered your own double.

And you stop thinking, because there are things even stronger than the imagination: the habits that force you to get up, look for a bathroom off this room without finding one, go out into the hallway rubbing your eyelids, climb the stairs tasting the thick bitterness of your tongue, enter your own room feeling the rough bristles on your chin, turn on the bath faucets and then slide into the warm water, letting yourself relax into forgetfulness.

But while you're drying yourself, you remember the old lady and the girl as they smiled at you before leaving the room arm in arm; you recall that whenever they're together they always do the same things: they embrace, smile, eat, speak, enter, leave, at the same time, as if one were imitating the other, as if the will of one depended on the existence of the other . . . You cut yourself lightly on one cheek as you think of these things while you shave; you make an effort to get control of yourself. When you finish shaving you count the objects in your traveling case, the bottles and tubes which the servant you've never seen brought over from your boarding house: you murmur the names of these objects, touch them, read the contents and instructions, pronounce the names of the manufacturers, keeping to these objects in order to forget that other one, the one without a name, without a label, without any rational consistency. What is Aura expecting of you? you ask yourself, closing the traveling case. What does she want, what does she want?

In answer you hear the dull rhythm of her bell in the corridor telling you breakfast is ready. You walk to the door without your shirt on. When you open it you find Aura there: it must be Aura because you see the green taffeta she always wears, though her face is covered with a green veil. You take her by the wrist, that slender wrist which trembles at your touch . . .

"Breakfast is ready," she says, in the faintest voice you've ever heard.

"Aura, let's stop pretending."

"Pretending?"

"Tell me if Señora Consuelo keeps you from leaving, from living your own life. Why did she have to be there when you and I . . . Please tell me you'll go with me when . . ."

"Go away? Where?"

"Out of this house. Out into the world, to live together. You shouldn't feel bound to your aunt forever . . . Why all this devotion? Do you love her that much?"

"Love her?"

"Yes. Why do you have to sacrifice yourself this way?"

"Love her? She loves me. She sacrifices herself for me."

"But she's an old woman, almost a corpse. You can't . . ."

"She has more life than I do. Yes, she's old and repulsive . . . Felipe, I don't want to become . . . to be like her . . . another . . ."

"She's trying to bury you alive. You've got to be reborn, Aura."

"You have to die before you can be reborn . . . No, you don't understand. Forget about it, Felipe. Just have faith in me."

"If you'd only explain."

"Just have faith in me. She's going to be out today for the whole day."

"She?"

"Yes, the other."

"She's going out? But she never . . ."

"Yes, sometimes she does. She makes a great effort and goes out. She's going out today. For all day. You and I could . . ."

"Go away?"

"If you want to."

"Well . . . perhaps not yet. I'm under contract. But as soon as I can finish the work, then . . ."

"Ah, yes. But she's going to be out all day. We could do something."

"What?"

"I'll wait for you this evening in my aunt's bedroom. I'll wait for you as always."

She turns away, ringing her bell like the lepers who use a bell to announce their approach, telling the unwary: "Out of the way, out of the way." You put on your shirt and coat and follow the sound of the bell calling you to the dining room. In the parlor the widow Llorente comes toward you, bent over, leaning on a knobby cane; she's dressed in an old white gown with a stained and tattered gauze veil. She goes by without looking at you, blowing her nose into a handkerchief, blowing her nose and spitting. She murmurs, "I won't be at home today, Señor Montero. I have complete confidence in your work. Please keep at it. My husband's memoirs must be published."

She goes away, stepping across the carpets with her tiny feet, which are like those of an antique doll, and supporting herself with her cane, spitting and sneezing as if she wanted to clear something from her congested lungs. It's only by an effort of the will that you keep yourself from following her with your eyes, despite the curiosity you feel at seeing the yellowed bridal gown she's taken from the bottom of that old trunk in her bedroom.

You scarcely touch the cold coffee that's waiting for you in the dining room. You sit for an hour in the tall, arch-back chair, smoking, waiting for the sounds you never hear, until finally you're sure the old lady has left the house and can't catch you at what you're going to do. For the last hour you've had the key to the trunk clutched in your hand, and now you get up and silently walk through the parlor into the hallway, where you wait for another fifteen minutes—your watch tells you how long—with your ear against Señora Consuelo's door. Then you slowly push it open until you can make out, beyond the spider's web of candles, the empty bed on which her rabbit is gnawing at a carrot: the bed that's always littered with scraps of bread, and that you touch gingerly as if you thought the old lady might be hidden among the rumples of the sheets. You walk over to the corner where the trunk is, stepping on the tail of one of those rats; it squeals, escapes from your foot, and scampers off to warn the others. You fit the copper key into the rusted padlock, remove the padlock, and then raise the lid, hearing the creak of the old, stiff hinges. You take out the third portion of the memoirs—it's tied with a red ribbon—and under it you discover those photographs, those old, brittle, dog-eared photographs. You pick them up without looking at them, clutch the whole treasure to your breast, and hurry out of the room without closing the trunk, forgetting the hunger of the rats. You close the door, lean against the wall in the hallway till you catch your breath, then climb the stairs to your room.

Up there you read the new pages, the continuation, the events of an agonized century. In his florid language General Llorente describes the personality of Eugenia de Montijo, pays his respects to Napoleon the Little, summons up his most martial rhetoric to proclaim the Franco-Prussian War, fills whole pages with his sorrow at the defeat, harangues all men of honor about the republican monster, sees a ray of hope is General Boulanger, sighs for Mexico, believes that in the Dreyfus affairs the honor—always that word "honor"—of the army has asserted itself again.

The brittle pages crumble at your touch: you don't respect them now, you're only looking for a reappearance of the woman with green eyes. "I know why you weep at times, Consuelo. I have not been able to give you children, although you are so radiant with life . . ." And later: "Consuelo, you should not tempt God. We must reconcile ourselves. Is not my affection enough? I know that you love me; I feel it. I am not asking you for resignation, because that would offend you. I am only asking you to see, in the great love which you say you have for me, something sufficient, something that can fill both of us, without the need of turning to sick imaginings . . ." On another page: "I told Consuelo that those medicines were utterly useless. She insists on growing her own herbs in the garden. She says she is not deceiving herself. The herbs are not to strengthen the body, but rather the soul." Later: "I found her in a delirium, embracing the pillow. She cried, 'Yes, yes, yes, I've done it, I've re-created her! I can invoke her, I can give her life with my own life!' It was necessary to call the doctor. He told me he could not quiet her, because the truth was that she was under the effects of narcotics, not of stimulants." And finally: "Early this morning I found her walking barefooted through the hallways. I wanted to stop her. She went by without looking at me, but her words were directed to me. 'Don't stop me,' she said. 'I'm going toward my youth, and my youth is coming toward me. It's coming in, it's in the garden, it's come back . . .' Consuelo, my poor Consuelo! Even the devil was an angel once."

There isn't any more. The memoirs of General Llorente end with that sentence: *"Consuelo, le démon aussi 'etait un ange, avant . . ."*

And after the last page, the portraits. The portrait of an elderly gentleman in a military uniform, an old photograph with these words in one corner: *"Moulin, Photographe, 35 Boulevard Haussmann"* and the date *"1894."* Then the photograph of Aura, of Aura with her green eyes, her black hair gathered in ringlets, leaning against a Doric column with a painted landscape in the background: the landscape of a Lorelei in the Rhine. Her dress is buttoned up to the collar, there's a handkerchief in her hand, she's wearing a bustle: Aura, and the date *"1876"* in white ink, and on the back of the daguerreotype, in spidery handwriting: *"Fait pour notre dixième anniversaire de mariage,"* and a signature in the same hand, *"Consuelo Llorente."* In the third photograph you see both Aura and the old gentleman, but this time they're dressed in outdoor clothes, sitting on a bench in a garden. The photograph has become a little blurred: Aura doesn't look as young as she did in the other picture, but it's she, it's he, it's . . . it's you. You stare and stare at the photographs, then hold them up to the skylight. You cover General Llorente's beard with your finger, and imagine him with black hair, and you only discover yourself: blurred, lost, forgotten, but you, you, you.

Your head is spinning, overcome by the rhythms of that distant waltz, by the odor of damp, fragrant plants: you fall exhausted on the bed, touching your cheeks, your eyes, your nose, as if you were afraid that some invisible hand had ripped off the mask you've been wearing for twenty-seven years, the cardboard features that hid your true face, your real appearance, the appearance you once had but then forgot. You bury your face in the pillow, trying to keep the wind of the past from tearing away your own features, because you don't want to lose them. You lie there with your face in the pillow, waiting for what has to come, for what you can't prevent. You don't look at your watch again, that useless object tediously measuring time in accordance with human vanity, those little hands marking out the long hours that were invented to disguise the real passage of time, which races with a mortal and insolent swiftness no clock could ever measure. A life, a century, fifty years: you can't imagine those lying measurements any longer, you can't hold that bodiless dust within your hands.

When you look up from the pillow, you find you're in darkness. Night has fallen.

Night has fallen. Beyond the skylight the swift black clouds are hiding the moon, which tries to free itself, to reveal its pale, round, smiling face. It escapes for only a moment, then the clouds hide it again. You haven't got any hope left. You don't even look at your watch. You hurry down the stairs, out of that prison cell with its old papers and faded daguerreotypes, and stop at the door of Señora Consuelo's room, and listen to your own voice, muted and transformed after all those hours of silence: "Aura . . ."

Again "Aura . . ."

You enter the room. The votive lights have gone out. You remember that the old lady has been away all day: without her faithful attention the candles have all burned up. You grope forward in the darkness to the bed.

And "Aura . . ."

You hear a faint rustle of taffeta, and the breathing that keeps time with your own. You reach out your hand to touch Aura's green robe.

"No. Don't touch me. Lie down at my side."

You find the edge of the bed, swing up your legs, and remain there stretched out and motionless. You can't help feeling a shiver of fear: "She might come back any minute."

"She won't come back."

"Ever?"

"I'm exhausted. She's already exhausted. I've never been able to keep her with me for more than three days."

"Aura . . ."

You want to put your hand on Aura's breasts. She turns her back: you can tell by the difference in her voice.

"No . . . Don't touch me . . ."

"Aura . . . I love you."

"Yes. You love me. You told me yesterday that you'd always love me."

"I'll always love you, always. I need your kisses, your body . . ."

"Kiss my face. Only my face."

You bring your lips close to the head that's lying next to yours. You stroke Aura's long black hair. You grasp that fragile woman by the shoulders, ignoring her sharp complaint. You tear off her taffeta robe, embrace her, feel her small and lost and naked in your arms, despite her moaning resistance, her feeble protests, kissing her face without thinking, without distinguishing, and you're touching her withered breasts when a ray of moonlight shines in and surprises you, shines in through a chink in the wall that the rats have chewed open, an eye that lets in a beam of silvery moonlight. It falls on Aura's eroded face, as brittle and yellowed as the memoirs, as creased with wrinkles as the photographs. You stop kissing those fleshless lips, those toothless gums: the ray of moonlight shows you the naked body of the old lady, of Señora Consuelo, limp, spent, tiny, ancient, trembling because you touch her. You love her, you too have come back . . .

You plunge your face, your open eyes, into Consuelo's silver-white hair, and you'll embrace her again when the clouds cover the moon, when you're both hidden again, when the memory of youth, of youth re-embodied, rules the darkness.

"She'll come back, Felipe. We'll bring her back together. Let me recover my strength and I'll bring her back . . ."

Questions for Discussion

1. The second person ("you") is a rare narrative voice. What is your response to it in this story? To what extent does it create a different tone or atmosphere from first- or third-person points of view? Does the narrator become the reader? Explain.

2. In what ways is the narrator tempted in this story?

3. Why is the name "Aura" significant? What are the definitions of "aura"?

4. What are the gothic elements of this story?

5. Aura, Consuelo, and the narrator disagree about fundamental facts concerning the house, such as the presence of a garden, cats, and rats. What is the effect of this contradictory perception? How does it prepare us in some ways for the ending of the story?

6. The narrator is bright, learned, and knowledgeable, but to what extent is this a trap, a liability?

7. What ideas or themes does this story dramatize?

Suggestions for Writing

1. Write an essay in which you analyze and provide examples for the different kinds of temptations the narrator encounters.

2. Write an essay in which you explain the role of "the past" in this story.

3. Write a sketch or several scenes of a story in the second person. Then in your notebook describe the strengths and weaknesses of using such a point of view.

4. Read other works that involve a "double," such as Robert Louis Stevenson's "Doctor Jekyll and Mr. Hyde," Oscar Wilde's "Portrait of Dorian Gray," Edgar Allan Poe's "William Wilson," Mark Twain's "The Prince and the Pauper," or James Hogg's *Confessions of a Justified Sinner*. Then write an essay in which you place "Aura" in the context of these other works and in which you explain the attraction "the double" has for writers (and readers).

Uncle Sven and the Cultural Revolution

LARS GUSTAFSSON

Uncle Sven was a research engineer at the Iron Works and lived in one of the houses up on the hill.

He was the only person in Trummelsberg who knew exactly at which longitude and latitude he lived: in Trummelsberg, the sun rises exactly eight minutes, twenty-nine seconds later than in Stockholm, because of westerly time difference; accordingly, it sets eight minutes, twenty-nine seconds later.

Actually, all of this only applies at the summer solstice, since Trummelsberg is situated at a latitude of 59°12′N; consequently, it receives a somewhat larger portion of polar darkness in the winter than does the capital, due to the inclination of the earth's axis.

These calculations were caused by the circumstance that while Uncle Sven was pursuing his education, he had found an American wife—as the years went by, she turned into the most enchanting little blue-haired troll who, all her life, stubbornly refused to learn Swedish, so that the salespeople in the Konsum supermarket finally had to learn to speak American in order to understand what she wanted. She always played the violin in church on solemn occasions.

This American wife—her name, by the way, was Frankie—considered that it went without saying there should be roses in a garden, lots of roses: Queen Elizabeth, Pink, Trotter's Glory, and so forth.

Now Trummelsberg has never been a particularly good place for roses. No doubt the winters do something to them that isn't good for them, and what the winters don't do is done by all those peculiar red and black ants that thrive so nicely in the morainal sand of northern Västmanland.

After a number of growing seasons that were exceptionally poor for roses, Uncle Sven maintained that the latitude was quite impossible for them, that there wasn't a single person who had succeeded in growing anything but briar roses in Trummelsberg. Since his wife's answer was that it was absolute nonsense, in the States people grew roses way up in the Finger Lakes district, a slight marital dispute arose during which Sven quickly proved that New York is actually at the latitude of Madrid and Austin, Texas, the latitude where the Bay of Aqaba runs into the Red Sea, and that a confounded northern latitude such as Trummelsberg's is only to be found among the frozen rivers of Labrador. When Frankie stubbornly kept insisting that the placement of Europe in relation to the North Pole couldn't possibly be as bad as all that, Sven decided to tackle the problem in earnest.

Actually, it was quite a simple matter.

The south wall of the house, where the roses drooped from the trellis in the spring light, had an east-west orientation. With the aid of an old army compass and a declination chart, it was quite easy to figure out that the wall faced as due south as could reasonably be expected.

Using his grandfather's excellent cylinder escapement watch and the radio's time signal at one p.m., (the equivalent of noon, Greenwich Mean Time), with an eye on the shrinking shadow of the flagpole, it should be quite easy to determine in how many minutes and seconds following the time signal the shadow was at its shortest.

It turned out not to be that easy. The first day, the sun went behind a cloud right at one o'clock and stayed there for the rest of the afternoon.

The next day, there was brilliant sunshine, but this time the lab director at the Iron Works called to say it had been decided that Sven was going to China with Johansson from Sales to confer with a steel factory outside Shanghai.

Sven liked Johansson. They sometimes played golf together. In China, the Cultural Revolution was in full swing, for this was in the beginning of April 1968.

Uncle Sven had only a vague notion of China, and the words "Cultural Revolution" evoked only vague associations with amateur theatrical groups. His wife seldom passed up any of the amateur theatricals in the community, although she still, after thirty years, couldn't understand Swedish. As a young girl, she had been with an amateur group in Boston.

Anyway, there was nothing to do but to say yes. Big business deals were afoot, and if Sven could bring in his passport after lunch so they could send it special delivery to Stockholm, the two gentlemen might perhaps be able to leave as early as the following Thursday.

"Do you think I should bring my table tennis paddle," Sven said.

Johansson wondered if it would be any use bringing his golf clubs.

When he returned to the trellis, naturally the shadow had grown too long again. The third day it rained. The fourth, Uncle Sven had to go out for lunch. It had to do with the trip to China: what interested the Chinese steel syndicate was the possibility of forging propeller shafts thirty meters long from a special kind of steel.

"The Americans are doing it. The Germans have been doing it since 1905. It's feasible, but you've got to have the right tools," Sven said. "Do they really have that size equipment?"

The fifth day, everything went perfectly. Eight minutes, twenty-nine seconds. Determining latitude was easy when you had the exact meridian. The flagpole was excellent, because it provided the same precision as the giant theodolites of the old Indian princes, with whose aid it had been possible to calculate the latitude of distant stars. True, it became necessary to walk rather far into the neighbor's garden, watch and all. His neighbor, the former cabowner Hansson, was rather surprised when Sven started using his steel measuring tape to measure the distance from the base of the flagpole to a mark right in the middle of the carefully raked approach to Hansson's garage. This led to certain explanations, even to some harsh words, and Sven returned to a belated lunch feeling that Hansson had never really appreciated the difference between sine and hyperbolic sine. Nevertheless, by the time he was ready for coffee he had calculated his private latitude on his pocket calculator: 59 degrees, 12 minutes and 34 seconds North.

This was a substantial piece of information, and Frankie asked if she shouldn't heat up the coffee, which had gone cold.

Roses or no roses: her husband was a marvelous guy.

They didn't reach Shanghai until Sunday. Shanghai was a sea of red flags, posters, pictures of Mao, the streets so packed with short, amicably curious people with little red books in their hands that sometimes their taxi, whose springs had seen better days and which smelled more strongly of gasoline inside than out, got completely stuck in the crowds.

Their hotel, a somewhat nondescript but enormous building with endless corridors, was so large that there was a hall porter's desk on every floor. Sven and Johansson from Sales followed gratefully in the steps of their shy interpreter. The bag with Johansson's golf clubs was heavy and dragged on the hall carpet. He tried to make the dragging as unobtrusive as possible.

He hoped that the Shanghai golf courses would still be open, even though the Cultural Revolution was in progress.

They hardly had time to wash off the dust and dirt of travel before new gentlemen from the steel syndicate arrived to welcome them. One of them was such a distinguished personage that he was dressed in black wool instead of blue. The meeting took place over a cup of tea in the hotel lobby, so the golf clubs were not in evidence.

"Is either of you interested in sports?" asked the black-clad man with amiable courtesy.

Perhaps golf was an expression of the profoundest bourgeois decadence? Following a sudden impulse, Johansson said, "I play table tennis. I actually play quite a bit of table tennis."

"I hope," said the worthy representative of the Tien Ting steel syndicate, "that we shall be fortunate enough, during the weeks ahead of us, to be able to find a player who can offer you something which bears at least some resemblance to a sporting opposition."

A secretary made a quick notation.

In the streets, crowds of people eddied back and forth all night like the sea; the red flags seemed to have a life of their own under the streetlights, fluttering and moving: a large, frightening waterfall of people gravitating to some distant place.

The first conference took place punctually at eight o'clock. Slightly breathless after a taxi ride through an ocean of cyclists who did not seem to be adhering to any kind of human traffic regulations, the gentlemen from Trummelsberg arrived at the steel syndicate and were ushered into a conference room in a plain annex.

This, too, was surprisingly full of people. Everybody had the little red book in his hand. A secretary quickly passed a copy to each of the gentlemen from Trummelsberg who, after an interval of bewildered page-turning, found that the text was in English.

The gentleman in the black suit led them in song. Then followed a reading, during which one of the interpreters obliged Uncle Sven with the right page in the English edition.

In Sven's opinion, the book was essentially sound: it breathed forth profound optimism. When his turn came, he wet his fingers, found a good place, and read, "Say what you think, clearly and without reservation."

He looked around. Everyone seemed to approve.

Johansson found something about Party work on the next page; this turned out a bit strange. But the next time they came around to Uncle Sven, he was prepared and read in a strong, loud voice, his English heavily overlaid with a Västmanland accent. "Study diligently."

After twenty minutes and another song, they sat down at the conference table.

After another twenty minutes of reports, questions, and misunderstandings, Uncle Sven realized that the problem was simple and unsolvable.

If you want to make—that is to say, forge—propeller shafts thirty meters in length from steel billets, you have to have drop forges that can handle a length of thirty meters.

The longest drop forge the steel syndicate possessed could, with some dangerous modifications, manage six meters.

They actually supposed it would be possible to forge five of them, six meters each, and then weld the ends together.

If Uncle Sven had been at home in Trummelsberg, he'd have laughed out loud. Now he leaned across the table instead, rather red in the face, agitatedly leafing back and forth through his little book.

Never, in all his adult life, had he encountered such absolute insanity. To weld together a propeller shaft, an object that would have to tolerate the regular weight of hundreds of kilotons, hour after hour, month after month, at the most crucial spot in a ship, with unavoidable microscopic tensile stress, a very large torque—a shaft that would have to tolerate all this, welded together!

Evidently they had flown him around the world to make fun of him. The lab director was going to hear some straight talking when Sven returned home.

Angrily, he kept turning the pages of his little book.

It certainly was the most peculiar text he'd ever come across.

Only after a while did he become aware that the respectful silence in the room was due to the fact that everyone was waiting for him to speak.

The only thing that surfaced in his mind was the word *Kohlsauerstoffverfahren.*

What on earth was *Kohlsauerstoffverfahren?* He must have heard it on some earlier occasion.

Yes of course, in Fulda in 1931, at Professor Eiseleben's, during a lecture one Thursday morning after a formidable drinking party in a duelling students' fraternity. But what the hell did *Kohlsauerstoffverfahren* mean?

An extremely slow cooling-down process, prolonged day after day, while pulverized coal and oxygen were added, accomplishing the exchange which bonded the complex crystals more securely to each other until no joint could be detected, not even with a metallurgical X-ray microscope. But how was it done? His lecture notes from Fulda had been confiscated by Nazi customs agents on his way home at Christmas, 1933.

Had anything as strange as *Kohlsauerstoffverfahren* ever existed? Or was it something he had dreamt? If there ever had been such a process, why hadn't it been used? Why wasn't it *world-renowned?*

And, if it existed—and that was the most provoking thought—why in the world hadn't he thought of it during his twenty-two years in Trummelsberg but here instead, surrounded by a bunch of strange people who slavishly read from a red confirmation book? Why here?

"My dear friends," said Uncle Sven. "I do not wish to make a pronouncement today. The extent and difficulty of the problem force me to a thorough study of the *Quotations from Chairman Mao.*"

A sigh of approval went through the room. Evidently, this gentleman from the Trummelsberg Iron Works wasn't as uninformed as one would have imagined, considering his European bald head and always dirty glasses.

In the night he slept fitfully and had strange dreams. Once he was with Grandma Tekla at a revival meeting in the Mission House up on the hill at Halvarsviken; people were singing and bearing witness, and the cast-iron stove in the old Mission House was steaming. Another time, he was in the yard of the high school in Västerås, pursued by a mean physics teacher who insisted that he was the one who had thrown an iceball through the window of the lab right after Morning Prayer.

The old principal, Landtmanson, regarded him with large, clear, reproachful eyes behind his pince-nez. He shook his head. What a wicked young man! "But I really didn't throw any iceball," Uncle Sven complained to the silence of his Chinese hotel room, turning, for the twentieth time, on his Chinese hotel pillow, which was much too hard and full of sharp corners.

Brown-shirted Nazi students were singing and shouting. The echoes bounced between the old buildings in Fulda, and Sven didn't want to hear and put his fingers in his ears behind the tall, dusty windows of the university library. Fritz, the old janitor, in black tail coat with strange-looking sleeve protectors, moved up and down the aisles, carrying periodicals with slips of paper inserted into them.

If he could only remember the name of that damn periodical. Or who had written the article.

He woke again, in a cold sweat, and pulled the curtain to one side. Empty, abandoned in the dim light of dawn, the all too wide Chinese street stretched toward still whiter, still more monotonous districts. Incomprehensible characters on red cotton streamers fluttered from tall poles in the faint morning breeze. Two cyclists in blue broadcloth were on their way down the street with some kind of lunchboxes in their bike baskets. They weren't speaking to each other; they just kept pedaling energetically.

Well, it could look like that at home at the Works, too. "You have to be satisfied so long as things are going all right," his Papa used to say. And here he, Sven, lay, sweating and feeling as if he might be coming down with gastritis, with obvious rheumatism in his left shoulder, pondering how the People's Republic might increase the size of their merchant marine.

As an old member of the Mission congregation and resident of Bergslagen, he was used to trying to do what he could. He fell asleep at the first true light of dawn. And life suddenly seemed quite meaningless to him.

"Constructing apparatus for drop-forging that will be able to handle thirty-meter pieces will take at least twelve months. It's possible that it might be done a bit faster in the U. S., where they have experience with very large pieces in the engineering industry, but naturally you have to consider costs at this juncture."

Mr. Wong, a white-haired, clean-shaven, very pleasant man, listened attentively. He, too, was wearing the Mao button in his lapel. He had wise, somewhat tired, but smiling eyes.

"Sooner or later it will have to be done, of course. The Chinese ship-building industry has to learn to handle really large pieces. The cost must be weighed against what will be gained in experience. In all probability, you will run into some disappointments along the way. At any rate, the obstacle is fatal as far as a normal construction timetable is concerned. Trummelsberg's Iron Works would probably be able to deliver the propeller shafts in a somewhat shorter time, but the order would necessitate an adjustment there as well. On the other hand, they have been manufacturing propeller shafts in Trummelsberg as far back as World War I. Isn't it a fact that the German submarine fleet in World War I was driven by propellers marked with the famous H, the quality symbol that signified the Counts Hermanssons' quality industry?"

Mr. Wong remained politely silent.

He, Uncle Sven, realized of course that for his company it would mean a large order if their Chinese friends really wanted to entrust them with it. But estimates would take some time. One would have to make a rather extensive total projection. He was prepared to try to get the preliminary calculations started by telegram, but it would take at least a few weeks.

Mr. Wong nodded in consideration.

On the other hand it was written, "Say what you think, clearly and without reservation." And if he, Uncle Sven, was really going to say what he thought, clearly and without reservation, it might surprise his Chinese friends.

"How so?" asked Mr. Wong, and the young interpreter, happy to have something to do at last, obediently translated, "How so?"

The atmosphere was a bit strained. Uncle Sven made an unnecessary noise with the china lid of his teacup, only to find that the cup was empty. With a gesture which betrayed a certain, very slight, but still discernible impatience, Mr. Wong sent one of the secretaries to fill it in the anteroom.

"Well," said Uncle Sven, "it's easy to tell yourself that the world is old, that everything has already been done. And in one way Chairman Mao is quite right: perhaps the world is very young. Perhaps there are thousands of untried possibilities just around the corner. Perhaps it's only we who are tired, who have become used to giving up, calling resignation by the name of truth, calling everything that represents an obstacle reality and every hope, unreality.

"I can quite well imagine that the Chairman is right, that it's actually— without any use of violence of course," he added with a cautious sidelong glance through his horn-rimmed glasses, "—the right thing to do to make a revolution.

"But on the other hand, Chairman Mao is quite wrong. Everything has been done before. History is always the strongest. Whatever you think, there is always some old Chinese or Greek philosopher who has thought it before. Confucius, for instance, a truly admirable Chinese philosopher."

Silence prevailed in the room as the interpreter continued to intone his translation—he had a bit of trouble with Confucius, but quickly realized that the gentleman had meant K'ung Fu-tse. The silence fell a few degrees, but Uncle Sven continued polishing his glasses with a dazzling white handkerchief from the left-hand pocket of his wool suit.

"As a boy, you find the world ridiculous; you want to do something entirely different. As an old man, you discover that you have done the usual things. You were only a letter in a text that was discovered long ago. Just as the rarest characters reappear again and again in a text if only it's long enough, you always, sooner or later, find that you are the repetition of something that existed already." Wasn't it a fact that he himself, as a boy, had been expelled from school, so that he had to complete his studies in Germany, where darkness was falling with greater and greater swiftness? Shouldn't he know what rebellion meant, he who had once said "Shut up, you old fart" to Landtmansson, principal of the Västerås highschool—a murmur went through the assembly when the interpreters at last collected themselves sufficiently to render a translation of this enormity. Well, he could understand what the Chairman meant in his excellent little red book. It was correct and, at the same time, it was wrong.

Now to get right down to it, there was, if his memory served him right, in *Archiv für Metallurgie,* volume XXXII, 1927, an article in which the so-called Eisenfels Process was described, that is to say Professor Mauritz Eisenfels' so-called *Kohlsauerstoff-Verfahren,* a method for the production of extremely strong crystal bonding through post-treatment of forged steel through the continuous, slow addition of oxygen and deoxidized coal. As far as he, Uncle Sven, knew, this method had never been tried on a large scale, but there was absolutely nothing to stop you from trying. Like thousands of other ideas, this one had lain dormant after the professor disappeared into some concentration camp, in night and fog, behind barbed wire. In short, during a night of study of Comrade Chairman Mao's writings, he had become convinced that his friends were on the right track. It had to be possible to assemble a propeller shaft from separate forged-steel segments. If they were successful, they would be the first in the world to have accomplished this feat. He himself felt rather tired after a very restless night and now wished to retire to his hotel, but if he were needed for consultation, he would of course be at their disposal on the following day.

Respectfully, they accompanied him all the way to his waiting car. One secretary carried his briefcase, another his umbrella. In the conference room, secretaries and interpreters struggled frantically, comparing their notes.

The discussions in the Planning Committee of the steel syndicate assumed the proportions of a waterfall. Every telephone line was fraught to the breaking point.

Johansson from Sales had the opportunity, a bit later the same week, to play table tennis. The hall was quite large and "a few young people" had been found who at least should be able to offer "a somewhat sporting opposition."

Johansson lost the first game 21–2. He succeeded in making his opponent, an extremely polite and quiet young man, a bit nervous with his first two serves, since the opponent had never seen anything like it. After that he lost 21–0, 21–0.

He never was quite sure whether he had played one of the club's lesser talents or a candidate for the world championship, but as time went by, he tended to describe it as a match against a world champion.

The Works made Uncle Sven retire two years later. Those last two years, he was considered too old and tired for the demands of foreign travel. When he retired, he bought an excellent Japanese telescope. You might see him occasionally on winter evenings, in a fur jacket from his army days, with his fur cap pulled down over his ears, trying to aim his Barlow lense at the Black Cloud in Pegasus, at Andromeda's shining, mysterious disc, and at the evasive moons of Jupiter, where perhaps is germinating the only life in the solar system that would diminish our own solitude.

On the wall of his living room Uncle Sven has a reminder of his trip, an exquisite painting from the Ming period. It is called "On the Way to a Friend with a Lute," and it shows an old man being rowed by a boy across a mountain lake at sunset, to a small hut on a forested island. The lights in the hut have just been lit. The friend is standing on the dock waiting. The shadows of the mountains deepen.

Frankie, who occasionally dusts the picture, a gift from some steel syndicate in Shanghai, regards it with dreaming and uncertain eyes.

Just *how* tremendously valuable this gift is she has never comprehended.

Questions for Discussion

1. What is the connection between Frankie's wish for a rose garden and the Chinese's wish for long propeller shafts? What are the similarities in the way Uncle Sven handles the situations?

2. In what sense is Uncle Sven both a typical engineer and an extraordinary one?

3. To what extent do you agree with Uncle Sven's opinion about "new ideas"?

4. In what ways are the countries of America, Germany, and China associated with one another, in Uncle Sven's mind and in the story generally?

5. How would you characterize Uncle Sven's behavior in a foreign country? Is it respectful? Arrogant? Explain.

6. What is the significance of the painting Uncle Sven receives as a gift?

Suggestions for Writing

1. Write an essay in which you explore both the philosophical and practical sides of Uncle Sven's character.

2. Write an essay in which you explain how the rose garden and the propeller shafts either support or refute Uncle Sven's attitude toward history and new ideas.

3. Write a story that features a character who is both typical of his profession and extraordinary.

4. Speculate: How would an American engineer have handled a similar situation in China? Write about this briefly in your journal or notebook.

5. Find several articles on China's Cultural Revolution of the 1960s and then write a brief summary of the issues and changes involved. Specifically, why might Uncle Sven's mention of Confucius disturb his Chinese colleagues?

The Jewbird

BERNARD MALAMUD

The window was open so the skinny bird flew in. Flappity-flap with its frazzled black wings. That's how it goes. It's open, you're in. Closed, you're out and that's your fate. The bird wearily flapped through the open kitchen window of Harry Cohen's top-floor apartment on First Avenue near the lower East River. On a rod on the wall hung an escaped canary cage, its door wide open, but this black-type longbeaked bird—its ruffled head and small dull eyes, crossed a little, making it look like a dissipated crow—landed if not smack on Cohen's thick lamb chop, at least on the table, close by. The frozen foods salesman was sitting at supper with his wife and young son on a hot August evening a year ago. Cohen, a heavy man with hairy chest and beefy shorts; Edie, in skinny yellow shorts and red halter; and their ten-year-old Morris (after his father)—Maurie, they called him, a nice kid though not overly bright—were all in the city after two weeks out, because Cohen's mother was dying. They had been enjoying Kingston, New York, but drove back when Mama got sick in her flat in the Bronx.

"Right on the table," said Cohen, putting down his beer glass and swatting at the bird. "Son of a bitch."

"Harry, take care with your language," Edie said, looking at Maurie, who watched every move.

The bird cawed hoarsely and with a flap of its bedraggled wings—feathers tufted this way and that—rose heavily to the top of the open kitchen door, where it perched staring down.

"Gevalt, a pogrom!"

"It's a talking bird," said Edie in astonishment.

"In Jewish," said Maurie.

"Wise guy," muttered Cohen. He gnawed on his chop, then put down the bone. "So if you can talk, say what's your business. What do you want here?"

"If you can't spare a lamb chop," said the bird, "I'll settle for a piece of herring with a crust of bread. You can't live on your nerve forever."

"This ain't a restaurant," Cohen replied. "All I'm asking is what brings you to this address?"

"The window was open," the bird sighed; adding after a moment, "I'm running. I'm flying but I'm also running."

"From whom?" asked Edie with interest.

"Anti-Semeets."

"Anti-Semites?" they all said.

"That's from who."

"What kind of anti-Semites bother a bird?" Edie asked.

"Any kind," said the bird, "also including eagles, vultures, and hawks. And once in a while some crows will take your eyes out."

"But aren't you a crow?"

"Me? I'm a Jewbird."

Cohen laughed heartily. "What do you mean by that?"

The bird began dovening. He prayed without Book or tallith, but with passion. Edie bowed her head though not Cohen. And Maurie rocked back and forth with the prayer, looking up with one wide-open eye.

When the prayer was done Cohen remarked, "No hat, no phylacteries?"

"I'm an old radical."

"You're sure you're not some kind of a ghost or dybbuk?"

"Not a dybbuk," answered the bird, "though one of my relatives had such an experience once. It's all over now, thanks God. They freed her from a former lover, a crazy jealous man. She's now the mother of two wonderful children."

"Birds?" Cohen asked slyly.

"Why not?"

"What kind of birds?"

"Like me. Jewbirds."

Cohen tipped back in his chair and guffawed. "That's a big laugh. I've heard of a Jewfish but not a Jewbird."

"We're once removed." The bird rested on one skinny leg, then on the other. "Please, could you spare maybe a piece of herring with a small crust of bread?"

Edie got up from the table.

"What are you doing?" Cohen asked her.

"I'll clear the dishes."

Cohen turned to the bird. "So what's your name, if you don't mind saying?"

"Call me Schwartz."

"He might be an old Jew changed into a bird by somebody," said Edie, removing a plate.

"Are you?" asked Harry, lighting a cigar.

"Who knows?" answered Schwartz. "Does God tell us everything?"

Maurie got up on his chair. "What kind of herring?" he asked the bird in excitement.

"Get down, Maurie, or you'll fall," ordered Cohen.

"If you haven't got matjes, I'll take schmaltz," said Schwartz.

"All we have is marinated, with slices of onion—in a jar," said Edie.

"If you'll open for me the jar I'll eat marinated. Do you have also, if you don't mind, a piece of rye bread—the spitz?"

Edie thought she had.

"Feed him out on the balcony," Cohen said. He spoke to the bird. "After that take off."

Schwartz closed both bird eyes. "I'm tired and it's a long way."

"Which direction are you headed, north or south?"

Schwartz, barely lifting his wings, shrugged.

"You don't know where you're going?"

"Where there's charity I'll go."

"Let him stay, papa," said Maurie. "He's only a bird."

"So stay the night," Cohen said, "but no longer."

In the morning Cohen ordered the bird out of the house but Maurie cried, so Schwartz stayed for a while. Maurie was still on vacation from school and his friends were away. He was lonely and Edie enjoyed the fun he had, playing with the bird.

"He's no trouble at all," she told Cohen, "and besides his appetite is very small."

"What'll you do when he makes dirty?"

"He flies across the street in a tree when he makes dirty, and if nobody passes below, who notices?"

"So all right," said Cohen, "but I'm dead set against it. I warn you he ain't gonna stay here long."

"What have you got against the poor bird?"

"Poor bird, my ass. He's a foxy bastard. He thinks he's a Jew."

"What difference does it make what he thinks?"

"A Jewbird, what a chutzpah. One false move and he's out on his drumsticks."

At Cohen's insistence Schwartz lived out on the balcony in a new wooden birdhouse Edie had bought him.

"With many thanks," said Schwartz, "though I would rather have a human roof over my head. You know how it is at my age. I like the warm, the windows, the smell of cooking. I would also be glad to see once in a while the *Jewish Morning Journal* and have now and then a schnapps because it helps my breathing, thanks God. But whatever you give me, you won't hear complaints."

However, when Cohen brought home a bird feeder full of dried corn, Schwartz said, "Impossible."

Cohen was annoyed. "What's the matter, crosseyes, is your life getting too good for you? Are you forgetting what it means to be migratory? I'll bet a helluva lot of crows you happen to be acquainted with, Jews or otherwise, would give their eyeteeth to eat this corn."

Schwartz did not answer. What can you say to a grubber yung?

"Not for my digestion," he later explained to Edie. "Cramps. Herring is better even if it makes you thirsty. At least rainwater don't cost anything." He laughed sadly in breathy caws.

And herring, thanks to Edie, who knew where to shop, was what Schwartz got, with an occasional piece of potato pancake, and even a bit of soupmeat when Cohen wasn't looking.

When school began in September, before Cohen would once again suggest giving the bird the boot, Edie prevailed on him to wait a little while until Maurie adjusted.

"To deprive him right now might hurt his school work, and you know what trouble we had last year."

"So okay, but sooner or later the bird goes. That I promise you."

Schwartz, though nobody had asked him, took on full responsibility for Maurie's performance in school. In return for favors granted, when he was let in for an hour or two at night, he spent most of his time overseeing the boy's lessons. He sat on top of the dresser near Maurie's desk as he laboriously wrote out his homework. Maurie was a restless type and Schwartz gently kept him to his studies. He also listened to him practice his screechy violin, taking a few minutes off now and then to rest his ears in the bathroom. And they afterwards played dominoes. The boy was an indifferent checker player and it was impossible to teach him chess. When he was sick, Schwartz read him comic books though he personally disliked them. But Maurie's work improved in school and even his violin teacher admitted his playing was better. Edie gave Schwartz credit for these improvements though the bird pooh-poohed them.

Yet he was proud there was nothing lower than C minuses on Maurie's report card, and on Edie's insistence celebrated with a little schnapps.

"If he keeps up like this," Cohen said, "I'll get him in an Ivy League college for sure."

"Oh I hope so," sighed Edie.

But Schwartz shook his head. "He's a good boy—you don't have to worry. He won't be a shicker or a wifebeater, God forbid, but a scholar he'll never be, if you know what I mean, although maybe a good mechanic. It's no disgrace in these times."

"If I were you," Cohen said, angered, "I'd keep my big snoot out of other people's private business."

"Harry, please," said Edie.

"My goddamn patience is wearing out. That crosseyes butts into everything."

Though he wasn't exactly a welcome guest in the house, Schwartz gained a few ounces although he did not improve in appearance. He looked bedraggled as ever, his feathers unkempt, as though he had just flown out of a snowstorm. He spent, he admitted, little time taking care of himself. Too much to think about. "Also outside plumbing," he told Edie. Still there was more glow to his eyes so that though Cohen went on calling him crosseyes he said it less emphatically.

Liking his situation, Schwartz tried tactfully to stay out of Cohen's way, but one night when Edie was at the movies and Maurie was taking a hot shower, the frozen foods salesman began a quarrel with the bird.

"For Christ sake, why don't you wash yourself sometimes? Why must you always stink like a dead fish?"

"Mr. Cohen, if you'll pardon me, if somebody eats garlic he will smell from garlic. I eat herring three times a day. Feed me flowers and I will smell like flowers."

"Who's obligated to feed you anything at all? You're lucky to get herring."

"Excuse me, I'm not complaining," said the bird. "You're complaining."

"What's more," said Cohen, "even from out on the balcony I can hear you snoring away like a pig. It keeps me awake at night."

"Snoring," said Schwartz, "isn't a crime, thanks God."

"All in all you are a goddamn pest and free loader. Next thing you'll want to sleep in bed next to my wife."

"Mr. Cohen," said Schwartz, "on this rest assured. A bird is a bird."

"So you say, but how do I know you're a bird and not some kind of a goddamn devil?"

"If I was a devil you would know already. And I don't mean because of your son's good marks."

"Shut up, you bastard bird," shouted Cohen.

"Grubber yung," cawed Schwartz, rising to the tips of his talons, his long wings outstretched.

Cohen was about to lunge for the bird's scrawny neck but Maurie came out of the bathroom, and for the rest of the evening until Schwartz's bedtime on the balcony, there was pretended peace.

But the quarrel had deeply disturbed Schwartz and he slept badly. His snoring woke him, and awake, he was fearful of what would become of him. Wanting to stay out of Cohen's way, he kept to the birdhouse as much as possible. Cramped by it, he paced back and forth on the balcony ledge, or sat on the birdhouse roof, staring into space. In the evenings, while overseeing Maurie's lessons, he often fell asleep. Awakening, he nervously hopped around exploring the four corners of the room. He spent much time in Maurie's closet, and carefully examined his bureau drawers when they were left open. And once when he found a large paper bag on the floor, Schwartz poked his way into it to investigate what the possibilities were. The boy was amused to see the bird in the paper bag.

"He wants to build a nest," he said to his mother.

Edie, sensing Schwartz's unhappiness, spoke to him quietly.

"Maybe if you did some of the things my husband wants you, you would get along better with him."

"Give me a for instance," Schwartz said.

"Like take a bath, for instance."

"I'm too old for baths," said the bird. "My feathers fall out without baths."

"He says you have a bad smell."

"Everybody smells. Some people smell because of their thoughts or because who they are. My bad smell comes from the food I eat. What does his come from?"

"I better not ask him or it might make him mad," said Edie.

In late November Schwartz froze on the balcony in the fog and cold, and especially on rainy days he woke with stiff joints and could barely move his wings. Already he felt twinges of rheumatism. He would have liked to spend more time in the warm house, particularly when Maurie was in school and Cohen at work. But though Edie was good-hearted and might have sneaked him in in the morning, just to thaw out, he was afraid to ask her. In the meantime Cohen, who had been reading articles about the migration of birds, came out on the balcony one night after work when Edie was in the kitchen preparing pot roast, and peeking into the birdhouse, warned Schwartz to be on his way soon if he knew what was good for him. "Time to hit the flyways."

"Mr. Cohen, why do you hate me so much?" asked the bird. "What did I do to you?"

"Because you're an A-number-one trouble maker, that's why. What's more, whoever heard of a Jewbird! Now scat or it's open war."

But Schwartz stubbornly refused to depart so Cohen embarked on a campaign of harassing him, meanwhile hiding it from Edie and Maurie. Maurie hated violence and Cohen didn't want to leave a bad impression. He thought maybe if he played dirty tricks on the bird he would fly off without being physically kicked out. The vacation was over, let him make his easy living off the fat of somebody else's land. Cohen worried about the effect of the bird's departure on Maurie's schooling but decided to take the chance, first, because the boy now seemed to have the knack of studying—give the black bird-bastard credit—and second, because Schwartz was driving him bats by being there always, even in his dreams.

The frozen foods salesman began his campaign against the bird by mixing watery cat food with the herring slices in Schwartz's dish. He also blew up and popped numerous paper bags outside the birdhouse as the bird slept, and when he had got Schwartz good and nervous, though not enough to leave, he brought a full-grown cat into the house, supposedly a gift for little Maurie, who had always wanted a pussy. The cat never stopped springing up at Schwartz whenever he saw him, one day managing to claw out several of his tailfeathers. And even at lesson time, when the cat was usually excluded from Maurie's room, though somehow or other he quickly found his way in at the end of the lesson, Schwartz was desperately fearful of his life and flew from pinnacle to pinnacle—light fixture to clothes-tree to door-top—in order to elude the beast's wet jaws.

Once when the bird complained to Edie how hazardous his existence was, she said, "Be patient, Mr. Schwartz. When the cat gets to know you better he won't try to catch you any more."

"When he stops trying we will both be in Paradise," Schwartz answered. "Do me a favor and get rid of him. He makes my whole life worry. I'm losing feathers like a tree loses leaves."

"I'm awfully sorry but Maurie likes the pussy and sleeps with it."

What could Schwartz do? He worried but came to no decision, being afraid to leave. So he ate the herring garnished with cat food, tried hard not to hear the paper bags bursting like fire crackers outside the birdhouse at night, and lived terror-stricken closer to the ceiling than the floor, as the cat, his tail flicking, endlessly watched him.

Weeks went by. Then on the day after Cohen's mother had died in her flat in the Bronx, when Maurie came home with a zero on an arithmetic test, Cohen, enraged, waited until Edie had taken the boy to his violin lesson, then openly attacked the bird. He chased him with a broom on the balcony and Schwartz frantically flew back and forth, finally escaping into his birdhouse. Cohen triumphantly reached in, and grabbing both skinny legs, dragged the bird out, cawing loudly, his wings wildly beating. He whirled the bird around and around his head. But Schwartz, as he moved in circles, managed to swoop down and catch Cohen's nose in his beak, and hung on for dear life. Cohen cried out in great pain, punched the bird with his fist, and tugging at its legs with all his might, pulled his nose free. Again he swung the yawking Schwartz around until the bird grew dizzy, then with a furious heave, flung him into the night. Schwartz sank like stone into the street. Cohen then tossed the birdhouse and feeder after him, listening at the ledge until they crashed on the sidewalk below. For a full hour, broom in hand, his heart palpitating and nose throbbing with pain, Cohen waited for Schwartz to return but the broken-hearted bird didn't.

That's the end of that dirty bastard, the salesman thought and went in. Edie and Maurie had come home.

"Look," said Cohen, pointing to his bloody nose swollen three times its normal size, "what that sonofabitchy bird did. It's a permanent scar."

"Where is he now?" Edie asked, frightened.

"I threw him out and he flew away. Good riddance."

Nobody said no, though Edie touched a handkerchief to her eyes and Maurie rapidly tried the nine times table and found he knew approximately half.

In the spring when the winter's snow had melted, the boy, moved by a memory, wandered in the neighborhood, looking for Schwartz. He found a dead black bird in a small lot near the river, his two wings broken, neck twisted, and both bird-eyes plucked clean.

"Who did it to you, Mr. Schwartz?" Maurie wept.

"Anti-Semeets," Edie said later.

Questions for Discussion

1. In what ways is this story similar to traditional fables (stories involving animals with human attributes, such as speech)? In what ways is it not?

2. Many traditional fables have "morals" or "messages." Does "The Jewbird" have such a message? If so what is it?

3. Describe Schwartz's personality. In what way is "Schwartz" an appropriate name for the bird?

4. Why does Harry Cohen throw the bird out the window?

5. Describe the tone that's established by the first few sentences of the story.

Suggestions for Writing

1. Write an essay in which you interpret "The Jewbird" as a story about prejudice and irrational hatred.

2. Write an essay that compares and contrasts "The Jewbird" with a traditional fable, such as one by Aesop.

3. Write a fable.

4. Write a story about prejudice or anti-Semitism.

5. Write an essay in which you compare and contrast Edgar Allan Poe's "The Raven" with Bernard Malamud's "The Jewbird."

My Melancholy Face

HEINRICH   BÖLL

As I stood by the harbor to watch the gulls, my melancholy face attracted a policeman who walked the beat in this quarter. I was completely absorbed in the sight of the floating birds, who shot up and plunged down, looking in vain for something edible: the harbor was desolate, the water greenish, thick with dirty oil, and in its crusted skin floated all kinds of discarded rubbish. Not a ship was to be seen, the cranes were rusty, the warehouses decayed; it seemed that not even rats populated the black debris on the quai; it was quiet. For many years all connections with the outside had been cut off.

I had fixed my eyes on one particular gull whose flight I was watching. It hovered near the surface of the water, nervous as a swallow that senses the approach of a thunderstorm; only once in a while did it dare the screeching leap upward to unite its course with that of its companions. If I could have made one wish, I would have chosen bread to feed it to the gulls, to break crumbs and fix a white point for the purposeless wings, to set a goal toward which they would fly; to tighten this shrieking web of chaotic trails by a toss of a bread crumb, grasping into them as into a pile of strings that one gathers up. But like them, I too was hungry; tired too, yet happy in spite of my melancholy because it was good to stand there, hands in my pockets, and watch the gulls and drink sadness.

But suddenly an official hand was laid on my shoulder, and a voice said: "Come along!" With this, the hand tried to jerk me around by the shoulder. I stood where I was, shook it off, and said calmly: "You're crazy."

"Comrade," the still invisible person said to me, "I'm warning you."

"My dear sir," I replied.

"There are no 'sirs'," he cried angrily. "We're all comrades!" And now he stepped up beside me, looked at me from the side, and I was forced to pull back my happily roaming gaze and sink it into his good eyes: he was serious as a buffalo who has eaten nothing but duty for decades.

"What grounds . . . ," I tried to begin . . .

"Grounds enough," he said, "your melancholy face."

I laughed.

"Don't laugh!" His anger was genuine. At first I had thought he was bored, because there were no unregistered whores, no staggering sailors, no thieves or absconders to arrest, but now I saw that it was serious: he wanted to arrest me.

"Come along . . . !"

"And why?" I asked calmly.

Before I became aware of it, my left wrist was enclosed in a thin chain, and at this moment I realized that I was lost again. One last time I turned to the roving gulls, glanced into the beautiful gray sky, and tried, with a sudden twist, to throw myself into the water, for it seemed better to me, after all, to drown alone in this filthy water than to be strangled in some backyard by the myrmidons or be locked up again. But the policeman, with a jerk, drew me so close that escape was no longer possible.

"And why?" I asked again.

"There's a law that you have to be happy."

"I am happy," I cried.

"Your melancholy face . . . ," he shook his head.

"But this law is new," I said.

"It's thirty-six hours old, and you know very well that every new law goes into effect twenty-four hours after its proclamation."

"But I don't know it."

"That's no excuse. It was announced day before yesterday, over all the loudspeakers, in all the papers, and it was published in handbills to those," here he looked at me scornfully, "those who have no access to the blessings of the press or the radio; they were scattered over every street in the area. So we'll see where you've spent the last thirty-six hours, comrade."

He dragged me on. Only now did I feel that it was cold and I had no coat, only now did my hunger assert itself and growl before the gates of my stomach, only now did I realize that I was also dirty, unshaven, ragged, and that there were laws that said every comrade was obliged to be clean, shaved, happy, and well-fed. He shoved me in front of him like a scarecrow who, convicted of stealing, had to leave the home of its dreams on the edge of the field. The streets were empty, the way to the precinct not long, and although I had known they would find some reason to arrest me again, still my heart grew heavy, because he led me through the places of my youth, which I had wanted to visit after viewing the harbor: gardens that had been full of shrubs, lovely in their disorder, overgrown paths—all this was now planned, ordered, neat, laid out in squares for the patriotic leagues which had to carry out their exercises here Mondays, Wednesdays, and Saturdays. Only the sky had its former shape and the air was like in those days when my heart had been full of dreams.

Here and there in passing I saw that already in many of the love barracks the state sign had been hung out for those whose turn to participate in the hygienic pleasure was on Wednesday; also many bars seemed authorized to display the sign of drinking, a beer glass stamped out of lead with stripes of the patriotic colors of the area: light-brown, dark-brown, light-brown. No doubt joy reigned already in the hearts of those who had been entered in the state lists of Wednesday drinkers, and could partake of a Wednesday beer.

The unmistakable sign of zeal adhered to everyone who met us, the thin aura of industry surrounded them, probably all the more when they caught sight of the policeman; they all walked faster, showed a perfectly dutiful face, and the women who came out of the stores tried to give their faces an expression of that joy which was expected from them, for they were commanded to show joy, vigorous cheerfulness about the duties of the housewife, who was encouraged to refresh the public worker with a good meal in the evening.

But all these people avoided us skillfully, so that no one had to cross our path directly; wherever signs of life were evident on the street, they disappeared twenty steps ahead of us. Everyone tried to step quickly into a store or turn a corner, and many may have entered an unfamiliar house and waited uneasily behind the door until our steps had faded away.

Only once, just as we were passing a crossing, an older man met us; briefly, I recognized the badge of the schoolteacher on him; it was too late for him to dodge us, and he now tried, after he had first greeted the policeman according to the prescribed regulations (that is, he hit himself three times on the head with a flat hand as a sign of absolute humility), then he tried to fulfill his duty, which demanded that he spit in my face three times and call me the obligatory name: "Traitorous swine." He aimed well, but the day had been hot, his throat must have been dry, because only a few meager, rather unsubstantial drops hit me—which I—against regulations—automatically tried to wipe off with my sleeve; whereupon the policeman kicked me in the behind and hit me with his fist in the middle of my backbone, adding in a calm voice: "Stage 1," which meant the first, mildest form of punishment every policeman could use.

The schoolteacher hurried away quickly. Otherwise everyone succeeded in avoiding us; only one woman, a pale, puffy blonde, taking her prescribed airing beside a love barrack before the evening pleasure, quickly threw me a kiss and I smiled gratefully, while the policeman tried to act as though he hadn't noticed anything. They are urged to allow these women freedoms that would immediately bring any other comrade a heavy punishment. Since they contribute substantially to the improvement of general working morale, they are thought of as standing outside the law, a concession whose significance the state philosopher Dr. Dr. Dr. Bleigoeth branded in the obligatory Journal of (State) Philosophy as a sign of beginning liberalization. I had read it the day before on my way to the capital, when I found a few pages of the magazine in the outhouse of a farm. A student—probably the farmer's son—had glossed it with astute comments.

Luckily we were about to reach the police station, when the sirens started to sound, which meant that the streets would overflow with thousands of people whose faces bore an expression of mild joy (for it was "recommended" not to show too great a joy after work since it would indicate that work was a burden; jubilation, however, was to reign at the beginning of work, jubilation and song)—all these thousands of people would have had to spit at me. Actually the sirens indicated that it was ten minutes before closing, for everyone was expected to indulge in a thorough washing for ten minutes, in accordance with the slogan of the present Chief of State: Happiness and Soap.

At the door to the precinct of this quarter, a plain concrete structure, two guards were posted who bestowed upon me in passing the usual "physical measures": they hit me violently on the temples with their bayonets and cracked the barrels of their pistols against my collarbone, following the preamble to State Law No. 1: "Every policeman except the arresting officer is to prove himself before every apprehended (they mean arrested) as an individual power; to the arresting officer falls the good fortune of executing all necessary bodily measures during the interrogation." The State Law No. 1 itself has the following wording: "Every policeman *may* punish anyone; he *must* punish everyone who has been found guilty of a transgression. There is, for all comrades, no exemption from punishment, but a possibility of exemption from punishment."

We now walked through a long, bare corridor, with many large windows; then a door opened automatically, because in the meantime the guards had announced our arrival, since in those days when everyone was happy, good, orderly, and everyone exerted himself to consume the prescribed pound of soap a day, in those days the arrival of an apprehended (an arrested) was indeed an event.

We entered an almost empty room, which contained only a desk with a telephone and two chairs; I was to place myself in the middle of the room; the policeman took off his helmet and sat down.

At first it was silent and nothing happened; they always do it that way; that's the worst part; I felt how my face sagged more and more, I was hungry and tired, and even the last trace of that joy of melancholy had vanished, for I knew that I was lost.

After a few seconds a tall, pale man entered in the brownish uniform of the pre-examiner; he sat down without saying a word and looked at me.

"Occupation?"

"Simple Comrade."

"Born?"

"1.1 one," I said.

"Last employment?"

"Prisoner."

The two looked at each other.

"When and where released?"

"Yesterday, house 12, cell 13."

"Released to where?"

"To the capital."

"Papers."

I took my release paper out of my pocket and handed it over. He fastened it to the green card on which he had started to write my statements.

"Former offense?"

"Happy face."

The two looked at each other.

"Explain," said the pre-examiner.

"At that time," I said, "my happy face attracted a policeman on a day when general mourning was ordered. It was the anniversary of the death of the chief."

"Length of punishment?"

"Five."

"Conduct?"

"Bad."

"Reason?"

"Lack of initiative."

"That's all."

Then the pre-examiner stood up, walked up to me and knocked out exactly three front middle teeth: a sign that I should be branded as a backslider, a measure I had not reckoned with. Then the pre-examiner left the room and a heavy fellow in a dark brown uniform stepped in: the Interrogator.

They all beat me: the Interrogator, the Senior Interrogator, the Head Interrogator, the Preliminary and Final Judge, and also the policeman carried out all the physical measures, as the law commanded; and they sentenced me to ten years because of my melancholy face, just as five years ago they had sentenced me to five years because of my happy face.

But I must try to have no face at all any more, if I succeed in enduring the next ten years with happiness and soap.

Questions for Discussion

1. What are some of the most important elements of the story that help convey the sense of an all-powerful government?

2. Characterize the narrator's response to his predicament. How does he react to being arrested and beaten?

3. What seems to be the purpose of the laws in the society this story describes?

4. What is the narrator's solution to being arrested, and to what extent is it symbolic of being a citizen in such a state?

5. How does Böll's being German add resonance to this story?

Suggestions for Writing

1. Write an essay in which you analyze the connection between the individual and the state in this story.

2. Write an essay in which you treat "My Melancholy Face" as satire, analyzing the techniques Böll uses to deal with his subject ironically and humorously. Also, attempt to explain the extent to which satiric humor is different from other kinds of humor.

3. Write a satire about a situation in which an individual is coerced by an organization, a bureaucracy, or a government.

The Author

DONALD   BARTHELME

My deranged mother has written another book. This one is called "The Bough" and is even worse than the others. I refer not to its quality—it exhibits the usual "coruscating wit" and "penetrating social observation"—but to the extent to which it utilizes, as a kind of mulch pile, the lives of her children.

This one, as I say, is even worse than the others (two American Book Award nominations and a Literary Guild alternate). My poor brother Sampson, who appears as "Rafe," is found, in the first chapter, performing a laparoscopy upon a patient who had been under the impression she was paying for quite another procedure. My brother is a very busy and popular doctor, and a hiatus in his office staffing was responsible for this understandable if lamentable mixup. What the book does not say is that the laparoscopy disclosed a fair amount of endometriosis which was then dealt with in a highly skilled and professional manner, thus averting considerable patient disgruntlement. Mother never puts anything good about any of us into her books.

"Rafe"'s relations with "Molly" (read Callie, Sam's wife) are, as you might imagine, not spared. Some time ago Sam and Callie had a little disagreement about his conduct during the Miami OB-GYN meeting when he was missing for some hours during a presentation on ultrasound and she learned that he had been out drinking with a bunch of heavily armed survivalists who liked to shoot up life-size plywood cutouts of Gorbachev with their (more or less illegal) Ingram M-11s which they can fire one-handed with a can of Stroh's in the other. Girl survivalists were also present. O.K., so my brother Sam is a gun nut. Why tell everybody in the world? Intervention is what surgeons are all about. How my mother gleans these details is beyond me, as none of us has spoken to her since 1974, when "Fumed Oak" was published.

My mother's treatment of my sister Virginia—"Alabama" in the book (Mother's masks are clear glass)—is flatly vicious. Virginia has had some tough times of late, what with the accident and the fallout from the accident. In "The Bough" "Alabama" has a blood-alcohol reading of .18% immediately after the crash, and that happens to be the right number, as many of Virginia's friends have recognized. What is truly reprehensible is the (painfully accurate) analysis of my sister's character. Virginia did her dissertation on Emerson; so does "Alabama." That certain passages in "Alabama"' dissertation offer striking parallels to recent work by Joel Porte (Harvard University Press) and Eric Cheyfitz (Johns Hopkins University Press) is announced for the first time in "Bough;" I had not thought Mother that much of a scholar. The line in the book "They shouldn't let me go into a bar without training wheels on" is pure Virginia.

My other brother, Denis (the "good brother" in the book), has asked his lawyers to look into the legal aspects. They have told him that suing one's mother is an awkward business at best and the appearance of filial impiety more or less cancels, for jurors, any merit such a suit might possess. They also pointed out, very reasonably, that the public nature of such an action, involving a well-known author, would tend to call attention to some of the very things we are not anxious to emphasize: for example, Denis's practice of purchasing U.S. Army morphine Syrettes from disaffected Medical Corps master sergeants and the ingenious places he finds to hide them in the office (hollowed-out cigars, his computer's surge suppressor) and the consequences of this for his brokerage business, all finely detailed in "The Bough." I must say I have never read a more telling account of the *jouissance* produced by high-grade morphine. What busy little bee brought her this news?

"The Bough" is No. 9 this week on the Los Angeles *Times* list. Thus does Stamford provide titillation for Santa Barbara, by way of Mother's bee-loud glade in Old Lyme. Somehow she uncovered the specifics of my "theft" of several inconsequential medicine bundles (cloth, painted wood, feathers) from the Native American Institute, where I am the former curator-at-large. I say "theft" because I wish to be as hard on myself as possible in this matter; others might call it "creative deaccessioning," and the Ghost Dance material (drum charts, dance notation) received in exchange, which the board would never have realized the value of, will be my monument. Yes, the finder's fee charged to the transaction was quite substantial, in the high six figures, as Mother does not fail to note, but Willie Leaping Deer and I earned every penny of it. No one who fully understands the Ghost Dance, whose object was to render the participants impervious to the encroachments of the white man (rifle bullets included), would have hesitated for a moment. "Mark" has a ridiculous affair with a Dakota shaman of ambiguous sex, and none of that is true except the trance scene; furthermore, the chanting on that occasion involved no intoxicants save "Pinafore," which I was teaching Wokodah and which he greatly enjoyed.

It is not that we, my mother's children, lead or claim to lead exemplary lives. But couldn't she widen her horizons just a bit?

"Mother, why do you do this to us?" I asked her recently.

Mother is handsome still, and bears a carefully cultivated resemblance to Virginia Woolf.

"What?" she said. "Do what?"

I was holding up a copy of "The Bough." "This," I said, more or less pointing it at her.

"But you're *mine*," she said.

Questions for Discussion

1. What issues of "authorship," "fiction," and "fact" does the story raise, in your view?

2. How would you describe the narrator of "The Author"? What characterizes his voice and his preoccupations?

3. Interpret the last sentence of the story.

Suggestions for Writing

1. Write a monologue from the point of view of a character in one of your stories. Perhaps have the character talk about you the author.

2. Assume that someone has made you a character in a piece of fiction, changing what you consider to be facts about you. Write a notebook entry that expresses possible reactions you might have to this situation.

3. Write an essay that extrapolates what "The Author" suggests about the fiction-writing process.

The Murder

JOYCE   CAROL   OATES

A gunshot.

The crowd scrambles to its feet, turmoil at the front of the room, a man lies dying.

The smell of gunpowder is everywhere.

It has not happened. He stands there, alive, living. His shoulders loom up thick and square: the cut of his dark suit is jaunty. He is perfect. He shuffles a stack of papers and leans forward confidently against the podium. Those hands are big as lobster claws. He adjusts the microphone, bending it up to him. He is six and a half feet tall, my father, much taller than the man who has just introduced him, and this gesture—abrupt and a little comic—calls our attention to the fact.

Mr. Chairman, I want to point out no less than five irregularities in this morning's session.

That voice. It is in my head. I am leaning forward, anxious not to miss anything. What color is his suit exactly? I don't know. I am not in Washington with him; I am watching this on television. It is important that I know the color of his suit, of his necktie, across the distance. That voice! It is enough to paralyze me, safe here, safe here at home.

It is evident that the Sawyer report was not taken seriously by this committee . . . we wish to question the integrity of these proceedings. . . . A ripple of applause. His voice continues, gaining strength. Nothing has really begun yet—the men are jockeying for position, preparing themselves with stacks of papers, words, definitions. It has the air of a play in rehearsal, not yet ready to be viewed by the public, the dialogue only partly memorized, the actors fumbling to get hold of the story, the plot.

Look at him standing there. He speaks without hesitation, as if his role is written and he possesses it utterly. So sizable a man, my father!—the very soles of his shoes are enough to stamp out ordinary people. His voice is aristocratic. His voice is savage. Listen to that voice. *I request a definition of your curious phrase "creeping internationalism of American institutions"*—

Laughter. The camera shifts to show the audience in the gallery, a crowd of faces. I am one of those faces.

—most respectfully request a definition of "bleeding-heart humanists"—

Scattered laughter, the laughter of individuals. It is mocking, dangerous. The distinguished men of the committee sit gravely, unsmiling, and their counterparts in the audience are silent. Who are the people, like my father, who dare to laugh? They are dangerous men.

He was almost shot, some months ago. The man was apprehended at once.

He had wanted to kill my father, to warn my father. But the shot had gone wild; the future was untouched.

His voice continues. The session continues. When the camera scans the audience I lean forward, here in Milwaukee. I need to see, to *see*. Is his murderer there in the audience?

My father is a man who will be murdered.

There are reasons for his murder. Look. Look at my mother: she is striding towards this room, her face flushed and grim. She is seeking me out. Her hair is in crazy tufts, uncombed, gray hair with streaks of red.

She jerks the door open. "What the hell?" she cries. "Are you still watching that?"

She stands in the doorway of my room and will not enter. It is one of her eccentricities—not to enter my room.

"Have you been watching that all day?" she says.

"It's—it's a very important hearing—"

"Turn it off! You need to go out and get some air."

I get to my feet.

My fingers on the knob—my head bowed—I stand above my father. He is a handsome man, but he cannot help me. He is a very handsome man. People stare after him. In the street, in a hotel lobby, anywhere people stare.

He was born to be stared at by women.

I am prepared to take my place in this story.

I am twenty-three and I have a life somewhere ahead of me, waiting. You see my fresh, unlined face, these two enormous strands of black hair, the white part in the center of my skull, the eyes. Dark eyes, like his. You see the pale, rather plain face, the ears pierced with tiny golden dots, almost invisible. You are dismayed as I walk across the room because my shoulders are slumped as if in weariness. I am round-shouldered, and I have grown to an unwomanly height. Deep inside me is a spirit that is also round-shouldered. Smaller women dart ahead of me, through doors or into waiting arms. I lumber along after them, a smile on my face, perspiring inside my dark, plain clothes. I am weighed down by something sinister that gathers in my face, a kind of glower, a knowledge perhaps.

I wake suddenly, as always. I sit up in bed. I remember the hearings and wonder if anything has happened to him overnight. There are no sessions scheduled for today. I dress slowly and brush my hair. I am preparing myself for anything, and it may be to review the clippings on my bureau—articles on him or by him, some with photographs.

He has moved away permanently.

Always, he has traveled. I remember him carrying a single suitcase, backing away, saying good-bye. His hearty, happy good-byes! I would follow him on the globe in his old study, so many times, pressing my forefinger against the shape of the country. There, there he was. Precisely there.

He is going to visit. I know this. He is nearby. This morning he is nearby.

My mother: nearly as tall as I, in slacks and an old sweater, in old bedroom slippers, a cigarette in her mouth. She smokes perpetually, squinting against the smoke irritably; right now she is arguing on the telephone, one of her sisters.

They are both going on a trip around the world, leaving in August. She doesn't really want me to join her, but she keeps after me, nagging me, trying to make me give in. Her sturdy legs are too much for me, her thick thighs, her robust face, her pocketbooks and hats and shoes. She is on the telephone in the kitchen, hunched over, barking with sudden laughter, one side of her face squinting violently against the smoke.

The house: three floors, too large for my mother and me. You could drift through the downstairs and never find anything to sit on. A statue from Ceylon—a ram with sharp, cruel horns—canvases on the walls, like exclamations. A crystal chandelier hangs from the ceiling, large and dangerous. Over the parquet floor there is an immense Oriental rug, rich as a universe. On the mantel there are more statues, smaller ones, figures of human beings and sacred animals, and a large ornamental dagger in its fur sheath, everything filmed over lightly with dust. Everything is pushed together: there is hardly room to walk through it. We live in the back rooms. My mother strides out occasionally to add another table or lamp to the debris, her cigarette smartly in her mouth, the shrewd cold eye of a collector taking in everything, adding it up, dismissing it. We enter the house through the back door.

The street: a city street, town houses and apartment buildings and enormous old homes. On a weekday morning like today you expect to see a face high at one of the windows of these homes, an attic window maybe. You expect to hear a faint scream. We watch television along this street and read the newspapers, staring at the pictures of men in public life.

The water: Lake Michigan frosted and pointed at the shore, a look of polar calm, absolute cold, absolute zero. It is zero here. I can hear the waves beneath the ice. I can hear the waves at the back of my head, always. We who live on the edge of the lake never leave the lake: we carry it around with us in our heads. My father lived in this house for fifteen years, and so he must carry the sound of the waves in his head too.

I was conceived, of course, to the rhythm of Lake Michigan.

He is approaching this house, driving a large car. He eyes the house from a block away, respectful of the enemy. He brakes the car suddenly, because he sees a tall figure appear, coming around the side of the house, her shoulders hunched against the wind. She walks with the hard stride of a soldier getting from one point to another, wanting only to get from one point to another.

A car slows at the curb, and I stare at it, amazed. At such times I may be pretty. But the glower returns, the doubt.

"Audrey! Don't be alarmed, just get in . . . can you talk with me for a few minutes?"

We stare at each other. His face is melancholy for a moment, as if my flat stare has disappointed him. But then he smiles. He smiles and says, "Please get in! You must be freezing!"

"I didn't—I didn't know you were in town—"

"Yes, I am in town. I am here. Have you had breakfast yet?"

"No. Yes. I mean—"

"Get in. Or are you afraid your mother is watching?"

I cannot believe that he is here, that I am so close to him. "But what—what do you want?" I hear myself stammering. He gets out of the car, impatient with me, and seizes my hands. He kisses me, and I recoil from his fierce good humor.

"Forget about your unfortunate mother and come take a ride with me," he says. "Surely you can spare your father ten minutes?" And he gives me a shake, he grips my elbow in the palm of his big hand. There is nothing to do but give in. We drive off, two giant people in a giant automobile.

He says, "And now, my dear, tell me everything!—what you are doing with your life, what your expectations are, whether you can spare your father a month or so of your company—"

I begin to talk. My life: what is there to say about it? I have written him. I imagine him ripping open the envelopes with a big fatherly smile, scanning the first few lines, and then being distracted by a telephone, some person. In one hand he holds my letters. In the other hand he holds the letters from his women. He loses these letters. He crumples them and sticks them in his pockets or thrusts them into drawers, but he loses them in the end.

"And mother is planning—"

"No, never mind your mother. I am not interested in morbid personalities!" he cries.

His sideways grin, his face, his thick dark hair. I laugh at his words. They are not funny, and yet they win me to laughter.

"Audrey, I've moved into another dimension. You know that. You understand me, don't you?"

He squeezes my hand.

"I woke up missing you the other day," he says.

I stare at the dashboard of the car. My eyes are dazzled by the gauges, the dials. I can think of nothing to say. My body is large and heavy and cunning.

"Why are you looking away from me? You won't even look at me!" he says. "And that peculiar little smile—what is that?" He turns the rearview mirror above the windshield so that I can see myself.

"Do you hate me very much?" he says gently.

When I packed to leave that afternoon, my mother stood in the doorway and said in a level, unalarmed voice: "So you're going to live the high life with that bastard? So you're going to move out of here, eh? Please don't plan on coming back, then."

She was amused and cynical, smoking her cigarettes. I was opening and closing drawers.

"I don't mean . . . I don't want to hurt you . . . " I stammered.

"What?"

My suitcases are packed. I am making an end of one part of my life. In the background, beneath my mother's voice, there is the sound of water, waves.

"Women are such fools. I hate women," my mother says.

Some time ago a woman came to visit my mother. I was about fifteen then, and I had just come home from school; I remember that my feet were wet and my hair frizzy and bedraggled, an embarrassment as I opened the door. The woman stared at me. She had a long, powdered face, the lips drawn up sharply into a look of tired festivity. Something had gone on too long. She had been smiling too long. The eyes were bright and beautiful, the lashes black, the hair black but pulled sharply back from her face, almost hidden by a dark mink hat. Though it was winter, she looked warm. Her cheeks were reddened. The lips were coated with lipstick that had formed a kind of crust. She was glittering and lovely, and she reached out to take hold of my wrist.

"Audrey. You're Audrey . . . "

Her eyelids were pinkened, a dark dim pink. I smelled a strange fruity odor about her—not perfume, not powder—something sweet and overdone. Her bare fingers squeezed mine in a kind of spasm.

Then my mother hurried downstairs. The two women looked at each other gravely, as if recognizing each other, but for several seconds they said nothing. They moved forward, both with a slow, almost drugged air: they might have been hurrying to meet and only now, at the last moment, were they held back. "Am I too early?" the woman said.

"No. No. Of course not," my mother said.

The woman took off her coat and let it fall across a sofa—the bronze of her dress clashed with the things in the room. The woman was a surprise, a holiday, a treat.

"I can't seem to stop shivering," the woman laughed.

That evening my mother drank too much. She told me bitterly, "Women are such fools! I hate women."

We take a private car from the airport to the hotel. It is Washington, and yet my father doesn't telephone to say that he is back. "Tomorrow it all begins again," he says. "I want us to have a few hours alone." But he is energetic and eager for it to begin, and I am eager to be present, to watch him. I am scanning the crowds on the sidewalk, for he is in danger, someone could rush up to him at any moment.

He is in an excellent mood. He is bringing me into his life, checking me into the hotel, into a room next to his; he is my father, taking care of me, solicitous and exaggerated. The hotel reminds me of my mother's home—so much ornamentation, rugs thick and muffling, furniture with delicate curved legs.

"Well, this is my home. I live here most of the year," he declares.

We have drinks in the lounge. We chat. I ask him, "Has anyone ever tried to shoot you again?" He laughs—of course not! Who would want to shoot him? He smiles indulgently, as if I've said the wrong thing, and he turns to call the waitress over to him. Another martini, please. There is joy in the way he eats, the way he drinks.

It occurs to me that he is a man with many enemies.

"Why do you look so somber?" he asks me.

"I was worried—I was thinking—"

"Don't worry over me, please, I assure you I don't need it!" he laughs. He pats my hand with a hand that is just like it, though larger. "You sound like a—" and he pauses, his smile tightening as he tries to think of the right word. He is a man who knows words, he knows how to choose the right words, always, but he cannot think of the right word now. And so finally he says, strangely, "—like a woman."

Who is watching us?

Some distance away I see a woman . . . she is standing unnaturally still, alone, watching us. She stands soldily, her feet in low-heeled shoes, and she wears a dark coat buttoned up to the neck, very trim and spare. I find myself thinking in disappointment, *She isn't very pretty.* But really, I can't see her face across the crowded lobby. I feel dizzy with her presence. I would like to point her out to my father.

But he doesn't seem to notice her. He looks everywhere; it is a habit of his to scan everyone's face, to keep an eye on the entrance; but his gaze doesn't settle upon that woman.

We get into a taxi and ride off. It is a suspension of myself, this drifting along in the cab, between the hotel and the chamber where the hearings are taking place. From time to time my father asks me something, as if to keep me attached to him. Or he squeezes my hand.

Photographers move forward to take his picture. They maneuver to get my father and to exclude other people. My father, accustomed to attention, waves genially but does not slow down. He has somewhere to get to: he is a man who has somewhere to be, people waiting for him. I look around the sidewalk to see who is watching us here. I expect to see the woman again, but of course she could not have gotten here so quickly. Is his murderer in this crowd, the man who will leap forward someday and kill my father? Even my father's face, behind its bright mask, is a face of fear.

He too is looking for his murderer.

In the gallery one of his associates sits with me. *Your father is a wonderful man,* he tells me. The proceedings begin. People talk at great length. There is continual movement, spectators in and out, attorneys rising to consult with one another, committee members leaving and returning. I understand nothing will be decided. I understand that no one is here for a decision.

"Mr. Chairman," my father says, barely bothering to stand, "I wish to disagree . . . "

I look around the room, and there she is. She is standing at the very back. She is alone, listening to my father's words, standing very still. She is my secret, this woman! I watch her: her attention never moves from him.

She is staring at *him.* She doesn't notice anyone in the room except him. Her eyes are large, fawnish, very bright.

"Do you hate me very much?" he must ask them all.

Over the weekend we go to one party after another. My father is handsome and noisy with success. I sit and listen to him talking about the terrible, unfathomable future of the United States. I listen to his friends, their agreement. *Everything is accelerated, a totally new style evolves every four or five years now, it's seized upon, mastered, and discarded—a continual revolution,* he says. These conversations are important, they determine the conditions of the world.

"But do you think things are really so bad?" I ask my father when we are alone.

"Have you been listening to all that?" he teases.

I am dragged into taxis, out of taxis. The ceilings of the hotel corridors are very high. The menu for room service lists a bag of potato chips for one dollar. Always there is the sound of a machine whirring, a mechanism to clear the air. We meet in the coffee shop, and eventually we go out to the street, to get in a cab. Once I looked over the roof of the car and saw that woman again—I saw her clearly. She was staring at us. Her purse was large, and she carried it under her arm.

"There is someone—"

"What?" says my father.

"Someone is—"

But the taxi driver needs directions, and I really have nothing to say.

I am silent.

Evening: we are shown into a crowded room, a penthouse apartment. The height is apparent; everyone seems elongated, dizzy, walking on the tips of their toes. I watch my father closely; he stands in a circle of people. In this room, awaiting him, there is a woman, and she will look at him in a certain way. They will approach each other, their eyes locking. His elbows move as he gestures; he bumps into someone and apologizes with a laugh.

I find a place to sit. The evening passes slowly. I am sitting alone, and people move around me. I sit quietly, waiting. From time to time my father checks on me, my hair plaited and smooth, my face chaste, innocent.

"Not bored, are you, sweetheart?" he says.

Women are placed strategically in this room: one here, one there, one in a corner, one advancing from the left, one already at his side, leaning against him, her hand on his wrist, the little lips, the dainty nostrils.

I will go to my father and take his arm and tell him quite gently, *You are going to die.*

My face is silent, fixed, my lips frozen into a kind of smile learned from watching other women.

No, I will say nothing. I will not tell him. I am silent. The shot will be precise and as near to silence as a gunshot can be. It will tear into his heart from the corner of a crowded room.

It is a way of making an end.

Questions for Discussion

1. In what ways does Oates improvise upon and subvert some of the conventions of "crime" or "detective" fiction in this story? In what ways does she draw attention to the art of making fiction?

2. What is the connection between the narrator's preoccupation with women and her preoccupation with her father?

3. How are power and murder connected in this story?

4. What does Oates do in this story to make the murder seem inevitable in a variety of ways?

5. Is the narrator's father murdered? If so, who kills him and why?

6. Characterize the narrator—her voice, her obsessions, the nature of her life.

Suggestions for Writing

1. Write an essay in which you discuss the improvisations and variations on conventional detective fiction that Oates creates in "The Murder."

2. Write an essay in which you analyze the connection between the narrator's private life and obsession with a larger public world in which her father is powerful.

3. Write a story that plays deliberately and extensively with the conventions of a subgenre of fiction: science fiction, detective fiction, romance fiction, children's fiction, and so forth.

4. Write a story about a power struggle between a mother, a father, and a daughter or son.

The Censors

LUISA   VALENZUELA

P oor Juan! One day they caught him with his guard down before he could even realize that what he had taken as a stroke of luck was really one of fate's dirty tricks. These things happen the minute you're careless and you let down your guard, as one often does. Juancito let happiness—a feeling you can't trust—get the better of him when he received from a confidential source Mariana's new address in Paris and he knew that she hadn't forgotten him. Without thinking twice, he sat down at his table and wrote her a letter. *The* letter that keeps his mind off his job during the day and won't let him sleep at night (what had he scrawled, what had he put on that sheet of paper he sent to Mariana?)

Juan knows there won't be a problem with the letter's contents, that it's irreproachable, harmless. But what about the rest? He knows that they examine, sniff, feel, and read between the lines of each and every letter, and check its tiniest comma and most accidental stain. He knows that all letters pass from hand to hand and go through all sorts of tests in the huge censorship offices and that, in the end, very few continue on their way. Usually it takes months, even years, if there aren't any snags; all this time the freedom, maybe even the life, of both sender and receiver is in jeopardy. And that's why Juan's so down in the dumps: thinking that something might happen to Mariana because of his letters. Of all people, Mariana, who must finally feel safe there where she always dreamed she'd live. But he knows that the *Censor's Secret Command* operates all over the world and cashes in on the discount in air rates; there's nothing to stop them from going as far as that hidden Paris neighborhood, kidnapping Mariana, and returning to their cozy homes, certain of having fulfilled their noble mission.

Well, you've got to beat them to the punch, do what everyone tries to do: sabotage the machinery, throw sand in its gears, get to the bottom of the problem so as to stop it.

This was Juan's sound plan when he, like many others, applied for a censor's job—not because he had a calling or needed a job: no, he applied simply to intercept his own letter, a consoling but unoriginal idea. He was hired immediately, for each day more and more censors are needed and no one would bother to check on his references.

Ulterior motives couldn't be overlooked by the *Censorship Division,* but they needn't be too strict with those who applied. They knew how hard it would be for those poor guys to find the letter they wanted and even if they did, what's a letter or two when the new censor would snap up so many others? That's how Juan managed to join the *Post Office's Censorship Division,* with a certain goal in mind.

The building had a festive air on the outside which contrasted with its inner staidness. Little by little, Juan was absorbed by his job and he felt at peace since he was doing everything he could to get his letter for Mariana. He didn't even worry when, in his first month, he was sent to *Section K* where envelopes are very carefully screened for explosives.

It's true that on the third day, a fellow worker had his right hand blown off by a letter, but the division chief claimed it was sheer negligence on the victim's part. Juan and the other employees were allowed to go back to their work, albeit feeling less secure. After work, one of them tried to organize a strike to demand higher wages for unhealthy work, but Juan didn't join in; after thinking it over, he reported him to his superiors and thus got promoted.

You don't form a habit by doing something once, he told himself as he left his boss's office. And when he was transferred to *Section J*, where letters are carefully checked for poison dust, he felt he had climbed a rung in the ladder.

By working hard, he quickly reached *Section E* where the work was more interesting, for he could now read and analyze the letters' contents. Here he could even hope to get hold of his letter which, judging by the time that had elapsed, had gone through the other sections and was probably floating around in this one.

Soon his work became so absorbing that his noble mission blurred in his mind. Day after day he crossed out whole paragraphs in red ink, pitilessly chucking many letters into the censored basket. These were horrible days when he was shocked by the subtle and conniving ways employed by people to pass on subversive messages; his instincts were so sharp that he found behind a simple "the weather's unsettled" or "prices continue to soar" the wavering hand of someone secretly scheming to overthrow the Government.

His zeal brought him swift promotion. We don't know if this made him happy. Very few letters reached him in *Section B*—only a handful passed the other hurdles—so he read them over and over again, passed them under a magnifying glass, searched for microprint with an electronic microscope, and tuned his sense of smell so that he was beat by the time he made it home. He'd barely manage to warm up his soup, eat some fruit, and fall into bed, satisfied with having done his duty. Only his darling mother worried, but she couldn't get him back on the right road. She'd say, though it wasn't always true: Lola called, she's at the bar with the girls, they miss you, they're waiting for you. Or else she'd leave a bottle of red wine on the table. But Juan wouldn't overdo it: any distraction could make him lose his edge and the perfect censor had to be alert, keen, attentive, and sharp to nab cheats. He had a truly patriotic task, both self-denying and uplifting.

His basket for censored letters became the best fed as well as the most cunning basket in the whole *Censorship Division*. He was about to congratulate himself for having finally discovered his true mission, when his letter to Mariana reached his hands. Naturally, he censored it without regret. And just as naturally, he couldn't stop them from executing him the following morning, another victim of his devotion to his work.

Questions for Discussion

1. This story is very short—what is sometimes called a "short short." How has the scale of the story influenced the storytelling? That is, are plot, character, and other elements necessarily different in this story than they are in longer ones? Explain.

2. What does this brief tale suggest about the influence of "the state" (in the form of censorship) on our lives?

3. Is this a comic story or a serious one? Is it both? Neither? Explain.

4. To what extent is Juan's predicament believable? Should we take the story literally or not? Is the change Juan undergoes believable, and can you apply it to your own experience or that of others?

5. To what extent is this story a parable?

Suggestions for Writing

1. Write an essay in which you interpret this story symbolically, with Juan and the censors representing "kinds" of people, power, and moral predicaments.

2. Write an informal journal entry or a more formal essay about your own views of censorship. When, if ever, is censorship appropriate? What should be censored and why? To what extent does the American Constitution prohibit censorship? Should pornography be censored? Should an attack on the Constitution be censored? Is it ever appropriate for a government to censor private correspondence? Think of other questions and issues.

3. Write a "short-short story"—three or four pages, typewritten, double-spaced.

The Ghost Children of Tacoma

RICHARD   BRAUTIGAN

T he children of Tacoma, Washington, went to war in December 1941. It seemed like the thing to do, following in the footsteps of their parents and other grown-ups who acted as if they knew what was happening.

"Remember Pearl Harbor!" they said.

"You bet!" we said.

I was a child, then, though now I look like somebody else. We were at war in Tacoma. Children can kill imaginary enemies just as well as adults can kill real enemies. It went on for years.

During World War II, I personally killed 352,892 enemy soldiers without wounding one. Children need a lot less hospitals in war than grown-ups do. Children pretty much look at it from the all-death side.

I sank 987 battleships, 532 aircraft carriers, 799 cruisers, 2,007 destroyers and 161 transport ships. Transports were not too interesting a target: very little sport.

I also sank 5,465 enemy PT boats. I have no idea why I sank so many of them. It was just one of those things. Every time I turned around for four years, I was sinking a PT boat. I still wonder about that. 5,465 are a lot of PT boats.

I only sank three submarines. Submarines were just not up my alley. I sank my first submarine in the spring of 1942. A lot of kids rushed out and sank submarines right and left during December and January. I waited.

I waited until April, and then one morning on my way to school: BANG! my first sub., right in front of a grocery store. I sank my second submarine in 1944. I could afford to wait two years before sinking another one.

I sank my last submarine in February 1945, a few days after my tenth birthday. I was not totally satisfied with the presents I got that year.

And then there was the sky! I ventured forth into the sky, seeking the enemy there, while Mount Rainier towered up like a cold white general in the background.

I was an ace pilot with my P-38 and my Grumman Wildcat, my P-51 Mustang and my Messerschmitt. That's right: Messerschmitt. I captured one and had it painted a special color, so my own men wouldn't try to shoot me down by mistake. Everybody recognized my Messerschmitt and the enemy had hell to pay for it.

I shot down 8,942 fighter planes, 6,420 bombers and 51 blimps. I shot down most of the blimps when the war was first in season. Later, sometime in 1943, I stopped shooting down blimps altogether. Too slow.

I also destroyed 1,281 tanks, 777 bridges and 109 oil refineries because I knew we were in the right.

"Remember Pearl Harbor!" they said.

"You bet!" we said.

I shot the enemy planes down by holding out my arms straight from my body and running like hell, shouting at the top of my lungs: RAT-tattattattattattattat-tattattattattat!

Children don't do that kind of stuff any more. Children do other things now and because children do other things now, I have whole days when I feel like the ghost of a child, examining the memory of toys played back into the earth again.

There was a thing I used to do that was also a lot of fun when I was a young airplane. I used to hunt up a couple of flashlights and hold them lit in my hands at night, with my arms straight out from my body and be a night pilot zooming down the streets of Tacoma.

I also used to play airplane in the house, too, by taking four chairs from the kitchen and putting them together: two chairs facing the same way for the fuselage and a chair for each wing.

In the house I played mostly at dive-bombing. The chairs seemed to do that best. My sister used to sit in the seat right behind me and radio urgent messages back to base.

"We only have one bomb left, but we can't let the aircraft carrier escape. We'll have to drop the bomb down the smokestack. Over. Thank you, Captain, we'll need all the luck we can get. Over and out."

Then my sister would say to me, "Do you think you can do it?" and I'd reply, "Of course, hang onto your hat."

Your Hat
Gone Now These
Twenty Years
January 1,
1965

Questions for Discussion

1. What does this story suggest about how and why children "play war"?

2. Describe the tone of this story.

3. Like Luisa Valenzuela's "The Censors," Brautigan's story is a short-short one. Explore the differences and similarities in the way each handles this compressed form.

4. Referring to "playing war," the narrator says that "Children don't do that kind of stuff anymore." Is the narrator correct? In what ways do children play war differently now? In your view, should children "play war"? Why or why not?

5. What is the effect of the "statistics" the narrator gives us? And of the epitaph at the end?

Suggestions for Writing

1. Write an essay in which you analyze this story's attitude toward children and their views of war.

2. In a journal entry, compare and contrast the type of play you recall with the type that Brautigan remembers from his childhood.

The Lottery

SHIRLEY JACKSON

The morning of June 27th was clear and sunny, with the fresh warmth of a full-summer day; the flowers were blossoming profusely and the grass was richly green. The people of the village began to gather in the square, between the post office and the bank, around ten o'clock; in some towns there were so many people that the lottery took two days and had to be started on June 26th, but in this village, where there were only about three hundred people, the whole lottery took less than two hours, so it could begin at ten o'clock in the morning and still be through in time to allow the villagers to get home for noon dinner.

The children assembled first, of course. School was recently over for the summer, and the feeling of liberty sat uneasily on most of them; they tended to gather together quietly for a while before they broke into boisterous play, and their talk was still of the classroom and the teacher, of books and reprimands. Bobby Martin had already stuffed his pockets full of stones, and the other boys soon followed his example, selecting the smoothest and roundest stones; Bobby and Harry Jones and Dickie Delacroix—the villagers pronounced this name "Dellacroy"—eventually made a great pile of stones in one corner of the square and guarded it against the raids of the other boys. The girls stood aside, talking among themselves, looking over their shoulders at the boys, and the very small children rolled in the dust or clung to the hands of their older brothers or sisters.

Soon the men began to gather, surveying their own children, speaking of planting and rain, tractors and taxes. They stood together, away from the pile of stones in the corner, and their jokes were quiet and they smiled rather than laughed. The women, wearing faded house dresses and sweaters, came shortly after their menfolk. They greeted one another and exchanged bits of gossip as they went to join their husbands. Soon the women, standing by their husbands, began to call to their children, and the children came reluctantly, having to be called four or five times. Bobby Martin ducked under his mother's grasping hand and ran, laughing, back to the pile of stones. His father spoke up sharply, and Bobby came quickly and took his place between his father and his oldest brother.

The lottery was conducted—as were the square dances, the teenage club, the Halloween program—by Mr. Summers, who had time and energy to devote to civic activities. He was a round-faced, jovial man and he ran the coal business, and people were sorry for him, because he had no children and his wife was a scold. When he arrived in the square, carrying the black wooden box, there was a murmur of conversation among the villagers, and he waved and called, "Little late today, folks." The postmaster, Mr. Graves, followed him, carrying a three-legged stool, and the stool was put in the center of the square and Mr. Summers set the black box down on it. The villagers kept their distance, leaving a space between themselves and the stool, and when Mr. Summers said, "Some of you fellows want to give me a hand?" there was a hesitation before two men, Mr. Martin and his oldest son, Baxter, came forward to hold the box steady on the stool while Mr. Summers stirred up the papers inside it.

The original paraphernalia for the lottery had been lost long ago, and the black box now resting on the stool had been put into use even before Old Man Warner, the oldest man in town, was born. Mr. Summers spoke frequently to the villagers about making a new box, but no one liked to upset even as much tradition as was represented by the black box. There was a story that the present box had been made with some pieces of the box that had preceded it, the one that had been constructed when the first people settled down to make a village here. Every year, after the lottery, Mr. Summers began talking again about a new box, but every year the subject was allowed to fade off without anything's being done. The black box grew shabbier each year; by now it was no longer completely black but splintered badly along one side to show the original wood color, and in some places faded or stained.

Mr. Martin and his oldest son, Baxter, held the black box securely on the stool until Mr. Summers had stirred the papers thoroughly with his hand. Because so much of the ritual had been forgotten or discarded, Mr. Summers had been successful in having slips of paper substituted for the chips of wood that had been used for generations. Chips of wood, Mr. Summers had argued, had been all very well when the village was tiny, but now that the population was more than three hundred and likely to keep on growing, it was necessary to use something that would fit more easily into the black box. The night before the lottery, Mr. Summers and Mr. Graves made up the slips of paper and put them in the box, and it was then taken to the safe of Mr. Summers's coal company and locked up until Mr. Summers was ready to take it to the square next morning. The rest of the year, the box was put away, sometimes one place, sometimes another; it had spent one year in Mr. Graves's barn and another year underfoot in the post office, and sometimes it was set on a shelf in the Martin grocery and left there.

There was a great deal of fussing to be done before Mr. Summers declared the lottery open. There were the lists to make up—of heads of families, heads of households in each family, members of each household in each family. There was the proper swearing-in of Mr. Summers by the postmaster, as the official of the lottery; at one time, some people remembered, there had been a recital of some sort, performed by the official of the lottery, a perfunctory, tuneless chant that had been rattled off duly each year; some people believed that the official of the lottery used to stand just so when he said or sang it, others believed that he was supposed to walk among the people, but years and years ago this part of the ritual had been allowed to lapse. There had been, also, a ritual salute, which the official of the lottery had had to use in addressing each person who came up to draw from the box, but this also had changed with time, until now it was felt necessary only for the official to speak to each person approaching. Mr. Summers was very good at all this; in his clean white shirt and blue jeans, with one hand resting carelessly on the black box, he seemed very proper and important as he talked interminably to Mr. Graves and the Martins.

Just as Mr. Summers finally left off talking and turned to the assembled villagers, Mrs. Hutchinson came hurriedly along the path to the square, her sweater thrown over her shoulders, and slid into place in the back of the crowd. "Clean forgot what day it was," she said to Mrs. Delacroix, who stood next to her, and they both laughed softly. "Thought my old man was out back stacking wood," Mrs. Hutchinson went on, "and then I looked out the window and the kids was gone, and then I remembered it was the twenty-seventh and came a-running." She dried her hands on her apron, and Mrs. Delacroix said, "You're in time, though. They're still talking away up there."

Mrs. Hutchinson craned her neck to see through the crowd and found her husband and children standing near the front. She tapped Mrs. Delacroix on the arm as a farewell and began to make her way through the crowd. The people separated good-humoredly to let her through; two or three people said, in voices just loud enough to be heard across the crowd, "Here comes your Missus, Hutchinson," and "Bill, she made it after all." Mrs. Hutchinson reached her husband, and Mr. Summers, who had been waiting, said cheerfully, "Thought we were going to have to get on without you, Tessie." Mrs. Hutchinson said, grinning, "Wouldn't have me leave m'dishes in the sink, now, would you, Joe?" and soft laughter ran through the crowd as the people stirred back into position after Mrs. Hutchinson's arrival.

"Well, now," Mr. Summers said soberly, "guess we better get started, get this over with, so's we can go back to work. Anybody ain't here?"

"Dunbar," several people said. "Dunbar, Dunbar."

Mr. Summers consulted his list. "Clyde Dunbar," he said. "That's right. He's broke his leg, hasn't he? Who's drawing for him?"

"Me, I guess," a woman said, and Mr. Summers turned to look at her. "Wife draws for her husband," Mr. Summers said. "Don't you have a grown boy to do it for you, Janey?" Although Mr. Summers and everyone else in the village knew the answer perfectly well, it was the business of the official of the lottery to ask such questions formally. Mr. Summers waited with an expression of polite interest while Mrs. Dunbar answered.

"Horace's not but sixteen yet," Mrs. Dunbar said regretfully. "Guess I gotta fill in for the old man this year."

"Right," Mr. Summers said. He made a note on the list he was holding. Then he asked, "Watson boy drawing this year?"

A tall boy in the crowd raised his hand. "Here," he said. "I'm drawing for m'mother and me." He blinked his eyes nervously and ducked his head as several voices in the crowd said things like "Good fellow, Jack," and "Glad to see your mother's got a man to do it."

"Well," Mr. Summers said, "guess that's everyone. Old Man Warner make it?"

"Here," a voice said, and Mr. Summers nodded.

A sudden hush fell on the crowd as Mr. Summers cleared his throat and looked at the list. "All ready?" he called. "Now, I'll read the names—heads of families first—and the men come up and take a paper out of the box. Keep the paper folded in your hand without looking at it until everyone has had a turn. Everything clear?"

The people had done it so many times that they only half-listened to the directions; most of them were quiet, wetting their lips, not looking around. Then Mr. Summers raised one hand high and said, "Adams." A man disengaged himself from the crowd and came forward. "Hi, Steve," Mr. Summers said, and Mr. Adams said, "Hi, Joe." They grinned at one another humorlessly and nervously. Then Mr. Adams reached into the black box and took out a folded paper. He held it firmly by one corner as he turned and went hastily back to his place in the crowd, where he stood a little apart from his family, not looking down at his hand.

"Allen," Mr. Summers said. "Anderson. . . . Bentham."

"Seems like there's no time at all between lotteries any more," Mrs. Delacroix said to Mrs. Graves in the back row. "Seems like we got through with the last one only last week."

"Time sure goes fast," Mrs. Graves said.

"Clark. . . . Delacroix."

"There goes my old man," Mrs. Delacroix said. She held her breath while her husband went forward.

"Dunbar," Mr. Summers said, and Mrs. Dunbar went steadily to the box while one of the women said, "Go on, Janey," and another said, "There she goes."

"We're next," Mrs. Graves said. She watched while Mr. Graves came around from the side of the box, greeted Mr. Summers gravely, and selected a slip of paper from the box. By now, all through the crowd there were men holding the small folded papers in their large hands, turning them over and over nervously. Mrs. Dunbar and her two sons stood together, Mrs. Dunbar holding the slip of paper.

"Harburt. . . . Hutchinson."

"Get up there, Bill," Mrs. Hutchinson said, and the people near her laughed.
"Jones."

"They do say," Mr. Adams said to Old Man Warner, who stood next to him, "that over in the north village they're talking of giving up the lottery."

Old Man Warner snorted. "Pack of crazy fools," he said. "Listening to the young folks, nothing's good enough for *them*. Next thing you know, they'll be wanting to go back to living in caves, nobody work any more, live *that* way for a while. Used to be a saying about 'Lottery in June, corn be heavy soon.' First thing you know, we'd all be eating stewed chickweed and acorns. There's *always* been a lottery," he added petulantly. "Bad enough to see young Joe Summers up there joking with everybody."

"Some places have already quit lotteries," Mrs. Adams said.

"Nothing but trouble in *that*," Old Man Warner said stoutly. "Pack of young fools."

"Martin." And Bobby Martin watched his father go forward. "Overdyke. . . . Percy."

"I wish they'd hurry," Mrs. Dunbar said to her older son. "I wish they'd hurry."

"They're almost through," her son said.

"You get ready to run tell Dad," Mrs. Dunbar said.

Mr. Summers called his own name and then stepped forward precisely and selected a slip from the box. Then he called, "Warner."

"Seventy-seventh year I been in the lottery," Old Man Warner said as he went through the crowd. "Seventy-seventh time."

"Watson." The tall boy came awkwardly through the crowd. Someone said, "Don't be nervous, Jack," and Mr. Summers said, "Take your time, son."

"Zanini."

After that, there was a long pause, a breathless pause, until Mr. Summers, holding his slip of paper in the air, said, "All right, fellows." For a minute, no one moved, and then all the slips of paper were opened. Suddenly, all the women began to speak at once, saying, "Who is it?," "Who's got it?," "Is it the Dunbars?," "Is it the Watsons?" Then the voices began to say, "It's Hutchinson. It's Bill," "Bill Hutchinson's got it."

"Go tell your father," Mrs. Dunbar said to her older son.

People began to look around to see the Hutchinsons. Bill Hutchinson was standing quiet, staring down at the paper in his hand. Suddenly, Tessie Hutchinson shouted to Mr. Summers, "You didn't give him time enough to take any paper he wanted. I saw you. It wasn't fair!"

"Be a good sport, Tessie," Mrs. Delacroix called, and Mrs. Graves said, "All of us took the same chance."

"Shut up, Tessie," Bill Hutchinson said.

"Well, everyone," Mr. Summers said, "that was done pretty fast, and now we've got to be hurrying a little more to get done in time." He consulted his next list. "Bill," he said, "you draw for the Hutchinson family. You got any other households in the Hutchinsons?"

"There's Don and Eva," Mrs. Hutchinson yelled. "Make *them* take their chance!"

"Daughters draw with their husbands' families, Tessie," Mr. Summers said gently. "You know that as well as anyone else."

"It wasn't *fair*," Tessie said.

"I guess not, Joe," Bill Hutchinson said regretfully. "My daughter draws with her husband's family, that's only fair. And I've got no other family except the kids."

"Then, as far as drawing for families is concerned, it's you," Mr. Summers said in explanation, "and as far as drawing for households is concerned, that's you, too. Right?"

"Right," Bill Hutchinson said.

"How many kids, Bill?" Mr. Summers asked formally.

"Three," Bill Hutchinson said. "There's Bill, Jr., and Nancy, and little Dave. And Tessie and me."

"All right, then," Mr. Summers said. "Harry, you got their tickets back?"

Mr. Graves nodded and held up the slips of paper. "Put them in the box, then," Mr. Summers directed. "Take Bill's and put it in."

"I think we ought to start over," Mrs. Hutchinson said, as quietly as she could "I tell you it wasn't *fair*. You didn't give him time enough to choose. *Every*body saw that."

Mr. Graves had selected the five slips and put them in the box, and he dropped all the papers but those onto the ground, where the breeze caught them and lifted them off.

"Listen, everybody," Mrs. Hutchinson was saying to the people around her.

"Ready, Bill?" Mr. Summers asked, and Bill Hutchinson, with one quick glance around at his wife and children, nodded.

"Remember," Mr. Summers said, "take the slips and keep them folded until each person has taken one. Harry, you help little Dave." Mr. Graves took the hand of the little boy, who came willingly with him up to the box. "Take a paper out of the box, Davy," Mr. Summers said. Davy put his hand into the box and laughed. "Take just *one* paper," Mr. Summers said. "Harry, you hold it for him." Mr. Graves took the child's hand and removed the folded paper from the tight fist and held it while little Dave stood next to him and looked up at him wonderingly.

"Nancy next," Mr. Summers said. Nancy was twelve, and her school friends breathed heavily as she went forward, swishing her skirt, and took a slip daintily from the box. "Bill, Jr.," Mr. Summers said, and Billy, his face red and his feet overlarge, nearly knocked the box over as he got a paper out. "Tessie," Mr. Summers said. She hesitated for a minute, looking around defiantly, and then set her lips and went up to the box. She snatched a paper out and held it behind her.

"Bill," Mr. Summers said, and Bill Hutchinson reached into the box and felt around, bringing his hand out at last with the slip of paper in it.

The crowd was quiet. A girl whispered, "I hope it's not Nancy," and the sound of the whisper reached the edges of the crowd.

"It's not the way it used to be," Old Man Warner said clearly. "People ain't the way they used to be."

"All right," Mr. Summers said. "Open the papers. Harry, you open little Dave's."

Mr. Graves opened the slip of paper and there was a general sigh through the crowd as he held it up and everyone could see that it was blank. Nancy and Bill, Jr., opened theirs at the same time, and both beamed and laughed, turning around to the crowd and holding their slips of paper above their heads.

"Tessie," Mr. Summers said. There was a pause, and then Mr. Summers looked at Bill Hutchinson, and Bill unfolded his paper and showed it. It was blank.

"It's Tessie," Mr. Summers said, and his voice was hushed. "Show us her paper, Bill."

Bill Hutchinson went over to his wife and forced the slip of paper out of her hand. It had a black spot on it, the black spot Mr. Summers had made the night before with the heavy pencil in the coal-company office. Bill Hutchinson held it up, and there was a stir in the crowd.

"All right, folks," Mr. Summers said. "Let's finish quickly."

Although the villagers had forgotten the ritual and lost the original black box, they still remembered to use stones. The pile of stones the boys had made earlier was ready; there were stones on the ground with the blowing scraps of paper that had come out of the box. Mrs. Delacroix selected a stone so large she had to pick it up with both hands and turned to Mrs. Dunbar. "Come on," she said. "Hurry up."

Mrs. Dunbar had small stones in both hands, and she said, gasping for breath, "I can't run at all. You'll have to go ahead and I'll catch up with you."

The children had stones already, and someone gave little Davy Hutchinson a few pebbles.

Tessie Hutchinson was in the center of a cleared space by now, and she held her hands out desperately as the villagers moved in on her. "It isn't fair," she said. A stone hit her on the side of the head.

Old Man Warner was saying, "Come on, come on, everyone." Steve Adams was in the front of the crowd of villagers, with Mrs. Graves beside him.

"It ain't fair, it isn't right," Mrs. Hutchinson screamed, and then they were upon her.

Questions for Discussion

1. How does Jackson create suspense in this story?

2. "The Lottery," Jackson's first published story, is one of the most famous short stories of the twentieth century. How do you account for its stature?

3. Assuming that "The Lottery" is a suggestive or even symbolic story, how might we apply events of the tale to other kinds of human experience? What behavior, social codes, and psychology does the story represent?

4. What is the effect of the second lottery in the story—the lottery just among the Hutchinson family? And what is the effect of our learning that someone gives the young Hutchinson boy pebbles to throw?

Suggestions for Writing

1. Write an essay in which you interpret "The Lottery" symbolically.

2. Write an essay in which you interpret the meaning of the second lottery (among the Hutchinson family).

3. There is a huge discrepancy between the folksy, small-town behavior of the community and the horror of the lottery. Write a journal entry about the effect this has on you as a reader and on Jackson's possible purposes for constructing the story in this way. What does this discrepancy suggest about human behavior?

4. "The Lottery" depicts an extreme and extremely brutal ritual, but perhaps you have participated in a less extreme ritual that, in retrospect, seems senseless. Write a journal entry about your participation in such a ritual, assessing your motives at the time and explaining why your perspective on the event has changed.

5. "The Lottery" and Luisa Valenzuela's story "The Censors" are very different in some respects, but they are similar insofar as one might read each as a parable and insofar as each deals with the oppressive, arbitrary practices of a society. Write an essay in which you explore the differences and similarities of these two stories, and of course feel free to take issue with the similarities mentioned in this essay topic.

If There Is Justice

AMOS OZ

Rami Rimon came home for the weekend on leave.

His face was thinner. His skin had shrunk a little. His jaws seemed more prominent. The lines on his face were sharper. His mother's face struggling to get out. Fine creases ringed his mouth. The sun had etched wrinkles round his eyes. Twin furrows ran from his nose to the corners of his mouth.

He was wearing an impeccable greenish uniform, with his beret tucked in his pocket. His stout boots were shod with steel at toe and heel. His sleeves were rolled up to reveal hairy forearms, and his hands were covered with little scars. He was conscious of his manly appearance as he strode slowly across the yard with an air of studied indifference. The men and women he met greeted him warmly. He responded with an offhand nod. There were traces of gun grease under his fingernails, and his left elbow was dressed with a grubby bandage.

When the first tumult of hugs and kisses, received by Rami with a wavering smile, had died down, Fruma said:

"Well, you won't believe it, but I was just thinking of you the moment before you turned up. Mother's intuition."

Rami thought there was nothing strange in that. He had said in his letter that he would come on Friday afternoon, and she knew perfectly well what time the bus came. As he spoke, he put down his shabby kit bag, pulled his shirt outside his trousers, lit a cigarette, and laid a heavy hand on Fruma's shoulder.

"It's good to see you, Mom. I wanted to tell you that I'm really glad to see you again."

Fruma glanced at his dusty boots and said:

"You've lost so much weight."

Rami drew on his cigarette and asked about her health.

"Come inside and have a shower before dinner. You're all sweaty. Would you like a cold drink first? No. A warm drink would be better for you. Wait, though, the first thing is to take you along to the surgery. I want the nurse to have a look at your elbow."

Rami started to explain about the wound. It happened during a bayonet practice; the clumsy oaf of a section commander . . . but Fruma did not let him finish the story.

"There you go dropping your ash on the floor. I've just washed it in your honor. There are four ash trays in the house, and you . . . "

Rami sat down in his filthy clothes on the clean white bedspread and kicked off his boots. Fruma rushed to fetch her husband's old slippers. Her eyes were dry, but she tried to turn her face away from her son to hide the look he disliked so much. Rami, however, pretended not to have seen that strained look, as of a dam about to burst. He lay back on the bed, looked up at the ceiling, drew the ash tray that Fruma had put in his hand closer to him, and blew out a puff of smoke.

"The day before yesterday we crossed a river on a rope bridge. Two ropes stretched one above the other, one to walk on and the other to hold. With all our stuff on our backs, spade, blankets, gun, ammunition, the lot. Now, who do you suppose it was who lost his balance and fell in the water? The section commander! We all . . . "

Fruma eyed her son and exclaimed:

"You've lost at least ten pounds. Have you had any lunch? Where? No, you haven't. I'll dash across to the hall and get you something to eat. Just a snack—I'll make you a proper meal when you've had a rest. How about some raw carrot? It's very good for you. Are you sure? I can't force you. All right, then, have a shower and go to sleep. You can eat when you wake up. But perhaps I'd better take you to the surgery right away. Wait a minute. Here's a nice glass of orange juice. Don't argue, drink it."

"I jumped in the water and fished him out," Rami continued. "Then I had to dive in again to look for his rifle. Poor wretch! It was hilarious. It wasn't his first accident, though. Once, on an exercise . . ."

"You need some new socks. They're all falling apart," Fruma remarked as she pulled his dirty laundry out of the kit bag.

"Once, on an exercise, he fired his submachine gun by accident. Nearly killed the battalion commander. He's the clumsiest fool you can imagine. You can tell what he's like from his name. He's called Zalman Zulman. I've written a song about him, and we sing it all day long. Listen."

"But they don't feed you there. And you didn't write every other day, as you promised. But I saw in the letter box that you wrote to Noga Harish. That's life. Your mother works her fingers to the bone, and some child comes and collects the honey. It doesn't matter now. There's something I must know: Did she answer your letter? No? Just as I thought. You don't know what she's like. It was just as well you ditched her. Everybody knows what she is. The mistress of a man who's old enough to be her grandfather. It's disgusting. Disgusting. Have you got enough razor blades? It's disgusting, I tell you."

"Is it true they're starting to work the Camel's Field? That's going to cause a flare-up, all right. Provided, of course, the powers that be don't get cold feet. You know, Jewish sentimentality and all that. My buddies say . . ."

"Go and have a shower. The water's just right now. No, I heard every word. Test me. 'Jewish sentimentality.' There aren't many boys of your age with such an independent way of thinking. After your shower you can have a nap. Meanwhile, I'll ask the nurse to come here. That wound looks very nasty. You've got to have it seen to."

"By the way, Mom, did you just say that she . . ."

"Yes, son?"

"All right. Never mind. It doesn't matter now."

"Tell me, tell me what you need. I'm not tired. I can do anything you want me to."

"No, thanks, I don't need anything. I just wanted to say something, but it's not important. It's irrelevant. I've forgotten. Stop running around. I can't bear it. We'll talk this evening. Meanwhile, you must have a rest, too."

"Me! I'll rest in my grave. I don't need to rest. I'm not tired. When you were a baby, you had something wrong with your ears. A chronic infection. There weren't any antibiotics then. You cried all night, night after night. You were in pain. And you've always been a sensitive boy. I rocked your cradle all night, night after night, and sang you songs. One does everything for children, without counting the cost. You won't repay me. You'll repay it to your own children. I won't be here any more, but you'll be a good father, because you're so sensitive. You don't think about rest when you're doing something for your children. How old were you then? You've forgotten all about it. It was the time when Yoash started going to school, so it must have been when you were eighteen months old. You were always a delicate child. Here am I rambling on, and you need to sleep. Go to sleep now."

"By the way, Mom, if you're going to the surgery could you bring me some corn ointment. You won't forget, will you?"

At five o'clock Rami woke up, put on a clean white shirt and gray trousers, quietly helped himself to a snack, and then went to the basketball field. On the way he met Einav, limping awkwardly. She asked how he was. He said he was fine. She asked if it was a hard life. He said he was ready to face any hardship. She asked if his mother was pleased with him and answered her own question:

"Of course Fruma's pleased with you. You're so bronzed and handsome."

The field was floodlit, but the light was not noticeable in the bright twilight. The only living souls there were Oren's gang. Rami put his hands in his pockets and stood for a while without doing or saying anything. The Sabbath will go by. Empty. Without anything happening. With mother. Sticky. What do I need? A cigarette. That thin boy playing by himself over there in the corner is called Ido Zohar. Once I caught him sitting in the common room at night writing a poem. What was I saying? A cigarette.

Rami put the cigarette to his mouth and two planes roared by, shattering the Sabbatical calm, hidden in the twilight glow. The dying sun struck sparks off their fuselage. The metal shone back dazzlingly. In a flash Rami realized that they were not our planes. They had the enemy's markings on their wings. An excited shout burst from his throat.

"Theirs!"

Instinctively he looked down, just long enough to hear Oren's confused cry, but by the time he looked up again the drama was almost over. The enemy planes had turned tail and were fleeing from other planes that were approaching powerfully from the southwest, evidently trying to block their escape. Instantly, dark shapes fell through the air toward the orchards to the north. Both planes had jettisoned the spare fuel tanks fixed to their wings to speed their flight. Rami clenched his fists and growled through his teeth, "Let them have it." Before he had finished there was an answering burst of gunfire. Lightning flashed. After what seemed a long interval, there came a dull roll of thunder. The fate of the raid was settled in an instant. The enemy planes disappeared over the mountains, one of them trailing a cloud of white smoke mixed with gray. Their pursuers paused, circled the valley twice like angry hounds, then vanished into the darkening sky.

Oren shouted jubilantly:

"We hit one! We smashed one! We brought one down!"

And Rami Rimon, like a child, not like a soldier, hugged Oren Geva and exclaimed:

"I hope they burn! I hope they burn to death!"

He pounded Oren's ribs exultantly with his fists until Oren drew away groaning with pain. Rami was seized by demented joy.

His joy accompanied him to the dining hall, where a spirit of noisy excitement reigned. He made his way among the tables to where Noga Harish stood in her best dress, looking at the notice board. He put his hands on her shoulders and whispered in her ear:

"Well, silly girl, did you see or didn't you?"

Noga turned to face him with a condescending smile.

"Good Sabbath, Rami. You're very brown. It suits you. You look happy."

"I . . . I saw it all. From beginning to end. I was up at the basketball field. Suddenly I heard a noise to the east, and I realized at once that . . ."

"You're like my little brother. You're cute. You're happy."

These remarks encouraged Rami. He spoke up boldly:

"Shall we go outside? Will you come outside with me?"

Noga thought for a moment. Then she smiled inwardly, with her eyes, not with her mouth.

"Why not?" she said.

"Come on then," said Rami, and took hold of her arm. Almost at once he let it go.

When they were outside the dining hall, Noga said:

"Where shall we go?"

Strangely enough, at that moment Noga remembered something she had forgotten: Rami's full name was Avraham. Avraham Rominov.

"Anywhere," Rami said. "Let's go."

Noga suggested they sit down on the yellow bench, facing the door of the dining hall. Rami was embarrassed. People would see them there, he said. And stare at them. And talk.

Noga smiled again, and again she asked calmly, "Why not?"

Rami could find no answer to her question. He crossed his legs, took a cigarette out of his shirt pocket, tapped it three times on his matchbox, stuck in in the corner of his mouth, struck a match, shielded the flame with both hands even though there was no wind, inhaled deeply with half-closed eyes, blew out a long stream of smoke, and when all this was done, lowered his eyes to the ground once more. Finally, he gave her a sidelong glance and began:

"Well? What have you got to say for yourself?"

Noga replied that she hadn't been going to say anything. On the contrary, she thought it was he who was going to do the talking.

"Oh, nothing special. Just . . . What do you expect me to do?" he suddenly burst out violently. "Spend the whole evening, the whole Sabbath, my whole leave with my mother, like some mother's darling?"

"Why not? She's missed you badly."

"Why not? Because . . . All right. I can see I bore you. Don't think I can't live without you. I can get on quite well without you. Do you think I can't?"

Noga said she was sure he could manage perfectly well without her.

They fell silent.

Hasia Ramigolski and Esther Klieger-Isarov came toward them, chatting in Yiddish and laughing. When they caught sight of Noga and Rami their conversation stopped dead. As they walked past, Hasia said:

"Good evening. Shabbat Shalom." She dwelt suggestively on the stressed syllables.

Rami grunted, but Noga smiled and said gently:

"A very good evening to you both."

Rami said nothing for a while. Then he murmured:

"Well?"

"I'm listening."

"I hear they're going to start working on the hill," Rami said. "There's going to be trouble."

"It's so pointless."

Rami quickly changed the subject. He told the story of his section commander who had fallen in the water trying to demonstrate how to cross a river on a rope bridge. He went on to say that it wasn't the poor fool's first accident. "Once, on an exercise, he accidently fired his submachine gun and nearly killed the battalion commander. You can tell what he's like from his name. He's called Zalman Zulman, of all things. I've written a rhyme about him:

> *"Zalman Zulman's full of fun,*
> *Always letting off his gun.*
> *Zalman Zulman lost his grip,*
> *Took an unexpected dip.*
> *Zalman Zulman . . ."*

"Just a minute. Does he play an instrument?"

"Who?"

"Zalman. The man you were talking about. What's the matter with your elbow?"

"What's that got to do with it?" Rami asked indignantly.

"With what?"

"With what we were talking about."

"You were telling me about someone called Zalman. I asked if he played an instrument. You haven't answered my question."

"But I don't see what . . . "

"You're very brown. It suits you."

"It's hardly surprising. We train all day in the sun. Of course we get brown. Listen: we went on a fifty-mile route march, with all the kit, gun, pack, spade, and all at the trot. Eight of the people in my squad . . ."

"Chilly, don't you think?"

". . . collapsed on the way. And we had to carry them on stretchers. I . . ."

"I'm cold. Couldn't you finish the story tomorrow? If you don't mind terribly."

"What's the matter?" Rami considered, and then asked thickly, "What's up? Is somebody waiting for you? Are you rushing off to . . . to keep an appointment?"

"Yes, I've got to take my father his dinner. He isn't well."

"What, again?" Rami asked absently. Noga explained that he had a pain in his chest and the doctor had ordered him to go to bed.

"Next week he's got to go and have an examination. That's all. Shall we meet here again tomorrow afternoon?"

Rami did not answer. He lit another cigarette and threw the lighted match away behind the bench. Noga said good night and started to go. Then she stopped, turned, and said:

"Don't smoke too much."

At that moment five steps separated them. Rami asked irritably why she should care whether he smoked a lot or a little. Noga ignored his question and said:

"You're very brown. It suits you. Good night."

Rami said nothing. He sat alone on the bench until the dancing started in the square, as it did every Friday night at a quarter past nine.

When it was over, shortly before midnight, he set off for his mother's room. He changed his course, however, because he met Dafna Isarov, who asked him if he was going home to bed already, and Rami thought he detected a sneer in her voice. So he turned off the path. His feet guided him toward the cow shed, where he had worked before he was called up. And as he walked he talked to himself.

This could never have happened to Yoash. It's happened to me, though. Women understand only one language, brute force. But, as mother said, I was always a delicate child. Hell. Now they're laughing. Everybody wants something bad to happen to someone else so as to make life more interesting. It's like that everywhere; it's like that on the kibbutz and it's even like that in the army. You're a child you're a child you're a child. You're like my little brother. Maybe being brown does suit me, but it hasn't got me anywhere. She didn't insult me for once. She didn't even call me a horse. What did she do to me tonight, how did she make fun of me? My Rami is a delicate, sensitive boy. I wish I could die. That'd show them. I can bend this sprinkler with my bare hands. That'll drive Theodor Herzl Goldring mad. I've got stronger hands than Yoash. If only he weren't dead, I'd show him. Where am I going? Walking around like some Jack looking for his Jill. Leaping on the mountains, skipping in the hills, as that filthy old lecher would say. People like that ought to be put down. Like Arabs. Punch him in the face, he raises his hands to protect himself, you hit him in the stomach and give him a kick for good measure. All over. Here we are at the cow shed. Hey, Titan, good bull. Are you awake? Bulls sleep standing up because they can't lie down because of the iron ring. If they come to slaughter you, Titan, don't let them. Don't give in. Show your mettle. Don't be a ghetto bull. Give them a *corrida*. We mustn't give in without a struggle. We must be strong and quick and light and violent like a jet fighter. Swoop and dart and turn and soar like a knife flashing through the sky like a fighter. A fighter is such a powerful thing. I could have been a pilot, but Mother.

Strange that the moon is shining. The moon does strange things. Changes things strangely. Changes the colors of things. Silver. My Rami is a delicate sensitive child Rami writes poems like Izo Zohar he loves nature hell he loves plants and animals hope they burn to death. Her father has a pain in his chest. It's because of old Berger. Dirty old man. Her father taught us a poem by Bialik once, called "The Slaughter," where it says that there is no justice in this world. It's true. It's a ghetto poem, but it's true. He's lived his life, he's got grown-up children, he's found his niche. Why did he steal her from me? What have I done to him? And she said I was brown and handsome. If I'm brown and handsome, and he's old and fat, then why.

When I die, she'll know. It'll shatter her. The moon colors everything white. Silver. Listen, Noga, listen. I've also got a pain in my chest, I'm also in pain, so why don't you. I make fun of Zalman Zulman, she makes fun of me, they all make fun of me. It shows there isn't any justice in the world, only slaughter, Titan, worse than anything the Devil could invent. That's from the same poem. The man who's being slaughtered starts thinking about justice. The man who's slaughtering him thinks only about violence. My mistake was not to use force on her. Why, Titan, why didn't I use force, do you know why? I'll tell you. Because my Rami is a delicate boy curse them he loves nature hope they burn he loves plants and animals filthy whores. That sounds like planes overhead. It's after midnight. I love these planes, roaring along without lights. There's going to be a big war. I'll die. Then they'll know.

The fish ponds. A light in Grisha's hut. A pressure lamp. I can hear Grisha's voice. In the boat. Shouting to his fishermen. He's been in three wars and he's come out alive.

Maybe Dafna, his daughter. Ridiculous. They'd laugh. What's in this filthy shed? Barrels. Sacks of fish food. The fishermen's supper. If they find me here. Grisha's belt. A pistol. It's a revolver. Fancy leaving a revolver in an empty shed. They'll be coming back to eat soon. They'll laugh, they'll laugh. They'll say I went for a walk to look for inspiration. I know how it works. It has a revolving drum with six chambers. You put a bullet in each chamber. After each shot the drum revolves and brings another bullet in line with the barrel. That's how the revolver works. Now let's see how Rami Rimon works. A trial. Without a judge. I'm the judge. Now let's begin.

Rami takes a bullet out of the leather holster, a yellow metal case containing a little brown metal projectile. First of all, he puts the bullet in his mouth. A sharp, metallic taste. Then he puts the bullet in one of the chambers. He spins the drum without looking, because luck must be blind. He puts the gun to his temple. The chances are five to one. He squeezes the trigger. A dry thud. Rami inserts a second bullet. Spins the blind drum. Four to two. Gun to temple. Squeezes. Dry thud. Maybe I'm being silly. We'll soon know, Judge. I'm not trying to kill myself.

It's only an experiment. Up to five. A delicate sensitive child couldn't do this. A third bullet. Blind spin. Cold damp hand. I've touched something damp. If I can do this, I'm not a delicate sensitive child. Up to five. Gun to temple. Squeeze the trigger. Dry thud. I'm past halfway. Two more tries. Fourth bullet. Now the odds are against me. Now comes the test. Watch carefully, Judge. Spin. Slowly. The drum, slowly. Without looking. Slowly. Temple. You're crazy. But you're no coward. Slowly squeeze. It's cold here.

Now the fifth. Last one. Like an injection. Delicate sensitive child's trembling. Why? Nothing will happen because nothing's happened so far, even though according to the odds I should have died with the fourth bullet. Don't tremble, dear little delicate child who cried all night with earache, don't tremble, think of Grisha Isarov who's come out of three wars alive. Yoash wouldn't have trembled, because he was Yoash. Little ghetto boy, with a little cap and a gray coat and side curls. I want to know how many I. Not to kill myself. Four. That's enough. Madness to go on. No, we said five—five let it be. Don't change your mind, coward, don't lie, you said five, not four. Five let it be. Put the gun to your temple. Now squeeze, horse, squeeze, you're a ghetto child, you're a little boy, you're my little brother, squeeze. Wait a moment. I'm allowed to think first. Suppose I die here. She'll know. She'll know I wasn't joking. But they'll say "broken heart" they'll say "unrequited love" they'll say "emotional crisis." Sticky, very sticky. Hell. Squeeze. You won't feel a thing. A bullet in the brain is instant death. No time for pain. And afterward? Like plunging through the sky. An invisible fighter. It doesn't hurt. Perhaps I've already pressed the trigger and died perhaps when you die nothing changes. Other people see a corpse blood bones and you carry on as usual. I can try again. If I press the trigger, it's a sign I'm still alive. Afterward everything will be black and warm. When you die it's warm even though the body gets cold. Warm and safe like under a blanket in winter. And quiet. Squeeze. You've got a chance. Like when we used to play dice when I was little and sometimes I wanted very badly to throw a six and I threw a six. Now I want very badly to press the trigger but my finger won't press. Trembling. Careful you don't press it accidentally. Everything is different when the moon shines yellow. Can hear Grisha cursing next week we're going to the firing range that'll be interesting I'll be top of the class I'm an excellent shot now count up to three and shoot. Eyes open. No. Eyes closed. No. One, two, th- no. Up to ten. One, two, three, four, five, six, seven, eight, nine, t-.

But Rami Rimon did not try his luck the fifth time. He put down the revolver and went out into the fields and wandered about till his feet guided him back to the cow shed. Grisha won't notice. And if he does, he'll have a shock. I forgot to check the most important thing. I didn't look inside the gun to see what would have happened if I'd pressed the fifth time. Better not to know. Some things are better left undone.

A new thought occurred to Rami. It soothed him like a gentle caress. Not all men are born to be heroes. Maybe I wasn't born to be a hero. But in every man there's something special, something that isn't in other men. In my nature, for instance, there's a certain sensitivity. A capacity to suffer and feel pain. Perhaps

I was born to be an artist, or even a doctor. Some women go for doctors and others go for artists. Men aren't all cast in the same mold. It's true. I'm not Yoash. But Yoash wasn't me. I've got some things he didn't have. A painter, perhaps.

It'll be morning soon. Planes in the sky. Sad Zalman Zulman's full of fun, always letting off his gun. Zalman Zulman lost his grip, took an unexpected dip. Zalman Zulman, whore like me, looking for justice in the w.c. Zalman Zulman go to bed, time to rest your weary head.

I composed the poem. I can abolish it. It's an abolished poem.

Questions for Discussion

1. How do the descriptions of Rami in the first paragraphs help characterize him?

2. Characterize Rami's mother.

3. In what ways does Rami's state of mind change during the course of the story? Consider the plot in regard to this question.

4. What does Rami find out about himself during the game of Russian roulette?

Suggestions for Writing

1. Do some background reading on the Six-Day War of 1967. Then write an essay in which you explain how Oz's story illuminates life in Israel during that time.

2. Compare and contrast Oz's depiction of a soldier with Frank O'Connor's in "Guests of the Nation."

3. Write a journal entry or a brief essay about the significance of the game of Russian roulette in this story. You may want to contrast its use with that of the film *The Deerhunter* if you have seen that film.

Everyday Use

ALICE   WALKER

for your grandmamma

I will wait for her in the yard that Maggie and I made so clean and wavy yesterday afternoon. A yard like this is more comfortable than most people know. It is not just a yard. It is like an extended living room. When the hard clay is swept clean as a floor and the fine sand around the edges lined with tiny, irregular grooves, anyone can come and sit and look up into the elm tree and wait for the breezes that never come inside the house.

Maggie will be nervous until after her sister goes: she will stand hopelessly in corners, homely and ashamed of the burn scars down her arms and legs, eying her sister with a mixture of envy and awe. She thinks her sister has held life always in the palm of one hand, that "no" is a word the world never learned to say to her.

You've no doubt seen those TV shows where the child who has "made it" is confronted, as a surprise, by her own mother and father, tottering in weakly from backstage. (A pleasant surprise, of course: What would they do if parent and child came on the show only to curse out and insult each other?) On TV mother and child embrace and smile into each other's faces. Sometimes the mother and father weep, the child wraps them in her arms and leans across the table to tell how she would not have made it without their help. I have seen these programs.

Sometimes I dream a dream in which Dee and I are suddenly brought together on a TV program of this sort. Out of a dark and soft-seated limousine I am ushered into a bright room filled with many people. There I meet a smiling, gray, sporty man like Johnny Carson who shakes my hand and tells me what a fine girl I have. Then we are on the stage and Dee is embracing me with tears in her eyes. She pins on my dress a large orchid, even though she has told me once that she thinks orchids are tacky flowers.

In real life I am a large, big-boned woman with rough, man-working hands. In the winter I wear flannel nightgowns to bed and overalls during the day. I can kill and clean a hog as mercilessly as a man. My fat keeps me hot in zero weather. I can work outside all day, breaking ice to get water for washing; I can eat pork liver cooked over the open fire minutes after it comes steaming from the hog. One winter I knocked a bull calf straight in the brain between the eyes with a sledge hammer and had the meat hung up to chill before nightfall. But of course all this does not show on television. I am the way my daughter would want me to be: a hundred pounds lighter, my skin like an uncooked barley pancake. My hair glistens in the hot bright lights. Johnny Carson has much to do to keep up with my quick and witty tongue.

But that is a mistake. I know even before I wake up. Who ever knew a Johnson with a quick tongue? Who can even imagine me looking a strange white man in the eye? It seems to me I have talked to them always with one foot raised in flight, with my head turned in whichever way is farthest from them. Dee, though. She would always look anyone in the eye. Hesitation was no part of her nature.

"How do I look, Mama?" Maggie says, showing just enough of her thin body enveloped in pink skirt and red blouse for me to know she's there, almost hidden by the door.

"Come out into the yard," I say.

Have you ever seen a lame animal, perhaps a dog run over by some careless person rich enough to own a car, sidle up to someone who is ignorant enough to be kind to him? That is the way my Maggie walks. She has been like this, chin on chest, eyes on ground, feet in shuffle, ever since the fire that burned the other house to the ground.

Dee is lighter than Maggie, with nicer hair and a fuller figure. She's a woman now, though sometimes I forget. How long ago was it that the other house burned? Ten, twelve years? Sometimes I can still hear the flames and feel Maggie's arms sticking to me, her hair smoking and her dress falling off her in little black papery flakes. Her eyes seemed stretched open, blazed open by the flames reflected in them. And Dee. I see her standing off under the sweet gum tree she used to dig gum out of; a look of concentration on her face as she watched the last dingy gray board of the house fall in toward the red-hot brick chimney. Why don't you do a dance around the ashes? I'd wanted to ask her. She had hated the house that much.

I used to think she hated Maggie, too. But that was before we raised the money, the church and me, to send her to Augusta to school. She used to read to us without pity; forcing words, lies, other folks' habits, whole lives upon us two, sitting trapped and ignorant underneath her voice. She washed us in a river of make-believe, burned us with a lot of knowledge we didn't necessarily need to know. Pressed us to her with the serious way she read, to shove us away at just the moment, like dimwits, we seemed about to understand.

Dee wanted nice things. A yellow organdy dress to wear to her graduation from high school; black pumps to match a green suit she'd made from an old suit somebody gave me. She was determined to stare down any disaster in her efforts. Her eyelids would not flicker for minutes at a time. Often I fought off the temptation to shake her. At sixteen she had a style of her own: and knew what style was.

I never had an education myself. After second grade the school was closed down. Don't ask me why: in 1927 colored asked fewer questions than they do now. Sometimes Maggie reads to me. She stumbles along good-naturedly but can't see well. She knows she is not bright. Like good looks and money, quickness passed her by. She will marry John Thomas (who has mossy teeth in an earnest face) and then I'll be free to sit here and I guess just sing church songs to myself. Although I never was a good singer. Never could carry a tune. I was always better at a man's job. I used to love to milk till I was hooked in the side in '49. Cows are soothing and slow and don't bother you, unless you try to milk them the wrong way.

I have deliberately turned my back on the house. It is three rooms, just like the one that burned, except the roof is tin; they don't make shingle roofs any more. There are no real windows, just some holes cut in the sides, like the portholes in a ship, but not round and not square, with rawhide holding the shutters up on the outside. This house is in a pasture, too, like the other one. No doubt when Dee sees it she will want to tear it down. She wrote me once that no matter where we "choose" to live, she will manage to come see us. But she will never bring her friends. Maggie and I thought about this and Maggie asked me, "Mama, when did Dee ever *have* any friends?"

She had a few. Furtive boys in pink shirts hanging about on washday after school. Nervous girls who never laughed. Impressed with her they worshiped the well-turned phrase, the cute shape, the scalding humor that erupted like bubbles in lye. She read to them.

When she was courting Jimmy T she didn't have much time to pay to us, but turned all her faultfinding power on him. He *flew* to marry a cheap city girl from a family of ignorant flashy people. She hardly had time to recompose herself.

When she comes I will meet—but there they are!

Maggie attempts to make a dash for the house, in her shuffling way, but I stay her with my hand. "Come back here," I say. And she stops and tries to dig a well in the sand with her toe.

It is hard to see them clearly through the strong sun. But even the first glimpse of leg out of the car tells me it is Dee. Her feet were always neat-looking, as if God himself had shaped them with a certain style. From the other side of the car comes a short, stocky man. Hair is all over his head a foot long and hanging from his chin like a kinky mule tail. I hear Maggie suck in her breath. "Uhnnnh," is what it sounds like. Like when you see the wriggling end of a snake just in front of your foot on the road. "Uhnnnh."

Dee next. A dress down to the ground, in this hot weather. A dress so loud it hurts my eyes. There are yellows and oranges enough to throw back the light of the sun. I feel my whole face warming from the heat waves it throws out. Earrings gold, too, and hanging down to her shoulders. Bracelets dangling and making noises when she moves her arm up to shake the folds of the dress out of her armpits. The dress is loose and flows, and as she walks closer, I like it. I hear Maggie go "Uhnnnh" again. It is her sister's hair. It stands straight up like the wool on a sheep. It is black as night and around the edges are two long pigtails that rope about like small lizards disappearing behind her ears.

"Wa-su-zo-Tean-o!" she says, coming on in that gliding way the dress makes her move. The short stocky fellow with the hair to his navel is all grinning and he follows up with "Asalamalakim, my mother and sister!" He moves to hug Maggie but she falls back, right up against the back of my chair. I feel her trembling there and when I look up I see the perspiration falling off her chin.

"Don't get up," says Dee. Since I am stout it takes something of a push. You can see me trying to move a second or two before I make it. She turns, showing white heels through her sandals, and goes back to the car. Out she peeks next with a Polaroid. She stoops down quickly and lines up picture after picture of me sitting there in front of the house with Maggie cowering behind me. She never takes a shot without making sure the house is included. When a cow comes nibbling around the edge of the yard she snaps it and me and Maggie *and* the house. Then she puts the Polaroid in the back seat of the car, and comes up and kisses me on the forehead.

Meanwhile Asalamalakim is going through motions with Maggie's hand. Maggie's hand is as limp as a fish, and probably as cold, despite the sweat, and she keeps trying to pull it back. It looks like Asalamalakim wants to shake hands but wants to do it fancy. Or maybe he don't know how people shake hands. Anyhow, he soon gives up on Maggie.

"Well," I say. "Dee."

"No, Mama," she says. "Not 'Dee,' Wangero Leewanika Kemanjo!"

"What happened to 'Dee'?" I wanted to know.

"She's dead," Wangero said. "I couldn't bear it any longer, being named after the people who oppress me."

"You know as well as me you was named after your aunt Dicie," I said. Dicie is my sister. She named Dee. We called her "Big Dee" after Dee was born.

"But who was *she* named after?" asked Wangero.

"I guess after Grandma Dee," I said.

"And who was she named after?" asked Wangero.

"Her mother," I said, and saw Wangero was getting tired. "That's about as far back as I can trace it," I said. Though, in fact, I probably could have carried it back beyond the Civil War through the branches.

"Well," said Asalamalakim, "there you are."

"Uhnnnh," I heard Maggie say.

"There I was not," I said, "before 'Dicie' cropped up in our family, so why should I try to trace it that far back?"

He just stood there grinning, looking down on me like somebody inspecting a Model A car. Every once in a while he and Wangero sent eye signals over my head.

"How do you pronounce this name?" I asked.

"You don't have to call me by it if you don't want to," said Wangero.

"Why shouldn't I?" I asked. "If that's what you want us to call you, we'll call you."

"I know it might sound awkward at first," said Wangero.

"I'll get used to it," I said. "Ream it out again."

Well, soon we got the name out of the way. Asalamalakim had a name twice as long and three times as hard. After I tripped over it two or three times he told me to just call him Hakim-a-barber. I wanted to ask him was he a barber, but I didn't really think he was, so I didn't ask.

"You must belong to those beef-cattle peoples down the road," I said. They said "Asalamalakim" when they met you, too, but they didn't shake hands. Always too busy: feeding the cattle, fixing the fences, putting up salt-lick shelters, throwing down hay. When the white folks poisoned some of the herd the men stayed up all night with rifles in their hands. I walked a mile and a half just to see the sight.

Hakim-a-barber said, "I accept some of their doctrines, but farming and raising cattle is not my style." (They didn't tell me, and I didn't ask, whether Wangero (Dee) had really gone and married him.)

We sat down to eat and right away he said he didn't eat collards and pork was unclean. Wangero, though, went on through the chitlins and corn bread, the greens and everything else. She talked a blue streak over the sweet potatoes. Everything delighted her. Even the fact that we still used the benches her daddy made for the table when we couldn't afford to buy chairs.

"Oh, Mama!" she cried. Then turned to Hakim-a-barber. "I never knew how lovely these benches are. You can feel the rump prints," she said, running her hands underneath her and along the bench. Then she gave a sigh and her hand closed over Grandma Dee's butter dish. "That's it!" she said. "I knew there was something I wanted to ask you if I could have." She jumped up from the table and went over in the corner where the churn stood, the milk in it clabber by now. She looked at the churn and looked at it.

"This churn top is what I need," she said. "Didn't Uncle Buddy whittle it out of a tree you all used to have?"

"Yes," I said.

"Uh huh," she said happily. "And I want the dasher, too."

"Uncle Buddy whittle that, too?" asked the barber.

Dee (Wangero) looked up at me.

"Aunt Dee's first husband whittled the dash," said Maggie so low you almost couldn't hear her. "His name was Henry, but they called him Stash."

"Maggie's brain is like an elephant's," Wangero said, laughing. "I can use the churn top as a centerpiece for the alcove table," she said, sliding a plate over the churn, "and I'll think of something artistic to do with the dasher."

When she finished wrapping the dasher the handle stuck out. I took it for a moment in my hands. You didn't even have to look close to see where hands pushing the dasher up and down to make butter had left a kind of sink in the wood. In fact, there were a lot of small sinks; you could see where thumbs and fingers had sunk into the wood. It was beautiful light yellow wood, from a tree that grew in the yard where Big Dee and Stash had lived.

After dinner Dee (Wangero) went to the trunk at the foot of my bed and started rifling through it. Maggie hung back in the kitchen over the dishpan. Out came Wangero with two quilts. They had been pieced by Grandma Dee and then Big Dee and me had hung them on the quilt frames on the front porch and quilted them. One was in the Lone Star pattern. The other was Walk Around the Mountain. In both of them were scraps of dresses Grandma Dee had worn fifty and more years ago. Bits and pieces of Grandpa Jarrell's Paisley shirts. And one teeny faded blue piece, about the size of a penny matchbox, that was from Great Grandpa Ezra's uniform that he wore in the Civil War.

"Mama," Wangero said sweet as a bird. "Can I have these old quilts?"

I heard something fall in the kitchen, and a minute later the kitchen door slammed.

"Why don't you take one or two of the others?" I asked. "These old things was just done by me and Big Dee from some tops your grandma pieced before she died."

"No," said Wangero. "I don't want those. They are stitched around the borders by machine."

"That'll make them last better," I said.

"That's not the point," said Wangero. "These are all pieces of dresses Grandma used to wear. She did all this stitching by hand. Imagine!" She held the quilts securely in her arms, stroking them.

"Some of the pieces, like those lavender ones, come from old clothes her mother handed down to her," I said, moving up to touch the quilts. Dee (Wangero) moved back just enough so that I couldn't reach the quilts. They already belonged to her.

"Imagine!" she breathed again, clutching them closely to her bosom.

"The truth is," I said, "I promised to give them quilts to Maggie, for when she marries John Thomas."

She gasped like a bee had stung her.

"Maggie can't appreciate these quilts!" she said. "She'd probably be backward enough to put them to everyday use."

"I reckon she would," I said. "God knows I been saving 'em for long enough with nobody using 'em. I hope she will!" I didn't want to bring up how I had offered Dee (Wangero) a quilt when she went away to college. Then she had told me they were old-fashioned, out of style.

"But they're *priceless!*" she was saying now, furiously; for she has a temper. "Maggie would put them on the bed and in five years they'd be in rags. Less than that!" "She can always make some more," I said. "Maggie knows how to quilt."

Dee (Wangero) looked at me with hatred. "You just will not understand. The point is these quilts, *these* quilts!"

"Well," I said, stumped. "What would *you* do with them?"

"Hang them," she said. As if that was the only thing you *could* do with quilts.

Maggie by now was standing in the door. I could almost hear the sound her feet made as they scraped over each other.

"She can have them, Mama," she said, like somebody used to never winning anything, or having anything reserved for her. "I can 'member Grandma Dee without the quilts."

I looked at her hard. She had filled her bottom lip with checkerberry snuff and it gave her face a kind of dopey, hangdog look. It was Grandma Dee and Big Dee who taught her how to quilt herself. She stood there with her scarred hands hidden in the folds of her skirt. She looked at her sister with something like fear but she wasn't mad at her. This was Maggie's portion. This was the way she knew God to work.

When I looked at her like that something hit me in the top of my head and ran down to the soles of my feet. Just like when I'm in church and the spirit of God touches me and I get happy and shout. I did something I never had done before: hugged Maggie to me, then dragged her on into the room, snatched the quilts out of Miss Wangero's hands and dumped them into Maggie's lap. Maggie just sat there on my bed with her mouth open.

"Take one or two of the others," I said to Dee.

But she turned without a word and went out to Hakim-a-barber.

"You just don't understand," she said, as Maggie and I came out to the car.

"What don't I understand?" I wanted to know.

"Your heritage," she said. And then she turned to Maggie, kissed her, and said, "You ought to try to make something of yourself, too, Maggie. It's really a new day for us. But from the way you and Mama still live you'd never know it."

She put on some sunglasses that hid everything above the tip of her nose and her chin.

Maggie smiled; maybe at the sunglasses. But a real smile, not scared. After we watched the car dust settle I asked Maggie to bring me a dip of snuff. And then the two of us sat there just enjoying, until it was time to go in the house and go to bed.

Questions for Discussion

1. What are the key conflicts of this story?

2. What is the significance of the narrator's description of "television families"?

3. Describe the elder daughter's behavior on her return home. How does her mother react to this behavior? What form does her reaction take?

4. What does the quilt come to symbolize?

Suggestions for Writing

1. Write an essay that interprets the quilt as a symbol in "Everyday Use."

2. Write an essay that explores both the generational and the political/cultural conflicts in the story.

3. Write a paragraph in your notebook or journal about the character Maggie.

4. Write a story in which a family possession or heirloom takes on symbolic meaning.

5. Read Alice Walker's *The Color Purple* or *The Temple of My Familiar* and write an essay that analyzes "Everyday Use" in comparison with one of these books.

Errand

RAYMOND   CARVER

C hekhov. On the evening of March 22, 1897, he went to dinner in Moscow with his friend and confidant Alexei Suvorin. This Suvorin was a very rich newspaper and book publisher, a reactionary, a self-made man whose father was a private at the battle of Borodino. Like Chekhov, he was the grandson of a serf. They had that in common: each had peasant's blood in his veins. Otherwise, politically and temperamentally, they were miles apart. Nevertheless, Suvorin was one of Chekhov's few intimates, and Chekhov enjoyed his company.

Naturally, they went to the best restaurant in the city, a former town house called the Hermitage—a place where it could take hours, half the night even, to get through a ten-course meal that would, of course, include several wines, liqueurs, and coffee. Chekhov was impeccably dressed, as always—a dark suit and waistcoat, his usual pince-nez. He looked that night very much as he looks in the photographs taken of him during this period. He was relaxed, jovial. He shook hands with the maître d', and with a glance took in the large dining room. It was brilliantly illuminated by ornate chandeliers, the tables occupied by elegantly dressed men and women. Waiters came and went ceaselessly. He had just been seated across the table from Suvorin when suddenly, without warning, blood began gushing from his mouth. Suvorin and two waiters helped him to the gentlemen's room and tried to stanch the flow of blood with ice packs. Suvorin saw him back to his own hotel and had a bed prepared for Chekhov in one of the rooms of the suite. Later, after another hemorrhage, Chekhov allowed himself to be moved to a clinic that specialized in the treatment of tuberculosis and related respiratory infections. When Suvorin visited him there, Chekhov apologized for the "scandal" at the restaurant three nights earlier but continued to insist there was nothing seriously wrong. "He laughed and jested as usual," Suvorin noted in his diary, "while spitting blood into a large vessel."

Maria Chekhov, his younger sister, visited Chekhov in the clinic during the last days of March. The weather was miserable; a sleet storm was in progress, and frozen heaps of snow lay everywhere. It was hard for her to wave down a carriage to take her to the hospital. By the time she arrived she was filled with dread and anxiety.

"Anton Pavlovich lay on his back," Maria wrote in her *Memoirs*. "He was not allowed to speak. After greeting him, I went over to the table to hide my emotions." There, among bottles of champagne, jars of caviar, bouquets of flowers from well-wishers, she saw something that terrified her: a freehand drawing, obviously done by a specialist in these matters, of Chekhov's lungs. It was the kind of sketch a doctor often makes in order to show his patient what he thinks is taking place. The lungs were outlined in blue, but the upper parts were filled in with red. "I realized they were diseased," Maria wrote.

Leo Tolstoy was another visitor. The hospital staff were awed to find themselves in the presence of the country's greatest writer. The most famous man in Russia? Of course they had to let him in to see Chekhov, even though "nonessential" visitors were forbidden. With much obsequiousness on the part of the nurses and resident doctors, the bearded, fierce-looking old man was shown into Chekhov's room. Despite his low opinion of Chekhov's abilities as a playwright (Tolstoy felt the plays were static and lacking in any moral vision. "Where do your characters take you?" he once demanded of Chekhov. "From the sofa to the junk room and back"), Tolstoy liked Chekhov's short stories. Furthermore, and quite simply, he loved the man. He told Gorky, "What a beautiful, magnificent man: modest and quiet, like a girl. He even walks like a girl. He's simply wonderful." And Tolstoy wrote in his journal (everyone kept a journal or a diary in those days), "I am glad I love . . . Chekhov."

Tolstoy removed his woollen scarf and bearskin coat, then lowered himself into a chair next to Chekhov's bed. Never mind that Chekhov was taking medication and not permitted to talk, much less carry on a conversation. He had to listen, amazedly, as the Count began to discourse on his theories of the immortality of the soul. Concerning that visit, Chekhov later wrote, "Tolstoy assumes that all of us (humans and animals alike) will live on in a principle (such as reason or love) the essence and goals of which are a mystery to us. . . . I have no use for that kind of immortality. I don't understand it, and Lev Nikolayevich was astonished I didn't."

Nevertheless, Chekhov was impressed with the solicitude shown by Tolstoy's visit. But, unlike Tolstoy, Chekhov didn't believe in an afterlife and never had. He didn't believe in anything that couldn't be apprehended by one or more of his five senses. And as far as his outlook on life and writing went, he once told someone that he lacked "a political, religious, and philosophical world view. I change it every month, so I'll have to limit myself to the description of how my heroes love, marry, give birth, die, and how they speak."   .

Earlier, before his t.b. was diagnosed, Chekhov had remarked, "When a peasant has consumption, he says, 'There's nothing I can do. I'll go off in the spring with the melting of the snows.' " (Chekhov himself died in the summer, during a heat wave.) But once Chekhov's own tuberculosis was discovered he continually tried to minimize the seriousness of his condition. To all appearances, it was as if he felt, right up to the end, that he might be able to throw off the disease as he would a lingering catarrh. Well into his final days, he spoke with seeming conviction of the possibility of an improvement. In fact, in a letter written shortly before his end, he went so far as to tell his sister that he was "putting on a bit of flesh" and felt much better now that he was in Badenweiler.

Badenweiler is a spa and resort city in the western area of the Black Forest, not far from Basel. The Vosges are visible from nearly anywhere in the city, and in those days the air was pure and invigorating. Russians had been going there for years to soak in the hot mineral baths and promenade on the boulevards. In June 1904, Chekhov went there to die.

Earlier that month, he'd made a difficult journey by train from Moscow to Berlin. He traveled with his wife, the actress Olga Knipper, a woman he'd met in 1898 during rehearsals for *The Seagull*. Her contemporaries describe her as an excellent actress. She was talented, pretty, and almost ten years younger than the playwright. Chekhov had been immediately attracted to her, but was slow to act on his feelings. As always, he preferred a flirtation to marriage. Finally, after a three-year courtship involving many separations, letters, and the inevitable misunderstandings, they were at last married, in a private ceremony in Moscow, on May 25, 1901. Chekhov was enormously happy. He called Olga his "pony," and sometimes "dog" or "puppy." He was also fond of addressing her as "little turkey" or simply as "my joy."

In Berlin, Chekhov consulted with a renowned specialist in pulmonary disorders, a Dr. Karl Ewald. But, according to an eyewitness, after the doctor examined Chekhov he threw up his hands and left the room without a word. Chekhov was too far gone for help: this Dr. Ewald was furious with himself for not being able to work miracles, and with Chekhov for being so ill.

A Russian journalist happened to visit the Chekhovs at their hotel and sent back this dispatch to his editor: "Chekhov's days are numbered. He seems mortally ill, is terribly thin, coughs all the time, gasps for breath at the slightest movement, and is running a high temperature." This same journalist saw the Chekhovs off at Potsdam Station when they boarded their train for Badenweiler. According to his account, "Chekhov had trouble making his way up the small staircase at the station. He had to sit down for several minutes to catch his breath." In fact, it was painful for Chekhov to move: his legs ached continually and his insides hurt. The disease had attacked his intestines and spinal cord. At this point he had less than a month to live. When Chekhov spoke of his condition now, it was, according to Olga, "with an almost reckless indifference."

Dr. Schwöhrer was one of the many Badenweiler physicians who earned a good living by treating the well-to-do who came to the spa seeking relief from various maladies. Some of his patients were ill and infirm, others simply old and hypochondriacal. But Chekhov's was a special case: he was clearly beyond help and in his last days. He was also very famous. Even Dr. Schwöhrer knew his name: he'd read some of Chekhov's stories in a German magazine. When he examined the writer early in June, he voiced his appreciation of Chekhov's art but kept his medical opinions to himself. Instead, he prescribed a diet of cocoa, oatmeal drenched in butter, and strawberry tea. This last was supposed to help Chekhov sleep at night.

On June 13, less than three weeks before he died, Chekhov wrote a letter to his mother in which he told her his health was on the mend. In it he said, "It's likely that I'll be completely cured in a week." Who knows why he said this? What could he have been thinking? He was a doctor himself, and he knew better. He was dying, it was as simple and as unavoidable as that. Nevertheless, he sat out on the balcony of his hotel room and read railway timetables. He asked for information on sailings of boats bound for Odessa from Marseilles. But he *knew*. At this stage he had to have known. Yet in one of the last letters he ever wrote he told his sister he was growing stronger by the day.

He no longer had any appetite for literary work, and hadn't for a long time. In fact, he had very nearly failed to complete *The Cherry Orchard* the year before. Writing that play was the hardest thing he'd ever done in his life. Toward the end, he was able to manage only six or seven lines a day. "I've started losing heart," he wrote Olga. "I feel I'm finished as a writer, and every sentence strikes me as worthless and of no use whatever." But he didn't stop. He finished his play in October 1903. It was the last thing he ever wrote, except for letters and a few entries in his notebook.

A little after midnight on July 2, 1904, Olga sent someone to fetch Dr. Schwöhrer. It was an emergency: Chekhov was delirious. Two young Russians on holiday happened to have the adjacent room, and Olga hurried next door to explain what was happening. One of the youths was in his bed asleep, but the other was still awake, smoking and reading. He left the hotel at a run to find Dr. Schwöhrer. "I can still hear the sound of the gravel under his shoes in the silence of that stifling July night," Olga wrote later on in her memoirs. Chekhov was hallucinating, talking about sailors, and there were snatches of something about the Japanese. "You don't put ice on an empty stomach," he said when she tried to place an ice pack on his chest.

Dr. Schwöhrer arrived and unpacked his bag, all the while keeping his gaze fastened on Chekhov, who lay gasping in the bed. The sick man's pupils were dilated and his temples glistened with sweat. Dr. Schwöhrer's face didn't register anything. He was not an emotional man, but he knew Chekhov's end was near. Still, he was a doctor, sworn to do his utmost, and Chekhov held on to life, however, tenuously. Dr. Schwöhrer prepared a hypodermic and administered an injection of camphor, something that was supposed to speed up the heart. But the injection didn't help—nothing, of course, could have helped. Nevertheless, the doctor made known to Olga his intention of sending for oxygen. Suddenly, Chekhov roused himself, became lucid, and said quietly, "What's the use? Before it arrives I'll be a corpse."

Dr. Schwöhrer pulled on his big mustache and stared at Chekhov. The writer's cheeks were sunken and gray, his complexion waxen; his breath was raspy. Dr. Schwöhrer knew the time could be reckoned in minutes. Without a word, without conferring with Olga, he went over to an alcove where there was a telephone on the wall. He read the instructions for using the device. If he activated it by holding his finger on a button and turning a handle on the side of the phone, he could reach the lower regions of the hotel—the kitchen. He picked up the receiver, held it to his ear, and did as the instructions told him. When someone finally answered, Dr. Schwöhrer ordered a bottle of the hotel's best champagne. "How many glasses?" he was asked. "Three glasses!" the doctor shouted into the mouthpiece. "And hurry, do you hear?" It was one of those rare moments of inspiration that can easily enough be overlooked later on, because the action is so entirely appropriate it seems inevitable.

The champagne was brought to the door by a tired-looking young man whose blond hair was standing up. The trousers of his uniform were wrinkled, the creases gone, and in his haste he'd missed a loop while buttoning his jacket. His appearance was that of someone who'd been resting (slumped in a chair, say, dozing a little), when off in the distance the phone had clamored in the early-morning hours—great God in heaven!—and the next thing he knew he was being shaken awake by a superior and told to deliver a bottle of Moët to room 211. "And hurry, do you hear?"

The young man entered the room carrying a silver ice bucket with the champagne in it and a silver tray with three cut-crystal glasses. He found a place on the table for the bucket and glasses, all the while craning his neck, trying to see into the other room, where someone panted ferociously for breath. It was a dreadful, harrowing sound, and the young man lowered his chin into his collar and turned away as the ratchety breathing worsened. Forgetting himself, he stared out the open window toward the darkened city. Then this big imposing man with a thick mustache pressed some coins into his hand—a large tip, by the feel of it—and suddenly the young man saw the door open. He took some steps and found himself on the landing, where he opened his hand and looked at the coins in amazement.

Methodically, the way he did everything, the doctor went about the business of working the cork out of the bottle. He did it in such a way as to minimize, as much as possible, the festive explosion. He poured three glasses and, out of habit, pushed the cork back into the neck of the bottle. He then took the glasses of champagne over to the bed. Olga momentarily released her grip on Chekhov's hand—a hand, she said later, that burned her fingers. She arranged another pillow behind his head. Then she put the cool glass of champagne against Chekhov's palm and made sure his fingers closed around the stem. They exchanged looks—Chekhov, Olga, Dr. Schwöhrer. They didn't touch glasses. There was no toast. What on earth was there to drink to? To death? Chekhov summoned his remaining strength and said, "It's been so long since I've had champagne." He brought the glass to his lips and drank. In a minute or two Olga took the empty glass from his hand and set it on the nightstand. Then Chekhov turned onto his side. He closed his eyes and sighed. A minute later, his breathing stopped.

Dr. Schwöhrer picked up Chekhov's hand from the bedsheet. He held his fingers to Chekhov's wrist and drew a gold watch from his vest pocket, opening the lid of the watch as he did so. The second hand on the watch moved slowly, very slowly. He let it move around the face of the watch three times while he waited for signs of a pulse. It was three o'clock in the morning and still sultry in the room. Badenweiler was in the grip of its worst heat wave in years. All the windows in both rooms stood open, but there was no sign of a breeze. A large, black-winged moth flew through a window and banged wildly against the electric lamp. Dr. Schwöhrer let go of Chekhov's wrist. "It's over," he said. He closed the lid of his watch and returned it to his vest pocket.

At once Olga dried her eyes and set about composing herself. She thanked the doctor for coming. He asked if she wanted some medication—laudanum, perhaps, or a few drops of valerian. She shook her head. She did have one request, though: before the authorities were notified and the newspapers found out, before the time came when Chekhov was no longer in her keeping, she wanted to be alone with him for a while. Could the doctor help with this? Could he withhold, for a while anyway, news of what had just occurred?

Dr. Schwöhrer stroked his mustache with the back of his finger. Why not? After all, what difference would it make to anyone whether this matter became known now or a few hours from now? The only detail that remained was to fill out a death certificate, and this could be done at his office later on in the morning, after he'd slept a few hours. Dr. Schwöhrer nodded his agreement and prepared to leave. He murmured a few words of condolence. Olga inclined her head. "An honor," Dr. Schwöhrer said. He picked up his bag and left the room and, for that matter, history.

It was at this moment that the cork popped out of the champagne bottle; foam spilled down onto the table. Olga went back to Chekhov's bedside. She sat on a footstool, holding his hand, from time to time stroking his face. "There were no human voices, no everyday sounds," she wrote. "There was only beauty, peace, and the grandeur of death."

She stayed with Chekhov until daybreak, when thrushes began to call from the garden below. Then came the sound of tables and chairs being moved about down there. Before long, voices carried up to her. It was then a knock sounded at the door. Of course she thought it must be an official of some sort—the medical examiner, say, or someone from the police who had questions to ask and forms for her to fill out, or maybe, just maybe, it could be Dr. Schwöhrer returning with a mortician to render assistance in embalming and transporting Chekhov's remains back to Russia.

But, instead, it was the same blond young man who'd brought the champagne a few hours earlier. This time, however, his uniform trousers were neatly pressed, with stiff creases in front, and every button on his snug green jacket was fastened. He seemed quite another person. Not only was he wide awake but his plump cheeks were smooth-shaven, his hair was in place, and he appeared anxious to please. He was holding a porcelain vase with three long-stemmed yellow roses. He presented these to Olga with a smart click of his heels. She stepped back and let him into the room. He was there, he said, to collect the glasses, ice bucket, and tray, yes. But he also wanted to say that, because of the extreme heat, breakfast would be served in the garden this morning. He hoped this weather wasn't too bothersome; he apologized for it.

The woman seemed distracted. While he talked, she turned her eyes away and looked down at something in the carpet. She crossed her arms and held her elbows. Meanwhile, still holding his vase, waiting for a sign, the young man took in the details of the room. Bright sunlight flooded through the open windows. The room was tidy and seemed undisturbed, almost untouched. No garments were flung over chairs, no shoes, stockings, braces, or stays were in evidence, no open suitcases. In short, there was no clutter, nothing but the usual heavy pieces of hotel room furniture. Then, because the woman was still looking down, he looked down, too, and at once spied a cork near the toe of his shoe. The woman did not see it—she was looking somewhere else. The young man wanted to bend over and pick up the cork, but he was still holding the roses and was afraid of seeming to intrude even more by drawing any further attention to himself. Reluctantly, he left the cork where it was and raised his eyes. Everything was in order except for the uncorked, half-empty bottle of champagne that stood alongside two crystal glasses over on the little table. He cast his gaze about once more. Through an open door he saw that the third glass was in the bedroom, on the nightstand. But someone still occupied the bed! He couldn't see a face, but the figure under the covers lay perfectly motionless and quiet. He noted the figure and looked elsewhere. Then, for a reason he couldn't understand, a feeling of uneasiness took hold of him. He cleared his throat and moved his weight to the other leg. The woman still didn't look up or break her silence. The young man felt his cheeks grow warm. It occurred to him, quite without his having thought it through, that he should perhaps suggest an alternative to breakfast in the garden. He coughed, hoping to focus the woman's attention, but she didn't look at him. The distinguished foreign guests could, he said, take breakfast in their rooms this morning if they wished. The young man (his name hasn't survived, and it's likely he perished in the Great War) said he would be happy to bring up a tray. Two trays, he added, glancing uncertainly once again in the direction of the bedroom.

He fell silent and ran a finger around the inside of his collar. He didn't understand. He wasn't even sure the woman had been listening. He didn't know what else to do now; he was still holding the vase. The sweet odor of the roses filled his nostrils and inexplicably caused a pang of regret. The entire time he'd been waiting, the woman had apparently been lost in thought. It was as if all the while he'd been standing there, talking, shifting his weight, holding his flowers, she had been someplace else, somewhere far from Badenweiler. But now she came back to herself, and her face assumed another expression. She raised her eyes, looked at him, and then shook her head. She seemed to be struggling to understand what on earth this young man could be doing there in the room holding a vase with three yellow roses. Flowers? She hadn't ordered flowers.

The moment passed. She went over to her handbag and scooped up some coins. She drew out a number of banknotes as well. The young man touched his lips with his tongue; another large tip was forthcoming, but for what? What did she want him to do? He'd never before waited on such guests. He cleared his throat once more.

No breakfast, the woman said. Not yet, at any rate. Breakfast wasn't the important thing this morning. She required something else. She needed him to go out and bring back a mortician. Did he understand her? Herr Chekhov was dead, you see. *Comprenez-vous?* Young man? Anton Chekhov was dead. Now listen carefully to me, she said. She wanted him to go downstairs and ask someone at the front desk where he could go to find the most respected mortician in the city. Someone reliable, who took great pains in his work and whose manner was appropriately reserved. A mortician, in short, worthy of a great artist. Here, she said, and pressed the money on him. Tell them downstairs that I have specifically requested you to perform this duty for me. Are you listening? Do you understand what I'm saying to you?

The young man grappled to take in what she was saying. He chose not to look again in the direction of the other room. He had sensed that something was not right. He became aware of his heart beating rapidly under his jacket, and he felt perspiration break out on his forehead. He didn't know where he should turn his eyes. He wanted to put the vase down.

Please do this for me, the woman said. I'll remember you with gratitude. Tell them downstairs that I insist. Say that. But don't call any unnecessary attention to yourself or to the situation. Just say that this is necessary, that I request it—and that's all. Do you hear me? Nod if you understand. Above all, don't raise an alarm. Everything else, all the rest, the commotion—that'll come soon enough. The worst is over. Do we understand each other?

The young man's face had grown pale. He stood rigid, clasping the vase. He managed to nod his head.

After securing permission to leave the hotel he was to proceed quietly and resolutely, though without any unbecoming haste, to the mortician's. He was to behave exactly as if he were engaged on a very important errand, nothing more. He *was* engaged on an important errand, she said. And if it would help keep his movements purposeful he should imagine himself as someone moving down the busy sidewalk carrying in his arms a porcelain vase of roses that he had to deliver to an important man. (She spoke quietly, almost confidentially, as if to a relative or a friend.) He could even tell himself that the man he was going to see was expecting him, was perhaps impatient for him to arrive with his flowers. Nevertheless, the young man was not to become excited and run, or otherwise break his stride. Remember the vase he was carrying! He was to walk briskly, comporting himself at all times in as dignified a manner as possible. He should keep walking until he came to the mortician's house and stood before the door. He would then raise the brass knocker and let it fall, once, twice, three times. In a minute the mortician himself would answer.

This mortician would be in his forties, no doubt, or maybe early fifties—bald, solidly built, wearing steel-frame spectacles set very low on his nose. He would be modest, unassuming, a man who would ask only the most direct and necessary questions. An apron. Probably he would be wearing an apron. He might even be wiping his hands on a dark towel while he listened to what was being said. There'd be a faint whiff of formaldehyde on his clothes. But it was all right, and the young man shouldn't worry. He was nearly a grownup now and shouldn't be frightened or repelled by any of this. The mortician would hear him out. He was a man of restraint and bearing, this mortician, someone who could help allay people's fears in this situation, not increase them. Long ago he'd acquainted himself with death in all its various guises and forms; death held no surprises for him any longer, no hidden secrets. It was this man whose services were required this morning.

The mortician takes the vase of roses. Only once while the young man is speaking does the mortician betray the least flicker of interest, or indicate that he's heard anything out of the ordinary. But the one time the young man mentions the name of the deceased, the mortician's eyebrows rise just a little. Chekhov, you say? Just a minute, and I'll be with you.

Do you understand what I'm saying, Olga said to the young man. Leave the glasses. Don't worry about them. Forget about crystal wine glasses and such. Leave the room as it is. Everything is ready now. We're ready. Will you go?

But at that moment the young man was thinking of the cork still resting near the toe of his shoe. To retrieve it he would have to bend over, still gripping the vase. He would do this. He leaned over. Without looking down, he reached out and closed it into his hand.

Questions for Discussion

1. How would you describe the style of the story early on, when the narrator reports what Chekhov was doing (and writing) a few weeks before his death? To what extent does the style or tone of the story change as it proceeds?

2. Characterize Tolstoy's appearance in the story. What do we learn about him from Carver's depiction?

3. Characterize the death scene. What is memorable and unusual about it?

4. What is the role of the young man in the story? What does his preoccupation with the cork add to the story?

Suggestions for Writing

1. Write an essay in which you discuss the ways in which "Errand" is not just a story but also a tribute to Chekhov's fiction. What are the Chekhovian elements in "Errand"? What is both comic and tragic about the story?

2. Write an essay about the young man—his character, his reaction to Chekhov's death, his preoccupation with the cork. Explain his role in the story.

3. Write a story about the death of a famous person, not necessarily a writer. As Carver apparently did, do some research about this person's death, but do not limit yourself to "the facts."

4. Write an essay in which you compare and contrast Anton Chekhov's "Gooseberries" with Carver's "Errand," chiefly with regard to narrative strategies each story exhibits.

Overview: Additional Questions for Discussion and Suggestions for Writing

1. Of the stories in this section, which ones explore contemporary issues that most concern or interest you? From your point of view, how appropriately do they explore these issues?

2. Consider the stories not written by Americans in this section—stories by Frame, Munro, Atwood, Fuentes, Gustafsson, Böll, and Valenzuela. What issues, points of view, or narrative techniques are most memorable in these stories? In what ways and to what extent do these authors handle fictional material differently from the way some American writers do?

3. Identify conflicts, themes, or issues that seem strikingly similar between the stories by Americans in this section and the stories by the Canadians, the Swede, the German, the New Zealander, and the Latin Americans.

4. Of all the stories in this section, which one would you recommend to a friend and why?

5. Which of the stories in this section seem most "experimental"? What is the nature of the experiments? How successful are the experiments?

6. Contrast these stories with those in the first section and make some generalizations about how the short story has changed and developed in one hundred years (or more).

7. Of the styles, voices, and techniques represented in this section, which ones would you most like to imitate in your writing? Why?

8. Which of the stories in this section would you like to see adapted to film? Why does this particular story lend itself to the cinema? Whom would you cast in the film?

9. What are the most significant differences between the stories by Gilman and Chopin in Part I and the stories by contemporary women writers represented in this section? What similarities do you see?

10. One of the introductory essays mentions precursors to the short story: myths, fairy tales, fables, biblical narratives, and so on. Which of these contemporary writers draw on these sources in the form of their stories or by means of allusion? In what ways and with what degree of success do these authors make use of this earlier material?

11.   Which story or stories in this section best reflect(s) your values and
       ethics? Why?

Suggestions for Writing

1.   The stories by Ozick, Gustafsson, and Yamamoto explore to some extent
      conflicts between ethnic groups or worldviews. Write an essay in which
      you analyze these conflicts and compare the approaches these authors
      take.

2.   The stories by Yates, Updike, Munro, Yamamoto, and Brautigan involve
      children, adolescents, or teenagers. Write an essay in which you analyze,
      compare, and contrast the perspectives on American youth that these
      stories provide.

3.   Write an essay about "the outsider" in several of the stories from this
      section. The stories by Cheever, Munro, Yamamoto, Yates, Ozick,
      Gustafsson, Böll, and Malamud depict various kinds of characters who
      are "outside" a family, an institution, a state, or a culture. Develop a
      thesis in which you account for the significance of "the outsider" in these
      contemporary short stories.

4.   Write an essay that focuses on narrative experimentation in several of
      these stories, especially as they are contrasted with earlier stories in the
      anthology. What conventions in narrative form are these authors changing
      or ignoring? In what ways are they using language differently? You might
      begin by looking at the stories by Fuentes, Barthelme, and Ozick.

5.   Choose a story from this section that exhibits a narrative technique, a
      point of view, a setting, or a subject that particularly impressed you and
      write a story that imitates that element. Strive for your own original
      story, of course, but take your inspiration from this element you
      admired.

6.   To gain experience in the different effects and limitations of different
      points of view, choose any three stories from this section that you have
      read and rewrite the openings of the stories from different points of
      view. That is, change the point of view from second person to first
      person in "Aura" (for example), or in "Goodbye, My Brother" (for
      example) keep the story opening in first person, but write from
      Lawrence's point of view.

7.   Turn yourself into an anthropologist and think about the symbols in the
      stories written by Americans that seem most "American" (and define

"American" any way you wish). What places, objects, and so forth do these writers take from the American landscape and turn into symbols?

8. The stories by O'Connor and O'Brien deal with crucial historical events: the civil rights movement and its consequences and the Vietnam War. Choose a significant event that has occurred during your lifetime (it need not be on a scale comparable to these two events, of course) and write a story that involves the event directly or indirectly.

9. Write a speculative science fiction story.

10. Write a story that draws on the fable form (like Malamud's "Jewbird").

11. Write an essay that analyzes the ways in which several of these authors end or "close" their stories. Which kinds of "closure" do you find most satisfying and why?

Part Four

Emerging Voices

Emerging Voices:
AN INTRODUCTION

THE MEANING OF "EMERGING"

The "voices" in this section are "emerging" in several different senses of the word. In some cases, emerging refers to stories and authors who have been published very recently, but newness is not a quality all of these authors and stories share.

Some stories come from the pens (or cursors) of writers who are experienced but whose reputations have only recently acquired international status; this is true of writers like Liliana Heker and Elsa Joubert. Some stories come from authors who are well established as poets but whose contribution to short fiction is less well known. Tess Gallagher fits into this category. Still other authors are emerging in the sense that they provide fresh perspectives on political and social issues—or on episodes of history—that have been with the world for some time. Njabulo Ndebele's story from South Africa, Fiona Barr's story from Northern Ireland, and Shawn Wong's story of Chinese immigrants to America in the nineteenth century achieve such perspectives.

THE NUCLEAR AGE

"Emerging Voices," then, is really a subset of "Contemporary Voices," especially in the sense that many of these authors grapple with subject matter linked to the world of the 1950s and the 1960s. This is certainly true of Martin Amis and Rick Demarinis, for instance, who give us widely different stories that explore what it means to live in the nuclear age.

COMING-OF-AGE AND OTHER ILLUMINATIONS

Meanwhile, Jayne Anne Phillips, Liliana Heker, Alberto Rios, Tess Gallagher, and Matt Ellison show how inexhaustible the subject of coming-of-age remains for writers of short fiction. Although focusing on the experience of young women and men, these authors are also able to illuminate Mexican culture, the power of sibling intimacy, class conflict in South America, and small-town American life. Such illumination is also one effect of the stories by Louise Erdrich,

Shawn Wong, Jim Welch, and Sesshu Foster—stories that reveal the mysteries and pathos of Native American, Hispanic American, and Asian American experience and history.

POLITICAL CONFLICT

Njabulo Ndebele and Elsa Joubert give us powerful, poignant stories that spring from both sides of the racial line in South Africa, and Fiona Barr gives us a woman who speaks with "a voice" on the other side of a political line in Belfast, Northern Ireland. These writers accept the challenge and the necessity of confronting politics with art; the results are vivid, intelligent, and memorable.

One might say in general that the stories in this last section collectively have a more recognizable "political edge" than stories in earlier chapters. In many instances, the political concern of the story is only implicit or secondary, as in Rick Demarinis's "Under the Wheat" or Gyanranjan's "Our Side of the Fence and Theirs." Nonetheless, these "emerging voices" reveal an awareness of how complicated, urgent, and ever-changing global and national politics are—and how much influence such politics exert on writers worldwide.

WIT AND TERROR

The stories by DeFrees, King, and Day take place far from the world of political conflict; indeed, they spring from strange interior worlds of a woman obsessed with a serial killer, a factory worker's encounter with a monstrous hybrid species, and the afterlife of an Italian man whose chest has "knocked him down." These authors show that wit and terror remain inseparable bedfellows in the contemporary story and that the legacy of Kafka and Poe persists in marvelously improvised ways. Stephen King, of course, is as well established and popular as any writer of fiction nowadays, but his story "Graveyard Shift" represents the resurgence of horror fiction in the 1970s and 1980s and therefore finds a niche among "Emerging Voices." His story provides a good example of the elements of horror fiction, and it raises interesting questions about why the subgenre has found such a wide readership.

WOMEN'S EXPERIENCE

This section also shows how significant, even central, women writers have become to the world of short fiction. When we contrast the stories of these writers with those of Chopin and Gilman, we also see how varied the voices, subject matter, and narrative innovations of women writers have become in a comparatively brief span of literary history. The stories here by Hulme, Engberg, and Grafton also show how multifaceted and subtle feminist points of view can be, and how they influence our perspectives on everything from "family life" to animal intelligence to detective fiction.

THE FUTURE OF THE SHORT STORY

As new writers emerge, in what directions are they taking the genre of short fiction? Where is the short story headed at the close of the twentieth century?

The safe answer is "Everywhere." With regard to technique, subject matter, point of view, style, language, and innovation, the short story has become a restless, globe-trotting, ever-more-eclectic creature. It is not a form of literature that has ever really broken away from its nineteenth-century "parents": Poe, Hawthorne, Chekhov, de Maupassant, James, Gilman. In fact, in short fiction there is greater continuity between centuries than there is in the genres of poetry and the novel. And it is remarkable how many writers still pay homage—through explicit praise or by example—to these early voices, particularly Poe and Chekhov.

But if a revolutionary "break" with the past has not happened in this genre, constant and feverish improvisation has. In general it is a genre in which one will likely find a political "edge" these days, as noted earlier. But it is also one that thousands of authors still use to explore private agonies, family dramas, and personal histories. Above all it is a genre that still relies on conventions of conflict, character, and plot—and it is one in which conventions are never safe. After all, stories by John Updike and Donald Barthelme have often appeared in the same magazine. There seems to be plenty of room in the world of fiction for the traditions of realism, surrealism, and absurdism, as well as for thriving subgenres like science fiction, horror fiction, and detective fiction. Hybrid forms that include the characteristics of several modes or subgenres are not uncommon; they are a post-Modern literary equivalent to genetic engineering.

Another important development to mention in connection with these emerging voices is the extent to which short-story criticism and theory have matured in recent years. More than ever, the short story is drawing the attention of excellent scholars and critics who continue to redefine the form and treat it as a distinct and significant literary genre. *Short Story Theory at a Crossroads* (1989), edited by Susan Lohafer and Jo Ellyn Clarey, is but one of many recent books ushering in a new era of short-story criticism.

In many parts of the world, the attitude toward the weather is, "If you don't like it, just wait a few minutes." One might say the same thing about the "weather," the "climate," and "the landscape" of the short story, whether it is written in Pretoria, Montana, Los Angeles, London, Brazil, Seattle, Belfast, or New Zealand. It is one of the most vital and adaptable art forms on our planet, as these "emerging voices" suggest in a variety of ways.

Snares

LOUISE ERDRICH

It began after church with Margaret and her small granddaughter, Lulu, and was not to end until the long days of Lent and a hard-packed snow. There were factions on the reservation, a treaty settlement in the Agent's hands. There were Chippewa who signed their names in the year 1924, and there were Chippewa who saw the cash offered as a flimsy bait. I was one and Fleur Pillager, Lulu's mother, was another who would not lift her hand to sign. It was said that all the power to witch, harm, or cure lay in Fleur, the lone survivor of the old Pillager clan. But as much as people feared Fleur, they listened to Margaret Kashpaw. She was the ringleader of the holdouts, a fierce, one-minded widow with a vinegar tongue.

Margaret Kashpaw had knots of muscles in her arms. Her braids were thin, gray as iron, and usually tied strictly behind her back so they wouldn't swing. She was plump as a basket below and tough as roots on top. Her face was gnarled around a beautiful sharp nose. Two shell earrings caught the light and flashed whenever she turned her head. She had become increasingly religious in the years after her loss, and finally succeeded in dragging me to the Benediction Mass, where I was greeted by Father Damien, from whom I occasionally won small sums at dice.

"Grandfather Nanapush," he smiled, "at last."

"These benches are a hardship for an old man," I complained. "If you spread them with soft pine-needle cushions I'd have come before."

Father Damien stared thoughtfully at the rough pews, folded his hands inside the sleeves of his robe.

"You must think of their unyielding surfaces as helpful," he offered. "God sometimes enters the soul through the humblest parts of our anatomies, if they are sensitized to suffering."

"A god who enters through the rear door," I countered, "is no better than a thief."

Father Damien was used to me, and smiled as he walked to the altar. I adjusted my old bones, longing for some relief, trying not to rustle for fear of Margaret's jabbing elbow. The time was long. Lulu probed all my pockets with her fingers until she found a piece of hard candy. I felt no great presence in this cold place and decided, as my back end ached and my shoulders stiffened, that our original gods were better, the Chippewa characters who were not exactly perfect but at least did not require sitting on hard boards.

When Mass was over and the smell of incense was thick in all our clothes, Margaret, Lulu, and I went out into the starry cold, the snow and stubble fields, and began the long walk to our homes. It was dusk. On either side of us the heavy trees stood motionless and blue. Our footsteps squeaked against the dry snow, the only sound to hear. We spoke very little, and even Lulu ceased her singing when the moon rose to half, poised like a balanced cup. We knew the very moment someone else stepped upon the road.

We had turned a bend and the footfalls came unevenly, just out of sight. There were two men, one mixed-blood or white, from the drop of his hard boot soles, and the other one quiet, an Indian. Not long and I heard them talking close behind us. From the rough, quick tension of the Indian's language, I recognized Lazarre. And the mixed-blood must be Clarence Morrissey. The two had signed the treaty and spoke in its favor to anyone they could collar at the store. They even came to people's houses to beg and argue that this was our one chance, our good chance, that the government would withdraw the offer. But wherever Margaret was, she slapped down their words like mosquitoes and said the only thing that lasts life to life is land. Money burns like tinder, flows like water. And as for promises, the wind is steadier. It is no wonder that, because she spoke so well, Lazarre and Clarence Morrissey wished to silence her. I sensed their bad intent as they passed us, an unpleasant edge of excitement in their looks and greetings.

They went on, disappeared in the dark brush.

"Margaret," I said, "we are going to cut back." My house was close, but Margaret kept walking forward as if she hadn't heard.

I took her arm, caught the little girl close, and started to turn us, but Margaret would have none of this and called me a coward. She grabbed the girl to her, Lulu, who did not mind getting tossed between us, laughed, tucked her hand into her grandma's pocket, and never missed a step. Two years ago she had tired of being carried, got up, walked. She had the balance of a little mink. She was slippery and clever, too, which was good because when the men jumped from the darkest area of brush and grappled with us half a mile on, Lulu slipped free and scrambled into the trees.

They were occupied with Margaret and me, at any rate. We were old enough to snap in two, our limbs dry as dead branches, but we fought as though our enemies were the Nadouissouix kidnappers of our childhood. Margaret uttered a war cry that had not been heard for fifty years, and bit Lazarre's hand to the bone, giving a wound which would later prove the death of him. As for Clarence, he had all he could do to wrestle me to the ground and knock me half unconscious. When he'd accomplished that, he tied me and tossed me into a wheelbarrow, which was hidden near the road for the purpose of lugging us to the Morrissey barn.

I came to my senses trussed to a manger, sitting on a bale. Margaret was roped to another bale across from me, staring straight forward in a rage, a line of froth caught between her lips. On either side of her, shaggy cows chewed and shifted their thumping hooves. I rose and staggered, the weight of the manger on my back. I planned on Margaret biting through my ropes with her strong teeth, but then the two men entered.

I'm a talker, a fast-mouth who can't keep his thoughts straight, but lets fly with words and marvels at what he hears from his own mouth. I'm a smart one.

I always was a devil for convincing women. And I wasn't too bad a shot, in other ways, at convincing men. But I had never been tied up before.

"*Booshoo,*" I said. "Children, let us loose, your game is too rough!"

They stood between us, puffed with their secrets.

"Empty old windbag," said Clarence.

"I have a bargain for you," I said, looking for an opening. "Let us go and we won't tell Pukwan." Edgar Pukwan was the tribal police. "Boys get drunk sometimes and don't know what they're doing."

Lazarre laughed once, hard and loud. "We're not drunk," he said. "Just wanting what's coming to us, some justice, money out of it."

"Kill us," said Margaret. "We won't sign."

"Wait," I said. "My cousin Pukwan will find you boys, and have no mercy. Let us go. I'll sign and get it over with, and I'll persuade the old widow."

I signaled Margaret to keep her mouth shut. She blew air into her cheeks. Clarence looked expectantly at Lazarre, as if the show were over, but Lazarre folded his arms and was convinced of nothing.

"You lie when it suits, skinny old dog," he said, wiping at his lips as if in hunger. "It's her we want, anyway. We'll shame her so she shuts her mouth."

"Easy enough," I said, smooth, "now that you've got her tied. She's plump and good looking. Eyes like a doe! But you forget that we're together, almost man and wife."

This wasn't true at all, and Margaret's face went rigid with tumbling fury and confusion. I kept talking.

"So of course if you do what you're thinking of doing you'll have to kill me afterward, and that will make my cousin Pukwan twice as angry, since I owe him a fat payment for a gun which he lent me and I never returned. All the same," I went on—their heads were spinning—"I'll forget you bad boys ever considered such a crime, something so terrible that Father Damien would nail you on boards just like in the example on the wall in church."

"Quit jabbering." Lazarre stopped me in a deadly voice.

It was throwing pebbles in a dry lake. My words left no ripple. I saw in his eyes that he intended us great harm. I saw his greed. It was like watching an ugly design of bruises come clear for a moment and reconstructing the evil blows that made them.

I played my last card.

"Whatever you do to Margaret you are doing to the Pillager woman!" I dropped my voice. "The witch, Fleur Pillager, is her own son's wife."

Clarence was too young to be frightened, but his mouth hung in interested puzzlement. My words had a different effect on Lazarre, as a sudden light shone, a consequence he hadn't considered.

I cried out, seeing this, "Don't you know she can think about you hard enough to stop your heart?" Lazarre was still deciding. He raised his fist and swung it casually and tapped my face. It was worse not to be hit full on.

"Come near!" crooned Margaret in the old language. "Let me teach you how to die."

But she was trapped like a fox. Her earrings glinted and spun as she hissed her death song over and over, which signaled something to Lazarre, for he shook himself angrily and drew a razor from his jacket. He stropped it with fast, vicious movements while Margaret sang shriller, so full of hate that the ropes should have burned, shriveled, fallen from her body. My struggle set the manager cracking against the barn walls and further confused the cows, who bumped each other and complained. At a sign from Lazarre, Clarence sighed, rose, and smashed me. The last I saw before I blacked out, through the tiny closing pinhole of light, was Lazarre approaching Margaret with the blade.

When I woke, minutes later, it was to worse shock. For Lazarre had sliced Margaret's long braids off and was now, carefully, shaving her scalp. He started almost tenderly at the wide part, and then pulled the edge down each side of her skull. He did a clean job. He shed not one drop of her blood.

And I could not even speak to curse them. For pressing my jaw down, thick above my tongue, her braids, never cut in this life till now, were tied to silence me. Powerless, I tasted their flat, animal perfume.

It wasn't much later, or else it was forever, that we walked out into the night again. Speechless, we made our way in fierce pain down the road. I was damaged in spirit, more so than Margaret. For now she tucked her shawl over her naked head and forgot her own bad treatment. She called out in dread each foot of the way, for Lulu. But the smart, bold girl had hidden till all was clear and then run to Margaret's house. We opened the door and found her sitting by the stove in a litter of scorched matches and kindling. She had not the skill to start a fire, but she was dry-eyed. Though very cold, she was alert and then captured with wonder when Margaret slipped off her shawl.

"Where is your hair?" she asked.

I took my hand from my pocket. "Here's what's left of it. I grabbed this when they cut me loose." I was shamed by how pitiful I had been, relieved when Margaret snatched the thin gray braids from me and coiled them round her fist.

"I knew you would save them, clever man!" There was satisfaction in her voice.

I set the fire blazing. It was strange how generous this woman was to me, never blaming me or mentioning my failure. Margaret stowed her braids inside a birchbark box and merely instructed me to lay it in her grave, when that time occurred. Then she came near the stove with a broken mirror from beside her washstand and looked at her own image.

"My," she pondered, "my." She put the mirror down. "I'll take a knife to them."

And I was thinking too. I was thinking I would have to kill them.

But how does an aching and half-starved grandfather attack a young, well-fed Morrissey and a tall, sly Lazarre? Later, I rolled up in blankets in the corner by Margaret's stove, and I put my mind to this question throughout that night until, exhausted, I slept. And I thought of it first thing next morning, too, and still nothing came. It was only after we had some hot *gaulette* and walked Lulu back to her mother that an idea began to grow.

Fleur let us in, hugged Lulu into her arms, and looked at Margaret, who took off her scarf and stood bald, face burning again with smoldered fire. She told

Fleur all of what happened, sparing no detail. The two women's eyes held, but Fleur said nothing. She put Lulu down, smoothed the front of her calico shirt, flipped her heavy braids over her shoulders, tapped one finger on her perfect lips. And then, calm, she went to the washstand and scraped the edge of her hunting knife keen as glass. Margaret and Lulu and I watched as Fleur cut her braids off, shaved her own head, and folded the hair into a quilled skin pouch. Then she went out, hunting, and didn't bother to wait for night to cover her tracks.

I would have to go out hunting too.

I had no gun, but anyway that was a white man's revenge. I knew how to wound with barbs of words, but had never wielded a skinning knife against a human, much less two young men. Whomever I missed would kill me, and I did not want to die by their lowly hands.

In fact, I didn't think that after Margaret's interesting kindness I wanted to leave this life at all. Her head, smooth as an egg, was ridged delicately with bone, and gleamed as if it had been buffed with a flannel cloth. Maybe it was the strangeness that attracted me. She looked forbidding, but the absence of hair also set off her eyes, so black and full of lights. She reminded me of that queen from England, of a water snake or a shrewd young bird. The earrings, which seemed part of her, mirrored her moods like water, and when they were still rounds of green lights against her throat I seemed, again, to taste her smooth, smoky braids in my mouth.

I had better things to do than fight. So I decided to accomplish revenge as quickly as possible. I was a talker who used my brains as my weapon. When I hunted, I preferred to let my game catch itself.

Snares demand clever fingers and a scheming mind, and snares had never failed me. Snares are quiet, and best of all snares are slow. I wanted to give Lazarre and Morrissey time to consider why they had to strangle. I thought hard. One- or two-foot deadfalls are required beneath a snare so that a man can't put his hand up and loosen the knot. The snares I had in mind also required something stronger than a cord, which could be broken, and finer than a rope, which even Lazarre might see and avoid. I pondered this closely, yet even so I might never have found the solution had I not gone to Mass with Margaret and grown curious about the workings of Father Damien's pride and joy, the piano in the back of the church, the instrument whose keys he breathed on, polished, then played after services, and sometimes alone. I had noticed that his hands usually stayed near the middle of the keyboard, so I took the wires from either end.

In the meantime, I was not the only one concerned with punishing Lazarre and Clarence Morrissey. Fleur was seen in town. Her thick skirts brushed the snow into clouds behind her. Though it was cold she left her head bare so everyone could see the frigid sun glare off her skull. The light reflected in the eyes of Lazarre and Clarence, who were standing at the door of the pool hall. They dropped their cue sticks in the slush and ran back to Morrissey land. Fleur walked the four streets, once in each direction, then followed.

The two men told of her visit, how she passed through the Morrissey house touching here, touching there, sprinkling powders that ignited and stank on the hot stove. How Clarence swayed on his feet, blinked hard, and chewed his fingers. How Fleur stepped up to him, drew her knife. He smiled foolishly and asked her for supper. She reached forward and trimmed off a hank of his hair. Then she stalked from the house, leaving a taste of cold wind, and then chased Lazarre to the barn.

She made a black silhouette against the light from the door. Lazarre pressed against the wood of the walls, watching, hypnotized by the sight of Fleur's head and the quiet blade. He did not defend himself when she approached, reached for him, gently and efficiently cut bits of his hair, held his hands, one at a time, and trimmed the nails. She waved the razor-edged knife before his eyes and swept a few eyelashes into a white square of flour sacking that she then carefully folded into her blouse.

For days after, Lazarre babbled and wept. Fleur was murdering him by use of bad medicine, he said. He showed his hand, the bite that Margaret had dealt him, and the dark streak from the wound, along his wrist and inching up his arm. He even used that bound hand to scratch his name from the treaty, but it did no good.

I figured that the two men were doomed at least three ways now. Margaret won the debate with her Catholic training and decided to damn her soul by taking up the ax, since no one else had destroyed her enemies. I begged her to wait for another week, all during which it snowed and thawed and snowed again. It took me that long to arrange the snare to my satisfaction, near Lazarre's shack, on a path both men took to town.

I set it out one morning before anyone stirred, and watched from an old pine twisted along the ground. I waited while the smoke rose in a silky feather from the tiny tin spout on Lazarre's roof. I had to sit half a day before Lazarre came outside, and even then it was just for wood, nowhere near the path. I had a hard time to keep my blood flowing, my stomach still. I ate a handful of dry berries Margaret had given me, and a bit of pounded meat. I doled it to myself and waited until finally Clarence showed. He walked the trail like a blind ghost and stepped straight into my noose.

It was perfect, or would have been if I had made the deadfall two inches wider, for in falling Clarence somehow managed to spread his legs and straddle the deep hole I'd cut. It had been invisible, covered with snow, and yet in one foot-pedaling instant, the certain knowledge of its construction sprang into Clarence's brain and told his legs to reach for the sides. I don't know how he did it, but there he was poised. I waited, did not show myself. The noose jerked enough to cut slightly into the fool's neck, a too-snug fit. He was spread-eagled and on tiptoe, his arms straight out. If he twitched a finger, lost the least control, even tried to yell, one foot would go, the noose constrict.

But Clarence did not move. I could see from behind my branches that he didn't even dare to change the expression on his face. His mouth stayed frozen in shock. Only his eyes shifted, darted fiercely and wildly, side to side, showing all the agitation he must not release, searching desperately for a means of escape.

They focused only when I finally stepped toward him, quiet, from the pine.

We were in full view of Lazarre's house, face to face. I stood before the boy. Just a touch, a sudden kick, perhaps no more than a word, was all that it would take. But I looked into his eyes and saw the knowledge of his situation. Pity entered me. Even for Margaret's shame, I couldn't do the thing I might have done.

I turned away and left Morrissey still balanced on the ledge of snow.

What money I did have, I took to the trading store next day. I bought the best bonnet on the reservation. It was black as a coal scuttle, large, and shaped the same.

"It sets off my doe eyes," Margaret said and stared me down.

She wore it every day, and always to Mass. Not long before Lent and voices could be heard: "There goes Old Lady Coalbucket." Nonetheless, she was proud, and softening day by day, I could tell. By the time we got our foreheads crossed with ashes, she consented to be married.

"I hear you're thinking of exchanging the vows," said Father Damien as I shook his hand on our way out the door.

"I'm having relations with Margaret already," I told him, "that's the way we do things."

This had happened to him before, so he was not even stumped as to what remedy he should use.

"Make a confession, at any rate," he said, motioning us back into the church.

So I stepped into the little box and knelt. Father Damien slid aside the shadowy door. I told him what I had been doing with Margaret and he stopped me partway through.

"No more details. Pray to Our Lady."

"There is one more thing."

"Yes?"

"Clarence Morrissey, he wears a scarf to church around his neck each week. I snared him like a rabbit."

Father Damien let the silence fill him.

"And the last thing," I went on. "I stole the wire from your piano."

The silence spilled over into my stall, and I was held in its grip until the priest spoke.

"Discord is hateful to God. You have offended his ear." Almost as an afterthought, Damien added, "And his commandment. The violence among you must cease."

"You can have the wire back," I said. I had used only one long strand. I also agreed that I would never use my snares on humans, an easy promise. Lazarre was already caught.

Just two days later, while Margaret and I stood with Lulu and her mother inside the trading store, Lazarre entered, gesturing, his eyes rolled to the skull. He stretched forth his arm and pointed along its deepest black vein and dropped his jaw wide. Then he stepped backward into a row of traps that the trader had set to show us how they worked. Fleur's eye lit, her white scarf caught the sun as she turned. All the whispers were true. Fleur had scratched Lazarre's figure into a piece of birchbark, drawn his insides, and rubbed a bit of rouge up his arm until the red stain reached his heart. There was no sound as he fell, no cry, no word, and the traps of all types that clattered down around his body jumped and met for a long time, snapping air.

Questions for Discussion

1. How would you characterize the narrator Erdrich has created? What is his personality like? What approaches to people and problems does he take?

2. How would you describe the narrator's relationship with Father Damien? What does the confession reveal about the narrator's attitude toward Catholicism and toward his remorse?

3. What different approaches to revenge does the story reveal?

4. Why won't the narrator and his friends sign the treaty? To what extent are you sympathetic to their position?

Suggestions for Writing

1. Write a response to the last scene. Consider the following: What does Lazarre die from? What is visually and thematically significant about the death scene?

2. Write an essay in which you analyze the way the characters do harm to and exact revenge upon one another. In what ways are these actions both "practical" and "symbolic"? In your view, which actions are appropriate? Inappropriate?

3. Write a story that involves revenge. See if you can make it a fairly complicated depiction of revenge, just as the narrator's attitudes and actions in "Snares" are complicated.

4. Write briefly in your notebook or journal about the ways in which "Snares" depicts Native Americans differently from the way Hollywood films typically depict them.

One Whale, Singing

KERI HULME

The ship drifted on the summer night sea.

'It is a pity,' she thought, 'that one must come on deck to see the stars. Perhaps a boat of glass, to see the sea streaming past, to watch the nightly splendour of stars.' Something small jumped from the water, away to the left. A flash of phosphorescence after the sound, and then all was quiet and starlit again.

They had passed through krillswarms all day. Large areas of the sea were reddish-brown, as though an enormous creature had wallowed ahead of the boat, streaming blood.

'Whale-feed,' she had said, laughing and hugging herself at the thought of seeing whales again.

'Lobster-krill,' he had corrected, pedantically.

The crustaceans had swum in their frightened jerking shoals, mile upon mile of them, harried by fish that were in turn pursued and torn by larger fish.

She thought, it was probably a fish after krill that had leaped then. She sighed, stroking her belly. It was the lesser of the two evils to go below now, so he didn't have an opportunity to come on deck and suggest it was better for the coming baby's health, and hers, of course, that she came down. The cramped cabin held no attraction: all that was there was boneless talk, and one couldn't see stars, or really hear the waters moving.

Far below, deep under the keel of the ship, a humpback whale sported and fed. Occasionally, she yodelled to herself, a long undulating call of content. When she found a series of sounds that pleased, she repeated them, wove them into a band of harmonious pulses.

Periodically she reared to the surface, blew, and slid smoothly back under the sea in a wheel-like motion. Because she was pregnant, and at the tailend of the southward migration, she had no reason now to leap and display on the surface.

She was not feeding seriously; the krill was there, and she swam amongst them, forcing water through her lips with her large tongue, stranding food amongst the baleen. When her mouth was full, she swallowed. It was leisurely, lazy eating. Time enough for recovering her full weight when she reached the cold seas, and she could gorge on a ton and a half of plankton daily.

Along this coast, there was life and noise in plenty. Shallow grunting from a herd of fish, gingerly feeding on the fringes of the krill shoal. The krill themselves, a thin hiss and crackle through the water. The interminable background clicking of shrimps. At times, a wayward band of sound like bass organ-notes sang through the chatter, and to this the whale listened attentively, and sometimes replied.

The krill thinned; she tested, tasted the water. Dolphins had passed recently. She heard their brief commenting chatter, but did not spend time on it. The school swept round ahead of her, and vanished into the vibrant dark.

He had the annoying habit of reading what he'd written out loud. 'We can conclusively demonstrate that to man alone belongs true intelligence and self-knowledge.'
He coughs.
Taps his pen against his lips. He has soft, wet lips, and the sound is a fleshy slop! slop!
She thinks:

Man indeed! How arrogant! How ignorant! Woman would be as correct, but I'll settle for humanity. And it strikes me that the quality humanity stands in need of most is true intelligence and self-knowledge.

'For instance, Man alone as a species, makes significant artefacts, and transmits knowledge in permanent and durable form.'
He grunts happily.
'In this lecture, I propose to. . . . '

But how do they know? she asks herself. About the passing on of knowledge among other species? They may do it in ways beyond our capacity to understand . . . that we are the only ones to make artefacts I'll grant you, but that's because us needy little adapts have such pathetic bodies, and no especial ecological niche. So hooks and hoes, and steel things that gouge and slay, we produce in plenty. And build a wasteland of drear ungainly hovels to shelter our vulnerable hides.

She remembers her glass boat, and sighs. The things one could create if one made technology servant to a humble and creative imagination. . . . He's booming on, getting into full lecture room style and stride.
'. . . thus we will show that no other species, lacking as they do artefacts, an organized society, or even semblances of culture. . . .'

What would a whale do with an artefact, who is so perfectly adapted to the sea? Their conception of culture, of civilization, must be so alien that we'd never recognize it, even if we were to stumble on its traces daily.

She snorts.
He looks at her, eyes unglazing, and smiles.
'Criticism, my dear? Or you like that bit?'
'I was just thinking. . . .'

Thinking, as for us passing on our knowledge, hah! We rarely learn from the past or the present, and what we pass on for future humanity is a mere jumble of momentarily true facts, and odd snippets of surprised self-discoveries. That's not knowledge. . . .

She folds her hands over her belly. You in there, you won't learn much. What I can teach you is limited by what we are. Splotch goes the pen against his lips.

'You had better heat up that fortified drink, dear. We can't have either of you wasting from lack of proper nourishment.'

Unspoken haw haw haw.

Don't refer to it as a person! It is a canker in me, a parasite. It is nothing to me. I feel it squirm and kick, and sicken at the movement.

He says he's worried by her pale face.

'You shouldn't have gone up on deck so late. You could have slipped, or something, and climbing tires you now, you know.'

She doesn't argue any longer. The arguments follow well-worn tracks and go in circles.

'Yes,' she answers.

but I should wither without that release, that solitude, that keep away from you.

She stirs the powder into the milk and begins to mix it rhythmically.

I wonder what a whale thinks of its calf? So large a creature, so proven peaceful a beast, must be motherly, protective, a shielding benevolence against all wildness. It would be a sweet and milky love, magnified and sustained by the encompassing purity of water. . . .

A swarm of insect-like creatures, sparkling like a galaxy, each a pulsing light-form in blue and silver and gold. The whale sang for them, a ripple of delicate notes, spaced in a timeless curve. It stole through the lightswarm, and the luminescence increased brilliantly.

Deep within her, the other spark of light also grew. It was the third calf she had borne; it delighted her still, that the swift airy copulation should spring so opportunely to this new life. She feeds it love and music, and her body's bounty. Already it responds to her crooning tenderness, and the dark pictures she sends it. It absorbs both, as part of the life to come, as it nests securely in the waters within.

She remembers the nautilids in the warm oceans to the north, snapping at one another in a cannibalistic frenzy.

She remembers the oil-bedraggled albatross, resting with patient finality on the water-top, waiting for death.

She remembers her flight, not long past, from killer whales, and the terrible end of the other female who had companied her south, tongue eaten from her mouth, flukes and genitals ripped, bleeding to a slow fought-against end.

And all the memories are part of the growing calf.

More krill appeared. She opened her mouth, and glided through the shoal. Sudden darkness for the krill. The whale hummed meanwhile.

He folded his papers contentedly.

'Sam was going on about his blasted dolphins the other night dear.'

'Yes?'

He laughed deprecatingly. 'But it wouldn't interest you. All dull scientific chatter, eh?'

'What was he saying about, umm, his dolphins?'

'O, insisted that his latest series of tests demonstrated their high intelligence. No, that's misquoting him, potentially high intelligence. Of course, I brought him down to earth smartly. Results are as you make them, I said. Nobody has proved that the animals have intelligence to a degree above that of a dog. But it made me think of the rot that's setting in lately. Inspiration for this lecture indeed.'

'Lilley?' she asked, still thinking of the dolphins,

'Lilley demonstrated evidence of dolphinese.'

'Lilley? That mystical crackpot? Can you imagine anyone ever duplicating his work? Hah! Nobody has, of course. It was all in the man's mind.'

'Dolphins and whales are still largely unknown entities,' she murmured, more to herself than to him.

'Nonsense, my sweet. They've been thoroughly studied and dissected for the last century and more.' She shuddered. 'Rather dumb animals, all told, and probably of bovine origin. Look at the incredibly stupid way they persist in migrating straight into the hands of whalers year after year. If they were smart, they'd have organized an attacking force and protected themselves!'

He chuckled at the thought, and lit his pipe.

'It would be nice to communicate with another species,' she said, more softly still.

'That's the trouble with you poets,' he said fondly. 'Dream marvels are to be found from every half-baked piece of pseudo-science that drifts around. That's not seeing the world as it is. We scientists rely on reliably ascertained facts for a true picture of the world.'

She sat silently by the pot on the galley stove.

An echo from the world around, a deep throbbing from miles away. It was both message and invitation to contribute. She mused on it for minutes, absorbing, storing, correlating, winding her song meanwhile experimentally through its interstices—then dropped her voice to the lowest frequencies. She sent the message along first, and then added another strength to the cold wave that travelled after the message. An ocean away, someone would collect the cold wave, and store it, while it coiled and built to uncontrollable strength. Then, just enough would be released to generate a superwave, a gigantic wall of water on the surface of the sea. It was a new thing the sea-people were experimenting with. A protection. In case.

She began to swim further out from the coast. The water flowed like warm silk over her flanks, an occasional interjectory current swept her, cold and bracing, a touch from the sea to the south. It became quieter, a calm freed from the fights of crabs and the bickerings of small fish. There was less noise too, from the strange turgid craft that buzzed and clattered across the ocean-ceiling, dropping down wastes that stank and sickened.

A great ocean-going shark prudently shifted course and flicked away to the side of her. It measured twenty feet from shovel-nose to crescentic tailfin, but she was twice as long and would grow a little yet. Her broad deep body was still well fleshed and strong, in spite of the vicissitudes of the northwind breeding trek: there were barnacles encrusting her fins and lips and head, but she was unhampered by other parasites. She blew a raspberry at the fleeing shark and beat her flukes against the ocean's pull in an ecstasy of strength.

'This lecture,' he says, sipping his drink, 'this lecture should cause quite a stir. They'll probably label it conservative, or even reactionary, but of course it isn't. It merely urges us to keep our feet on the ground, not go hunting off down worthless blind sidetrails. To consolidate data we already have, not, for example, to speculate about so-called ESP phenomena. There is far too much mysticism and airy-fairy folderol in science these days. I don't wholly agree with the Victorians' attitude, that science could explain all, and very shortly would, but it's high time we got things back to a solid factual basis.'

'The Russians,' she says, after a long moment of non-committal silence, 'the Russians have discovered a form of photography that shows all living things to be sources of a strange and beautiful energy. Lights flare from fingertips. Leaves coruscate. All is living effulgence.'

He chuckles again.

'I can always tell when you're waxing poetic.' Then he taps out the bowl of his pipe against the side of the bunk, and leans forward in a fatherly way.

'My dear, if they have, and that's a big if, what difference could that possibly make. Another form of energy? So what?'

'Not just another form of energy,' she says sombrely. 'It makes for a whole new view of the world. If all things are repositories of related energy, then humanity is not alone. . . .'

'Why this of solitariness, of being alone. Communication with other species, man is not alone, for God's sake! One would think you're becoming tired of us all!'

He's joking.

She is getting very tired. She speaks tiredly.

'It would mean that the things you think you are demonstrating in your paper. . . .'

'Lecture.'

'Work . . . those things are totally irrelevant. That we may be on the bottom of the pile, not the top. It may be that other creatures are aware of their place and purpose in the world, have no need to delve and paw a meaning out.

Justify themselves. That they accept all that happens, the beautiful, the terrible, the sickening, as part of the dance, as the joy or pain of the joke. Other species may somehow be equipped to know fully and consciously what truth is, whereas we humans must struggle, must struggle blindly to the end.'

He frowns, a concerned benevolent frown.

'Listen dear, has this trip been too much. Are you feeling at the end of your tether, tell us truly? I know the boat is old, and not much of a sailer, but it's the best I could do for the weekend. And I thought it would be a nice break for us, to get away from the university and home. Has there been too much work involved? The boat's got an engine after all . . . would you like me to start it and head back for the coast?'

She is shaking her head numbly.

He stands up and swallows what is left of his drink in one gulp.

'It won't take a minute to start the engine, and then I'll set that pilot thing, and we'll be back in sight of land before the morning. You'll feel happier then.'

She grips the small table.

Don't scream, she tells herself, don't scream.

Diatoms of phantom light, stray single brilliances. A high burst of dolphin sonics. The school was returning. A muted rasp from shoalfish hurrying past. A thing that curled and coiled in a drifting aureole of green light.

She slows, buoyant in the water.

Green light: it brings up the memories that are bone deep in her, written in her very cells. Green light of land.

She had once gone within yards of shore, without stranding. Curiosity had impelled her up a long narrow bay. She had edged carefully along, until her long flippers touched the rocky bottom. Sculling with her tail, she had slid forward a little further, and then lifted her head out of the water. The light was bent, the sounds that came to her were thin and distorted, but she could see colours known only from dreams and hear a music that was both alien and familiar.

(Christlookitthat!)

(Fuckinghellgetoutahereitscomingin)

The sound waves pooped and spattered through the air, and things scrambled away, as she moved herself back smoothly into deeper water.

A strange visit, but it enabled her to put images of her own to the calling dream.

Follow the line to the hard and aching airswept land, lie upon solidity never before known until strained ribs collapse from weight of body never before felt. And then, the second beginning of joy. . . .

She dreams a moment, recalling other ends, other beginnings. And because of the web that streamed between all members of her kind, she was ready for the softly insistent pulsation that wound itself into her dreaming. Mourning for a male of the species, up in the cold southern seas where the greenbellied krill swarm in unending abundance. Where the killing ships of the harpooners lurk. A barb sliced through the air in an arc and embedded itself in the lungs, so the whale blew red in his threshing agony. Another that sunk into his flesh by the heart. Long minutes later, his slow exhalation of death. Then the gathering of light from all parts of the drifting corpse. It condensed, vanished . . . streamers of sound from the dolphins who shoot past her, somersaulting in their strange joy.

The long siren call urges her south. She begins to surge upward to the sweet night air.

She says, 'I must go on deck for a minute.'

They had finished the quarrel, but still had not come together. He grunts, fondles his notes a last time, and rolls over in his sleeping bag, drawing the neck of it tightly close.

She says wistfully, 'Goodnight then,' and climbs the stairs heavily up to the hatchway.

'You're slightly offskew,' she says to the Southern Cross, and feels the repressed tears begin to flow down her cheeks. The stars blur.

Have I changed so much?
Or is it this interminable deadening pregnancy?
But his stolid, sullen, stupidity!
He won't see, he won't see, he won't see anything.

She walks to the bow, and settles herself down, uncomfortably aware of her protuberant belly, and begins to croon a song of comfort to herself.

And at that moment the humpback hit the ship, smashing through her old and weakened hull, collapsing the cabin, rending timbers. A mighty chaos. . . .

Somehow she found herself in the water, crying for him, swimming in a circle as though among the small debris she might find a floating sleeping bag. The stern of the ship is sinking, poised a moment dark against the stars, and then it slides silently under.

She strikes out for a shape in the water, the liferaft? the dinghy?

And the shape moves.

The humpback, full of her dreams and her song, had beat blindly upward, and was shocked by the unexpected fouling. She lies, waiting on the water-top.

The woman stays where she is, motionless except for her paddling hands. She has no fear of the whale, but thinks, 'It may not know I am here, may hit me accidentally as it goes down.'

She can see the whale more clearly now, an immense zeppelin shape, bigger by far than their flimsy craft had been, but it lies there, very still. . . .

She hopes it hasn't been hurt by the impact, and chokes on the hope.

There is a long moaning call then, that reverberated through her. She is physically swept, shaken by an intensity of feeling, as though the whale has sensed her being and predicament, and has offered all it can, a sorrowing compassion.

Again the whale makes the moaning noise, and the woman calls, as loudly as she can, 'Thank you, thank you', knowing that it is meaningless, and probably unheard. Tears stream down her face once more.

The whale sounded so gently she didn't realize it was going at all.

'I am now alone in the dark,' she thinks, and the salt water laps round her mouth. 'How strange, if this is to be the summation of my life.'

In her womb the child kicked. Buoyed by the sea, she feels the movement as something gentle and familiar, dear to her for the first time.

But she begins to laugh.

The sea is warm and confiding, and it is a long long way to shore.

Questions for Discussion

1. How fairly does this story represent the scientific point of view toward whales, dolphins, and animal intelligence?

2. Hulme takes a risk in this story by actually trying to represent the point of view of a whale. How successful, in your view, is she in this representation? How would you characterize the representation?

3. What do you make of the relationship between the narrator and her husband? Why are most of her responses to him "interior"? Why won't she debate him more?

4. How successful is the resolution to the story?

Suggestions for Writing

1. Why does the whale's sinking of the boat change the woman's attitude toward being pregnant? How believable is this change in her? Write a response to these questions in your notebook or journal.

2. Literature and the cinema contain memorable encounters between human beings and large sea creatures. Some of the most famous encounters take place in Herman Melville's *Moby Dick,* Jules Verne's *Ten Thousand Leagues Under The Sea,* and in the films *Jaws, Leviathan,* and *The Abyss.* Write an essay in which you compare and contrast Hulme's story with one or more of these books or films (or with another art work—even a painting—with which you are familiar).

3. An "anthropocentric" description of an animal is one that gives human thoughts and emotions to an animal. How anthropocentric is Hulme's representation of a whale's point of view? If you were to make the point of view even more like a whale's, what might you change, add, or delete?

4. Write a story that involves an encounter between a person and an animal in the wild. As Hulme does, try to make the encounter somewhat different from those we have frequently seen in action/adventure books and films.

She Didn't Come Home

SUE GRAFTON

September in Santa Teresa. I've never known anyone yet who doesn't suffer a certain restlessness when autumn rolls around. It's the season of new school clothes, fresh notebooks, and finely sharpened pencils without any teeth marks in the wood. We're all eight years old again and anything is possible. The new year should never begin on January 1. It begins in the fall and continues as long as our saddle oxfords remain unscuffed and our lunch boxes have no dents.

My name is Kinsey Millhone. I'm female, thirty-two, twice divorced, "doing business" as Kinsey Millhone Investigations in a little town ninety-five miles north of Los Angeles. Mine isn't a walk-in trade like a beauty salon. Most of my clients find themselves in a bind and then seek my services, hoping I can offer a solution for a mere thirty bucks an hour, plus expenses. Robert Ackerman's message was waiting on my answering machine that Monday morning at nine when I got in.

"Hello. My name is Robert Ackerman and I wonder if you could give me a call. My wife is missing and I'm worried sick. I was hoping you could help me out." In the background, I could hear whiney children, my favorite kind. He repeated his name and gave me a telephone number. I made a pot of coffee before I called him back.

A little person answered the phone. There was a murmured child-size hello and then I heard a lot of heavy breathing close to the mouthpiece.

"Hi," I said, "can I speak to your daddy?"

"Yes." Long silence.

"Today?" I asked.

The receiver was clunked down on a tabletop and I could hear the clatter of footsteps in a room that sounded as if it didn't have any carpeting. In due course, Robert Ackerman picked up the phone.

"Lucy?"

"It's Kinsey Millhone, Mr. Ackerman. I just got your message on my answering machine. Can you tell me what's going on?"

"Oh wow, yeah . . . "

He was interrupted by a piercing shriek that sounded like one of those policeman's whistles you use to discourage obscene phone callers. I didn't jerk back quite in time. "Shit, that hurt."

I listened patiently while he dealt with the errant child.

"Sorry," he said when he came back on the line. "Look, is there any way you could come out to the house? I've got my hands full and I just can't get away."

I took his address and brief directions, then headed out to my car.

Robert and the missing Mrs. Ackerman lived in a housing tract that looked like it was built in the forties before anyone ever dreamed up the notion of family rooms, country kitchens, and his 'n' hers solar spas. What we had here was a basic drywall box; cramped living room with a dining L, a kitchen and one bathroom sandwiched between two nine-by-twelve-foot bedrooms. When Robert answered the door I could just about see the whole place at a glance. The only thing the builders had been lavish with was the hardwood floors, which, in this case, was unfortunate. Little children had banged and scraped these floors and had brought in some kind of foot grit that I sensed before I was even asked to step inside.

Robert, though harried, had a boyish appeal; a man in his early thirties perhaps, lean and handsome, with dark eyes and dark hair that came to a pixie point in the middle of his forehead. He was wearing chinos and a plain white T-shirt. He had a baby, maybe eight months old, propped on his hip like a grocery bag. Another child clung to his right leg, while a third rode his tricycle at various walls and doorways, making quite loud sounds with his mouth.

"Hi, come on in," Robert said. "We can talk out in the backyard while the kids play." His smile was sweet.

I followed him through the tiny disorganized house and out to the backyard, where he set the baby down in a sandpile framed with two-by-fours. The second child held on to Robert's belt loops and stuck a thumb in its mouth, staring at me while the tricycle child tried to ride off the edge of the porch. I'm not fond of children. I'm really not. Especially the kind who wear hard brown shoes. Like dogs, these infants sensed my distaste and kept their distance, eyeing me with a mixture of rancor and disdain.

The backyard was scruffy, fenced in, and littered with the fifty-pound sacks the sand had come in. Robert gave the children homemade-style cookies out of a cardboard box and shooed them away. In fifteen minutes the sugar would probably turn them into lunatics. I gave my watch a quick glance, hoping to be gone by then.

"You want a lawn chair?"

"No, this is fine," I said and settled on the grass. There wasn't a lawn chair in sight, but the offer was nice anyway.

He perched on the edge of the sandbox and ran a distracted hand across his head. "God, I'm sorry everything is such a mess, but Lucy hasn't been here for two days. She didn't come home from work on Friday and I've been a wreck ever since."

"I take it you notified the police."

"Sure. Friday night. She never showed up at the babysitter's house to pick the kids up. I finally got a call here at seven asking where she was. I figured she'd just stopped off at the grocery story or something, so I went ahead and picked 'em up and brought 'em home. By ten o'clock when I hadn't heard from her, I knew something was wrong. I called her boss at home and he said as far as he knew she'd left work at five as usual, so that's when I called the police."

"You filed a missing persons report?"

"I can do that today. With an adult, you have to wait seventy-two hours, and even then, there's not much they can do."

"What else did they suggest?"

"The usual stuff, I guess. I mean, I called everyone we know. I talked to her mom in Bakersfield and this friend of hers at work. Nobody has any idea where she is. I'm scared something's happened to her."

"You've checked with hospitals in the area, I take it."

"Sure. That's the first thing I did."

"Did she give you any indication that anything was wrong?"

"Not a word."

"Was she depressed or behaving oddly?"

"Well, she was kind of restless the past couple of months. She always seemed to get excited around this time of year. She said it reminded her of her old elementary school days." He shrugged. "I hated mine."

"But she's never disappeared like this before."

"Oh, heck no. I just mentioned her mood because you asked. I don't think it amounted to anything."

"Does she have any problem with alcohol or drugs?"

"Lucy isn't really like that," he said. "She's petite and kind of quiet. A homebody, I guess you'd say."

"What about your relationship? Do the two of you get along okay?"

"As far as I'm concerned, we do. I mean, once in a while we get into it but never anything serious."

"What are your disagreements about?"

He smiled ruefully. "Money, mostly. With three kids, we never seem to have enough. I mean, I'm crazy about big families, but it's tough financially. I always wanted four or five, but she says three is plenty, especially with the oldest not in school yet. We fight about that some . . . having more kids."

"You both work?"

"We have to. Just to make ends meet. She has a job in an escrow company downtown, and I work for the phone company."

"Doing what?"

"Installer," he said.

"Has there been any hint of someone else in her life?"

He sighed, plucking at the grass between his feet. "In a way, I wish I could say yes. I'd like to think maybe she just got fed up or something and checked into a motel for the weekend. Something like that."

"But you don't think she did."

"Unh-uh and I'm going crazy with anxiety. Somebody's got to find out where she is."

"Mr. Ackerman . . . "

"You can call me Rob," he said.

Clients always say that. I mean, unless their names are something else.

"Rob," I said, "the police are truly your best bet in a situation like this. I'm just one person. They've got a vast machinery they can put to work and it won't cost you a cent."

"You charge a lot, huh?"

"Thirty bucks an hour plus expenses."

He thought about that for a moment, then gave me a searching look. "Could you maybe put in ten hours? I got three hundred bucks we were saving for a trip to the San Diego Zoo."

I pretended to think about it, but the truth was, I knew I couldn't say no to that boyish face. Anyway, the kids were starting to whine and I wanted to get out of there. I waived the retainer and said I'd send him an itemized bill when the ten hours were up. I figured I could put a contract in the mail and reduce my contact with the short persons who were crowding around him now, begging for more sweets. I asked for a recent photograph of Lucy, but all he could come up with was a two-year-old snapshot of her with the two older kids. She looked beleaguered even then, and that was before the third baby came along. I thought about quiet little Lucy Ackerman whose three strapping sons had legs the size of my arms. If I were she, I knew where I'd be. Long gone.

Lucy Ackerman was employed as an escrow officer for a small company on State Street not far from my office. It was a modest establishment of white walls, rust and brown plaid furniture with burnt orange carpeting. There were Gauguin reproductions all around and a live plant on every desk. I introduced myself first to the office manager, a Mrs. Merriman, who was in her sixties, had tall hair, and wore lace-up boots with stiletto heels. She looked like a woman who'd trade all her pension monies for a head-to-toe body tuck.

I said, "Robert Ackerman has asked me to see if I can locate his wife."

"Well, the poor man. I heard about that," she said with her mouth. Her eyes said, "Fat chance!"

"Do you have any idea where she might be?"

"I think you'd better talk to Mr. Sotherland." She had turned all prim and officious, but my guess was she knew something and was dying to be asked. I intended to accommodate her as soon as I'd talked to him. The protocol in small offices, I've found, is ironclad.

Gavin Sotherland got up from his swivel chair and stretched a big hand across the desk to shake mine. The other member of the office force, Barbara Hemdahl, the bookkeeper, got up from her chair simultaneously and excused herself. Mr. Sotherland watched her depart and then motioned me into the same seat. I sank into leather still hot from Barbara Hemdahl's backside, a curiously intimate effect. I made a mental note to find out what she knew, and then I looked, with interest, at the company vice president. I picked up all these names and job titles because his was cast in stand-up bronze letters on his desk, and the two women both had white plastic name tags affixed to their breasts, like nurses. As nearly as I could tell, there were only four of them in the office, including Lucy Ackerman, and I couldn't understand how they could fail to identify each other on sight. Maybe all the badges were for clients who couldn't be trusted to tell one from the other without the proper ID's.

Gavin Sotherland was large, an ex-jock to all appearances, maybe forty-five years old, with a heavy head of blond hair thinning slightly at the crown. He had a slight paunch, a slight stoop to his shoulders, and a grip that was damp with sweat. He had his coat off, and his once-starched white shirt was limp and wrinkled, his beige gabardine pants heavily creased across the lap. Altogether, he looked like a man who'd just crossed a continent by rail. Still, I was forced to credit him with good looks, even if he had let himself go to seed.

"Nice to meet you, Miss Millhone. I'm so glad you're here." His voice was deep and rumbling, with confidence-inspiring undertones. On the other hand, I didn't like the look in his eyes. He could have been a con man, for all I knew. "I understand Mrs. Ackerman never got home Friday night," he said.

"That's what I'm told," I replied. "Can you tell me anything about her day here?"

He studied me briefly. "Well, now I'm going to have to be honest with you. Our bookkeeper has come across some discrepancies in the accounts. It looks like Lucy Ackerman has just walked off with half a million dollars entrusted to us."

"How'd she manage that?"

I was picturing Lucy Ackerman, free of those truck-busting kids, lying on a beach in Rio, slurping some kind of rum drink out of a coconut.

Mr. Sotherland looked pained. "In the most straightforward manner imaginable," he said. "It looks like she opened a new bank account at a branch in Montebello and deposited ten checks that should have gone into other accounts. Last Friday, she withdrew over five hundred thousand dollars in cash, claiming we were closing out a big real estate deal. We found the passbook in her bottom drawer." He tossed the booklet across the desk to me and I picked it up. The word VOID had been punched into the pages in a series of holes. A quick glance showed ten deposits at intervals dating back over the past three months and a zero balance as of last Friday's date.

"Didn't anybody else double-check this stuff?"

"We'd just undergone our annual audit in June. Everything was fine. We trusted this woman implicitly and had every reason to."

"You discovered the loss this morning?"

"Yes, ma'am, but I'll admit I was suspicious Friday night when Robert Ackerman called me at home. It was completely unlike that woman to disappear without a word. She's worked here eight years, and she's been punctual and conscientious since the day she walked in."

"Well, punctual at any rate," I said. "Have you notified the police?"

"I was just about to do that. I'll have to alert the Department of Corporations, too. God, I can't believe she did this to us. I'll be fired. They'll probably shut this entire office down."

"Would you mind if I had a quick look around?"

"To what end?"

"There's always a chance we can figure out where she went. If we move fast enough, maybe we can catch her before she gets away with it."

"Well, I doubt that," he said. "The last anybody saw her was Friday afternoon. That's two full days. She could be anywhere by now."

"Mr. Sotherland, her husband has already authorized three hundred dollars' worth of my time. Why not take advantage of it?"

He stared at me. "Won't the police object?"

"Probably. But I don't intend to get in anybody's way, and whatever I find out, I'll turn over to them. They may not be able to get a fraud detective out here until late morning anyway. If I get a line on her, it'll make you look good to the company *and* to the cops."

He gave a sigh of resignation and waved his hand. "Hell, I don't care. Do what you want."

When I left his office, he was putting the call through to the police department.

I sat briefly at Lucy's desk, which was neat and well organized. Her drawers contained the usual office supplies; no personal items at all. There was a calendar on her desktop, one of those loose-leaf affairs with a page for each day. I checked back through the past couple of months. The only personal notation was for an appointment at the Women's Health Center August 2, and a second visit last Friday afternoon. It must have been a busy day for Lucy, what with a doctor's appointment and ripping off her company for half a million bucks. I made a note of the address she'd penciled in at the time of her first visit. The other two women in the office were keeping an eye on me, I noticed, though both pretended to be occupied with paperwork.

When I finished my search, I got up and crossed the room to Mrs. Merriman's desk. "Is there any way I can make a copy of the passbook for that account Mrs. Ackerman opened?"

"Well, yes, if Mr. Sotherland approves," she said.

"I'm also wondering where she kept her coat and purse during the day."

"In the back. We each have a locker in the storage room."

"I'd like to take a look at that, too."

I waited patiently while she cleared both matters with her boss, and then I accompanied her to the rear. There was a door that opened onto the parking lot. To the left of it was a small rest room and, on the right, there was a storage room that housed four connecting upright metal lockers, the copy machine, and numerous shelves neatly stacked with office supplies. Each shoulder-high locker was marked with a name. Lucy Ackerman's was still securely padlocked. There was something about the blank look of that locker that seemed ominous somehow. I looked at the lock, fairly itching to have a crack at it with my little set of key picks, but I didn't want to push my luck with the cops on the way.

"I'd like for someone to let me know what's in that locker when it's finally opened," I remarked while Mrs. Merriman ran off the copy of the passbook pages for me.

"This, too," I said, handing her a carbon of the withdrawal slip Lucy'd been required to sign in receipt of the cash. It had been folded and tucked into the back of the booklet. "You have any theories about where she went?"

Mrs. Merriman's mouth pursed piously, as though she were debating with herself about how much she might say.

"I wouldn't want to be accused of talking out of school," she ventured.

"Mrs. Merriman, it does look like a crime's been committed," I suggested. "The police are going to ask you the same thing when they get here."

"Oh. Well, in that case, I suppose it's all right. I mean, I don't have the faintest idea where she is, but I do think she's been acting oddly the past few months."

"Like what?"

"She seemed secretive. Smug. Like she knew something the rest of us didn't know about."

"That certainly turned out to be the case," I said.

"Oh, I didn't mean it was related to that," she said hesitantly. "I think she was having an affair."

That got my attention. "An affair? With whom?"

She paused for a moment, touching at one of the hairpins that supported her ornate hairdo. She allowed her gaze to stray back toward Mr. Sotherland's office. I turned and looked in that direction, too.

"Really?" I said. "No wonder he was in a sweat," I thought.

"I couldn't swear to it," she murmured, "But his marriage has been rocky for years, and I gather she hasn't been that happy herself. She has those beastly little boys, you know, and a husband who seems determined to spawn more. She and Mr. Sotherland . . . Gavie, she calls him . . . have . . . well, I'm sure they've been together. Whether it's connected to this matter of the missing money, I wouldn't presume to guess." Having said as much, she was suddenly uneasy. "You won't repeat what I've said to the police, I hope."

"Absolutely not," I said. "Unless they ask, of course."

"Oh. Of course."

"By the way, is there a company travel agent?"

"Right next door," she replied.

I had a brief chat with the bookkeeper, who added nothing to the general picture of Lucy Ackerman's last few days at work. I retrieved my VW from the parking lot and headed over to the health center eight blocks away, wondering what Lucy had been up to. I was guessing birth control and probably the permanent sort. If she were having an affair (and determined not to get pregnant again in any event), it would seem logical, but I hadn't any idea how to verify the fact. Medical personnel are notoriously stingy with information like that.

I parked in front of the clinic and grabbed my clipboard from the backseat. I have a supply of all-purpose forms for occasions like this. They look like a cross between a job application and an insurance claim. I filled one out now in Lucy's name and forged her signature at the bottom where it said "authorization to release information." As a model, I used the Xerox copy of the withdrawal slip she'd tucked in her passbook. I'll admit my methods would be considered unorthodox, nay illegal, in the eyes of law-enforcement officers everywhere, but I reasoned that the information I was seeking would never actually be used in court, and therefore it couldn't matter *that* much how it was obtained.

I went into the clinic, noting gratefully the near-empty waiting room. I approached the counter and took out my wallet with my California Fidelity ID. I do occasional insurance investigations for CF in exchange for office space. They once made the mistake of issuing me a company identification card with my picture right on it that I've been flashing around quite shamelessly ever since.

I had a choice of three female clerks and, after a brief assessment, I made eye contact with the oldest of them. In places like this, the younger employees usually have no authority at all and are, thus, impossible to con. People without authority will often simply stand there, reciting the rules like mynah birds. Having no power, they also seem to take a vicious satisfaction in forcing others to comply.

The woman approached the counter on her side, looking at me expectantly. I showed my CF ID and made the form on the clipboard conspicuous, as though I had nothing to hide.

"Hi. My name is Kinsey Millhone," I said. "I wonder if you can give me some help. Your name is what?"

She seemed wary of the request, as though her name had magical powers that might be taken from her by force. "Lillian Vincent," she said reluctantly. "What sort of help did you need?"

"Lucy Ackerman has applied for some insurance benefits and we need verification of the claim. You'll want a copy of the release form for your files, of course."

I passed the forged paper to her and then busied myself with my clipboard as though it were all perfectly matter-of-fact.

She was instantly alert. "What is this?"

I gave her a look. "Oh, sorry. She's applying for maternity leave and we need her due date."

"Maternity leave?"

"Isn't she a patient here?"

Lillian Vincent looked at me. "Just a moment," she said, and moved away from the desk with the form in hand. She went to a file cabinet and extracted a chart, returning to the counter. She pushed it over to me. "The woman has had a tubal ligation," she said, her manner crisp.

I blinked, smiling slightly as though she were making a joke. "There must be some mistake."

"Lucy Ackerman must have made it then if she thinks she can pull this off." She opened the chart and tapped significantly at the August 2 date. "She was just in here Friday for a final checkup and a medical release. She's sterile."

I looked at the chart. Sure enough, that's what it said. I raised my eyebrows and then shook my head slightly. "God. Well. I guess I better have a copy of that."

"I should think so," the woman said and ran one off for me on the desktop dry copier. She placed it on the counter and watched as I tucked it onto my clipboard.

She said, "I don't know how they think they can get away with it."

"People love to cheat," I replied.

It was nearly noon by the time I got back to the travel agency next door to the place where Lucy Ackerman had worked. It didn't take any time at all to unearth the reservations she'd made two weeks before. Buenos Aires, first class on Pan Am. For one. She'd picked up the ticket Friday afternoon just before the agency closed for the weekend.

The travel agent rested his elbows on the counter and looked at me with interest, hoping to hear all the gory details, I'm sure. "I heard about that business next door," he said. He was young, maybe twenty-four, with a pug nose, auburn hair and a gap between his teeth. He'd make the perfect co-star on a wholesome family TV show.

"How'd she pay for the tickets?"

"Cash," he said. "I mean, who'd have thunk?"

"Did she say anything in particular at the time?"

"Not really. She seemed jazzed and we joked some about Montezuma's revenge and stuff like that. I knew she was married, and I was asking her all about who was keeping the kids and what her old man was going to do while she was gone. God, I never in a million *years* guessed she was pulling off a scam like that, you know?"

"Did you ask why she was going to Argentina by herself?"

"Well, yeah, and she said it was a surprise." He shrugged. "It didn't really make sense, but she was laughing like a kid, and I thought I just didn't get the joke."

I asked for a copy of the itinerary, such as it was. She had paid for a round-trip ticket, but there were no reservations coming back. Maybe she intended to cash in the return ticket once she got down there. I tucked the travel docs onto my clipboard along with the copy of her medical forms. Something about this whole deal had begun to chafe, but I couldn't figure out quite why.

"Thanks for your help," I said, heading toward the door.

"No problem. I guess the other guy didn't get it either," he remarked.

I paused, midstride, turning back. "Get what?"

"The joke. I heard 'em next door and they were fighting like cats and dogs. He was pissed."

"Really?" I asked. I stared at him. "What time was this?"

"Five-fifteen. Something like that. They were closed and so were we, but Dad wanted me to stick around for a while until the cleaning crew got here. He owns this place, which is how I got in the business myself. These new guys were starting and he wanted me to make sure they understood what to do."

"Are you going to be here for a while?"

"Sure."

"Good. The police may want to hear about this."

I went back into the escrow office with mental alarm bells clanging away like crazy. Both Barbara Hemdahl and Mrs. Merriman had opted to eat lunch in. Or maybe the cops had ordered them to stay where they were. The bookkeeper sat at her desk with a sandwich, apple, and a carton of milk neatly arranged in front of her, while Mrs. Merriman picked at something in a plastic container she must have brought in from a fast-food place.

"How's it going?" I asked.

Barbara Hemdahl spoke up from her side of the room. "The detectives went off for a search warrant so they can get in all the lockers back there, collecting evidence."

"Only one of 'em is locked," I pointed out.

She shrugged. "I guess they can't even peek without the paperwork."

Mrs. Merriman spoke up then, her expression tinged with guilt. "Actually, they asked the rest of us if we'd open our lockers voluntarily, so of course we did."

Mrs. Merriman and Barbara Hemdahl exchanged a look.

"And?"

Mrs. Merriman colored slightly. "There was an overnight case in Mr. Sotherland's locker, and I guess the things in it were hers."

"Is it still back there?"

"Well, yes, but they left a uniformed officer on guard so nobody'd walk off with it. They've got everything spread out on the copy machine."

I went through the rear of the office, peering into the storage room. I knew the guy on duty and he didn't object to my doing a visual survey of the items, as long as I didn't touch anything. The overnight case had been packed with all the personal belongings women like to keep on hand in case the rest of the luggage gets sent to Mexicali by mistake. I spotted a toothbrush and toothpaste, slippers, a filmy nightie, prescription drugs, hairbrush, extra eyeglasses in a case. Tucked under a change of underwear, I spotted a round plastic container, slightly convex, about the size of a compact.

Gavin Sotherland was still sitting at his desk when I stopped by his office. His skin tone was gray and his shirt was hanging out, big rings of sweat under each arm. He was smoking a cigarette with the air of a man who's quit the habit and has taken it up again under duress. A second uniformed officer was standing just inside the door to my right.

I leaned against the frame, but Gavin scarcely looked up.

I said, "You knew what she was doing, but you thought she'd take you with her when she left."

His smile was bitter. "Life is full of surprises," he said.

I was going to have to tell Robert Ackerman what I'd discovered, and I dreaded it. As a stalling manoeuver, just to demonstrate what a good girl I was, I drove over to the police station first and dropped off the data I'd collected, filling them in on the theory I'd come up with. They didn't exactly pin a medal on me, but they weren't as pissed off as I thought they'd be, given the number of civil codes I'd violated in the process. They were even moderately courteous, which is unusual in their treatment of me. Unfortunately, none of it took that long and before I knew it, I was standing at the Ackermans' front door again.

I rang the bell and waited, bad jokes running through my head. Well, there's good news and bad news, Robert. The good news is we've wrapped it up with hours to spare so you won't have to pay me the full three hundred dollars we agreed to. The bad news is your wife's a thief, she's probably dead, and we're just getting out a warrant now, because we think we know where the body's stashed.

The door opened and Robert was standing there with a finger to his lips. "The kids are down for their naps," he whispered.

I nodded elaborately, pantomiming my understanding, as though the silence he'd imposed required this special behavior on my part.

He motioned me in and together we tiptoed through the house and out to the backyard, where we continued to talk in low tones. I wasn't sure which bedroom the little rugrats slept in, and I didn't want to be responsible for waking them.

Half a day of playing papa to the boys had left Robert looking disheveled and sorely in need of relief.

"I didn't expect you back this soon," he whispered.

I found myself whispering too, feeling anxious at the sense of secrecy. It reminded me of grade school somehow: the smell of autumn hanging in the air, the two of us perched on the edge of the sandbox like little kids, conspiring. I didn't want to break his heart, but what was I to do?

"I think we've got it wrapped up," I said.

He looked at me for a moment, apparently guessing from my expression that the news wasn't good. "Is she okay?"

"We don't think so," I said. And then I told him what I'd learned, starting with the embezzlement and the relationship with Gavin, taking it right through to the quarrel the travel agent had heard. Robert was way ahead of me.

"She's dead, isn't she?"

"We don't know it for a fact, but we suspect as much."

He nodded, tears welling up. He wrapped his arms around his knees and propped his chin on his fists. He looked so young, I wanted to reach out and touch him. "She was really having an affair?" he asked plaintively.

"You must have suspected as much," I said. "You said she was restless and excited for months. Didn't that give you a clue?"

He shrugged one shoulder, using the sleeve of his T-shirt to dash at the tears trickling down his cheeks. 'I don't know," he said. "I guess."

"And then you stopped by the office Friday afternoon and found her getting ready to leave the country. That's when you killed her, isn't it?"

He froze, staring at me. At first, I thought he'd deny it, but maybe he realized there wasn't any point. He nodded mutely.

"And then you hired me to make it look good, right?"

He made a kind of squeaking sound in the back of his throat and sobbed once, his voice reduced to a whisper again. "She shouldn't have done it . . . betrayed us like that. We loved her so much . . ."

"Have you got the money here?"

He nodded, looking miserable. "I wasn't going to pay your fee out of that," he said incongruously. "We really did have a little fund so we could go to San Diego one day."

"I'm sorry things didn't work out," I said.

"I didn't do so bad, though, did I? I mean, I could have gotten away with it, don't you think?"

I'd been talking about the trip to the zoo. He thought I was referring to his murdering his wife. Talk about poor communication. God.

"Well, you nearly pulled it off," I said. Shit, I was sitting there trying to make the guy *feel* good.

He looked at me piteously, eyes red and flooded, his mouth trembling. "But where did I slip up? What did I do wrong?"

"You put her diaphragm in the overnight case you packed. You thought you'd shift suspicion onto Gavin Sotherland, but you didn't realize she'd had her tubes tied."

A momentary rage flashed through his eyes and then flickered out. I suspected that her voluntary sterilization was more insulting to him than the affair with her boss.

"Jesus, I don't know what she saw in him," he breathed. "He was such a pig."

"Well," I said, "if it's any comfort to you, she wasn't going to take *him* with her, either. She just wanted freedom, you know?"

He pulled out a handkerchief and blew his nose, trying to compose himself. He mopped his eyes, shivering with tension. "How can you prove it, though, without a body? Do you know where she is?"

"I think we do," I said softly. "The sandbox, Robert. Right under us."

He seemed to shrink. "Oh, God," he whispered, "Oh, God, don't turn me in. I'll give you the money, I don't give a damn. Just let me stay here with my kids. The little guys need me. I did it for them. I swear I did. You don't have to tell the cops, do you?"

I shook my head and opened my shirt collar, showing him the mike. "I don't have to tell a soul, I'm wired for sound," I said, and then I looked over toward the side yard.

For once, I was glad to see Lieutenant Dolan amble into view.

Questions for Discussion

1. Compare and contrast Kinsey Millhone with Sherlock Holmes and/or Philip Marlowe if you have read the stories featuring them in this anthology. Also, generally compare and contrast Millhone with other fictional detectives with whom you are familiar.

2. In this story both the detective and the victim are women. To what extent, if any, does this circumstance change the nature of this detective story?

3. How would you describe Millhone's interaction with the murderer at the end of the story? What is unusual about what they have to say to one another?

4. In your view, what is the purpose of the first two paragraphs of this story? What information do we find there?

Suggestions for Writing

1. One might argue that this story depicts a network of women—the detective and several informants—solving a crime involving men and solving it in spite of (or without the aid of) the police, chiefly men. Using this argument as a *working* thesis, develop an essay. You will likely alter and perhaps even disagree with this working thesis, and you may want to bring in the Holmes and Marlowe stories (by Conan Doyle and Chandler) as you develop your analysis.

2. Outline the plot of a detective story (not a novel!). Then write in your journal or notebook about conventions you had to consider (or dismiss), plot devices or characters you felt obligated to include, and any other elements the outline made you aware of.

3. The first-person point of view is extremely popular with detective writers. Why? Write a response to this question in your journal or notebook.

A Daughter's Heart

SUSAN   ENGBERG

T he early Saturday morning that Kathleen came home from college for spring vacation, she found her father polishing the brass doorknobs and plates in the front vestibule. "Oh, this is fine," Chris said. He set down the bottle of tarnish remover and the rag and embraced her heartily. He was tall, but only slightly taller than she, and his leanness surprised her; it seemed that before there had been more of him.

"Hello, hello," she exclaimed. She disentangled herself from duffel bag and backpack and hugged her father again, setting them both a little off balance. Her body was stronger than ever from a daily regime of running and exercises, but feelings and gestures were still hard for her to put together without awkwardness. This particular morning, life's potential seemed so vast as to be almost uncontainable; she felt she might fly apart from the inner press of it.

Most of the night on the train she had been awake, talking intensely with the young man who chanced to sit next to her, a divinity student, it turned out, who had had so many of the same questions as she that four hundred miles had seemed insubstantial. Was creation necessary to the Divine? they both wanted to know. Tom, his name had been. Kat had dozed off for only an hour, just before dawn, but she wasn't tired now, not at all. Here was her father, and the moment of reunion was alive with delight.

"May I have a turn?" asked her mother's amused, warm voice. Here were Tina and Carol, too, coming down the stairs, still in their bathrobes. They were all together in the familiar entrance hall, around them the papered walls, the polished banisters, the small desk at the foot of the stairs, the daylight. How clear it seemed! Kat hugged everyone vigorously. She had so much to tell them!

"I think we could have a real breakfast now," said Chris to Miriam. Kat saw the look they gave each other through the excited greetings of their daughters. It was like a note so low and steady she could barely make it out; she only knew it was there.

They had tea and toast and jam and scrambled eggs at the table beside the sunny kitchen window. Quick birds flew now and then to the feeder just outside the glass, built one fall years ago by Chris. The bright air was intermittently snow-flurried, as if with particles of precipitated light. Kat sighed with an upsurge of happiness. Plants flourished in the windows; the large room was fragrant with toast and the cookies her mother was in the midst of baking; the sunlight touched everything, their faces, their hands, the dishes of red and purple jams, the amber tea.

She poured out her life for them—philosophy, French, biology, literature, her runs along the river path, her room in the scholars' house, the repertory symphony, the new good food group, the meditation society, her ideas for travel next summer—and she must hear about them, all the news this minute, entire: Tina's dancing, Carol's editorship of the school paper, her mother's new job in the high school office, her father's counseling and current graduate courses. Hearing their voices was like being inside a familiar piece of music once more; like music their voices reassured her that life was meant to flow inside its forms, to enlarge but not break the heart. Oh, she wanted them to talk and talk until nothing was unsaid that should be said.

"But aren't you exhausted?" her mother finally asked. "Don't you want to nap this morning?"

"I couldn't possibly." Kat laughed, but then the telephone rang, and Carol jumped up; her father said he should be getting on with the paper he was writing; her mother took out the last sheet of cookies and turned off the oven; Tina stretched gracefully back in her chair, long hair loose, lovely slender face fifteen years old now, one small glisten of butter at the corner of her mouth. Breakfast was over.

Kat washed the dishes with her mother. She ran through the cold to the trash can and on her way back crumbled a heel of bread ceremoniously into the feeder. The brilliant fine snow seemed to be whirling out of nowhere, falling, then lifting, as if the center of gravity were everywhere at once. A run to the lake with her father was what she wanted today, just like their jogs of last summer, when they would be out and back in the mornings before anyone else was even awake.

Upstairs in her room Kat unpacked her bags, books mostly, a few bulky sweaters and pairs of blue jeans, a small gray heap of what her mother would probably refer to gently and reprovingly as untidy linen. She laid out the books on her desk and shoved most of the clothes back into the duffel bag in the corner. Clothes were merely an irritant. The largest of the sisters, Kat had simplified her wardrobe when she had gotten away from home to the few garments that felt comfortable on her body—jeans in the winter, gym shorts in the summer, and for concerts a long cotton skirt sewn by her mother.

"Is this all you've got?" Tom had asked her that morning as he had helped her hoist her duffel to her shoulder in the station, and she had been proud of the compactness of her load and the strength of her body. "Only what's necessary," she had said laughing, but then a moment later, turning into the thronging station, she had collided with a hurrying businessman and bumbled onto an upward-moving escalator, when what she really needed was to go down, toward the street and the commuter trains. Gliding back to the level where they had parted, she had looked for Tom, for a young man in a blue down jacket with sand-colored hair and a reddish beard, but he was gone. Streams of strangers had been crossing from one opening or another across the great dusky room, or loitering at the snack bars and newsstand; daylight had appeared only high up, among the grimy clerestories of the vaulted ceiling.

Now in her own bedroom at last, Kat pushed the curtains fully apart and gazed out onto the suburban neighborhood roofs. Her hands shook slightly. Minute tremors passed now and then through her body. The light shivered with snow, turned gray for an instant, and returned to brightness. Here she was. What was her father doing?

His study was at the end of the upstairs hallway; it was a porch, really, overlooking the street, and wherever there weren't windows, he had over the years built shelves for his accumulating books. There were also a large worktable and chair and several filing cabinets and a reading chair of comfortable depth, into which Kat herself had often retreated. This morning, however, the chairs were unused; her father stood at a window, a length of sash cord over his shoulder and various tools and pieces of molding strewn around him. Kat hung quietly in the doorway until he turned around. "Well, here's my girl," he said. "All unpacked?"

She nodded. "Would you like to take a run with me, Father? I've been doing four miles every day at school, faithfully."

"That's discipline!" he exclaimed approvingly. "If I hadn't et so much toast I'd say yes. Later I'll go. Come here a minute, will you, and snake this cord over the pulley to me? All right, that's it, almost . . . there, I've got it. Now hand me that counterweight, please. What a job! Every window in this house suddenly seems to have at least one broken cord."

"Do you always have to take the window apart like that?" asked Kat.

"No other way, tedious as it seems."

"Can't you hire someone to do it?"

Chris laughed shortly as he continued to work. "I can probably do it better and certainly cheaper. Now that army knife, please, and then we'll see if we can get this all back together."

Kat straddled the arm of the chair and handed him tools. Outside the window the reddish maple buds seemed swollen, tossed in the capricious air within the secure limits of their branches' pliancy, unflurried by the drafts of spinning snow. Kat squinted. All this brilliance was almost too much for eyes that were unrested. In summer this porch was a cool shaded bower, as timeless as green repetitive summer days that began and ended with the same sweet sounds, dove calls, other bird calls, coming out of nowhere. There was no way to measure the hours Kat had spent in this chair, enjoying the sweet latent fullness of immobility. It had been a way of putting herself in her father's care, even when he was absent.

"That should do it for this one," said Chris. "One down and eleven to go. Are you going to be my helper or what? You're looking a little tired around the edges."

She looked up at his face. "What's the paper you're writing now?"

"Forster," he said, "and a few of the ones after him who have tussled with India."

"Mmm." Kat's eyes scanned his orderly desk. He still kept his pencils and pens in the marmalade jar. Neat stacks of papers were as usual held in place by some of the glass paperweights he had inherited from his mother, Grandmother Birks, wife of Reverend Birks. The glass collection had been handed down when the manse was dismantled several years ago; for these milky green and pink and yellow plates and pitchers and bowls Chris had built special tiered shelves in front of the dining room windows. He had built the dictionary stand, too, on which the unabridged book now lay open, the printed columns appearing to Kat from where she sat blurred and yet enticingly orderly, all that knowledge so easily contained within two covers.

"Lexicography must be a blissful occupation," her father had said to her one day last summer.

"Then why don't you do it?" she had asked.

"I may, I may yet," he had answered.

Kat slid down into the easy chair and watched as her father gathered up his tools and moved to another window. He always seemed to be busy at something, she mused, but what was it that was strongest in his mind? His work over the past years had been as a guidance counselor in the schools. Now he was back in school himself, as enthusiastic over some of his courses as Kat was with her own.

"Well, what about India? Why do you say 'tussled'?" she demanded.

"Because of the perspective it affords us," he answered, "the extreme perspective, so that there's that much more to integrate."

Kat took a deep breath and plumped herself more heavily into the chair. "Father, may I ask you something?"

"Anything at all."

"Do you remember if you ever used to be afraid of your mind?"

"Afraid of my mind?"

"Yes." Kat found it difficult to continue. She leaned back her head and let her eyes rest on the tossing branches of the maple. Her body tightened as if a sudden electric current had jammed all its connections. "Yes, afraid of where it might take you," she finally said with a shaking voice.

"Of where it might take me?" Chris put down his screwdriver and came to sit near her in the straight desk chair. "Tell me what it feels like," he suggested. He had picked up one of the glass paperweights, and after holding it for a few moments he passed it down to Kat, a magnified pansy that she remembered clearly from her grandparents' house. Its familiar weight felt good in her hand. She rubbed her fingers over the surface.

"It sometimes seems as if my mind has a mind of its own," she said. "A lot of the time I can't concentrate. I daydream too much. I never know what I'm going to think next. Everything seems so much larger than it ever did before. I mean, there's no end to what I could be thinking, is there?

"The time I waste is just incredible!" she blurted out after a pause. "Sometimes I think I'm going to split apart."

"But you've been doing very well," her father protested. "Your record shows that you've put your mind on your work admirably well. You needn't worry about what happens to drift through when you relax a little. Your business is the direction that you're going, isn't it?"

"Yes, but it's as if I'm going in all directions at once. Oh, I don't know!" Kat pressed her eyes shut. She had cried many times with her father before, but today she didn't want to cry. She wanted to be clear. What she saw behind her eyes was herself, a lumbering, long-haired girl sprawled gracelessly in a chair. She opened her eyes and laughed.

"My dear girl," her father said, "if I could make sure of giving you one thing it would be the assurance that the confusions you feel are caused by the wonderful depth of the questions you're asking. You are blessed, my dear, and you have my blessing too, for whatever it may be worth."

Kat looked intently at her father's face. His beard had turned even grayer this year, and his thin face looked tired today. A small amount of money had come to him at the death of his parents, Kat knew, but she wasn't sure how much. An image came to her suddenly, perhaps touched off by the glass weight that she kept passing from one palm to another, of a pair of balance scales, of a pair of chairs like scales, containing her father and herself, she ponderously lower and he above, appearing erect, light, almost transparent in his love. The image troubled her. His provision for her over the years had been so gracious, so natural and seemly, as never to be disquieting. She had never before considered in such a concrete way the possible toll of her life on his, measure for measure of finite energy.

"I've taken up too much of your time!" she said. "You'll never get your paper written."

"It's not every day my girl comes home," said Chris firmly. He was smiling at her. "You make your mother and me very happy, you know, just by letting us watch you grow. We're grateful to you."

In an instant she was up and had her arms around his neck; she kissed him and breathed in his nearness, and in a rush she thought how her well-being still seemed to depend quite literally on his words; without his presence it might happen that she would fall, that she would become in the lapse of time a burden to herself.

The telephone rang a good deal during the day. Two boys and a girl, dressed identically in jeans and flannel shirts and hiking boots, came at noon to pick up Carol for an expedition to the city and stayed long enough, lounging bulkily in the living room, to eat an entire tray of fresh cookies. Kat had broken off from playing the piano and was on the couch, fiddling with a wooden puzzle, one of the many objects—books, magazines, records, games of skill, well-crafted puzzles, the large globe, the piano, the photograph albums—that were on hand to entice the interest. Young people loved this comfortable room; Kat's own friends had often come for a few minutes and stayed for hours. Some of them had told Miriam troubles and questions that would have been unspeakable in their own homes. They had never seemed to mind when Chris quoted poetry to them, or even scriptures. Around her parents they had often become, Kat had observed, more settled in their behavior than was usual and yet at the same time more lively. Gradually over the years she had become aware of what a gift it was her parents had, of what was there for others to receive.

"Fill the tray, will you please, Kathleen?" asked Miriam. She was sitting close by at her sewing machine in the dining room. The ironing board was set up, too, and pressed linens lay piled on the table. A dancing costume was being sewn for Tina, who sat on the floor at her mother's feet with a piece of hand sewing; now and then she artfully changed her posture, so as to give a stretching exercise to one set of muscles or another.

Kathleen plodded to the kitchen and back with the cookie tray. By now she was quite tired indeed but felt held in place by the charming rhythms of family life. She sank deeply into the couch and ate several more cookies. For a blank moment she couldn't even remember what it was she had been hoping to do that day. She knew it involved her father, who was upstairs now in his study, with the door shut.

Carol and her friends took another round of turns on the balance labyrinth box and then surged into the hallway, clumped about finding jackets, and called out high-spirited thanks and farewells. Doors banged. It was a run she had wanted, Kat remembered, out into the open with her father, down through neighborhood streets to the beach, up the shore to the breakwater point, and back again with the victory of exertion.

The sewing machine whirred and clicked beneath Miriam's intent profile. Tina put down her sewing. Her cheeks were flushed. Kat had been told at breakfast how serious the dancing was becoming for Tina now. Encouraged by her teachers, she traveled every Saturday down into the city for additional classes. Perhaps she would go straight from high school to dancing school, who knew? Chris had said. Now Tina rose neatly from the floor, stretched, and floated up the stairs. Kat could hear her stopping to knock at her father's door.

"Kathleen," said Miriam, "what is your clothes situation right now? Do you have anything that needs mending?"

"No. Thank you, Mother."

"What about your underwear, would you like to soak it a bit in some bleach?"

"No, everything is fine, thank you," said Kat as she watched her mother measuring and pinning the hem of the dancing skirt. From upstairs came the murmur of voices.

"And your new room at school?" asked Miriam, looking up at her daughter over the rims of her glasses. "It does sound as if you like it."

"It's lovely to be in a house," Kat agreed. She told her mother about the pine tree outside her window and how the small birds chirped among its branches at sunset; she told her about some of the other girls and about the washing machine in the basement and the cozy kitchen where they could fix snacks whenever they liked.

Miriam's hands efficiently continued with their task. One pin after another was pushed into the soft material; a needle was threaded; daughters were being clothed, readied. She sat almost in the doorway between the two rooms, framed, against a background of colored glass objects and windows of daylight. The spaces around the glass pieces seemed to Kat to pulse with brightness; something inside her was pulsing too, giddily. She rubbed her eyes and then leaned back and closed them. The house was quiet.

"I really do think you should nap for a while, Kathleen. Why don't you just lie down where you are? There's an afghan behind you."

"I don't want to nap."

Miriam laughed. "That's what you've been telling me all your life. Everything will still be here when you wake up, you know."

"Who says?" teased Kat.

Miriam laughed again. "I do," she answered. "I'll keep watch." She dipped her needle over and over into the cloth.

Kat took off her shoes and lay down on the couch. She would read magazines, she decided, while she was waiting for her father to come to a stopping point.

"Are you hungry?" asked Miriam.

"Nothing right now, thanks. I want to run with Father."

"You're going out this afternoon?"

"I guess so." Kat set a pile of magazines on her chest and opened one to an account of a tribal wedding, color photographs from far away in Africa. There were certain things the women did in preparation for the ceremony and certain things the men did. Everyone seemed to be having a good time.

Kat turned another page. "Mother, is Father happy to be back in school?"

"He seems to be."

"Wasn't he happy before?"

"He was dissatisfied. It has been very hard for him to make his job what he wants it to be."

"Will he be getting a new job?"

"We'll see."

"Do you really like your job?"

Miriam laughed. "At my age I'm pleased to have some work." She bit free her sewing thread and held up the finished skirt. "Now there," she said, "how does that look?"

"Very nice," said Kat. "You must be proud of Tina."

"Of course," answered Miriam, "and of you too."

"Don't you ever get tired of being our mother and doing all these things?"

"Sometimes."

"Do you ever want to quit?"

"Goodness, Kathleen!" her mother exclaimed. "This is what God has given me. I do what I can in the time that I have."

"But don't you ever wonder which thing to do next?"

"No, I don't," said Miriam, somewhat impatiently. "I leave that to your father. Why are you asking me all these questions? Do we seem unhappy to you?"

"No," said Kathleen with a sigh. "I was just wondering." She put the magazines away and rolled onto her side, facing her mother, her large-limbed, inert body bent to fit the couch. The comfort of this familiar place seemed to be draining from her whatever energy she had left. She watched her mother stand up and drape the dancing costume on a hanger. She heard the faint ticking of the iron as it began to warm up. Miriam shook out something and hung it over the ironing board. There were footsteps, her father's voice, something about light bulbs.

"Now?" asked Miriam. "You can do that later, can't you?"

"Might as well now," answered Chris.

Kat heard him thud down the basement stairs, and when he returned he was carrying a ladder.

"She's asleep?" he whispered to his wife.

Kat closed her eyes. She heard her parents kissing, then her father clattering up the stairs with the ladder. The ironing board creaked and knocked, like a boat against close moorings, and like a diver heady with gravity, her mind plunged down beneath the surface of the light.

Watch out for the guards, a dream voice babbled, but she couldn't stop to listen.

When she woke up, she was alone, but someone had covered her with the afghan. The laundry and sewing had been put away. A bowl of fruit rested on the table in a pool of its own reflection.

Kat began to cry, very suddenly and without knowing why, and then as suddenly stopped. She stood up unsteadily, alone, it seemed, in the downstairs of the house. No one was in the kitchen, but a piece of red beef stood on the stove ready to cook. The sunlight was on the other side of the house now. The faucet dripped.

A recent picture of her parents was among the many pinned to the bulletin board by the refrigerator. In it they were at a party of some sort, seated at a table with a number of other people, all of the same generation. Kathleen bent closer to peer at the photograph. Many of the other people were overweight and flushed. There were a number of brightly printed clownish garments. Some of the faces looked tan, as if they had traveled to other climates; most were laughing broadly at the camera. Chris and Miriam, however, sat slender and calm and a little pale, with sweet steady smiles and clear eyes.

Kat began to cry again. Through her tears she looked at the other pictures on the board and then she read through the family calendar for the month of April and the grocery list and a list in her father's handwriting of household chores. *To Do,* the paper was headed: *garden seeds, brass hardware, sweep basement, ceiling lights, window sashes, outdoor trim, clean gutters;* the list continued to the bottom of the page in several colors of ink, with some of the items crossed off.

When there was nothing left to examine, Kathleen blew her nose, took a drink of water, and wandered back through the house to the stairs. On her mother's desk in the hallway was a pile of bills, ready to be mailed. There was another photograph, in a frame, which Kat had seen so many times she didn't stop now to look but started on up the stairs. In that photograph three evidently happy children faced the camera, dressed for church, long brown hair braided. They stood on the steps of the house next door to the church where Grandfather and Grandmother Birks had lived for so many years. A lilac tree had bloomed beside that porch, Kat remembered, and it continued to bloom in the photograph on her mother's desk at the foot of the stairs.

The upper hallway was darkened because of the many closed doors. There were more photographs on these walls, her own graduation face among them, smiling freshly in the dimness, honor student, pride to her family, hope of the future. Kat glanced into this seamless, startling face and quickly turned away. From behind her she heard a murmur of voices in her parents' room and then everything was quiet.

Very quietly in her own room she pulled off her jeans and dressed in her running clothes. She tied back her hair without needing a mirror. She put on her shoes outside the house, sitting on the front steps beneath the maple tree and the windows of her father's study. And then she took off into the late afternoon. No snow remained in the sky or on the ground, but when she reached the lake a last ridge of winter ice rimmed the beach. Whitecaps were giving off sideways spume; deep in the distance, blue-gray water leveled off into purple. Kat ran strongly, without feeling tired. It would be clear tonight. Last night, too, it had been clear during the train ride. She and her new friend had watched the full moon rising. Above the flat agricultural land it had appeared slightly flattened, gigantic, orange, close, oriental. She had looked over her shoulder at it; she had felt it following her; she had seen herself on a plain of earth beneath stars, being called upon to take in the moon, to let herself be overtaken. Tom had watched it too. He had stopped talking, turned out the little reading light above their seat, and leaned across her to get a better view.

Her own heart had felt as full as the moon, enlarged with light, brimming over in waves like music, and yet still miraculously whole, still alive: to be going home! to be containing such a sight! to be rushing along without seeming to move beneath that presence in the sky! Kat took a deep breath and continued running at her own pace all the way to the breakwater point and home.

Questions for Discussion

1. One might argue that the conflict is revealed very gradually and subtly in this story, but how does the first paragraph at least suggest a conflict?

2. Describe this family. How do they react to the daughter's return?

3. At one point in the story, the daughter looks at her father's face, thinks of a small inheritance he has received, thinks of scales. What kind of awareness is she arriving at in this scene?

4. Why does the daughter wake up from her nap and begin to cry? In what ways has the story prepared us for that moment? In what ways has it not?

Suggestions for Writing

1. Write an essay in which you analyze the last scene, involving the daughter running and the moon, in relation to the rest of the story. What is significant about the imagery here? How does the last scene resolve the story? What change in the daughter does it show?

2. "This story is too nice. The daughter gets along great with everyone in her family. Her mother and father tell her how important she is. She is smart and attractive." Write a response to this devil's-advocate point of view in your notebook or journal. In what way is this "nice" story also about trouble?

3. Write a journal entry or a story about going home. You might use your own experience, or you might think of a time when a brother or a sister first came home from college.

Bess

JAYNE   ANNE   PHILLIPS

Y̶ou have to imagine: this was sixty, seventy, eighty years ago, more than the
lifetimes allotted most persons. We could see no other farms from our house, not
a habitation or the smoke of someone's chimney; we could not see the borders of
the road anymore but only the cover of snow, the white fields, and mountains
beyond. Winters frightened me, but it was summers I should have feared.
Summers, when the house was large and full, the work out-of-doors so it seemed
no work at all, everything done in company—summers all the men were home,
the farm was crowded, lively; it seemed nothing could go wrong then.

Our parents joked about their two families, first the six sons, one after the
other; then a few years later the four daughters, Warwick, and me. Another
daughter after the boy was a bad sign, Pa said; there were enough children. I was
the last, youngest of twelve Hampsons, and just thirteen months younger than
Warwick. Since we were born on each other's heels, Mam said, we would have
to raise each other.

The six elder brothers had all left home at sixteen to homestead somewhere
on the land, each going first to live with the brother established before him. They
worked mines or cut timber for money to start farms and had an eye for women
who were not delicate. Once each spring they were all back to plant, garden with
Pa, and the sisters talked amongst themselves about each one.

By late June the brothers had brought their families, each a wife and several
children. All the rooms in the big house were used, the guesthouse as well, swept
and cleaned. There was always enough space because each family lived in two big
rooms, one given to parents and youngest baby and the other left for older
children to sleep together, all fallen uncovered across a wide cob-stuffed
mattress. Within those houses were many children, fifteen, twenty, more. I am
speaking now of the summer I was twelve, the summer Warwick got sick and
everything changed.

He was nearly thirteen. We slept in the big house in our same room, which
was bay-windowed, very large and directly above the parlor, the huge oak tree
lifting so close to our window it was possible to climb out at night and sit hidden
on the branches. Adults on the porch were different from high up, the porch lit in
the dark and chairs creaking as the men leaned and rocked, murmuring, drinking
homemade beer kept cool in cellar crocks.

Late one night that summer, Warwick woke me, pinched my arms inside my
cotton shift, and held his hand across my mouth. He walked like a shadow in his
white nightclothes, motioning I should follow him to the window. Warwick was
quickly through and I was slower, my weight still on the sill as he settled himself,

then lifted me over when I grabbed a higher branch, my feet on his chest and shoulders. We climbed into the top branches that grew next the third floor of the house and sat cradled where three branches sloped; Warwick whispered not to move, stay behind the leaves in case they look. We were outside Claude's window, seeing into the dim room.

Claude was youngest of the older brothers and his wife was hugely with child, standing like a white column in the middle of the floor. Her white chemise hung wide round her like a tent and her sleeves were long and belled; she stood, both hands pressed to the small of her back, leaning as though to help the weight at her front. Then I saw Claude kneeling, darker than she because he wasn't wearing clothes. He touched her feet and I thought at first he was helping her take off her shoes, as I helped the young children in the evenings. But he had nothing in his hands and was lifting the thin chemise above her knees, higher to her thighs, then above her hips as she was twisting away but stopped and moved toward him, only holding the cloth bunched to conceal her belly. She pressed his head away from her, the chemise pulled to her waist in back and his one hand there trying to hold her. Then he backed her three steps to the foot of the bed and she half leaned, knees just bent; he knelt down again, his face almost at her feet and his mouth moving like he was biting her along her legs. She held him just away with her hands and he touched over and over the big globed belly, stroking it long and deeply like you would stroke a scared animal. Suddenly he stood quickly and turned her so her belly was against the heaped sheets. She grasped the bed frame with both hands so when he pulled her hips close she was bent prone forward from the waist; now her hands were occupied and he uncovered all of her, pushing the chemise to her shoulders and past her breasts in front; the filmy cloth hid her head and face, falling even off her shoulders so it hung halfway down her arms. She was all naked globes and curves, headless and wide-hipped with the swollen belly big and pale beneath her like a moon; standing that way she looked all dumb and animal like our white mare before she foaled. All this time she was whimpering, Claude looking at her. We saw him, he started to prod himself inside her very slow, tilting his head and listening . . . . I put my cool hands over my eyes then, hearing their sounds until Warwick pulled my arms down and made me look. Claude was tight behind her, pushing in and flinching like he couldn't get out of her, she bawled once. He let her go, stumbling; they staggered onto the bed, she lying on her back away from him with the bunched chemise in her mouth. He pulled her to him and took the cloth from her lips and wiped her face.

This was perhaps twenty minutes of a night in July 1900. I looked at Warwick as though for the first time. When he talked he was so close I could feel the words on my skin distinct from night breeze. "Are you glad you saw," he whispered, his face frightened.

He had been watching them from the tree for several weeks.

In old photographs of Coalton that July 4, the town looks scruffy and blurred. The blue of the sky is not shown in those black-and-white studies. Wooden sidewalks on the two main streets were broad and raised; that day people sat along them as on low benches, their feet in the road, waiting for the parade. We were all asked to stay still as a photographer took pictures of the whole scene from a nearby hillside. There was a prayer blessing the new century and the cornet band assembled. The parade was forming out of sight, by the river; Warwick and Pa had already driven out in the wagon to watch. It would be a big parade; we had word that local merchants had hired part of a circus traveling through Bellington. I ran up the hill to see if I could get a glimpse of them; Mam was calling me to come back and my shoes were blond to the ankles with dust. Below me the crowd began to cheer. The ribboned horses danced with fright and kicked, jerking reins looped over low branches of trees and shivering the leaves. From up the hill I saw dust raised in the woods and heard the crackling of what was crushed. There were five elephants; they came out from the trees along the road and the trainer sat on the massive harnessed head of the first. He sat in a sort of purple chair, swaying side to side with the lumbering swivel of the head. The trainer wore a red cap and jacket; he was dark and smooth on his face and held a boy close his waist. The boy was moving his arms at me and it was Warwick; I was running closer and the trainer beat with his staff on the shoulders of the elephant while the animal's snaky trunk, all alive, ripped small bushes. Warwick waved; I could see him and ran dodging the men until I was alongside. The earth was pounding and the animal was big like a breathing wall, its rough side crusted with dirt and straw. The skin hung loose, draped on the limbs like sacking crossed with many creases. The enormous creature worked, wheezing, and the motion of the lurching walk was like the swing of a colossal gate. Far, far up, I saw Warwick's face; I was yelling, yelling for them to stop, stop and take me up, but they kept on going. Just as the elephants passed, wind lifted the dust and ribbons and hats, the white of the summer skirts swung and billowed. The cheering was a great noise under the trees and birds flew up wild. Coalton was a sea of yellow dust, the flags snapping in that wind and banners strung between the buildings broken, flying.

Warwick got it in his head to walk a wire. Our Pa would not hear of such foolishness, so Warwick took out secretly to the creek every morning and practiced on the sly. He constructed a thickness of barn boards lengthwise on the ground, propped with nailed supports so he could walk along an edge. First three boards, then two, then one. He walked barefoot tensing his long toes and cradled a bamboo fishing pole in his arms for balance. I followed along silently when I saw him light out for the woods. Standing back a hundred feet from the creek bed, I saw through dense summer leaves my brother totter magically just above the groundline; thick ivy concealed the edges of the boards and made him appear a jerky magician. He still walked naked since the heat was fierce and his trousers too-large hand-me-downs that obstructed careful movement. He walked parallel to the creek and slipped often. Periodically he grew frustrated and jumped cursing into the muddy water. Creek bottom at that spot was soft mud and the water perhaps five feet deep; he floated belly-up like a seal and then crawled up the bank mud-streaked to start again. I stood in the leaves. He was tall and coltish then, dark from the sun on most of his body, long-muscled; his legs looked firm and strong and a bit too long for him, his buttocks were tight and white. It was not his nakedness that moved me to stay hidden, barely breathing lest he hear the snap of a twig and discover me—it was the way he touched the long yellow pole, first holding it close, then opening his arms gently as the pole rolled across his flat still wrists to his hands; another movement, higher, and the pole balanced like a visible thin line on the tips of his fingers. It vibrated as though quivering with a sound. Then he clasped it lightly and the pole turned horizontally with a half rotation; six, seven, eight quick flashes, turning hard and quick, whistle of air, snap of the light wood against his palms. Now the pole lifted, airborne a split second and suddenly standing, earthward end walking Warwick's palm. He moved, watching the sky and a wavering six feet of yellow needle. The earth stopped in just that moment, the trees still, Warwick moving, and then as the pole toppled in a smooth arc to water he followed in a sideways dive. While he was under, out of earshot and rapturous in the olive water, I ran quick and silent back to the house, through forest and vines to the clearing, the meadow, the fenced boundaries of the high-grown yard and the house, the barn where it was shady and cool and I could sit in the mow to remember his face and the yellow pole come to life. You had to look straight into the sun to see its airborne end and the sun was a blind white burn the pole could touch. Like Warwick was prodding the sun in secret, his whole body a prayer partly evil.

One day of course he saw me watching him, and knew in an instant I had watched him all along; by then he was actually walking a thick rope strung about six feet off the ground between two trees. For a week he'd walked only to a midpoint, as he could not rig the rope so it didn't sag and walking all the way across required balance on the upward slant. That day he did it; I believe he did it only that once, straight across. I made no sound but as he stood there poised above me his eyes fell upon my face; I had knelt in the forest cover and was watching as he himself had taught me to watch. Perhaps this explains his anger—I see still, again and again, Warwick jumping down from the rope, bending his knees to an impact as dust clouds his feet but losing no balance, no stride, leaping toward me at a run. His arms are still spread, hands palm-down as though for support in the air and then I hear rather than see him because I'm running, terrified— shouting his name in supplication through the woods as he follows, still coming after me wild with rage as I'd never seen anyone. Then I was nearly out of breath and just screaming, stumbling—

It's true I led him to the thicket, but I had no idea where I was going. We never went there, as it was near a rocky outcropping where copperheads bred, and not really a thicket at all but a small apple orchard gone diseased and long dead. The trees were oddly dwarfed and broken, and the ground cover thick with vines. Just as Warwick caught me I looked to see those rows of small dead trees; then we were fighting on the ground, rolling. I fought with him in earnest and scratched his eyes; already he was covered all over with small cuts from running through the briars. This partially explains how quickly he was poisoned but the acute nature of the infection was in his blood itself. Now he would be diagnosed severely allergic and given antibiotics; then we knew nothing of such medicines. The sick were still bled. In the week he was most ill, Warwick was bled twice daily, into a bowl. The doctor theorized, correctly, that the poison had worsened so as to render the patient's blood toxic.

Later Warwick told me, if only I'd stopped yelling—now that chase seems a comical as well as nightmarish picture; he was only a naked enraged boy. But the change I saw in his face, that moment he realized my presence, foretold everything. Whatever we did from then on was attempted escape from the fact of the future.

"Warwick? Warwick?"

In the narrow sun porch, which is all windows but for the house wall, he sleeps like a pupa, larva wrapped in a woven spit of gauze and never turning. His legs weeping in the loose bandages, he smells of clear fluid seeped from wounds. The seepage clear as tears, clear as sweat, but sticky on my hands when my own sweat never sticks but drips from my forehead onto his flat stomach where he says it stings like salt.

"Warwick. Mam says to turn you now."

Touching the wide gauze strips in the dark. His ankles propped on rolls of cloth so his legs air and the blisters scab after they break and weep. The loose gauze strips are damp when I unwrap them, just faintly damp; now we don't think he is going to die.

He says, "Are they all asleep inside?"

"Yes. Except Mam woke me."

"Can't you open the windows. Don't flies stop when there's dew?"

"Yes, but the mosquitoes. I can put the netting down but you'll have that dream again."

"Put it down but come inside, then I'll stay awake."

"You shouldn't, you should sleep."

Above him the net is a canopy strung on line, rolled up all the way round now and tied with cord like a bedroll. It floats above him in the dark like a cloud the shape of the bed. We keep it rolled up all the time now since the bandages are off his eyes; he says looking through it makes everyone a ghost and fools him into thinking he's still blind.

Now I stand on a chair to reach the knotted cords, find them by feel, then the netting falls all around him like a skirt.

"All right, Warwick, see me? I just have to unlatch the windows."

Throw the hooks and windows swing outward all along the sun-porch walls. The cool comes in, the lilac scent, and now I have to move everywhere in the dark because Mam says I can't use the lamp, have kerosene near the netting—

"I can see you better now," he says, from the bed.

I can tell the shadows, shapes of the bed, the medicine table, the chair beside him where I slept the first nights we moved him to the sun porch. Doctor said he'd never seen such a poison, Warwick's eyes swollen shut, his legs too big for pants, soles of his feet oozing in one straight seam like someone cut them with scissors. Mam with him day and night until her hands broke out and swelled; then it was only me, because I don't catch poison, wrapping him in bandages she cut and rolled wearing gloves.

"Let me get the rose water," I whisper.

Inside the tent he sits up to make room. I hold the bowl of rose water and the cloth, crawl in and it's like sitting low in high fields hidden away, except there isn't even sky, no opening at all.

"It's like a coffin, that's what," he'd said when he could talk.

"A coffin is long and thin," I told him, "with a lid."

"Mine has a ceiling," Warwick said.

Inside everything is clean and white and dry; every day we change the white bottom sheet and he isn't allowed any covers. He's sitting up—I still can't see him in the dark, even the netting looks black, so I find him, hand forehead nose throat.

"Can't you see me. There's a moon. I see you fine."

"Then you've turned into a bat. I'll see in a moment, it was light in the kitchen."

"Mam?"

"Mam and three lamps. She's rolling bandages this hour of the night. She doesn't sleep when you don't."

"I can't sleep."

"I know."

He only sleeps in daytime when he can hear people making noise. At night he wakes up in silence, in the narrow black room, in bandages in the tent. For a while when the doctor bled him he was too weak to yell for someone.

He says, "I won't need bandages much longer."

"A little longer," I tell him.

"I should be up walking. I wonder if I can walk, like before I wondered if I could see."

"Of course you can walk, you've only been in bed two weeks, and a few days before upstairs—"

"I don't remember when they moved me here, so don't it seem like I always been here."

Pa and two brothers and Mam moved him, all wearing gloves and their forearms wrapped in gauze I took off them later and burned in the wood stove.

"Isn't always. You had deep sleeps in the fever, you remember wrong." I start at his feet, which are nearly healed, with the sponge and the cool water. Water we took from the rain barrel and scented with torn roses, the petals pounded with a pestle and strained, since the doctor said not to use soap.

The worst week I bathed him at night so he wouldn't get terrified alone. He was delirious and didn't know when he slept or woke. When I touched him with the cloth he made such whispers, such inside sounds; they weren't even words but had a cadence like sentences. If he could feel this heat and the heat of his fever, blind as he was then in bandages, and tied, if he could still think, he'd think he was in hell. I poured the alcohol over him, and the water from the basin, I was bent close his face just when he stopped raving and I thought he had died. He said a word.

"Bessie," he said.

Bless me, I heard. I knelt with my mouth at his ear, in the sweat, in the horrible smell of the poison. "Warwick," I said. He was there, tentative and weak, a boy waking up after sleeping in the blackness three days. "Stay here, Warwick. Warwick."

I heard him say the word again, and it was my name, clearly.

"Bessie," he said.

So I answered him. "Yes, I'm here. Stay here."

Later he told me he slept a hundred years, swallowed in a vast black belly like Jonah, no time anymore, no sense but strange dreams without pictures. He thought he was dead, he said, and the moment he came back he spoke the only word he'd remembered in the dark.

Sixteen years later, when he did die, in the mine—did he say a word again, did he say that word? Trying to come back. The second time, I think he went like a streak. I had the color silver in my mind. A man from Coalton told us about the cave-in. The man rode out on a horse, a bay mare, and he galloped the mare straight across the fields to the porch instead of taking the road. I was sitting on the porch and saw him coming from a ways off. I stood up as he came closer; I knew the news was Warwick, and that whatever had happened was over. I had no words in my mind, just the color silver, everywhere. The fields looked silver too just then, the way the sun slanted. The grass was tall and the mare moved through it up to her chest, like a powerful swimmer. I did not call anyone else until the man arrived and told me, breathless, that Warwick and two others were trapped, probably suffocated, given up for dead. The man, a Mr. Forbes, was surprised at my composure. I simply nodded; the news came to me like an echo. I had not thought of that moment in years—the moment Warwick's fever broke and I heard him speak—but the moment returned in an instant. Having felt it once, that disappearance, even so long before, I was prepared. Memory does not work according to time. I was twelve years old, perceptive, impressionable, in love with Warwick as a brother and sister can be in love. I loved him then as one might love one's twin, without a thought. After that summer I understood too much. I don't mean I was ashamed; I was not. But no love is innocent once it has recognized its own existence.

At eighteen I went away to a finishing school in Lynchburg. The summer I came back, foolishly, I ran away west. I eloped partially because Warwick found fault with anyone who courted me, and made a case against him to Mam. The name of the man I left with is unimportant. I do not really remember his face. He was blond but otherwise he did resemble Warwick—in his movements, his walk, his way of speaking. All told, I was in his company eight weeks. We were traveling, staying in hotels. He'd told me he was in textiles but it seemed actually he gambled at cards and roulette. He had a sickness for the roulette wheel, and other sicknesses. I could not bear to stand beside him in the gambling parlors; I hated the noise and the smoke, the perfumes mingling, the clackings of the wheels like speeded-up clocks and everyone's eyes following numbers. Often I sat in a hotel room with a blur of noise coming through the floor, and imagined the vast space of the barn around me: dark air filling a gold oval, the tall beams, the bird sounds ghostly, like echoes. The hay, ragged heaps that spilled from the mow in pieces and fell apart.

The man who was briefly my husband left me in St. Louis. Warwick came for me; he made a long journey in order to take me home. A baby boy was born the following September. It was decided to keep my elopement and divorce, and the pregnancy itself, secret. Our doctor, a country man and friend of the family, helped us forge a birth certificate stating that Warwick was the baby's father. We invented a name for his mother, a name unknown in those parts, and told that she'd abandoned the baby to us. People lived so far from one another, in isolation, that such deceit was possible. My boy grew up believing I was his aunt and Warwick his father, but Warwick could not abide him. To him, the child was living reminder of my abasement, my betrayal in ever leaving the farm.

The funeral was held at the house. Men from the mine saw to it Warwick was laid out in Coalton, then they brought the box to the farm on a lumber wagon. The lid was kept shut. That was the practice then; if a man died in the mines his coffin was closed for services, nailed shut, even if the man was unmarked.

The day after Warwick's funeral, all the family was leaving back to their homesteads having seen each other in a confused picnic of food and talk and sorrowful conjecture. Half the sorrow was Warwick alive and half was Warwick dead. His dying would make an end of the farm. I would leave now for Bellington, where, in a year, I would meet another man. Mam and Pa would go to live with Claude and his wife. But it was more than losing the farm that puzzled and saddened everyone; no one knew who Warwick was, really. They said it was hard to believe he was inside the coffin, with the lid nailed shut that way. Touch the box, anywhere, with the flat of your hand, I told them. They did, and stopped that talk.

The box was thick pine boards, pale white wood; I felt I could fairly look through it like water into his face, like he was lying in a piece of water on top of the parlor table. Touching the nailed lid you felt first the cool slide of new wood on your palm, and a second later the depth—a heaviness inside like the box was so deep it went clear to the center of the earth, his body contained there like a big caged wind. Something inside, palpable as the different air before flash rains, with clouds blown and air clicking before the crack of downpour.

I treated the box as though it were living, as though it had to accustom itself to the strange air of the house, of the parlor, a room kept for weddings and death. The box was simply there on the table, long and pure like some deeply asleep, dangerous animal. The stiff damask draperies at the parlor windows looked as though they were about to move, gold tassels at the hems suspended and still.

The morning before the service most of the family had been in Coalton, seeing to what is done at a death. I had been alone in the house with the coffin churning what air there was to breathe. I had dressed in best clothes as though for a serious, bleak suitor. The room was just lighted with sunrise, window shades pulled halfway, their cracked sepia lit from behind. One locust began to shrill as I took a first step across the floor; somehow one had gotten into the room. The piercing, fast vibration was very loud in the still morning: suddenly I felt myself smaller, cramped as I bent over Warwick inside his white tent of netting, his whole body afloat below me on the narrow bed, his white shape in the loose bandages seeming to glow in dusk light while beyond the row of open windows hundreds of locusts sang a ferocious pattering. I could scarcely see the parlor anymore. My vision went black for a moment, not black but dark green, like the color of the dusk those July weeks years before.

Questions for Discussion

1. How does the first paragraph introduce a sense of trouble-to-come, of doom?

2. Describe Bess's and Warwick's reaction to seeing Claude and his wife make love. How does this experience shape the relationship between Bess and Warwick? How does "voyeurism" function throughout the story?

3. "After that summer I understood too much." What is your interpretation of what the narrator means by this sentence?

4. One might argue that "Bess" is made up of several remarkably vivid, self-contained scenes: spying on Claude and his wife; the parade; the wire-walking; Warwick's illness; Bess visiting his coffin. Visually and thematically, what connects these scenes?

Suggestions for Writing

1. Write an essay that analyzes the sister-brother relationship in "Bess." What is universal about the relationship? What is unusual about it? How does it shape Bess's life? To what extent is it an unhealthy relationship? A "normal" one?

2. What is the significance of the locust in the last scene of the story? Write a brief response to this question in your notebook.

3. Write a scene that captures a vivid moment from your childhood. Rather than telling us how you felt then or feel now about this memory, let the images "do the talking." Make the scene as vivid and suggestive as possible.

The Civil Engineer

MATT ELLISON

We lived in a faded olive-green house with pink screen doors on the edge of town. Sundays, after Messiah Lutheran was built, Mom and I went there. Dad stayed at the Roman Catholic church.

I didn't mind church so much after that. The pews had red velvet kneelers. Behind the altar were tall panes of glass which rose to a peak way over our heads. They looked out to the east the way Indians faced their teepees. At the inauguration service, Mom bent over and said in my ear, "Eric, that's Don Sederholm." She pointed out a lanky man who looked young enough to be my older brother. "He designed Messiah Lutheran. He's the architect."

Pastor Knudsen thanked him and asked him to come up in front of everyone. "He's not Lutheran," Mom whispered, "but he ought to be." He stood under the high windows of the altar. The morning sun spilled over his hair. He had a crewcut like me. I was surprised to see a wide smile shine across his face. You didn't applaud when you were in church but the mass of us smiled back. You couldn't look at him and not smile back.

That spring Mr. Sederholm took a house down the block from us on Sage Brush Drive. Saturday mornings he swam at the one outdoor pool in town. His blond arms hooked the aqua water as he did the crawl from one end to the other. "Mr. Sederholm swims a mile every time he comes," Mom said, carefully toweling her short hair long after we had gotten out. Mr. Sederholm climbed out of the pool. Sun sparkled on his wet skin. Mom shielded her eyes to him.

"Good heavens, Don, what will you do this winter?"

A serious look enveloped him. He ran his hand across his head.

"Good question, Mrs. Fallang," he said.

In the Friday *Tribune* Mom showed me an article. Mr. Sederholm had petitioned the city council to enclose the pool. He had submitted a free design and a feasibility study. A sketch showed how the structure could be built inexpensively with fiberglass. It said all that in the *Tribune*.

Next week, Mom and I sat in the car after we left the pool. Mr. Sederholm walked towards his old car. Mom took off her sunglasses. "Donny," she hailed with a little wave, "you should come to church more often."

"Thank you, Mrs. Fallang," he said. He folded his arms and rocked back on his heels. "You're probably right."

Mom backed up our car. As she looked over her bare shoulder she said to me, "He needs to socialize more. He's so young and just starting out, with a family to support. He needs to meet the right people."

I hated Spanish rice. It had baked-up peppers and other crusty things. Dad cleared his plate to the kitchen. "I hope for your sake you finish it," Mom said, rising. "Or your strawberry shortcake will just go to waste." For hours I watched the whipped cream soften down on the strawberries the way I liked, but I could not eat Spanish rice. By 9:00 I was still trying to gag down bites. Dad polished his dress boots in the living room.

"Evelyn, we can't afford a carport," he said. "I don't care if Carol Keisling and her husband can or not. We can't."

"But Lloyd, I think if we ask that architect, what's his name, Eric, that Don Sederholm, maybe he'll come up with a cheap design, then we could see."

I stood to clear my plate. The whipped cream had dissolved; the shortcake was soggy anyway.

"If we can't afford the carport, how do you figure we can afford an architect?"

"Maybe Donny would design something just so we could estimate."

"Donny?" Dad said.

"Eric, eat one more bite, then you can have your dessert," she said. "You'd think one bite would kill him."

"Donny?" Dad said.

"Mr. Sederholm. He's a friend of the church. I'm sure he wouldn't charge."

Sunday I was playing on one of the frames that thrust out of the ground into a pinnacle over Messiah Lutheran, the ones that held the wide panels of windows. The laminated beams were as thick as a chimney but rose higher than the county courthouse. At their base, my arms could just spread from one edge of the beam to the other. I leaned sideways on one foot hugging it while Mom chatted. Mr. Sederholm had to keep saying hello to all the women of the congregation as they left.

"I'm sure Eric wouldn't mind, would you, Eric?"

"No really, Evelyn, Hope and I can't afford a babysitter just to go out to the movies."

"But Eric would just love it and he doesn't need money for it, do you Eric?" Mom said.

"For Christ's sake, Evelyn," he said, then put a knuckle in the corner of his mouth. "What I mean is, well, no. I'm saying no. Really. Isn't tomorrow a school day for him?"

"I wouldn't mind," I said. I slid down the thick beam to his feet.

Two new saplings were planted in the Sederholms' front yard. In the backseat of an old red DeSoto parked in the driveway was an identical pair of little car seats. At the backdoor I stood under a newly built porch with a fiberglass skylight in the roof. The window frames were cut into alternating V's jutting from the wainscotting to the roof line.

"Come in, you must be Eric." Mrs. Sederholm's lips matched the color of their car. "Donny, Eric's here." She pulled on my arm so I would come in. "He's in the basement working."

When Mr. Sederholm came up he wrote the number of the restaurant and the Starlight drive-in and the times they would be at each on a bright yellow notepad on the kitchen table. He used a little plastic card to line up his printing. It looked like cuneiform writing on tablets I saw in our encyclopedia.

"If there's any problem at all I want you to call right away." He impressed this on me by clasping my shoulders with his hands. His hands were strong. "Have them page us at the drive-in if you have to."

Mrs. Sederholm brought me to see the twins. Two baby girls slept in two small beds, each with a guard rail. She showed me one then the other. "This is Sandra, we call her Sandy," she whispered. "This is Debby." She led me out. "We named them after movie stars."

Opening the screen door, Mr. Sederholm kissed Mrs. Sederholm. I didn't mind. She adjusted her earrings. They sparkled. They couldn't wait to go out.

"The girls shouldn't wake up at all," she said. "I hope you won't be bored."

There were LIFE magazines and Charlie Brown books everywhere, and a bowl of M&Ms in the middle of the coffee table.

"No," I said. "My folks don't go to movies. I like to get out."

It was dark. I didn't know where I was. I woke up when I heard a car pull up on the gravel. I thought they were my parents when they first came in. They made me take a ride home with Mr. Sederholm because it was so late. "It's only two blocks," I said, but I had to let him. Before I got out he gave me money. I knew not to take it because Mom had arranged it for free.

"Take it," he said. "And thanks. Hope and I had such a good time."

Mom got Mr. Sederholm to ride with us Saturdays to go swimming. He like to talk. We liked him. When it was raining he wouldn't let us go in till it stopped. We sat in the car.

"Your work is so elegant," Mom said. "I just wish Lloyd had your eye."

"It's mostly a matter of knowing what you really want."

"You make it sound so simple. I don't even have a clue, except I just have a feeling it's something like they did at that house, oh you know, what's their name, the Keisling's house."

"You mean a carport?" He smiled. "For a simple addition, it's an easy way to make your house look extravagant."

"That's just what I was hoping. Isn't that exciting? I'm sure Donny's ideas would be even more elegant, don't you think, Eric?"

Mr. Sederholm looked quickly out the window up at the sky which was clearing. The rain had not stopped.

"It's not that I wouldn't love to design something for you, Evelyn. It's just that we're trying to make it a policy . . . you know. Hope and I still have trouble just making ends meet. So I . . . that's the only problem, if you know what I mean.

"Oh I understand," Mom said. "Believe me, Lloyd and I hardly have a cent ourselves."

The Sederholms began to ask me over every Saturday. Mrs. Sederholm worried about the money but they went out anyway. She loved to go to the drive-in in the old DeSoto and he loved to take her. I liked to make myself at home. They talked like I was one of them.

"I feel bad about asking her for money to do their carport."

"But honey, you just can't keep doing so much free work any more."

"I know, but Evelyn, I mean Mrs. Fallang, thinks a few sketches would persuade her husband."

"Oh?"

Mrs. Sederholm opened the screen door for him.

"Hope, I made it clear to her."

"I hope you made it very clear. You know how you are."

"If you knew her you'd know how hard it is honey."

He stepped out. This time they didn't kiss.

"I do know her, Donny. She's very attractive, isn't she?"

"Hope, that's not what I meant."

"Eric, isn't that your mother I've seen, the pretty one?"

"I guess so," I said. "I'm just sort of used to her."

"Help yourself to anything, Eric," Mr. Sederholm said as the screen door closed. "It's just hard for me to say no, sweetheart, that's all it is."

Sometimes I put the girls to sleep. I told them about the bear who came over the mountain. To see what he could see. Donny had showed me how. Then I hung out. First I read the new LIFE magazine. Then if there wasn't a new Charlie Brown I re-read the old ones. I loved Charlie Brown. One night I discovered they had got cable TV. I always ate just half the M & M's. Once Sandy woke up. I felt scared when I heard her cry, but I didn't want them to have to come home. I wanted to stay. There was a bottle in the fridge. She liked it when I read her Charlie Brown while she sucked on her bottle. She fell back to sleep.

I discovered Donny's office in the basement. Hundreds of clear plastic triangles hung from the ceiling the way I used to hang my model planes. Something was plugged in that I figured out was an electric pencil sharpener. Big wads of green rubber turned out to be erasing pads. He had three big tables that raised in the back with knobs and had long ruler things hooked up to wires on either side. Wide sheets of crinkly white paper were stacked everywhere. I found a squat grey cabinet stacked with drawers wider than my bunkbed and as narrow as a yardstick. In the top drawer were compasses, ones that expanded and ones with arms that bent at angles and ones as large as the blackboard compasses at school. I found all kinds of mechanical pencils, colored inks and pens, and a cardboard box labeled 'templates' full of paper-thin metal sheets with cutouts and grooves.

The lower drawers were labeled "blueprints". They were full of large blue-type paper. I pulled them out. On the very top were the blueprints marked "FALLANG JOB." I looked at each one. I loved them. I loved the blue, I loved the print; man, I loved them all. All the straight lines, and the way some were heavy and some were soft and they all crossed together at so many different angles. Blueprints. I said the word. I held them so much my fingers colored. I licked the blue from my fingers. It didn't come off. I ran to the washroom. It didn't wash off. I didn't worry. Donny wouldn't mind.

So when Donny spread our carport plans before my parents for them to review, I already knew them by heart. I felt they were mine. I didn't care, I snuck in right beside him as he explained the details. I feasted my eyes. An architect not only drew the carport in careful straight lines from every side, but grew little trees and shrubs all over. Green grass and blossoming acaraganas. Windows that danced with light and a handsome abstract car parked inside, with a gleaming silver driveway leading up to it like it was Oz.

And that was just the beginning. Not only did these blueprints dazzle, but they had power. By the time summer school started, Adrian Doll came by with all his tools and a big truck full of lumber. Adrian Doll read Donny's blueprints. He cut wood. He read them again. After class I smelled him cutting wood and it smelled like lilacs. He cut with grace, and quickly. I sat in the clumps of sheetgrass back of our yard and drank water and watched the walls lift up. Day by day supports appeared, concrete was poured and smoothed, beams hoisted up out of nowhere. I saw these blueprints in action, they made things happen. Adrian Doll, who never said one word to me, who I was sure couldn't speak, he mounted these blueprints on the side of the house like a painting. He studied them and did what they said. When he left for the day he carefully rolled them like treasure maps into a blue cardboard tube. I circled until dark through the nearly completed construction just to smell the fresh cabinet wood, the musty wet odor of the joint compound, the flashy smell of the cement, the acrid electrical wiring. I pressed my hands on the wall to feel the prickly sensation of raw wood. I climbed on the panels to the airy open bays where windows would go. Things were really looking good; I saw wide horizons of the wheatfields opening up in every direction.

Blueprints. Every night I said it out loud because it was magic. It seared into my dreams. I dreamed I wore a white robe made of blueprints. I woke and thought: I am becoming an architect. Because an architect does blueprints. Donny does them. Donny is happy because he knows how to make blueprints. I will be like Donny.

Mom didn't have to say "Come on, Eric, you haven't got all day." I whisked through Saturday afternoon and the job jar so that, instead of complaining there was nothing to do, I swung open the hall closet doors. I jungle-gymmed my way up the shelves of sheets and towels to the one foot by two foot opening in the ceiling. I muscled my way through and began crawling through the attic. The attic was low and hot. Faded pink fiberglass lay in-between the rafters like a bank of murky sun-drenched clouds. Light burst in through two metal air vents one at either end. You had to walk carefully. One misstep and FOOM! your foot would go right through the sheetrock into Mom and Dad's bedroom. I would test it. I would put one foot squarely on the sheetrock and add my weight little by little, then I stopped.

The original blueprints to the whole house were left up in the attic. They were rolled up with rubber bands around them. I took them. I kept them under my bed. The elevation drawings of the front of our house were like a portrait. The big picture windows loomed out at me: I am the god of your house. Study me.

And when I found in our living room under a stack of newspapers a snap-closed box and opened it, I knew what it was. Donny used these kind of things, compasses, mechanical pencils, a silver canister for leads, rulers. He had left it. I held it. It was old. It was not his good set. I knew what to do. I took it. Donny would want me to. I didn't tell anyone. I wouldn't let them make me give it back.

Deep in my room I began to make drawings. First, a fiberglass porch. Then more plans. Daily I drew and redrew, measuring the basement, saying, we put the sofa over here and the TV here, and the laundry chute goes from my parents' floor and empties on this side of the basement, instead of into my room, because I can't stand the way their dirty clothes fall from the trap door in their closet into a heap in my room. I drew and drew. Each drawing showed me new possibilities. In the Sears and Monkey Ward summer editions I poured over the maps of America showing in colored contours which of their trees would grow where. I stretched the boundaries far enough north to include cherry trees and oaks. I knew from the new leaves on the Sederholm's saplings that many things would grow here that weren't supposed to. I saw how a wild rose hedge would create a living fence, so we could get a dog. We could have another baby, a girl, and let her play in the yard when it wasn't hot. I threw out the oil-stained 6 by 6 railroad ties Dad had drug home to terrace the bluff in back. I used flagstones and added Russian olives and juniper.

"Dad," I said "look what we should do." I showed him page after page. I had carefully lettered all the exact dimensions with the little ruler in the snap box.

"What do you think?"

"Pretty nice, Eric."

"No, I mean can we do it?"

"Do what?"

"This. Any of it. Can we?"

"Ask the boss," he said.

I did. I did ask the boss. I showed her all the same drawings.

"Mom. What do you think of my blueprints?"

"Eric, these aren't blueprints."

"I know, Mom, but just say they were. What do you think?"

She looked at the top one.

"How did you do these?"

"What do you mean?"

"I mean, what did you use to draw these? These lines? You don't know how to draw like that."

"Forget it," I said.

"Evelyn, what is this?" Dad stepped inside with a handful of letters.

"What is what?"

"This bill. It's from Don Sederholm."

"Oh?" Mom rose abruptly. "Let me see that."

"This bill is for 150 dollars. Goddammit, Evelyn, what is this?"

"Lloyd, don't talk to me like that. I have no idea what this is all about."

"He's charging us."

"Lloyd, I can't believe this any more than you. I most certainly never said we could afford this. Who does he think he is?"

"I'm going to see about this, I'll tell you that."

He picked up his boots and polish and stomped into the hall. I grabbed my blueprints and left for the door.

"Now where are you going," Mom said.

"Just out."

"Did you see today's paper?"

"No."

She showed me an article from the *Tribune*. It said the town council had rejected the plan for covering the pool. The town couldn't levy the money for several years.

"I don't think you should be going over to the Sederholm's so often."

"Why not?"

"Please don't. Is that clear?"

She went back to the paper.

At first I didn't understand. Then on Saturday I figured it out. I got up to go swimming but we weren't going. Donny didn't come by. I didn't get any call that night to babysit for the girls. It was obvious. He knew about the drafting set. He found out I had stolen it. That's why he was charging so much money. He was that mad.

I retreated to my room. I stopped going to summer school. Instead, I redesigned everything. Nothing could stop me. I mapped the city. I designed a college for our town. I drafted bus routes and airports for jets to come. I laid out a hospital so people wouldn't have to drive all the way to Billings. I made a relief map in plaster of the state using vacation maps from the glove compartment of our Dodge. I painted green where there were forests and sienna where there was rangeland; snow topped the peaks of the highest mountains and aqua filled all the major lakes and rivers. The largest towns weren't big enough. I used a large open space in the eastern plains to start a new city. I moved our town there. Streets were wide enough so there we wouldn't have traffic like I had seen in LIFE. There was one park for every neighborhood. Poor people from all the big cities which were having race riots were moved to this city. It became the fourth largest city in the country. The government was all architects. Everything was designed. Everyone went to a special camp in the Bob Marshall wilderness before they could live there. In the camp you learned to like work. You and other people worked together for fun, so when you went to the city you kept working with each other for fun only for real. Everybody began to be happy. They sent their kids to the camp in the mountains. The kids never learned to hate work. They were taught to pretend that work was play. So they played very hard. When they moved to our city they didn't know how to hate work. They only knew how to play. It became the first largest city in the country. Every one wanted to come. The architects who ruled would only allow more people when there were enough streets and houses and parks to fit them. They held elections to name the city.

Regular school was about to begin. I was almost done. Mom made me come out of my room to buy new clothes. I saw no more work had been done on our carport. The bays for the windows looking out onto the harvested wheatfields hung empty. There were no latches on the cabinet doors. Adrian Doll didn't come by. I asked what happened. Dad said if Adrian Doll could do carpentry so could he. He dragged 2 by 4's, four or five at a time, to the basement. He used a dull blue handsaw he had sitting around to cut those 2 by 4's lengthwise. It took him hours. I watched his muscles and they looked like horse legs rolling with sweat and patchy hair.

The carport sat. Mom had been parking the Dodge there and oil drips scarred the cement. Tire ruts gouged out the lawn leading to the carport. The grass died. There was no gleaming silver driveway. It looked like shit. Because we didn't use the blueprints. You needed blueprints.

Mom had a new chore. We painted and painted. Oil-base, putrid, nauseating enamels. We smeared them, flat pink, yellow, green over all the routed wood panels lining the outside of the carport. Inside blasted and sealed, lacquers and thinners. We cleaned out brushes with bacon fat, and greased it on our arms and legs to clean off. We finished and hated it. We had ruined it. Because we had no blueprints.

The swimming pool was closing. On our way there on the last week-end, Mom and I passed the Sederholms' house.
"Those trees won't last the winter," she pointed. "He of all people ought to know that."
Not the trees but something about the house seemed different. I turned my head as we drove by.
"It's too bad about him," she said.
"Why?" I asked.
"That he has to move."
"He does?"
"Oh, I thought you knew."
"Why?"
"He can't get work. Architecture just doesn't pay any more. He can't even make a living at it."

I sat alone in my room. Laundry from the ceiling fell on my head. I tore up my blueprints. They weren't blueprints. They were jerky lines on typewriter paper. They hadn't made anything happen. I was no architect. I couldn't read the marks on the architect rule. I couldn't make the cars abstract. I couldn't draw trees. I couldn't even do shading. I couldn't be like Donny Sederholm. And I couldn't make things happen. I was no architect. I was a thief. I stole instruments that weren't mine. That I didn't need. That I didn't even know how to use. From some one who did need them, who did know how to use them. Some one who needed them to make a living.

All evening I sat under the fiberglass skylight while some other babysitter watched their TV inside. Very late, I heard the DeSoto crackle the gravel of the driveway.

"Eric, for crying out loud. What's wrong?"

I handed Donny the small black drafting case. Despite all my plans, it was hard to say the words. I couldn't think of what to say first. I told him that all the leads were lost or broken. I was trying to tell him that I was going to buy more before they moved, but it turned out I couldn't tell him. I couldn't tell him because I burst out crying.

Later, I sat with them in the kitchen eating M&Ms.

"I was so sure I told her I was leaving it for Eric," Donny said.

"Maybe you did," Mrs. Sederholm said.

"I just didn't make myself clear again," he said.

Before I went home that night, I wanted to tell him how bad I felt that architecture didn't pay anymore, but I knew how bad he must already feel. I asked Mrs. Sederholm specially to drive me home. I told her.

"But, honey, Donny's doing fine," she said.

"I know, but I know he can't get any work, either."

"Eric, what are you talking about?" she said.

"I found out architecture doesn't pay anymore."

"Oh, really, since when?"

She stopped the car in front of my house.

"That's why you have to move, isn't it?" I said.

She looked at me funny.

"We're moving because Donny's going to be a partner in a larger firm."

"I thought you were broke."

"Well, we're not rolling in dough," she laughed.

"But Mom said. . . "

"Oh? What did she say?"

The old DeSoto idled in my front yard. My house looked better in the dark. A blue light from the street lamp fell in the car. I didn't have much to say. I held the drafting set tightly in my hands. Mrs. Sederholm took a deep breath.

"I do feel bad now that I didn't call you anymore to baby-sit. I'm sorry to say it, but I was pretty mad at your mother."

"Why?"

She patted her fingers on the back of the seat.

"Let's just say I didn't think your mother was very nice to us. Maybe Donny wasn't very nice to her either, I don't know. It's just too bad when you're mad at someone it has to affect people you like. Anyway, you better run home."

Half way up the lawn, I stopped as she turned the car around.

"Mrs. Sederholm?"

She rolled down her window.

"When are you moving?"

"About the end of the month, I guess. Why?"

"I was hoping you and Mr. Sederholm would have to go to the drive-in once before you left."

She smiled at me, sort of the way Donny smiled that day in Messiah Lutheran.

"Honey," she said, "I'll call you Saturday."

When I finished high school, I got into Carnegie-Mellon. I graduated in civil engineering. I work for the largest private construction firm in the country. I travel a lot and read a lot of blueprints. I'm not an architect but I get the job done.

Questions for Discussion

1. How would you characterize the narrator? What sort of young man is he?

2. Describe the town and the narrator's attitude toward it.

3. What ironies emerge from the relationships between Eric, the Sederholms, and Eric's parents?

4. Interpret the brief utopian daydream that the narrator has toward the end of the story. What does it add to the story?

Suggestions for Writing

1. Write an essay in which you discuss the blueprints as a symbol in this story. What do "blueprints" add to the characterization, themes, and overall comic tone of the story?

2. Write a journal entry about an adult occupation with which you were infatuated when you were young—just as Eric is fascinated with "blueprints" in this story.

Back Yard

ELSA   JOUBERT

I live on the periphery of an existence which I don't understand.

There are superficial points of contact: a few words to the petrol-pump attendant, good morning to the man who delivers the milk. And there is the Black woman who works in my house.

She is closer to me than a sister, and she is more intimately acquainted with my private life than a sister could ever be.

But I do not know her.

Even the name I call her is a functional title, chosen for practical reasons. It is not rooted in her identity as my name is in mine. I have not been informed of her real name; I would not be able to pronounce it.

She is my link with the unknown, a bridge I negotiate with great difficulty.

My home is my fortress. I know the walls that enclose every room. I move from room to room. I shift a chair, straighten a mirror against the wall, I pick flowers and arrange them in a vase. I caress my house with touch and glance.

But now she is here I am no longer alone.

She came to live in the room in the back yard and her territory is demarcated.

I planted large shrubs to screen the room from my view. In the evening when I close the window that faces her room, I hear voices behind the shrubs, or a rustling sound as though someone has come out of the room to urinate in the shrubbery.

I don't say anything and I don't look out. I draw the curtains closed.

But when morning comes I open the curtains again.

The life in that room in my back yard is bound up with my life. Without that life, I'm like a body that casts no shadow; my property and my house feel deserted; I wander aimlessly; the flowers droop in their vases and the mirrors on my walls reflect blurred images.

I seek the life in the room in my back yard so I may know it. With the fingers of the blind, I grasp the door which is so firmly shut against me. I cannot see.

For God's sake, just walk in and have a look, my husband tells me. Why the nerves?

He goes to work and I stay behind.

My children go to school and I stay behind.

My visitors leave and I stay behind.

I and the life of the Black woman in my back yard.

It is not a solitary life, but one of multiplicity. This is the first thing I have to learn. Her life is involved with another, and this second life with others, and I, through them, with an amorphous body that has entered my life. Most of the time the room in my back yard surges with the strangers who are entertained there. It seems as though the walls are flexible, they've lost their rigidity and can expand and contract like a canvas bag.

And these strangers have a radar which I don't understand. It warns them of my approach along the nearby garden path, the approach of danger. The noise level drops, the bulging contracts, the buzz, the drone of conversation fades into silence. The walls shrink back into themselves, become solid, the room just a room and the door firmly shut.

If I walked on, if I came along the cement path, turned the handle and opened the door, what would I see? Perhaps a man on the bed, a woman on the chair, a child on the floor, a second child hiding among the clothes behind the door, and another man on a bench at the window—the fat man whom I know.

And they'd gaze at me as if they were carved out of wood.

And the mugs of coffee, or the bowls of cold congealed food, or the children's helpings served on torn-off bits of paper, would also freeze; disappearing in the silence. Becoming nothing before my eyes.

And I would see nothing. I would look at the ceiling and say: Oh, isn't Flora here? Or Emma, or Agnes, or Evangelina. That's what I would say if I went in.

But I don't go in. I walk past the closed wooden door, past the silent fixed walls of the small rectangular room. I tread on a dry twig on the path to make quite sure they're aware of my presence, and turn the hose-pipe on to the fruit trees in this dry patch of back garden. Then, talking to myself, I walk away.

If I was to wait, if I was to wait concealed, I would see the strangers start moving again, and then, as if my coming was a danger signal, begin to leave the room. The black figures would slip away across the back garden behind the shrubs. Those who had more confidence and carried briefcases or wore hats would pass through the side gate back to the freedom of the streets.

As I water the flowers in the no man's land of my front garden, I greet the ones with briefcases and they return the greeting.

And sometimes, in the intimacy of my back garden, I greet the ones who slip away, and they too return the greeting. And they learn to trust and they dare to come from their dark world into mine and say with eyes blinking in the bright light, Help me.

The fat one whom I know stands at the back door.

'Oh, madam . . .' His eyes are shiny, round and empty as marbles. 'Oh, madam.' He digs in his ear with a finger. He lowers his hands and produces his pass from a trouser pocket.

He shows it to me, childlike in his pleasure.

'It's there. Honestly, it's there.' His finger goes back to digging in his ear. 'But it's wrong.'

The pass is tattered. The stamps are not in order. Flora—he's her brother—has been battling to get him to put it right but he won't listen to her.

'They must just catch him and take him away to Bethal,' says Flora. 'He can plant potatoes there. They hit you with the spade-handle there. That'll teach him a lesson.'

He laughs at the idea he should be hit with a spade-handle. His thick lips draw back to show the pink flesh within and the yellow roots of his large teeth. He laughs and shakes his head at himself and his own stupidity.

'But I went there, madam, like Flora said I should. To the permit office, as she said.'

'And I told you to ask for Tebe because he'd help you,' said Flora.

He laughed again and had another dig in his ear. 'I forgot the name, madam, and I asked for Febe, and they told me they didn't know anyone by that name.'

'He's a *mampara*,' said Flora. 'He just stood there at the office. Wasted my bus-fare.'

I took the pass and paged through it. I read: Work permit and new pass 23 September.

It was now April of the following year. I felt the desperation rise up in me. 'Can't you do what it says here? He's been at home for six months. And here it says you should have come to get a new pass and permit on the twenty-third of September.'

Now Flora too was scratching her ear. She opened her mouth to speak and then shut it again.

He began to laugh again, about his own stupidity, and he mumbled: 'Oh, madam . . .' But I'd seen the darkness fill his eyes and I felt the chill of fear.

It was only then that I realized: like Flora, he could not read.

The old man too had drawn a letter from his pocket. The old man who'd found his way here from the location at dead of night or in the small hours of the morning. The old man who'd used his knobkerrie to heave himself on to his feet from the straight-backed chair in a dark corner of the room in my back yard. The old man who'd steadied himself with a hand on the concrete wall as he climbed laboriously up the steps to my back door.

He didn't say much. He took off his hat as though he was preparing to pray.

'You talk,' he said to Flora.

His eyelids were sunken, he was thin and bowed, his hair was damp, flattened by his hat. There were threads of white in his beard and his mouth was small and meek.

'He is my uncle,' Flora told me.

The old man held his knobkerrie under his arm so he could use both hands to unfold the sheet of cheap thin blue paper. He gave it to me so I could read what was written on it in pencil.

'We have had it read,' said Flora. 'I can tell the madam what it says. It's from his grandchild. Her father and mother are both dead. But her father wasn't from the Cape and when he died, his brother took the girl back to the country to grow up. But now she wants to come back to her grandpa and get work in town. It's dry in the country, she's hungry and there's no work. The old man has been sending her money but he's old now and he can't carry on.'

'Does she have the right papers?'

The old man produced another document. It was a school form, much folded, yellow with age, bearing a faded stamp. I could just make out the name of the school and Patience Makebe, Standard One, but it must have been a while ago and the date was so faded I couldn't decipher it.

I gave them a lift to the permit office.

Flora wanted to find Tebe so she pushed through the queue, obliging us to follow. They let us through because I was there. We came to Tebe's work station. He was a small, lightly built Black man in a suit with a white shirt, a tie, and spectacles. I wondered if he was related to Flora, or perhaps a boy friend, because he stood up the minute he saw her and led us through an even longer queue, through waiting-rooms where people sat as though they'd been there for centuries, patiently, purposefully, organically part of their benches. Some looked at us, others had their eyes closed as though they were asleep.

The White official was tired and irritable. Tebe, bringing yet another bunch of people, made him angry and Flora, who kept interrupting, added to the aggravation. He took out a handkerchief and mopped his brow. There was a wide gap between his desk and the bench against the wall where we sat.

Flora was hardly seated before she stood up again, talking.

'Sit down,' he shouted at her. 'Keep quiet.'

There was an immeasurable chasm between the large empty wooden desk he sat behind and our bench against the wall. He drew a piece of paper towards him and picked up his pen, waiting.

Flora pulled the letter out of her bodice, unfolded it and put it on the desk in front of him. I tried to say something but the official shut me up.

'Does she have papers?'

The old man took out the yellowed form he'd folded up and put back in his pocket.

The official read the form. He read the letter.

He tapped the name on the letter and the name on the form. Nhlanda Rhoda was mentioned in the letter, Patience on the form . . . which one were we talking about?

The old man spoke to Flora in their language, quietly as though he dared not speak over the desk. When he looked up again, his eyes were expressionless, as though any certainty or optimism he might have entertained had waned.

'The teacher was a nun and she gave her another name,' Flora explained.

'And these are all the papers she has, these . . .' Exasperated, he didn't even finish his own sentence. But he took pity on the old man. 'Look, she can't come here without papers. Hasn't she got anything else? A birth certificate?'

The old man shook his head, he didn't know. He reached for the yellow rectangle of paper on the desk.

'This isn't sufficient,' said the official. 'This . . . this Patience. How do I know it's the same girl?' He indicated the letter. 'And even if I knew'—he pointed to the stamp—'when was she there? Where was it? The school probably doesn't exist any longer.' Then, at the end of his tether: 'How am I supposed to know who you want the form for, or even that Nhlanda Rhoda ever even existed?'

'We'd better go,' I said.

We pushed our way outside through the people. My hands were sweating and the smell of people made me claustrophobic. The steering wheel was stiff under my hands, the car was stuffy and smelly. The old man didn't come back with us. He didn't get into the car, simply took off his hat and bowed slightly as if in prayer.

'I'll just send some more money for food,' he said.

I nodded. 'Yes. Send some more money for food.'

There's a mysterious radar link between my back yard and the back yards all around mine.

There's a network running right through town, invisible lines joining one back yard room to another, joining suburbs, and joining the suburbs to the Black locations. Like a spiderweb—invisible until the light catches it, or dust collects on it, or smoke coats it with soot—these lines of communication only became visible in a time of crisis.

Rosy drank.

Rosy, who was relieving Flora. Rosy, who wore her dresses long and sometimes asked to go early so she could attend a church service. Sometimes she sang right through Saturday night.

But now and then I'd hear something falling in the kitchen and when I got to her I could see something had snapped in Rosy. Her headscarf would be awry, and when she stirred the saucepan, the food would splash over the stove, because her movements had lost their co-ordination.

Then I'd send her to her room to sleep it off and I'd finish the supper myself.

That was when the weakness was containable, bearable, overlookable.

But when she finished off everything that was strong and piquant in the house (we'd taken to locking up the liquor much earlier), when Rosy grew silent and preoccupied, then we knew something was brewing, just as you know bad weather's on the way when the wind drops, or mugginess rises from the tarmac or the perspective of trees and buildings in the distance is flattened.

Then all we could do was wait.

And one morning Rosy was no longer there. She was gone. She had disappeared somewhere in the limbo which the Black locations seemed to us.

An uncomfortable feeling hung over our house, like a cloud. Contact with the darkness, the unknown. A stranger had entered our world of whitewashed walls, swags of red bougainvillaea and shiny verandahs; of laid tables and a warming oven full of dishes ready to be served; of freshly made-up beds and a bale of pressed laundry to be put away.

Was the stranger fear, guilt, regret, or love?

We loved Rosy. We shared our food and our clothes with her. We told her of our hopes and fears.

Why then the stranger who came to live with us in our house when Rosy was off somewhere in her own limbo?

I did the housework. I chatted with the milkman. I bought a new vegetable knife. I was busy.

Then being busy made me restless.

And I became aware of the radar that was operating from my empty back yard to the back yards nearby, to far-flung neighbourhoods, over the mountain, as far as the workshops in the industrial area, delivery vans, garage allotments to the unknown darkness of the men's hostels in the Black locations.

And late, after nine on the third night after she'd gone, there was a knock at the door. A young Black man asking, cap in hand, 'Madam, is Rosy back?'

The phone rings . . . From whose house? While which White woman is out—just nipped down to the shops, or to get the post? 'This is Agnes, madam. Is Rosy back?'

Or a bleep bleep in the telephone receiver and the sound of a coin being inserted, but the receiver clicks and I hear nothing. And there it is again: bleep bleep, another coin in the slot, the call comes through and a gruff male voice asks: 'Madam, I speaking Rosy? Rosy not there?' And then: 'Madam, I find out. I let you know.'

Rosy is part of a peculiar amorphous body that feels her absence, that feels somewhere in its intuitive radar: a line is down, someone somewhere in the network has fallen.

And after another two or three days another Black woman came and knocked at the door. It was late—after ten. Where had she come from? Which kitchen had she to clean first? At which bus stop had she stood and waited? She had a young girl with her.

'She'll help you, madam, until Rosy is back.'

And this young girl, hardly more than a child, who I didn't know, knew me, knew the way round the back to the room in the back yard, and she knew which loose brick in the wall to look under for the key to Rosy's room, and the Black woman said: 'It's all right, madam, you can let her stay in the room.' Rosy's uniforms didn't fit her too well, straining to remain buttoned over her young bosom. I gave her a T-shirt to wear under the uniform. The next day she set to work at the kitchen sink with the confidence of experience. The strong black hands wrung out the tea towels and polished the stainless steel, and once again I saw that special dry shine only a Black hand can get on my sink.

Rosy reappeared after a week. She was brought by the same strange Black woman. They came in the evening and Rosy hid behind her as they stood in the shadow on the verandah. 'She's not completely fit yet, madam, but she's all right. She'll be able to work tomorrow.'

Rosy was embarrassed, her face was ashen and she'd lost weight. The dress I knew so well looked as though it was hanging on a scarecrow. Even her shoulders seemed narrower.

Later when I had a cup of tea in the kitchen with the Black woman, she told me what had happened.

'We looked for him, madam. He's got his problems too and sometimes they get on top of him.'

I know about Rosy's problems. I gave her school fees for her youngest child in Cradock, the child who'd been living with foster parents from birth. We'd sent food because they'd written that she was thin and wouldn't eat. I told Rosy not to distress herself over the son in Port Elizabeth who wouldn't work. She should stop sending money to pay his fines and bail him out of prison. They wrote to tell her he was to be declared a habitual criminal if he was involved in another stabbing. Couldn't his father lend a hand? I suggested—but she hadn't seen the father for ages and the son was thirteen the last time he'd seen him. He was the child of her youth, and, because she was working, he too had grown up with foster parents. I told her: What can you do? Upsetting yourself doesn't achieve anything.

Until last week when the letter came and I opened it for her because her hands were shaking too much and it said: her son had killed and was to hang.

'It's a good thing we found her, madam,' the Black woman told me. 'They're looking for her at the office. The papers came saying she had to come and see her son one last time before he hangs.

'Madam, I think she's afraid to see this child who is to hang.'

The woman sitting on the edge of the bed in the dimness of the room in my back yard is still a child herself. A child who looks up at me with no fear or self-consciousness in her eyes, but a radiant composure, an unshakeable sense of being. As my eyes grow accustomed to the dimness and she turns to me, I see the great swollen belly resting on her knees.

She wears an overall of Flora's or Rosy's or Agnes's. The shoulders are too wide and drop almost to her elbows. An adult garment on a child's body.

A child's body? She clasps her stomach with her hands. The hands hold the stomach protectively as if they have a primal knowledge which the child does not have yet.

The delicate hands of a child are the hands of the ancients.

Her face is thin and angular. She is wasting away while her baby grows. What source did she draw on for strength to let the baby grow?

Flora had called me from the house to the room. 'Madam, Nhlanda has come back.'

'Nhlanda?'

'Patience . . . she's going to have a baby. The man of the house is dead and the widow doesn't want to look after her so they sent Nhlanda to us.'

It was oddly poetic: the girl who came from nowhere with no papers, and the baby she would bear.

There was an order in the chaos. There was a light in this darkness, and I allowed the brightness of the dark unknown to flood over me.

The advent of the child she would bear was poetic, in spite of the problems she brought with her—where would she be confined, what clinic would accept her at this late stage, which hospital would admit her without papers, who would support the child, buy its clothes?

Even my mother-in-law, who was strict about this kind of thing and didn't believe in 'spoiling' people, volunteered to provide the nappies.

My one daughter crocheted a matinée jacket and my youngest found a doll she could spare.

Was there ever a child so lacking in papers? Was there ever a life so guilelessly conceived. To be born and set on its way in the world?

We'd hide the baby if they came looking for it.

We'd comfort him with milk if he screamed. We would wrap him up if he was cold and we'd wash him when he was dirty.

Was there ever a baby who would come into the world so uninvited?

We went away for a week's holiday and on our return we found the back yard was deserted again. The cat sat on the high back garden wall and watched us with wild hungry eyes.

The room in the back yard looked strangely small, as though it stood alone on an open space, four white walls and a sloping roof and three steps leading up to the door. It stood abandoned and whitewashed and lonely. The door was tightly shut, the windows too, and the curtains were drawn. Two freshly laundered uniforms and two aprons hung on the line. The pegs had shifted up in the wind so they were bundled wretchedly together against the pole.

The key to the room lay on the table in the back yard. That was all. When we unlocked the door we found nothing but a stuffy smell and the neatly folded bedding.

There was a layer of dust on the newspaper lining the drawer in the small chest. It looked as though it had lain there undisturbed for a long long time—even years. When I drew the curtains, the rings dragged as though they'd rusted from years of hanging in one position. The dark burnt patch on the dressing table suggested someone had used a small stove there.

And the servants from next door came to tell us that they'd packed their things and left with the bundles and boxes on their heads one night. Flora, Nhlanda, a strange man, and a boy.

The room in my back yard is empty.

Another Black woman is moving in this afternoon.
I live on the periphery of an existence I do not understand.

Translated by Catherine Knox

Questions for Discussion

1. "I live on the periphery of an existence which I don't understand." This sentence begins and ends the story. Explain your sense of what the narrator means by it.

2. How would you characterize the narrator's relationship and attitude toward the black women who work for her?

3. In what ways is the narrator both powerful and powerless in relation to the other men and women in the story?

4. How would you describe the tone of this story? What emotions (on the part of the narrator) does the tone convey?

5. From this story what did you learn about the social and political situation in South Africa?

Suggestions for Writing

1. Write an essay about the last section of the story, which features the young pregnant woman. What larger issues might this woman and her situation represent, even symbolize? What is the narrator's relationship to her? Why did the young woman (and the others) leave?

2. Does the narrator understand more than she pretends to? Write a response to this question in your journal or notebook.

3. Write an essay in which you compare and contrast this story with Njabulo S. Ndebele's story "Death of a Son." Specifically, compare and contrast the two women narrators.

The Stolen Party

LILIANA HEKER

As soon as she arrived she went straight to the kitchen to see if the monkey was there. It was: what a relief! She wouldn't have liked to admit that her mother had been right. *Monkeys at a birthday?* her mother had sneered. *Get away with you, believing any nonsense you're told!* She was cross, but not because of the monkey, the girl thought; it's just because of the party.

"I don't like you going," she told her. "It's a rich people's party."

"Rich people go to Heaven too," said the girl, who studied religion at school.

"Get away with Heaven," said the mother. "The problem with you, young lady, is that you like to fart higher than your ass."

The girl didn't approve of the way her mother spoke. She was barely nine, and one of the best in her class.

"I'm going because I've been invited," she said. "And I've been invited because Luciana is my friend. So there."

"Ah yes, your friend," her mother grumbled. She paused. "Listen, Rosaura," she said at last. "That one's not your friend. You know what you are to them? The maid's daughter, that's what."

Rosaura blinked hard: she wasn't going to cry. Then she yelled: "Shut up! You know nothing about being friends!"

Every afternoon she used to go to Luciana's house and they would both finish their homework while Rosaura's mother did the cleaning. They had their tea in the kitchen and they told each other secrets. Rosaura loved everything in the big house, and she also loved the people who lived there.

"I'm going because it will be the most lovely party in the whole world, Luciana told me it would. There will be a magician, and he will bring a monkey and everything."

The mother swung around to take a good look at her child, and pompously put her hands on her hips.

"Monkeys at a birthday?" she said. "Get away with you, believing any nonsense you're told!"

Rosaura was deeply offended. She thought it unfair of her mother to accuse other people of being liars simply because they were rich. Rosaura too wanted to be rich, of course. If one day she managed to live in a beautiful palace, would her mother stop loving her? She felt very sad. She wanted to go to that party more than anything else in the world.

"I'll die if I don't go," she whispered, almost without moving her lips.

And she wasn't sure whether she had been heard, but on the morning of the party she discovered that her mother had starched her Christmas dress. And in the afternoon, after washing her hair, her mother rinsed it in apple vinegar so that it would be all nice and shiny. Before going out, Rosaura admired herself in the mirror, with her white dress and glossy hair, and thought she looked terribly pretty.

Señora Ines also seemed to notice. As soon as she saw her, she said:

"How lovely you look today, Rosaura."

Rosaura gave her starched skirt a slight toss with her hands and walked into the party with a firm step. She said hello to Luciana and asked about the monkey. Luciana put on a secretive look and whispered into Rosaura's ear: "He's in the kitchen. But don't tell anyone, because it's a surprise."

Rosaura wanted to make sure. Carefully she entered the kitchen and there she saw it: deep in thought, inside its cage. It looked so funny that the girl stood there for a while, watching it, and later, every so often, she would slip out of the party unseen and go and admire it. Rosaura was the only one allowed into the kitchen. Señora Ines had said: "You yes, but not the others, they're much too boisterous, they might break something." Rosaura had never broken anything. She even managed the jug of orange juice, carrying it from the kitchen into the dining room. She held it carefully and didn't spill a single drop. And Señora Ines had said: "Are you sure you can manage a jug as big as that?" Of course she could manage. She wasn't a butterfingers, like the others. Like that blonde girl with the bow in her hair. As soon as she saw Rosaura, the girl with the bow had said:

"And you? Who are you?"

"I'm a friend of Luciana," said Rosaura.

"No," said the girl with the bow, "you are not a friend of Luciana because I'm her cousin and I know all her friends. And I don't know you."

"So what," said Rosaura. "I come here every afternoon with my mother and we do our homework together."

"You and your mother do your homework together?" asked the girl, laughing.

"I and Luciana do our homework together," said Rosaura, very seriously.

The girl with the bow shrugged her shoulders.

"That's not being friends," she said. "Do you go to school together?"

"No."

"So where do you know her from?" said the girl, getting impatient.

Rosaura remembered her mother's words perfectly. She took a deep breath.

"I'm the daughter of the employee," she said.

Her mother had said very clearly: "If someone asks, you say you're the daughter of the employee; that's all." She also told her to add: "And proud of it." But Rosaura thought that never in her life would she dare say something of the sort.

"What employee?" said the girl with the bow. "Employee in a shop?"

"No," said Rosaura angrily. "My mother doesn't sell anything in any shop, so there."

"So how come she's an employee?" said the girl with the bow.

Just then Señora Ines arrived saying *shh shh,* and asked Rosaura if she wouldn't mind helping serve out the hotdogs, as she knew the house so much better than the others.

"See?" said Rosaura to the girl with the bow, and when no one was looking she kicked her in the shin.

Apart from the girl with the bow, all the others were delightful. The one she liked best was Luciana, with her golden birthday crown; and then the boys. Rosaura won the sack race, and nobody managed to catch her when they played tag. When they split into two teams to play charades, all the boys wanted her for their side. Rosaura felt she had never been so happy in all her life.

But the best was still to come. The best came after Luciana blew out the candles. First the cake. Señora Ines had asked her to help pass the cake around, and Rosaura had enjoyed the task immensely, because everyone called out to her, shouting "Me, me!" Rosaura remembered a story in which there was a queen who had the power of life or death over her subjects. She had always loved that, having the power of life or death. To Luciana and the boys she gave the largest pieces, and to the girl with the bow she gave a slice so thin one could see through it.

After the cake came the magician, tall and bony, with a fine red cape. A true magician: he could untie handkerchiefs by blowing on them and make a chain with links that had no openings. He could guess what cards were pulled out from a pack, and the monkey was his assistant. He called the monkey "partner." "Let's see here, partner," he would say, "turn over a card." And, "Don't run away, partner: time to work now."

The final trick was wonderful. One of the children had to hold the monkey in his arms and the magician said he would make him disappear.

"What, the boy?" they all shouted.

"No, the monkey!" shouted back the magician.

Rosaura thought that this was truly the most amusing party in the whole world.

The magician asked a small fat boy to come and help, but the small fat boy got frightened almost at once and dropped the monkey on the floor. The magician picked him up carefully, whispered something in his ear, and the monkey nodded almost as if he understood.

"You mustn't be so unmanly, my friend," the magician said to the fat boy.

"What's unmanly?" said the fat boy.

The magician turned around as if to look for spies.

"A sissy," said the magician. "Go sit down."

Then he stared at all the faces, one by one. Rosaura felt her heart tremble.

"You, with the Spanish eyes," said the magician. And everyone saw that he was pointing at her.

She wasn't afraid. Neither holding the monkey, nor when the magician made him vanish; not even when, at the end, the magician flung his red cape over Rosaura's head and uttered a few magic words . . . and the monkey reappeared, chattering happily, in her arms. The children clapped furiously. And before Rosaura returned to her seat, the magician said:

"Thank you very much, my little countess."

She was so pleased with the compliment that a while later, when her mother came to fetch her, that was the first thing she told her.

"I helped the magician and he said to me, 'Thank you very much, my little countess.' "

It was strange because up to then Rosaura had thought that she was angry with her mother. All along Rosaura had imagined that she would say to her: "See that the monkey wasn't a lie?" But instead she was so thrilled that she told her mother all about the wonderful magician.

Her mother tapped her on the head and said: "So now we're a countess!"

But one could see that she was beaming.

And now they both stood in the entrance, because a moment ago Señora Ines, smiling, had said: "Please wait here a second."

Her mother suddenly seemed worried.

"What is it?" she asked Rosaura.

"What is what?" said Rosaura. "It's nothing; she just wants to get the presents for those who are leaving, see?"

She pointed at the fat boy and at a girl with pigtails who were also waiting there, next to their mothers. And she explained about the presents. She knew, because she had been watching those who left before her. When one of the girls was about to leave, Señora Ines would give her a bracelet. When a boy left, Señora Ines gave him a yo-yo. Rosaura preferred the yo-yo because it sparkled, but she didn't mention that to her mother. Her mother might have said: "So why don't you ask for one, you blockhead?" That's what her mother was like. Rosaura didn't feel like explaining that she'd be horribly ashamed to be the odd one out. Instead she said:

"I was the best-behaved at the party."

And she said no more because Señora Ines came out into the hall with two bags, one pink and one blue.

First she went up to the fat boy, gave him a yo-yo out of the blue bag, and the fat boy left with his mother. Then she went up to the girl and gave her a bracelet out of the pink bag, and the girl with the pigtails left as well.

Finally she came up to Rosaura and her mother. She had a big smile on her face and Rosaura liked that. Señora Ines looked down at her, then looked up at her mother, and then said something that made Rosaura proud:

"What a marvelous daughter you have, Herminia."

For an instant, Rosaura thought that she'd give her two presents: the bracelet and yo-yo. Señora Ines bent down as if about to look for something. Rosaura also leaned forward, stretching out her arm. But she never completed the movement.

Señora Ines didn't look in the pink bag. Nor did she look in the blue bag. Instead she rummaged in her purse. In her hand appeared two bills.

"You really and truly earned this," she said handing them over. "Thank you for all your help, my pet."

Rosaura felt her arms stiffen, stick close to her body, and then she noticed her mother's hand on her shoulder. Instinctively she pressed herself against her mother's body. That was all. Except her eyes. Rosaura's eyes had a cold, clear look that fixed itself on Señora Ines's face.

Señora Ines, motionless, stood there with her hand outstretched. As if she didn't dare draw it back. As if the slightest change might shatter an infinitely delicate balance.

Questions for Discussion

1. How does the opening section, including the disagreement about the monkey, reveal the basic conflict between mother and daughter?

2. How does the interrogation of Rosaura by the blond girl foreshadow what happens at the end of the story?

3. Why doesn't Rosaura receive a gift?

4. What does Rosaura receive instead of a gift and why? What does she learn from the action of Señora Ines?

5. Heker leaves us not with Rosaura's reaction but with Señora Ines's gesture, frozen in time. What is the significance of this last image, in your view?

Suggestions for Writing

1. Write an essay that combines a technical and thematic analysis of Heker's story by assessing the way Heker expresses social conflict chiefly through dialogue.

2. In your journal, write briefly about Rosaura's mother's behavior in the story. Should she, for example, have prevented her daughter from going to the party? Why or why not?

3. In your journal or notebook, write about a time when you misread a social situation or were involved in a "collision" of assumptions (false or otherwise) about social status.

4. Speculate: Will Rosaura become just like her mother, or will she take the experience of the party and mature in a different direction? Just how will this experience affect her in the long run? Write briefly about this in your journal or notebook.

A Chagall Story

RICHARD   CORTEZ   DAY

One afternoon in Via della Spada, Guido Iannotti's chest knocked him over. He had been knocked over by lots of things in his long life. He remembered particularly a certain brown horse with a mean eye and a mule's trick of kicking sideways. Mamma, he almost hadn't gotten up that time. But never before had his own chest knocked him down.

As he lay there on the street, he saw faces bending over him—Paolo the greengrocer from around the corner, Fulvia from the bakery—and farther back a circle of others, acquaintances from the quarter, passersby, a tourist or two. How serious they all were! Fulvia, with both hands to her cheeks, said, *"È morto?"* and Paolo replied, *"Morto, sì."*

Dead? Guido Iannotti dead? If they would give him a few minutes, let him rest a little, he would scramble to his feet and do a dance. But as he saw himself there on the stones, mouth open, gulping like a fish, he had to admit that they might have a point. The sickly gray color of his face, the caved-in cheeks: even at eighty a man should look better than that. Perhaps if someone would straighten his hat . . .

An ambulance nosed into the narrow street, siren howling, and the crowd parted respectfully. But it kept right on going. Guido rose to follow it with his eyes. *Madonna Santa*, it was on another mission! He looked down and saw a second ambulance, this one silent, stopping beside the form on the sidewalk. Two men got out, in no rush at all. They lifted him as if he weighed no more than a picture of himself. "Hey, easy—watch my hat!" he said.

One of the men picked up his hat and tossed it in after him. Guido dove for a look. He saw his shoe soles, like the letter *V*, and, within the *V*, the yellow flower in his buttonhole and the bottom of the jaw he'd been shaving for more than sixty years. The men closed the doors. They got in and drove away. Guido watched. No, they weren't heading for the hospital.

Fulvia, with flour on her cheeks, crossed herself. The passersby moved on. Paolo went back into his shop, where a customer was testing the pears. "Hey, signora," he said, "buy first, then squeeze!" Within a few minutes, life was back to normal in Via della Spada. Guido was gone and forgotten.

"So, I'm a spirit," he said. "So this is what it's like." He knocked a ripe pear onto the floor right under Paolo's nose. Paolo squinted and scratched his head. *"Aou,* I'm invisible," Guido said. He rolled three tomatoes out of the box, knocked another pear to the floor, and flung a bunch of grapes at Paolo's feet. Paolo was the kind who hid inferior fruit under the good ones, who shortchanged you unless you counted every lira, who weighed his hand with the vegetables. Guido had bought that hand a thousand times. He turned the cashbox upside down and let the bills flutter. Paolo rolled his eyes, crossed himself, howled like a dog.

This was sport. This was revenge. How he'd longed to get even with that tyrant Paolo. He felt better than he'd felt for a long while. Where was the old ache in his hip? They must have carted it off in the ambulance. He felt like getting out and doing things. But since he wasn't sure how much time he had before going to heaven, he thought he should get home and put his affairs in order. He had always made duty his first priority. He didn't want to leave a mess for his daughter—it wouldn't be right.

In Via del Moro, how often he'd cursed the darkness. It wasn't a street, it was a slit between rows of houses. It might have been fine for an astronomer— you could set your clock by the flash the sun made as it passed over—but for the people who had to live there, well, he was surprised they weren't as blind as moles. What did they need eyes for? They got where they were going by touching the walls.

The stairway to his apartment had been his cross to bear. Eight flights, eighty-eight steps, and with what reward at the top? A cramped dungeon of a place, a kind of subcellar, as if they'd built the house upside down. He and his wife had raised three children there, the whole family pale as mushrooms, and then their daughter, Lisa, and her husband had moved in and raised their two, and now one of those two had come back with *her* husband, to raise yet more children in the gloom. There had always been plenty of children. Laura, bless her, had died ten years ago because of her weight. To climb the stairs, she'd had to work twice as hard as Guido. Finally, her heart gave out.

This time, he skipped up the steps and wasn't even winded. In the apartment he saw that the family had already heard. News travels fast in the Santa Maria Novella quarter; Lisa was already wearing black. But what was this? Her husband, Marco, who was too lazy to work and get an apartment of his own, was going through the dresser, throwing Guido's things out, putting his own clothes in the drawers. And look, there on the bed, all his personal belongings—his letters, the pictures he'd saved, Laura's wedding ring, his documents, his keys, his pocketknife, his own wedding ring! Lisa and Marco were going through everything, moving into his room, and him not even decently buried yet. Look at them, stretching out on the bed, bouncing, testing it! His own family, the ungrateful wretches!

But then a thought crossed his mind. Could there have been a funeral already, and he'd missed it? Perhaps they'd put him in the ground with proper ceremonies and tears, with the jonquil in his buttonhole, with his hat resting on his chest. While he'd been kicking fruit around Paolo's shop, perhaps the funeral had come and gone. In this spirit life, he could see, he was still a puppy. He had a lot to learn. Where, for example, did one catch the bus for heaven? Shouldn't there be an angel picking him up about now, or at least a notice pinned up somewhere?

He left his family to their predictable concerns. Life was for the living, and he wanted no part of it. Let Lisa and her husband have the sagging bed, the old backbreaker; let them go on dragging their bodies up the stairs. That was life? All that labor? And for what? Free as a bird, he took a few turns around Piazza Santa

Maria Novella, keeping an eye out for the angel. On a cornice of the church, he sat next to a pigeon. Down below, two priests strolled in the April sunshine. There were young lovers, hurrying businessmen, gawking tourists. He dove from the ledge, swooped low, and like a lark fired up and over the buildings to the train station. Perhaps it wouldn't be a bus, but one of those trains, a funicular, like he'd ridden on his honeymoon at Vesuvius.

But there was nothing at the station, either. If he could find some other spirits . . . Where in Florence would spirits hang out? He sailed over the Arno and tried Santa Maria del Carmine, then Santo Spirito. Nothing doing. He swung back across the river to the big cathedral, the Duomo, and alighted on the main altar. There was a mass in progress. To get some attention, he hovered right over the priest's head, then blew out one of the candles, but the priest went right on with his sermon. Guido fanned his notes onto the floor, but he kept talking, the old fool. All is vanity, remember that you too will die, and so forth. The idiot. Guido, with exquisite pleasure, spiraled up into the dome, then plunged and did hair-raising turns at floor level around the rows of columns. Then he shot from the church right through a ten-foot-thick stone wall. He didn't get a scratch.

At Santa Croce and San Miniato al Monte, he fared no better than at the other churches. Nothing but people, no angels, no other spirits. Had he missed the helicopter? Where was the elevator? He drifted into All Saints' for a look around, and there, in the right transept, in a glass case, he saw the *corpo incorrotto,* the uncorrupted remains, of Saint Giacomo Melanzane, who had been archbishop of Florence from A.D. 1389 until 1439.

The body wasn't exactly fresh, but it was still recognizable as a man's, though the face was shrunken, leathery, and brown, and the miter had tipped a bit forward on the brow. But there were the eyes, the nose, and the down-turned, sour-looking mouth. In fact, the saint, in Guido's estimation, looked pretty much like he himself would have looked with a few hundred more years on him.

But miracle of miracles! The eyes opened a little and looked sideways. With the smallest of gestures, but unmistakable in meaning, the head moved: come here.

"In there?" Guido said.

The saint nodded. With some distaste, Guido went through the glass.

It wasn't too bad. The see-through coffin, though not large, contained the two of them easily, and there was only a faint dusty smell, like very dry leaves. He said, "Thank you, Your Reverence. I was beginning to think I was alone in the universe."

"You are. And call me Giacco. It's good of you to call. I haven't had a decent conversation in God knows how long. It's too bad we can't have coffee. That's the one thing I miss most. I like it strong, black, sweet—almost syrup. It puts hair on your chest. Remember the taste? Remember how the first swallow goes straight to your brain?"

"Yes, I remember," Guido said. "But what I want to know is, how do I get to heaven? I seem to be stuck here, between two worlds. I must have missed something."

"Heaven? Ha, there isn't any."

"There isn't? Just hell, then? I thought . . ."

"No hell, either. I don't know where those notions come from—it was long before my time. Anyway, they're false."

"But there must be an afterlife. Look, we're talking, and we're both dead."

"We're that, all right. Look at me. Would you believe I used to be over six feet tall? You're lucky—they plopped you right in the ground. They tanned me like a horsehide and left me to be stared at. It's humiliating. The loathing, the disgust on people's faces—it's like being a leper. Everyone turns away."

"But you're Saint Melanzane. I thought saints were enthroned in splendor, close to God."

"You've been in the Baptistery, I see. Idiot artists! What thrones? What God? Anyway, where would you set up a throne? It's just air up there. It's less than air. What would you stand a throne on?"

"Then this is all there is?"

"It could be worse. Cheer up. Have you tried hovering and swooping? Sailing's a lot of fun. You can go through walls, you know, and play tricks on people."

"I've done all that. It's—forgive me—kind of boring, isn't it? Where are all the other spirits? There must be millions of us, somewhere."

"You're new at this. You've got to stop thinking of where and when, for there aren't any. Millions, you say? Billions—quadrillions. They're out in the universe, mostly. You almost never meet one. No, this is it—you're on your own. Do what you can with what you've got."

"But, Your Reverence—"

"Stop that. Do I look like a thing to be revered?"

"Well then, Giacco. The universe—you admit there is one. But you say there's no God. So where did the universe come from?"

"Oy, one of those. Just my luck. I never see anyone, and when someone comes along, he turns out to be a philosopher! Sludge, that's where it came from. A big gob of sludge."

"Then who created the sludge?"

"How do I know? It created itself, then diversified. It turned itself into sun and moons, trees, birds, bugs, and people, not to mention lions and lambs. It's all sludge, when you break it down."

"The soul?"

"Sludge."

"Christ? Mary? The Apostles?"

"Yep. Say, there's a nun in a box over at Santissima Annunziata. Saint Ambrosia, I think her name is. Why don't you coast over and have a chat with her? She might like some company. If I remember right, she was a real student of these questions. Augustine, Jerome, Aquinas—they were her boys. Pop over there, she's a laugh a minute, or used to be."

"All right, I'll go see her," Guido said. "But is this all you do, lie here and grump, until you get another body to inhabit?"

"Get another body? Does that happen?"

"I don't know, Giacco—you're the archbishop. I've heard of it, that's all I can say. It's called reincarnation."

"Wouldn't you know? As if once wasn't enough. Twice yet. But maybe it won't happen. I've never heard of it. Can we choose a body, do you think, or do we take potluck? What if it was a cow or pig? Or a toad? What if it was a woman? Imagine that!"

"Maybe it won't happen," Guido said. "Don't be upset. I'm sorry I brought it up."

"Another body, Jesus." He fell silent for a few moments. Then he brightened. "Say, would you like to go out for a while, hover some? We could shoot down to Rome. The Vatican's nice—very well kept up. Or we could swing down around Africa—"

"No thanks," Guido said. "I want to find my wife if I can. Her name is Laura—gray-haired, overweight? You haven't seen her, have you?"

"Ha. You've got lots to learn about the way things work. You're still too close to life—you think the way people think. What's a wife? Sludge—in a shape of sorts, soft, squishy, with a pocket to reach into and pull babies out of, eh? What say we whip out to Mars and back? Want to race?"

"Another time maybe. I think I'll hang around some. Maybe I'll come across her."

"Fat chance."

"Well, see you later."

"There isn't any. You're a case. There should be a school for infants like you. Later, before, after, once upon a time: you'll stop thinking like that. Take a swoop or two out in the universe. Come back smarter, kid."

Guido eased through the glass, through the side wall of the church, and shot up over the city. He did a parabola, falling to, through, the roof of Santissima Annunziata. Ah, there below the altar, in a glass coffin, was the nun that Giacco had mentioned. Now for some answers. "Psst," he said. "Psst, Ambrosia!" She lay, or her body did, in classic repose, hands folded on her breast. Where her spirit was, who could say? Maybe she'd gone for a spin. Maybe she was lost in theological speculation. He couldn't get a word out of her.

He noticed a very old but familiar-looking woman kneeling at the altar before the coffin. "Mamma?" he said. He hovered before the wrinkled face. Then he saw the rings—her own, Laura's, and one on her right thumb, his. Could it be? This ancient creature was his daughter Lisa, whom he'd just left that morning in Via del Moro.

Her husband had died? Her daughter, too? For her to be wearing the rings, the whole family must have died. Had there been an epidemic? Were all the Iannottis dead?

He fired from the church and zipped straight to Via del Moro. In the apartment he found a strange young woman nursing a baby. Lisa must have moved. He didn't recognize any of the furniture. Thoughtfully, he cruised Via delle Belle Donne, Via della Spada, and the other streets in the maze off Piazza Santa Maria Novella. Paolo was gone, his shop converted to a shoestore, and though Fulvia's bakery was still there, he knew neither the owner nor the customers. On the facade of the church, pigeons still perched, but who knew how many generations of pigeons had lived and died since he'd lived in the quarter?

Had lived? Did live! He was more alive now than ever! Like a hummingbird, he shot straight up into the haze above the city. That meandering path of blue light down there—it was his beloved river, the Arno—and the big patch of green: what else but Cascine Park, where he and Laura had walked on Sunday when they were young. The red tile roofs, the broad boulevards, the parks, the labyrinthine narrow streets: that was Florence down there, filling the valley, busy as an anthill, lovely. With a city that complex and fascinating, why would he want a universe!

He tipped forward and shot down into it. This was where she would be—she'd loved the city as much as he did. Yellow was her color. Laura and yellow. Why else had he worn a yellow flower in his buttonhole for all those years? There, just above that border of jonquils—Laura?

No, but this was where she would come to—this park. The universe might be endless, but so was eternity. That improved the odds considerably. He wove among the yellow flowers, wove a pattern in the air above the grass, constructing an attractive design. The jonquils moved in the April breeze. He hovered brightly, giving off all the light he had.

Questions for Discussion

1. What does Guido Iannotti discover "the afterlife" to be like?

2. What does Guido discover about himself, his family, his friends, and his city after he dies?

3. Is the conversation between Saint Melanzane and Guido sacrilegious? Explain.

4. What does the saint mean when he tells Guido that he is "still too close to life"?

5. Interpret the ending. What does it show us about what Guido has learned? What emotional response does it draw out of you?

6. Find an art book with reproductions of works by Marc Chagall (born 1887) and then explain how this story *is* a "Chagall story."

Suggestions for Writing

1. Any story about an afterlife might be said to be a religious story. Write an essay about "A Chagall Story" that addresses the religious and spiritual implications of it.

2. "A story in which a guy flies around after he's dead is just plain unrealistic and silly." In your journal or notebook, take issue with this devil's-advocate statement, not just to make a case for Day's story, but to justify "unrealistic" fiction in general.

3. Write an essay about the depiction of time and space in this story as contrasted with that of Ray Bradbury's story "2002: Night Meeting." What are some significant differences and similarities between these two speculative stories?

4. One thing Guido gains from being "knocked down by his chest" is the ability to fly around his city. Grant yourself the same wish (without being knocked down by your chest—or anything else), and write a description of this bird's-eye view of your town or city. Where would you choose to go? How would you perceive your town or city differently—not just in terms

of a physical vantage point but of an emotional or conceptual one? Make the imagery as vivid as you can.

5. To some extent, Day's story is a meditation on a city, as is Cynthia Ozick's story "The Butterfly and the Traffic Light." Write an essay in which you compare and contrast these two stories, particularly in the way they illuminate American and Italian cities.

Each Year Grain

SHAWN   HSU   WONG

I am the son of my father and I have a story to tell about my history and about a dream. I had the dream inside of a tree. I was child, walking through a forest of giant shade and I found a huge stump of a once giant redwood burned hollow so that you could step inside and look up and see the sky. I suddenly shouted into the charcoal darkness, into the soft charred soul of this tree. My shout was absorbed so quickly, I knew the tree was listening. And I spoke to the tree in my dream. The tree showed me its rings of growth and as I ran my fingers over each year grain, the tree showed me the year I was born and my history.

I asked the tree to show me the year I was born and the year of my father's birth and the tree said that it would not only show that year but would begin farther back in my history and show me my great-grandfather's country, the country that he came to, the land where he toiled day after day and the land where he was buried.

I came running down the grassy hills as fast as the wind moves down the waves of grass from shade to light. I came running down the long meadow of tumbling yellow greens racing wind across drifting grasses. I came running into a dream Appoloosa-like.

"Your great-grandfather's country was a rich land, the river's sand had gold dust in it. The water was fresh and clear, the sand sparkling beneath the surface of the water like the shiny skin of the trout that swam in the deep pools. This was California's gold country of the 1850's and your great-grandfather was there to reap the riches that California offered and to return home a rich man to live in comfort with his family."

I knew by the feeling of the land in my dream that great-grandfather did not live to return to China, nor to reap any riches. Instead he died here in northern California buried in the dark moist earth. And I heard my great-grandfather's voice in the wind speak, "Do not send my bones back to China. Bury me here beneath my tears."

The hawk glides in hot drafts of summer dust wind and drops the furry body of his meal into the brittle meadow grasses below and the body becomes the grass of next spring growing wet from light snow. And the land that makes each spring birth again is held moist in my hands. California north.

"Your great-grandfather was humiliated by the land and the people to which he gave his life. But unlike the other Chinese who died here and had their bones sent back to China, so that at least that much of them would return home away from the land that humiliated them and the life they loathed, your great-grandfather felt that since this land was important enough for him to give his life to, he should not leave and that his sons should follow him to this country, and his soul would protect them."

Woodsmoke drifts from Shasta, Trinity, Siskiyou, north to the wild Klamath River. Drift woodsmoke, bend and fall with the river near the people that live in your California heart! Klamath, Salmon, Eel, river running to a space where woodsmoke lives in the deep clover and moss on the breath of wind that passes down through the unmoving redwoods. California northcoast. Woodsmoke dissolves in a forest of mist from the sea cold, falling from jagged cliffs wearing by age. Points and coasts like Reyes, Bolinas, Monterey, take Sur Country energy into the black night ocean and repeat over and over the same silence.

I could see the gold country land in my dreams and I loved its sun, its wood, and the dark, loose and cool earth where my feet could dig in like roots. Then another vision came into my dream. It was not the same land.

And the tree spoke to me, "One of the men you see working here was your great-grandfather building the railroad. It was the work that broke him and the work that he desperately held on to—to make a little place in this country. His brother was murdered."

My great-grandfather who drove rail spikes and laid track was speaking to me. "I left for San Francisco one month before my brother. In those days some ships were bringing us in illegally. They would drop a lifeboat outside the Golden Gate with the Chinese in it. Then the ship would steam in and at night the lifeboat would come in quietly and unload. If they were about to be caught, my people would be thrown overboard. But, you see, they couldn't swim because they were chained together. My brother died on that night and now his bones are chained to the bottom of the ocean. No burial ever. Now I am fighting to find a place in this country.

"We do not have our women here. My wife is coming to live here. We are staying. Nothing was sweet about those days I lived alone in the city, unless you can find sweetness in that kind of loneliness. I slept in the back of a kitchen by the grimy window where the light and noises of the wet city streets were ground in and out of me like the cold. The bed was so small I could hardly move away from my dreams. And when I awakened with the blue light of the moon shining in, there would be no dreams. That one moment when I wake, losing my dreams, my arms and heart imagining that she was near me moving closer and I float in her movements and light touch. But the blue light and the noise was always there and I would have nothing in my hands."

Great-grandfather's wife was a delicate, yet a strong and energetic lady. Insisting in her letters to Great-grandfather to let her come and join him. The loneliness was overpowering him, yet he resisted her pleas, telling her that life was too dangerous for a woman. "The people and the work move like hawks around me, I feel chained to the ground, unable even to cry for help. The sun blisters my skin, the winters leave me sick, the cold drains us. I look into the eyes of my friends and there is nothing, not even fear."

Upon receiving his letter, Great-grandmother told her friends that she was leaving to join her husband, saying that his fight to survive was too much for a single man to bear. And so she came and was happy and the hawks had retreated.

She lived in the city and gave birth to a son while Great-grandfather was still working in the Sierras building the railroad. He wrote to her, saying that the railroad would be finished in six months and he would return to the city and they would live together again as a family.

During the six months, the hawks came back into his vision. "The hawks had people faces laughing as they pulled me apart with their sharp talons, they had no voices just their mouths flapping open, a yellow hysteria of teeth." He knew that this was the beginning of sickness for his lover, he sensed her trouble and moments of pain, no word from her was necessary. "Your wounds are my wounds," he would say in the night, "the hawks that tear our flesh are disturbed by the perfect day, the pure sun that warms the wounds, I am singing and they cannot tear us apart."

She saw the sun as she woke that morning after waking all night long in moments of pain. The sun was so pure. She thought that this could not be the city, its stench, its noise replaced by this sweet air. She knew that this air, this breath, was her husband's voice. The ground was steaming dry, the humus became her soul, alive and vital with the moving and pushing of growth. She breathed deeply, the air was like sleep uninterrupted by pain, there was no more home to travel to, this moment was everything that loving could give and that was enough. She was complete and whole with that one breath, like the security of her childhood nights sleeping with mother, wrapping her arms around her, each giving the other the peace of touch, pure sun. There was a rush of every happiness in her life that she could feel and touch and as she let go, she thought of their son, and the joy of his birth jarred her and she tried desperately to reach out to wake, to hold on to that final fear, to grasp his childhood trust, but the smell of the humus, the moist decaying leaves struck by sunlight and steaming into her dreams was too much and she was moving too fast into sleep.

Great-grandfather had dreams, making vows to his son, seeing dark legends that moved on him like skeletons stomping down the metal spiral staircase of her grave. The hollow sounds of their white silk capes flapping in an updraft of hot dust.

"I shall take my son away from these hawks who cause me to mourn. I cannot cry. My tears leave scars on my face. There is no strength in pity. I will take my son away, move deeper into this country. I have heard stories about the South that there is no winter, only sun."

The images were strength for him. He had dreams of the South and they moved upon him like legends of faith. The hot dry dust and heat cleansing his skin, warming his back. The swamps were the visions of life's blood, there was something vital and deep red in the hiss of hot animal mouths and the humid steaming life that rose up to embrace him. There was a julep woman there for him, cool and she was the touch of green. She was silence, soft as meadow loam, sweet as a stream that he could lie in, letting her waters rush over his body, hearing the sound of leaves in the wind. The dream always ended with the scream of white fire. It was the magnolia. A huge magnolia tree afire, branches of flames moving around each white magnolia blossom. He saw them drop into the dust, a ball of white fire. The smell of the magnolia burning always woke him that smell lingering into morning like charred flesh, so cold.

> *Magnolia, magnolia your white blood*
> *Is the fire of moons.*
> *Your flower is winter to my flesh.*

For Great-grandfather it was not enough anymore to say he was *Longtime Californ'*. He had lost faith in the land. He fell into deeper depressions, not from mourning his wife's death, but more from his loss of faith in the country. He had been defeated when he had vowed not to lose ground to the harsh land and cruel people. It was his son that finally carried him through, helped return the faith so that at least he would die at peace.

> Slide, tumble down wide open tall grass hills, feel the warm sun on your face as you spin from earth to sky, fingers reaching into the moist earth and laugh uncontrolled or cry, it doesn't matter, just keep tumbling down that steep hill and finally when you roll slowly to a stop stained green stained brown and exhausted you will notice while catching your breath that you may have startled a blue heron which lifts its great wings up then down again rising from the meadow loam down the sun washed valley of tall trees. Watch until the low sun engulfs its silent flying guest. The moment is yours, take it with you into your own loneliness where sight becomes feeling. Instantaneously.

"The country that accepted your great-grandfather and his son now rejected them. The railroad was finished and the Chinese were chased out of the mines. They were allowed to live but not marry. The law was designed so that the Chinese would gradually die out, leaving no sons or daughters."

Questions for Discussion

1. In what way does the opening paragraph, featuring "the dream in the tree," establish a pattern or set a tone for the rest of the story? Put another way, what is significant about the dream's taking place "in a tree"?

2. There are four sections of the story that are set off typographically from the rest of the narrative. How is the language of these sections different? Who "speaks" these sections? In your view, what do they add to the story?

3. How would you describe the narrator's grandfather's relationship with the California land?

4. Summarize the plight of Chinese immigrants of the grandfather's generation as revealed in this story.

5. In what ways does the story celebrate California and, by implication, America? In what ways does it "indict" California and America?

Suggestions for Writing

1. Write an essay about the narrative structure of "Each Year Grain." How is it conventional? How is it experimental? In your view, how successful is this structure and why?

2. In your notebook, write several brief monologues "spoken" by your grandfather, grandmother, great uncle, or great aunt. Try to let these monologues explain the person's experience in America (or another country that was home).

3. Gather some information from books and articles about the experience of the Chinese immigrants in California in the nineteenth century. Then write an essay analyzing Wong's perspective on this experience. What does his fictional account add to your sense of this history?

Under the Wheat

RICK DEMARINIS

Down in D-3 I watch the sky gunning through the aperture ninety-odd feet above my head. The missiles are ten months away, and I am lying on my back, listening to the sump. From the bottom of a hole, where the weather is always the same cool sixty-four degrees, plus or minus two, I like to relax and watch the clouds slide through the circle of blue light. I have plenty of time to kill. The aperture is about fifteen feet wide. About the size of a silver dollar from here. A hawk just drifted by. Eagle. Crow. Small cumulus. Nothing. Nothing. Wrapper.

Hot again today, and the sky is drifting across the hole, left to right, a slow thick wind that doesn't gust. When it gusts, it's usually from Canada. Fierce, with hail the size of eyeballs. I've seen wheat go down. Acres and acres of useless straw.

But sometimes it comes out of the southeast, from Bismarck, bringing ten-mile high anvils with it, and you find yourself looking for funnels. This is not tornado country to speak of. The tornado path is to the south and west of here. They walk up from Bismarck and farther south and peter out on the Montana border, rarely touching ground anywhere near this latitude. Still, you keep an eye peeled. I've seen them put down gray fingers to the west, not quite touching but close enough to make you want to find a hole. They say it sounds like freight trains in your yard. I wouldn't know. We are from the coast, where the weather is stable and always predictable because of the ocean. We are trying to adjust.

I make five-hundred a week doing this, driving a company pick-up from hole to hole, checking out the sump pumps. I've found only one failure in two months. Twenty feet of black water in the hole and rising. It's the company's biggest headache. The high water table of North Dakota. You can dig twelve feet in any field and have yourself a well. You can dig yourself a shallow hole, come back in a few days and drink. That's why the farmers here have it made. Except for hail. Mostly they are Russians, these farmers.

Karen wants to go back. I have to remind her it's only for one year. Ten more months. Five-hundred a week for a year. But she misses things. The city, her music lessons, movies, the beach, excitement. We live fairly close to a town, but it's one you will never hear of, unless a local goes wild and chainsaws all six members of his family. The movie theater has shown "Bush Pilot," "Red Skies of Montana," "Ice Palace," and "Kon Tiki," so far. These are movies we would not ordinarily pay money to see. She has taken to long walks in the evenings to work out her moods, which are getting harder and harder for me to pretend aren't there. I get time-and-a-half on Saturdays, double-time Sundays and Holidays, and thirteen dollars per diem for the inconvenience of relocating all the way from Oxnard, California. That comes to a lot. You don't walk away from a gold mine like that. I try to tell Karen she has to make the effort, adjust. North Dakota isn't all that bad. As a matter of fact, I sort of enjoy the area. Maybe I am more adaptable. We live close to a large brown lake, an earthfill dam loaded with northern pike. I bought myself a little boat and often go out to troll a bit before the carpool comes by. The freezer is crammed with fish, not one under five pounds.

There's a ghost town on the other side of the lake. The houses were built for the men who worked on the dam. That was years ago. They are paintless now, weeds up to the rotten sills. No glass in the windows, but here and there a rag of drape. Sometimes I take my boat across the lake to the ghost town. I walk the overgrown streets and look into the windows. Sometimes something moves. Rats. Gophers. Wind. Loose boards. Sometimes nothing.

When the weather is out of Canada you can watch it move south, coming like a giant roll of silver dough on the horizon. It gets bigger fast and then you'd better find cover. If the cloud is curdled underneath, you know it means hail. The wind can gust to one-hundred knots. It scares Karen. I tell her there's nothing to worry about. Our trailer is on a good foundation and tied down tight. But she has this dream of being uprooted and of flying away in such a wind. She sees her broken body caught in a tree, magpies picking at it. I tell her the trailer will definitely not budge. Still, she gets wild-eyed and can't light a cigarette.

We're sitting at the dinette table looking out the window, watching the front arrive. You can feel the trailer bucking like a boat at its moorings. Lightning is stroking the blond fields a mile away. To the southeast, I can see a gray finger reaching down. This is unusual, I admit. But I say nothing to Karen. It looks like the two fronts are going to butt heads straight over the trailer park. It's getting dark fast. Something splits the sky behind the trailer and big hail pours out. The streets of the park are white and jumping under the black sky. Karen has her hands up to her ears. There's a stampede on our tin roof. Two TV antennas fold at the same time in a dead faint. A jagged Y of lightning strikes so close you can smell it. Electric steam. Karen is wild, screaming. I can't hear her. Our garbage cans are rising. They are floating past the windows into a flattened wheat field. This is something. Karen's face is closed. She doesn't enjoy it at all, not at all.

I'm tooling around in third on the usual bad road, enjoying the lurches, rolls, and twists. I would not do this to my own truck. The fields I'm driving through are wasted. Head-on with the sky and the sky never loses. I've passed a few unhappy-looking farmers standing in their fields with their hands in their pockets, faces frozen in an expression of disgust, spitting. Toward D-8, just over a rise and down into a narrow gulch, I found a true glacier. It was made out of hail stones welded together by their own impact. It hadn't begun to melt yet. Four feet thick and maybe thirty feet long. You can stand on it and shade your eyes from the white glare. You could tell yourself you are inside the arctic circle. What is this, the return of the Ice Age?

Karen did not cook tonight. Another "mood." I poke around the fridge. I don't know what to say to her anymore. I know it's hard. I can understand that. This is not Oxnard. I'll give her that. I'm the first to admit it. I pop a beer and sit down at the table opposite her. Our eyes don't meet. They haven't for weeks. We are like two magnetic north poles, repelling each other for invisible reasons. Last night in bed I touched her. She went stiff. She didn't have to say a word. I took my hand back. I got the message. There was the hum of the air-conditioner and nothing else. The world could have been filled with dead bodies. I turned on the lights. She got up and lit a cigarette after two tries. Nerves. "I'm going for a walk, Lloyd," she said, checking the sky. "Maybe we should have a baby?" I said. "I'm making plenty of money." But she looked at me as if I had picked up an ax.

I would like to know where she finds to go and what she finds to do there. She hates the town worse than the trailer park. The trailer park has a rec hall and a social club for the wives. But she won't take advantage of that. I know the neighbors are talking. They think she's a snob. They think I spoil her. After she left I went out on the porch and drank eleven beers. Let them talk.

Three farm kids. Just standing outside the locked gate of D-4. "What do you kids want?" I know what they want. A "look-see." Security measures are in effect, but what the hell. There is nothing here yet but a ninety-foot hole with a tarp on it and a sump pump in the bottom. They are excited. They want to know what ICBM stands for. What is a warhead? How fast is it? How do you know if it's really going to smear the right town? What if it went straight up and came straight down? Can you hit the moon? "Look at the sky up there, kids," I tell them. "Lie on your backs, like this, and after a while you sort of get the feeling you're looking *down,* from on top of it." The kids lie down on the concrete. Kids have a way of giving all their attention to something interesting. I swear them to secrecy, not for my protection, because who cares, but because it will make their day. They will run home, busting with secret info. I drive off to D-9, where the sump trouble was.

Caught three lunkers this morning. All over twenty-four inches. It's seven a.m. now and I'm on Ruby Street, the ghost town. The streets are all named after stones. Why I don't know. This is nothing like anything we have on the coast. Karen doesn't like the climate or the people and the flat sky presses down on her from all sides and gives her bad dreams, sleeping and awake. But what can I *do?*

I'm on Onyx Street, number 49, a two-bedroom bungalow with a few pieces of furniture left in it. There is a chest of drawers in the bedroom, a bed with a rotten gray mattress. There is a closet with a raggedy slip in it. The slip has brown water stains on it. In the bottom of the chest is a magazine, yellow with age. *Secret Confessions.* I can imagine the woman who lived here with her husband. Not much like Karen at all. But what did she do while her husband was off working on the dam? Did she stand at this window in her slip and wish she were back in Oxnard? Did she cry her eyes out on this bed and think crazy thoughts? Where is she now? Does she think, "This is July 15, 1962, and I am glad I am not in North Dakota anymore"? Did she take long walks at night and not cook? I have an impulse to do something odd, and do it.

When a thunderhead passes over a cyclone fence that surrounds a site, such as the one passing over D-6 now, you can hear the wire hiss with nervous electrons. It scares me because the fence is a perfect lightning rod, a good conductor. But I stay on my toes. Sometimes, when a big cumulus is overhead stroking the area and roaring, I'll just stay put in my truck until it's had its fun.

Because this is Sunday, I am making better than twelve dollars an hour. I'm driving through a small farming community called Spacebow. A Russian word, I think, because you're supposed to pronounce the *e*. No one I know does. Shade trees on every street. A Russian church here, grain elevator there. No wind. Hot for nine a.m. Men dressed in Sunday black. Ladies in their best. Kids looking uncomfortable and controlled. Even the dogs are behaving. There is a woman, manless I think, because I've seen her before, always alone on her porch, eyes on something far away. A "thinker." Before today I've only waved hello. First one finger off the wheel, nod, then around the block once again and the whole hand out the window and a smile. That was last week. After the first turn past her place today she waves back. A weak hand at first, as if she's not sure that's what I meant. But after a few times around the block she knows that's what I meant. And so I'm stopping. I'm going to ask for a cup of cold water. I'm thirsty anyway. Maybe all this sounds hokey to you if you are from some big town like Oxnard, but this is not a big town like Oxnard.

Her name is Myrna Dan. That last name must be a pruned-down version of Danielovitch or something because the people here are mostly Russians. She is thirty-two, a widow, one brat. A two-year old named "Piper," crusty with food. She owns a small farm here but there is no one to work it. She has a decent allotment from the U.S. Government and a vegetable garden. If you are from the coast you would not stop what you were doing to look at her. Her hands are square and the fingers stubby, made for rough wooden handles. Hips like gateposts.

No supper again. Karen left a note. "Lloyd, I am going for a walk. There are some cold cuts in the fridge." It wasn't even signed. Just like that. One of these days on one of her walks she is going to get caught by the sky which can change on you in a minute.

Bill Finkel made a remark on the way in to the dispatch center. It was a little personal and coming from anybody else I would have called him on it. But he is the lead engineer, the boss. A few of the other guys grinned behind their hands. How do I know where she goes or why? I am not a swami. If it settles her nerves, why should I push it? I've thought of sending her to Ventura to live with her mother for a while, but her mother is getting senile and has taken to writing mean letters. I tell Karen the old lady is around the bend, don't take those letters too seriously. But what's the use when the letters come in like clockwork, once a week, page after page of nasty accusations in a big, inch-high scrawl, like a kid's, naming things that never happened. Karen takes it hard, no matter what I say, as if what the old lady says is true.

Spacebow looks deserted. It isn't. The men are off in the fields, the women are inside working toward evening. Too hot outside even for the dogs who are sleeping under the porches. Ninety-nine. I stopped for water at Myrna's. Do you want to see a missile silo? Sure, she said, goddamn rights, just like that. I have an extra hard hat in the truck but she doesn't have to wear it if she doesn't want to. Regulations at this stage of the program are a little pointless. Just a hole with a sump in it. Of course you can fall into it and get yourself killed. That's about the only danger. But there are no regulations that can save you from your own stupidity. Last winter when these holes were being dug, a kid walked out on a tarp. The tarp was covered with light snow and he couldn't tell where the ground ended and the hole began. He dropped the whole ninety feet and his hardhat did not save his ass. Myrna is impressed with this story. She is very anxious to see one. D-7 is closest to Spacebow, only a mile out of town. It isn't on my schedule today, but so what. I hand her the orange hat. She has trouble with the chin strap. I help her cinch it. Piper wants to wear it too and grabs at the straps, whining. Myrna has big jaws. Strong. But not in an ugly way.

I tell her the story about Jack Stern, the Jewish quality control man from St. Louis who took flying lessons because he wanted to be able to get to a decent size city in a hurry whenever he felt the need. This flat empty farm land made his ulcer flare. He didn't know how to drive a car, and yet there he was, tearing around the sky in a Bonanza. One day he flew into a giant hammerhead—thinking, I guess, that a cloud like that is nothing but a lot of water vapor, no matter what shape it has or how big—and was never heard from again. That cloud ate him and the Bonanza. At the airport up in Minot they picked up two words on the emergency frequency, *Oh no,* then static.

I tell her the story about the motor-pool secretary who shot her husband once in the neck and twice in the foot with a target pistol while he slept. Both of them pulling down good money, too. I tell her the one about the one that got away. A northern as big as a shark. Pulled me and my boat a mile before my twelve-pound test monofilament snapped. She gives me a sidelong glance and makes a buzzing sound as if to say, *That* one takes the cake, Mister! We are on the bottom of D-10, watching the circle of sky, lying on our backs.

The trailer *stinks.* I could smell it from the street as soon as I got out of Bill Finkel's car. Fish heads. *Heads!* I guess they've been sitting there like that most of the afternoon. Just the big alligator jaws of my big beautiful pikes, but not the bodies. A platter of them, uncooked, drying out, and getting high. Knife fork napkin glass. I'd like to know what goes on inside her head, what passes for thinking in there. The note: "Lloyd, Eat your fill." Not signed. Is this supposed to be humor? I fail to get the point of it. I have to carry the mess to the garbage cans without breathing. A wind has come up. From the southeast. A big white fire is blazing in the sky over my shoulder. You can hear the far-off rumble, like a whale grunting. I squint west, checking for funnels.

Trouble in D-7. Busted sump. I pick up Myrna and Piper and head for the hole. It's a nice day for a drive. It could be a bearing seizure, but that's only a percentage guess. I unlock the gate and we drive to the edge of it. Space age artillery, I explain, as we stand on the lip of D-7, feeling the vertigo. The tarp is off for maintenance and the hole is solid black. If you let your imagination run, you might see it as bottomless. The "Pit" itself. Myrna is holding Piper back. Piper is whining, she wants to see the hole. Myrna has to slap her away, scolding. I drain my beer and let the can drop. I don't hear it hit. Not even a splash. I grab the fussing kid and hold her out over the hole. "Have yourself a *good* look, brat," I say. I hold her by the ankle with one hand. She is paralyzed. Myrna goes so white I have to smile. "Oh wait," she says. "Please, Lloyd. No." As if I ever would.

Myrna wants to see the D-flight control center. I ask her if she has claustrophobia. She laughs, but it's no joke. That far below the surface inside that capsule behind an eight-ton door can be upsetting if you're susceptible to confinement. The elevator is slow and heavy, designed to haul equipment. The door opens on a dimly-lit room. Spooky. There's crated gear scattered around. And there is the door, one yard thick to withstand the shock waves from the Bomb. I wheel it open. Piper whines, her big eyes distrustful. There is a musty smell in the dank air. The lights and blower are on now, but it will take a while for the air to freshen itself up. I wheel the big door shut. It can't latch yet, but Myrna is impressed. I explain to her what goes on in here. We sit down at the console. I show her where the launch "enabling" switches will be and why it will take two people together to launch an attack, the chairs fifteen feet apart and both switches turned for a several second count before the firing sequence can start, in case one guy goes berserk and decides to end the world because his old lady has been holding out on him, or just for the hell of it, given human nature. I show her the escape hole. It's loaded with ordinary sand. You pull this chain and the sand dumps into the capsule. Then you climb up the tube that held the sand into someone's wheat field. I show her the toilet and the little kitchen. I can see there is something on her mind. Isolated places make you think of weird things. It's happened to me more than once. Not here, but in the ghost town on the other side of the lake.

Topside the weather has changed. The sky is the color of pikebelly, wind rising from the southeast. To the west I can see stubby funnels pushing down from the overcast, but only so far. It looks like the clouds are growing roots. We have to run back to the truck in the rain, Piper screaming on Myrna's hip. A heavy bolt strikes less than a mile away. A blue fireball sizzles where it hits. Smell the ozone. It makes me sneeze.

This is the second day she's been gone. I don't know where or how. All her clothes are here. She doesn't have any money. I don't know what to do. There is no police station. Do I call her mother? Do I notify the FBI? The highway patrol? Bill Finkel?

Everybody in the carpool knows but won't say a word, out of respect for my feelings. Bill Finkel has other things on his mind. He is worried about rumored economy measures in the Assembly and Check-Out program next year. It has nothing to do with me. My job ends before the phase begins. I guess she went back to Oxnard, or maybe Ventura. But how?

We are in the D-flight control center. Myrna, with her hardhat cocked to one side, wants to fool around with the incomplete equipment. Piper is with her grandma. We are seated at the control console and she is pretending to work her switch. She has me pretend to work my switch. She wants to launch the entire flight of missiles, D-1 through D-10, at Cuba or Panama. Why Cuba and Panama? I ask. What about Russia? Why not Cuba or Panama? she says. Besides, I have Russian blood. Everyone around here has Russian blood. No, it's Cuba and Panama. Just think of the looks on their faces. All those people lying in the sun on the decks of those big white holiday boats, the coolies out in the cane fields, the tin horn generals, and the whole shiteree. They'll look up trying to shade their eyes but they won't be able to. What in hell is this all about, they'll say, then *zap*, poof, *gone*.

I feel it too, craziness like hers. What if I couldn't get that eight-ton door open, Myrna? I see her hardhat wobble, her lip drop. What if? Just what *if?* She puts her arms around me and our hardhats click. She is one strong woman.

Lloyd, Lloyd, she says.

Yo, I say.

Jesus. *Jesus.*

Easy, easy.

Lloyd!

Bingo.

It's good down here—no *rules*—and she goes berserk. But later she is calm and up to mischief again. I recognize the look now. Okay, I tell her. What *next,* Myrna? She wants to do something halfway nasty. This, believe me, doesn't surprise me at all.

I'm sitting on the steel floor listening to the blower and waiting for Myrna to finish her business. I'm trying hard to picture what the weather is doing topside. It's not easy to do. It could be clear and calm and blue or it could be wild. There could be a high thin overcast or there could be nothing. You just can't know when you're this far under the wheat. I can hear her trying to work the little chrome lever, even though I told her there's no plumbing yet. Some maintenance yokel is going to find Myrna's "surprise." She comes out, pretending to be sheepish, but I can see that the little joke tickles her.

Something takes my hook and strips off ten yards of line then stops dead. Snag. I reel in. The pole is bent double and the line is singing. Then something lets go but it isn't the line because I'm still snagged. It breaks the surface, a lady's shoe. It's brown and white with a short heel. I toss it into the bottom of the boat. The water is shallow here, and clear. There's something dark and wide under me like a shadow on the water. An old farmhouse, submerged when the dam filled. There's a deep current around the structure. I can see fence, tires, an old truck, feed pens. There is a fat farmer in the yard staring up at me, checking the weather, and I jump away from him, almost tipping the boat. My heart feels tangled in my ribs. But it's only a stump with arms.

The current takes my boat in easy circles. A swimmer would be in serious trouble. I crank up the engine and head back. No fish today. So be it. Sometimes you come home empty-handed. The shoe is new, stylish, and was made in Spain.

I'm standing on the buckled porch of 49 Onyx Street. Myrna is inside reading *Secret Confessions:* "What My Don Must Never Know." The sky is bad. The lake is bad. It will be a while before we can cross back. I knock on the door, as we planned. Myrna is on the bed in the stained, raggedy slip, giggling. "Listen to this dogshit, Lloyd," she says. But I'm not in the mood for weird stories. "I brought you something, honey," I say. She looks at the soggy shoe. "That?" But she agrees to try it on, anyway. I feel like my own ghost, bumping into the familiar but run-down walls of my old house in the middle of nowhere, and I remember my hatred of it. "Hurry up," I say, my voice true as a razor.

A thick tube hairy with rain is snaking out of the sky less than a mile away. Is it going to touch? "They never do, Lloyd. This isn't Kansas. Will you please listen to this dogshit?" Something about a pregnant high school girl, Dee, locked in a toilet with a knitting needle. Something about this Don who believes in purity. Something about bright red blood. Something about ministers and mothers and old-fashioned shame. I'm not listening, even when Dee slides the big needle in. I have to keep watch on the sky, because there is a first time for everything, even if this is not Kansas. The wind is stripping shingles from every roof I see. A long board is spinning like a slow propeller. The funnel is behind a bluff, holding back. But I can hear it, the freight trains. Myrna is standing behind me, running a knuckle up and down my back. "Hi, darling," she says. "Want to know what I did while you were out working on the dam today?" The dark tube has begun to move out from behind the bluff, but I'm not sure which way. "Tell me," I say. "Tell me."

Questions for Discussion

1. How would you describe the narrative structure of this story? To what extent is there a traditional plot? What is the chief conflict?

2. When does the story take place, and what is our only clue of this?

3. The narrator does not talk explicitly about nuclear war, but how many other images of and references to different kinds of disaster are there in the story? Which ones are most memorable? Why?

4. What is your assessment of this narrator? What are his sympathetic and unsympathetic qualities? By combining this kind of character with the issue of nuclear weapons, what effect does Demarinis achieve?

Suggestions for Writing

1. One might argue that "Under the Wheat" is a story that refuses to make its theme explicit; its narrator merely reports his day-to-day activities and terrible accidents about which he has heard. Write an essay that attempts to reveal and explain ideas or themes that you believe the story dramatizes, even if indirectly.

2. What is the function of the narrator's marriage—and his attitude toward his wife—in the story?

3. "Under the Wheat" includes several vivid depictions of storms. In your notebook write a description of severe or unusual weather from the point of view of a narrator who may be quite different from you. That is, the description will tell us both about the weather and, indirectly, about the narrator.

Graveyard Shift

STEPHEN KING

Two A.M., Friday.

Hall was sitting on the bench by the elevator, the only place on the third floor where a working joe could catch a smoke, when Warwick came up. He wasn't happy to see Warwick. The foreman wasn't supposed to show up on three during the graveyard shift; he was supposed to stay down in his office in the basement drinking coffee from the urn that stood on the corner of his desk. Besides, it was hot.

It was the hottest June on record in Gates Falls, and the Orange Crush thermometer which was also by the elevator had once rested at 94 degrees at three in the morning. God only knew what kind of hellhole the mill was on the three-to-eleven shift.

Hall worked the picker machine, a balky gadget manufactured by a defunct Cleveland firm in 1934. He had only been working in the mill since April, which meant he was still making minimum $1.78 an hour, which was still all right. No wife, no steady girl, no alimony. He was a drifter, and during the last three years he had moved on his thumb from Berkeley (college student) to Lake Tahoe (busboy) to Galveston (stevedore) to Miami (short-order cook) to Wheeling (taxi driver and dishwasher) to Gates Falls, Maine (picker-machine operator). He didn't figure on moving again until the snow fell. He was a solitary person and he liked the hours from eleven to seven when the blood flow of the big mill was at its coolest, not to mention the temperature.

The only thing he did not like was the rats.

The third floor was long and deserted, lit only by the sputtering glow of the fluorescents. Unlike the other levels of the mill, it was relatively silent and unoccupied—at least by the humans. The rats were another matter. The only machine on three was the picker; the rest of the floor was storage for the ninety-pound bags of fiber which had yet to be sorted by Hall's long gear-toothed machine. They were stacked like link sausages in long rows, some of them (especially the discontinued meltons and irregular slipes for which there were no orders) years old and dirty gray with industrial wastes. They made fine nesting places for the rats, huge, fat-bellied creatures with rabid eyes and bodies that jumped with lice and vermin.

Hall had developed a habit of collecting a small arsenal of soft-drink cans from the trash barrel during his break. He pegged them at the rats during times when work was slow, retrieving them later at his leisure. Only this time Mr. Foreman had caught him, coming up the stairs instead of using the elevator like the sneaky sonofabitch everyone said he was.

"What are you up to, Hall?"

"The rats," Hall said, realizing how lame that must sound now that all the rats had snuggled safely back into their houses. "I peg cans at 'em when I see 'em."

Warwick nodded once, briefly. He was a big beefy man with a crew cut. His shirtsleeves were rolled up and his tie was pulled down. He looked at Hall closely. "We don't pay you to chuck cans at rats, mister. Not even if you pick them up again."

"Harry hasn't sent down an order for twenty minutes," Hall answered, thinking: *Why couldn't you stay the hell put and drink your coffee?* "I can't run it through the picker if I don't have it."

Warwick nodded as if the topic no longer interested him.

"Maybe I'll take a walk up and see Wisconsky," he said. "Five to one he's reading a magazine while the crap piles up in his bins."

Hall didn't say anything.

Warwick suddenly pointed. "There's one! Get the bastard!"

Hall fired the Nehi can he had been holding with one whistling, overhand motion. The rat, which had been watching them from atop one of the fabric bags with its bright buckshot eyes, fled with one faint squeak. Warwick threw back his head and laughed as Hall went after the can.

"I came to see you about something else," Warwick said.

"Is that so?"

"Next week's Fourth of July week." Hall nodded. The mill would be shut down Monday to Saturday—vacation week for men with at least one year's tenure. Layoff week for men with less than a year. "You want to work?"

Hall shrugged. "Doing what?"

"We're going to clean the whole basement level. Nobody's touched it for twelve years. Helluva mess. We're going to use hoses."

"The town zoning committee getting on the board of directors?"

Warwick looked steadily at Hall. "You want it or not? Two an hour, double time on the fourth. We're working the graveyard shift because it'll be cooler."

Hall calculated. He could clear maybe seventy-five bucks after taxes. Better than the goose egg he had been looking forward to.

"All right."

"Report down by the dye house next Monday."

Hall watched him as he started back to the stairs. Warwick paused halfway there and turned back to look at Hall. "You used to be a college boy, didn't you?"

Hall nodded.

"Okay, college boy, I'm keeping it in mind."

He left. Hall sat down and lit another smoke, holding a soda can in one hand and watching for the rats. He could just imagine how it would be in the basement—the sub-basement, actually, a level below the dye house. Damp, dark, full of spiders and rotten cloth and ooze from the river—and rats. Maybe even bats, the aviators of the rodent family. *Gah.*

Hall threw the can hard, then smiled thinly to himself as the faint sound of Warwick's voice came down through the overhead ducts, reading Harry Wisconsky the riot act.

Okay, college boy, I'm keeping it in mind.

He stopped smiling abruptly and butted his smoke. A few moments later Wisconsky started to send rough nylon down through the blowers, and Hall went to work. And after a while the rats came out and sat atop the bags at the back of the long room watching him with their unblinking black eyes. They looked like a jury.

Eleven P.M., Monday.

There were about thirty-six men sitting around when Warwick came in wearing a pair of old jeans tucked into high rubber boots. Hall had been listening to Harry Wisconsky, who was enormously fat, enormously lazy, and enormously gloomy.

"It's gonna be a mess," Wisconsky was saying when Mr. Foreman came in. "You wait and see, we're all gonna go home blacker'n midnight in Persia."

"Okay!" Warwick said. "We strung sixty lightbulbs down there, so it should be bright enough for you to see what you're doing. You guys"—he pointed to a bunch of men that had been leaning against the drying spools—"I want you to hook up the hoses over there to the main water conduit by the stairwell. You can unroll them down the stairs. We got about eighty yards for each man, and that should be plenty. Don't get cute and spray one of your buddies or you'll send him to the hospital. They pack a wallop."

"Somebody'll get hurt," Wisconsky prophesied sourly. "Wait and see."

"You other guys," Warwick said pointing to the group that Hall and Wisconsky were a part of. "You're the crap crew tonight. You go in pairs with an electric wagon for each team. There's old office furniture, bags of cloth, hunks of busted machinery, you name it. We're gonna pile it by the airshaft at the west end. Anyone who doesn't know how to run a wagon?"

No one raised a hand. The electric wagons were battery-driven contraptions like miniature dump trucks. They developed a nauseating stink after continual use that reminded Hall of burning power lines.

"Okay," Warwick said. "We got the basement divided up into sections, and we'll be done by Thursday. Friday we'll chain-hoist the crap out. Questions?"

There were none. Hall studied the foreman's face closely, and he had a sudden premonition of a strange thing coming. The idea pleased him. He did not like Warwick very much.

"Fine," Warwick said. "Let's get at it."

Two A.M., Tuesday.

Hall was bushed and very tired of listening to Wisconsky's steady patter of profane complaints. He wondered if it would do any good to belt Wisconsky. He doubted it. It would just give Wisconsky something else to bitch about.

Hall had known it would be bad, but this was murder. For one thing, he hadn't anticipated the smell. The polluted stink of the river, mixed with the odor of decaying fabric, rotting masonry, vegetable matter. In the far corner, where they had begun, Hall discovered a colony of huge white toadstools poking their way up through the shattered cement. His hands had come in contact with them as he pulled and yanked at a rusty gear-toothed wheel, and they felt curiously warm and bloated, like the flesh of a man afflicted with dropsy.

The bulbs couldn't banish the twelve-year darkness; it could only push it back a little and cast a sickly yellow glow over the whole mess. The place looked like the shattered nave of a desecrated church, with its high ceiling and mammoth discarded machinery that they would never be able to move, its wet walls overgrown with patches of yellow moss, and the atonal choir that was the water from the hoses, running in the half-clogged sewer network that eventually emptied into the river below the falls.

And the rats—huge ones that made those on third look like dwarfs. God knew what they were eating down here. They were continually overturning boards and bags to reveal huge nests of shredded newspaper, watching with atavistic loathing as the pups fled into the cracks and crannies, their eyes huge and blind with the continuous darkness.

"Let's stop for a smoke," Wisconsky said. He sounded out of breath, but Hall had no idea why; he had been goldbricking all night. Still, it was about that time, and they were currently out of sight of everyone else.

"All right." He leaned against the edge of the electric wagon and lit up.

"I never should've let Warwick talk me into this," Wisconsky said dolefully. "This ain't work for a *man*. But he was mad the other night when he caught me in the crapper up on four with my pants up. Christ, was he mad."

Hall said nothing. He was thinking about Warwick, and about the rats. Strange, how the two things seemed tied together. The rats seemed to have forgotten all about men in their long stay under the mill; they were impudent and hardly afraid at all. One of them had sat up on its hind legs like a squirrel until Hall had gotten in kicking distance, and then it had launched itself at his boot, biting at the leather. Hundreds, maybe thousands. He wondered how many varieties of disease they were carrying around in this black sumphole. And Warwick. Something about him—

"I need the money," Wisconsky said. "But Christ Jesus, buddy, this ain't no work for a *man*. Those rats." He looked around fearfully. "It almost seems like they think. You ever wonder how it'd be, if we was little and they were big—"

"Oh, shut up," Hall said.

Wisconsky looked at him, wounded. "Say, I'm sorry, buddy. It's just that . . ." He trailed off. "Jesus, this place stinks!" he cried. "This ain't no kind of *work for a man!*" A spider crawled off the edge of the wagon and scrambled up his arm. He brushed it off with a choked sound of disgust.

"Come on," Hall said, snuffing his cigarette. "The faster, the quicker."

"I suppose," Wisconsky said miserably. "I suppose."

Four A.M., Tuesday.
Lunchtime.

Hall and Wisconsky sat with three or four other men, eating their sandwiches with black hands that not even the industrial detergent could clean. Hall ate looking into the foreman's little glass office. Warwick was drinking coffee and eating cold hamburgers with great relish.

"Ray Upson had to go home," Charlie Brochu said.

"He puke?" someone asked. "I almost did."

"Nuh. Ray'd eat cowflop before he'd puke. Rat bit him."

Hall looked up thoughtfully from his examination of Warwick. "Is that so?" he asked.

"Yeah." Brochu shook his head. "I was teaming with him. Goddamndest thing I ever saw. Jumped out of a hole in one of those old cloth bags. Must have been big as a cat. Grabbed onto his hand and started chewing."

"Jee-*sus*," one of the men said, looking green.

"Yeah," Brochu said. "Ray screamed just like a woman, and I ain't blamin' him. He bled like a pig. Would that thing let go? No sir. I had to belt it three or four times with a board before it would. Ray was just about crazy. He stomped it until it wasn't nothing but a mess of fur. Damndest thing I ever saw. Warwick put a bandage on him and sent him home. Told him to go to the doctor tomorrow."

"That was big of the bastard," somebody said.

As if he had heard, Warwick got to his feet in his office, stretched, and then came to the door. "Time we got back with it."

The men got to their feet slowly, eating up all the time they possibly could stowing their dinner buckets, getting cold drinks, buying candy bars. Then they started down, heels clanking dispiritedly on the steel grillwork of the stair risers.

Warwick passed Hall, clapping him on the shoulder. "How's it going, college boy?" He didn't wait for an answer.

"Come on," Hall said patiently to Wisconsky, who was tying his shoelace. They went downstairs.

Seven A.M., Tuesday.

Hall and Wisconsky walked out together; it seemed to Hall that he had somehow inherited the fat Pole. Wisconsky was almost comically dirty, his fat moon face smeared like that of a small boy who has just been thrashed by the town bully.

There was none of the usual rough banter from the other men, the pulling of shirttails, the cracks about who was keeping Tony's wife warm between the hours of one and four. Nothing but silence and an occasional hawking sound as someone spat on the dirty floor.

"You want a lift?" Wisconsky asked him hesitantly.

"Thanks."

They didn't talk as they rode up Mill Street and crossed the bridge. They exchanged only a brief word when Wisconsky dropped him off in front of his apartment.

Hall went directly to the shower, still thinking about Warwick, trying to place whatever it was about Mr. Foreman that drew him, made him feel that somehow they had become tied together.

He slept as soon as his head hit the pillow, but his sleep was broken and restless: he dreamed of rats.

One A.M., Wednesday.

It was better running the hoses.

They couldn't go in until the crap crews had finished a section, and quite often they were done hosing before the next section was clear—which meant time for a cigarette. Hall worked the nozzle of one of the long hoses and Wisconsky pattered back and forth, unsnagging lengths of the hose, turning the water on and off, moving obstructions.

Warwick was short-tempered because the work was proceeding slowly. They would never be done by Thursday, the way things were going.

Now they were working on a helter-skelter jumble of nineteenth-century office equipment that had been piled in one corner—smashed rolltop desks, moldy ledgers, reams of invoices, chairs with broken seats—and it was rat heaven. Scores of them squeaked and ran through the dark and crazy passages that honeycombed the heap, and after two men were bitten, the others refused to work until Warwick sent someone upstairs to get heavy rubberized gloves, the kind usually reserved for the dye-house crew, which had to work with acids.

Hall and Wisconsky were waiting to go in with their hoses when a sandy-haired bullneck named Carmichael began howling curses and backing away, slapping at his chest with his gloved hands.

A huge rat with gray-streaked fur and ugly, glaring eyes had bitten into his shirt and hung there, squeaking and kicking at Carmichael's belly with its back paws. Carmichael finally knocked it away with his fist, but there was a huge hole in his shirt, and a thin line of blood trickled from above one nipple. The anger faded from his face. He turned away and retched.

Hall turned the hose on the rat, which was old and moving slowly, a snatch of Carmichael's shirt still caught in its jaws. The roaring pressure drove it backward against the wall, where it smashed limply.

Warwick came over, an odd, strained smile on his lips. He clapped Hall on the shoulder. "Damn sight better than throwing cans at the little bastards, huh, college boy?"

"Some little bastard," Wisconsky said. "It's a foot long."

"Turn that hose over there." Warwick pointed at the jumble of furniture. "You guys, get out of the way!"

"With pleasure," someone muttered.

Carmichael charged up to Warwick, his face sick and twisted. "I'm gonna have compensation for this! I'm gonna—"

"Sure," Warwick said, smiling. "You got bit on the titty. Get out of the way before you get pasted down by this water."

Hall pointed the nozzle and let it go. It hit with a white explosion of spray, knocking over a desk and smashing two chairs to splinters. Rats ran everywhere, bigger than any Hall had ever seen. He could hear men crying out in disgust and horror as they fled, things with huge eyes and sleek, plump bodies. He caught a glimpse of one that looked as big as a healthy six-week puppy. He kept on until he could see no more, then shut the nozzle down.

"Okay!" Warwick called. "Let's pick it up!"

"I didn't hire out as no exterminator!" Cy Ippeston called mutinously. Hall had tipped a few with him the week before. He was a young guy, wearing a smut-stained baseball cap and a T-shirt.

"That you, Ippeston?" Warwick asked genially.

Ippeston looked uncertain, but stepped forward. "Yeah. I don't want no more of these rats. I hired to clean up, not to maybe get rabies or typhoid or somethin'. Maybe you best count me out."

There was a murmur of agreement from the others. Wisconsky stole a look at Hall, but Hall was examining the nozzle of the hose he was holding. It had a bore like a .45 and could probably knock a man twenty feet.

"You saying you want to punch your clock, Cy?"

"Thinkin' about it," Ippeston said.

Warwick nodded. "Okay. You and anybody else that wants. But this ain't no unionized shop, and never has been. Punch out now and you'll never punch back in. I'll see to it."

"Aren't you some hot ticket," Hall muttered.

Warwick swung around. "Did you say something, college boy?"

Hall regarded him blandly. "Just clearing my throat, Mr. Foreman."

Warwick smiled. "Something taste bad to you?"

Hall said nothing.

"All right, let's pick it up!" Warwick bawled.

They went back to work.

Two A.M., Thursday.

Hall and Wisconsky were working with the trucks again, picking up junk. The pile by the west airshaft had grown to amazing proportions, but they were still not half done.

"Happy Fourth," Wisconsky said when they stopped for a smoke. They were working near the north wall, far from the stairs. The light was extremely dim, and some trick of acoustics made the other men seem miles away.

"Thanks." Hall dragged on his smoke. "Haven't seen many rats tonight."

"Nobody has," Wisconsky said. "Maybe they got wise."

They were standing at the end of a cozy, zigzagging alley formed by piles of old ledgers and invoices, moldy bags of cloth, and two huge flat looms of ancient vintage. "Gah," Wisconsky said, spitting. "That Warwick—"

"Where do you suppose all the rats got to?" Hall asked, almost to himself. "Not into the walls—" He looked at the wet and crumbling masonry that surrounded the huge foundation stones. "They'd drown. The river's saturated everything."

Something black and flapping suddenly dive-bombed them. Wisconsky screamed and put his hands over his head.

"A bat," Hall said, watching after it as Wisconsky straightened up.

"A bat! A bat!" Wisconsky raved. "What's a bat doing in the cellar? They're supposed to be in trees and under eaves and—"

"It was a big one," Hall said softly. "And what's a bat but a rat with wings?"

"Jesus," Wisconsky moaned. "How did it—"

"Get in? Maybe the same way the rats got out."

"What's going on back there?" Warwick shouted from somewhere behind them. "Where are you?"

"Don't sweat it," Hall said softly. His eyes gleamed in the dark.

"Was that you, college boy?" Warwick called. He sounded closer.

"It's okay!" Hall yelled. "I barked my shin!"

Warwick's short, barking laugh. "You want a Purple Heart?"

Wisconsky looked at Hall. "Why'd you say that?"

"Look." Hall knelt and lit a match. There was a square in the middle of the wet and crumbling cement. "Tap it."

Wisconsky did. "It's wood."

Hall nodded. "It's the top of a support. I've seen some other ones around here. There's another level under this part of the basement."

"God," Wisconsky said with utter revulsion.

Three-thirty A.M., Thursday.

They were in the northeast corner, Ippeston and Brochu behind them with one of the high-pressure hoses, when Hall stopped and pointed at the floor. "There, I thought we'd come across it."

There was a wooden trapdoor with a crusted iron ringbolt set near the center.

He walked back to Ippeston and said, "Shut it off for a minute." When the hose was choked to a trickle, he raised his voice to a shout. "Hey! Hey, Warwick! Better come here a minute!"

Warwick came splashing over, looking at Hall with that same bird smile in his eyes. "Your shoelace come untied, college boy?"

"Look," Hall said. He kicked the trapdoor with his foot. "Sub-cellar."

"So what?" Warwick asked. "This isn't break time, col—"

"That's where your rats are," Hall said. "They're breeding down there. Wisconsky and I even saw a bat earlier."

Some of the other men had gathered round and were looking at the trapdoor.

"I don't care," Warwick said. "The job was the basement, not—"

"You'll need about twenty exterminators, trained ones," Hall was saying. "Going to cost the management a pretty penny. Too bad."

Someone laughed. "Fat chance."

Warwick looked at Hall as if he were a bug under glass. "You're really a case, you are," he said, sounding fascinated. "Do you think I give a good goddamn how many rats there are under there?"

"I was at the library this afternoon and yesterday," Hall said. "Good thing you kept reminding me I was a college boy. I read the town zoning ordinances, Warwick—they were set up in 1911, before this mill got big enough to co-opt the zoning board. Know what I found?"

Warwick's eyes were cold. "Take a walk, college boy. You're fired."

"I found out," Hall plowed on as if he hadn't heard, "I found out that there is a zoning law in Gates Falls about vermin. You spell that v-e-r-m-i-n, in case you wondered. It means disease-carrying animals such as bats, skunks, unlicensed dogs—and rats. Especially rats. Rats are mentioned fourteen times in two paragraphs, Mr. Foreman. So you just keep in mind that the minute I punch out I'm going straight to the town commissioner and tell him what the situation down here is."

He paused, relishing Warwick's hate-congested face. "I think that between me, him, and the town committee, we can get an injunction slapped on this place.

You're going to be shut down a lot longer than just Saturday, Mr. Foreman. And I got a good idea what *your* boss is going to say when he turns up. Hope your unemployment insurance is paid up, Warwick."

Warwick's hands formed into claws. "You damned snot-nose, I ought to—" He looked down at the trapdoor, and suddenly his smile reappeared. "Consider yourself rehired, college boy."

"I thought you might see the light."

Warwick nodded, the same strange grin on his face. "You're just so smart. I think maybe you ought to go down there, Hall, so we got somebody with a college education to give us an informed opinion. You and Wisconsky."

"Not me!" Wisconsky exclaimed. "Not me, I—"

Warwick looked at him. "You what?"

Wisconsky shut up.

"Good," Hall said cheerfully. "We'll need three flashlights. I think I saw a whole rack of six-battery jobs in the main office, didn't I?"

"You want to take somebody else?" Warwick asked expansively. "Sure, pick your man."

"You," Hall said gently. The strange expression had come into his face again. "After all, the management should be represented, don't you think? Just so Wisconsky and I don't see *too* many rats down there?"

Someone (it sounded like Ippeston) laughed loudly.

Warwick looked at the men carefully. They studied the tips of their shoes. Finally he pointed at Brochu. "Brochu, go up to the office and get three flashlights. Tell the watchman I said to let you in."

"Why'd you get me into this?" Wisconsky moaned to Hall. "You know I hate those—"

"It wasn't me," Hall said, and looked at Warwick.

Warwick looked back at him, and neither would drop his eyes.

Four A.M., Thursday.

Brochu returned with the flashlights. He gave one to Hall, one to Wisconsky, one to Warwick.

"Ippeston! Give the hose to Wisconsky." Ippeston did so. The nozzle trembled delicately between the Pole's hands.

"All right," Warwick said to Wisconsky. "You're in the middle. If there are rats, you let them have it."

Sure, Hall thought. And if there are rats, Warwick won't see them. And neither will Wisconsky, after he finds an extra ten in his pay envelope.

Warwick pointed at two of the men. "Lift it."

One of them bent over the ringbolt and pulled. For a moment Hall didn't think it was going to give, and then it yanked free with an odd, crunching snap. The other man put his fingers on the underside to help pull, then withdrew with a cry. His hands were crawling with huge and sightless beetles.

With a convulsive grunt the man on the ringbolt pulled the trap back and let it drop. The underside was black with an odd fungus that Hall had never seen before. The beetles dropped off into the darkness below or ran across the floor to be crushed.

"Look," Hall said.

There was a rusty lock bolted on the underside, now broken. "But it shouldn't be underneath," Warwick said. "It should be on top. Why—"

"Lots of reasons," Hall said. "Maybe so nothing on this side could open it—at least when the lock was new. Maybe so nothing on that side could get up."

"But who locked it?" Wisconsky asked.

"Ah," Hall said mockingly, looking at Warwick. "A mystery."

"Listen," Brochu whispered.

"Oh, God," Wisconsky sobbed. "I ain't going down there!"

It was a soft sound, almost expectant; the whisk and patter of thousands of paws, the squeaking of rats.

"Could be frogs," Warwick said.

Hall laughed aloud.

Warwick shone his light down. A sagging flight of wooden stairs led down to the black stones of the floor beneath. There was not a rat in sight.

"Those stairs won't hold us," Warwick said with finality.

Brochu took two steps forward and jumped up and down on the first step. It creaked but showed no sign of giving way.

"I didn't ask you to do that," Warwick said.

"You weren't there when that rat bit Ray," Brochu said softly.

"Let's go," Hall said.

Warwick took a last sardonic look around at the circle of men, then walked to the edge with Hall. Wisconsky stepped reluctantly between them. They went down one at a time. Hall, then Wisconsky, then Warwick. Their flashlight beams played over the floor, which was twisted and heaved into a hundred crazy hills and valleys. The hose thumped along behind Wisconsky like a clumsy serpent.

When they got to the bottom, Warwick flashed his light around. It picked out a few rotting boxes, some barrels, little else. The seep from the river stood in puddles that came to ankle depth on their boots.

"I don't hear them anymore," Wisconsky whispered.

They walked slowly away from the trapdoor, their feet shuffling through the slime. Hall paused and shone his light on a huge wooden box with white letters on it. "Elias Varney," he read, "1841. Was the mill here then?"

"No," Warwick said. "It wasn't built until 1897. What difference?"

Hall didn't answer. They walked forward again. The subcellar was longer than it should have been, it seemed. The stench was stronger, a smell of decay and rot and things buried. And still the only sound was the faint, cavelike drip of water.

"What's that?" Hall asked, pointing his beam at a jut of concrete that protruded perhaps two feet into the cellar. Beyond it, the darkness continued and it seemed to Hall that he could now hear sounds up there, curiously stealthy.

Warwick peered at it. "It's . . . no, that can't be right."

"Outer wall of the mill, isn't it? And up ahead . . ."

"I'm going back," Warwick said, suddenly turning around.

Hall grabbed his neck roughly. "You're not going anywhere, Mr. Foreman."

Warwick looked up at him, his grin cutting the darkness. "You're crazy, college boy. Isn't that right? Crazy as a loon."

"You shouldn't push people, friend. Keep going."

Wisconsky moaned. "Hall—"

"Give me that." Hall grabbed the hose. He let go of Warwick's neck and pointed the hose at his head. Wisconsky turned abruptly and crashed back toward the trapdoor. Hall did not even turn. "After you, Mr. Foreman."

Warwick stepped forward, walking under the place where the mill ended above them. Hall flashed his light about, and felt a cold satisfaction—premonition fulfilled. The rats had closed in around them, silent as death. Crowded in, rank on rank. Thousands of eyes looked greedily back at him. In ranks to the wall, some fully as high as a man's shin.

Warwick saw them a moment later and came to a full stop. "They're all around us, college boy." His voice was still calm, still in control, but it held a jagged edge.

"Yes," Hall said. "Keep going."

They walked forward, the hose dragging behind. Hall looked back once and saw the rats had closed the aisle behind them and were gnawing at the heavy canvas hosing. One looked up and almost seemed to grin at him before lowering his head again. He could see the bats now, too. They were roosting from the roughhewn overheads, huge, the size of crows or rooks.

"Look," Warwick said, centering his beam about five feet ahead.

A skull, green with mold, laughed up at them. Further on Hall could see an ulna, one pelvic wing, part of a ribcage. "Keep going," Hall said. He felt something bursting up inside him, something lunatic and dark with colors. *You are going to break before I do, Mr. Foreman, so help me God.*

They walked past the bones. The rats were not crowding them; their distances appeared constant. Up ahead Hall saw one cross their path of travel. Shadows hid it, but he caught sight of a pink twitching tail as thick as a telephone cord.

Up ahead the flooring rose sharply, then dipped. Hall could hear a stealthy rustling sound, a big sound. Something that perhaps no living man had ever seen. It occurred to Hall that he had perhaps been looking for something like this through all his days of crazy wandering.

The rats were moving in, creeping on their bellies, forcing them forward. "Look," Warwick said coldly.

Hall saw. Something had happened to the rats back here, some hideous mutation that never could have survived under the eye of the sun; nature would have forbidden it. But down here, nature had taken on another ghastly face.

The rats were gigantic, some as high as three feet. But their rear legs were gone and they were blind as moles, like their flying cousins. They dragged themselves forward with hideous eagerness.

Warwick turned and faced Hall, the smile hanging on by brute willpower. Hall really had to admire him. "We can't go on, Hall. You must see that."

"The rats have business with you, I think," Hall said.

Warwick's control slipped. "Please," he said. "Please."

Hall smiled. "Keep going."

Warwick was looking over his shoulder. "They're gnawing into the hose. When they get through it, we'll never get back."

"I know. Keep going."

"You're insane—" A rat ran across Warwick's shoe and he screamed. Hall smiled and gestured with his light. They were all around, the closest of them less than a foot away now.

Warwick began to walk again. The rats drew back.

They topped the miniature rise and looked down. Warwick reached it first, and Hall saw his face go white as paper. Spit ran down his chin. "Oh, my God. Dear Jesus."

And he turned to run.

Hall opened the nozzle of the hose and the high-pressure rush of water struck Warwick squarely on the chest, knocking him back out of sight. There was a long scream that rose over the sound of the water. Thrashing sounds.

"Hall!" Grunts. A huge, tenebrous squeaking that seemed to fill the earth. "HALL, FOR GOD'S SAKE—"

A sudden wet ripping noise. Another scream, weaker. Something huge shifted and turned. Quite distinctly Hall heard the wet snap that a fractured bone makes.

A legless rat, guided by some bastard form of sonar, lunged against him, biting. Its body was flabby, warm. Almost absently Hall turned the hose on it, knocking it away. The hose did not have quite so much pressure now.

Hall walked to the brow of the wet hill and looked down.

The rat filled the whole gully at the far end of that noxious tomb. It was a huge and pulsating gray, eyeless, totally without legs. When Hall's light struck it, it made a hideous mewling noise. Their queen, then, the *magna mater*. A huge and nameless thing whose progeny might someday develop wings. It seemed to dwarf what remained of Warwick, but that was probably just illusion. It was the shock of seeing a rat as big as a Holstein calf.

"Goodbye, Warwick," Hall said. The rat crouched over Mr. Foreman jealously, ripping at one limp arm.

Hall turned away and began to make his way back rapidly, halting the rats with his hose, which was growing less and less potent. Some of them got through and attacked his legs above the tops of his boots with biting lunges. One hung stubbornly on at his thigh, ripping at the cloth of his corduroy pants. Hall made a fist and smashed it aside.

He was nearly three-quarters of the way back when the huge whirring filled the darkness. He looked up and the gigantic flying form smashed into his face.

The mutated bats had not lost their tails yet. It whipped around Hall's neck in a loathsome coil and squeezed as the teeth sought the soft spot under his neck. It wriggled and flapped with its membranous wings, clutching the tatters of his shirt for purchase.

Hall brought the nozzle of the hose up blindly and struck at its yielding body again and again. It fell away and he trampled it beneath his feet, dimly aware that he was screaming. The rats ran in a flood over his feet, up his legs.

He broke into a staggering run, shaking some off. The others bit at his belly, his chest. One ran up his shoulder and pressed its questing muzzle into the cup of his ear.

He ran into the second bat. It roosted on his head for a moment, squealing, and then ripped away a flap of Hall's scalp.

He felt his body growing numb. His ears filled with the screech and yammer of many rats. He gave one last heave, stumbled over furry bodies, fell to his knees. He began to laugh, a high, screaming sound.

Five A.M., Thursday.

"Somebody better go down there," Brochu said tentatively.

"Not me," Wisconsky whispered. "Not me."

"No, not you, jelly belly," Ippeston said with contempt.

"Well, let's go," Brogan said, bringing up another hose. "Me, Ippeston, Dangerfield, Nedeau. Stevenson, go up to the office and get a few more lights."

Ippeston looked down into the darkness thoughtfully. "Maybe they stopped for a smoke," he said. "A few rats, what the hell."

Stevenson came back with the lights; a few moments later they started down.

Questions for Discussion

1. Judging from King's story, what are some key elements of a "horror story"?

2. How important is setting (time, place) in this story? What does it add to the story?

3. How would you describe the characters in this story?

4. Are King's descriptions excessive? Why or why not?

Suggestions for Writing

1. Using King's story as evidence, write an essay in which you argue for or against the inherent value of "horror fiction."

2. Write an essay in which you compare and contrast King's story with Poe's "The Tell-Tale Heart." How does each author work within the subgenre of psychological horror differently?

3. Write a one-page imitation of Stephen King's writing.

A Pair of Glasses

TESS GALLAGHER

Her grandmother would put on glasses to read labels on cans when the girl went to the market with her. The grandmother would read the brand names and the prices out loud to the girl. The girl could not read much yet herself, but sometimes she pretended she could. The grandmother would read a word, and the girl would say it to herself and stare at the word—trying to hold it in her mind. They would go down the aisles this way, the girl pushing the cart and saying the brand names and prices. At the counter the grandmother would take her billfold out of her purse, hand the purse to the girl and take off the glasses.

"Here, put these away for me, honey," she'd say, and the eyeglasses would come into the girl's hands. It was always an important moment, to be holding the glasses. Under the lenses the girl's fingers seemed larger, and as if they had a life of their own. When she looked down, her shoes leapt up at her from the floor. Once when her grandmother had to leave the counter for a moment, the girl had put the purse in the shopping basket and opened up the eyeglasses. She set them on the bridge of her nose and held them there, looking around at the blurred faces of the other shoppers. It was a wonderful, dizzying feeling and it gave her the idea that the wearing of glasses was a way of seeing that only a few people were privileged to have. When the grandmother returned with the missing grocery item, she took the eyeglasses from the girl.

"You're going to break those, honey. Here, let's put them away." Then the glasses had gone back inside the purse until the next shopping trip.

Neither the girl's father nor her mother wore eyeglasses. The nearest thing to glasses in the house was a pair of field glasses her father kept in the corner cabinet. He used these when he went deer hunting and also to watch ships passing through the inlet of water which their house faced. Once the girl had stood in a chair at the window and her father had stood behind her holding the field glasses to her eyes. The glasses were heavy.

"Can you see now?" he asked her. He twisted the lenses and the girl stared into the glasses until she could begin to see an object taking shape. When she could tell what it was, she jumped up in the chair until her nose knocked against the metal bridge of the glasses.

"A boat! A boat with a man in it," she reported. Then her father said sternly, "Now you're getting silly. Stand still or I'll put them away." Then the girl stood still and watched the waves lapping the side of the boat. The man stood up and turned sideways so the girl could see he was reeling on a fishing pole.

"He's got a fish!" the girl said, pressing her eyes into the metal rims of the field glasses.

"Let me see," her father said, and lifted the glasses from her. Then she could see only a far black speck on the bluegray water.

"I don't think he's got anything," her father said after he'd held the glasses on the speck a long time. "If he did, he lost it." Finally her father put the glasses back into their leather case.

The girl liked the smell of the leather case. Sometimes she would beg to be allowed to put the field glasses away, just for the pleasure of how perfectly the lenses slid into the darkness of the case. Then she snapped the case shut and her father swung the glasses up to the top of the corner cabinet, until the next time he wanted to watch something on the water.

No one in the girl's class at school wore eyeglasses, but on the playground she saw several children who did wear them. This set them apart from the others—as if they might be smarter or able to see things she couldn't. She began to yearn for the company of those who wore glasses.

At recess the girl played jump-rope with an older girl who wore glasses. The other girl's name was Brenda, and Brenda loved to jump double-dutch. The girl was especially good at turning the ropes for double-dutch, so Brenda often asked her to get a partner and turn the ropes while she jumped. Besides the glasses, which had blue plastic rims, Brenda had pigtails which her mother often tied with blue ribbons. The girl thought the sight of Brenda jumping double-dutch with her blue-rimmed glasses and the blue hair-ribbons bouncing on her pigtails between the whipping sound of the ropes was the most wonderful sight she could imagine.

Then one day while the girl was turning the ropes, one of Brenda's pigtails caught in the ropes and the blue-rimmed glasses went flying. The girl dropped her end of the ropes and ran over to the glasses before anyone else could reach them. She picked them up. But when she saw the crack across one lens she started to cry. Brenda was upset too and the girls wept into each other's hair with the eyeglasses pressed between them. The next day Brenda came to school without the glasses and she seemed then, to the girl, to have passed back into the ranks of the ordinary.

It was late October and leaves covered the sidewalk. The girl walked to school in the crisp morning air. On her way she gathered a bouquet of the brightest orange and red leaves she could find. She gave these to her teacher, Miss Binki. Miss Binki was very tall and slender, but one feature of her appearance held the girl's amazement, and she supposed that all the other students were similarly fascinated. Miss Binki had pointed breasts that pushed her sweater out. The girl stared with her mouth open as the breasts moved around the schoolroom, hovering over her classmates' shoulders when Miss Binki stooped beside them to help with their work. Some days the breasts seemed more prominent than others. These were days when Miss Binki apparently felt like setting a good example for her students. It was then she would show them how to stand tall and straight with their shoulders back and chests out. Good posture was important, Miss Binki said, and Miss Binki saw to it that they practiced it by walking around the room with encyclopedias balanced on their heads.

The girl carried the volume *Bu–Cz* on her head. When she passed Miss Binki's desk the woman smiled at her. It was at this minute the girl lost her balance and the book tumbled from her head across Miss Binki's desk and into her lap. Miss Binki very calmly picked up the book, walked around the desk and placed it back on the girl's head. After a moment, the girl continued walking.

Once, before leaving for school in the morning, the girl asked her mother if there wasn't something she could take to Miss Binki as a present. Her mother went into the fruit cellar and brought up a jar of raspberry jam. The girl carried the jam to school and placed it on Miss Binki's desk before the teacher arrived.

"Who brought me this nice jar of jam?" Miss Binki asked the class once they were all seated at their desks. The girl was too shy to answer. Then one of the boys who'd seen the girl put the jam on the desk began to point his finger and call, "She did, she did!" Later, on the playground, this same boy called her "teacher's pet" and chanted this until the girl left the playground.

It was about this time that the girl, in the presence of grown-ups, began to rub at her eyes with the heel of her hand and to blink when the grown-ups talked to her. At school the children were cutting out pilgrims—the men in their tall black hats, the women in bonnets. The girl preferred to draw. She drew a turkey with a tail showing all the colors in the rainbow. She drew a pilgrim holding the turkey by the feet, and she added a pair of spectacles to the pilgrim. She told Miss Binki that this was so he could see all the beautiful colors of the tail feathers. But in the girl's reading group she complained that she couldn't see the letters plainly, and she asked to be moved closer to the blackboard.

Miss Binki sent a note home with the girl in a sealed envelope. Not long after that, the girl's father and mother dressed up in their good clothes and drove the girl to an eye doctor for an examination. At first the girl thought this doctor must be a kind of dentist and that he intended to pull her eyes out. She put her fists over her eyes and braced against the wall of the office. She wouldn't go into the examination room. But finally she took her father's hand and went into the room, which held various machines and charts. After a short while, the doctor came in. The girl noticed that he was wearing a pair of spectacles himself, and then that he was wearing a white jacket with several pens clipped to his pocket. The doctor turned off the lights in the room and positioned himself in front of the girl. He began to flash sharp pinpoints of light into her open eyes. Then he asked her if she knew the alphabet. The girl said she did. The doctor began to project different-sized letters of the alphabet onto a large screen on one wall of the examination room. The girl knew something serious was taking place. Her parents were worried about her eyesight. They had brought her to a man who gave out eyeglasses to those with poor eyesight. The girl hoped more than anything that her eyesight would be found poor enough so the doctor would prescribe a pair of eyeglasses for her.

When the letter *C* flashed onto the screen the girl knew it was *C,* but she said "*O.*" An *h* appeared and she said it was a *b.* If there was an open space to the letter, she closed it and made another letter out of it. Sometimes she couldn't think what to do, so she just said she couldn't see what the letter was. She was certain she'd demonstrated that she had terrible eyesight. Leaving the examination room, she bumped into things as the bright daylight streamed down on her.

She sat with her mother in the waiting room while the doctor talked to her father. Finally her father came out.

"You talk to him," her father said to her mother.

Then the girl sat with her father until her mother reappeared. Her mother was nodding to what the doctor was saying. "We'll talk it over," her mother told the doctor. "We'll see."

The girl felt worried and happy at the same time. She got into the car with her parents and stared out the window as they passed all the familiar stores and houses of the town. When they arrived home her parents went inside and into the kitchen, where they made coffee and sat at the kitchen table. They were quiet and the girl supposed they were thinking of what to do about her bad eyes. She wondered why they hadn't had her fitted for eyeglasses right then and there at the doctor's office—why she was being allowed to walk around in such a condition. Then her father called her over to the table and told her to sit with them.

"The doctor says you've got an eye disease," her father said. "It could get worse, and it could get better. But there are treatments, and if that doesn't work there's an operation they can do." Her father looked at her mother and then took a sip from his coffee. "But it costs a lot of money," he said. "There's no way we can pay for such things," her father said.

"Here, honey," her mother said. "Here's a glass of milk. Sit over here next to me and drink it." The girl moved over next to her mother, took the glass of milk and looked into it as if it had betrayed her. She felt too sad to drink anything, but she took several large gulps of milk.

"We'll just have to hope the trouble isn't as serious as the doctor thinks," her mother said. "Maybe it will clear up."

In the days and weeks that followed, the girl tried to remember that she had bad eyes, but she often forgot and became perfectly able to see words on the blackboard. Miss Binki praised her and several times said how glad she was that the girl's eyesight was improving. This forgetfulness did not mean that the girl had given up the idea of getting her own pair of glasses.

On a trip to the dimestore with her grandmother to buy hair ribbons, the girl had spotted rows and rows of eyeglasses between the handkerchief and yarn displays. When she picked up a pair and peered through them, the shelves in the store had loomed up around her until the pit of her stomach ached. She begged her grandmother to buy her a pair.

"Those glasses are for old people like me," her grandmother said. "Those are reading glasses for very weak, tired eyes like mine."

A few days before Christmas the girl's father asked her to name a few things she might like to find under the Christmas tree when she opened her gifts.

"A pair of glasses," the girl said. "Like those in the dimestore."

"Oh, I don't know about that," her father said and laughed. Then he looked at her and said, "Is that what you really want?"

"Yes," the girl said. "A pair of eyeglasses."

On Christmas Eve the girl opened her gifts with her parents and grandmother watching. She got a pair of rain boots, more hair ribbons and a bag of peppermint candies. But no eyeglasses. Then her father left the room and came back with a small package.

"Here," he said. "Maybe this will cheer you up."

Inside the wrapping paper was a pair of eyeglasses from the dimestore. The girl was so happy she forgot all her other gifts. She unfolded the eyeglasses and tried them on.

"They're a little big," her mother said. "Maybe we should take them back and get a smaller pair."

"No, no," the girl cried. "They fit me. They fit fine." She got up from the chair she'd been sitting in and took a few steps into the room. The glasses wiggled on her nose as she walked, and the room seemed to tilt back and forth. The Christmas tree lights blurred into each other and blazed against her face as she stared at them. The faces of her parents and her grandmother seemed odd to her, like masks, and she drew back from this vision. But mostly she was pleased with what she saw when she looked out through the eyeglasses. She felt as if she had grown larger, and although she knew this wasn't so, she loved the feeling because she thought it made her seem older.

The next day she wore the glasses all day. She was disappointed that there were no children in the neighborhood she could show them to. School would begin again in a few days, she knew, but in the meantime she was the only one except her family who knew she had a pair of eyeglasses. That evening, her mother came in to say good night and discovered the girl in bed with her glasses on.

"What do you expect to see while you're asleep?" her mother asked, and took the glasses from her. But the next day her mother gave them back. The girl put them on when the mailman came. She met him on the porch.

"Are you the doctor of the house?" he asked. "Oh no, you're the professor. Here's some mail to answer," he said. The girl came back into the house carrying the mail and feeling very proud because the mailman had noticed that she had her own pair of eyeglasses.

School was starting again after the Christmas vacation, and the girl's father said to her that morning, "Now have a little sense, honey. Don't take those glasses to school." So the girl had been all day at school without her eyeglasses. She ran all the way home after school and hurried into the house. She found the eyeglasses in the drawer of her nightstand where she'd put them for safekeeping. She spit onto each of the lenses and then polished them with the hem of her skirt. She put the glasses on and went out into the yard to lie on her back and stare up at the clouds. But the sky was so bright she closed her eyes and daydreamed instead.

The next day she slipped the eyeglasses into her lunch bucket and took them to school. She sat in her seat in Miss Binki's class and put them on. She felt very special and different from the other children as she sat with her glasses on. It did not matter that she could hardly see to write her name at the top of her paper. She was happy and proud to be wearing eyeglasses.

Miss Binki kept looking in the girl's direction, and the girl supposed that Miss Binki was admiring her glasses. Then Miss Binki came up beside the girl's desk and spoke to her.

"Did you get a new pair of glasses?" Miss Binki asked. "Are your eyes bothering you again, dear?"

"Yes," the girl said. "I got some glasses for Christmas."

"May I see them?" Miss Binki asked.

The girl did not hesitate. She wanted Miss Binki to admire her glasses. She handed them up to her and watched Miss Binki try them on.

"Oh my! Oh dear," Miss Binki said. "Your eyes can't be *this* bad. You're going to ruin your eyes, dear, wearing these glasses." Miss Binki removed the brown-rimmed glasses from her nose and slipped them into her dress pocket. Then she took a step away. The girl could not believe what was happening. She sat gazing at the pocket into which her glasses had disappeared.

"I'll save them for you," Miss Binki said. "You can have them back at the end of the year." She walked to her desk and the girl saw her take the eyeglasses out and place them into her desk drawer and turn a key. It was a drawer into which the girl had seen many forbidden items disappear. Things of an altogether different nature from her eyeglasses—a succession of slingshots, marbles, toys, candy bars—all to be collected by their owners at the end of the school year.

The girl went home in tears. She told her mother and father what had happened. She thought surely they would go to Miss Binki and get her eyeglasses back. But the girl's father only shook his head and said, "It's good enough for you. I guess you'll learn to listen now."

After that the girl had periods where she forgot entirely about the glasses. But there were other times when she would fasten her attention on them there in Miss Binki's desk drawer, and she would be unable to think of anything else. She knew that the end of school was months away.

The girl's opinion of Miss Binki began to change. She no longer seemed the beautiful young woman all the children loved for her pointed breasts and bright red lipstick. The girl had noticed something decidedly sharp, even harsh, about the woman's features. There were lines under her eyes. Miss Binki called for quiet more and more often. Several times a day children were banished to the cloakroom for misbehaving. But the girl continued to conduct herself quietly and patiently in the hope that she would do nothing further to bring disfavor to herself.

Finally it had come, the last day of school, and the children were told to form a line at Miss Binki's desk. She was handing back the last of their schoolwork. It was also the moment at which the children who'd had their belongings appropriated would have them returned. The girl was fully prepared to forgive Miss Binki when her eyeglasses were returned to her. She was thinking this, that she would apologize, when suddenly her turn came and she found herself standing before Miss Binki. The teacher had put on her best posture for these final moments at her desk with her students. Her head was erect and her back was straight.

"Here you are, dear," Miss Binki said, handing the girl the bundle of drawings and scribblings. She smiled at the girl. "Have a good summer."

"My glasses," the girl said.

"I knew there was something," Miss Binki said. "But I almost forgot." She reached into her desk drawer and brought out the eyeglasses. "Yes, here are your glasses. I don't think they'll hurt your eyes now. You have a good summer, dear."

The girl took the glasses and ran with them out into the schoolyard. She dropped her papers and fitted the eyeglasses to her head. But something was wrong. The world stayed the same. There was no miraculous fuzziness and the girl felt the same as she'd always felt—too small and too young. Her stomach did not leap and swerve with each step she took. Her glasses had somehow lost their magic in Miss Binki's desk drawer. The girl put her hand up to touch the lenses and was surprised when her finger went through the frame into her eye. She gave a little cry and took off the glasses. Then she saw that the lenses had been removed from the frames. The girl held the glasses and stuck her finger through the frame into one of the eye spaces and twirled the eyeglasses in disbelief. Then she put the glasses back on to make sure. She could see other children coming gaily in little groups out of the school building. She saw her papers blowing crazily across the schoolyard. She was seeing with her own good eyes through the plastic rims.

There was a tight feeling in her chest as she walked slowly home wearing the empty frames. There were moments when her eyes welled up, and it seemed that the lenses had miraculously returned to the glasses. But when she reached her fingers up through the rims and wiped her eyes, she found she could see quite normally. She thought of Miss Binki bent over her eyeglasses, purposely removing the lenses. As she imagined this, a hot feeling came up in her. It was a feeling so terrible that the girl stopped where she was on the sidewalk and shouted, "I hate her! I hate her!" A man who was sitting with his dog on his front porch looked at her and the girl felt the awful feeling pour out of her until she became afraid and began to run as fast as she could, holding the eyeglass frames to her face with one hand.

When the girl reached home she didn't go into the house but went instead around to the backyard and sat in the swing. She kicked herself high into the air in the swing, then higher, until she felt she might fly out over the rooftops. Gradually the feeling of hatred left her. After a while she climbed down from the swing and went into the house for supper.

"What did I tell you," her father said at the supper table. The empty frames lay near her plate. "I guess that serves you right, doesn't it," her father said.

"Even if the teacher meant well—and I'm sure she did," her mother said, "it was a mean thing to do." The girl's mother went to the stove and took up the rest of the fried potatoes. But the girl knew her mother couldn't understand.

The girl didn't say anything. She chewed her food slowly and felt she had fallen into the company of people who hated eyeglasses. She didn't know why this was so. She squinted at her plate. It seemed a great effort to lift food to her mouth. She was glad when at last her plate was empty.

Questions for Discussion

1. In what ways are glasses important to the girl in this story? Why are they so important to her? What might the glasses symbolize?

2. How well do her parents, her friends, and her teacher understand how important glasses are to her?

3. How is the tone of this story affected by the use of "the girl" in place of a name? How does this decision on the part of Gallagher affect your response to this character?

4. Describe what you think the girl learns from the teacher's behavior regarding the glasses. And from her parents' reaction.

Suggestions for Writing

1. Write an essay that analyzes the pair of glasses as a symbol, both in the girl's life and for the reader. To what extent do the glasses symbolize universal aspects of growing up?

2. In your journal or notebook, write briefly about the character of the teacher. When she first appears in the story, is the reader's response to her likely to be different from the girl's response to her? Why or why not? How and why does the teacher change in the eyes of the girl?

3. Write a story that springs from an episode in your life that changed your attitude toward a person you had formerly admired. Of course, feel free to fictionalize this experience as you develop it into a story; you need not stick to all of the "facts."

The Iguana Killer

ALBERTO   ALVARO   RIOS

S apito had turned eight two weeks before and was, at this time, living in Villahermosa, the capital city of Tabasco. He had earned his nickname because his eyes bulged to make him look like a frog, and besides, he was the best fly-catcher in all Villahermosa. This was when he was five. Now he was eight, but his eyes still bulged and no one called him anything but "Sapito."

Among their many duties, all the boys had to go down to the Rio Grijalva every day and try to sell or trade off whatever homemade things were available and could be carried on these small men's backs. It was also the job of these boys to fish, capture snails, trick tortoises, and kill the iguanas.

Christmas had just passed, and it had been celebrated as usual, very religious with lots of candle smoke and very solemn church masses. There had been no festivities yet, no laughing, but today would be different. Today was the fifth of January, the day the children of Villahermosa wait for all year. Tomorrow would be the *Día de los Reyes Magos,* the Day of the Wise Kings, when presents of all sorts were brought by the Kings and given to friends. Sapito's grandmother, who lived in Nogales in the United States, had sent him two packages. He had seen them, wrapped in blue paper with bearded red clown faces. Sapito's grandmother always sent presents to his family, and she always seemed to know just what Sapito would want, even though they had never met.

That night, Sapito's mother put the packages under the bed where he slept. It was not a cushioned bed, but rather, a hammock, made with soft rattan leaves. Huts in Villahermosa were not rented to visitors by the number of rooms, but, instead, by the number of hooks in each place. On these hooks were hung the hammocks of a family. People in this town were born and nursed, then slept and died in these hanging beds. Sapito could remember his grandfather, and how they found him one afternoon after lunch. They had eaten mangoes together. Sapito dreamed about him now, about how his face would turn colors when he told his stories, always too loud.

When Sapito woke up, he found the packages. He played up to his mother, the way she wanted, claiming that the *Reyes* had brought him all these gifts. *Look and look, and look here!* he shouted, but this was probably the last time he would do this, for Sapito was now eight, and he knew better, but did not tell. He opened the two packages from Nogales, finding a baseball and a baseball bat. Sapito held both gifts and smiled, though he wasn't clearly sure what the things were. Sapito had not been born in nor ever visited the United States, and he had no idea what baseball was. He was sure he recognized and admired the ball and knew what it was for. He could certainly use that. But he looked at the baseball bat and was puzzled for some seconds.

It was an iguana-killer. *"¡Mira, mamá! un palo para matar iguanas!"* It was beautiful, a dream. It was perfect. His grandmother always knew what he would like.

In Villahermosa, the jungle was not far from where Sapito lived. It started, in fact, at the end of his backyard. It was not dense there, but one could not walk far before a machete became a third hand, sharper, harder, more valuable than the other two in this other world that sometimes kept people.

This strong jungle life was great fun for a boy like Sapito, who especially enjoyed bringing coconuts out of the tangled vines for his mother. He would look for monkeys in the fat palm trees and throw rocks at them, one after the other. To get back, the monkeys would throw coconuts back at him, yelling terrible monkey-words. This was life before the iguana-killer.

Every day for a week after he had gotten the presents, Sapito would walk about half a mile east along the Río Grijalva with Chachi, his best friend. Then they would cut straight south into the hair of the jungle.

There is a correct way to hunt iguanas, and Sapito had been well-skilled even before the bat came. He and Chachi would look at all the trees until the tell-tale movement of an iguana was spotted. When one was found, Sapito would sit at the base of the tree, being as quiet as possible, with baseball bat held high and muscles stiff.

The female iguana would come out first. She moved her head around very quickly, almost jerking, in every direction. Sapito knew that she was not the one to kill. She kept the little iguanas in supply—his father had told him. After a few seconds, making sure everything was safe, she would return to the tree and send her husband out, telling him there was nothing to worry about.

The male iguana is always slower. He comes out and moves his head to one side and just stares, motionless, for several minutes. Now Sapito knew that he must take advantage, but very carefully. Iguanas can see in almost all directions at once. Unlike human eyes, both iguana eyes do not have to center in on the same thing. One eye can look forward, and one backward, like a clown, so that they can detect almost any movement. Sapito knew this and was always careful to check both eyes before striking. Squinting his own eyes which always puffed out even more when he was excited, he would not draw back his club. That would waste time. It was already kept high in the air all these minutes. When he was ready, he would send the bat straight down as hard and as fast as he could. Just like that. And if he had done all these things right, he would take his prize home by the tail to skin him for eating that night.

Iguanas were prepared like any other meat, fried, roasted, or boiled, and they tasted like tough chicken no matter which way they were done. In Tabasco, and especially in Villahermosa, iguanas were eaten by everybody all the time, even tourists, so hunting them was very popular. Iguana was an everyday supper, eaten without frowning at such a thing, eating lizard. It was not different from the other things eaten here, the turtle eggs, *cahuamas,* crocodile meat, river snails. And when iguanas were killed, nobody was supposed to feel sad. Everybody's father said so. Sapito did, though, sometimes. Iguanas had puffed eyes like his.

But, if Sapito failed to kill one of these iguanas, he would run away as fast as he could—being sad was the last thing he would think of. Iguanas look mean, they have bloodshot eyes, and people say that they spit blood. Sapito and his friends thought that, since no one they knew had ever been hurt by these monsters, they must not be so bad. This was what the boys thought in town, talking on a summer afternoon, drinking coconuts. But when he missed, Sapito figured that the real reason no one had ever been hurt was that no one ever hung around afterward to find out what happens. Whether iguanas were really dangerous or not, nobody could say for certain. Nobody's parents had ever heard of an iguana hurting anyone, either. The boys went home one day and asked. So, no one worried, sort of, and iguanas were even tamed and kept as pets by the old sailors in Villahermosa, along with the snakes. But only by the sailors.

The thought of missing a hit no longer bothered Sapito, who now began carrying his baseball bat everywhere. His friends were impressed more by this than by anything else, even candy in tin boxes, especially when he began killing four and five iguanas a day. No one could be that good. Soon, not only Chachi, but the rest of the boys began following Sapito around constantly just to watch the scourge of the iguanas in action.

By now, the bat was proven. Sapito was the champion iguana-provider, always holding his now-famous killer-bat. All his friends would come to copy it. They would come every day asking for measurements and questioning him as to its design. Chachi and the rest would then go into the jungle and gather fat, straight roots. With borrowed knives and machetes, they tried to whittle out their own iguana-killers, but failed. Sapito's was machine made, and perfect.

This went on for about a week, when Sapito had an idea that was to serve him well for a long time. He began renting out the killer-bat for a *centavo* a day. The boys said yes yes right away, and would go out and hunt at least two or three iguanas to make it worth the price, but really, too, so that they could use the bat as much as possible.

For the next few months, the grown-ups of Villahermosa hated Sapito and his bat because all they ate was iguana. But Sapito was proud. No one would make fun of his bulging eyes now.

Sapito was in Nogales in the United States visiting his grandmother for the first time, before going back to Tabasco, and Villahermosa. His family had come from Chiapas on the other side of the republic on a relative-visiting vacation. It was still winter, but no one in Sapito's family had expected it to be cold. They knew about rain, and winter days, but it was always warm in the jungle, even for these things.

Sapito was sitting in front of the house on Sonoita Avenue, on the sidewalk. He was very impressed by many things in this town, especially the streetlights. Imagine lighting up the inside *and* the outside. It would be easy to catch animals at night here. But most of all, he was impressed by his rather large grandmother, whom he already loved very much. He had remembered to thank her for the iguana-killer and the ball. She had laughed and said, *"Por nada, hijo."* As he sat and thought about this, he wrapped the two blankets he had brought outside with him tighter around his small body. Sapito could not understand or explain to himself that the weather was cold and that he had to feel it, everyone did, even him. This was almost an unknown experience to him since he had never been out of the tropics before. The sensation, the feeling of cold, then, was very strange, especially since he wasn't even wet. It was actually hurting him. His muscles felt as if he had held his bat up in the air for an hour waiting for an iguana. Of course, Sapito could have gone inside to get warm near the wood-burning stove, but he didn't like the smoke or the smell of the north. It was a different smell, not the jungle.

So Sapito sat there. Cold had never been important in his life before, and he wasn't going to let it start now. With blankets he could cover himself up and it would surely pass. Covered up for escape, he waited for warmness, pulling the blankets over his head. Sometimes he would put out his foot to see if it was okay yet, the way the lady iguana would come out first.

Then, right then in one fast second, Sapito seemed to feel, with his foot on the outside, a very quiet and strange moment, as if everything had slowed. He felt his eyes bulge when he scrunched up his face to hear better. Something scary caught hold of him, and he began to shiver harder. It was different from just being cold, which was scary enough. His heartbeat was pounding so much that he could feel it in his eyes.

He carefully moved one of the blankets from his face. Sapito saw the sky falling, just like the story his grandmother had told him the first day they had been there. He thought she was joking, or that she didn't realize he was already eight, and didn't believe in such things anymore.

Faster than hitting an iguana Sapito threw his blankets off, crying as he had not cried since he was five and they had nicknamed him and teased him. He ran to the kitchen and grabbed his mother's leg. Crying and shivering, he begged, "*¡Mamá, por favor, perdóneme!*" He kept speaking fast, asking for forgiveness and promising never to do anything wrong in his life ever again. They sky was falling, but he had always prayed, really he had.

His mother looked at him and at first could not laugh. Quietly, she explained that it was *nieve,* snow, that was falling, not the sky. She told him not to be afraid, and that he could go out and play in it, touch it, yes.

Sapito still didn't know exactly what this *nieve* was, but now his mother was laughing and didn't seem worried. In Villahermosa, *nieve* was a good word, it meant ice cream. There was a *nieve* man. Certainly the outside wasn't ice cream, but the white didn't really look bad, he thought, not really. It seemed, in fact, to have great possibilities. Sapito went back outside, sitting again with his blankets, trying to understand. He touched it, and breathed even faster. Then, closing his eyes, which was not easy, he put a little in his mouth.

Sapito's family had been back in Villahermosa for a week now. Today was Sunday. It was the custom here that every Sunday afternoon, since there were no other amusements, the band would play on the *malecón,* an area something like a park by the river, where the boats were all loaded.

Each Sunday it was reserved for this band—that is, the group of citizens that joined together and called themselves a band. It was a favorite time for everyone, as the paddle boat lay resting on the river while its owner played the trumpet and sang loud songs. The instruments were all brass, except for the marimba, which was the only sad sounding instrument. Though it was hit with padded drumsticks, its song was quiet, hidden, always reserved for dusk. Sapito had thought about the marimba as his mother explained about snow. Her voice had its sound for the few minutes she spoke, and held him. Before the marimba, before dusk, however, the brass had full control.

As dusk came, it was time for the *verbenas,* when the girls, young and old, would come in and walk around the park in one direction and the boys would walk the opposite way, all as the marimba played its songs easily, almost by itself. On these Sundays no one was a man or a woman. They were all boys and girls, even the women who always wore black. This was when all the flirting and the smiling of smiles bigger than people's faces took place. Sapito and Chachi and the rest of the smaller boys never paid attention to any of this, except sometimes to make fun of someone's older sister.

An old man, Don Tomasito, the baker, played the tuba. When he blew into the huge mouthpiece, his face would turn purple and his thousand wrinkles would disappear as his skin filled out. Sapito and his friends would choose by throwing fingers, and whoever had the odd number thrown out, matching no one else, was chosen to do the best job of the day. This had become a custom all their own. The chosen one would walk around in front of Don Tomasito as he played, and cut a lemon. Then slowly, very slowly, squeeze it, letting the juice fall to the ground. Don Tomasito's lips would follow.

On this first Sunday afternoon after he had returned, Sapito, after being chased by Señor Saturnino Cantón, who was normally the barber but on Sunday was the policeman, pulled out his prize. Sapito had been preparing his friends all day, and now they were yelling to see this new surprise. This was no iguana-killer, but Sapito hoped it would have the same effect.

Some of the people in Villahermosa used to have photographs of various things. One picture Sapito had particularly remembered. Some ladies of the town, who always made their own clothes, once had a picture taken together. They were a group of maybe ten ladies, in very big dresses and hats, some sitting and some standing. What Sapito recalled now was that they were all barefoot. They were all very serious and probably didn't think of it, but now, Sapito, after traveling to the north and seeing many pictures at his grandmother's house, thought their bare feet were very funny, even if shoes were hard to get and couldn't be made like dresses could. Sapito knew about such things now. He remembered that people in Nogales laughed at him when he was barefoot in the snow.

But now, Sapito had a photograph, too. This was his surprise. Well, what it was, really, was a Christmas card picturing a house with lots of snow around. He had gotten the picture from his grandmother and had taken great care in bringing it back home. He kept the surprise under his shirt wrapped in blue paper against his stomach, so it would stay flat. Here was a picture of the *nieve,* just like he had seen for himself, except there was a lot more of it in the picture. An awful lot more.

At the end of this Sunday, making a big deal with his small hands, he showed this prize to his friends, and told them that *nieve,* which means both snow and ice cream in the Spanish of those who have experienced the two, would fall from the sky in Nogales. Any time at all. His bulging eyes widened to emphasize what he was saying, and he held his bat to be even more convincing.

No one believed him.

"Pues, miren, ¡aquí está!" He showed them the picture, and added now that it was a picture of his grandmother's house where he had just visited.

When Chachi asked, as Sapito had hoped, if it came down in flavors, he decided that he had gone this far, so why not. *"Vainilla,"* he stated.

As the months went by, so did new stories, and strawberry and pistachio, and he was pretty sure that they believed him. After all, none of them had ever been up north. They didn't know the things Sapito knew. And besides, he still owned the iguana-killer.

Three months after the snow-picture stories had worn off, Señora Casimira, with the help of the town midwife, had a baby girl. The custom here was that mother and baby didn't have to do any work for forty days. No one ever complained. Mostly the little girls would help in the house, doing the errands that were not big enough to bother the boys or the big girls with. They'd throw water out front to quiet the dust. Neighbors would wash the clothes.

For the boys, usually because they could yell louder and didn't want to work with the girls, their job was to go and bring charcoal from the river, to bring bananas and coconuts, and whatever other food was needed. Every morning Sapito and his friends would stand outside the door of Señora Casimira's house, with luck before the girls came, and call in to her, asking if she needed anything. She would tell them yes or no, explaining what to bring if something was necessary.

Spring was here now, and today was Saturday. Sapito thought about this, being wise in the way of seasons now, as he looked down on the Casimira *choza,* the palm-thatched hut in which they lived. Señor Casimira was sure to be there today, he figured. There was no need to hang around, probably. Sapito had saved a little money from renting the killer-bat, and he suggested to his friends that they all go to Puerto Alvarado on the paddle boat. They were hitting him on the back and laughing yes! even before he had finished.

The Río Grijalva comes down from the Sierra Madre mountains, down through the state of Tabasco, through Villahermosa, emptying through Puerto Alvarado several miles north into the Gulf of Mexico. The boys looked over at the Casimira *choza,* then backward at this great river, where the paddle boat was getting ready to make its first trip of the day to Puerto Alvarado. They ran after it, fast enough to leave behind their shadows.

Sapito and his friends had been in Alvarado for about an hour when they learned that a *cahuama,* a giant sea turtle, was near by. They were on the rough beach, walking toward the north where the rocks become huge. Some palm trees nodded just behind the beach, followed by the jungle, as always. Sometimes Sapito thought it followed him, always moving closer.

Climbing the mossy rocks, Chachi was the one who spotted the *cahuama.* This was strange because the turtles rarely came so close to shore. In Villahermosa, and Puerto Alvarado, the money situation was such that anything the boys saw, like iguanas or the *cahuama,* they tried to capture. They always tried hard to get something for nothing, and here was their chance—not to mention the adventure involved. They all ran together with the understood intention of dividing up the catch.

They borrowed a rope from the men who were working farther up the shore near the palm trees. *"¡Buena suerte!"* one of the men called, and laughed. Sapito and Chachi jumped in a *cayuco,* a kayak built more like a canoe, which one of the fishermen had left near shore. They paddled out to the floating turtle, jumped out, and managed to get a rope tied around its neck right off. Usually, then, a person had to hop onto the back of the *cahuama* and let it take him down into the water for a little while. Its burst of strength usually went away before the rider drowned or let go. This was the best fun for the boys, and a fairly rare chance, so Sapito, who was closest, jumped on to ride this one. He put up one arm like a tough cowboy. This *cahuama* went nowhere.

The two boys climbed back into the *cayuco* and tried to pull the turtle, but it still wouldn't budge. It had saved its strength, and its strong flippers were more than a match for the two boys now. Everyone on shore swam over to help them after realizing that yells of how to do it better were doing no good. They all grabbed a part of the rope. With pure strength against strength, the six boys sweated, but finally outpulled the stubborn *cahuama,* dragging it onto the shore. It began flopping around on the sand until they managed to tip it onto its back. The turtle seemed to realize that struggling was a waste of its last fat-man energy, and started moving like a slow motion robot, fighting as before but, now, on its back, the flippers and head moved like a movie going too slow.

The *cahuama* had seemed huge as the boys were pulling it, fighting so strong in the water, but it was only about three feet long when they finally took a breath and looked. Yet, they all agreed, this *cahuama* was very fat. It must have been a grandfather.

Chachi went to call one of the grown-ups to help. Each of the boys was sure that he could kill a *cahuama* and prepare it, but this was everybody's, and they wanted it cut right. The men were impressed as the boys explained. The boys were all nervous. Maybe not nervous—not really, just sometimes they were sad when they caught *cahuamas* because they had seen what happens. Like fish, or iguanas, but bigger, and bigger animals are different. Sad, but they couldn't tell anyone, especially not the other boys, or the men. Sapito looked at their catch.

These sailors, or men who used to be sailors, all carried short, heavy machetes, specially made for things taken from the sea. Chachi came back with a man who already had his in hand. The blade was straight because there was no way to shape metal, no anvil in Alvarado. The man looked at Sapito. *"Préstame tu palo,"* he said, looking at Sapito's iguana-killer. Sapito picked it up from where he had left it and handed it to the man, carefully. The fisherman beat the turtle on the head three times fast until it was either dead or unconscious. Then he handed the bat back to Sapito, who was sort of proud, and sort of not.

The man cut the *cahuama's* head off. Some people eat the head and its juice, but Sapito and his friends had been taught not to. No one said anything as it was tossed to the ground. The flippers continued their robot motion.

He cut the side of the turtle, where the underside skin meets the shell. He then pulled a knife out of his pocket, and continued where the machete had first cut, separating the body of the turtle from the shell. As he was cutting he told the boys about the freshwater sac that *cahuamas* have, and how, if they were ever stranded at sea, they could drink it. They had heard the story a hundred times, but nobody knew anybody who really did it. The boys were impatient. Then he separated the underpart from the inside meat, the prize. It looked a little redder than beef. The fins were then cut off—someone would use their leather sometime later.

The man cut the meat into small pieces. The boys took these pieces and washed them in salt water to make the meat last longer. Before cooking them, they would have to be washed again, this time in fresh water to get all the salt off. In the meantime, the saltwater would keep the meat from spoiling. One time Sapito forgot, or really he was in too much of a hurry, and he took some *cahuama* home but forgot to tell his mother. It changed colors, and Sapito had to go get some more food, with everybody mad at him. The boys knew that each part of the *cahuama* was valuable, but all they were interested in now was what they could carry. This, of course, was the meat.

The man gave each of the boys some large pieces, and then kept most of it for himself. The boys were young, and could not argue with a grownup. They were used to this. The fisherman began to throw the shell away.

"*No, por favor, damelo,*" Sapito called to him. The man laughed and handed the shell to Sapito, who put his pieces of meat inside it and, with the rest of the boys, wandered back to the river to wait for the paddle boat. The shell was almost too big for him. The boys were all laughing and joking, proud of their accomplishment. They asked Sapito what he was going to do with the shell, but he said that he wasn't sure yet. This wasn't true. Of course, he was already making big, very big, plans for it.

They got back early in the afternoon, and everyone went home exhausted. Sapito, before going home, went into the jungle and gathered some green branches. He was not very tired yet—he had a new idea, so Sapito spent the rest of the afternoon polishing the shell with sand and the hairy part of some coconuts, which worked just like sandpaper.

When it was polished, he got four of the best branches and whittled them to perfection with his father's knife. Sapito tied these into a rectangle using some *mecate,* something in between rope and string, which his mother had given him. The shell fit halfway down into the opening of the rectangle. It was perfect. Then, onto this frame, he tied two flat, curved branches across the bottom at opposite ends. It moved back and forth like a drunk man. He had made a good, strong crib. It worked, just right for a new-born baby girl.

Sapito had worked hard and fast with the strength of a guilty conscience. Señora Casimira just might have needed something, after all. It was certainly possible that her husband might have had to work today. All the boys had known these facts before they had left, but had looked only at the paddle boat—and it had waved back at them.

Sapito took the crib, hurrying to beat the jungle dusk. Dusk, at an exact moment, even on Sundays, owned the sky and the air in its own strange way. Just after sunset, for about half an hour, the sky blackened more than would be normal for the darkness of early night, and mosquitoes, like pieces of sand, would come up out of the thickest part of the jungle like tornadoes, coming down on the town to take what they could. People always spent this half hour indoors, Sundays, too, even with all the laughing, which stopped then. This was the signal for the marimba's music to take over.

Sapito reached the *choza* as the first buzzings were starting. He listened at the Casimira's door, hearing the baby cry like all babies. The cradle would help. He put it down in front of the wooden door without making any noise, and knocked. Then, as fast as he could, faster than that even, he ran back over the hill, out of sight. He did not turn around. Señora Casimira would find out who had made it. And he would be famous again, thought Sapito, famous like the other times. He felt for the iguana-killer that had been dragging behind him, tied to his belt, and put it over his right shoulder. His face was not strong enough to keep away the smile that pulled his mouth, his fat eyes all the while puffing out.

Questions for Discussion

1. What elements of "The Iguana Killer" are exotic to you, and which ones are familiar or universal?

2. Why does Sapito react the way he does to the snow, and why does he fabricate things about the snowstorm to his friends when he returns to Villahermosa?

3. How would you characterize Sapito? What are the memorable qualities of his personality?

4. What motivates Sapito to kill iguanas and to make a crib out of the turtle shell? How sympathetic is this motivation?

5. In what ways is the period of time depicted by the story a formative time in Sapito's life?

Suggestions for Writing

1. Write an essay in which you discuss the universal aspects of Sapito's behavior in this story. In what ways is Sapito a fairly typical young person? In what ways is he not? To what extent is this story accessible to an audience unfamiliar with the particulars of Sapito's way of life?

2. In your notebook write briefly about the baseball bat—"the iguana killer"— as a possible symbol in this story. What does it represent for Sapito? For the reader?

3. In your journal write about a gift you received as a child that took on enormous value and meaning for you—something that may have seemed insignificant to everyone else. Account for the extraordinary meaning this gift took on.

4. Write an essay in which you compare and contrast Sapito of "The Iguana Killer" with Yoneko of "Yoneko's Earthquake," by Hisaye Yamamoto. You may want to begin your analysis of the stories by focusing on how "formative" each experience is for these characters.

Death of a Son

NJABULO S. NDEBELE

At last we got the body. Wednesday. Just enough time for a Saturday funeral. We were exhausted. Empty. The funeral still ahead of us. We had to find the strength to grieve. There had been no time for grief, really. Only much bewilderment and confusion. Now grief. For isn't grief the awareness of loss?

That is why when we finally got the body, Buntu said: "Do you realize our son is dead?" I realized. Our awareness of the death of our first and only child had been displaced completely by the effort to get his body. Even the horrible events that caused the death: we did not think of them, as such. Instead, the numbing drift of things took over our minds: the pleas, letters to be written, telephone calls to be made, telegrams to be dispatched, lawyers to consult, "influential" people to "get in touch with," undertakers to be contacted, so much walking and driving. That is what suddenly mattered: the irksome details that blur the goal (no matter how terrible it is), each detail becoming a door which, once unlocked, revealed yet another door. Without being aware of it, we were distracted by the smell of the skunk and not by what the skunk had done.

We realized something too, Buntu and I, that during the two-week effort to get our son's body, we had drifted apart. For the first time in our marriage, our presence to each other had become a matter of habit. He was there. He'll be there. And I'll be there. But when Buntu said: "Do you realize our son is dead?" he uttered a thought that suddenly brought us together again. It was as if the return of the body of our son was also our coming together. For it was only at that moment that we really began to grieve; as if our lungs had suddenly begun to take in air when just before, we were beginning to suffocate. Something with meaning began to emerge.

We realized. We realized that something else had been happening to us, adding to the terrible events. Yes, we had drifted apart. Yet, our estrangement, just at that moment when we should have been together, seemed disturbingly comforting to me. I was comforted in a manner I did not quite understand.

The problem was that I had known all along that we would have to buy the body anyway. I had known all along. Things would end that way. And when things turned out that way, Buntu could not look me in the eye. For he had said: "Over my dead body! Over my dead body!" as soon as we knew we would be required to pay the police or the government for the release of the body of our child.

"Over my dead body! Over my dead body!" Buntu kept on saying.

Finally, we bought the body. We have the receipt. The police insisted we take it. That way, they would be "protected." It's the law, they said.

I suppose we could have got the body earlier. At first I was confused, for one is supposed to take comfort in the heroism of one's man. Yet, inwardly, I could draw no comfort from his outburst. It seemed hasty. What sense was there to it when all I wanted was the body of my child? What would happen if, as events unfolded, it became clear that Buntu would not give up his life? What would happen? What would happen to him? To me?

For the greater part of two weeks, all of Buntu's efforts, together with friends, relatives, lawyers and the newspapers, were to secure the release of the child's body without the humiliation of having to pay for it. A "fundamental principle."

Why was it difficult for me to see the wisdom of the principle? The worst thing, I suppose, was worrying about what the police may have been doing to the body of my child. How they may have been busy prying it open "to determine the cause of death?"

Would I want to look at the body when we finally got it? To see further mutilations in addition to the "cause of death"? What kind of mother would not want to look at the body of her child? people will ask. Some will say: "It's grief." She is too grief-stricken.

"But still . . . ," they will say. And the elderly among them may say: "Young people are strange."

But how can they know? It was not that I would not want to see the body of my child, but that I was too afraid to confront the horrors of my own imagination. I was haunted by the thought of how useless it had been to have created something. What had been the point of it all? This body filling up with a child. The child steadily growing into something that could be seen and felt. Moving, as it always did, at that time of day when I was all alone at home waiting for it. What had been the point of it all?

How can they know that the mutilation to determine "the cause of death" ripped my own body? Can they think of a womb feeling hunted? Disgorged?

And the milk that I still carried. What about it? What had been the point of it all?

Even Buntu did not seem to sense that the principle, the "fundamental principle," was something too intangible for me at that moment, something that I desperately wanted should assume the form of my child's body. He still seemed far from ever knowing.

I remember one Saturday morning early in our courtship, as Buntu and I walked hand-in-hand through town, window-shopping. We cannot even be said to have been window-shopping, for we were aware of very little that was not ourselves. Everything in those windows was merely an excuse for words to pass between us.

We came across three girls sitting on the pavement, sharing a packet of fish and chips after they had just bought it from a nearby Portuguese cafe. Buntu said: "I want fish and chips too." I said: "So seeing is desire." I said: "My man is greedy!" We laughed. I still remember how he tightened his grip on my hand. The strength of it!

Just then, two white boys coming in the opposite direction suddenly rushed at the girls, and, without warning, one of them kicked the packet of fish and chips out of the hands of the girl who was holding it. The second boy kicked away the rest of what remained in the packet. The girl stood up, shaking her hand as if to throw off the pain in it. Then she pressed it under her armpit as if to squeeze the pain out of it. Meanwhile, the two boys went on their way laughing. The fish and chips lay scattered on the pavement and on the street like stranded boats on a river that had gone dry.

"Just let them do that to you!" said Buntu, tightening once more his grip on my hand as we passed on like sheep that had seen many of their own in the flock picked out for slaughter. We would note the event and wait for our turn. I remember I looked at Buntu, and saw his face was somewhat glum. There seemed no connection between that face and the words of reassurance just uttered. For a while, we went on quietly. It was then that I noticed his grip had grown somewhat limp. Somewhat reluctant. Having lost its self-assurance, it seemed to have been holding on because it had to, not because of a confident sense of possession.

It was not to be long before his words were tested. How could fate work this way, giving to words meanings and intentions they did not carry when they were uttered? I saw that day, how the language of love could so easily be trampled underfoot, or scattered like fish and chips on the pavement, and left stranded and abandoned like boats in a river that suddenly went dry. Never again was love to be confirmed with words. The world around us was too hostile for vows of love. At any moment, the vows could be subjected to the stress of proof. And love died. For words of love need not be tested.

On that day, Buntu and I began our silence. We talked and laughed, of course, but we stopped short of words that would demand proof of action. Buntu knew. He knew the vulnerability of words. And so he sought to obliterate words with acts that seemed to promise redemption.

On that day, as we continued with our walk in town, that Saturday morning, coming up towards us from the opposite direction, was a burly Boer walking with his wife and two children. They approached Buntu and me with an ominously determined advance. Buntu attempted to pull me out of the way, but I never had a chance. The Boer shoved me out of the way, as if clearing a path for his family. I remember, I almost crashed into a nearby fashion display window. I remember, I glanced at the family walking away, the mother and the father each dragging a child. It was for one of those children that I had been cleared away. I remember, also, that as my tears came out, blurring the Boer family and everything else, I saw and felt deeply what was inside of me: a desire to be avenged.

But nothing happened. All I heard was Buntu say: "The dog!" At that very moment, I felt my own hurt vanish like a wisp of smoke. And as my hurt vanished, it was replaced, instead, by a tormenting desire to sacrifice myself for Buntu. Was it something about the powerlessness of the curse and the desperation with which it had been made? The filling of stunned silence with an utterance? Surely it ate into him, revealing how incapable he was of meeting the call of his words.

And so it was, that that afternoon, back in the township, left to ourselves at Buntu's home, I gave in to him for the first time. Or should I say I offered myself to him? Perhaps from some vague sense of wanting to heal something in him? Anyway, we were never to talk about that event. Never. We buried it alive deep inside of me that afternoon. Would it ever be exhumed? All I vaguely felt and knew was that I had the keys to the vault. That was three years ago, a year before we married.

The cause of death? One evening I returned home from work, particularly tired after I had been covering more shootings by the police in the East Rand. Then I had hurried back to the office in Johannesburg to piece together on my typewriter the violent scenes of the day, and then to file my report to meet the deadline. It was late when I returned home, and when I got there, I found a crowd of people in the yard. They were those who could not get inside. I panicked. What had happened? I did not ask those who were outside, being desperate to get into the house. They gave way easily when they recognized me.

Then I heard my mother's voice. Her cry rose well above the noise. It turned into a scream when she saw me. "What is it, mother?" I asked, embracing her out of a vaguely despairing sense of terror. But she pushed me away with an hysterical violence that astounded me.

"What misery have I brought you, my child?" she cried. At that point, many women in the room began to cry too. Soon, there was much wailing in the room, and then all over the house. The sound of it! The anguish! Understanding, yet eager for knowledge, I became desperate. I had to hold onto something. The desire to embrace my mother no longer had anything to do with comforting her; for whatever she had done, whatever its magnitude, had become inconsequential. I needed to embrace her for all the anguish that tied everyone in the house into a knot. I wanted to be part of that knot, yet I wanted to know what had brought it about.

Eventually, we found each other, my mother and I, and clasped each other tightly. When I finally released her, I looked around at the neighbors and suddenly had a vision of how that anguish had to be turned into a simmering kind of indignation. The kind of indignation that had to be kept at bay only because there was a higher purpose at that moment: the sharing of concern.

Slowly and with a calmness that surprised me, I began to gather the details of what had happened. Instinctively, I seemed to have been gathering notes for a news report.

It happened during the day, when the soldiers and the police that had been patrolling the township in their Casspirs began to shoot in the streets at random. Need I describe what I did not see? How did the child come to die just at that moment when the police and the soldiers began to shoot at random, at any house, at any moving thing? That was how one of our windows was shattered by a bullet. And that was when my mother, who looked after her grandchild when we were away at work, panicked. She picked up the child and ran to the neighbors. It was only when she entered the neighbor's house that she noticed the wetness of the blanket that covered the child she held to her chest as she ran for the sanctuary of neighbors. She had looked at her unaccountably bloody hand, then she noted the still bundle in her arms, and began at that moment to blame herself for the death of her grandchild. . .

Later, the police, on yet another round of shooting, found people gathered at our house. They stormed in, saw what had happened. At first, they dragged my mother out, threatening to take her away unless she agreed not to say what had happened. But then they returned and, instead, took the body of the child away. By what freak of logic did they hope that by this act their carnage would never be discovered?

That evening, I looked at Buntu closely. He appeared suddenly to have grown older. We stood alone in an embrace in our bedroom. I noticed, when I kissed his face, how his once lean face had grown suddenly puffy.

At that moment, I felt the familiar impulse come upon me once more, the impulse I always felt when I sensed that Buntu was in some kind of danger, the impulse to yield something of myself to him. He wore the look of someone struggling to gain control of something. Yet, it was clear he was far from controlling anything. I knew that look. Had seen it many times. It came at those times when I sensed that he faced a wave that was infinitely stronger than he, that it would certainly sweep him away, but that he had to seem to be struggling. I pressed myself tightly to him as if to vanish into him; as if only the two of us could stand up to the wave.

"Don't worry," he said. "Don't worry. I'll do everything in my power to right this wrong. Everything. Even if it means suing the police!" We went silent.

I knew that silence. But I knew something else at that moment: that I had to find a way of disengaging myself from the embrace.

Suing the police? I listened to Buntu outlining his plans. "Legal counsel. That's what we need," he said. "I know some people in Pretoria," he said. As he spoke, I felt the warmth of intimacy between us cooling. When he finished, it was cold. I disengaged from his embrace slowly, yet purposefully. Why had Buntu spoken?

Later, he was to speak again, when all his plans had failed to work: "Over my dead body! Over my dead body!"

He sealed my lips. I would wait for him to feel and yield one day to all the realities of misfortune.

Ours was a home, it could be said. It seemed a perfect life for a young couple: I, a reporter; Buntu, a personnel officer at an American factory manufacturing farming implements. He had traveled to the United States and returned with a mind fired with dreams. We dreamed together. Much time we spent, Buntu and I, trying to make a perfect home. The occasions are numerous on which we paged through *Femina, Fair Lady, Cosmopolitan, Home Garden, Car,* as if somehow we were going to surround our lives with the glossiness in the magazines. Indeed, much of our time was spent window-shopping through the magazines. This time, it was different from the window-shopping we did that Saturday when we courted. This time our minds were consumed by the things we saw and dreamed of owning: the furniture, the fridge, TV, videocassette recorders, washing machines, even a vacuum cleaner and every other imaginable thing that would ensure a comfortable modern life.

Especially when I was pregnant. What is it that Buntu did not buy, then? And when the boy was born, Buntu changed the car. A family, he would say, must travel comfortably.

The boy became the center of Buntu's life. Even before he was born, Buntu had already started making inquiries at white private schools. That was where he would send his son, the bearer of his name.

Dreams! It is amazing how the horrible findings of my newspaper reports often vanished before the glossy magazines of our dreams, how I easily forgot that the glossy images were concocted out of the keys of typewriters, made by writers whose business was to sell dreams at the very moment that death pervaded the land. So powerful are words and pictures that even their makers often believe in them.

Buntu's ordeal was long. So it seemed. He would get up early every morning to follow up the previous day's leads regarding the body of our son. I wanted to go with him, but each time I prepared to go he would shake his head.

"It's my task," he would say. But every evening he returned, empty-handed, while with each day that passed and we did not know where the body of my child was, I grew restive and hostile in a manner that gave me much pain. Yet Buntu always felt compelled to give a report on each day's events. I never asked for it. I suppose it was his way of dealing with my silence.

One day he would say: "The lawyers have issued a court order that the body be produced. The writ of *habeas corpus*."

On another day he would say: "We have petitioned the Minister of Justice."

On yet another he would say: "I was supposed to meet the Chief Security Officer. Waited the whole day. At the end of the day they said I would see him tomorrow if he was not going to be too busy. They are stalling."

Then he would say: "The newspapers, especially yours, are raising the hue and cry. The government is bound to be embarrassed. It's a matter of time."

And so it went on. Every morning he got up and left. Sometimes alone, sometimes with friends. He always left to bear the failure alone.

How much did I care about lawyers, petitions and Chief Security Officers? A lot. The problem was that whenever Buntu spoke about his efforts, I heard only his words. I felt in him the disguised hesitancy of someone who wanted reassurance without asking for it. I saw someone who got up every morning and left not to look for results, but to search for something he could only have found with me.

And each time he returned, I gave my speech to my eyes. And he answered without my having parted my lips. As a result, I sensed, for the first time in my life, a terrible power in me that could make him do anything. And he would never ever be able to deal with that power as long as he did not silence my eyes and call for my voice.

And so, he had to prove himself. And while he left each morning, I learned to be brutally silent. Could he prove himself without me? Could he? Then I got to know, those days, what I'd always wanted from him. I got to know why I have always drawn him into me whenever I sensed his vulnerability.

I wanted him to be free to fear. Wasn't there greater strength that way? Had he ever lived with his own feelings? And the stress of life in this land: didn't it call out for men to be heroes? And should they live up to it even though the details of the war to be fought may often be blurred? They should.

Yet it is precisely for that reason that I often found Buntu's thoughts lacking in strength. They lacked the experience of strife that could only come from a humbling acceptance of fear and then, only then, the need to fight it.

Me? In a way, I have always been free to fear. The prerogative of being a girl. It was always expected of me to scream when a spider crawled across the ceiling. It was known I would jump onto a chair whenever a mouse blundered into the room.

Then, once more, the Casspirs came. A few days before we got the body back, I was at home with my mother when we heard the great roar of truck engines. There was much running and shouting in the streets. I saw them, as I've always seen them on my assignments: the Casspirs. On five occasions they ran down our street at great speed, hurling tear-gas canisters at random. On the fourth occasion, they got our house. The canister shattered another window and filled the house with the terrible pungent choking smoke that I had got to know so well. We ran out of the house gasping for fresh air.

So, this was how my child was killed? Could they have been the same soldiers? Now hardened to their tasks? Or were they new ones being hardened to their tasks? Did they drive away laughing? Clearing paths for their families? What paths?

And was this our home? It couldn't be. It had to be a little bird's nest waiting to be plundered by a predator bird. There seemed no sense to the wedding pictures on the walls, the graduation pictures, birthday pictures, pictures of relatives, and paintings of lush landscapes. There seemed no sense anymore to what seemed recognizably human in our house. It took only a random swoop to obliterate personal worth, to blot out any value there may have been to the past. In desperation, we began to live only for the moment. I do feel hunted.

It was on the night of the tear gas that Buntu came home, saw what had happened, and broke down in tears. They had long been in the coming. . .

My own tears welled out too. How much did we have to cry to refloat stranded boats? I was sure they would float again.

A few nights later, on the night of the funeral, exhausted, I lay on my bed, listening to the last of the mourners leaving. Slowly, I became conscious of returning to the world. Something came back after it seemed not to have been there for ages. It came as a surprise, as a reminder that we will always live around what will happen. The sun will rise and set, and the ants will do their endless work, until one day the clouds turn gray and rain falls, and even in the township, the ants will fly out into the sky. Come what may.

My moon came, in a heavy surge of blood. And, after such a long time, I remembered the thing Buntu and I had buried in me. I felt it as if it had just entered. I felt it again as it floated away on the surge. I would be ready for another month. Ready as always, each and every month, for new beginnings.

And Buntu? I'll be with him, now. Always. Without our knowing, all the trying events had prepared for us new beginnings. Shall we not prevail?

Questions for Discussion

1. How does the death of the son change the relationship between the man and the wife?

2. How does the death of the son illuminate for the reader the racial and political conflict in South Africa?

3. Characterize how the women, including the narrator, respond to the violence and oppression with which their lives are filled. (At one point, for instance, the narrator says, ". . . that anguish had to be turned into a simmering kind of indignation. The kind of indignation that had to be kept at bay only because there was a higher purpose at that moment: the sharing of concern." What do you think she means by these statements?)

4. In what sense is the narrator stronger than Buntu? How does she account for her strength?

5. Interpret the ending of the story. What is significant about the imagery? What is the cause of the narrator's hopefulness?

Suggestions for Writing

1. Write an essay about this story in which you analyze the significance of "speech" and "silence" throughout the story.

2. Write an essay about this story in which you assess the ways in which the personal tragedy of the narrator and her husband illuminates the public strife in South Africa.

3. Write an essay in which you discuss the ways in which the story is about women's and men's different ways of dealing with tragedy, oppression, and anger.

4. Write an essay in which you compare and contrast this story with Elsa Joubert's "Back Yard."

The Wall-Reader

FIONA BARR

"Shall only our rivers run free?" The question jumped out from the cobbled wall in huge white letters, as The People's taxi swung round the corner at Beechmount. "Looks like the paint is running freely enough down here," she thought to herself as other slogans glided past in rapid succession. Reading Belfast's grim graffiti had become an entertaining hobby for her, and she often wondered, was it in the dead of night that groups of boys huddled round a paint tin daubing walls and gables with tired political slogans and cliches? Did anyone ever see them? Was the guilty brush ever found? The brush is mightier than the bomb, she declared inwardly, as she thought of how celebrated among journalists some lines had become. "Is there a life before death?" Well, no one had answered that one yet, at least, not in this city.

The shapes of Belfast crowded in on her as the taxi rattled over the ramps outside the fortressed police barracks. Dilapidated houses, bricked-up terraces. Rosy-cheeked soldiers, barely out of school, and quivering with high-pitched fear. She thought of the thick-lipped youth who came to hijack the car, making his point by showing his revolver under his anorak, and of the others, jigging and taunting every July, almost sexual in their arrogance and hatred. Meanwhile, passengers climbed in and out at various points along the road, manoeuvring between legs, bags of shopping and umbrellas. The taxi swerved blindly into the road. No Highway Code here. As the woman's stop approached, the taxi swung up to the pavement, and she stepped out.

She thought of how she read walls—like tea-cups, she smiled to herself. Pushing her baby in the pram to the supermarket, she had to pass under a motorway bridge that was peppered with lines, some in irregular lettering with the paint dribbling down the concrete, others written with felt-tip pen in minute secretive hand. A whole range of human emotions splayed itself with persistent anarchy on the walls. "One could do worse than be a reader of walls," she thought, twisting Frost's words. Instead, though, the pram was rushed past the intriguing mural with much gusto. Respectable housewives don't read walls!

The 'Troubles,' as they were euphemistically named, remained for this couple as a remote, vaguely irritating wart on their life. They were simply ordinary (she often groaned at the oppressive banality of the word) middle-class, and hoping the baby would marry a doctor, thereby raising them in their autumn days to the select legions of the upper class. Each day their lives followed the same routine—no harm in that sordid little detail, she thought. It helps structure one's existence. He went to the office, she fed the baby, washed the rapidly growing mound of nappies, prepared the dinner and looked forward to the afternoon walk. She had convinced herself she was happy with her lot, and yet felt disappointed at the pangs of jealousy endured on hearing of a friend's glamorous job or another's academic and erudite husband. If only someone noticed her from time to time, or even wrote her name on a wall declaring her existence worthwhile: "A fine mind" or "I was once her lover." That way, at least, she would have evidence she was having impact on others. As it was, she was perpetually bombarded with it. Marital successes, even marital failures evoked a response from her. All one-way traffic.

That afternoon she dressed the baby and started out for her walk. 'Fantasy time,' her husband called it. 'Wall-reading time' she knew it to be. On this occasion, however, she decided to avoid those concrete temptations and, instead, visit the park. Out along the main road she trundled, pushing the pram, pausing to gaze into the hardware store's window, hearing the whine of the Saracen as it thundered by, waking the baby and making her feel uneasy. A foot patrol of soldiers strolled past, their rifles, lethal even in the brittle sunlight of this March day, lounged lovingly and relaxed in the arms of their men. One soldier stood nonchalantly, almost impertinent, against a corrugated railing and stared at her. She always blushed on passing troops.

The park is ugly, stark and hostile. Even in summer, when courting couples seek out secluded spots like mating cats, they reject Musgrave. There are a few trees, clustered together, standing like skeletons, ashamed of their nakedness. The rest is grass, a green wasteland speckled with puddles of gulls squawking over a worm patch. The park is bordered by a hospital with a military wing which is guarded by an army billet. The beauty of the place, it has only this, is its silence.

The hill up to the park bench was not the precipice it seemed, but the baby and pram were heavy. Ante-natal self-indulgence had taken its toll—her midriff was now most definitely a bulge. With one final push, pram, baby and mother reached the green wooden seat, and came to rest. The baby slept soundly with the soother touching her velvet pink cheeks, hand on pillow, a picture of purity. The woman heard a coughing noise coming from the nearby gun turret, and managed to see the tip of a rifle and a face peering out from the darkness. Smells of cabbage and burnt potatoes wafted over from behind the slanting sheets of protective steel.

"Is that your baby?" an English voice called out. She could barely see the face belonging to the voice. She replied yes, and smiled. The situation reminded her of the confessional. Dark and supposedly anonymous. "Is that you, my child?" She knew the priest personally. Did he identify her sins with his "Good morning, Mary," and think to himself, "and I know what you were up to last night!" She blushed at the secrets given away during the ceremony. Yes, she nervously answered again, it was her baby, a little girl. First-time mothers rarely resist the temptation to talk about their offspring. Forgetting her initial shyness, she told the voice of when the baby was born, the early problems of all-night crying, now teething, how she could crawl backwards and gurgle.

The voice responded. It too had a son, a few months older than her child, away in Germany at the army base at Munster. Factory pipes, chimney tops, church spires, domes all listened impassively to the Englishman's declaration of paternal love. The scene was strange, for although Belfast's sterile geography slipped into classical forms with dusk and heavy rain-clouds, the voice and the woman knew the folly of such innocent communication. They politely finished their conversation, said goodbye, and the woman pushed her pram homewards. The voice remained in the turret, watchful and anxious. Home she went, past vanloads of workers leering out at the pavement, past the uneasy presence of foot patrols, past the church. "Let us give each other the sign of peace," they said at Mass. The only sign Belfast knew was two fingers pointing towards Heaven. Life was self-contained, the couple often declared, just like flats. No need to go outside.

She did go outside, however. Each week the voice and the woman learned more of each other. No physical contact was needed, no face-to-face encounter to judge reaction, no touching to confirm amity, no threat of dangerous intimacy. It was a meeting of minds, as she explained later to her husband, a new opinion, a common bond, an opening of vistas. He disclosed his ambitions to become a pilot, to watching the land, fields and horizons spread out beneath him—a patchwork quilt of dappled colours and textures. She wanted to be remembered by writing on walls, about them that is, a world-shattering thesis on their psychological complexities, their essential truths, their witticisms and intellectual genius. And all this time the city's skyline and distant buildings watched and listened.

It was April now. More slogans had appeared, white and dripping, on the city walls. "Brits out. Peace in." A simple equation for the writer. "Loose talk claims lives," another shouted menacingly. The messages, the woman decided, had acquired a more ominous tone. The baby had grown and could sit up without support. New political solutions had been proposed and rejected, interparamilitary feuding had broken out and subsided, four soldiers and two policemen had been blown to smithereens in separate incidents, and a building a day had been bombed by the Provos. It had been a fairly normal month by Belfast's standards. The level of violence was no more or less acceptable than at other times.

One day—it was, perhaps, the last day in April—her husband returned home panting and trembling a little. He asked had she been to the park, and she replied she had. Taking her by the hand, he led her to the wall on the left of their driveway. She felt her heart sink and thud against her. She felt her face redden. Her mouth was suddenly dry. She could not speak. In huge angry letters the message spat itself out.

"TOUT."

The four-letter word covered the whole wall. It clanged in her brain, its venom rushed through her body. Suspicion was enough to condemn. The job itself was not well done, she had seen better. The letters were uneven, paint splattered down from the cross T, the U looked a misshapen O. The workmanship was poor, the impact perfect.

Her husband led her back into the kitchen. The baby was crying loudly in the livingroom but the woman did not seem to hear. Like sleepwalkers, they sat down on the settee. The woman began to sob. Her shoulders heaved in bursts as she gasped hysterically. Her husband took her in his arms gently and tried to make her sorrow his. Already he shared her fear.

"What did you talk about? Did you not realise how dangerous it was? We must leave." He spoke quickly, making plans. Selling the house and car, finding a job in London or Dublin, far away from Belfast, mortgages, removals, savings, the tawdry affairs of normal living stunned her, making her more confused. "I told him nothing," she sobbed, "what could I tell? We talked about life, everything, but not about here." She trembled, trying to control herself. "We just chatted about reading walls, families, anything at all. Oh Sean, it was as innocent as that. A meeting of minds we called it, for it was little else."

She looked into her husband's face and saw he did not fully understand. There was a hint of jealousy, of resentment at not being part of their communication. Her hands fell on her lap, resting in resignation. What was the point of explanation? She lifted her baby from the floor. Pressing the tiny face and body to her breast, she felt all her hopes and desires for a better life become one with the child's struggle for freedom. The child's hands wandered over her face, their eyes met. At once that moment of maternal and filial love eclipsed her fear, gave her the impetus to escape.

For nine months she had been unable to accept the reality of her condition. Absurd, for the massive bump daily shifted position and thumped against her. When her daughter was born, she had been overwhelmed by love for her and amazed at her own ability to give life. By nature she was a dreamy person, given to moments of fancy. She wondered at her competence in fulfilling the role of mother. Could it be measured? This time she knew it could. She really did not care if they maimed her or even murdered her. She did care about her daughter. She was her touchstone, her anchor to virtue. Not for her child a legacy of fear, revulsion or hatred. With the few hours' respite the painters had left between judgement and sentence she determined to leave Belfast's walls behind.

The next few nights were spent in troubled, restless sleep. The message remained on the wall outside. The neighbours pretended not to notice and refused to discuss the matter. She and the baby remained indoors despite the refreshing May breezes and blue skies. Her husband had given in his notice at the office, for health reasons, he suggested to his colleagues. An aunt had been contacted in Dublin. The couple did not answer knocks at the door. They carefully examined the shape and size of mail delivered and always paused when they answered the telephone.

The mini-van was to call at eleven on Monday night, when it would be dark enough to park and pack their belongings and themselves without too much suspicion being aroused. The firm had been very understanding when the nature of their work had been explained. They were Protestant so there was no conflict of loyalties involved in the exercise. They agreed to drive them to Dublin at extra cost, changing drivers at Newry on the way down.

Monday finally arrived. The couple nervously laughed about how smoothly everything had gone. Privately, they each expected something to go wrong. The baby was fed, and played with, the radio listened to and the clock watched. They listened to the news at nine. Huddled together in their anxiety, they kept vigil in the darkening room. Rain had begun to pour from black thunderclouds. Everywhere it was quiet and still. Hushed and cold they waited. Ten o'clock, and it was now dark. A blustery wind had risen, making the lattice separation next door bang and clatter. At ten to eleven, her husband went into the sitting room to watch for the mini-van. His footsteps clamped noisily on the floorboards as he paced back and forth. The baby slept.

A black shape glided slowly up the street and backed into the driveway. It was eleven. The van had arrived. Her husband asked to see their identification and then they began to load up the couple's belongings. Settee, chairs, television, washing machine—all were dumped hastily, it was no time to worry about breakages. She stood holding the sleeping baby in the livingroom as the men worked anxiously between van and house. The scene was so unreal, the circumstances absolutely incredible. She thought: "What have I done?" Recollections of her naivety, her insensibility to historical fact and political climate were stupifying. She had seen women who had been tarred and feathered, heard of people who had been shot in the head, boys who had been knee-capped, all for suspected fraternising with troops. The catalogue of violence spilled out before her as she realised the gravity and possible repercussions of her alleged misdemeanor.

A voice called her, "Mary, come on now. We have to go. Don't worry, we're all together." Her husband led her to the locked and waiting van. Handing the baby to him, she climbed up beside the driver, took back the baby as her husband sat down beside her and waited for the engine to start. The van slowly manoeuvred out onto the street and down the main road. They felt more cheerful now, a little like refugees seeking safety and freedom not too far away. As they approached the motorway bridge, two figures with something clutched in their hands stood side by side in the darkness. She closed her eyes tightly, expecting bursts of gunfire. The van shot past. Relieved, she asked her husband what they were doing at this time of night. "Writing slogans on the wall," he replied.

The furtiveness of the painters seemed ludicrous and petty as she recalled the heroic and literary characteristics with which she had endowed them. What did they matter? The travellers sat in silence as the van sped past the city suburbs, the glare of police and army barracks, on out and further out into the countryside, past sleeping villages and silent fields, past whitewashed farmhouses and barking dogs. On to Newry where they said goodbye to their driver as the new one stepped in. Far along the coast with Rostrevor's twinkling lights opposite the bay down to the Border check and a drowsy soldier waving them through. Out of the North, safe, relieved and heading for Dublin.

Some days later in Belfast the neighbours discovered the house vacant, the people next door received a letter and a cheque from Dublin. Remarks about the peculiar couple were made over hedges and cups of coffee, the message on the wall was painted over by the couple who had bought the house when it went up for sale. They too were ordinary people, living a self-contained life, worrying over finances and babies, promotion and local gossip. He too had an office job, but his wife was merely a housekeeper for him. She was sensible, down to earth, and not in the least inclined to wall-reading.

Questions for Discussion

1. Characterize Belfast as seen through the eyes of the narrator.

2. What is the effect of her referring to the soldier as "the voice"?

3. Why is it wrong and dangerous for the narrator and the soldier to speak? Why are the narrator and her husband driven from the neighborhood?

4. Who are the Provos and what does the wall divide?

Suggestions for Writing

1. Read John Conroy's *Belfast Diary: War as a Way of Life* (Boston: Beacon Press, 1987) or other books about Belfast and Northern Ireland. Then write an essay in which you analyze the way Barr's story presents a personal side of the political turmoil in Northern Ireland.

2. What do "the wall" and "the voice" represent to the narrator? Write a response to this question in your notebook or journal.

3. Write an essay about "The Wall-Reader" and the stories by Elsa Joubert and Njabulo Ndebele in this section. All three stories concern private lives in countries torn apart by political conflict. In what ways do these authors approach "the private and the public" differently? In your view which story is most compelling?

The Street of the Fathers

SESSHU FOSTER

Their fathers drank together. They labored on the landscaping crew, and spent their paychecks in the bars of east San Jose. Then they returned to the weariness of clapboard houses, dusty lots, broken down cars and children in the streets, women busy as every day. His father found her father a house for rent on the same block, with torn yellow shades across the windows and old apricot trees in back which sometimes bloomed but never bore fruit.

Her father brought her mother and her brothers and sisters and herself across the mountains on the Tioga Road from the reservation east of the Sierras. His mother helped her mother feed everyone that first night, gave her Tupperware, lent her the sewing machine to make curtains, and then the house lost that dead yellow look of a place where a laborer did no more than sleep.

His own father was to become a sentimental drunk. Her father, however, turned out to be a mean drunk. Alcoholism broke both families before the children were grown, though both men were nice enough when sober. Both men worked very hard and were capable of much warmth and personal charm. It was too bad that was not the way that he remembered them in the end. Yet both had impressed him much as he grew up, so that at one end of the universe for him there would always be the street of the fathers.

Everyone called her family "the Indians" because even though they lived like everyone else in the mostly Mexican neighborhood, including the whites and the one Vietnamese family, when their relatives showed up from anywhere on the West Coast they stayed as long as they wanted, to party and fight. Only the Ochoas who knew everybody from church had more parties, but their festivities were regular, like the Vote Democrat sign stuck in their dead lawn every two years.

They grew up like cousins, with his mother putting ice on her mother's broken face, and taking in her brothers and sisters when there was trouble, and her mother ordering him around like he was one of her own, on beer runs to the Chinese market, or to fetch the men at which bar or whose garage or on a hillside or field somewhere on the edge of town where there might be new development.

She grew up to be broad shouldered as her mother, with her mother's high broad cheek bones and her father's black eyes and black hair. Even apart from her name, Chicanos could sense a difference with her that was not first apparent. When she got to be fifteen, her dark stare made him nervous, because she was like his cousin and also he did not think that girls liked him very much. He was not a pretty boy with the spoiled confidence they seemed to like.

Years of high school did not teach him much more than to waste time. He did make a lot of friends who practiced new ways of wasting time together. During the recession of 1971-73, the fathers acted like broken men, without jobs, and the mothers could not hold things together alone. In his senior year, when there was no money, for fun he spent the night with one of her best friends, so that afterwards they never shared the easy affection of cousins again.

On the day he graduated, he got a little drunk that night with some friends who had dropped out, and when they had to fight the Ramos brothers and their friends who came down to shut them up, he got the piss kicked out of him. He figured they let him have it because he graduated after all, though he did not get it bad like the time Steve Ramos stabbed him through both hands. This time there was just the sweet taste of his torn cheek inside his mouth and blood crusting in his nostrils and then he had to lift his head to see good through his swollen eye. None of it, the little bruises and dry blood in his hair and the ache in his limbs was anything. It was his little goodbye to all that bullshit, he figured. He and his friends drank the rest of their beer in an orchard before he walked home.

Late that night he stood holding himself up against her back fence, calling her name.

He heard her shush him from the black shadows of the porch and did not believe she was going to talk to him now. He stood in the street light and it felt like a bath of hot moonlight.

"I bet Tony has a hot date tonight. Is Monica out tonight with the Valedictorian?"

"I don't know," he said. He tried to see where her voice was coming from. His heart pounded as he saw her, dressed in her father's torn T-shirt, come through the thick weeds under the fruit trees. She stood in the shadows by a rusting box springs.

"Are you my date?" she asked, "You didn't ask me out to the prom, but I heard you didn't even go to the prom."

"They wouldn't let freshmen like you into the prom."

"Oh yeah? To what do I owe this honor tonight?"

"I just came by to say . . . hi, or goodbye. One of those."

"The way you look." She shook her head sharply, "We gonna meet Tony and Geronimo or Macho Kim at the American Playland?"

"Come here a minute," he said, his voice suddenly husky. "In the fall I'm going to the university."

She chuckled, "Well, tonight you better go back to the cot on the laundry porch at your mother's house. She'll kill you if she catches you like this."

"Come here," he said. She stepped into the light and he caught his breath on how the shirt hung from her breasts and hips.

"How much of this are you gonna remember tomorrow?" she smirked, but she stepped up to the edge of the fence.

He wanted to kiss her so he stepped forward and leaned down and banged his mouth on the fence. Then he could not see, so he stepped back with one hand to his mouth, and waited for his vision to clear. His mouth began to bleed again.

She clucked. "Come here," she said.

He could not see her eyes, but he stepped forward. She took one of his hands and put it on her shoulder, so he could steady himself. Then she took his head in both hands and tilted it back in the light. At that point all he could see was brightness.

"You want a piece of steak for that face?"

"I'm okay," he said. He thought of his father and grinned in spite of the sting of his split lip. "I'm following in the old man's foot steps, but his footprints are full of broken glass."

She put her hand on the back of his head and on tiptoe, kissed his cheek. "Congratulations," she said.

She looked at her hand and wiped it on her shirt. "Now you go home and get some sleep."

After she was gone, he walked along the ruts in the alley with the broken glass sparkling and a dark barking and the gravel grinding underfoot and the light and pain growing in his head till he felt like he was wire-walking alone high on the Golden Gate Bridge.

He had wanted to say something to the freshman to make her his that summer, but she was cool with him and avoided talking to him alone. The university in Hayward promised him money in the fall but it was not enough to live on so he took the bus there and found a job and a place to stay. When he was back in town, his mother said that the freshman had invited him to her sixteenth birthday party and really hoped that he could make it.

His sister picked out a sweater for him to take as a gift, and as he carried it in a little package in one hand up the block, he was nervous. Cars were parked along the street and there was music and laughter and talk of people spilling down the front steps and out onto the lawn. It was bigger than the Ochoas last quincianere, and lots of her family were there from out of town, and his brothers and sisters were all there already. He stepped around people, smoke from the barbeque swirling past him, as he went up the stairs. She was inside, on the couch. When he came in, she said something to the girls around her and they all laughed. She had the laughing look on her face as she hugged him and took the present. She took his wrist and got him something to drink and left him talking with her brothers, who said their father had left early with a carload of men, and their mother was in the back putting the little kids to sleep. Later, when people started dancing, he got out of the noise by going back into the kitchen for more to drink.

As always, there was beer in the refrigerator.

"There you are," she said, smiling, into the kitchen.

"I was wondering if you'd have time for me tonight," he smiled.

"Oh, you can see me anytime," she said, putting her hand on his arm. "Excuse me," she added. He stiffened and moved away from the refrigerator. She got out a six-pack of 7 Up.

"The dancers are getting thirsty," she explained as she went back into the living room.

He followed her. The night was warm and all the windows were open and you could hear the cars pull up and leave on the gravel out front. A girl grabbed him and asked him to dance. He hated to dance and she knew it and she sent all her pretty friends to ask him to dance. And when he started turning them down they flirted with him and he looked up and saw her grinning at him from across the room.

Later that year she said hi to him in the supermarket, but by the time he paid at the check-out stand she was gone. Then he got busy with school at the university and he began thinking of her as a kid from the old neighborhood, as someone from his childhood, from the time when his parents lived together as man and wife. But when he returned to visit his mother and brothers and sisters he still hoped that he would run into her.

She had just finished with high school herself when his mother told him that her father had gone for good. His own father had gotten an old army truck to help her mother move the family back to the reservation, and would he help them. He took the bus back on a Friday and walked across town to the neighborhood. The next morning, as the sun started to heat up, he helped his father tie the refrigerator, stove, furniture, and boxes of kids' clothes and toys on the back of the truck. He saw she had almost nothing. A few cardboard boxes of clothes and things and books. Some of her things went to his sisters.

Her aunt came and picked up the family in her little Japanese car. He and his father drove the Tioga Road over the pass with one of her brothers. They unloaded the belongings at a trailer on the reservation owned by the tribe. It stood on a sandy lot with two others on a dirt road lined with cottonwood trees. They were the only green in the dry wind at this time of year. Beyond the trees there was a big empty field which looked like it had once been planted in alfalfa, across the highway from the country road maintenance sheds and their heavy equipment. Beyond that was a low range of rough hills, with a rutted jeep track zigzagging into them behind a barbed wire cattle fence.

She was quiet and reserved and he could not think of much to say. Her mother said the tribe kept the trailers for people who came and went. The other two were empty, with the sand lots brushed clean by the wind. In back of the trailer he could see a clothes line made of rusting steel wire, which the wind made hum.

He and his father and her brother muscled in the old Frigidaire and then the stove and connected them to the gas. They figured out how to light the pilots on all the appliances, and he noticed a layer of dust on all the windowsills and below the windows on the floor. The wind whined as it blew against the windows and around the corners of the trailer. The little kids fought over the boxes of toys and things and her mother kept her busy, telling her what to do with the kids and boxes. His father's face was red from beer and as always, he worked hard cheerfully. His father heaved the old heavy sofa off the truck bed and the two younger men grabbed one end and hustled it into the trailer across that sandy yard. His father's remarks made everybody laugh, and her mother folded out the couch and made the bed up with sheets for the kids.

When he and his father stood ready at the empty truck, her mother lined all the kids up and had them say goodbye and thank you. She smiled at him and he hoped he smiled as well as she did.

"Maybe you'll write to me," she said.

"I will write," he said.

And then he and his father hit the road over the Tioga Pass. And he did write to her and she never answered his letters. His mother said she saw her back in San Jose once, and she'd said hi to everybody. What the hell, he thought. She grew up and I grew up and everybody grows up. It wasn't like we <u>every</u> had anything together to start with. Neither of us did anything wrong did we? And he worked hard and studied hard and played hard and by the time he'd finished at the university he had known a lot of nice women. He put himself through school and helped out his mother after his father stopped sending any money.

He did not think of her often after that. He still had a thing about black haired women. When he saw them he expected them to turn around and it would be her. He would find himself staring at the back of some woman's head without knowing why, and sometimes he remembered why, and sometimes he didn't. More than ten years later, he was in a country of black haired women when he saw her for the last time.

He had his second university degree by then and his corporate job and several days of all-day meetings ahead of him and he worked for people for whom he felt nothing. He went to bed that night perfectly clean and perfectly well-fed, lying in pastel printed sheets in a 14th floor hotel room above Osaka, Japan. He did not like the idea of the days ahead and he did not like this antiseptic room whose plastic color scheme seemed like it had been designed by Fisher Price Toys, so he turned off all the lights and lay on the cool bed in the dark. He stared for a long time at the lights of the electric skyline of the city which embraced that deep black bay. The night seemed starless above that brilliance and its black glass did not reflect him.

And before the morning had broken he dreamed about her.

He dreamed that he and his father moved them back into the old neighborhood in East Sanjo. He marveled how the trees seemed the same full green as in summers ago. He and his father worked cheerful and hard till past twilight, exhilarated by the run together over the mountains, as they had been in the past. They put the refrigerator and stove and sofa and boxes all back into the clapboard house with the weeds and dying fruit trees, as if they could set everything up like it had once been. Then his father drove out of the yard in the big olive truck for a bar somewhere, so when it got late for convenience he was given a blanket to sleep on the floor of her room. The sofa would be there if his father came back. When everyone had gone to sleep, he climbed into her warm bed. She said nothing, but looked at him with wide eyes. He began rubbing her back and breasts with his hands. "No," she said wearily, and got out of bed. She took a blanket and went out on the couch where her family would see her in the morning and know that he had not been good with her.

At about 5 AM he woke with his throat dry from the air conditioning and he regretted having awoken. Against the blue night there was the same skyline, delineated by crystalline blue lamps and white arc lights and a tall industrial crane silhouetted atop the steel girders of a new structure.

Questions for Discussion

1. What is the significance of the title? How do "the fathers" determine what happens to the narrator and the young woman?

2. Characterize the narrator. What sort of person is he in high school? What sort of person does he become?

3. Why is he haunted by the memory of her?

4. What is the significance of the dream and the last image that conclude the story?

Suggestions for Writing

1. Write an essay in which you analyze "The Street of the Fathers" as a "nostalgia" story. What make him yearn for the past? What does the past represent to him? Is his memory of the neighborhood entirely pleasant? What role do "the fathers" play in his nostalgia? How do you interpret the dream at the end of the story?

2. Write a story that springs from your memories of a neighborhood in which you lived. Feel free to fictionalize, however.

3. Write a sketch in your notebook about a neighborhood in which you lived.

4. Write an essay in which you compare and contrast this story with "Yoneko's Earthquake" by Hisaye Yamamoto. Or write one in which you compare and contrast this story with "Bess" by Jayne Anne Phillips.

Fools Crow

J A M E S   W E L C H

It was a sunny, windless day and the seven children pulling their buffalo rib sleds to a steep hill beyond the horse herds talked and teased each other. The two girls, at twelve winters, were the oldest. They had been sent to keep an eye on the younger ones, but they were not happy, for the five boys made jokes about the size of their breasts and the skinnyness of their legs. One Spot, in particular, was cruel to them. He liked these times when he didn't have to follow his older brother around, and so he bullied the younger boys and made the girls chase him. He boasted of his hunting skill and tried to rub snow in another boy's face. When one of the girls hit him with a small skin of pemmican, it stung his cheek but he didn't cry. He called the girl Skinny Weasel and he liked her, although she was a year older than he was. She liked One Spot's brother, Good Young Man, but he was more interested in hunting than girls. He was off hunting the bighorns with Fools Crow now in the foothills of the Backbone. They would be gone for two or three sleeps. One Spot had been jealous of Good Young Man's fortune, but Fools Crow had promised him a set of horns. He picked up a handful of snow and threw it at Skinny Weasel. His cheek stung but he liked her.

None of them noticed the wolf that had emerged from behind a clump of drifted-over greasewood until he was fifty paces to the side of them. He was large and gray and his eyes were golden in the brilliant sun. Snow clung to one side of him as though he had been lying down. As he walked, his tail drooped and dragged on the deep snow and a sound, somewhere between a growl and a grunt, came up from his chest.

It was this sound that Skinny Weasel's girlfriend heard, and when she looked over she saw the animal's gait was shakey and listed to one side. He had his head down, but she noticed his tongue hanging almost to the snow. Then she saw the whiteness around his mouth and she thought he had been eating snow. Her first impulse was to turn and run, but then the big-mouth began to veer away from them. She watched him out of the corner of her eye as the wolf circled behind them. Then she said something to Skinny Weasel in a low voice and the girls stopped and turned. It was at this point that one of the boys let out a cry of fear, for he had just seen the wolf.

The wolf looked up at them and coughed and bared his fangs, making chewing motions as though he were trying to rid himself of a bone or hairball. He watched listlessly as the children ran, all but One Spot, who stood in the deep snow with his hands on his hips. He taunted the big-mouth with a war song that he had learned from Fools Crow.

The other children stopped near the base of the big hill and turned to watch. The wolf covered the thirty paces with such speed that they didn't have a chance to cry out a warning. By the time One Spot had turned to run, the wolf was upon him, knocking him face-down in the snow, standing over him, growling, the hair on his back standing up and shining in the sunlight. The children screamed as they watched the wolf attack the bundled-up child as he tried to crawl away. He struck repeatedly at the blanket, his low growl now a roar of fury. At last he found One Spot's head and sank his fangs into the exposed skin behind the ear. The child screamed in pain and turned over, only to feel a fang knock against his cheek bone, opening it up. Then the fangs were twisting and pulling at the cheek, gnashing into the soft flesh. One Spot felt the wetness and the hot breath. He saw for one brief instant the yellow eye and the laid-back ear—then he sank into the red darkness and deep snow.

Skinny Weasel was crying as she watched the wolf stagger away. In his charge and attack he had used up the last of his energy. Now his throat was swollen shut and the saliva hung in long strands from his mouth. He began a wide circle, always veering to his right, his eyes now seeing nothing, his breath coming in harsh barks, his tongue and tail once again hanging and dragging on the snow. Skinny Weasel watched him disappear behind a stand of willows near the river; then she ran to the limp, ragged form in the snow field. When she rolled him over, she bit her lips to keep from screaming. A flap of ragged skin lay back over One Spot's eye, exposing the clean white bone of his cheek. One ear lobe hung from a thin piece of skin and there was a large mat of blood in the hair. She thought she heard a rattle deep in the boy's throat. With a shudder, she placed the flap of skin down over the cheek bone. Then she and the others managed to lift him onto his sled. Skinny Weasel's girlfriend covered him up with her own blanket. Then the two girls pulled the sled through the deep snow back toward camp. The sun was still high and the sweat was cool on the girls' bodies.

By the time Fools Crow and Good Young Man got back from their hunting trip, four days later, One Spot was able to sit up and take some meat. But most of the time he lay in his robes and thought of the yellow eye and the laid-back ear, the harsh breath and the snapping teeth. Every time he closed his eyes, he saw the bounding wolf and he cried out in his weakness and pain. Heavy Shield Woman had slept little, despite the fact that Killdeer and another woman had attempted to take over the nursing of her son. Now she sat in a listless trance and thought of the many things that had happened to her family. She didn't really think, but images of White Quiver and Killdeer and Good Young Man entered her head and they all seemed far away, as though she had lost them all. Even when she looked down at One Spot, in one of his rare moments of peace, she saw the black pitchy substance that held his cheek in place and she thought that he had gone away from her too. Only Killdeer was there to talk with, but Heavy Shield Woman didn't talk. She answered questions without elaboration and she didn't volunteer any conversation. In some ways, she felt a lingering guilt (she had felt it for some time) about her role as medicine woman at the Sun Dance ceremonies. She thought she could not be a virtuous woman, for she felt no happiness or peace since her husband was returned to her. Her virtue (if that was what it was) resulted from a drab emptiness in her life, a day-to-day barrenness of spirit relieved only by moments of pleasure at the antics of her sons and Killdeer's swelling belly. But these moments were short-lived and only increased her over-all sadness, as she thought of their futures, her own future. She knew she would never see White Quiver again and that thought almost gave her relief; but then she would think of the happiness they had shared, the times they had lain together, the pride in his eyes each time she delivered him a son, and she would become consumed with a restless fury. Many times she thought of going to Three Bears and telling him what was in her heart and renouncing her role as medicine woman. In her mind she had already done so. Now when the girls looked to her for guidance, she averted her eyes and said nothing. She began to avoid them, for she was sure they would see in her eyes what she felt in her heart.

But Fools Crow and Good Young Man did not know any of this as they rode into camp with the carcasses of two bighorns. True to his word Fools Crow had a set of horns tied to the frame of one of the pack horses. He rode first to his own lodge and dumped one of the bighorns in the snow beside the entrance. Then he led the other pack horse to Heavy Shield Woman's lodge, kicking a black dog in the ribs when he became too curious. As he loosened the rawhide strings that held the animal down, Killdeer emerged from her mother's lodge. She came forward and squeezed his upper arm and smiled. She called to her brother, Good Young Man, who sat exhausted on his horse, ready to drive the pack horses back to the herd. Wearily, he rolled onto his belly and slid off the horse. He had planned to return to the camp in triumph because he had shot one of the bighorns with Fools Crow's rifle, but now he felt the stiffness in his legs and wanted only to lie down and sleep.

But Killdeer motioned him close, and then she told them about One Spot's encounter with the wolf. Even as she explained that he was all right, her voice shook and she looked at the snow at Fools Crow's feet. Good Young Man listened to his sister, first with fear, and then relief. He had forgotten about being tired, and when his sister paused, he ducked into the lodge.

Killdeer looked into her husband's eyes. "The children he was with think the wolf might have the whitemouth. They say he was acting funny, walking sideways in a big circle, his tail dragging in the snow. They think he had the foam on the mouth, but they couldn't tell if it was that, or if he was eating snow."

"Did he breathe different?"

"Skinny Weasel said it was like a harsh bark in his throat."

"Maybe it was a bone caught."

"Maybe," said Killdeer, but her voice was doubtful.

"Is your mother in the lodge?"

"She is out gathering firewood."

Fools Crow entered the lodge, with Killdeer right behind him. Good Young Man knelt beside his brother, holding his hand. One Spot looked at Fools Crow: then he grinned.

"I sang my war song," he said.

"But did you have your weapons?" Fools Crow got down on his knees and ruffled the boy's hair.

"No," the boy said sheepishly.

"Hai-ya! What warrior goes out empty-handed?"

"He would kill this wolf with his bare hands. He would be a great warrior," said Good Young Man with a smile.

"If I had my knife—"

"If he had his knife! Listen to him talk!" Fools Crow laughed. "And now you have your first battle wounds. Let me see." Fools Crow leaned over the boy's face. The patch of skin held by the black pitch looked a pale purple and was slightly swollen. He almost lost his whole cheek, thought Fools Crow. As it is, it will always be swollen and discolored, but it will at least be there. The earlobe was completely bitten off and would cause no trouble. But behind the ear, in a patch of cut-off hair, there were several puncture wounds. The whole area was an angry red, except for the small white circles around each fang mark. These were draining, but the area was swollen and tender-looking. It scared Fools Crow to look at these wounds, but he didn't say anything.

"He has nightmares," said Killdeer. "He gets very little sleep because of them."

"Sleep-bringer will visit soon. All warriors have bad dreams after battle—they will pass." Fools Crow looked down at One Spot. "You must not think of this wolf as your enemy. He did only what wolves will do. The big-mouth is a sacred power-animal, and if he visits you in your dreams, it is only because he wishes to help you. Someday, he will become your secret helper."

"When I am old enough for my vision?"

"Yes. Then he will come to you and give you some of his secret medicine. But for now, you must think of him as your brother and treat him with great respect. Do you understand that?"

"But why did he attack me?"

"This one was—sick. I think he didn't know what he was doing. But wolves are unpredictable. It is best to leave them alone, even if they are our brothers—like the real-bear."

"Will I have a scar forever?"

"Do you remember the story of Poia—Scarface?"

"Yes. He came from Sun Chief and instructed our people in the Sun Dance. Afterward, Sun Chief made him a star in the sky, just like his father, Morning Star."

"But before all that, he was a boy just like you, with a scar on his face—"

"But the people laughed at him and scorned him!"

"In those days, the people were not wise. Now we honor Poia. Of all the Above Ones, he is most like us, and so you must think of your scar as a mark of honor. You will wear it proudly and the people will be proud of you. And they will think highly of you because you did not kill your brother, the wolf." Fools Crow laughed. "We will tell them you took pity on this big-mouth."

One Spot thought for a moment, his dark eyes narrowed and staring up at the point where the lodge-poles came together. He heard some children run by but he didn't envy them. Finally he said, "Yes, I took pity on my brother. But if I had my weapons, I surely would have killed him."

One Spot did not get over his dreams, but now instead of attacking him, the wolf turned away or stopped, sometimes lifting his lip to growl, other times simply staring at the boy through golden eyes. But he always kept his distance and One Spot, in spite of his fear, began to look forward to the wolf's visits, for he was memorizing every aspect of the animal, from his silver-tipped fur to the way his long ears flickered when One Spot shouted at him. For seven sleeps he dreamed of the big-mouth and on the eighth day, he was well enough to walk down to the river to throw rocks. Good Young Man stayed with him, never leaving the lodge to play with friends or even to visit Killdeer and Fools Crow. Together, he and his mother had skinned and quartered the bighorn. The meat was strong but good and would last a long time. Heavy Shield Woman also seemed to be improving. For the first time in many sleeps she went to visit a friend who lived on the other side of camp. The friend was very glad to see her for she had been concerned about Heavy Shield Woman. They ate and talked until well after dark and the friend noticed that Heavy Shield Woman smiled and laughed more than she had in some time and talked less about her bad fortune. When the friend's husband came home, with a fat blackhorn cow he had killed on the Cutbank, Heavy Shield Woman remembered that she had not fed One Spot and Good Young Man. She looked up at the stars as she hurried along the icy path to her lodge and the cold air was fresh in her chest.

When she entered the lodge, Good Young Man looked up anxiously. He was kneeling by his brother's side. "One Spot seems to be sick again. He seems to have difficulty swallowing. He moves his jaws and is thirsty all the time but he can't drink."

Heavy Shield Woman ran to One Spot and sank to her knees. His forehead glistened in the firelight and his throat seemed to jump and quiver on its own. He looked up at her and his eyes were wide with fear. He tried to speak but the effort made him swallow and he cried out in pain. In panic he began to thrash around under the buffalo robe. Heavy Shield Woman held him and spoke soothing words to him, but he didn't seem to hear or know her.

"Good Young Man, put on the water to heat—build up the fire first—then run for, for Fools Crow and Killdeer. Run fast."

One Spot had quieted down a little, but when Heavy Shield Woman looked down at him, she saw the saliva bubbling around his mouth. His eyes were dark and unseeing.

When Good Young Man returned with Fools Crow and Killdeer, Heavy Shield Woman was mopping the sick boy's face with a cloth dampened in the warm water. Suddenly One Spot began to tremble violently and make noises in his throat. He tried to kick the robe off, but Fools Crow held his legs.

"It is the whitemouth," he said. "The wolf has infected him."

"Oh, I feared it. I knew it would happen. I saw it once as a girl. But we must do something!" Heavy Shield Woman moaned as she remembered how her girlfriend had died of a kit-fox bite. She had never forgotten it, and now she was seeing it again.

"Killdeer! Hold his legs while I get Mik·api." But before he left, he glanced at One Spot's face and he shuddered.

Fools Crow was gone for a long time. Killdeer helped her mother hold down the struggling boy. He did not recognize either of them, but the strange noise in his throat seemed a cry for help. Killdeer sank back on her heels once when her brother suddenly stopped and held himself rigid. She wiped the sweat from her forehead, and only then did she realize that she had been crying.

At last, Fools Crow entered the lodge. His chest was heaving and his face was crimson.

"Where's Mik·api?" Killdeer held her breath.

"I searched the camp—but he was not to be found."

He looked down and Heavy Shield Woman was looking up at him with a blankness in her eyes. He suddenly thought that he had not looked at her this way since he had married Killdeer—nor had she looked at him. But now this taboo did not matter.

"We need a green hide," he said. "Mik·api once told me how to do this."

Heavy Shield Woman looked down at her son who was beginning to stir again. A trickle of blood from the crescent scab on his cheek ran down his neck. She wiped the saliva from his mouth. "Morning Eagle had just returned from his hunt. He brought back a blackhorn."

Fools Crow ran across a small icy field to Morning Eagle's lodge. He told the hunter what he needed and the two men began to skin the blackhorn. They worked quickly, not caring if they punctured the skin or left too much meat on it.

When they finished, Fools Crow draped the skin over his shoulder and began to trot back to Heavy Shield Woman's lodge. He was surprised to see so many people standing around. They had been talking among themselves, but he hadn't heard a word.

Back in the lodge the two women undressed the violent boy while Fools Crow spread the green hide, skin side up, on the other side of the fire. Good Young Man helped him clear away the spot. Fools Crow clapped him on the shoulder and squeezed. Then he helped the women carry One Spot over to the hide. He was taken aback by the strength in the small body and he understood how much effort it had taken the women to hold him down. But they managed to lay him on the smooth cool skin, with his arms pinned to his sides, and roll him up. Only his head stuck out of the furry bundle. Killdeer looked down and could not believe that the contorted face, the white foamy mouth which uttered such strange harsh sounds, belonged to her younger brother. But she knew that when a bad spirit entered one's body, the body no longer belonged to the person but became the embodiment of that spirit. And so, as she looked at the face, she grew calm, for she felt that now the spirit had been trapped, her husband would drive it away with the medicine he learned from Mik·api. She helped her mother to the far side of the fire and squatted to watch.

Fools Crow, who had stopped by his lodge for his parfleche of medicines, took out a small bundle of sweetgrass and threw some into the fire. Then he lit braids and purified both the out-of-his-mind boy and himself. He began to chant in a steady rhythm that matched his own heartbeat. As he chanted he passed his hands over the boy. His eyes were closed and the steady rhythm of his voice seemed to place the boy under a spell. One Spot had stopped struggling and the noise in his throat became less a cry of fear and pain. Then Fools Crow removed a burning stick from the fire and touched it against the furry hide. There was a hiss and the lodge was suddenly filled with the stink of burning hair. Heavy Shield Woman started, but Killdeer held her close. Still chanting, Fools Crow burned off more of the curly hair. He did this several times until the hair was black and crinkly, then he turned the boy over, and the movement made One Spot cry out. But now Fools Crow began to pass the burning stick over the green robe, lighting long strips of hair and the smell made Killdeer feel faint. She looked beyond her mother to Good Young Man, but he was watching intently, mesmerized by the moving stick of fire. Again Fools Crow turned the boy over until he was lying on his stomach. The boy made no sound and Killdeer became frightened. But when she was his eyes flicker, she let out a deep breath.

Once Fools Crow stopped to wipe One Spot's sweat-drenched head. He looked into the boy's eyes, but they were opaque and without recognition. Then he turned him again and burned off the last of the hair.

When he finished, Fools Crow threw a bundle of sage onto the fire to purify the air. As he did this he said a prayer to the Above Ones and to the Medicine Wolf to take pity on the boy and to restore him to health. Then he instructed the women to unwrap him and bathe him with warm water. While they did this, he took some sticky-root and tastes-dry and ground it up into a paste.

The women placed the small limp body on a robe and Fools Crow swabbed the paste on the boy's throat. They covered him with another robe.

Fools Crow sent the two women back to his own lodge, there to prepare some broth and meat. He said he would send Good Young Man to fetch them when they were needed. Heavy Shield Woman was reluctant to leave, but Killdeer talked her out of the lodge. The sudden draft of cold air swirled through the lodge and dried the sweat on Fools Crow's face. The lodge smelled of burnt hair and sage and sticky-root.

Good Young Man built up the fire and gave Fools Crow a drink of water. He dipped another cupful and looked questioningly at his younger brother, but the medicine man shook his head and motioned the youth to sit on the other side of the fire.

For the rest of that night Fools Crow beat on his small drum, which was nothing more than a piece of tough neck hide stretched over a willow frame. His stick was made of ash, rounded at one end and feathered at the other. He accompanied the slow beat with a monotonous song, and in spite of his fascination, Good Young Man eventually fell asleep. Four times before dawn he was awakened by a shrill whistle—short, furious blasts—and started to his feet to see Fools Crow crouching, blowing his eagle-bone pipe over the length of the still form of One Spot. Then he would watch for a while before drifting off again.

Sometime after first light, he awoke and it was quiet. He threw back the robe and sat up. Fools Crow still knelt beside his brother, but now he was hunched over, his head down. Good Young Man watched his broad back move up and down with his breathing. Then he slid from beneath the robe and tended to the fire. It was nearly out, but he coaxed a flame out of some dry twigs. When he had the fire crackling, he crept around and looked down at the face of his younger brother. In the half-light of dawn, the face looked pale and shiny, like the back-fat of a blackhorn. Only the skin on the cheek that had been torn away had some color. It was a dull purple, fading to bright pink along the scar. Good Young Man got down on all fours and looked closer. He looked at the chest beneath the robe. Nothing moved. He became frightened and in his fear, he blew on the face. The eyes seemed to move beneath the lids. He blew again, and this time the eyes opened and the brows came down in irritation.

Questions for Discussion

1. In what sense is the story about Fools Crow? In what sense is it not?

2. Characterize the point of view of the children at the beginning of the story. To what extent is it a universal point of view? To what extent is it a particularly Native American point of view?

3. What is "whitemouth"?

4. In what sense does this story illuminate Native American culture in general? What did you find particularly illuminating about the story in this regard?

5. Explain the ending of the story. What happens? How is the ending both subtle and dramatic?

Suggestions for Writing

1. Write an essay about the multiple points of view in this story. What does the use of several points of view add to the story? What points of view are particularly effective?

2. What does the way the family reacts to One Spot's ailment reveal about Native American culture in general? Write a response to this question in your notebook or journal.

Our Side of the Fence and Theirs

GYANRANJAN

Mukherji has been transferred and no longer lives in our neighborhood. The new people who moved in have no contact with us. They appear to be Punjabis, but maybe not. It's hard to know anything about them.

Ever since they arrived, I've been strangely anxious to find out about them. For some reason I can't stand staying detached. Even on journeys I have to get acquainted with the other travelers. Perhaps it's just my nature. But no one at our house is indifferent to those people. We're respectable, honorable people. Having young women in the home, we're forced to understand everything and to be constantly aware. We're full of curiosity, and keep forming impressions based on the activities of our new neighbors.

I'd like to invite the whole family over to our house and be able to come and go at their place. But probably they're completely unaware of my feelings. Their life is an unusual one. They spend a good part of the day sitting around on chairs set on the firm ground near the veranda of their house. Those chairs remain outside all the time, even at night. They're very careless, but the chairs have never been stolen.

On one side of our house, there's a government office and a high brick wall. Behind us is the back of a two-story apartment building and, in front, the main street. As a result, we have no real proximity with any other family. The new neighbors seem like certain people found in big cities who establish no connection with others and keep strictly to themselves. Both this city and the neighborhood are quiet and peaceful. People come and go at a leisurely pace and stroll around casually, since life has no great urgency. That's why we find our neighbors strange.

I went outside. Those people were having morning tea, at the late hour of nine. Besides the husband and wife, there's one girl who must be their daughter. One always sees these same three people, never a fourth. The daughter may not be pretty, but she's a well-mannered young woman. If she used the right makeup, she might even look pretty. I've noticed that she laughs a lot—and frequently. Her mother and father laugh also. They always look happy. What sorts of things do they talk about, and why are they always laughing? Are their lives so full of delightful circumstances which keep them laughing? Or are they insensitive to the harsh, realistic circumstances of life? Amazed, I compare my family with the neighbors.

They startle me by suddenly bursting into laughter. I'd been concentrating on the rose beds, but now my trowel stopped. Their laughter seemed unable to stop. The girl rose from the chair and stood up, handing her teacup to her mother for fear of spilling it. Instead of standing straight, she was doubled over.

Something funny in the conversation, perhaps a joke, must have set off the explosion of laughter. The girl, helpless with laughter, was unaware that her dupatta had slipped off one shoulder. The movement of her bosom was visible—free and unrestrained. This was too much! Her mother should have scolded her for that carelessness. What kind of person was she not to mind? But maybe, unlike me, none of them had even looked in that direction.

Daily a kind of mild compulsion grips me, and my helpless fascination about the new neighbors grows. I'm not the only one. Puppi is very curious too, and keeps praising the material of that girl's kurtas. My brother's wife also glances periodically from the kitchen toward their house, and Granny even knows when the neighbors have bought water chestnuts or squash and when the stove has been lit. Nevertheless, those people don't show a scrap of interest in us.

The girl never looks in our direction, nor do her parents. It doesn't even seem intentional. So the thought of them conversing with us is remote and unimaginable. Perhaps they don't need us in their world. Maybe they consider us inferior. Or maybe they fear trouble because of our proximity. I don't know to what extent that could be true, however, since the sight of a young man in the vicinity doesn't seem to fill her parents with the fear which my father feels for Puppi at the sight of my friends.

We never hear a radio at their place, while ours blares constantly. There's bare ground in front of their house, with not even a blade of grass. Our house has a lawn, along with a vegetable garden and beds of strong-smelling flowers. Why doesn't that girl make friends with my sister and my sister-in-law? Why don't her parents mix with mine? Why don't they notice us drinking tea out of cups prettier than theirs? What they ought to do is add us to their list of acquaintances. They should be interested in everything of ours. Next to the fence, on our side, there's a big tall tamarind tree with fruit six inches long hanging from it. Girls are crazy about tamarind fruit, and yet this neighbor girl never even looks over longingly. She's never given me the satisfaction of breaking a piece of fruit off the tree.

I keep waiting. . . .

Our neighbors evidently have no problem that might make them want to seek our help. Perhaps the little internal problems that exist in our home and others don't exist in theirs, which is astonishing. None of the three ever appears worried. The girl's father must frown occasionally, and at times her mother must get upset, but nothing can be seen or heard from our place. Possibly the girl has some secret and private corner in her heart—some complication or emotional conflict. Maybe so, maybe not. Nothing definite can be known.

A light usually burns at night in their middle room, where Mukherji and his whole family used to sleep. Apparently even indoors they sit together and talk. They must have an endless supply of stories and material for conversation. A sigh slips from my lips. In our house the talk deals only with the weather, mosquitoes, the birth of children, the new wives of relatives, kitchen matters, and ancient divine heroes who obliterate the present.

The fence between our houses is a barrier only in name. It's only a foot-high ridge of dirt with some berry bushes, a long stretch of dry twisted wild cactus, and some unknown shrubs with white ants clustered around the roots. In between, the ridge is broken in several places. Paths have formed, used by the fruit and vegetable sellers as well as the sweeper woman and the newspaper vendor. The postman and milkman have been using these paths for years. Despite the damage from dogs and cats coming and going and from animals grazing on the plants, the fence remains much the same as ever. Until a short time ago, Mukherji's daughter Shaila used to take this route bringing books over to me. It's such a convenient and simple fence that we can easily ride bicycles through the gaps from one side to the other without dismounting. And previously we used to pass through that way, but no longer, because our neighbors interpret a fence as something uncrossable.

They've been living here for three months. . . .

I often move my desk outdoors for study. At this time of year the outside air is lovely, like ice water in an intense summer thirst. But studying there is difficult. My eyes leap the fence and my mind hovers around the neighbors' house. A young and unattached girl. Cheerful and fearless parents. If only I'd been born in that home! That's the way my mind wanders.

At times the neighbor girl sits outside all alone, doing some work or doing nothing. Occasionally she strolls over to the wall on the other side of her house. Elbows propped on the wall, she watches the street. Then she returns. Loafers from other neighborhoods come into our area a lot. Not that there's any lack of them in our neighborhood too. But she always seems innocent and free, walking with small swaying steps.

At our place, in contrast, my sister-in-law takes Puppi along even when she goes outside to get flowers for worship. She's scared outside the house and in it too. She's kept scared. A sharp eye is kept on Puppi also. One time the neighbor girl's father put his hand on his wife's shoulder in the course of conversation, and Puppi was immediately called into the house on some pretext. That scene produced an uproar at our place. Such shamelessness! Gradually people in our house have begun considering the neighbors quite dangerous.

With the passing of time, the attraction toward the neighbors has changed into dislike, though they might as well be nonexistent as far as we're concerned. In time, however, our family has made the neighbors a focal point for all the evils in the world. Our eyes cross the fence thousands of times in what has become a part of our daily routine. A new distress has crept into our minds, added to our other worries. I, too, waste a lot of time, but not a glance from there ever falls this way.

Somewhere nearby a diesel engine, finding no signal to proceed, stands shrieking. The novelty of the sound is startling. For a while all of us will talk about nothing but the diesel engine.

Yesterday those neighbors had not been home since noon. A few guests were staying at their place, but there was no hustle and bustle—just the usual carefree atmosphere. I rose and went inside. Sister-in-law was drying her hair. Then, I don't know why, she teased me slyly, connecting me with the neighbor girl. Smiling to myself, I went outdoors. Just then the girl and her mother returned, probably from the bazaar, carrying some packages. The father must have remained behind.

Both that evening and this morning people kept coming and going there. But it couldn't be considered a large number of people. Their house has the atmosphere of some ordinary festival celebration—just faintly. We were all astonished when the milkman reported that the daughter's marriage took place last night. It was some man from the other side of town. She'd had an Arya Samaj wedding. My sister-in-law threw me a teasing look of sympathy, and I started laughing. I laughed openly and freely, thinking what dreamers we all are.

Now and then three or four people would arrive at their house. They'd go inside, then come out a little later and go away. They were mostly serious and restrained people. At times children gathered, shouting and running around, but otherwise there was no commotion—as though everything were taking place easily and smoothly. There was no way to know just what was happening, nor how.

At our house this has been a day of great uneasiness. After several hours, the girl emerged. She was wearing a sari, maybe for the first time. She stepped out on the veranda straightening her sari and carrying a coconut. Her swaying walk was restricted considerably by the sari and she moved forward with an eye on each step. She hadn't veiled herself in any way, nor, even with her husband walking so close to her, did she show any of the embarrassment and coquettishness of a traditional bride. Her husband looked like some friend of mine. No one was weeping and wailing. Several times the girl's mother kissed her warmly on both cheeks. The father patted her head. The girl's eyes could no longer conceal a shimmer of tears reflecting her excitement over the new life ahead.

Squirrels were darting across the fence from one corner to the other. Mother expressed amazement to me over the girl's failure to cry. According to her, the girl had become hardened by her education and had no real love or attachment for her mother and father. "They're all like that these days . . . with not one tear for those who struggled and sacrificed to raise them."

I was not interested in listening to such things. I observed that Mother was enjoying the sun, shifting her position to stay in the patches of sunshine. Then Father made a pronouncement—"In the old days, girls would cry all the way to the edge of the village. Anyone who didn't was beaten and forced to cry. Otherwise her life at her husband's home could never be happy." Father feels very distressed that things are no longer like that. "The old days are passing and men's hearts have become machines, just machines!" At such times his voice grows sharp, and the wreckage of Kali Yug, this Age of Darkness, dances before his eyes.

A few small isolated fragments of cloud have appeared in the sky over our home and then passed on. The parents and relatives reached the gate and were waiting to give the girl a last farewell. The boy's party had brought a Herald car for the groom which looked like a colorful room. That colorful room glided slowly away and was gone.

Granny was the most astounded of all and kept muttering to herself. This marriage made no sense at all to her. "No fanfare, no uproar, no feasting. What's the point of such stinginess! And besides, not even asking the neighbors on such an occasion. What's happening to mankind? Good god!"

Having said good-bye to the girl, the people walked back to the house. Each carried out a chair and sat down outdoors. Ever since the girl's departure, her mother had been a little sad and subdued. A few people kept her company, probably trying to cheer her up. My friend Radhu swore that he could prove the girl was a woman of the world. I felt only the sadness of an intense loss. A sort of strange emptiness—an emptiness at being left behind and an emptiness produced by Radhu's loose talk about the girl. Absolutely unfounded! Maybe talking about a girl's misconduct provides a kind of depraved satisfaction. But perhaps in one corner of my mind, I, too, like my family, can't tolerate the behavior of the neighbors.

Night is sloughing off the cover of evening. The people who were seated around a table across the fence have risen and dispersed. As usual, a light is burning in the middle room of the neighbors' house. Their night has become peaceful and quiet as usual, and there's no way to know how they're feeling about the absence of one member of the family. At our house, though, the bazaar of neighbor-criticism is doing a heated business.

Questions for Discussion

1. How would you describe the narrator and his attitude toward the neighbors?

2. In what ways do the neighbors offend the narrator? Are you sympathetic to his response to them?

3. To what extent does the story comment indirectly about the differences not just between neighbors but between ethnic groups, nations, and cultures?

4. What does the story suggest about Indian families—their structure and importance?

Suggestions for Writing

1. Write an essay about the way this story comments about the role of "perception" and "prejudice" in conflict between people.

2. Write an essay in which you compare and contrast Gyanranjan's story with Robert Frost's poem "Mending Wall."

3. Write an entry in your notebook or journal about a memorable event involving neighbors.

4. If you live in a dormitory or similar group-living arrangement, write in your notebook about how this story illuminates certain conflicts in such an arrangement.

The Ventriloquist's Dummy

MADELINE DEFREES

Every day when Frieda Tremblay takes the bus downtown she spends the entire 28 minutes looking for the Green River Killer. She always tries for a seat a little more than halfway back, on the side opposite the driver. Over the fluttering page of an open book, she studies each man's face without ever meeting the eyes of a suspect, and she matches his features, one by one, with the newspaper drawing that hangs in her memory as if it had always been there.

Frieda has already planned what she will do if she finds the Killer. She will ring the bell for the next stop near a telephone. Then she will pass the note she carries in her purse to the bus driver. She imagines him stalling for time, fussing with the signs on the front of the bus, checking to see whether the schedules are in the right boxes, while she, Frieda Tremblay, phones 9-1-1 and later gets her picture in the paper.

Lately this plan has run into a problem: bus drivers no longer qualify for automatic trust. One of them has just been charged with killing a woman who wouldn't be hounded into giving him a date. Frieda remembers the shy, sweet face of Jorie Sundahl, there on the front page. The driver had worked for Metro 16 years, and Jorie had tried eight times to get police or the transit authorities to pay attention to her phone calls. They started paying attention right after the bus driver sought her out in a remote duplex and stabbed her.

While her husband was alive, Frieda went everywhere in a cab because Ed drove one. He would drop her off at work before starting his shift and pick her up at the restaurant when their work day ended. She's glad he isn't around to read about the cab that appears again and again in attempts to trace the killer's movements. Always impatient with police questioning, Ed would be sure to get himself in trouble by being disrespectful to an officer.

In spite of the shortening winter days, Frieda finds the bus ride home even better for her purposes than the morning ride. Outbound passengers pay on leaving the bus, every rider framed for a few seconds in the patch of light near the door, as the man fumbles for change or flashes a pass with his picture.

It has taken Frieda a few days to dislodge the old drawing and replace it with the latest composite of the Green River Killer, which police call "the best yet because it comes from an eyewitness." The young woman in question had been left for dead but recovered to add her testimony to the thickening file of the special task force. Frieda knows the description by heart: *white, 25 to 30 years old, 5-feet-9 to 6-foot-1 . . . thin build . . . shoulder length, sandy-colored hair, blue eyes, a thin mustache and a ruddy complexion scarred by acne.*

Without being too obvious, she studies two blond men of the right age riding the bus this morning. At least three others have to be considered. She never dismisses candidates with dark hair or red, or persons without mustaches, solely on that basis. The Killer can read newspapers, too, and he would certainly take steps to protect himself. Frieda's own hair is the color of cornmeal mush with a clump of platinum curls wilting on the crown.

The victims are mostly women in their 20's. Frieda is 56, but when she first started dyeing her hair, a friend told her she looked centuries younger. Most of the murdered women had been prostitutes or "linked to prostitution." Frieda doesn't know what the link might be, but you can't go downtown without standing close to a prostitute, and that's a link of sorts. Besides, the world is so mixed-up, especially in the city, that even she was recently denied credit against all evidence of her spotless record and her five years' service as a Mormon missionary in the worst part of Las Vegas. If she can't be trusted to pay her bills, she could conceivably by mistaken for a streetwalker.

Frieda doesn't even care about the reward money, though she could use the thousand or more it must come to by now. What she cares about is making the world safe for democracy. She's always liked the ring of that phrase, attainable or not.

Already Frieda has ruled out the two blond men. One is barely five feet tall and the complexion of the other is positively ashen. Does the Killer use Rose Blush Illusion Foundation as he goes on his deadly rounds? It is not out of the question.

Frieda glances into the rearview mirror in time to intercept the bus driver's huge wink at a young girl sitting next to her mother and sister on the side benches. The girl reminds Frieda of Brooke Shields. She is a sexy 14 with a sulky charm in the curve of lip and cheek. Since the mother seems to be daydreaming, Frieda keeps watch to see whether the girl eggs him on, but the child might as well be inside one of those teen-insulated bubbles, her pale blue eyes moving lazily over something beyond the passing landscape. She just continues mechanically chewing gum, exposing her tonsils, knees crossed to show firm thighs and bare ankles in tight jeans. She holds a cheap copy of *Summer Love* in one dimpled hand.

Now the bus driver is talking to the mother, bold as you please, and teasing the younger child. Even at seven, she seems coquettish. The nerve of that man! Frieda memorizes his features when he isn't looking. Blue eyes, dark hair combed straight back, unhealthy pallor, slight paunch.

Frieda begins to wish she hadn't sold Ed's cab. She could have taken out the meter, removed the top sign and painted out the others. She had always left the driving to Ed, but now, with taxi and bus drivers going berserk, she might be safer with the wheel of the Olds in her own hands.

Suddenly Frieda reins in her gaze. In the seat just ahead of her, a man with expensively-styled hair, iron-gray at the temples, is reading the *Times*. He has folded the newspaper into neat quarters and is perusing a story about the Green River Killer. That makes Frieda examine him sharply. Trim mustache, well-cut suit of inconspicuous color, white shirt, conservative tie. When Frieda discovers the deep scars on the firm line of cheekbone and jaw she has to be careful not to betray her excitement.

It's hard to tell how tall the man is, but he looks shorter than the Killer is supposed to be. There are, of course, platform shoes of the kind she has seen Blacks wear, and a really clever criminal might have other resources unknown to ordinary citizens.

Near the bridge, the man stuffs the newspaper in a briefcase and moves lightly to the front of the bus. As she watches him, Frieda is surprised to discover that they have changed bus drivers, apparently while she was concentrating on the man riddled by acne. Now she realizes that the woman with the two daughters is no longer on board. With so much to keep track of, Frieda isn't sure how much longer she can manage. She thinks about how she will report the bus driver, keeping her voice calm and her facts straight. She wishes she had noticed the exact street where he got off. She can only do so much—she works hard all day at the restaurant—and lately this other job is more demanding. Tomorrow is her day off, and she is ready for it.

About noon, still in her purple robe and slippers, Frieda looks out the front window and is annoyed to see a pair of men with the serious look of door-to-door evangelists. She opens the door prepared to send them packing.

"Seattle Police," says the man in the navy windbreaker, flashing a badge instead of a Bible. He has short blond hair, a pimpled receding chin, and the kind of glasses that change with the light. Just now they are murky and overcast.

Frieda is so startled by this appearance that she forgets to check everything carefully. The man could be showing her a pop bottle cap for all the attention she gives the badge, which he has already returned to an inside pocket. These men don't look like plainclothes detectives on TV. They certainly don't look like regular policemen. Out of uniform, they look as if they'd been sitting at the counter in a bar all day, ordering a beer every twenty minutes or so and watching the football game.

"Does your husband drive a cab?" asks the second man, the one in a two-piece cinnamon suit. His thick dark mustache looks fake to Frieda even though she tends to be receptive to cosmetic enterprise.

"If he does," Frieda says, "I'd worry a lot. His license expired five years ago—two years before he died." The blond man makes a few pencilled notes, impassive as a secretary taking dictation.

"Is anyone else driving the cab?" the man in brown asks.

"*That* I wouldn't know," Frieda says. "I'm too busy at the restaurant to shadow that beat-up Olds." She hopes her answer has the authority of a private eye, that all those TV cop shows she watches will pay off. She needs a friend on the force, an ear she can count on when the time comes.

Waiting for the bus next morning, Frieda watches a slim, middle-aged man in a brown uniform approach her stop. When he gets close enough she reads the emblem on his left arm—"Northwest Protective Service." Frieda's heart knocks like a missing motor at this proof of Divine Providence.

"Do you belong to a special unit of the police?" Frieda asks when the man glances her way.

"No . . . no . . . I don't. It's a private god service."

Frieda wishes the man would speak legibly. "It's *what?*" she asks, not really prepared for this revelation.

"A private god service," he repeats, just as the bus pulls to the curb and swallows up what might have been a religious experience.

The Brooke Shields lookalike is on the bus again. This time she is alone, but there is a different driver, and Frieda is somewhat disappointed to note that he behaves himself.

It has been a hard day at the restaurant. Frieda's feet ache worse than usual and she decides to stop at the Red Cross store on her way home and buy a pair of shoes with better arches.

The man who comes to wait on her must be six-foot-six, and having to communicate with inhabitants of the lower air has given his head a peculiar set as if it were stuck on Horizontal Hold.

"Is there something I can help you with?" he asks, and there is a strange familiarity in the ordinary words, the odd way his head tilts, one of the hardest positions in Jane Fonda's easier exercises. From that angle, he lowers the lids as he speaks, steering the conversation with his eyes shut. Some corporate giant's success manual may have warned him that customers are intimidated by tall men.

Frieda is relieved when the man, probably a department manager, sends someone else to help her try on the shoes. Between fittings, she keeps the tall man in view, and she thinks he's watching her, though she can't be sure because of his peculiar manner.

The next evening while the bus waits at a red light, Frieda looks down at the cab in the next lane and sees the manager from the shoe department folded like a ventriloquist's dummy in the back seat. His head tilts to the left, and that directs his gaze somewhere in the vicinity of the bus window where Frieda is sitting. She lets a sharp little intake of breath escape before her native caution asserts itself, and she looks away. Is it possible the man is following her? The red light turns green, the bus moves forward, the cab moves beside it.

Fortunately, two other women get off at Frieda's stop, five blocks from where she lives. This is a friendly neighborhood—mostly families and retired couples—but not immune to crime. Just last week, a burglary was reported on the next street. The district weekly carries a special column for items from the police blotter—mostly domestic violence and burglaries near the bottom of the hill—and Frieda walks briskly in spite of her fatigue. The two women talk excitedly about a recent wedding, the sound of their voices reassuring.

When the women turn at the intersection, Frieda is suddenly blinded by the brights of an oncoming car descending the hill. As she crosses the street, the car turns in at a driveway, then backs and reverses direction. She has to keep herself from breaking into a run.

The instant she lets herself in the front door and switches on the light, the telephone rings. "Hello," Frieda says. Then, louder, "*Hello.*" The line is open, but the silence is total. Not even heavy breathing. Frieda says *Hello* two more times, then slams down the phone. Before she can take off her coat, it rings again.

"Hello?" she says, thinking it may be a bad connection. Nothing. Again Frieda hangs up, and when the phone rings a third time she refuses to answer. After three rings it stops.

Lately Frieda has taken to buying both the *P-I* and the *Times*. Most of her coffee customers tip a quarter, and she stashes the coins in her uniform pocket, ready for the vending machines at the bus stop. At home she skims morning and evening papers looking for new leads in the Green River case. She clips out the stories and pastes them neatly in a notebook with a green cover. The recently-published task force number is posted on the bulletin board above her phone.

It is cold tonight, and Frieda is warming up a bowl of yesterday's chili. She has closed the venetian blinds in the front room and turned on a dim lamp by the window. The kitchen always makes her feel like a tropical fish, its curtainless greenhouse windows and fluorescent lights exposing her to anyone who might wander up the driveway to the back of the house. A really inquisitive prowler could get a fluoroscopic view.

Looking for a moment through the eyes of such a man, Frieda sees her spine articulated on a brightly-lit screen, the dark lumbar blotch of one ruptured disk. She sees her heart pumping wildly, the gently-swelling lungs, the floating kidneys (a matched pair), and the once-energetic ovaries, now sadly retired.

Police say that the killer is someone so ordinary that no one would suspect him. And he is smart—too smart in all his widely-scattered attacks to leave one solid clue. Hundreds of reports have poured in on the special line, and every lead has been followed up without substantial progress. Several callers have mentioned a cab. Frieda shivers again, recalling the two plainclothesmen who knocked at her door. If they were plainclothesmen. They could have been drug addicts using a police cover, looking for someone to rob. Next time she would inspect their badges *and* their cards.

Frieda is re-reading today's Green River story for the third time when the doorbell rings. She goes to the front entryway and shouts through the closed door: "Who is it?"

There is a shuffle of feet on the front porch. She hears the one word *Times*. Maybe, "We're from the *Times*" or, "Do you want the *Times?*" She isn't going to open the door, but she switches on the front porch light to give the neighbors a better view of anyone trying to break in, and goes back to the kitchen. After a minute or two, she returns to the hall and is terrified to hear voices.

"Go *away!*" Frieda calls through the slender barrier. She hopes the door is locked—the deadbolt is unreliable—and she is afraid any tampering may appear as a welcoming sign. "Go away! Leave me alone!"

"Ma'am," comes the angry reply, "all you have to do is say *No, OK?*" and she hears the sound of feet descending the steps.

At work next day Frieda asks for a private talk with the restaurant manager. Sitting across from Ted Gould in his panelled cubbyhole off the kitchen, she twists her ring, adjusts her glasses and asks whether the manager has noticed that Sandy, the cook, is acting strangely. Sandy has worked at the restaurant nine years, and Frieda has been there only six weeks, but she thinks that makes her more objective.

"Strange . . . *how?*" the manager wants to know. He shifts some papers around with both hands, eyes straying towards the door.

"Well," Frieda sags helplessly in her chair, then lets it all out in a whispered rush: "He sort of *stabs* the potatoes when he's making french fries, and he squeezes the avocados too hard, and if you're waiting for an order, he wheels around too fast and shoves it in your face and says something like, 'Here! Deliver the poison!' " Frieda leans back, exhausted by this impersonation.

The manager's face flushes. Ruddy. Yes, ruddy, but he is a smooth talker. "Frieda," he says, "Sandy has an odd sense of humor, but he's harmless as a babe. I think you take him too seriously. It's the fear talking."

If it *is* the fear, the interview with the manager doesn't hush it up. Complicity. That is the technical name. Frieda is no dummy. Complicity means that one crook, masquerading as an ordinary citizen, is in league with other crooks, looking, if possible, even more like ordinary citizens. Frieda plans to call the Green River number as soon as she gets home.

She will tell them about the plainclothesmen looking for her dead husband, about the bus driver who flirts with an underage girl. She will report the tall man from the shoe store who followed her bus in a cab, and the man disguised as a private guard at the bus stop. She will recommend a thorough investigation of the restaurant, especially the manager and the cook, and she will show police the block where the car turned around to keep her in view as she hurried home after dark. She has nothing to go on for the pair from the *Times,* but she would recognize the louder of the two voices, especially if it came through a door.

Frieda feels a strange kind of eagerness to have it all over, and she is so lost in thought that she hardly notices the thin young man who gains steadily on her. Just past a streetlight, his shadow joins hers on the jagged grass and, for a few steps, seems almost an extension of her own, then breaks off suddenly when she hears him and turns. He passes her hurriedly, and it is as if fear itself had eased out of her and led the way so she would know for once she didn't have to worry, that she would come home safely as the one so nearly taken. She could recall that shadow as if it had a face.

Questions for Discussion

1. Characterize Frieda Tremblay. What is memorable about her personality and the way she thinks?

2. To what extent is Frieda "paranoid" in the popular sense of that term? To what extent are her fears justified?

3. What motivates Frieda to involve herself in police investigations?

4. Explain the importance of the end of the story. To what extent does it resolve the story? How does Frieda react to being followed by the young man, and how do you explain her reaction?

Suggestions for Writing

1. Write an essay about the notion of "complicity" in this story. In what sense does Frieda "comply"? In what sense does the story show noncriminals to be criminals? How does the title express the idea of complicity?

2. To what extent do you sympathize with Frieda, and to what extent does she seem strange or weird to you? Write a response in your notebook or journal to these questions.

3. In your journal or notebook, write briefly about the effect of the present tense in this story.

Bujak and the Strong Force or God's Dice

MARTIN AMIS

Bujak? Yeah, I knew him. The whole street knew Bujak. I knew him before and I knew him after. We all knew Bujak—sixty years old, hugely slabbed and seized with muscle and tendon, smiling at a bonfire in the yard, carrying desks and sofas on his back, lifting a tea-chest full of books with one hand. Bujak, the strongman. He was also a dreamer, a reader, a babbler. . . . You slept a lot sounder knowing that Bujak was on your street. This was 1980. I was living in London, West London, carnival country, what the police there call the *front line*. DR. ALIMANTADO, SONS OF THUNDER, RACE WAR, NO FUTURE: dry thatched dreadlocks, the scarred girls in the steeped pubs. Those black guys, they talked like combative drunks, all the time. If I went up to Manchester to stay with my girlfriend, I always left a key with Bujak. Those hands of his, as hard as coal, the nails quite square and symmetrical, like his teeth. And the forearms, the Popeye forearms, hefty and tattoo-smudged and brutal, weapons of monstrous power. Large as he was, the energies seemed impacted in him, as though he were the essence of an even bigger man; he stood for solidity. I am as tall as Bujak, but half his weight. No, less. Bujak once told me that to create a man out of nothing would require the equivalent energy of a thousand-megaton explosion. Looking at Bujak, you could believe this. As for me, well, a single stick of TNT might do the job—a hand grenade, a firecracker. In his physical dealings with me (you know, the way someone moves across a room toward you, this can be a physical event) he showed the tender condescension that the big man shows to the small. Probably he was like that with everyone. He was protective. And then, to good Bujak, thoughtful, grinning Bujak, the worst thing happened. A personal holocaust. In the days that followed I saw and felt all of Bujak's violence.

His life went deep into the century. Warrior caste, he fought in Warsaw in 1939. He lost his father and two brothers at Katyn. He was in the resistance—all his life he was in the resistance. In that capacity he visited (and this is a story of violence, of visitation) many neat tortures on Nazi collaborators. He rose up with the Armia Kraiova and was imprisoned in December 1944. During the postwar years he worked in a touring circus, a strongman, bending bars, butting brick walls, tugging trucks with his teeth. In 1956, the year of my birth, he was there for the Polish October, and for the November in "Hungaria." Then the United States, the halls, queues, and cubicles of Ellis Island, with wife, mother, small daughter. His wife Monika was hospitalized in New York for a minor condition; she came down with a hospital supergerm and died overnight. Bujak worked as a longshoreman in Fort Lauderdale. He took and gave many crunchy beatings—strikebreakers, mob men, union goons. But he prospered, as you're meant to do, in America. What brought him to England, I think, was a certain kind of (displaced)

Polish nostalgia or snobbery, and a desire for peace. Bujak had lived the twentieth century. And then, one day, the twentieth century, a century like no other, came calling on him. Bookish Bujak himself, I'm sure, saw the calamity as in some sense postnuclear, Einsteinian. It was certainly the end of his existing universe. Yes, it was Bujak's Big Crunch.

I first met Bujak one wintry morning in the late spring of 1980—or of PN 35, if you use the postnuclear calendar that he sometimes favored. Michiko's car had something wrong with it, as usual (a flat, on this occasion), and I was down on the street grappling with the burglar tools and the spare. Compact and silent, Michiko watched me sadly. I'd managed to loosen the nuts on the collapsed wheel, but the aperture for the jack was ominously soft and sticky with rust. The long-suffering little car received the vertical spear in its chassis and stayed stoically earthbound. Now I have to say that I am already on very bad terms with the inanimate world. Even when making a cup of coffee or changing a light bulb (or a fuse!), I think—What is it with objects? Why are they so aggressive? What's their beef with *me?* Objects and I, we can't go on like this. We must work out a compromise, a freeze, before one of us does something rash. I've got to meet with their people and hammer out a deal.

"Stop it, Sam," said Michiko.

"Get a real car," I told her.

"Please, just stop. Stop it! I'll call a towtruck or something."

"Get a real car," I said and thought—yeah, or a real boyfriend. Anyway, I was throwing the tools into their pouch, dusting my palms and wiping away my tears when I saw Bujak pacing across the road toward us. Warily I monitored his approach. I had seen this hulking Bohunk or throwback Polack from my study window, busying himself down on the street, always ready to flex his primitive can-do and know-how. I wasn't pleased to see him. I have enough of the standard-issue paranoia, or I did then. Now I've grown up a little and realize that I have absolutely nothing to fear, except the end of the world. Along with everybody else. At least in the next war there won't be any special wimps, punchbags, or unpopularity contests. Genocide has had its day and we're on to something bigger now. Suicide.

"You a Jew?" asked Bujak in his deeply speckled voice.

"Yup," I said.

"Name?"

And number? "Sam," I told him.

"Short for?"

I hesitated and felt Michi's eyes on my back.

"Is it Samuel?"

"No," I said. "Actually it's Samson."

The smile he gave told me many things, most obviously that here—here was a happy man. All eyes and teeth, the smile was ridiculous in its gaiety, its candor. But then happiness is a pretty clownish condition, when you stop to think about it. I mean, round-the-clock happiness, it's hardly an appropriate response. To me, this gave him an element of instability, of counterstrength, of violence. But Bujak here was clearly happy, in his universe. Bujak, with his happiness accessory.

"Jews usually good up here," he said, and knocked a fingertip on his shaved head. "No good with their hands."

Bujak was good with *his* hands: to prove it, he bent forward and picked up the car with them.

"You're kidding," I said. But he wasn't. As I got to work he was already shooting the breeze with Michiko, nonchalantly asking her if she'd lost any family at Nagasaki or Hiroshima. Michi had, as it happened—a cousin of her father's. This was news to me but I felt no surprise. It seems that everyone loses someone in the big deaths. Bujak changed stance freely, and, at one point, lifted a forgetful hand to scratch his skull. The car never wavered. I watched Bujak as I worked, and saw that the strength he called on owed nothing to the shoulders or the great curved back—just the arms, the arms. It was as if he were raising the lid of a cellar door, or holding up a towel while a little girl dressed on the beach. Then he roughly took the tire iron from my hands and knelt on one knee to rivet the bolts. As the grained slab of his head loomed upward again Bujak's eyes were tight and unamused, and they moved roughly too across my face. He nodded at Michi and said to me, "And who did you lose?"

"Uh?" I said. If I understood his question, then the answer was none of his business.

"I give money to Israel every year," he said. "Not much. Some. Why? Because the Polish record on the Jews is disgraceful. After the war even," he said, and grinned. "Quite disgraceful. Look. There is a tire mender in Basing Street. Tell them Bujak and they will make it for you fairly."

Thanks, we both said. Off he went, measuring the road with his strides. Later, from my study window, I saw him pruning roses in the small front garden. A little girl, his granddaughter, was crawling all over his back. I saw him often, from my study window. In those days, in 1980, I was trying to be a writer. No longer. I can't take the study life, the life of the study. This is the only story I'll ever tell, and this story is true. . . . Michiko was sold on Bujak right away and dropped a thank-you note through his door that same afternoon. But it took a while before I had really made terms with Bujak.

I asked around about this character, as you will when you're playing at writing. Like I said, everybody knew Bujak. In the streets, the pubs, the shops, they spoke of him as a fixer and handyman, omnicompetent: all the systems that keep a house going, that keep it alive—Bujak could handle them, the veins, the linings, the glands, and the bowels. He was also marked down as a definite eccentric, a stargazer, a "philosopher"—not, I gathered, a valued calling in these parts—and on occasion as an out-and-out *nutter* (one of those words that never sound right on American lips, like *quid* and *bloody*). People gave Bujak his due as a family man: once Michi and I glimpsed him quite far afield, outside the Russian church on the junction of St. Petersburg Place and Moscow Road, erect in his suit, with his mother, his daughter, and his granddaughter; I remember thinking that even huge Bujak could show the fussed delicacy you get from living in a house full of ladies. But most eagerly and vehemently, of course, they spoke of Bujak the peacekeeper, the vigilante, the rough-justice artist. They spoke of skirmishes, vendettas, one-man wars, preemptive strikes. Standing there in the pub, the shoulderless and bespectacled American with his beer mug awkwardly poised, or peering over a counter, or standing on a corner with milk carton and newspaper under my arm, I was indulged with tales of Bujak and the strong force.

The time he caught two black kids prying at a neighbor's basement window and sent them twirling into the street with two flicks of his wrist, like someone mucking out a trench. Or what he did to their big brothers when they jumped him in Golbourne Road the following night. Any brawler or burglar nabbed by Bujak soon wished himself under the hosepipe in some nice safe slammer. He took on all comers. Feuding with the council, he once dragged a skip full of rubbish a hundred yards from his front door. He went out one night and upended a truck after a row about a generator with some local building contractors. The Bujak women could walk the All Saints Road at any hour and expect no bother. And Bujak himself could silence a pub just by walking past it. He was popular, though. He was the community man, and such community as the street had devolved upon Bujak. He was our deterrent.

And it wasn't enough. . . . Now, in 1985, it is hard for me to believe that a city is anything more or other than the sum of its streets, as I sit here with the Upper West Side blatting at my window and fingering my heart. Sometimes in my dreams of New York danger I stare down over the city—and it looks half made, half wrecked, one half (the base perhaps) of something larger torn in two, frayed, twangy, moist with rain or solder. And you mean to tell me, I say to myself, that this is supposed to be a *community?* . . . My wife and daughter move around among all this, among the violations, the life-trashers, the innocent murderers. Michiko takes our little girl to the daycare center where she works. Daycare—that's good. But what about dawn care, dusk care, what about night care? If I just had a force I could enfold them with, oh, if I just had the strong force. . . . Bujak was right. In the city now there are loose components, accelerated particles—something *has* come loose, something is wriggling, lassoing, spinning toward the edge of its groove. Something must give and it isn't safe. You ought to be terribly careful. Because safety has left our lives. It's gone forever. And what do animals do when you give them only danger? They make more danger, more, much more.

It was 1980, the birth year of Solidarity, and Bujak was Polish. This combination of circumstances led me to assume that Bujak was liberal in his sentiments. Actually it didn't follow. As I proudly strolled with him to the timber yard or the home-improvement stores off the Portobello Road, Bujak would fume against the blacks, the *czarnuchy,* as they strutted and gabbled round about us. The blacks were fine, he grinningly argued, in a context of sun, surf, and plentiful bananas; but in a Western city they were just children—understandably angry children too. Once he stopped dead to marvel at two gay punks in NO FUTURE T-shirts, with hair like old ladies' bonnets, as they walked toward us hand in hand. "It's incredible, isn't it," he said, rolling the *r.* With the faggots, Bujak saw their plight, and their profusion, as an Einsteinian matter also. He confessed to the fantasy of leading a cavalry charge against the streets and their strange ensembles—the sound of the hooves, the twirling cutlasses. "A desire which I suppress of course. But if I could just press a button," he added, greedily eyeing the *pedaly,* the *czarnuchy,* the street dwellers as they turned and gesticulated and reshuffled and moved on.

Violence in a man is usually the overspill of something else. You know how it is. You see these guys. I appear to have an almost disabling sensitivity to violence in other men, a fallout detector for those spots of waste or exorbitance that spill over into force. Like a canary in a prewar coalmine, I check out early when there is violence, when there is poison in the air. What is this propensity? Call it *fear,* if you like. *Fear* will do fine. The raised voice in the restaurant and its sour tang of brutality and booze, the look a man will give his wife which demotes her on the human scale, which prepares her for the human disgrace of violence, the pumping leg, the fizzing eye, the public bar at ten fifty-five. I see all this—my body sees it, and gives me adrenaline, gives me sweat. I faint at the sight of blood. I faint at the sight of a Band-Aid, an aspirin. This sense of critical fragility (myself, my wife, my daughter, even the poor planet, baby blue in its shawls), it drove me from my study in the end. The study life is all thought and anxiety and I cannot take the study life anymore.

Late at night, over at Bujak's large, aromatic, icon-infested apartment (the blue glow of saints, candles, vigils), I scanned the big Pole for the excrescences of violence. His mother, old Roża, made the tea. The old woman ("rouge" with an *a* on the end), she calmed me with her iconic presence, the moist hair grained like silver, as Bujak talked about the strong force, the energy locked in matter. Grinning in the gloom, Bujak told me what he had done to the Nazi collaborator in Warsaw, in 1943. Boy, I thought; I bet the guy didn't do much collaborating after that. However, I couldn't conceal my distaste. "But aren't you glad?" urged Bujak. No, I said, why should I be? "You lost two grandparents to these people." Yeah, I said. So? That doesn't change anything. "Revenge," said Bujak simply. Revenge is overrated, I told him. And out of date. He looked at me with violent contempt. He opened his hands in an explanatory gesture: the hands, the arms, the policemen of his will. Bujak was a big fan of revenge. He had a lot of time for revenge.

I once saw him use those hands, those arms. I saw it all from my study window, the four-paneled screen (moon-spotted, with refracting crossbar) through which the world came in at me then. I saw the four guys climb from the two cars and steady themselves in front of Bujak's stoop. Did I hear a scream from within, a cry of warning or yearning? . . . Bujak's daughter gave the old man a lot of grief. Her first name was Leokadia. Her second name was trouble. Rural-looking yet glamorous, thirty-three, tall, plump, fierce, and tearful, she was the unstable element in Bujak's nucleus. She had, I noticed, two voices, one for truth, and one for nonsense, one for lies. Against the brown and shiny surface of her old-style dresses, the convex and the concave were interestingly disposed. *Her* daughter, little Boguslawa, was the by-blow of some chaotic twelve-hour romance. It was well known on the street that Leokadia had round heels: the sort of girl (we used to say) who went into a hot flush every time she saw an army personnel carrier. She even made a pitch at me, here at the flat one time. Needless to say, I failed to come across. I had my reasons: fear of reprisals from Michiko and Bujak himself (they both loomed in my mind, incongruously equal in size); also, more basically, I'm by no means sure I could handle someone like Leokadia in the cot. All that breast and haunch. All those freckles and tears. . . . For six months she had been living with a man who beat her, lithe little Pat, sinewy, angular, wired very tight. I think she beat him too, a bit. But violence is finally a masculine accomplishment. Violence—now that's man's work. Leokadia kept going back to Pat, don't ask me why. I don't know. They don't know. There she goes again, ticking back to him on her heels, with black eye, grazed cheek, wrenched hair. Nobody knows why. Not even they know. Bujak, surprisingly, stayed out of it, held his distance, remained solid—though he did try to keep the little girl, Boguslawa, safely at home, out of the turbulence. You would often see old Roża ferrying the kid from one flat to the other. After her second spell in the hospital (cracked ribs this time) Leokadia called it a day and went home for good. Then Pat showed up with his pals and found Bujak waiting.

The three men (I saw it all) had an unmistakable look about them, with that English bad-boy build, proud guts and tapering legs that bent backward from the knee down, sparse-haired with old-young faces, as if they had done their aging a lot quicker than one year at a time. I don't know whether these guys would have frightened anybody much on the American circuit, but I guess they were big enough and their intention was plain. (Did you read about the Yablonsky murders? In the States these days, if you're on the list, they come in and do the whole family. Yes, they just nuke you now.) Anyway, they frightened me. I sat writhing at my desk as Pat led them through the garden gate. I hated the flares of his jeans, the compact running shoes, the tight Fred Perry. Then the front door opened: bespectacled Bujak, wearing braces over his vest, old, huge. In a reflex that spelt seriousness and scorn, the men loosened their shoulders and let their hands dangle in readiness. Words were exchanged—demand, denial. They moved forward.

Now I must have blinked, or shut my eyes, or ducked (or fainted). I heard three blows on a regular second beat, clean, direct, and atrocious, each one like an ax splitting frozen wood. When I looked up, Pat and one of his friends were lying on the steps; the other guys were backing away, backing away from the site of this incident, this demonstration. Expressionlessly Bujak knelt to do something extra to Pat on the floor. As I watched, he tugged back the hair and carefully poked a neutronium fist into Pat's upturned face. I had to go and lie down after that. But a couple of weeks later I saw Pat sitting alone in the London Apprentice; he was shivering remorsefully in the corner behind the jukebox; the pleated welt on his cheek bore all the colors of flame, and he was drinking his beer through a straw. In that one blow he had taken payment for everything he had given Leokadia.

With Bujak, I was always edging into friendship. I don't know if I ever really made it. Differences of age aren't easy. Differences of strength aren't easy. Friendship isn't easy. When Bujak's own holocaust came calling, I was some help to him; I was better than nothing. I went to the court. I went to the cemetery. I took my share of the strong force, what little I could take. . . . Perhaps a dozen times during that summer, before the catastrophe came (it was heading toward him slowly, gathering speed), I sat up late on his back porch when all the women had gone to bed. Bujak stargazed. He talked and drank his tea. "Traveling at the speed of light," he said one time, "you could cross the whole universe in less than a second. Time and distance would be annihilated, and all futures possible." No shit? I thought. Or again: "If you could linger on the brink of a singularity, time would be so slow that a night would pass in forty-five seconds, and there would be three American elections in the space of seven days." Three American elections, I said to myself. Whew, what a boring week. And why is *he* the dreamer, while I am bound to the low earth? Feeling mean, I often despised the dreaming Bujak, but I entertained late-night warmth for him too, for the accretions of experience (time having worked on his face like a sculptor, awful slow), and I feared him—I feared the energy coiled, seized, and locked in Bujak. Staring up at our little disk of stars (and perhaps there are better residential galaxies than our own: cleaner, safer, more gentrified), I sensed only the false stillness of the black nightmap, its beauty concealing great and routine violence, the fleeing universe, with matter racing apart, exploding to the limits of space and time, all tugs and curves, all hubble and doppler, infinitely and eternally hostile. . . . This evening, as I write, the New York sky is also full of stars—the same stars. There. There is Michiko coming down the street, hand in hand with our little girl. They made it. Home at last. Above them the gods shoot crap with their black dice: threes and fives and ones. The Plough has just rolled a four and a two. But who throws the six, the six, the six?

All peculiarly modern ills, all fresh distortions and distempers, Bujak attributed to one thing: Einsteinian knowledge, knowledge of the strong force. It was his central paradox that the greatest—the purest, the most magical—genius of our time should have introduced the earth to such squalor, profanity, and panic. "But how very like the twentieth century," he said: this was always going to be the age when irony really came into its own. I have cousins and uncles who speak of Einstein as if he were some hero ballplayer captaining a team called the Jews ("the mind on him," "look at the mind on the guy"). Bujak spoke of Einstein as if he were God's literary critic, God being a poet. I, more stolidly, tend to suspect that God is a novelist—a garrulous and deeply unwholesome one too. . . . Actually Bujak's theory had a lot of appeal for me. It was, at least, holistic. It answered the big question. You know the question I mean, and its cumulative disquiet, its compound interest. You ask yourself the question every time you open a newspaper or switch on the TV or walk the streets among sons of thunder. New formations, deformations. You know the question. It reads: *Just what the hell is going on around here?*

The world looks worse every day. Is it worse, or does it just look it? The world gets older. The world has seen and done it all. Boy, is it beat. It's suicidal. Like Leokadia, the world has done too many things too many times with too many people, done it this way, that way, with him, with him. The world has been to so many parties, been in so many fights, lost its keys, had its handbag stolen, drunk too much. It all adds up. A tab is presented. Our ironic destiny. Look at the modern infamies, the twentieth-century sins. Some are strange, some banal, but they all offend the eye, covered in their newborn vernix. Gratuitous or recreational crimes of violence, the ever-less-tacit totalitarianism of money (money—what *is* this shit anyway?), the pornographic proliferation, the nuclear collapse of the family (with the breeders all going critical, and now the children running too), the sappings and distortions of a mediated reality, the sexual abuse of the very old and the very young (of the weak, the weak): what is the hidden denominator here, and what could explain it *all?*

To paraphrase Bujak, as I understood him. We live in a shameful shadowland. Quietly, our idea of human life has changed, thinned out. We can't help but think less of it now. The human race has declassed itself. It does not live anymore; it just survives, like an animal. We endure the suicide's shame, the shame of the murderer, the shame of the victim. Death is all we have in common. And what does that do to life? Such, at any rate, was Bujak's damage check. If the world disarmed tomorrow, he believed, the species would still need at least a century of recuperation, after its entanglement, its flirtation, after its thing with the strong force.

Academic in any case, since Bujak was insuperably convinced that the end was on its way. How could man (that dangerous creature—I mean, look at his *record*), how could man resist the intoxication of the Perfect Crime, one that destroys all evidence, all redress, all pasts, all futures? I was enough of a peacenik, optimist, and funker to take the other view. A dedicated follower of fear, I always thought that the fat brute and the big bastard would maintain their standoff: they know that if one fist is raised then the whole pub comes down anyway. Not a masterpiece of reassurance, I agree—not at ten fifty-five on a Saturday night, with the drink still coming.

"Deterrence theory," said Bujak, with his grin. "It's not just a bad theory. It's not even a theory. It's an insanity."

"That's why you have to go further."

"You are a unilateralist?"

"Well yeah," I said. "Someone's got to make a start sometime. Make a start. England is historically well placed to give it a try. So the Russians take Europe, maybe. But that risk must be smaller than the other risk, which is infinite."

"This changes nothing. The risk is unaltered. All you do here is make life easier to part with."

"Well, I just think you have to make a start."

Our arguments always ended on the same side street. I maintained that the victim of a first strike would have no reason to retaliate, and would probably not do so.

"Oh?" said Bujak.

"What would be the point? You'd have nothing to protect. No country, no people. You'd gain nothing. Why add to it all?"

"Revenge."

"Oh yeah. The heat of the battle. But that's not a *reason.*"

"In war, revenge is a reason. Revenge is as reasonable as anything. They say nuclear war will not be really *war* but something else. True, but it will feel like war to those who fight it."

On the other hand, he added, nobody could guess how people would react under the strong force. Having crossed that line the whole world would be crazy or animal and certainly no longer human.

One day in the fall of 1980 Bujak traveled north. I never knew why. I saw him on the street that morning, a formidable able sight in the edifice of his dark blue suit. Something about his air of courtly gaiety, his cap, his tie, suggested to me that he was off to investigate an old ladyfriend. The sky was gray and gristly, with interesting bruises, the street damp and stickered with leaves. Bujak pointed a tight umbrella at his own front door. "I come back tomorrow night," he said. "Keep an eye on them."

"Me? Well, sure. Okay."

"Leokadia, I learn, is pregnant. Two months. Pat. Oh, Pat—he really was too bad." Then he shrugged powerfully and said, "But I'm pleased. Look at Boguslawa. Her father was an animal too. But look at her. A flower. An angel from heaven."

And off he went, pacing out the street, content, if necessary, to walk the whole way. That afternoon I looked in on the girls and drank a cup of tea with old Roża. Christ, I remember thinking, what is it with these Polacks? Roża was seventy-eight. By that age *my* mother had been dead for twenty years. (Cancer. Cancer is the *other* thing—the third thing. Cancer will come for me too, I guess. Sometimes I feel it right in front of me, fizzing like television inches from my face.) I sat there and wondered how the quality of wildness was distributed among the Bujak ladies. With pious eyes and hair like antique silver, Roża was nonetheless the sort of old woman who still enjoyed laughing at the odd salacious joke—and she laughed very musically, one hand raised in gentle propitiation. "Hey, Roża," I would say: "I got one for you." And she would start laughing before I began. Little Boguslawa—seven, silent, sensitive—lay reading by the fire, her eyes lit by the page. Even the brawny beauty Leokadia seemed steadier, her eyes more easily containing their glow. She spoke to me now as levelly as she used to before we had that awkward tangle in my apartment. You know, I think the reason she put out for the boys so much was the usual thing about trying to accumulate approval. Approval is funny stuff, and some people need a lot more of it than others. Also she was obviously very rich in her female properties and essences; being prudent isn't so easy for girls kitted out like that. Now she sat there equably doing nothing. The red flag was down. All was calm with her dangerous floods and tides. A moony peace—Michi was like that herself sometimes, when our child was on the way. Our little one. Expecting. I stuck around for an hour or so and then crossed the road again, back to my study and its small life. I sat and read *Mosby's Memoirs* for the rest of the evening; and through my window I did indeed keep an eye on the Bujak front door. The next day was Friday. I looked in on the ladies to drop off a key before heading north myself—to Manchester and to Michiko. Meanwhile, energetic actors, vivid representatives of the twentieth century—Einstein's monsters—were on their way south.

At midnight on Saturday Bujak returned. All I know about what he found I got from the newspapers and the police, together with a couple of stray details that Bujak let slip. In any event I will add nothing; I will add nothing to what Bujak found. . . . He had no premonition until he placed his key in the lock and saw that the door was open and gave softly to his touch. He proceeded in deep silence. The hall had an odd smell to it, the smell of cigarette smoke and jam. Bujak tipped open the living-room door. The room looked like half of something torn in two. On the floor an empty vodka bottle seemed to tip slightly on its axis. Leokadia lay naked in the corner. One leg was bent at an impossible angle. Bujak moved through the terrible rooms. Roża and Boguslawa lay on their beds, naked, contorted, frozen, like Leokadia. In Leokadia's room two strange men were sleeping. Bujak closed the bedroom door behind him and removed his cap. He came closer. He leaned forward to seize them. Just before he did so he flexed his arms and felt the rustle of the strong force.

This happened five years ago. Yes, I'm here to tell you that the world is still around, in 1985. We live in New York now. I teach. The students come to me, and then they leave. There are gaps, spaces in between things big enough for me to glimpse the study life and know again that I can't take it. My daughter is four years old. I was present at the birth, or I tried to be. First I was sick; then I hid; then I fainted. Yeah, I did real good. Found and revived, I was led back to the delivery room. They placed the blood-fringed bundle in my arms. I thought then and I think now: How will the poor little bitch make it? How will she *make* it? But I'm learning to live with her, with the worry bomb, the love bomb. Last summer we took her to England. The pound was weak and the dollar was strong—the bold, the swaggering dollar, plunderer of Europe. We took her to London, London West, carnival country with its sons of thunder. Bujak country. I'd called my landlady and established that Bujak, too, was still around, in 1984. There was a question I needed to ask him. And Michi and I wanted to show Bujak our girl, little Roża, named for the old woman.

It was old Roża whom I had thought of most fixedly, during the worst car journey of my life, as we drove from Manchester to London, from fair weather into foul, into Sunday weather. That morning, over coffee and yogurt in her cubicle, Michi handed me the smudged and mangling tabloid. "Sam?" she said. I stared at the story, at the name, and realized that the rat life is not somewhere else anymore, is not on the other side but touches your life, my life. . . . Cars are terrible things and no wonder Bujak hated them. Cars are cruel creatures, vicious bastards, pitiless and inexorable, with only this one idea, this A-to-B-idea. They made no allowances. Down we slid through the motorway wheel-squirt. Neighbors gathered as we parked, the men bearing umbrellas, the women with their arms folded, shaking their heads. I crossed the street and rang the bell. And again. And for what? I tried the back door, the kitchen porch. Then Michiko called me. Together we stared through the living-room window. Bujak sat at the table, hunched forward as if he needed all the power of his back and shoulders just to hold position, just to keep his rest energy seized, skewered. Several times I knocked on the glass. He never moved. There was a noise in my ear and the seconds fussed and fussed, slower than a fuse. The street felt like a cave. I turned to Michi and her four-lidded eyes. We stood and watched each other through the heavy rain.

    Later, I was some help to him, I think, when it was my turn to tangle with the strong force. For some reason Michiko could bear none of this; the very next day she bowed out on me and went straight back to America. Why? She had and still has ten times my strength. Perhaps that was it. Perhaps she was too strong to bend to the strong force. Anyway, I make no special claims here. . . . In the evenings Bujak would come and sit in my kitchen, filling the room. He wanted proximity, he wanted to be elsewhere. He didn't talk. The small corridor hummed with strange emanations, pulsings, fallout. It was often hard to move, hard to breathe. What do strong men feel when their strength is leaving them? Do they listen to the past or do they just hear things—voices, music, the cauldron bubble of distant hooves? I'll be honest and say what I thought. I thought, Maybe he'll have to kill me, not because he wants to or wishes me harm, but because he has taken so much harm himself. This would free him of it, for a while. Something had to give. I endured the aftermath, the radiation. That was the only thing I had to contribute.

Also I went with him to court, and was at his side throughout *that* injury, that serial injury. The two defendants were Scotsmen, bail beaters from Dundee, twentyish, wanted—not that it made much difference who they were. There was no plea of insanity, nor indeed any clear sign of it. Sanity didn't enter into the thing. You couldn't understand anything they said so a policeman translated. Their story went like this. Having had more pints of beer than were perhaps strictly good for them, the two men took up with Leokadia Bujak on the street and offered to walk her home. Asked inside, they in turn made passionate love to the young woman, at her invitation, and then settled down for a refreshing nap. While they slept, some other party had come in and done all these terrible things. Throughout Bujak sat there, quietly creaking. He and I both knew that Leokadia might have done something of the kind, on another night, in another life, Christ, she might have done—but with these dogs, these superdogs, underdogs, threadbare rodents with their orange teeth? It didn't matter anyway. Who *cared*. Bujak gave his evidence. The jury was out for less than twenty minutes. Both men got eighteen years. From my point of view, of course (for me it was the only imponderable), the main question was never asked, let alone answered: it had to do with those strange seconds in Leokadia's bedroom, Bujak alone with the two men. Nobody asked the question. I would ask it, four years later. I couldn't ask it then. . . . The day after sentencing I had a kind of a breakdown. With raw throat and eyes and nose streaming I hauled myself onto a jet. I didn't even dare say good-by. At Kennedy what do I find but Michiko staring me in the face and telling me she's pregnant. There and then I went down on my lousy knees and begged her not to have it. But she had it all right—two months early. Jesus, a new horror story by Edgar Allan Poe: The Premature Baby. Under the jar, under the lamp, jaundice, pneumonia—she even had a heart attack. So did I, when they told me. She made it in the end, though. She's great now, in 1985. You should see her. It is the love bomb and its fallout that energize you in the end. You couldn't begin to do it without the love. . . . That's them on the stairs, I think. Yes, in they come, changing everything. Here is Roża, and here is Michiko, and here am I.

Bujak was still on the street. He had moved, from 45 to 84, but he was still on the street. We asked around. The whole street knew Bujak. And there he was in the front garden, watching a fire as it flexed and cracked, the snakeheads of flame taking sudden bites from the air—snakes of fire, in the knowledge garden. After all, we coped with fire, when it came; we didn't all get broiled and scorched. He looked up. The ogre's smile hadn't changed that much, I thought, although the presence of the man was palpably reduced. Still old and huge in his vest, but the mass, the holding energy softened and dispersed. Well, something had to give. Bujak had adopted or been adopted by or at any rate made himself necessary to a large and assorted household, mostly Irish. The rooms were scrubbed, bare, vigorous, and orderly, with all that can-do can do. There was lunch on the sun-absorbing pine table: beer, cider, noise, and the sun's phototherapy. The violence with which the fiftyish redhead scolded Bujak about his appearance made it plain to me that there was a romantic attachment. Even then, with the old guy nearer seventy than sixty, I thought with awe of Bujak in the sack. Bujak in the bag! Incredibly, his happiness was intact—unimpaired, entire. How come? Because, I think, his generosity extended not just to the earth but to the universe—or simply that he loved all matter, its spin and charm, redshifts and blueshifts, its underthings. The happiness was there. It was the strength that had gone from him forever. Over lunch he said that, a week or two ago, he had seen a man hitting a woman on the street. He shouted at them and broke it up. Physically, though, he was powerless to intercede—*helpless,* he said, with a shrug. Actually you could feel the difference in the way he moved, in the way he crossed the room toward you. The strength had gone, or the will to use it.

Afterward he and I stepped out onto the street. Michiko had ducked out of this last encounter, choosing instead to linger with the ladies. But we had the girl with us, little Roża, asleep on Bujak's shoulder. I watched him without fear. He wouldn't drop the folded child. He had taken possession of Roża with his arms.

As if by arrangement we paused at number 45. Black kids now played in the garden with a winded red football. Things were falling away between Bujak and me, and suddenly it seemed that you could say what you liked. So I said, "Adam. No offense. But why didn't you kill them? *I* would have. I mean, if I think of Michi and Roża . . . " But in fact you cannot think it, you cannot go near it. The thought is fire. "Why didn't you kill the sons of bitches? What stopped you?"

"Why?" he asked, and grinned. "What would have been the reason?"

"Come on. You could have done it, easy. Self-defense. No court on earth would have sent you down."

"True. It occurred to me."

"Then what happened? Did you—did you feel too weak all of a sudden? Did you just feel too weak?"

"On the contrary. When I had their heads in my hands I thought how incredibly easy to grind their faces together—until they drowned in each other's faces. But no."

But no. Bujak had simply dragged the men by the arms (half a mile, to the police station in Harrow Road), like a father with two frantic children. He delivered them and dusted his hands.

"Christ, they'll be out in a few years. Why *not* kill them? Why not?"

"I had no wish to add to what I found. I thought of my dead wife Monika. I thought—they're all dead now. I couldn't add to what I saw there. Really the hardest thing was to touch them at all. You know the wet tails of rats? Snakes? Because I saw that they weren't human beings at all. They had no idea what human life was. No idea! Terrible mutations, a disgrace to their human molding. An eternal disgrace. If I had killed them then I would still be strong. But you must start somewhere. You must make a start."

And now that Bujak has laid down his arms, I don't know why, but I am minutely stronger. I don't know why—I can't tell you why.

He once said to me: "There must be more matter in the universe than we think. Else the distances are horrible. I'm nauseated." Einsteinian to the end, Bujak was an Oscillationist, claiming that the Big Bang will forever alternate with the Big Crunch, that the universe would expand only until unanimous gravity called it back to start again. At that moment, with the cosmos turning on its hinges, light would begin to travel backward, received by the stars and pouring from our human eyes. If, and I can't believe it, time would also be reversed, as Bujak maintained (will we move backward too? Will we have any say in things?), then this moment as I shake his hand shall be the start of my story, his story, our story, and we will slip downtime of each other's lives, to meet four years from now, when, out of the fiercest grief, Bujak's lost women will reappear, born in blood (and we will have our conversations, too, backing away from the same conclusion), until Boguslawa folds into Leokadia, and Leokadia folds into Monika, and Monika is there to be enfolded by Bujak until it is her turn to recede, kissing her fingertips, backing away over the fields to the distant girl with no time for him (will that be any easier to bear than the other way around?), and then big Bujak shrinks, becoming the weakest thing there is, helpless, indefensible, naked, weeping, blind and tiny, and folding into Roża.

Questions for Discussion

1. How would you characterize the analogy this story develops between Bujak's response to his "personal holocaust" and the politics of nuclear armament?

2. To what extent is it significant—with regard to the twentieth-century world—that one character is Jewish, one is Japanese, and one is Polish in this story?

3. Summarize the argument about "revenge" that Bujak and the narrator have midway through the story. What personal experience and personal qualities inform each side of the argument?

4. In what ways does Amis connect Einsteinian physics with everyday, street-level life throughout the story? What is your response to encountering these ideas in the story?

Suggestions for Writing

1. "Violence in a man," says the narrator, "is usually the overspill of something else." Write a response in your journal or notebook that explains what you think he means by this statement and the extent to which you find the statement valid.

2. "But violence is finally a masculine accomplishment. Violence—now that's man's work," says the narrator. Write a response to this statement in your journal or notebook. To what extent is violence a male "accomplishment?"

3. Write an essay about the change Bujak undergoes after his family is murdered. Why does he undergo the change? What reasons does he give? What moral and political implications does it suggest?

4. Write an essay that examines the way in which Amis weaves references to Einsteinian physics into the story. What meaning do they add to the story? How accessible are they? How does the theory of the Big Bang and the Big Crunch inform the ending of the story?

5. Write an essay in which you discuss the ways in which European politics form part of the background to the essay and the background to Bujak's behavior.

6. In what ways has the story made you think differently about violence and "strong force"? Write briefly in response to this question in your journal or notebook.

7. Write a story that involves a choice about whether to participate in an act of violence or not.

Overview: Additional Questions for Discussion and Suggestions for Writing

1. Select any three stories from this section and any three from "Early Voices" and list several significant ways in which these stories show how the short story has changed. Consider such elements as subject matter, narrative technique, and language.

2. Several of these stories concern political conflict, including Fiona Barr's, Elsa Joubert's, Martin Amis's, and Njabulo Ndebele's. Considering these stories and other "political" stories or novels you have read, speculate about what fiction adds to one's understanding of political conflicts. In what sense is a story different from an essay in this regard? What problems might writers encounter when they write fiction about political conflict?

3. "Early Voices" contains stories that have endured for over one hundred years. Select two or three stories from "Emerging Voices" that you think might endure that long and explain your selection.

4. Make a list of the stories you have read from this section and then list as many common themes as you can.

5. Of all the stories in this section, which one seems most traditional in its narrative technique? In what sense is it traditional? To what extent is its being traditional a strength (or a weakness)?

6. Chekhov, Kafka, Joyce, and Hemingway are four writers who influenced the development of short fiction enormously. In the stories from "Emerging Voices" that you have read, where do you find the influence of these writers? How does the influence manifest itself?

7. Of all the stories in this section, which one would you recommend to a parent for reading and why?

8. Which of the stories in this section seems to represent a worldview or an area of experience that is closest to your own? Why?

9. Which of the stories in this section was most successful at illuminating for you an experience or a worldview that is significantly different from your own? Why?

10. Contrast Grafton's story with Conan Doyle's Sherlock Holmes story. How much has "the detective story" changed or stayed the same in about 100 years?

<h1 style="text-align: center;">Suggestions for Writing</h1>

1. The stories by Engberg, Phillips, Heker, Gallagher, and Foster concern young women. Write an essay about two, three, four, or all of these stories and focus on the depiction of young women's experience.

2. Write an essay in which you compare and contrast the ways in which DeFrees and Grafton deal with "crime" in their respective stories.

3. Write an essay about the four detective stories in this anthology: the stories by Conan Doyle, Chandler, Oates, and Grafton.

4. The stories by Erdrich, Wong, Rios, Foster, and Welch spring from North American cultures that are not Anglo Saxon in origin. Write an essay about any or all of these stories and assess the ways in which this fiction enriches your sense of "North America" and its several cultures. How effectively *does* fiction illuminate culture, in your view? To what extent did these stories reinforce or erase cultural stereotypes?

5. Some stories in this section spring from a "rural" experience, including those by Erdrich, Phillips, Wong, Gallagher, Rios, and Ellison. Others express an "urban" or "suburban" experience, including those by Grafton, Engberg, DeFrees, and Foster. Choose one or more stories from each category and write an essay that compares and contrasts them.

6. Select stories by Americans from "Early Voices" and "Emerging Voices" and write an essay in which you explain how the stories reveal ways in which America has changed (or stayed the same).

7. To some extent, the stories by Erdrich, Hulme, Joubert, Heker, Ndebele, and Barr all present women's views of serious political conflicts. Write an essay about several of these stories and analyze these perspectives on politics.

8. From all four sections, select a total of 10 or 12 stories *not* written by Americans; stories that you would recommend including in an anthology of "short stories from around the world." Then in your notebook, write a brief "justification" for your selection and an explanation of your criteria for selection.

9. Which stories in this anthology are the most important ones for an

aspiring fiction writer to read? In your notebook list your choices and explain their importance to a writer.

10.   Drawing on examples from this anthology and from other reading you have done, write your own essay about "the evolution of the short story."

Biographical Notes

ALEICHEM, Sholem (1859–1916). Sholem Aleichem is the pseudonym of Sholem Rabinowitz, who is considered to be one of the key founders of modern Yiddish literature. Aleichem was a Russian Jew who grew up in the Ukraine and began writing comic and satiric pieces for newspapers in 1883. He left Russia in 1905 following a czarist reaction to an aborted revolution. Aleichem's stories draw on a rich oral tradition, and many of them feature comic episodes narrated in monologues by garrulous, earthy speakers. Several of the characters from his tales formed the basis for the famous musical *Fiddler on the Roof.*

AMIS, Martin (1950–). Amis is English but also spent a year of his boyhood in Princeton, New Jersey. He has contributed articles to *The Observer, The New Statesman,* and other periodicals, and his books of fiction include *Money, The Rachel Papers,* and *Other People: A Mystery Story.* His nonfiction includes *Invasion of the Space Invaders* and *The Moronic Inferno and Other Visits to America.* Much of Amis's writing reveals a satirist's commitment to exposing folly, and he is a particularly astute observer of American life.

ANDERSON, Sherwood (1876–1941). Anderson was born in Ohio and grew up in several midwestern towns. When he was nineteen, he left home to live and work in Chicago and then enlisted to fight in the Spanish-American War. After the war, he briefly pursued a business career, but a nervous collapse in 1912

led him to give up business and write full time. His fourth book, *Winesburg, Ohio* (1919), contained a series of interwoven stories and found a wide readership that established Anderson's reputation. Anderson published two more novels and three collections of short stories before his death in 1941.

ATWOOD, Margaret (1939–). Atwood is one of numerous Canadian writers who have given Canada an even greater literary profile abroad than it previously had in this century. Atwood is adept at both novels and short stories. Her novels include *Surfacing* (1972) and *The Handmaid's Tale* (1987), and her most highly acclaimed collection of stories is *Bluebeard's Egg* (1985). Although much of her writing addresses issues related to feminism, Atwood's work also has a broad range of other themes and characters.

BARR, Fiona (1955–). Barr is one of many Irish women writers who are making an enormous impact on the Irish literary scene, as well as finding an audience in Europe and America. In America, Barr's work has appeared in *The Midland Review* and in the anthology *Territories of the Voice,* edited by Louise DeSalvo and others.

BARTHELME, Donald (1931–1989). Barthelme was one of the most innovative writers of short fiction in his time, and in some ways he was the quintessential postmodernist. Much of his fiction deliberately undermines literary conventions, plays with language, and immerses itself in various kinds of surrealism. The result is often a striking combination of the shocking and the funny, the tragic and the absurd. Much of Barthelme's fiction appeared in *The New Yorker;* he taught at Boston University, the University of Houston, and other colleges. *Sixty Stories* appeared in 1981. *Forty Stories* appeared in 1987.

BEATTIE, Ann (1947–). Ann Beattie's short fiction, much of which has appeared in *The New Yorker* magazine, has drawn critical and popular acclaim. Many of her stories examine the lives of middle-class white Americans plagued by various kinds of *angst.* Beattie's stories are also known for their striking use of imagery and their polished prose style. Her books include *Distortions, Chilly Scenes of Winter* (a novel), and *Secrets and Surprises.* Her stories have also appeared in such magazines as *Canto, Ploughshares,* and *Mississippi Review.*

BÖLL, Heinrich (1917–). Böll is among the writers credited with starting a new German literature after World War II, and he began his career by writing stories concerning soldiers. As he developed he turned into a much fiercer critic of society and its institutions. His books include *View of a Clown, 18 Stories,* and *Billiards at Halfpast Nine.* Böll was born and grew up in Köln.

BOROWSKI, Tadeusz (1922–1951). The Polish writer Borowski belonged to the Warsaw underground movement during the Second World War. He was captured by Germans and spent two years in the Auschwitz and Dachau concentration-camps. (His parents had been incarcerated in Soviet labor camps during the previous decade.) Borowski committed suicide in 1951, leaving behind many stories that would be collected in the volume *This Way for the Gas, Ladies and Gentlemen.*

BRADBURY, Ray (1920–). Bradbury is one of the most respected writers of science fiction ever, and this reputation may be traced to the enormous success and impact of *The Martian Chronicles* (1950). He writes a kind of science fiction that stresses perception, ethics, and social issues more than technology or high adventure. His other books

include *The Illustrated Man* (1951), *Fahrenheit 451* (1953), and *The Stories of Ray Bradbury* (1980).

BRAUTIGAN, Richard (1937–1986). In some ways, Brautigan was a quintessentially "sixties" writer who celebrated the counterculture life, borrowed conventions from several genres, and fashioned wry, surrealistic novels, sketches, and stories. *Trout Fishing in America* (1967) launched Brautigan's popular career, though he had been writing for some time before the publication of that book. Other books include *The Abortion, Revenge of the Lawn,* and *In Watermelon Sugar.*

CARVER, Raymond (1939–1988). Carver grew up in Oregon and came to a writing career only after working in mills and holding odd jobs. He studied at Humboldt State University in California and at the University of Iowa. In the 1970s his stories began to have enormous impact both on casual readers of fiction and critics. His unpretentious prose and his preoccupation with working-class characters attracted many imitators, and he was—unfairly, perhaps—credited with starting a new wave of so-called minimalist prose. His interests and his style were more varied than one might imagine at first glance, however. He produced five volumes of stories, including *Cathedral* and *Where I'm Calling From.*

CATHER, Willa (1873–1947). Cather was born in Virginia but grew up in Nebraska, where three of her best-known novels are set: *O Pioneers!* (1913), *The Song of the Lark* (1915), and *My Antonia* (1918). Before devoting herself to writing fiction, Cather worked as a journalist and high-school teacher. Her collections of short fiction include *Youth and the Bright Medusa* (1932).

CHANDLER, Raymond (1888–1959). Chandler was born in Chicago but spent much of his boyhood in England. There he attended Dulwich College and worked for two newspapers. Chandler fought in World War I and returned to the United States in 1919, settling in California and serving as a director of oil companies. He turned to writing relatively late—at age 45—and published his first detective stories in *Black Mask.*

His first novel, *The Big Sleep,* appeared in 1939 and was later made into a motion picture. With Dashiell Hammett and Ross MacDonald, Chandler is considered to be one of the "big three" hard-boiled detective writers, and his detective Philip Marlowe is almost as famous as Sherlock Holmes. His letters, which are fascinating, have also been published.

CHEEVER, John (1912–1982). Cheever was born in Massachusetts and moved to New York City when he was eighteen. His career, like that of John Updike, is strongly associated with the magazine *The New Yorker,* where Cheever published many of his stories. If anything, Cheever's reputation is even more strongly linked than Updike's to his short fiction. *The Enormous Radio and Other Stories* (1953), Cheever's second collection of stories, established his reputation, and *The Stories of John Cheever* (1978) remains one of the most impressive collections of short fiction produced this century. It won the Pulitzer Prize. Cheever's novels include *The Wapshot Chronicle* (1957), *Bullet Park* (1969), and *Falconer* (1977).

CHEKHOV, Anton (1860–1904). Chekhov is widely considered to be one of the most innovative and important writers of short fiction. He was born in Taganrog, Russia, and studied medicine at the University of Moscow. He began writing fiction for newspapers and journals chiefly as a way to supplement his income, but he became more artistically ambitious when he received financial support from publisher and patron of the arts Aleksey Suvorin. By the time he was twenty-eight, Chekhov had written about six hundred stories. In the 1890s Chekhov began writing for the stage; his plays include *Uncle Vanya* (1897) and *The Cherry Orchard* (1904). In his fiction and drama, Chekhov is adept at exploring the emotional "interior" life as well as the consequences of social change.

CHOPIN, Kate (1851–1904). Chopin was born and raised in St. Louis, but after her marriage to a cotton broker in 1870, she spent many years in Louisiana. After the death of her husband, Chopin returned to St. Louis in 1882 and published her first novel, *At Fault,* eight years later. Two collections of short stories appeared within a few years, and it was at this time that Chopin translated stories by Guy de Maupassant. Her masterpiece is considered to be *The Awakening* (1899), but because this novel dealt frankly with adultery, it scandalized readers and critics, damaging her career.

CONRAD, Joseph (1857–1924). Conrad was born Josef Teodor Konrad in Poland. As a young man, Conrad worked as a merchant seaman, sailing to far-flung continents and surviving two shipwrecks. Later he commanded British merchant ships in Asia and mastered English. In much of his fiction, Conrad addresses complex moral and psychological issues within the context of adventure tales. His novels include *Nostromo* (1904) and *Lord Jim* (1900), as well as the longer stories "Heart of Darkness," which informed the motion picture *Apocalypse Now,* and "The Secret Sharer."

CRANE, Stephen (1871–1900). Crane was born in New Jersey, attended Syracuse University briefly, and worked as a journalist in New York City. *The Red Badge of Courage,* the novel that established his reputation, was published in 1895 but was actually written after Crane had completed *Maggie: A Girl of the Streets* (1896). After the publication of these works, Crane served as a correspondent during the Spanish-American War and went on to write a handful of enduring stories, including "The Open Boat" and "The Blue Hotel." Crane is often associated with naturalism, a worldview that sees human beings as victims of accidental, arbitrary forces in nature and less able to determine their fates than they often believe.

DAY, Richard Cortez (1947–). Day teaches at Humboldt State University in Arcata, California. His stories have appeared in *Redbook, The Kenyon Review,* and *The New England Review. When in Florence,* his first collection of short stories, appeared in 1986. He is currently working on a second collection.

DeFREES, Madeline (1919–). DeFrees was born and grew up in Oregon, and until 1973 she was a member of the

Sister of the Holy Names of Jesus and Mary. She published her earlier prose and poetry under the name of Sister Mary Gilbert. Her recent books of poetry include *When Sky Lets Go* and *Magpie on the Gallows.* Two new books of poetry about to be published are *Light Station* and *Island in the Sound.* She is also working on an autobiography. De-Frees has taught at the University of Montana and the University of Massachusetts.

DeMARINIS, Rick (1947?–). Demarinis's fiction has appeared in many anthologies and periodicals, including *The Graywolf Annual* and *The Iowa Review.* His most recent book of fiction is *The Coming Triumph of the Free World,* which was published in 1988.

De MAUPASSANT, Guy (1850–1893). De Maupassant was born in the region of Normandy in France. He served in the military during the Franco-Prussian War (1870–1871) and later worked in the government. In the decade of the 1870s, Maupassant became acquainted with Turgenev, Zola, and Flaubert in Paris and actually studied with Flaubert. His first published story was "Boule de Suif," which appeared in 1880. The story drew wide acclaim, and fueled by this success, de Maupassant went on to write six novels and several hundred stories. In the late 1880s, de Maupassant became mentally ill, and it is widely believed that his illness resulted from a venereal disease. He attempted to commit suicide in 1892, was committed to an asylum, and died in 1893.

DOYLE, Arthur Conan (1859–1930). Conan Doyle will always be remembered as the creator of the world's most famous private detective, Sherlock Holmes. Doyle himself was a Scottish doctor who volunteered as a physician in South Africa during the Boer War. Like his detective, Doyle was a curious combination of the rational and irrational, for he loved the science of medicine but was also deeply interested in psychic experiences and the occult. The novel *A Study in Scarlet* gave birth to Holmes in 1887, and Doyle wrote Holmes stories for the next forty years. He "killed off" Holmes at one point but was convinced to revive him when readers demanded more tales.

Doyle's non-Holmes works include *Micah Clarke* (1889) and *The White Company* (1890).

ELLISON, Matt (1958–). Ellison was born and raised in Montana. He received a B.A. from the University of Montana and has also studied writing at Columbia University. He has been in residence at the Ragdale Foundation in Lake Forest, Illinois, and now works as a computer programmer in New York City.

ELLISON, Ralph (1914–). Ellison was born in Oklahoma City. At age twenty-two he went to New York City to participate in the Federal Writers Project, where he met Langston Hughes and Richard Wright, among others. He edited *Negro Quarterly,* served in the Merchant Marines during World War II, and began to write what would become his epic novel and one of the most highly acclaimed works of fiction in American literary history: *Invisible Man* (1952). Since then Ellison has published many stories and essays and has taught at New York University.

ENGBERG, Susan (1940–). Engberg lives in Milwaukee, Wisconsin. Her stories have appeared in *Sewanee Review, Massachusetts Review, Ploughshares,* and other magazines. A story of hers has also won an O. Henry award. *A Stay by the River,* her first collection of short fiction, appeared in 1985.

ERDRICH, Louise (1954–). Erdrich grew up in Wahpeton, North Dakota, a region where much of her fiction is set. She is the author of *Love Medicine* and *The Beet Queen* (novels), *Jacklight* (a book of poems), and numerous short stories, one of which won an O. Henry Prize and another which appeared in *The Best Short Stories of 1988.* Erdrich lives in New Hampshire with her husband, Michael Dorris, with whom she sometimes collaborates.

FAULKNER, William (1897–1962). Faulkner was born in Mississippi and embarked on his writing career in his mid-twenties. His stories and novels intermingle numerous fictional families, places, and situations to such an extent that Faulkner's "world" takes on mythic dimensions. Faulkner's work provides one of the most complex views of the American South as that region moved into the modern age. His use of stream-of-consciousness techniques and his rich, verbose diction made him a preeminent if quirky stylist. His novels include *The Sound and the Fury* (1929), *Light in August* (1932), and *Go Down, Moses and Other Stories* (1942), which contains the remarkable long story "The Bear." Faulkner also collaborated on screenplays, including one for *The Big Sleep,* and published numerous short stories in commercial magazines.

FOSTER, Sesshu (1956–). Foster lives in Los Angeles, California, where he teaches in the Los Angeles Unified School District. Foster received a B.A. in creative writing from the University of California, Santa Cruz, and his work has appeared in several literary magazines, including *The Northwest Review* and *Willow Springs.* He has coedited an anthology of urban multicultural poetry, and his own book of poetry, *Angry Days,* appeared in 1987.

FRAME, Janet (1924–). Frame is one of New Zealand's most important and accomplished writers, and she is a novelist with a worldwide reputation. Her novels include *Living in the Maniototo* (1984), and her collections of short fiction include *You Are Now Entering the Human Heart* (1983). She has also written a multivolume autobiography and has published poetry in numerous magazines.

FUENTES, Carlos (1929–). Fuentes is the son of a career Mexican diplomat, so he traveled and studied widely as he grew up. In the 1950s he joined the Communist party. He broke with the party in 1962, and since then he has served as Mexico's ambassador to France. Since the 1960s, however, he has devoted much of his energy to writing novels and stories. Recent books include *Terra Nostra* (1975), *Hydra Head* (1978), and *The Old Gringo* (1985), which was turned into a motion picture. Among his collections of short stories are *Burnt Water* and *Songs of the Blind.* Fuentes's writing addresses many questions of politics, economics, and history—chiefly in his native Mexico.

GALLAGHER, Tess (1946–). Gallagher grew up in the state of Washington and attended the University of Washington. She is an extremely versatile writer,

publishing acclaimed books of poetry, fiction, and nonfiction. A collection of stories entitled *The Lover of Horses* appeared in 1986. Her books of poetry include *Instructions to the Double* and *Willingly.* Gallagher has also coedited a special issue of *Ploughshares,* and she wrote the introduction to her husband Raymond Carver's last book of poems, *A New Path to the Waterfall.* Gallagher has taught at Syracuse University.

GILMAN, Charlotte Perkins (1860–1935). Gilman was born in Connecticut and studied at the Rhode Island School of Design. She married Charles Stetson in 1884, and they had a daughter. Shortly thereafter Gilman suffered a nervous breakdown, and in 1888 she left Stetson and moved to Pasadena. In 1900 she married a cousin, George Gilman, and started her career as a writer andlecturer on social issues, including feminism. She wrote several books of nonfiction, and her novels include *What Diantha Did* (1910) and *The Crux* (1911). "The Yellow Wallpaper" remains her best-known short story, and like much of her writing, it deals with the collision between social forces and the individual experience of a woman.

GRAFTON, Sue (1940–). Grafton is the author of several mystery novels featuring the private investigator Kinsey Millhone, including *'E' Is for Evidence.* With Marcia Muller, Sara Paretsky, and several other women mystery writers, Grafton has introduced new kinds of female private investigators to the tradition and has carved out a niche that is significantly different from the one inhabited by such writers as Agatha Christie, Dorothy Sayers, and P. D. James.

GUSTAFSSON, Lars (1936–). Gustafsson is one of several contemporary Swedish writers whose work has reached a worldwide audience through translation. His stories are among the most original being written today, combining wideranging intellect, quirky wit, and an outlook that can change from cynicism to affability in a single story. Gustafsson has taught in America, and four of his books have been translated into English; these include *Stories of Happy People* and *Death of a Beekeeper.*

GYANRANJAN. Born in Allahabad, India, in 1936, Gyanranjan is the son of a renowned writer. He published his first short story in 1960, and his reputation quickly grew. Two collections of his stories appeared in 1968 and 1971, and he continues to work in the short-story form. In America, his work has appeared in several anthologies, including *Ourselves Among Others: Cross-Cultural Readings for Writers.*

HAWTHORNE, Nathaniel (1804–1864). Hawthorne was born in Salem, Massachusetts, and was a classmate of Longfellow at Bowdoin College in Maine, where he graduated in 1825. His first book, *Twice-Told Tales,* was published in 1837. For a time he lived near Thoreau and Emerson in Concord, Massachusetts. *Moses from an Old Manse,* another collection of short stories, appeared in 1846, and *The Scarlet Letter,* the novel that established Hawthorne's reputation permanently, was published in 1850. The descendant of a prominent Puritan family, Hawthorne is known for his exploration of moral and spiritual issues. In addition to working as a writer, Hawthorne also was employed in the United States Custom House in Boston, and he served as a consul in England and Italy. His other novels include *The House of the Seven Gables* (1851) and *The Blithedale Romance* (1852).

HEKER, Liliana (1950–). Heker is an Argentinian who published her first book of stories, *Those Who Beheld the Burning Bush,* while she was in her teens. Heker edited the literary magazine *El Ornitorrinco (The Platypus)* during many of the worst years of Argentina's military dictatorships, and she has spoken powerfully for the role of writers in their nations' politics. Heker's work has appeared in many anthologies, including *Other Fires* (1985), edited by Alberto Manguel.

HEMINGWAY, Ernest (1899–1961). Hemingway is often well known even to those who have not read his work because he cultivated a popular image of the robust, "macho" man of adventure. He was born in Oak Park, Illinois, and worked as a journalist for the *Kansas City Star.* He worked as an ambulance driver in

France and Italy during World War I and was gravely wounded. After the war Hemingway lived in Paris, moved from journalism to fiction, and became acquainted with other American expatriates, including Gertrude Stein, who dubbed the group "the Lost Generation." Hemingway developed a lean, "cool" style that owes much to journalism and that shares some characteristics with hard-boiled detective fiction. His novels include *The Sun Also Rises* (1926), *For Whom the Bell Tolls* (1940), and *The Old Man and the Sea* (1952). Like his contemporaries Faulkner, Joyce, and Lawrence, Hemingway made remarkable achievements in both short and long fiction.

HENRY, O. (1862–1910). O. Henry is the pen name of William Sidney Porter, who was born in North Carolina. Porter worked as a bank teller in Texas and later went to prison for embezzling funds, and it was there that he began to write fiction. After serving a four-year sentence, Porter went to New York City in 1901 and quickly became a popular writer of short tales; it is said that at the peak of his career, he wrote a story a week. *The Complete Works of O. Henry* appeared in 1953. One of the most respected prizes for short fiction in America honors O. Henry.

HUGHES, Langston (1902–1967). Hughes was a native of Joplin, Missouri, but grew up in Ohio. After attending Columbia University for a year, Hughes came in contact with the writers, musicians, and artists who were forming what would later be called the Harlem Renaissance of the 1920s. Hughes's poetry absorbed the rhythms of jazz, and all of his writing explores the predicament of blacks in twentieth-century America. In addition to poetry and short fiction, Hughes wrote criticism, history, and humorous sketches, many of which feature the comic figure Jesse B. Simple. Hughes's books include *Weary Blues* (1926), *Montage of a Dream Deferred* (1951), and *Laughing to Keep from Crying* (1952).

HULME, Keri (1947–). Hulme is a Maori who grew up in Christchurch and Moreraki in New Zealand. Her first novel, *The Bone People* (1983), found an audience worldwide and identified her as an important new novelist, but she had been writing poetry and stories for several years. The novel won the Pegasus Prize for Literature as well as the New Zealand Book Award. Her work has also appeared in *Some Other Country: New Zealand's Best Short Stories* and other anthologies.

HURSTON, Zora Neale (1901?–1960). Hurston grew up in Florida, attended Howard University in the early 1920s, and lived in New York City in the late 1920s. There she met Langston Hughes and other members of what would be called the Harlem Renaissance, and she eventually collaborated with Hughes on the work *Mule Bone*. Hurston later studied anthropology at Barnard College and returned to Florida to record oral histories. Hurston is the author of two classic works of fiction—*The Eatonville Anthology* (1927), a collection of stories, and *Their Eyes Were Watching God* (1937), a novel. Hurston's work was rediscovered posthumously by feminist critics, but during the last decades of her life she received little recognition or money. She died in Florida.

JACKSON, Shirley (1919–1965). Jackson wrote many novels and stories, but there is no question that she will be remembered chiefly for a single powerful story, "The Lottery." She was born in San Francisco and went to college at Syracuse. Her novels include *Hangsaman* (1951) and *We Have Always Lived in a Castle* (1962).

JAMES, Henry (1843–1916). James is thought to be one of the most important American novelists, short-story writers, and theorists of fiction. He was born in New York City and educated by private tutors in America and Europe. His first novel, *Roderick Hudson,* was published serially in *The Atlantic Monthly* in 1875. From that point on, James produced an enormous volume of fiction, including *Daisy Miller* (1879), *Portrait of a Lady* (1881), and *The Golden Bowl* (1904). After about 1866, James lived abroad, feeling out of place in American culture. Many of his novels and stories draw from this "expatriate" experience in a variety of ways. All of his work exhibits a preoccupation with complicated human psychology.

JOUBERT, Elsa (1922–). Joubert is a South African author who has written several novels and travelogues in Afrikaans. In 1978 she published *Die Swerfjare van Poppie Nongena,* a novel about a black domestic servant and her family. The novel became a best-seller, was translated into English as *Poppie,* and won an award from the Royal Society of Literature in London. Joubert has also published a collection of short fiction entitled *Milk* (1980), and her work appears in *The Penguin Book of Southern African Stories,* edited by Stephen Gray.

JOYCE, James (1882–1941). Joyce was born in Dublin and attended University College there. Early in his intellectual development, Joyce rejected Catholicism and thereby began the process that would make him a literal and figurative exile from his own Irish background. His important early works are the short-story collection *Dubliners* and the novel *Portrait of the Artist as a Young Man* (1916). His masterwork is the complex, multilayered, and highly allusive novel *Ulysses* (1922), which is one of the most important contributions to the artistic movement now known as modernism.

KAFKA, Franz (1883–1924). Kafka was Czechoslovakian and led something of a double life: He pursued an ordinary career as a civil servant, but his private life was filled with self-doubt and tortuous neuroses. The self-doubt spilled over into his writing; just before he died, he instructed his literary executor to destroy his manuscripts, but the executor disobeyed him. Kafka's fiction is among the most original ever written and often combines a simple, parable-like structure with startling surrealism. His short novels include *The Metamorphosis* (1915) and *The Penal Colony* (1919). He also published two collections of stories during his life. He died of tuberculosis in Berlin.

KAWABATA, Yasunari (1899–1972). Kawabata attended Tokyo Imperial University and later joined a group of writers known as the New Impressionists, who to some extent defined themselves in opposition to proletarian writers. Owing to the translations by E. G. Seidensticker, Kawabata's work—including the novels *Snow Country* and *The Sound of the Mountain*—has been widely read in Europe and the Americas. Kawabata received the Nobel Prize for Literature in 1968. He committed suicide in 1972.

KING, Stephen (1947–). King was born in Portland, Maine. He is considered to be the American master of an enormously popular subgenre, horror fiction. He has written at least twenty novels, including *Carrie, The Dead Zone,* and *Misery,* some of which have been turned into motion pictures. He also wrote the story "Stand by Me," which was the basis of a motion picture. King's stories have been gathered in four collections, one of which is *Night Shift.*

KODA, Aya (1904–). Koda is the daughter of Rohan Koda, who was an important figure in Japanese literature in the late nineteenth and early twentieth centuries. In fact, her literary career began when newspapers coaxed her to write recollections of her father following his death. From these sketches she moved on to write short stories. She lives in Tokyo.

LAWRENCE, D. H. (1885–1930). Lawrence was born in a coal-mining district in England's industrial midlands, and this working-class background informs much of his fiction. Lawrence was preoccupied by what he saw as the deadening effects of industrial society on passion, instinct, sexuality, and human liberty. His novels include *The Rainbow* (1915), *Women in Love* (1920), and *Lady Chatterley's Lover* (1928). The latter scandalized many readers because of its frank depiction of a passionate and unconventional love affair. Lawrence was also a superb poet and a provocative essayist. His marriage to the aristocrat Frieda von Richthofen Weekley was ironic, given his attitudes toward social classes and conventions, and it took the couple to such far-flung places as Australia, Tahiti, and Taos, New Mexico. He died of tuberculosis.

MALAMUD, Bernard (1914–1986). Malamud was born and grew up in New York City and became one of America's most original and surprising writers. His novel *The Natural* (1956) mixed baseball, mythology, comedy, and tragedy. Subsequent novels include *A New Life* (1961),

The Fixer (1966), and *God's Grace* (1982). Malamud's novels and stories often express a belief in humans' ability not just to survive but to prevail despite enormous obstacles of spirit and circumstance. His stories are collected in such books as *Rembrandt's Hat* and *Idiots First.* Malamud taught at Oregon State University and Bennington College.

MANSFIELD, Katherine (1888–1923). Mansfield grew up in New Zealand, where many of her stories are set, and moved to England when she was twenty-one. There she met and eventually married the writer John Middleton Murry and became part of a modernist literary circle that included D. H. Lawrence. With Murry she edited several magazines, including *The Blue Review,* and her short stories quickly drew wide acclaim. Unlike her contemporaries Virginia Woolf, James Joyce, and Lawrence, Mansfield did not move on to a substantial career as a novelist, but her powerful, inventive short fiction has endured. She died of tuberculosis.

MELVILLE, Herman (1819–1891). Melville is of course best known for his monumental novel *Moby Dick* (1851). He grew up in New York City, the son of a merchant. In his youth, Melville worked as a farmhand, a bank messenger, and a schoolteacher. In 1839 he sailed to England as a merchant seaman, and in 1841 he left a brief career as a legal scrivener to sail the South Pacific, where he participated in a mutiny, lived among cannibals, and learned to harpoon. His early novels, including *Typee* (1846), spring from these adventures and were quite successful. Later novels like *Moby Dick* (1851) and *Pierre* (1852) did not find a popular audience and were not well received by critics, circumstances that embittered Melville. The short novel *Billy Budd* was not discovered until the 1920s. Melville's most famous short story, "Bartleby the Scrivener," was published in 1856.

MUNRO, Alice (1931–). Munro was born in Winham, Ontario, and attended the University of Western Ontario. She helped found and operate a bookstore in Victoria, British Columbia, and started publishing short stories in the 1950s. Along with Margaret Atwood, she is one of Canada's best-known and most widely acclaimed writers of fiction. Her collections of short fiction include *Something I've Been Meaning To Tell You* (1974), *Who Do You Think You Are?* (1978), and *The Moons of Jupiter* (1983). Munro's stories contain rare mixtures of pathos and wit and often detail the frustrations and problems of middle-class Canadian women. Munro's novel *The Beggar's Maid* won the Governor General's Literary Award in 1979.

NDEBELE, Njabulo S. (1948–). Ndebele is a lecturer in African, Afro-American, and English literature at the University College of Roma, Lesotho. He earned an M.A. from Cambridge and a Ph.D. from the University of Denver. His collection of stories *Fools* (1983) won the Noma Award, and he is a highly regarded literary figure as well as an important critic of postcolonial oppression. In America, Ndebele's work has appeared in *Triquarterly* and other magazines.

O'BRIEN, Tim (1946–). O'Brien is a native of Minnesota who studied at Macalester College. After graduating in 1968, he was drafted into the army and served in the Vietnam War. After the war he studied at Harvard University and worked for *The Washington Post.* In 1976 he began writing fiction full time and has produced several novels dealing with the Vietnam War from different angles. His books include *If I Die in a Combat Zone, Northern Lights,* and *Going After Cacciato* (1978), which is his most highly acclaimed novel to date. A more recent book that does not deal with Vietnam directly is *The Nuclear Age* (1985).

O'CONNOR, Flannery (1925–1964). O'Connor was one of the most fiercely original writers of her time. She was born and grew up in Georgia and began publishing when she was still in college. Her fiction draws heavily on her Catholic background, exhibits a fascination with the grotesque, and addresses key issues of morality and justice. Her novel *Wise Blood* appeared in 1952, and *The Complete Stories* was published in 1971. She died in Milledgeville, Georgia, at the age of thirty-nine.

O'CONNOR, Frank (1903–1966). Frank O'Connor is the pen name of Michael

John O'Donovan, who was born in Cork, Ireland. Although O'Connor wrote novels, travel literature, and criticism, his reputation rests almost exclusively on his short stories, many of which he tirelessly revised, even after they were published. He was associated with the Irish Literature Revival, an artistic movement that asserted a distinct Irish heritage and nationality and whose most notable member was William Butler Yeats. Many of O'Connor's stories appeared in American magazines during the 1930s and are now most accessible in *Collected Stories* (1981). O'Connor's study of the short story, *The Lonely Voice* (1963), is a classic and remains useful to critics and writers alike.

OATES, Joyce Carol (1938–). It has become standard practice to call Oates an incredibly prolific writer, and she is. But she is more than prolific; she is an enormously talented and versatile writer of novels, short stories, poetry, and nonfiction. Oates was born in New York, studied at Syracuse and the University of Wisconsin, and began publishing novels in the mid-1960s. Since then she has produced dozens of volumes of fiction, poems, and criticism. Her novels include *The Assassins* (1975) and *You Must Remember This* (1987). Collections of stories include *By the North Gate* and *The Wheel of Love.* Oates teaches at Princeton University.

OZ, Amos (1939–). Amos Oz is one of Israel's best-known writers. His original last name was Klausner. He broke with his father's conservative Zionism and joined a kibbutz, changing his name to "Oz" at that time. (The name means "strength" in Hebrew.) He has studied at Oxford and Hebrew Universities, and he fought in the 1967 Six-Day War. Many of his stories and novels concern kibbutz life, and Oz continues to live with his family on Kibbutz Hulda, located between Jerusalem and Tel Aviv.

OZICK, Cynthia (1928–). Ozick was born and grew up in the Bronx, and she studied at New York University and Ohio State University. Her first novel, *Trust,* appeared in 1966, and her first collection of short stories, *The Pagan Rabbi and Other Stories,* appeared five years later. One of Ozick's interests is the lives of Jews who have immigrated to America, and in general she is concerned with themes of identity and survival. Her recent work includes the novella *The Messiah of Stockholm* (1987).

PHILLIPS, Jayne Anne. (1952–). Phillips was born in Virginia and now lives in Massachusetts. She is the author of a collection of short stories, *Black Tickets,* and of the novels *Fast Lanes* and *Machine Dreams.* Her short stories have appeared in numerous magazines, and her story "Bess" appeared in the anthology *New American Fiction: The Writers Select Their Own Favorites.*

PIRANDELLO, Luigi (1867–1937). Pirandello was born in Sicily and most of his stories and plays are closely linked to that region of Italy. Pirandello studied in Rome and Bonn and settled in Rome to begin a writing career. Financial crises and his wife's struggle with mental illness vitiated his personal life, however, and affected his writing. Pirandello wrote several novels and several hundred short stories, and his forty plays include *Six Characters in Search of an Author* (1927) and *Henry IV* (1922). Many stories, like "War," and many of his plays reflect his interest in a realistic mode, but he also wrote experimentally, including plays that were labeled "theater of the grotesque." Pirandello lived for a time in both France and America.

POE, Edgar Allan (1809–1849). Poe was orphaned at age two and raised by John Allan in Richmond, Virginia. He briefly studied at the University of Virginia but was asked to leave because of gambling debts. He subsequently enlisted in the army and spent a brief period at West Point. His first book was *Tamerlane and Other Poems* (1827), and he also wrote reviews and articles for the *Southern Literary Messenger* and other magazines. He is often credited with inventing the modern detective story, but he is probably best known for his tales of horror and madness as well as for important reviews and essays, including "The Philosophy of Composition." *Tales of the Grotesque and Arabesque* appeared in 1839; *The Raven and Other Poems* was published in 1845.

PORTER, Katherine Anne (1890–1980). Porter was born in Texas and educated in a Catholic convent and several private schools. She married at sixteen, divorced at twenty-one, and then went to work for several newspapers in Chicago, Denver, and San Antonio. She went to Mexico to study art in 1920 and took part in revolutionary political movements. Her first collection of stories, *Flowering Judas,* appeared in 1930 and received critical and popular acclaim. Two other collections appeared in 1939 and 1944, and in the 1950s Porter taught at Stanford University. Her *Collected Stories* (1965) won the Pulitzer Prize. Porter published one novel (*Ship of Fools,* 1962) and many essays, but her reputation rests exclusively on her highly original short stories.

RIOS, Alberto (1955–). Rios teaches at Arizona State University in Tempe. He was born in Nogales, Arizona, and received an M.F.A. in creative writing at the University of Arizona. *Whispering to Fool the Wind,* a book of poems, won the Walt Whitman Award in 1981. *The Iguana Killer* won the 1984 Western States Book Award.

STEINBECK, John (1902–1968). Steinbeck was born in Salinas, California, a region that figured significantly in his writing. Steinbeck studied at Stanford and worked in a variety of jobs before establishing his writing career with three novels that appeared in the 1930s: *Tortilla Flat, In Dubious Battle* (1936), and *The Grapes of Wrath* (1939). The latter novel is considered to be *the* fictional account of the Great Depression and its effect on people forced to migrate out of the Dust Bowl. Later novels include *East of Eden* and *Cannery Row;* Steinbeck also wrote several books of nonfiction and collections of short fiction. He was awarded the Nobel Prize for Literature in 1962.

TOLSTOY, Leo (1828–1910). Tolstoy's family was from the Russian nobility. He studied briefly at Kazan University but then joined the army. Three autobiographical novels were published in the 1850s, and in 1856 Tolstoy resigned from the army. He married in 1862 and began his monumental novel *War and Peace* (1869). His other major novel,

Anna Karenina, appeared in 1876. In the late 1880s Tolstoy experienced a religious conversion and dedicated himself to a radical form of Christianity. Several volumes of nonfiction were devoted to this subject and appeared in the 1880s and 1890s. Although Tolstoy's reputation depends upon his two great novels, "The Death of Ivan Ilych" demonstrates his power in short fiction.

TURGENEV, Ivan (1818–1883). Along with his countryman Chekhov, Turgenev is often credited with advancing the "revolt against plot" in short fiction because he was often less interested in a clear thread of action than in evoking a place or a mental state. He also gained a reputation for depicting Russian peasants with generosity and understanding. Turgenev studied at the University of Moscow, the University of St. Petersburg, and the University of Berlin. His first collection of short stories, *A Sportsman's Sketches,* sometimes translated as *Hunting Sketches* (1852), remains a landmark one. His best-known novel is *Fathers and Sons* (1862). In part because of difficulty with official censors, Turgenev spent most of his time abroad after 1855, and in Paris he met Henry James, Guy de Maupassant, and Flaubert.

UPDIKE, John (1932–). Updike is one of America's most prolific novelists and one who has achieved both popular and critical acclaim. When he was only twenty-three, he joined the staff of *The New Yorker* magazine and published his first stories there. One of his earliest novels, *Rabbit, Run* (1960), remains one of his most acclaimed. His third novel featuring Rabbit Angstrom (*Rabbit Is Rich,* 1981) won the Pulitzer Prize and the National Book Award. Updike's other novels, many of which examine the lives of middle-class "WASP" Americans, include *Couples, Of the Farm, The Centaur,* and *The Witches of Eastwick.* He has also published several collections of short stories, many of which appeared first in *The New Yorker,* and he has published volumes of verse.

VALENZUELA, Luisa (1938–). Valenzuela was born in Buenos Aires in 1938 and wrote her first story when she was seventeen. Carlos Fuentes has called her "the heiress of Latin American fiction," and her novel *He Who Searches* has been compared with Garcia Marquez's *One Hundred Years of Solitude,* particularly in the way it creates a "fantastical realism." Valenzuela's other works include *Clara, The Lizard's Tail,* and a recent collection of short fiction, *The Open Door.* Valenzuela's work is frequently translated into English.

WALKER, Alice (1944–). Alice Walker is one of the premier American writers now living, and her reputation is based in part on the award-winning novel *The Color Purple.* Walker was born in Georgia and graduated from Sarah Lawrence College. She was a social worker in New York City and has taught literature and writing at Jackson State College, Tougaloo College, Wellesley, and Yale. Her other books include *Meridian, In Love and Trouble: Stories of Black Women,* and *The Temple of My Familiar.*

WELCH, James (1949–). Welch lives in Missoula, Montana, where he also attended the University of Montana, studying with Richard Hugo and Madeline DeFrees. He is the author of three novels and a book of poetry. Welch was born on the Blackfoot Reservation in Browning, Montana, and much of his writing illuminates the lives and history of Native Americans from that region. Welch has taught at the University of Washington and at Cornell University.

WELTY, Eudora (1909–). Welty is a native of Jackson, Mississippi and is considered to be one of the most accomplished writers of short fiction in the twentieth century. During the Depression, Welty worked for newspapers and radio stations in a position created by the Works Progress Administration. Welty has published several volumes of award-winning fiction, including *A Curtain of Green and Other Stories* (1941) and *The Collected Stories of Eudora Welty* (1980). She has also written three novels, including *The Optimist's Daughter,* which won the Pulitzer Prize in 1972. Welty's fiction is firmly set in the South, demonstrating a powerful sense of that region's conflicts and many voices.

WONG, Shawn Hsu (1949–). Wong was born in Oakland, California, and grew up in Berkeley. He has edited special issues of the *Bulletin of Concerned Asian Scholars* and *The Yardbird Reader.* He also coedited an important anthology of contemporary Asian American writing: *Aiiieeeeee!,* which appeared in 1974. A sequel appeared in 1985. Wong writes short fiction, novels, and essays, and he teaches at the University of Washington in Seattle.

YAMAMOTO, Hisaye (1921–). Yamamoto was born in Redondo Beach, California, and much of her work deals with Asian American life in that region. Partly because she devoted time to raising a family, Yamamoto's output of fiction has been comparatively slim, and yet the stories she has written have received acclaim for their astonishing originality. As "Yoneko's Earthquake" suggests, Yamamoto is a master of point of view, and she can produce fiction that is both poignant and humorous. Her stories also offer a striking, detailed portrait of Japanese American life in agrarian California.

YATES, Richard (1930?–). Yates began publishing short stories in the mid-1950s, and since then he has become something of "a writer's writer"—enormously respected among writers and editors but somewhat less well known than such contemporaries as John Updike or John Cheever. Nonetheless, his collection of short stories entitled *Eleven Kinds of Loneliness* remains a classic. Kurt Vonnegut called it "one of the ten best short-story collections ever written by an American." Yates's novels include *Revolutionary Road, Disturbing the Peace,* and *A Good School.* A more recent collection of short stories is *Liars in Love* (1981). Yates lives in Boston.

Glossary of Critical and Literary Terms

ACTION: The occurrences in a story. It is important not to confuse this kind of action with that of "action story" or "action movie." Action in a story includes any event or incident and need not be limited to adventurous or violent behavior.

ALLEGORY: A story, novel, narrative poem, or play in which characters, plot, and even setting represent specific ideas, religious themes, spiritual conflicts, or values. When we read Hawthorne's "Young Goodman Brown," for instance, we may interpret Goodman Brown's state of mind as representative of religious obsession in general, not just as a single character's obsession. Allegorical literature to some extent spins parallel threads of action, the literal (a single character with a religious obsession) and the symbolic (religious obsession in general). See *symbol.*

ALLUSION: A *reference* that a work of literature makes to other specific characters, persons, events, things, or so forth, in art or life. An allusion attempts to draw on a shared body of knowledge and can be explicit or implicit. A short story containing the line "The world was all before them" is alluding to Milton's *Paradise Lost* and, indirectly, to the Bible. "You won't have me to kick around anymore" alludes to a remark by Richard Nixon after he lost an election in California. This term should not be confused with "illusion."

AMBIGUITY: A word, sentence, scene, or section of a narrative that may be reasonably interpreted in two or more ways. Some writers *intend* ambiguity as a way of representing a situation that is complicated or uncertain. Other writers are ambiguous by mistake, creating what they think will be a simple scene (for example) but one which turns out to confuse readers.

ANACHRONISM: A person, product, event, or term that is "out of time" or chronologically wrong. A character in 1837 cannot use the colloquial street language of 1990, for example, without being anachronistic.

ANTAGONIST: The rival, enemy, opponent, or opposing force against which a main character or protagonist struggles. Just as a protagonist need not be all good, an antagonist need not be all bad. "Good guys" and "bad guys" are but one simplistic and extreme example of protagonists and antagonists. See *protagonist.*

ANTICLIMAX: A resolution, scene, crisis, or conflict that seems unsatisfying, empty, unimportant, dull, or undeveloped. If a character reacts to a situation in a less forceful, believable, dramatic, or engaging way than we anticipate, we are apt to call the reaction "anticlimactic." One task of reading is to determine whether an anticlimax, like an ambiguity, serves an artistic purpose or is simply a flaw. Anticlimax does not refer only to the point in a story where there should be a crisis or climax; resolutions and other moments in a story can be anticlimactic.

ANTIHERO: A character whose beliefs and actions are in contrast to those of a traditional hero. Such a character need not be evil or corrupt and can be quite the opposite. For example, Melville's Bartleby is a "good" character who nonetheless exhibits antiheroic qualities.

ARCHETYPE: A repeated, even ancient, pattern of action, conflict, character, or theme. Literary critics borrowed the term from the psychologist Carl Gustav Jung (1875–1961), who claimed that individuals were tied to a "collective unconscious" or collective memory that the entire human race shared. A story featuring the ritual initiation of a boy into manhood or a girl into womanhood might be called "archetypal" because it repeats (retells) an event common to many civilizations.

ATMOSPHERE: What restaurants and stories have in common. The mood or figurative "weather" of a narrative. The fog, gaslight, and carriages of Sherlock Holmes's London create a famous (and much borrowed) atmosphere.

AUTHORIAL INTRUSION: A bald statement or interpretation that strikes readers as an intrusion of the author into her or his own narrative. The "moral" at the end of a fable is a conventional intrusion that we expect, but such intrusions now are apt to be seen as symptoms of an author's impatience or heavy-handedness.

BELIEVABLE: Refers to the degree to which we accept a story as figuratively true. An action in a story is believable if it strikes readers as something the character would do, given what the readers have learned about the character. Ray Bradbury's Martian stories are not *literally* believable (colonies on Mars don't actually exist), but the characters and situations in them are believable or "acceptable" to most readers. The critic Samuel Taylor Coleridge spoke of "a willing suspension of disbelief," the willingness of readers to accept the terms of literature and participate in the story. When readers get angry with a fictional character's behavior, the character is so believable that the readers have participated fully in the fiction. People who talk about soap opera characters as if they were real people have similarly suspended their disbelief.

BURLESQUE: A kind of satire that makes fun of situations, actions, events, or persons by means of exaggeration. See *caricature* and *satire.*

CANON: A body of literature regarded as important or central in a nation or a culture; the works of literature that have "endured." Because a canon is created by people, it is subject to biases and prejudices. To some extent, the canon of English and American literature has always been in flux because new works are always being written and because readers cannot agree on what ought to endure—on what is a "classic." One product of the "global community" of the twentieth century is the increasing availability of translated literature. Another is the disappearance of barriers between Western and Eastern cultures. Also, in America and elsewhere more women and persons of color have influenced literature and criticism and broadened the diversity of culture. As a result of these and other developments, the notion of a *single* literary canon or literary tradition is more impractical than ever.

CARICATURE: A kind of satire that makes fun of a person—and chiefly a person's appearance—by means of distortion and exaggeration. Editorial cartoonists often create caricatures of famous persons by making a large nose even larger or an identifying hairstyle extreme. Some authors produce caricatures not for satiric reasons but because of racist, sexist, or ethnocentric points of view. See *flat* and *stereotype.*

CENTRAL: In fiction, what is crucial, important, or key. Sammy is the "central" character of Updike's "A & P." Sammy's having to deal with the appearance of "Queenie" in the store is the "central" action of the story. Stokesie and Lengel are "secondary" or "peripheral" characters. Sammy's having to deal with rude customers is a "secondary" action.

CHARACTER: Refers either to the person(s) in a story or to the quality of personality a character has. Julian is a character in Flannery O'Connor's "Everything That Rises Must Converge." His character is marked in part by arrogance.

CHRONOLOGY: The time scheme of a story. The chronology of Conrad's "The Secret Sharer" is several days; that of de Maupassant's "The Necklace" is many years. Stories may take chronological leaps, skipping hours, days, months, years. A chronology in a story may be straightforward, or it may be rearranged. A *flashback* is one way to rearrange a "straight" or "linear" chronology.

CLICHE: A trite, overused, or "worn out" expression, idea, situation, theme, or character type. "Looking for a needle in a haystack" is a worn-out expression or cliche referring to an impossible search. See *stereotype*.

CLIMAX: The moment in a scene or a story when the action is most intense or most complicated. "Crisis" or "crucial moment" are equivalent terms. Often a climax is the point at which a main character *must* choose or take action of some kind.

CLOSURE: This term refers to the tactics and strategies authors use to end narratives.

COMPLICATION: The entanglement or difficulty or problem that springs from a conflict between characters or between a character and a situation or force. A complication might be said to occur between the time when a conflict is introduced in a story and the time when a climax is reached.

COMPRESSION: Refers to the scale of a poem, story, novel, or play. Generally, a short story has to be more compressed than a novel, working with fewer characters, situations, images, and words. In terms of compression, therefore, the demands of writing a story are similar to those of writing lyric poetry.

CONFLICT: The key problem, trouble, entanglement, or struggle in a story. A basic conflict: one character wants something from another character who does not want to relinquish it. Conflicts can occur within characters as well as between them. Conflicts produce complications, crises, and resolutions (defined elsewhere).

CONNOTATION: A secondary or suggestive meaning of a word. For example, "gay" used to denote "happy"; then it acquired the suggestive meaning of "homosexual"; now, in most cases, it denotes "homosexual." "Loose" denotes the opposite of tight, but one connotation of "loose" is "sexually promiscuous." See *denotation*.

CONVENTION: Any aspect of literature that has been established, including standard punctuation of dialogue, keeping a story in one verb tense, and using a title. "Conventional" can be a negative term, referring to a story (for example) that uses a conflict that strikes one as being worn out.

CRISIS: See *climax*.

CRITICISM: The art and craft of interpretation. When we read a story and write a response to it, we are practicing criticism. Unlike "*a* criticism," criticism is not necessarily negative. One can write criticism that praises a work of art. See specific kinds of criticism: *feminist, formalist, Marxist, historical, Freudian.* See also *deconstruction* and *archetype*.

DECONSTRUCTION: A comparatively recent form of criticism that is deeply skeptical of literature's capacity to determine the response of readers and to represent reality. From this perspective, a reader reacts to a printed text and mentally rearranges or "deconstructs" it, as opposed to looking for a meaning that the author may have intended. Critics who work from this point of view think of themselves as "entering" works of literature as if the works were complicated buildings or even labyrinths. They doubt whether *a* meaning of a story can be determined, and they see language less as a conduit of meaning than as a complex, confusing, even contradictory system of "signs." Deconstruction makes criticism a playful, chaotic process that challenges the tenets of nearly every other way of reading literature.

DENOTATION: The primary meaning of a word or term. "To strike" is the denotation of "hit." One connotation of "hit" is an assassination. A denotation is essentially the dictionary definition, without the more recent suggestiveness that a word or term has acquired. Dictionary definitions change, however, and connotations can become denotations over time. See *connotation*.

DENOUEMENT: A term equivalent to "resolution." See *resolution*.

DIALOGUE: The words characters say to one another in a story. Conventionally, this speech is set off by quotation marks.

DIDACTIC: A story is didactic if it forcefully and overtly sets out to teach a lesson or convey a moral stance. Fables are one kind of didactic story; biblical parables are another. See *authorial intrusion*.

DISCONTINUITY: In fiction, "discontinuity" refers to several ways in which authors intentionally confuse or disrupt a clear flow of plot, a clear sense of chronology, a unified point of view, or so on. In some cases, discontinuity is a result of flawed writing, but many writers during and after the Modern period believed that circumstances required art to involve itself with discontinuity. A stream-of-consciousness narrative is often discontinuous. See *surrealism.*

DISTANCE: In most cases, "distance" refers either to the psychic distance between the narrator of a story and the characters and events or to the psychic distance between the reader and the story. If a story strikes us as unbelievable, there is a distance between story and reader and "distance" is a negative term. If a narrator strikes us as being objective or cold, there is distance between the narrator and the action of the story, but this distance may seem appropriate. In this case, "distance" is merely descriptive, not negative.

DOUBLE: Fiction and other art forms often explore twin personalities, split personalities, literal and figurative twins, and so on, particularly as a way of exploring psychological, religious, or moral problems. A shorthand way of describing this motif is to say that this or that story involves a "double," or in German, a "doppelgänger." Poe's story "William Wilson," Stevenson's story "Dr. Jekyll and Mr. Hyde," Hogg's novel *Confessions of a Justified Sinner,* and Conrad's "The Secret Sharer" exemplify the use of the double.

DRAMATIC: Literally, this means "like drama" or "like a play." It can also refer to a story that presents a clear, vivid conflict. Or, used even more loosely, it can mean "exciting," as in "The ending was dramatic."

EPIPHANY: Originally a religious term referring to the "manifestation" of Christ to the wise men. James Joyce used the term to refer to a certain moment of revelation in a story or a novel, when a character "sees into" the nature of her or his personality, life, city, culture, or era. Such revelations for Joyce need not be beneficent and are quite often moments of disillusionment when hope or pride are stripped away. The term is particularly useful to readers of the short story because short fiction from the nineteenth century forward is so often concerned with psychological crises and moments of discovery and introspection.

EPISODE: One part of a narrative.

EPISODIC: Whereas "episode" merely refers to one part of a narrative, "episodic" is often a negative term. An episodic story is usually one that is loosely, even incoherently organized, featuring many scenes that seem strung together without much purpose.

EXISTENTIALISM: This term describes an intellectual movement that is both philosophical and literary, beginning with Kierkegaard and continuing with such writers as Sartre, Heidegger, and Camus. The existential worldview sees people as entirely responsible for their own actions and their fate and is implicitly antithetical to religious worldviews based on faith in a deity. Camus's novel *The Stranger* is an example of a work influenced by this worldview. Hemingway's short story "A Clean, Well-Lighted Place" suggests a similar influence.

EXPERIMENTAL FICTION: Almost an infinitely broad term referring to fiction that attempts to alter, distort, or subvert any literary conventions, including those of plot, conflict, character, and verisimilitude (defined elsewhere). However, one era's experiment can become another era's convention. Donald Barthelme's story "The Author" is experimental in the sense that it is deliberately enigmatic, playing with language and thwarting conventional notions of clarity.

EXPOSITION: The part of a story that provides background or other essential information about a character.

FEMINIST CRITICISM: Refers to criticism that assesses the depiction of women in literature and that defines traditions of literature by women. This type of criticism also questions versions of literary history that overlook, trivialize, or misread literature by women.

Feminist criticism has rediscovered a great deal of neglected literature by women, and it has sometimes merged with other kinds of interpretation that stress the socioeconomic, political, or psychological issues related to gender. Feminist criticism has also revealed the "canon" and traditions of literature to be shaped—and distorted—by perspectives that may claim to be objective but that are biased or prejudicial. See *canon*.

FICTION: Prose narrative in which "fact" is transformed by invention and imagination. "Short fiction" usually refers to narratives that are much shorter than one hundred pages and typically shorter than fifty. Many short stories concentrate on one or two main characters in a single conflict, so that "short" refers to the scope of the narrative as well as to sheer length. Critics continue to explore and debate the differences between novels and short stories.

FIRST PERSON: A kind of narration that is presented by an "I" speaker. Joyce's "Araby" is in the first person.

FLASHBACK: A break in the straightforward chronological development of a story; a return to an early time in a story's chronology. A narrative may start by describing a character who is eighteen years old, and then it may feature a flashback in which we see the character when she is ten.

FLAT: When applied to characterization in stories, this term refers to shallowness. Minor or secondary characters often should be "flat" or one-dimensional. However, if a main character seems insufficiently complex, particular, or engaging, "flatness" can be a flaw in the view of some readers. See *round* and *stereotype*.

FORESHADOWING: A suggestion of events or situations to come. The bullwhip in Hurston's story "Sweat" might be seen as a foreshadowing of the snake that appears later in the story.

FORM: This term is almost too broad to define, but it can refer to the shape a story takes. For instance, if you told someone you were writing a love story, they might want to know what "form" your particular love story would take. The term also applies to the structure of a story—its scenes, organization, plot,

and so forth. See *convention* and *formalist criticism*.

FORMALIST CRITICISM: The study of literature as an artifice or "art object" distinct from the author's biography and the historical context. Formalist criticism stresses patterns of imagery, metaphors and similes, symbols, paradoxes, ironies, and other topics that spring from literature perceived chiefly as an arrangement of words. "New Criticism" in the early twentieth century was an American school of formalism. New Critics reacted in part to nineteenth-century criticism that stressed the connection between a work and its author's biography.

FREUDIAN CRITICISM: Criticism that draws heavily on the psychoanalytic writings of Sigmund Freud (1856–1939) and his ideas about repression, compulsive behavior, the subconscious mind, sexual taboos, and forces in the personality (id, ego, superego). Just as some psychologists and psychiatrists interpret patients' anecdotes and dreams clinically, Freudian critics "listen" to literary stories as expressions of psychological conflict or symptoms of emotional problems. In turn, psychologists are more interested than ever in the way patients shape experience with stories.

GENRE: A type or kind of literature, such as poetry, drama, or fiction. Faulkner's *The Sound and the Fury* belongs to the genre of fiction; his "A Rose for Emily" belongs to the genre of short fiction. A subgenre is a category within a genre; for example, short detective fiction is a subgenre of short fiction. Particularly since the nineteenth century, short fiction has been treated as a genre distinct from fiction (novels), although the two obviously share many characteristics.

GOTHIC: Refers to many different historical periods and styles of art and architecture. In connection with fiction, it suggests the mysterious, the "dark," the desolate, the grotesque, the morbid, or the horrific. Poe's fiction is often described as "gothic," and the horror fiction that he inspired in such current writers as Stephen King and Clive Barker relies on gothic elements. "Gothic romance" refers to a particular kind of formula fiction in which sentimental tales of love are set in castles or other situations that are exotic.

HERO: Refers specifically to a character that exhibits heroic qualities: strength, courage, wisdom, power, adaptability. The term refers more generally to a main character, a central character, or protagonist—who, ironically, may or may not exhibit heroic qualities of the sort mentioned. That is, a "hero" in the sense of a "main character" may be a coward.

HISTORICAL CRITICISM: Criticism that studies literature in connection with authors' lives and historical eras, social movements, economic factors, and specific events, such as wars, migrations, and revolutions. See *Marxist criticism* and *feminist criticism.*

ILLUSION: Appearance, not reality. In a story, a character may be living according to an illusion, and the conflict may spring from the character's having to confront this falsehood. Julian's mother in Flannery O'Connor's "Everything That Rises Must Converge" lives her life under the illusion that blacks and whites are not socially equal, and that condescending to blacks is appropriate behavior. The story involves the shattering of the illusion. It is important not to confuse "illusion" with "allusion." See *allusion.*

IMAGERY: May refer to figures of speech, such as similes or metaphors (defined elsewhere); may refer more broadly to any "images" the words in a story bring to our minds; or may refer even more generally to any concrete detail (not necessarily visual) in a story. Updike's "A & P" begins "In walks these three girls in nothing but bathing suits." The sentence creates an image in our minds. In contrast, later in the story the sentence "Then everybody's luck begins to run out" is an abstract sentence that creates no visual detail in our minds; it presents a general idea that will be fleshed out with examples. In the same story, Updike's character compares shoppers in a supermarket with "sheep"; in this case the concrete image is metaphorical. See *metaphor.*

INTERIOR MONOLOGUE: A character speaking to himself or herself. One kind of interior monologue is stream-of-con-

sciousness; Porter's "The Jilting of Granny Weatherall" includes stream-of-consciousness passages that function as interior monologue.

IRONY: The difference between what is said and what is meant, between what is attempted and what is achieved, or between what a character knows and what a reader knows. Sarcasm is one form of verbal irony, such as when we respond to bad news by saying "Oh, that's just *great.*" Dramatic irony occurs when the reader or other characters know something the main character does not, as in O. Henry's "Gift of the Magi," where one secret purchase nullifies the worth of another, and where the reader sees that the characters are working at cross purposes.

LIMITED OMNISCIENT: A point of view that is essentially in the third person ("She opened the door" or "He looked across the room"), describes the actions of several characters, but enters the thoughts of only one character. In a sense, the narrative is "filtered" through the mind of only one character. Hawthorne's "Young Goodman Brown" is told from this point of view.

MARXIST CRITICISM: Criticism that draws heavily on the writings of Karl Marx, especially his critique of capitalism and industrial society. Such criticism sees literature in part as an expression of certain social classes, social values, and economic struggles. Sometimes the term is also used loosely to describe any criticism that emphasizes socioeconomic conflicts but that may not draw directly from Marx's work or that of Friedrich Engels.

METAPHOR: Used loosely, any figure of speech (such as "used loosely") or comparison. More specifically, a comparison between two things without the use of "like" or "as": "The cold wind cut through his thin coat." Here the wind is compared metaphorically to a sharp blade. In "A Rose for Emily," Faulkner compares Emily metaphorically to a body submerged in water to give us an image of her appearance and to begin to suggest how she belongs to an earlier era. See *simile.*

MOTIF: A theme, idea, symbol, plot, conflict, situation, or character type that recurs in literature, art, folklore, music, or so forth. Joyce's story "Araby" uses the motif of unrequited love. Updike's story "A & P" makes ironic use of a chivalric motif by having Sammy attempt to be "Queenie's" "prince" and "save" her.

MOTIVE: The desire or other cause that drives characters to do what they do.

MYTH: In a broad sense, a system of beliefs to which a culture subscribes. "Myth" may also refer to *one* story in such a system, such as *the* myth of the Yellow Woman or *the* myth of Prometheus, both of which are single elements of Native American and Ancient Greek worldviews, respectively. The work of the scholar Joseph Campbell is indispensable for understanding connections between the myths of different cultures.

NARRATOR: The character or "voice" that tells the story. Updike is the author of "A & P," but Sammy is the narrator, speaking as an "I" distinct from Updike. Tolstoy is the author of "The Death of Ivan Ilych," but a third-person "speaker" tells the story from various characters' point of view. See *first person, second person, third person, limited omniscient, omniscient, objective, central, peripheral,* and *unreliable.*

NATURALISM: Applied to literature, a literary movement that grew out of realism (defined elsewhere); naturalistic writers used subject matter that was often considered sordid, wrote in a style that seemed nearly scientifically objective, and suggested in their stories that a person's influence over his or her fate was dubious. Stephen Crane's works—including *The Red Badge of Courage,* "The Open Boat," and "The Blue Hotel"—are often cited as examples of naturalism. See *realism.*

OBJECTIVE: Applied to narration, a third-person narrator who reports actions and events in a voice that seems detached or "cold" or "journalistic." The narrator in Hemingway's "A Clean, Well-Lighted Place" might be described as "objective."

OMNISCIENT: An omniscient point of view "knows all." It is a third-person narrative voice that can describe the actions, ideas, and feelings of every character in the story. It gives the writer enormous freedom to "wander" among various perspectives, but such freedom can cause a story to lose focus and direction. Tolstoy uses this point of view effectively in "The Death of Ivan Ilych," in part because one of his purposes is to represent a *variety* of responses to one person's death. By comparison, Hawthorne's "Young Goodman Brown" is in a third-person narrative voice that is limited to one character. See *limited omniscient.*

PACE: The speed of a story. A story that seems to drag in places may contain excessive detail, lengthy, purposeless dialogue, or nondescript scenes. Stories can also move too fast, of course, chiefly by seeming to leap over important scenes or to rush to a crisis or to a resolution without sufficient *exposition.*

PARODY: Satire that makes fun of a work of literature or an author's style. For example, there is an annual contest for stories that imitate and make fun of the spare style of Ernest Hemingway. See *satire, burlesque,* and *caricature.*

PERIPHERAL: Applied to narration, a character who is not always involved directly in the key action. Dr. Watson narrates the stories of Sherlock Holmes, but Holmes is the central character; therefore, we might call Watson a peripheral narrator. Such narration may be awkward because the point-of-view character is relatively passive and yet must be near the action to describe it. Such narration may also be useful for expressing complicated psychological conflicts or situations, such as voyeurism.

PLOT: The sequence of events in a story. Five different authors working with the same basic story ("character X falls in love with character Y and takes him to Tahiti, where they . . .") would emphasize different elements, create a different sequence of episodes, and thereby produce five different plots. "Plot," therefore, is *not* synonymous with "story." For example, Flannery O'Connor's "Everything That Rises Must Converge" is the "story" of a mother and son who are forced to confront their racism and arrogance. The "plot" of the story is the specific sequence of scenes and descriptions that O'Connor's narrator provides.

POINT OF VIEW: In connection with essays and editorials, means "opinion" or "thesis," but in fiction refers to the perspective or angle from which the story is told. Consequently, when we identify the point of view of a story, we determine the "person" (first, second, or third) as well as the character(s) through which the story is told. Updike's "A & P" is told in the first person from Sammy's perspective, for example.

PROTAGONIST: The central character of a story. See *antagonist* and *hero*.

REALISM: When applied to literature, usually refers to a broad movement in the nineteenth century to depict "life as it is really lived," meaning, in part, that literary characters were based on ordinary persons in ordinary, even mundane, occupations. The term is sometimes contrasted with such modes of literature as romance, fantasy, or allegory, in which characters are often supernatural, "larger than life," and pointedly *extra*ordinary. However, because "life as it is really lived" is a matter of opinion, the claims of realism to be "more accurate" are difficult to prove. The stories of de Maupassant, Chekhov, and James are often considered examples of realism. See *naturalism* and *verisimilitude*. Used very loosely, the term "realistic" is often synonymous with "believable," as in the statement, "This story seemed realistic to me."

RESOLUTION: The resolution of a story is the specific way in which the conflict, crisis, problem, or struggle turns out. In Joyce's "Araby," the resolution occurs after the boy reaches the bazaar and becomes disillusioned. "Resolution," then, is the aftermath or result of a confrontation or any other kind of conflict. It is important to remember that resolutions in fiction do not have to be appropriate or right; a character can make a choice that would be inappropriate or wrong in life but that fits the story. See *conflict*.

ROUND: A character who is complex and particularized, with a variety of qualities that interest us. See *flat*.

SATIRE: A category of art including works that make fun of people, events, ideas, or other works of art, usually by means of exaggeration, distortion, or other techniques that make the reader laugh at a subject. Parody, burlesque, and caricature (defined elsewhere) are types of satire. Some claim that satirists want to call attention to problems, flawed persons, or bad ideas and thereby "correct" them; others claim that satirists attack their subject only for the sport of it. Editorial cartoons are usually satiric in nature.

SECOND PERSON: A rare narrative voice: "You. . . ." Fuentes's "Aura" is in the second person.

SENTIMENTAL: When applied to literature, usually means "overly sentimental," meaning that the work attempts to elicit an emotional response from the reader that is disproportionate to the story presented, that it attempts—in a cheap way—to be a tearjerker, or that it has a happy ending that is either forced or trite.

SETTING: The time, place, and cultural context of a story. John Steinbeck's "Chrysanthemums" is set on a farm in the Salinas Valley of California in the early part of the twentieth century.

STEREOTYPE: An oversimplified (or "stock") character or situation. The villain dressed all in black is a stereotypical character, entirely predictable. Some stereotypes spring from an unthinking repetition of literary conventions; others spring from racist, sexist, or provincial points of view. See *caricature* and *round*.

STORY: May refer to *a* story published in a magazine or book, or to the general idea of that story. For example, O. Henry's "The Gift of the Magi" is *a* story, but it is also "the story of a newlywed couple whose attempts to buy gifts for one another fail but in failing demonstrate the couple's love." See *plot*.

STREAM-OF-CONSCIOUSNESS: One narrative technique—which can be used in first, second, or third person—that attempts to imitate or approximate the complicated, random, associative, or haphazard "flow" of human thoughts. Writers working with this technique still shape and order the narrative, but they try to create the impression of the mind's intricate, unpredictable flow.

STYLE: A broad term referring to an author's distinctive way of writing. In describing someone's style, we are likely to emphasize vocabulary, diction, and sentence structure as well as overall perception of people and places. "The Hemingway style," for instance, refers to his clipped, spare style. Hemingway provided plain descriptions and often used simple and compound sentences. Also, his vocabulary and diction were far less rich than those of Faulkner, for example.

SYMBOL: An object, person, or act that takes on added abstract, philosophical, religious, or cultural significance. A wedding ring is literally a band of gold, but it is also a symbol for certain values, traditions, obligations, and commitments. The bus in Flannery O'Connor's "Everything That Rises Must Converge" is literally a mode of transportation the characters share, but it also symbolizes the history of the civil rights movement in America during the 1950s and early 1960s.

SURREALISM: An approach to art that owes some of its notions to French symbolist poetry of the nineteenth century and to the depth psychology of Freud, Jung, and others. "Depth psychology" refers to intricate theoretical models of the human mind, specifically of the subconscious mind. Surrealistic literature (and art) manipulates imagery, chronology, and conventions to approximate the logic (or illogic) of dreams, in which many experiences are fused. Films and music videos draw heavily on surrealistic techniques, in part because the splicing of film and video lends itself to juxtaposition, jumbled chronology, and other dreamlike characteristics. See *Freudian criticism, symbol, archetype,* and *stream-of-consciousness.*

THEME: The key idea, issue, political viewpoint, or implied "comment" that a story suggests to us. Some readers might say that one theme of Conrad's "Secret Sharer" is "the search for identity," even though the story is not "about" identity in the way an essay might be. See *didactic.*

THIRD PERSON: A narrative voice that speaks of "he," "she," or "they." Tolstoy's "Death of Ivan Ilych" is in the third person.

TONE: Difficult to define, partly because it refers to the "impression" created by a story. Essentially, "tone" describes the figurative "sound" of a story, the attitude created by *all* of its verbal techniques.

TOPICAL: When applied to literature, suggests that a work has deliberately dealt with a current political or social issue. One advantage of topical literature is that it does attempt to address and make sense of the world around it. One disadvantage of topical literature is that it may not appeal to an audience who reads it years later; another is that it may lack perspective on the topic or issue.

UNRELIABLE NARRATOR: A narrator who gives us information we do not trust. All narrator's have limitations that color what they present, but an unreliable narrator is significantly untrustworthy. For example, we often "read past" what a child narrator says because he or she may be innocent of certain things. If a narrator is insane, we have to reinterpret nearly everything she or he says to get to the "real" story. The narrator of Poe's "The Tell-Tale Heart" is unreliable. Of course, unreliability assumes that the reader first believes in the concept of a narrator. Deconstructive criticism generally dismisses the idea of a narrator and sees literature as a construct of words, "spoken" by no one. See *deconstruction.*

VERISIMILITUDE: The quality of reality a story creates. If a writer describes a street in Chicago in a way that strikes a reader from Chicago as "accurate," "true," or "right," then the story has achieved verisimilitude. As this example implies, however, the degree of verisimilitude depends as much on the reader's response as it does on the writer's presentation. The term belongs to a tradition of criticism that emphasizes "mimesis," or the way art accurately reflects life. See *realism.*

VOICE: The narrative voice of a story. The voice of "The Secret Sharer" belongs to the captain, not to the author, Conrad. Critics also use "voice" to describe authors as spokespersons: Ralph Ellison is one voice of black Americans' experiences, for example; James Baldwin is another.

Selected Checklist of Anthologies, Books on Writing, Collections of Short Fiction, Magazines

Note: This list is for those who want to continue writing as well as those who want to study or teach the art of short fiction in the years ahead. It is not by any means a comprehensive list, and it is designed only to begin to enlarge your sense of the art. Add to it according to your own tastes and discoveries.

Contents:
I. Anthologies
II. Books on Writing and Short Fiction
III. Short Fiction (American and Canadian)
IV. Short Fiction (English, Irish, Australian, New Zealander)
V. Short Fiction (Asian, Continental, Latin American)
VI. Magazines and Publications on Publishing
A. Mass-Market Magazines
B. Small Literary Magazines
C. Publications on Publishing

I. ANTHOLOGIES

Alexander, Meena, ed. *Truth Tales: Contemporary Stories by Women of India.* New York: Feminist Press, 1989.

Atwood, Margaret and Robert Weaver, eds. *The Oxford Book of Canadian Short Stories.* New York: Oxford Univ. Press, 1988.

Bellow, Saul, ed.. *Great Jewish Short Stories.* New York: Dell, 1985.

Birch, Cyril, trans. *Stories from a Ming Collection: The Art of the Chinese Storyteller.* New York: Grove Press, 1968.

Brink, Andre and J. M. Coetzee, eds. *A Land Apart: A Contemporary South African Reader.* New York: Penguin, 1986.

Cahill, Susan, ed. *New Women and New Fiction: Short Stories Since the Sixties.* New York: Mentor, 1986.

Cahill, Susan. *Women and Fiction: Short Stories by and about Women.* New York: Mentor, 1975.

Cassill, R. V. *The Norton Anthology of Short Fiction.* Third edition. New York: Norton, 1986.

Charters, Anne, ed. *The Story and Its Writer.* New York: St. Martin's Press, 1983.

Chin, Frank, ed. *Aiiieeee!: An Anthology of Asian American Writers.* Washington, D.C.: Howard Univ. Press, 1983.

Clerc, Charles and Louis Leiter, eds. *Seven Contemporary Short Novels.* Glenview,

Ill.: Scott, Foresman, 1982. (Roth, Mc-Cullers, Vonnegut, Morrison, Kosinski, Atwood, Bellow).

Conlon, Faith, Rachel Da Silva, and Barbara Wilson, eds. *The Things That Divide Us: Short Fiction by Women.* Seattle: Seal Press, 1985.

Ellison, Emily and Jane B. Hill, eds. *Our Mutual Room: Modern Literary Portraits of the Opposite Sex.* Atlanta: Peachtree Publishers, 1988.

Fadiman, Clifton. *The World of the Short Story: A 20th Century Anthology.* Boston: Houghton Mifflin, 1986.

Flores, Angel. *Great Spanish Short Stories.* New York: Dell, 1962.

Forkner, Ben and Patrick Samway, S.J., eds. *A Modern Southern Reader.* Atlanta: Peachtree Publishers, 1988.

Forkner, Ben and Patrick Samway, S.J., eds. *Stories of the Modern South.* New York: Penguin, 1981.

Forkner, Ben. *Modern Irish Short Stories.* New York: Viking, 1980.

Fulton, Bruce and Ju-Chan Fulton, trans. *Words of Farewell: Stories By Korean Women Writers.* Seattle: Seal Press, 1989.

Garnett, Constance and Nathan Haskell Dole, trans. *Four Great Russian Short Novels.* New York: Dell, 1959.

Godwin, Gail, ed. *Best Short Stories of 1985.* Boston: Houghton Mifflin, 1986.

Gray, Stephen, ed. *The Penguin Book of Southern African Fiction.* New York: Penguin, 1985.

Grossman, William, ed. *Modern Brazilian Short Stories.* Berkeley, Univ. of California Press, 1967.

Halpern, Daniel, ed. *The Art of the Tale: An International Anthology of Stories 1945–85.* New York: Viking, 1986.

Hampl, Patricia, ed. *The Houghton Mifflin Anthology of Short Fiction.* Boston: Houghton Mifflin, 1988.

Hanson, Katherine, ed. *An Everyday Story: Norwegian Women's Fiction.* Seattle: Seal Press, 1984.

Henry, Dewitt, ed. *The Ploughshares Reader: New Fiction for the 80's.* Wainscott, N.Y.: Pushcart Press, 1985.

Hibbet, Howard, ed. *Contemporary Japanese Literature: An Anthology of Fiction, Film, & Other Writings Since 1945.* New York, Knopf, 1977.

Hills, L. Rust and Tom Jenks. *The Esquire Fiction Reader II.* New York: Wampeter/Esquire Press, 1986.

Hills, L. Rust, ed. *Great Esquire Fiction: The Finest Stories from the First Fifty Years.* New York: Penguin, 1983.

Howe, Irving and Ilana Wiener Howe, eds. *Short Shorts: An Anthology of the Shortest Stories.* New York: Bantam, 1982.

Howes, Barbara, ed. *Eye of the Heart: Short Stories from Latin America.* New York: Avon, 1973.

Isherwood, Christopher. *Great English Short Stories.* New York: Dell, 1957.

Klinkowitz, Jerome and John Somer, eds. *Innovative Fiction: Stories For The Seventies.* New York: Dell, 1972.

Koppelman, Susan, ed. *"May Your Days Be Merry and Bright" and Other Christmas Stories By Women.* Detroit: Wayne State Univ. Press, 1988.

Koppelman, Susan, ed. *The Other Woman: Stories of Two Women and a Man.* New York: Feminist Press, 1984.

Lindberg, Stanley W. and Stephen Corey, eds. *Necessary Fictions: Selected Stories from the Georgia Review.* Athens: Univ. of Georgia Press, 1986.

Lucas, Alex. *Great Canadian Short Stories.* New York: Dell, 1971.

Madden, David. *The World of Fiction.* Ft. Worth: Holt, Rinehart and Winston, 1990.

Mancini, Pat, ed. *Contemporary Latin American Short Fiction.* New York: Fawcett, 1979.

Mitchell, Edward and Rainer Schulte, eds. *Continental Short Stories: The Modern Tradition.* New York: Norton, 1968.

Mizener, Arthur, ed. *Modern Short Stories.* New York: Norton, 1979.

Morris, Joan. *Modern Japanese Stories.* New York: Tuttle, 1962.

Murphey, George, Jr., ed. *Best Short Fiction of 1985.* New York: Bantam, 1986.

Murray, Jan, ed. *The New Penguin Book of Scottish Short Stories.* New York: Penguin, 1983.

Norris, Gloria, ed. *New American Short Stories: The Writers Select Their Own Favorites.* New York: New American History Library, 1986.

Oosthuizen, Ann, ed. *Stepping Out: Short Stories of Friendship Between Women.* London and New York: Pandora, 1986.

Patrick, William, ed. *Mysterious Sea Stories.* New York: Bantam, 1986.

Pickering, James H., ed. *Fiction 100: An Anthology of Short Stories.* Fourth edition. New York: Macmillan, 1985.

Piekarski, Vicki, ed. *Westward the Women: Anthology of Western Stories by Women.* Albuquerque: Univ. of New Mexico Press, 1988.

Pritchett, V. S., ed. *The Oxford Book of Short Stories.* New York: Oxford Univ. Press, 1988.

Raffel, Burton, ed. *The Signet Classic Book of Contemporary American Short Stories.* New York: New American Library, 1985.

Richards, Alun, ed. *The Penguin Book of Welsh Short Stories.* New York: Penguin, 1981.

Richards, David. *The Penguin Book of Russian Short Stories.* New York: Penguin, 1981.

Sargent, Pamela, ed. *Women of Wonder: Science Fiction Stories by Women about Women.* New York: Vintage, 1985.

Sennett, Dorothy, ed. *Full Measure: Modern Short Stories On Aging.* St. Paul: Graywolf, 1988.

Simpson, Lewis P., ed. *Selected Stories from The Southern Review 1965–1985.* Louisiana: Louisiana State Univ. Press, 1988.

Skaggs, Calvin, ed. *The American Short Story,* Vol. I. New York: Dell, 1986.

Skaggs, Calvin, ed. *The American Short Story,* Vol. II. New York: Dell, 1987.

Solomon, Barbara, ed. *American Wives: An Anthology of Short Fiction.* New York: Mentor, 1986.

Solomon, Barbara, ed. *The Experience of American Women: An Anthology of Stories.* New York: Mentor, 1978.

Spender, Stephen, ed. *Great German Short Stories.* New York: Dell, 1960.

Stegner, Wallace and Mary Stegner, eds. *Great American Short Stories.* New York: Dell, 1979.

Stewart, Frank, ed. *Passages to the Dream Shore: Contemporary Stories of Hawaii.* Honolulu: Univ. of Hawaii Press, 1988.

Taggard, Ernestine, ed. *Twenty Grand: Great American Short Stories.* New York: Bantam, 1971.

Trimmer, Joseph and C. Wade Jennings, eds. *Fictions.* San Diego: Harcourt, Brace, Jovanovich, 1988. Second edition.

Tyler, Anne, ed. *The Available Press/PEN Short Story Collection.* New York: Ballantine Books, 1985.

Tyler, Anne, ed. *Best Short Stories of 1983.* Boston: Houghton Mifflin, 1984.

Updike, John, ed. *Best Short Stories of 1984.* Boston: Houghton Mifflin, 1985.

Walker, Scott, ed. *The Graywolf Annual.* Saint Paul: Graywolf, 1985.

Walker, Scott, ed. *The Graywolf Annual Two: Short Stories by Women.* Saint Paul: Graywolf, 1986.

Walker, Scott, ed. *The Graywolf Annual Four: Short Stories by Men.* Saint Paul: Graywolf, 1988.

Warren, Robert Penn and Albert Erskine, eds. *Short Story Masterpieces.* New York: Dell, 1972.

Washington, Mary Helen, ed. *Black-Eyed Susans/Midnight Birds: Short Stories by and about Black Women.* New York: Doubleday, 1989.

II. BOOKS ON WRITING AND SHORT FICTION

Bates, H. E. *The Modern Short Story.* Boston: The Writer, 1972.

Berg, Stephen, ed. *In Praise of What Persists.* New York: Harper Colophon, 1984. (Essays by 24 writers).

Booth, Wayne C. *The Rhetoric of Fiction.* Chicago: Univ. of Chicago Press, 1961.

Bruck, Peter. *The Black American Short Story in the 20th Century.* Amsterdam: B. R. Gruner, 1977.

Burnett, Hallie and Whit Burnett. *Fiction Writer's Handbook.* New York: Harper & Row, 1975. Preface by Norman Mailer.

Burnett, Hallie. *On Writing the Short Story.* New York: Barnes & Noble, 1983.

Burroway, Janet. *Writing Fiction: A Guide to Narrative Craft.* Boston: Little, Brown, 1986. Second edition.

Crowley, Donald, ed. *The American Short Story 1850–1945: A Critical History.* Boston: Twayne, 1979.

Dembo, L. S., ed. *Interviews with Contemporary Writers.* Second Series, 1972–1982. Madison: Univ. of Wisconsin Press, 1983.

Dostoievsky, Fyodor. *The Diary of a Writer.* Layton, Utah: Peregrine Smith Books, 1988.

Flora, Joseph M., ed. *The British Short Story, 1890–1945: A Critical History.* Boston: Twayne, 1980.

Forster, E. M. *Aspects of the Novel.* New York: Harcourt Brace Jovanovich, 1927/ 1947.

Gardner, John. *On Becoming a Novelist.* New York: Harper & Row, 1983.

Gardner, John. *The Art of Fiction.* New York: Vintage, 1982.

Garland, Susan. *The Short Story Cycle: A Genre Companion and Reference Guide.* Westport: Greenwood Press, 1988.

Gass, William. *Fiction and the Figures of Life.* New York: Knopf, 1970.

Goldberg, Natalie. *Writing Down the Bones.* London: Shambhala, 1986.

Haycraft, Howard. *The Art of The Mystery Story.* New York: Carroll and Graf.

Haycraft, Howard. *Murder for Pleasure: The Life and Times of the Detective Story.* New York: Carroll and Graf.

Hendin, Josephine. *Vulnerable People: A View of American Fiction Since 1945.* New York: Oxford, 1978.

Hills, Rust. *Writing in General and the Short Story in Particular.* New York: Bantam, 1979.

Hugo, Richard. *The Triggering Town.* New York: Norton, 1978.

James, Henry. *The Art of Fiction and Other Essays.* Edited by Morris Roberts. London: Oxford Univ. Press, 1948.

Josipovici, Gabriel. *The World and the Book: A Study of Modern Fiction.* London: Paladin, 1973.

Kilroy, James, ed. *The Irish Short Story: A Critical History.* Boston: Twayne, 1980.

Knott, William C. *The Craft of Fiction.* New Jersey: Prentice-Hall, 1973.

Kundera, Milan. *The Art of the Novel.* New York: Grove, 1986.

Lohafer, Susan. *Coming To Terms with The Short Story.* Baton Rouge: LSU Press, 1983.

Lohafer, Susan and Jo Ellyn Clarey, eds. *Short Story Theory at a Crossroads.* Baton Rouge: LSU Press, 1989.

Lubbock, Percy. *The Craft of Fiction.* New York: Viking, 1957.

May, Charles E., ed. *Short Story Theories.* Athens: Ohio Univ. Press, 1976.

Oates, Joyce Carol. *(Woman) Writer: Occasions and Opportunities.* New York: Dutton, 1988.

O'Connor, Frank. *The Lonely Voice: A Study of the Short Story.* Cleveland: World, 1963.

Paulson, Suzanne Morrow. *Flannery O'Connor: A Study of the Short Fiction.* Boston: Twayne, 1988.

Peden, Margaret Sayers, ed. *The Latin American Short Story*. Boston: Twayne, 1986.

Plimpton, George, ed. *Writers at Work: The Paris Review Interviews*. New York: Viking and Penguin (continuous).

Porter, Katherine Anne. *The Days Before*. New York: Harcourt, Brace, 1952.

Pritchett, V. S. *Chekhov: A Spirit Set Free*. New York: Random House, 1988.

Richter, David H. *The Borzoi Book of Short Fiction*. New York: Alfred A. Knopf, 1983.

Robison, James Curry. *Peter Taylor: A Study of the Short Fiction*. Boston: Twayne, 1988.

Sachs, Murray, ed. *The French Short Story in the Nineteenth Century*. New York: Oxford, 1969.

Sloane, William. *The Craft of Writing*. Julia Sloane, ed. New York: Norton, 1979.

Stegner, Wallace. *Teaching the Short Story*. Davis: Univ. of California Press, 1965.

Stephens, Michael Gregory. *The Dramaturgy of Style: Voice in Short Fiction*.

Carbondale: Southern Illinois Univ. Press, 1986.

Stevick, Philip, ed. *The American Short Story 1900–45: A Critical History*. Boston: Twayne, 1981.

Tanner, Tony. *City of Words: American Fiction, 1950–1970*. New York: Harper & Row, 1971.

Vannatta, Dennis, ed. *The British Short Story, 1945–1980: A Critical History*. Boston: Twayne, 1982.

Voss, Arthur. *The American Short Story: A Critical Survey*. Norman: Univ. of Oklahoma Press, 1973.

Weaver, Gordon, ed. *The American Short Story 1845–1930: A Critical History*. Boston: Twayne, 1983.

Weixlmann, Joe. *American Short-Fiction Criticism and Scholarship, 1959–1977: A Checklist*. Athens: Univ. of Ohio Press, 1982.

West, Ray B. *The Short Story in America, 1900–1950*. Chicago: Regenery, 1952.

Woolf, Virginia. *A Writer's Diary*. New York: Harcourt, Brace, 1954.

III. SHORT FICTION (AMERICAN AND CANADIAN)

Adams, Alice. *Beautiful Girl*. New York: Knopf, 1978.

Adams, Alice. *Return Trips*. New York: Knopf, 1984.

Adams, Gail. *The Purchase of Order*. Athens: Univ. of Georgia Press, 1988.

Anderson, Sherwood. *The Triumph of the Egg*. New York: Viking, 1921 and 1949.

Apple, Max. *The Oranging of America and Other Stories*. New York: Viking, 1976.

Baldwin, James. *Going to Meet the Man*. New York: Dial Press, 1965.

Bambara, Toni Cade. *Gorilla, My Love*. New York: Random House, 1972.

Bambara, Toni Cade. *The Sea Birds Are Still Alive*. New York: Vintage.

Banks, Russell. *The New World*. Urbana: Univ. of Illinois Press, 1978.

Barth, John. *Lost in the Funhouse*. Boston: Atlantic, 1967.

Barthelme, Donald. *Unspeakable Practices, Unnatural Acts*. New York: Farrar, Straus, Giroux, 1965.

Barthelme, Frederick. *Two Against One*. New York: Weidenfeld and Nicholson, 1988.

Beattie, Ann. *Secrets and Surprises*. New York: Warner, 1978.

Beattie, Ann. *The Burning House*. New York: Warner, 1982.

Beattie, Ann. *Where You'll Find Me and Other Stories*. New York: Collier/Macmillan, 1987.

Bell, Madison Smartt. *Zero DB And Other Stories*. New York: Ticknor and Fields, 1987.

Bellow, Saul. *Mosby's Memoirs and Other Stories*. New York: Viking, 1968.

Bontemps, Arna. *The Old South.* New York: Dodd, Mead, 1933.

Bowles, Paul. *Collected Stories 1939–1976.* Santa Barbara: Black Sparrow, 1983.

Boyle, Kay. *The White Horses of Vienna and Other Stories.* 1964.

Boyle, T. Coraghessan. *Descent of Man.* Boston: Little, Brown, 1978.

Boyle, T. Coraghessan. *Greasy Lake and Other Stories.* New York: Vintage, 1984.

Bradbury, Ray. *The Martian Chronicles.* Garden City: Doubleday, 1958.

Brodkey, Harold. *Stories in an Almost Classical Mode.* New York: Knopf, 1988.

Brown, George Mackay. *Time to Keep and Other Stories.* New York: Vanguard, 1987.

Brown, Rosellen. *Street Games.* New York: Doubleday, 1974.

Busch, Frederick. *Domestic Particulars: A Family Chronicle.* New York: New Directions, 1976.

Busch, Frederick. *Hardwater Country.* New York: Knopf, 1979.

Busch, Frederick. *Manual Labor.* New York: New Directions, 1982.

Calisher, Hortense. *The Collected Stories.* New York: Arbor House, 1975.

Carver, Raymond. *Cathedral.* New York: Knopf, 1984.

Carver, Raymond. *What We Talk About When We Talk About Love.* New York: Knopf, 1981.

Carver, Raymond. *Where I'm Calling From.* New York: Atlantic Monthly Press Vintage, 1988.

Capote, Truman. *Breakfast at Tiffany's: A Short Novel and Three Stories.* New York: Random House, 1958.

Cather, Willa. *Willa Cather's Collected Short Fiction, 1892–1912.* Lincoln: Univ. of Nebraska Press, 1965.

Cheever, John. *The Stories of John Cheever.* New York: Knopf, 1978.

Chestnutt, Charles W. *The Wife of His Youth and Other Stories.* Ann Arbor: Univ. of Michigan Press, 1987.

Colwin, Laurie. *Passion and Affect.* New York: Viking, 1974.

Conley, Robert J. *The Witch of Goingsnake and Other Stories.* Norman: Univ. of Oklahoma Press, 1988.

Conroy, Frank. *Midair.* New York: Owl/Holt, 1987.

Coover, Robert. *Pricksongs and Descants.* New York: Dutton, 1969.

Crane, Stephen. *Pictures from Life: Stories by Stephen Crane.* Selected and introduced by Thomas A. Gullason. Syracuse, N.Y.: Syracuse Univ. Press, 1988.

Deaver, Philip K. *Silent Retreats.* Athens: Univ. of Georgia Press, 1988.

Demarinis, Rick. *The Coming Triumph of the Free World.* New York: Viking, 1988.

Dove, Rita. *Fifth Sunday.* University of Alabama: Calaloo Fiction Series, 1985.

Dreiser, Theodore. *Free and Other Stories.* New York: Boni & Liverwright, 1918.

Dubus, Andre. *Finding a Girl in America: Ten Stories and a Novella.* Boston: Godine, 1980.

Dubus, Andre. *Selected Stories.* Boston: David Godine, 1988.

Dumas, Henry and Eugene B. Redmond, eds. *Goodbye, Sweetwater: New and Selected Stories.* New York: Thunder's Mouth Press, 1988.

Elkin, Stanley. *Stanley Elkin's Greatest Hits.* New York: Dutton, 1980.

Farrell, James T. *An Omnibus of Short Stories.* New York: Vanguard, 1967.

Faulkner, William. *Selected Short Stories.* New York: Modern Library, 1956.

Faulkner, William. *Uncollected Stories of William Faulkner.* Edited by Joseph Blotner. New York: Random House, 1979.

Fitzgerald, F. Scott. *All the Sad Young Men.* New York: Scribner's, 1926.

Frucht, Abby. *Fruit of the Month*. Iowa: Univ. of Iowa Press, 1987.

Gallant, Mavis. *From the Fifteenth District*. New York: Random House, 1979.

Gallant, Mavis. *Home Truths*. New York: Laurel/Dell, 1987.

Garrett, George. *The Magic Striptease*. Garden City: Doubleday, 1973.

Gilchrist, Ellen. *Drunk with Love and Other Stories*. New York, 1987.

Glasgow, Ellen. *The Collected Stories of Ellen Glasgow*. Baton Rouge: Louisiana State Univ. Press, 1963.

Godwin, Gail. *Dream Children*. New York: Knopf, 1976.

Godwin, Gail. *Mr. Bedford and the Muses*. New York: Knopf, 1984.

Gordon, Caroline. *The Collected Stories of Caroline Gordon*. New York: Farrar, Straus, Giroux, 1981.

Goyen, William. *The Collected Stories of William Goyen*. New York: Doubleday, 1972.

Hall, Donald. *The Ideal Bakery and Other Stories*. New York: Harper, 1987.

Hannah, Barry. *Airships*. New York: Knopf, 1978.

Hannah, Barry. *Captain Maximus*. New York: Penguin, 1981.

Hegi, Ursula. *Unearned Pleasures and Other Stories*. Univ. of Idaho Press, 1988.

Helprin, Mark. *A Dove of the East and Other Stories*. New York: Knopf, 1975.

Helprin, Mark. *Ellis Island and Other Stories*. New York: Knopf, 1982.

Hemingway, Ernest. *The Short Stories of Ernest Hemingway*. New York: Scribner's, 1927.

Hempel, Amy. *Reason to Live*. New York: Knopf, 1985.

Henry, O. *The Best Short Stories of O. Henry*. New York: Vintage.

Hirshfield, Jane. *Of Gravity & Angels*. Middletown, Conn.: Wesleyan Univ. Press, 1988.

Hood, Mary. *How Far She Went*. Athens: Univ. of Georgia Press, 1980.

Hughes, Langston. *The Ways of White Folks*. New York: Knopf, 1947.

Irving, Washington. *Selected Works*. New York: Modern Library, 1952.

Jackson, Shirley. *The Lottery; or, The Adventures of James Harris*. New York: Farrar, Straus, Giroux, 1966.

James, Henry. *The Complete Tales of Henry James*. 12 vols. Philadelphia: Lippincott, 1961–64.

James, Henry. *Great Short Works of Henry James*. New York: Perennial/Harper & Row, 1966.

Johnson, Charles. *The Sorcerer's Apprentice*. New York: Penguin, 1986.

Klinkowitz, Jerry. *"Short Season" and Other Stories*. Baltimore: Johns Hopkins Univ. Press, 1988.

Klass, Perri. *I Am Having an Adventure: Stories*. New York: Plume/NAL, 1987.

Kraf, Elaine. *The Princess of 72nd Street*. New York: New Directions, 1979.

London, Jack. *Great Short Works of Jack London*. New York: Perennial/Harper & Row, 1966.

Malamud, Bernard. *Idiots First*. New York: Farrar, Straus, Giroux, 1963.

Malamud, Bernard. *Rembrandt's Hat*. New York: Farrar, Straus, Giroux, 1973.

Martoni, Michael. *Safety Patrol*. Baltimore: Johns Hopkins Univ. Press, 1989.

Mason, Bobbie Ann. *Shiloh and Other Stories*. New York: Harper & Row, 1982.

McCarthy, Mary. *Cast a Cold Eye*. New York: Harcourt, Brace, 1950.

McCluskey, John Jr., ed. *The City of Refuge: The Collected Stories of Rudolph Fisher*. Columbia: Univ. of Missouri Press, 1987.

McCullers, Carson. *The Ballad of the Sad Cafe and Other Stories*. Boston: Houghton Mifflin, 1955.

Meinke, Peter. *The Piano Tuner*. Athens: Univ. of Georgia Press, 1986.

Melville, Herman. *Great Short Works of Herman Melville.* New York: Perennial/Harper & Row, 1966.

Miller, Sue. *Inventing the Abbots.* New York: Dell, 1987.

Morris, Wright. *Collected Stories: 1948–1986.* New York: Harper & Row, 1987.

Munro, Alice. *The Beggar Mind.* New York: Knopf, 1979.

Munro, Alice. *The Progress of Love.* New York: Penguin, 1987.

Nabokov, Vladimir. *Tyrants Destroyed and Other Stories.* New York: McGraw-Hill, 1975.

Oates, Joyce Carol. *The Seduction, and Other Stories.* Santa Barbara, Calif.: Black Sparrow, 1975.

O'Connor, Flannery. *The Complete Stories.* New York: Farrar, Straus, Giroux, 1971.

O'Hara, John. *The O'Hara Generation.* New York: Random House, 1969.

O'Hara, John. *Selected Short Stories.* New York: Vintage.

Olsen, Tillie. *Tell Me A Riddle.* Philadelphia: Lippincott, 1961.

Ozick, Cynthia. *The Pagan Rabbi and Other Stories.* New York: Dutton, 1971.

Paley, Grace. *Enormous Changes at the Last Minute.* New York: Farrar, Straus, Giroux, 1974.

Paley, Grace. *The Little Disturbances of Man.* New York: Penguin, 1984.

Phillips, Jayne Anne. *Dark Tickets.* New York: Random House, 1982.

Phillips, Jayne Anne. *Fast Lanes.* New York: Seymour Lawrence/Delacorte, 1987.

Poe, Edgar Allan. *Great Short Works of Edgar Allan Poe.* New York: Perennial/Harper & Row, 1966.

Porter, Katherine Anne. *Collected Stories.* New York: Harcourt Brace Jovanovich, 1965.

Powers, J. F. *The Prince of Darkness.* New York: Vintage.

Price, Raynolds. *The Names and Faces of Heroes.* New York: Atheneum, 1963.

Purdy, James. *Children Is All.* New York: New Directions, 1962.

Rios, Alberto Alvaro. *The Iguana Killer: Twelve Stories of the Heart.* Moscow, Idaho: Confluence Press, 1984.

Roth, Philip. *Goodbye, Columbus and Five Short Stories.* Boston: Houghton Mifflin, 1959.

Salinger, J. D. *Franny and Zooey.* Boston: Little, Brown, 1961.

Sanford, Winifred M. *Windfall and Other Stories.* Dallas: Southern Methodist Univ. Press, 1988.

Schwartz, Lynne Sharon. *The Melting Pot and Other Subversive Stories.* New York: Penguin, 1987.

Shaw, Irwin. *Irwin Shaw Stories: Five Decades.* New York: Bantam/Dell, 1984.

Simpson, Mona. *Anywhere But Here.* New York: Knopf, 1987.

Smiley, Jane. *The Age of Grief: A Novella and Stories.* New York: Knopf, 1987.

Singer, Isaac Bashevis. *Gimpel the Fool and Other Stories.* New York: Noonday, 1957.

Singer, Isaac Bashevis. *Selected Short Stories of Isaac Bashevis Singer.* New York: Modern Library, 1966.

Singer, Isaac Bashevis. *An Isaac Bashevis Singer Reader.* New York: Farrar, Straus, Giroux, 1971.

Southern, Terry. *Red Dirt, Marijuana and Other Tastes.* New York: NAL, 1967.

Stafford, Jean. *The Collected Stories of Jean Stafford.* New York: FSG, 1969.

Steinbeck, John. *The Long Valley.* Garden City, N.Y.: Sun Dial, 1941.

Stuart, Jesse. *A Jesse Stuart Reader.* New York: McGraw-Hill, 1963.

Sukenick, Ronald. *The Death of the Novel and Other Stories.* New York: Dial, 1969.

Tallent, Elizabeth. *In Constant Flight: Stories.* New York: Owl/Holt, 1987.

Targan, Barry. *Harry Belten and the Mendelssohn Violin Concerto.* Iowa City, Iowa: Univ. of Iowa Press, 1975.

Targan, Barry. *Surviving Adverse Seasons.* Urbana: Univ. of Illinois Press, 1979.

Taylor, Peter. *Collected Stories.* New York: Penguin, 1980.

Taylor, Peter. *In The Miro District.* New York: Carroll and Graf, 1979.

Taylor, Peter. *The Old Forest and Other Stories.* New York: Knopf, 1985.

Twain, Mark. *Great Short Works of Mark Twain.* New York: Perennial/Harper & Row, 1966.

Updike, John. *The Music School and Other Stories.* New York: Vintage.

Updike, John. *Museums and Women and Other Stories.* New York: Knopf, 1985.

Updike, John. *The Same Door.* New York: Knopf, 1959.

Vonnegut, Kurt, Jr. *Welcome to the Monkey House.* New York: Delacorte, 1968.

Walker, Alice. *In Love and Trouble: Stories of Black Women.* New York: Harcourt Brace Jovanovich, 1973.

Welty, Eudora. *The Collected Stories.* New York: Harcourt Brace Jovanovich, 1980.

Wharton, Edith. *The Collected Stories of Edith Wharton.* 2 vols. Edited by R. W. B. Lewis. New York: Scribner's, 1968.

Whelan, Gloria. *Playing with Shadows.* Urbana: Univ. of Illinois Press, 1988.

Williams, Joy. *Taking Care.* New York: Vintage, 1978.

Williams, Tennessee. *Eight Mortal Ladies Possessed.* New York: New Directions, 1974.

Williams, William Carlos. *The Doctor Stories.* Edited by Robert Coles. New York: New Directions, 1969.

Williams, William Carlos. *Make It Light: Collected Stories.* New York: Random House, 1950.

Wolfe, Thomas. *From Death to Morning.* New York: Scribner's, 1935.

Wolff, Tobias. *The Barracks Thief and Other Stories.* New York: Vintage, 1984.

Wolff, Tobias. *In the Garden of the North American Martyrs.* New York: Ecco, 1981.

Wright, Richard. *Uncle Tom's Children: Five Long Stories.* New York: Harper, 1938.

Yates, Richard. *Eleven Kinds of Loneliness.* Boston: Little, Brown, 1962.

IV. SHORT FICTION (AUSTRALIAN, BRITISH, INDIAN, IRISH, NEW ZEALANDER, SOUTH AFRICAN)

Anderson, Jessica. *Stories From the Warm Zone and Sydney Stories.* New York: Viking, 1987.

Barnard, Marjorie. *The Persimmon Tree and Other Stories.* New York: Penguin, 1978.

Bates, H. E. *A Month by the Lake and Other Stories.* New York: New Directions, 1987.

Bowen, Elizabeth. *The Collected Stories.* New York: Knopf, 1974.

Conrad, Joseph. *The Heart of Darkness and The Secret Sharer.* New York: Bantam Classics, 1976.

Conrad, Joseph. *Sea Stories.* New York: Carroll and Graf, 1978.

Doyle, Arthur Conan. *The Complete Sherlock Holmes.* New York: Doubleday, 1930. (Frequently reprinted).

Farmer, Beverly. *Milk.* New York: Penguin, 1984.

Forster, E. M. *The Celestial Omnibus and Other Stories.* New York: Vintage, 1971.

Gordimer, Nadine. *Selected Stories.* New York: Penguin, 1975.

Gordimer, Nadine. *Six Feet of the Country.* New York: Penguin, 1980.

Grace, Patricia. *Waiariki and Other Stories.* New York: Penguin, 1981.

Gray, Stephen. See under *Anthologies.*

Greene, Graham. *Collected Stories.* New York: Viking, 1952.

Hardy, Thomas. *The Distracted Preacher and Other Tales.* New York: Penguin, 1979.

Isherwood, Christopher. *The Berlin Stories.* New York: New Directions, 1965.

Jolley, Elizabeth. *Woman in a Lampshade.* New York: Penguin, 1984.

Joyce, James. *Dubliners.* London: Heubsch, 1916. (Widely available).

Kiely, Benedict. *A Letter to Peachtree.* Boston: Godine, 1988.

Lawrence, D. H. *The Complete Stories.* New York: Viking Penguin, 1961.

Lavin, Mary. *Selected Stories.* New York: Penguin, 1981.

Lessing, Doris. *A Man and Two Women.* New York: Simon and Schuster, 1961.

Mansfield, Katherine. *The Garden Party and Other Stories.* London, 1922.

Norris, Leslie. *The Girl from Cardigan: Sixteen Stories.* Layton, Utah: Peregrine Smith Books, 1988.

O'Brien, Edna. *The Fantastic Heart: Se-lected Stories.* New York: Farrar, Straus, Giroux, 1984.

O'Connor, Frank. *Collected Stories.* New York: Knopf, 1981.

Pritchett, V. S. *Collected Stories.* New York: Random House, 1982.

Pritchett, V. S. *More Collected Stories.* New York: Random House, 1986.

Sillitoe, Alan. *The Loneliness of the Long-Distance Runner.* New York: Knopf, 1959.

Stead, Christina. *Ocean of Story.* New York: Penguin, 1965.

Thomas, Dylan. *The Collected Stories.* New York: New Directions, 1970.

Trevor, William. *Collected Stories.* New York: Penguin, 1985.

Trevor, William. *Lovers of Their Time and Other Stories.* New York: Viking, 1978.

Verma, Nirmal. *The World Elsewhere.* St. Paul: Readers International, 1988.

White, Patrick. *The Burnt Ones.* New York: Penguin, 1975.

Woolf, Virginia. *A Haunted House.* New York: Harcourt/Brace, 1940.

See also Part I, Anthologies

V. SHORT FICTION (ASIAN, CONTINENTAL, LATIN AMERICAN)

Bachman, Ingeborg. *The Thirtieth Year: Stories.* New York: Holmes & Meier, 1987.

Böll, Heinrich. *18 Stories.* New York: McGraw Hill, 1966.

Borges, Jorge Luis. *Labyrinths and Other Writings.* New York: Vintage, 1971.

Buzatti, Dino. *Restless Nights: Stories.* Berkeley, Calif.: North Point Press, 1987.

Camus, Albert. *Exile and the Kingdom.* New York: Knopf, 1958.

Chekhov, Anton. *The Darling and Other Stories.* New York: Macmillan, 1916 and 1944. (See also Penguin collections of his short fiction edited by Ronald Wilks.)

Chekhov, Anton. *Late-Blooming Flowers and Other Stories.* New York: Carroll and Graf, 1980.

Cortazar, Julio. *Blow Up and Other Stories.* New York: Vintage, 1973.

de Balzac, Honore. *Selected Short Stories.* New York: Penguin, 1972.

de la Fontaine, Jean. *Selected Fables.* New York: Penguin, 1972.

de Maupassant, Guy. *Selected Short Stories.* New York: Penguin, 1979.

Dostoyevsky, Fyodor. *The Best Short Stories of Fyodor Dostoyevsky.* New York: Vintage, 1974.

Endo, Shusaku. *Stained Glass Elegies.* New York: Dodd, Mead, 1982.

Fuentes, Carlos. *Burnt Water: Selected Stories.* New York: Farrar, Straus, Giroux, 1985.

Grin, Alexander. *Selected Short Stories.* Ann Arbor: Ardis Publications, 1987.

Gustafsson, Lars. *The Death of a Beekeeper.* New York: New Directions, 1987.

Gustafsson, Lars. *Funeral Music for Freemasons: Stories.* New York: New Directions, 1982.

Gustafsson, Lars. *Stories of Happy People.* New York: New Directions, 1986.

Jie, Zhang. *Love Must Not Be Forgotten.* San Francisco: China Books, 1986.

Kafka, Franz. *The Complete Stories.* New York: Schocken, 1971.

Kawabata, Yasunari. Translated by Dunlop and Holman. *Palm-of-the-Hand Stories.* Berkeley, Calif.: North Point Press, 1988.

Landolfi, Thomaso. *Words in Commotion and Other Stories.* New York: Penguin, 1985.

Marquez, Gabriel Garcia. *Leaf Storm and Other Stories.* New York: Harper & Row, 1971.

Mishima, Yukio. *Death in Midsummer and Other Stories.* New York: New Directions, 1966.

Pacheco, Jose Emilio. *Battles in the Desert and Other Stories.* New York: New Directions, 1975.

Pushkin, Alexander. *The Captain's Daughter and Other Stories.* New York: Vintage, 1972.

Rilke, Rainer Maria. *The Selected Stories.* New York: Vintage, 1976.

Robbe-Grillet, Alan. *Snapshots.* New York: Grove Press, 1962.

Tolstoy, Leo. *The Death of Ivan Ilych and Other Stories.* London: Oxford, 1935.

Turgenev, Ivan. *The Hunting Sketches.* New York: Signet, 1962.

Waiser, Robert. *Selected Stories.* New York: Vintage, 1977.

VI. MAGAZINES AND PUBLICATIONS ON PUBLISHING

A. Mass-Market Magazines

Atlantic Monthly

Cosmopolitan

Esquire

Harper's

Ladies Home Journal

McCall's

Mademoiselle

Ms.

The Nation

The New Yorker

Redbook

Vanity Fair

Vogue

B. Small Literary Magazines

Allegheny Review (for undergraduate literature)

Antaeus

Arizona Quarterly

California Quarterly

Carolina Quarterly

Chicago Review

Fiction Network Magazine

Georgia Review

Granta

Iowa Review

Iris: A Journal About Women

Kansas Quarterly

The Kenyon Review

Laurel Review

Malahat Review

Massachusetts Review

Missouri Review

New England Quarterly

Nimrod

Northwest Review

Ontario Review

Paris Review

Partisan Review

Ploughshares

Seattle Review

Sequoia

Sewanee Review

Shenandoah

Sierra Journal

South Carolina Review

Southern Review

Story Quarterly

Texas Review

Triquarterly

Virginia Quarterly Review

Webster Review

Whetstone

Willow Springs

Wind: Literary Journal

C. Publications on Publishing

The Writer (magazine)

Writer's Digest (magazine)

Poets and Writers (newsletter)

Chronicle of the Associated Writing Programs

Writer's Market (book)

Novel and Short Story Writer's Market (book)

International Directory of Little Magazines and Small Presses

Copyright Acknowledgments

Index of Authors

AUTHOR   **PAGE**

Aleichem, Sholem 229
Amis, Martin 888
Anderson, Sherwood 371
Atwood, Margaret. 597
Barr, Fiona. 854
Barthelme, Donald 657
Beattie, Ann. 536
Böll, Heinrich 651
Borowski, Tadeusz 353
Bradbury, Ray 605
Brautigan, Richard. 671
Carver, Raymond 700
Cather, Willa 407
Chandler, Raymond. 445
Cheever, John. 500
Chekhov, Anton 150
Chopin, Kate 190
Conrad, Joseph. 257
Crane, Stephen. 236
Day, Richard Cortez 792
DeFrees, Madeline 881
Demarinis, Rick 805
Doyle, Arthur Conan 206
Ellison, Matt. 767
Ellison, Ralph 422
Engberg, Susan. 748
Erdrich, Louise. 717
Faulkner, William 331
Foster, Sesshu 860

Frame, Janet 516
Fuentes, Carlos 612
Gallagher, Tess. 828
Gilman, Charlotte Perkins 193
Grafton, Sue. 735
Gustafsson, Lars. 634
Gyanranjan. 875
Hawthorne, Nathaniel 50
Heker, Liliana. 787
Hemingway, Ernest. 318
Henry, O. 224
Hughes, Langston 430
Hulme, Keri 726
Hurston, Zora Neale 435
Jackson, Shirley 674
James, Henry 159
Joubert, Elsa 778
Joyce, James. 300
Kafka, Franz. 323
Kawabata, Yasunari 474
King, Stephen. 814
Koda, Aya 357
Lawrence, D. H.. 305
Malamud, Bernard. 643
Mansfield, Katherine 469
Maupassant, Guy de 86
Melville, Herman 60
Munro, Alice 521
Ndebele, Njabulo. 846
O'Brien, Tim 583
O'Connor, Flannery. 571

O'Connor, Frank 339
Oates, Joyce Carol 660
Oz, Amos 682
Ozick, Cynthia 563
Phillips, Jayne Anne 758
Pirandello, Luigi 349
Poe, Edgar Allan 45
Porter, Katherine Anne 379
Rios, Alberto Alvaro 836
Steinbeck, John 387

Tolstoy, Leo 110
Turgenev, Ivan 93
Updike, John 494
Valenzuela, Luisa 668
Walker, Alice 692
Welch, James 866
Welty, Eudora 396
Wong, Shawn Hsu 800
Yamamoto, hisaye 541
Yates, Richard 551

Index of Titles

"A & P," John Updike 494
"Araby," James Joyce 300
"Aura," Carlos Fuentes 612
"The Author," Donald
    Barthelme 657
"Back Yard," Elsa Joubert 778
"Bartleby the Scrivener: A Story
    of Wall Street," Herman
    Melville 60
"Bess," Jayne Anne Phillips 758
"Bezhin Meadow," Ivan
    Turgenev 93
"The Black Kimono," Aya
    Koda 357
"The Blue Hotel," Stephen
    Crane 236
"Bujak and the Strong Force,"
    Martin Amis 888

"The Butterfly and the Traffic
    Light," Cynthia Ozick 563
"The Censors," Luisa
    Valenzuela 668
"A Chagall Story," Richard
    Cortez Day 792
"Chrysanthemums," John
    Steinbeck 387
"Civil Engineer," Matt Ellison . . . 767
"A Clean, Well-Lighted Place,"
    Ernest Hemingway 318
"A Daughter's Heart," Susan
    Engberg 748
"Death of a Son," Njabulo
    Ndebele 846
"The Death of Ivan Ilych," Leo
    Tolstoy 110

"Doctor Jack-o'-lantern," Richard
Yates. 551

"Each Year Grain," Shawn Hsu
Wong. 800

"The Egg," Sherwood
Anderson 371

"Errand," Raymond Carver 700

"Everyday Use," Alice Walker . . 692

"Everything That Rises Must
Converge," Flannery
O'Connor 571

"The Fly," Katherine
Mansfield 469

"Fools Crow," James Welch. . . . 866

"The Ghost Children of
Tacoma," Richard Brautigan. . 671

"The Gift of the Magi," O.
Henry 224

"Goodbye, My Brother," John
Cheever. 500

"Gooseberries," Anton
Chekhov. 150

"Graveyard Shift," Stephen
King 814

"Guests of the Nation," Frank
O'Connor 339

"The Horse Dealer's Daughter,"
D. H. Lawrence 305

"A Hunger Artist," Franz Kafka . 323

"If There Is Justice," Amos Oz. . 682

"The Iguana Killer," Alberto
Alvaro Rios 836

"Insulation," Janet Frame. 516

"In the White Night," Ann
Beattie. 536

"The Jewbird," Bernard
Malamud 643

"The Jilting of Granny
Weatherall," Katherine Anne
Porter 379

"King of the Bingo Game," Ralph
Ellison 422

"The Lottery," Shirley Jackson. . 674

"Miles City, Montana," Alice
Munro 521

"The Mole," Yasunari
Kawabata. 474

"The Murder," Joyce Carol
Oates. 660

"My Melancholy Face," Heinrich
Böll 651

"The Necklace," Guy de
Maupassant 86

"On Account of a Hat," Sholem
Aleichem 229

"On the Road," Langston
Hughes 430

"One Whale, Singing," Keri
Hulme 726

"Our Side of the Fence and
Theirs," Gyanranjan 875

"A Pair of Glasses," Tess
Gallagher 828

"Paul's Case," Willa Cather 407

'Petrified Man," Eudora Welty . . 396

"The Pupil," Henry James 159

"Rape Fantasies," Margaret
Atwood 597

"A Rose for Emily," William
Faulkner. 331

"A Scandal in Bohemia," Arthur
Conan Doyle. 206

"The Secret Sharer," Joseph
Conrad. 257

"She Didn't Come Home," Sue
Grafton 735

"Snares," Louise Erdrich 717

"The Stolen Party," Liliana
Heker 787

"The Story of an Hour" Kate
Chopin 190

"The Street of the Fathers,"
Susshu Foster 860

"The Supper," Tadeus
Borowski 353

"Sweat," Zorah Neale Hurston . . 435

"The Tell-Tale Heart," Edgar
Allan Poe 45

"The Things They Carried," Tim
O'Brien 583

"2002: Night Meeting," Ray
Bradbury 605

"Uncle Sven and the Cultural
Revolution," Lars
Gustafsson 634

"Under the Wheat," Rick
Demarinis 805

"The Ventriloguist's Dummy,"
Madeline DeFrees 881

"The Wall-Reader," Fiona Barr . . 854

"War," Luigi Pirandello 349

"The Wrong Pigeon," Raymond
Chandler 445

"The Yellow Wallpaper,"
Charlotte Perkins Gilman 193

"Yoneko's Earthquake," Hisaye
Yamamoto 541

"Young Goodman Brown,"
Nathaniel Hawthorne 50